International Acclaim for Battlefield Earth
Epic Saga of Adventure in the Yea

One of the n

"A superlativ and pacing... epic in siz as anything he ever wrote... if you you'll like Hubbard."

PUBLISHER'S WEEKLY

"Pure entertainment and pure science fiction... a series of wild adventures in which the pace never slackens... Action all the way."

HERALD EXPRESS

"For science fiction gourmets this saga of the year 3, 000 is a feast of unlimited courses: Intergalactic war; suspense; adventure; domination of the Earth by a crude alien race, 'Battlefield Earth' is a blockbuster adventure by a masterhand at storytelling."

WESTERN EVENING HERALD

"...huge, rollicking saga... the pace starts fast and never lets up."

ATLANTA JOURNAL – CONSTITUTION

"... this latest work guarantees him a place beside the greatest authors in the field. Not to be missed."

ABERDEEN EVENING EXPRESS

"Think of the 'Star Wars' sagas and 'Raiders of the Lost Ark', mix in the triumph of 'Rocky I', 'Rocky II', and 'Rocky III' and you have captured the exuberance, style and glory of 'BATTLEFIELD EARTH'"

BALTIMORE EVENING SUN

"A cracking good read for everyone."

HARTLEPOOL MAIL

AMONGST THE MANY CLASSIC WORKS
BY L. RON HUBBARD:

Beyond the Black Nebula
Buckskin Brigades
The Conquest of Space
The Dangerous Dimension
Death's Deputy
The Emperor of the Universe
Fear
Final Blackout
Forbidden Voyage
The Incredible Destination
The Kilkenny Cats
The Kingslayer
The Last Admiral
The Magnificent Failure
The Masters of Sleep
The Mutineers
Ole Doc Methuselah
Ole Mother Methuselah
The Rebels
Return to Tomorrow
Slaves of Sleep
To The Stars
The Traitor
Triton
Typewriter In The Sky
The Ultimate Adventure
The Unwilling Hero

L. Ron Hubbard

BATTLEFIELD Earth

A SAGA OF THE YEAR 3000

L. Ron Hubbard

Battlefield Earth

A SAGA OF THE YEAR 3000

N. E™ PUBLICATIONS UK Ltd.

BATTLEFIELD EARTH: A SAGA OF THE YEAR 3000

THIS BOOK CONTAINS THE COMPLETE TEXT OF THE ORIGINAL HARDCOVER EDITION.

ISBN 1-870451-17-1
Printed in England
First Paperback Edition Published for the
United Kingdom

Second printing 1987

Cover art: Gerry Grace

This brand-new novel is dedicated to Robert A. Heinlein, A. E. van Vogt, John W. Campbell, Jr., and all the merry crew* of science fiction and fantasy writers of the thirties and forties—The Golden Age—who made science fiction and fantasy the respected and popular literary genres they have become today.

*Stars of that time include, in part: Forrest J Ackerman, Poul Anderson, Isaac Asimov, Harry Bates, Eando Bender, Alfred Bester, James Blish, Robert Bloch, Nelson Bond, Anthony Boucher, Leigh Brackett, Ray Bradbury, Fredric Brown, Arthur J. Burks, Edgar Rice Burroughs, Karel Čapek, E. J. Carnell, Cleve Cartmill, Arthur C. Clarke, Hal Clement, Groff Conklin, Ray Cummings, L. Sprague de Camp, Lester del Rey, August Derleth, Ralph Milne Farley, Hugo Gernsback, Mary Gnaedinger, H. L. Gold, Edmond Hamilton, Robert E. Howard, E. Mayne Hull, Aldous Huxley, Malcolm Jameson, David H. Keller, Otis Adelbert Kline, C. M. Kornbluth, Henry Kuttner, Fritz Leiber, Murray Leinster, Willy Ley, Frank Belknap Long, H. P. Lovecraft, R. W. Lowndes, J. Francis McComas, Laurence Manning, Leo Margulies, Judith Merril, Sam Merwin, Jr., P. Schuyler Miller, C. L. "Northwest Smith" Moore, Alden H. Norton, George Orwell, Raymond A. Palmer. Frederik Pohl, Fletcher Pratt, E. Hoffman Price, Ed Earl Repp, Ross Rocklynne, Eric Frank Russell, Nathan Schachner, Idris Seabright (Margaret St. Clair). Clifford D. Simak, C. A. Smith, E. E. "Doc" Smith, Olaf Stapledon, Theodore Sturgeon, John Taine, William F. Temple. F. Orlin Tremaine, Wilson Tucker, Jack Vance, Donald Wandrei, Stanley G. Weinbaum, Manly Wade Wellman, H. G. Wells, Jack Williamson, Russell Winterbotham, Donald A. Wollheim, Farnsworth Wright, S. Fowler Wright, Philip Wylie. John Wyndham, Arthur Leo Zagat, and all their illustrators They are all worth rereading, every one.

INTRODUCTION

Recently there came a period when I had little to do. This was novel in a life so crammed with busy years, and I decided to amuse myself by writing a novel that was *pure* science fiction.

In the hard-driven times between 1930 and 1950, I was a professional writer not simply because it was my job, but because I wanted to finance more serious researches. In those days there were few agencies pouring out large grants to independent workers. Despite what you might hear about Roosevelt "relief," those were depression years. One succeeded or one starved. One became a top-liner or a gutter bum. One had to work very hard at his craft or have no craft at all. It was a very challenging time for anyone who lived through it.

I have heard it said, as an intended slur, "He was a science fiction writer," and have heard it said of many. It brought me to realize that few people understand the role science fiction has played in the lives of Earth's whole population.

I have just read several standard books that attempt to define "science fiction" and to trace its history. There are many experts in this field, many controversial opinions. Science fiction is favored with the most closely knit reading public that may exist, possibly the most dedicated of any genre. Devotees are called "fans," and the word has a special prestigious meaning in science fiction.

Few professional writers, even those in science fiction, have written very much on the character of "sf." They are usually too busy turning out the work itself to expound on what they have written. But there are many experts on this subject among both critics and fans, and they have a lot of worthwhile things to say.

However, many false impressions exist, both of the genre and of its writers. So when one states that he set out to write a work of *pure* science fiction, he had better state what definition he is using.

It will probably be best to return to the day in 1938 when I first entered this field, the day I met John W. Campbell, Jr., a day in the very dawn of what has come to be known as The Golden Age of science fiction. I was quite ignorant of the field and regarded it, in fact, a bit diffidently. I was not there of my own choice. I had been summoned to the vast old building on Seventh Avenue in dusty, dirty, old New York by the very top brass of Street and Smith publishing company—an executive named Black and another, F. Orlin Tremaine. Ordered there with me was another writer, Arthur J. Burks. In those days, when the top brass of a publishing company—particularly one as old and prestigious as Street and Smith—"invited" a writer to visit, it was like being commanded to appear before the king or receiving a court summons. You arrived, you sat there obediently, and you spoke when you were spoken to.

We were both, Arthur J. Burks and I, top-line professionals in other writing fields. By the actual tabulation of A. B. Dick, which set advertising rates for publishing firms, either of our names appearing on a magazine cover would send the circulation rate skyrocketing, something like modern TV ratings.

The top brass came quickly to the point. They had recently started or acquired a magazine called *Astounding Science Fiction*. Other magazines were published by other houses, but Street and Smith was unhappy because its magazine was mainly publishing stories about machines and machinery. As publishers, its executives knew you had to have *people* in stories. They had called us in because, aside from our A. B. Dick rating as writers, we could write about *real people*. They knew we were busy and had other commitments. But would we be so kind as to write science fiction? We indicated we would.

They called in John W. Campbell, Jr., the editor of the magazine. He found himself looking at two adventure-story writers, and though adventure writers might be the aristocrats of the whole field and might have vast followings of their own, they were *not* science fiction writers. He resisted. In the first place, calling in top-liners would ruin his story budget due to their word rates. And in the second place, he had his own ideas of what science fiction was.

Campbell, who dominated the whole field of sf as its virtual czar until his death in 1971, was a huge man who had majored in physics at Massachusetts Institute of Technology and graduated from Duke University with a Bachelor of Sciences degree. His idea of getting a story was to have some professor or scientist write it and then doctor it up and publish it. Perhaps that is a bit unkind, but it really was what he was doing. To fill his pages even he, who had considerable skill as a writer, was writing stories for the magazine.

The top brass had to directly order Campbell to buy and to publish what we wrote for him. He was going to get *people* into his stories and get something going besides *machines*.

I cannot tell you how many other writers were called in. I do not know. In all justice, it may have been Campbell himself who found them later on. But do not get the impression that Campbell was anything less than a master and a genius in his own right. Any of the stable of writers he collected during this Golden Age will tell you that. Campbell could listen. He could improve things. He could dream up little plot twists that were masterpieces. He well deserved the title that he gained and kept as the top editor and the dominant force that made science fiction as respectable as it became. *Star Wars*, the all-time box office record movie to date (exceeded only by its sequel), would never have happened if science fiction had not become as respectable as Campbell made it. More than that—Campbell played no small part in driving this society into the space age.

You had to actually work with Campbell to know where he was trying to go, what his idea was of this thing called "science fiction." I cannot give you any quotations from him; I can just tell you what I felt he was trying to do. In time we became friends. Over lunches and in his office and at his home on weekends—where his wife Doña kept things smooth—talk was always of stories but also of science. To say that Campbell considered science fiction as "prophecy" is an oversimplification. He had very exact ideas about it.

Only about a tenth of my stories were written for the fields of science fiction and fantasy. I was what they called a high-production writer, and these fields were just not big enough to take everything I could write. I gained my original reputation in other writing fields during the eight years before the Street and Smith interview.

Campbell, without saying too much about it, considered the bulk of the stories I gave him to be not science fiction but fantasy, an altogether different thing. Some of my stories he eagerly published as science fiction—among them *Final Blackout*. Many more, actually. I had, myself, somewhat of a science background, had done some pioneer work in rockets and liquid gases, but I was studying the branches of man's past knowledge at that time to see whether he had ever come up with anything valid. This, and a love of the ancient tales now called *The Arabian Nights*, led me to write quite a bit of fantasy. To handle this fantasy material, Campbell introduced another magazine, *Unknown*. As long as I was writing novels for it, it continued. But the war came and I and others went, and I think *Unknown* only lasted about forty months. Such novels were a bit hard to come by. And they were not really Campbell's strength.

So anyone seeking to say that science fiction is a branch of fantasy or an extension of it is unfortunately colliding with a time-honored professional usage of terms. This is an age of mixed genres. I hear different forms of music mixed together like soup. I see so many different styles of dance tangled together into one "dance" that I wonder whether the choreographers really know the different genres of dance anymore. There is abroad today the concept that only *conflict* produces new things. Perhaps the philosopher Hegel introduced that, but he also said that war was necessary for the mental health of the people and a lot of other nonsense. If all new ideas have to spring from the conflict between old ones, one must deny that virgin ideas can be conceived.

So what would *pure* science fiction be?

It has been surmised that science fiction must come from an age where science exists. At the risk of raising dispute and outcry—which I have risked all my life and received but not been bothered by, and have gone on and done my job anyway—I wish to point out some things:

Science fiction does *not* come after the fact of a scientific discovery or development. It is the herald of possibility. It is the plea that someone should work on the future. Yet it is not prophecy. It is the dream that precedes the dawn when the inventor or scientist awakens and goes to his books or his lab saying, "I wonder whether I could make that dream come true in the world of real science."

You can go back to Lucian, second century A.D., or to Johannes Kepler (1571–1630)—who founded modern dynamical astronomy and who also wrote *Somnium*, an imaginary space flight to the moon—or to Mary Shelley and her Frankenstein, or to Poe or Verne or Wells and ponder whether this was really science fiction. Let us take an example: a man invents an eggbeater. A writer later writes a story about an eggbeater. He has *not*, thereby, written science fiction. Let us continue the example: a man writes a story about some metal that, when twiddled, beats an egg, but no such tool has ever before existed in fact. He has now written science fiction. Somebody else, a week or a hundred years later, reads the story and says, "Well, well. Maybe it could be done." And makes an eggbeater. But whether or not it was possible that twiddling two pieces of metal would beat eggs, or whether or not anybody ever did it afterward, the man still has written science fiction.

How do you look at this word "fiction"? It is a sort of homograph. In this case it means two different things. A professor of literature knows it means "a literary work whose content is produced by the imagination and is not necessarily based on fact; the category of literature comprising works of this kind, including novels, short stories, and plays." It is derived from the Latin *fictio*, a making, a fashioning, from *fictus*, past participle of *fingere*, to touch, form, mold.

But when we join the word to "science" and get "science fiction," the word "fiction" acquires two meanings in the same use: 1) the science used in the story is at least partly fictional; and 2) any *story* is fiction. The *American Heritage Dictionary of the English Language* defines science fiction as "fiction in which scientific developments and discoveries form an element of plot or background; especially a work of fiction based on prediction of future scientific possibilities."

So, by dictionary definition and a lot of discussions with Campbell and fellow writers of that time, science fiction has to do with the material universe and sciences; these can include economics, sociology, medicine, and suchlike, all of which have a material base.

Then what is fantasy?

Well, believe me, if it were simply the application of vivid imagination, then a lot of economists and government people and such would be fully qualified authors! Applying the word "imaginative" to fantasy would be like calling an entire library "some words." Too simplistic, too general a term.

In these modern times many of the ingredients that make up "fantasy" as a type of fiction have vanished from the stage. You hardly even find them in encylopedias anymore. These subjects were spiritualism, mythology, magic, divination, the supernatural, and many other fields of that type. None of them had anything really to do with the real universe. This does not necessarily mean that they never had any validity or that they will not again arise; it merely means that man, currently, has sunk into a materialistic binge.

The bulk of these subjects consists of false data, but there probably never will come a time when *all* such phenomena are explained. The primary reason such a vast body of knowledge dropped from view is that material science has been undergoing a long series of successes. But I do notice that every time modern science thinks it is down to the nitty-gritty of it all, it runs into (and sometimes adopts) such things as the Egyptian myths that man came from mud, or something like that. But the only point I am trying to make here is that there is a whole body of phenomena that we cannot classify as "material." They are the nonmaterial, nonuniverse subjects. And no matter how false many of the old ideas were, they still existed; who knows but what there might not be some validity in some bits of them. One would have to study these subjects to have a complete comprehension of all the knowledge and beliefs possible. I am not opening the door to someone's saying I believe in all these things: I am only saying that there is another realm besides dedicated—and even simple-minded—materialism.

"Fantasy," so far as literature is concerned, is defined in the dictionary as "literary or dramatic fiction characterized by highly fanciful or supernatural elements." Even that is a bit limited as a definition.

So fantasy could be called any fiction that takes up elements such as spiritualism, mythology, magic, divination, the supernatural, and so on. *The Arabian Nights* was a gathering together of the tales of many, many countries and civilizations—not just of Arabia as many believe. Its actual title was *A Thousand and One Nights of Entertainment*. It abounds with examples of fantasy fiction.

When you mix science fiction with fantasy you do not have a pure genre. The two are, to a professional, separate genres. I notice today there is a tendency to mingle them and then excuse the result by calling it "imaginative fiction." Actually they don't mix well: science fiction, to be credible, has to be based on some degree of plausibility; fantasy gives you no limits at all. Writing science fiction demands care on the part of the author; writing fantasy is as easy as strolling in the park. (In fantasy, a guy has no sword in his hand; bang, there's a magic sword in his hand.) This doesn't say one is better than the other. They are simply very different genres from a professional viewpoint.

But there is more to this: science fiction, particularly in its Golden Age, had a mission. I cannot, of course, speak for my friends of that period. But from Campbell and from "shooting the breeze" with other writers of the time, one got the very solid impression that they were doing a heavy job of beating the drum to get man to the stars.

At the beginning of that time, science fiction was regarded as a sort of awful stepchild in the world of literature. But worse than that, science itself was not getting the attention or the grants or the government expenditures it should have received. There has to be a *lot* of public interest and demand before politicians shell out the financing necessary to get a subject whizzing.

Campbell's crew of writers were pretty stellar. They included very top-liner names. They improved the literary quality of the genre. And they began the boom of its broader popularity.

A year or so after The Golden Age began, I recall going into a major university's science department. I wanted some data on cytology for my own serious researches. I was given a courteous reception and was being given the references when I noticed that the room had been gradually filling up. And not with students but with professors and deans. It had been whispered around the offices who was in the biology department, and the next thing I knew, I was shaking a lot of hands held out below beaming faces. And what did they want to know: What did I think of this story or that? And had I seen this or that writer lately? And how was Campbell?

They had a literature! *Science fiction!*

And they were proud of it!

For a while, before and after World War II, I was in rather steady association with the new era of scientists, the boys who built the bomb, who were beginning to get the feel of rockets. They were all science fiction buffs. And many of the hottest scientists around were also writing science fiction on the side.

In 1945 I attended a meeting of old scientist and science fiction friends. The meeting was at the home of my dear friend, the incomparable Bob Heinlein. And do you know what was their agenda? How to get man into space fast enough so that he would be distracted from further wars on Earth. And they were the lads who had the government ear and authority to do it! We are coming close to doing it. The scientists got man into space and they even had the Russians cooperating for a while.

One can't go on living a naive life believing that everything happens by accident, that events simply follow events, that there is a natural order of things and that everything will come out right somehow. That isn't science. That's fate, kismet, and we're back in the world of fantasy. No, things do get planned. The Golden Age of science fiction that began with Campbell and *Astounding Science Fiction* gathered enough public interest and readership to help push man into space. Today, you hear top scientists talking the way we used to talk in bull sessions so long ago.

Campbell did what he set out to do. So long as he had his first wife and others around him to remind him that science was for *people,* that it was no use to just send machines out for the sake of machines, that there was no point in going into space unless the mission had something to do with people, too, he kept winning. For he was a very brilliant man and a great and very patient editor. After he lost his first wife, Doña, in 1949—she married George O. Smith—and after he no longer had a sounding-board who made him keep people in stories, and when he no longer had his old original writing crew around, he let his magazine slip back, and when it finally became named *Analog,* his reign was over. But The Golden Age had kicked it all into high gear. So Campbell won after all.

When I started out to write this novel, I wanted to write *pure* science fiction. And not in the old tradition. Writing forms and styles have changed, so I had to bring myself up to date and modernize the styles and patterns. To show that science fiction is not science fiction because of a particular kind of plot, this novel contains practically every type of story there is—detective, spy, adventure, western, love, air war, you name it. All except fantasy; there is none of that. The term "science" also includes economics and sociology and medicine where these are related to material things. So they're in here, too.

In writing for magazines, the editors (because of magazine format) force one to write to exact lengths I was always able to do that—it is a kind of knack. But this time I decided not to cut everything out and to just roll her as she rolled, so long as the pace kept up. So I may have wound up writing the biggest sf novel ever in terms of length. The experts—and there are lots of them to do so—can verify whether this is so.

Some of my readers may wonder that I did not include my own serious subjects in this book. It was with no thought of dismissal of them. It was just that I put on my professional writer's hat. I also did not want to give anybody the idea I was doing a press relations job for my other serious works.

There are those who will look at this book and say, "See? We told you he is just a science fiction writer!" Well, as one of the crew of writers that helped start man to the stars, I'm very proud of also being known as a science fiction writer. You have satellites out there, man has walked on the moon, you have probes going to the planets, don't you? Somebody had to dream the dream, and a lot of somebodies like those great writers of The Golden Age and later had to get an awful lot of people interested in it to make it true.

I hope you enjoy this novel. It is the only one I ever wrote just to amuse myself. It also celebrates my golden wedding with the muse. Fifty years a professional—1930–1980.

And as an old pro I assure you that it is *pure* science fiction. No fantasy. Right on the rails of the genre. Science is for people. And so is science fiction.

Ready?

Stand by.

Blast off!

L. Ron Hubbard
October 1980

See the ad on the last page of this book for details

PART 1

— 1 —

"Man,' said Terl, 'is an endangered species."

The hairy paws of the Chamco brothers hung suspended above the broad keys of the laser-bash game. The cliffs of Char's eyebones drew down over his yellow orbs as he looked up in mystery. Even the steward, who had been padding quietly about picking up her saucepans, lumbered to a halt and stared.

Terl could not have produced a more profound effect had he thrown a meat-girl naked into the middle of the room.

The clear dome of the Intergalactic Mining Company employee recreation hall shone black around and above them, silvered at its crossbars by the pale glow of the Earth's single moon, half-full on this late summer night.

Terl lifted his large amber eyes from the tome that rested minutely in his massive claws and looked around the room. He was suddenly aware of the effect he had produced, and it amused him. Anything to relieve the humdrum monotony of a ten-year* duty tour in this gods-abandoned mining camp, way out here on the edge of a minor galaxy.

In an even more professorial voice, already deep and roaring enough, Terl repeated his thought. "Man is an endangered species."

Char glowered at him. "What in the name of diseased crap are *you* reading?"

Terl did not much care for his tone. After all, Char was simply

* Time, distance, and weight have been translated in all cases throughout this book to old Earth time, distance, and weight systems for the sake of uniformity and to prevent confusion in the various systems employed by the Psychlos.—*Translator*

one of several mine managers, but Terl was chief of minesite security. "I didn't read it. I thought it."

"You must've got it from somewhere," growled Char. "What *is* that book?"

Terl held it up so Char could see its back. It said, "General Report of Geological Minesites, Volume 250,369." Like all such books it was huge but printed on material that made it almost weightless, particularly on a low-gravity planet such as Earth, a triumph of design and manufacture that did not cut heavily into the payloads of freighters.

"Rughr," growled Char in disgust. "That must be two, three hundred Earth-years old. If you want to prowl around in books, I got an up-to-date general board of directors' report that says we're thirty-five freighters behind in bauxite deliveries."

The Chamco brothers looked at each other and then at their game to see where they had gotten to in shooting down the live mayflies in the air box. But Terl's next words distracted them again.

"Today," said Terl, brushing Char's push for work aside, "I got a sighting report from a recon drone that recorded only thirty-five men in that valley near that peak." Terl waved his paw westward toward the towering mountain range silhouetted by the moon.

"So?" said Char.

"So I dug up the books out of curiosity. There used to be hundreds in that valley. And furthermore," continued Terl with his professorial ways coming back, "there used to be thousands and thousands of them on this planet."

"You can't believe all you read," said Char heavily. "On my last duty tour—it was Arcturus IV—"

"This book," said Terl, lifting it impressively, "was compiled by the culture and ethnology department of the Intergalactic Mining Company."

The larger Chamco brother batted his eyebones. "I didn't know we had one."

Char sniffed. "It was disbanded more than a century ago. Useless waste of money. Yapping around about ecological impacts and junk like that." He shifted his bulk around to Terl. "Is this some kind of scheme to explain a nonscheduled vacation? You're going to get your butt in a bind. I can see it, a pile of requisitions this high for breathe-gas tanks and scoutcraft. You won't get any of *my* workers."

"Turn off the juice," said Terl. "I only said that man—"

"I know what you said. But you got your appointment because you are clever. That's right, clever. Not intelligent. Clever. And I can see right through an excuse to go on a hunting expedition. What Psychlo in his right skull would bother with the things?"

The smaller Chamco brother grinned. "I get tired of just dig-dig-dig, ship-ship-ship. Hunting might be fun. I didn't think anybody did it for—"

Char turned on him like a tank zeroing in on its prey. "Fun hunting those things! You ever *see* one?" He lurched to his feet and the floor creaked. He put his paw just above his belt. "They only come up to here! They got hardly any hair on them except their heads. They're a dirty white color like a slug. They're so brittle they break up when you try to put them in a pouch." He snarled in disgust and picked up a saucepan of kerbango. "They're so weak they couldn't pick this up without straining their guts. And they're *not* good eating." He tossed off the kerbango and made an earthquake shudder.

"You ever see one?" said the bigger Chamco brother.

Char sat down, the dome rumbled, and he handed the empty saucepan to the steward. "No," he said. "Not alive. I seen some bones in the shafts and I heard."

"There were thousands of them once," said Terl, ignoring the mine manager. "Thousands! All over the place."

Char belched. "Shouldn't wonder they die off. They breathe this oxygen-nitrogen air. Deadly stuff."

"I got a crack in my face mask yesterday," said the smaller Chamco brother. "For about thirty seconds I thought I wasn't going to make it. Bright lights bursting inside your skull. Deadly stuff. I really look forward to getting back home where you can walk around without a suit or mask, where the gravity gives you something to push against, where everything is a beautiful purple and there's not one bit of this green stuff. My papa used to tell me that if I wasn't a good Psychlo and if I didn't say sir-sir-sir to the right people, I'd wind up at a butt end of nowhere like this. He was right. I did. It's your shot, brother."

Char sat back and eyed Terl. "You ain't really going hunting for a *man,* are you?"

Terl looked at his book. He inserted one of his talons to keep his place and then thumped the volume against his knee.

"I think you're wrong," he mused. "There *was* something to these creatures. Before we came along, it says here, they had towns on every continent. They had flying machines and boats. They even appear to have fired off stuff into space."

"How do you know that wasn't some other race?" said Char. "How do you know it wasn't some lost colony of Psychlos?"

"No, it wasn't that," said Terl. "Psychlos can't breathe this air. It was man all right, just like the cultural guys researched. And right in our own histories, you know how it says we got here?"

"Ump," said Char.

"Man apparently sent out some kind of probe that gave full directions to the place, had pictures of man on it and everything. It got picked up by a Psychlo recon. And you know what?"

"Ump," said Char.

"The probe and the pictures were on a metal that was rare everywhere and worth a clanking fortune. And Intergalactic paid the Psychlo governors sixty trillion Galactic credits for the directions and the concession. One gas barrage and we were in business."

"Fairy tales, fairy tales," said Char. "Every planet I ever helped gut has some butt and crap story like that. Every one." He yawned his face into a huge cavern. "All that was hundreds, maybe thousands of years ago. You ever notice that the public relations department always puts their fairy tales so far back nobody can ever check them?"

"I'm going to go out and catch one of these things," said Terl.

"Not with any of my crews or equipment you ain't," said Char.

Terl heaved his mammoth bulk off the seat and crossed the creaking floor to the berthing hatch.

"You're as crazy as a nebula of crap," said Char.

The two Chamco brothers got back into their game and intently laser-blasted the entrapped mayflies into smoky puffs, one by one.

Char looked at the empty door. The security chief knew no Psychlo could go up into those mountains Terl really was crazy There was deadly uranium up there.

But Terl, rumbling along a hallway to his room, did not consider himself crazy. He was being very clever as always. He had started the rumors so no questions would get out of hand when he began to put into motion the personal plans that would make him wealthy and powerful and, almost as important, dig him out of this accursed planet.

The man-things were the perfect answer. All he needed was just one and then he could get the others. His campaign had begun and begun very well, he thought.

He went to sleep gloating over how clever he was.

— 2 —

It was a good day for a funeral, only it seemed there wasn't going to be one.

Dark, stormy-looking clouds were creeping in from the west, shredded by the snow-speckled peaks, leaving only a few patches of blue sky showing.

Jonnie Goodboy Tyler stood beside his horse at the upper end of the wide mountain meadow and looked with discontent upon the sprawled and decaying village.

His father was dead and he ought to be properly buried. He hadn't died of the red blotches and there was no question of somebody else catching it. His bones had just crumbled away. So there was no excuse not to properly bury him. Yet there was no sign of anyone doing so.

Jonnie had gotten up in the dawn dark, determined to choke down his grief and go about his correct business. He had yelled up Windsplitter, the fastest of his several horses, put a cowhide rope on his nose, and gone down through the dangerous defiles to the lower plain and with a lot of hard riding and herding pushed five wild cattle back up to the mountain meadow. He had then bashed out the brains of the fattest of them and ordered his Aunt Ellen to push the barbecue fire together and get meat cooking.

Aunt Ellen hadn't cared for the orders. She had broken her sharpest rock, she said, and couldn't skin and cut the meat, and certain men hadn't dragged in any firewood lately.

Jonnie Goodboy had stood very tall and looked at her. Among

people who were average height, Jonnie Goodboy stood half a head taller, a muscular six feet shining with the bronzed health of his twenty years. He had just stood there, wind tangling his corn-yellow hair and beard, looking at her with his ice-blue eyes. And Aunt Ellen had gone and found some wood and had put a stone to work, even though it was a very dull one. He could see her now, down there below him, wrapped in the smoke of slow-roasting meat, busy.

There ought to be more activity in the village, Jonnie thought. The last big funeral he had seen was when he was about five years old, when Smith the mayor had died. There had been songs and preaching and a feast and it had ended with a dance by moonlight. Mayor Smith had been put in a hole in the ground and the dirt filled in over him, and while the two cross-sticks of the marker were long since gone, it had been a proper respectful funeral. More recently they had just dumped the dead in the black rock gulch below the waterpool and let the coyotes clean them up.

Well, that wasn't the way you went about it, Jonnie told himself. Not with his father, anyway.

He spun on his heel and with one motion went aboard Windsplitter. The thump of his hard bare heel sent the horse down toward the courthouse.

He passed by the decayed ruins of cabins on the outskirts. Every year they caved in further. For a long time anybody needing a building log hadn't cut any trees: they had just stripped handy existing structures. But the logs in these cabins were so eaten up and rotted now, they hardly even served as firewood.

Windsplitter picked his way down the weed-grown track, walking watchfully to avoid stepping on ancient and newly discarded food bones and trash. He twitched his ear toward a distant wolf howl from up in a mountain glen.

The smell of new blood and the meat smoke must be pulling the wolves down, thought Jonnie, and he hefted his kill-club from where it dangled by a thong into his palm. He'd lately seen a wolf right down in the cabins, prowling around for bones, or maybe even a puppy or a child. Even a decade ago it wouldn't have happened. But every year there were fewer and fewer people.

Legend said that there had been a thousand in the valley but Jonnie thought that was probably an exaggeration There was plenty of food. The wide plains below the peaks were overrun with wild cattle, wild pigs, and bands of horses. The ranges above were alive with deer and goats. And even an unskilled hunter had no trouble getting food. There was plenty of water due to the melting snows and streams, and the little patches of vegetables would thrive if anybody planted and tended them.

No, it wasn't food. It was something else. Animals reproduced, it seemed, but man didn't. At least not to any extent. The death rate and the birth rate were unbalanced, with death the winner. Even when children were born they sometimes had only one eye or one lung or one hand and had to be left out in the icy night. Monsters were unwanted things. All life was overpowered by a fear of monsters.

Maybe it was this valley.

When he was seven he had asked his father about it. "But maybe people can't live in this place," he had said.

His father had looked at him wearily. "There were people in some other valleys, according to the legends. They're all gone, but there are still some of us."

He had not been convinced. Jonnie had said, "There's all those plains down there and they're full of animals. Why don't we go live there?"

Jonnie had always been a bit of a trial. Too smart, the elders had said. Always stirring things up. Questions, questions. And did he believe what he was told? Even by older men who knew a lot better? No. Not Jonnie Goodboy Tyler. But his father had not brought any of this up. He had just said wearily, "There's no timber down there to build cabins."

This hadn't explained anything, so Jonnie had said, "I bet I could find something down there to build a cabin with."

His father had knelt down, patient for once, and said, "You're a good boy, Jonnie. And your mother and I love you very much. But nobody could build anything that would keep out the monsters."

Monsters, monsters. All his life Jonnie had been hearing about the monsters. He'd never seen one. But he held his peace. The oldsters believed in monsters, so they believed in monsters.

But thinking of his father brought an unwelcome wetness to his eyes.

And he was almost unseated as his horse reared. A string of

foot-long mountain rats had rushed headlong from a cabin and hit Windsplitter's legs.

What you get for dreaming, Jonnie snapped to himself. He put Windsplitter's four hoofs back down on the path and drummed him forward the last few yards to the courthouse.

— 3 —

Chrissie was standing there, her leg being hugged as always by her younger sister.

Jonnie Goodboy ignored her and looked at the courthouse. The old, old building was the only one to have a stone foundation and stone floor. Somebody had said it was a thousand years old, and though Jonnie didn't believe it, the place sure looked it. Even its seventeenth roof was as sway-backed as an overpacked horse. There wasn't a log in the upper structure that wasn't gaping with worm holes. The windows were mainly caved in like eyeholes in a rotted skull. The stone walkway close to it was worn half a foot deep by the bare horny feet of scores of generations of villagers coming here to be tried and punished in the olden days when somebody had cared. In his lifetime Jonnie had never seen a trial, or a town meeting for that matter.

"Parson Staffor is inside," said Chrissie. She was a slight girl, very pretty, about eighteen. She had large black eyes in strange contrast to her corn-silk hair. She had wrapped around herself a doeskin, really tight, and it showed her breasts and a lot of bare leg.

Her little sister, Pattie, a budding copy of the older girl, looked bright-eyed and interested. "Is there going to be a real funeral, Jonnie?"

Jonnie didn't answer. He slid off Windsplitter in a graceful single motion. He handed the lead rope to Pattie, who ecstatically uncoiled herself from Chrissie's leg and snatched at it. At seven Pattie had no parents and little enough of a home, and her sun rose and set only on Jonnie's proud orders.

"Is there going to be meat and a burying in a hole in the ground and everything?" demanded Pattie.

Jonnie started through the courthouse door, paying no heed to the hand Chrissie put out to touch his arm.

Parson Staffor lay sprawled on a mound of dirty grass, mouth open in snores, flies buzzing about. Jonnie stirred him with his foot.

Parson Staffor had seen better days. Once he had been fat and inclined to pomposity. But that was before he had begun to chew locoweed—to ease his toothaches, he said. He was gaunt now, dried up, nearly toothless, seamed with inlaid grime. Some wads of weed lay on the stones beside his mouldy bed.

As the toe prodded him again, Staffor opened his eyes and rubbed some of the scum out of them in alarm. Then he saw it was Jonnie Goodboy Tyler, and he fell back without interest.

"Get up," said Jonnie.

"That's this generation," muttered the parson. "No respect for their elders. Rushing off to the bushes, fornicating, grabbing the best meat pieces."

"Get up," said Jonnie. "You are going to give a funeral."

"A *funeral?*" moaned Staffor.

"With meat and sermons and dancing."

"Who is dead?"

"You know quite well who's dead. You were there at the end."

"Oh, yes. Your father. A good man. Yes, a good man. Well, maybe he was your father."

Jonnie suddenly looked a little dangerous. He was standing there at ease, but he was wearing the skin of a puma that he himself had slain and he had his kill-club on a wrist thong. The club seemed to jump of its own volition into his palm.

Parson Staffor abruptly sat up. "Now don't take it wrong, Jonnie. It's just that things are a little mixed up these days, you know. Your mother had three husbands one time and another, and there being no real ceremonies these days—"

"You better get up," said Jonnie.

Staffor clawed for the corner of an ancient, scarred bench and pulled himself upright. He began to tie the deerskin he usually wore, and obviously had worn far too long, using a frayed woven-grass rope. "My memory isn't so good these days, Jonnie. One time I could remember all kinds of things. Legends, marriage ceremonies, hunt blessings, even family quarrels." He was looking around for some fresh locoweed.

"When the sun is straight up," said Jonnie, "you're going to call the whole village together at the old graveyard and you're—"

"Who's going to dig the hole? There has to be a hole, you know, for a proper funeral."

"I'll dig the hole," said Jonnie.

Staffor had found some fresh locoweed and began to gum it. He looked relieved. "Well, I'm glad the town doesn't have to dig the hole. Horns, but this stuff is green. You said meat. Who is going to kill and cook it?"

"That's all taken care of."

Staffor nodded and then abruptly saw more work ahead. "Who's going to assemble the people?"

"I'll ask Pattie to tell them."

Staffor looked at him reproachfully. "Then there's nothing for me to do until straight-up. Why'd you wake me up?" He threw himself back down on the dirty grass and sourly watched Jonnie walk out of the ancient room.

— 4 —

Jonnie Goodboy sat with his knees to his chest, his arms wrapped around them, staring into the remains of the dance fire.

Chrissie lay on her stomach beside him, idly shredding the seeds from a large sunflower between her very white teeth. She looked up at Jonnie from time to time, a little puzzled but not unduly so. She had never seen him cry before, even as a little boy. She knew he had loved his father. But Jonnie was usually so tall and grand, even cold. Could it be that under that good-looking, almost pretty face he felt emotions for her, too? It was something to speculate about. She knew very well how she felt about Jonnie. If anything happened to Jonnie she would throw herself off the cliff where they sometimes herded wild cattle to their death, an easy way to kill them. Life without Jonnie Goodboy would not only not be worth living, it would be completely unbearable. Maybe Jonnie did care about her. The tears showed *something*.

Pattie had no such troubles. She had not only stuffed herself with roast meat, she had also stuffed herself with the wild strawberries that had been served by the heap. And then during the dancing she had run and run and run with two or three little boys and then come back to eat some more. She was sleeping so heavily she looked like a mound of rags.

Jonnie blamed himself. He had tried to tell his father, not just when he was seven, but many times thereafter, that something was wrong with this place. Places were *not* all the same. Jonnie had been—was—sure of it. Why did the pigs and horses and cattle in the plains have little pigs and horses and cattle so numerously and so continuously? Yes, and why were there more and more wolves and coyotes and pumas and birds up in the higher ranges, and fewer and fewer men?

The villagers had been quite happy with the funeral, especially since Jonnie and a couple of others had done most of the work.

Jonnie had not been happy with it at all. It wasn't good enough.

They had gathered at sun straight-up on the knoll above the village where some said the graveyard had been. The markers were all gone. Maybe it had been a graveyard. When Jonnie had toiled—naked so as not to stain his puma-skin cloak and doe britches—in the morning sun, he had dug into something that might have been an old grave. At least there was a bone in it that could have been human.

The villagers had come slouching around and there had been a wait while Pattie tore back to the courthouse and awakened Parson Staffor again. Only twenty-five of them had assembled. The others had said they were tired and asked for any food to be brought back to them.

Then there had been an argument about the shape of the grave hole. Jonnie had dug it oblong so the body could lie level, but when Staffor arrived he said it should be straight up and down, that graves were dug straight up and down because you could get more bodies into a graveyard that way. When Jonnie pointed out that there weren't any burials these days and there was plenty of room, Staffor told him off in front of everybody.

"You're too smart," Staffor rapped at him. "When we had even half a council *they* used to remark on it. Every few council meetings, some prank of yours would come up. You'd ridden to the high ridge and killed a goat. You'd gone clear up Highpeak and gotten lost in a blizzard and found your way back, you said, by following the downslope of the ground. *Too* smart. Who else trained six horses? Everybody knows graves should be straight up and down."

But they had buried his father lying flat anyway, because nobody else had wanted to do more digging and the sun was now past straight-up and it was getting hot.

Jonnie hadn't dared suggest what he really wanted to do. There would have been a riot.

He had wanted to put his father in the cave of the ancient gods, far up at the top of the dark canyon, a savage cleft in the side of the tallest peak. When he was twelve he had strayed up there, more trying out a pony than going someplace. But the way up the canyon had been very flat and inviting. He had gone for miles and miles and miles and then he had been abruptly halted by giant, vertical doors. They were of some kind of metal, heavily corroded. One couldn't see them from above or even from the canyon rims. They were absolutely huge. They went up and up.

He had gotten off his pony and climbed over the rubble in front of them and simply stared. He had walked all around in circles and then come back and stared some more.

After a while he had gotten brave and had walked up to them. But push as he might, he couldn't open them. Then he had found a latch-like bar and he had pried it off and it fell, just missing his foot. Rusted but very heavy.

He had braced his shoulder against one door, sure that it was a door, and pushed and pushed. But his twelve-year-old shoulder and weight hadn't had much effect on it.

Then he had taken the fallen bar and begun to pry it into the slight crack, and after a few minutes he had gotten a purchase with it.

There had been a horrible groaning sound that almost stood his hair up straight, and he dropped the bar and ran for the pony.

Once he was mounted, his fright ebbed a bit. Maybe it was just a sound caused by the rusted hinges. Maybe it wasn't a monster.

He had gone back and worked some more with the bar, and sure enough it was just the door groaning on the pins that held it.

An awful smell had come out of the cracked opening. The smell itself had made him afraid. A little light had been let in and he peeked inside.

A long flight of steps led down, remarkably even steps And they would have been very neat, except . .

The steps were covered by skeletons tumbled every which way. Skeletons in strips of clothing—clothing like he had never seen.

Bits of metal, some bright, had fallen among the bones.

He ran away again, but this time not as far as the pony. He had suddenly realized he would need proof.

Bracing his nerve to a pitch he had seldom before achieved, he went back and gingerly stepped inside and picked up one of the bits of metal. It had a pretty design, a bird with flying wings holding arrows in its claws, quite bright.

His heart almost stopped when the skull he had removed it from tipped sideways and went to powder before his very gaze, as though it reproached him with its gaping eyes for his robbery and then expired.

The pony had been in a white-coat lather when he pulled up in the village.

For two whole days he said nothing, wondering how best to ask his questions. Previous experience in asking questions had made him cautious.

Mayor Duncan was still alive at that time. Jonnie had sat quietly beside him until the big man was properly stuffed with venison and was quiet except for a few belches.

"That big tomb," Jonnie had said abruptly.

"What big what?" Mayor Duncan had snorted.

"The place up the dark canyon where they used to put the dead people."

"What place?"

Jonnie had taken out the bright bird badge and shown it to Mayor Duncan.

Duncan had looked at it, twisting his head this way and that, twisting the badge this way and that.

Parson Staffor, brighter in those days, had reached across the fire in a sudden swoop and grabbed the badge.

The ensuing interrogation had not been pleasant: about young boys who went to places that were forbidden and got everybody in trouble and didn't listen at conferences where they had to learn legends and were too smart anyway.

Mayor Duncan, however, had himself been curious and finally pinned Parson Staffor into recounting an applicable legend.

"A tomb of the old gods," the parson had finally said. "Nobody has been there in living memory—small boys do not count. But it was said to exist by my great-grandfather when he was still alive—and he lived a long time. The gods used to come into these mountains and they buried the great men in huge caverns. When the lightning flashed on Highpeak, it was because the gods had come to bury a great man from over the water.

"Once there were thousands and thousands living in big villages a hundred times the size of this one. These villages were to the east, and it is said there is the remains of one straight east where thousands lived. And the place was flat except for some hills. And when a great man died there the gods brought him to the tomb of the gods."

Parson Staffor had shaken the badge. "This was placed on the foreheads of the great when they were laid to rest in the great tomb of the gods. And that's what it is, and ancient law says that nobody is supposed to go there and everybody had better stay away from there forever—especially little boys." And he had put the badge in his pouch, and that was the last Jonnie ever saw of it. After all, Staffor was a holy man and in charge of holy things.

Nevertheless, Jonnie thought his father should have been buried in the tomb of the gods. Jonnie had never been back there again and thought of it only when he saw lightning hit Highpeak.

But he wished he had buried his father there.

"Are you worried?" asked Chrissie.

Jonnie looked down at her, his reverie broken. The dying fire wove a reddish sheen into her hair and sparked in her dark eyes.

"It's my fault," said Jonnie.

Chrissie smiled and shook her head. Nothing could be Jonnie's fault.

"Yes, it is," said Jonnie. "There's something wrong with this place. My father's bones . . . in the last year they just crumbled like that skeleton's in the tomb of the gods."

"The tomb of the what?" said Chrissie idly. If Jonnie wanted to talk nonsense it was all right with her. At least he was talking to her.

"I should have buried him there. He was a great man. He taught me a lot of things—how to braid grass-rope, how to wait for a puma to crouch before you stepped aside and hit him as he sprang: they can't turn in mid-air, you know. How to cut hide into strips . . ."

"Jonnie, you aren't guilty of anything."

"It was a bad funeral."

"Jonnie, it's the only funeral I remember."

"No, it was not a good funeral. Staffor didn't preach a funeral sermon."

"He talked. I didn't listen because I was helping gather strawberries, but I know he talked. Did he say something bad?"

"No. Only it didn't apply."

"Well, what did he say, Jonnie?"

"Oh, you know, all that stuff about god being angry with the people. Everybody knows that legend. I can quote it myself."

"Quote it."

Jonnie sniffed a little impatiently. But she was interested and it made him feel a little better.

" 'And then there came a day when god was wroth. And wearied he was of the fornicating and pleasure dallying of the people. And he did cause a wondrous cloud to come and everywhere it struck; the anger of god snuffed out the breath and breathing of ninety-nine out of a hundred men. And disaster lay upon the land and plagues and epidemics rolled and smote the unholy, and when it was done the wicked were gone and only the holy and righteous, the true children of the lord, remained upon the stark and bloodied field. But god even then was not sure and so he tested them. He sent monsters upon them to drive them to the hills and secret places, and lo the monsters hunted them and made them less and less until at last all men remaining were the only holy, the only blessed, the only sure righteous upon Earth. Hey man!' "

"Oh, that one. You say it very nicely, Jonnie."

"It's my fault," said Jonnie morosely. "I should have made my father listen. There is something wrong with this place. I am certain that if he had listened and we moved elsewhere, he would be alive today. I *feel* it!"

"Where else is there?"

"There's that whole great plain out there. Weeks of riding on it, I am sure And they say man once lived in a big village out there."

"Oh, no, Jonnie. The monsters."

"I've never seen a monster."

'You've seen the shiny flashing things that sail overhead every few days."

"Oh, those. The sun and moon sail overhead too So do the stars And even shooting stars."

Chrissie was frightened suddenly. "Jonnie, you're not going to *do* something?"

"I am. With first light I am going to ride out and see if there really was a big village in the plains."

Chrissie felt her heart contract. She looked up at his determined profile. It was as though she was sinking down, down into the earth, as though she lay in today's grave.

"Please, Jonnie."

"No, I'm going."

"Jonnie, I'll go with you."

"No, you stay here." He thought fast, something to deter her. "I may be gone for a whole year."

Water got into her sight. "What will I do if you don't come back?"

"I'll come back."

"Jonnie, if you don't come back in a year, I'll come looking for you." Jonnie frowned. He scented blackmail.

"Jonnie, if you're leaving, you see those stars up there? When they come back to the same place next year and you haven't returned, I will come looking."

"You'd be killed out in the plains. The pigs, the wild cattle . . ."

"Jonnie, that is what I will do. I swear it, Jonnie."

"You think I'd just wander off and never return?"

"That's what I will do, Jonnie. You can go. But that's what I will do."

— 5 —

The first dawn light was painting Highpeak rose. It was going to be a beautiful day.

Jonnie Goodboy was completing the packing of a lead horse. Windsplitter was sidling about, biting at the grass but not really eating. He had his eye on Jonnie. They were obviously going somewhere, and Windsplitter was not going to be left out.

Some wisps of smoke were coming from the breakfast fire of the Jimson family nearby. They were roasting a dog. Yesterday at the funeral feast nearly a score of dogs had gotten into an idiot fight. There had been plenty of bones and meat as well. But the pack had gotten into a fight and a big brindle had been killed. Looked like the Jimson family would have meat all day.

Jonnie was trying to keep his mind on petty details. And off Chrissie and Pattie, who were standing there watching him quietly.

Brown Limper Staffor was also there, idling about in the background. He had a clubfoot and should have been killed at birth, but he was the only child the Staffors had ever had, and Staffor was parson after all. Maybe mayor, too, since there wasn't any now.

There was no affection whatever between Jonnie and Brown Limper. During the funeral dancing, Brown had sat on the sidelines making sneering remarks about the dancing, about the funeral, about the meat, about the strawberries. But when he had made a remark about Jonnie's father—''Maybe never had a bone in the right place,''—Jonnie had hit him a backhand cuff. Made Jonnie ashamed of himself, hitting a cripple.

Brown Limper stood crookedly, a faint blue bruise on his cheek, watching Jonnie get ready, wishes of bad luck written all over him. Two other boys of similar age—there were only five in the whole village who were in their late teens—wandered up and asked Brown what was going on. Brown shrugged.

Jonnie kept his mind carefully on his business. He was probably taking too much, but he didn't know what he'd run into. Nobody knew. In the two buckskin sacks he was roping on either side of the lead horse he had flint stones for fire, rat's nests for tinder, bundles of cut thongs, some sharp-edged rocks that were sometimes hard to find and cut indifferently well, three spare kill-clubs—one heavy enough to crush a bear's skull just in case—some warm robes that didn't stink very much, a couple of buckskins for spare clothes . . .

He gave a start. He hadn't realized Chrissie had come within a foot of him. He hoped he wouldn't have to talk.

Blackmail, that's what it was—plain as possible and all bad. If she'd said she would kill herself if he didn't come back, well, one could have put that down to girl vaporings. But threatening to follow him in a year put another shadow on it entirely. It meant he would have to be cautious. He'd have to be careful not to get himself killed. It was one thing to worry about his own life; he didn't care a snap for risk or danger. But the thought of Chrissie going down on the plains if he didn't come back made him snow-cold at the pit of his stomach. She'd be gored or mauled or eaten alive and every agonizing second of it would be Jonnie's fault. She had effectively committed him to caution and care—just what she intended.

She was holding something out to him. Two somethings. One was a large bone needle with a thong hole in it, and the other was a skin awl. Both were worn and polished and valuable.

"They were mama's," said Chrissie.

"I don't need anything."

"No, you have them."

"I won't need them!"

"If you lose your clothes," she wailed, "how are you going to sew?"

The crowd had thickened. Jonnie didn't need any outbursts He snatched the needle and awl out of her hand and unlashed the neck of a sack and dropped them in, made sure they hadn't missed and dropped out, and then relashed the sack.

Chrissie stood more quietly. Jonnie turned and faced her. He was a little bit shocked. There wasn't even a smudge of color in her face. She looked like she hadn't slept and had tick fever as well.

Jonnie's resolution wavered. Then beyond Chrissie he saw Brown Limper tittering and talking behind his hand to Petie Thommso.

Jonnie's face went tight. He grabbed Chrissie and kissed her hard. It was as though he had taken a board from an irrigation trough; the tears went down her cheeks.

"Now look," said Jonnie. "Don't you follow me!"

She made a careful effort to control her voice. "If you don't come back in a year, I will. By all the gods on Highpeak, Jonnie."

He looked at her. Then he beckoned to Windsplitter, who sidled over. With one smooth spring he mounted, the lead rope of the other horse gripped in his hand.

"You can have my other four horses," said Jonnie to Chrissie "Don't eat them; they're trained." He paused. "Unless you get awful hungry, of course, like in the winter."

Chrissie hung on to his leg for a moment and then she stepped back and sagged.

Jonnie thumped Windsplitter with a heel and they moved off This was going to be no wild free ride to adventure. This was going to be a tiptoe scout with care Chrissie had seen to that!

At the entrance to the defile he looked back. About fifteen people were still standing there watching him go. They all looked dejected. He used a heel signal to make Windsplitter rear and waved his hand. They all waved back with sudden animation.

Then Jonnie was gone down the dark canyon trail to the wide and unknown plains.

The rest of the people drifted off. Chrissie still stood there, hoping with a wild crazy hope that he would ride into sight, returning.

Pattie tugged at her leg. 'Chrissie. Chrissie, will he come back?''

Chrissie's voice was very low, her eyes like ashes in a dead fire. ''Goodbye,'' she whispered.

— 6 —

Terl belched. It was a polite way to attract attention, but the belch didn't make much impression through the whine and howl of machines in the transport department maintenance dome.

Zzt's concentration on his work became more marked. Minesite 16's transport chief had little use for the security head. Every time a tool or a car or fuel turned up missing—or something was broken—it got attention from security.

Three crashed cars were strewn about in various stages of reassembly, one of them very messy with splotches of green Psychlo blood in the interior upholstery. The big drills that dangled from the ceiling rails pointed sharp beaks this way and that, idling in their programming. Lathes with nothing in their jaws spun waiting for something to twist and shave. Belts snarled and slapped at each other.

Terl watched the surprisingly nimble talons of Zzt disassemble the small concentric shells of a high-speed jet engine. Terl had hoped to detect a small tremble or two in Zzt's paws—if the transport chief's conscience was bothering him it would be much easier to do business. There was no tremble.

Zzt finished the disassembly and threw the last ring on the bench. His yellow orbs contracted as he looked at Terl. ''Well? What have I done now?''

Terl lumbered closer and looked around. "Where are your maintenance men?"

"We're fifteen mechanics under complement. They were transferred to operations over the last month. I know it and you know it. So why are you here?"

As chief of security, Terl had learned through experience not to be very straightforward. If he simply asked for a manual reconnaissance plane, the transport chief would demand the emergency voucher, not get it, and say "No transport." And there were no emergencies for security on this dull planet. Not real ones. In hundreds of years of operation, there had not been the slightest security threat to Intergalactic Mining operations here. A dull security scene, and consequently the chief of that department was not considered very important. Apparent threats had to be manufactured with guile as their sole ingredient.

"I've been investigating a suspicion of conspiracy to sabotage transport," said Terl. "Kept me busy for the last three weeks." He eased his bulk back against a wrecked car.

"Don't lean on that recon. You'll dent its wing."

Terl decided it was better to be friendly and rumbled over to a stool at the bench where Zzt was working. "Confidentially, Zzt, I've had an idea that could get us some outside personnel. I'm working on it, and that's why I need a manual recon."

Zzt batted his eyebones and sat down on another stool, which creaked despairingly under his thousand-pound bulk.

"This planet," said Terl confidingly, "used to have a sentient race on it."

"What race was that?" asked Zzt suspiciously.

"Man," said Terl.

Zzt looked at him searchingly. A security officer was never noted for his sense of humor. Some had been known to bait and entrap and then file charges. But Zzt couldn't help himself His mouthbones started to stretch, and even though he sought to control them, they spread and suddenly his laugh exploded in Terl's face. Zzt hastily got it under control and turned back to his bench to resume work.

"Anything else on your mind?" asked Zzt, as an afterthought.

This was not going well, thought Terl. Well, that's what happened when you were frank. It just didn't mix with security.

"This suspicion of conspiracy to sabotage transport," said

Terl as he looked around at the wrecked cars with half-lowered eyebones, "could reach to high places."

Zzt threw down a wrench with a clang. A low snarl rumbled in him. He sat there, staring in front of him. He was thinking.

"What do you really want?" he asked at last.

"A recon plane. For five or six days."

Zzt got up and yanked a transport schedule clipboard off the wall and studied it. He could hear Terl almost purring.

"You see this schedule?" said Zzt, pushing it under Terl's nose.

"Well, yes."

"Do you see where it has six drone recons assigned to security?"

"Of course."

"And do you see where this has been going on for—" Zzt peeled back sheet after sheet, "—blast! For centuries I suppose."

"Have to keep a minesite planet under surveillance," said Terl complacently.

"Under surveillance for what?" said Zzt. "Every scrap of ore was spotted and estimated long before your and my living memory. There's nothing out there but mammals. *Air* organisms."

"There might be a hostile landing."

"Here?" sneered Zzt. "Company probes in outer space would detect it ages before it ever arrived here. Terl, transport has to fuel and maintain and recondition those drones two and three times a year. You know and I know the company is on an economy wave. Tell you what."

Terl waited sourly to be told.

"If you will let us cancel those recon drones, I'll put a tri-wheel ground cycle at your disposal for a limited time."

Terl let out a small shrill scream.

Zzt amended his bargain. "A ground car at your disposal when ordered."

Terl lumbered over to the crashed vehicle that had blood on its seats. "Wonder if this was caused by faulty maintenance."

Zzt stood there, unrelenting. The crash had been caused by too much kerbango on duty.

"One recon drone programmed to cover the whole planet once a month," said Zzt. "One ground car at your permanent disposal."

Terl looked at the other wrecks but couldn't think of anything. These investigations were done and dead. Teach him to close investigations!

He wandered back to Zzt. "One drone recon programmed to cover the whole planet once a month. One *armored* and *firepower* ground car at permanent disposal with no questions on ammunition, breathe-gas, or fuel requisitions."

Zzt took the forms from the bench drawer and made them out. He shoved the papers and clipboard at Terl.

As he signed, Terl thought to himself that this transport chief really ought to be looked into. Maybe for ore robbery!

Zzt took the papers back and removed from the switchboard the combination keycard of the oldest and rattiest ground car that was gathering dust in the garage dome. He coupled it with a coupon book for ammo, another for breathe-gas, and another for fuel.

The deal would never actually become part of recorded history as a deal, for the dates of the orders were carefully not coincident. Neither suspected that they had just materially altered the future of the planet. And not for the better of Intergalactic. But that is sometimes the way with large commercial companies.

When Terl had left to get his Mark II (armored, firepower) ground car, Zzt thought to himself that it was wonderful what lies executives told just to be able to go hunting. Kill-mad they all were. Machine kill-mad, too. from the jam-ups he had to repair. What a story! Man a sentient race indeed! He laughed and got back to work.

— 7 —

Jonnie Goodboy Tyler galloped free across the vast ocean of grass, Windsplitter exuberantly stretching his legs, the lead horse rollicking along behind.

What a day. Blue sky and the wind a cooling freshness on his face.

Now two days out, he had come down from the mountains, through the foothills, and into the vastest plain he had ever imagined. He could still see the tiniest tip of Highpeak behind him, and with the sun it kept him true on course and reassured him that he could find his way home whenever he wanted.

Total security! The herds of wild cattle were many, but he had been living with those all his life. A few wolves, but what were wolves? No bear, no puma so far. Why, in all reverence to the gods, did anybody ever stay cooped up in the mountains?

And monsters—what monsters? Phagh! Crazy tales!

Even that shiny, floating cylinder that had gone overhead every few days the whole of his life was overdue down here. It had come from west to east with the regularity of every other heavenly body, but even it seemed to have stopped. On his present course he would have seen it.

In short, Jonnie Goodboy Tyler was suffering from a bad case of overconfidence. And the first disaster that hit him had to do with pigs.

Pigs were usually easy to kill—if you were a bit nimble and watched out for charges of the boars. And a small suckling pig was exactly what one could use for supper.

Right there ahead of him, clear in the late-afternoon light, was a compact herd of pigs out in the open. There were big ones and small ones, but they were all fat.

Jonnie pulled Windsplitter to a halt and slid off. The wind was not quite right, a bit too downwind to the pigs. They'd smell him if he approached directly.

With a bent-knee run, he brought himself silently around them until the wind was at right angles.

He stopped and hefted his club. The tall grass was nearly to his waist.

The pigs were rooting around a shallow depression in the plain, where water stood in the wet months, making a temporary marsh. There must be roots to be had there, Jonnie supposed. There were dozens of pigs, every one with his snout down.

With a crouching gait, staying below the grass tops, Jonnie went forward, closing the distance yard by yard.

Only a few feet separated him now from the outermost fringe of pigs. Silently he rose until his eyes were just above the level of the grass. A small porker was only three arm-spans from him, an easy throw.

"Here's for supper," breathed Jonnie and heaved his kill-club straight and true at the head of the pig.

Dead on, a direct hit. The pig let out an earsplitter and dropped.

But that wasn't all that happened. Instant confusion roared.

Hidden from Jonnie by the tall grass and slightly behind him and to his right, a five-hundred-pound boar who had become tired of eating had lain down for a nap.

The squeal of the hit pig acted like a whip on the whole herd, and away they went in an instant charge, straight upwind at Jonnie's horses.

For the big boar, to see was to charge.

Jonnie felt like he had been struck by a mountain avalanche. He was knocked flat and squashed in instants so close together they felt like one.

He rolled. But the whole sky over him was filled with boar belly. He didn't see but he sensed the teeth and tusks trying to find him.

He rolled again, the savage squeals mixing with the roaring pound of the blood in his ears.

Once more he rolled and this time he saw daylight and a back.

In the blink of an eye he was on the boar's back.

He reached an arm across the throat.

The boar spun around and around like a bucking horse.

Jonnie's arm tightened until he could feel his sinews crack.

And then the boar, strangled, dropped into a limp, jerking pile.

Jonnie unloaded quickly and backed up. The boar was gasping its breath back. It lurched to unsteady feet, and, seeing no opponent, staggered off.

Jonnie went over and picked up the small pig, keeping an eye on the departing boar. But the boar, although it cast about and made small convulsive charges, still couldn't see anybody, and after a bit it trotted in the direction the herd had taken, following the trampled grass.

There was no herd in sight.

And there were no horses!

No horses! Jonnie stood there with the dead pig. He had no sharp rock to cut it. He had no flints to start a fire and roast it. And he had no horses.

It might be worse. He looked at his legs, expecting to see tusk gashes. But he found none. His back and face ached a bit from the collision of the charge and his own collision with the ground, but that was all.

Mentally kicking himself, more ashamed than scared, he made off in the direction of the trail of crushed grass. After a while his depression wore off a bit, to be replaced by optimism. He began to whistle a call. The horses would not have just gone on running in front of the pigs. They would have veered off somewhere.

Just as darkness was falling he spotted Windsplitter calmly cropping grass. The horse looked up with a "Where have you been?" and then, with a plainly mischievous grin, as though he had intended to all the time, came over and bumped Jonnie with his muzzle.

It took another ten minutes of anxious casting about to locate the lead horse and the packs.

Jonnie went back a short way to a little spring they'd passed and made camp. There he made himself a belt and a pouch, and into the latter he put tinder and a flint and some small, sharp-edged stones. He put a stronger thong on the big kill-club and fastened it to the belt. He wasn't going to be caught empty-handed a second time in this vast prairie. No indeed.

That night he dreamed of Chrissie being strangled by pigs, Chrissie mauled by bears, Chrissie crushed to a pulp under stampeding hoofs while he stood helpless in the sky where the spirits go, unable to do a damned thing.

— 8 —

The "Great Village" where "thousands had lived" was obviously another one of those myths, like monsters. But he would look for it nonetheless.

By the half-light of the yellowing dawn, Jonnie was again trotting eastward.

The plain was changing. There were some features about it that didn't seem usual, such as those mounds. Jonnie detoured from his way into the sun to look at one of them.

He stopped, leaning forward with a hand braced on Windsplitter's shoulder, to study the place.

It was a little sort of hill, but it had a hole in the side. A rectangular hole. Otherwise the mound was all covered with dirt and grass. Some freak of nature? A window opening?

He slid off his horse and approached it. He walked around it. Then he paced it out. It was about thirty-five paces long and ten paces wide. Hah! Maybe the mound was rectangular too!

An old, splintered stump stood to one side and Jonnie appropriated a jagged piece of it.

He approached the window and, using the scrap of wood, began to push away the grass edges. It surprised him that he seemed to be digging not in earth but in loose sand.

When he got the lower part of the rectangle cleared, he could get right up to it and look into it.

The mound was hollow.

He backed up and looked at his horses and then around at the countryside. There wasn't anything menacing there.

He bent over and started to crawl into the mound

And the window bit him!

He straightened right up and looked at his wrist.

It was bleeding.

It wasn't a bad cut. It was that he was cut at all that startled him.

Very carefully he looked at the window.

It had teeth!

Well, maybe they weren't teeth. They were dull-bright and had a lot of colors in them and they stood all around the outside edges of the frame. He pulled one of them out—they were very loose. He took a bit of thong from his belt and tried it.

Wonder of wonders, the tooth readily cut the thong, far better than the best rock edge.

Hey, he thought, delighted, look what I got! And with the greatest care—for the things did bite unless you were careful—he removed the splinters, big and small, from the frame and stacked them neatly. He went to his pack and got a piece of buckskin and wrapped them up. Valuable! You could cut and skin and scrape something wonderful with these things. Some kind of rock. Or this mound was the skull of some strange beast and these were the remains of its teeth. Wonderful!

When he had them all and they were carefully stowed in his pack—except one nice bit he put in his belt pouch—he returned to the task of entering the mound.

There was nothing to bite him now and he climbed through the rectangle. There wasn't any pit. The level of the inside seemed to be a bit higher than the outside ground.

A sudden flurry startled him half out of his wits. But it was just a bird that had a nest in here, and it left through the window with a rustle of wings. Once outside, it found a place to sit and began to scold and scold.

Jonnie fumbled his way through the dimness. There wasn't much there, mainly rust. But there *had* been things there; he could tell from the rust piles and wall marks.

Walls? Yes, the place had walls. They were of some sort of rough stone or something, very evenly fitted together in big square blocks.

Yes, these were walls. No animal made anything like this.

And no animal made anything like this tray. It must have been part of something else, now turned to reddish powder. At the bottom of the powder were some circular discs about as big as three thumbnails. And at the bottom of the pile of discs was one that was almost bright.

Jonnie picked it up and turned it over. He caught his breath.

He moved over to the window where there was better light. There could be no mistake.

It was the big bird with spread wings and arrows gripped in its claws.

The same sign he had found in the tomb.

He stood in quivering excitement for a bit and then calmed down. He had it now. The mystery was solved. And he went back out the window and showed Windsplitter.

"God house," said Jonnie. "This is where they stayed while waiting to take great men up to the tomb. Pretty, isn't it?"

Windsplitter finished chewing a mouthful of grass and gave Jonnie a shove in the chest. It was time they were going.

Jonnie put the disc in his belt pouch. Well, it was no Great Village, but it proved definitely that there were things to find out here in the plains. Walls, imagine that. Those gods could build walls.

The bird stopped scolding in some relief as Jonnie mounted up and moved away. It looked after the little cavalcade and then, with a couple more criticisms, went back inside the ancient ruin.

— 9 —

Terl was as happy as a baby Psychlo on a diet of straight kerbango. Although it was late in the day, he was on his way!

He steered the Mark II ground car down the ramp, through the atmosphere port, and into the open air.

There was a warning plaque on the ledge in front of the driver's seat:

> BATTLE READINESS MUST BE OBSERVED AT ALL TIMES! Although this tank is compression contained, personal face masks and independent breathing systems must be kept in place. Personal and unauthorized battle use prohibited. (signed) Political Department, Intergalactic Mining Company, Vice-Director Szot.

Terl grinned at the sign. In the absence of political officers—on a planet where there was no indigenous politics—and in the absence of a war department—on a planet that had nothing to war against—the chief of security covered both those functions. That this old battle car existed on the planet at all meant that it must be very, very old and in addition must have gotten there as a result of fixed allocations of vehicles to company stations. Clerks in Planet 1, Galaxy 1 offices were not always well advised when they wrote their endless directives and orders to the far-flung outposts of the commercial empire. Terl threw his personal face mask and tank onto the gunner's seat beside him and rubbed a thankful paw over his craggy face.

What a lark! The old car ran like a well-greased digger. Small, not more than thirty feet long and ten feet high, it skimmed above the ground like a low-flying wingless bird. Cunning mathematics had contoured it so that every exterior surface would make a hostile projectile glance off at an angle. Missile-proof glass slots gave a fine view of the terrain. Even the blast muzzles of its artillery were cleverly recessed. The interior upholstery, though worn and cracked in places, was a beautiful soothing shade of purple.

Terl felt good. He had five days of jet fuel and breathe-gas and five days of rations in their ten-pound packs. He had cleaned up every scrap of paper in his baskets and had started no new "emergencies." He had a "borrowed" shaft analysis picto-recorder that would take great pictures when put to other uses. And he was on his way!

A break in the dull life of a security chief on a planet without insecurities. A planet that wasn't likely to produce many opportunities for an ambitious security chief to get promotion and advancement.

It had been a gut blow when they ordered him to Earth. He wondered at once what he had done, whom he had accidentally insulted, whose bad side he had gotten on, but they assured him that none of these was the case. He was young. A Psychlo had a life span of about 190 years, and Terl had been only 39 when he had been appointed. It was pointed out to him that few ever became security chiefs at such a tender age. It would show in his record that he had been one. And when he came back from the duty tour, they would see. Plums, like planets you could breathe on, went to older Psychlos.

He had not been fooled, really. Nobody in security personnel pool, Planet 1, Galaxy 1 had wanted anything at all to do with this post. He could hear the future assignment interview now.

"Last post?"

"Earth."

"Where?"

'Earth, rim star, third planet, secondary galaxy 16."

"Oh. What did you accomplish on that post?"

"It's all in the record."

"Yes, but there's nothing in the record."

"There *must* be something. Let me see it."

"No, no. Confidential company record."

And then the final horror: "Employee Terl, it just happens that we have an opening in another rim star system, Galaxy 32. It's a quiet place, no indigenous life and no atmosphere at all. . . ."

Or even worse: "Employee Terl, Intergalactic has been dropping for some time on the exchange and we have orders to economize. I'm afraid your record doesn't recommend continued employment. Don't call us. We'll call you."

He already had a bit of scribble on the wall. A month ago he'd received word that his tour of duty had been extended and there was no mention of his relief. A little bit of horror had touched him, a vision of a 190-year-old Terl tottering around on this same planet, long forgotten by friends and family, ending his days in a dome-crazy stupor, lowered into a slit-trench grave, and ticked off the roster by a clerk who kept the records neat—but didn't know a single face on them.

Such questionable fates required action—big action.

There were better daydreams: waiting in a big entrance hall, uniformed ushers at attention but one of them whispering to another, "Who's that?" And the other, "Don't you know? That's *Terl*." And the big doors opening—"The president of the company is waiting to thank you, sir. Please come this way. . . ."

According to the mine surveys there was an ancient highway to the north of here. Terl flipped the ground car onto auto and spread out a big map. There it was, running east and west. And west was where he wanted to go. It would be busted up and overgrown, maybe even hard to spot. But it would have no steep grades and it would run squarely up into the mountains. Terl had drawn a big circle around the target meadow.

There was the "highway" ahead.

He threw the controls to manual and fumbled a bit. He hadn't driven one of these things since security school years ago, and his uncertain control made the car yaw.

He zoomed up the side embankment of the road and yanked back the throttles and pawed the brakes. The car slammed to earth in a geysering puff of dust, square in the center of the highway. It was a pretty jolting stop but not bad, not bad. He'd get better at it.

He picked up his face mask and tank and donned them. Then he hit the decompression button so the tanks would recontain the breathe-gas without waste. There was a momentary vacuum, a trifle uncomfortable on the hearing bones, and then with a sign, the outside air entered the cab.

Terl swung open the top hatch and stood up on the seat the tank creaking and shuddering under his repositioned weight. The wind felt cool outside the borders of his face mask.

He gazed around with some distaste. This sure was wide country. And empty The only sound was the whisper of wind in the grass. And the sound of silence, vast silence. Even a far-off bird call made the silence heavier.

The earth was tan and brown. The grass and occasional shrubs were green. The sky was an expansive blue, specked with white puffs of clouds. A strange country. People on home planet wouldn't believe it. No purple anywhere.

With a sudden inspiration Terl reached down into the car and grabbed the picto-recorder. He aimed it in a sweeping circle, letting it grind away. He'd send his folks a spool of this. Then they'd believe him when he said it was one horns-awful of a planet and maybe sympathize with him.

"My daily view," he said into the recorder as he finished the sweep. The words rumbled through his mask, sounding sad.

There *was* something purple. Straight west there were some mountains and they looked purple. He put the picto-recorder down and grinned at the mountains so far away. This was better than he thought. No wonder men lived up in the mountains. They were purple. Maybe the men were a bit sentient after all. He hoped so, but not any great confidence; he was probably optimistic. But it gave some substance to his nebulous plans.

Still looking westward, he suddenly caught sight of a landscape feature between himself and the mountains: a distant skyline silhouetted against the declining sun. He shifted a lever on his face mask glass to get magnification. The skyline leaped closer. Yes, he was right. There was a ruined city. Fuzzy and broken but the buildings still very tall. And quite extensive.

The wind fluttered his mine map as he looked at it. The ancient highway ran straight west into it. Reaching down, he took a massive tome off the pile he had on the rear crew seat and opened it to a marked place. There was an insert drawing on the page—some cultural artist had sketched it a few centuries ago.

The company had used air-breathing Chinkos for cultural posts on planets where there was air. The Chinkos had come from Galaxy 2, beings as tall as Psychlos but thread-thin and delicate. They were an old race, and the Psychlos didn't like to admit they had learned what they knew of cultural arts from them. But they had been easy to transport, despite breathing air and being feather-light. And they were cheap. Alas, they were no more, not even in Galaxy 2, having initiated a strike of all things. Intergalactic had wiped them out. But that was long after the culture and ethnology department had been terminated on Earth. Terl had never seen a Chinko. Remarkable beings, drawing pictures like this. Colorful too. Why would anybody *draw* something?

He compared the distant skyline to the sketch. Aside from a bit of blunting and crumbling in the ensuing years, they were the same.

The text said, "To eastward of the mountains lies the ruin of a man-city, remarkably well preserved. It was man-called 'Denver.' It is not as aesthetically advanced as those in the middle or eastern part of the continent. The usual miniature doors have little or no ornamentation. The interiors are no more than slightly oversized dollhouses. Utility rather than artistry seems to have been the overall architectural purpose. There are three cathedrals, which were apparently devoted to the worship of different heathen gods, showing that the culture was not monosectarian even though it may have been dominated by priesthoods. One god, 'bank,' seems to have been more general in worship. There was a man-library remarkably well stocked with books. The department sealed some of the library rooms after removing to archives the only important volumes—those on mining. As no ore bodies were evident under the foundations and no valuable ore materials were employed by the indigenous population in its construction, the man-city remains in a remarkable state of preservation, aided in part by the dry climate. The cost of further restoration is being requisitioned."

Terl laughed to himself. No wonder the culture and ethnology department had been phased out on this planet, if it was applying for credits to reconstruct man-cities! He could hear the counterblast from the directors now. They'd fair put a shaft through the heads of such arty types.

Well, it was data he might use in his plans. Who knew?

He got back to the business at hand. There was the highway stretching out. He was right in the middle of it. It was a couple of hundred feet wide at this point and it could be clearly discerned. It probably had two or three feet of sand on top of it, but the growing grass was uniform and the shrubs to either side, not being able to put down roots directly on it, defined between their two edge rows a straight course.

Terl took another look around. There were some cattle, a small herd of horses in the distance. Nothing worth shooting—since no Psychlo could eat meat of that metabolism—nothing dangerous enough to offer sport. It was luxurious to have time to think about hunting and even to be equipped for it—and even more luxurious not to do it! He had a bigger game going anyway.

He dropped down into the driver's seat and punched the buttons to close the top. The unbreathable air exhausted from the cab and was replaced by proper gas. He took off his face mask, contrary to regulations, and dropped it on the gunner's seat. The purple interior was a relief to his nerves.

This confounded planet! It even looked bad through the purple tint of the windscreens.

He glanced again at the map. Now was the time for some luck. He knew he couldn't go up into the mountains themselves due to the uranium the recon drones always indicated in that area. But the recon drones also reported that these man-things sometimes came down to the mountain foothills, which were safe enough.

Terl thought over his plans again. They were beautiful plans. Personal wealth, personal power. The recon drones had told him more than others knew. The scans had pointed out a vein of almost solid gold, uncovered by a landslide after Intergalactic surveys were finalized. A delicious, fabulously rich vein of gold in plain sight, a vein about which the company was ignorant—since the landslide was recent and Terl had destroyed the records. A joke on Zzt to propose no more recon drones over the area!

The uranium count in that area of the mountains was formidable and so no Psychlo could mine it. Even a few bits of uranium-dust could explode Psychlo breathe-gas.

Terl smiled at his own genius. All he needed was a man-thing and then a few more man-things. *They* could mine it, and to blast with uranium. Somehow he would get the gold off the planet and home, and he had ideas about how he could do that too. Then wealth and power! And no more of this place!

All the security chief had to do was keep others from suspecting what he was really doing, to advertise quite other reasons. But Terl was an expert at that.

If he were truly lucky he could catch a man-thing this side of the meadow. He did not have too much time to lie in wait. He *felt* lucky.

The sun was very low, thanks to his late start. He'd lie up in that man-city for the night, sleeping in the car.

He sent the Mark II skimming along the ancient highway

— 10 —

A skyline!

Jonnie Goodboy Tyler pulled up with a yank so sudden he startled Windsplitter into a rear.

There it was, straight east. It wasn't hills or mountains. It wasn't some trick of the eye. It was sharp and rectangular.

He had been so unconvinced.

When he had left the ancient ruin, he found a very easy way to travel. It was almost as if the ruin with the window had once had a broad path leading to it.

There were shrubs on the right and shrubs on the left, two rows about two hundred feet apart that dwindled eastward into the distance. Underfoot there was fairly even grass. You had to watch it a bit because there were shallow gullies in places. When you looked down between these little gullies, there was something gray-white. Jonnie had inspected it with care. He had gotten down and dug at the edges of such a crack and it seemed that the gray-white stuff was continuous.

Just like the inner walls of the ruin.

Maybe it was a wall of the ancients, fallen over sideways. But no, it would have cracked as it fell.

Outside the courthouse at home, level stones had been laid as pavement. But who wanted a pavement two hundred feet wide? And hours-journey long? For what?

This big path had not been used for a long time. If it was a path. It went between hillocks that had been sliced into and it went across water courses—although it was pretty irregular and broken in these.

He had been excited for a while, but then he got used to it and devoted his attention mainly to keeping Windsplitter from tripping in the little gullies.

When he was a little boy, one of the families had had a wheeled cart they hauled firewood in, and he had been told that once there had been a lot of carts, even one that was pulled by a mare. Well, you could sure roll a cart on this wide turf. And roll it fast and far.

But as to the Great Village, he was coming to believe as the afternoon wore on that somebody had probably seen that god house back there and multiplied it in his imagination.

And then suddenly there it was!

But was it?

He put Windsplitter up to a trot regardless of the little gullies. In the clear air the skyline wasn't coming his way very fast. It even appeared to be receding.

He stopped. Maybe it was a trick of the eye after all. But no, the lines it made were up and down and flat on top and there was an awful lot of it.

It wasn't hills or mountains. Only building sides could be that regular.

He started up again, more sedately, remembering now to be careful. And after a while he could see that he was getting closer.

The sun was coming down and he wasn't there yet. The prospect of entering that place in the dark was definitely not cheering. Who knew what it might be full of? Ghosts? Gods? People?

Monsters? Ah, no. Not monsters. They were just the stuff mamas frightened their kids to sleep with.

He pulled off the path where it crossed a stream and made camp. He warmed up some of his roasted pork and then cut it with one of the sharp, shiny things he had taken out of the window.

My, he marveled, imagine anything cutting like that. It would make life a real pleasure. You had to watch it not to cut your own fingers, as he had already done twice, slightly. Maybe you could bed the cutting edge in wood or something for a handle. Then you would really have something.

After supper he built up his fire to keep the wolves off—a couple were sitting over there now, amber-eyed in the reflected firelight and looking hungry.

"Run away," shouted Jonnie, "or I'll be wearing your hides.' But the wolves just sat there.

Windsplitter and the lead horse didn't want to go away from the fire. The wolves made them nervous. So Jonnie picked up a couple of rocks, fist-sized, from the nearby stream bed.

He wasn't interested in hunting wolves, but his horses had to find grass

He threw a pork bone about ten feet beyond the fire and in the direction of the wolves.

Big rangy things they were. One slunk forward, belly low, snarling to reach the pork bone. In a moment the wolf's attention would be fixed on the bone.

Jonnie's arm blurred. The far wolf caught the rock squarely between his eyes.

Jonnie's arm blurred again. The near wolf didn't jump in time and he too was a dead wolf.

Jonnie said to Windsplitter, "I got to do all the work, is that it?" And he walked over to the far wolf and hauled the carcass to the fire. Then he dragged the closer one in. Nope, neither one had a pelt worth taking at this time of the year. And they had ticks too.

"Go on and eat," he told the horses.

He built up the fire again, just in case the wolves had friends, and rolled up his robes. Tomorrow was going to be *the* day.

— 11 —

Jonnie approached the Great Village cautiously.

He was up before first light, and the yellow dawn found him in the outskirts of the place, peering, halting, looking closer at the strange sights, nervous.

Sand lay over everything, and grass and even scrub grew in the wide paths between the buildings.

He gave a start every time a rabbit or a rat came tearing out of the ancient structures, disturbed by his footfalls. Even though the hoofs were muffled by the grass and sand, the silence of the place was so intense that any disturbance of it seemed overloud.

He had never heard an echo before to notice it. The return of sound caused him a great deal of worry. For a little while he thought there must be another horse walking in the distance. But at last he worked it out.

He hit his wrist kill-club against the one in his belt and promptly heard the same sound repeated softly like a mockery. He waited but no further mock occurred. Then he hit the clubs together again and the same sound returned. He decided it didn't happen unless he did it first.

He looked about him. To both his left and his right were the tall remains of buildings, very tall indeed. Pitted by wind erosion, discolored by endless centuries of weather, they still stood, flat and even and imposing. Astonishing. Whoever could build such things? Gods, perhaps?

He eyed the massive size of the building blocks. No man could lift one by himself.

Jonnie sat his horse in the middle of what must have been the main path of the "Great Village." He frowned, straining to comprehend the building of such a place. Many men? But how could they reach so high?

He concentrated laboriously. Gradually he could conceive that if one built up steps of logs, and if many, many men put ropes around a block, and if they carried it up the steps and then took the steps away, they might have done it. Marvelous, dizzy, and dangerous. But it was possible.

Satisfied that it didn't need gods or monsters to have made this place, and therefore very relieved, he continued his exploration.

He wondered whether some odd kind of tree had grown along this path. He got down and looked at the stump of one. It was hard and jagged. It had been hollow and it was deep in the strange rock. It wasn't wood. It was a reddish metal, and when you scraped away the red powder, underneath was black. He looked up and down both sides of the wide path. The placing of these things was very precise. Although he couldn't figure out what they were for, it was obvious that, like buildings, they were placed objects.

The innumerable windows surrounded him, seeming to stare back at him. The morning sun had come now and it shone into those that faced it. Here and there were vast surfaces of the shiny stuff he had collected from the mound on the plain. It was not clear; it was whitish and bluish like the cataracts on an old man's eyes. But there were whole sheets of it in some places. He began to realize it was some kind of covering, perhaps to keep out the cold and heat and yet let in light. People at home sometimes did that, using the tissue of animal stomachs. But those who had built the Great Village had access to some kind of rock or hard substance that came in sheets. They must have been very clever people.

He saw a great yawning doorway ahead of him. The doors had fallen away and lay there half-buried in the sand. The inside of the building gaped darkly.

Jonnie walked his horse through the door and looked about in the dimness. Debris was scattered all about, rotted and decayed beyond identification. But a waist-high series of platforms stood; they were of a remarkably white stone that had bluish veins in it.

He leaned down from his horse and stared at the walls behind them. There were heavy, heavy doors set into it, two of them ajar, one of them wide open. Big wheels of still bright metal were inset into them.

Jonnie stepped to the platforms of white stone and dropped to the other side. Cautiously he approached the open niche.

There were shelves, and on the shelves, tangled with rotted remains of some kind of sacking, were mounds and mounds and mounds of discs. Some were a dull gray, almost tarnished away, but one pile was bright yellow.

Jonnie picked up a disc. It was as wide across as two fingernails and remarkably heavy. He turned it over and his eyes bugged.

Here was that bird again! Talons gripping a bundle of arrows. Hastily he pawed into the other mounds, looking at disc after disc. Most of them had a bird on one side. The face of a man, the faces of different men, were on the other.

Face of a *man!*

And some of them had women on them.

This was not a god symbol. This was a man symbol.

The bird with the arrows belonged to *man!*

The shock of it sent him reeling. He supported himself against the wall of the niche for minutes. He felt his head buzzing with the readjustment of ideas.

These doors to the niches were man-made. The Great Village was man-made. The doors of the tomb in the mountains were of similar material even if larger.

The tomb was not a god tomb. The mound out on the plain was also man-made.

Man had once built things—he was certain of it.

And it would take many men to make this Great Village. Therefore there must have been many men at one time.

He rode his horse out of the place in a deep daze. His most basic ideas and values had suffered severe shifts and it took a lot of getting used to. What legends were true? Which ones were false?

There was the legend of the Great Village and here it was. Man had obviously made it and had lived here in forgotten times.

Maybe the legend of god getting angry with man and wiping him out was true. And maybe it wasn't. Maybe it had just been a big storm.

He looked around the paths and buildings. There was no evidence of a storm: the buildings were still standing. Many even had that strange thin sheeting in the windows. There were no bodies about, but from a time so long ago, bones wouldn't last.

And then he saw a structure that had its doors firmly closed and sheets of metal fastened where the windows should be, and looking closer, he saw that a huge metal clamp sealed the place. He got down and inspected the clamp.

It was of a different age than the village: there was no tarnish on it at all. It was old, but not that old.

Something or someone at some time had pushed aside the sand in front of the doors. It was grass-grown sand but it had been disturbed.

Jonnie frowned. This building was not like the rest. It was in a fair state of preservation. Somebody had put metal sheets on the windows and the metal was quite different from any in the rest of the town: it showed no signs of corrosion.

Somebody had given this building special treatment.

He backed up to get a better overall view. It was indeed a different kind of building. Fewer windows. Block solid.

As an experienced tracker, Jonnie studied the time differences here. Long, long after the "village" had been abandoned, somebody had made access to this place, made a path, even dug a path in and out of the doors and then fastened the doors thoroughly. But even that had been a long time ago.

Curious, he scanned the front façade. One of the metal window covers was loose. It was higher than his head so he stood on his horse and pried at it. It gave a little bit. Encouraged, he shoved the handle of his kill-club into the crack, and with a protesting whine the cover suddenly sprang loose, startling Windsplitter, who moved off.

Jonnie held on to the ledge, his feet dangling.

He pulled himself up. The transparent sheeting under the cover was still in place. He took his kill-club and managed to hit it.

The crash and tinkle of the stuff as it fell was shockingly loud in this quiet place.

Experienced now with the cutting quality of this stuff, Jonnie hung on to the ledge with one arm and cleaned up the jagged bits from one side of the frame and dusted off the ledge.

He pulled himself through.

The place was so dark that it took quite a while to see anything. Light was coming through in thin cracks where other windows remained covered. At length his eyes adjusted and he dropped cautiously down into the huge room. Now that he was not blocking the window's light he could see quite well.

Dust and sand were only a filmy cover over things. There were tables and tables and tables and chairs and chairs and chairs, all marshaled in orderly rows. But they were not the interesting things.

Almost every wall was covered with shelving. The stacks of shelves even protruded out into the room. Somebody had covered them with a sheeting you could see through. Something lay under the sheeting on every shelf.

Jonnie approached cautiously. He carefully removed the fastenings to the sheeting and looked behind it.

Queer, thick rectangles stood on these shelves. Rows of them. At first he thought it was all one piece and then he found that one could remove a single rectangle. He took one off the shelf.

It almost fell to pieces in his hands!

Awkwardly, he juggled to hold it together and then succeeded. What a strange object! It was a box that wasn't a box. The covers slid sideways away from each other, enclosing a packet of thin, remarkably thin slices that had black marks on them, lots of little, tiny black marks all in orderly rows. What a strange object! How complicated!

He put the first one back on the shelf and took a second, smaller one. It too fell open.

Jonnie found himself staring at a *picture*.

It didn't have depth. At first it seemed to, but his finger told him it was just a flat plane. The object there was a big red circle, much bigger than a strawberry, much smoother. It had a stem. And alongside it there was a black tent with a crossbar in the middle of it.

He turned the sheet. There was a picture of a bee. No bee was ever that big, but this was certainly a bee. It too looked three-dimensional until his finger told him it wasn't. And a black thing beside it had two bulges on it.

Jonnie turned another sheet. There was a cat—a small cat, to be sure, but it was definitely a cat. And it had a curved black thing beside it like a new moon.

A few pages later there was a picture of a fox. And beside it was a black pole with two flags coming off it.

Suddenly a quiver went through Jonnie. He held his breath. He grabbed the first object he had taken and pried it open again. There was the tent. There was the bee's black mark. Yes—and there was the pole with two flags.

He held the two rectangles, his head in a whirl. He stared at them.

There was a meaning here. Foxes? Bees? Cats? Tents, bulges, new moons?

These things had meanings in them!

But about what? Animals? Weather?

He could sort all that out later. He crowded the two rectangles into his belt pouch. Anything that was connected to weather and animals had value. Rectangles with meaning in them. The idea made bright lights pop in your skull.

He replaced the protective sheet, went back out the window, replaced the metal covering as well as he could, and whistled Windsplitter over, dropping down to the horse's back.

Jonnie looked around him expansively. Who knew what things of enormous value were in the Great Village? He felt rich, excited.

There was no reason at all for his people to stay cooped up there in the mountains. Here was shelter and to spare. Here was firewood growing in the streets. Here were rooms and rooms and rooms!

And come to think of it, he felt better since he had been away from the mountain meadow. Better physically.

And it hadn't taken a year—actually just a few days.

He gathered up the lead rope of his pack horse and they trotted briskly along the wide paths toward the eastern part of the Great Village.

Although his eyes were busy taking it all in, his mind was engrossed in organizing a migration from the mountains down to this place: what he would have to pick up for evidence to convince them; what he was going to say to Staffor; how they could transport their goods . . . maybe build a cart? Maybe there were carts right here in the Great Village. He could round up some horses. These piles of red dust he saw along either side of the wide paths from time to time might once have been carts of a sort. It was hard to figure out what shape they had really had, they were so caved in. The impression of a wheel. Sheets of translucent rock. No, they hadn't been horse carts, or had they? He began to look at such objects more closely.

And then he saw the insect.

— 12 —

It was very bright daylight now. And there it sat. There could be no mistaking it.

Alien.

Surely it must be an insect. Only cockroaches looked like that. Or beetles. No, cockroaches.

But there were no cockroaches that big. Not thirty feet long and ten feet high and maybe twelve feet side to side.

A horrible brown color. And smooth.

Jonnie had stopped, the lead horse bunched up behind. The thing was sitting squarely in the middle of the wide path. It seemed to have two eyes in front, slitted. There was nothing like this on the plains or in the mountains, and he had seen nothing like it in the Great Village center. It looked new, with very little dust on it, and shiny.

He felt it was alive. There was something about it. Yes, alive. Not inanimate metal but a living thing. Then he saw what made him think so.

There had been a slight rocking motion. Something moved behind the slitted eyes.

Jonnie, making no sudden movements, turned Windsplitter and, pulling the lead horse, began to move away in the direction from which he had approached. He had already noted that these paths were mostly rectangular and that you could go all the way around a group of buildings and come back to the same place.

There was open country to the east, not very far. He would go down a side path and then circle back and get out into the plains. Hopefully he could outrun it. If it moved.

There was an earsplitting roar!

Jonnie glanced back in terror. The thing rose up three feet above the ground. Dust flew from below it. It began to inch forward. It was alive!

He put Windsplitter into a gallop straight down the street. He passed one corner path, two. The thing was falling behind. It was now two corners back.

He swerved Windsplitter up a side path, yanking the lead horse with him. They reached another corner and again he turned. Up ahead were two tall buildings. He'd keep going and reach the open country. He'd make it.

And then suddenly there was a sheet of flame. Ahead of him the right-hand building exploded apart. Its top slid slowly down and into the street ahead, blocking it.

Spattered with dust, Jonnie hauled up short.

He could hear the roaring of the thing somewhere beyond the rubble. He listened, holding his breath. The position of the roar was changing. It was shifting to the right.

He traced it with his ears. It was going on down the other street. Now it was level with him. Now it was getting behind him.

The thing had somehow blocked the street ahead of him and then gone on, planning to come up behind him.

He was trapped.

Jonnie looked at the smoking mound of fresh rubble ahead of him. It rose twenty feet above the pavement, a steep barricade.

There was no panic in him now. He slowed the hard pounding of his heart. The thing to do was wait until the monster was right in the street behind him—then go over that barricade.

He sidled Windsplitter back to get a good run.

The thing was roaring down the side path behind him. Now it was turning. He glanced back. There it was, wisps of smoke coming out of its nostrils.

Jonnie put the heel to Windsplitter. He yanked on the lead rope.

"EEYAH!" shouted Jonnie.

The horses sprinted at the barricade. Rough and full of loose stones. Dangerous.

Up they scrambled. Rubble slid. Pray the gods no broken legs.

Up they went.

They hit the top. One glance back showed the thing rolling up to the very bottom of the barricade.

Jonnie sent the horses down in a turmoil of tumbling debris.

They hit the street before them at a run and kept running.

The walls racketed with the thunder of their run. Jonnie swerved through a checkerboard of paths, edging to the open country.

He could not hear the roaring thing now over the powerful thud of the running hoofs.

Further and further. The buildings were thinning. He saw open country between two structures to his right and skidded down off the embankment and raced for freedom.

As soon as he had free running space everywhere but toward the town, he slowed.

Windsplitter and the lead horse were blowing and puffing. He walked them until they caught their breath, casting his eyes restlessly up and down the edges of the town behind them.

Then he caught the roaring again. He strained his eyes, watching.

There it was!

It slid out from among the buildings and started straight toward him.

He put the horses up to a trot.

The thing was closing the distance.

He put the horses up to a run.

The thing not only closed the distance but started to pass him.

Jonnie swerved at right angles.

The thing banked into a turn and flashed by him, went well ahead, turned and blocked his way.

Jonnie pulled up. There it was, ugly, roaring, gleaming.

He turned around and began to run away from it.

It let out a blasting roar, scorched by him and again stopped, blocking his way.

Jonnie's face tightened into determination.

He took his biggest kill-club from his belt. He put the thong solidly on his wrist. He cast off the lead horse.

Walking Windsplitter, he went up ahead of the thing. It didn't move. He went about a hundred feet in front of the thing. It didn't move. He carefully spotted the position of a slitted eye.

He began to whirl the kill-club. It swooshed in the air.

He put a heel to Windsplitter and they raced straight at the thing.

The kill-club, carried with the full speed of the running horse, whooshed down straight at the slitted eye.

The crash of impact was deafening.

Jonnie slowed beyond the thing. It had not moved.

He trotted Windsplitter back to the original position, a hundred feet in front of the thing. He turned and made ready for a second run.

The lead horse came up behind him to its habitual place. Jonnie glanced at it and then back at the thing. He calculated the distance and the run to strike at the other slitted eye.

He touched a heel. Windsplitter plunged forward.

And then a great gout of yellow bloomed out from between the eyes. Jonnie was struck a blow like all the winds of Highpeak rolled into one.

Windsplitter caught the full force of it. Up into the air went horse and rider. Down they came with a shuddering crash against the earth.

— 13 —

Terl didn't know what he was looking at.

He had bunked down in the car in the outskirts. He had the old Chinko map of the ancient city, but he had no curiosity about it.

With a few shots of kerbango, he had eased himself off into sleep, intending to be gone with the dawn, through the city and into the mountains. Senseless, even risky, to go on in the dark.

The car, however, had grown hot with the morning sun before he awoke. And now he stared out at an odd thing in the street before him. Maybe it had been the footfalls that had awakened him.

He didn't know what it was. He had seen horses—they were always falling down mine shafts. But he had never before seen a horse with two heads.

That's right. Two heads. One in front and one in the middle.

And a second animal of similar sort behind. Only this one only had a second body in the middle, as if the second head was bent down out of sight.

He batted his eyebones. He shifted over into the driver's seat and stared more intently through the armored windshield.

The two beasts had now turned around and were walking the other way, so Terl started up and began to follow.

It became apparent to him at once that the beasts knew he was after them. He took a hasty look at his ancient street map, thinking he could flash around a couple of blocks and head them off.

But instead it was the beasts who turned.

Terl saw they would dead-end and knew they would circle a block. It was elementary indeed to handle that.

He glanced again at his map and spotted the right buildings to make a barricade.

The firepower of the old Mark II was not very heavy but it was surely enough for that. He adjusted the force lever with a fumbling and inexperienced paw and steered the tank into position. He hit thc fire button.

The resulting explosion was extremely satisfactory. A whole building tipped over to make a barricade.

He jockeyed his throttle and wheeled around and went down the street, turned, and sure enough! There they were. He had his quarry trapped.

Then he sat with slack jawbones to see the beasts go straight up over the smoking rubble and vanish from view.

Terl sat there for a minute or two. Was this any part of what he was trying to accomplish? He was puzzled by the beasts but they didn't have anything to do with the business he was in.

Oh, well. He had lots of time, and hunting was hunting after all. He pushed a button and fired off an antennae capsule set to hover three hundred feet up and then turned on his picture screen.

Sure enough, there were the beasts, tearing along, zigzagging around blocks. He watched their progress while he ate some breakfast. That done, he took a small shot of kerbango, engaged the drive train, and following the picture was soon out in open country with his quarry in plain sight.

He raced around in front and blocked them. They turned. He did it again.

What were they? The second beast still had his head down, but the one in the lead definitely had two heads. Terl decided he had better not talk about this in the recreation room They'd roast him.

He watched with curiosity when the beast in the front stopped, took a stick out of his belt, and began a run at him. His curiosity turned to amazement. The thing was going to attack him. Incredible!

The crash of the club against the windshield was deafening. His earbones rang with the assault. And that wasn't all. There was an immediate atmosphere sizzle.

A wave of dizziness hit Terl. Bright lights popped in his skull. Air! Air was getting into the cab!

This old Mark II had seen better days. The supposedly armored windscreen had come loose in its mounts. Terl gaped at it in disbelief. The side gasket had given way!

He panicked. Then his eye caught the sign about face masks and he hastily snatched the mask and flask of breathe-gas off the gunner's seat and snapped it over his face, opening the valve. He inhaled deeply and the dizziness lessened. He took three deep breaths to clean the damned air out of his lungs.

Terl stared anew at the strange beast. It was lining up for another run!

His paws fumbled with the firepower. He wanted no recoil of the blast blowing back through the opened windscreen and he pulled the force lever low to "stun." He hoped it was enough.

The beast started the run. Terl hit the fire button.

It was enough all right. The ions sizzled and glared. The beasts were slammed back, lifted clean off the ground. They fell.

Terl watched intently to make sure they kept on lying where they had fallen. Good! They did.

He let out a shuddering sigh into his mask, winding down. And then he sat up straight in new amazement. He had thought, when they were hit, that he was dealing with two four-legged beasts. But lying on the ground they had come apart!

Terl swung a side door wide and crawled out. He checked his belt gun and then rumbled over to the game he had hit.

Three beasts, maybe four!

The two four-legged beasts were two. On the one behind, a bundle of something had fallen apart. That maybe made three. The nearer one definitely was two different beasts.

What a confusion!

He shook his head, trying to clear it. The effects of air were not wearing off fast enough: little bright sparks were still popping in front of his eyes.

He lumbered over to the more distant one, pushing the tall grass away. It was a horse. He had seen plenty of horses; the plains were full of them. But this horse had had a bundle tied on its back. Simple as that. The bundle had come loose. He kicked it. It wasn't anything alive, just some skins, some animal hides, and nonsense bits of other things.

He walked back toward the tank through the high grass.

The other thing was also a horse. And over to the right where it had fallen clear . . .

Terl pushed back the grass. Well, luck of the gold nebula! It was a *man*.

The Psychlo turned the man over. What a small, puny body! Hair on the face and head but nowhere else. Two arms, two legs. White-brown skin.

Terl was unwilling to admit that Char's description fitted. In fact, he resented the fact that it did come close and promptly rejected it.

The chest was moving—only slightly, true—but it was still alive. Terl felt fortunate indeed. His excursion was successful without his even going up into the mountains.

He picked the man up with one paw and went back to the tank, throwing the man into the gunner's seat, which engulfed it. Then he set to work repairing the windscreen gasket with some permastick. The whole side of the glass had been dislodged, and although the glass itself was not even scratched, that had been quite a blow. He looked down at the small body swallowed in the seat. A fluke. It was the age of this tank, the brittleness of its gaskets. Sure was a ratty car; he'd find something wrong and put it in Zzt's records—misplaced parts or something. He went over the other gaskets, the doors, and the other screen. They seemed all right, if brittle. Well, he wasn't going underwater and there would surely be no more attacks from things like that.

Terl stood up on the driver's seat and looked all around the horizon. All clear. No more of these beasts.

He banged down the top and settled himself. His paw hit the compression change, and the hiss of air exhausting from the cab and the gurgle of breathe-gas entering was welcome. His face mask was sweaty in the growing heat of the day and he hated the thing. Oh, for a proper-atmosphere planet, a planet with right gravity, with purple trees—

The man-thing went into a sudden convulsion.

Terl drew back, alarmed. It was turning blue and jerking about. The last thing he wanted was a raving mad animal inside the cab.

Hastily he adjusted his face mask, reversed the compression, and kicked open the side door. With one bat of his paw he knocked the thing back out onto the grass.

Terl sat there watching it. He was afraid his plans were going up in a puff. The thing must have been more heavily affected by the stun blast than he knew. Crap, they were weak!

He opened the cab top and looked over at one of the horses.

He could see its sides moving. It was breathing and wasn't in any convulsion. It was even recovering. Well, a horse was a horse, and a man might be . . .

He suddenly got it. The man-thing couldn't breathe breathe-gas. The bluish color was fading; the convulsions had stopped. The chest was panting as the thing gulped in air.

That gave Terl a problem. Blast if he was going to ride back to the minesite in a face mask.

He got out of the car and went to the farther horse. It was recovering, too. The sacks were lying near it. Terl rummaged through one and came up with some thongs.

He went back and picked up the man-thing and slammed it up on top of the car. He arranged it so its arms stuck out to each side. Tying piece after piece of thong together he made a long rope. He tied one end to one wrist of the thing, passed the rope under the car—grunting a bit as he lifted it up to do so—and tied the other wrist. He yanked it good and tight. Then he pushed at the man-thing experimentally to see whether it would fall off.

Very good. He threw the sacks onto the gunner's seat and got in, closed up, and restarted the atmosphere change.

The nearest horse was lifting its head, struggling to get up. Aside from surface blood boils caused by the stun gun, it seemed to be all right, which meant that the man-thing would probably recover.

Terl stretched his jawbones in a grin. Well, it was coming out all right after all.

He started up the car, turned it, and headed back toward the minesite.

■

PART 2

— 1 —

Terl was all efficiency, great plans bubbling in his cavernous skull.

The old Chinkos had had a sort of zoo outside the compound, and despite the years that had intervened since the Chinkos were terminated here, the cages were still there.

There was one in particular that was just right. It had a dirt floor and a cement pool, and netting of heavy mesh strung all around it. They had had some bears there that they said they were studying, and although the bears had died after a while, they had never escaped.

Terl dumped the new beast into the cage. The thing was still only semiconscious, getting over the shock of breathe-gas most likely. Terl looked at it lying there and then looked around. This had to be just right, all precautions taken.

The cage door had a lock on it. It was open to the sky and there was no netting over the top—what bear could climb a thirty-foot set of bars?

But there was a possibility that this new beast might tamper with the cage door. It wasn't probable. But the door didn't have a good lock on it.

Terl had dumped the bags in the cage, having no place else to put them. And the long thong rope he had used was lying on the bags.

He decided it would be wise to tie the beast up. He passed the thong around the neck of the thing and tied it there with a simple rigger knot and tied the other end to a bar.

He stood back and checked things again. It was fine. He went out and closed the cage door. He'd have to put a better lock on it. But it would do just now.

Satisfied with himself, Terl ran the car into the garage and went to his office.

There was not much to do. A few dispatches, just forms, no emergencies. Terl finished up and sat back. What a dull place. Ah, well, he had started wheels rolling to get off it, to get back home.

He decided he had better go out and see how the man-thing was getting along. He picked up his breathe-mask, put a new cartridge into it, and went out through the offices. There were a lot of empty desks these days. There were only three secretarial-type Psychlos there, and they didn't pay much attention to him.

Outside the compound, he reached the gate of the cage. He stopped, his eyebones rattling.

The thing was clear over to the gate!

He went in with a growl, picked the thing up, and put it into its original place.

It had untied the knot.

Terl looked at it. Plainly it was terrified of him. And why not? It only came up to his belt buckle and was about a tenth of his weight.

Terl put the thong back around its neck. Being a mining company worker, accustomed to rigs and slings, Terl knew his knots. So this time he tied a double-rigger knot. That would hold it!

Cheerful once more, Terl went to the garage and got a water hose and began to wash down the Mark II. As he worked, he turned over various plans and approaches in his head. They all depended on that man-thing out there.

On a sudden hunch, he went back outside to look into the cage. The thing was standing inside the door!

Terl crossly barged in, carried it back to its original position, and stared at the rope. It had untied a double-rigger knot.

With fast-working paws, Terl fixed that. He put the rope around its neck and tied it with a bucket-hoist knot.

The thing looked at him. It was making some funny noises as if it could talk.

Terl walked out, fastened the door, and got out of sight. He wasn't a security chief for nothing. From a vantage point behind a building, he levered his face mask glass to telephoto and observed.

The thing, in no time at all, untied the complex bucket-hoist knot!

Terl rumbled back before it could get to the door. He went in, plucked the thing up, and put it back on the far side of the cage.

He wound the rope around and around its neck and then tied it with a double-bucket knot so complex that only a veteran rigger could loosen it.

Once more he went off to an unseen distance.

Again believing itself unobserved, what was the thing doing now?

It reached into a pouch it was wearing, took out something bright, and cut the rope!

Terl rumbled off to the garage and rummaged about through centuries of castoffs and debris until he found a piece of flexirope, a welding torch, a welding power cartridge, and a short strip of metal.

When he got back, the thing was over by the door again, trying to climb the thirty-foot bars.

Terl did a very thorough job. He made a collar out of the metal and welded it hotly around the neck. He welded the flexirope to the collar and welded the other end into a ring, hooking the ring over a bar thirty feet above the dirt floor of the cage.

He stood back. The thing was grimacing and trying to hold the collar away from its neck, for it was still hot.

That'll hold it, Terl told himself.

But he hadn't finished. He wasn't a security chief for nothing. He went back to his office storeroom and broke out two button cameras, checked them, and switched them to the wavelength of his office viewer.

Then he went back to the cage and put one button camera way up in the bars, pointing down, and put the other one out at a distance where it could view the exterior.

The thing was pointing at its mouth and making sounds. Who knew what that meant?

Only now did Terl feel relaxed.

That night he sat smugly in the employee recreation room, responding to no questions, quietly drinking his kerbango in a very self-satisfied way.

— 2 —

Jonnie Goodboy Tyler stared in despair at his packs across the yard.

The sun was hot.

The collar on his burned neck hurt.

His throat was parched with thirst. And he felt hungry.

In those packs, just inside the cage door, there was a pig bladder of water. There was some cooked pork, if it hadn't spoiled. And there were hides he could rig for shade.

At first he had just been trying to get out.

The very idea of being caged made him feel ill. Sicker even than the lack of water and food.

It was all so unknown. The last he really remembered was starting to charge the insect and being blown into the air. Then this. No, wait. There was something after he was first stunned.

He had started to come to, lying on something soft and smooth. He had seemed to be inside the insect. He had seen a huge *something* next to him. And then there was a sensation like breathing fire straight into his lungs that pulled every nerve short and threw him into a convulsion.

There was another glimpse of an occurrence. He had flickeringly regained consciousness for a few moments. He seemed to be tied to the top of the insect speeding across the plain. And then the back of his head bumped and the next he knew he was in here—in this cage!

He put it together. He had hurt the insect, but not fatally. It had eaten him, but then spit him up. It had carried him on its back to its lair.

But the real shock was the monster.

It was true, he knew now, that he had always been "too smart." He had doubted his elders. He had doubted the Great Village and there it had been. He had doubted the monsters and here one was.

When he had come to and found himself looking up at that thing, his head had reeled. He felt himself literally bending the bars behind him to get away. A monster!

Eight or nine feet tall, maybe more. About three and a half feet wide. Two arms. Two legs. A shiny substance for a face and a long tube from the chin down to the chest. Glowing amber eyes behind the shiny front plate.

The ground shook as it approached. A thousand pounds? Maybe more.

Huge booted feet dented the earth.

And it had furry paws and long talons.

He had been certain it was going to eat him right then. But it hadn't. It had tied him up like a dog.

There was something strange about this monster's perceptions. Every time he had tried to get untied and out of the cage, the monster had shown up again. As though it could see when it wasn't around to see.

Possibly those little spheres had had something to do with it. The monster held them in its paws like small detachable eyes. One was up there now, glittering, way up in the corner of the cage. Like a little eye. The other one was out there stuck onto a nearby building side.

But the monster had caught him trying to get out before it planted those eyes.

What was this place? There was a constant rumble from somewhere, a muted roar similar to the one the insect had made. The thought of more of those insects chilled him.

There was a big stone basin in the middle of the cage, a few feet deep with steps up one side. Lots of sand was in the bottom of it. A grave? A place to roast meat? No, there were no charred sticks or ashes in it.

So there were monsters. When he stood in front of it, his face was just above the level of its belt buckle. Belt buckle? Yes, a shiny thing that held a belt together. It suddenly dawned on Jonnie that the monster was wearing a covering that wasn't its own skin. A slippery, shiny purple substance. It wasn't its own hide. Like clothes you'd cut out of a hide. Pants. A coat. A collar. It wore clothes.

Ornaments on the collar. And a device of some sort on the belt buckle. That device was stamped on his mind's eye, right now. It was a picture of ground on which stood small square blocks. Vertical shafts were going up from the square blocks. Out of the shafts seemed to be coming clouds of smoke, and smoke in curls lay all over the top of the picture. The idea of clouds of smoke stirred some memory in him, but he was too hungry and too thirsty and too hot to wrestle with it.

The ground under him began to shake in measured tread. He knew what this was.

The monster came to the door. It was carrying something. It came in and loomed over him. It threw down into the dirt some soft, gooey sticks of something. Then it just stood there.

Jonnie looked at the sticks. They weren't like anything he had ever seen.

The monster made motions, pointing from the sticks to his face. That failing, the monster took up a stick and squashed it against Jonnie's mouth, saying something in a rumbling roaring voice. A command.

Jonnie got it. This was supposed to be food.

He worked a bit of it around in his mouth and then swallowed it.

Abruptly and immediately he was violently ill. He felt like his whole stomach was going to rush back out of his mouth. Before he could control them, his limbs went into the beginning of a convulsion.

He spat. Too thirsty to have much saliva, he tried to get rid of the stuff, all of it, every bit of it, every tiny piece of the acid taste of it.

The monster just backed up and stood there staring at him.

"Water," pleaded Jonnie, getting control of his shaking limbs and voice. "Please. Water." Anything to wash this horrible stuff out.

He pointed to his mouth. "Water."

The monster just went on standing there. The eyes back of the faceplate were slitted, glowing with an eerie fire.

Jonnie composed himself stoically. It was wrong to look weak and beg. There was such a thing as pride. He drew his face into stillness.

The monster leaned over and checked the collar and the flexirope, turned around and went back out, closed the gate with a firm clang, wired it shut and left.

The evening shadows were growing long.

Jonnie looked at his packs by the gate. They might as well be on the top of Highpeak!

A cloak of misery settled over him. He had to assume Windsplitter was gravely injured or dead. And he had to assume that in a few days he himself probably would die of thirst or hunger.

Twilight came.

And then with a shock he realized Chrissie's promise to find him would wind up in her certain death. He caved in.

The little bright eye, up in the corner of the cage, stared down unwinkingly.

— 3 —

The following day, Terl probed around the disused quarters of the old Chinkos.

It was unpleasant work. The quarters were outside the pressurized Psychlo domes of the minesite and he had to wear a breathe-mask. The Chinkos were air-breathers. And while the quarters had been sealed off, a few hundred years of neglect and weather leaks had left their marks.

There were rows and rows of bookcases. Lines and lines of filing cabinets full of notes. Old scarred desks, rickety and frail to begin with, collapsing into themselves. Piles of junk in lockers. And everything filmed over with white dust. Good thing he didn't have to breathe it.

What funny beings the Chinkos had been. They were the Intergalactic Mining Company's answer to some protests by more warlike and able worlds that mining was wrecking planetary ecologies. And, the company being plush and profitable at that time, some knothead of a director in Intergalactic's main office had created the culture and ethnology department, or C and E. Maybe it was originally named the ecological department, but Chinkos could paint, and some Intergalactic director's wear-the-claws wife had begun to make a private fortune selling Chinko work on other planets and got the name changed. There was very little that didn't show up in the secret files of the security department.

It was the strike the Chinkos had invented, not the corruption, that caused the final wipeout. Corruption at director level was very paws-off for security. A strike was not.

But the Chinkos here had been gone long before that, and this place looked it. What, after all, was worth culturing on this planet? There weren't enough indigenous populations left to bother with. And who had cared anyway? But like any bureaucracy, the Chinkos had been busy. Look at those hundreds of yards of cabinets and books.

Terl was looking for a manual on the feeding habits of man. Surely these busy Chinkos had studied that.

He pawed and pawed. He opened and flipped hundreds of indexes. He got down and poked into lockers. And while he got a very good idea of what there was in these rambling offices and lockers, he couldn't find one single thing about what man ate. He found what bears ate. He found what mountain goats ate. He even found a treatise, scholarly composed, printed and reeking with wasted expense, on what some beast known as a "whale" ate, a treatise that ended up laughably enough with the fact that the beast was totally extinct.

Terl stood in the middle of the place, disgusted. No wonder the company had phased out C and E on Earth. Imagine roaring around, burning up fuel, keeping a whole book-manufacturing plant steaming like a digger shovel, wearing out eyesight. . . .

It wasn't all in vain, though. He had learned from the aged and yellowed map he now gripped in his hand that there were a few other groups of men left on this planet. At least there had been a few hundred years ago.

Some were in a place the Chinkos called "Alps." Several dozen, in fact. There had been about fifteen up in the ice belt the Chinkos called "North Pole" and "Canada." There had been an unestimated number at a place called "Scotland" and there had been some in "Scandinavia." And also in a place called "Colorado."

This was the first time he had seen the Chinko name for this central minesite area. "Colorado." He looked at the map with some amusement. "Rocky Mountains." "Pike's Peak." Funny Chinko names. The Chinkos always did their work in painfully severe Psychlo, faithful to their ore. But they had had funny imaginations.

This was getting him no place, however, although it was good to know, for the sake of his planning, that there had been a few more men around.

He would have to rely on what he should have relied on in the first place—security. The techniques of security. He would put them to work.

He walked out and closed the door behind him and stared around at this non-Psychlo alien world. The old Chinko offices, barracks, and zoo were up on the high hill back of the minesite. Close by but higher. The arrogant bastards. One could see all around from this place. One could see the ore transshipment platform as well as the freighter assembly field; the place didn't look very busy down there. Intergalactic would be sending some sizzlers down the line unless quotas were met. He hoped he wouldn't have too many investigations ordered by the home office.

Blue sky. Yellow sun. Green trees. And the wind that tugged at him full of air.

How he hated this place.

The thought of staying made him grit his fangs.

Well, what do you expect in an alien world?

He'd finish that investigation ordered about a lost tractor and then put his tried-and-true security technology to work on that man-thing.

That was the only way out of this hellhole.

— 4 —

Jonnie watched the monster.

Thirsty, hungry, and with no hope, he felt adrift in a sea of unknowns.

The thing had come into the cage, its footsteps shaking the earth, and had stood there for some time just looking at him, small glints of light in its amber eyes. Then it had begun to putter around.

Right now it was testing the bars, shaking them, apparently verifying that they were firm. Satisfied, it rumbled all around the perimeter inspecting the dirt.

It stood for a while looking at the sticks it had tried to make Jonnie eat. Jonnie had pushed them as far away as possible since they had a bad, pungent smell. The monster counted them. Aha! It could count.

It spent some time examining the collar and rope. And then it did a very strange thing. It unhooked the rope's far end from the bar top. Jonnie held his breath. Maybe he could get to his packs.

But the monster now hooked the rope on a nearby bar. He dropped a loop over the bar indifferently and then moved off to the door.

It spent some time at the door, rewinding the wires that kept it closed, and did not seem to notice that when it turned its back on the door, one of the wires sprang free.

The monster rumbled off toward the compound and disappeared.

Lightheaded with thirst and hunger, Jonnie felt he was having delusions. He was afraid to hope. But there it was: the rope could be removed, and the gate fastening might be loose enough to open.

He made very sure the monster was really gone.

Then he acted.

With a flip of the rope he got the far end off the bar.

Hastily he wrapped the length around his body to get it out of his way and tucked the end into his belt.

He dove for his packs.

With shaking hands he ripped them open. Some of his hope died. The water bladder had burst, probably from the earlier impact, and there was only dampness there. The pork, wrapped in hide that retained the sun's heat, was very spoiled, and he knew better than to eat it.

He looked at the door. He would try.

Grabbing a kill-club and rope from the pack and checking his belt pouch for flints, Jonnie crept to the door.

No sign of the monster.

The wires of the fastening were awfully big. But age had weakened them. Even so they tore and bruised his hands as he feverishly sought to open them.

Then they were open!

He pushed against the door.

In seconds he was sprinting through the shrubs and gullies to the northwest.

Keeping low, taking advantage of every bit of cover so as to remain hidden from the compound, he nevertheless went fast.

He had to find water. His tongue was swollen, his lips cracked.

He had to find food. He felt the lightheaded unreality that came with the beginnings of starvation.

Then he had to get back to the mountains. He had to stop Chrissie.

Jonnie went a mile. He examined his backtrail. Nothing. He listened. No sound of the insect, no feel of monster feet shaking the earth.

He ran two miles. He stopped and listened again. Still nothing. Hope flared within him.

Ahead he could see greenery, a patch jutting out of a gully, a sign of water.

His breath hoarse and rattling in his chest, he made the edge of the gully.

No scene could be more heartwarming. A speck of blue and white. The cheerful burble of a small brook running through the trees.

Jonnie lunged forward and a moment later plunged his head into the incalculably precious water.

He knew better than to drink too much. He just kept rinsing his mouth. For minutes he plunged his head and chest in and out of the stream, letting the water soak in.

Gone was the taste of that terrible gooey stick. The freshness and cleanness of the brook were almost as joyful as its wetness.

He drank a few cautious swallows and then sank back, catching his breath. The day looked brighter.

The backtrail was still quiet. The monster might not discover he was gone for hours. Hope surged again.

Far off to the northwest, just a little bit above the curve of the plain, were the mountains. Home.

Jonnie looked around him. There was an old rickety shack on the other side of the stream bed, the roof sunk down to its foundation.

Food was his concern now.

He took more swallows of water and stood up. He hefted his kill-club and walked through the stream toward the ancient shack.

While running, he had seen no game. Perhaps it was cleared out in the vicinity of the compound. But he didn't need big game. A rabbit would do. He had better take care of this fast and keep going.

Something moved in the shack. He crept forward, silent.

In a scurry several big rats raced out of the shack. Jonnie had started his throw and then stopped. Only in the dreariest of a starving winter would one eat rats.

But he had no time and he saw no rabbits.

He picked up a rock and threw it against the shack. Two more rats streamed out and he threw his kill-club straight and true.

A moment later he was holding a dead rat in his hand, a big one.

Did he dare light a fire? No, no time for that. Raw rat? Ugh.

He took a piece of the sharp, clear stuff from his pouch and stepped back to the stream. He cleaned and washed the rat.

Hunger or no hunger, it took some doing to bite into the raw rat meat. Almost gagging, he chewed and swallowed. Well, it was food.

He ate very slowly so that he wouldn't get any sicker than he felt at eating raw rat.

Then he drank some more water.

He wrapped a last piece of the rat in a scrap of hide and put it in his pouch. He kicked some sand over the debris he had left.

He stood up straight and looked at the distant mountains. He took a deep breath, bracing himself to start again on his run.

There was a low whistle in the air and something fell over him.

He rolled.

It was a net.

He couldn't get free.

The more he tried to get out of it, the more tangled up he became. He stared wildly around.

Through an opening he saw the truth.

The monster, without haste, was moving forward out of the trees, taking in the slack of the rope to which the net was attached.

The thing exhibited no emotion. It moved as though it had all the time in the world.

It wrapped Jonnie up in the net and tucked the whole bundle under its arm and then began to rumble along back toward the compound.

— 5 —

Terl, fiddling with forms at his desk, felt very cheerful.

Things were working out fine, just fine. Security techniques were always best. Always. He now knew exactly what he had wanted to know: the thing drank water and drank it by plunging its head and shoulders into a stream or pond. And more importantly, it ate raw rat.

This made things very easy. If there was any animal available near the compound, it was rat.

He guessed he could teach the old Chinkos a thing or two. It was elementary to let the man-thing loose and elementary to keep him under surveillance with a flying scope. It was, of course, a little trying to be out in the open wearing a breathe-mask and yet make speed over the ground. That man-thing didn't run very fast compared to a Psychlo, but it had been a bit of an exertion. It was hard to exert oneself while wearing a breathe-mask.

But he hadn't lost his skill in casting nets, old-fashioned though it might be. He hadn't wanted to use a stun gun again: the thing seemed frail and went into convulsions.

Well, he was learning.

He began to wonder how many raw rats a day the thing had to consume. But he could find that out easily.

He looked with boredom at the report before him. The lost tractor had been found along with its Psychlo driver at the bottom of a two-mile-deep mine shaft. They ate up a lot of personnel these days. There'd be a yowl from the main office about replacement costs. Then he cheered up. This fitted very well into his plans.

He checked around to make sure he had no more work to do and put his desk in order for the end of day.

Terl went over to a cabinet and took out the smallest blast gun he could find. He put a charge cartridge in it and set it to minimum power.

He took some rags and cleaned up his face mask and put a new cartridge in it.

Then he went outside.

Not a hundred yards north of the compound he saw his first rat. With the accuracy that had won him an honored place on his school shoot team, even though the thing was in streaking motion, he blew its head off.

Fifty feet farther, another rat leaped out of a culvert and he decapitated it in midair. He paced off the distance. Forty-two Psychlo paces. No, he hadn't lost his touch. Silly things to be hunting, but it still took a master's touch.

Two. That would be good enough to start with.

Terl looked around at the hateful day. Yellow, blue, and green. Well, he'd get quit of this.

Feeling very cheerful, he rumbled up the hill to the old zoo.

His mouthbones stretched in a grin. There was the man-thing crouched down at the far side of the cage, glaring at him. *Glaring* at him? Yes, it was true. It was the first time Terl had noticed it had emotions.

And what else had it been doing?

It had gotten to the packs—he remembered the thing clutching at them when he had returned it to the cage yesterday—and it was now sitting on them. It had been doing something else. It had been looking down at a couple of books. Books? Now where the crap nebula had it gotten books? Didn't seem possible it could have gotten into the old Chinko quarters. The collar, the rope were all secure. He'd investigate that in due course. The thing was still here, which was what was important.

Terl advanced, smiling behind his mask. He held up the two dead rats and then tossed them to the man-thing.

It didn't jump hungrily at them. It seemed to withdraw. Well, gratitude wasn't something you found in animals. No matter. Terl wasn't after gratitude from this thing.

Terl went over to the old cement bear pool. It didn't seem to be cracked. He traced the piping. The piping seemed to be all right.

He went outside the cage and fumbled around in the undergrowth, looking for the valves, and finally found one. He turned it. Hard to do with a valve that old. He was afraid his great strength would just twist the top off.

From the nearby garage he got some penetrating oil and went back and worked the valve over. Finally he got it open. Nothing happened.

Terl traced the old water system to a tank the Chinkos had

built. He shook his head over the crudity of it. It had a pump but the charge cartridge was long expended. He freed up the pump and put a new cartridge in it. Intergalactic was never one for innovations, thank the stars. The cartridges the pump needed were the same ones still in use.

He got the pump whirring but no water came. Finally he found the pond. The old pipe was simply not in the water, so with one stamp of his boot he put it back in.

Up at the tank the water began to run in. And down in the cage the pool began to fill swiftly. Terl grinned to himself. A mining man could always handle fluids. And here too he hadn't lost his touch.

He went back into the cage. The big center pool was filling rapidly. It was muddy and swirling since it had been full of sand. But it was wet water!

The pool filled up to the top and slopped over, spilling across the floor of the cage.

The man-thing was hastily picking up its things and jamming them into the bars to escape the inundation.

Terl went back outside and shut off the valve. He let the tank on the hill fill and then shut that off.

The cage was practically awash. But the water was draining off through the bars. Good enough.

Terl slopped over to the man-thing. It was clinging to the bars to keep out of the water. It had the hides way up, jammed over the cross braces. To keep them dry?

It was holding on to the books with one hand.

Terl looked around. Everything was in order now. So he had better look into these books.

He started to take them out of its hand but it held on. With some impatience, Terl smashed at its wrist and caught the two books as they fell.

They were man-books.

Puzzled, Terl leafed through them. Now where could this thing have picked up man-books? He drew his eyebones together, thinking.

Ah, the Chinko guidebook! There had been a library in that town. Well, maybe this animal had lived in that town.

But books? This was better and better. Maybe, like the Chinkos had said, these animals could grasp meaning. Terl could not read the man-characters but they obviously were readable.

This first one here must be a child's primer. The other one was some kind of child's story. Beginner books.

The animal was looking stoically away in another direction. It was useless, of course, to try to talk to it—

Terl halted his thought in mid-blink.

Better and better for his plans! It *had* been talking! He remembered now. What he had thought were growls and squawks like you get from any animal had been reminiscent of words!

And here were books!

He made the thing look at him by turning its head. Terl pointed to the book and then at the thing's head.

It gave no sign of understanding.

Terl pushed the book up close to its face and pointed at its mouth. No sign of recognition occurred in the eyes.

It either wasn't going to read or it couldn't read.

He experimented some more. If these things could actually talk and read, then his plans were sure winners. He turned the pages in front of its face. No, no sign of recognition.

But it *had* books in its possession. It *had* books, but it couldn't read. Maybe it had them for the pictures. Ah, success. Terl showed it a picture of a bee and there was a flicker of interest and recognition. He showed it the picture of the fox and again that flick of recognition. He took the other book with pages of solid print. No sign of recognition.

Got it. He put the small books in his breast pocket.

Terl knew what to do. He knew every piece of everything in the old Chinko quarters and that included man-language discs. They had never written up what man ate but they had gone to enormous trouble with man-language. Typically Chinko. Miss the essentials and soar off into the stratosphere.

He knew tomorrow's program. Better and better.

Terl checked the collar, checked the rope, securely locked up the cage, and left.

— 6 —

It had been a damp, cold, thoroughly miserable night.

Jonnie had clung to the bars for hours, loathe to sit down or even step down. Mud was everywhere. The gush of water had taken the sand and dirt in the pool and spread it all over the cage and the dirt of the floor had avidly soaked it up. The mud became ankle deep.

But at last, exhausted, he had given in and slept lying in the mud.

Midmorning sun was drying it somewhat. The two dead rats had floated away out of reach and Jonnie didn't care.

Already dehydrated from his previous experience, he felt the hot sun increase his thirst. He looked at the muddy pool, contaminated with slime from the cage. He could not bring himself to drink it.

He was sitting miserably against the bars when the monster appeared.

It stopped outside the door and looked in. It was carrying some metallic object in its paws. It looked at the mud and for the moment Jonnie thought it might realize he couldn't go on sitting and sleeping in the mud.

It went away.

Just as Jonnie believed it would not come back, it reappeared. This time it was still carrying the metal object, but it was also carrying a huge rickety table and an enormous chair.

The thing made tricky work getting through the door with all that load, a door too small for it in the first place. But it came on in and put the table down. Then it put the metal object on the table.

Jonnie had at first believed that the huge chair was for him. But he was quickly disabused. The monster put the chair down at the side of the table and sat down on it: the legs of it sunk perilously into the mud.

It indicated the mysterious object. Then it took the two books out of its pocket and threw them on the table. Jonnie reached for them. He had not thought he would ever see them again and he had begun to make out of them a kind of sense.

The monster cuffed his hand and pointed at the object. It waved a paw across the top of the books in a kind of negative motion and pointed again at the object.

There was a sack on the back of the object and it had discs in it about the diameter of two hands.

The monster took out one of the discs and looked at it. It had a hole in the middle with squiggles around it. The monster put the disc on top of the machine. There was a rod there that fitted into the middle of the disc.

Jonnie was extremely suspicious, his hand bruised from the cuff. Anything this monster was up to would be devious, treacherous, and dangerous. That had been adequately proved. The game was to bide one's time, watch, and learn—and out of that possibly wrest freedom.

The monster now pointed to two windows on the front of the object. Then it pointed to a single lever that stuck out from the front of it.

The monster pushed the lever down.

Jonnie's eyes went round. He backed up.

The object *talked!*

Clear as a bell, it had said, [''Excuse me . . .'']

The monster pulled the lever up and it stopped talking.

Jonnie drew back further. The monster clouted him between the shoulder blades and drove him up to the table so hard the edge hit his throat. The monster raised a cautionary finger at him.

It shoved the lever up, and by standing on tiptoe Jonnie could see that the disc went backward from the way it had gone.

The monster pulled the lever down again. The object said, [''Excuse me, but I am . . .''] The monster centered the lever and the machine stopped. Then it pushed the lever up and the machine went backward again.

Jonnie tried to look under the machine and back of it. The thing wasn't alive, surely. It didn't have ears or a nose or a mouth. Yes, it did have a mouth. A circle low down in front of it. But the mouth didn't move. Sound just came out of it. And it was talking Jonnie's language!

The monster pushed the lever down again and the object said, [''Excuse me, but I am your . . .''] This time Jonnie saw that some odd squiggles had been showing up in the top window and a strange face in the lower window.

Once more the monster pushed the lever up and the disc on top went backward. Then the monster centered the lever. It pointed a talon at Jonnie's head and then at the object.

Jonnie noticed then that the monster had been moving the lever off center, all positions to the left. The monster now moved the lever all the way over to the right and down, and different squiggles appeared but the same picture showed, and the machine said something in some strange tongue.

The monster backed it up and put the lever in the left-right center and down. Different squiggles, same lower picture, but an entirely different set of sounds.

Behind the face mask the monster seemed to smile. It repeated the last maneuver again and pointed to itself. Jonnie suddenly understood that that was the monster's language.

Jonnie's interest was immediate, intense, and flaming.

He reached up and pushed the monster's paw away. It was hard to reach because the table was so high and big, but Jonnie made nothing of that.

He moved the lever up and to the left. Then he moved it down. The machine said, [''Excuse me, but I am your instructor . . .''] Then Jonnie did the same operation in the right-hand position and it said something that was language but strange. Then he did it in the center position and it spoke again in the language of the Psychlos.

The monster was looking at him closely, even suspiciously. It bent way over and peered back into Jonnie's face. The flickering, amber eyes slitted. Then it made a doubtful motion toward the machine as though it would pick it up and carry it off.

Jonnie slapped the huge hands away and fastened again on the lever. He put it in the left track and let it roll.

[''Excuse me,''] the machine said, [''but I am your instructor if you will forgive such arrogance. I do not have the honor to be a Psychlo. I am but a lowly Chinko.''] The face in the bottom window bowed twice and put a hand over its eyes.

[''I am Joga Stenko, Junior Assistant Language Slave in the Language Division of the Department of Culture and Ethnology, Planet Earth.''] Squiggles were running rapidly in the upper window.

[''Forgive my presumption, but this is a course of study in reading and speaking the man-languages of English and Swedish.]

[''On the left-hand track of the record, I hope you will have no trouble in finding English. On the right-hand track you will find the same text in Swedish. On the center track the same text is in Psychlo, the Noble Language of Conquerors.]

[''The written equivalent in each case appears in the upper window and suitable pictures appear in the lower window.]

[''You will pardon my humble pretensions of learnedness. All wisdom abides in the Governors of Psychlo and one of their major companies, the great and mighty Intergalactic Mining Company, on which let there be profit!'']

Jonnie centered the lever. He was breathing hard. The language was stilted, oddly pronounced, and many of the words he did not know. But he grasped it.

He looked more closely at the object. He frowned, concentrating heavily. And then he grasped that it was a machine, a not-live thing. That meant that the insect had been not live either.

Jonnie looked at the monster. Why was this thing doing this? What fresh dangers and privations did it have in mind? There was no kindness in those amber eyes. They were like a wolf's eyes seen in firelight.

The monster pointed toward the machine and Jonnie pulled the lever down to the left.

[''Excuse me,''] it said, [''but we will begin with the necessary alphabet. The first letter is A. Look at the upper window.''] Jonnie did and saw the marks.

[''A . . . pronounced *ay*. Its sound it also *a* as in 'pat,' *ay* as in 'pay,' *ay* as in 'care,' *ah* as in 'father.' Look at it well, excuse me please, so you can always recognize it. The next letter of the alphabet is B. Look at the window. It always has the sound of *b* as in bat . . .'']

The monster batted his hand up and opened the primer to the first page. It tapped a talon on A.

Jonnie had already made the connection. Language could be written and read. And this machine was going to teach him how to do it. He centered the lever and pulled it down and there it was evidently spouting an alphabet in Psychlo. The little face in the lower window was showing mouth formations to say the sounds. He swung the lever over to the right and it was saying an alphabet in . . . Swedish?

The monster stood up, looking the four feet down to Jonnie. It took two dead rats from its pocket and dangled them in front of Jonnie.

What was this? A reward? It made Jonnie feel like a dog being trained. He didn't take them.

The monster made a sort of shrugging motion and said something. Jonnie couldn't understand the words. But when the monster reached over to pick up the machine, he knew what they must have been. Something like, "Lesson's over for the day."

Jonnie instantly pushed the arms away from the machine. He moved over defiantly and stood there, blocking the reach. He wasn't sure what would happen, if he'd be batted halfway across the cage. But he stood there.

So did the monster. Head on one side, then the other.

The monster roared. Jonnie did not flinch. The monster roared some more and Jonnie divined, with relief, that it was laughing.

The monster's belt buckle, showing the clouds of smoke in the sky, was a few inches below Jonnie's eyes. It connected with the ancient legend that told of the end of Jonnie's race. The laughter beat at Jonnie's ears, a growling thunder of mockery.

The monster turned around and went out, still laughing as it locked the gate.

There was bitterness and determination on Jonnie's face. He had to know more. Much more. Then he could act.

The machine was still on the table.

Jonnie reached for the lever.

— 7 —

The summer heat dried out the mud.

White clouds spotted the skies above the cage.

But Jonnie had no time for them. His whole concentration was on the teaching machine.

He had gotten the huge chair shifted around and by lifting the seat height with folded skins, he could hunch over the table, close facing the old Chinko who, in the picture, fawned in an agony of politeness as he taught.

Mastering the alphabet in English was quite a trick. But mastering it in Psychlo was even worse. Far far easier to trail game by its signs and know, almost to the minute, how long ago it had passed and what it was doing. These signs and symbols were fixed deathless on a screen and the meanings that they gave were unbelievably complex.

In a week, he thought he had it. He had begun to hope. He had even commenced to believe that it was easy. "B is for Bats, Z is for Zoo, H is for Hats and Y is for You." And by going over the same text in Psychlo, the Bats, Zoos, Hats and Yous became (a little incomprehensibly) Pens, Shovels, Kerbango and Females. But when he finally grasped, under the Chinko's groveling tutelage, that Psychlo words for Hats, Zoos and Bats would start with different letters, he knew he had it.

He at length could lie back and rattle off the alphabet in English. Then he could, with a bit of squinting, sit up and rattle off the Psychlo alphabet in Psychlo. And with all the different nuances of how they sounded.

Jonnie knew he mustn't take too long at this. The diet of raw meat would eventually do him in; he was close to semi-starvation since he could barely bring himself to eat it.

The monster would come and watch him a little while each day. While he was there, Jonnie was silent. He knew he must sound funny while he drilled. And the monster's laughter made the back of his hair stand up. So he would be very quiet under that scrutiny from outside the cage.

It was a mistake. The monster's eyebones behind the breathe-mask plate were coming closer and closer together with a growing frown.

The triumph of the alphabet was short-lived. At the end of it, the monster, one beautiful bright day, yanked open the door of the cage and came roaring in like a storm!

It yelled at Jonnie for minutes on end, the cage bars shaking. Jonnie expected a cuff but he didn't cringe when the monster's paw snaked out.

But it was reaching for the machine, not Jonnie. It yanked the lever down into a second stage that Jonnie had never suspected.

A whole new set of pictures and sounds leaped out!

The old Chinko said, in English, "I am sorry, honored student and forgive my arrogance, but we will now begin the drill of progressive cross-association of objects, symbols and words."

And there was a new sequence of pictures! The sound for H

the picture of H began to follow one another at a slow interval. Then the Psychlo letter that had an H-like sound began to repeat, in sound and picture. And then they went faster and faster until they were an almost indistinguishable blur!

Jonnie was so astonished he did not realize the monster had left.

Here was a new thing. The lever was so big and resistive he had not realized that all this lurked just beyond another thrust of pressure.

Well, if a little push DOWN would do that, what happened with a little push UP?

He tried it.

It almost blew his head off.

It took him quite a space of travel of the sun-made bar shadows to get brave enough to try it again.

Same thing!

It almost knocked him off the chair.

Holding back, he stared at the thing suspiciously.

What was it that came out of it?

Sunlight?

He tried it again and let it hit his hand.

Warm.

Tingling.

Carefully staying off to the side, he saw that pictures were appearing in the frames. And he heard, in the weirdest way, sort of with his head, not his ears, "Beneath the level of your consciousness, the alphabet will now go in. A,B,C . . ."

What was this? Was he "hearing" through his hand? No, that couldn't be! He wasn't hearing at all except for that meadowlark.

Soundless somethings were coming from the MACHINE!

He moved a little further back. The impression was less. He moved closer: he felt that his brains were frying.

"Now we will do the same sounds in Psychlo. . . ."

Jonnie went over to the furthest extension of his chain and sat down against the wall.

He thought and thought about it.

He grasped at last that the cross-association drill of symbols sounds and words was to get him very fast and then faster and faster so he did not have to grope for what he had been taught but would be able to use it without hesitation.

But this shaft of "sunlight" coming out of the machine?

He got braver. He went back and found a disc that must be very advanced and put it on. Bracing himself, he grimly pushed the lever all the way up.

Suddenly he KNEW that if all three sides of a triangle were equal, all its enclosed three angles were also equal.

He backed up. Never mind what a triangle was or an angle, he now KNEW.

He went back and sat down against the wall. Suddenly he reached out with his finger and drew in the dust a three pointed shape. He poked a finger at each inside bend. He said, wonderingly, "They're equal."

Equal what?

Equal each other.

So what?

Maybe it was valuable.

Jonnie gazed at the machine. It could teach him in the ordinary way. It could teach him by speeding the lesson up. And it could teach him very smoothly and instantly with a beam of "sunlight."

Abruptly an unholy joy began to light his face.

Alphabet? He had to learn the whole civilization of the Psychlos!

Did that monster realize why he wanted it?

Life became a long parade of discs, stacks of discs. Every hour not needed for sleep was spent at the table—with straight picture learning, with progressively speeding cross-association, with the piercing beams of "sunlight."

Half-starved, his sleep was restless. Nightmares of dead Psychlos were intertwined with raw rats chasing mechanical horses that flew. And the discs went round and round.

But Jonnie kept on, kept on cramming years of education into weeks and months. There was so MUCH to know! He had to grasp it ALL!

And with only one goal in mind: vengeance for the destruction of his race! Could he learn enough fast enough to accomplish his purpose?

— 8 —

Terl had felt smug right up to the moment he received the summons from the Planetary Director. He was nervous now, waiting for the appointment to occur.

The weeks had fled on, the summer fading into the chill of autumn. The man-animal was doing well. Its every waking moment seemed to be spent crowded up against the Chinko language and technical instruction machine.

It hadn't begun to talk yet, but of course it was just an animal and stupid. It hadn't even grasped the principle of progressive speed cross-association until it had been shown. And it didn't even have enough sense to stand squarely in front of the instantaneous conceptual knowledge transmitter. Didn't it realize you had to get the full wave impulse to get it through your skull bones? Stupid. It would take months at this rate to get an education! But what could you expect of an animal that lived on raw rat!

Still, sometimes when he went in the cage, Terl had looked into those strange blue eyes and had seen danger. No matter. Terl had decided that if the animal proved dangerous, he could simply use it to get things started, and then at the first sign it was getting out of hand it could be vaporized fast enough. One button push on a hand-blaster. Zip-bang, no man-animal. Very easily handled.

Yes, things had been going very well until this summons. Such things made one nervous. There was no telling what the Planetary Director might have found out, no telling what tales some employee might have carried to him. A security chief was ordinarily not much consulted. In fact, by a devious chain of command, a security chief was not directly under the Planetary Director on all points. This made Terl feel better. In fact, there had been cases where a security chief had removed a Planetary Director—cases involving corruption. But still, the Planetary Director remained the administrative head and was the one who filed reports, reports that could transfer one, or continue one on post.

The summons had come late the night before and Terl had not slept very well. He had tumbled around in his bed, imagining conversations. At one time he had actually gotten up and combed through his office files wondering what he had on the Planetary Director, just in case. That he couldn't recall or find anything depressed him. Terl only felt operational when he had big leverage in terms of potential blackmail.

It was almost with relief that he saw the appointment time arrive and he rumbled into the office of the top Psychlo.

Numph, Planetary Director of Earth, was old. Rumor had it that he was a discard from the Central Company Directorate. Not for corruption, but just for bumbling incompetence. And he had been sent as far away as they could send him. An unimportant post, a rim star in a remote galaxy, a perfect place to send someone and forget him.

Numph was sitting at his upholstered desk, looking out through the pressure dome at the distant transshipment center. He was gnawing absently on a corner of a file folder.

Terl approached watchfully. Numph's executive uniform was neat. His fur, turning blue, was impeccably combed and in place. He didn't look particularly upset, though his amber cyes were introverted.

Numph didn't look up. "Sit down," he said absently.

"I come in response to your summons, Your Planetship."

The old Psychlo turned to his desk. He looked wearily at Terl. "That's obvious." He didn't much care for Terl, but he didn't dislike him either. It was the same with all these executives, definitely not first team. Not like the old days, other planets, other posts, better staffs.

"We're not showing a profit," said Numph. He threw the folder down on his desk. Two kerbango saucepans rattled, but he did not offer any.

"I should imagine this planet is getting mined out," said Terl.

"That's not it. There's plenty of deep-down ore to keep us going for centuries. Besides, that's the concern of the engineers, not security."

Terl didn't care to feel rebuked. "I've heard that there's an economic depression in a lot of the company's markets, that prices are down."

"That could be. But that's the concern of the economics department at the home office, not security."

This second rebuke made Terl a bit restless. His chair groaned alarmingly under his bulk.

Numph pulled the folder to him and fiddled with it. Then he looked wearily at Terl.

"It's costs," said Numph.

"Costs," said Terl, getting his own back a bit, "has to do with accounting, not security."

Numph looked at him for several seconds. He couldn't make up his mind whether Terl was being insolent. He decided to ignore it. He threw the folder back down.

"Mutiny is," said Numph.

Terl stiffened. "Where's the mutiny?" Not the slightest rumor of it had reached him. What was going on here? Did Numph have his own intelligence system that bypassed Terl?

"It hasn't occurred yet," said Numph. "But when I announce the pay cuts and drop all bonuses, there's liable to be one."

Terl shuddered and leaned forward. This affected him in more ways than one.

Numph tossed the folder at him. "Personnel costs. We have three thousand seven hundred nineteen employees on this planet scattered over five active minesites and three exploratory sites. That includes landing field personnel, freighter crews, and the transshipment force. At an average pay of thirty thousand Galactic credits a year, that's C111,570,000. Food, quarters, and breathe-gas is averaged at fifteen thousand credits each; comes to C55,785,000. The total is C167,355,000. Add to that the bonuses and transport and we have nearly exceeded the value of our output. That doesn't count wear and tear, and it doesn't count expansion."

Terl had been dimly aware of this and in fact had used it as an argument—a false one—in furthering his own personal plan.

He did not think the time was ripe to spring his project. But he had not anticipated that the powerful and rich Intergalactic Company would go so far as to cut pay and wipe out bonuses. While this affected him directly, he was far more interested in his own plan of personal wealth and power.

Was it time to open up a new phase in his own scheme? The animal was actually doing pretty well. It probably could be trained for the elementary digging venture. It could be used to recruit other animals. He was pretty well convinced it could do the necessary mining, dangerous though it was.

Stripping that vein out of the blizzard-torn, sheer cliff would be quite a trick and might be fatal to some of the animals involved. But who cared about that? Besides, the moment the stuff was gotten out, the animals would have to be vaporized so the secret could never leak.

"We could increase our output," said Terl, fencing in toward his target.

"No, no, no," said Numph. "That's pretty impossible." He sighed. "We're limited on personnel."

That was cream to Terl's earbones.

"You're right," said Terl, heading Numph further into the trap. "Unless we solve it, it will lead straight into mutiny."

Numph nodded glumly.

"In a mutiny," said Terl, "the first ones the workers vaporize are the executives."

Again Numph nodded, but this time there was a flicker of fear in the depths of his amber eyes.

"I'm working on it," said Terl. It was premature and he hadn't intended to spring it, but the time was now. "If we could give them hope that the cuts weren't permanent and if we imported no new personnel, the threat of mutiny would be reduced."

"True, true," said Numph. "We are already not bringing in any additional or new personnel. But at the same time our installations are working very hard, and there's already some grumbling."

"Agreed," said Terl. He plunged. "But what would you say if I told you that right this minute I was working on a project to halve our work force within two years?"

"I'd say it would be a miracle."

That was what Terl liked to hear. Plaudits from one and all in the home office would be his yet.

Numph was looking almost eager.

"No Psychlo," said Terl, "likes this planet. We can't go outside without wearing masks—"

"Which increases costs in breathe-gas," said Numph.

"—and what we need is a work force of air-breathers that can do elementary machine operation."

Numph sank back, doubt hitting him. "If you're thinking of . . . what was their name . . . Chinkos, they were all wiped out ages back."

"Not Chinkos. And I congratulate Your Planetship on his knowledge of company history. Not Chinkos. There is a potential local supply."

"Where?"

"I am not going to say any more about it right now, but I want to report that I am making progress and that it is very hopeful."

"Who are these people?"

"Well, actually, they are not 'people,' as you would say. But there are sentient beings on this planet."

"They think? They talk?"

"They are very manually adept."

Numph pondered this. "They talk? You can communicate with them?"

"Yes," said Terl, biting off a bit more than he really knew. "They talk."

"There's a bird down on the lower continent can talk. A mine director there sent one. It could swear in Psychlo. Somebody didn't replace the air cartridge in its dome and it died." He frowned. "But a bird isn't manually—"

"No, no, no," said Terl, cutting off the bumbling. "These are little short things, two arms, two legs—"

"Monkeys! Terl, you can't be serious—"

"No, not monkeys. Monkeys could never operate a machine. I am talking about man."

Numph looked at him for several seconds. Then he said, "But there are only a very few of them left, even if they could do what you say."

"True, true," said Terl. "They have been listed as an endangered species."

"A what?"

"A species that is about to become extinct."

"But a few like that would not resolve our—"

"Your Planetship, I will be frank. I have not counted how many there are left—"

"But nobody has even seen one for ages. Terl . . ."

"The recon drones have noted them. There were thirty-four right up in those mountains you see there. And they exist on other continents in greater numbers. I have reason to believe that if I were given facilities I could round up several thousand."

"Ah, well. Facilities . . . expense . . ."

"No, no. No real expense. I have been engaged on an economy program. I have even reduced the number of recon drones. They breed fast if given a chance—"

"But if nobody has even seen one . . . what functions could they replace?"

"Exterior machine operators. Over seventy-five percent of our personnel is tied up in just that. Tractors, loading rigs. It's not skilled operation."

"Oh, I don't know, Terl. If nobody has even seen one—"

"I have one."

"What?"

"Right here. In the zoo cages near the compound. I went out and captured one—took a bit of doing, but I made it. I was rated high in marksmanship at the school, you know."

Numph puzzled over it. "Yes . . . I did hear some rumor there was a strange animal out in the zoo, as you call it. Somebody, one of the mine directors, I think . . . yes, Char it was, laughing about it."

"It's no laughing matter if it affects pay and profits," glowered Terl.

"True. Very true. Char always was a fool. So you have an animal under testing that could replace personnel. Well, well. Remarkable."

"Now," said Terl, "if you will give me a blanket requisition on transport—"

"Oh, well. Is there any chance of seeing this animal? You know, to see what it could do. The death benefits we have to pay on equipment accidents would themselves tip the profit-loss scale if they didn't exist. Or were minimized. There's also machine damage potential. Yes, the home office doesn't like machine damage."

"I've only had it a few weeks and it will take a little time to train it on a machine. But yes, I think I could arrange for you to see what it could do."

"Fine. Just get it ready and let me know. You say you're training it? You know it is illegal to teach an inferior race metallurgy or battle tactics. You aren't doing that, are you?"

"No, no, no. Just machine operation. The push-pull of buttons and levers is all. Have to teach it to talk to be able to give it orders. I'll arrange for a demonstration when it's ready. Now if you could just give me a blanket requisition—"

"When I've seen the test there will be time enough," said Numph.

Terl had risen out of his chair, the prepared sheets of

requisitions half out of his pocket. He put them back. He'd have to think of some other way—but he was good at that. The meeting had come off pretty well. He was not feeling too bad. And then Numph dropped the mine bucket on him.

"Terl," said Numph. "I certainly appreciate this backup. Just the other day there was a dispatch from home office about your continued tour of duty here. They plan in advance, you know. But in this case they needed a security chief with field experience on home planet. I'm thankful I turned it down. I recommended you for another ten-year tour of duty."

"I had only two years left to run," gagged Terl.

"I know, I know. But good security chiefs are valuable. It will do your record no harm to show you are in demand."

Terl made it to the door. Standing in the passageway he felt horribly ill. He had trapped himself, trapped himself right here on this cursed planet!

The glittering vein of gold lay in the mountains. His plans were going well in all other ways. It would take perhaps two years to get those forbidden riches, and the end of this duty tour would have been a personal triumph. Even the man-thing was shaping up. Everything had been running so well.

And now ten years more! Diseased crap, he couldn't stand that!

Leverage. He had to have leverage on Numph. Big leverage.

— 9 —

The explosion had been sharp and loud. Completely unlike the dull roar that every five days regularly shook the cage and compound.

With some skill and agility, Jonnie had found that he could go up the bars, using a cage corner, and, bracing himself there, look far and wide across the plains to the mountains and down on the domed compound of the Psychlos. Feet braced against the crossbars, he could almost relax in this precarious position.

Winter had come. The mountains for some time now had been white. But today they were invisible under white-gray skies.

To the east of the compound there lay a curious huge platform.

It was surrounded by widely spaced poles and wires. It had a flooring that was bright and shiny, some sort of metal. At its southern edge there was a domed structure from which Psychlos came and went. At the northern side of it was a different kind of field, a field where strange, cylindrical craft arrived and departed.

The craft would land with a cloud of dust. Their sides would open and rock and chunks of things would spill out and the vessel would rise again into the air and fly away, dwindling to nothingness beyond the horizon.

The dumped material would be pushed onto a belt that ran between towers, carrying the load over to the huge area of bright and shiny flooring.

Through the days, craft after craft would come, and by the fifth day there would be an enormous pile of material mounded up on the platform.

It was then that the most mysterious thing would occur. At exactly the same time of the day, exactly every fifth day, there would be a humming. The material on the platform would glow briefly. Then there would be a roar like a low thunderclap. And the material would vanish!

It was this one feature, of all the mysteries that surrounded him on his post at the top of the bars, that riveted his attention.

Where did it go? There it would be, a small mountain of material. And then—hum-roar-bang—it would be gone. Nothing ever reappeared on that shiny platform. The material was brought in by those flying objects, taken over by the belt. And there it vanished.

Jonnie had seen it happen often enough now that he could predict the minute, hour, and day. He knew the dome to the south would light up, the wires around the platform would vibrate and hum, and then roar-bang, the piled material would be gone.

But that wasn't what had happened down there today. One of the machines that pushed the material onto the belt had blown up. A swarm of Psychlos were down there around it now. They were doing something with the driver. And a couple more were putting out a fire on the machine itself.

The machines had big blades in front and were covered with a transparent dome where the driver sat. But the dome was off that one now, apparently blown off.

A squat vehicle came up. The driver had been stretched out on the ground. They now put the body in a basket and put it into the squat vehicle, which was driven away.

Another machine with a blade came over and pushed the damaged vehicle off to one side out of the way, and then went back to pushing material onto the belt. The Psychlos went back to their machines and the dome.

An accident of some sort, thought Jonnie. He hung there for a while but nothing else was going on.

Yes, there was. His cage bars were trembling. But this was near to hand and ordinary. It was footsteps of the Psychlo who kept him caged. Jonnie slid down to the floor.

The monster came to the door and unfastened it and entered. He glared at Jonnie.

The monster was quite unpredictable of late. He seemed calm one time and ruffled and impatient the next.

Right now he was very impatient. He made a savage gesture at Jonnie and then at the language machine.

Jonnie took a deep breath. Every waking hour for months he had been at that machine, working, working, working. But he had never spoken a word to the monster.

He did so now. In Psychlo, Jonnie said, "Broke."

The monster looked at him curiously. Then it went over to the machine and pushed down the lever. It didn't work. The monster shot a glare at Jonnie as though Jonnie had broken it and then picked the machine up and looked under it. That was quite a feat in Jonnie's eyes, for he himself couldn't budge it an inch on the table.

The machine had just quit that morning, shortly before the explosion. Jonnie moved closer to see what the monster was doing. It removed a small plate in the bottom and a little button dropped out. The monster read some numbers on the button and then laid the machine on its side and left the cage.

He came back shortly with another button, put it in the same place, and put the plate back on. He righted the machine and touched the lever. The disc turned and the machine said, ["Forgive me, but addition and subtraction . . ."] And the monster put it in neutral.

The monster pointed a talon at Jonnie and then urgently back at the machine.

Jonnie plunged again. In Psychlo he said, "Know all those. Need new records."

The monster looked at the thick original sheaf of recordings, hundreds of hours of them. It looked at Jonnie. Its face was grim back of its face mask. Jonnie was not sure he wasn't going to get knocked halfway across the cage. Then the monster seemed to make up its mind.

It yanked the pack of discs out of the back of the machine and left. Shortly it returned with a new, thicker stack of discs and shoved them into the storage compartment of the machine. It took the old disc off and put the next sequentially numbered one on. Then it pointed at Jonnie and back at the machine. Plainly, Jonnie was supposed to get to work and get to work now.

Jonnie took a deep breath. In Psychlo he said, "Man does not live on raw rat meat and dirty water."

The monster just stood there staring at him. Then it sat down in the chair and looked at him some more.

— 10 —

Terl knew leverage when he saw it.

As a veteran security officer, he depended on leverage at every turn. And advantage. And blackmail. A method of forcing compliance.

And now it was turned around. This man-thing had sensed that it had leverage.

He sat there studying the man-thing. Did it have any inkling of the plans? No, of course not. Possibly he had been too insistent, day after day, so that this thing sensed he wanted something of it.

Possibly he had been too indulgent. He had gone to the trouble every day or two to go out and shoot rats for it. And earlier, hadn't he gotten it water? And look at all the cunning and difficulty of establishing what it ate.

Here it stood, brave and strong, telling him it didn't eat that. Terl looked at it more closely. Well, not brave and strong. It looked pretty sickly, really. It had a worn robe around it and yet it was almost blue with the coldness of the day. He glanced over at the pond. It was frozen over, dirt and all.

He looked around further. The cage wasn't as dirty as it might have been. The thing evidently buried its jobs.

"Animal " said Terl, "you had better get to work if you know what is good for you." Bluster sometimes made it even when one didn't have leverage.

"The winter weather," said Jonnie in Psychlo, "is bad for the machine. At night and in rain or snow I keep it covered with a deerhide from my pack. But the dampness is not good for it. It is becoming tarnished."

Terl almost laughed. It was so funny to hear this animal actually speaking Psychlo. True, there was some accent, probably Chinko. No, maybe not Chinko, since all the polite phrases, the "forgive-mes" and "pardon-mes" Terl had heard when he checked the records, were not there. Terl had never met a Chinko since they were all dead, but he had met a lot of subject races on other planets and they were carefully servile in their speech. As they should be.

"Animal," said Terl, "you may know the words but you do not understand a proper attitude. Shall I demonstrate?"

Jonnie could have been launched on a flight to the bars with one sweep of those huge paws.

He drew himself up. "My name is not 'animal.' It is Jonnie Goodboy Tyler."

Terl absolutely gaped at him. The effrontery. The bald gall of this thing!

He hit him.

The collar almost broke Jonnie's neck as the rope brought him up short.

Terl stalked out of the cage and slammed the door. The ground shook like an earthquake as he stamped away.

He had almost reached the outer door of the compound when he stopped. He stood there, thinking.

Terl looked at the gray-white world, felt the cold glass of his face mask cutting his gaze. Blast this stinking planet.

He turned around and walked back to the cage. He opened the door and went over to the man-thing. He picked it up, wiped the blood off its neck with a handful of snow, and then put it standing in front of the table.

"My name," said Terl, "is Terl. Now what were we talking about?" He knew leverage when he saw it.

But never in their association thereafter did he ever address Jonnie as anything other than "animal." A Psychlo after all could not ignore the fact that his was the dominant race. The greatest race in all universes. And this man-thing—ugh.

■

PART 3

— 1 —

Zzt was banging around in the transport repair shop, throwing down tools, discarding parts, and generally making an agitated din.

He caught sight of Terl standing nearby and he turned on him in an instant attack.

"Are you at the bottom of this pay cut?" demanded Zzt.

Mildly, Terl said, "That would be the accounting department, wouldn't it?"

"Why has my pay been cut?"

"It's not just your pay, it's also mine and everybody else's " said Terl.

"I've got three times the work no help, and now half the pay!"

"The planet is running at a loss, I'm told," said Terl.

"And no bonuses," said Zzt.

Terl frowned. This was not the time or place for a favor. Leverage. He had no leverage at all these days.

"Been a lot of machines blowing up lately," said Terl.

Zzt stood and looked at him. There was more than a hint of threat in that. One never knew about this Terl.

"What do you want?" said Zzt.

"I'm working on a project that could solve all this," said Terl. "That could get our pay and bonuses back."

Zzt ignored that. When a security chief sounded like he was doing favors, watch it.

"What do you want?" said Zzt.

"If it's successful, we'd even get more pay and bonuses."

'Look, I'm busy. You see these wrecks?"

"I want the loan of a small mine car puller,' said Terl

Zzt barked a sharp, sarcastic laugh. "There's one. Blew up yesterday down at the transshipment area. Take that."

The small bladed vehicle had its whole canopy blown off and the green bloodstains had dried on its panel. Its interior wiring was charred.

"What I want is a small pulling truck," said Terl. "A simple one." Zzt went back to throwing tools and parts around. A couple narrowly missed Terl.

"Well?"

"You got a requisition?" said Zzt.

"Well—" began Terl.

"I thought so," said Zzt. He stopped and looked at Terl "You sure you haven't got anything to do with this pay cut?"

"Why?"

"Rumor around you were talking to the Planet Head."

"Routine security."

"Hah!"

Zzt attacked the wrecked, bladed vehicle with a hammer to remove the remains of its pressure canopy.

Terl walked away. Leverage. He had no leverage.

In deep gloom he stood in a hallway between domes, lost in thought. He did have a solution of sorts. And there were signs of unrest. He made a sudden decision.

A compound intercomm was near to hand. He took hold of it and called Numph.

"Terl here, Your Planetship. Could I have an appointment in about an hour? . . . I have something to show you . . . Thank you, Your Planetship. One hour."

He hung up, pulled his face mask off a belt hook, donned it, and went outside. Soft snowflakes were drifting down.

At the cage he went straight over to the far end of the flexirope and untied it.

Jonnie had been working at the instruction machine and he watched Terl warily. Terl, coiling up the rope, did not fail to notice that the man-thing was now using the chair to sit in. A bit arrogant but it was good news, really. The thing had one of its hides rigged to the bars to keep snow off a sleeping place. There was another one tented over the machine and work place.

Terl yanked at the rope. "Come along," he said.

"You promised I could build a fire. Are we going out to get firewood?" asked Jonnie.

Terl yanked on the rope and forced Jonnie to follow him. He went straight to the old Chinko offices and booted open the door.

Jonnie looked around the place with interest. They were not inside the domes. This was an air-filled place. Dust lay in a blanket and stirred as they walked through the interior. There were papers scattered about, even books. There were charts on the walls. Jonnie saw that this was where the desk and chair had come from, for many just like them stood about.

Terl opened a locker and brought out a face mask and bottle. He hauled Jonnie close to him and slammed the mask over his face.

Jonnie batted it off. It was quite large. It was also full of dust. Jonnie found a rag in the locker and wiped the mask out. He examined the fastenings and discovered they were adjustable.

Terl was rummaging around and finally came up with a small pump. He put a fresh power cartridge in the pump, connected it to the bottle, and began filling it with air.

"What is this?" asked Jonnie.

"Shut up, animal."

"If it is supposed to work like yours, why do you have different bottles?"

Terl kept on pumping up the air bottle. Jonnie threw down the mask and sat down against the locker door, looking the other way.

The amber eyes slitted. More mutiny, thought Terl. Leverage, leverage. He didn't have any.

"All right," said Terl, disgusted. "That is a Chinko air mask. Chinkos breathed air. You breathe air. You have to have it to go in the compound or you'll die. My bottles contain proper breathe-gas and the compound domes are filled with breathe-gas, not air. Now, satisfied?"

"You can't breathe air," said Jonnie.

Terl controlled himself. "*You* can't breathe breathe-gas! Psychlos come from a proper planet that has proper breathe-gas. You, animal, would die there. Put on that Chinko mask."

"Did the Chinkos have to wear these in the compound?"

"I thought I told you."

"Where are the Chinkos?"

"Were, *were*," said Terl, thinking he was correcting the thing's grammar. It already spoke with an accent. High and squeaky, too. Not a proper bass. Irritating.

"They're not here anymore?"

Terl was about to tell him to shut up when a streak of sadism took over. "No, they're not here anymore! The Chinkos are dead—the whole race of them. And you know why? Because they tried to strike. They refused to work and do as they were told."

"Ah," said Jonnie. It came together for him. One more piece of evidence that added up to the smoke on the belt buckle design. The Chinkos had been another race; they had worked long and hard for the Psychlos; their reward had been extermination. It bore out his estimate of the Psychlo character.

Jonnie looked around at the shambles; the Chinkos must have been killed a long time ago.

"See this gauge?" said Terl, pointing to the air bottle he had now filled. "It registers one-zero-zero when the bottle is full. As it is used up, this needle goes down. When it gets as low as five you're in trouble and will run out of air. There's an hour of air in the bottle. Watch the gauge."

"Seems like there should be two bottles and one should carry the pump," said Jonnie.

Terl looked at the air bottle and saw it had clamps on it for a mate and there was a pocket for the pump. He had not bothered to look at the labels and directions on the bottle.

"Shut up, animal," Terl said. But he filled a second bottle, joined it to the first, and put the pump in the slot between them. Roughly he put the mask and rig on Jonnie.

"Now hear me, animal," said Terl. "We are going inside the compound and *I* am going to talk to a very important executive, His Planetship himself. You are to speak not one word and you are going to do exactly what you are told to do. Understand, animal?"

Jonnie looked at him through the Chinko faceplate.

"If you don't obey," said Terl, "all I have to do is pull your face mask loose and you'll go into convulsions." Terl didn't like the look he always got from those ice-blue eyes. He yanked the lead rope.

"Let's go, animal."

— 2 —

Numph was nervous. He looked at Terl uncertainly as the security chief entered.

"Mutiny?" said Numph.

"Not so far," said Terl.

"What do you have there?" said Numph.

Terl yanked on the lead rope to pull Jonnie from behind him. "I wanted to show you the man-thing," said Terl.

Numph sat forward at his desk and stared. A nearly naked, unfurred animal. Two arms, two legs. Yes, there was fur. On its head and lower face. Strange ice-blue eyes. "Don't let it pee on the floor," said Numph.

"Look at its hands," said Terl. "Manually adept . . ."

"You *sure* there's no mutiny?" said Numph. "The news was released this morning. I haven't heard any response from two continents yet, the minesites there."

"They probably aren't very pleased, but no mutiny yet. If you look at these hands—"

"I'll watch the ore output carefully," said Numph. "They might try to cut that down."

"Won't mean anything. We're pretty short of personnel," said Terl. "There are no maintenance mechanics left in transport. They've all been transferred to operations to up production."

"I'm told there's widespread unemployment on the home planet. Maybe I should pull in more personnel."

Terl sighed. Bumbling fool. "With reduced pay and no bonuses and this planet being as awful as it is, I shouldn't think you'd get many takers. Now this animal here—"

"Yes, that's so. I should have brought in more personnel before we cut the pay. You sure there's no mutiny?"

Terl plunged. "Well, the best way to halt a mutiny is to promise upped production. And within a year, I think we can replace fifty percent of our outside machine and vehicle operators with *these*." Damn, he wasn't getting through.

"It hasn't peed on the floor, has it?" said Numph, leaning forward to look. "Really, that thing smells *bad*."

"It's these untanned hides it wears. It doesn't have any proper clothes."

"Clothes? Would it wear clothes?"

"Yes, I believe it would, Your Planetship. All it has right now is hides. As a matter of fact, I have a couple of requisitions here—" He advanced to the desk and laid them there for signature. Leverage, leverage. He didn't have any leverage on this fool.

"I just had this place cleaned," said Numph. "Now it will have to be ventilated thoroughly. What are these things?" he added, looking at the requisitions.

"You wanted a demonstration that this man-thing could operate machines. One of those is for general supplies and the other is for a vehicle."

"They're marked 'urgent.' "

"Well, we have to raise hope fast if we want to avoid a mutiny."

"That's so." Numph was reading the whole requisition form even though he had seen thousands of them.

Jonnie stood patiently. Every detail of this interior was being taken in. The breathe-gas ports, the material of the dome, the strips that held it together.

These Psychlos didn't wear masks inside, and for the first time he was seeing their faces. They were almost human faces except they had bones for eyebrows and eyelids and lips. They had amber orb eyes like those of wolves. He was beginning to be able to read their emotions as they related to their expressions.

When they had come down the compound halls they had passed several Psychlos, and these had looked at him with curiosity, but they had looked at Terl with outright hostility. Apparently he had some special job or rank that wasn't popular. But then all the relationships among these people were hostile, one to another.

Numph eventually looked up. "You really think one of those things could run a machine?"

"You said you wanted a demonstration," said Terl. "I have to have a vehicle to train it."

"Oh," said Numph. "Then it isn't trained yet. So how do you know?"

Damn, thought Terl. This fool was worse than he had thought. But wait. There was something bothering Numph. There was something Numph was not talking about. The intuition of a security chief always sensed it. Leverage, leverage. If he could know this, maybe he'd have leverage. He'd have to keep his eyes and ears open. "It learned to operate an instruction machine very quickly, Your Planetship."

"Instruction?"

"Yes, it can read and write its own language now, and can speak, read, and write Psychlo."

"No!"

Terl turned to Jonnie. "Greet His Planetship."

Jonnie fastened his eyes on Terl. He said nothing.

"Speak!" said Terl loudly, and in an undertone added, "You want that face mask ripped off?"

Jonnie said, "I think Terl wants you to sign the requisitions so that I can be trained to operate a machine. If you ordered it, you should sign it."

It was as though he had said nothing at all. Numph was looking out the window, thinking about something. Then his nostrils flared. "That thing certainly stinks."

"It will be gone," said Terl, "just as soon as I get the requisitions signed."

"Yes, yes," said Numph. He dashed initials on the forms.

Terl took them quickly and started to leave.

Numph leaned forward and looked. "It didn't pee on the floor, did it?"

— 3 —

Terl had had no sleep and two fights already today, and he was in no mood for a third.

The snow was drifting down on a gray-white day, covering the half-wrecked, small, bladed vehicle, deepening on the broad expanse beyond the zoo. The man-thing looked utterly ridiculous in the huge Psychlo seat. Terl snorted.

The first fight had been over the uniform requisition. The clothing shop foreman—a mangy half-wit named Druk—had maintained that the requisition was forged: he had even said that knowing Terl he did not doubt it; and he had had the effrontery to verify it with an administrator. Then Druk had said he didn't have any uniforms that size and he wasn't in the habit of outfitting midgets and neither was the company Cloth yes, he had cloth. But it was executive cloth.

Then the animal had spoken up and said that under no circumstances would it wear purple. Terl had batted it. But it got up and said the same thing again. Leverage, leverage, damn not having leverage on this animal.

But Terl had had an inspiration and had gone out to the old Chinko quarters and found a bale of the blue stuff the Chinkos had once worn. The tailor said it was trash, but he could think of no more arguments.

It had taken an hour to hack out and fuse together two uniforms for the man-thing. And then it had refused to wear a regulation company buckle on the belt—almost had a fit in fact. Terl had had to go back to the Chinko quarters and dig around until he found what must have been an artifact—a small gold military buckle with an eagle and arrows on it. At least that made an impression on the man-thing. Its eyes had just about popped out.

The second fight had been with Zzt.

First Zzt wouldn't talk at all. Then he finally condescended to look at the requisition. He pointed out that there were no registration numbers in the blanks provided and maintained that this authorized him to provide anything he cared to at his own discretion. He said Terl could have the wrecked bladed vehicle. It was a write-off but it still ran. That was what had brought on the actual blows.

Terl had hit Zzt hard and they had gone around and around for almost five minutes, blow and counterblow. Terl had finally tripped over a tool dolly and gotten himself kicked.

He had taken the wrecked bladed vehicle. He had to walk beside it, running it, to get it out through the garage atmosphere port.

He now had the animal on it and it looked like another fight.

"What's this green stuff all over the seat and floor?" said Jonnie. The gently falling snow was covering it but it turned patches of the snow pale green as it dissolved.

At first Terl wasn't going to answer. Then his sadistic streak got the better of him. "That's blood."

"It isn't red."

"Psychlo blood isn't red; it's *real* blood and it's a proper color—green. Now shut up, animal. I'm going to tell you how—"

"What's all this charred stuff around the edges of this big circle?" And Jonnie pointed to the edges where the canopy had once been.

Terl hit him. Jonnie almost flew off the huge high seat where he had been standing. But with some agility he caught hold of a roll bar and didn't fall.

"I have to know," said Jonnie when he caught his breath. "How can I be sure somebody didn't press the wrong button and blow this thing up?"

Terl sighed. The arms of the man-thing weren't long enough to reach the controls and he'd have to stand up on the floor plates to run it. "They didn't push any wrong button. It just blew up."

"But how? Something must have made it blow up." Then he realized that this was the vehicle that had killed a Psychlo down on the landing field. He himself had heard it explode.

Jonnie pushed away some snow and sat down on the seat and looked the other way.

"All right!" snarled Terl. "When these vehicles are run by Psychlo operators they have a transparent hood over them. That is needed for breathe-gas. You won't be using any canopy or breathe-gas, animal, so it won't blow up."

"Yes, but why *did* it blow up? I have to know if I'm going to run the thing."

Terl sighed, long and shudderingly. Exasperation made his fangs grate. The animal was sitting there looking the other way.

"Breathe-gas," said Terl, "was under the canopy. They were loading gold ore and it must have had a trace of uranium in it. There must have been a leak in the canopy or a crack and the breathe-gas touched the uranium and exploded."

"*Ur*anium? *Ur*anium?"

"You're pronouncing it wrong. It's *uranium*."

"How do you say it in English?"

That was enough. "How the crap nebula would *I* know?" snapped Terl.

Jonnie carefully didn't smile. Uranium, uranium, he said to himself. It blew up breathe-gas!

And he had incidentally learned that Terl could not speak English.

"Which controls are which?" said Jonnie.

Terl was mollified a trifle. At least the animal wasn't looking the other way. "This button stops it. Learn that button good, and if anything else goes wrong, push it. This bar turns it to the left, that one to the right. This lever lifts the front blade, that one tilts it, the next one angles it. The red button backs it up."

Jonnie stood on the floor plates. He made the front blade lift, tilt, and angle, peering over the hood each time to see what was happening. Then he made the blade lift well up.

"See that grove of trees over there?" said Terl. "Start it toward them, dead slow."

Terl walked beside the vehicle. "Now stop it." Jonnie did. "Now back it up." Jonnie did. "Now go forward in a circle." Jonnie did.

Although Terl seemed to think this was a small vehicle, the seat was fifteen feet off the ground. The blade was twenty feet wide. And when it started up it shook not only itself but the ground, such was its heavy power.

"Now start pushing snow," said Terl. "Just a couple of inches off the top."

It was very difficult at first getting the blade to bite in varying degrees while the machine rolled forward.

Terl watched. It was cold. He had had no sleep. His fangs ached where Zzt had landed a good one. He clambered up on the vehicle and took Jonnie's rope and wrapped it around a roll bar, tying it at a distance where Jonnie wouldn't be able to get to it.

Jonnie stopped the vehicle, ready for a breather.

"Why didn't Numph hear me speaking?" asked Jonnie

"Shut up, animal."

"But I have to know. Maybe my accent is too bad."

"Your accent is awful but that isn't the reason. You had a face mask on and Numph is a bit deaf." This was a plain, outright security chief lie.

Numph had been able to hear all right and the animal's face mask had not muffled his speech a bit. Numph had been distracted by something else. Something Terl didn't know. And the reason Terl had had no sleep was that he had spent the entire night rummaging through dispatches, records, and Numph's files trying to get to the bottom of it. Leverage. Leverage. That's what Terl needed. He had found nothing of importance, nothing at all. But there *was* something.

Terl felt dead on his feet. He was going in to take a nap. "I have some reports to write," said Terl. "You just keep this thing going around and practice with it. I'll be out soon."

Terl took a button camera out of his pocket and stuck it on the after roll bar, out of the animal's reach. "Don't get any ideas. This vehicle only goes at a walk." And he left.

But the nap, aided by a heavy shot of kerbango, was a bit longer than he intended, and it was nearly dark when he came lumbering hurriedly back.

He stopped and stared. The practice field was all chewed up. But that wasn't the amazing thing. The animal had neatly knocked down half a dozen trees and pushed them all the way up the hill to the cage where they were now stacked. More—he had used the blade drop to slice up the trees into sections a few feet long and slit them.

The animal was sitting on the seat now, hunkered down out of the keening wind that had sprung up.

Terl untied the rope and Jonnie stood up.

"What's that all about?" said Terl, pointing at the chopped-up trees.

"Firewood," said Jonnie. "Now that I'm untied I will carry some into the cage."

"Firewood?"

"Let's say I'm tired of a diet of *raw* rat, my friend."

That night, having eaten his first cooked food in months and thawing the winter chill from his bones before the pleasant fire on the cage floor, Jonnie heaved a sigh of relief.

The new clothes were hung up on sticks to dry. He sat cross-legged, digging into his pouch.

He drew out the gold metal disc and then he reached for the gold belt buckle he had just acquired. He studied them.

The bird with the arrows was essentially the same on each one And now he could read the squiggles.

The disc said, ["The United States of America"].

The belt buckle said, ["The United States Air Force"].

So his people long ago had been a nation. And it had had a force of some sort devoted to the air.

The Psychlos wore belt buckles that said they were members of the Intergalactic Mining Company.

With a smile that would have frightened Terl had he seen it, Jonnie supposed that he was as of this minute a member, the only member, of the United States Air Force.

He put the buckle carefully under a piece of robe he used for a pillow and lay for a long time looking at the dancing flames.

— 4 —

The mighty planet Psychlo, "king of the galaxies," basked beneath the forceful rays of triple suns.

The courier stood to the side of Intergalactic's transshipment receipt area, waiting. Above him the mauve skies domed the purple hillsides of the horizon. All about him spread the smoke-spewing factories, the power lines, the tense and crackling might of the company. Machines and vehicles boiled in purposeful turmoil throughout the multilayered roads and plains of the vast compound. In the distance lay the pyramidal shapes of the Imperial City. Spotted among the outlying hills were the compounds of many other companies—factories that spewed out their products to whole galaxies.

Who would be elsewhere? thought the courier. He sat astride his small ground-go, momentarily idle in his daily rounds, waiting. Who would want to live and toil on some forgotten light-gravity planet, wearing a mask, working under domes, driving pressurized vehicles, digging in alien soil? Or, drafted, fighting some war on territory nobody cared about anyway? Not this Psychlo, that was for sure.

A shrieking whistle pierced the day: the warning signal to get clear of the transshipment receipt platform, chasing away a fleet of blade, brush, and vacuum vehicles that had been clearing it.

The courier automatically checked his own proximity. Good, he was outside the danger area.

The network of lines and cables about the platform hummed. Then they shrieked into a crescendo that ended with a roaring explosion.

Tons of ore materialized on the platform surface, teleported in an instant across the galaxies.

The courier gazed through the momentarily ionized air. Look at that. The incoming ore had a crust of whitish substance overlying it. The courier had seen it before from time to time. Somebody said it was called "snow." Trickles of water took the place of the flakes. Imagine having to work and live on a crazy planet like that.

The all-clear signal sounded and the courier gunned his ground-go forward to the new ore heap. The receipt foreman rumbled out to the new pile of ore.

"Look at that," said the courier. "Snow."

The receipt foreman had seen it all, knew it all, and held junior couriers in contempt. "It's bauxite, not snow."

"It had some snow on it when it landed."

The receipt foreman scrambled over to the right side of the pile and fished around. He brought up a small dispatch box. Standing on the ore, he noted the box number on his clipboard and then brought it over to the courier.

Blade vehicles were charging in on the new pile. The receipt foreman impatiently handed the clipboard to the courier, who signed. The box was thrown at him. He threw back the clipboard and it caught the receipt foreman on his massive chest.

The courier gunned his ground-go and swiftly threaded his way through the incoming machines, speeding toward the Intergalactic Central Administration Compound.

A few minutes later a clerk, carrying the box, walked into the office of Zafin, Junior Assistant to the Deputy Director for Secondary Uninhabited Planets. The office was little more than a cubicle, for space at Intergalactic Central housed three hundred thousand administrative personnel.

Zafin was a young ambitious executive. "What's that box doing wet?" he said.

The clerk, who was about to set it down among papers, hastily withdrew it, got out a cloth, and dried it. He looked at the label. "It's from Earth; must be raining there."

"Typical," said Zafin. "Where's that?"

The clerk tactfully hit a projector button and a chart flared on the wall. The clerk shifted the focus, peered, and then put a claw on a small dot.

Zafin wasn't bothering to look. He had opened the dispatch box and was sorting the dispatches to different departments under him, zipping an initial on those that required it. He was almost finished when he held up a dispatch that required some work and couldn't just be initialed. He looked at it with distaste.

"Green flashed urgent," said Zafin.

The clerk took it apologetically and read it. "It's just a request for information."

"Too high a priority," said Zafin. He took it back. "Here we have three wars in progress and somebody from . . . where?''

''Earth,'' said the clerk.

''Who sent it?''

The clerk took the dispatch back and looked. ''A security chief named . . . named Terl.''

''What's his record?''

The clerk put his talons on a button console and a wall slot clattered and then spat out a folder. The clerk handed it over.

''Terl,'' said Zafin. He frowned, thinking. ''Haven't I heard that name before?''

The clerk took back the folder and looked at it. ''He requested a transfer about five months ago our time.''

''Steel trap brain,'' said Zafin. ''That's me.'' And he meant it. He took the folder back. ''Never forget a name.'' He leafed through the papers. ''Must be a dead, dull place, Earth. And now a dispatch with wrong priority.''

The clerk took the folder back.

Zafin frowned. ''Well, where's the dispatch?''

''On your desk, Your Honor.''

Zafin looked at it. ''He wants to know what connections . . . Numph? Numph?''

The clerk worked the console and a screen flashed. ''Intergalactic Director, Earth.''

''This Terl wants to know what connections he has in the main office,'' said Zafin.

The clerk pushed some more buttons. The screen flashed. The clerk said, ''He's the uncle of Nipe, Assistant Director of Accounting for Secondary Planets.''

''Well, write it on the dispatch and send it back.''

''It's also marked confidential,'' said the clerk.

''Well, mark it confidential,'' said Zafin. He sat back, thinking. He turned his chair and looked out the window at the distant city. The breeze was cool and pleasant. It dissipated some of his irritation.

Zafin turned back to his desk. ''Well, we won't discipline this what's-his-name . . .''

''Terl,'' said the clerk.

''Terl,'' said Zafin. ''Just put it in his record that he assigns too high priorities to nonsense. He's simply young and ambitious and doesn't know much about being an executive. We don't need a lot of excess and incorrect administration around here! You understand that?"

The clerk said that he did and backed out with the box and its contents. He wrote into Terl's record, "Assigns too high priorities to nonsense; young, ambitious, and unskilled as an executive. Ignore further communications."

The clerk grinned wickedly in his own little cubicle as he realized the description also fit Zafin. He put the answer to Terl's dispatch on it in a precise, clerkly calligraphy and didn't even bother to file a copy. In a few days it would be teleported back to Earth.

The mighty, imperious, and arrogant world of Psychlo hummed on.

— 5 —

The day for the demonstration had arrived and Terl went into a flurry of activity.

Up early, he had again put the animal through its paces. He had made it drive the blade machine up and down and up and down and around and around. Terl had pushed it so hard that the machine had finally run out of fuel. Well, he could fix that.

He went to see Zzt.

"You don't have a requisition," said Zzt.

"But it's just a fuel cartridge."

"I know, I know. But I have to account for them."

Terl grated his fangs. Leverage, leverage, all was leverage, and he didn't have anything at all on Zzt.

Suddenly Zzt halted what he was doing. There was a flicker of a smile on his mouthbones. It made Terl suspicious. "Tell you what I will do," said Zzt. "After all, you did give up five recon drones. I'll just check out that blade machine."

Zzt put on a face mask and Terl followed him outside.

The animal was sitting on the machine, collared, the lead rope firmly fastened to a roll bar. It was kind of bluish and shivering in the bitter wind of late winter. Terl ignored it.

The hood popped up as Zzt released the catches. "I'll just make sure it's all functional," he said, his voice muffled by his face mask and further muffled because his head was in the motor mounts. ''Old machine.''

''It's a wrecked machine,'' said Terl.

''Yes, yes, yes,'' said Zzt, busily pulling and pushing connections. ''But you got it, didn't you?''

The animal was watching everything Zzt did. It was standing there on the top edge of the instrument panel looking down. ''You left a wire loose,'' said the animal.

''Ah, so I did,'' said Zzt. ''You talk?''

''I think you heard me.''

''Yes, I did hear you,'' said Zzt. ''And I also heard no proper, polite phrases.''

Terl snorted. ''It's just an animal. What do you mean, polite phrases? To a mechanic?''

''Well, there,'' said Zzt, ignoring Terl. ''I think that will be fine in there.'' He pulled out a power cartridge and shoved it into the casing and screwed on the cap. ''Start it up.''

Terl reached over and pushed a button and the machine seemed to run all right.

Zzt turned it off for him. ''I understand you're giving some kind of a demonstration today. I never seen no animal drive. Mind if I come out and watch?''

Terl eyed him. He didn't have any leverage on Zzt and all this cooperation and interest was out of character. But he couldn't put a talon on anything wrong. ''Come ahead,'' he grunted. ''It'll take place here in an hour.''

He would kick himself later, but right now he had a lot on his mind.

''Could I get warmed up?'' said Jonnie.

''Shut up, animal,'' said Terl, and he rushed off into the compound.

Nervously Terl waited in the outer office of Numph. One of the clerks had announced him but there had been no invitation to enter.

Finally, after forty-five minutes, he scowled another clerk into announcing him again and this time he was signaled to enter.

Numph had nothing on his desk but a saucepan of kerbango He was looking at the mountain view through the canopy wall. Terl scratched his belt to make a small noise. Numph eventually turned around and gave him an absent look.

"The demonstration you ordered can take place right away," said Terl. "Everything is all ready, Your Planetship."

"Does this have a project number?" said Numph.

Terl hastily made up a number. "Project thirty-nine A, Your Planetship."

"I thought that had to do with new site recruitment."

Terl had saved himself by adding an A, which no projects had. "That was probably thirty-nine. This is thirty-nine A. Substitution of personnel—"

"Ah, yes. Transferring more personnel from home."

"No, Your Planetship. You remember the animal, of course."

Recollection cut into Numph's fog. "Ah, yes. The animal." And he just sat there.

Leverage, leverage, thought Terl. He had no leverage on this old fool. He had combed the offices inside and out and could find none. The home office had merely said he was the uncle of Nipe, Assistant Director of Accounting for Secondary Planets. All this meant, apparently, was that he had his job by influence and was a known incompetent. At least that was all Terl could make out of it.

Obviously, Numph was not going to stir. Terl could see his plans crumbling. He would wind up just vaporizing that damned animal and forgetting it. And all for lack of leverage.

Behind his impassive face, Terl was thinking so hard sparks were flashing internally.

"I'm afraid," said Numph, "that—"

Hastily Terl interrupted. Don't let him say it. Don't let him condemn me to this planet! The inspiration was on his lips in a miraculous bypass of his thinking.

"Have you heard from your nephew lately?" he said. He meant it socially. He was about to add a lie that he had known Nipe in school.

But the effect was out of proportion. Numph jerked forward and looked at him closely. It was not much of a jerk. But it was enough. There was something there!

Terl said nothing. Numph kept looking at him, seeming to wait. Was Numph afraid? He had started to say so, but that was a figure of speech.

"There's no reason to be afraid of the animal," said Terl, smoothly, easily, deliberately misinterpreting things. "It doesn't bite or scratch."

Numph just kept on sitting there. But what was that in his eyes?

"You ordered the demonstration and it's all ready, Your Planetship."

"Ah, yes. The demonstration."

"If you'll just get a mask and come outside . . ."

"Ah, yes. Of course."

The Intergalactic head of the planet drank off the kerbango in steady gulps, got up, and took his face mask off the wall.

He went into the hall and signaled some of his staff to put on their breathe-masks and follow, and then, with many slit-eyed, darting glances at Terl, he walked with him to the outside air. A mystified Terl was jubilant nevertheless. The old fellow positively reeked with fear. The plan was going to come off!

— 6 —

Jonnie sat high on the blade machine. The aching cold wind blew puffs of snow, momentarily obscuring the compound. Jonnie's attention was caught by the approaching crowd. Their combined footfalls made the earth shake.

The place chosen for the demonstration was a small plateau jutting out from the compound. It was a few thousand square feet in extent but ended in a sharp-edged cliff that dropped more than two hundred feet into a ravine. There was room to maneuver but one had to stay away from that edge.

Terl came stomping toward him through the light snow. He stepped up on a lower frame of the blade machine to put his huge face near Jonnie's.

"See that crowd?" said Terl.

Jonnie looked at them. They were gathered by the compound. Zzt was over to their left.

"See this speaker?" said Terl. He jostled a speaking-horn thing in his hand. He had used it before in the drilling.

"See this blaster?" said Terl, and he patted a belt handgun he had buckled on, a huge thing.

"If you do one thing wrong," said Terl, "or foul up in any

way, I will gun you right off that rig. You'll be very dead. Splattered dead."

Terl reached up and made sure the leash was secure; he had wrapped it around the roll bar and welded the end to the rear bumper. It didn't leave much room for Jonnie to move.

His instructions had gone unheard by the small crowd. Now Terl approached them and turned, stood with his huge feet apart, seemed to swell, and yelled, "Start it up!"

Jonnie started it up. He felt uneasy; a sixth sense was biting him, like when you had a puma behind you that you hadn't seen. It wasn't Terl's threats. It was something else. He looked over the crowd.

"Raise the blade!" roared Terl, through the horn.

Jonnie did.

"Lower the blade!"

Jonnie did.

"Roll it ahead."

Jonnie did.

"Back it up."

Jonnie did.

"Put it in a circle."

Jonnie did.

"Now build a mound of snow from all angles!"

Jonnie started maneuvering, handling the controls, taking light scrapes of snow, pushing them to a center. He was doing better than just making a mound; he was building a square-sided pile and leveling off its top. He worked rapidly, backing up, pushing in more snow. The precisely geometric mound took shape.

He had just one more run to make inward, a run that would carry him toward the cliff a few hundred feet away.

Suddenly the controls did not respond. There had been a prolonged whirring whine in the guts of the control box. And every knob and lever on the control panel went slack!

The blade machine yawed to the right, yawed to the left.

Jonnie hammered at the slack controls. Nothing bit! The blade abruptly rose high in the air.

The machine rumbled relentlessly forward and rose up to the top of the pile, almost summersaulted over backward. At the top, it slammed down flat. Then it almost did a forward flip as it went down the other side.

It was rolling straight toward the cliff edge!

Jonnie punched the kill button time after time but it had no effect on the roaring engine.

He fought the controls. They stayed slack.

Wildly he looked back at the crowd. He got a fleeting impression of Zzt off to the side. The brute had something in its paw.

Jonnie strained at the collar that held him to this deadly machine.

He tugged at the flexirope. It was as unyielding as ever.

The cliff edge was coming nearer.

There was a manual blade control to his left, held by a hook. Jonnie fought to get the hook loose. If he could drop the blade it might stick and hold. The hook wouldn't let go.

Jonnie grabbed in his pocket for a fire flint and banged the flint against the hook. The hook let go. By its own weight the scraper blade came down in a swooping arc and gouged into the rocky earth.

The machine rocked and slowed.

There was a small explosion under the hood. An instant later smoke shot up in the air. And a split second after that a roaring tongue of flame rose.

The cliff edge was only a few feet away. Jonnie stared at it for an instant through the growing sheets of flame. The machine edged forward, buckling its scraper blade.

Jonnie whirled to the roll bar behind him. The flexirope was wrapped around and around it. Pressing the rope against the metal he attacked it with the flint. He had tried it before with no success. But on the verge of being yanked in flames two hundred feet down, hope was all he had left.

His back was getting scorched. He turned to face front. The instrument panel was beginning to glow red hot.

The machine inched closer to the edge.

Small explosions sounded as instruments burst. The searing metal of the panel's upper edge was glowing with heat.

Jonnie grabbed what slack he had on the flexirope and held it against the red-hot metal edge. The rope began to melt!

It took all his will power to hold his hands there. The flexirope dripped molten drops.

The machine teetered. At any moment the blade was going to go into vacant space to shoot the machine into thin air.

The flexirope parted!

Jonnie went off the machine in a long dive and rolled.

With a shuddering groan, the last support of the blade snapped.

Flames geysered. As though shot from a catapult, the machine leaped into empty space.

It struck far below on the slope, bounced, plunged to a stop, and was consumed in fire.

Jonnie pressed his burned hands into the cooling snow.

— 7 —

Terl was looking for Zzt.

When the machine finally went over, Terl had looked around in sudden suspicion. But Zzt wasn't there.

The crowd had laughed. Especially at the last part of it when the machine went. And their laughter was like daggers in Terl's ears.

Numph just stood there, shaking his head. He seemed almost cheerful when he commented to Terl, "Well, just shows you what animals can do." Only then had he laughed. "They pee on the floor!"

They had drifted back to their offices and Terl was now searching the transport compound. In the underground floors, he walked past rows and rows of out-of-use vehicles, battle planes, trucks, blade scrapers . . . yes, and ground cars, some of them quite posh. It had not struck him before how villainous was Zzt's pawing off on him of that old wreck of a Mark II.

He searched fruitlessly for half an hour and then decided to try the repair room again.

Seething, he stomped into it and stared around.

His earbones picked up a tiny whisper of metal on metal.

He knew that sound. It was the safety slide being pulled back on a blaster.

"Stand right there," said Zzt. "Keep your paws well away from your belt gun."

Terl turned. Zzt had been standing just inside a dark tool locker.

Terl was boiling. "You installed a remote control when you 'fixed' that motor!"

"Why not?" said Zzt. "And a remote destruct charge as well."

Terl was incredulous. "You admit it!"

"No witnesses here. Your word, my word. Means nothing."

"But it was your own machine!"

"Written off. Plenty of machines."

"But why did you do it?"

"I thought it was pretty clever, actually." He stepped forward, holding the long-barreled blast gun in one hand.

"But why?"

"You let our pay and bonuses be cut. If you didn't do it, you let it be done."

"But look, if I could make animal operators, profits would come back."

"That's your idea."

"It's a good idea!" snapped Terl.

"All right. I'll be frank. You ever try to keep machines going without mechanics? Your animal operators would have just messed up equipment. One just did, didn't it?"

"*You* messed that up," said Terl. "You realize that if this occurred on your report, you'd be out of work."

"It won't occur on my report. There are no witnesses. Numph even saw me walk off before the thing went wild. He would never forward the report. Besides, they all thought it was funny."

"Lots of things can be funny," said Terl.

Zzt motioned with the blaster barrel. "Why don't you just walk out of here and have a nice crap."

Leverage. Leverage, thought Terl. He was fresh out of it.

He left the garage.

— 8 —

Jonnie was a mound of misery in the cage.

The monster had pitched him in there before going off.

It was cold but Jonnie could not hold a flint in his hands to start a fire. His fingers were a mass of blisters. And somehow, right then, he didn't want much to do with fire.

His face was scorched, eyebrows and beard singed away. Some of his hair was gone. The old Chinko uniform cloth must have been fireproof—it had not ignited or melted, thus saving body burns.

Bless the Chinkos. Poor devils. With their polite phrases and brightness they had yet been exterminated.

That was one lesson to be learned. Anyone who befriended or sought to cooperate with the Psychlos was doomed from the beginning.

Terl had not made one motion in the direction of that burning vehicle to salvage him, knowing he was tied to it. Compassion and decency were no part of the Psychlo character. Terl had even had a gun and could have shot the flexirope in half.

Jonnie felt the ground rumble. The monster was in the cage. A boot toe turned him over. Slitted, amber eyes appraised him.

"You'll live," grunted Terl indifferently. "How long will it take you to get well?"

Jonnie said nothing. He just looked up at Terl.

"You're stupid," said Terl. "You don't know anything about remote controls."

"And what could I have done, tied to the seat?" said Jonnie.

"Zzt, the bastard, put a remote control under the hood. And a firebomb."

"How was I supposed to see that?"

"You could have inspected."

Jonnie smiled thinly. "Tied to the cab?"

"You know now. When we do it again I'll—"

"There won't be any 'again,' " said Jonnie.

Terl loomed over him, looking down.

"Not under these conditions," said Jonnie.

"Shut up, animal!"

"Take off this collar. My neck is burned."

Terl looked at the frayed flexirope. He went out of the cage and came back with a small welding unit and a new coil of rope. It wasn't flexirope. It was thinner and metallic. He burned off the old rope and welded the new one on, ignoring Jonnie's effort to twist away from the flame. He fixed the far end of the new rope into a loop and dropped it over a high cage bar out of reach.

With Jonnie's eyes burning holes in his back, Terl went out of the cage and locked the door.

Jonnie wrapped himself in the dirty fur of a robe and lay in sodden misery beneath the newly fallen snow.

■

PART 4

— 1 —

It had been a very bad winter in the mountains; snowslides had early blocked the passes into the high meadow.

Chrissie sat quietly and forlornly in front of the council in the courthouse. The wind whined and moaned through the gaps in the walls, and the fire that had been built in the center of the room sent harried palls of smoke into the faces of the council.

Parson Staffor lay very ill in a nearby hut. The winter had sapped what little vitality he had and his place was taken by the older Jimson man they were now calling parson. Jimson was flanked by an elder named Clay and by Brown Limper Staffor, who seemed to be acting as a council member even though he was far too young and clubfooted—he had begun to sit in for Parson Staffor when he became ill and had just stayed on, grown into a council member now. The three men sat on an old bench.

Chrissie, across the fire from them, was not paying much attention. She had had a horrible nightmare two nights ago—a nightmare that had yanked her, sweating, out of sleep and left her trembling ever since. She had dreamed that Jonnie had been consumed in fire. He had been calling her name and it still sounded in her ears.

"It's just plain foolishness," Parson Jimson was saying to her. "There are three young men who want to marry you and you have no right whatever to refuse them. The village population is dwindling in size; only thirty have survived the winter. This is not a time to be thinking only of yourself."

Chrissie numbly realized he was talking to her. She made an effort to gather the words in: something about population. Two babies had been born that winter and two babies had died. The young men had not driven many cattle up from the plains before the pass closed and the village was half-starved. If Jonnie had been here . . .

"When spring comes," said Chrissie, "I'm going down on the plains to find Jonnie."

This was no shock to the council. They had heard her say it several times since Jonnie left.

Brown Limper looked through the smoke at her. He had a faint sneer on his thin lips. The council tolerated him because he didn't ever say much and because he brought them water and food when meetings were too long. But he couldn't resist. "We all know Jonnie must be dead. The monsters must have got him."

Jimson and Clay frowned at him. He had been the one who brought to their attention the fact that Chrissie refused to marry any of the young men. Clay wondered whether Brown Limper didn't have a personal stake in this.

Chrissie rallied from her misery. 'His horses didn't come home."

"Maybe the monsters got them, too," said Brown Limper.

"Jonnie did not believe there were any monsters," said Chrissie. "He went to find the Great Village of the legend."

"Oh, there are monsters, all right," said Jimson. "It is blasphemy to doubt the legends."

"Then," said Chrissie, "why don't they come here?"

"The mountains are holy," said Jimson.

"The snow," said Brown Limper, "closed the passes before the horses could come home. That is, if the monsters didn't get them, too."

The older men looked at him, frowning him to silence.

"Chrissie," said Parson Jimson, "you are to put aside this foolishness and permit the young men to court you. It is quite obvious that Jonnie Goodboy Tyler is gone."

"When the year has gone by," said Chrissie, "I shall go down to the plains."

"Chrissie," said Clay, "this is simply a suicidal idea."

Chrissie looked into the fire. Jonnie's scream echoed in her ears from the nightmare. It was completely true, what they said: she did not want to live if Jonnie was dead. And then the sound of the scream died away and she seemed to hear him whisper her name. She looked up with a trace of defiance.

"He is not dead," said Chrissie.

The three council members looked at each other. They had not prevailed. They would try again some other day.

They ignored her and fell to discussing the fact that Parson Staffor wanted a funeral when he died. There wouldn't be much in the way of food and there were problems of digging in the frozen ground. Of course he was entitled to a funeral, for he had been parson and maybe even mayor for many years. But there were problems.

Chrissie realized she was dismissed, and she got up, eyes red with more than smoke, and walked to the courthouse door.

She wrapped the bearskin more tightly about her and looked up at the wintry sky. When the constellation was in that same place in spring she would go. The wind was cutting keen and she pulled the bearskin even tighter. Jonnie had given her the bearskin and she fingered it. She would get busy and make him some new buckskin clothes. She would prepare packs. She would not let them eat the last two horses.

When the time came she would be all ready to go. And she would go.

A blast of wind from Highpeak chilled her, mocked her. Nevertheless, when the time came she would go.

— 2 —

Terl was in a furious burst of activity. He hardly slept. He left the kerbango alone. The doom of years of exile on this cursed planet haunted him; each time he slowed his pace he collided with the horrible thought and it jabbed him into even greater efforts.

Leverage, leverage! He conceived himself to be a pauper in leverage.

He had a few things on employees here and there, but they were minor things: peccadillos with some of the Psychlo female clerks, drunkenness on the job leading to breakage, tapes of mutterings about foremen, personal letters smuggled into the teleportation of ore, but nothing *big*. This was not the kind of thing personal fortunes were easily built from. Yet here were thousands of Psychlos, and his experience as a security officer told him the odds in favor of finding blackmail material were large. The company did not hire angels. It hired miners and mining administrators and it hired them tough; in some cases, particularly on a planet like this—no favored spot—the company even winked at taking on ex-criminals. It was a criticism of himself, no less, that he could not get more blackmail than he had.

This Numph. Now *there* was one. He had potential leverage on Numph but Terl did not know what it was. He knew it had something to do with the nephew Nipe in home office accounting. But Terl could not dig out what it really was. And so he dared not push it. The risk lay in pretending to be wise to it and then, by some slip, revealing he didn't have the data. The leverage would go up in smoke, for Numph would know Terl had nothing. So he had to use it so sparingly that it was almost no use at all. Blast!

As the days and weeks of winter went on, a new factor arose. His requests for information from the home planet were not being answered. Only that one scrap about Nipe, that was all. It was a trifle frightening. No answers. He could send green flash urgents until he wore out his pen and there wasn't even an acknowledgment.

He had even become sly and reported the discovery of a nonexistent hoard of arms. Actually it was just a couple of muzzle-loading bronze cannon some workman had dug up in a minesite on the overseas continent. But Terl had worded the report in such a way that it was alarming, although it could be retracted with no damage to himself: a routine, essential report. And no acknowledgment had come back. *None*.

He had investigated furiously to see whether other departmental reports got like treatment—they didn't. He had considered the possibility that Numph was removing reports from the teleportation box. Numph wasn't.

Home office knew he existed, that was for sure. They had confirmed the additional ten-year duty stretch, had noted Numph's commendation affirmative, and had added the clause of *company optional extension*. So they knew he was alive, and there could not possibly be any action being taken against him or he would have intercepted interrogatories about himself. There had been none.

So, without any hope of home office cooperation, it was

obviously up to Terl to dig himself out. The ancient security maxim was ever present in his mind now: where a situation is needed but doesn't exist, *make one*.

His pockets bulged with button cameras and his skill in hiding them was expert. Every picto-recorder he could lay his paws on lined the shelves of his office—and he kept his door locked.

Just now he was glued to a scope, observing the garage interior. He was waiting for Zzt to go to lunch. In his belt Terl had the duplicate keys to the garage.

Open beside him was the book of company regulations relating to the conduct of personnel (Security Volume 989), and it was open to Article 34a-IV (Uniform Code of Penalties).

The article said: "Wherein and whereas theft viciously affects profits . . ." and there followed five pages of company theft penalties, ". . . and whereas and wherefore company personnel also have rights to their monies, bonuses, and possessions . . ." and there followed one page of different aspects of it, ". . . the theft of personal monies from the quarters of employees by employees, when duly evidenced, shall carry the penalty of vaporization."

That was the key to Terl's present operation. It didn't say theft went on record. It didn't say a word about when it happened as related to when it was to be punished. The key items were "when duly evidenced" and "vaporization." There was no judicial vaporization chamber on this planet, but that was no barrier. A blast gun could vaporize anyone with great thoroughness.

There were two other clauses in that book that were important: "All company executives of whatever grade shall uphold these regulations"; and "The enforcement of all such regulations shall be vested in the security officers, their assistants, deputies, and personnel." The earlier one included Numph—he could not even squeak. The latter one meant Terl, the sole and only security officer—or deputy or assistant or personnel—on this planet.

Terl had spot-watched Zzt for a couple of days now and he knew where he kept his dirty workcoats and caps.

Aha, Zzt was leaving. Terl waited to make sure the transport chief did not come back because he had forgotten something. Good. He was gone.

With speed, but not to betray himself or alarm anyone by rushing if met in the halls, Terl went to the garage.

He let himself in with a duplicate key and went directly to the washroom. He took down a dirty workcoat and cap. He let himself out and locked the door behind him.

For days now Terl had also watched, with an artfully concealed button camera, the room of the smaller Chamco brother. He had found what he wanted. After work, the smaller Chamco brother habitually changed from his mine clothes in his room and put on a long coat he affected for dinner and an evening's gambling in the recreation area. More: the smaller Chamco brother always put and kept his cash in the cup of an antique drinking horn that hung on the wall of his room.

Terl now scanned the minesite patiently. He finally spotted the smaller Chamco brother exiting from the compound, finished with lunch, and boarding the bus to the teleportation transshipment area where he worked. Good. Terl also scanned the compound corridors. They were empty in the berthing areas during work time.

Working fast, Terl looked from a stilled picto-recorder frame of Zzt to the mirror before him and began to apply makeup. He thickened his eyebones, added length to his fangs, roughed the fur on his cheeks, and labored to get the resemblance exact. What a master of skills one had to be in security.

Made up, he donned the workcoat and cap.

He took five hundred credits in bills from his own wallet. The top one he marked: "Good luck!" very plainly. He scribbled several different names on it with different pens.

He connected a remote control to a picto-recorder that was registering the Chamco room, checked everything, and checked the mirror too.

One more look at the live view of the garage. Yes, Zzt was back, puttering around with a big motor. That would keep him busy for a while.

Terl sped down the corridors of the berthing compound. He entered the smaller Chamco brother's room with a passkey. He checked the drinking horn on the wall. Yes, it had money in it. He put in the five hundred credits. He went back to the door. Ready!

He touched the remote control in his pocket.

Imitating the rolling walk of Zzt, he went over to the drinking horn and with stealthy movements took out the five hundred credits, looked around as though fearful of being observed, counted the money—the marked bill plainly in view—and then crept out of the room, closing and locking the door.

A berthing attendant saw him from a distance and he ducked.

He got back to his room and swiftly removed the makeup. He put the five hundred credits back in his wallet.

When the screen showed him Zzt had gone for dinner, he returned the cap and workcoat to the washroom.

Back in his own quarters, Terl rubbed his paws.

Leverage. Leverage. Stage one of this lever was done, and he was going to pull it and good.

— 3 —

It was a night that was long remembered by the employees in the recreation area of the minesite.

They were not unused to seeing Terl drunk, but tonight—well! The attendant shoveled panful after panful of kerbango at him and he took them all.

Terl had begun the evening looking depressed, and that was understandable since he wasn't very popular lately—if he ever had been. Char had watched him slit-eyed for a while, but Terl was obviously just bent on getting drunk. Finally Terl seemed to rouse himself and did a bit of paw-gripping—a game whose object was to see which player couldn't stand it any more and let go—with some of the mine managers. Terl had lost in every case; he was getting drunker and drunker.

And now Terl was heckling the smaller Chamco brother into a game of rings. It was a gambling game. A player took a ring and put it on the back of the paw and then with the other paw snapped it off and sailed it at a board. The board had pegs with numbers, the bigger numbers all around the edges. The one that got the biggest number won. Then stakes were put up again and another round occurred.

The smaller Chamco brother hadn't wanted to take him on. Terl was usually very good at rings. Then his drunken condition became too alluring and the Chamco let himself be persuaded.

They started by putting up ten-credit bets—steep enough for the recreation area. Chamco got a ninety and Terl a sixteen.

Terl insisted upon raising the bets and the Chamco couldn't refuse, of course.

The ring shot by the smaller Chamco brother sizzled through the atmosphere and clanged over a four peg. The Chamco groaned. Anything could beat that. And lately he had been saving his money. When he got home—in just a few months now—he was going to buy a wife. And this bet had been thirty credits!

Terl went through contortions of motions, put the ring on the back of his paw, sighted across it, and then with the other paw sent it like a ray blast at the board. A three! Terl lost.

As the winner, the smaller Chamco brother couldn't quit. And Terl had taken another pan of kerbango, leering around at the interested gallery, and upped the bets.

The onlookers placed some side bets of their own. Terl was reeling drunk. He did have a reputation with this game, which made the odds lower, but he was so obviously drunk that he even faced the wrong direction and had to be turned in the right one.

The smaller Chamco brother got fifty. Terl got two. "Ah, no, you don't quit now," Terl said. "The winner can't quit." His words were slurred. "I bet . . . I bet one hun— . . . hundred credits."

Well, with pay halved and bonuses gone, nobody was going to object to winning easy money, and the smaller Chamco went along.

The audience roared at Terl's bungling as loss after loss occurred. And the smaller Chamco brother found himself standing there with four hundred fifty credits.

Terl reeled over to the attendant and got another saucepan of kerbango. As he drank it he went through his pockets, turning them out one by one. Finally he came up with a single bill, a bit crumpled and marked all over.

"My good-luck money," sobbed Terl.

He lurched over to the firing position in front of the board. "Chamco Two, just one more crap-little bet. You see this bill?"

The smaller Chamco brother looked the bill over. It was a good-luck bill. Mine employees taking off for far places after a final party sometimes exchanged good-luck bills. Everybody signed everybody else's bill. And this had a dozen signatures on it.

"I'm betting my good-luck bill," said Terl. "But you got to promise you won't spend it and that you'll trade it back to me on payday if I . . . I lose it?"

The smaller Chamco brother had gotten money-hungry by now. He was picking up nearly two weeks' pay, and the wage cuts had hurt. Yes, he'd promise to do that.

As winner, the smaller Chamco brother went first. He had never been very good at rings. He fired and ouch! It was a one. Anything, but anything, would beat it.

Terl stared at it. He went drunkenly forward and looked at it closely. He reeled back to the firing line, faced the wrong way, had to be turned, and then zip! He got off a sizzler.

It hit the blank wall.

With that, Terl passed out. The attendant, helped by the Chamcos and Char and couple of others, got Terl on a banquet serving trolley that groaned and bent. They wheeled him in a triumphal parade to his quarters, got the key out of his pocket, brought him in, and dumped him on the floor. They were pretty drunk, too, and they went away chanting the funeral dirge of the Psychlos in a most feeling way.

When they were gone, Terl crawled to the door and closed and locked it.

He had taken counter-kerbango pills after dinner, and all he had to do now was get rid of the excess, which he did, tickling his throat with a talon over the wash basin.

Quietly then, with great satisfaction, he undressed and got into bed and had a beautiful sleep full of beautiful dreams concerning the beautiful future of Terl.

— 4 —

Jonnie heard the monster enter the cage and close the door.

In the past few weeks Jonnie's hands and face had healed and his hair; eyebrows, and beard had grown out. His reflection in the water from the snow he had melted in a pan told him that. He couldn't see any scars on his hands but they still looked red where they had been burned.

He was wrapped in a robe, facing away from the door, and he didn't look around. He had worked late with the instruction machine.

"Look over here, animal," said Terl. "See what I brought you."

There was something different in the monster's voice. It seemed jovial if that were possible. Jonnie sat up and looked.

Terl was holding up four rats by their tails. Lately the nearby rat population had been cut down and Terl had been shooting rabbits and bringing them in, a very welcome change indeed. Yet here were more rats and the monster thought it was a favor.

Jonnie lay down again. Terl threw the rats over by the fire. One wasn't quite dead and started to crawl away. Terl flashed his handgun from its holster and blew its head off.

Jonnie sat up. Terl was putting the gun away.

"Trouble with you, animal," said Terl, "you have no sense of appreciation. Have you finished the discs on basic electronics?"

Actually, Jonnie had. Terl had brought the discs weeks ago, along with some discs on higher mathematics. He didn't bother to answer.

"Anybody that could be fooled by remote controls couldn't ever really operate machines," said Terl. He had harped on this before, omitting the truth that it was he who had been fooled.

"Well, here are some other texts. And you better wrap your rat brain around them if you ever expect to handle machines—mining machines."

Terl threw three books at him. They looked huge but they were featherweight. One hit Jonnie but he caught the other two. He looked at them. They were Psychlo texts, not Chinko translations. One was *Control Systems for Beginning Engineers*. Another was *Electronic Chemistry*. The third was *Power and its Transmission*. Jonnie wanted the books. Knowledge was the key out of captivity. But he put the books down and looked at Terl.

"Get those into your rat brain and you won't be sending machines over cliffs," said Terl. Then he came nearer and sat down in the chair. He looked closely at Jonnie. "When are you really going to start cooperating?"

Jonnie knew this was a very dangerous monster. a monster that wanted something that hadn't been named.

"Maybe never," said Jonnie.

Terl sat back, watching Jonnie closely. "Well, never mind, animal. I see you pretty well recovered from your burns. Your fur is growing back." Jonnie knew Terl had no interest in that and wondered what was coming next.

"You know, animal," said Terl, "you sure had me fooled that first day." Terl's eyes were watchful but he seemed to be just rambling along. "I thought you were four-legged!" He laughed very falsely. "It sure was a surprise when you fell apart into *two* animals." He laughed again, amber eyes very cunning. "Wonder what happened to that horse."

Before he could stop himself, Jonnie experienced a wave of sorrow over Windsplitter. He choked it off instantly.

Terl looked at him. Then he got up and wandered over to the cage door. To himself Terl was thinking: the horse is a key to this. He had been right. The animal was attached emotionally to that horse. Leverage, leverage. It came in many guises and its use was power.

Terl appeared to be laughing. "You sure had me fooled that first day. Well, I've got to be going. Get busy on those books, rat brain." He went out. "That's a good one; *rat brain.*"

Jonnie sat staring after him. He knew he had betrayed something. And he knew Terl was up to something. But what? Was Windsplitter alive?

Uneasy, Jonnie built up the fire and began to look over the books. And then he was gripped in a sudden wave of excitement: he had found "uranium" listed in the index of *Electronic Chemistry*.

— 5 —

Terl was not at all surprised to see the smaller Chamco brother come nervously into his office.

"Terl," he said hesitantly. "You know that good-luck credit note you lost to me. Well, I won't be able to exchange—"

"What are you talking about?" said Terl.

"That good-luck credit note. You lost it to me and I promised to exchange it with you. I wanted to tell you—"

"Wait a minute," said Terl. He fished out his wallet and looked into it. "Hey, you're right. It isn't here."

"You lost it to me playing rings and I promised to exchange it back. Well—"

"Oh, yes. I have some dim recollection of it. That was quite a night. I was drunk, I guess. What about it?"

The smaller Chamco brother was nervous. But Terl seemed so open and pleasant he was emboldened. "Well, it's gone. Stolen."

"Stolen!" barked Terl.

"Yes. Actually the five hundred credits I won and a hundred sixty-five more besides. The good-luck bill was among—"

"Hey, now. Slow up. Stolen from where?"

"My room."

Terl got out an official pad and began to make notes "About what time?"

"Maybe yesterday. Last night I went to get some drinking money and I found—"

"Yesterday. Hmmm." Terl sat back thoughtfully and gnawed at the top of his pen, "You know this isn't the first theft reported from rooms. There were two others. But you're in luck."

"How so?"

"Well, you realize of course that I am responsible for security." Terl made an elaborate demonstration of searching through piles of junk on his back bench. He turned to the smaller Chamco brother. "I shouldn't let you in on this." He looked thoughtful, then seemed to make a sudden decision. "I can trust you to keep this secret."

"Absolutely," said the smaller Chamco brother.

"Old Numph worries all the time about mutinies."

"He should after that pay cut."

"And so—well, you understand, I wouldn't do this on my own initiative-but it just so happened that your room was under surveillance yesterday—along with several other rooms, of course."

This did not much shock the Chamco. The company often put work areas and quarters under surveillance.

Terl was fumbling through stacks of discs among the clutter. "I haven't reviewed them. Actually, never intended to. Anything to keep management happy . . . ah, yes. Here it is. What time yesterday?"

"I don't know."

Terl put the disc on a player and turned on the screen. "You're just lucky."

"I should say so!"

"We'll just scan through this disc. It was on for two or three days . . . I'll give it a fast-forward."

"Wait!" said the smaller Chamco brother. "Something flashed by."

Terl obligingly reversed it. "Probably just you going in and out. I never review these things. It takes so long and there's so much to do. Company regulations—"

"Wait! Look at that!"

Terl said. "Here?"

"Yes. Who's that?"

Terl brightened up the screen.

"That's Zzt!" cried the Chamco. "Look what he's doing! Searching the room. Hah! He found it. Crap! Look at that! There's your bill!"

"Incredible," said Terl. "You sure are lucky there was a mutiny scare on. Where you going?"

The Chamco had made an angry dive at the door, "I'm going down and beat the crap out of that low—"

"No, no," said Terl. "That won't get your money back." And it wouldn't either, for the money was nestling in a wad under Terl's front belt. He had taken it from the room soon after the Chamco had hidden it. "This has become an official matter because it was detected on an official disc, during an official surveillance."

Terl opened a book of regulations, Volume 989, to Article 34a-IV. He turned several pages and then spun the book about and showed the Chamco where it said "theft of personal monies from the quarters of employees by employees," and "when duly evidenced" and "vaporization."

The smaller Chamco read it. He was surprised. "I didn't know it was that stiff."

"Well, it is. And this is official, so don't go rushing off to take the law into your own hands."

Terl took a blast rifle out of the rack and handed it to the smaller Chamco. "You know how to use this. It's fully charged. You're now a deputy."

The smaller Chamco was impressed. He stood there fumbling with the catches and made sure the safety was on. "You mean I can kill him?"

"We'll see. This is official."

Terl picked up the disc and a smaller portable screen and player and the book of regulations, then looked around to see whether he had everything. "Come along. Stay behind me and say nothing."

They went to the quarters and found an attendant. Yes, the attendant had seen Zzt coming out of Chamco's room. Yes, he knew Zzt by sight. He didn't recall whether it was the thirteenth or the fourteenth of the month. But he'd seen him. He was cautioned to say nothing, for "it was official and had to do with mutiny surveillance," and the attendant obligingly signed the witness report, vowing to himself to be sure to keep quiet. He didn't care much for executives anyway.

And so it was that Terl, followed by the smaller Chamco brother with a blast rifle in ready position, came to the maintenance area of the garage. Terl snapped a small button camera on the wall and pushed its remote.

Zzt looked up. He had a heavy wrench in his paw. He looked at the blast rifle and the set faces. Fear stirred in him.

"Put down that wrench," said Terl. "Turn around and hold onto that chain-lift rail with both paws."

Zzt threw the wrench. It missed. Terl's paws batted him across three dollies. The Chamco danced around trying to get in a shot.

Terl put his boot on Zzt's neck. He waved the Chamco back.

His body obscuring the Chamco's view, Terl knelt and, with a rapid sleight of paw, "extracted" the wad of bills from Zzt's rear pocket.

Terl handed them to the Chamco. "Are these your bills?"

Zzt had rolled over and stared up at them from the greasy floor.

The Chamco counted. "Six hundred fifty credits. And here's the good-luck bill!" He was ecstatic.

Terl said, "You're witness to the fact they were in his back pocket."

"Absolutely!" said the Chamco.

"Show that bill to the camera on the wall," said Terl.

"What is this?" roared Zzt.

"Back up and keep that blast rifle ready," said Terl to the Chamco. Then, keeping himself out of the fire path to Zzt, he laid the things he had carried on the bench. He opened the book of regulations and pointed it out to Zzt.

Zzt angrily read it aloud. He faltered toward the end and turned to Terl. "Vaporize! I didn't know that!"

"Ignorance is no excuse, but few employees know all the

regulations. That you didn't know it is probably why you did it."

"Did what?" cried Zzt.

Terl turned on the disc. Zzt looked at it, confused, incredulous. He saw *himself* stealing the money!

Before Zzt could recover, Terl showed him the attendant's signed statement.

"Do I vaporize him now?" begged the Chamco, waving the rifle about and fumbling off the safety catch.

Terl waved a conciliatory paw. "Chamco, we know you have every right—no, actually the duty—to carry out the execution." He looked at Zzt, who was standing there stunned. "Zzt, you're not going to do this sort of thing again, are you?"

Zzt was shaking his head, not in answer but in dumbfounded confusion.

Terl turned back to Chamco. "You see? Now, listen, Chamco, I can understand your anger. This is a first-time mistake for Zzt. You've got your money back—and by the way, we'll exchange that bill now. I'll need it for the evidence file."

The Chamco took the note Terl offered and handed over the good-luck bill. Terl held the bill up to the wall camera running on remote and then laid it down on the statement.

"You see, Chamco," said Terl, "I can keep this file open, but in a safe place where it can be found if anything happens to either of us. It can be activated at any time. And *would* be activated if further offenses occurred." His voice took on a pleading tone. "Zzt has been a valuable fellow in the past. As a favor to me, lay aside your revenge and let it lie."

The Chamco was thoughtful, his bloodlust cooling.

Terl glanced at Zzt and saw no attack signals. He put out his paw to the Chamco. "Give me the rifle." The Chamco did and Terl put on the safety slide. "Thank you," said Terl. "The company is indebted to you. You can go back to work."

The Chamco smiled. This Terl was sure a fair and efficient Psychlo. "I sure appreciate your getting my money back," said the Chamco and left.

Terl turned off the camera he had put on the wall and restored it to his pocket. Then he picked up the things on the bench and made them into a neat package.

Zzt was standing there restraining the tremble that threatened to engulf him. The aura of death had gripped him all too nearly. Stark terror flared in his eyes as he looked at Terl. He was not seeing Terl. He was seeing the most diabolical devil ever drawn in the mythology of the Psychlos.

"All right?" said Terl quietly.

Zzt sank slowly down on a bench.

Terl waited a bit but Zzt didn't move. "Now to business," said Terl. "I want certain things assigned to my department. A Mark III ground car, executive. Two battle planes, unlimited range. Three personnel freighters. And fuel and ammunition without inventory. And a few other things. In fact, I just happen to have the requisitions right here for you to sign. Oh, yes, there are some blank ones, too. All right?"

Zzt did not resist the pen as it was pushed between his claws. The thick sheaf of requisitions was slipped onto his knee. Lifelessly he began to sign each one.

That night a very cheerful Terl, who said he felt lucky even though a bit drunk, won all six hundred fifty credits back from the smaller Chamco brother in a very narrowly contested game of rings.

Terl even bought kerbango for the whole crowd out of his winnings as a good-night gesture. They cheered him when he happily rumbled off to a well-earned sleep.

He dreamed beautiful dreams wherein leverage made him wealthy, crowned him king, and got him far away from this accursed planet.

— 6 —

Jonnie laid down his book and stood, stretching. There was more than a smell of spring in the air. The snow had run off and only lingered in shady places. The air was crystal, the sky a beautiful blue. There was a surging tension in his limbs and muscles. It was one thing to be cooped up in winter. It was quite another to sit in a cage in spring.

He saw what had distracted him a few moments before. Terl drove up to the cage gate in a long, sleekly gleaming, black tank. It purred quietly, hiding awesome power behind its gun muzzles and slitted ports.

Terl bounded out and the ground shook. He was very jovial. "Get your clothes on, animal. We're going for a drive."

Jonnie was dressed in buckskin.

"No, no, no," said Terl. "Clothes! Not hides. You'll stink up my new ground car. How do you like it?"

Jonnie was suddenly alert. Terl asking for opinion or admiration was not the Terl he knew. "I'm dressed," said Jonnie.

Terl was unhooking the leash from the cage. "Oh, well. What's the difference? I can stand it if you can. Get your air mask. You'll be inside, and I am damned if I'll drive around in one. Bring your clubs, too."

Now Jonnie *was* alert. He put on a belt and a pouch with flints and the bits of glass for cutting. He put the thong of the kill-club over his wrist.

Terl checked the air bottles and playfully snapped the elastic of Jonnie's mask as he put it on him. "Now get in, animal. Get in. Some ground car, eh?"

Indeed it was, thought Jonnie, as the gunner's seat engulfed him. Blazing purple fabric, gleaming instrument panel, and shining control buttons.

"I checked her all out for remotes," said Terl. He laughed and laughed at his joke as he climbed in. "You know what I'm referring to, rat brain. No over the cliff on fire today." He hit a button and the doors closed and sealed. He turned on the breathe-gas louvers and the atmosphere changed in a blink. "Crap, were you stupid!" he laughed some more.

The ground car went hurtling toward the open, four feet above the earth, accelerating to two hundred miles per hour in a breath, almost breaking Jonnie's spine.

Terl unsnapped his face mask and threw it aside. "You see those doors? Don't ever hit a latch or try to open one when I'm not wearing a mask, animal. This thing would wreck with no driver."

Jonnie looked at the latches and buttons and noted the information carefully. What a good idea.

"Where are we going?" he asked.

"Oh, just a drive, just a drive. Seeing the sights."

Jonnie doubted that. He was watching every control action Terl was making. He could identify most of the levers and buttons already.

They sped north and then in a long curve headed south of

west. Despite the blur of speed, Jonnie could see they were following some ancient, grass-overgrown highway. By the sun he marked their course.

Through the heavily plated gunner's slits he could see a mass of ancient buildings and a field. A high mountain lay beyond. A range lay to the west. The ground car slowed and drew up a distance from the largest building. Jonnie looked at the desolate scene of ruin.

Terl reached into the ground car bar and drew himself a small pan of kerbango. He drank it off and smacked his mouthbones and belched. Then he put on his face mask and hit the door button. "Well, get out, get out and see the sights."

Jonnie shut off his air and removed his mask. Terl flipped the leash to give it length and Jonnie got out. He looked around. In a nearby field there were some mounds of what had been machines, perhaps. The structures before him were impressive. Near where they stood was a sort of trench, long overgrown, curving. The grass was tall and the wind from the mountains moaned lonesomely.

"What was this place?" said Jonnie.

Terl stood with his elbow braced against the top of the car, indolent, very casual. "Animal, you are looking at the primary defense base of this planet during the days of man."

"Yes?" prompted Jonnie.

Terl reached into the car and brought out a Chinko guidebook and threw it at him. A page was marked. It said, "A short distance from the minesite lies an impressive military ruin. Thirteen days after the Psychlo attack, a handful of men stood off a Psychlo tank for over three hours, using primitive weapons. It was the last resistance that was overcome by the Psychlos." That was all it said.

Jonnie looked around.

Terl pointed at the curved trench. "It happened right here," he said, with a sweep of his paw. "Look." He dealt out more leash.

Jonnie crept over to the trench. It was hard to see where it began and ended. It had some stones in front of it. The grass was very tall, moving in the wind.

"Look good," said Terl.

Jonnie moved down into the trench. And then he saw it. Although a great time had passed, there were scraps of metal that had been guns. And there were scraps of uniforms, mainly buried, hardly more than impressions.

Suddenly he was gripped by the vision of desperate men, fighting valiantly, hopelessly. He glanced across the field before the trench and could almost see the Psychlo tank coming on, withdrawing, coming on, battering them at last to death.

Jonnie's heart rose, swelled in his chest. Blood hammered in his ears.

Terl leaned indolently against the car. "Seen enough?"

"Why have you shown me this?"

Terl barked a laugh behind his mask. "So you won't get any ideas, animal. This was the number-one defense base of the planet. And just one measly Psychlo tank knocked it to bits in a wink. Got it?"

That wasn't what Jonnie had gotten. Terl, who couldn't read English had not read the still-plain letters on the building. Those letters said, ["United States Air Force Academy"].

"Well, put on your mask and get in. We have other things to do today."

Jonnie got in. It had not been the "primary defense base." It was just a school. And that handful of men had been schoolboys, cadets. And they'd had the guts to stand off a Psychlo tank, outgunned, hopeless, for three hours!

As they moved off, Jonnie looked back at the trench. His people. Men! He found it hard to breathe. They had not died tamely. They had fought.

— 7 —

Terl drove straight north, following the overgrown bed of an old highway. For all his joviality he was thinking very hard. Fear and leverage. If you didn't have leverage you could make fear work. He felt he had already accomplished a little bit: the animal had seemed impressed back there. But he had a lot to do to get both fear and leverage and get enough of them to break this animal and cow it completely.

"Comfortable?" asked Terl.

Jonnie snapped out of his daydream and became instantly alert. This was not the Terl he knew. Casual. Chatty even. Jonnie was on his guard.

"Where are we going?" he said.

"Just a little drive. New ground car. Doesn't she run well?"

The tank ran well all right. The plate on the panel said "Mark III General Purpose Tank, Executive, 'The Enemy Is Dead,' Intergalactic Mining Company Serial ET-5364724354-7. Use Only Faro Power Cartridges and Breathe-Gas. 'Faro is the Breath and Power of Life.' "

"Is 'Faro' part of Intergalactic?" said Jonnie.

Terl took his eyes off driving for a moment and looked suspiciously at Jonnie. Then he shrugged, "Don't you bother your little rat brain about the size of Intergalactic, animal. It's a monopoly that stretches across every galaxy. It's a size and scope you couldn't grasp if you had a thousand rat brains."

"It's all run from home planet, isn't it?"

"Why not," said Terl. "Something wrong with that?"

"No," said Jonnie. "No. Just seems an awfully big company to be run from one planet."

"That isn't all Psychlo runs," said Terl. "There's dozens of companies the size of Intergalactic and Psychlo runs them all."

"Must be a big planet," said Jonnie.

"Big and powerful," said Terl. Might as well add a little more fear. "Psychlo can and has crushed every opposition that ever stood in her path. One Imperial check mark on an order and a whole race can go phuttt!"

"Like the Chinkos?" said Jonnie.

"Yes." Terl was bored.

"Like the human race here?"

"Yes, and like one rat-brained animal will go phuttt if it doesn't shut up," said Terl in sudden irritation.

"Thank you," said Jonnie.

"That's better. Even becoming properly polite!" Terl's good humor returned, but it wouldn't have had he realized that the "thank you" had been for vital information.

Abruptly their headlong pace swept them into the outskirts of the city.

"Where are we?" said Jonnie.

"They called it 'Denver.' "

Aha, thought Jonnie. The Great Village had been named Denver. If it had a name to itself, that implied that there were other Great Villages. He reached for the Chinko guidebook of the area and was just reading about the library when the ground car came to a stop.

"Where's this?" inquired Jonnie, looking around. They were at the eastern edge of the town and slightly to the south.

"Knew you had a rat brain," said Terl. "This is where you—" he laughed suddenly and that made it hard to talk, "—where you attacked a tank!"

Jonnie looked around. It was indeed the place. He looked through all the slits, taking in the area. "What are we doing here?"

Terl grinned in what he was quite certain was his most friendly grin. "We're looking for your horse! Isn't that nice?"

Jonnie thought fast. There was more to this. He had better be very calm. He saw no bones but that meant nothing, for wild animals would have been at work. He looked at Terl and realized the brute actually believed a horse would wait around. Windsplitter most probably had trotted on after them a while and then wandered back toward home in the mountains.

"There are countless animals out in the open here," said Jonnie. "Picking out those two horses—"

"Rat brain, you don't have a grip on machines. It shows. Look here." Terl turned on a large screen set into the instrument panel. The immediate vicinity showed up on it. Terl turned a knob and the scene was viewable from different directions.

Then Terl pushed a button and there was a dull pop like a small explosion in the top of the car. Looking up through the overhead port Jonnie saw a spinning object fly up in the air a hundred feet. Terl pushed a lever up and the object went up. Terl pulled the lever down and the object came lower. What it was seeing registered on the viewscreen.

"That's why you can't get away," said Terl. "Look." He changed a lever on the screen and the image became enlarged. He pushed a button marked "Heat search" and the screen and spinner above went onto automatic.

Jonnie watched as groups of animals were zeroed in, enlarged, reduced; other groups found and inspected up close; more animals spotted and examined . . .

"Just sit and watch that," said Terl, "and tell me if you see your horse." He laughed. "Security chief of Earth running a lost-and-found department for an animal owned by an animal." He laughed more loudly at his own joke.

There were cattle and cattle and cattle. There were wolves—small ones from the nearby mountains and huge ones down from the north. There were coyotes. There was even a rattler. There were no horses at all.

"Well," said Terl, "we'll just drive along to the south. You keep your eyes open, animal, and you'll get your horse back."

They drove at a leisurely pace. Jonnie watched the scope. Time went on. Still no horses, none at all.

Terl began to get irritated. Leverage, leverage. His luck was out today!

"No horses," said Jonnie. And he knew very well that if he had seen Windsplitter he would have kept still.

Terl finally looked at the scope. Ahead of them was a small hill, rocky on top, with a lot of trees distributed around it and darkness in among the trees. There were cattle, some with rather big horns just to the north of it in the open. Fear, then. The day wouldn't be wasted. He swerved the car into the trees and stopped.

"Get out," said Terl. He put on his breathe-mask and hit the door buttons. He threw out the leash and then reached into the huge compartment under the seat and drew out a blast rifle along with a bag of grenades.

Jonnie stood in the open and took off his mask. He switched tanks before he put it on the seat. It had been a long drive.

Terl took a position at the edge of the trees, the rocks behind him, the open plain in front. "Come here, animal," he said.

The leash was trailing. Jonnie walked over to Terl. He wasn't going to give the monster a chance to gun him down.

"I'm going to give you a little exhibition," said Terl. "I was top shot in my school. You ever notice how neat the rat heads were blown off? Some of them were fifty paces away. You're not listening, animal."

No, Jonnie was not listening. He had caught a whiff of something and he looked at the rocks behind them. There was an opening in them. A cave? There was the whiff again.

Terl reached down and jerked the leash, almost snapping Jonnie off his feet. Jonnie got up from his knees and looked again toward the cave. He gripped the kill-club in his fist.

With an expert motion, Terl snapped a grenade onto the end of the blast rifle. "Watch this!"

There were a half-dozen cattle about eighty paces out on the plain. Two of them were heavy horned bulls, old and tough. The other four were cows.

Terl lifted the blast rifle muzzle-high and fired. The grenade soared in a long arc over the top of the cattle and landed well beyond them. It exploded in a bright green flash. One cow went down, hit by a fragment.

The others leaped and began to run. They ran away from the sound and straight toward Terl.

Terl leveled the blast rifle. "Those hoofs are moving," he said. "So you won't think it's an accident."

The bulls were coming on in a headlong rush, the cows behind them. The ground shook. The distance was closing quickly.

Terl began to fire in quick single shots.

He broke the legs of the following cows and they tumbled to earth bawling.

He broke the right front leg of the farthest bull. The other was almost upon them.

One final shot and Terl broke the right front leg of the nearest bull, which skidded to a crumbled heap, mere feet in front of them.

The air was shattering with the bawls of pain from the cattle.

Terl grinned as he looked at them. Jonnie looked back at him in horror. That grin behind the faceplate was of pure joy.

Jonnie felt revulsion for the monster. Terl was— Jonnie suddenly realized there was no word for "cruel" in the Psychlo language. He turned toward the cattle.

Walking out in front with his kill-club to put them out of their agony, he heard a new sound, a rustling rumble.

Jonnie whirled. Coming away from the cave, awakened and angered by all the racket, charging straight at Terl's back, was the biggest grizzly bear Jonnie had ever seen.

"Behind you!" he yelled. But his voice was drowned in the bawling of the cattle. Terl just stood there grinning.

A moment later the bear roared.

Terl heard it and started to turn. But he was too late.

The grizzly hit him in the back with an impact that sent out a shock wave.

The blast rifle, driven from Terl's paws, soared into the air toward Jonnie. He caught it in his left hand

But Jonnie wasn't thinking of the blast rifle as any more than a club. And he had his own kill-club up and striking before the bear could aim a second blow at Terl. The kill-club caught the grizzly square on the brain pan. The bear staggered, distracted and stunned.

Jonnie sailed in again.

The bear struck out with a massive clawed blow. Jonnie went under it. The kill-club hit again on the brain pan.

The bear reared up and struck at the kill-club as it came in again. The thong snapped.

Jonnie grasped the rifle by the barrel. The grizzly came at him with gaping jaws.

The rifle stock crashed into the bear's teeth.

Jonnie struck again on the brain pan.

With a dwindling roar the bear went down.

It stayed down, its limbs twitching in death.

Jonnie backed up. Terl was lying on his side, conscious. His mask was in place. His eyes behind the faceplate were wide and staring.

Jonnie backed up farther. Thank god the leash hadn't caught on anything and tripped him during the fight. He snapped the leash to him. Then he turned his attention to the gun. It had little labels on its controls. The safety catch was off. There was a charge under the trigger. It was scratched but not otherwise damaged.

Jonnie looked at Terl. Terl looked back, his claws flexing and unflexing, waiting. He was certain the animal would level the gun and kill him. His paw stole down to his belt gun.

If Jonnie saw the movement toward the belt gun he ignored it. He turned his back on Terl. He located the sights on the blast rifle and then, with six shots, put the crippled cattle out of their misery.

Jonnie put on the safety catch. He reached into his pouch and got a piece of sharp-edged glass and walked over to the bear and began to skin it.

Terl lay and looked at him. At length he realized he had better check himself out. A pain in his back, a rip in his collar, a bit of green blood on his paw. He tested his back. It was nothing serious. He went over to the car and sat down on a seat with the doors open and hunched there, still looking at Jonnie.

"You're not going to carry that hide inside this car," said Terl.

Jonnie didn't look up from his skinning. "I'll lash it on top."

At length Jonnie bundled up the hide and went over to the youngest cow. Working deftly with the sharp glass, he took out the tenderloin and tongue, cut a haunch, and wrapped them in the bear hide.

Jonnie took some thongs from his pouch and lashed the hide with its meat to a gunmount on the car top.

Then he handed the blast rifle to Terl. "The safety is on," he said. He was cleaning himself up with handfuls of grass.

Terl looked at him. Fear? Fear be damned. This animal had no fear in him.

Leverage. It had to be leverage. Lots of it!

"Get in," said Terl. "It's getting late."

— 8 —

The following day, Terl was again a blur of activity. He was getting ready for another interview with Numph.

He rushed about doing mutiny interviews, recording each one on a type of tape that could be cut and spliced. It was a very artful task, requiring the greatest care. He approached numbers of employees on the job, inside the compound and out.

The interviews went very smoothly and rapidly.

Terl would ask, "What company regulations do you know concerning mutiny?" The employees, sometimes startled, always suspicious, would quote what they knew or thought they knew concerning mutiny.

The security chief would then request, "In your own words, tell me your opinion of mutiny." The employees would of course get long-winded and reassuring: "Mutiny is a very bad thing. Executives would cause vaporizations wholesale and no one would be safe. I sure never intend to advocate or take part in any mutiny."

The interviews went on and on through the day, Terl rushing about, mask on outside, mask off inside. Recording, recording, recording. He always wound up an interview shaking his head and smiling and saying it was just routine and they knew how it was with management being what it was and he, Terl, was on the employee's side. But he left a bit of worry in his wake, employees vowing to themselves to have nothing whatever to do with any mutiny, pay cut or no pay cut.

From time to time, passing through his office, Terl would look at the image of the cage where the high button cameras still performed their guard duty. Curiosity and a vague unease made him keep checking.

The animal seemed very industrious. It had been up with first light. It had worked and worked, scraping the bear hide clean, and had taken old ashes and worked them into it. The hide was now hanging, pinned to the bars.

Then the fire had been built up and an odd network of branches, sort of racks, had been made, around the fireplace. The beef was cut into long, thin strips and hung on the racks near the fire. Leaves from the chopped-up trees kept being put on the fire, creating a great deal of smoke, and the smoke was winding around the meat.

Terl could not quite make out what the animal was really doing. But toward the end of the day he thought he knew. The animal was observing some kind of religious ritual having to do with spring. He had read something about this in the Chinko guidebooks. They had dances and other silly things. The smoke was supposed to carry the spirits of slain animals to the gods. Yesterday they had certainly slain enough animals. The thought of it made Terl's back twinge.

He had never believed any of these Earth creatures could actually hurt a Psychlo, but that grizzly bear had shaken his confidence slightly. It had been an awfully big bear—it weighed almost as much as Terl himself.

Probably come sunset, the animal down there in the cage would build the fire up and begin to dance or something. He concluded it wasn't up to anything dangerous and kept on with his headlong interviewing.

That night the recreation hall saw nothing of Terl. And he also forgot to see whether the animal danced. He was too busy with his tapes.

Working with an expertise only a trained security chief cherished, Terl was editing tapes, slicing out single words and even phrases and juggling them about.

By his readjusting of word positions and scrapping of whole paragraphs, employees began to say things on the reels that were building up that could hang them.

A typical answer would become, "I intend to advocate mutiny. In any mutiny it would be safe to vaporize executives." It was painstaking work. And the reels built up.

Finally he copied them onto new, clean discs that would show no sign of editing or splicing, and with the east graying he sat back, finished.

Yawning, he puttered around, cleaning up, destroying the originals and the scraps, waiting for breakfast time. He realized he had forgotten to keep an eye on the animal to see whether it danced.

Terl decided he needed sleep more than breakfast and laid himself down for a short nap. His appointment with Numph was not until after lunch.

Later he was to tell himself that it was because he had missed both breakfast and lunch that he made the blunder.

The interview began well enough. Numph was sitting at his upholstered desk sucking at an after-lunch saucepan of kerbango. He was his usual bumbling self.

"I have the results of the investigation you requested," Terl began.

"What?"

"I interviewed a lot of local employees."

"About what?"

"Mutiny."

Numph was immediately alert.

Terl put the disc player on Numph's desk and made ready to play the "interviews," saying, "These are all very secret, of course. The employees were told that no one would hear about it and they did not know the interviews were recorded."

"Wise. Wise," said Numph. He had laid the saucepan aside and was all attention.

Terl let the discs spin one after another. The effect was everything he had hoped for. Numph looked grayer and grayer. When the discs were finished Numph poured himself a saucepan full of kerbango and sucked it down in one whoosh. Then he just sat there.

If ever he had seen guilt, Terl decided, he was seeing it now. Numph's eyes were hunted.

"Therefore," said Terl, "I advise that we keep all this secret. We must not let them know what each is actually thinking, for it would lead them to conspire and actually mutiny."

"Yes!" said Numph.

"Good," said Terl. "I have prepared certain papers and orders about this." He put the sheaf on Numph's desk. "The first one is an order to me to take what measures I deem necessary to handle this matter."

"Yes!" said Numph and signed it.

"The second one is to strip all arsenals of all minesites and keep all weapons under lock and key."

"Yes!" said Numph and signed it.

"This next one is to retrieve any battle planes from other minesites and localize them under seals, except those I might need."

"Yes," said Numph and signed it.

Terl removed that which had been signed and left Numph staring at the next one.

"What's this?" said Numph.

"Authority to round up and train man-animals on machine operation so that company ore shipments can be kept rolling in event of deaths of company employees or refusals to work."

"I don't think it's possible," said Numph.

"It's only a threat to force employees back to work. You know and I know it is not really feasible."

Numph signed it doubtfully and only because it said: "Emergency plan, strategic alternative ploy. Objective: employee dissuasion from strike."

And then Terl made his blunder. He took the signed authorization and added it to the rest. "It permits us to handle forced reduction of employees," he commented. Afterward he realized he need not have said a thing.

"Oh?" said Numph.

"And I am sure," Terl had gone on, confirming his blunder, "I am very certain that your nephew Nipe would heartily approve of it."

"Approve of what?"

"Reduction of employee numbers," Terl rattled on.

And then Terl saw it. There was a relieved look on Numph's face—a knowing look—a look of realization that gave Numph *great* satisfaction.

Numph gave Terl an almost amused glance. Relief seemed to soak into him. Confidence took the place of fear.

Terl knew he had messed it up. He had had only a hint of the leverage connected to Nipe. And right now he had been guilty of exposing that he was only pretending he knew. Numph knew that Terl really didn't know. And Terl never had really known what Numph was up to. A real blunder.

"Well," said Numph, suddenly expansive, "you just run along now and do your job. I'm sure everything will work out just fine."

Terl stopped outside the door. What the blast *was* the leverage? What was the real story behind it? Numph was no longer afraid. Terl could hear him chuckling.

The security chief threw off the black cloud that threatened. He moved off. At least he had the animals and he could carry on. And when he had finished with them he could vaporize them. He wished he could also vaporize Numph!

Leverage, leverage. He had none on Numph. And he had none at all on the animal.

Terl would have to get busy.

— 9 —

The transshipment air was a loud clatter of hurtling shapes under the spring sun. A freighter had just roared in and the ore it spilled was racketing onto the field. The blade machines were nudging about, hurrying the ore to the conveyors. The giant buckets clanked and rattled, halting jerkily to spill their contents on the conveyor belt. Huge fans roared to blast dust in the air. A fall of ore flowed onto the transshipment platform.

Jonnie sat amid the din, chained to the controls of the dust analyzer, sprayed with fanned dirt and half-deafened from the clamor.

What he was doing was cross-testing the consecutive loads on the belt for uranium. The fans beat a fog of ore particles into the air at this point in the progressive steps. It was Jonnie's job to throw a lever that sent beams through the whirlwind, check the panel to see whether a purple or a red light went on, and throw levers that sent the ore on for transshipment (purple), or dumped it to the side and sounded an alarm (red). When the red came on, it was urgent to dump.

He was not operating independently. He was closely supervised by Ker, the assistant operations officer of the minesite. Ker was protected by domed headgear. Jonnie was catching the hurricane of dust and din full in the eyes and face. He did not even have goggles. Ker walloped him on the shoulder to indicate that this bucketful could be sent on, and Jonnie thrust at the levers.

Ker had been carefully chosen by the security chief as the very fellow to instruct the animal in the operation of minesite machinery. And Terl had his reasons.

A midget for a Psychlo, Ker was only seven feet tall. He was a "geysermouth," as they called it, since he chattered incessantly; nobody bothered to listen to him. He had no friends but tried to make them. He was reputedly dim-witted even though he knew his machines well. If these reasons were not enough, Terl had leverage: he had caught Ker in a compromising situation involving two female Psychlo clerks in an out-of-bounds operations office. Terl had picto-recorded but not reported it, and Ker and the females had been very grateful. There were other things: Ker was a habitual criminal who had taken employment on Earth one jump ahead of arrest, and Terl had fixed up a name change. Before the animal idea had occurred to Terl, he had tried to work out something involving Ker, but it would have been impossible for a Psychlo to go into those mountains, and he had been forced to abandon taking Ker into his confidence.

But Ker had his uses. He was chattering away now, voice dimmed by the helmet he wore and by the din. "You have to be sure to detect every scrap of radiation dust. Not one isotope must get through to the platform."

"What would it cause?" shouted Jonnie.

"There'd be a spark-flash on the home planet, like I told you. The teleportation platform there would get disrupted and we'd catch blazes. It's just the dust. You have to make sure there's none in the dust. No uranium!"

"Has it ever happened?" shouted Jonnie.

"Blast no!" roared Ker. "And it never will.'

"Just *dust?*" said Jonnie.

"Just dust."

"What about a solid piece of uranium?"

"You won't detect that."

"Would anything detect it?"

"We never ship it!"

They got along pretty well. At first Ker had thought the animal was a peculiar thing. But it seemed friendly and Ker didn't have any friends. And the animal asked questions constantly and Ker loved to talk. Better an animal audience than none at all. Besides, it was a favor to Terl and staved off possible disclosures.

Terl brought the man-thing down each morning, tied it up to the machine it would operate, and picked it up each night. Ker, much cautioned and threatened with the consequences if Jonnie got loose, had the right to untie the animal and put it on another machine.

The regular operator this morning was glad of a break. The post was extremely dangerous and had killed several Psychlos in past decades. One usually got danger pay for it, but that was now suspended with the economy wave.

The freighter load was handled. The last bucketful went by on the conveyor belt position and the whole area drifted down to momentary idleness. The regular operator came back, looking suspiciously at his equipment.

"Did it break anything?" said the regular operator with a talon jerk at Jonnie.

"It hasn't broke anything around here yet," said Ker defensively.

"I heard it blew up a blade scraper."

"Oh, that scraper was one that had already blown up," said Ker. "You know the one a few months ago that got Waler."

"Oh, that one. The one that got a hairline crack in its canopy?"

"Yeah," said Ker. "That one."

"I thought this animal blew it up."

"That's just that Zzt making excuses for lack of maintenance."

Nevertheless the regular operator carefully checked over his uranium detection station.

"Why are you so nervous about it?" said Jonnie.

"Hey," said the regular operator, "it talks Psychlo!"

"He could have a leak in his helmet," explained Ker to Jonnie. "Or you could have left some dust on the controls."

Jonnie looked at the regular operator "You ever have a helmet blow up?"

"Blazes, no! I'm still alive, ain't I? And I ain't going to have any breathe-gas blow up around me. Get off my machine. Another freighter is coming in."

Ker untied the animal and led it over to the shade of a power pylon. "That about completes you on the transshipment machinery. Tomorrow I'm going to start you on actual mining."

Jonnie looked around. "What's that little house over there?"

Ker looked. It was a small domed structure with a bunch of cooling coils on the back of it. "Oh, the morgue. Company orders require all dead Psychlos to get returned to home planet."

Jonnie was interested. "Sentiment? Families?"

"Oh, no. Blazes, no. Nothing silly like that. They got some dumb idea that if an alien race had dead Psychlos to fool around with they could work out the metabolism and get up to mischief. Also, it's a sort of nose count. They don't want names riding on a payroll after a guy is dead—somebody else could collect the pay. It used to be done."

"What happens with them—the corpses?"

"Oh, we let them collect and then schedule their teleportation back, just like any other package. When they get them home they bury them. The company has its own cemetery on Psychlo."

"Must be quite a planet."

Ker glowed with a smile. "You can say that! None of these damned helmets or canopies. Unlimited breathe-gas! The whole atmosphere is breathe-gas. Wonderful. Good gravity, not thin like this. Everything a gorgeous purple. And females aplenty! When I get out of here—maybe—if Terl fixes it so I can—I'm going to have ten wives and just sit all day chomping kerbango and rolling the females."

"Don't they have to import all the breathe-gas here?"

"Yes, indeed. You can't make it on other planets. It takes certain elements that seldom exist off Psychlo."

"I should think the home planet would run out of atmosphere."

"Oh, no!" said Ker. "The elements are in the rocks and even the core and it just makes more and more. See those drums over there?"

Jonnie looked at a pyramid of drums that had evidently just come in on reverse teleportation from Psychlo. Trucks with lifts were loading them. And just as he looked, a truck was shifting some barrels aboard the last freighter in.

"Those drums are going back overseas," said Ker.

"How many minesites are there?" said Jonnie.

Ker scratched where his dome met his collar. "Sixteen. I think."

"Where are they located?" said Jonnie, being very casual.

Ker started to shrug and then had a happy thought. He reached into a rear pocket and brought out a sheaf of papers. He had used the back of a map to make some work assignment notes on. He unfolded it. Although it was covered with creases and dirt it was quite plain. It was the first time Jonnie had seen a map of the whole planet.

With a searching talon, Ker counted. "Yep. Sixteen with two substations. That's the lot."

"What's a substation?"

Ker pointed up at the pylon. Other pylons marched southwest into the distance until they were dwindling specks. "That power line comes in from a hydroelectric installation several hundred miles from here. It's an ancient dam. The company changed all the machinery in it and it gives us all our power here for transshipment. It's a substation."

"Any workers there?"

"Oh, no. All automatic. There's another substation on the overseas south continent. It's not manned either."

Jonnie looked at the map. He was excited but showed none of it. He counted five continents. Every minesite was precisely marked.

He reached over and took a pen out of Ker's breast pocket. "How many machines do I still have to be checked out on?" asked Jonnie.

Ker thought about it. "There's drillers . . . hoists . . ."

Jonnie reached over and took the map and folded it so there was a fresh blank space on the back. He began to list the machines as Ker called them out.

When the list was finished, Jonnie gave Ker his pen but casually put the map in his pouch.

Jonnie stood up and stretched. He hunkered back down and said, "Tell me some more about Psychlo. Sure must be an interesting place."

The assistant operations officer chattered on. Jonnie listened intently. The data was a valuable flood and the map in his pouch crackled comfortingly.

When just one man was taking on the whole empire of the

Psychlos in the hope of freeing his people, every scrap of information had value beyond price.

The engulfing roar of company operations thundered around them in enormous power.

■

PART 5

— 1 —

Eyes on the sky of an evening, noting the slow yearly wheel of the constellations, Jonnie knew he would have to escape.

In about three weeks the year would be up. He had a horrible vision of Chrissie coming into the plains and, if she survived there, blundering onto the minesite.

There were many obstacles. It would be almost insurmountably difficult, given the search tools of the Psychlos. But he set about planning his road to freedom with stubborn relentlessness.

Complicating his plans was the self-set goal of an Earth free of Psychlos and the resurrection of the human race.

Lying awake, he saw the cage revealed in all its ugliness by a rising moon, and he almost ridiculed himself for his own timidity.

Here he was, collared like a dog, chained up, locked behind bars, subject to swift detection and swifter pursuit. Yet he knew that even if he died trying he would more than try.

First he must escape.

A key to possible freedom came to him only two days later. Freedom, at last, from his collar.

For some reason Terl had insisted that he be trained in electronic repair. The explanation Terl gave was thin: sometimes the controls of a machine broke, sometimes the remote control systems went awry, and the operator had to handle it. That Terl had done the explaining was enough to disqualify the reason. But more than that, in all the time Jonnie had been training on machines, he had never seen an operator touch electronic repair. When something went wrong somebody came screeching in on a tri-wheeled cart from the electronics section and fixed it fast. That Terl insisted that Jonnie know how to do it—Ker had not objected for an instant—was one more piece of the puzzle that was Terl. Whatever Terl wanted of him eventually would happen somewhere where there were no electronics repairmen.

So Jonnie sat, dwarfed on a bench, learning circuits and diagrams and components. They didn't give him too much trouble. The electrons went here, got changed there, and wound up doing something else over at this place. The little wires and components and pieces of binding metal all made pretty good sense.

It was the *tools* that mystified him at first. There was a thing like a little knife that had a big handle—big to Jonnie, small to a Psychlo—that did the most remarkable thing. When you turned a switch to the proper number in its heel and put the blade down on a piece of wire, the wire fell apart. And when you reversed it and touched it to the wires you were now holding together, they became one piece once more. It only happened when you were splitting or binding the same type of metal. You had to use a binding substance when handling two different types of metal that you wanted to join.

When Ker wandered off for one of his frequent snacks and Jonnie was tied up alone for the moment in the electronics shop, he tested the tool against the frayed end of the leash.

It came apart, cleanly cut.

Jonnie reversed the switch, held the cut pieces together, and touched the tool to it.

They went back together with no trace of the cut.

Jonnie knew without trying it that it would do the same thing to his metal collar.

He looked at the door to make sure Ker was not coming back and no one else coming in, and then he swept his eyes over the rest of the room. There was a tool cupboard at the far end. He knew better than to have the knife he was using vanish. Jonnie parted his leash, raced to the tool cupboard, and opened it. It was a messy pile of parts, wires, and tools. He rummaged in it frantically. Seconds sped by. Then he saw what he was looking for at the bottom—an old tool of the same kind.

From far off he could feel the rumble of returning feet.

He rushed back to his bench and with the newly found tool put his leash ends back together again. It worked!

Ker returned, lazy and disinterested. Jonnie had already slid the tool down into the cuff of his moccasin.

"You're doing pretty good," said Ker, looking at his work.

"Yes, I'm doing pretty good," said Jonnie.

— 2 —

Terl was deep into the puzzle of Numph. Somehow and some way Terl knew he had gotten onto something, and then somehow and some way, he had messed it up.

The thing kept him awake nights and gave him a headache.

For some of the things he was now going to be seen doing, he had to have the insurance of big leverage on Numph.

He had lazied along with the fake "mutiny" measures. They weren't important anyway. He had caused the few battle planes on the other minesites to be flown in and parked. He had picked up their arsenals and had them under seal. He had taken over control of the single remaining recon drone. On its last pass over the high mountains he had gloated.

The beautiful vein was still there, naked to view, exposed a hundred feet down a two-thousand-foot cliff. Pure white quartz studded with wires and knobs of gleaming yellow gold! A fortuitous earthquake had caused the cliff face to shear off and fall into the dark depths of the canyon, exposing the fortune. The ancient volcano higher up must have spewed out a geyser of pure liquid gold in some ancient eruption and then covered it shallowly. A stream had cut the canyon through the ages and now the slide.

The site had a few disadvantages. The approaches to it showed uranium in some form or another, which put it out of bounds for a Psychlo. It rested in a cliff face so sheer that it could only be mined from a lowered platform. The rest of two thousand feet would gape dizzyingly below and the canyon winds would batter at the mining stage. Room for machinery at the top of the cliff was minimal and precarious. Several miners' lives would be expendable at such a site.

Terl only wanted the cream of it. No mining in depth down to the next pocket. Just that pocket right there, the one that was exposed. There must be a ton of gold in sight.

At Psychlo prices—where very scarce gold ran at very high prices—it was worth nearly a hundred million credits. Credits that could bribe and buy and open the doors to unlimited personal power.

He knew how to get it out. He had even worked out how to transship it to home planet and get it to arrive there undetected and recoverable.

He looked at the recon drone photos again and then falsified their date and place markings with a clever bit of forgery and hid them deep in otherwise innocuous, boring files.

To guarantee it, he needed leverage on Numph. Then in the event of any slip or mishap he would be protected.

There was also the matter of getting his ten-year sentence—he thought of it as a sentence—contracted down to just another year on this cursed planet.

Whatever Numph had going involved Nipe and Nipe's home-planet post in accounting. Terl had gotten that far. He sat hunched over his desk thinking.

He needed leverage on the animal, and it would have to be big—big enough to force the animal to dig without supervision and, not only that, to deliver. Well, the animal's learning was going well and plans for other animals were all in place. He would come up with something; Terl believed in his own luck. The animals somehow would do it and then he would vaporize them and get the gold to home planet.

The unknown was Numph. With a single order he could dismiss the animals or have them killed. He could simply withdraw permission to use the machinery. And soon the bumbling old fool, seeing no mutiny, would withdraw the blanket authorizations. The "mutiny" was too thin.

Terl looked at the clock. It was within two hours of transshipment time.

He got up, took his breathe-mask off a peg, and a few minutes later was at the transshipment platform.

Terl stood there in the swirling dust and din of preshipment time. The dispatch-box courier had already been there, and the box, sealed and ready, lay on a corner of the platform. Char came over, interrupted in his preparation for transshipment firing and unfriendly.

"Routine check of dispatch transmission," said Terl. "Security business." He showed him the blanket authorization.

"You'll have to be fast," shouted Char. "No time to wait around." He glanced at his clock.

Terl scooped up the dispatch box and took it over to the car he had arrived in. He unlocked it with his master key and laid it on the seat. Nobody was watching. Char was back harassing blade machine operators to neaten up the ore.

Terl adjusted the button camera on his collar tab and speedily riffled through the sheaves. They were routine reports, routine day-to-day recounting of operational data.

Terl had done all this before and it hadn't yielded anything, but there was always hope. The Planetary Director had to initial everything and sometimes added data and comments.

The button camera whirred and in short order every sheet had been recorded.

Terl put them back in the box, locked it, and took it over to the platform.

"Everything all right?" said Char, relieved not to have another detail pushed too close to firing time.

"No personal mail, nothing," said Terl. "When do you send the dead ones back?" He indicated the morgue.

"Semiannually as always," said Char. "Get your car out of here. This is a big shipment and we're in a hurry."

Terl went back to his office. Without really hoping, he put the report copies onto a screen, one after the other, studying them.

He was only interested in the ones that had Numph's writing on them. Somehow, somewhere, there was a secret communication in these reports that only Nipe in accounting could decipher; of that Terl was certain. There was no other way to get a communication back to home planet.

When he finally got this—and when he got a real lever on the animal—he could launch his private mining mission.

Terl sat late, missing dinner, studying these and older dispatch box copies until his amber eyes were dulled to a dim flicker.

It was here someplace. He was certain of it.

— 3 —

Collecting things that would aid his escape was not easy.

At first Jonnie had thought he might handle the two button cameras that overlooked his cage—one inside and one outside. If he could bypass these, then at night he could open his collar and freely get about and prepare.

He had spent valuable time studying button cameras in the electronics shop. They were simple devices. They had a small mirror to catch the image, and the image became transmitted electrons; the pattern was simply picked up and recorded on a disc. There was no power in the button camera; power was transmitted to it on a closed circuit from the receiver.

He tried to modify his instruction machine to perform the same function. His object was to record a view of the cage with him in it. Then, with a quick switchover, he could leave the button cameras transmitting *that* picture while he himself was elsewhere. But there were two cameras, viewing from different angles. He only had one recorder.

Terl caught him one day with the instruction machine in pieces. He was bringing in a rabbit he had shot.

The monster stood there for a while and finally said, "Teach an animal a trick and it has to work it on everything. I think you've wrecked that playing machine."

Jonnie went on reassembling it.

"Put it back together so it works and you can have this rabbit."

Jonnie ignored him. But when he had the machine back together, Terl threw down the rabbit.

"Don't monkey with things that don't need fixing," Terl said with the air of good-god-what-you-have-to-teach-an-animal.

But later Jonnie got a break. The problem was body-heat detection equipment. If in some way he could nullify such surveillance, then he hoped he could get to the mountains. He doubted he could be traced, if the heatseeking equipment could be fooled.

Ker had him running a drill into the side of a mine shaft over at the actual mine. It was an abandoned hole, about fifty feet in diameter. Ker had lowered the drill platform down into the hole. At that point a rock outcropping was exposed. Under the platform was an ore net.

The drill was heavy, having been built for Psychlos. Jonnie's muscles bulged as he bucked the bit into the outcropping. He had a phone in his ear and Ker was chattering away into it.

"Don't push steady. Just lean on it and let up, time after time. After you got a hole drilled, trip the second trigger and the drill will expand and break off the ore. Keep the net in place to catch it as it falls. Now just keep that sequence going. . . ."

"It's hot!" Jonnie had yelled back up at him. And it was hot. The drill, spinning at high revs, was heating the wall and in itself was almost glowing with friction.

"Oh," said Ker. "You haven't got a heat protector." He fished around in his pockets amid papers and bits of old snacks and finally dug out a very small package. He put it in a lowering cup and let it down on a line.

Jonnie opened it up. It was a sheet of thin, transparent stuff. It had two sleeves.

"Put it on," yelled Ker.

Jonnie was amazed that so much area could be compressed into such a small package. The garment was built for a Psychlo and the sleeves were enormous, and it was much too long. He took some tucks in it and put it on over his head and down the front of his body.

He resumed bucking the drill. It was amazing. The reflected heat from the wall and the drill bit did not reach him.

After Ker finally decided Jonnie could use the drill and handle the rig and Jonnie was back on level ground, he went through the motions of giving back the heat shield.

"No, no," said Ker. "Throw it away. It's disposable. They get dirty and torn. A driller usually carries half a dozen. I don't know why I forgot. But I ain't been a driller for years."

"It's the only one I got," said Jonnie.

"And you're sure a driller," said Ker.

Jonnie neatly repackaged it and put it in his pouch. He was betting that no heat detector could detect through it. If he wore it and kept it from gaping, the spinning scanner would be blind to it. He hoped.

The food problem he had solved. The smoked beef was compact and would keep him from starving if he was running so fast that he had no time to hunt.

He carefully patched up moccasins and made sure he had an extra pair. Terl observed that, too.

"You don't have to wear those, you know," Terl said one evening as he came out to check the cage locks. "There are old Chinko boots that could be cut down. Didn't they give you any boots with your clothes?"

The following day the compound tailor came out, complaining in his breathe-mask, and measured Jonnie for boots. "I am not a bootmaker!" he protested. But Terl had shown him the blanket requisition, so the tailor also measured Jonnie for a heavy knee-length overcoat and cold-weather cap. "It is coming on to summer," said the tailor. "It's not the time of year for winter clothing." But he had done the measuring anyway and very soon the boots and clothing were delivered to the cage. "Freaky executives," the tailor had muttered during the final try-on. "Dressing up animals!"

It made Jonnie uneasy that Terl was being obliging. He carefully checked all his preparations over to see whether any could give away his plans to escape. He decided not. Terl seemed very preoccupied these days, indifferent. Or was that a pose?

The thing that was really giving Jonnie a problem was how to get his hands on a gun.

Before all the "mutiny" precautions, some of the workers he had seen had worn relatively small, compact handguns at their belts. He had supposed they used them for plinking or shooting game. Terl still wore his—a rather bigger one—but the others seemed to have stopped.

Jonnie wondered how far he could trust Ker. The "midget" was definitely Terl's creature. But from some of the tales Ker had chattered on with, he was distinctly criminal: he told how he had rigged certain games of chance, how he had looted ore boxes "as a joke," how he had gotten a female to believe her father needed money and "relayed it for her."

One day they were waiting for a machine to be idle so it could be used in practice and Jonnie decided to make a test. He still had the two discs he had gotten in the Great Village. He knew now that one was a silvery coin and the other a gold coin.

He took the silver coin out of his pocket and began flipping it.

"What's that?" Ker wanted to know. Jonnie gave it to him and Ker scratched it with a talon. "I dug some of these up once in a wrecked town on the southern continent," said Ker. "You must have gotten this locally, though."

"Why?" said Jonnie, alert that perhaps Ker could read English letters.

"It's fake," said Ker. "An alloy of copper with a nickel-silver plating. A real coin—and I saw some once—is solid silver." He handed it back, losing interest.

Jonnie took out the yellow coin and started flipping it.

Ker caught it in the air before it could fall back into Jonnie's hand. His interest was sudden and intense "Hey, where did you get this?'' Ker dented the edge with a talon tip and looked at it closely.

''Why?'' said Jonnie innocently. ''Is it worth something?''

A very sly look came into Ker's eye. The coin he was holding and trying to be casual about was worth four thousand credits! Gold, alloyed just enough to be used in coinage without undue wear. Ker steadied his hand and looked very, very casual. ''Where'd you get this?''

''Well,'' said Jonnie, ''it came from a very dangerous place.''

''There are more of them?'' Ker was quivering a little bit. He was holding in his paw three months' pay! All in one little coin. And as an employee he could legally possess it as a ''souvenir.'' On Psychlo it could buy a wife. He tried to remember how many coins it took for them to cease to be ''souvenirs'' and become company property. Ten? Thirteen? So long as they were old and obviously mintage, not some fake made by a miner.

''The place is so dangerous one couldn't go there without at least a belt gun.''

Ker looked at him searchingly. ''Are you trying to get me to give you a belt gun?''

''Would I do something like that?''

''Yes,'' said Ker. This animal was very, very quick on machines. Quicker in fact than Psychlo trainees.

Ker looked longingly at the gold coin or medallion or whatever it had been. He said nothing. Then he handed it back to Jonnie and just sat there, his amber eyes shadowed in the depths of his breathe-gas dome.

Jonnie took the coin back. ''I'm careless with things like this. I can't buy anything, you know. I keep it in a hole just to the right of the cage door as you come in.''

Ker sat there for a while. Then he said, ''The next machine is ready.''

But that night, while Terl was making his rounds of the minesite and was distant from his viewing screen, the gold coin disappeared from the hole where Jonnie had put it, and in the morning, when Jonnie dug there, covering the action with his body, a small handgun and spare charges were in the hole instead.

Jonnie had a gun.

— 4 —

A remaining hurdle was *knowledge*.

The Chinkos were good teachers, and they could stack real learning onto a disc and get it assimilated like lightning flashes. But basically they had been working for Psychlos and trying to teach Psychlos, and they omitted a lot of things that Psychlos either already knew or could not have much interest in. This left gaps.

Jonnie had picked up inferences that there was uranium in the mountains to the west. Mostly he guessed this because no active mining ever seemed to have been undertaken there by the Psychlos. From the accident he had witnessed and for other reasons, he suspected uranium was deadly to the Psychlos. But he didn't know for sure and he didn't know how.

He was utterly dismayed, in studying the text on electronic chemistry, to find there were many, many different atomic formations of uranium.

Sitting at his fire, grinding away at texts and the instruction machine alternately, Jonnie was disturbed by the ground-shake that always preceded Terl. It was simply the monster's nightly rounds.

"What are you studying so hard, animal?" asked Terl, looming over him.

Jonnie decided to plunge, to take a chance. He looked the many feet up to Terl's mask. "It's the mountains to the west," said Jonnie.

Terl looked at him suspiciously for a little while.

"There's not much in here about them," said Jonnie.

Terl was still suspicious. What had this animal guessed?

"I was born and raised there," said Jonnie. "There's data on mountains everywhere else on the planet but hardly any on those right there." He pointed to where faint moonlight shone on the bold snowcaps. "The Chinkos took a lot of books out of the library. Man-books. Are they here?"

"Oh," snorted Terl in relief. "Man-books. Ha."

Terl was rather more pleased than otherwise. This fitted into his own concentrations. He left and came back shortly with a battered table and a disorderly armload of books that avalanched down on it. They were frail books, very ancient, and some broke their backs or came apart with his mishandling.

"I am nothing but an animal attendant," said Terl. "If mauling through this gibberish makes you happy, be happy." He paused at the cage door after he went out and locked it. "Just remember one thing, animal. The junk you'll find in those man-books didn't have anything in them to defeat Psychlos." Then he laughed. "Probably lots of recipes on how to prepare raw rat, though." He rumbled off to the compound, his laughter fading.

Jonnie touched the books reverently. And then with hope he began to inspect them. They mostly concerned mining. His first find was a text on chemistry. It contained a table of "elements" that gave the atomic formation of every element man had known.

With a sudden puzzlement he grabbed the Psychlo text on electronic chemistry. It too had a table on the atomic formation of elements.

He put them side by side in the flickering firelight.

They were different!

Both tables were apparently based on the "periodic law," by which the properties of the chemical elements recur periodically when the elements are arranged in increasing order of their atomic numbers. But there were elements on the man-table that did not occur on the Psychlo table. And the Psychlo table had dozens more elements. The Psychlo table also had many more gases listed and did not seem to specialize in oxygen.

Jonnie floundered through it, not too adept at getting the abbreviations related to the substances, more used to reading Psychlo than English.

Yes, the Psychlos listed radium and even gave it an atomic number of eighty-eight, but they noted it as a rare element. And they had dozens of elements numbered and listed above eighty-eight.

Nothing made it plainer than the difference in these tables that he was dealing with an alien planet in an alien universe. Some of the metals were compatible. But on the whole the distribution was different and even atomic formation seemed at variance.

At length he suspected that both tables were imperfect and incomplete and, with a spinning head, gave it up. He was a man of action, not a Chinko!

He turned to his next huge question. Were there uranium mines in the mountains?

At length he found some charts and listings. He had been certain that there must be uranium mines—man-mines—in those mountains. But all he found were notations that where they had existed they were mined out.

What? No uranium mines? No active ones, anyway.

Yet he was dead certain that there must be uranium in those mountains. Otherwise, why would the Psychlos avoid them? Maybe they just thought there was. No, there must be uranium in those mountains.

Some of his plans began to crumble at the edges and he fell into something like despair.

He began to search in the books, looking for any references at all to uranium.

And then he hit, as Ker would say, pay dirt of a sort.

It was a book on mine toxicology, a subject he made out as "poisons in mines affecting miners." And there it was in the index: "Uranium; radiation poisoning."

For the next half-hour he struggled through the entry. It seemed that you had better damn well be clothed in lead shielding when you fooled around with radium or uranium or radiation. All sorts of terrible things happened if you weren't. Rashes, hair falling out, burns, blood changes . . .

And then he had it: people bombarded with radiation experienced changes in their genes and chromosomes, and birth defects and sterility resulted.

That was what was wrong with his people.

That was why children seldom came and why those that did were often imperfect at birth.

That was the reason for the lethargy of some of them.

And that could also be the "red sickness." And the crumbling away of his father's bones.

It was all there. It described exactly what was happening to his people. Why they did not multiply.

There was radiation in the village valley!

He went back hurriedly to the mine maps. No, there was not even a worked-out uranium mine anywhere around the village.

But radiation was what it was. The symptoms were unmistakable.

He knew now why the Psychlos stayed away from there. But if there were no mines, where was the radiation coming from? The sun? No, not that. Goats on the higher ridges had no trouble multiplying and he had never seen a deformed goat.

Well, he had an answer of sorts. It was not a clean-cut one. There was radiation but no mines.

It struck him abruptly that man must have had a way of detecting radiation; he seemed to know so much about it. Eventually he found that, too. It was called a "Geiger counter" after somebody named "Geiger," who was born and died on dates that Jonnie had no trace or inkling of. It seemed that radiation or "ionizing particles," if present, passed through a gas. The radiation generated a current in the gas that made a needle react. Radiation somehow generated a current in certain gases.

The schematic diagrams were unintelligible to him until he found a table that gave the abbreviations. He could then translate them across into Psychlo, which he did laboriously. He wondered whether he could make a Geiger counter. He decided, given the Psychlo electronics shop, that he could. But after he escaped, that wouldn't be available. Despair began to creep in on him.

He finally put the books away and in the small hours fell into an exhausted sleep. He had nightmares. Chrissie mauled and smashed to bits. His people wasted and truly extinct. And the world of the Psychlos come alive and laughing at him.

— 5 —

But it wasn't the whole world of the Psychlos laughing. It was Terl.

Mid-morning sunlight filled the cage as Jonnie awoke. Terl was standing at the second table, turning over the man-books and laughing.

Jonnie sat up in his robes.

"You finished with these, animal?"

Jonnie went over to the artificial pond and washed his face. A month back he had persuaded Terl to keep a trickle running in so he could get clean water at the intake. It was cold and refreshed him.

There was a shattering crash in the air and for a moment he

thought something had blown up. But it was only the recon drone passing overhead.

For some days now it had been making mid-morning sweeps. Ker had explained to him what it was. It was an ore detection, activity surveillance craft, capable of taking continuous pictures. It was regulated by remote control.

All his life Jonnie had seen such craft overhead and had supposed they were natural phenomena such as meteors or the sun and moon. But those had passed every few days and this one was passing daily. The old ones did not rumble in the distance as they approached and did not make an explosion as they went by. This one did. Ker hadn't really known why, but it had to do with speed. They were very fast. You couldn't turn one in the air or stop one. You could only guide it, and it had to go all the way around the planet to get back. So this one—if it was the same one—was circling the planet daily. The harsh boom was very unpleasant.

Terl looked up at it and then carefully ignored it. Minesite personnel didn't like it.

"Why every day?" said Jonnie, looking up at it. It was an element in his escape planning. It only took pictures but that would be enough.

"I said," snarled Terl, "are you finished with these books?"

The recon drone was fading, its rumble losing itself across the eastern plains. Its path had been from the mountains.

Jonnie made a breakfast of cold meat and water. Terl stacked the books up in his arms and went to the cage door.

Terl halted, indifferently. "If you're so keen on data about those mountains," said Terl, "there's a whole relief map of them in the library of that town up north. You want to look at it?"

Instantly alert, Jonnie nevertheless kept on with his breakfast. An accommodating Terl always has something else in mind. But this was a chance Jonnie had scarcely dared hope for.

In his planning he had gone over ways to get Terl to take him out in the car. It would be a simple matter to throw a door catch, swing a blast of air into the car, hit the emergency stop button, and hold a gun on Terl. Desperate, but it was a chance.

"I got nothing to do today," said Terl. "Your machine training has ended. We might run up to the town. Look at that relief map. Do a little hunting. Maybe look some more for your horse."

A rambling Terl was not within Jonnie's experience. Did the monster know something?

"I want to show you something, anyways," said Terl. "So get your things together and I'll be by in about an hour and we'll take a ride. I've got to check some things. I'll be back. Be ready, animal."

Jonnie scrambled. This was a bit premature and it upset his planning, but he looked on it as a heaven-sent chance. He had to get away and get to his people, both to stop Chrissie, if she attempted to keep her promise, and to move the village to a safer place. There were only two weeks left before the constellation returned to its place.

He put the small gun in his belt pouch, put the metal cutter alongside his ankle, packed a supply of smoked beef. He dressed in buckskin.

When the hour was up, a vehicle rumbled into sight and stopped. Jonnie stared at it, wondering what was going on. This was not the Mark III tank. It was a simple equipment truck normally used for transporting machinery. It had an enclosed, pressurized cab. The back was large and open, surrounded by stakes. Its only similarity to a tank was that it had no wheels but skimmed a varying distance up to three feet above ground.

Then Jonnie realized that this might work to his advantage. It had no heat-seekers, no guns.

Terl got out and opened the cage. "Throw your things into the back, animal. And ride in the back." He unfastened the leash and boosted Jonnie over the tailgate. He took out a pocket welder and fastened the leash to the cab.

"This way," said Terl, "I won't have to smell those hides!" He was laughing when he got into the cab, took off his mask, and turned on its system. Suddenly Jonnie realized he had no way of immobilizing Terl—he couldn't open the door on him.

The truck skimmed away. It was slower than the tanks and it was not as well cushioned against the ground, for it was now running very underloaded.

Jonnie held on, his head ducked below the forward cab level. The eighty-mile-an-hour wind of passage roared over his head and against the truck's upright stakes.

He was thinking fast. Somehow he could play this so as to get the truck as well. Its controls weren't any different, of that he was certain from the quick glance he had had. All Psychlo controls were simple levers and buttons.

What a relief it would be to get rid of this collar. His heart was thudding expectantly. Once again, if he made no mistakes, he would be free!

— 6 —

It was no more than 1:00 when they thudded to a halt outside the library in the town. Terl got out, shaking the vehicle with his weight.

He was still conversational when he unfastened the leash. "See anything of your horse?"

"Not a thing," said Jonnie.

"Too bad, animal. This truck is the very thing to carry a horse, or ten horses for that matter."

Terl went to the library door and with a tool undid the lock. He gave the leash a yank and sent Jonnie in ahead of him.

The place was a quiet tomb of dust, the interior the same as Jonnie had last seen it. Terl was looking around.

"Ha!" said Terl. "So that's how you got in before!" He was pointing to the disturbed dust under a window and the unchanged impressions of footprints across the floor. "You even put the guard screens back! Well," he added, looking around, "let's find data on the western mountains."

Jonnie was aware of the changes in himself. Those blotches of white he had seen before were signs, very plain and easy to read. He saw that his previous visit had occurred beside the ["Children's Section"] and that the shelves he had first approached were marked ["Child Education"].

"Wait a minute," said Terl. "I don't think you know how to read a library index. Come over here, animal." He yanked on the leash he had let run long. He was standing by stacks of small drawers. He bent over and opened one. "According to the Chinkos, every book has a card and the cards are in here in these drawers. Alphabetical. Got it?"

Jonnie looked at the drawers. Terl had pulled one out that was all [''Q'']. The cards were musty and grayed but readable. ''Anything there about mountains?'' said Terl.

Tense as he was, Jonnie had to repress a smile. Here was more proof that Terl couldn't read English. ''The drawer you have there is about vehicles,'' said Jonnie.

''Yes, I can see that,'' said Terl. ''Go through it and find 'mountains.''' He moved off, elaborately interested in some ancient posters on the wall, holding the leash.

Jonnie started opening drawers. Some were stuck; others had their front tabs missing. But he finally found the drawers for [''M'']. He began to go through the cards. He came to [''Modern Military Science''].

''I've found something,'' said Jonnie. ''May I have a pen to write the numbers?''

Terl handed him a pen several sizes too big for Jonnie's hand and then gave him some folded sheets. Terl wandered off again. Jonnie wrote down the numbers of several books.

''I have to go over to the shelves now,'' said Jonnie. And Terl paid out more line.

After a little while, and after a minor battle with a ladder that had sunk into and stuck to the floor, Jonnie got up to a higher shelf and raised the protective sheet. In a moment he was swiftly scanning through a section of a book headed *[Defense Systems of the United States]*.

''Anything about mountains?'' said Terl. Jonnie bent down and showed him a page entitled [''MX1 Anti-Nuclear Silos''].

''Yep,'' said Terl.

Jonnie handed him the book. ''We better take this one. There's some more.''

In rapid order he fought the ladder along the shelves and took out another half-dozen books: *[Nuclear Physics, Congressional Hearings on Missile Installations, The Scandals of Nuclear Mismanagement, Nuclear Deterrent Strategy, Uranium—Hope or Hell]* and *[Nuclear Waste and Pollution]*. There were more but he felt rushed, and the seven books were heavy for a man about to run.

''I don't see any pictures,'' said Terl.

Jonnie quickly pushed the ladder along. He grabbed a book, *[Colorado, Scenic Wonderland]*, glanced at it, and gave it to Terl.

''That's more like it, animal.'' Terl was pleased with the

gorgeous views of mountains, particularly since many were purple and the aging ink had turned bluish. "More like it."

Terl put the books in a sack. "Let's see if we can locate the relief map." He gave the leash a yank that almost tumbled Jonnie off the ladder. But Terl didn't lead the way to another floor right then. He wandered over to the door first and seemed to be listening. Then he came back and went up some stairs.

There was a relief map laid out on display, possibly not a permanent fixture. Terl knelt down and looked at it searchingly.

Jonnie, keyed up as he was, was made very uneasy by the colored relief map. It showed the nearby mountains very accurately by his estimation. The passes and Highpeak were plain. And there was the meadow of the village in plain sight. Of course the map had been made ages before there was a village. But still, there it was. It made Jonnie nervous. He knew the recon drone must have spotted it long since and that Terl undoubtedly had pictures of it.

There, also, was the long canyon, and Jonnie knew he was looking at the location of what he had taken to be an ancient tomb. He looked as closely as he could without calling it to Terl's attention. No, there was no tomb or anything else marked at the head of that canyon. As a slight diversion, he traced out with his finger some of the letters: [ROCKY MOUNTAINS, PIKE'S PEAK, MOUNT VAIL].

Then he saw that he needn't have bothered to dissemble. Terl's attention was glued on a deep, long canyon. A talon was carefully tracing a cliff face and the river below it. The monster, seeing Jonnie was watching, quickly traced some other canyons in the same way. But he came back to that one canyon.

Terl stiffened for a moment, head jerking up. Then he became very bland. "Seen all you want, animal?"

Jonnie was happy to get him away from the relief map. It was too much like Terl staring down at Jonnie's people.

Terl went down the stairs toward the front door, pools of ancient dust stirring as he walked.

The sound of their footsteps had obscured it. Jonnie was certain he heard the hoofstrike of a horse!

— 7 —

Terl was standing just outside the library, looking down the grass-grown street.

Jonnie shifted his position to see what Terl was looking at. He went rigid with shock.

A hundred yards away, there was Windsplitter!

And somebody on him and three other horses behind him.

Terl was just standing there watching the street.

The moment had come. It was not coordinated. But Jonnie knew he was having his last chance.

He snapped the metal tool out of his ankle cuff and slashed the leash.

It parted.

Like a streak of light Jonnie sprinted out of the door past Terl. Suddenly yanking talons caught in the buckskin. It ripped.

Zigzagging like a hare, Jonnie headed for the nearest tree cover, momentarily expecting a pistol blast in the back.

He halted with his back braced against a broad aspen.

It was Chrissie!

And not only Chrissie, there was Pattie.

A sob surged up through Jonnie.

"Go back!" he screamed. "Chrissie! Go back! Run!"

But Chrissie pulled up, staring. The three horses behind her bunched up.

Chrissie's glad cry rang out. "Jonnie!"

Pattie yelled with delight. "Jonnie! Jonnie!"

And Windsplitter started to trot toward him.

"Go back!" screamed Jonnie. "Run! Oh my god, *run!*"

They halted, perplexed, their gladness turning into alarm. At a distance behind Jonnie they could see a *thing*. They started to turn the horses.

Jonnie crouched and whirled. Terl was still standing in the library door. Jonnie grabbed the handgun from his pouch and threw the safety off. He let the handgun show.

"If you fire on them you're dead!" he shouted.

Terl just stood there

There was a turmoil of horses behind Jonnie. He risked a glance back. Windsplitter had reared. He had seen no reason not to approach his master. He was fighting to come forward.

"Run, Chrissie! Run!" screamed Jonnie.

Terl was walking forward, rumbling, indolent. He had not drawn his gun.

"Tell them to ride up closer," called Terl.

"Stand where you are!" shouted Jonnie. "I'll shoot!"

Terl leisurely strolled forward. "Don't get them hurt, animal.'

Jonnie stepped out from the tree. The handgun was extended. He was sighting it on Terl's mask tube.

"Be reasonable, animal," said Terl. But he stopped.

"You knew they would be here today!" said Jonnie.

"Yes," said Terl. "I've been tracking them by recon drone for days. Ever since they left your village. Put the gun away, animal."

Behind him Jonnie could hear the horses milling. If only they would run!

Terl, paw staying clear of his gun, was reaching for his breast pocket.

"Stay still or I'll shoot!" called Jonnie.

"Well, animal, you can go ahead and pull the firing catch if you like. The electrical connector has a dummy wire in it."

Jonnie looked at the gun. He took a deep breath and lined it up. He clenched the trigger.

Nothing happened.

Terl finished his motion to his breast pocket. He took out the gold coin and tossed it in the air and caught it. "I, not Ker, sold you the gun, animal."

Jonnie pulled a kill-club from his belt. He braced himself for a charge.

Terl's paw motion was swifter than the eye. His belt gun was out. It fired a sharp bark.

An inhuman scream racketed out behind Jonnie. He glanced back. A pack horse was down, threshing.

"Your friends will be next," said Terl.

Jonnie lowered the club.

"That's better," said Terl. 'Now help me round these creatures up so we can get them in the truck."

— 8 —

The truck bumped southward with its cargo of freight and despair.

Collared and cinched up to a bracing, Jonnie looked over the scene in misery.

Pattie, bruised from a fall in the melee, was sitting bolt upright, arms lashed to her sides and her back lashed to a truck stake. She was in shock and her face was gray-white. She was eight now.

The wounded horse, still bleeding from a deep blast penetration in its right shoulder, still burdened with its pack, lay on its side, legs kicking slightly from time to time. Terl had simply picked it up and dumped it into the truck bed. Jonnie worried that it might kick out and break the left leg of another horse. It was one of Jonnie's old string, named Blodgett.

The three other horses were snubbed tight to the truck stakes and their nostrils were flaring in fear as the plain fled fast below the vehicle.

Chrissie was lashed to a bracing across from Jonnie. Her eyes were shut. Her breathing was shallow.

Questions had surged in Jonnie but he blocked them with tight lips. His own plans looked futile to him. He blamed himself for delaying his escape. He might have known that Terl had it all worked out. Hatred of the monster choked his throat.

At length Chrissie opened her eyes and looked at him. She saw he was watching Pattie.

"I couldn't leave her," said Chrissie. "She followed and I took her back twice, but the third time we were too far out in the plain; it was better to go on."

"Just rest, Chrissie," said Jonnie.

The horse Blodgett moaned as the truck banged over some rough ground.

"I know I was early," said Chrissie. "But Windsplitter came home. He was on the plain below the pass, and some of the boys were out to drive some cattle up and they saw him and Dancer and brought them in." Dancer was the lead horse Jonnie had taken, a mare.

Chrissie was quiet for a while. Then: "Windsplitter had a fresh scar on him like a puma had raked him and it looked like perhaps he might have run off and left you. I thought maybe you were hurt."

Yes, thought Jonnie. Windsplitter could have wandered back last year and when he tried to mount up through the passes found them blocked with snow. He would have wandered back to winter on the plain, followed by Dancer. There was a deep furrow, now healing, on Windsplitter's rump.

"It's all right," said Jonnie soothingly.

"I couldn't stand the idea of you lying down there hurt," said Chrissie.

The truck bumped on for a while.

"Jonnie, there *was* a Great Village," said Chrissie.

"I know," said Jonnie.

"Jonnie, that's a monster, isn't it?" She twitched her head toward the cab.

"Yes," said Jonnie. "It won't harm you." Any lie to calm her.

"I heard you speak its language. It has a language, and you talk it."

"I've been its captive for almost a year," said Jonnie.

"What will it do? To Pattie? To us?"

"Don't worry too much about it, Chrissie." Yes, god alone knew what the monster would do to them now. There was no reason to tell her this had messed up his escape. It wasn't her fault. It was his own. He had delayed too long.

The truck swerved across a broken bridge and jolted on.

Jonnie decided he had better tell her something to calm her. "It apparently wants something from me. I will have to do it now. It won't really harm you. Just threats. When I've done whatever it is, it will let us go." He didn't like to lie. He had felt all along that Terl would kill him when he had served his unknown purpose.

Chrissie managed a shaky smile. "Old Mr. Jimson is parson and mayor now. We got through the winter all right." She was silent for a while. "We only ate two of your horses."

"That's good, Chrissie."

"I made you some new buckskins," said Chrissie. "They're in that pack."

"Thank you, Chrissie."

Pattie, her eyes dilated, suddenly screamed, "Is it going to eat us?"

"No, no, Pattie," said Jonnie. "It doesn't eat living things. It's all right, Pattie."

She subsided.

"Jonnie." Chrissie paused. "You're alive. That's the main thing, Jonnie." Tears welled out of her eyes. "I thought you were dead!"

Yes. He was alive. They were alive. But he didn't know for how long. He thought of Terl breaking the legs of the cattle.

The truck rattled through an expanse of brush.

"Jonnie," said Chrissie. "You're not mad at me, are you?"

Oh, dear god. Mad at you. Oh god, no. He couldn't talk. He shook his head.

The roar of the mine became louder in the distance.

— 9 —

They had been left in the truck throughout the chilly night. Terl had simply put a couple of button cameras on it, one at each end, and had gone off to his quarters.

But it was midmorning now and Terl had been bustling about the cages since before dawn. Jonnie had not been able to turn his head enough to see what he was doing; the collar and leash had never been so tight.

Terl came to the back of the truck and dropped its gate. He led the horses out and tied the lead ropes to a tree. Then he bodily shoved the wounded horse off the truck and when it hit the ground shoved it further out of the way. It was trying to stand and he cuffed it, knocking it down again.

He came onto the bed and unfastened Pattie. He had a collar in his paw and he clamped it around Pattie's throat. He pulled out a welding torch and welded it shut and then welded a lead to it. Picking the little girl up with one swoop, he went off with her.

Presently he came back. Chrissie shrank away from him. He had another collar and he welded it on. Jonnie had a closer look at it as the leash was fastened. This collar had a red bulge on its side. Jonnie realized that Pattie's had had one too.

Terl looked at Jonnie's eyes. They were ice-blue and deadly. "Your turn in a moment, animal. No need to be cross. A whole new life is opening up for you." He scooped up Chrissie and packed her off the truck.

He was gone for some time. Jonnie heard the cage door opening and shutting as though being tested.

Then the truck rocked as Terl's enormous weight came onto it again.

He looked down at Jonnie. "Any more dummy wires?" he said. "You sure you're not sitting on a blast rifle that has its action dummy wired?" Terl laughed at his own joke. "You know, I am going to knock the crap out of Ker for not teaching you any better." He was fumbling with Jonnie's leash and lashings. "Rat brain," said Terl.

The recon drone rumbled in from the distance and passed over with an earsplitting roar. Jonnie glared at it as it passed.

"Good," said Terl, approving. "You know what spotted her and so you know what will spot you now, if you get up to anything I don't like. Beautiful pictures we get with that thing. Tiniest detail. Get off the truck."

Jonnie was yanked toward the cage. Terl had indeed been busy. Several things were changed. One of them was his instructor machine and table. It now sat outside the cage. Terl yanked him to a halt.

Chrissie and Pattie were tied to an iron rod that had been inset into the side of the pool. Chrissie was trying to massage some feeling back into Pattie's arms and legs, and the little girl was crying with the pain of returning blood.

"Now, animal," said Terl, "I am giving you a briefing tour, so pay very close attention." Terl pointed to an electric connector box on a nearby wall. His talon indicated a heavy wire coming from it that led to the top bars of the cage, wound around each one, enclosed the whole cage high up, and returned to the box. Each cage bar now had insulator wrappings around the bottom.

Terl yanked Jonnie over to a clump of bushes. A coyote was lying there, its head muffled in wrappings, snarls coming from it. Terl put on an insulator glove and picked up the coyote.

"Now tell those two other animals to watch this carefully," said Terl.

Jonnie said nothing.

"Well, no matter," said Terl. "I see they are watching."

With his gloved paw, Terl held up the struggling coyote and launched it at the bars.

There was a searing puff of light.

The coyote shrieked.

An instant later it was a charred, crackling mess on the bars, turning black.

Terl chuckled. "Animal, tell them if they touch those bars, that's what will happen."

Jonnie told them never to touch the bars.

"Next," said Terl, taking off the glove and putting it in his belt, "we have a real treat for you."

Terl reached into his pocket and took out a compact switch box. "You know all about remotes, animal. Remember your tractor! This is a remote." He pointed at the two girls. "Now look closely and you will see they are wearing a different kind of collar. See that red bulge on the side of the collar?"

Jonnie did, all too clearly. He felt sick.

"That," said Terl, "is a small bomb. It is enough to shatter their necks and blow their heads off. Understand, animal?"

Jonnie glared.

"This switch," said Terl, pointing to his remote control box, "is the small animal. *This* switch," and he pointed to another, "sets off the collar of the other animal. This box—"

"And what is the third switch?" said Jonnie.

"Well, thank you for asking. I didn't think I was getting through to your rat brain. This third switch ignites a general charge in the cage that you do not know the location of and that will blow up the whole lot."

Terl was smiling behind his faceplate, his amber eyes slitted, flickering, watching Jonnie.

At length he continued. "This control box is always on my person. There are also two other remotes in places you don't know about. Now, is all that very clear to you?"

"It's clear to me," said Jonnie, repressing his shaking anger, "that one of the horses can come over and get electrocuted. It's also clear that you could accidentally trip those controls."

"Animal, we are standing here jabbering and omitting the fact that I have truly befriended you."

Jonnie was very alert.

Terl took out a metal cutter and snipped off Jonnie's collar. He then mockingly handed him its remains and the leash.

"Run around," said Terl. "Feel liberty. Frisk!"

Terl moved off and started picking up some odds and ends of tools he had strewn about while working. The stench of the electrocuted coyote was rank in the air.

"And what do *I* pay for this?" said Jonnie.

Terl came back. "Animal, you must have realized by now—in spite of your rat brain—that your best course is to cooperate with me."

"In what way?"

"That's better, animal. I like to see gratitude."

"In what way?" repeated Jonnie.

"The company has some projects that need doing. They are very confidential, of course. And you are standing there pledging your full cooperation. Right?"

Jonnie looked at him.

"And when they are all done," said Terl, "why, I will stagger you with gifts, and you can return to the mountains."

"With them," said Jonnie, pointing at Chrissie and Pattie.

"Of course, and with your four-legged companions as well."

Jonnie knew a false Terl when he saw one.

"Of course," said Terl, "if you try to get away—which I think by now you have found impossible—or if you seek to mess me up or if you don't succeed, why then, very easy, the little one loses its head. And if you repeat your mistake in any way, the bigger one loses *its* head. And if you go off the cable completely, the whole place blows up. Now do I have your promise of cooperation?"

"I can move around all I please?"

"Of course, animal. I'm tired of hunting rats for you. And I'm sure not going to hunt rats for those two in there!" Terl laughed, the soul of joviality.

"I can go into the cage?"

"When I'm standing outside with my little remote control box watching. Yes."

"I can ride around the country?"

"As long as you wear this," said Terl. He pulled out of his pocket a button camera with a loose neck band and dropped it over Jonnie's head. "If it shuts off or gets beyond a five-mile range, why, I just push the first switch."

"You're not a monster. You're a devil."

But Terl saw clearly he had won. "So you promise?"

Jonnie dejectedly looked at the remote control box bulge in Terl's pocket. He looked at the two girls who were now gazing at him trustingly.

"I promise to do the project," said Jonnie. It was as far as he could be stretched.

But it was enough for Terl. He almost gaily tossed his tools into the back of the truck and drove off.

Jonnie walked over to the cage, careful not to touch the bars, and began a cautious low-key explanation of what was going on. He felt like a cheat as he did so. If ever he had seen treachery, it had been in Terl's eyes.

■

PART 6

— 1 —

Leverage, leverage, Terl told himself as he went through company papers in his office.

He *must* solve this riddle of Numph. With enough on the Planetary Director, Terl could begin his own project in earnest. Wealth and power on home planet beckoned from the future. Only Numph could drop a mine bucket on him. And Terl was determined that once his project was completed, he was not going to spend ten more years on this cursed planet. With enough on Numph, all he had to do was finish the project, obliterate all evidence (including vaporizing the animals), get his employment terminated, and there he'd be, wallowing in luxury at home. But Numph was getting a little restive; in the last interview a couple of days ago Numph had complained of the noise of the recon drone in its daily pass-by, and veiling it as a sort of compliment, he noted that the "mutiny" was not showing up on his lines. There *was* something on Numph. Terl was fervidly certain of it.

He was thumbing through a company publication, "Metal Markets of the Galaxies," which was issued several times a year. It was supposed to go to the sales department but there was none on this planet, since it sent its ore directly to home planet and had no sales except to the home company. Yet the publication was sent routinely to all minesites through the galaxies, and Terl had fished this latest copy out of the incoming dispatch box.

So many credits for this metal and so many credits for another. Such and such credits for unsmelted ore of what percent. It was very dull. But Terl laboriously went through it, hopeful of some clue.

From time to time he watched his live screens, keeping check on the animal. The button camera around its neck was working well, and in the vicinity of the cage and nearby plateau he had a broader view. It was a test to see whether the animal really was going to behave. The control box that monitored the cameras lay handy on Terl's littered desk.

The animal so far had been very well behaved. Terl was struck by its orderly sense of priorities.

It had somehow managed to turn the wounded horse over and get the packs off it. It had gotten some pitch from a tree and sealed the wound. It must have been effective, for the horse was now standing on shaky legs, a bit dazed but munching at the tall grass.

The animal had then staked out the other three horses, using a plaited type of rope that had come from the packs. One particular horse tried to follow the man-thing around, nudging with its nose. It struck Terl very odd that the man-thing talked to it, that the man-thing had also talked to the wounded horse. Very peculiar. Terl couldn't understand the language and listened intently to see whether the horses talked back. Maybe they did. Supersonic? They must say something, because the man-thing sometimes answered them. Was it a different tongue than the man-thing used to the two female creatures in the cage? Terl guessed there might be several such languages. Well, it was no matter and not important. He was no Chinko, he decided, with contempt for the old race.

Terl had next been distracted by the screen views of the animal when it mounted up on a horse and went down to the work area. From what he could see via the button camera the animal wore, the Psychlo workmen ignored him after a brief glance. The machines went right on tearing around as always.

The man-thing rode up to Ker. Terl got very interested and turned up the volume. Ker tried to edge away.

The animal said something peculiar: "It's not your fault."

Ker stopped backing up. He looked confused.

"I forgive you," said the animal.

Ker just stood there staring. Terl couldn't get a very good look at Ker due to the shadows of the dome Ker wore, but it seemed to Terl that Ker looked relieved. Terl took careful note of that as a sort of trick: it was not the kind of behavior he had ever thought about.

And then Terl really was startled. The animal borrowed a blade machine from Ker. Char came over and objected, and Ker waved him off. The animal tied the horse to trail after the machine and drove the vehicle back up to the plateau. Ker had looked positively threatening at Char. Had the animal started a fight between the two Psychlos? How had the animal managed that?

Well, Terl thought, he was just imagining things, and the screen views had been jumpy and the sound very flawed due to the roar of machinery. And Terl went back to the real puzzle of Numph.

The next time Terl remembered to check, he saw that the animal had used the blade machine to knock down a half-dozen trees and pile them up near the cage. It was using the blade controls to axe up the trees in lengths. Terl was pleased it could operate a machine like that. It would have need of such skill.

Terl got involved with bauxite quotations through the galaxies and didn't pay any more attention until nearly nightfall.

The animal had returned the blade machine and was now almost finished with a fence. It had built a fence of sorts all around the cage! Terl was puzzled until he remembered the animal's saying the horses might touch the bars. Of course! It was protecting the females from flash in case the horses short-circuited the bars.

After another hour of studying prices, Terl got his face mask and went down to the cage area.

He found that the animal had built itself a little hut from the tree branches and now had the instruction machine and table and packs in it and was kindling a fire in front of it. Terl hadn't really recognized that man-things could create houses without dressed timber or stones.

The man-thing got a branch burning and, with some other things in its hand, went over to the cage. It had left a zigzag opening before the door—to bar the horses and still let a man-thing through.

Terl threw a switch and cut off the juice to the bars and let the animal in the cage. It handed the female the burning brand, put down some other things, came out again, and got some wood and took it in.

It was very uninteresting to Terl. He noted idly that the females had cleaned up the old robes, dismantled the meat-drying rack, and neatened the place up. He checked their collars and leashes and the firmness of the pin to which they were tied. They shrank from him as if he were a disease. It amused him.

After he had pushed the animal out and was locking the cage door, from nowhere an idea hit him. Terl hastily turned on the juice again and went tearing back to his office.

Throwing down his face mask, Terl yanked a huge calculator into the center of the desk. Talons rattled on the key buttons. Reports to home office concerning ore tonnage shipped flashed on the screen and went into the calculator.

Ripping through the sales price publication and battering its data into the machine, working with an intense fury, Terl calculated the home office values of Earth ore shipped.

He stared at the screen. He sat back, stunned.

The operational cost of Intergalactic on Earth and the current market value of the ore shipped told one incredible fact. Not only were Earth operations *not* losing money, but ore-sold values were five hundred times the operating cost. This planet was incredibly profitable.

Economy wave! By the crap nebula, for this planet could afford to pay five, ten, or fifteen times the wages and bonuses.

Yet Numph had cut them.

It was quite one thing for the company to make an enormous profit. But it was quite another for Numph to lie about it.

Late into the night Terl worked. He went over every report Numph had sent to the home office in past months. They seemed very usual, very much in order. The pay columns, however, were a bit fishy. They listed the employee's name and grade and then said simply, "Usual pay for grade" in a symbol form, and under bonuses they said, "As designated." Very funny sort of accounting.

One could say, of course, that this mine area was not an administration center and was short of personnel and that the home office should finish the reports—after all, the home office accounting section was not only well staffed but also totally automated. Here they just handed out the credits across a pay table to the employees; a lot of them couldn't write anyway, and there were no signed receipts. It was this omission that made it necessary to return bodies of workers killed.

Then, about midnight, Terl found something funny about the vehicle reports. Vehicles in use for each five-day work period were customarily reported by their serial numbers. The first oddity was that *Numph* was reporting vehicles in use. Hardly a function for the Planetary Head—but Terl knew Numph's writing.

Suddenly Terl found a vehicle he knew was *not* in use. It was one of twenty battle planes he had had returned from other minesites: those twenty sat outside in a nearby field, there being no room left in the garage. Yet there it was: "Battle Plane 3-450-967 G." Numph had noted it in use for the past period.

On report after report, Terl examined those in-use listings. He noticed that they varied in position from one to another; the sequence was different in every report.

Terl smelled *code*.

By dawning light he had it.

Using serial numbers of the countless vehicles on the planet, one could choose the last three digits and, by plain substitution of numbers for letters, write pretty much what one pleased.

With expanding joy he read the first message he had decoded. It said: "No complaints here. Bank difference as usual."

Terl did another calculation.

He was exuberant. These reports went to Nipe, Numph's nephew in home-office accounting. The total pay and bonuses of Earth should have been around one hundred sixty-seven million Galactic credits. Actually *no* bonuses were being paid and only half the salary.

It meant that Nipe, on home planet, was reporting full pay and bonuses and was banking to the personal account of himself and Numph close to one hundred million Galactic credits a year. Their own combined pay would not exceed C75,000. Their swindle was making them nearly one hundred million a year.

There was the evidence: the code, the incomplete accounts.

Terl's office shook as he paced back and forth, hugging himself.

Then he paused. How about making Numph and Nipe cut him in? They would. They would have to.

But no. Good as he was as a security chief, Terl realized that if he could untangle the scheme so could somebody else. It was big money but dangerous money. Nipe and Numph stood a fair chance of failure, and if caught they would be vaporized out of hand. Terl wanted no part of that. So far he was not culpable. He could not be blamed for not catching on, for it was not part of his department to do accounting. No complaints had come his way. He had written orders from Numph to be alert for mutiny, but no orders from anyone to police home office.

No, Terl would be content with his own one hundred million,

thank you. It was very smooth. He had it all worked out. It was not company ore. No company employees would be used. He could call it an experiment and even show he was ordered to do it. Nothing would go into company records. The last little part of it was risky—getting it to home planet—but he could even worm out of that if caught. And he wouldn't be caught.

Let Numph and Nipe have their fortune—and their risk. He would preserve these records just long enough to convince Numph if he needed to, and then he would destroy them.

Oh, did he look forward to his next interview with Numph!

— 2 —

"I see you have acquired some more animals," said Numph querulously the next afternoon.

A jolly Terl had gotten the interview with a bit of persuasion. He was not popular with Numph's office staff. And he definitely didn't seem very popular with Numph.

The Planetary Director sat there behind his upholstered desk. He was not looking at Terl but gazing with distaste upon the awesome mountain scenery in the distance.

"Just as you authorized," said Terl.

"Humph," said Numph. "You know, I really don't see any traces of this mutiny of yours."

Terl had put a cautionary paw across his own mouthbones. Numph noticed it and turned to face him.

The security chief had brought a lot of papers and some equipment with him. He now raised a warning talon to Numph and then reached down and picked up the equipment.

Numph watched while the security chief passed a probe all over the office, up along the curving canopy beams, beside the edges of the rug, over the desk, and even under the chair arms. Each time Numph sought to question, Terl put up a cautionary talon. Plainly the security chief was making sure there were no button cameras or picto-recorder diaphragms anywhere about.

Terl looked through the canopy and examined the outside carefully. No one was around. Finally he smiled in reassurance and sat down.

"I don't like that recon drone crashing by every morning," said Numph "It gives me a headache."

Terl made a notation. "I will change its course at once, Your Planetship."

"And these animals," said Numph. "You're getting a positive zoo out there. Just this morning Char said you had added six more!"

"Well, actually," said Terl, "the project requires more than fifty. Also some machines to train them and authorization—"

"Absolutely not!" said Numph.

"It will save the company a great deal of money and increase its profits—"

"Terl, I am going to issue an order to vaporize those things. If home office were to hear—"

"It's confidential," said Terl. "It's a surprise. How grateful they will be when they see their payroll and bonuses shrink and their profits soar."

Numph frowned, feeling himself on very sure ground. Terl knew the blunder he had made before. Numph, left to his own crooked course, would have enormously increased the number of personnel brought here from Psychlo. Every extra employee greatly padded Numph's pocket.

"I have other ways of increasing ore shipments," said Numph. "I am considering doubling our work force with employees from home planet. There are plenty out of work there."

"But that will reduce profits," said Terl innocently. "You told me yourself that profits were a battle just now."

"More ore, more profits," said Numph belligerently. "And they go on half-pay when they arrive. That's final."

"Now these authorizations I have here," said Terl, undisturbed, "to train up a native, indigenous work force—"

"Did you hear me?" said Numph angrily.

"Oh, yes, I heard you," smiled Terl. "*My* concern is for the company and the increase of its profits."

"You imply mine is not?" challenged Numph.

Terl laid his work papers on the desk in front of Numph. At first the Planetary Director started to sweep them away with a paw. Then he sat suddenly still, frozen. His eyes stared. His paws began to tremble. He read the profit estimations. He read the circled absence of actual pay information. He read the vehicle numbers, and then he read the message, "No complaints here. Bank difference as usual."

Numph looked up at Terl. Staring, frozen terror crept into his eyes.

"By company regulations," said Terl, "I have the right to replace you."

Numph was staring at the gun in Terl's belt. His eyes were hypnotized with shock.

"But actually, I don't care much for administration. I can see that someone in your position, faced with growing old and with no future, might find other ways to solve his problems. I am very understanding."

Numph's terror-filled eyes lifted to Terl's chest, waiting.

"The crimes of someone on home planet are not in my duty sphere," said Terl.

There was a flicker in Numph's eyes. Incredulity.

"You have always been a good administrator," continued Terl. "Mainly because *you let other employees do exactly what they think best serves company interests*."

He swept up the evidence. "Out of regard for you, these will be put away where none can see them—unless something happens to me, of course. I will report nothing to home office. I know nothing about this. Even if you say I do, there will be no evidence and you won't be believed. If you get vaporized because of it, it will be entirely because of mistakes you make on other lines. They will not include me."

Terl got up, followed by Numph's stricken eyes.

A huge sheaf of requisitions and order forms was laid on Numph's desk. "For your signature!" said Terl.

They were blank. They were undated. They were forms from the Planetary Director's own office.

Numph started to say, "But they're blank. You could put anything on these. Personal money, machines, mines, change operations, even transfer yourself off the planet!" But his voice wouldn't work. And then he realized that his brain wouldn't function either.

The pen was pushed between his claws, and for the next fifteen minutes Numph signed his name over and over and over again, slowly, almost witlessly.

Terl picked up the sheaf of signed blanks. He would be very sure that none of these got loose while they were not filled in!

"All for the good of the company," said Terl. He was smiling. He put the thick sheaf in a securely locked case, put the evidence in a big envelope, picked up his equipment. "To remove you would ruin the career of a valuable employee. As your friend I can only seek to minimize damage to the company. I am pleased to tell you that you are in no danger of any kind from me. You must believe that. I am a faithful company employee but I protect my friends."

He gave a little bow and left.

Numph sat like a dumped sack of ore, nerveless, incapable of reaction.

Only one thought kept going round and round and round in his head. The security chief was an untouchable demon, a demon who, forever after, could do exactly as he wished. Numph never thought of even trying to stop him. He was and forever after would be in the complete power of Terl. He was too paralyzed to even think of warning Nipe. From here on out, Terl would be the real head of this planet, doing exactly as he pleased.

— 3 —

It had been a good hunt and Jonnie was going back to the compound.

That morning he had looked with sorrow at the dejected bearing of the two girls. What little they could do to clean up their squalid cage they had done. They had tried to put on bright faces when he talked to them through the two barricades. Pattie had come out of it a bit more, but she hadn't laughed when he told her she would marry the king of the mountains—it was an old personal joke. She had suddenly burst into tears, and Chrissie, trying to comfort her, had begun to cry too.

Something had to cheer them up or at least keep them busy, Jonnie thought.

He got the horses and with Windsplitter stepping out had ridden away from the compound. Dancer and the third horse—named Old Pork after his habit of grunting—trailed behind. Blodgett was better, but it would be some time before the wounded horse could run.

Jonnie was looking for deer. With venison to smoke and a hide to tan and strip, the girls would get their minds off their worries.

Some of his own guilt and bitterness dimmed as he raced across the plain, Windsplitter eager, the other two pounding along behind. The wind had wiped some of his pessimism away. The illusion of freedom stimulated him. Perhaps there was hope.

He had done better than one deer. He had come hammering into an arroyo and found himself within feet of antelope. And shortly after, one cleaned antelope was on the back of Old Pork.

Not a half-hour later he had gotten his deer, a young buck.

With both pack horses laden and trailing behind him, he was looking for kinnikinnick, a wild plant that gave good flavor to venison. It was really too early for the berries to form, but the leaves were good.

His attention was drawn to a humming sound far behind him. He halted, examining the sky. There it was, a tiny dot getting bigger. It was heading either toward him or toward the compound.

The horses had gotten used to machinery sounds, and there was not much to choose at the moment between the buzz overhead and the mutter of noise in the compound not three miles ahead of them.

Jonnie's curiosity turned to a feeling of unrest. Where was that object going? It was very low, not traveling very fast now.

Suddenly he knew it was heading for him.

There had been a row of planes in a field near the compound. Twenty of them that Terl had ferried in and left in the open. This was one of them.

It was about a hundred feet up. almost stopped. The roar was making the horses nervous.

Jonnie kicked Windsplitter ahead and started straight for the compound.

The plane drew off, turned, and then with a shattering burst of speed dove on him.

The earth before the horses erupted in explosions of dirt.

Windsplitter reared and tried to spin away. Clods battered the horses.

Jonnie's ears ached with the explosions. He turned the horses in another direction, to the right.

The earth erupted in a long line in front of him.

Windsplitter began to plunge in terror. One of the pack horses broke loose.

Jonnie wheeled and began to race to the north.

In front of him the ground again erupted.

He tried to get his horse to go through the hanging curtain of dust. Windsplitter turned and tried to run away to the south.

This time the plane plunged down and settled across their path.

Terrified, Windsplitter reared. Jonnie got him under control.

Terl was sitting in the open door of the plane, laughing. He roared, moving back and forth, pounding his chest to get his breath.

With considerable trouble, Jonnie got the two pack horses together. He dismounted to straighten their packed meat.

"You looked so funny," gasped Terl, straightening his face mask.

The horses were rolling their eyes, trembling. But Jonnie's eyes were not rolling—had they been blast guns, Terl would have been dead.

"I just wanted to show you how easy it is to stop you if you ever got out of hand," said Terl. "Just one of those gun blasts, aimed *at* you and not in front of you, would have made you a pale pink mist!"

Jonnie had tied the pack horse lead ropes to Windsplitter's neck. He stood there, soothing Windsplitter with a stroking hand.

"I'm celebrating," said Terl. "Send those horses back to the compound and get in."

"I don't have an air mask," said Jonnie, "and that interior will be breathe-gas."

"I brought your air mask," said Terl, reaching inside and holding it up. "Get in."

Jonnie had Windsplitter calm now. He took hold of the horse's ear. "Go to Chrissie," he said.

Windsplitter cast a glance at the plane and then, glad enough, started off toward the compound, pulling the pack horses with him.

Yes, Terl told himself. The animal did have a language with other animals.

Jonnie put on the air mask and pulled himself up into the plane.

— 4 —

Badly as it had started, Jonnie could not believe the sensation of flight.

He was lost in the huge copilot seat and the belt that was supposed to keep him in would not contract enough to do so. But he braced himself with a grip on a handhold and watched the Earth race away from him.

He felt awe. Was this how it was to be an eagle? Is that how the world looked from the sky?

The panorama of the mountains to the west began to open in relief. And in a few moments he realized they were now higher than Highpeak, seen whitely in the cold clear air.

For fifteen minutes he was enthralled. They were at a height of about four miles. He had never realized there was so much world! Or that one could feel so thrilled.

Then Terl said, "You can operate any of the mine machines, can't you, animal? Now this is no different except that it goes in three dimensions, not just two. Those controls in front of you duplicate these. Fly it!"

Terl's paws came off the controls.

The plane immediately flopped over. Jonnie was thrown against the door. The plane staggered and began a sickening dive.

Jonnie had not paid any attention to what Terl was doing with the controls before. They were a maze of levers and buttons. He gripped the security belt and got himself into position to reach things. He started pushing buttons.

The plane went crazy. It soared, it swooped. The ground rushed up and sped away.

Terl's laughter cut above the roar. Jonnie began to realize the creature was a bit high on kerbango. Celebrating indeed.

With a steadying concentration, Jonnie looked at the controls. As on all Psychlo equipment, everything was marked. Some of the terms he didn't know. But he spotted an additional button alongside every button familiar in mining machinery. He grasped that the third set was for the third dimension.

The main thing, he instinctively knew, was not to get too close to that ground! He found a button for altitude and punched it. Although the plane was staggering, the ground began to fall away.

This was too close to a win for Terl. "I'll take over," he said. 'I got high honors as a pilot at the school. Watch me land on that cloud!"

A ragged top puff of cloud was ahead of them. Terl punched some buttons and stopped the plane on a flat place in the mist. "Trouble is, rat brain, you didn't watch what I was doing. You were too busy gawking at the scenery. But I guess if rats had been meant to fly, they'd be birds!" He laughed at his own joke, reached behind his seat, and unstrapped a sealed container of kerbango. He took a chomp on it and put it back. "First lesson. Don't ever leave anything adrift in a plane. It'll fly around and bat your brains out. Not," he added with more laughter, "that rats have brains!"

He took off and made Jonnie repeat the operation of landing and stopping. After the third attempt, Jonnie made it without being half down in the cloud.

Jonnie took off and started to fly toward the mountains. Terl instantly—and Jonnie thought a bit fearfully—batted his hands away from the copilot controls and with his own turned the plane back.

"Not while I'm with you," growled Terl, his mood changed.

"Why not over the mountains?" asked Jonnie.

Terl scowled. "Whenever you fly over those mountains, just make very sure you got no breathe-gas loose anyplace. Understand?"

Jonnie understood. He suddenly understood a lot more than Terl thought he did.

"Why are you teaching me to fly?" asked Jonnie, more to distract Terl from his line of thinking than because he believed Terl would tell him. He was right.

"Any miner has to know how to fly," said Terl. Jonnie knew that wasn't true. Ker could fly, he was sure, since Ker had said so. But Ker had also said other miners were only interested in going underground, not above it.

It was mid-afternoon when they landed the battle plane at the end of the row. Jonnie had been right. It was the twentieth plane. Terl inched it into precise position. He put on his breathe-mask, opened the door. and gave Jonnie a shove to get out.

"Don't get any ideas that you can start one of these things," said Terl. "They require a special key to unlock the computers." He dangled a key in front of Jonnie. "I keep the one to this plane right here beside the remote control box." He took the box out and looked at it. "Yep, all switches still open." He showed Jonnie the box. "And no dummy wires!" he laughed loudly. "That's pretty good. No dummy wires!"

Jonnie went off to round up his horses. Windsplitter had gone to Chrissie and the three horses were standing outside the wooden barrier.

Pattie yelped to see him. He realized they had been worried by the horse showing up without him.

"Got an antelope and a deer!" Jonnie called into the cage. "I was a little delayed looking for kinnikinnick. I found some, not very much, but it will flavor the meat."

Chrissie was very pleased. "We can strip and smoke the meat," she called across the two barriers. "There's plenty of ashes here and we can tan the hides." Jonnie felt better.

Pattie called, "Jonnie, there's a huge grizzly bear skin in here. Did you kill it, Jonnie?"

Yes, Jonnie had killed it. But he was not so sure that he hadn't killed the wrong beast!

Later that evening when Terl came to let him, supervised, into the cage, he gave the girls the skinned meat and hides to handle. He touched them reassuringly, hiding his wince at the way the collars chafed their throats.

When he came out and Terl had locked up and turned the juice back on, Terl said, "I'm just an animal attendant. But I don't wire dummy wires!"

He threw a stack of books at Jonnie before he rumbled away. "Get your rat brain around these, animal. Tonight. Ker will take up your instruction in the morning, so don't go chasing off on a rat hunt."

Jonnie looked at the books. He was dimly getting an idea of what Terl must want out of him.

The books were: *Beginner's Flight Manual* and *Teleportation in Relation to Manned and Drone Flight*. The latter was clearly marked, *Secret. Not for Alien Race Distribution*. Could it be, thought Jonnie, that Terl was acting well outside the business of the company? If so, it was doubly certain he and the girls would be killed when they had served their purpose. Terl would not leave witnesses around.

— 5 —

Jonnie and Ker were engaged in ferrying mining machines and equipment to the "defense base." The order to do so had come early that morning from Terl.

The machinery freighter plane was parked with doors agape and ramps let down in the open field near the battle planes.

A remarkably cowed Zzt checked off a drilling machine as it was run up the ramp by Ker. He raised the ramps and closed the doors.

Jonnie buckled himself into the copilot's seat and Ker slid behind the controls. The freighter lifted abruptly and spun to the west. Ker flew low and kept the ship steady, for none of the machinery was lashed.

Jonnie did not even look at the ground flowing by—they had made this short trip several times. He was tired. For a week he had been practicing flying all day and studying all night, and it was beginning to show.

His headache, however, came from the text *Teleportation in Relation to Manned and Drone Flight*. The flight part of it was far less interesting than teleportation. He felt that if he could grasp that, he might be able to do something to avert the fate he knew would come someday.

The mathematics of the text were quite beyond him. They were Psychlo mathematics a long way in advance of what he had studied. The symbols made his head spin.

The history section at the start of the book was perfunctory. It simply stated that a hundred thousand years ago a Psychlo physicist named En had untangled the riddle. Prior to this, it was thought that teleportation consisted of converting energy and matter to space and then reconverting it in another place so it would assume its natural form. But this had never been proven. En had apparently found that space could exist entirely independent of time, energy, or mass and that all these things were actually separate items. Only when combined did they make up a universe

Space was dependent only upon three coordinates When one

dictated a set of space coordinates one shifted space itself. Any energy or mass contained in that space thereupon shifted with that space shift.

In the matter of a motor such as this freighter had, it was just an enclosed housing in which space coordinates could be changed. As the coordinates changed, the housing was forced to go along, and this gave the motor power. That explained why these planes were run by a switchboard and not a thrust through the air. They didn't have to have wings or controls. Much smaller housings in the tail and on each side had similar sets of coordinates fed into them to climb and bank. A series of coordinates were progressively fed to the main motor and it simply went forward or backward as the housed space occupied each set of coordinates in turn.

Teleportation over vast distances worked the same way. Matter and energy were pinned to the space, and when it was exchanged with another space, they simply changed too. Thus matter and energy would seem to disappear in one place and appear in another. They didn't actually change. Only the space did.

Jonnie could see now how Earth had been attacked. Informed in some way of its existence, possibly from some Psychlo station in this universe, the Psychlos had only to fish in its coordinates.

They evidently used a recorder of some sort. They cast the recorder out to a test set of coordinates and then got it back and looked at the pictures. If the recorder vanished they knew they had sent it into the mass of the planet. Then they just had to adjust the coordinates for a new recorder cast.

In that way they had sent the killer gas. When it dissipated, they had followed it with Psychlos and weapons.

That was how Earth had been wiped out and conquered. But it didn't tell Jonnie how to reverse the process. Any Psychlo station out there could teleport new gas or even an army to Earth at will. That was the point that was giving him a headache.

"You're not very chatty," said Ker, circling to land at the old defense base, going dead slow because of loose machinery. Jonnie came out of it. He pointed at the button camera that hung around his neck.

"Forget it," said Ker to his astonishment. "They only have a range of about two miles." He pointed at his work jacket pocket flap. A much smaller button camera with the symbol of the company on it was actually serving as a real button.

"Not five or more?" asked Jonnie.

"Crap no," said Ker. "The security measures of this company are a pain. There's no recorder in this plane. I checked. What the splintered asteroid are we doing hauling this machinery over to this old defense base?" He looked down. "It doesn't even look like a defense base anyway."

And it didn't. It was just some buildings, not even a landing field. No bunkers anyone could see. Some kind of a strange series of pointed things standing up at one end.

"Terl gives the orders," said Jonnie, a bit resigned.

"Blast, no. These weren't Terl's orders. I saw them. They were signed by the head of the planet. Terl was even complaining. He said he wondered whether old Numph had gone off his computers."

It gave Jonnie new data, but not what Ker thought. Terl was covering his tracks. This was *Terl's* project. It made him uneasy.

"This stuff," said Ker, with a backward jerk of his head, "is supposed to be practice equipment. But for who? It's perfectly good mining equipment. Hold on, we're going to land." He punched the console buttons and the freighter crept down and landed easily and level.

Ker put on his face mask. "Another funny thing. There's no supply of breathe-gas with any of this stuff. Just what was left in their tanks. You're the only one I know that can operate these machines without breathe-gas in the canopies. You going to operate all these machines?" He laughed. "It'd sure run your butt off! Let's unload."

They spent the next hour lining the machines up in an open field near the largest building. There were drillers and flying platforms, cable reelers, ore netters, blade scrapers, and a single transport truck. With the items brought in earlier loads there were over thirty machines now.

"Let's prowl," said Ker. "We been fast. What's in this big building?"

It consisted only of rooms, rooms, and rooms. Each with bunks and lockers. There were what may have been washrooms. Ker was prowling for loot. But broken windows and wind and snow had not left much. Dust and indistinguishable debris were thick.

"Already been prowled," was Ker's finding. "Let's look elsewhere."

Ker clumped through the entrance of another building. Jonnie saw that it had been a library, but without Chinko protection it was mainly litter. A thousand years of cockroaches had dined on paper.

A queer, broken structure that once had had seventeen points—Jonnie counted them—seemed to have been some kind of a monument. Ker entered a door that was no longer there. A cross was still hanging on a wall.

"What's that thing?" said Ker.

Jonnie knew it was a church cross. He said so.

"Funny thing to have in a defense base," said Ker. "You know, I don't think this *was* a defense base. More like a school."

Jonnie looked at Ker. The midget Psychlo might be thought dim-witted, but he was dead on the mark. Jonnie did not tell him there were signs all over the place that said ["United States Air Force Academy"].

They wandered back to the freighter. "I bet we're establishing a school," said Ker. "I bet that's what it is we're doing. But who's going to be taught? Not Psychlos with no breathe-gas, that's for sure. Put up the ramps, Jonnie, and we'll get out of here."

Jonnie did, but he didn't climb up to the cockpit. He looked around for water and firewood. He had an idea he'd be camping out here. Yes, there was a stream coming down from a nearby snow-capped peak. And there was plenty of firewood in the trees.

He walked out and looked at the trench where the last battle had been fought against the Psychlos. The grass was tall and waving in a lonesome-sounding wind.

He climbed to the freighter cockpit, deeply troubled.

— 6 —

At evening when he opened the cage, Terl sounded excited. "Tell your horses and females goodbye, animal. Tomorrow at dawn we're going on a long trip."

Jonnie stopped with his arms full of the firewood he had been taking in "How long?"

"Five days, a week. It depends," said Terl. "Why do you want to know?"

"I have to leave them food . . . a lot of things."

"Oh," said Terl indifferently. "Am I going to have to stand here and wait?" He made up his own mind. He locked up the cage again and turned on the juice. "I'll come back later." He rumbled off hurriedly.

Well, here it goes, Jonnie told himself. What devilry was going to take place now?

Fortunately, that day he had gotten a fat young bull. He swiftly went about his work. He quartered it and rolled up two quarters in the hide, putting it outside the door.

"Chrissie!" he called. "Put me together enough smoked meat for a week. Also think about what you'll need for that time."

"You're leaving?" Was there a trace of panic in Chrissie's voice?

"Just for a little while."

Both girls looked apprehensive. They seemed so forlorn in there. Jonnie cursed to himself. "I'll be sure to come back," he said. "Get busy with the food."

He inspected Blodgett's wound. Blodgett could walk now, but torn muscles had ended her running days.

The grazing problem for the horses was a little rough. He did not want to turn them loose, but he couldn't stake them to a week's grazing all in one spot. He finally settled it by letting them loose but instructing Pattie to call them to the barrier a couple of times a day to talk to them. Pattie promised she would.

He prepared a belt pouch with flint and tinder, cutting glass, and a few odds and ends. He folded up a complete suit of buckskins. He made a pack of these and two kill-clubs.

When Terl came back later in the evening and opened the cage door, Jonnie rapidly moved in what Chrissie would need. She could smoke beef and work with hides. It would keep them busy. He took the packet she had prepared.

"You will be all right, Jonnie?" she asked.

He didn't feel like smiling, but he smiled. "I'll make it my first business in all cases," he said. "Now don't you worry. Put some of that tallow on Pattie's neck and it will help the chafing."

"Come on," said Terl irritably, outside the cage.

"How do you like the glass to cut things with?" said Jonnie.

Chrissie said, "It is very good if you don't cut yourself."

"Well, be careful."
"Hey," said Terl.
Jonnie gave Pattie a kiss on the cheek. "Now you take good care of your sister, Pattie."
He put his arms around Chrissie and hugged her. "Please don't worry."
"For crap, come out of that cage," said Terl.
Chrissie's hand trailed down Jonnie's arm. He drew away until only their fingers were touching.
"Be careful, Jonnie." Tears were rolling down her cheeks.
Terl yanked him out and banged the cage door behind him. While Jonnie closed the wood barrier, Terl turned on the juice.
"At dawn," said Terl, "I want you down at the landing field ready to go. Personnel Freighter Ninety-One. Wear decent clothes and boots that won't stink the ship up. Bring your air pump and plenty of bottles and an extra mask. Is that understood, animal?" He rumbled off, practically trotting. Terl was a busy fellow these days. The ground-shake died out.
Later Jonnie picked some wild flowers and berries in the dark and tried to throw them between the bars. But the electric current simply arched and sizzled them before they could get through. It made things seem even worse.
He went to bed at last, dispirited, certain that the future was going to be very rough, if not fatal.

— 7 —

They were aloft at last, flying just to the east of north, rising rapidly to an altitude of over ten miles. Terl loomed over the control panel, silent and withdrawn. Jonnie sat at the copilot console, the seat belt wrapped around him twice, air mask tending to mist. It was growing very cold in the flight cab.
They were late getting off because Terl had personally gone over every fitting and unit of the plane as though suspicious that someone might have sabotaged it. The actual ship number was eighteen digits long and only ended in ninety-one. It was an old ship, a castoff from some war on some other planet, and it showed its scars in dents and sears. It had a forward flight

compartment like any freighter, but it was armored and fitted with batteries of air-to-air and air-to-ground blast guns.

The huge body of the plane, now empty, was fitted to carry not ore but fifty company attack troops—there were huge benches, bins for supplies, racks for their blast guns. There were many ports, all armored. The plane had not carried troops or even been flown for ages.

Seeing that breathe-gas compression would be off in the compartment, Jonnie had thought it might be better to ride there, but Terl put him in the copilot seat. Now he was glad. This altitude probably had little air in it, and the cold was seeping into the cab with icy fingers.

Below them the mountains and plains spread out, apparently not moving at any great speed even though the plane was well above hypersonic.

Soon Jonnie knew he was looking at the top of the world. Pale green misty sea and white vastnesses of ice were all across the northern horizon. They were not going to cross the North Pole, but nearly.

The chattering console computer was rolling itself out a tape of their successive positions. Jonnie looked at it. They were turning in a curve to head more easterly.

"Where are we going?" said Jonnie.

Terl didn't answer for some time. Then he yanked an Intergalactic Mining chart of the planet from a seat pocket and threw it at Jonnie. "You're looking at the world, animal. It's round."

Jonnie unfolded the chart. "I know it's round. Where are we going?"

"Well, we're not going up there," said Terl, pointing a talon toward the north. "That's all water in spite of its looking solid. Just ice. Don't never land there. You'd freeze to death."

Jonnie had a chart open. Terl had drawn a red, curving course line from the area of departure, up across a continent, then across a large island and then down to the top of another island. Typical of a mining map, it was all in numbers and without names. He translated rapidly in his head back to Chinko geography. Using ancient names, the course lay up over Canada, across the top of Greenland, past Iceland and down to the north tip of Scotland. On the mine map, Scotland was 89-72-13.

After punching in a new series of coordinates, Terl put the ship on automatic and reached back of his seat for a container of kerbango. He slurped some into his container cover and chewed it down.

"Animal," said Terl above the roar of the ship, "I am about to recruit fifty man-things."

"I thought we were almost gone."

"No, rat brain. There are some groups in various inaccessible places on the planet."

"And," said Jonnie, "having gotten them, we are going to take them back to the 'defense base.' "

Terl looked at him and nodded. "And you're going to help."

"If I'm going to help, maybe we better talk over how we are going to do this."

Terl shrugged. "Simple. There's a village up in the mountains where you sec that red circle. This is a battle plane. We just dive in with stun blasts and then walk around and load the ones we want aboard."

Jonnie looked at him. "No."

Hostile, Terl said, "You promised—"

"I know what I promised. I'm saying 'no' because your plan won't work."

"These guns can be set to 'stun.' They don't have to be put on a 'kill' setting."

"Maybe you better tell me what these men are going to do," said Jonnie.

"Why, you're going to train them on machines. I thought you could figure that out yourself, rat brain. You've been ferrying the machines. So what's wrong with this plan?"

"They won't cooperate," said Jonnie.

With a frown, Terl studied that. Leverage, leverage. It was true that he wouldn't have leverage. "We'll tell them that if they don't cooperate we'll shoot up their village for keeps."

"Probably," said Jonnie. He looked at Terl with disgust and laughed.

It stung Terl. Jonnie was sitting back now, looking at the map. Jonnie saw that they were avoiding a minesite located in the southwest of England. He wagered with himself that Terl would come down to wave top in the last run into Scotland.

"Why won't it work?" demanded Terl.

"If I've got to train them, you better let me walk in and get them."

Terl barked a laugh. "Animal, if you walked into that village they would drill you like a sieve. Suicide! What a rat brain!"

"If you want any help from me," said Jonnie, offering the map, "you'll land up here on this mountain and let me walk in the last five miles."

"And then what will you do?"

Jonnie did not want to tell him. "I'll get you fifty men."

With a shake of his head, Terl said, "Too risky. I didn't spend over a year training *you* just to have to start all over!" Then he realized he might have said too much. He looked suspiciously at Jonnie, thinking: the animal must not consider itself valuable.

"Crap!" said Terl. "All right, animal. You can go ahead and get yourself killed. What's one animal more or less? Where's the mountain?"

Well short of northern Scotland, Terl brought the personnel freighter down to wave top. They skimmed the gray-green water, eventually roared up the side of a cliff, shot inland battering the scrub and trees, and came to a halt under the shoulder of a mountain.

Jonnie won his own bet. Terl had avoided the minesite in the south.

— 8 —

Jonnie stepped down into a different land.

The barren mountain and its scrub seemed to swim in a soft mist; everything was hazed and faintly blue. It seemed a very beautiful place, but it had dark gorges and inaccessible summits, and there was a secretness about it as though its softness concealed a harsh threat. He had not realized a land could be so different from the bold mountains of his home.

He had changed to buckskin. He hung a kill-club on his belt.

"It's over there about five miles," said Terl, pointing south. "Very rough terrain. Don't get any ideas about vanishing. There's a whole ocean and continent between you and your country. You'd never make it back." He took out the control box and laid it on the seat behind him. He pointed at it.

"Could be," said Jonnie, "that by tomorrow morning I'll

come back and get you to move into the village. So don't move off."

"Tomorrow noon," said Terl, "I'll come down and collect fifty men, my way. If you're still alive, duck under something to avoid the stun guns. Damned fool."

"See you tomorrow morning," said Jonnie, moving off.

"Goodbye, rat brain," said Terl.

Jonnie found a faint trail that went south and, alternately running and walking, wove his way through the gullies and brush and barren fields.

It was not a very promising land for food. He did not start any deer but he saw an old trace of one. There was not much grazing to be had. Far off on another mountain he thought he saw some sheep, just a few of them, more like a small cloud than animals.

He caught a glimpse of water through the scrub ahead and went up a gully, intending to get a better look. Yes, there was an inland body of water ahead. He trotted back to the trail.

Abruptly, three pointed stakes jabbed out of cover. He stopped. Very, very slowly he put up his hands, palms out to show they were empty of weapons.

A guttural, wheezing voice said, "Take his club. Be swift noo."

One spear lowered, and a heavyset youth with a black beard stepped forward and a bit fearfully yanked the club from Jonnie's belt. The youth retreated around behind him and pushed him. The other spears made way.

"Look saucy noo," the wheezing voice said, "dinna let him runaway."

They came to a small clearing and Jonnie looked at them. There were four: two with black hair and dark eyes, a third with blond hair and blue eyes and taller than the rest, plus an old man who seemed to be in charge.

Their dress was partly woven cloth and partly hides. They wore patterned skirts of some rough fabric that fell to their knees. On their heads they had bonnets.

"It's a thief from the Orkneys," said one.

"Na, I ken Orkneymen," said another.

"Could be he's a Swede," said the blonde one. "But no, no Swede dresses so."

"Hush yer prattle," said the old one. 'Look in his pouch an' mayhap ye'll find the answer."

Jonnie laughed. "I can give you the answer," he said.

They recoiled on the defensive.

Then a black-haired one crept forward and looked closely into his face.

"He's a Sassenach! Hear the accent!"

The old man brushed the speaker aside with impatience. "Na, the Sassenachs be dead these mony centuries. Except for those already here."

"Let's go down to the village," said Jonnie. "I'm a messenger."

"Ah," said a black-bearded one. "Clanargyll! They want to talk of peace."

"Noo, noo, noo," said the old man. "He wears no such plaid." He squared himself off in front of Jonnie. "Messenger you be from whom?"

"You'll fall over on your backside," laughed Jonnie, "when I tell you. So let's go down to the village. My message is for your parson or mayor."

"Ah, it's a parson we have. But you'll be meaning Chief of the Clan, Fearghus! Git ahind him you boys and push him along."

— 9 —

The village sprawled on the shore of what they said was Loch Shin. It looked temporary, as though the inhabitants could easily pick up belongings and flee to a mountainside. A great many racks stood about with fish drying on them. A few children peeked, afraid, from behind fallen walls. No vast number of people came out to watch the group enter the village, but there was a feeling of eyes watching.

Here too the mist softened the land. The waters of the loch lay placid and extensive in the quiet day.

They put Jonnie in the front chamber of the only whole stone house apparent. It had an inner room, and the old man went in. There was considerable murmuring of voices from in there as Jonnie waited. A scrawny child peeked at him from behind a tattered cloth curtain, its blue eyes intense. He put out a hand toward it to beckon it closer, and it vanished in a flurry of curtain.

There was evidently a back door, and Jonnie heard it open and close several times. The murmuring in the inner room intensified; more people were coming into it from the back.

At length the old man came to Jonnie. "He'll see you noo," he said and pointed to the inner chamber.

Jonnie went in. About eight men had assembled and taken seats along the walls. They had spears and clubs beside them or in their hands.

Seated on a large chair against the back wall was a big black-haired, black-bearded power of a man. He had a short skirt that showed the bony knees of strong legs. He wore a pair of white crossbelts, pinned together at the center of the X with a large silver badge. A bonnet sat squarely on his head and he held a large, ancient sword across his knees. Jonnie knew he must be looking at Chief of the Clan, Fearghus.

Fearghus looked about at his council to see that they were all there and alert. He stared at the newcomer.

"A messenger," said Fearghus, "from whom?"

"Have you had any trouble with the monsters?" said Jonnie.

A shock went through the group.

"I take it you mean the demons," said Fearghus.

"Would you mind telling me any trouble you have had?" said Jonnie.

This threw them into an uproar. Fearghus held up an imperious hand. Quiet fell.

"Young man," said Fearghus, "since you give us no name, as you claim to be a messenger, although you have not said from whom—though I suppose you will tell us in good time—I will do you the courtesy of answering your question." Jonnie was getting the notes of the accent and followed easily. The Chief talked in his throat and clipped off the words.

"Since the days of the myths," said Fearghus, "we have had nothing but trouble with the demons. The myths tell us they raised a cloud across the land and all peoples died except a very few. I am sure you know these myths since they are religious and you appear to be a properly, politely, religious man.

"All to the south of us, no men dare live. There is a fortress of the demons five hundred miles to the south and west. And from time to time, they foray out and hunt men. They kill them without reason or compunction.

"At this moment you find us in the fishing village, for the fish are running. We sit here and work at risk. As soon as we have a little food, we will retire further into the Highlands. We have always been a proud people, we of the Clanfearghus. But no one can fight the demons. Now that I have answered you, please continue."

"I am here," said Jonnie, "to recruit fifty young, valiant men. They will be taught certain skills and will perform certain tasks. It will be dangerous. Many of them may die. But in the end, should God grant us fortune and we are true to our task, we may defeat the demons and drive them from this world."

It caused an explosion. The council had withdrawn into themselves at their Chief's recitation of ancient history and they had been made fearful. But the idea of someone combating the demons was so outrageous they exploded.

Jonnie sat quietly until the Chief thumped the chair arm with his sword hilt. The Chief looked at a council member. "You wished to speak, Angus?"

"Aye. There is another myth, that once long ago when Scots were thousands, a great crusade went south and they were crushed."

"That was before the demons," shouted another council member.

"Nobody has ever fought the demons!" yelled another.

A grizzled council member stood forward and the Chief recognized him as Robert the Fox. "I do not deny," he said, "that it would be worthy cause. We starve in the Highlands. There is little grazing for sheep. We dare not plow and plant crops as our ancestors once did in these rocky glens, for the myths tell us demons fly through the air and have eyes, and some say that the strange metal cylinder that passes overhead on some days is itself a demon.

"But I also tell you," he continued, "that this stranger, clothed in what I take to be buckskin, signifying a hunter, speaking a strangely accented speech, smiling and courteous and no Argyll, has voiced an idea that in all my long life, I have never heard before. His words cause the mind to flare with sudden vision. That he can propose such a vision of daring and boldness proves that in some way he must be a Scot! I recommend we listen." He sat down.

Fearghus was musing. "We could not let all our young men go. Some would have to be from the Campbells, some from the Glencannons. But never mind. Stranger, you have not told us either your name or from whom you are a messenger."

Jonnie braced himself. "I am Jonnie Goodboy Tyler. I am from America."

There was chatter. Then Robert the Fox said, "Legends say it was a land of the ancients where many Scots went."

"Then he *is* a Scot," said another council member.

The Chief held up his hand to quiet them. "That doesn't tell us from whom you are a messenger."

Jonnie looked calm. He didn't feel calm. "I am a messenger from mankind—before we become extinct forever."

He saw a flicker of awe in some, a flicker of wonder in others.

The Chief leaned forward again. "But how did you get here?"

"I flew here."

The Chief and the others digested this. The Chief frowned then. "In these times only the demons can fly. How did you get here from America?"

"I own a demon," said Jonnie.

— 10 —

He had to get to Terl before the monster took off and blasted the village. The sun was arcing up perilously close to the deadline: noon.

Jonnie ran uphill on the trail, his heart overworked. Bushes whipped by. Stones rolled under his pounding feet.

It had been a wild night and a hard-worked morning.

The clan Chief had sent runners and riders thundering across the Highlands to summon other Chiefs. They came from far glens and hidden caves of the mountains, bearded, kilted, cautious, and suspicious—enemies, many of them, one to another.

The Chiefs of the MacDougals, Glencannons, Campbells, and many others had come. Even the Chief of the Argylls. A subdued English lord from a group in the lower hills had come. The King of a tiny Norse colony on the east coast had strode in late.

It was after midnight when Jonnie could talk to them all.

He leveled with them. He explained that Terl had personal plans of his own, independent of the company, and was using his power to further his own ambitions. He told them that Terl conceived himself to be using Jonnie, and through Jonnie, men, to carry out his project, and that quite possibly Terl would slaughter the lot of them when he had finished with them.

Jonnie began to realize, as he spoke to the intent faces around the flickering council fire, that he must be dealing with some Scot love of guile. For when he told them he had an outside chance of turning the tables and using Terl, only then did the Chiefs begin to nod and smile and hope.

But when he told them about Chrissie, held as a hostage against his good behavior, and that part of his own plan was to rescue her, he had them. A streak of romanticism, which had survived all their defeats and humblings, welled up in them. While they could agree to a long-shot objective with their minds, they rose to the rescue of Chrissie with their hearts. What does she look like? Black eyes and corn-silk hair. How was she formed? Beautiful and comely. How did she feel? Crushed with despair, hardly daring to hope for rescue. They were angered by the collar, disgusted with the leash, violent about the cage. They shook their chiefly weapons in the flashing firelight and made speeches and quoted legends.

Beacon fires had been set flaming in the hills, their Chiefs signaling a gathering of the clans. They sent their warlike messages until the dawn.

A meadow was the assigned meeting place, and by noon the clans would be there.

Questions and introductions and ceremony had detained Jonnie until after eleven of the morning, and he looked up with a shock to see that he had very little time indeed to get to the plane and stop Terl from committing a folly that would ruin the future.

With a sharp pain in his side from exertion, Jonnie pounded up the steep, twisting trail, swift feet spurning the ground. He hardly dared take time to check the sun. He could not be sure whether Terl was keeping the appointment by a clock or by the heavens. He dreaded any moment to hear ahead of him the roar of the plane taking off for a lethal pass over the village.

More than five miles and all uphill! And over a very bad trail.

Jonnie heard the beginnings of a start-up ahead of him. He was almost there. He burst through the brush at the edge of the plateau. The plane was already beginning to rise.

He yelled, waving his arms, racing forward. If he missed, all his work would be undone.

The plane hovered, feet off the ground, turning toward the village.

Jonnie threw his kill-club the last thirty feet to strike the fuselage and attract attention.

The plane settled back. Jonnie collapsed on the ground, drawing air in loud, hoarse breaths. The roar of the plane turned off and Terl opened the door.

"Did they chase you out?" said Terl into his face mask. "Well, get in, animal, and we'll go down and carry out a proper plan."

"No," said Jonnie as he crawled up into the seat, still panting. His feet were bruised from stones and he inspected them. "It's all set."

Terl was derisive. "All night I saw fires burning on the tops of the hills. I was sure they were roasting you for a feast!"

"No," said Jonnie. "They lit fires to call in candidates for the work group."

Terl plainly did not see how this could be.

"We have to be very careful," said Jonnie.

Terl could agree with that.

"They're going to meet in a meadow about three miles from here."

"Ah, you got them to get together so we could blast them better."

"Look, Terl, we can succeed only if we do this exactly right."

"You sure are wheezing. Tell me the truth, are they chasing you?"

Jonnie threw down a moccasin and it made a loud snap. "Blast it! It's all arranged! Only we have to finish it. There will be hundreds in that meadow. I want you to land at the upper edge of it. I'll show you where. And then you must sit in the door of the plane and do absolutely nothing. Just sit there. I will choose from the candidates. We will get them aboard and leave by tomorrow morning."

"You're giving *me* orders?" shouted Terl.

"That's how it was arranged." He was putting his moccasins

back on. "You must just sit there in the plane door so you can watch and make sure it all goes well."

"I understand," said Terl with a sudden grin. "You have to have me there to frighten them into submission!"

"Exactly," said Jonnie. "Can we go down there now?"

— 11 —

There had never been so many together within memory, Robert the Fox said.

Over a thousand Scots, with a few English and some Norsemen, crowded the broad meadow. They had brought some food and drink. They had brought arms—just in case. And they had brought their pipers. The panorama was of colored kilts, ponies, shifting groups of men, and smoke from fires, and over all lay the skirling whine and shriek of bagpipes.

There was a momentary surge back when the plane landed on the little knoll overlooking the meadow. But on Jonnie's instructions the Chiefs had briefed their people well. And when the huge Terl took his position within the open plane door, there was no unseemly panic. The men left a wide distance between the plane and themselves, however. The obvious fear Terl saw on some of the faces confirmed for him that the animal had been right: he was needed there to overawe them.

Jonnie kept one eye on Terl. He could not be sure that Terl's sadism would not cause some sort of incident.

Over five hundred young men were part of the throng. Their Chiefs had already talked to them and they gathered now in a central group below Jonnie.

Jonnie sat on a horse lent him by Chief Glencannon so he could be seen by all. He sat the mount easily even though it had a saddle and bridle, things Jonnie had never seen before and that he considered effete for one who never had trouble with horses.

The Chiefs and heads of groups stood with their young men. Outside these groups and at the edge of the crowd stood pipers. A few women, some young, some old, and older men sat on the grass where a knoll side overlooked the scene. A few children raced about, running into legs.

Jonnie began. He already knew they had been briefed. His job was made much easier by a high literacy level among these people. They had not lost the art of reading and writing and they knew a lot of history, mainly their own myths and legends.

"You all know why I am here. I want fifty young men who are able, courageous, and strong, to go on a crusade to rid the world of the demon up there who does not speak or understand our language. When I ask you to look at him and shrink back in fear, please do so."

"I amna afeered of naething!" said one young man.

"Just act so when I ask you to. I will not for a moment believe, and neither will your friends, that you are afraid. All right?"

The young man said it was.

"I feel it is necessary to tell you the character of this demon so you can help me. He is treacherous, vicious, sadistic, and devious. He lies from choice even when the truth will serve. When I point now, cower back and look terrified."

Jonnie pointed. The crowd, on cue, looked up at Terl in the plane door and cowered back.

Terl grinned behind his face mask. This was more like it.

"The mining company that conquered this planet in ages past has equipment and technology beyond those of man. Planes in the air, machines to drill the earth, gases and guns that can slaughter whole cities. Man has been deprived of his planet by these creatures. The men who volunteer to come with me will learn to use those tools, fly those planes, man those guns!

"Our chances are not in our favor. Many of us may die before this is through.

"Our race is growing fewer in numbers. In coming years we may be gone forever. But even though the odds are against us, at least let it be said that we took this small last chance and *tried*."

The crowd went into a raving, excited roar of enthusiasm. The pipes took it up and screamed. Drums pounded.

Into the din, Jonnie shouted, "I want fifty volunteers!"

All volunteered instantly. Not just the five hundred young men but the whole thousand in the meadow.

When he could again be heard above the shrilling pipes and shouting voices, Jonnie announced a series of tests he would give during the afternoon. The Chiefs turned to their people to organize it and Jonnie dropped down from the horse.

"Mon, MacTyler," cried the grizzled old man who had first captured Jonnie, "ye are a true Scot!"

And Jonnie found, as he assisted in straightening out the turmoil for the tests, that his name had indeed changed to *Mac*Tyler. There were even some arguments as to which clan his people had originally belonged to, but it was at length decided that the MacTylers had been distributed evenly among all the clans before they went to America.

The only problem with the tests was in trying to disqualify someone. Jonnie had the young men, one after another, walk a straight line with closed eyes to make sure their sense of balance was good; he made them run a distance to be certain their wind was excellent; he made them look at letters at a distance to make sure their sight was passing. Only a couple of the Norsemen were as tall as Jonnie, but the scattering of black beards and blond beards was about equal. Jonnie assumed that refugees from Scandinavia or the lower countries and even from Ireland had changed their blood over the centuries, but it certainly had not changed the hard-core ethnology of the Highlands, which had held out now against all corners and defeats for thousands of years.

The men got tired of just being examined. Some fights broke out from complaints of losers. And the Chiefs organized competitions to settle things.

The selections went well into darkness and were finally completed by firelight.

But Jonnie did not wind up with fifty. He finished with eighty-three. For diplomacy, Jonnie requested the Chiefs to select an older man as their representative, one in whom they felt confidence; they chose Robert the Fox as a veteran of many raids and very learned. So that made fifty-one.

Apparently it would be unseemly not to have pipers, so two of those were chosen, and these claimed they needed a drummer so one of those was selected. This made fifty-four.

Then some old women elbowed themselves to the front and demanded to know who was going to mend torn kilts, scrape hides, dry fish, care for wounded, and cook? and Jonnie found himself with new arguments and elections and five old widows of indeterminate age but universally attested skills. This made fifty-nine.

Since the Chiefs had been told there was a lot of study involved, Jonnie found himself confronting a small but determined schoolmaster who claimed it took an iron rod to make young men, who had appetites only for hunting and women, study. And the Chiefs said he must go too: number sixty.

But the question of death had stirred up a row from three parsons. Who would care for the souls of these young men? And also keep them respectful? There was a further quarrel as to which of the three it would be, and the lucky one drew the long straw. This made sixty-one.

Jonnie had his own plan to take care of. All of those chosen were bright. But he had to have three very bright ones who also came somewhere near his height and build, who could learn Psychlo quickly, and who could at a distance or over poor radio connections look and sound vaguely like him. He found about a dozen and asked the Chiefs, schoolmaster, and parson which of these were quick studies. They named the three. And that made sixty-four.

A scholarly old fellow showed up who lamented the fact that no one would be writing the history that would become legend. It turned out he was the dean of literature of a sort of underground university that had been eking along for centuries, and on the argument that he had two capable replacements for himself in the school and—due to his age and poor health—was expendable anyway, he could not be left behind by the MacTyler. Robert the Fox thought that very necessary, so that made sixty-five.

Eighteen outright, uncontestable ties had shown up in the contests the Chiefs had arranged, and when it looked like blood would be spilled over it, Jonnie gave in. And that made eighty-three.

He woke up Terl, who had been hitting the kerbango pretty heavily since sunset and was lying like a mountain across the plane seats.

"We have eighty-three," said Jonnie. "The plane takes fifty Psychlos, and eighty-three humans won't occupy that space or make up that weight. I want to make sure you do not object to eighty-three."

Terl was foggy and sleepy. "The casualty rate of such a project is high. We have to make it appear that they are just training all winter when they are operating, so the extra numbers are fine. Why'd you wake me up for a silly question like that, animal?" And he went back to sleep. Jonnie had culled another piece of Terl's project from this. Up to now he hadn't any real hard data on Terl's plans. Praise all for kerbango, thought Jonnie as he went off.

He had the historian draw up a roster of the Anguses and Duncans and all their parade of names, and sent them off in the night to hasten pell-mell to their homes and get heavy and light clothing and sleeping blankets, personal gear, and a few days' worth of food to tide them over until he could round up cattle. They must be back at dawn, and those who didn't have them borrowed horses, for in some cases it was a long ride both ways.

Jonnie had a final meeting with the Chiefs. "We have caused quite a row up here in the Highlands, and although the local minesite is five hundred miles away, it would be a good thing now for your people to be quiet and undemonstrative for the coming year."

The English lord thought that was a very good idea. The Chiefs agreed to it.

"There is a distinct possibility," said Jonnie, "that we will fail. And that I will never see you again and the group will be killed."

They brushed this off. Brave men always risked death, didn't they? And they'd not blame MacTyler. The bad thing would be not to try. That would be what couldn't be forgiven.

In the midnight chill, Jonnie talked to those who had not been chosen, thinking he would leave disappointment there. But he found the Chiefs had already told them that when the mission succeeded they would be a recovery corps in charge of policing and reorganizing England, Scandinavia, Russia, Africa, and China, and they were already scheduling study, training, and organizing to do that at the end of a year. And the non-chosens were wild with enthusiasm.

Fearghus was spokesman as he calmly outlined it to Jonnie. It worked on a clan system, of course.

My god, gaped Jonnie, these Scots thought big!

"Don't fret, MacTyler. We're behind ye."

Jonnie, exhausted, stretched out under the fuselage of the freighter, wrapped in a woolen blanket handwoven in the tartan of Clanfearghus, and fell into a hopeful sleep. For the first time since the death of his father, he did not feel alone.

■

PART 7

— 1 —

The first trouble came from Terl. He had a hangover after his solo binge, and he had been irritated close to anger at the comings and goings and delays.

At first light, Jonnie began to load them as they arrived singly and in groups from their errands to their homes. The people in the meadow had not left but had slept on the ground around fires—no one was going to miss the departure. More Scots, having missed the gathering of the clans due to distance or infirmity, had come in, and the number had doubled.

Jonnie began showing them how to tie down their gear in the military supply locks of the personnel freighter, and how to fasten themselves into the seats, two to a seat, and adjust the belts. He had gotten about six fully settled when two of them promptly got out of their seats again and started showing newcomers where to stow their gear and how to handle the belts.

Some apologized for seeming to bring so little but times had been hard, they said. It was no longer safe to raid in the lowlands. Some thought perhaps they were bringing too much, but one never knew, did one?

Some were a bit late and streamed in in a breathless rush, the historian worriedly checking off their names.

The old women came in a clatter of kettles. The parson arrived rolling a keg—in case someone became ill. Jonnie strapped it down tightly, curious: he had never seen whiskey before.

The sun was getting higher. Terl roared from the cab, "Get these filthy animals loaded!" People became very quiet; Jonnie winked at them and they relaxed and got loading going once more.

Finally, they were all there. All eighty-three of them.

Jonnie said: "This flight will take several hours. We will go very high. It will be very cold and the air will be thin. Endure it somehow. If you feel lightheaded it will be from lack of air, so make an effort to breathe more often. Keep yourselves tightly strapped in. This plane can turn in all directions and even upside down. I am now going to the forward cab to help fly this thing. Remember that one day soon many of you will also be able to fly machines, so observe things closely. Robert the Fox is in charge here. Questions?"

There wasn't one. He had made them more confident in their new environment. They seemed cheerful, not afraid.

"Take it up, MacTyler!" said Robert the Fox.

Jonnie waved at the crowd out of the side door and they roared back. He slammed and locked the door.

He settled himself in the copilot seat, wound the security belt around himself twice, put on his air mask, and got out the map. Terl was looking sourly at the crowd.

With vicious sudden gestures, Terl recompressed the cab with breathe-gas and ripped off his mask. And Jonnie saw his amber eyes were shot with green. Terl had been going heavy on the kerbango. There was an evil twist to his mouthbones.

He was rumbling something about "late" and "having no leverage on these blasted animals" and "teach a lesson."

Jonnie stiffened in alarm.

The plane vaulted skyward at a speed enough to crush him into his seat. It was at three thousand feet in the wink of an eye. Jonnie's map and hands were pressed painfully downward into the copilot control panel.

Terl's talons snapped at some more buttons. The ship started over on its side.

"What are you doing?" shouted Jonnie.

"I'm going to set an example!" roared Terl. "We've got to show them what will happen if they disobey."

The thick mob in the meadow was a small dot below them as the plane turned downward. Suddenly Jonnie knew that Terl was going to blast them.

The ground came screaming up, the crowd getting large.

"No!" screamed Jonnie.

Terl's talons were reaching out for the fire buttons.

Jonnie heaved the map.

Open, it pinned itself against Terl's face, cutting off his vision.

The ground was coming up with speed.

Jonnie hit his own controls with staccato fingers.

Two hundred feet up, the plane abruptly changed course to level. Its inertia sucked it down to only yards above the crowd's heads.

Like a javelin it shot forward.

Ahead of them, the trees leaping larger, was the mountainside.

Jonnie's fingers stabbed keys.

Branches hit the underbody. The plane rocketed up the mountainside only feet from the ground.

It shot into the clear as they passed the mountain crest. Jonnie leveled it and stabbed it at the distant beaches.

He reversed the tape that had taken them on the incoming voyage and fed it into the autopilot.

The sea sped by only yards below them. They were in the clear, undetectable by any minesite observation post, heading for home.

Jonnie. bathed in sweat, sat back.

He looked at Terl. The monster had gotten the map off his face. Flames were flickering in his green-shot eyes.

"You almost killed us," said Terl.

"You would have spoiled everything," said Jonnie.

"I've got no leverage on these animals," snapped Terl. He looked over his shoulder to beyond the cab rear wall. "How," he added with nasty sarcasm, "do you intend to keep them obedient? With little baby toys?"

"They've been obedient enough so far, haven't they?" said Jonnie.

"You ruined this whole trip for me," said Terl. He relapsed into moody silence. At length, he rubbed at his aching head and fumbled around for his kerbango. He brought up an empty container and threw it down. Jonnie clipped it into a rack so it wouldn't go adrift. Terl found another one under the seat. He chewed off a slug of it and sat there gloomily.

"Why," asked Terl, at length, "were they cheering yesterday?"

"I told them the end of the project would see them highly paid," said Jonnie.

Terl thought that over. Then, "They were cheering because of pay?"

"More or less," said Jonnie.

Terl was suspicious. "You didn't promise any gold, did you?"

"No, they don't know anything about gold. Their currency is horses and such things."

"High pay, eh?" said Terl. He was suddenly very jovial. The kerbango was taking effect. He had just had a wonderful thought. High pay. He knew exactly the pay they would get. Exactly. At the muzzle end of a blast gun. He cheered up enormously.

"You fly this thing pretty good, rat brain, when you're not trying to kill everybody." This struck Terl as very, very funny and he laughed from time to time all the way home. But that was not what pleased him. How stupid these animals were! High pay, indeed. No wonder they'd lost the planet! He had his leverage. He'd never heard such enthusiasm!

— 2 —

Forty-eight hours after their arrival at the "defense base," Jonnie was very glad he had Robert the Fox along. He had to handle a threatened war.

Two of the young men, amid all the flurry of settling in, had yet found time to discover the remains of a weapons cargo. A truck, in the last days of man's civilization, had apparently run into a road cutbank and a cave-in had covered it. There it had remained for more than a thousand years until Scot hands uncovered it.

Jonnie had just come in to the base with a group driving wild cattle before them. He had been very busy settling the group in. He had lots of help. No one required much in the way of orders. They had swept out and apportioned off an old dormitory. They had dug latrines. The parson had made the chapel useful. And the old women had found a place that could be protected from deer and cattle and, being near the water, was ideal for a vegetable garden; Jonnie had used a drilling machine to plow it up and the women assured him that now nobody would get scurvy—they had brought seeds, and radishes and lettuce and spring onions would be up in no time in this sunlight and deep soil. The schoolmaster had appropriated the ancient academic building and had a schoolroom set up.

The Scots had proven remarkably ingenious with machinery;

they seemed to know what some of these pipes and wires were all about, having heard of them and read of them in their books.

Thus Jonnie was not too startled to find a youth—Angus MacTavish—holding out an ancient piece of metal to him and requesting permission to "make this and the rest of the lot serviceable." Jonnie had not thought that among all this bustle anyone would have time to dig up an old wrecked man-truck and its contents.

"What is this thing?" said Jonnie.

The youth showed him some stamped letters. The object was covered with what must have been a very thick grease that, down the ages, had become rock-hard but had preserved the object. The letters, which the youth had cleaned off, said ["Thompson submachine gun. . . ."] It had a company name and serial number.

"There's case on case of them," said Angus. "A whole truckload. And airtight boxes of ammunition. When the grease comes off these, they might be fired. The truck must have run off the road and gotten buried in the cave-in. May I clean it up and test it, MacTyler?"

Jonnie absently nodded and went on with the cattle. He was thinking about getting over to the base and getting a horse. There were plenty of wild horses but they needed to be broken, and driving in cattle for food on foot was not the safest occupation he knew of. He was also speculating about using one of these small Psychlo trucks to do the job. Food shortage had been a problem for the Scots and there was no reason they could not be very well fed; it would make them even tougher and more able to stand the work ahead.

He was not prepared for the deputation that came to him as he finished supper. A mess hall had been set up, and although the women were cooking outside, eating was being done inside—off broken tables with much eroded cutlery. Robert the Fox was sitting there with him.

Angus MacTavish held out the weapon to him. "It works. We cleaned it and figured out how to load and operate it, and the ammunition will fire."

Jonnie could see that others in the mess hall were giving them their silent attention.

"There's lots of these and lots of ammunition," said Angus MacTavish. "If you climb the hill and look over to the east, off in the distance you can see the Psychlo minesite." He smiled. "A group could sneak over tonight and blow them to pieces!"

There was an instant cheer from the rest.

Young men from other tables stood up and crowded around.

Jonnie had a horrible vision of slaughtered Scots and blasted plans.

Robert the Fox caught Jonnie's eye. He seemed to want a nod and Jonnie gave him one. He stood up.

The old veteran was one of the few Scots who had ever seen a Psychlo up close before the freighter had arrived. Raiding for cattle down into the lowlands where cattle now wandered amid ruins, Robert the Fox had once encountered a party of Psychlo hunters from the minesite in Cornwall. The Psychlos had wiped out the other members of the party. But Robert, clinging to the belly of a horse, had been able to flee the carnage unobserved. He was well aware of the power of the Psychlo weaponry and the murderous character they exercised.

"This young man," said Robert the Fox, pointing to Angus MacTavish who was standing there holding his man-machine gun, "has done very well. It is a credit to be resourceful and brave." The young man beamed. "But," continued Robert the Fox, "it is one of the great wisdoms that one best succeeds at what one prepares totally. One minesite destroyed will not end the power of the Psychlos. Our war is against the entire Psychlo empire and for this we must work hard and prepare." He became conspiratorial, "We must not wipe out just one base and alert them to our intent."

That did it. The young men thought this was very wise and happily finished their dinner of roasts and steaks.

"Thank you," said Jonnie to Robert the Fox. The precipitate war was averted for the moment.

A bit later, in the lingering twilight, Jonnie took the older men down to show them the trench.

He had begun to realize he had a sort of council It consisted of Robert the Fox, the parson, the schoolmaster, and the historian.

Jonnie probed about in the grass, looking for iron bits, and at last he uncovered the almost totally eroded frame of a weapon that might have been similar to the Thompson. It was very hard to tell what make it was, but it had been a gun.

Jonnie told his council the history of the spot according to Psychlo records.

They hardly needed to get the point. Such weapons had not stopped the Psychlos.

Then the historian—Doctor MacDermott—looked about curiously. "But where are the remains of the tank?"

"It defeated them," said Jonnie.

"Now that is very odd," said the historian. "Not that they were defeated here, but that there's no rusting remains of any Psychlo battle equipment."

"This was a defeat," said Jonnie. "The Psychlos may have suffered damage, maybe not. But they would have taken any damaged equipment from the field."

"No, no, no," said the historian. And he told them about a handwritten romance in the university library about a similar battle. It had occurred on a line between two ancient villages known as Dumbarton and Falkirk, at the narrowest point above where England and Scotland had once met, just below the Highlands. "And the remains of Psychlo tanks can be detected there to this very day."

"That's true," said Robert the Fox. "I have seen them."

The historian said, "No Psychlo has ever come north of that point—not until you, MacTyler, flew in your demon. It is the only reason we can still exist in the Highlands."

"Tell me more of this romance," said Jonnie.

"Oh, it is quite badly written," said the historian. "A curiosity, not literature. It was scribbled by a private in the Queen's Own Highlanders who escaped north from the battle. A sapper, I think he was. They handle land mines."

"Land mines?" said the parson. "Mines for ore?"

"No, no," said the historian. "I think they used the word 'mine' for explosives buried in the earth—when the enemy crossed them, they exploded. The private used the term 'tactical nuclear weapons.' He goes on about how a fragment of a regiment that had been in bunkers escaped the gassing and withdrew north. The captain, I think, had a girl in the Highlands. And they laid a string of mines from Dumbarton to Falkirk. Psychlo tanks in pursuit hit them and these mines exploded. The Psychlos were not out of tanks or troops. They simply withdrew south and they never came back to recover their dead or their equipment. The romance says it was due to the spirit of Drake intervening, for drums could be heard. . . ."

"Wait," said Jonnie. "Those were nuclear weapons

"Whatever those are," said the parson.

"Uranium," said Jonnie. "There must still be a band of uranium dust between those two towns." He explained to them about Psychlo breathe-gas.

"Aye, it fits," said Robert the Fox.

The historian looked enlightened and drew his shabby old cloak around his shrunken shoulders. "It sounds like the magic ring of fire, or the geometric signs the creatures of the netherworld dare not cross."

Jonnie looked at the eroded remains of the weapon in his hands and then along the trench. "These poor men didn't have any uranium, didn't even really know about Psychlos. They had only these."

"They died like brave men," said the parson, removing his cap.

The others also removed theirs.

"We just have to be sure," said Jonnie. "we don't wind up like them!"

"Aye," said Robert the Fox.

Jonnie laid the remains of the gun down and they walked back thoughtfully toward the cooking fires. The wail of a piper was soft in the night wind.

— 3 —

Terl was working with maps of the mountains. He had the latest recon drone pictures of the lode and he was trying to find any trails or roads that came near this deep gash. It was one awfully difficult operation, and when he thought about the animals undertaking something that would make an experienced Psychlo miner cough, it put spots in front of his eyes. The site was simply not accessible by ground travel.

His newly acquired secretary, Chirk, came in. She was stupid enough not to be any menace and good-looking enough to be decorative. She got drunk with economical speed and had other advantages. Her utility was in blocking off callers and shuffling administration papers back for somebody else to handle. Since he was now in reality the top Psychlo on the planet, he shouldn't be bothered with trivial details. Overload the already crushed Numph, was his motto.

"The animal is here to see you," she trilled.

Terl had hastily covered up the maps when her paws touched the door. He scraped them into a top drawer and out of sight. "Send it in."

Wearing his air mask and clothing of Chinko cloth, Jonnie came in. He had a long list in his hand.

Terl looked at him. Things were working out pretty well. The animal was on his good behavior, despite having no button camera surveillance now. They had an arrangement whereby Jonnie could come over every few days and take care of food for the girls and confer.

Jonnie had suggested a radio link, but Terl had become very cross and adamant. *No* radio. That was final. The animal could walk his feet off if he wanted to say anything to Terl. Terl knew there were plenty of receivers in the minesite, and radio might tip his paw and blow his security.

"I have a list," said Jonnie.

"I can see that," said Terl.

"I want piping and Chinko cloth and the tools to cut and sew it together and some pumps and shovels—"

"Give it to Chirk. Sounds like you're rebuilding the whole defense base. Typical animal. Why don't you get busy with machine instruction?"

"I am," said Jonnie. And it was very true. He had been spending ten hours a day with the youths and schoolmaster.

"I'll send over Ker," said Terl.

Jonnie shrugged. Then he indicated the list. "There's a couple of items here that should be cleared with you. The first is the Chinko instruction machines. There are about six of them in the old Chinko quarters. The equipment controls are all in Psychlo and so are the manuals. I want to take those and all their discs and books."

"So?" said Terl.

Jonnie nodded. "The other item is flying trucks."

"You've got flying platforms."

"I think we should have some flying personnel carriers and flying trucks. I've been to see Zzt and he has a whole garage floor full of them."

To Terl's suspicious mind came the sudden feeling that the

animal was looking through the desk top at the maps in the drawer. It was very true that there were no roads to that place. All carrying, he realized, would have to be by air—and it would be difficult flying at that. But a flying truck or a personnel carrier had the same controls as a battle plane and fewer guns. There was a hard rule that no alien race could be trained in battle. Then Terl thought of the inaccessible lode. Well, a mining truck was not a battle plane, that was for sure. Besides, he controlled the planet and he made the rules.

"How many you want?" said Terl, reaching for the list. "Hey! You've written twenty! And tri-wheel ground cars . . . three ground cars . . ."

"The order was to train them on equipment, and if I haven't got the equipment—"

"But twenty!"

Jonnie shrugged. "Maybe they're hard on equipment."

Terl barked a sudden laugh as he remembered the animal nearly going over the cliff in the burning blade scraper. It tickled him.

He drew out one of the blanks Numph had signed and punched the animal's list in above the signature.

"How much time have I got?" asked Jonnie.

Terl was too secretive to come flat out with times. The times actually coincided with the semiannual firing of personnel and dead Psychlos. He calculated rapidly. Nine months total. Maybe three months for training to the next transshipment, and six months for mining to the second in the early spring of next year. Better give it an edge.

"Two months to get them all trained," said Terl.

"That's awfully fast."

Terl took the remote control box out of his pocket and tapped it and put it back. He laughed.

Jonnie frowned, his face mask obscuring the dangerous light that had leaped into his eyes.

He took a tight hold on his temper and voice. "I could use Ker to help ferry this stuff."

"Tell Chirk."

"Also," said Jonnie, "I need some experience operating over those mountains. The updrafts and downdrafts are very strong and in winter they'll be worse. I don't want you getting ideas if I fly around up there."

Terl put his paws protectively on the desk top as though to block a view into the drawer. Then he realized he was getting jumpy. Still, the longer he kept things in the dark, the less chance there was of the animal's talking to other personnel. He began to weave an elaborate fantasy to explain to others why animals were flying in the mountains.

"You seem to know an awful lot," he said suddenly.

"Only what you've told me," said Jonnie.

"When?"

"Different times. Over in Scotland."

Terl stiffened. True, he had been unguarded. Very unguarded if this stupid rat brain had picked it up. . . .

"If I hear just one leak of this real project—through Ker or anybody else—" he tapped the control box in his pocket, "the smaller female is going to have a collar explosion!"

"I know that," said Jonnie.

"So get out," said Terl. "I'm far too busy for all this chatter."

Jonnie had Chirk copy the requisition on a duplicator and asked her to call Ker to help ferry the equipment. "Here you are, animal," she said when she was through and handed him the copies.

"My name is Jonnie."

"Mine is Chirk." She batted her painted eyebones. "You animals are kind of funny and cute. How can you be so much fun to hunt like some of the employees say? You certainly don't *look* dangerous. And I don't think you are even edible. *Crazy* planet! No wonder poor Terl hates it so. We're going to have a *huge* house when we go home next year."

"A huge house?" said Jonnie, looking up at this rattlebrain in wonder.

"Oh, yes. We'll be rich! Terl says so. Tah-tah, Jonnie. Bring me a sack of goodies when you want a favor next time."

"Thank you, I will," said Jonnie.

He went out with his warehouse-size list to get busy. He knew he had a new piece of the puzzle. Terl would not be here more than a year. Terl was going home and going home "rich."

— 4 —

"I am sorry, gentlemen," said Jonnie to his council.

They were seated on some bashed-up chairs in what had become Jonnie's combined quarters and office—a spacious room that overlooked most of the area, chosen because it had whole windows.

Jonnie pointed to the stacks of books. "I have searched through everything I can find and am unable to locate it."

Robert the Fox, Doctor MacDermott, the parson, and the schoolmaster sat glumly looking at him. He never tried to fool them about anything. One thing about MacTyler—he was honest with them.

Things had been going well, too. Almost too well. The young men were progressing marvelously in their ability to handle equipment. There had been only one casualty with the flying trucks—two trainees had been attacking each other's trucks in the air in simulated combat and one of the young lads had punched a wrong button at the wrong time and hit the ground. He was lying in the infirmary now, leg properly set by the parson and attended by the clucking old widows; the flying truck, according to Ker who came over to fix it, was fit only to be cannibalized.

The three young men who looked like Jonnie had bruised hands from the schoolmaster's ruler; the schoolmaster kept them at the instruction machines from dawn to noon when they went off to study vehicles; they were learning Psychlo under heavy pressure and doing it very well.

Several young men had caught wild horses and broken them to ride, and they rounded up wild cattle and shot deer so there was no lack of food. Radishes and lettuce brightened their fare, proud trophies of the old women's garden.

In fact everyone was working like fury and the place looked like an ant hill all day.

"Perhaps," said Doctor MacDermott, "we could help you look." He gestured at the books. "If you'd tell us exactly what it is we're to be locating."

"It's uranium," said Jonnie. "The key to this battle is uranium."

"Ah, yes," said Doctor MacDermott. "It isn't harmful to humans but is deadly to Psychlos."

"It *is* harmful to humans," said Jonnie, pointing to a toxicology text. "Given too much exposure to it some humans die rather frightfully. But it apparently ignites the breathe-gas of Psychlos and makes it explode. It is uniformly fatal to them.

"These mountains," he continued, sweeping his hand toward the mountains outlined by the sunset behind them, "are supposed to have been full of uranium. I know definitely the Psychlos believe they are. You can't force a Psychlo up into them.

"The demon Terl is going to send us into those mountains to find, probably, gold. He has undoubtedly spotted some. We may or may not mine the gold. Probably we would have to, to keep going. But we could *also* mine uranium."

"And you can't locate any," said Doctor MacDermott.

Jonnie shook his head. "There's even lists of uranium mines. But they're all marked 'mined out,' 'mine closed,' that sort of thing."

"Must have been very valuable," said Robert the Fox.

"They list a lot of uses for it," said Jonnie. "Mainly military."

The parson rubbed his nose thoughtfully. "Would your own village people know anything?"

"No," said Jonnie. "They're one of the proofs that there is uranium up there. That's why I have not taken you gentlemen there, much as I would like to. I'm certain their illnesses and inability to reproduce have a lot to do with uranium."

"It doesn't seem to have affected you, MacTyler," smiled the parson.

"I wandered a lot and was not home much of the time. And some are affected more than others, perhaps."

"Heredity," said Doctor MacDermott. "Over the centuries some of you may have developed a resistance or an immunity. They would not know?"

Jonnie shook his head. "I haven't gone up there because I don't want to stir them up—the recon drone flies daily. But one day soon I must find a way to move them. And a place to move them to. No, they would know nothing about uranium or they would have long since quit that valley."

"We do have to solve this problem," he continued. "It is the center of every plan."

Doctor MacDermott held out his hand. "Deal those books

around and we will put aside some of our sleep and help you look.''

Jonnie started handing them books in rotation.

''I think,'' said Robert the Fox, ''we should send out some scouts. It is basic in the planning of any successful raid that one sends out some scouts first. How do you recognize this uranium?''

''Indicators are there in the mine books,'' said Jonnie. ''But the main tool we do not have. It's called a 'Geiger counter,' and though I've looked it up and have a vague idea of how one is made, the point is we don't have one.''

''Perhaps,'' said the schoolmaster, ''there may be one in some of these old villages. Do they have directories for factories?''

''I doubt such an instrument would be worth much after a thousand years,'' said Doctor MacDermott. ''But I do see there a . . . goodness, but this has almost gone to pieces . . . a telephone? book . . . to ['Dev . . . Denve . . .']. Telephones,'' he added for the others, ''used to exist in cities. Here . . . ['instruments . . . International Business Machines Research?'] Oh, drat. The address can't be made out.''

''The writing exists on many buildings there,'' said Jonnie.

Robert the Fox leaned forward. ''As I say, it takes a scout. Scout before raid is the watchword. We must be very careful that the demons do not suspect us of snooping about.''

''They have body heat detectors,'' said Jonnie. ''That's how you escaped them clinging under a horse. They knew horses were running away. But the recon drone takes only pictures, and one should get under cover when he hears the rumble far off. The sound of a ground car, however, means real danger, for they have spinners that fly up in the air and look for heat. I have some covers that we can throw over ourselves to block heat, but we have to be very, very careful. I think it's best that I go.''

''Na, na,'' said Robert the Fox, his accent thickening into dialect from sudden alarm. ''We canna ha' ye dae thet, laddie.''

The rest of the council also shook their heads.

The parson said, ''You keep yourself safe, MacTyler. That's why we're here—to help you.''

''The small demon . . .'' said Jonnie.

''The one that came to fix the flying machine?''

''The same,'' said Jonnie. ''His name's Ker. He told me an order had been issued, he said by the planet head, to forbid all hunting parties in this whole area and to restrict them all to the mining areas and compound. There was some talk, Ker said, of coming over here for some sport. So there aren't any demons wandering around and it's perfectly safe to go up to the Great Village on a scout—so long as we don't stay in sight of the recon drone."

"Scouts," said Robert the Fox firmly, "are not done by Chiefs. Raids, perhaps. Scouts, no! We will send young Angus MacTavish. All those in favor?" And Jonnie was firmly voted down.

Thus it was that young Angus MacTavish went scouting to Denver in a small ground car in the dark that night. He was peculiarly adept at operating machinery: he had taken piping and brought the water closer, and he had worked out how the water mains and sewers worked, and he had even gotten a couple of inside toilets working, to the amazement of his friends.

He was gone forty-eight hours and came back with a lot of wonders to report. But the International Business Machines Research Laboratories were in ruins that bore no fruit. There was nothing there even vaguely resembling the Geiger counter that had been described to him. He had also located a "Bureau of Mines," but it had only decayed records. He discovered a "Prospector's Outfitter," and though he had found some stainless steel sample picks that he brought back, and an assortment of stainless steel knives that delighted the old women in their work, there had been no Geiger counter there either.

The council met again and grimly decided to carry on and get ready anyway, and the parson said a prayer that pleaded with the good lord to have pity on them and lead them somewhere, somehow, to a Geiger counter and uranium.

They also decided to send out more scouts, but without too much hope.

— 5 —

Jonnie awoke in the middle of the night to the abrupt realization that he knew where a uranium detector existed. The ore duster at the transshipment area! He had even spent apprentice time on it.

So, despite Robert the Fox's prohibition against his scouting, Jonnie was on a scout, dangerous or not.

Every few days he saw Chrissie. Each time he did, he made it a habit to ride around the minesite idly just to accustom the Psychlos to his being there. He would sit Windsplitter and wander around.

Today Chrissie and Pattie looked very forlorn. Jonnie had brought fresh meat and more deerskin for them to tan and sew. He had cut plenty of firewood—one of the Scots had unearthed a stainless steel axe from a village ruin, and it made such work remarkably fast. He placed all this outside the wooden barrier to be taken in when Terl was "not busy" and could come out.

It was frustrating to talk through the wooden barrier and the cage bars. Chrissie and Pattic held up some buckskin shirts and breeches for him to admire and then repackaged them for him to take. He called to them that they looked fine. Pattie exhibited a new arrangement for their pitiful shelter—they could fasten nothing to the bars—and he said it looked much better.

What was he doing, they wanted to know. He said he was working. And was he all right? Yes, he was fine. And were things going well? Just fine. Difficult to carry on a conversation across a space of forty feet through two screening barricades and under the surveillance of at least two button cameras. Difficult to be calm and reassuring when what he really wanted to do was blow the place up and get them out of there.

He had a picto-recorder on a strap around his neck. With a couple of buckskin thongs he had steadied it to his chest so that with a slight motion of his hand he could start and stop it without raising it to his eye. He had practiced doing that and had gotten pretty accurate at pointing it without looking through the finder. He requisitioned a dozen of the things and plenty of miniature discs. As he talked he took pictures of the girls and the cage from several angles, pictures of the switch box and wires. It was a risk, he knew.

He told Chrissie and Pattie he would be back and rode casually to a high point above the Chinko quarters. Seemingly idle, he took broad panoramas, both wide-angle and telephoto, of the minesite. He took pictures of the twenty battle planes lined up in the field, the distant cartridge fuel dump, and, beyond that, the breathe-gas storage dump. He took pictures of the morgue a hundred yards beyond the transshipment area. And he covered the freighter landing area and ramps and conveyor belt and control tower.

Then luck! He saw a freighter on its way in with a load of ore. He idled down off the knoll. As he passed the cage, he felt a sudden need for cautiousness. He dismounted and slipped the discs he had already taken into the waiting pack, making it appear that he was just putting in some flowers.

Remounted, he wandered on down to the ore-dusting area. He let Windsplitter pause near tasty clumps of grass and at last came to the dust-coated area of transshipment.

The freighter had not unloaded yet. Employees were coming out and getting onto their machines. He rode up to the ore-dusting machine. The operator was not there. A hook was swinging from a crane and he pretended to duck it. But in actual fact he leaned over and pulled out a wire from the back of the machine's controls. He did not know its circuit, but with luck he would very soon.

The operator knew him slightly from his apprentice days but glanced at him with normal Psychlo disdain. ''You better get that horse out of here! Ore coming in.''

Jonnie backed Windsplitter off.

The freighter discharged with a dusty roar. The blade machines raced about neatening up the pile. The first load was ready for the buckets on the conveyor belt.

A red light flared.

A horn went off.

The ore duster operator cursed and banged at his controls.

All activity stopped.

The air around the operator's dome and mask might well have turned blue from his cursing.

Char came rumbling like a tank out of the dome of the transshipment control office, shouting as he came.

Far off was the faint moan of another freighter coming in from an overseas minesite.

It was not a transshipment firing day, but schedules were about to ball up on freighter discharge.

Char was shouting for electronics repair, and somebody in the dome, on the loudspeaker system, was demanding to know where the duty electronics was.

Jonnie could have told them where duty electronics was. He'd seen the employee walking toward the compound fifteen minutes ago.

Char was raving at the operator on the ore duster. The operator was hammering paws on the control panel.

Jonnie slid off his horse and went to them. "I can fix it."

With a roar that had concussion in it, Char told him to get the———out of there!

"No, I can fix it," said Jonnie.

A voice coming closer said, "Let him fix it. I trained him." It was Ker.

Char was distracted by the new interruption. He whirled to storm abuse at the midget Psychlo.

Picto-recorder running, Jonnie slid up to the front of the ore duster control panel. He snapped it open. He stood at right angles to the layout of components and pretended to study it. Then he reached in and touched a couple of points, doing nothing to them. Given pictures of this, he could build it!

He closed the box.

He rapidly connected the wire he had earlier loosened.

Char turned back to him after chomping on Ker.

"It's fixed," said Jonnie. "It was just a loose wire."

Ker yelled to the operator, "Try it now!"

The operator did and the ore duster purred.

"See?" said Ker. "I trained him myself."

Jonnie got back on Windsplitter, using the motion to turn off his picto-recorder.

"It's working now," said the operator.

Char looked venom at Jonnie. "You keep that horse out of this area. If this was a firing time he'd land in Psychlo!" He went off muttering something about damned animals.

The conveyor belt and buckets and machines were roaring away again, making haste to clear the load before the new freighter came in. The old one took off.

Windsplitter wandered down toward the morgue. This building, remarkable for its refrigerator coils, stood well back. Jonnie turned and looked from it back at the compound. It was a straight course from here, across the transshipment platform and up the hill to the cage.

"And *what*," said a voice, "are you doing down here with a picto-recorder?"

It was Terl. He had stepped out of the morgue and had a list in his hand. In the dark reaches of the building, coffins were stacked. Terl had been checking Psychlo corpses scheduled for return home at the semiannual firing.

"Practicing," answered Jonnie.

"For what?" growled Terl.

"Sooner or later you'll want me to take picture for you up in the—"

"*Don't* talk about that around here!"

Terl tossed his list back of him toward the morgue and stepped close to Jonnie. He yanked the picto-recorder off Jonnie's chest, snapping the holding straps. The thongs bit into Jonnie's back as they resisted just before they gave.

Turning the machine over, Terl snapped the disc out of it, threw it in the dust, and stamped on it with his boot heel.

He poked sharp talons into Jonnie's belt and flipped out four more discs.

"They're just blanks," said Jonnie.

Terl threw those into the dust and ground them under a heavy toe.

He shoved the picto-recorder back at Jonnie. "It's a company rule not to record a transshipment area."

"When you want me to take pictures," said Jonnie, "I hope you'll be able to make them out."

"I *better* be able to," snarled Terl illogically and stamped back into the morgue.

Later, when Jonnie was let in to take Chrissie supplies, he had no trouble slipping the earlier discs from his incoming pack to Chrissie's outgoing pack.

But they weren't the circuit diagrams that would detect uranium.

Out of plain revenge that night he showed his whole crew the earlier pictures he had taken. He showed them all the locations of the whole transshipment area. He would have to do it again later when proper plans were formed. But for now he wanted to show them pictures of Chrissie and Pattie.

The shots showed the girls, showed the collars, showed the switch box to the bars. But mainly it showed their faces, the faces of a little girl and a beautiful woman.

The Scots watched the pictures, attentive to the geography of the transshipment area, the battle planes, the breathe-gas dump, the fuel dump, the morgue, and the platform. But when they saw the pictures of Chrissie and Pattie they began with pity and ended with rage.

Robert the Fox had to speak again to prevent them from tearing over right then and ripping the place to pieces. The pipers played a mournful lament.

If the Scots had been enthusiastic before, they were deadly determined and angry now.

But Jonnie lay unable to sleep that night. He had had it right in the camera—the circuit of a uranium detector. He had not memorized it. He had counted upon getting the pictures. He blamed himself for depending on machines. Machines were all right but they did not replace man.

There would come a day of reckoning with Terl. He vowed it bitterly.

— 6 —

In the clear, cold noon they were on their way for a first look at the lode. Jonnie, Robert the Fox, the three who looked similar to Jonnie, and the two Scot mining shift leaders who had been appointed sped along in the small personnel carrier, high above the grandeur of the Rockies.

Terl had come early that morning, threatening and secretive. His ground car had been spotted some time since by a posted sentry and Jonnie had been warned.

Wrapped in a puma skin against the dawn chill, Jonnie met the ground car as it stopped. Breakfast was just over in the mess hall and a warning had been sent to stay inside. The grounds were nearly deserted and there was nothing to distract Terl's attention.

He got out, tightening his breathe-mask, and stood there tossing the remote control box idly into the air and catching it in his paw.

"Why," said Terl, "are you interested in a uranium detector?"

Jonnie frowned and looked mystified—or tried to.

"I heard after you left the other day that you 'repaired' the ore duster. With a picto-recorder around your neck? Ha!"

Jonnie decided on a sudden verbal attack. "You expect *me* to go up into those mountains without knowing what to avoid? You expect me to go tearing around getting myself wrecked—"

"Wrecked?"

"Physically wrecked from uranium contamination—"

"See here, animal, you can't talk this way to *me!*"

"—when you know very well that I could be made sick if I didn't avoid uranium dust! You've told me there's uranium up there! And you expect me—!"

"Wait a minute," said Terl. "What are you talking about?"

"Mining toxicology!" snapped Jonnie.

The kilted sentry who had called him was standing by the mess hall door, looking daggers and dirks at Terl.

"Sentry!" shouted Jonnie. "Grab a book, any book in English, and bring it here! Fast!"

Jonnie turned back to Terl. The running footsteps of the sentry could be heard inside the building. Terl put the control box back in his pocket so his gun paw could be free just in case.

The sentry rushed out with an ancient volume labeled [*The Poems of Robert Burns*]. He had snatched it from the parson who was reading at breakfast. It would have to do.

Jonnie snapped it open. He put his finger on a line that said, ["Wee, sleekit, cowrin, tim'rous beastie, . . ."]

"See there!" he demanded of Terl. "In the presence of uranium, a man's hair falls out, his teeth fall out, his skin develops red blotches, and his bones crumble! And it happens in just a few weeks of exposure."

"You don't explode?" said Terl.

"It doesn't say anything here about explosion, but it says that continuous exposure to uranium dust can be fatal! Read it yourself!"

Terl looked at a line that said something about, ["O, what a panic's in thy breastie!"] and said, "So it does. I didn't know that."

"You know it now," said Jonnie. He closed and thumped the book. "I found this by accident. You didn't tell me. Now are you going to let me have a detector or aren't you?"

Terl looked thoughtful. "So your bones turn to dust, do they? And it takes a few months?"

"Weeks," said Jonnie.

Terl began to laugh. His paw dropped from his belt gun and he swatted himself in the chest, catching his breath. "Well," he said at length, "I guess you'll just have to take your chances, won't you?"

It hadn't worked. But Terl was totally off the scent now. Actually feeling more secure.

"That wasn't what I came over here for, anyway," said Terl. "Can we go some place less public?"

Jonnie handed the book back to the sentry with a wink to reassure him. The Scot had enough sense not to grin. But Terl was rummaging around the ground car.

He beckoned Jonnie to follow and took him back of the chapel where there were no windows. He had a big roll of maps and photos and he sat down on the ground. He motioned for Jonnie to hunker down.

"Your animals are all trained?" said Terl.

"As well as can be expected."

"Well, notice you've had a couple extra weeks."

"They'll do."

"All right, now. We have to come to the time to be real miners!" He rolled out the map. It was a patch-up of sectional running shots from a recon drone, and it condensed about two thousand square miles of the Rocky Mountains from Denver to the west. "You can read one of these?"

"Yes," said Jonnie.

Terl snapped the head of a canyon with his talon. "It's *there*." Jonnie could almost feel the surge of greed in Terl. His voice was a conspiratorial mutter. "It's a lode of white quartz with streamers of pure gold in it. It's a freak. Exposed by a landslide in recent years." And he took a large photograph out of the pack.

There it was, a diagonal slash of white in the red side of a canyon. Terl took a closer shot and showed it. Fingers of pure gold could be seen threading through the quartz.

Jonnie would have spoken but Terl held up his paw to stop him. "You fly over and take a close look at it. When you've seen it and gotten it oriented as a mining problem, you come back and see me and I will clarify any questions as to procedure." He tapped the location on the larger map. "Memorize that spot." Jonnie noted that the map bore no markings. Clever Terl. No clues if the map went adrift.

He sat there and let Jonnie study the map.

Jonnie knew these mountains, but he had never had a detailed picture of them from this angle: above.

Terl put all his papers away except the map. "Hold on to that." He stood up.

"How long do we have to get it out?" said Jonnie.

"Day 91 of the coming year. That's six and a half months away."

"That's also winter," said Jonnie.

Terl shrugged. "It's always winter up there. Ten months of winter and two months of fall." He laughed. "Fly over and look at it, animal. Take a week or two to study it out. And then come over and we'll have a private meeting. And this is confidential, do you hear? Outside of your animals, *say nothing*."

Terl had gone off playing catch with the control box. His ground car roared away back to the compound.

A couple of hours later Jonnie's party was flying high above the Rockies.

"That's the first time," said one of the Scots behind Jonnie, "that I knew Robbie Burns was toxic."

Jonnie turned. He thought the sentry must have gotten aboard. "You speak Psychlo that well?"

"Of course," said the Scot and showed the ruler bruises or the back of his hand. He was one of the lads chosen because of his resemblance to Jonnie. "I was putting an ear to a window on the second floor above you. He can't understand English, can he?"

"One of our very few advantages," said Jonnie. "I didn't get the uranium detector."

"Well," said Robert the Fox, "it's a very optimistic man that thinks he can win all the battles. What are all those villages down there?"

It was true. There were old towns here and there throughout this section of the mountains.

"They're deserted," said Jonnie. "I've been to some of them. No population but rats. Mining ghost towns."

" 'Tis a sad thing" said Robert the Fox. "All this space and all kinds of food and no people. And over in Scotland there's little space that will grow anything and hardly any food at all. It's a dark chapter in history we've been through."

"We'll change it," said a young Scot behind him.

"Aye," said Robert the Fox. "If we have any luck. All this great broad world full of food and no people! What are the names of those grand peaks down there?"

"I don't know," said Jonnie. "If you look on the mine map

you'll see they just give them numbers. I think they had names once but people forgot. That one over there we just call 'Highpeak.' "

"Hey!" said a young Scot. "There's sheep down on that mountainside!" He was using a hand telescope.

"They're called bighorns," said Jonnie. "It's quite a feat to hunt one down. They can stand on a ledge not bigger than your hand and sail off and land on another one not wider than two fingers."

"And there's a bear!" said the Scot. "What a big one!"

"The bears will go into hibernation soon," said Jonnie. "I'm surprised one is out at this altitude."

"Some wolves are following him," said the Scot.

"Laddies," said Robert the Fox, "we are hunting bigger game! Keep your eye out for the canyon."

Jonnie spotted it shortly before one o'clock.

— 7 —

It was a startling sight. The grandeur of the scene in this thin, cold air made one feel small.

Out of a river, a thin, silver thread in the depths far below, reared a reddish, massive wall of rock rising sheer and raw. Narrowly across from it was its echoing face. Down through the eons the river, finding a softer strata between the two faces, had gnawed its turbulent way to make at last this gigantic knife slice in the all but impregnable stone. A thousand feet deep, a hundred yards wide, the enormous wound gaped.

All around it rose majestic peaks, hiding it from the world.

The sparkling white line of quartz, many feet thick, marked it with a brief, diagonal line. And in that quartz, imbedded and pure, gold shone and beckoned.

It had in its reality a much greater impact than any photograph. It was like a jewel band set upon the wrinkled skin of a hag.

One could see far below where a portion of the cliff face had fallen; the fragments lay like crashed pebbles in the depths. The river had eaten too deep under the cliff and an earthquake had shaken a slice of the face loose.

Snow had not fallen yet, for the year was dry, and there was nothing to impede the view. Jonnie dropped the plane lower.

And then the wind hit them.

Funneled up the long gorge, compressed and screaming to get free, the turbulent currents tore at the cliff.

With fingers racing across the overlarge keys of the console, Jonnie fought to keep the light personnel plane in position.

It was not a dazzling lode at that moment. It was a brutal, elemental wall that could crush them if they touched it.

Jonnie leaped the plane a thousand feet up, clear of the updrafts, and steadied it. He turned to one of the Scots, the one who looked like him and who had spoken of Burns. His name was Dunneldeen MacSwanson. "Can you handle this plane?"

Dunneldeen came forward. Robert the Fox went to a rear seat and strapped himself into the copilot seat.

In these teleportation drives, there were a number of corrections that had to be constantly watched. Some were built in to the computers; some were preprogrammed for any flight. Space itself was absolute and motionless, having no time, energy, or mass of its own. But to stay in one place relative to the mass around one, it was necessary to parallel the track of such mass. The world turned daily, and that was a near thousand-mile-an-hour correction. The earth orbited the sun and that required second-to-second correction. The solar system was precessing, and even if the correction was minute, it had to be compensated for. The whole solar system was en route to somewhere else at a blinding speed. The universe itself was twisting in relation to other universes. These factors and others made control of the ship a dicey business in normal times. Down there in that canyon it was a nightmare.

The irregular external buffetings of the wind upset the inertia of the motor housing and made instant shifts of coordination continual.

Dunneldeen had been schooled and trained in all this. But he had seen Jonnie's fingers flying over that console and knew it was no routine flight. In the first place the Psychlo keys allowed for wide talons and wider paws, and it required a snapping tension in the wrists to compensate for these spacings with human hands.

Dunneldeen looked down at the canyon top. "It is no 'roam in the gloamin',' " he said. "But I can try!" He started down.

Jonnie unwrapped his seat belt and had them pass a small contrivance called a core gun to him. By firing a small rotating borer, the gun would take a one-inch diameter chunk out of a rock face, the length of the core varying by how long one let the borer stay there before hauling it back on a line. With it one obtained a cylindrical sample of a vein or rock.

"Start taking pictures," he yelled at the rest of them. They had three picto-recorders aboard, an instrument that measured depth below surfaces, and one that measured densities while drawing a pattern. The instruments were "light" Psychlo prospecting tools, but being Psychlo, they required a lot of muscle.

The Scots took the equipment and began individually operating through the slots in the side of the fuselage.

Jonnie lowered his own port and readied the core gun. "Take us in as close to the vein as you can get without risking us."

"Aye!" said Dunneldeen. "There's the rub. Ready? *Down* we go!"

They shot back into the chasm. Jonnie could hear Dunneldeen's fingers on the console keys: they sounded like a miniature of that Thompson. Then the sound was blotted out by the shrieking howl of the canyon wind.

They swerved. The wall came within inches and swept back to yards. It danced up and down. The scream of the motors began to match the wind as they raced to correct positions.

Jonnie forced himself to concentrate. He wanted a core on the first shot, for it took time to rewind. The sparkling lode danced and leaped in his sights. He pressed the trigger. With a bark and sizzle of paying out line, the corer hit the lode.

Dead on!

He triggered the rotator. The line whipped up and down in the wind.

The plane suddenly slid sideways in a sickening swoop and almost hit the opposite wall. The core came out and dangled below the ship. Jonnie reeled the looping, twisting line in.

"Take her up!" he shouted.

Dunneldeen vaulted the ship up two thousand feet to quieter air. He sat there, limp, his arms and wrists aching, sweat heavy on his forehead. "Ooo, mon! 'Tis like danc'n' wi' the devil's wife!" he panted, relapsing to dialect.

"Did you get your readings and pictures?" Jonnie called over his shoulder.

The instrument men had gotten their depths and densities. But those operating the picto-recorders, struck by the awesome scene and seeing much more of it to take, said no, they wanted another crack at it.

"I'll take her," said Jonnie.

"The devil's wife?" said Dunneldeen. "Na, MacTyler. I have a feeling I'll be dancing this dance again some other day. I'll keep her, thank you." He yelled back over his shoulder: "What do you want?"

They wanted the slide debris at the canyon bottom.

"I hope you all made your peace with the parson before we left," said Dunneldeen. "Here we go!"

They plummeted to the bottom of the gorge and made a pass. The boiling white froth of the river fanged at the fallen fragments. They were mainly under water.

The plane fought back up the narrow gorge slowly so the picture takers could track it on both sides. Dunneldeen's hands were a blur on the controls. The bucking ship screamed as its motors over-revved.

"Something is getting hot," called Robert the Fox. And it had become warm in the cabin despite the altitude. It was the motor housings, overworked in compensating for the lunging and changing inertia of the ship.

They drew opposite the top of the cliff. Jonnie looked at it while the picto-recorders were busy.

There was no flat surface there where one could set down a ship. There was no space where one could operate a lowered drilling platform. It was all pinnacles and clefts.

Jonnie saw something else and called for vertical shots down the cliff face. The cliff was not vertical. It fell away inward. Anything lowered from above would hang fifteen to twenty feet away from the face of the cliff. How could one hope to rig ore nets?

They went directly above it and Jonnie saw something else. "Shoot more verticals of that top!" he called.

Yes, he saw it plainly now. There was a crack inset about thirty feet from the top edge of the cliff, parallel to it. Another such crack had caused the fall of rock that bared the lode. But here was a *second* one. Just waiting for another earthquake. The whole lode would pitch into the gorge.

They went up two thousand feet and the picto-recorder operators had to be content with general scenery. It was impressive enough in its gigantic beauty.

"By your leave, MacTyler," said Dunneldeen, "if it's home we're going now, I'll exchange with Thor."

Jonnie nodded, and a near-duplicate of him, who was nicknamed Thor due to his Swedish background slid over the seat top, matched his motions to Dunneldeen's, and took over. Dunneldeen dragged himself back to the rear. "It's a reel a bit fast for the piper," he said. "Are we going to have to operate in *that?*"

The core in Jonnie's hand was part white quartz and part gold. It was a very pretty thing. This was a lure that had wooed Terl, that had given them their chance. He wondered how many lives it would take.

"Head for home," he told Thor.

They were very quiet on the way back.

— 8 —

Jonnie was very edgy as he walked Windsplitter around the minesite as casually as he could. What he was doing was dangerous, but one could not have told it from the easy way he sat his horse. It was a semiannual firing day and the personnel at the minesite were hurried, snappish, and preoccupied.

Jonnie had a picto-recorder hidden in a tree that overlooked the site and he had a remote control hidden in his pouch. He had gotten a long-play disc into the recorder, but that would not permit it to run for hours untended. He had to get all the data he could. Robert the Fox would not have approved, for this was a scout pure and simple. And if Terl spotted the picto-recorder or detected the remote, there could be repercussions.

Jonnie had delayed reporting to Terl, taking advantage of the "week or so" order. He had heard by accident of this semiannual firing from Ker the chatterer.

Ker had come over at Jonnie's request to inspect the personnel carrier motor. Jonnie needed the data. If it was faulty that was one thing, but if it was only underpowered for the job at the lode that was another.

So Ker had come to the base, growling a bit about it: he was an operations officer, not a mechanic. But Terl had sent him.

The midget Psychlo's temper was sweetened, however, by Jonnie's handing him a small gold ring a scout had found on the "finger" of a corpse long gone to dust.

"Why give me this?" said Ker, suspiciously.

"Souvenir," said Jonnie. "Not very valuable."

It was valuable. It was a month's pay.

Ker dented it slightly with a fang. Pure gold.

"You want something, don't you," Ker decided.

"No," said Jonnie. "I've got two so I gave you one. We've been shaftmates quite a while now." This was a Psychlo mining term for a pal who pulled one out of a cave-in or a fight.

"We have, haven't we," said Ker.

"Besides, I might want somebody killed," Jonnie added.

This sent Ker off into a gale of laughter. He appreciated a good joke. He put the ring in his pocket and got busy on the motor.

Half an hour later he came over to where Jonnie lolled in the shade. "Nothing wrong with that motor. If it got hot, it was just being overdriven. You want to watch it, though. You keep running one that hard and it will go up in smoke."

Jonnie thanked him. Ker hunkered down in the building's shade. They talked, mostly Ker chattering. Ker got on the subject of being pushed by schedules and Jonnie eased in casually with his question. "What happens on Day 91 of the new year?"

"Where'd you get that?"

"Saw it posted at the minesite."

Ker scratched his greasy neck fur. "You must have read wrong. It would be Day 92. That's a semiannual firing date. One's happening in just seven days, you know. What a lot of bother."

"Something different about it?"

"Aw, you must have seen a couple when you were in the cage down there. You know, semiannual firing."

Jonnie may have seen it, but at that time he didn't know what he was looking at. He put on a stupid look.

"It's a slow firing," said Ker. "No ore. Personnel incoming and outgoing. Including the dead ones."

"Dead ones?"

"Yeah, we're shipping dead Psychlos home. They want them accounted for because of pay and they don't want them looked into by aliens, I guess. Nutty company rules. Lot of trouble. They put them in coffins and hold them down in the morgue and then . . . crap, Jonnie. You've seen the morgue. Why am I telling you?''

''Better than working,'' said Jonnie.

Ker barked a laugh. ''Yep, that's true. Anyway, a slow firing means a three-minute build-up and then zip. On a semiannual day, the home planet sends in the personnel and then they hold a tension between here and home planet, and a couple of hours later we fire off returning personnel and dead bodies.

''You know,'' he continued, ''you don't want to fool around on ordinary transshipments. I see you around on that horse sometimes. Ordinary firing is all right for dispatches and ore, but a live body would get ripped up in the transition. You'd come apart. On a slow firing the bodies come through great, live or dead. If you're trying to get to Psychlo, Jonnie, don't do it with the ore!'' He laughed and thought it very funny. A human, breathing air and built for light gravity, wouldn't live two minutes on Psychlo.

Jonnie laughed with him. He had no intention of ever going to Psychlo. ''They really bury those dead bodies on Psychlo?''

''Sure enough. Names, markers, and everything. It's in the employee contract. Of course the cemetery is way out of town in an old slag heap, and nobody ever goes there. But it's in the contract. Silly, ain't it?''

Jonnie agreed it was.

Ker left in very good spirits. ''Remember to tell me who you want killed.'' And he went into howls of laughter and drove off in his old truck.

Jonnie looked up to the window above him where Robert the Fox had been running a recorder out of sight. ''Turn it off.''

''Off,'' said Robert the Fox, leaning out and looking down at Jonnie.

''I think I know how Terl is going to ship the gold to Psychlo. In coffins!''

Robert the Fox nodded. ''Aye, it all fits. He'll load them here, and then most likely when he goes home he will just dig them up some dark Psychlo night with nobody the wiser. What a ghoul!''

And so Jonnie, sitting Windsplitter at the firing site, was making very sure he had all the data on a semiannual just in case it was needed.

The incoming load had not arrived and Terl was rumbling around getting things organized. He had medical personnel and administrative clerks waiting to receive the incoming employees. He was very sure that there would be quite a few, for Numph was in pocket for every new worker and he had said he was bringing in lots of employees.

The network of wires around the staging area was being checked out by technicians. A white light went on. Jonnie, sitting Windsplitter up the slope, touched his remote to start his concealed picto-recorder.

A red light over the operations dome began to flash. A horn wailed. A bullhorn roared, "Stand clear!"

The wires started to hum. Jonnie glanced at a Psychlo watch, big as a turnip on his wrist. He marked the time.

There was a building roar. Trees began to quiver from ground vibration. An electrical pulse beat in the air.

All employees had withdrawn from the platform. All machines and motors were off. There was nothing but that growing roar.

A huge purple light over the dome flashed on.

The platform area wavered like heat waves. Then three hundred Psychlos materialized on it.

They stood in a disorderly mass with their baggage. Breathe-gas helmets were on their heads. They staggered a trifle, looking around. One of them dropped to his knees.

An intermittent white light began to pulse. "Coordinates holding!" the bullhorn roared.

Minesite medical rushed in with a stretcher for the one who had collapsed. Baggage carriers converged on the platform. Administrative personnel rushed the newcomers into a solid mass on a field and then got them into a snake line.

Terl took a list from an incoming executive and began to pat down uniforms for weapons and contraband, working fast. A detector in his hand played on baggage. Terl occasionally extracted an item and tossed it to a growing pile of forbidden articles. He was working very fast, like a huge tank battering away at the line, dislodging odd bits from it.

Personnel people were sorting new employees toward freighters or toward the berthing section of the compound. The newcomers looked like half-asleep giants, accustomed to this sort of thing, paying little heed, not even protesting when Terl took things away from them, not challenging any of the assignments of the personnel people, not resisting, not helping.

To Jonnie on the knoll this mass of creatures were in discreditable contrast to the Scots who were interested in things and alive.

Then Jonnie came alert. Terl was about two-thirds down the line. He had stopped. He was looking at a new arrival. Terl backed up and then suddenly gave a wave for the rest of the line to pass on and didn't inspect any more. He let everybody through.

A few minutes later the newcomers were in compound barracks or sitting in waiting personnel carriers to go to other minesites.

The bullhorn roared, "Coordinates holding and linked in second stage." The white light on the dome began to flash intermittently. The personnel transports started up and took off.

Jonnie realized that interference was being held down on the coordinate frequence. Knowing what he did now about teleportation, he realized that motors could not run during a firing. It was an important point. Teleportation motors interfered with the teleportation in transshipment.

That was why the Psychlos didn't locally teleport ore on the planet from one point to another but used freighters. A small motor was one thing, but teleportation of ore was reserved for transport between planets and universes.

Apparently if any motor were running around the transshipment area while those wires were humming and building up, it would mess up the firing due to overly disturbed local space.

Jonnie knew he was now watching a holding between the space of Psychlo and the space of this planet. A secondary holding was just keeping coordinates punched in, and he could visualize the operators in that control tower punching consoles with staccato paws to keep this planet and Psychlo lined up for the second firing.

It was the second one Jonnie was interested in. It apparently would not take place for a while. He turned off his picto-recorder remote.

After a wait—he timed it and found it was one hour and thirteen minutes—the white light on the dome began a very rapid flashing. The bullhorn bawled, "Stand by for return firing to Psychlo!"

A semiannual seemed to use up far more electricity. Technicians had auxiliary bus bars closed on the high poles. There was still a faint hum in the air.

Sweepers rolled and whirred over the firing platform, cleaning it, getting rid of scraps the new personnel may have dropped.

Jonnie noticed that the conveyor belt detectors were not manned and all the ore apparatus was standing still, neglected. He had hoped to pass by the ore duster with the sample from the lode in his pocket and see whether the ore duster registered any uranium mixed in with the gold. But he couldn't. The thing wasn't running.

Terl came rumbling down toward the morgue. Jonnie turned on his picto-recorder. Psychlos were getting busy again around the firing platform. The bullhorn bawled: "Coordinates holding and linked in second stage." They were still lined up with Psychlo.

Jonnie envisioned that far-off planet, universes away, purple and heavy like a huge discolored boil, infecting and paining the universes. He knew there were scraps of its space right in front of him, linked to the space of Earth. Psychlo: a parasite larger than the host. Voracious, pitiless, without even a word for "cruelty."

Terl was now opening up the morgue. Small lift trucks dashed by him and into it. Terl stood there watching, a list in his hand. The first lift truck came out. Terl looked at the closed coffin number and checked his list. The truck with the huge coffin borne in its claws sped to the firing platform and dumped its burden with a thud. The coffin teetered and then fell flat.

A second truck came out of the morgue with another coffin. Terl read the number and checked it off, and that coffin was carried up and dumped on the firing platform. Then rapidly a third and a fourth truck repeated the action. The first truck was bringing another coffin out.

Jonnie watched while sixteen coffins were piled, this way and that, carelessly, on the platform.

A line of returning personnel were dropped off a flatbed ground truck with their baggage near Terl at the morgue. He went through their clothing and glanced into their effects. There were twelve of them. As they finished, the lift trucks moved them and their baggage to the firing platform.

The white light went steady. "Coordinates on first stage!" bawled the bullhorn. "Motors off!"

The twelve departing Psychlos stood there or sat on their

mounds of baggage. The sixteen coffins were mixed up with the baggage.

It suddenly struck Jonnie that nobody waved or said goodbye. It meant nothing to anyone here that these creatures were going home. Or maybe it did, he thought, looking more closely. The machine operators around seemed to be moving with more savage jerks; one couldn't see well into their helmets, or at this distance, but Jonnie felt they resented the homegoers.

A red light over the operations area began to flash. A horn wailed. The bullhorn bawled, "Stand clear!"

The wires began to hum. Jonnie glanced at his watch.

The tree leaves quivered. The ground vibrated. The hum of the wires gradually and slowly built to a roar.

Two minutes went by.

On went the purple light.

A wavering haze appeared over the platform.

The personnel and coffins were gone.

Then Jonnie noticed an undulating wave of sound and a quiver in the wires. It was almost like a recoil.

A different horn went off. A white light flashed. The bullhorn bawled, "Firing completed. Start motors and resume normal actions."

Terl was locking the morgue. He came rumbling up the slope. Jonnie turned off his picto-recorder remote and started to move off. Terl seemed to be very distracted but the movement caught his eye.

"Don't hang around here!" snapped Terl.

Jonnie guided the horse toward him.

In a low guttural, Terl said, "You must not be seen around here anymore. Now clear out."

"What about the girls?"

"I'll take care of it, I'll take care of it."

"I wanted to give you the report."

"Shut up!" Terl looked around. Was he frightened? He drew close to the horse's shoulder, bringing his eyes to the level of Jonnie's head. "I'll come over and see you tomorrow. Hereafter, don't come *near* this place."

"I—"

"Go over to your car and get to your base. Right now!" And Terl made sure that he did.

It took a very dicey scout that night to recover the picto-recorder from the tree. But with a heat shield to prevent detection, Jonnie did it.

What was up with Terl?

■

PART 8

— 1 —

"It looks like it will be almost impossible to get out," said Jonnie. "And it's going to take an awful lot of advice and skill."

He was uneasy about the state Terl was in. Their conference was already two days late.

They were meeting in an abandoned mine drift, a workings fifty feet underground and a mile south of the "defense base." It was dusty; the timbers sagged; it was a dangerous place to be due to the possibility of cave-in.

Terl had come silently to the base, having parked his ground car some distance away under brush in a ravine and walked the rest of the distance in the night, a mining heat shield over his head. Silently, with gestures, he had made the night sentry—who almost shot him, so mysteriously did he materialize in the dark—get Jonnie. He had then led Jonnie to this abandoned drift and checked around them with a probe.

But the monster did not seem to be attending to what was going on. Jonnie had shown him the pictures of the lode on a portable viewer he had brought and explained about the overheating motor, about the wind. Terl had emitted a few mutters but little else.

For Terl was a very worried Psychlo. When the crowd had arrived at the semiannual, Terl had been efficiently going down the line checking them out. He was almost two-thirds finished when he found himself face to face with *him*.

The newcomer had his head down and the dome firing helmet was not too clean to see through, but there was no mistaking.

It was Jayed!

Terl had seen him once while a student at the school. There

had been a crime nobody ever learned about and Jayed had been the agent who appeared to handle it.

He was not a company agent. He was a member of the dreaded Imperial Bureau of Investigation, the I.B.I. itself.

There was no mistaking him. Round jowled face, left front fang splintered, discolored mouth and eyebones, mange eroding his paws. It was Jayed all right.

It was such a shock that Terl had not been quick-witted enough to go on with his inspection. He had simply passed on the rest of the line. Jayed didn't seem to notice—but the great I.B.I. never missed anything.

What was he there for? Why had he come to this planet?

On the incoming receipt forms he was listed as "Snit" and designated as "general labor." This meant to Terl that Jayed must be undercover.

But why? Was it Numph's messing with payrolls? Or—and Terl shuddered—was it the animals and the gold?

His first impulse was to load up blast rifles and rush over and wipe out the animals, return the vehicles, and claim it was all Numph's idea and that he had had to step in and handle it.

For two days, however, Terl waited around to see whether Jayed would sidle up to him and confide. He gave the fellow every chance. But Jayed simply went into the general labor force at the local mine.

Terl didn't dare put a button camera near him. Jayed would detect that. He didn't dare interrogate the workers around Jayed to see what questions the agent was asking. Jayed would hear it right back.

No button cameras appeared in Terl's area. Probes detected no remote devices beaming in on him.

A very tense Terl had then decided to be very wary and wait for the first outgoing dispatch box, for Jayed might possibly put a report into it.

Sitting there, looking at the lode on the screen, Terl gradually forced himself to focus his eyes. Yes, it did appear difficult. He knew it would be.

"You say wind?" said Terl.

"Overheats the motors. A flying drill platform would not be able to hold itself in place long enough to do any effective work."

The miner in Terl stirred. "Long spike rods driven into the

cliff side. One could build a platform on that. It's precarious but the rods sometimes hold."

"One would have to have a place to land on top."

"Blast a flat place out."

Jonnie flipped a slide and showed him the crack, the possibility of the whole lode sheering off and plummeting to the bottom of the gorge. "Can't blast."

"Drills," said Terl. "Possibly flatten a place with just drills. Tedious but it could be done. Fly back of the cliff edge and drill toward the chasm." But he was drifting off, abstracted.

Jonnie realized that Terl was scared of something. And he realized something else: if this project were abandoned, Terl's first action would be to kill all of them, either to cover evidence or just out of plain sadism. Jonnie decided it was up to him to keep Terl interested.

"That might work," said Jonnie.

"What?" said Terl.

"Drilling from back of the chasm toward it, keeping a ship out of the wind while it hovers."

"Oh, that. Yes."

Jonnie knew he was losing him.

To Terl, it wasn't a screen in front of him—it was the face of Jayed.

"I haven't shown you the core," said Jonnie. He tilted the portable lamp and brought the core out of his pocket.

It was an inch in diameter and about six inches long, pure white quartz and gleaming gold. Jonnie tipped it about so it sparkled.

Terl came out of his abstraction. What a beautiful specimen!

He took hold of it. With one talon he delicately dented the gold. Pure gold!

He fondled it.

Suddenly he saw himself on Psychlo: powerful and rich, living in a mansion, doors open to him everywhere. Talons pointing on the street with whispers. "That's *Terl!*"

"Beautiful," said Terl. "Beautiful."

After a long time, Jonnie said, "We'll try to get it out."

Terl stood up in the narrow drift, and dust eddied in the lamp. He still fondly gripped the core.

"You keep it," said Jonnie.

Suddenly it was as though the core were hot. "No, no, no!" said Terl. "You must hide it! Bury it in a hole."

"All right. And we'll try to mine the lode."

"Yes," said Terl.

Jonnie breathed a pent-up sigh of relief.

But at the drift entrance before they parted, Terl said, "No radio contacts. None. Do not overfly the compound. Skim the mountains on the east; fly low leaving and arriving at this base. Make a temporary second base in the hills and do your shifts from that.

"And stay away from the compound! I'll see the females are fed."

"I should go over and tell them they won't be seeing me."

"Why?"

"They worry." Jonnie saw that Terl couldn't comprehend that and amended it quickly. "They might make a fuss, create a disturbance."

"Right. You can go once more. In the dark. Here, here's a heat shield. You know where my quarters are. Flash a dim light three times."

"You could just let me take the girls over to the base."

"Oh, no. Oh, no, you don't." Terl patted his remote control. "You're still under my orders."

Jonnie watched as he rumbled off and vanished in the night. Fear was preying on Terl. And in that state Terl would vacillate and change his mind.

It was a troubled Jonnie who went back to the base.

— 2 —

They were overflying the lode area, Jonnie, Robert the Fox, the three near-duplicates, and the shift leaders. They were high up. The air was crystal and the mountains spread grandly about them. They were looking for a possible landing site back from the chasm.

"Aye, 'tis the devil's own problem," said Robert the Fox.

"Impossible terrain," said Jonnie.

"No, I don't mean that," said Robert the Fox. "It's this Terl demon. On the one hand we have to keep this mining going and fruitful, and on the other, the last thing we want is for him to succeed. I know very well he'd kill us all if he lost hope. But I'd rather be dead than see him win."

"Time is on our side," said Jonnie, turning the plane for another pass over the edge.

"Aye, time," said Robert the Fox. "Time has a nasty habit of disappearing like the wind from a bagpipe. If we haven't made it by Day 91, we're finished."

"MacTyler!" called Dunneldeen from the back. "Put your eyes on that space about two hundred feet back from the edge. A bit west. It looks flatter."

There was a bark of laughter from the others. Nothing was flat down there. From the edge and back the terrain was tumbled like a miniature Alps, all stone outcrops and sharp-toothed boulders. No place was flat enough even to set this plane down.

"Take over, Dunneldeen," said Jonnie. He slid sideways and let the Scot into the pilot's seat. Jonnie made sure he had control and then went into the back.

He picked up a coil of explosive cord and began to put himself into harness. The others helped him. "I want you to hold about ten feet above that spot. I'll go down and have a try at blasting it flat."

"No!" said Robert the Fox. He gestured at David MacKeen, a shift leader. "Take that away from him, Davie! You're not to be so bold yourself, MacTyler!"

"Sorry," said Jonnie. "I know these mountains."

It was so illogical that it stopped Robert the Fox. He laughed. "You're a bonnie lad, MacTyler. But a bit wild."

Dunneldeen had them hovering over the spot and Jonnie wrestled with the door to get it open. "Proves I'm a Scot," he said.

The others didn't laugh. They were too tense with concern. The plane was making small jumps and jerks and the sharp ground bobbed up and down below. Even here, two hundred feet from the edge, there was wind.

Jonnie was lowered to the ground and let the pickup rope go slack. Not too much blast or that cliff would sheer off again. It might even break off downward. Jonnie examined the ground and chose a sharp tooth. He girdled it with explosive cord, getting it as low and level as possible. He set the fuse.

At a wave of his hand, the pickup rope tightened and yanked him into the air. He hung there, spinning in the wind.

The explosive cord flashed and the roar racketed around the mountains, echoing.

They lowered him again into the wind-whipped dust and with a spike gun he drove a spike into the rock he had blasted loose. A line came down to him and he put it through the eye of the spike. If he had judged correctly the tooth should sheer away.

He was hauled up higher. The plane's motors screamed. The rock came away.

They lowered the pickup line and he cut the haul cord with a clipper.

The huge rock bounded into a hollow, leaving a flat place where it had stood.

For an hour, grounded and hauled away alternately, Jonnie worked. Some of the blasted rock fell into nearby hollows. Gradually a flattish platform fifty feet in diameter materialized two hundred feet back from the cliff edge.

The plane landed.

David, the shift leader, crept over the broken ground to the crack thirty feet in from the edge. The wind buffeted his bonnet. He put a measuring instrument down into the crack that would tell them if it widened in the future.

Jonnie went over to the edge of the cliff and with Thor holding his ankles tried to look under it and see the lode. He couldn't. The cliff face was not vertical.

The others clambered around seeing what they could.

Jonnie came back to the plane. His hands were scraped. This place had to be worked with mittens. He'd ask the old women to make some.

"Well," said Robert the Fox. "We got down."

The daily recon drone rumbled in the distance. They had their orders. The three near-duplicates of Jonnie dove for the plane and out of sight. Jonnie stood out in the open.

There was plenty of time. The sharp crack of the sonic boom hit them like a club as the recon drone went overhead. The plane and ground shook. The drone dwindled in the distance.

"I hope the vibrations of that thing," said Dunneldeen, emerging, "don't split the cliff."

Jonnie gathered the others around him. "We have a supply point now. First thing to do is pound in a security fence so nothing can slide off, and construct a shift shelter. Right?"

They nodded.

"Tomorrow," said Jonnie, "we'll bring two planes. One loaded with equipment and the other equipped to drive rods. We'll try to construct a working platform to mine the lode, balanced on rods driven into the cliff just below the vein. Survey up here right now what equipment we need for safety reels, ore buckets, and so on."

They got to work to mine the gold they didn't want but had to have. Gold was the bait in the trap.

— 3 —

Jonnie lay in the dead grass on a knoll and studied the far-off compound through a pair of Psychlo infrared night glasses. He was worried about Chrissie.

Two months had gone by and he felt their chances were worsening. The only blessing was that the winter snows were late: but not the winter cold, and the wind sighing through the night was bitter.

The huge night glasses were icy to the touch. The binocular character of them made them hard to use—the two eyepieces, being Psychlo, were so far apart he could only use one at a time.

The faint light of the dying moon reflected from the snow-capped peak behind him and gave a faint luminescence to the plain.

He was trying to see her fire. From this vantage point he knew by experience that he should be able to. So far he could not find even the tiniest pinpoint of it.

The last time he had seen her, two months ago, he had piled the cage with wood, given her some wheat to boil, and even a few late radishes and lettuces, all from the old women's garden. She had a fair supply of smoked meat, but it would not last forever.

He had tried rather unsuccessfully to cheer her up and give her confidence he himself was not feeling.

He had also given her one of the stainless steel knives the scout had found, and she had pretended to be amazed and delighted with it and the way it could scrape a hide and cut thin strips of meat.

In all these two months, he had not heard from Terl. Forbidden to go to the compound, having no radio contact, he had waited in vain for Terl to come to the base.

Perhaps Terl thought they had moved. True, they had put an emergency camp near the minesite down in a hidden valley. They had moved extra machines, supplies, and the three shifts for the lode and one of the old women to cook and wash for them. There was an abandoned mining village there and it was a short flight to the lode.

The efforts to mine the vein were not going well. They had driven the steel bars into the cliff and tried to build a platform, but the wind, meeting resistance, kept flexing the rods at the point of contact with the cliff and the section there would become red hot. It was daredevil work. Two rods had already broken and only safety lines had saved Scots from plummeting a thousand feet to their deaths. Two months' work in bitter and ferocious winds. And they had only a few pounds of wire gold to show for it—gold grabbed, as it were, on the fly.

This was the fifth night he had lain here and looked in vain for the fire that should be there.

Five nights before, not seeing the fire, they had sent a scout.

There had been a row with the council and the others when they found he was determined to slip down there himself. They had literally barred the door on him. Robert the Fox had become cross with him and shouted into his ears that Chiefs didn't scout. They might raid, but never scout. It was too dangerous for him; he was not expendable. He had argued and found the rest of the council taking Robert's side. And when other Scots heard the raised voices they came and stood around the council—as they had a right to do, they said—and added their arguments against his taking senseless risks with his person.

It had been quite a row. And they were right.

They had sent, as a compromise, young Fearghus. He went off like a shadow through the cold moonlight and they waited out the hours.

Somehow young Fearghus got home. He was badly wounded. The flesh of his shoulder was seared like beef. He had gotten almost to the small plateau in front of the cage. The moon had set by then. There was no fire in the cage. But there was something new at the compound—sentries! The area was patrolled by one armed Psychlo near the cages and one or more guards walking the perimeter of the compound.

The guard at the cage had fired at a shadow. Fearghus had gotten away only by howling like a wolf in pain, for the sentry supposed he had shot a wolf, common enough on the plains.

Fearghus was in the makeshift hospital now, shoulder packed in bear grease and herbs. He would get well, clucked over by one of the old women. He was triumphant rather than cowed, for he had proven the majority opinion right.

The other Scots, singly and in groups, informed MacTyler that the point was proven beyond any doubt. A Chief must not go on scout; raid yes, scout no.

The parson had consoled Jonnie. In Jonnie's quarters when they were alone, the parson had patiently explained. "It isn't that they feel you can't do it, nor even actually that maybe they themselves couldn't go on if something happened to you. It's just that they're fond of you, laddie. It's you who gave us the hope."

Lying in the tall grass using binoculars built for an alien face, Jonnie did not feel much hope.

Here they were, a tiny group of a vanishing race, on a planet itself small and out of the way, confronting the most powerful and advanced beings in the universes. From galaxy to galaxy, system to system, world to world, the Psychlos were supreme. They had smashed every sentient race that had ever sought to oppose them, and even those that had tried to cooperate. With advanced technology and a pitiless temperament, the Psychlos had never been successfully opposed in all the rapacious eons of their existence.

Jonnie thought of the trench, of the sixty-seven cadets with pathetically inadequate weapons trying to stop a Psychlo tank and dying for it, taking with them the last hope of the human race.

No, not the last hope, thought Jonnie. A thousand or more years later, here were the Scots and himself. But what a *forlorn* hope. One casual sortie from that compound with one old Psychlo ground tank and the hope would be ended.

Yes, Jonnie and the Scots could probably attack that compound. They could probably wipe out several minesites and even end this present operation. But the Psychlo company would sweep in and extort a revenge that would end it all forever.

Yes, he had a potential weapon. But not only did he have no uranium; he didn't even have a detector. He had nothing at all to tell him where to look or even whether something was uranium. He and the Scots had a very forlorn hope indeed.

He put the binoculars on maximum magnification. One last sweep on that sleeping compound way over there. Nightlights, green pinpoints under the domes. But no yellow-orange fire.

He was about to give it up for the night when his sweeping glasses picked up the fuel dump. There were piled the cartridges that powered the machines. A bit distant, safely away in case of a blowup, was the explosives magazine—plenty of explosives for mining, but even blowing the whole thing up would not really jar the compound. And there were the battle planes, twenty of them lined up on a ready line. Across the transshipment area from the battle planes and distant from all the rest, but closer to the cage area, was the breathe-gas dump. The company didn't care how much breathe-gas it stockpiled; in huge drums and small mask bottles, there must be enough breathe-gas there to last the mining operation fifty years. It was piled higgledy-piggledy. It was never checked out—machine operators simply picked up canisters for their canopies and masks. There was too much of it to require conservation.

The glasses swept on. Jonnie was looking for sentries now. He found one of them. The Psychlo was waddling lazily through the dark between the breathe-gas dump and the transshipment platform. Yes, there was another one: up on the plateau near the cage.

Suddenly Jonnie swept the glasses back to the breathe-gas dump. Aside from a half-dozen trodden paths the place was surrounded by tall weeds and grass, and the undergrowth and ground cover stretched out to the horizon.

He brought the glasses back to the breathe-gas dump.

Suddenly, with a surge of hope, he knew he had his uranium detector.

Breathe-gas!

A small bottle of it would let out through its regulator the minute quantities required for masks.

If one let a little breathe-gas escape in the vicinity of radiation, it would make a small explosion.

A Geiger counter reacted when the radiation activated gas in a tube, or so the old books told him. Well, breathe-gas didn't just react: it exploded violently.

Dangerous sort of instrument perhaps. But with care it just might work.

Jonnie snaked back off the knoll.

Twenty minutes later, at the base, he was saying to the council: "A Chief mustn't go on a scout. Right?"

"Aye," they all agreed, glad he had gotten the point at last.

"But he can go on a raid," said Jonnie.

They became stiffly alert.

"I may have solved the uranium detector problem," said Jonnie. "Tomorrow night, we are going on a raid!"

— 4 —

Jonnie crept toward the plateau near the cage. The moon had set; the night was dark. The sounds of distant wolves mingled with the moan of the icy wind. He heard above it the click of equipment as the sentry moved.

Things had definitely not gone well tonight. The first plan had been aborted, making for last-minute changes. All afternoon a mixed herd of buffalo and wild cattle had been ideally located on the plain.

It was said that when a winter was going to be a very bad one, buffalo drifted down from the vastnesses of the north. Or perhaps it was a sort of migration to the south that would happen anyway. The wolves, long and gray, a different kind of wolf, came with them.

The wolves were still out there but the buffalo and cattle were not. The plan had been to stampede the mixed herd across the compound and create a diversion. It happened now and then and would not be suspicious. But just as the raid was about to be launched, the herd had taken it into their heads to trot castward and were now too far away to be of any use. It was a bad omen. It meant hastily changed plans and a raid with no diversion. Dangerous.

Twenty Scots were scattered out there on the plain, among them Dunneldeen. They were caped and hooded—as was Jonnie—with the heat-deflecting fabric used in drilling. A mixture of powdered grass and glue made from hoofs had been painted over the costume: with this, infrared would read them like part of the surrounding grass; even visually they could be mistaken for the general terrain.

The Scots were under specific orders to converge upon the breathe-gas dump, separately pick up cases of small pressure cylinders, and get back to the base.

The trick was to raid an enemy who would never know he had been raided. They must not suspect at the compound that the "animals" were hostile. It was a raid that must look like no raid. The Scots must not take any weapons, must not collide with any sentries, must not leave any traces.

There was some protest that Jonnie was going to go to the cage. He explained, not really believing it, that this way he would be *behind* any sentries who might converge upon the dump if a disturbance was noted.

Jonnie gripped a kill-club and stole forward toward the plateau. And his next ill chance was awaiting him.

The horses were not there. Perhaps nervous because of the wolves or seeking better grazing, they had wandered off. Through the glasses, Jonnie had seen two of them last night.

He had planned to creep up the last distance by guiding a horse alongside of him. All his horses were trained to strike with their front hoofs on command, and if the sentry were alerted and had to be hit, it would look like the Psychlo had simply tangled with a horse.

No horses. Wait. A dim increase in blackness in the black at the bottom of the cliff ahead of him. Jonnie sighed with relief as the crunch of dry grass being munched came to him.

But when he arrived, it was only Blodgett, the horse with the crippled shoulder, probably not given to much wandering due to the lameness.

Oh, well. Better Blodgett than none at all. The horse nuzzled him in greeting but obeyed the order to be silent.

With a hand on Blodgett's jaw, causing the horse to stop a bit every few feet, walking back of the horse's shoulder and protected from any detector the sentry might be carrying, Jonnie quietly approached the cage. If he could get within striking distance of the sentry—and if Blodgett remembered the training—and if the lame shoulder permitted, Jonnie intended to take out the sentry.

The Psychlo was looming up under the reflected glow of a

dim, green light burning somewhere in the dome. There was no fire in the cage.

Twenty feet. Fifteen feet. Ten feet . . .

Suddenly the sentry turned, alert. Ten feet! Way out of striking distance.

But just as Jonnie was about to launch the kill-club he saw that the sentry was listening back of himself. There was a tiny whisper of crackling sound. Jonnie knew what it was: a radio intercomm plugged into the sentry's ear. Some other sentry had spoken to him over it.

The Psychlo hefted the six cumbersome feet of his blast rifle. He muttered something inside his own helmet dome, answering.

The other sentry must be down by the dump. Had a Scot been seen? Was the operation blown?

The cage sentry went lumbering off to the other side of the compound, in the direction of the dump.

Whatever was going on down there, Jonnie had his own mission. He moved quickly up to the wooden barrier.

"Chrissie!" he whispered as loudly as he dared into the darkness of the cage.

Silence.

"Chrissie!" he hissed more urgently.

"Jonnie?" a whisper came back. But it was Pattie's voice.

"Yes. Where is Chrissie?"

"She's here . . . Jonnie!" There were tears in back of Pattie's whisper. "Jonnie, we don't have any water. The pipes froze." She sounded very weak herself, possibly ill.

There was an odor in the air and in the green dimness Jonnie spotted a pile of dead rats outside the door. Dead rats that had not been taken in and were rotting.

"Do you have any food?"

"Very little. And we have had no firewood for a week."

Jonnie felt a fury rising in himself. But he must be fast. They had no time. "And Chrissie?"

"Her head is hot. She just lies here. She doesn't answer me. Jonnie, please help us."

"Hold on," said Jonnie hoarsely. "In a day or two you'll get help, I promise. Tell Chrissie. Make her understand."

He could do little right now. "Is there ice in the pool?"

"A little. Very dirty."

"Use the heat of your body to melt it. Pattie, you must hold on for a day or two."

"I'll try."

"Tell Chrissie I was here. Tell her—" What did girls want to hear, what could he say? "Tell her that I love her." It was true enough.

There was a sharp sound down by the dump. Jonnie knew he couldn't stay. Something, somebody was in trouble down there.

Gripping Blodgett's mane to drag the horse along, Jonnie ran silently to the other side of the compound.

He stared down the hill toward the dump. He knew exactly where it was but there were no lights. Yes, there was a light!

A sentry flashlight flicked across the dump.

Two sentries were down there. The silhouettes against the dump showed they were a hundred feet this side of it.

Jonnie covered himself with the horse and went down the hill.

A light flicked at him, dazzling. It passed on.

"Just one of those damned horses," said a voice ahead of him. "I tell you there's something to the right of that dump."

"Turn on your scanner!"

A thudding sound came from the dump like a box being overturned.

"There *is* something over there," said the sentry.

They started to advance, flashlight playing before them. It silhouetted them to Jonnie. He crept the horse forward.

Jonnie saw what had happened. A messily stacked tier of boxes had overturned when someone touched one.

With better night sight than the light-blinded sentries, he saw a Scot move and then begin to run away.

No. A sentry saw it. The sentry was raising the blast rifle to fire.

What a bad night! The Psychlos would know the animals were raiding them. A wounded or dead Scot in a heat camouflage cape would give it all away. The Psychlos would retaliate. They'd wipe out the base.

Twenty feet away the sentry was shoving off the safety catch, aiming.

The kill-club struck him like a lightning bolt in the center of his back.

Jonnie was racing forward, unarmed now.

The other sentry turned. The light hit Jonnie.

The Psychlo raised his blast rifle to fire.

Jonnie was past him! Grasping the muzzle of the huge gun, he spun it out of his paws.

Jonnie reversed the weapon to use the butt. There must be no shots to wake the compound.

The Psychlo turned and tried to grab him. The rifle butt crunched into the sentry's stomach and he folded.

Jonnie thought he was home free but he wasn't. The ground shook. A third sentry came running up. The light from the fallen flashlight shone on the huge rushing legs. The third sentry had a belt gun drawn. He was five feet away, raising the weapon to fire.

Holding the blast rifle by its muzzle, Jonnie whirled the butt into the third one's helmet.

There was a crack of splitting helmet glass. Then a hoarse intake of hostile air.

The Psychlo went down. The first one was trying to get up and bring a weapon to bear.

Jonnie crashed the butt of the rifle down on his chest and his helmet came loose. He choked a strangled gasp as the air hit him.

My god! Jonnie agonized. Three sentries to explain! Unless he acted, they were for it and washed up the whole way. He forced the rages of combat back to calmness. He heard Blodgett running off.

Somewhere up in the compound a door slammed. This place would be swarming.

He stamped out the flashlight.

Raking through his pockets he searched for a thong. He found one, found two. He pieced them together.

He reached down and got hold of the first sentry's blast rifle. He tied the extended thong to the trigger.

Then with all his might he plunged the muzzle of the blast rifle into the ground, choking its bore with dirt and leaving it erect.

He hunched down behind the protection of the first sentry's body.

There were running feet coming down from the compound. Doors were slamming. They would be here any instant.

He made sure he was protected both from sight of the compound and from the blast and pulled the thong.

The choked blast rifle exploded like a bomb.

The corpse before him jolted.

Geysered dirt and rocks began to fall back.

But Jonnie was gone.

Two hours later, with his side aching from running, Jonnie came back to the base.

Robert the Fox had seen that no unusual lights were on and had the place organized in case of pursuit. As the raiders came in, one by one, he had their boxes of breathe-gas carefully hidden in a basement and collected them in a silent group in the faintly lit auditorium. He had fifteen Scots standing by with submachine guns and passenger ships lined up in case they had to evacuate. The camouflaged capes had been removed and hidden. No evidence left in sight; no precaution untaken; withdrawal, if called for, already organized. Robert the Fox was an efficient veteran of many a raid in his own homeland.

"Did we leave anyone?" panted Jonnie.

"Nineteen came back," said Robert the Fox. "Dunneldeen is still out there."

Jonnie didn't like it. He looked around at the nineteen raiders in the hall. They were concentrating on getting themselves back to normal, straightening their bonnets, picking grass off themselves, winding down.

A runner from the lookout with night glasses posted on top of a building came in with the message: "No pursuit visible. No planes have taken off."

"That was one devil of an explosion," said Robert the Fox.

"It was a blast rifle that blew up," said Jonnie. "When the barrel is clogged they blow back and explode their whole magazine of five hundred rounds."

"Sure made the echoes ring," said Robert the Fox. "We heard it over here, miles away."

"They are loud," said Jonnie. He sat panting on a bench. "I've got to figure out how to get a message to Terl. Chrissie is ill, and they're without water. No firewood."

The Scots tensed. One of them spat the word "Psychlos!"

"I'll figure a way to get a message," said Jonnie. "Any sign of Dunneldeen?" he called to a messenger at the door.

The messenger went off to the lookout.

The group waited. Minutes ticked on. Half an hour went by. They were strained. Finally Robert the Fox stood up and said, "Well, bad as it is, we better—"

There was the thud of running feet.

Dunneldeen came racing through the door and sank down panting. He was not just panting, he was also laughing.

"No sign of pursuit!" the messenger shouted in.

The tension vanished.

Dunneldeen delivered a box of breathe-gas vials and the parson rushed it off to hide it in case of search.

"No planes have taken off," the messenger yelled into the room.

"Well, for now, laddies," said Robert the Fox, "unless the devils are waiting for daylight—"

"They won't come," said Dunneldeen.

Others were drifting into the room. Submachine guns were being uncocked. Pilots came in from the passenger standby planes. Even the old women were peering in the door. Nobody knew yet what had gone wrong out there.

Dunneldeen had his breath and the parson was moving around serving out small shots of whiskey.

"I stayed behind to see what they would do," said the cheerful Dunneldeen. "Ooo, and you should have seen our Jonnie!" He gave a highly colored account. He had been one of the last ones to reach the dump, and when he touched a box a whole pile of them fell over. He fled, zigzagging, but circled back in case Jonnie needed help. "But help, he needed no help!" And he told them how Jonnie had killed the three Psychlos "with his bare hands and a rifle butt" and had "blown the whole lot sky-high." And he'd "looked like a David fighting *three* Goliaths."

There wouldn't be any pursuit. "I hid behind the horse two hundred feet away and moved it closer when the Psychlos all met at the bodies. The horse wasn't hit in the blast but a piece of gun must have slashed into a buffalo that was standing near the dump."

"Yes, I saw the buffalo." "I ran into it going in." "Is that what that shadow was?" murmured various raiders.

"Some big Psychlo—maybe your demon, Jonnie—came down," continued Dunneldeen, "and flashed lights around. And they figured out the buffalo had overturned the boxes and the sentries had gone hunting on watch—oh, they were cross at the sentries for that—and stumbled and dug a blast rifle into the dirt and it went off and killed them."

Jonnie expelled a sigh of relief. He hadn't known about the buffalo but he had intended them to think the rest of it. He had even recovered the burned-off thong. The explosion would have masked the other damage, and he'd found his kill-club in a mad last-second scramble before escape. Yes, there was no evidence.

"What a raid!" exulted Dunneldeen. "And ooo what a bonnie Chief our Jonnie is!"

Jonnie sipped at the whiskey the parson gave him to hide his embarrassment.

"You're a scamp," said Robert the Fox to Dunneldeen. "You might have been caught."

"Ah, bit we haed tae know noo, didn't we?" laughed Dunneldeen, unabashed.

They wanted to parade the pipers. But Robert the Fox would give no clue to the eyes of a watching enemy that tonight was any different. He sent them to bed.

Well, thought Jonnie, as he settled down in the wool plaid blanket, they had their uranium detector, perhaps.

But that didn't help Chrissie. No radio. No personal contact. How was he going to force Terl to come over?

— 5 —

A haggard, nervous Terl approached the rendezvous. He drove his armored ground car with one paw and held the other on the firing triggers of the fully charged heavy guns.

He had not figured out Jayed's presence on Earth. The Imperial Bureau of Investigation agent had been assigned to a lowly ore-sorting post by personnel; Terl had not dared suggest any assignment. An ore sorter only worked when there was ore coming up at the end of shifts, and a fellow could disappear off the post for hours and not be missed and reappear as though he'd been there all the time. Terl dared not put surveillance equipment near him for Jayed was a past master at that, after decades in the I.B.I.

Terl had tried to get Jayed involved with Chirk, his secretary. He offered Chirk wild promises if she could get Jayed into bed with her—with a button camera of the smallest size imbedded in a mole. But Jayed had paid no attention to her. He had just gone on shuffling about, head down, giving the exact appearance of an employee up to absolutely nothing. But what else? That was how the I.B.I. would work.

With shaking paws Terl had ransacked the dispatch boxes to home planet. There was nothing from Jayed in them. No new types of reports, no strange alterations of routine paper. Terl had spent agonizing nights going through the traffic. He could find nothing.

Rumbling about, feeling like he was spinning, Terl had tried to figure out whether the I.B.I. had invented some new means of communication. The company and the Imperial government did not invent things—they had not, to Terl's knowledge, for the last hundred thousand years. But still, there could always be something he didn't know about. Like writing on ore samples being shipped through. But it would take specially designated ore and there was no departure he could find.

The Imperial government was usually only interested in the company's ore volumes—the government got a percentage. But it could also intervene in matters of serious crime or intended crime.

Terl could not find what Jayed was doing. And the appearance of a deadly secret agent on the base, with falsified papers, had not permitted Terl a single relaxed moment for the past two months.

He did his own work with a fury and an impeccable thoroughness quite foreign to him. He got through investigations at once. He answered all dispatches at once. Anything questionable in his files was buried or destroyed at once. Terl had even personally overhauled and fueled and charged the twenty battle planes in the field so that he would appear alert and efficient.

He had filed a banal report about the animals. There were dangerous posts in mining, slopes one could not get into, and as an experiment "ordered by Numph" he had rounded up a few animals to see whether they could run simpler machine types. The animals were not dangerous; they were actually stupid and slow to learn. It did not cost the company anything and it might increase their profits in case the experiment worked out. It was not very successful yet anyway. Nothing was taught the animals about metallurgy or warfare, both because of company policy and because they were too stupid. They ate rats, a vermin plentiful on this planet. He sent the report through with no priority. He was covered. He hoped.

But fifteen times a day Terl decided that he should wipe out the animals and return the machines to storage. And fifteen times a day he decided to go on with it just a little longer.

The sentry affair had disturbed him, not because Psychlos had been killed (he needed the dead bodies for his plans), but because one of the sentries, when Terl put the body in a coffin for transshipment next year, had had a criminal brand burned into the fur of his chest. This three-bar brand was put on criminals by the Imperial government. It represented someone "barred from justice procedures, barred from government assistance, and barred from employment." It meant the personnel department on the home planet was careless. He had made an innocuous report of it.

For a flaming moment of hope he thought perhaps Jayed might be investigating that or looking for some such. But when he had a fellow employee mention it casually to Jayed, no interest had been shown.

Terl simply could not find out what Jayed was looking for, nor why Jayed was there. The tension and uncertainty of it had brought him near to perpetual hysteria.

And this morning, out of the blue, the animal had done something that literally stood Terl's fur on end with terror.

As was his usual practice, Terl was stripping the day's photos from the recon drone receiver, when he found himself looking at a photo of the minesite with a sign in it.

There, sharp and clear, at the lode, was the animal steadying a huge twelve-by-twelve-foot sign. It was resting on a flat place the animals had made back of the lode. In clearest Psychlo script it said:

URGENT
Meeting Vital.
Same place. Same time.

That was bad enough! But a machine tarpaulin seemed to have fallen over the last part of the sign. There was another line. It said:

The w. . . .

Terl couldn't read the rest of it.

The stupid animal apparently had not noticed part of its sign was obscured.

With shaking claws, Terl had tried to find another frame in the sequence that looked back of the tarpaulin. He could not.

Panic gripped him.

Gradually his scattered wits collected down to seething anger. The panic died out as he realized that his was the only recon drone receiver on the planet; the telltale on the side of it that showed whether anything else was receiving was mute. He daily watched these photos and had exactly tracked the progress at the lode. The animal he had captured always seemed to be there with a crew. While all these animals looked alike, he thought he could recognize the blond beard and size of the one he had trained. This usually reassured him, for it seemed to mean the animal was busy and not wandering around elsewhere.

The progress at the lode was minimal but he knew the problems of mining it, and he also knew they might solve them without his advice. He had months to go—four months more, actually—before Day 92.

He got over his panic and shredded the photos. Jayed had no possible access to them.

But to directly link Terl with the project was not to be allowed. He began to imagine that the sign had started with his name and regretted having shredded it so fast. He should have made sure. Maybe it did start: "Terl!"

Terl was not introspective enough to realize that he was bordering upon insanity.

The darkness spread like a black sack over the tank. He had been driving on instruments without lights. It was treacherous terrain: an old city had been here once, but it was now just a honeycomb of abandoned mine holes where the company had followed an old deposit centuries before.

Something showed on his detector screen right ahead. Something live!

His paw rested alertly on the firing knob, ready to blast. He cautiously made sure he was headed away from the compound and masked by a hill and ancient walls. Then he turned on a dim inspection light.

The animal was sitting on a horse at the rendezvous point. It was a different horse, a wild horse nervous because of the tank. The dim, green tank light bathed the rider. There was another, someone else! No, it was just another horse . . . it had a large pack on its back.

Terl swept his scanners around. No, there was nobody else here. He looked back at the animal. Terl's paw quivered an inch above the firing lever. The animal did not seem to be alarmed.

The interior of the tank was compressed with breathe-gas but Terl also had on a breathe-mask. He adjusted it.

Terl picked up an intercom unit and pushed it through the atmosphere-tight firing port. The unit fell to the ground outside the tank. Terl picked up the interior unit.

"Get down off that horse and pick up this intercom," ordered Terl.

Jonnie slid off the half-broken horse and approached the tank. He picked the unit off the ground and looked through the tank ports for Terl. He could see nothing. The interior was dark and the glass was set to block a view in.

Through the intercom, Terl said, "Did you kill those sentries?"

Jonnie held the outside unit to his face. He thought fast. This Terl was in a very strange state. "We haven't lost any sentries," he said truthfully.

"You know the sentries I mean. At the compound."

"Have you had trouble?" said Jonnie.

The word "trouble" almost made Terl's head spin. He didn't know what trouble he had, or what kind of trouble, or from where. He got a grip on himself.

"You obscured the last part of that sign," he said accusingly.

"Oh?" said Jonnie innocently. He had obscured it on purpose so that Terl would come. "It meant to say, 'The winter is advancing and we need your advice.' "

Terl simmered down. Advice. "About what?" He knew about what. It was next to impossible to get out that gold. But there had to be a way. And he *was* a miner. Top student of the school, actually. And he studied the recon drone pictures daily. He knew the flexing rods would not let them build a platform. "You need a portable shaft stairway. You've got one in your equipment. You nail it to the outside face and work from it."

"All right," said Jonnie. "We'll try it." He had Terl calmer now that he was on a routine subject of interest.

"We also need some protection in case of uranium," said Jonnie.

"Why?"

"There's uranium in those mountains," said Jonnie.

"In the gold?"

"I don't think so. In the valleys and around." Jonnie thought he had better emphasize that Terl was barred from those places, and also he was desperate for the data. He could not experiment with uranium without protection from it. "I've seen men turn blotchy from it," he added, which was true but not of his present crew.

This seemed to cheer Terl up. "No crap?" he said.

"What gear protects one?"

Terl said, "There's always radiation around on a planet like this and a sun like this. Small amounts. That's why these breathe-masks have leaded glass in their faceplates. That's why all the canopies are leaded glass. You don't have any."

"It's lead that protects one?"

"You'll just have to take your chances," said Terl, amused, feeling better.

"Can you turn a light up here?" asked Jonnie. There was a thump as he laid a sack on the flat section in front of the windscreen.

"I don't want any lights."

"Do you think you were followed?"

"No. That spinning disc on the roof is a detection wave-neutralizer. You needn't worry about our being traced."

Jonnie looked up at the top of the tank. In the very dim light he could see a thing planted there. It looked like a fan. It was running.

"Turn a light on this," said Jonnie.

Terl looked at his screens. There were no telltales. "I'll drive ahead under that tree."

Jonnie steadied the ore sack as Terl slowly put the car under a mask of evergreens. He stopped again and turned on a light that lit up the area in front of the windshield.

With a lift of his arm, Jonnie spilled about ten pounds of ore onto the tank bonnet. It flashed under the light. It was white quartz and wire gold. And it shone and glittered as though it had jewels in it as well. Eight pounds of it was pure wire gold from the lode.

Terl sat and stared through the windscreen at it. He swallowed hard

"There's a ton of it there," said Jonnie. "If it can be gotten out. It's in plain view."

The Psychlo just sat and looked at the gold through the windscreen. Jonnie scattered it so it shone better.

He picked up the intercom again. "We're keeping our bargain. You must keep yours."

"What do you mean?" said Terl, detecting accusation.

"You promised to give food and water and firewood to the females."

Terl shrugged. "Promises," he said indifferently.

Jonnie put his arm around the gold and started to sweep it back into the ore sack and withdraw it.

The motion was not lost on Terl. "Quit it. How do you know they *aren't* being cared for?"

Jonnie let the gold lie. He moved over so the light touched his face. He tapped a finger against his forehead. "There's something you don't know about humans," said Jonnie. "They have psychic powers sometimes. I have psychic powers with those females." It would not do to tell Terl that it was the absence of a fire or a scout that alerted him. All's fair in love and war, as Robert the Fox would say, and this was both love and war.

"You mean without radios, right?" Terl had read about this. He hadn't realized these animals had it. Damned animals.

"Right," said Jonnie. "If she is not well cared for and if she isn't all right, I *know*!" He tapped his head again.

"Now I have a pack here," said Jonnie. "It has food and water and flints and firewood and warm robes and a small tent. I'm going to lash it on top of this tank and right away when you get back, you're to put it in the cage. Also get the cage cleaned up, inside and outside, and fix the water supply."

"It's just the tank," said Terl. "It goes empty, needs to be topped up. I've been busy."

"And take those sentries away. You don't need sentries!"

"How did you know there were sentries?" said Terl suspiciously.

"You just told me so, tonight," said Jonnie into the intercom. "And my psychic powers tell me they tease her."

"You can't order me around," bristled Terl.

"Terl, if you don't take care of the females, I just might take it into my head to wander up to those sentries and mention something I know."

"What!" demanded Terl.

"Just something I know. It wouldn't cause you to be fired but it would be embarrassing."

Terl suddenly vowed he had better get rid of those sentries.

"You'll *know* if I don't do these things?" said Terl.

Jonnie tapped his own forehead in the light.

But the threat had unsettled Terl's spinning wits. On an entirely different tack he demanded, "What'll you do with the gold if you don't deliver it?"

"Keep it for ourselves," said Jonnie, starting again to put it back in the bag.

Terl snarled deep and threateningly. His amber eyes flared in the darkness of the tank. "I'll be damned if you will!" he shouted. Leverage, leverage! "Listen! Did you ever hear of a drone bomber? Hah, I thought not. Well, let me tell you something, animal: I can lift off a drone bomber and send it right over that site, right over your camp, right over any shelter, and bomb you out of existence. All by remote! You're not as safe as you think, animal!"

Jonnie just stood there, looking at the blank, black windows of the tank as the words avalanched through the intercom.

"You, animal," snarled Terl, "are going to mine that gold and you're going to deliver that gold and you are going to do it all by Day 91. And if you don't I'll blast you and all animals on this planet to hell, you hear me, to hell!" His voice ended in a shriek of hysteria and he stopped, panting.

"And when Day 91 comes, and we've done it?" said Jonnie.

Terl barked a sharp, hysterical laugh. He felt he really had to get control of himself. He sensed he was acting strangely. "Then you get paid!" he shouted.

"You keep your side of the bargain," said Jonnie. "We'll deliver it."

Good, thought Terl. He had cowed the animal. This was more like it. "Put that pack on the tank," he said magnanimously. "I'll fill the water tank and clean up the place and take care of the sentries. But don't forget my remote control box, eh? You act up and dead females!"

Jonnie tied the vital pack on the vehicle roof. In the process of doing so he removed the wave-neutralizer and put it behind a tree. Terl would think it had been knocked off by the tree branches, perhaps. It might be useful.

Terl had turned the bonnet light off and Jonnie put the ore back in the sack. He knew Terl wouldn't take it with him.

Without saying goodbye, Terl drove off and the tank vanished.

Minutes later, when it was hidden from view and miles away, Dunneldeen climbed out of a mine hole where he had been holding a submachine gun in sweaty hands. He had realized the weapon would do nothing to that tank, but they had not expected Terl to stay in the armored vehicle. Although they would not have shot him, they thought he might have tried to kidnap Jonnie if the girls were dead. Dunneldeen gave a short whistle. Ten more Scots bobbed into view from mine holes, putting their guns on safety.

Robert the Fox came down the hill from an old ruined wall. Jonnie was still standing there looking off toward the compound.

"That demon," said Robert the Fox, "is on the verge of insanity. Did ye ken how his talk darted this way and that? The hysteria in his laughter? He's hard driven by something we don't know about."

"We didn't know about the drone bombers," said Dunneldeen.

"We know now," said Robert the Fox. "MacTyler, you know this demon. Wouldn't you say he was borderline daft?"

"Do you suppose he meant to blast you when he drove in?" asked Dunneldeen. "But you handled it very well, Jonnie MacTyler."

"He's dangerous," said Jonnie.

Two hours later he saw a fire start, a tiny pinpoint of light in the distant cage. Later a scout would confirm the removal of the sentries and he himself would check on the water and Chrissie.

An insane Terl was making this a much more hazardous game they were playing. A treacherous Terl was one thing. A maniac Terl was quite another.

■

PART 9

— 1 —

The snows were late, but when they came they made up for it with a violent, howling vengeance that almost stopped the work at the lode.

The staircase was not working. Jonnie had helped all he could, flying an overheating platform to drive in the pins, hanging from safety wires over the yawning chasm, encouraging the others. They had almost made it, had even taken out another ninety pounds in gold, when the first real storm of winter hit them. Under winds of near hurricane force, driving frozen pellets as hard as bullets, almost shaking the very mountains themselves, the staircase had collapsed. Fortunately it had just been abandoned during a shift change when it went, and there were no casualties.

They were waiting now for a lull in the storm to see what else they could do.

It was mandatory that they appear industrious, for it was the opinion of Robert the Fox that Terl would not act violently unless it appeared there was no hope. But just now the driving snow masked any pictures the recon drone might take in its daily overfly.

Besides, it was not vital, they all assured him, that Jonnie be there. Long ago the planning had provided that three who looked like him keep up the appearance that he was always there. One of these three was always visible to the recon drone—each one to his own watch. It had even been Thor who had held up the sign, not Jonnie. Three watches were vital, for no crew could stand it for more than two hours in this bitter cold.

So Jonnie was not there today. Through the driving storm, he and three others were heading for a place once called "Uravan."

The historian, Doctor MacDermott, was developing quite a knack for picking up information out of the tattered remains of books. He even had a young Scot, an accomplished scout, assigned to him now just to go off and dig up ancient maps and books. And MacDermott had found a reference that said that Uravan had [''one of the world's largest uranium deposits'']. It was supposed to be west and slightly south of the base about two hundred twenty miles, just beyond and a bit southwest of an enormous, distinctive plateau.

Uranium!

So Jonnie and one of the pilots and Angus MacTavish were on their way in a personnel plane. Who knew, they might be lucky.

Angus MacTavish was delighted. He was the one who figured out man-mechanics and got things working.

Jonnie had trained him and another half-dozen Scots in electronics and they were all good at that and mechanics, but it was Angus MacTavish who was the star. Pugnacious, never knowing the meaning of defeat, a bundle of enthusiastic black-haired optimism, Angus was quite certain they would find mountains of uranium right there, all ready to shovel into a bag and cart off.

Jonnie didn't think so. In the first place they had no protection from radiation yet, so they were a long way from shoveling anything. But a uranium mine might have enough left around to test breathe-gas. He wisely refrained from dampening Angus's enthusiasm. All they were out for was, in fact, a scout to find a place to test breathe-gas.

The storm made visibility very poor. The passenger craft bucketed along, battered by the machine-gunning of occasional local storms. The plane had damn-all in the way of instruments and it was all contact flying. A time or two a peak would flash by a mite too close, but from way up high it was a carpet of turbulent whiteness and one might lose his bearings. Fortunately the storm was blowing eastward and its worst furies were past by the time they had gone a hundred miles.

They burst out of a cloud into clear weather. The panorama of the western Rockies spread out, glistening in the late morning sun, breathtaking in its beauty.

''Scotland may be the best land in the world,'' said the copilot, ''but 'tis never like this!''

Jonnie punched their speed up to about five hundred, and the white vast world fled by. He spotted the plateau, estimated from the ancient schoolbook map he held where Uravan might be. Even in the snow they could make out where an ancient, curving road had been. He spotted the southeast point where the road forked and, down to treetop level and counting the white-coated remains of towns, brought them to the mounds and dumps that must be Uravan. He landed in front of some buildings, the plane crunching into the fresh snow.

Angus MacTavish was out of the door like a running buck, his kilt flying behind him. He dashed into one ruined building after another and suddenly came speeding back.

His voice thin in the sharp air, he yelled, " 'Tis Uravan!" He held up some tattered scraps of paper.

Jonnie reached in back and got out a breathe-gas cartridge and the equipment. He and Angus had worked half the night making a remote control that would turn the regulator on and off. All they had to do was find a hot radiation spot, back off, turn on the remote, and see whether they got a flash of exploding breathe-gas. Jonnie also got out some shovels, climbing ropes, and mine lamps.

Running all over the place like a hunting hound, Angus was tracking down likely spots. There were ore dumps. There had been fences but these had long since rusted away.

They tried repeatedly. They would scoop out an old dump and put the breathe-gas cartridge down, back off, release some breathe-gas, and see whether it flashed in a small explosion.

After a dozen tries, Angus became convinced it must be a spent cartridge. He switched it on in front of his face and promptly turned blue with coughing. No, it wasn't a spent cartridge. They went down in pits. They scrambled into drifts long since unsafe.

They used up five cartridges of breathe-gas.

No explosions.

Jonnie felt a bit disheartened. He let Angus and the pilot go on with the experiments while he wandered around through the ruins. It was all so badly decayed there was difficulty in recognizing what the buildings had been used for. How Angus had found paper simply added up to Angus: it must have been protected by being preserved under something.

Then Jonnie started to get suspicious. In all this area he had only found one pitiful remnant that might have been a body, merely teeth fillings and buttons lying in a certain pattern in a room.

No remains of file cabinets. No distinguishable remains of machinery aside from some decayed hoists. But no bodies save that one.

He went back to the plane and sat down. This place had been mined out *before* the Psychlo attack. And it had been mined out with such care that the waste dumps weren't even hot.

Angus came streaming back shouting: "It works! It works!" He was carrying something that had been framed.

Jonnie got out and looked at it. One corner of the ancient frame was not charred. Inset into the dilapidated mounting was a piece of ore. It had a brass plate under it, mostly undecipherable. There must have been a leaded glass face on the frame once, for a scrap of it remained in a corner.

He carried it over to a rock and sat down and studied it. The ore was brown and black. It had been mounted as an exhibit on a lead background. He held the inscription this way and that. He couldn't make out more than that it was the ["first"] something. And then a person's name he couldn't make out either. He turned the plate in another way and then saw the letters at the top more plainly. They said ["PITCHBLENDE"].

"Look!" said Angus. "Let me show you."

He took the frame from Jonnie and put it about thirty feet away. He pointed the breathe-gas cartridge at it and came back to Jonnie. He flipped on a remote switch. The breathe-gas emission exploded!

"I'll do it again," yelped Angus. He turned the switch full on and left it on. He wouldn't have had time to turn it off anyway.

The bottle, its emitting snout flaming like a rocket engine, took off and went about ten feet. The pilot and Angus shouted with delight.

"Pitchblende," said Jonnie, who had done a lot of homework. "That's uranite ore. It's the source of a lot of radioactive isotopes. Where'd you get it?"

They dragged him off to the broken shambles of a building that was so collapsed they had to tug and pull at a lot of roof to get at anything else in it.

Covered with dust and hot from work despite the chill air, Jonnie at last went out and sat down on what had once been a porch.

A museum. A small museum it had been. Other specimens were there. Rose quartz, hematite, things that weren't from this immediate place. There wasn't even any evidence that the pitchblende had been from here.

"The test for breathe-gas works!" said the irrepressible Angus.

Jonnie felt depressed. He knew it worked. He had seen a blade scraper canopy blow up and kill a Psychlo long ago when some radioactive dust hit it.

"I'm glad it works," he said. "But even if there is any uranium left under us it's too deep for us to get to. Collect some more lead and wrap that specimen up. We'll take it home."

"Let's look around here some more!" said Angus.

Jonnie had to wait out the storm to the east anyway. "Go ahead," he said.

But he knew it was mined out. Only one body and a museum.

Where in heaven's name was he going to find uranium—lots of it? *Where?*

— 2 —

Jonnie gazed with horror into the deep canyon. There was a flying drill platform down there, close to the river, and it was in real trouble.

It was the day after their return from Uravan. The storm had blown over, leaving a sparkling, white-coated day. But at these altitudes it was bitterly cold, and the canyon, as ever, was funneling winds into torrents of turbulence.

Two Scots, one of them Dunneldeen, the other a black-haired youth named Andrew, were down on that platform trying to recover the staircase, which had fallen nine hundred feet down into the frozen river. Sixty feet long and built of rods, it had pierced the river ice, leaving an end on the bank.

They had grappled the end with a hook lowered from the flying drill platform and had tried to fly the staircase up and out of the river. It was caught underwater. Now sprays coming up through the broken ice were coating the platform with water that instantly froze, increasing the platform's weight by the moment.

He knew what they were trying to do. They were trying to

look busy for the benefit of the recon drone that would be there in a moment or two. The rest of the shift crew were strung out along the chasm's edge untangling the masses of cables and drums that had been scrambled by the storm. Dunneldeen and Andrew had gone down there to look busy salvaging the staircase.

Jonnie had been returning in the small passenger plane to work out some new method of getting the gold. He didn't have a copilot. He had only old Doctor MacDermott, the historian, who had begged a ride so that he could come up to the lode and write the saga of the storm. The ancient Scot, who had considered himself expendable at the recruiting, was a very wise and valued dean of literature, but he was not in the slightest bit trained in their work and frail beyond estimation, with hardly the muscle and skill one needed. There was no time at all to drop down and pick up a trained and agile Scot from the site on the cliff.

They were using local radios. All the items of equipment had them built in, for their range and the range of mine intercoms was only a mile. The transmissions were also masked by the mountains to the east. The radio down there on the platform was evidently open.

"Throw off the reel brakes, Andrew!" Dunneldeen was saying tensely. "The motors are overheating."

"They wilna disengage. 'Tis this spray!"

"Andrew! Disengage the hooks to that staircase!"

"They wilna budge, Dunneldeen! And the thing is stuck under the ice!"

The whine of the overloaded motors was also coming through the open mikes.

Jonnie knew what was going to happen. They couldn't fly the platform free. They couldn't drop down into the rolling, freezing water. And that platform was going to go up in flames any moment.

Such a platform had rudimentary flying controls, usually covered by a lead glass canopy. But the humans didn't use the canopies and Dunneldeen was down there in the midst of flying spray that was coating not only himself but also the controls with instant ice.

The recon drone would be by in another second or two. It must see efforts to mine, not disaster. Jonnie could hear its nearing rumble outside his open side port.

Its hypersonic explosion would occur any moment now The

instant it went by he would have to somehow get those two off that platform.

"Doctor Mac," shouted Jonnie into the rear of the plane. "Get ready. You're about to be a hero!"

"Oh my goodness," said Doctor MacDermott.

"Open the side door and throw out two life lines!" shouted Jonnie. "Make sure our ends are secure to this ship."

The old man scrambled about, grabbing at unfamiliar coils and tangles of cables in the rear.

"Hold on!" shouted Jonnie.

He sent the passenger craft plummeting a thousand feet into the racketing, wind-blasting roar of the chasm. The walls flashed by.

Doctor MacDermott's stomach stayed a thousand feet up. The nearby white and red blur of canyon walls streaked past the open door and he stared at it open-mouthed, barely able to hold on.

Jonnie cracked open the plane's radio. "Dunneldeen!" he yelled into the mike. "Stand by to abandon that thing!"

There was the crack of the sonic boom. The recon drone had passed.

Dunneldeen's fur-hooded face was looking up, and Jonnie realized it was not for the passenger plane but for the benefit of the drone so Terl would suppose it was Jonnie there.

Smoke was coming from the platform motor housings, blue smoke, different from the geysers of spray.

The ice-pressured river was taking full advantage of the hole just made to geyser its way to freedom.

Andrew was pounding on the encrusted winch with a sledge. Then he dropped the sledge and seized a bottle of burning gas and tried to open its controls in order to burn the cable in two. The bottle was thick with ice and and would not open.

The passenger plane came down to twenty-five feet from the top of the platform, Jonnie madly punching control buttons to hold it there. Smoke from the burning motors of the platform swirled, chokingly, into the plane above.

"Doctor Mac!" shouted Jonnie. "Throw out those life lines!"

The old man fumbled with the coils. He could not tell one cable from another. Then he found an end. He pitched it out the door.

Scrambling, he let about fifty feet uncoil and then fastened the cable to a clamp in the plane as best he could. Jonnie maneuvered the cable end over the spray-battered platform.

"I cannot find another cable end!" wailed Doctor MacDermott.

Jonnie shouted into the mike, "Grab that rope!"

"You, Andrew!" shouted Dunneldeen.

Twenty feet of cable from the plane coiled down on the platform and was promptly covered with spray that instantly turned to ice.

Andrew took a turn of cable around his arm.

"Don't put it around your arm!" shouted Jonnie. If Dunneldeen were below him the tightening of the rope would break or sever Andrew's arm. "Put it around that sledge hammer!"

Tongues of flame were coming from the motor housing of the platform.

Andrew managed to break the sledge loose from the ice. He took two turns of cable around the head of it.

"Grab hold!" yelled Jonnie.

Andrew grabbed the slippery sledge handle with his mittened hands.

Jonnie jumped the passenger plane up twenty feet, pulling Andrew up and leaving the end of the cable dangling over Dunneldeen.

"The captain abandons ship!" said Dunneldeen and grabbed the cable end.

Jonnie put the passenger plane up slowly. It would not do to whip-snap the two men off into the roiling river to be swept under the ice.

Andrew was hanging to the sledge twenty feet below the passenger plane. Dunneldeen was dangling forty feet below on the same rope.

"I think this clamp is slipping!" wailed Doctor MacDermott in the back.

The iced mittens of the men below were certainly slipping. It was impossible to raise them a thousand feet to the top of the gorge. Jonnie looked wildly at the river.

The flying platform below exploded in a violence of orange flame.

The passenger plane bucked in the concussion.

Jonnie looked down at the men. The flames had hit Dunneldeen. His leggings were on fire!

Jonnie swept the plane downriver. With frantically racing fingers he brought it to forty-five feet above the snow-coated ice of the stream. Was that ice thick enough?

He dipped the plane. Dunneldeen struck the deep snow. Jonnie dragged him a hundred feet through the drifts on the river to put the fire out.

He saw a shelf beside the river, narrow and snow-covered.

Bringing the plane within feet of the canyon wall, he lowered Dunneldeen onto it and then dropped further.

Andrew's gloves, which had been slipping down the sledge handle inch by inch, let go, and he fell the last ten feet. He almost went off the ledge. Dunneldeen grabbed him.

Jonnie, battling the wind, turned the plane around and brought the open door to the ledge.

The two men scrambled in, helped by Doctor MacDermott.

Andrew reeled in the cable and got the side door shut. Jonnie vaulted the plane two thousand feet up and maneuvered to land at the pad on the top.

Doctor MacDermott was stammering with apologies to the two men. "I could not find a second rope."

"Think nothing of it," said Dunneldeen. "I even got a sleigh ride out of it!"

Doctor MacDermott was clucking over his charred leggings, terribly relieved to find Dunneldeen was just singed and not badly burned.

"I had my chance to be a hero," said Doctor MacDermott "and I muffed it!"

"You did just fine," said Andrew. "Just fine."

Jonnie got out of the plane and walked over to the canyon edge. They followed him. The shift crew was also staring down, their faces shiny from the perspiration of strain. It had been a wild thing to watch.

Shaking his head, Jonnie looked down a thousand feet to where the edge of the staircase was imbedded in the bank. The flying platform had vanished under the ice. The snow around the place was pockmarked with the impacts of broken bits and blackened from the explosion.

Jonnie faced Dunneldeen and the crew. "That," said Jonnie, "is that!"

The shift boss and Dunneldeen said, almost in chorus, "But we can't quit!"

"No more of these acrobatics in thin air," said Jonnie. "No

more hanging over this edge with our hearts in our throats. Come with me."

They followed him back to the pad. He pointed straight down. "Below us," said Jonnie, "that vein is extending into the cliff. It's a pocket vein. Pockets of gold probably occur every few hundred feet. We're going to put a shaft down to that vein. Then we're going to drift along that vein underground to the cliff edge and try to recover that gold from behind!"

They were silent. "But that fissure out there . . . we can't blast: it would knock the face of the cliff off."

"We're just going to have to use drills. Point drills to go in with parallel holes. Then vibrating spades to literally cut the rock. It will take time. We can work hard and maybe get there."

Underground? It dawned on them it was a great idea.

The shift boss and Dunneldeen started making plans to fly in drilling machinery and scrapers and bucket conveyors. Waves of relief began to spread. The shift change crew flew in and when they heard about it they cheered. They had hated hanging by their heels in greedy space with little return to show.

"Get it set up and rolling before the next pass-over of the drone," said Jonnie. "Terl's gone crazy but he's a miner. He'll see what we're doing and hold off. It's like taking rock out with teaspoons, so we'll work this all three shifts around the clock. It'll be easier to work underground in this weather anyway. We'll use the dig-out to enlarge this flat space. Now where's a transit so we can get the exact direction down and over for the dig?"

The sound of the plane revved up. Dunneldeen was going back for pilots and equipment.

We might make it yet, thought Jonnie.

— 3 —

A worried Zzt watched Terl and a swarm of mechanics working over the old bomber drone.

The huge underground garages and hangars resounded with the whine of drills and clang of hammers.

Since the last semiannual personnel intake, Zzt had gotten his mechanics back; aside from exchanging recon drones for refueling every three days (a drone he considered useless), his work was not backlogged. Terl had left the transport chief and section alone until now. Terl himself had serviced the twenty battle planes in the outside field. So aside from this present unexpected project, Zzt had little about which to complain.

But *this* idiocy! The bomber drone? He knew he had better speak.

Terl was in the huge plane's control room working with presets of buttons. He was covered with grease and sweat. He had a small remote keyboard in his hand, and he was punching settings into the main panels of the ship.

"Scotland . . . Sweden," Terl was saying, consulting his tables and notes and pushing ship buttons. There were no seats in the place for it would never be piloted, and Terl was hunched uncomfortably on a balance motor housing.

". . . Russia . . . Alps . . . Italy . . . China . . . no. Alps . . . India . . . China . . . Italy . . . Africa . . ."

"Terl," said Zzt timidly.

"Shut up," snapped Terl, not even looking up. ". . . Amazon . . . Andes . . . Mexico . . . Rocky Mountains! Rocky Mountains one, two, and three!"

"Terl," repeated Zzt. "This bomber drone has not been flown in a thousand years. It's a wreck."

"We're rebuilding it, aren't we?" snarled Terl, finishing his presets and standing up.

"Terl, maybe you don't know that this was the original conquest drone. It was the one that gassed this planet before our takeover."

"Well, I'm loading it with gas canisters, ain't I?"

"But Terl, we've already conquered this planet a thousand or more years ago. You release kill gas now, even in just a few places, and it might hit our own minesites."

"They use breathe-gas," snapped Terl, shouldering by Zzt and walking back into the huge plane. Workmen were trundling up big gas canisters from deep underground storage. They had to burnish them gingerly to get the crud of ages off them. Terl energetically directed the workers hooking them in place. "Fifteen canisters! You've only brought fourteen. Get another one!" Some workmen rushed off and Terl was hooking wires up to the canister release valves, muttering to himself, checking color coding.

"Terl, they only kept this drone as a curiosity piece. These things are dangerous. It's one thing to remote-guide a recon drone with its small motors—they don't override the controls! But this thing has motors like a dozen ore freighters. The signals it sends back to a remote get overridden by its own motors. It could charge around and release gas almost anyplace. They're too erratic for competent use. And once you start them you can't stop them. Like transshipment firing, they're irreversible."

"Shut up," said Terl.

"In the regulations," persisted Zzt, "it says these things only get used in 'most extreme emergency!' There is no emergency, Terl."

"Shut up," said Terl, going on with his wire matching.

"And you've ordered it permanently parked in front of the automatic firing bay. We need that for servicing ore freighters. This is a *war* drone, and they only use them for primary attack on a planet and *never* use them afterward except in a withdrawal. There is no war, and we're not withdrawing from this planet."

Terl had had enough. He threw down his notes and loomed over Zzt. "*I* am the best judge of these things. Where there is no war department on a planet, the security chief has that post. My orders are final. This drone gets parked at the hangar firing door and don't you move it! As to control," he shook the small one-foot-square box in front of Zzt's face, "all it needs is the date setting and fire buttons pushed in and there's nothing erratic after that! This drone will go and do what it's supposed to do! And it stays on standby!"

Zzt backed up. Dollies were moving the huge old relic over to the firing door where it would be in the way of everything and leave no other door to service freighters.

"Those were awfully funny locations you were punching in," Zzt said faintly.

Terl was holding a big wrench. He walked closer to Zzt. "They're man-names for planet locations. They're the places where *man*-animals were left."

"That little handful?" ventured Zzt.

Terl screamed something and threw the wrench at him. Zzt ducked and it went clanging across the hangar floor, making workers dodge.

"You're acting kind of insane, Terl," said Zzt.

"Only alien races ever go insane!" screamed Terl.

Zzt stood aside as they dollied the ancient drone to the firing door.

"It's going to stay right there," yelled Terl at nobody in particular. "It'll get fired anytime in the next four months." And for sure on Day 93, he smiled to himself.

Zzt wondered for a moment whether he ought to shoot Terl when they were in some quiet place. Terl had restored weapons to the employees, refilled the weapon racks in compound halls, let them wear belt guns again. Then he remembered that Terl had an envelope parked somewhere "in case of death."

Later, Zzt mentioned it privately to Numph. Zzt liked to hunt and the bomber drone would wipe out most of the game again. Numph had also liked to hunt once.

But Numph just sat there and looked woodenly at him.

The bomber drone, the one originally shipped in to gas and conquer the planet, remained standing at the firing door, in everybody's way, filled with lethal gas, preset, just requiring a few punches of the remote Terl kept in his own possession.

Zzt shuddered every time he passed it. Terl had obviously gone stark raving mad.

That night in his quarters Terl did feel spinny. Another day and he had gotten absolutely no clue as to what Jayed was up to, what the agent was looking for.

Terl followed the recon drone photos. The animals were burrowing underground now, which was smart. They might possibly make it, and if they didn't he had his answers.

He looked in on the females every evening, throwing wood and meat at them. Sometimes he found packages outside the cage door—he chose not to think about how they got there—and threw them in too. He'd fixed the water, but so it overflowed. The bigger one was sitting up again. He never saw them without being nagged by the puzzle of "psychic powers"; he wondered which one of them sent out the impulses and whether they could be read on a scope. Oh, well, as long as the animals up in the mountains worked, he'd keep these females alive. It was good leverage.

But on Day 93, ha! He could not count on the animals not talking. He could not count on the company or government not catching up with him. The animals had to go, and this time *all* of them.

Terl fell asleep floundering around in a half-conceived possibility. Jayed was denying him gold. It was Jayed's fault. But how did one commit the perfect murder of a top agent of the I.B.I.? It made one's head spin to try to work it out. Meantime he would be the model of efficiency. He had to look like the greatest, most cautious and alert security chief the company had ever known.

Was he crazy, really? No. Just clever.

— 4 —

Jonnie was going home.

In a canyon above the village meadow, they unloaded four horses and a pack from the freight plane. The breath of the horses hung about them in small, thin puffs. The horses, very recently wild, had not liked the ride and stamped about and snorted when their blindfolds were removed. The air was clear and frosty at this altitude. Snow from the recent storm covered the world and silenced it.

Angus MacTavish and Parson MacGilvy were with Jonnie. A pilot had come along so that the plane could be moved in case the visit lasted longer than a day. The recon drone had already gone by when they took off from the base and the plane should not be there when it passed again.

A week ago Jonnie had awakened in the night with the sudden realization that he might know where some uranium was. His own village! He had no great hope for it, but the signs were there in the illness of his people. Possibly there was no great amount, but also possibly there was more than that single rock from Uravan. He felt a trifle guilty for having to have an ulterior motive to go home, for there were other reasons. His people should be moved, both because of their continuous exposure to radiation and also because they should not be exposed in any future bombing.

Jonnie and his men had scoured the mountains for another possible home, and only yesterday had they found one. It was an old mining town on the western slope, lower in altitude, open through a narrow pass to a western plain. A brook ran down the street in the town center. Many of the buildings and houses still retained glass. Wild cattle and game were plentiful. But even better there was a large, half-mile-long tunnel behind the town that could serve as refuge. A coal deposit was on the hill nearby. The place was beautiful. It had no trace of uranium in it.

Jonnie did not think the people of the village would move. He had tried before as a youth and even his father had thought he was just being restless. But he had to try again.

Angus and the parson had insisted on coming with him. He had explained the dangers of exposure to radiation to them and had not wanted to put them at risk. But Angus simply waved a breathe-gas bottle and promised to check it out ahead of them and not be foolish about it, and the parson, being a wise and experienced member of the clergy, knew Jonnie might need help.

They knew better than to simply fly a plane into the meadow. The people had seen recon drones all their lives, but a plane close up might terrify them.

Part of last night had been spent planning. Angus and the parson had been briefed: there would be no action that might alarm the people, no talk of monsters, no frightening tidings about Chrissie. It would be strange enough to be seen entering from the upper canyon, for the pass on the eastern side of the meadow and all such passes were now choked with snow.

And so they rode, three mounted men and a heavily-laden pack horse, down into the meadow. The horse's hoofs made little sound in the loose snow. The deserted cabins on the outskirts were dilapidated and forlorn. Only a whiff of pungent woodsmoke was in the air. Where were the dogs?

Jonnie drew up. The corral where horses were kept was empty. Then he listened carefully and heard a stamp in the old barn sheds beyond: there was a horse there, possibly more than one. He looked toward the pens where wild cattle were usually driven in before the first snow: there were not many cattle there, not enough to last through the winter.

Angus slid down and, as he had promised, did a test for radiation. There was no reaction directly ahead of them.

Where were the dogs? True, they were not used to anything coming in the back door of the valley. But it was strange.

Jonnie rode on toward the courthouse below them. Angus made another test ahead of them. There was no reaction.

An old hound came out of a ruin and looked at them with half-blind eyes. It came forward cautiously, belly deep in the snow. It approached Jonnie, sniffing hard, wisps of vapor rising from its nose.

Then it began to wag its tail, coming closer, wagging harder and harder until the tail was almost whipping the dog's face as he doubled on himself with greeting. The hound began to yelp with welcome.

Three or four more dogs sounded down in the village center.

Jonnie dismounted to pat the hound. It was Panther, one of his family's dogs. He walked on, leading the horse, the dog rheumatically trying to cavort about him.

A gaunt-eyed child peered at them from the corner of a building and then ran off, stumbling and falling in the snow.

Jonnie stopped at the courthouse and looked in. The door was off its hinges and the place was empty and cold; snow had drifted well into the main room. He came out and surveyed the scene of the quiet, ruined village.

He saw smoke coming from the roof of his family's house and walked over to it. He knocked.

There were sounds within and then the door cracked open. It was his Aunt Ellen. She just stood there, staring through the slit. Then, "Jonnie?" and then "But you're dead, Jonnie!"

She opened the door wide and stood there crying.

After a little she wiped her eyes with a doeskin apron. "Come in, Jonnie. I kept your room . . . but we gave your things to the young men. . . . Come in, the cold is getting in the house."

"Is there illness in the village?" said Jonnie, thinking of his companions.

"Oh, no. Nothing unusual. There was a deer seen on the hills and the men are all up there trailing it. There's not too much food, Jonnie. Not since you went away." Then she realized it sounded like an accusation. "I mean . . ."

She was crying again. Jonnie felt a tug at his heartstrings. She was growing old before her time. She was gaunt, her face bones showing too plainly.

Jonnie brought in Angus and the parson and they warmed themselves at the fire. Aunt Ellen had never seen a stranger before in her life and she was a little frightened. But she acknowledged the introductions and then busied herself getting them some hot soup made from boiled bones, and they said it was very good. She stopped flashing questioning glances at Jonnie and was pleased with them.

"Chrissie found you?" she finally ventured to ask.

"Chrissie is alive," said Jonnie. "So is Pattie." No alarm, don't alarm them.

"I'm so glad! I was so worried. But she would ride off! Your horse eventually came back, you know." She started to cry again and then came over and gave Jonnie a violent hug. She went off to prepare beds for them in case they spent the night.

Jonnie went out and found the small child who had spotted them and sent him up the hill to recall the party that had been after the deer.

It was past four when he finally got the town council assembled. He was surprised that it was only old Jimson and Brown Limper Staffor. The third member had died recently and no other was appointed. Jonnie had gotten a fire going in the courthouse and propped the door back up.

He introduced Angus and the parson, and the "town council" acknowledged them a bit worriedly: like Aunt Ellen they had never before seen strangers. But Angus and the parson withdrew inconspicuously to the side.

Jonnie made his business known to the town council. No alarm. He told them he had discovered the valley was unhealthy and that was why they had so few children and so many deaths, and that he had originally gone off to find a better location and had finally done so. The new town was very nice: it had water available in the main street and less snow and more game and better houses and even some black rock that burned very hot, and it was a very nice place. It was a good plea and very well presented.

Old Jimson was interested and looked very favorable. He consulted with Brown Limper as was correct.

Brown Limper held old grudges against Jonnie. Look what had happened. Jonnie had gone off and this had drawn away Chrissie and Pattie—probably to their deaths—and now here was Jonnie Goodboy Tyler turned up a year and a half or more later with some demand that they move their homes. These *were* their homes. They had always been safe here. And that was that.

They took a vote. It was a tie. The town council didn't know what to do.

"There used to be a village assembly, a town meeting," said Jonnie.

"There hasn't been one in all my life," said Brown Limper

"Yes, I know of those," said Jimson. "One was held thirty years ago to change the location of the stock pens."

"As the council is tied," said Jonnie, "it should call a town meeting."

Brown Limper didn't like it, but there was nothing else they could do. By this time several people had drifted by from curiosity and Jonnie had no trouble sending word out to collect the people into the courthouse.

It was five and dark when they all came. Jonnie had gotten more wood and built up the fire. He knew better than to light a miner's lamp for illumination.

When at last he looked at them, sitting on benches and on the floor, faces bathed in the firelight of the smoky room, he felt very bad. They were a beaten people. They were gaunt, some of them ill. The children were too quiet. There were only twenty-eight now.

A flaming rage at the Psychlos surged up in him.

He made himself very calm. He smiled at them when he felt more like weeping.

Jonnie began, with the council's permission, by opening up his pack.

There were gifts. He handed out some dried meat, some bundles of kinnikinnick for food flavoring, and some very live flints that would strike long trains of sparks. The people found these very acceptable and thanked him. Then Jonnie took out some stainless steel axes and showed them what they would do by cutting a large piece of firewood with one blow. The people were impressed. Jonnie handed them out as presents. That done, he got out a bundle of stainless steel knives. When he showed how they cut—warning them not to cut their fingers—the women were quite excited. He handed those around.

Finally he got down to business and told them all about the new town and how easy it would be to move—he didn't tell them they would be flown to it, for he knew he would have sacrificed credibility.

No one asked questions when they were invited. Jonnie had a foreboding.

He took a triangle of broken glass from his pouch and showed them that you could see through it. He told them that in the new town a lot of the windows had this in them and it let light in and kept the cold out. He passed the glass around. A little boy cut himself on it slightly and the glass was quickly handed back.

He told them this valley was making them ill. That it had a poison in it that made it difficult to have children.

With a pleading look on his face, he let old Jimson put it to a vote. All those in favor of moving. Count. All those in favor of staying here. Count.

Three in favor. Fifteen against. They wouldn't count the children.

Jonnie would not let it go. He rose. "Please tell me," he demanded of them, "why you take this decision?"

An elderly man, Torrence Marshall, rose, looked around to see whether it was all right, and then spoke. "This is our home. We are safe here. We thank you for the gifts. We are glad *you* are home." He sat down.

Brown Limper looked smug. The people wandered off quietly to their suppers.

Jonnie sat down. He held his head in his hands, defeated.

He felt the parson's hand on his shoulder. " 'Tis seldom," said the parson, "that a man is a king in his own country."

"It's not that," said Jonnie. "It's just that . . ." He couldn't finish. Over and over in his head went the words: "My poor people. Oh, my poor people."

Later that night, he went up to the knoll where the cemetery had been. He searched through the snow until he found the cross of his father's grave. It had fallen over. He put it back in place and scratched the name on it. For a long cold time he stood looking down at the slight mound. His father had seen no sense in moving the village.

Were all his people going to die here? The bitter winter wind moaned down from Highpeak.

— 5 —

"Wake up, Jonnie! Wake up! It *flashed!*"

Jonnie pried himself awake. It was still dark, though dawn was late at this season of the year. It was disorienting to find himself in his own room with Angus shaking him and a miner's light burning on the table.

Suddenly he grasped the import of what Angus was saying and got up and began to get into his buckskins.

Angus had awakened very early and had been thirsty, and Aunt Ellen had heard him clattering around the buckets. There had been no water and Angus didn't like eating snow, so Aunt Ellen had said she would go get some water. But Angus said no, he'd get the water if she showed him where it was, and she pointed out the spring where everybody got their water on the edge of the village, and he took a hide bucket and went. Because he'd promised Jonnie not to go anywhere without testing, he'd taken a vial of breathe-gas and the remote, and he had been tossing the breathe-gas bottle thirty feet ahead of him and turning it on and off and WHAM, it flashed!

Hopping about with excitement, Angus was handing Jonnie bits of clothing to rush him on. He pushed Jonnie out the door and they walked toward the spring at the village edge.

Angus stopped him. He triggered the remote.

WHAM!

There was a flash and thud of breathe-gas exploding.

The parson, awakened by the commotion, joined them. Angus did it again for his benefit.

A sudden chill came over Jonnie, and not from the morning cold. That flash was right alongside the path where the villagers went two and three times a day for water. And more. As a little boy he had been a mutineer on a subject of what work he would do. He was a *man*, he had said—illogically since he had begun this soon after he could walk—and he would *hunt*, but he would not sweep floors or bring water. And he never had fetched water from that spring. He had even watered his horses at another spring way up the slope. The chill came from his certainty that he himself was not immune to radiation. He had simply never gone to that spring. By a fluke he had escaped contamination. All because hide buckets slopped on him.

But the villagers, particularly the children and women and older people who did draw water, were daily being hit with radiation. He felt a deeper chill for his people.

Angus wanted to dash up and dig under the snow. Jonnie, aided by the parson, held him back.

"We've no protective shields," said Jonnie. "We need lead, lead glass, something. But let's mark this out so it becomes a prohibited zone, and then let's look further."

They found by cautious sallies that the radiation from that spot extended, with enough force to explode breathe-gas, about thirty feet in all directions. Angus apparently had hit it dead center. They marked the ring with ashes taken from an abandoned cabin hearth, and with an axe Jonnie collected some stakes and drove them in to form a circle. Jonnie took some plaited rope and wound it around the stakes.

Jimson, along with some others attracted by the explosions, wanted to know what they were doing. Jonnie left it to the parson. As he worked he heard fragments of the parson's explanation. Something about spirits. But whatever it was Jimson shortly began to route people around the spot in a businesslike way. Jonnie was sure it would become taboo to walk within that circle. It was only a few steps further to avoid it altogether.

Dawn was there. They had to work fast to be out of there before midday, and there might be other spots. The recon drone passed near here and lately was overflying around noon. He wanted no pictures of this operation on Terl's screens. A circle of rope was nothing; it would look like a stock corral. Tracks were nothing. People and horses and dogs wandered around. But the plane up the canyon and three differently garbed people were something else.

While they chewed some breakfast Aunt Ellen brought them, Jonnie looked out across the expansive meadow. What a lot of ground to cover!

He made up his mind. It was a risk, but very brief exposures, according to toxicology texts, could be tolerated.

He got an air mask and bottles out of the gear Angus had brought. He filled his pockets with breathe-gas flasks. He got a bucket of ashes. He got on one of their horses.

"I am going to crisscross this meadow at a dead run," he told Angus and the parson. "Back and forth and back and forth on paths thirty feet apart. I'll be holding a breathe-gas vial in my hand, turned slightly on. Every time it flashes, I'll throw down a handful of ashes and then hold up my arm. Now, parson, I want you to stand on that knoll and make a sketch of this valley, and you, Angus, tell him each time I hold up my hand. Got it?"

They got it. The parson went up to the knoll with a pad and pen and Angus following him.

The three young men who had voted to move wanted to know

whether they could help. Jonnie told them yes, they could have fresh horses ready.

Jonnie looked around. All was ready. The red-gold sun made the snow glisten. He made sure his air mask was tight, opened the breathe-gas vial, and put a heel to the horse.

Only a minute later the vial in his hand flashed. He threw down ashes, raised his arm, and sped on at a dead run. Angus's yell floated to him on the still air. The parson was marking it on his sketch.

Back and forth, back and forth across the meadow. A flash, a handful of ashes, a raised hand, the echo of Angus's yell and the thud of the flying hoofs.

He took a new horse, opened a new bottle, and was off again.

Villagers gazed dully on the scene. Jonnie Goodboy had often done strange things. Yes, he *was* quite a horseman. Everybody knew that. It was a bit of a mystery why he kept lighting a torch every now and then. But old Jimson had some explanation from the clergyman who had come with Jonnie—a real clergyman from some village named Scotland. They hadn't known there was any nearby village. Oh, yes, there had been. It was a long time ago. It was a couple of ridges over. Well, in all this snow one didn't get a chance to get about much. But Jonnie Goodboy sure could ride, couldn't he? Look at the snow fly!

Two hours, four lathered horses, sixteen vials of breathe-gas, and a tired Jonnie later, they got ready to take their leave. They were a bit pressed for time, too pressed to evaluate the map.

They had decided to leave the horses as a gift and would have to walk to the plane.

The parson was explaining to Jimson that people must stay well away from those ash marks, and Jimson respectfully said he would see to it even if Brown Limper was skeptical.

Aunt Ellen was looking frightened. "You're leaving again, Jonnie." She was trying to work out how to tell him that he was the only family she had.

"Would you like to come with me?" said Jonnie.

Well no. This was their home, Jonnie. He should come back. Going to wild places was in his blood, she guessed.

He promised to try to come back and then gave her some gifts he had saved until last: a great big stainless steel kettle and three knives and a fur robe with sleeves in it!

She pretended to like that very much, but she was crying when he turned back at the edge of the upper path and waved. She had a horrible feeling she would never see him again.

— 6 —

It was an intense hum of intent men in the room of the old mining town near the lode. Several groups were hard at work.

It had amused the Scots very much to take over the offices of the [''Empire Dauntless Mining Corporation'']. The building had been almost intact and when cleaned up made an acceptable operations room.

Jonnie half-suspected that somebody had rebuilt the town after the lead lode mine had played out. It was too unlike other towns. He tried to figure out why anyone would reconstruct a town after its ore was gone, but evidence certainly showed someone had. Next door was a place called the [''Bucket of Blood Saloon''] that the parson had gravely put ''off limits.'' It still had its glasses and mirrors intact, and paintings of nearly nude dancing girls and cupids could dimly be made out. Across the street was an office labeled [''Wells Fargo''] and another one labeled [''Jail''].

They all lived in the [''London Palace Elite Hotel''], which had labeled suites named after men who must have been famous in mining. Three of the old widows queened it over a coal-burning galley Angus had explained to them. It had running water—luxury!

The [''Empire Dauntless''] offices contained what must have been working models of the mine, and they had found [''history pamphlets''] in it that talked about the good old wild days of a boom camp and [''bad men'']. Also curious little leaflets that said [''Tour Schedules''] and had a daily time and place scheduled for a [''bank hold-up'']. Paintings of prospectors and mine discoverers and [''bad men''] had been cleaned off and put back on the walls.

Robert the Fox and two pilots were studiously going over possible plans to hijack an ore freighter. They had no craft that could possibly fly to Scotland or Europe, for their mine equipment could only go a few hundred miles. They had been going around and around this problem ever since the night the demon had told them about "bomber drones." They felt they had a responsibility to alert not only the Scots but other peoples they might find traces of. They dared not alert the Psychlos they were up to anything. To intercept in the air, leaving the Psychlos to believe the freighter had gone down over the sea, was the only thing they kept coming up with. But to silence the Psychlo pilot radio, to board a freighter plane to plane in midair. were some of the things they couldn't work out.

Another group—two of the leaders who were off shift, with Thor and Dunneldeen and some of the miners—were going over mining progress. They had gotten down to the lode and were drifting along it inch by inch toward the cliff. The quartz they were taking out was pure and beautiful, but it had no gold in it. Jonnie had explained to them, from references, that it was a lode with pockets. Wire gold veins only had pockets of gold every few hundred feet. It was not continuous valuable ore. They were getting tired of mining pure white quartz with no gold to show for it. They were trying to figure out how close they were to the fissure in the cliff. It had widened a tiny amount, which worried them.

The historian, Doctor MacDermott, was off by himself, chair tilted against a wall, reading industriously from things his scout had lately brought in from a collapsed school library in a little mining town.

Jonnie, Angus, the parson, and the schoolmaster were clustered over the parson's sketch of the valley.

The positions of the live radiation points were in a line. At first Jonnie had thought it might be a vein of uranite popping to the surface at intervals. But the points were too regular.

"They are roughly one hundred feet apart," said Jonnie. "In a straight line."

They were staring at the map, thinking, when Doctor MacDermott came over.

"It's something funny I've got here, MacTyler," said the historian, shaking his book. "The Chinko guidebook was mistaken about the Air Force Academy."

Jonnie shrugged. "They often said things just to please the Psychlos."

"But they called the Academy a primary defense base."

"I know," said Jonnie. "They wanted it to sound big because it was the last battle fought on the planet."

"But there *was* a 'primary defense base,' " said the historian, shaking the book he held.

Jonnie looked at it. It was [''Regulations Regarding and Governing the Evacuation of School Children in Event of Atomic War, Department of Civil Defense''].

"Apparently," said the historian, "the children were to be kept in school until the town mayor was flown out of the city . . . no . . . ah, here it is: ['and that all orders thereafter shall be issued from the primary defense base']."

"But we don't know where that was," said Jonnie.

The old man scuttled back to his pile of books. "Yes, we do!" He came back with a volume concerning congressional hearings into cost overruns of military budgets. MacDermott opened the volume to where he had marked it. He read, "['Question by Senator Aldrich: The Secretary of Defense then freely admits that the overrun of one point six billion dollars in the construction of the primary defense base in the Rocky Mountains was incurred without congressional authority. Is that correct, Mr. Secretary?']" MacDermott showed Jonnie and slapped the book shut. "So the Chinkos were wrong while they were being right. There *was* a 'primary defense base' and it was in the Rocky Mountains." He smiled primly and started back to his chair.

Jonnie went very still.

The tomb!

The iron doors, the dead troops on the stairs.

The tomb!

"Doctor Mac," Jonnie called. "Come back here."

He showed him the sketch. "You told us a story once about a line of nuclear mines laid by the Queen's Own Highlanders from Dumbarton to Falkirk."

The historian nodded. He was looking at the sketch. "Did you find some wrecked remains of Psychlo tanks?" he said.

"No," said Jonnie. "But look. This line goes exactly across the exit from the pass from the lower plains. They're exactly spaced. They're in an exact straight line."

"But with no tanks—" said the parson.

"They never exploded!" said Jonnie. "Time has just made them fall apart."

"How did you guess this?" said the historian.

Jonnie smiled. It was a little bit hard to speak. He indicated the sketch to cover his surge of emotion. After a moment he said,

"That pass leads up from the western plain to the meadow. And behind that meadow there is a canyon that goes up into the mountains, and way up that canyon is the primary defense base of the ancient government of man!" He filled in the rest of the sketch.

Other groups had sensed something was happening. They began drifting over.

Jonnie felt like crying. He swallowed hard.

"I wondered where they sent all the uranium they'd mined. I knew it must be *somewhere*. . . ."

The parson touched his arm, not wanting him to run into a future failure with a crash. "They would not have it in the base, laddie."

"But the base records will tell us where it is!" said Jonnie. "It would have maps, wires of communication . . . I know we'll crack this *there!*"

Angus had been staring at the sketch. "Ooh!" he was saying to himself. "Land mines! And I was just going to burrow in!"

Robert the Fox was already gathering up those in charge to begin their expedition to the tomb.

The historian was diving for references that would tell them the perils of entering tombs.

"Don't fret, laddie," said the parson to Jonnie, who was just sitting there staring. "Dawning will tell us if it's true."

■

PART 10

— 1 —

The doors were cracked open, just as he had left them so many years ago. Lying there, crusted with snow but just where he had dropped it, was the iron bar he had used to open the doors. The smell might or might not be there, for he was now wearing an air mask.

They had left just as soon as they could see to fly, and Jonnie had spotted them down accurately just before the door. Behind him in the canyon the Scots were unloading gear. The plane would have to leave and they would have to obliterate all tracks with snow before the recon drone came over on its daily round.

The calm voice of Robert the Fox was directing them: "Have you got the lamps? Check out the spare air bottles. Where is Daniel? Easy with those explosives. . . ."

A Scot came up with a sledge hammer to open the door wider and Angus rushed over and pushed him aside. "No. No. No. 'Tis just wanting a bit of penetrating oil." Angus was popping the bottom of an oilcan. His voice sounded muffled through the air mask.

They were all getting air masks on. The historian had found it was very unhealthy to enter tombs. Something called "spores" sometimes came off bone dust of the long dead and made a man cough his lungs out.

"Mind if I slip in first, Jonnie?" said Angus. Jonnie took his shoulder pack so Angus could slide through. The mine lamp played on the interior. "Och! Enough dead men!" His oilcan was popping on hinges. "Try it, Jonnie."

Jonnie put his shoulder to the doors and they swung back, shooting a blast of light down the stairs. Angus had stepped out of the way and was now wading on littered corpses, puffs of bone dust rising around his boots.

They all stood for a moment, looking down the steps, awed.

On this graveyard of a planet, they were no strangers to dead remains. They lay in structures and basements in abundance wherever there was any protection from wild animals or the weather, corpses more than a thousand years dead.

But reaching down this long flight of stairs were the remains of several hundred men. Protected from the air until a dozen years ago, their clothing, arms, and equipment were somewhat preserved, but the bones had gone to powder.

"They fell forward," said Robert the Fox. "Must have been a regiment marching *in*. See? These two fellows at the top of the steps must have been closing the doors."

"The gas," said Jonnie. "They opened the doors to let the regiment in, looks like, and the gas hit them from the canyon."

"Wiped the place out," said Robert the Fox. "Listen, all of you. Don't go in there without a tight air mask."

"We ought to bury these men," said the parson. "They each have little tags on them," he picked one up. [" 'Knowlins, Peter, Private USMC No. 35473524. Blood Type B.' "]

"Marines," said the historian. "We've got a military base here all right."

"Do you suppose," said the parson to Jonnie, "that village of yours could once have been a marine base? It is different than other towns."

"The village has been rebuilt a dozen times," said Jonnie. "Robert, let's go in."

"Remember your priorities," said Robert to the group. "Inventory only. Don't touch records until they're identified. This is a big place. Don't stray or get lost."

"We ought to bury these bodies," said the parson.

"We will, we will," said Robert. "All in good time. Gunners forward. Flush out and destroy any animals."

Five Scots carrying submachine guns raced down the steps, alert for bears or snakes in hibernation or stray wolves.

"Ventilation team, stand by," said Robert, and glanced over his shoulder to make sure the three assigned to carry the heavy mine ventilation fans were there and ready.

There was an uneven burst of fire below. The sub-Thompson

ammunition was dud two rounds out of five, and to get a sustained burst one had to recock the bolt in mid-fire.

Robert's small limited-range radio crackled. "Rattlesnakes. Four. All dead. End com."

"Aye," said Robert the Fox into the mike.

There was another ragged burst of fire.

The radio crackled. "Brown bear. Hibernating. Dead. End com."

"Aye," said Robert.

"Second set of doors, tight locked."

"Explosives team," Robert called over his shoulder.

"Naw, naw!" said Angus. "We may need those doors!"

"Go ahead," said Robert. "Belay explosives team, but stand by." Into the mike, "Mechanic en route."

They waited. The radio crackled. "Doors open." A pause. "Area beyond seems airtight. Probably no hostile animals beyond. End com."

"Ventilation team. Forward," said Robert.

The last man on that team was carrying a cage of rats.

Presently a current of air began to come out of the tomb.

The radio crackled: "Rats still alive. End com."

"There you are, MacTyler," said Robert.

Jonnie checked his face mask and walked down through the dust of the stairs. He heard Robert firing the rest of the teams behind him and then giving orders to clean up the outside area and dust all traces with snow when the planes left. The orders sounded way off and thin in the booming caverns of the primary defense base of a long-dead nation.

— 2 —

Jonnie's miner's lamp played upon the floors and walls of what seemed like endless corridors and rooms.

The place was huge. Offices, offices, offices. Barracks. Storerooms. Their footsteps resounded hollowly, disturbing the millennia-long sleep of the dead.

The first find was a stack of duplicated routing plans for the base. A Scot found them in a reception desk drawer. They were not very detailed, apparently intended to route visiting officers around. The Scot got permission to distribute and, racing up, miner's lamp bobbing, shoved a copy into Jonnie's hand.

Level after level existed. There was not just a maze at one level but also mazes down, down, and down.

He was looking for an operations office, someplace where dispatches might mount up, where information was collected. Operations . . . operations . . . where would that be?

Behind him an argument broke out. It was Angus and Robert the Fox at the other end of the corridor.

Angus's voice was raised. "I *know* it's all by elevators!"

There was a murmur from Robert.

"I *know* it's all electrical. I've been through all this before at the first school! Electrical, electrical, electrical! It takes generators. And they're just piles of congealed rust! Even if you got one to run, there's no fuel—it's just sludge in the tanks. And even if you put in juice, those light bulbs won't work and the electric motors are frozen solid."

Robert murmured something.

"Sure the wires may be all right. But even if you got juice in them, all you'd have is an intercom and we've *got* that. So stick to miner's lamps! I'm sorry, Sir Robert, but there's just so much dinosaur you can revive from a pile of bones!"

Jonnie heard Robert laughing. He himself differed a little bit with Angus's point of view. They did not know that there weren't emergency systems that might work some other way, and they did not know that there might not be other fuels in sealed containers that might still function. The chances were thin, but they could not be ruled out. They were despairingly going to rig mine cables to get to the other levels when a Scot found ramps and stairwells going down.

Operations . . . operations . . .

They found a communications console, the communicator's remains at the desk. Under the dust that had been his hand was a message:

["URGENT. Don't fire. It isn't the Russians."]

"Russians? Russians?" said a Scot. "Who were the Russians?"

Thor had come, absent without leave from his shift at the lode but intending to get back. He was part Swedish "They're some people that used to live on the other side of Sweden. They were run by the Swedes once."

"Don't disturb any messages," said Robert the Fox.

Operations . . . operations . . .

They found themselves in an enormous room. It had a huge map of the world on a middle table. Apparently clerks with long poles pushed little models around on the map. There were side-wall maps and a balcony overlooking it. Miner's lamps flicked over maps, models, and the remains of the dead. Impressive and well preserved. There were lots of clocks, all stopped long ago.

A crude, hastily made cylinder model rested on the map just east of the Rockies. A long pole was still touching it, the last action of a dead arm. Another map on the wall was plotting the course of something and the last ["X"] was straight above this base.

It was too much data to sort out in a moment. Jonnie went on looking.

They found themselves in a nearby room. It had lots of consoles. ["Top Secret"] had been the name of this room.

One console said ["Local Defense"] and had a chart and map over it. Jonnie went to it and looked closely. ["TNW Minefields"], he read.

Then suddenly he found himself looking at marks of the string mines in the meadow below them. ["TNW 15"].

There was a firing button: ["TNW 15"]. But there were rows and rows of these buttons.

TNW? TNW?

The reedy voice of the historian piped up behind him. " 'TNW' means 'tactical nuclear weapons.' Those are the mines!"

Angus came over. "Och! Electrical firing buttons. You push the console button and up they go."

"Might also be fused for contact," said Jonnie cautiously. "No wonder the Psychlos thought these mountains were radioactive!"

"What's a 'silo'?" said the parson at another board. "It says ['Silo 1,' 'Silo 2'] and so on."

"A silo," said Thor, "is where you keep wheat. They used to have them in Sweden. You put wheat in them for storage."

"I can't imagine why they'd be that interested in wheat. Look at the way these buttons are marked. ['Standby,' 'Ready,' 'Fire']."

The historian was hastily riffling through a dictionary he

habitually carried. He found it. ["'1. A cylindrical upright storage facility for wheat, grain, and other foodstuffs. 2. A large, underground structure for the storage and launching of a long-range ballistic missile.' "]

Jonnie reached out and grabbed the parson's wrist. "Don't touch that console! It could contain emergency systems about which we know nothing." He turned, excited. "Robert, get this whole board and layout picto-recorded. We have to know the exact location of every silo on that board. Those missiles might have uranium in them!"

— 3 —

They were in a storeroom area now. Angus had found a huge ring of keys and was scampering ahead of Jonnie, opening doors. Robert the Fox was following more sedately; he had his worn old cape wrapped very tightly about him for it was bitterly cold in this place—probably the temperature seldom rose much, even in summer. Robert's radio crackled occasionally as some Scot elsewhere reported in—the radios worked well underground, designed for miner use.

Jonnie had not yet found all he wanted by a long shot. The planning of a battle against an enemy whose battle tactics were all but unknown was a chancy business. And he did not yet know exactly how the Psychlos had done it. So he had half an ear to Robert's radio and was not paying all that much attention to Angus.

They were at a heavy door that said ["Arsenal"] and Angus was changing keys about to open it. Some faint hope that it might contain nuclear weapons rose in Jonnie. The door opened.

Boxes! Cases! Endless rows of them!

Jonnie played his lamp over the stencils. He did not know what all these letters meant: this military certainly loved to obscure things under letters and numbers.

Angus danced up with a book, fluttering the well-preserved pages. [" 'Ordnance, Types and Models'!"] he crooned. "All the numbers and letters will be here. Even pictures!"

"Inventory that," said Robert the Fox to a Scot beside him who was making lists.

"Bazooka!" said Angus. "There, up there! Those long boxes! ['Antitank, armor-piercing missile projectiles']."

"Nuclear?" asked Jonnie.

"Non-nuclear. Says so."

"I think," said Robert, "this is just their local arsenal for possible base use. They wouldn't be supplying the whole army from this spot."

"Lots of it," said Angus.

"Enough for a few thousand men," said Robert.

"Can I open a box?" asked Angus to Robert.

"One or two for now just to ascertain condition," said Robert and waved a couple of the following Scots forward to assist.

Angus was flipping through the catalogue, miner's lamp dancing on the pages. "Ah, here! ['Thompson submachine gun' . . .]" He stopped and looked up at the boxes. He shook his head and looked back at the page. "No wonder!"

"No wonder what?" prompted Robert, a bit impatient. The recon drone must have passed overhead by this time, and they had had no lunch and needed a break to recharge their air bottles outside.

"That ammunition we found was very well preserved. Airtight. Well, it maybe had to be. This sub-Thompson was a century out of date when we found the truckload. They must have just been sending them to the cadets to practice with. They were relics!"

Jonnie was not about to try to fight Psychlos with sub-Thompsons. He started to pass on.

Boxes were being opened behind him. Angus raced up. His lamp was shining on an all-metal, lightweight hand rifle. It was block-solid covered with grease that ages ago had formed into a tight, hard cast.

"Mark fifty assault rifle!" said Angus. "The last thing they issued! I can clean these up so they purr!"

Jonnie nodded. It was a sleek weapon.

["MAGAZINE"] said the door ahead of him. It was a doubly thick door. Meant ammunition. Maybe tactical nuclear weapons?

Angus let another Scot open it for him. He was back there rummaging in cases.

A box right ahead, standing among vast tiers of boxes, said ["Ammunition, Mark 50 Assault"]. Jonnie took a jimmy out of his belt and pried open the top. It was not airtight. The cardboard dividers were decayed and stained. The brass was okay and the bullet clean, but the primer at the bottom told its tale. The ammunition was dud. He called Angus and showed him the cartridge.

They went on looking for nuclear weapons.

More storerooms and more storerooms.

And then pay dirt!

Jonnie found himself looking at literally thousands of outfits, neatly arranged on shelves, even with sizes, complete with shoes and face-plated helmets, packed in a kind of plastic that was airtight and nearly imperishable: [''COMBAT RADIATION PROTECTION UNIFORMS''].

His excited hands ripped open a package. Lead-impregnated clothing. Lead-glass faceplates.

And in mountain camouflage: gray, tan, and green.

Riches! The one thing that would let them handle radiation!

He showed Robert the Fox. Robert put it on the radio as real news but told the others to go on with their own searches and inventories.

They were on their way outside for food and air when another piece of news came through. It was Dunneldeen. Apparently he had relieved Thor, who had to go on shift at the mine. Dunneldeen wasn't even supposed to be there. ''We got some great big huge security safes here,'' Dunneldeen's voice came over the radio. ''No combination. One is marked ['Top Secret Nuclear'] and ['Classified Personnel Only.' 'Manuals.'] We need an explosives team. End com.''

He guided them to him. Robert the Fox looked at Angus and Angus shook his head. ''No keys,'' said Angus.

The explosives team rigged nonflame blasting cartridges to the hinges and everyone went into the next corridor while the explosives team trailed wire. They held their ears. The concussion was head-splitting. A moment later they heard the crash of a door hitting the floor. The fire member of the team raced in with an extinguisher but it was not needed.

Lamps beamed through the settling dust.

Presently they were holding in their hands operations manuals, maintenance manuals, repair manuals, hundreds and hundreds of separate manuals that gave every particular of every nuclear device that had been built, how to set it, fire it, fuse and defuse it, store it, handle it, and safeguard it.

"Now we've got everything but the nuclear devices," said Robert the Fox.

"Yes," said Jonnie. "You can't shoot with papers!"

— 4 —

It must have been night outside, but nothing could be darker than the deep guts of this ancient defense base. The black seemed to press in upon them as though possessed of actual weight. The miner's lamps were darting shafts through ink.

They had come down a ramp, gone through an air-sealed door, and found an enormous cavern. The sign said ["Heliport"]. The time-decayed bulks of collapsed metal that stood along the walls had been some kind of planes, planes with large fans on top. Jonnie had seen pictures of them in the man-books: they were called "helicopters." He stared at the single one sitting in the middle of the vast floor.

The small party of Scots with him were interested in something else. The doors! They were huge, made of metal, reaching far right and far left and up beyond their sight. Another entrance to the base—a fly-in entrance for their type of craft.

Angus was scrambling around some motors to the side of the doors. "Electrical. Electrical! I wonder if these poor lads ever thought there would be a day when you had to do something manually. What if the power failed?"

"It's failed," said Robert the Fox, his low voice booming in the vast hangar.

"Call me the lamp boys," said Angus. And presently the two Scots who were packing lamps, batteries, wires, and fuses for their own lighting trotted down the ramp, pushing their gear ahead of them on a dolly they had found.

Hammering began over by the motors that operated the doors.

Robert the Fox came over to Jonnie. "If we can get those doors to open and close we can fly in and out of here. There's a sighting port over there and it shows the outside looks like a cave opening, overhung, not visible to the drone."

Jonnie nodded. But he was looking at the center helicopter. The air was different here; he could feel it on his hands. Drier. He went over to the helicopter.

Yes, there was his eagle. With arrows in its claws, dim but huge on the side of this machine. Not like the other machines, which had minor insignia. He made out the letters: [''President of the United States'']. This was a special plane!

The historian answered his pointing finger. ''Head of the country. Commander in Chief of the Armed Forces.''

Jonnie was puzzled. Yes, possibly he had gotten here on that day of disaster a thousand or more years ago. But if so, where was he? There had been no such sign on the offices. He walked around the hangar. Ha! There was another elevator, a smaller one in a different place. He looked further and found a door to a stairwell that led upward. The door was hard to open, apparently air-sealed. He got through it and mounted upward. Behind him the hammer and clang of the group faded and died. There was only the soft pat of his feet on the stairs.

Another air-sealed door at the top, even harder to open.

This was an entirely different complex. It stood independent of the rest of the base. And due to dry air and seals and possibly something else, the bodies were not dust. They were mummified. Officers on the floor, slumped over desks. Only a few.

Communication and file rooms. A briefing room with few chairs. A bar with glasses and bottles intact. Very superior grade of furnishings. Carpets. All very well preserved. Then he saw the door symbol he was looking for and went in.

The sign was on the splendid polished desk. A huge eagle plaque on the wall. A flag, with some of its fabric still able to stir when he caused a faint breeze opening the door.

The man was slumped over the desk, mummified. Even his clothing still looked neat.

Jonnie looked under the parchment hand and without touching it slid out the sheaf of papers.

The top date and the hour were two days later than the ones that ended in the operations room in the other complex.

The only explanation Jonnie could think of was that the ventilation systems didn't join: when gas hit the main base, the system was turned off here. And they had not dared turn it back on.

The president and his staff had died from lack of air.

Jonnie felt strangely courteous and respectful as he removed more papers from the desk and trays. He held in his hands the last hours of the world, report by report. Even pictures and something from high up called [''satellite pictures''].

He hastily skimmed through the reports to make sure he had it all.

A strange object had appeared over London without any trace of where it came from.

Teleportation, filled in Jonnie.

It had been at an altitude of 30,000 feet.

Important, thought Jonnie.

It had dropped a canister and within minutes the south of England was dead.

Psychlo gas. The myths and legends.

It had cruised eastward at 302.6 miles per hour.

Vital data, thought Jonnie.

It had been attacked by fighter planes from Norway; it had not fought back; it had been hit with everything they had without the slightest evidence of damage to it.

Armor, thought Jonnie.

An interchange on something called the [''hotline''] prevented a nuclear missile exchange between the United States and Russia.

The ''Don't fire; it isn't the Russians'' message on the desk in the other complex, thought Jonnie.

It was hit with nuclear weapons over Germany without the slightest apparent damage.

No pilots, thought Jonnie. It was a drone. No breathe-gas in it. Very heavy motors.

It had then toured the major population centers of the world, dropping canisters and wiping out populations.

And wiped out the other complex of this base without even knowing or caring that it was there, thought Jonnie. On the operations map of the other complex, they had plotted it only just to the east of this location.

It then went on to obliterate the eastern part of the United States. The reports had come in from [''Dew Line''] stations in the Arctic and some parts of Canada. It continued on its almost leisurely way to wipe out all population centers in the southern hemisphere. But at this point something else began to happen. Isolated observers and satellites reported tanks of a strange design materializing one after the other in various parts of the world and mopping up fleeing hordes of human beings.

Stage two; teleportation, thought Jonnie.

Military reports, out of sequence and incomplete, were shuffled in with the reports of the tanks. All major military airfield installations, whether gassed out of existence or not, were being blown to bits by strange, very fast flying craft.

Battle planes teleported in at the same time as the tanks.

Reports of some tanks exploding, some battle planes exploding. Reasons not known.

Manned craft, thought Jonnie. Breathe-gas hitting areas of radiation caused by firing on the drone with nuclear weapons.

The drone spotted by satellite landing near Colorado City, Colorado. Causes most structures there to collapse.

Preset remote control, thought Jonnie. Even their central command minesite had been picked out. Whole area carefully plotted and observed by casting picto-recorders. Rough, uncontrolled landing of drone near preplanned command area.

Tank spotted by satellite shooting at pocket of cadets wearing flight oxygen masks at the Air Force Academy. Report by acting commander of corps of cadets. Then no further communication.

The last battle, thought Jonnie.

Efforts from the com room to contact somebody, anybody, anywhere, via a remote antennae located three hundred miles to the north. Antennae location bombed by enemy battle plane.

Radio tracking, thought Jonnie.

Unspotted, but with their air shut off, the president and his aides and staff had lasted two more hours until they died of asphyxiation.

Jonnie put the papers respectfully in a protecting mine bag.

Feeling a bit strange for speaking, he said to the corpse, "I'm sorry no help came. We're something over a thousand years late." He felt very bad.

His gloom would have followed him as he left the dreary, dark, cold quarters had not the barking, cheery voice of Dunneldeen sprung from the radio at his belt. Jonnie halted and acknowledged.

"Jonnie, laddie!" said Dunneldeen. "You can stop worrying yourself about scraping uranium out of the dirt! There's a full nuclear arsenal, complete with assorted bombs, intact, just thirty miles north of here! We found the map and a plane just checked it out! Now all we've got to worry about is blowing off our innocent little heads and exploding this whole planet in the bargain!''

— 5 —

Disaster struck in the form of an earthquake on Day 32 of the new year.

Shortly after midnight, the tremor awakened Jonnie. Equipment on his bureau in the London Palace Elite Hotel rattled together and he sat up in his bed. The prolonged throb of vibration was still occurring!

The old building groaned.

The rumble of the earthquake traveled on. It was followed by a second, lesser tremor a half-minute later, and then that was gone.

It was not too unusual in the Rockies. No damage seemed to be done in the old mining town.

Uneasy but not really alarmed, Jonnie pulled on buckskin pants and moccasins and, throwing a puma skin over his shoulders, sprinted through the snow to the Empire Dauntless.

The duty sentry's light was on. The young Scot was tapping a buzzer key that activated the communication system to the mine: it was a directional laser radio, limited to an exact width and undetectable beyond these mountains.

The Scot looked up. His face was a bit white. ''They don't answer.'' He tapped the key again more rapidly as though his finger by itself could shoot the beam through. ''Maybe the receiver pole got twisted in the quake.''

In minutes, Jonnie had a relief crew routed out, spare ropes and winches assembled, blankets and stimulants packaged and being loaded on the passenger plane. Strained faces turned repeatedly toward the mine even though it was far out of their line of sight. They were worried for the mine duty shift: Thor, a shift leader named Dwight, and fifteen men.

The night was black as coal; even the stars were masked by high, invisible clouds. It was no mean stunt flying these mountains in the dark. The instruments of the mine plane glowed green as the ship vaulted upward. The image screen painted a blurred picture of the terrain ahead. Jonnie adjusted it to sharpness. Beside him a copilot made some console plane weight corrections. Jonnie was depending on his eyes to avoid the first mountain slope. He flipped on the plane's beam lights. They struck the snow slope and he eased the plane up over it.

He *knew* things had been going too well.

They had been making real progress in their preparations. They were far from ready, but what they had accomplished had been miraculous.

He hunted ahead for the next mountainside, checking the viewscreen. Good lord, it was dark! He checked his compass. The men in the back were tense and silent. He could almost feel what they were thinking.

The top knoll flipped by under them. A little too close. Where was the next one?

The assault rifles he had at first considered worthless were proving the very thing. With a great deal of ingenuity they had salvaged the ammunition. They had drawn out the bullets from the case and tapped out the primer. By careful experimentation they had found out how to substitute a blasting cap in the bottom of the shell case. At first they had thought they would also need powder and had blown up a rifle trying it—no casualties. It turned out that the blasting cap was enough to fire a bullet at high velocity.

Jonnie swerved the plane to avoid a suddenly looming cliff and went a little higher. If he went too high he could lose his way entirely if lights were out at the mine. His lights might also become visible at the compound. Stay low. Dangerous, but stay low.

Then they had taken the bullets and drilled a small hole in the nose and, wearing radiation suits, inserted a grain of radioactive material from a TNW. They had covered this with a thin bit of melted lead. In this way a man could carry the ammunition without danger of radiation hitting him.

But when it was fired, oh my! They tried it on breathe-gas in a glass bottle, and did that breathe-gas explode.

Too low. Jonnie had recognized a lone scrub on a ridge. He lifted the plane over it. They were on course. Hold down the speed. Don't have another disaster flying in the dark.

The bullets were also armor-piercing to some degree and,

when fired into a breathe-gas vial two hundred yards away, caused a violent reaction that brought concussion all the way back to them.

They put every available Scot onto an assembly line converting bullets and they had cases and cases of them now.

A hundred assault rifles and five hundred magazines had been cleaned to perfection. They fired without a stutter or dud.

No good against a tank or a thick, lead-glass compound dome, but those assault rifles would be deadly to individual Psychlos. With breathe-gas in their blood streams they would literally explode.

He spotted the river that ran out of the gorge. He eased down, following it, the plane's lights flashing on the uneven ice and snow.

They'd been so happy about the assault rifles that they had gone to work on the bazookas. They had found some nuclear artillery shells and had converted their noses over to the bazooka noses, and now they had armor-piercing, nuclear bazookas. There were still a number of those left to make.

Yes, it had been too smooth, too good to be true.

There were no lights on the mine pad ahead.

There was no one visible there at all.

He set the plane down on the pad.

The passengers boiled out of it.

Their lights darted this way and that.

One of them who had run to the chasm edge called back, his voice thin in the cold darkness: "Jonnie! The cliff face has gone!"

— 6 —

A light shone down from the present edge and confirmed it. The fissure, thirty feet back from the old edge, had simply opened in the earthquake and fallen into the gorge.

The cliff face was no longer overhanging but sloped up toward them.

In the light, the wide edge of the broken-off quartz lode was visible. It was pure white. No gold in the remaining vein. The pocket of gold was gone!

But Jonnie was thinking right now of the crew. They had not reached the fissure, for the avalanche had exposed no tunnel.

They were somehow trapped under them, if they were still alive.

Jonnie raced back to the shaft edge. It yawned blackly, a large circle of emptiness, silent. The shaft was about a hundred feet deep.

He looked around, flashing his light. "The hoist! Where is the hoist?"

The entire apparatus used to take out ore and lower and raise men was missing.

Lights played down the mountain. It was not on the slope.

Jonnie approached the hole more closely. Then he saw the slide marks of the cross timbers that had supported the hoist cage over the hole.

The hoist was down there in the shaft.

"Be very quiet, everyone," said Jonnie. Then he bent over and cupped his hands and shouted down, "Down there! Is anyone alive?"

They listened.

"I thought I heard something," said the parson, who had come along.

Jonnie tried again. They listened. They could not be sure. Jonnie turned on his belt radio and spoke into it. No answer. He saw Angus in the rescue team. "Angus! Drop an intercom on a cable down into that hole."

While Angus and two others were doing that, Jonnie pulled a picto-recorder out of the rescue gear. He found more cable and extended its leads.

Angus had rigged and lowered the intercom. Jonnie signaled to the parson. The place was broadly lit now with lamps the relief crew had put on poles. The parson's hand was shaking as he held the intercom mike.

"Hello the mine!" said the parson.

The intercom mike down there should pick up voices if there was any reply. There wasn't.

"Keep trying," said Jonnie. He paid out the line of the picto-recorder and lowered it into the hole. Robert the Fox stepped forward from the relief group and took charge of the portable screen.

At first there was just the shaft wall sliding by as the picto-recorder went down. Then a piece of timber, then a tangle of cable. Then the hoist!

Jonnie rotated the cable and shifted the remote control to wide-angle.

The hoist was empty.

A sigh of relief joined the night wind as the tense group saw that no one had been killed in the hoist.

Jonnie worked the remote to look over the hoist. It was hard to tell, but it did not appear there was anybody crushed under the fallen hoist.

The picto-recorder swung idly on its cable ninety feet below them. Eyes strained at the viewscreen, begging it for data.

"No drift hole!" said Jonnie. "The drift hole isn't visible! When the hoist fell it caved in the entrance to the drift down there!"

Pressing a flying platform into service, they flew a three-man crew down to the bottom of the drift. Robert the Fox wouldn't let Jonnie go down on it.

One of the men dropped down from the platform and fixed lifting hooks into the cage cable and they pulled it back up to the top of the hole.

They rigged a crane, pulleys, and a winch, and thirty-three minutes later—clocked by the historian who also had sneaked aboard the relief plane—they had the hoist out of the shaft and sitting off to the side.

Jonnie put the picto-recorder back down and it confirmed his guess. The shaft end of the level drift down there was blocked. knocked shut when the hoist fell.

They rigged buckets to crane cable and very shortly they had four men down at the bottom. Jonnie ignored Robert and went this time.

They tore at the rocks with their hands, filling up buckets that shot aloft to be replaced by empty ones. More tools and welcome sledges came down.

Two hours went by. They changed three of the men twice. Jonnie stayed down there.

They worked in a blur of speed. The rattle of rocks and thud of sledges freeing them resounded in the dusty hole bottom. The rockfall was thicker than they had hoped.

Two feet into the drift. Three feet. Four feet. Five feet. Maybe the whole drift had collapsed!

They changed crews. Jonnie stayed down there.

Three hours and sixteen minutes after their arrival at the bottom, Jonnie heard a distant whisper of sound. He held up his hand for silence. "In the mine!" he shouted.

Very faintly it came back: ". . . air hole . . ."

"Repeat!" shouted Jonnie.

It came back, ". . . make . . ."

Jonnie grabbed a long mine drill. He looked for the thinnest place he could imagine in the white rock wall before him, socked the rock drill point into it, and signaled the man on the drill motor. "Let her spin!"

They bucked the drill into it with the pressure handles. The others would hear it in there and get out of the way.

With a high scream the drill went through.

They dragged it out.

"Air hose!" yelled Jonnie. And they fed the hose through the drill hole and turned the air compressor on. Air from the drift squealed back past the sides of the hose and into the rescue crew's faces.

Twenty-one minutes later they had the top of the rockfall cleared and could drag men out.

They had to drop the gap farther to get the last one. It was Dunneldeen and he had a broken ankle and broken ribs.

Seventeen men, only one with a serious injury.

They passed them to the top silently in the hoist buckets.

A dust- and sweat-covered Jonnie was the last one up. The parson threw a blanket around him. The salvaged crew were bundled up, sitting in the snow, most of them drinking something hot that one of the old women had sent in a huge jug. The parson had finished setting the ankle of Dunneldeen and, helped by Robert the Fox, was taping up the ribs.

Finally Thor said, "We lost the lode."

Nobody said anything.

— 7 —

With dawn making a faint, pale line in the east, Jonnie looked down into thc abyss.

The pure white lode showed not the slightest trace of gold. It was in plain sight.

When the recon drone came over, Terl would have a picture of this. Far, far below, as yet invisible in the darkness, a new fall of rock would tell the story.

Jonnie tried to guess Terl's reaction. It was difficult to do so, for Terl was undoubtedly over his own edge into madness.

How many hours did Jonnie have until the drone? Not many.

The air was unaccountably still. The morning wind had not started up. The dawn light was reflected back from the surrounding majestic peaks.

Jonnie ran over to a flying platform and gestured to a pilot to join him. He lifted it up, put it over the edge of the chasm, and dropped it like a rocket to the bottom. He braked it and hovered.

Turning on the beam lights of the platform he examined the mass of fallen rock. Some of it had gone through the river ice. Some of it made a new bank for the stream. He played the light through the debris. It was an enormous mass.

Hopefully, he looked for some slightest whiteness that would indicate a piece of the lode.

None!

A ton of gold perhaps. But now it was buried under a mountain of rockfall, possibly even plunged into the river bottom.

The debris was so peaked and broken one couldn't even land on it. He tossed around the idea of clearing a flat place. But it would take hours and the winds would be here soon.

He had to face it. The gold was *gone*.

The morning wind was beginning to blow now. He couldn't stay down here and live to tell about it. If he had another short period of morning quiet he might do something. But they'd used up their time.

He sent the flying platform screaming up to the cliff top. It was already being buffeted by turbulent air. He landed.

He told Robert the Fox, "Get these men back to the town."

Jonnie walked back and forth. The parson looked at him in sympathy. "We aren't done yet, laddie," said the parson. The whole group looked to be in the shock of disappointment.

Robert the Fox was looking at Jonnie. They were loading the saved crew and two pilots were at the controls of the plane. Dunneldeen was being eased gently aboard.

"I'm going to do it!" said Jonnie suddenly.

Robert the Fox and the parson walked over.

"Terl," said Jonnie, "doesn't know how close that drift was to the inside of the lode. He doesn't know that we hadn't already mined the back of it. If he sees that white quartz out there he'll know we didn't get to it before the slide. Thor!" he shouted. "How close were you to the fissure?"

Thor asked the shift leader and they did some calculations. "About five feet," Thor finally shouted from the plane.

"I'll blow it in," said Jonnie. "It doesn't matter now if we blast. I'm going to blow the last end of the drift so it looks like it was through! Take that plane back fast and get me explosives and a shot-holer gun!"

He rattled off the exact explosives needed and the plane with the salvaged crew vibrated, ready to take off.

"And bring in the next shift!" shouted Jonnie. "We've very little time till the recon drone pass-over. Fly fast!" It was daylight now and they could. The plane roared off the pad.

Jonnie didn't wait for it to get back before he started to work. He went down the shaft, carrying some tools, got out of the bucket at the bottom, and made his way over the rubble and into the drift.

The crew's equipment was still lying about. The lamps were still on. Jonnie picked up a drill and began to make six-inch-deep holes all around the extreme edges of the white quartz. Two Scots picked up other drills and began to help him when they saw what he was doing: he was putting in shot holes.

While he worked he had others of the rescue team clear the remaining equipment out of the drift and take it above. No reason to waste that. Only the shift radio had been smashed in the rockfall. This drift would never be used again and it might well blow to bits.

He was surprised the plane came back so fast. He was in radio contact with the surface and he told them what he wanted down there.

Very shortly the explosives arrived. He put powerful, molding explosive into each one of the shot holes. Then on top of that he put a giant concussion-fired blasting cap. On top of all that he packed neutral goo. It was rigged so it would blow outward toward the cliff face.

He went back up to the surfacc, talking on the radio as he was hoisted aloft. They had a harness and cable rigged and he went out to the cliff edge, shrugging into the harness. He ignored Robert the Fox's request that somebody else do it; they had not used explosives that much and Jonnie knew them well.

Using a winch and safety wires, they lowered him over the edge. He found it very easy to go down the cliff face now that it was slightly inclined. He signaled when he was opposite the lode and they halted the lowering winch.

Bouncing himself about with his moccasins against the cliff, he looked for the pinhole. From inside he had put a very thin drill all the way through to the outside.

There was the tiny hole! It marked the top center of the inside ring of shot holes.

The shot-holer gun bounced down to him. This was the dicey part. The gun might set off the inside blast with concussion, and if it did he'd be blown off the cliff by the explosion. But he had no time to just drill.

He made a plaited cable of blasting cord. With the shot-holer set at minimum power he made holes for pins in the lode. Getting himself adjusted up and down by the winch and with a thousand feet of chasm gaping below him, he wound the blasting cord through the pins. Presently he had a big circle on the vein.

He fixed an electric firing wire to the cord and let it pay out as they reeled him up.

He was pressed for time. It would be at most half an hour before the recon drone came over and the smoke must be cleared.

The firing wire was run to the plane. He made everyone including himself get into the plane in case more cliff went.

"Stand by!" he shouted.

He pressed the firing button.

Smoke and flame flashed on the cliff face. White quartz and country rock blasted toward the other wall of the canyon.

The ground shook.

No more cliff fell.

Jonnie took the plane up and into the height and position the recon drone would be.

They had a black hole in the cliff side. It looked like the drift had reached the lode.

They landed again to look busy with equipment. The smoke of the blast dissipated in the mountain air.

The rumble of the drone grew louder in the distance.

— 8 —

A very hungover Terl sat beside the drone receiver in his office, woodenly taking the lode scans out of the roller.

He had slept the sleep of the very drunk both last night and this morning, and he had not felt any earthquake, nor had anyone informed him of it since the compound was proof against such slight tremors, and it had been much more severe in the mountains.

What little pleasure he got in life these days was looking at the scan photos, even though they showed only a bit more waste ore around the shaft and a little activity.

He was no closer to solving the puzzle of Jayed than he had been when the fellow arrived. The endless searching and trying to figure out the reasons I.B.I. might have an interest here had cost Terl weight, had sunken in and dulled his eyes, and had put a tremor in his talons when he lifted the all-too-frequent kerbango saucepans to his mouthbones. His hatred of this planet with its accursed blue skies and white mountains deepened day by day. This routine moment at the scanner, taken only after locking all doors and checking with a debug probe, was his only hopeful instant in the day.

Terl raised the scan picture to the light. It took him a moment or two to realize it was different today. Then he quivered with abrupt shock.

The face of the cliff had avalanched.

There was no *lode* there.

He didn't have yesterday's pictures. He always tore them up promptly. He tried to estimate how much of the face was gone.

The incline of it was different. He couldn't estimate how deep the sheer-off had cut into the cliff.

There was a hole. That would be the drift. They had been drifting along the vein.

He was about to put the photo down to think about it when he noticed the mineral side scan trace. The primary purpose of a recon drone was not surveillance. It scanned ceaselessly for minerals and recorded them on a tracc. This trace was different.

Indeed it *was* different. He knew the lode trace: the jagged spectrum of *gold*. He quickly ran the trace into the analyzing machine.

Sulphur? There was no sulphur in that lode. That gold was not a sulphide gold compound. Carbon? Flourine? What in the name of the crap nebula . . . none of these minerals were in that area!

He wondered whether he was looking at the six-common-mineral formula of what the Psychlos called "trigdite." None of the explosives or fuels were imported from Psychlo. They were dangerous to transship and easy to make on this planet. The little factory stood about ten miles south of the compound, served by the power lines from the distant dam, and every now and then a crew went down to combine the elements into fuel cartridges and explosives. So all these elements were present on this planet.

He ran it through the scanner again to get the exact balance of the mix.

Trigdite!

Terl's unbalanced wits instantly leaped to a wrong conclusion. Trigdite was the commonest trace one got around any Psychlo mine. It would almost be unusual not to find it as it hung in the rocks and air after blasting.

He leaped from his chair and ripped the scan photo to bits in savage paws. He threw down the fragments. He stamped on them. He pounded his fists against the wall.

The vicious rotten animals had blown the face of the cliff off! Just to spite him! Just to get even with him! They'd destroyed his lode!

He collapsed in the chair.

He heard a knocking at his door and Chirk's worried voice. "Whatever is the matter, Terl?"

Suddenly he realized he must get control of himself. He must be very cold, very clever.

"The machine broke," he shouted, a clever explanation.

She went away.

He felt cool, dispassionate, masterful. He knew exactly what he would do, knew it step by step. He would have to remove all possible threats to his life. He would have to cover all traces.

First he would commit the perfect crime. He had worked it all out.

Then he would release the drone and exterminate the animals.

His talons were still shaking a bit. He knew it would make him feel much better if he went out and killed the two females. He had that planned for Day 94. He would make a couple of explosive collars for the horses and then he would lead the horses up to the cage and show the females the red blob on the horses' collars was the same as on theirs, and then he would hit a switch and explode a horse's head off. The females would go into terror. Then he'd do it to the other horse. Then he'd pretend to let them loose but step back and blow the smaller female's head off. The amount of terror he could generate would be delicious. He felt he needed such a boost now. Then he remembered the animal's "psychic powers." That animal up in the hills would know about it and might do something to avoid getting killed.

No, attractive and needful to his nerves as it might be, he must not indulge himself. He must be cool, masterful and clever.

He had better set the perfect crime in motion right this instant.

He got up with deliberate, calm determination and went about it.

— 9 —

The perfect crime began by appointing Ker the deputy head of the planet. It was all done within the hour and distributed and posted. The company rules allowed for a deputy, there was none and it was only logical that one be appointed.

To do this, Terl used the already signed order pages he had gotten from Numph.

In the evening, Terl took Numph aside, swearing him to strict secrecy and hinting his swindle with pay and bonus funds might be at risk, and got him to make an appointment with a new employee named Snit.

He did not inform Numph that "Snit" was the cover name of Jayed of the Imperial Bureau of Investigation.

Terl impressed on Numph that no one must know of the appointment. It must take place at the hour just before midnight in the administration compound. He also didn't mention that the offices would be deserted at that time.

Telling Numph it was all for his own protection, Terl arranged to be standing behind a curtain in Numph's office when Jayed arrived.

With very expert care, Terl had oiled and charged an assassin gun, a silent weapon. He had also prepared two remote explosion blasting caps.

Just before the appointment time, Terl told Numph to be sure his handgun was loaded and ready in his lap. This frightened Numph a little, but Terl said, "I'll be right behind this curtain protecting you."

Numph was at the desk, gun in lap; Terl was behind the curtain. The hour of the appointment arrived. So far Terl had been calm and masterful, but as he waited his nerves were playing him tricks and making his eyebones twitch. What if Jayed didn't come?

A dreadful minute went by. Then another. Jayed was late.

Then, what a relief to Terl, the slither of footsteps in the outside hall. Of course! Jayed must have been putting a probe to the area to see whether it was free of surveillance devices. What a fool, thought Terl illogically. Terl had already done that and very thoroughly too. There were no surveillance devices here.

The door slid quietly open and Jayed came in. His head was down. He had not even bothered to change out of his tattered ore-sorter clothes.

"You sent for me, Your Planetship," muttered Jayed.

As he had been coached, Numph said, "Are you certain that no one knows you are here?"

"Yes, Your Planetship," mumbled Jayed. What an act, thought Terl contemptuously.

He stepped out from behind the curtain and walked forward. "Hello, Jayed," said Terl.

The fellow was jolted. He looked up. "Terl? Is it Terl?" I.B.I. agents were trained. They never forgot a face. Terl knew the fellow had not seen him for years and years and then only as a security student at the mine school when Jayed had been investigating a crime there. One interview. But it didn't fool Terl. He knew Jayed must have studied and studied the photographs and records of every executive here, and especially the security chief's. Terl smiled disdainfully.

Then Jayed saw the assassin pistol at Terl's side. He stepped back. He raised his mangy paws. "Wait. Terl! You don't understand—!"

What was he trying to do? Open his shirt? Reach for a secret weapon?

It made no difference. Terl stepped into position and raised the gun, putting it on a direct line from Numph to Jayed.

Terl fired one, accurate, deadly shot into Jayed's heart.

Jayed was trying to say something. Some protest. He was dead, crumpled and mangy on the green-stained carpet.

Terl thrilled a bit with the murder. Jayed had been *afraid*! But this was no time for self-indulgence.

A calm masterful Terl turned to Numph.

Numph was sitting there in terror. Terl thought it was delicious. But he had a job to do.

"Don't worry, Numph," said Terl. "That fellow was an agent of the I.B.I. come to smoke you out. He hasn't. You're safe. I have saved your life."

Numph tremblingly laid his own gun down on the desk top. He was panting but much relieved.

Terl walked up on the side of Numph that held the gun. He raised the assassin gun quickly.

Numph's eyes shot wide, his mouth opened in incredulity.

Terl pushed the muzzle of the silent weapon against Numph's head and pulled the firing catch.

The jolt knocked Numph sideways. Green blood began to pour from a wound that went all the way through his head.

A calm, completely in charge, cool Terl steadied the body and then tipped it forward so that it fell across the desk. He arranged the still twitching arm so that it might have fired the shot. The twitches stopped. Numph was dead.

Working with precision and care, he put a remote-controlled blast cap in the barrel of Numph's gun.

Terl produced a new weapon from his boot. He went over to Jayed's body and put the stiffening paw around the butt on it.

Into the muzzle of Jayed's gun, he put the second remote-control cap.

He looked around. It was all in order.

Walking casually but very silently, he went out to the nearly empty recreation hall, entering as though just coming in from outside, even taking his breathe-mask off. He ordered a saucepan of kerbango from the attendant. It was Terl's usual routine. He was a little surprised to notice he needed it.

After a few minutes, when the yawning attendant was hinting he wanted to close up and was letting down a blind in preparation for the morrow, Terl casually put his hand in his pocket.

He pressed the first remote. Far off there was a muzzled explosion. The attendant looked up, listening, looking toward the other end of the compound.

Terl pressed the second remote.

There was another explosion.

"That sounded like gunfire," said the attendant.

A door slammed somewhere. Somebody else had heard it.

"It did, didn't it," said Terl.

He stood up. "Sounded like it was in the compound! Let's see if we can find it."

With the attendant in his wake, Terl started running through the berthing areas, opening doors. "Did a shot go off in here?" he was barking at startled, just-awakened Psychlos. Some of them had heard the shots, too.

"Where did it sound like it came from?" Terl was demanding of people out in the halls.

Some pointed toward the administration building. Terl thanked them and efficiently went plowing in that direction, followed by a crowd of Psychlos.

He industriously searched through the offices, turning on lights. The crowd was also searching.

Somebody yelled from Numph's corridor, "They're in here. They're in here!"

Terl let a lot of fellows get there first. Then he went plowing through them. "Who is it? Where?"

They babbled at him, pointing in through the open door. The two bodies were in view.

Char was regarding them sourly from just inside the door. He made as if to walk forward. Terl swept him back.

"Don't touch anything!" commanded Terl. "As security chief, I am in charge here. Back!"

He bent over the bodies one after the other. "Anybody recognize this one?" he said, pointing to Jayed's body.

After a moment and craning necks, "I think his name's Snit," from a personnel officer. "I really don't know."

"They're both dead," said Terl. "Call for some stretchers. I'll record this." There was a picto-recorder on Numph's desk, as always. Terl whirred it at the room and each body. "I'll want statements from all of you."

Somebody had called the medical staff. They had heard the shots and were prompt. They loaded the bodies on the stretchers.

"Take them directly to the morgue unless you want to examine them first," said Terl.

"They're both dead," said the medical chief. "Blast gun wounds."

"Move along," said Terl efficiently to the crowd. "It's all over."

Tomorrow morning he would write his report, all backed by witnessed statements: An agent of the I.B.I., recognized by the keen eye of Terl, had not seen fit to announce himself to the planet's security chief but, proceeding alone, had apparently visited Numph late in the evening and possibly had attempted a foolhardy, single-handed arrest. Numph had shot him with a hidden gun and then committed suicide. Terl had now followed through, seeing whether Numph were guilty of some crime, had continued an investigation begun long since, and had found a pay swindle, papers, and evidence to hand. Meanwhile, Terl respectfully submitted all was under control; a competent, experienced deputy Numph had earlier appointed was now on the job; etc. Bodies en route at next semiannual firing, Day 92.

Tomorrow afternoon, as soon as he had verified the animals were still there, he would launch the drone and obliterate "the foolish experiment Numph had been engaged upon." All evidence would be covered, all tracks obliterated. Whatever Jayed had been after, it made no difference now.

Terl felt very calm, very cool, very masterful. He had brought off the perfect crime.

It was odd that he couldn't sleep and kept twitching.

■

PART 11

— 1 —

It was the consensus of opinion at the mountain site that they all should be very visible and look busy for the flyover of the drone today.

Jonnie was very concerned. It was absolutely vital that Terl continue with his gold scheme. All their own plans depended on it utterly.

They had weighed various alternates to their own strategy but none of them was good. They could fly into the old defense base now—Angus had gotten the heliport door to work—but they only used it for supplies. It was a long way from ready. The parson's idea that they should bury the dead there was shelved due to the magnitude of the task and their own few numbers. The parson had decided the place was really a tomb anyway. Later, perhaps, when they had freed the planet—if they succeeded in that—they could bury the dead. Now their energies must be devoted to the living and a possible future. So they really couldn't withdraw into the old primary defense base. It wasn't ready and they were not defeated. Not yet anyway.

Keeping Terl going on with his plan was their single hope. But Jonnie was very concerned. In that last interview he realized Terl was no longer sane, if he ever had been.

Gold was the bait in the trap for Terl. So Jonnie added to their plans.

They worked in a rush from the last passing of the drone yesterday to prepare for its passing today.

The lode core he had blasted out had hit the opposite side of the canyon and rebounded back in shattered pieces to lie upon the top of the new rockfall at the canyon bottom.

Jonnie fashioned a remote-control box for a blade scraper machine they could afford to lose.

Robert the Fox fashioned a lifelike dummy to strap into the seat. The dummy's hands in mittens were rigged to move back and forth when the machine ran. Knowing the macabre was Terl's favorite dish, he also wadded up scraps of discarded clothing and patterned it with steer blood.

They rigged an ore net to the end of a crane cable and filled it with white quartz from the upper tunnel. Taking what wire gold they had, they encrusted the top of the lode with the specimens.

In the black, brief period of no wind at dawn, they cabled the blade scraper down to the top of the rockfall.

An operator hidden in a cleft at the top of the cliff on the opposite side of the canyon, from which perch the blade scraper could be seen, made the scraper make a flat place (at risk of its toppling into the river) and dig into the pile.

The ore net, with its carefully prepared load, was craned down to the side of the blade scraper.

It was ready long before the drone came, so Jonnie gathered them at the top of the shaft.

"Wire gold goes in pockets," he told them. "It says so in the old man-manuals on mining. There is a possibility that there is another pocket in this vein. It could be two hundred, five hundred feet up the vein from the cliff. It could have little gold, it could have much.

"What we've got to do now is reverse direction on the vein and drift along it into the mountain. It will be much faster since we can blast now.

"So rig this cage again so it doesn't slip and get to work mining up that vein. We have about sixty days left until Day 92. Probably we will have to deliver the gold by Day 86. So get going and hope!"

"And pray," added the parson.

— 2 —

A very masterful Terl sat in the morning sunlight of his office, pen held in claws, carefully not trembling. He was about to write the report and round off his perfect crime.

His day was efficiently planned. He would write the report, get the latest recon pictures after the drone passed over, and, if the animals were there, fire the drone. Zzt was nattering to anybody that would listen that it blocked the hangar firing gate and he could not get ore freighters in and out to service them, and so Terl would get Zzt to insist he fire it to save space. Then he would see Ker and threaten him into being cooperative as the new Planet Head.

But Terl somehow felt unhappy. This morning sunlight, dancing across his rug, even though filtered by the colored lead glass of the canopy, was a reminder he was still on this accursed planet. Gone were his dreams of a wealthy Terl, living in luxury on Psychlo. But no matter. One had to do what one had to do.

For the tenth time he started to write the report. So far, he had not gotten through the first line of the heading, much less the report. Something was nagging him.

Ah, yes! He didn't have Jayed's badge or badge number! The agent had been reaching into his shirt, undoubtedly to show him the badge and identification disc of an I.B.I. operative. Also, if he knew the medical department, they had just dumped the bodies on the benches and he had better put them on ledges.

By plan he would have to have ten bodies. He now had five, counting the three guards that had blown themselves up. He sighed. It *had* been a beautiful plan: put the gold in the coffins, ship them home, and when he returned there, dig up the coffins some dark Psychlo night, melt them down, and lord it over everyone as a very rich fellow! Well, that was all finished now. The arrival of Jayed had ended it. And the treacherous animals had betrayed him.

He needed the badge and I.B.I. identification number. He would feel better if he cuffed Jayed's body a time or two. He picked up a breathe-mask and went out of the compound.

As he passed the cage of the females he noticed a bundle of food and firewood had been left outside the gate. He gave it a kick and would have passed on when he realized that "psychic powers" might prematurely alert the animals in the mountains. He shut off the electrical circuit with his remote, opened the cage door, and threw the bundle violently at the two females. It landed in their fire and the small one scrambled to salvage it before it burned. He noticed the other one was holding a stainless steel man-knife from some old ruin. He went over and wrested it out of her hand. Then, remembering "psychic powers," he attempted to pat her on the head. She didn't seem to like it.

Terl put the knife in his belt, went out, reconnected the juice, and stuffed the remote in his breast pocket. The younger one was saying something in man-language, something undoubtedly harsh. Treacherous creatures, these animals. Well, all that would be handled soon. After the gas drone had done its work he'd be through with this pair. And good riddance.

He rumbled on down to the morgue, and sure enough the medicals had just dumped the bodies and not even on a bench! He turned on the lights, closed the door, and hoisted a thousand pounds of Numph onto a shelf. Even in death the old bungler looked stupid, an expression of amazement still on his face. Not all the blood had dried yet and Terl got it on his hands. He wiped them off on Numph's coat.

Jayed's body was surprisingly light, not more than seven hundred pounds. Terl plunked it down on a table and cuffed it.

"Blast you," said Terl to the corpse. "If you hadn't shown up my future would have been a beautiful dream." He cuffed the face again.

Mange. The creature had mange. Terl looked at the corpse sourly. Then he reached over and, with clenched fangs, gripped its throat and choked it. He threw the head back and it hit the table with a thud. Terl cuffed it again.

He took hold of himself. He had to be calm, cool, competent. Where was the badge? He patted the jacket and couldn't feel any lump.

Maybe Jayed had carried the badge in his boots. Hollow soles were an I.B.I. specialty. He pulled the boots off and examined them. No hollow soles.

Blast it, the fellow carried his badge somewhere! Terl patted the ragged trousers. Nothing. He stood back from the corpse.

What a pitiful spectacle this Jayed was! The clothes were full of holes. The fur was diseased.

Where was it! He *had* been reaching for something! Terl ripped the bloodied shirt and jacket with a jerk that bared the chest. He examined the rags that had torn off in his paws. Nothing in them. Then he noticed the chest. He stared.

The three horizontal bands! The brand of a criminal.

The rags fell from Terl's talons. He bent closer, staring at the chest.

No mistake.

The criminal brand.

He bent closer and scraped at it. No, it was actually burned in!

He gave it an expert appraisal. It was about a year old.

Hastily he turned and seized the right ankle of the corpse. Yes! The shackle scars, complete with the barb marks, of the Imperial prison. A closer look. Also about a year old.

Terl backed up to the wall and stared at the corpse.

It was not an unfamiliar story. An official or an agent had committed a crime in the performance of duty or had been stupid enough to tamper with a crime committed by the aristocracy, had been drummed out of his position and thrown into the Imperial prisons.

Suddenly Terl knew exactly what Jayed had done. He had used his talents to escape. He had forged papers as "Snit" and he had worked his way through the personnel lineup of Intergalactic Mining and gotten himself shipped to the farthest outpost of the company.

Jayed had been on the run!

It hit Terl like a thunderbolt. Jayed had not been investigating anything here! Jayed was in hiding. His gesture to his chest was to show Terl the brand and put himself at Terl's mercy. And it would have worked! Terl could have used him in devious ways.

All these months of worry!

All about nothing.

Terl looked at the pitiful, mangy creature on the table. It was a good thing the door was closed because for quite a while Terl couldn't stop laughing.

— 3 —

Once more that day, Terl was sitting at his desk. He was relaxed, at ease. There was a saucepan of kerbango there and he wasn't even chewing on it.

His pen moved easily on the report. This changed the whole thing. It was very simple.

Despite warning Numph to be watchful—copy of warning enclosed—due to the number of criminals in the work force, a criminal whose papers said his name was "Snit" had gotten into the offices with probable intent to rob and walked in on Numph, who had shot him. Before he died the criminal had shot Numph. Witnessed statements to hand and enclosed. The personnel department in the home office could possibly institute physical examinations as this was the second branded criminal received in recent drafts of personnel. It was, of course, necessary for the company to make a profit and understandable that this was a very out-of-the-way planet, but it had only one security officer. But the matter was actually of no great importance, and one would not venture to criticize the practices of the home office since they knew what they were doing. Situation well in hand. A recently appointed deputy had competently assumed the duties of Planet Head. The crime was simple and routine. Bodies en route at next semiannual firing.

That was that. An expansive Terl finished packaging the evidence and picto-recorder discs. Nobody would be interested anyway. He called Chirk and, with a playful paw on her rump, gave her the package to log and include in the dispatch box. She left and he glanced at the clock. He was overdue at the receiving machine. He went over to it and punched the coordinates of the pictures he wanted and they came whirring forth. He glanced at them casually: the drone firing schedule had to be confirmed. Yes, they were up there at the minesite, working with the cage. . . .

Suddenly he sat forward and spread the pictures out.

They had a blade scraper operating down at the bottom of the cliff, turning over the rubble!

Yes! A crane was raising an ore net . . what was that in the basket?

He punched rapid keys on the machine and got a closer-view picture. He looked at it. He looked at the analysis squiggle at the side: he didn't have to analyze that; he knew it! It was *gold*.

They were recovering the lode out of the slide!

He stood up and examined the pictures more closely. What was this over at the side of the slide? Ah, the mangled remains of dead bodies. They'd lost a crew in the drift and with stupid sentimentality they were also digging them out. Why bother? They didn't have to ship them to home planet. Who cared about the corpses of animals? But wait, that meant they must have been up to the lode from behind.

And what were they doing with the cage? Still mining? Ah, pockets. They must have spotted another pocket on that vein up inside the mountain. The mining man in Terl told him that was a good possibility.

He looked at the gold in that ore net. Several hundred pounds of it? He crashed down in his chair and smiled. He began to chuckle.

That drone. He didn't have to fire it. It could wait till Day 93. Then for sure, but not now. No, by the crap nebula, not now!

How wonderful he felt. It had been ages since his head hadn't ached. He reached out a paw. The talons were steady as bedrock.

— 4 —

Terl bounced up, pulsing with good cheer and energy. He grabbed some equipment and packages.

He still had a schedule, but it was different.

He sailed through the compound and into the office of the Planet Head.

Attendants had finished mopping up blood, but there were some stains left. The atmosphere was a bit sharp with cleaning fluids.

There sat Ker. The midget Psychlo looked a bit funny and depressed, lost in the immensity of the chair back of the vast square yardage of the desk.

"Good afternoon, Your Planetship," caroled Terl.

"Would you close the door, please?" said Ker faintly.

Terl took a probe out from under his arm and waved it about to make sure the place hadn't been bugged overnight. He was almost careless about it. He felt free!

"I'm not very popular," said Ker. "People haven't been very polite to me so far. They wonder why Numph appointed me his deputy. I wonder myself. I'm an operations officer, not an administrator. And now all of a sudden I'm head of the planet."

Terl, with a wonderful smile on his mouthbones, stepped closer. "Now what I'm going to tell you, Ker, I will deny emphatically I ever said, and there is no record and you'll forget this conversation."

Ker was instantly alert. As a hardened criminal he knew better than to trust security chiefs. Ker wriggled in the chair that was too big for him.

"Numph," said Terl, "didn't appoint you."

Ker got very alert!

"*I* did," said Terl. "And as long as you do exactly what I tell you to do, without ever telling anyone I told you to do it, you will be fine. More than fine. Wonderful!"

"They'll just send in a new Planet Head on Day 92," said Ker. "That's only a couple of months off. And he'll find out if I've done anything wrong . . . yes, and he may find out I'm not welcome in certain universes."

"No, Ker. I don't think you'll be replaced. In fact, I am very, very certain you will not be. You're good for this post for years."

Ker was wary and puzzled, but Terl seemed so confident that he listened cautiously.

Terl opened an envelope and fanned out the evidence he had gathered on Numph. Ker looked at it with slowly widening eyes.

"A hundred-million-credit-a-year swindle," said Terl. "Of which Numph got half. You're not only here for years but you'll be rich enough when you do go home to buy your record clean and live in luxury."

The Psychlo midget studied it. It was a little hard to grasp at first. Nipe, Numph's nephew, was crediting full pay to the employees of this planet but was in fact diverting half the pay and all the bonuses into private accounts for himself and Numph.

He finally got that. All he had to do was to continue to deny bonuses and pay only half-pay.

"Why are you doing this?" said Ker. "Do you get a slice of this? Is that it?"

"Oh, no. I don't even want a quarter of a credit of it. It's all yours. But, of course, I am really doing it because I am your friend. Haven't I always protected you?"

"You've got enough blackmail on me already to get me vaporized," said Ker. "Why this, too?"

"Now, Ker," said Terl reprovingly. Then he decided it was time to level. "I want you to issue any order I tell you to, and to give me an order in six months to go home."

"That's fine," said Ker. "I can even issue orders not to countermand any orders you issue. But I still don't see that I won't be relieved in two months."

Terl got down to business. "This is the code Numph used. Vehicles-in-use numbers. You won't be relieved. Nipe, his nephew, has influence. This is your first coded message to Nipe." He put it on the desk, reminding himself to destroy his own handwritten version as soon as Ker had it encoded in his.

The message said: "Numph assassinated by escaped criminal. New situation created. He appointed me especially to carry on. Arrangements are as always. Deposit his share to my numbered account Galaxy Trust Company. Condolences. Happy future association. Ker."

"I don't have a numbered account," said Ker.

"You will, you will. I have all the papers for you and they will go out in the next transshipment. Foolproof."

Ker looked back at the message. For the first time since the murders he began to smile. He sat back, seeming to get bigger. Suddenly he reached forward and slapped paws with Terl, symbolizing full-hearted agreement.

When Terl left him, Ker had swelled up so much he was practically filling the chair.

The only reservation Terl had, as he swept on to his next scheduled action, was that the dim-witted little midget might overreach himself with pomposity and make some clownish mistake. But he'd keep an eye on him. He'd keep a close eye on him. And who cared what happened to Ker once Terl was off this planet!

Any potential alliance Jonnie might have had with Ker was wholly and totally severed.

— 5 —

Terl's next actions were carefully observed by keen Scottish eyes in the hills.

Late the previous afternoon Terl had gone tearing off in an executive tank at high speed. He had headed toward the ancient city to the north and entered it.

About noon he left the ruins there and came roaring down the remains of the overgrown highway to the Academy.

Terl got out of the tank, faceplate of the breathe-mask glinting in the sun, and strode in a free and relaxed fashion in the direction of the sentry who came forward.

There was very little at the Academy now; a housekeeping unit and three Scot sentries, usually light-duty invalids recovering from some mishap.

This one had his arm in splints and in a sling. "What can I do for you, sir?" said the sentry in acceptable Psychlo.

Terl looked around. No vehicles left here—no, there was the tail of a small passenger plane. Must have them all up at the mine. Probably even running out of them.

He looked at the sentry. Probably running out of personnel, too, if Terl knew anything about the dangers of mining. Well, no matter. There were still some of them left alive.

He was wondering how to communicate with this animal. It had not registered on him that he had been addressed in Psychlo, simply because he didn't believe it. Animals were stupid.

Terl made gestures with his paws, indicating the height and beard of the head animal. He went through a pantomime of looking around, sweeping his arm toward himself and pointing at the spot beside him. Very difficult to get anything across to an animal.

"You probably mean Jonnie," said the sentry in Psychlo.

Terl nodded absently and wandered off. He'd probably have to wait until they flew up to the mine and brought him back, but that was quite all right.

He realized with an expansive good feeling that he now had lots of time; but more than that, he had freedom. He could go where he pleased and do what he pleased. He flexed his arms and wandered off. It might be an accursed planet but he had space now. It was as though invisible walls had been moved off him and miles away.

Some horses were grazing in a nearby park. Terl, to pass the time, practiced drawing his belt gun and firing. One by one he broke their legs. The resulting screaming of the agonized mounts was quite satisfactory. He was just as fast on the draw as ever, just as accurate. At two hundred yards, even! A black horse. Four draws, four fires. The horse was a skidding cloud of snow. What a caterwaul! Delicious.

Jonnie's voice behind him was a bit hard to hear in the racket but it didn't surprise Terl. He turned easily, mouthbones wreathed in a smile behind the faceplate.

"Want to try?" said Terl, pretending to hand over the gun.

Jonnie reached for it. Terl laughed an enormous laugh and put it back in his belt.

Jonnie had long since been waiting for Terl: from the moment Terl had started on this route from the city, he had known Terl would call here and he had flown down from the mine. It had seemed better not to let Terl know he was under observation and he had intended to delay a bit longer. But the screaming of the tortured horses had sickened him.

This was a much-changed Terl, very like his old self.

"Let's walk," said Terl.

With a signal of the hand that Terl did not see, an angry Jonnie sent a Scot to slit the throats of the tortured, maimed horses and put them out of their misery. He steered Terl around the corner of a building to block his view of the action.

"Well, animal," said Terl. "I see you are getting along just fine. I suppose you are trying for a second pocket."

"Yes," said Jonnie, controlling his anger, "we don't have quite enough gold yet." *That* was an understatement. All the gold they had he was carrying in a bag right this minute.

"Fine, fine," said Terl. "Need any equipment? Any supplies? Just say the word. Got a list with you?" Jonnie didn't. "No, well all you have to do is put a list in those bundles you keep leaving outside the cage and I'll just have them run right over to you. Label it 'training supplies,' of course."

"Fine," said Jonnie.

"And if you want to talk to me, just flash a light through the glass at my quarters, three short flashes and I'll come out and we can talk. Right?''

Jonnie said that was fine. There were some mining points that came up every now and then.

''Well, you just ask the right party,'' said Terl, patting himself on the chest. ''What I don't know about mining has never been written up!'' He laughed loudly.

Indeed this was a different Terl, thought Jonnie. Something had taken the pressure off him.

They were still out in a field and hidden from view by a knoll.

''Now to business,'' said Terl. ''On Day 89 you are to deliver my gold to this building in the old city up there.'' He took a picture out of his pocket and showed it to Jonnie.

It said on the building: [''United States Mint'']. Jonnie started to take it but Terl pulled it back and showed him three other views: the street, the building from two sides.

''Day 89,'' said Terl. ''Two hours after sunset. Don't be seen. There's a room I've fixed up. Put it in there.''

Jonnie studied the views. Obviously Terl was not going to give him physical possession of them. There were some mounds he knew were old cars, and back of the building was a bigger mound, probably a truck. The doors of the place were sound and closed, but undoubtedly Terl had them unlocked.

''Have you got a flatbed ground truck?'' asked Terl. ''No? I'll give you one.'' He became impressive, commanding. ''Now listen carefully: you and two other animals, no more, are to arrive at that exact time. You, *personally*. Tell the others you won't return until Day 93 and you'll bring them their pay. From Day 89 to 93 I have some other things for you to do. Understand? You personally and two animals, no more; the rest stay at the mine. Right?''

Jonnie said that was understood. They were standing well-screened from any view behind some bushes. ''Do you want to see a sample of what was hauled up?''

Yes, Terl certainly did. So Jonnie threw down a piece of heavy cloth and spilled wire gold onto it. It glowed softly in the sunlight.

Terl glanced up to be sure there was no overhead surveillance and then hunkered down. He fondled the nets of gold, some of the quartz still sticking to it. He spent some time at it and then stood up with a paw signal to put it away. Jonnie did so. Carefully. It was all they had.

Gazing at the bag, Terl let out a long sigh into his breathe-mask. ''Beautiful,'' he said. ''Beautiful.''

He came out of it. ''So on Day 89, I get a ton of gold, right?'' He patted his pocket where the remote control lay. ''And then on Day 93 you get your payoff!''

''Why the delay?'' said Jonnie. ''That's four days.''

''Oh, you've got a few things to do,'' said Terl. ''But never fear, animal. Come Day 93 you will be paid off. With interest. Compounded. I promise you very faithfully!'' He laughed a huge guffaw into his mask, and Jonnie knew that Terl might be feeling high today but he was not entirely sane.

''You'll get everything that's coming to you, animal!'' said Terl. ''Let's walk back to the car.''

Never in his whole life had Terl felt so good. He recalled from the Scotland trip how eager they were for pay. This animal was going to get paid on Day 89! Then he could kill the females. With no fear of ''psychic powers.'' Delicious!

''Goodbye, animal,'' he said, and drove off in great spirits.

— 6 —

The next weeks were filled with tension. They were driving along the vein in hopes of a second pocket but as yet saw only white quartz, no gold. And without gold, nothing else was going to work.

The incident of the horse herd caused an uproar among them. They had trained those horses and they had become pets, left at the Academy where there was grazing, waiting for better days. The Scots were outraged, not only because of the loss but because of the sickening way it had been done. It brought home to all of them the nature of the enemy. Were all Psychlos like that? Yes, unfortunately. Lookouts had spotted other crippled animals around the compound. Didn't this put the girls in great danger? Yes, but one had to grit one's teeth and make sure their plan came off on schedule. By all that was holy, they mustn't muff a single thing! It was like playing a violent kind of chess with maniacs.

In other areas than the gold they were making progress.

Angus had made keys to everything in sight. It was very risky: heat-shielded bodies, silent feet in the snow of night, impressions in wax, dusted-over tracks. There was double jeopardy in this, for any discovery might not only cost the man his life but also alert the Psychlos that something was intended.

They had a good break in studying the old battle of a thousand years ago. The records were all in order now, all satellite overviews of it in sequence.

Jonnie and Doctor MacDermott had been going over them, looking for something that might help. There were numerous reports on the battle planes in that one-sided struggle.

An oddity was that a Psychlo battle plane had dive-bombed a tank in downtown Denver, but there was no tank detailed to downtown Denver according to U.S. Army statements on it. This attracted Jonnie's attention and led him to discover a second report on the same plane.

After bombing the tank that the report said was not there, the battle plane took off at high speed to the northwest and was sighted colliding with a snow-covered mountainside. It didn't explode. The spotting gave the exact position.

They looked it up on their maps. It was only about three hundred miles to the north of them.

Dunneldeen verified it with an overfly and metal detector, and the battle plane was still there, buried—all but a tip of its tail—in perpetual snows.

Using two flying ore platforms, they dug it out and airlifted it at night, to avoid detection, to the old base, and there in the heliport, subjected it to minute study.

The battle plane was unserviceable but it contained a host of information that could not be gained by a stealthy scout to the compound. The two Psychlo pilots had been killed on impact but their equipment, though decayed, was intact.

They went over every detail of the breathe-masks. They found there was a compartment that contained jet-driven backpacks as a form of parachute in case of necessary bailout. The security belts were no different from those used in the mine vehicles. The pilots also wore belt guns.

The controls of the plane were identical to the passenger

mining ships. The only additions were the gun triggers and switches for a magnetic "grappler."

Examining the skids on which the plane stood, they found, indeed, that they were electromagnetic. The plane could be fixed with this to any metal surface and obviated the necessity of tying it down.

They also located the key slots and determined the type of keys.

They cleaned it up as best they could and used it for drilling their pilots.

The dead, mummified Psychlos were dissected by the parson to ascertain where their vital organs were located. Their hearts were in back of their belt buckles and their lungs were high in their shoulders. Their brains were very low in the back of the head and the rest of the head was bone. The parson then buried them with proper solemnity.

They were busy on many projects. They built a large-scale model of the compound in the huge loft of the Empire Dauntless Mining building and drilled every team member.

They marked out approximate distances in a meadow—without betraying anything to a drone—and timed everything: how fast did one have to go to get from this place to that, what were the starting times from zero time in order to converge simultaneously. There was much information they did not have and could not get, so they made up for it with flexibility.

A problem they had to solve was replacing the horses. By rounding up and training wild ones, and working very fast, a small group was able to do this.

They had all become excellent marksmen with the assault rifles and bazookas.

With the relentless drilling by Robert the Fox, that past master of raids, they were really getting someplace.

"If we miss," Robert the Fox repeatedly told them, "and slip up on the tiniest detail, those plains out there will once again be crawling with transshipped Psychlo tanks and the sky studded with battle planes. The home planet of the Psychlos would retaliate with ferocity. We would have no course open save to withdraw into the old military base and probably perish of asphyxiation when they resort to gas. We have one thin chance. We must *not* miss in any tiniest detail. Let's go through it all again."

A strike force of only threescore men taking on the whole Psychlo Empire? They would harden their determination and go through the drill again. And again and again.

But they did not yet have the vital, crucial chip: the *gold*.

— 7 —

They labored in the mine twenty-four hours a day with three shifts. Inward further and further they drove along the barren, white quartz vein.

And then on Day 60 the vein faulted. Some ancient cataclysm had shifted it up or down, to the right or left. Suddenly there was just country rock before them. No more vein.

The possibility that they would lose it had not been missing from their calculations. For weeks now they had been sending out scouts to locate any stored gold within their range of recovery.

They had been given hope by Jonnie's earliest discovery of a gold coin in a bank vault in Denver. But most of the coins left were just curiosities, worthless souvenirs: they were silver-plated copper. Only five more gold coins were in that vault, and these few ounces were a long way from making up a ton of gold.

A few bits from what must have been jewelry shops added another pitiful two ounces.

Mining company officials at old mines through the mountains had no gold in their vaults, though they found plenty of receipts: the receipts all said [''Shipped] (so many) [ounces to the U.S. Mint, Denver''] or [''Shipped] (such and such) [poundage of concentrate to the smelter''].

In a perilous journey in a plane, carrying heavy supplies of fuel in reserve, Dunneldeen, a copilot, and a gunner, flying by night to escape drone detection, went all the way to the eastern coast to a place once called New York. They found the buildings mostly knocked down but some gold vaults: tunneled into and empty.

They also visited a place the historian had found called Fort Knox, but it was just a gutted ruin.

Dunneldeen had accumulated a remarkable fund of information and picto-recorder shots: bridges gone, tumbled rubble, wild game, wild cattle and varmints abundant, no trace of people, and they had had some hair-raising experiences.

But they got no gold.

They had to come to the conclusion that the Psychlos, as much as a thousand years ago, had thoroughly gutted this planet of gold. They must have even taken it from corpses in the streets, rings from fingers and fillings from teeth. Possibly this, along with the Psychlo sport of hunting humans on days off, accounted for the thoroughness of population wipeout. There was evidence that in the early days of conquest they had even massacred people just for their rings and fillings. They began to understand Terl a little better in his dangerous enterprise to possess the yellow metal for himself. To the humans, the metal meant very little: they had no experience of using it in trade; it was pretty and didn't tarnish and was easily pounded into shape, but stainless steel had a lot more utility. Their own ideas of trade and thrift had to do with useful items that were real wealth.

None of this got them any closer to getting a ton of gold. They frantically test-drilled for the lost vein.

On Day 70 they found the vein again. It had been shifted by some past upheaval two hundred thirty-one feet to the north and only thirty feet from the surface.

They wiped off their sweating faces, the droplets tending to freeze in the bitter winter winds of these altitudes, made a new level area for equipment and a new shaft, and began to drift again along the white quartz. The vein had thinned down to about three feet in width. They drove on, filling the dark air of the drift with white chips and blast fumes.

Jonnie went back to studying the battle reports. They must know Psychlo tactics very precisely. He was once again struck with the oddity of this attack on a "tank" in Denver where no tank existed. He narrowed down the location on the faded satellite photos—they had kept coming off the machine even after the president was dead. Yes, there was smoke at that place.

They had scouted out Denver thoroughly. Typically, Terl had not intended to work in the U.S. Mint to refine his gold; he had set up a place in the basement of the remains of a smelter a few minutes' drive away. He was just using the U.S. Mint as a receipt point.

But all the gold invoices they found in the mines said, ["U.S. Mint"], and it seemed to Jonnie that where so much gold was funneled in, there might be further traces there, in case they missed at the lode. Also this tank that didn't exist to the U.S. military might have been guarding the mint.

In a swift foray, he and Dunneldeen swooped down to the U.S. Mint. They had made very sure there were no ground cars or planes as the afternoon faded. They landed in a park in the cover of giant trees and sped on silent feet to the mint.

The place was still. It had been scouted before, but once more they went over it just in case the Psychlos had missed a vault. Inside they found nothing.

They lingered outside in the darkness. Dunneldeen amused himself by prying into the mounds that had once been cars, wondering what they looked like in the days when they could run. Jonnie was thinking about the views Terl had shown him. He went around to the back and played a mine lamp on the ground so it would reflect a dim light up.

Shortly, he was looking at the largest mound. It came to him that this must be the tank the battle plane had destroyed. The nonexistent tank.

He lifted some turf—blown sand and grass had overlaid it. He cut the turf very carefully so it could be laid back and leave no sign of disturbance. The thing wasn't an ordinary car. It was so thickly built that it had endured the rust of time. The metal was twisted where it had burned out. He had never seen anything like this. It had a slot one might fire out of, but that would be its closest resemblance to a tank. The window frames had bars over them, a bit like a cage. What was this thing? He pried a section of metal aside with a mine crowbar and got inside. The interior had been blackened by fire and floor plates had warped. He pried up a floor plate.

Half a minute later a smiling Jonnie was making a bird call and beckoning for Dunneldeen. He took the Scot inside.

As one might piece together, when the Psychlo attack came, the U.S. Mint had sought to evacuate its vaults.

GOLD! How much?

In extremely heavy ingots, there it had lain neatly for a thousand years. Overlooked, for everyone thought it was a tank.

They estimated its weight with excited heftings. And then their excitement dimmed.

"It's less than a tenth of a ton," said Dunneldeen. "Would Terl be satisfied with that?"

Jonnie didn't think so. In fact he knew Terl wouldn't. It was also far less than suited their own project.

"A tenth of a loaf is better than none," said Dunneldeen.

They packed the two hundred pounds of gold in the plane and put the "tank" back together and scattered snow on it and around it to cover tracks.

They now had about three hundred pounds in gold.

They needed a ton.

It was enough to make one take up alchemy, the mythical conversion of lead to gold, said the historian when they returned. And in fact he spent hours that night fruitlessly studying just that.

The parson made a visit to Jonnie's village to prepare the people for the possibility of withdrawal into the old base. He told Jonnie his Aunt Ellen sent her love and for him to be very careful in the wild places he went. Jonnie detected the parson was sweet on Aunt Ellen and privately wished him luck.

They felt bad they couldn't warn other peoples on this planet.

If they failed, man might indeed become extinct.

— 8 —

The shift that went on duty at the end of Day 86 began like any other shift. The vein had been narrowing lately—pinching out. They tried not to be hopeful, but shift ends, when they had not found the pocket yet, were always a bitter disappointment.

Dunneldeen, recovered from the cave-in, was operating a chattering spade bit, sweat streaming off him in the closed, hot confines of the drift. He had a sudden illusion that a drop of sweat had turned color as it dropped into his eye. He switched off the spade bit to clear his vision. He looked again in front of him through the swirling smoke and white dust. The illusion was still there.

But it wasn't an illusion!

A single, round spot of glowing yellow marked the shining white vein.

He put the spade bit against it and turned it on. The chattering edge bit further. He shut it off and walked closer to the vein.

He stood stock-still and then let out a blasting whistle to stop the shift.

He pointed. And then bedlam broke loose!

It was *gold!*

They had finally hit the second pocket!

The shift abruptly left off shouting and every bit and drill they had down there began to cut into the vein.

The wire gold began to blossom against the white.

An excited call went to the duty watch in town, and in a handful of minutes they had the third shift helping them.

The town went wild.

Every Scot and even two of the old widows helped form a human bucket line out of the mine; weighing, sacking, and loading bag after bag of mixed wire gold and quartz. To the devil with the odd bits of rock. The gold was like twisted springs and small cages of gleaming yellow.

Before sunset on Day 88 they had the whole pocket out.

Sixteen hundred forty-seven pounds, it weighed out, subtracting the rock.

Adding to that the three hundred six pounds they already had, it made one thousand nine hundred fifty-three pounds.

It was short of a ton but it would have to do.

The project was on its way!

They began to oil their assault rifles.

The parson prayed long and earnestly for their success. There were no parallels for odds such as these.

— 9 —

Terl waited, trying to be casual, in front of the U.S. Mint. It was two hours after sunset on Day 89. It was good and dark; there would be no moon these next three nights.

The weather on this cursed planet was on the edge of spring. There had already been a warm day or two. All the snow was gone. It was reasonably warm tonight and he had been prepared to wait. Animals were pretty stupid about time.

He was leaning against a flatbed truck he had driven in from the base. It was a shabby relic, not even on the inventory. It wouldn't be missed. He had prepared it carefully.

But, right on time, there were the animals.

With only a pinpoint of light, pointed at the ground, their vehicle rolled up and stopped a few feet from Terl.

It was heavily laden. So they had kept their part of the bargain after all. Yes, animals certainly were stupid.

There were three man-things in the cab. But Terl couldn't restrain his eagerness. He walked over to the flatbed and began to poke talons and a light into the sacks. Wire gold! Unrefined, unmelted, a bit of the white quartz clinging . . . no, here were some melted chunks.

He remembered himself and stood back and played a radiation detector on the sacks. Clean.

He estimated the load by a practiced glance at the pistons that supported the body over the driving mechanism. Allowing for the slight weight of the man-things—maybe four hundred pounds—and for the debris, he must have about nineteen hundred pounds here. Recent trade papers told him that gold in its scarcity at home had soared to eighty-three hundred twenty-one Galactic credits an ounce. This load was worth about . . . he was very good at figures in his head . . . about C189,718,800.00. Several dozen fortunes!

Wealth and power!

He felt very expansive.

The animals hadn't gotten out of the cab. Terl went to the side of it and flashed a subdued light into it. These fellows all had black beards!

Actually, it was Dunneldeen, Dwight, and another Scot.

Terl went through a pantomime seeking to ask where the animal Jonnie was.

The pantomime might or might not have been comprehensible, but Dwight, who spoke Psychlo, knew exactly what was meant. Purposely speaking in broken Psychlo, Dwight said, "Jonnie not can come. Him have accident. Him hurt foot. He say we come. Much apology."

Terl was a bit taken aback by the information. It upset his planning. But yes, in the recon drone pictures this afternoon he had noticed an overturned blade scraper at the site and had seen no sign of the blonde-bearded Jonnie who for months had always been visible. Well, no matter. It didn't upset much. It just delayed getting rid of the females. A hurt foot wouldn't stop that animal's "psychic powers" if he touched the females ahead of time. And if aroused, they could cause mischief. No mischief that he, Terl, couldn't handle.

"We help transfer sacks to other truck," said Dwight.

Terl had never intended that. "No," he said, making wide explicit motions—rather hard to see in the dark—"we just swap trucks. You get it? I keep your truck. You take this truck."

The three Scots piled out of the huge cab of the Psychlo truck they had brought and got into Terl's.

Dunneldeen took the controls. He started the motors and made a wide sweep in the street, turning back the way they had come.

Terl stood with a waiting smile upon his mouthbones.

The truck went up to the corner and turned into a side street, out of sight of Terl.

Dunneldeen hastily punched in the numbers to keep it going down the slope.

He looked sideways to make sure Dwight and the other Scot had the door open.

"Go!" he barked.

The other two dove out the door.

Dunneldeen shot his own door open and in a rolled ball hit the soft turf of the street.

He glanced back. The other two were up and running for cover, a pair of darker blurs in the dark.

He yanked a heat-detector shield out of his belt and began to run to an alley. He made it.

The flatbed went on down the street for another hundred yards.

It exploded with a battering, violent concussion that blew in the buildings on both sides of the street.

Back at the gold-laden flatbed, Terl chuckled. He could hear the patter of pieces beginning to hit as they returned to earth for blocks around. There was a roaring sigh as some buildings collapsed. He was pleased. He would have been more pleased if the animal had been in it. He didn't have to go and look. He wouldn't have found anything anyway. The distance-fused demolition charge had been placed under the cab seats.

Terl got in the laden truck and drove to the smelter he had rigged.

He had done number five of seven alternate, possible actions in boobytrapping and sending the truck back. It had been dicey precalculating the options.

The teams in antiheat capes drew back from the surrounding buildings. They collected Dunneldeen and the other two and went off for stage two. Would they be this fortunate next time? Dicey indeed outguessing a mad Psychlo.

— 10 —

The workroom in the ancient smelter had been all set up by Terl. The windows had been shuttered and the doors made snug. The only piece of equipment of the original man-setup that he was using was the huge metal cauldron in the middle of the floor, and this too he had reworked, surrounding it with Psychlo speed-heaters.

Tools, molds, and molecular sprays were all laid out.

The marking equipment was that of the morgue down at the compound.

Terl parked the flatbed in front of the unlighted door and with practically no effort at all carried in ore sacks six or eight at a time and emptied them into the cauldron.

He hid the flatbed, came in and barred the door, and checked to see that all the shutters were in place. He did not notice a newly drilled hole in one. He turned on the portable lights.

With practiced ease he darted the point of a probe around the interior to make sure there were no bugs or button cameras. Satisfied, he laid the equipment aside.

The instant it clattered to the bench, an unseen hand unfastened an ancient ventilator door and placed two button cameras in advantageous positions. The ventilator door, well oiled, was shut again. A bit of dust, dislodged in the action, drifted down across a lamp beam.

Terl looked up. Rats, he thought. Always rats in these buildings.

He turned on the speed heaters of the cauldron and the wire gold and lumps began to settle down and shrink. Bubbles began to form. One had to be careful not to overheat gold; it went into gaseous form and much could be lost in vapors. The roof beams of this old smelter must be saturated in gold gas that had recondensed. He watched the thermometers carefully.

The yellow-orange content of the cauldron went liquid and he turned the heaters to maintain.

The molds were all laid out. They were for coffin lids ordinarily used in manufacture, for coffins were a local product, made in the shops of the compound.

Terl held a huge ladle in mittened paws and began to transfer liquid gold into the first lid mold.

Two hundred pounds of gold per coffin. Ten coffin lids. He worked fast and expertly, taking care to spill none. The hiss of the molten metal striking the molds was pleasant to his earbones.

How easy all this was! The company insisted on lead coffins. Now and then an employee died in a radiation accident on some far planet, and after some messy experiences such as coffins falling apart in transshipment or creating minor accidents with radiation, the company, fifty or sixty thousand years ago, had laid down exact rules.

Lead was a glut on the market on Psychlo. They had lots of that. They also had plenty of iron and copper and chrome. What were scarce were gold, bauxite, molybdenum, and several other metals. And what was absent, thank the evil gods, was uranium and all its family of ores. So the coffins were always made of lead, stiffened up with an alloy or two such as bismuth.

He only had to make lids. There were stacks and stacks of coffins in the morgue. One of the reasons he had to be secretive was that it would look a bit silly for him to be making more coffins and bringing them in.

Presently he had nine lid molds full. It was a bit tricky on the tenth. The cauldron was down to the bottom and a residue of rock was mixed in the dregs.

He had to be speedy with all this for it had to be done before dawn. He speed-chilled the dregs and dumped in a demijohn of acid to dissolve the rock and sediment left. Then he speed-warmed it again. The clouds of boiling acid looked good to him. He was in a breathe-mask, so who cared. He spooned the dissolved dregs out and reheated the gold.

By scraping very carefully, he was able to get the last lid fairly full. He made up the weight with a bit of melted lead.

While the lid molds cooled, he cleaned up the cauldron and ladle and made sure there were no splatters on the floor.

The lids weren't cooling fast enough and he put a portable fan to them. He gingerly tapped one. Good!

With care he tapped the lids out of the molds and laid them on a bench. He got out a molecular spray and fed a lead-bismuth rod into it and began to paint the gold with a lead-bismuth covering. About seven lead-bismuth rods later he had ten leadlike coffin lids.

He took off his mittens and gathered up the marking equipment that usually stayed in the morgue. He pulled a list from his pocket.

With great neatness he marked ten names, company worker serial numbers, and dates of death on the lids.

It had taken some trouble getting ten bodies. There were the three sentries blown up by the exploding gun. There was Numph. There was Jayed, blast him. But a mine safety program being run over in medical had kept casualties down from normal, and there had been only three mine deaths since the last semiannual firing. This left Terl two bodies short.

One he had acquired by casually dropping a blasting cap into a shot hole before they tamped in the explosive. He had thought to get two or three with this but he only got the explosives expert.

The other one had been rather involved. He had loosened the steering bar of a tri-wheeler. The things were quite high-speed and ran around lots of obstacles. But he had had to wait three boring days until it finally spilled and killed the admin personnel riding it.

So he had his ten names.

He punched them into the soft metal of the lids with the marker. He inspected them. Two showed gold through and that would not do. He got out his molecular spray and sprayed lead-bismuth over them. Fine.

He made a test with a claw point. The covering didn't scratch. It would probably also stand up to the handling of fork trucks.

He then took a marker and made a small "X," hard to see unless you looked for it, on the lower left-hand corner of each lid.

Time was getting on. He rapidly scooped up his equipment and disengaged the speed heater from the cauldron. He looked around. He had everything.

He turned out the lights, pulled the truck in front of the door, and loaded two or three lids at a time. He dumped the equipment on it.

He went back in, took a bag of dust and scattered it around the room, flashed his lamp about one more time to make sure, closed the doors, and happily drove off.

In the smelter, the ventilator opened and the button cameras were retrieved with a quick hand. The hole in the shutter was repaired.

Terl drove rapidly to the compound. It was now very late but he had, as of recent weeks, made a practice of driving about the compound as though doing rounds and the sound of the motor would alert no one.

It was very dark.

He stopped at the morgue. Without lights he carried the ten lids inside. Then he drove the truck to the nearby scrap dump and dug the equipment into and under another pile of scrap.

He walked back to the morgue, closed the door, and turned on the lights. He probed the place for bugs.

He did not notice a small hole drilled through the thick wall or the button camera that appeared there right after his probe.

Terl lined up ten coffins from the stacks of empties. He took off their lids and dumped them back of the stack. He moved the ten around so they would be in position to be picked up by the forklifts on Day 92.

From the shelves he yanked down the ten bodies and dumped them with thuds into the coffins.

Jayed's was the last one. "Jayed, you silly crunch, what a crap lousy I.B.I. agent you were. It ain't smart, Jayed, to come in here worrying your betters. And what did you get for it?" Terl picked up the lid he'd made, checked the name. "A coffin and a grave burying you under the phony name of Snit."

The glazed eyes seemed to regard him reproachfully.

"No, Jayed," said Terl. "It will do no good to argue. None at all. Neither your murder, nor that of Numph, will ever be traced to me. Goodbye, Jayed!" He slammed the coffin lid down on Jayed.

He covered the rest of the coffins with his lids. He checked the small "Xs."

He took a tool that cold-bonded metal and sealed the lids down to the coffins. He put the tool on the shelf. He took the name-marking tool out of his pocket and put it where it belonged.

He looked around and stood straighter. So far all was perfect.

And he was all ready, a whole day early for the semiannual firing. He reached for the light.

He did not hear the whisper against stone as the button camera was withdrawn from the hole or the squish of cement as the hole was blocked.

Terl opened the door. It was getting dimly light.

He walked across the open space, the firing platform, and up the hill to his quarters.

Behind him at the morgue, two caped figures slipped away into the ravine.

Four hours later on this Day 91, Jonnie, Robert the Fox, the council, and team members concerned went over and over the picto-recorder pictures. They must not miss the tiniest possibility or the largest option. They could not afford to miss. The fate, not just of themselves, but of galaxies depended upon making *no* mistakes.

■

PART 12

— 1 —

The recreation hall of the compound was ablaze with light and bursting with noise. It was jammed full of Psychlos and they were mostly drunk. It was a grand party on the evening of the semiannual firing. Char and two other executives were going home.

It was something to celebrate: the end of a duty tour on this accursed planet. Attendants rushed about with saucepans of kerbango held six or eight at a time in their paws. Female Psychlo clerks, released from the cowed decorum that was their normal lot, joked and got their bottoms smacked. A couple of fights had already started and ended without anyone discovering what the fight had been about. Games of chance and marksmanship were a tangle of disorganized confusion.

Jokes of a bawdy and discreditable nature were being buffeted at the departing executives. ''Have a saucepan on me at the Claw in Imperial City!'' ''Don't buy more wives than you can handle in one night!'' ''Tell them a thing or two at the home office about what it's like out here, the mangy slobs!''

The atmosphere was so convivial that even Ker was included, and the midget sat with pompous importance trying to judge a contest of how many bites a minute could be taken from a saucepan with the participant's paws held behind him.

Five executives were chanting a school yell that went, ''Psychlo, Psychlo, Psychlo, kill'm, kill'm, kill'm,'' over and over, tunelessly but loud.

Down back of the firing platform a train of pack horses, hoofs muffled with furred hide, moved silently out of a ravine and through the dark toward the unlit morgue. The greenish compound glow reached toward them unrevealingly. A faint clink of metal as Angus MacTavish unlocked the morgue door with a master key.

Char was very drunk, drunk and reeling. He walked unsteadily over to Terl—who looked drunk but was cold and tensely sober.

"That's a goo' idea," said Char. He was always a nasty drunk and the more he drank the nastier he got.

"What is?" said Terl through the uproar.

"Tell'm a thing or two at the home office," hiccuped Char.

Terl went very still. Char did not see his eyes narrow and flame. Then Terl said in a drunken slur, "I got a little presen' for you, Char. C'm outside for a minute."

Char lifted his eyebones. "Ain' gotta mask."

"Thersh masks beshide the door port," said Terl.

Unobserved by the rest, Terl steered him to the hall and they got into masks in a tangled fashion. Terl went through the atmosphere lock, dragging Char behind.

Terl led him down near the zoo cages. There was no fire burning. It was too late. There was no bundle in front of the cage.

The spring chill of the exterior revived Char a trifle and he returned to being nasty. "Animals," he said. "You're a animal lover, Terl. I never did like you, Terl."

Terl was not listening to him. What was that down by the morgue? He peered more closely. There were animals down there!

"You're awful clever, Terl. But you're not clever enough to fool *me!*"

Terl took a couple of steps toward the morgue, trying to see in the dark. He took out a pocket torch and flashed it in that direction. Brown hide? Hard to see.

Then he got a better view of it. A small herd of buffalo. They'd been drifting north for days now. Mixed in with some horses. He turned the torch off. The casually walking hoofs were distant, tiny thuds. Louder were the squeaks and crunches of the new spring grass being pulled up as the herd grazed its way along. An owl was hooting off somewhere. Usual nonsense of this accursed planet. He gave his attention back to Char.

Terl put his arm around Char's shoulder and guided him back to a point where the circles of the compound domes made a recess as they met. It was very dark here, hidden from all views

"What didn't fool you, friend Char?" asked Terl.

The owl hooted again.

Terl looked around. There were no vantage points from which they could be seen.

Char was sneering. "The blast cap smoke," he said, putting his face mask very close to Terl's. He reeled and Terl held him up.

"What about it?" said Terl.

"Why, that wasn't no blast gun that went off in old Numph's office. That was a blasting cap. Y'think an old mine boss like me can't smell the difference between a blast *gun* and a blast *cap!*"

Terl's paw was reaching for the small of his own back, under the jacket. He'd been trying to work out a way to furnish a reason for launching the gas drone day after tomorrow. He suddenly had it, and without stirring up any psychic powers either.

"Appointin' Ker, that miserable excuse, just hours before. Oh!" exclaimed the hostile Char. "You are clever enough for *some* people, but I see through you, Terl. I see through you."

"Why, what did you think?" said Terl.

"Think! I didn't have time to think! When I get home I can tell them a thing or two. You ain't so smart, Terl. Think I don't know one smoke for another? And people will agree with me when I get home!"

Terl shoved ten inches of stainless steel knife into Char's heart. It was the knife Jonnie had given Chrissie.

He lowered the sagging body down to the ground. He took a nearby scrap of discarded tarpaulin and covered it.

Terl went back to the cage and looked in. The girls were sleeping.

The buffalo herd was still moving quietly past the morgue.

Terl went back inside. There was more to do tonight but just now the party must not realize he had been absent. He joined the Psychlos who were chanting. They were very drunk.

Down at the morgue men moved carefully so as not to disturb the buffalo they had drifted in on the place from the plain. The horses were unloaded and gone.

Nobody had observed the murder of Char. It was not possible to get that close to the domes without being seen. Those in the morgue continued their work, unaware that a new factor had been entered into planning, one they did not know about and had not predicted.

The farewell party continued to racket noise out of the compound, unaware that their guest of honor was missing.

— 2 —

Jonnie lay in a coffin at the near end of the morgue. The lid was slightly propped open to give him air and an interior view. On the outside roof a button camera brought the exterior scene to a hand viewer resting beside him in the dark confines. He was dressed in Chinko blue but he wore moccasins, the better to speed him today.

For today in the space of just two exact minutes he had to cover certain exact grounds and do very drilled and exact things and do them in an exact time, or the whole project would fail and he would be dead. And Chrissie and Pattie would die as well. And all the Scots and others left on Earth.

He heard the transshipment area control tower warning horn for the incoming phase.

"Motors off. Stand clear!"

The humming came on. The ground vibrated. The coffin lid trembled. The humming built up and up.

Suddenly two hundred new incoming Psychlos appeared on the platform along with their baggage.

The humming dropped. A faint vibration remained.

"Coordinates holding and linked up with second stage."

The whole area came to life. One hour and thirteen minutes would elapse now until they fired back to Psychlo.

Personnel department members were herding the incoming draft off to the side and getting them in line.

Terl eyed the assemblage. The last time a draft had come in he had had a bad shock, and now he wasn't taking any chances. He was half-expecting to find a new Planet Head in this lot, somebody to replace Ker, and he might have to think fast. He walked down the line, not looking at baggage for contraband. He was just looking at faces through their domed transport helmets, checking off the names. Two hundred. More of old Numph's nonsense to get as many on the swindle payroll as he could. Terl went down the whole line. He breathed a sigh of relief. No replacement here for Ker, just the usual gutter sweepings from the slums of Psychlo plus an oddball junior executive and a couple of graduates from the mine school. Routine. Not one in the lot that could qualify as a Planet Head. All a bit lethargic. No agents from I.B.I. either!

Terl raised a paw to personnel and they divided some off for waiting transport planes destined for other minesites and some to berthing here. They loaded them on flatbeds with their baggage and they were gone.

That was a relief to Terl. He approached the morgue. That blasted horse of the animal's that was always hanging around the compound was grazing in back of the morgue. "Get away from here!" Terl yelled at the horse and made paw motions to shoo him off. The horse looked at Terl indifferently. and when Terl went to open the door it came even closer.

Terl unlocked the morgue door and threw it wide.

There were ten coffins lying there, ready to be scooped up by lift machines. He checked for the small "X" marks on the covers. Nothing like taking precautions. Every lid had its little "X" mark.

He patted one of them fondly. He took a deep breath. Maybe eight or ten months from now he would be digging these up some dark Psychlo night in the isolated and dreary cemetery on Psychlo. And it would be riches, power! The fruits of his project were hard won. They wouldn't be that hard to spend!

The first lift came, thrust its prongs under a coffin. Terl went back outside. He checked off the name on his records. The second coffin, the third, the fourth . . . Terl looked at the fourth one, a bit puzzled. How come he had spelled Jayed's false name wrong? Not "Snit" but "Stni." He checked for the "X." That was there all right. Well, to crap with it. He'd enter the error on the record. One good false name deserved another. The ex-agent was good and dead. That's all that mattered.

The lifts were dumping the coffins any which way on the platform. Terl watched, a bit apprehensive at the rough handling. But none landed upside-down.

Nine of the coffins were lying out there now. The lift superintendent stopped his machine beside Terl to let him check off number ten, the last one he was carrying.

"These coffins seem awful heavy," commented the superintendent.

Terl looked up, masking any alarm. They were only about a hundred pounds overweight, not enough to notice and certainly not enough to make much difference to a lift machine. The coffins should weigh about seventeen hundred each, even with those lids.

"Your power cartridge is probably half-discharged," said Terl.

"Maybe," said the superintendent. The coffins seemed like three thousand pounds. But he rolled the machine and dumped the tenth one on the platform.

The personnel department flatbed for outgoing personnel came up. Its driver was looking a little harassed. There were five Psychlos and their baggage on the truck, two of them returning executives and the other three ordinary miners going home. The driver gave Terl the list.

"You'll have to change that list," said the driver. "Char is supposed to be on it. He was scheduled to go home today and all of us in personnel have been running around looking for him, and we can't find him. His baggage is here but we can't find Char."

"Which is his baggage?" asked Terl. The driver pointed to a separate pile and Terl swept it off the truck with one sweep of his arm.

"We looked everywhere," said the driver. "Shouldn't we hold up the firing?"

"You know you can't do that," said Terl quickly. "Did you look in the beds of the female admin people?"

The driver let out a guffaw. "I guess we should have done that. That was *some* party last night."

"We'll fire him off in six months," said Terl and wrote, "Fires later," on the document after Char's name and signed it.

The personnel flatbed went off to dump the passengers on the platform. They stood about in a group, making sure their firing helmets were on tight. They were several feet away from the coffins.

Terl glanced at his watch. One hour and eleven minutes. Two more minutes to go.

"Coordinates holding on second stage!" came from the bullhorn over the operations dome. The white light was flashing.

Terl walked back closer to the morgue. That blasted horse was poking around the door. Terl made shooing motions with his paws. The horse moved off a few steps and began to graze again.

It was a relief to see those coffins out there. Terl stood gazing upon them fondly. About one minute to go.

Then his hair seemed to stand on end. From within the morgue, the empty deserted morgue, came a voice!

— 3 —

When the last coffin had gone out the open door, Jonnie had silently slid out of his coffin. He had three kill-clubs thrust in his belt and he was holding a fourth, the heaviest one. He laid a picto-recorder player in the middle of the floor with one flashing motion and backed up behind the door. The shadow of Terl outside lay across the floor.

The recorder started to play. It was a recording of Terl's own voice. It said, "Jayed, you silly crunch, what a crap lousy I.B.I. agent you were."

It was playing loud enough to be heard outside.

The shadow of Terl contracted, turning.

The recorder said, "It ain't smart, Jayed, to come in here worrying your betters. . . ."

Terl lunged through the door, slamming it shut with a frantic hand. He raised his boot to stamp the recorder into oblivion.

Jonnie dove forward. With a motion he had drilled and drilled with a dummy, the kill-club crashed into Terl's skull.

With his other hand, even as Terl fell forward, Jonnie ripped up the pocket flap and got the remote control box to the cage.

A horn was going outside. "Coordinates holding on first stage. Motors off!"

Jonnie hit Terl again. The body collapsed. Jonnie ripped the breathe-mask off Terl's face and threw it clear to the far end of the morgue where it landed with a clatter. He bent over Terl. Green blood was running down the side of the monster's head. The feet were drumming. Then Terl was still. There was no breathing. The eyes seemed glazed. He would have liked to put a shot in Terl. He took the belt gun. But he didn't dare shoot. Until those wires out there started to hum, they could stop the firing.

The instant the wires began to hum he knew the process was irreversible.

The bullhorn bawled, "Stand clear!"

The wires had begun to hum.

Jonnie's two minutes had begun, and they might well be his last two minutes alive. He had clicked on the stopwatch on his wrist.

He flashed out the door and twisted the lock closed behind him. In these two minutes, nobody would fire a gun since it might hit wires or mess up coordinate settings.

He took in the scene. Windsplitter was only three paces away from where he was supposed to be. Jonnie was on him and with one heel jab they were running.

In a flying blur they raced to the platform!

The humming was intensifying. Anything that stayed on that platform was going to go to Psychlo where you couldn't even breathe the atmosphere. And a very messy arrival this would be if all went well.

Windsplitter's hoofs hit the metal of the platform and he reared to a stop as Jonnie dove for the first coffin.

His fingers sought a little round ring that imperceptibly stood out, just under the lid at the top end. He pulled it and a strip came away in his hand. One!

Second coffin. Ring found. Pull. Strip in hand. Two!

The third coffin. Ring. Strip. Three!

A hysterical Psychlo voice came on the bullhorn. "Clear the platform! Clear the platform!"

The small group of Psychlos beyond the coffins woke up to something strange going on. They stared. One of the executives, hungover from the party, raised his arm to point.

Fourth, fifth, and sixth rings!

In these coffins were ten "planet buster" nuclear missile bombs, forbidden by treaties because they could crack the planet's crust and spray the world with fallout.

Packed around them were the "dirtiest" early, radioactive atomic bombs, outlawed because of their extreme pollution potential.

The seventh ring was bent. Jonnie fumbled with it.

"Grab him!" screamed the executive on the platform.

The five Psychlos moved to attack.

Jonnie threw his kill-club at the executive. He went down.

Jonnie yanked two more kill-clubs from his belt and hurled them in a blur of speed. Two more Psychlos went down.

He got back to number seven. He untwisted it and got it out.

He grabbed number eight and pulled it.

There was a suicide squad of Scots in the bushes, standing by in case at the last moment Jonnie failed. He had forbidden it but they insisted. He had timed the run. He wanted no dead Scots.

Jonnie had refused to simply let the fuses be set. If the firing had been canceled they would have blown Earth out of existence. They had to be sure the irreversible action of actual firing was in progress before these fuse strips were pulled.

Nine strips in hand!

The two remaining Psychlos had been further away but they were coming now.

"Strike!" shouted Jonnie at Windsplitter.

The horse reared and struck the nearest Psychlo.

The last monster on the platform reached to grab Jonnie.

Ten!

Jonnie struck with the kill-club and smashed the Psychlo's helmet.

The reaching talons tore his sleeve. He struck again.

He leaped to the back of Windsplitter.

"Run!"

Someone on the control porch had come out with a blast rifle but did not dare shoot.

The humming wires were building up to crescendo.

Jonnie was off the platform and racing up the hill to the cage. His watch said forty-two seconds left to go. He had never known time to flow so slowly! Or so fast!

He had not gone to Psychlo.

But blast rifles were waiting to cut him down.

He had already switched the remote control box he had recovered so as to shut off the current to the bars. He had gotten out the metal severing tool so he could slash off the girls' collars.

Windsplitter plunged to a halt before the cage door. Jonnie threw himself off the horse.

He paused for an instant.

The cage door was open! The wood barrier was torn aside!

Where were the girls? Their effects were all here.

Not up? There was a mound under the robes. Ah, they must still be asleep.

He rushed in, metal tool ready to cut the collars, shouting their names.

No motions in the robes.

He threw the furs aside.

He was staring at the corpse of Char. It lay on its back and the stainless steel knife he had given Chrissie was sticking out of Char's middle.

He had no time for speculation. He was out of the cage, staring about. Old Pork and Dancer were not there. Could it be possible the girls had actually killed Char and escaped? Not likely! Not with this remote box in Terl's possession.

Seconds were ticking away. Blast rifles were waiting.

He leaped on Windsplitter and dashed for the edge of the bluff. They started a small avalanche as they halted halfway down the slope.

Jonnie sprang off and made sure they were covered from sight.

The humming came to top crescendo. The strange quiver was in the air. He recognized the feeling.

The shipment had shimmered and vanished from the platform!

— 4 —

Now would come the usual minor recoil that followed a semi-annual firing.

Jonnie counted the seconds. He was panting heavily from his sprint. Windsplitter beside him was blowing, trembling.

Suddenly the ground shook. The air was rent with a splintering crash. A flash lit the sky.

Recoil? Sounded more like the place had blown up!

Jonnie scrambled to the top of the cliff and peered over the edge.

Too much recoil!

By fuse the nuclear weapons should not have gone off on Psychlo for another ten seconds.

The operations dome was still in the air, flames geysering from it.

The network of wires around the platform was melting.

Machines in the area were sent skidding. Psychlo operators were tumbled to the earth.

Wild, aura-like, sheet lightning bloomed over the transshipment scene!

The compound domes were rocked but seemed intact.

The concussion was racketing across the plains.

It was too soon for the bombs to go off on Psychlo. What had happened? Had they missed their target and landed their lethal cargo on some nearer space? Did this mean Psychlo armament from the home planet could still appear in the sky and crush them?

But right now the question was: had this messed up their assault plans?

He looked anxiously toward the row of battle planes. The instant after recoil was their cue.

He looked toward the nearby ravines. Scot teams in camouflage radiation dress were due to sprint out of cover and take position with their weapons.

That recoil might also be radioactive, and here he was with no radiation battle suit.

Yay! There went the battle planes! Sixteen of them had been manned, each with a pilot and copilot. They had hidden in the planes all night. Keys to them had been placed on each seat.

Up soared the battle planes! A blasting, combined roar of heavy motors. Thirty-two Scot pilots and copilots.

Fifteen planes peeled off and darted at hypersonic toward their destinations. One plane for each distant minesite on the planet. The mission was to batter and destroy them and prevent a counterattack here. One plane to act as air cover for this central minesite. Radio silence was the watchword. No warning!

Jonnie looked at the remaining planes on the ground to see whether they had been battered. He noted they were a bit turned. They seemed all right. . . .

Wait! Something was wrong. There should be four planes left there. They only had thirty-two pilots and copilots. But there were three planes left, not four!

He raised himself above the cliff edge again and swept the scene.

And there it was.

The whole side wall of the morgue had been battered out, and the coffin with which it had been done lay in the rubble!

Terl had somehow come to life and hammered his way out of the morgue.

Jonnie looked up.

Where there should have been one battle plane up there for this minesite, there were two! Jonnie grabbed for Windsplitter. Something was wrong. The horse had gone lame in its plunge down the cliff. It was three hundred yards to those planes.

With a glare at the sky, Jonnie was running down the hill, putting all his strength into it.

A blast rifle spat at him from the compound. He raced on through a cloud of dirt.

Where were the assault teams? Had they been knocked flat?

Racing, Jonnie headed for the nearest battle plane, shots streaking the air about him. More blast rifles were firing from the compound.

He got to the plane door and got it half open. A blast rifle shot slammed it shut. He dove under the plane and went in the other door.

The key. The key! Where had Angus put this plane's key? He was scrambling through the edges of the seats. The recoil jolt had jarred the key off the seat. A blast rifle splattered a shot onto the windscreen. There was the key! On the floor!

The instant before he touched the starters, he heard the chunk of a bazooka go. Then the flailing chatter of assault rifles.

The motors barked and he raced his hands over the console. The plane flashed upward to two thousand feet.

He caught a glimpse of the attack groups moving in. Two bazooka teams. Four assault rifle parties. They had been protected in the ravines in which they had crouched all night, covered with antiheat shields.

Jonnie flipped on the viewscreens. Where was Terl?

— 5 —

A few miles to the north, Terl and the minesite cover plane were engaged in a dance of battle.

Jonnie slammed his battle plane toward the two ships. Suddenly they moved farther north. One plane was running away to the north. The other took off in pursuit. Two Scots running away? No! Jonnie suddenly understood what was happening. It was a trick! Terl was pretending to run away to lure the Scots into a trap maneuver.

Radio silence. Damn radio silence!

The Scots fell for it.

Before Jonnie could get there, Terl had looped back and deadly fingers of flame were raking the Scots' ship.

The target flamed! It roared toward the ground.

Two men ejected, right and left, from the burning plane. Their jet packs smoked as they bit and arrested their falls. They were sailing some distance apart.

If Jonnie could get behind Terl while he was still concentrating on the plane . . . yes! Terl dove to shoot one of the pilots, unable to resist a sadistic touch.

The pilot was hit and spun back upward.

Jonnie was right behind Terl. He pressed his gun trips and the artillery blasters knifed into the ship.

Then abruptly Terl's plane was gone!

A quick glance at the viewscreens. Terl was above him.

But Terl didn't shoot.

Abruptly Jonnie realized that Terl was going to ignore him and try to get back to the compound and shoot up the ground troops.

The keynote of Psychlo battle tactics was outguessing with a plane's keyboard. The planes could dart so quickly and at such changing speeds that one had to divine what the other would do and do it first.

Jonnie snapped his battle plane in front of Terl's. For an instant he could see the facemasked Psychlo through the armored windscreen. It *was* Terl. A madly efficient Terl, a Terl who for all his insanity was a past master at flying and a top marksman. Jonnie wondered whether he could match this maniac.

Terl went to the right. Jonnie had outguessed him and gone the same direction. Terl went farther right. Jonnie had outguessed him and was in front of him with ready firing guns.

Terl went up. Jonnie's hands on the keyboard did not outguess him and Terl was almost able to dart past and return to rake the compound assault teams. Jonnie corrected and almost rammed Terl from below.

Why hadn't he battered the monster's head off in the morgue? But there had been no time.

Terl went low to the right, then to the left, then to the right. Rhythmical. Easy to predict. Jonnie was in front of him every time.

Too late, Jonnie realized it was a trap. The fourth time, Terl's guns were firing at the place Jonnie was about to be. Only the slip of a finger on a key saved him from being blasted out of the sky.

Abruptly Terl seemed to abandon his effort to get through to the compound. He headed straight north.

Down below, the burning plane sent up soaring piles of black smoke.

Was this another Terl trick? Luring him off?

Ears blasted by the scream of tortured motors, Jonnie swept his eyes across his viewscreens. Where was Terl going and why? With a sudden hunch he flipped on a heat detection screen.

Chrissie and Pattie, riding to the north! Their horses' bellies to the ground as they raced along.

Leverage. Jonnie suddenly realized Terl was trying to get back his leverage! If he could recover his hostages he might bring pressure on Jonnie.

Jonnie flipped open the local command radio. Sure enough—Terl's voice!

"If you don't go down there and land, animal, I'll kill them both."

Terl was right ahead of him, dropping down to about four thousand feet.

Jonnie hit his keys. He estimated exactly where Terl would be.

Jonnie's battle plane slammed into the back of Terl's. Jonnie closed the switch for the magnetic grips. The skids of his plane locked to the back of Terl's.

Half-deafened by the thud of contact, Jonnie stepped up his speed control to hypersonic. His motors shrieked. He punched in coordinates to compare with six feet underground directly below them.

He glanced over the side to see that the riders were clear of that spot. They were.

The motors of both ships were screaming in discord, fighting against one another in howling dissonance. They jerked and wrestled in the sky, suspended in space. The motors began to get hot. Very shortly they would burn and explode.

Jonnie reached back for the jet packs. The straps had already been shortened. He shrugged into it. He made sure he still had Terl's belt gun.

He took one final glance at the keyboard. Locked in. Six feet underground, directly below, four thousand feet down, speed control at hypersonic.

Jonnie dove out the plane door. The air bit at him as he plummeted down.

His jets barked alive and the descent slowed. By swinging his legs, he went up to a higher altitude.

He looked at the locked and fighting ships.

He had expected that Terl would bail out. The outcome was inevitable. The ships would explode. He was counting on Terl's having no belt gun, and he intended to hunt him down in a jet pack or on the ground. But Terl didn't bail out. Jonnie could see him battering away at his control console.

Jonnie, holding in space with his backpack jets, had the sickening feeling he had made a mistake. Terl, after all, knew Psychlo tactics backward.

What Terl was doing in that jerking, fighting mess where one ship's motors fought the other's, was trying to outguess the settings of the plane that rode his back. If he could, both motors would agree. Possibly, then, a quick roll and reversal of the settings would throw the other ship off his back.

The smoke from those conflicting motors was already beginning to rise in the battle plane Jonnie had bailed out of.

Suddenly Terl got the combination! Both ships' motors smoothed into shrieking agreement.

But Jonnie's combination was straight down and six feet under, hypersonic.

At an abrupt two thousand miles an hour, both ships hurtled toward the earth.

In an instant, Terl apparently realized that this set of console coordinates was sudden death.

Jonnie could see him in the cabin, moving urgently.

With only five hundred feet to go, Terl frantically punched in the reverse combination. His ship motors went into a fighting howl.

The inertia of the mass carried it down to within twenty feet of the ground before the descent halted.

But the force on the hot motors was too great for them to overcome.

Both ships burst into an orange ball of fire!

Terl's body hurtled out of the door and struck rolling.

The ships struck!

With a swing of his legs Jonnie headed downward into a dive. With a thumb on the jet pack throttle, he guided himself to land about a hundred feet from the fiercely flaming wreck.

Terl was still rolling.

— 6 —

Jonnie shed his jet backpack. It was almost expended anyway. Not taking his eyes from Terl, he drew the belt gun and slid off its safety.

Terl had been on fire for a moment. He was not now. He had rolled it out in the damp spring grass. He was fifty feet away. He was lying motionless. He had a breathe-mask on.

Jonnie approached cautiously. This was a very treacherous beast. He walked within forty feet. Thirty feet. Terl was just lying there, inert.

A statement Robert the Fox had made drifted through Jonnie's head: "Plan well, but when battle is joined, expect the unexpected! And cope with it!" Terl's escape had scrambled their plans. The compound down there was without air cover. The lord alone knew what was going on. The sound of gunfire was rattling and thudding in the distance. The mutter of flames came from the burning planes nearby.

Jonnie didn't look. He had his eyes on Terl, watchful. He stopped. Twenty-five feet was close enough. He could not quite see through the faceplate. Terl was singed. There was some dried green blood on his jacket.

Suddenly Terl's hand blurred and a small gun appeared in it like magic.

Jonnie dropped at the first hint of motion and fired.

There was a flash as Terl's gun exploded in his paw. Then he was up and starting to run.

There were questions Jonnie wanted answered. His first snap shot had been lucky and had hit the gun. He drew a careful bead on Terl's right leg. "Here's one for the horses," flashed through his head. He fired.

The leg buckled and Terl went down. The foot stayed twisted in the wrong direction.

Jonnie walked over to where the exploded gun lay. It was a very slim weapon. Was this what was called an "assassin gun"?

Terl was lying there, motionless.

"Quit shamming, Terl," said Jonnie.

Terl suddenly laughed and sat up.

"Why didn't you die in the morgue?"

"Animal," said Terl, putting his foot right-way to but carefully sitting quiet under the menace of the gun twenty feet away. "I can hold my breath for four minutes!"

He was too cheerful. His leg was bleeding through his pants. He was singed. But he was too cheerful. Jonnie *knew* there was something else. He backed up.

Moving so that he could keep Terl in view out of the corner of his eye, he glanced around the plain. The compound was behind them, possibly twenty miles. Gunfire was coming faintly from that direction. He knew he should make some effort to help them.

Where were the girls? Probably they had gone on. No! There they were! Jonnie hadn't expected that. They were coming back. Riding at a slow trot, cautiously, they were coming back. They were about a mile away.

It hit Jonnie suddenly. The shock of not finding them in the cage, the fear that they were still in that holocaust down there, had stayed suspended. He was swept by a tide of relief. They were all right!

Jonnie waved his arm to signal them to come on in.

Still alert to Terl, Jonnie scanned farther afield. One of the pilots that had bailed out had come in this direction. He peered. Yes! There was somebody moving about four miles to the south—hard to see due to camouflage dress—but a trained eye such as Jonnie's detected by the motion of things, not only by contrasts.

Terl was laughing again. "You'll never get away with it, animal. Psychlo will be into this place in a swarm!"

Jonnie didn't answer. He waved the girls in. The horses were shying as they came around the burning wreck. Chrissie was mounted on Old Pork, Pattie on Dancer. The horses weren't blowing, so their earlier riding must not have been so fast.

The girls were unable to believe it was Jonnie. Chrissie stayed mounted, some distance away. She was ghastly pale. Her neck was raw red from the collar now gone. "Jonnie? Is that you, Jonnie?" He looked different in the blue clothing. Pattie had no doubts. She sprang from the back of Dancer and raced to Jonnie and put her arms around his waist, her hair coming up to his pocket. "See? See?" she was shouting back to Chrissie. "I told you Jonnie would come! I told you and told you!"

Chrissie was sitting her horse and crying.

"You got the monster!" said Pattie, excited, pointing at Terl.

"Don't get between me and him," said Jonnie, caressing her hair but holding the gun on Terl. He should be at the compound; he must not dally here.

Jonnie didn't want the girls near him in case Terl moved. He had a sudden idea. "Chrissie! Look down to the south there about four miles."

Chrissie took a grip on herself and wiped her eyes. Jonnie wanted her to do something. She looked. She tried to speak, then cleared her throat and tried again. "Yes, Jonnie." She looked harder. "It's something moving."

"It's a friend," said Jonnie. "Ride down there as fast as you can whip up Old Pork and bring him back here!"

Chrissie straightened up. She guided Old Pork well around Terl and then lit out to the south, her hair streaming back as Old Pork raced away.

The gunfire was picking up in volume to the south. Being gentle with Pattie and walking sideways while keeping a gun on Terl, Jonnie got to a position where he could see the compound. They stood on a slightly higher rise than it.

In the clear afternoon air he could see it, in miniature, but vividly.

White water was spraying two or three hundred feet in the air. It looked like a waterfall in reverse. Then he knew what had happened. The automatic fire sprinkler system had let go.

Those Scots down there were fighting in a torrent of water!

What he was afraid of was that the Psychlos would get out a tank or some additional battle planes. He surveyed the sky. It was free of planes.

As he watched he saw a flash of fire and then the distant "boomp" came to them, the sound bazookas make. He was not sure the bazookas could get through a Psychlo tank.

They needed air support down there! And here he was twenty miles away! There wasn't another single pilot in those assault teams. They had committed their all.

He shifted the gun impatiently. Terl was sitting there laughing again. By rights he should simply shoot him full of daylight. But he had a feeling Terl knew something, and was up to something more.

"How'd the girls get away?" said Jonnie to Terl.

"Why, animal, how can you doubt me? I promised you I'd let them loose as soon as you delivered the gold. I simply kept my word this morning. I didn't suspect you'd be so false you would . . ."

"Come off it, Terl. Why'd you let them loose?"

Terl laughed again, more loudly.

Pattie had gone over to get Dancer who was wandering off. She was coming back. "I don't know why this nasty-old-awful-thing did it. But just before dawn, he cut off our collars and told us to get on the horses and ride away. We went about ten miles and hid, thinking maybe you'd show up. We had no place to go. Then this afternoon the whole place seemed to blow up, bang, bang, and we rode toward the mountains."

Suddenly Jonnie added it up. He spoke to Terl. "So you murdered Char, did you, and left him in the cage with that man-knife in him so that man could be blamed for his death. The question is, Terl, how were you going to wipe out the humans?

Terl had been looking at his watch. He reached toward his pocket. Jonnie abruptly made him desist.

"Just two talons," said Terl, holding them up.

Jonnie indicated he could but was very watchful.

Terl plucked something that was about a foot square from his side pocket, moving very delicately and gingerly under the watchful gun. It was a large remote computer board. Thin. Familiar in machine operation but a bit bigger and dirtier than usual.

With a laugh Terl tossed it toward Jonnie, who backed up in case it exploded.

"You took the wrong remote off me, rat brain."

Jonnie stared down at it, not comprehending. The keyboard only had date, hour, and fire on it. It had no stop or correction tab.

"It's irreversible," said Terl. "Once punched and activated, the board is worthless. This morning before the semiannual, I used it up."

Terl glanced at his watch. "In about ten minutes now, you'll all collect your pay whether you messed up Psychlo or not!" He went into a gale of laughter. "You were after the wrong remote!"

The laughter made him sputter in his face mask. "And here you are," he finally managed, "twenty miles away and you can't do a thing about it. And couldn't anyway!"

He pounded his paws in the dirt, he was laughing so hard.

— 7 —

At that exact moment Zzt in the underground hangars was almost out of his wits.

Ever since that wild recoil had occurred at the end of the semiannual, things had been in chaos.

The rumor had been flying about that it was *humans* out there. *Men!* Zzt knew better. Those silly slugs could do nothing. It was undoubtedly Tolneps, landing in here from their system. Zzt, although his thinking was interrupted every few seconds by curses at Terl, had it all worked out. The Tolneps had buggered up the teleportation bands to paralyze counterattack and were in here after the still not inconsiderable mineral content of this planet. There had been trouble with the Tolneps before and the last war with them was inconclusive. They were short, about half the size of a Psychlo, and they could breathe almost anything. And were immune to Psychlo gas barrages, worse luck. Therefore he was rigging a Mark 32 low-flying ground strafer, the most heavily gunned plane in the hundreds of planes in these hangars.

And damn and blast that Terl. *He* was supposed to be in charge of defense! And where were the standby, alert battle planes? Out in the weather. And where were the tanks? Snug and rusting in the underground tank park! And where were the reserves at other minesites? Pulled in here!

Damn Terl! There was no fuel cartridge or ammunition supply inside the compound. Zzt was illogical in blaming Terl for this, since it was against company rules to store them inside a compound.

They were nearly a half-mile from here, and two parties of Psychlos that had tried to get to the dump had been slaughtered. And that was another thing that proved it was Tolneps. The Psychlos who had been hit simply exploded into a pale green flash. Only Tolneps could invent weapons like that!

So he had to scavenge in the old planes and ground cars for half-used cartridges and ammunition charges. Oh, there was quite a bit to be found, but it couldn't be depended on.

He had come to physical blows with the two Chamco brothers, blast them. They were readying up a heavy armored tank. Two tanks that had gotten out that violent afternoon had been blown to cinders. So the Chamcos were rigging one of the old brutes of the Basher class: "Bash our Way to Glory." Nothing could penetrate its hide and its guns wrecked things for miles. The Chamcos were salvaging fuel and ammunition cartridges for it, and they had the nerve, the twisted metal nerve, to maintain that the attackers were Hockners from Duraleb, a system Psychlo had completely whipped two hundred years ago.

The battle had been over who got the cartridges, and that pompous midget Ker had come down and given them both half. Another Terl mess!

The cartridges didn't fit the Mark 32. Zzt had spent valuable time machining a false case around them to get them into the tubes. Damn Terl!

He had told his men to *move that damned drone* two hours ago. Damn Terl!

Now here he was. He had found a copilot: one of the executives in the draft that had just arrived, rated combat on a Mark 32, named Nup; a dimwit—but that's what you got on an out-of-the-way planet like this—who thought it was a typical Bolbod attack, based on a rumor he had heard in the kerbango shops lately in the Imperial City that a conquest of the Bolbods was intended.

Zzt had collected a combat breathe-mask, gotten a shoulder bag of extra vials, gotten his sidearms, put spare rations in his pocket, and last but not least put his favorite wrench into the side of his boot, a wrench that sometimes came in handy in any kind of fight or situation.

The Mark 32 motors turned over easily. It purred. In no time at all he would be out there and that would be the very positive end of this attack! Damn Terl!

Zzt let off the skid grips and taxied the Mark 32, "Hit 'Em Low, Kill 'Em," toward the firing door. Mechanics leaped to get out of his way. The place was in a turmoil of Psychlos trying to get planes ready with nothing. And that damned drone was still standing there.

Ordinarily you could fire three planes at once through that door. It was high enough even to add a fourth. But that ancient relic of a gas drone was so wide and so tall it was blocking the whole door. Just what he'd told Terl. Damn Terl! There was *no* way he could get the Mark 32 past it.

Zzt leaned out the door and screamed for the shift foreman. He came rushing up. Zzt almost bit him. "Move that damned drone! Two hours ago I—"

"It won't dolly," panted the foreman. He pointed. Four dolly trucks had been trying to push it away. "It won't move!"

Zzt gave his equipment bag a hoist onto his shoulder and sprang down. "You imbecile crunch! The only inside control that thing has is its mag-grapnels. Why haven't you let it off! Those big skis are magnetically locked to this platform! Why don't you learn—"

"It's a very old drone," chattered the foreman, his wits starting to crumble under Zzt's glare.

Zzt rushed to the door of the drone. It was a huge door, big enough to load a dozen gas canisters at a time. Somebody had put a rolling ladder there and Zzt ran up it, his equipment clattering, and pried at the door. It was locked! An armored door itself the size of a plane.

"Where's the key?" screamed Zzt.

"Terl had it!" the foreman shouted up at him. "We've looked everywhere for Terl. We can't find him!"

Damn Terl! "Have you searched his rooms?" Zzt yelled down from the rolling ladder.

"Yes. Yes. Yes!" cried the foreman. "We—"

At that moment a higher-pitched voice bit into the row of the hangar. "Yoohoo!" It was Chirk. Zzt stared in daggers of hostility. The cheap twit!

But she was holding a single huge key. "I found this in his desk," she caroled.

"Where are the other keys to this thing?" shouted Zzt. "The preset box keys."

"That's the only one there was in the desk," lilted Chirk.

It gave Zzt an instant's pause. He didn't want this damned old relic firing itself off in the hangar with no way to get out. But he had to *move* it. This was the door key they were passing up to him.

He glared at the key. Three toggles. Pitted. The shaft almost in two. Terl could at least have made a new key! But oh no, it was paws off.

He shoved the key, all twenty pounds of it, at the lock hole. He twisted it with a curse. Damn Terl!

The rusty, magnetic clenchers gave. The key fell apart.

Zzt flung it to the platform below, narrowly missing Chirk. At least the door was open.

He struggled to swing it back. Even the hinges were decayed and stiff. It opened to reveal the enormous interior.

Zzt got a torch. There were no lights in this thing. It was never meant to have a pilot in it. It was just tons and tons and tons of gas canisters, engines, and armor.

He thought belatedly he might have robbed some fuel from it. Too late now.

He lumbered forward to the control compartment. He had better throw them off. But no! They were armor-locked solid. They couldn't be unset without a key. And this metal wouldn't surrender to anything. It was armored! Damn Terl!

He darted his light around. There was the magnetic grip release, the only interior control, put there so hangar and firing people could lock and unlock it when moving it about with tractors.

Zzt reached for the release brake.

Before he could touch it, it moved!

He froze, looking at it in horror. Yes, there was a click in the preset box. He dove for the door.

The forward jerk of the motors threw him off his feet. He scrambled for the exit.

Too late!

The hangar door was fleeing by. It was already yards down to the ground. He didn't dare jump.

The drone took off, its rusty side door flapping in the wind.

Zzt led out a shuddering groan. Damn Terl!

Well, at least they could get the battle planes out and end the Tolnep attack.

And all this on half-pay and no bonuses.

Probably that was Terl's doing, too.

— 8 —

Jonnie, twenty miles away, saw the drone launch. It was a huge thing. The gas drone? He went ice cold.

The flash of an explosion bloomed on the side of it. He knew it would be a bazooka firing. There was a team there to prevent the launching of planes. A second flash against the hull as the boom of the first one drifted faintly to them. Neither had the slightest effect upon the drone. It rose in stately massiveness to two thousand feet as it turned. Still climbing, it headed northwest.

It went by them to the east, looming in the sky, so big it looked close even though two miles away. It was ragged and patched and dented, evidences of former combat on its discolored hide. A tense Jonnie clocked it at about three hundred miles an hour. A battle plane had fired just behind it. Bazooka missiles hit the plane, exploded in two flares of light. It continued sedately on its way, following the drone. As it passed over them he saw it was a different type of battle plane. The Psychlo numbers "32" were on its side and then the smoke logos of the Psychlos. An escort?

The heavy roars beat at the earth.

When they had gone, Terl said, "Why not admit it, animal? You're licked. When the Psychlos counterattack from home planet, you'll already be gone. So why not toss that gun over here and we can make a deal?"

Jonnie ignored him. He was carefully tracking the compass course of the drone relating it to the afternoon sun. He watched it as long as he could as it droned away to the northeast. It was not turning further. Be calm, he told himself. Don't panic.

"Where's it going first?" he said to Terl. A battle plane could do two thousand miles an hour. You can catch it. Be calm.

"Throw the gun over and I'll tell you all about it," said Terl.

Terl's motions alarmed Pattie. "Don't believe anything he says," she pleaded. "He promised us food and didn't bring it. He even made out to us two or three times that you were dead!"

"You'll tell me about it," said Jonnie, "or I'll start shooting off your feet." He aimed his gun.

"Do it!" said Pattie. "He's a nasty old brute! A devil!"

Jonnie was glancing in the direction Chrissie had gone. She was taking an awful long time coming back. He couldn't leave the girls out here alone and certainly not with Terl alive. Be calm, he told himself. You can catch up with it.

"All right," said Terl as though resigned. "I'll give you the places it's going.

"In proper order," said Jonnie, raising the gun suggestively.

"You'd get a kick out of shooting me up, wouldn't you?" said Terl.

"I don't get any enjoyment out of hurting things the way—"

"That's because you're a rat brain," laughed Terl.

All this Psychlo talk between Jonnie and Terl was making Pattie very nervous. "Don't listen to him, Jonnie, just shoot him," she demanded, grabbing Jonnie's gun arm.

"All right," said Terl. "It's first target is the bottom of Africa. The next is China. The next is Russia. Then it is preset to fly to Italy and then right here."

Good, thought Jonnie. He didn't mention Scotland. It's heading over the Arctic on that course. Scotland. That's its first target. And it would be because the Psychlos couldn't get up there, or thought they couldn't. Thank you, Terl.

"Good," he said aloud. "For information received, you live a while longer." It would take it seventeen hours to get to Scotland. Look calm. You can catch it.

Chrissie was coming down. They had been hidden by a dip in the plains. The horse was at a walk. And he saw why as she came near.

It was Thor. She was holding him upright in front of her on the horse. She had removed her buckskin jacket and used it for bandages. Thor's antiradiation suit was stained with blood around the left shoulder. She had torn it away there and used buckskin and grass to staunch the blood flow. Thor's left arm was broken, bound in rough sticks for splints. It was he who had been shot out of the sky when he was using the jet pack.

With Chrissie's help Thor slid off the horse. He was gray from blood loss and stood unsteadily. He looked at Jonnie ruefully. "I'm sorry, Jonnie."

"It was my fault, not yours," said Jonnie. "Ease him down on that rock, Chrissie."

Thor looked at Terl. He had seen the monster close up only a couple of times. Thor was wearing a .457 caliber Smith and Wesson revolver from the old base arsenal loaded with radiation bullets. He suddenly recognized Terl and grabbed for his gun to shoot him.

"No, no," said Jonnie. "Keep the gun drawn and train it on him and shoot him the moment he looks like he's going to move, particularly his hands. Can you sit there okay?"

Thor was about fifty feet from Terl. He eased down further and got the gun trained on Terl.

"Now, Terl," said Jonnie, "that gun he is holding can put a hole in you a horse could dive through. It has special explosive bullets, worse than your own blast gun. Got it?" Be calm in front of these people. You can catch up with it.

He turned to Pattie. He gave her the huge blast pistol to hold. He showed her where the trigger was and she determinedly walked back of a rock so she could support the gun with it.

"I point it like this?"

"And keep it on him." You have time, he told himself. Do a good job here.

"Why not kill him?" said Thor.

"He leaks information," said Jonnie.

Terl couldn't understand what they were saying but he got their drift.

Jonnie took out a knife and, keeping out of the line of possible fire, made Terl swivel around. He inserted the knife at Terl's collar and cut the cloth down the back. He went around front, watching Terl's eyes for a telltale clench signaling action and pulled the coat sleeves off. He ripped the cloth down the side of each of Terl's legs. He darted a shallow stab at Terl when he sought to spring. Terl subsided. Jonnie got Terl's boots and pants off. He took his watch. He took his cap. The only thing Terl had left was his breathe-mask and Jonnie even took the emergency vials off that. Terl glared.

There he sat, his fur matted with sweat, his claws twitching to rake Jonnie.

Jonnie took the belt and made Terl put his paws behind him and cinched the belt as tight as he could around the wrists. Then he took Old Pork's bridle and tied the wrists and belt and then passed the rope under the mask tube. He cinched it up. If Terl tried to wrestle his wrists loose he would choke himself. Do a good job, Jonnie told himself. Don't panic. In a battle plane you can catch the drone.

He had been working very fast. He now stepped away from Terl and quickly went through the clothes. Sure enough, Terl had two more weapons secreted. A knife and a second assassin gun.

Jonnie fired a round with the assassin gun. It was silent. The bush he aimed at began to burn. He gave the light gun to Pattie and took the belt gun back.

"Let me shoot him now," said Pattie.

Thor said to Terl, in Psychlo, "The little girl over there is begging to shoot you."

"I'll be quiet here," said Terl.

"Don't go near him. Light a fire from that wreck over here to the side, Chrissie, so that Thor stays warm and you can see this area." He turned to Thor. "Who was with you?"

"Glencannon," said Thor. "He's over there in the hills somewhere. I think he tried to get closer to the base. I tried to reach him on this mine radio twice. He's got one but he doesn't answer. They've only a five-mile range." He looked curious. "Where are you going?"

At that moment there was an explosion flash at the compound. A battle plane had come out of the hangar and apparently been hit with a bazooka. It soared in a flame ball and crashed at the sound of the bazooka and then the plane explosion reached them. A second battle plane came out and met the same fate.

"See?" said Jonnie. "I'll send back a mine car for you." Be calm. At two thousand miles an hour you can catch that drone.

The girls looked numbly at Jonnie.

But what could he do? He had meant to send them to the Academy base, but Thor was in no shape to travel at all. Why not kill Terl? No, that would solve nothing. Sound calm to these people. The speed of the drone was three hundred two miles an hour, he remembered from the messages he had taken from the hand of a president a thousand years dead. A battle plane could go hypersonic at two thousand miles an hour. Even if it were halfway to Scotland, he could catch it hours before it arrived.

He swung up on Dancer. The base was about twenty miles away. Make it in an hour or so of hard riding.

"We can still make a deal, animal," said Terl. "If you sent uranium to Psychlo, you're really messed up. It's been tried before. They have a force field around their receipt platform and if any uranium flashes on Psychlo, that force field triggers solid to enclose their whole platform. The flashback occurs at the sending point just like you saw today. Psychlo will be attacking this place, animal. You'll need me to mediate."

Jonnie looked at him. He raised his hand in farewell to the girls and Thor and thumped a heel into Dancer, and she streaked off through the declining sunlight.

Ahead of him pulsed and flickered the battle at the compound. He had wasted time. He could not have done anything else. Be calm, he told himself. Don't panic. A battle plane could catch that drone.

As he raced across the plain, he put out of his mind a thought that kept crowding in. Not all the armed forces of the United States in its days of power had been able to do anything at all to that gas drone. Not with planes, missiles, atomic bombs, or even suicide crashes.

You have time. You can catch up with it. Don't panic.

■

PART 13

— 1 —

One thing at a time, Jonnie told himself. Do each thing properly. Each one as it comes up and each one in its turn. He had read that in a book from the man-library. He had been looking for cures for radiation and he found some. And he'd also found a book about how to handle confusion. It came from too many things at once. And that was certainly happening now! The drone, the possibility of a Psychlo counterattack, the outcome of the compound battle still in question. No reports yet of the attacks on other minesites. One could easily get confused, make a mistake, even panic. Stay calm. One thing at a time.

Dancer had been racing flat-out southward. That was not the right thing to do. He could founder her. He began to alternate a trot with a run. She was breathing better. The light was failing. Something as silly as a tripped horse could wreck everything. Trot, run, trot, run. Twenty miles. They would make it.

He had a mine radio in his pocket, small by Psychlo standards. At ten miles he began to call Glencannon, Thor's pilot. Jonnie spoke into the mike as he rode.

At about eleven miles, Glencannon's voice came back. "Is that you, MacTyler?" The voice sounded a bit weak.

"Can you see a running horse from where you are?" said Jonnie.

There was a long pause. Then, "Yes, you're about three miles northeast of me. You got Terl?"

"Yes, but he's all tied up at the moment."

There was a silence and then a short, barking laugh. Some of the tension had gone out of Glencannon's voice when he spoke next: "What was he after up there?"

Long story. No time now. Just be calm. Jonnie said aloud, "The girls are safe. Thor is hurt but all right."

A sigh of relief at the other end.

"Can you still pilot a plane?" said Jonnie.

Pause. "My ribs are a bit caved in and I have a twisted ankle. That's what's taking so long getting back to the compound. But yes, MacTyler, of course I can still pilot a plane."

"Keep traveling toward the compound. Have a light ready to flash. I'll send a mine car for you. They'll need air cover."

"I have a light. I'm sorry about the air cover."

"It was my fault," said Jonnie. "Good luck."

Dancer alternately trotted and ran. Keep calm. Things were not hopeless. They had a fighting chance. There were bright spots. They had agreed not to blow up the whole compound. The historian wanted the library, Angus wanted the machine shops. They evidently hadn't sent any radioactive bullets into the domes. Except for the drone and its escort they still apparently had air control.

At five and a half miles he began calling Robert the Fox at the compound, hoping somebody was monitoring the mine radio. The schoolmaster answered; Jonnie was surprised for there were several classified as noncombatants: the parson, the old women, the historian, and the schoolmaster. Jonnie shortly heard a relieved Robert the Fox.

"The girls are safe," said Jonnie. There was a pause at the other end as Robert the Fox apparently passed the word along. When the mike opened next from that end, Jonnie heard some cheering in the background. The news was evidently popular.

"We're holding out here," said Robert the Fox. "I have to talk to you about something when you get here, but not on this open line."

Dancer skirted a clump of trees. It was getting pretty dark.

"Those apes can't talk English," said Jonnie.

"No matter, still can't talk about it. When will you be here?"

"About fifteen minutes," said Jonnie.

"Come in through the ravine to the north. There's a lot of heavy return fire near the compound."

"Right," said Jonnie. "Are the planes okay?"

"We pulled them back to better cover in the ravine. We don't have pilots."

"I know. Listen now. Have somebody put the following items in one plane: warm clothing, a robe, mittens for me; something to eat; some plain, nonradioactive limpet mines; an assault rifle;

an air mask with plenty of air bottles—I'll be flying at one hundred fifty thousand feet."

There was a silence at the other end and Jonnie prompted: "Got that?"

"Yes," said Robert the Fox. "It will be done." He certainly didn't sound very eager.

"Send out a couple of mine cars," said Jonnie. He gave the locations. "Better send a man or two to help bring in Terl."

"Terl?" said Robert the Fox.

"It's the naked truth," said Jonnie. "Get that plane ready. I'll be taking off just as soon as I arrive."

A silence. Then, "Will do." He went off the air.

About five minutes later, a mine car passed him going north in the twilight. It was the parson, one of the old women, and a Scot with his arm in a sling. The parson raised his hand in a benediction—no, it was a salute! They were off to get Thor and the girls and Terl. A great length of hoist chain was flying out behind the mine car. Jonnie glanced back. The old woman was carrying a blast rifle.

The sound of the fire exchange was getting loud. The spray of the fire system was shooting two hundred feet in the air. Under it winked the blue-green of blast rifles. The stuttering orange flashes of assault weapons were plainer in the floodlights that were on all over the compound.

Jonnie sped Dancer down into the opening of the ravine and pulled to a halt beside the two remaining planes. Streaks of blast rifle shots laced the sky above their heads. The horse was blowing heavily, covered with lather, but not foundered. One thing at a time, Jonnie told himself. You can catch the drone.

— 2 —

Robert the Fox had his old cape thrown over his antiradiation battle dress. His grizzled hair was singed on one side. His face was composed but there was a hint of concern. He grabbed Jonnie's wrist and gave it a hearty shake of welcome.

Jonnie looked at the singed hair. "How are casualties?"

"Light," said Robert the Fox. "Surprisingly light. They don't want to show themselves to us. It impeded their aim. And it's like fighting in a rainstorm. Look, you're not wearing antiradiation—''

''That water is washing radiation away as fast as you fire it in,'' said Jonnie. ''I have something to do. There's no breathe-gas in that drone. I don't need radiation cover.''

''Jonnie, can't that drone wait until the minesites have been flattened? It will take the drone up to eighteen hours to get where it's going overseas. We tracked it on the search equipment of this plane. Which is to say, we tracked the escort. The drone has wave cancellers.''

Jonnie opened the plane door. It was all ready. There was bread and meat on the seat. An old woman popped up beside him and handed him a cup of steaming herb tea that smelled suspiciously of whiskey. When he looked at her, questioning her presence in this battle zone, she said, ''They can't eat bullets!'' and laughed a cackling laugh.

Robert's hand was detaining him. ''We still have radio silence successfully in.'' They had agreed to give the remote minesite attack pilots twelve hours of radio silence to let them finish off the outlying areas with total surprise if possible. ''That's more than they need. We can shorten it and they can converge on that drone—''

''It's headed for Scotland,'' said Jonnie. ''That's its first stop.''

''I know.''

Jonnie finished off the hot drink and started to climb into the plane.

The detaining hand again. ''There's something I've got to tell you.'' When Jonnie had stopped to listen, he continued, ''We may not have hit Psychlo.''

''I know,'' said Jonnie.

''That means that we may need all the planes and equipment we can get here. They're in hangars under us. We don't have men enough to take the place by assault and we mustn't destroy it.''

''You can work this out with Glencannon. You'll have a pilot in half an hour or so. You can bash it in from the air.'' He made to get into the plane and again Robert's hand was on his sleeve.

''We had a funny thing happen, just before sunset,'' said Robert. ''A tank surrendered!''

— 3 —

vas a very happy man. The Cornwall compound Isles was dead ahead, lit up like the one-time cities en.

lrawn straws for Cornwall. This was the minesite hunting parties and made it death for Scots to go ychlos at this place, over the centuries, had gunned beyond count just for sport on their days off. There ale of a raiding party captured and tied to trees and by tiny bit and man by man for eighteen agonizing any tales like it.

is copilot Dwight had drawn the long straw to the r fellow pilots. They had drilled the navigation. No er gotten within a hundred miles of this minesite in sand years and little was actually known of it, but sorbed what there was.

lain all night, quite relaxed, warmly dressed for flying. They had heard the warning horns go for the of the semiannual. They had piled into their seats, ng at the consoles.

ed and thrilled, they had watched Jonnie's incredible nething had gone wrong as he reached the cage and asn't so good. No rescue. But Jonnie had piled down dge of the bluff, safe as a wee bairn in his truckle bed blast rifles went.

oil had been a bit disconcerting for it had slewed the of position with concussion. But all was well. They had eir plane into the sky on schedule. They had seen the radio towers collapse in a tangle of cables behind by both the concussion of recoil and bazooka fire. A ur radio silence had begun successfully. Ample time for st minesite to be reached without any warning.

thousand miles an hour, one hundred thousand feet up, shifted the clock and come down to normal Psychlo levels to a nighttime minesite. There it was!

Jonnie stepped back onto the ground. He might as well spend this time getting into the warm clothing needed at high altitudes and he proceeded to do so. "Go on."

Robert took a deep breath, but before he went on a runner came up to tell him the historian had delivered a new load of ammunition from the Academy. Robert told him to see it was passed out. The blast fire needles continued to lash overhead in the now quite dark night.

"The tank is a 'Bash our Way to Glory.' It's down there at the other end of the ravine. Oh, don't be alarmed. It's in our hands. It came out of the garage port and came right straight toward us. We hit it with bazookas and they didn't even dent it. But it didn't fire back. It went right straight down to the end of the ravine there and threw out an intercom through an atmosphere lock and said it wanted to talk to the 'Hockner Leader.' It wanted a guarantee of safety in return for cooperation."

Jonnie was getting into the warm boots. "Well, go on."

"It's a kind of weird scene," continued Robert. "When they got a safety guarantee they came out of the tank. They said they were the Chamco brothers. We got interrogation going. They said they knew Terl had sold out. It seems there was a mine manager named Char, a friend of theirs, who turned up missing at the firing. Well, this Char told the Chamco brothers that there'd been a murder. That Terl had murdered the head of the planet so he could appoint a new Planet Head named Ker. And that Ker, this afternoon, had denied them ammunition for the tank. The Chamcos claim Terl and Ker have sold out to some race called the 'Hockners of Duraleb' and even launched the drone to wipe out the other minesites."

"I suppose it's mostly correct," said Jonnie. "Except the parts about the Hockners and the drone. The Psychlos have a lot of enemies, but according to their histories they defeated the Hockners a couple of hundred years ago. Listen, Sir Robert, in all due respect, I've got to be going!"

"There's more," said Robert the Fox. "They haven't got tank and plane fuel in there, and we've cut down four sorties of theirs to get to the fuel and ammunition dump way over there. But they have plenty of blast rifle ammunition. We don't have men enough for an assault—"

"What else?" said Jonnie. "Sounds like good news, not bad."

"Well, it's not all good news. It seems there's sixteen levels of compound under us. Each level stretches for acres. Quarters, shops, garages, hangars, offices, workrooms, libraries, supply warehouses—"

"I didn't know it was that much, but that's not bad news either."

"Wait. If that thing were to be hit with radiation this whole assault force would be blown to bits. We're fighting on a loaded bomb. We must *save* those planes and equipment if we have to defend Earth. And we need them for reconstruction if we really did blow up Psychlo."

"You'll have air support shortly," said Jonnie. "You can withdraw—"

"Well, the Chamco brothers say they know what will happen in there. That we'll flood the place with air! They said they know how 'us Hockners' took the Duraleb system back. They say there aren't enough breathe-gas masks and vials but the recirculating system has plenty. These Chamco brothers are design and maintenance engineers. They promised to help us if we paid them. They say the whole planet has been on half-pay and no bonuses. And they don't want to be killed in an 'air flood' as they called it."

Jonnie had on the warm clothing and was finishing a sandwich of oat bread and dried venison. "Sir Robert, as soon as you get air support you can plan something—"

"The Chamco brothers told us the breathe-gas recirculating system was exterior to the base and air-cooled, and they were tricked into admitting all one had to do was shoot up the intake pipes from the cooling system and the pumps would fill the whole compound with air."

"You got it all solved," said Jonnie.

"Yes, but we need the intakes shot up at long range from the air."

"That shouldn't take long. As soon as Glencannon gets here—"

"Well, I think you ought to do it," said Robert. "It's not very dangerous and if you fire from about a half-mile off—"

"I can do that as I take off."

"But you should come back down here to verify—"

Suddenly Jonnie knew what Robert was up to. Robert the Fox was going to wait until all planes could converge on that drone. And that *was* taking a chance. The planes to other minesites

might be in trouble thems
keep me from making a si
The veteran spread his
too much already to get y
pleading.
Jonnie swung up into the
"Then I'm coming with y
"You're going to stay rig
A mine car ricocheted into
halt. The driver grabbed an a
get back into the battle. Gle
over to them.
"Damn!" said Robert the F
"What's the matter?" said
the greeting. "I'm all right. I
and put something around this
Robert the Fox put an arm a
was something else," he said.
We've got a job for you. A lot
the old Chinko quarters—"
"Goodbye, Sir Robert," Jonn
"Good luck," said Robert
suicide-crash the drone if everythi
to see him again. Then he turned a
waiting runners. He had a little tr
Jonnie sent the plane soaring o
spotted and hit, and was on his
combined military powers of Earth
way to do it all alone.
Waiting until the drone was—w
land was cutting it a bit close. If a
might blow gas canisters, and a
Scotland and Sweden as well. The
attack in force. But even that guaran
had ever tried a head-on smash at the
plane traveling at maximum with all
of collision. As a last resort, that wou
He hadn't said anything about it to
man hadn't guessed it.

Dunneldeen
of the British
must have be
They had
that sent out
south. The P
down people
was even a t
shot tiny bit
days. And m
He and h
envy of thei
Scot had ev
over a thou
they had ab
They ha
stratospher
final firing
hands waiti
Wide-ey
sprint. So
that part w
under the
before the
The rec
plane out
vaulted th
planetwid
them, hit
twelve-ho
the farthe
At tw
they had
approach

Scanners and viewscreens alight, they found no sign of hostile action, no guard planes in the air.

Lighted steam was coming out of some shafts in the hills that must be five miles deep. Smelter chimneys belched curling, green smoke. Warehouses stood in bold outline. And there were the glowing domes of the compound! Target one.

But Dunneldeen, being Dunneldeen, was quick to take advantage of sudden opportunities even when they were not quite specified in planning.

The silly apes down there lit up the whole landing area for him! It gleamed like a bloody stage. They thought he was simply some nonscheduled Psychlo flight. Bless radio silence.

And Dunneldeen saw something else. Strung on massive power poles, coming down from the north, was their power supply. And right there, in the full glare of the landing area, was the obvious master pole. The freaks cared nothing about an aerial navigation menace. It was the master pole. The lines from the north came down into it. The local light cables all routed out from it to the buildings and compound. There was a big open space for landing and take-off in the middle of this spider's web.

Right at the side of the landing stage was a huge wheel. Dunneldeen recognized it. The master wheel that, when spun, withdrew the master bus bar from the circuit.

By Dunneldeen's opportunist mentality, it was simply too good to miss. Why let them have lots of light while they rushed about manning their defense weapons and trying to get out to their planes? Why not simply throw the whole thing into total chaos? And then go up and, with infrared screens, shoot the place to bits. Their own plane had a wave neutralizer, copied from one stolen from a ground car, and they could turn it on and those apes wouldn't know what to shoot at. Further, if this battle plane took off it would seem like it was a defense plane.

Dunneldeen spoke rapidly to a startled but agreeable Dwight. Just as casually as though they were a visiting plane, they landed right beside the big wheel. Dunneldeen hitched the assault rifle strap over his shoulder, opened the door of the plane, stepped down, walked over to the bus bar wheel, and gave it its first spin.

It all went okay just up to that point. But now a Psychlo in a little guardhouse they had not spotted, only ten feet from that bus bar, stepped out and stared at Dunneldeen.

"The Tolneps!" screamed the guard.

Before Dunneldeen could get the assault rifle into position the guard had closed the door and hit a siren. A bullhorn opened up enough to blast one's eardrums in. "Tolnep attack! All posts! Tolneps! Gun positions!"

Regardless of what Tolneps might be, Dunneldeen spun the bus bar wheel so fast it screamed. He realized then why it was so close to the landing stage. They darkened the place for attack precautions. And had a guardhouse right handy to do it.

Dunneldeen raced back to the plane. He dove in. Dwight's assault rifle opened up as guards boiled out of a stairwell. They dissolved into luminous green flashes.

The battle plane soared. Dunneldeen threw on the wave neutralizer and infrared screens.

They reverted to plan.

With guns set to "No Flame, Maximum Concussion" they roared across the compound.

The domes squashed like punctured balloons.

They raced across the lines of warehouses and knocked their roofs flat.

For good measure they made another pass, this time dropping nonradiation, antipersonnel bombs.

One gun opened up at them and the plane took a jolt. They flashed down and squashed the gun with a single blast.

And that was the end of the base. The Psychlo Intergalactic Mining Company did not believe in lavishing money on safety equipment in any department, apparently. And hadn't Jonnie said something about Terl calling in all the armaments from these bases?

From what they could gather, standing by way up in the air, the creatures in the compound had been unable to get the masks on before the domes were smashed, for there certainly wasn't any mob coming out.

They hung around for a while, occasionally knocking out an isolated vehicle and a stray guard.

It really was quiet down there after that.

Then they saw something on their radar screen. It was an incoming transport. Abruptly they recalled transport plane engines leaving after the incoming firing. This thing had been slow-poking its way home and they had passed it. Good!

Dunneldeen, much to Dwight's dismay, landed beside the bus bar and turned it on.

They just sat there. The landing lights were now on. Any Psychlo employee left alive was not concentrating on coming out.

The transport plane landed. The Psychlos got out, fooled around with baggage. Then the pilot got out. The Psychlos walked in a mob toward the compound. Then they began to feel something was wrong and stopped. The Psychlo pilot reached for his belt gun.

Dunneldeen and Dwight cut them down with assault rifles.

Dunneldeen flew Dwight over to the fuel dump. They knew what fuel cartridge the transport took, for it was a duplicate of the plane that had brought Jonnie to Scotland. Dwight got the fuel cartridges. Dunneldeen brought him back to the transport plane. Dwight took the old cartridges out and put new ones in. Dunneldeen shot a guard car that had survived and came racing toward them. It blew up.

Dunneldeen got into the air. Dwight flew the transport up. Dunneldeen shot the master power pole to bits in a fanfare of sparks and flashes.

Seeing that Dwight was well clear, Dunneldeen flew to a point about ten feet above the breathe-gas dump. He dropped a low-yield, lead-shielded, time-fused radioactive mine on it. He soared up and the dump roared in a lovely green-blue flash.

He again checked to see where Dwight had gotten to, saw he was safe. Dunneldeen soared to ten thousand feet, nosed the plane over, sighted, and fired at the explosives dump. It went up like a miniature volcano. Absolutely beautiful.

He dropped back and verified that the compound had not exploded. This was part of their orders. The machinery and stored planes were apparently intact.

With no atmosphere to breathe and no fuel to fly, with ninety percent of its personnel probably dead, the minesite in Cornwall was a write-off. That paid for a lot of crimes.

Dunneldeen fell in beside the transport. "What's a Tolnep?" asked Dunneldeen. Dwight didn't know either, but Dunneldeen supposed he did look strange in a Chinko air mask and U.S. Air Force stratosphere flying gear.

They had already agreed on a new and wonderful plan Dunneldeen had thought up. They had almost six hours of radio silence left. Orders complete and time on their hands.

Dunneldeen was related to the Chief of Clanfearghus, and besides there was a lass he had not seen for nearly a year.

They hoped the other fourteen minesite attack planes had done as well. Of course, perhaps not with the same *style*.

They headed for Scotland.

— 4 —

Zzt had sunk into deep apathy.

The gas drone roared on, deafening, cold, and dark.

That silly dimwit Nup!

Zzt had thought at first that the engine sounds he heard were just some rattles in this old relic, but after a while his trained ear could pick the sound out separately from the din in here. He listened in different parts of the cheerless drone and then at the flapping door. It was the Mark 32! The Mark 32, "Hit 'Em Low, Kill 'Em," heavy armored, ground strafer.

Nup was flying escort to the drone?

Zzt had puzzled and puzzled on it and in fact had done little else. At first Zzt was all hope. He thought Nup had followed him out of the hangar intending to lower a ladder to the open door and snatch him out of here. But Nup seemed to be utterly unaware of the fact that there *was* an open door and was flying on the opposite side of the drone from it.

True, Zzt had not briefed him at all. The busted lamp bulb had mostly been talking about Bolbods and rumors in Psychlo that they were the next target. What nonsense! Zzt went over it carefully. No, in the rush of trying to get out and at those attacking Tolneps with a ground strafer, he had simply raced around asking whether anyone had been checked out on a Mark 32 and had slammed Nup into the copilot seat and then had had to go attend to that drone.

He dimly remembered his last words to Nup. They were, "Come on!" And he had been surprised when Nup hadn't run after him to the drone.

Instead of mopping up the Tolneps, Nup was out there flying escort in a ground strafer. He might have been checked out but he certainly didn't know what it was for. Why, with that Mark 32 he could batter down a whole city! And nothing could penetrate its hide. It was a support plane, a support plane for ground troops. No ground fire could touch it. No interceptor ships could even scratch its hide. And what was Nup doing with it? Riding escort to a drone that needed none. Zzt got bitter. Damn Terl and damn Nup!

Then as the huge drone with its deafening engines rolled along to the devils-knew-what destination, Zzt began to realize that Nup didn't know he was aboard!

A bit later, when he looked at his watch, Zzt realized that that Mark 32 was going to run out of fuel. Wherever they were in this dark night, that Mark 32 was a write-off. He hadn't put fuel in it for such a trip because he didn't have cartridges, and a Mark 32 had no great range anyway, being intended for local use.

Well, Zzt had plenty of breathe-gas. He had a gun, he had a wrench.

For a while he monkeyed around with the preset box armor, thinking he might be able to open it and change it. But without keys or the means to make them, not even a piece of blast artillery could open it. When they said "armored" they sure meant these damned old gas drones.

So he had finally slumped down on the cold plates in the forward end of the ship and in apathy decided to last it out. In a day or two or three this thing would land. There was nothing in it to cushion anyone from the rough landings these made, but Zzt imagined he would survive it.

Just sit and wait. That was all he could do.

Damn Terl! Damn Nup! Damn the company!

And all on half-pay and no bonuses.

— 5 —

Jonnie was searching for the drone.

Every viewscreen was flashing.

Down below the cold Arctic spread out, visible in the screens, invisible to direct sight. He remembered it from his last trip across it. A forbidding array. Once down in it you were dead: if not from direct cold on an ice flow, then from immersion in those waters.

As nearly as he could judge, the gas drone was somewhere ahead only a few minutes now. Shortly he should have it on his screen.

He was a little bit disturbed about the girls and Thor. He had not seen them on his screens as he went by. Of course he was by then very high. The spot of light he saw might be their fire, but it also might be the planes still burning. He had wasted too much time already and help was on the way to them. He remembered their numb faces when they realized he was leaving them there. But they must be all right. Probably they were at the Academy or the compound by now. Maybe the parson had been driving very fast. A mine ground car could do over sixty on rough terrain.

He hoped the other planes had reached the minesites and done their jobs. There was still five hours of radio silencc yet to go. He wished he could open up on this radio and yell to them, "Hey, anybody that's done in his minesite, get up here to such and such coordinates and help blast this confounded drone." But he didn't dare. It might cost some of them their lives by alerting their targets. They all had extra fuel and then some. They all had spare ammunition. But if any had had to delay or were waiting for an optimal moment to pounce on a minesite and he opened up, it could throw their lives away. He wasn't about to kill any Scots to save his own hide. When radio silence opened and Robert didn't hear from him, Robert would converge them to handle the drone. Late, maybe, but a second chance. He hoped it wouldn't come to that for their friends in Scotland would be endangered.

Maybe he was searching for something that was wave cancelled. That escort ship was his hope. Maybe it had peeled off or gone somewhere else. *Its* blip should be visible!

Ah, now. What was that tiny spark of green on the viewscreen? Another iceberg? No, the height telltale read four thousand two hundred twenty-three feet. Speed? Speed?

Three hundred two miles per hour!

He had the escort on the screen.

His gloved hands danced on the console. He braked down from hypersonic, dropping abruptly to five thousand feet in a descent as fast as a firing rocket. He cushioned at the bottom, feeling a trifle squashed for a moment. Easy, take it easy. Size up this escort.

He got it bright and clear in infrared. There was the drone beside it. One thing at a time. This escort was first target.

What *was* that plane? He had never seen anything like it before. Lowslung, flat, minimum skids . . . it looked like it was mainly armor!

Suddenly he realized that his guns might not even dent it. He had seen a tank bazooka flash against its side without affecting it in the least. He had a sinking feeling. Not only was the drone renowned as impregnable, but here was an escort ship that—

His mind raced with possibilities. Robert the Fox sometimes said, "When you only have two inches of claymore use ten feet of guile." What did that escort know about *him?*

He reached for the local command radio switch. The range was only about twenty miles.

A torrent of angry Psychlo words hit him: "It's about time somebody showed up! I should have been relieved of this job hours ago! What kept you?" Angry. Very angry!

Jonnie opened his transmit switch. He lowered the pitch of his voice as much as possible. "How are things?"

"The drone's all right and why shouldn't it be? I've been escorting it, haven't I? You certainly run a messed-up planet here! It's not like this on Psychlo! I should hope not! You're late! What's your name?"

Jonnie hastily dredged up a name that was common to twenty percent of the Psychlos. "Snit. Could I ask who I'm talking to?"

"Nup, Executive Administrator Nup! Use 'Your Executiveship' when you address me! Crap planet."

"Did you arrive recently, Your Executiveship?" asked Jonnie.

"Just today, Snit. And how am I greeted? With a crummy Bolbod attack anyone could handle! Wait," suspiciously, "you have a very strange accent. Like . . . like . . . yes, like a Chinko instruction disc! That's what it is. You're not a Bolbod, are you?" The click of firing buttons pulled off safety to standby.

"I was born here," said Jonnie truthfully.

A sharp nasty laugh. "Oh, a colonial!" Silence for a moment. "Were you briefed on this mission?"

"A little bit, Your Executiveship. But orders have been changed. That's what I was sent to tell you."

"You're not relieving me?" Very hostile.

"The destination has been changed!" said Jonnie. "There's radio silence. They had to send me with the word."

"Radio silence?"

"Planetary wide, Your Executiveship."

"Ah, then it is a Bolbod attack! They operate everything on radio! I knew it."

"I'm afraid so, Your Executiveship."

"Well, if you're not going to relieve me, what am I expected to do? I am almost out of fuel! Where's the nearest minesite!"

Jonnie thought very fast.

"Your Executiveship, the orders were that if you were almost out of fuel—" Good lord, where could he send him? That Mark 32 was the only thing that one could home in on in a search! "—I was to tell you to land with magnetic grapnels on top of the drone . . . right at the front end."

"What?" Incredulous.

"Then drop off when we come close to the next minesite. You've got a map there?"

"No. I haven't got a map. You run things very badly on this planet. Not like Psychlo. It should be reported."

"There's an attack on."

"Nothing can dent this plane. It's a ground strafer. I don't know why it's being sent on escort."

"How much fuel do you have, Your Executiveship?"

A pause. Then, "Crap! It's only ten minutes' worth! You almost killed me with your lateness."

"Well, just land on the extreme front end of the drone—"

"Why the front end? I should land in the middle. If I land on the front end it will unbalance the weight distribution of the drone."

"It's the way it's loaded this trip. They omitted part of the load in the front. They said specifically the front end."

"This is a pretty heavy plane!"

"Not for the drone. You better get moving, Your Executiveship. That water is cold down there. Ice, too! And you'll need fuel to off-load. It's only a few hours to the next minesite."

Jonnie watched his screens. He couldn't see the plane in direct sight. With a bit of anxiety, he opened up the view to include the monstrous drone.

He felt faint with relief when the Mark 32 dove ahead, sat

down on the top-front section of the drone, and put on its magnetic grips. They held!

The heat indicator of the viewscreen showed the Mark 32 had shut off its motors.

Jonnie watched. He expected the drone to nose down, possibly to crash. It did sag. Then its engines started to compensate and it rolled gently, thundering along, still going on its lethal way. Nup had landed off-center, inducing a continuous roll, right to left, left to right. It would roll to the right, and the balance motors would compensate and bring it back too far to the left and then overcompensate in the other direction. Only about ten degrees each way. But this did not at all change the steadfast course the drone was following. A very slow roll. Was it also crabbing slightly?

— 6 —

With Nup out of the way, at least for now, Jonnie got down to the business of seeing what could be done to halt the drone.

He drew off a bit to give his screens better play on it. It looked like a derelict! Here was a mark where an atomic bomb had hit it, there was a scar where possibly a plane had crashed into it leaving the charred remnants of oil and fuel. There a row of minute dents where surface-to-air or air-to-air missiles had struck it. But such marks were notable only for their stains, not for any damage they had done.

He flew the battle plane down under it. He looked at the big skids used for parking and storing. No joy there.

He brought the battle plane alongside it again. He felt like a hummingbird flapping along with a buzzard.

Probably when the last mission of this thing was completed and it had crashed, demolishing the then-known city of "Colorado Springs," the company had just let it lie there until it had built hangars and, as an afterthought, had probably flown water tanks over it and way above it and washed the radiation off of it and then stored it.

A chilling thought as to why they must have done that. Psychlos had no room for sentiment or art in any form. They would not have kept it for any other reason than that they couldn't dismantle it on this planet. Psychlo alone would have the massive shops to do that. They certainly didn't want it back. It had done its job. They wouldn't leave it out where it could be measured up by some enemy agent. They had kept it because the company couldn't destroy it on this planet. What it was built of, the devil only knew!

Well, he tried to cheer himself, Nup's plane skids had stuck to it. These magnetic so-called skids were actually whole-molecule reorientation fields. The molecules in the surface of one substance became, with the field, comingled with the molecules of the other substance like a temporary weld. So this thing was built of molecular metal, possibly some unknown—to this planet—metal, alloyed with some other strange metal. It even could be that the combination of such metals was, while molecular, irreversible and couldn't be melted or pounded apart once mixed. Maybe the Psychlos had something that, when certain elements were mixed together, could not then be "unmixed" by flame, electrical arcs, radiation, or anything. Maybe even laminated layers of such metals, each one protecting the one under it.

A very *chilling* thought. Jonnie did not consider himself even a kindergarten-level metallurgist, but he recalled the prohibition the Psychlos had of ever teaching an alien race anything about that subject. And here he was trying to solve it, flying along in the night, without texts, without a calculator, and without even the mathematics to use it if he had it.

What would destroy that drone? And before it reached even the coast of Scotland..

He had thought a Psychlo was a monster when he first saw one. Now he was really looking at a monster. An ultimate in indestructibility.

Out of the tail of his eye he thought he saw something move on the viewscreen. He looked at it closely. There it was again. A rhythmic pulse under the bottom of the drone. He counted it out. Once every twenty seconds, regular as his watch. Suddenly he realized he had been studying just one side of the drone. He guessed he was feeling a bit overwhelmed. Well! Easily remedied. He hit his console with rapid fingers and flick, he was over on the other side of the drone.

This side had been away from him when he first saw the thing from the plains after it fired. Nup had been flying on the other side also.

He trimmed in his viewscreens.

What! The huge loading door was unlatched. And since Nup had landed on the nose, making the drone roll and crab periodically, the door was swinging open and closed.

A door.

Unlatched.

He televiewed it with quivering fingers. It had the broken stub of a key in it.

He viewed the whole mammoth door. It was open when the plane rolled down on that side, then was closed by the rushing air and gravity when the plane rolled back.

Every twenty seconds.

He suddenly regretted the tenderheartedness that had caused him to refuse a companion on this voyage. It would be dangerous, but hanging from a dangling wire ladder, it would be possible to drop down and into that door. No, it would require a pilot to run the plane and somebody going into that drone who knew enough to paralyze it if possible. And he had no pilots, and Glencannon couldn't be spared.

Open, closed, open, closed.

Size? He looked at the door. He compared his own ship's span and depth. This ship could *fly* into that door! Top and bottom a very narrow squeeze. Plenty to spare on the sides.

Yikes! Fly this ship sideways at three hundred two miles per hour? And then in?

Well, it was standard battle tactics to fly sideways with these teleportation motor drives. There was no wing support area needed such as birds used. When you shut off these motors, the ship didn't glide anywhere. It just dropped like a stone. It was leveled with small teleportation balance motors, not fins.

Yes, in theory one could fly sideways and then dart forward and in.

But the *timing!* Ouch. That rolling drone was moving the opening up and down about thirty feet each roll.

He'd try it.

But that slamming door had to be taken off first. The way it swung, it barred the available opening.

Jonnie decided he would first try to shoot the hinges off. He dropped the battle plane back, setting the firing controls to "Needle Width," "Flame," and "Single Shot."

He lined up the plane and sights, fingers dancing on the console, one foot extended to the floor firing button—always hard to reach in a plane built for nine- or ten-foot-tall Psychlos. Even Ker had trouble with floor controls.

Line up, door open, hinge exposed. Stamp!

A needle of hot flame hit the hinge. It didn't sever. The door began to swing shut again.

His local command channel burst into life. "What the crap are you doing?" cried Nup, alarmed.

"I don't have a copilot, Your Executiveship. I have to shoot the door open to change the controls and destination."

"Oh." Then, as Jonnie was lining up for the next try, "You be careful of company property, Snit! Willful damage is a vaporizing offense."

"Yes, Your Executiveship." Jonnie fired the next try.

The hinge glowed briefly. The door hid it from view again. The door didn't sag. Maybe the hinge was binding. Jonnie looked at the infrared target scope. Yes, there were two hinges, one up, one lower.

He lined up on the lower hinges. Door open, hinge in scope. Stamp! Flash!

The door still didn't fall off.

Maybe if he alternated his shots, upper hinge, lower hinge, one then the other.

He drew off a bit to flex his fingers. The other scopes showed ice and sea endlessly below him. Nothing else in the sky.

Back to it. Upper. Stamp! Flash! Lower. Stamp! Flash! Over and over. But a shot possible only every forty seconds.

This was *time*-consuming! Well, he wasn't too pressed for time. Not yet anyway.

Stamp! Flash! Wait. Stamp! Flash! Wait.

Those hinges would get cherry red but they didn't sever.

Getting nowhere, Jonnie drew off. Then, with a bright inspiration, he took a position above the drone and slightly to the other side so he could fire into the *back* of the door as it rolled open. He changed his gun setting to "Broad," "No Flame," and "Continuous."

He sighted carefully. The next time the door swung open he stamped on the firing button and sent a string of flashes against the inside of the door. It swung open. He shifted his plane over to the side gradually as he fired. Despite reverse roll the door was forced open and then, despite a three-hundred-two-mile-an-hour rush of air, suddenly sprang back under the hammering and lay against the hull. Wide open!

Jonnie stopped firing.

The door stayed open. Wide open, pinned back to the hull.

He examined the hinges by throwing the sight to tele. They were a bit twisted, probably from the shots. It was the hinges that precariously held the door open. Would it close again? Maybe. It was vibrating from wind force.

Watchfully, Jonnie drew off. His fingers raced on the console as he sought to correct for flying sideways. He got the sequence of combinations that did it. He inched the plane exactly opposite the yawning doorway.

Up went the doorway, down went the doorway. Yikes, this had to be timed!

He thought he had better just sit there and study it for a bit. He turned on the plane's lights to get direct visual. You couldn't do this on instruments alone.

The black pit lit up. He could see inside. Yes, there was an area just inside the door. A flat platform. Probably needed for loading canisters. Ow! Canisters were stacked just in front of that platform. Would they explode if hit in an overshoot?

He calculated the distance and combination on the console. Then, with a sudden inspiration, he braced his foot against the magnetic grip setting lever. The jar of any impact would cause his foot, jolted, to set the magnetic skids.

He took a deep breath. He looked around him to be sure there were no loose objects. He moved the belted revolver they had issued him so its holster wouldn't punch him in the stomach if he jackknifed forward. The lanyard from the revolver was around his neck. He pulled it a bit to the side so it wouldn't catch on the control console if he pitched forward, for if it did, it could choke him. He laid a soft map case on the upper part of the console in case his head hit with the sudden stop.

Jonnie took another deep breath. He adjusted his air mask.

He watched the door. His fingers dancing on the console to get in the exact position, he zeroed in on the doorway. Count, count, count. How far would the doorway move up after he started forward?

He spread four fingers of his right hand across the huge keyboard to the four buttons that would start him. He spread four fingers of his left hand across the buttons that would stop him.

Up, up, up. Right hand ready. Punch!

The battle plane stabbed into the open door.

Crunch, down with the fingers of his left hand. Stop.

Crash!

He had not quite cleared the top of the door and a wide peel of metal screeched away.

His foot was jolted on the grip lever and the grips went on.

Jonnie's head slammed against the map case.

Lights flashed in his skull.

Blackness.

— 7 —

During all this time, Zzt had been fluctuating between hope and suspicion.

The antics of that plane puzzled him. He knew he had no friends. Who would want to rescue him? He couldn't think of anybody. Char had been his shaftmate, and Char had vanished and was undoubtedly dead, for who would miss a chance to go home? And Char had not shown up at the firing. Terl. Probably Terl had killed him. So it was not Char. Who else was there? Nobody. So who *was* interested in rescuing him? It was a highly suspicious circumstance.

That dimwit Nup had apparently landed on top of the drone to keep from going down into the ice below—and it was ice; one could feel the Arctic in this awful chill. Ice felt a certain way in the atmosphere. Terrible planet. One couldn't blame Nup for that. Common enough tactic for one plane to land on another when shot up or out of fuel, and get carried to safety. So it wasn't any real credit to Nup to think of it. But the crazy fool had landed off-center, and it was making the drone crab but mainly roll. And that roll was making Zzt sick at his stomach.

When he realized that somebody was evidently interested in the door, he had searched in his bag for a molecular metal cutter and found to his dismay he didn't have one. Not that it would have worked on this laminated molecular plating. But he would have tried.

Then whoever it was had let loose shots into the place.

Somebody was trying to kill him! He'd been right in believing he had no friends.

The interior had huge frames on the inside of the skin and Zzt had hastily drawn himself flat against the hull to take advantage of the projection of the wide frame.

He peered out cautiously. Then he relaxed a bit. The target was the hinges. Somebody was trying to get the door off. Zzt knew the hinges wouldn't part, but at the same time it was interesting indeed that somebody would try to part them. Why? How come somebody wanted to remove the door? That didn't make any sense at all.

Every mining plane, whatever else it was used for, followed a mining tradition. Every employee was basically a miner. Mining techniques, procedures, and equipment were into the mining company like kerbango was into the bloodstream and far more permanently. Hoists, lifts, cable ladders, safety lines, hooks, nets . . . they even shoveled paper around with scoops that looked like mine shovels. It was totally inconceivable that that plane out there didn't have a cable ladder and safety wires.

So why didn't it just lower a cable ladder and safety wire to him and let him time those door swings and dart up the ladder to the plane? They could lower him a jet backpack and even pick him out of the air.

All this was so routine to Zzt that the idea of anybody having to remove a door to make it wide open was a strange precaution.

Was somebody trying to steal a canister? That was impossible. They were all locked in. Everything in this damned derelict was armored, inside and out. Such ships were hell to repair, and he had resented the time Terl had taken. You couldn't get at anything in it. It was just a one-time-use rig, built to be expended. So nobody could steal anything here.

Were they trying to send it elsewhere? Well, you couldn't do that without keys, and he had no keys.

So what was going on?

The battering barrage that got the door all the way open and warped it in that position made it easier to lower a cable ladder. All right! Where was the ladder and safety wire? Nothing came dangling down into the huge open maw.

Zzt had just moved forward to peek when blinding lights flashed on, throwing the interior into a blaze of dirt motes and floating rust dust shaken loose in the firing.

He heard a plane's motor suddenly race.

He didn't even have time to get behind the protective frame.

Before his half-blinded eyes a *plane* shot in the door!

The floor plates shook! Metal shrieked.

The plane had crashed on the loading stage platform directly inside the door.

Zzt stumbled backward, expecting it to blow up. But its motor suddenly died and the peculiar fang-setting-on-edge sound of molecular cohesion pierced the dying whine of components. The thing had set its skid grips with a timing and precision Zzt had never seen before.

Staggered by the concussion and already sick with the rolling, Zzt lurched to his feet. It still had its lights on. He peered through this glare to see the pilot. He couldn't make it out. He staggered forward, hand on his belt gun. He still couldn't see the pilot. The armored glass door . . . the pilot was sitting up slowly.

A small being! A mask! A strange fur coat collar!

Zzt let out a near hysterical shriek. "A Tolnep!"

In blind confusion, Zzt drew and fired his belt gun. He fired again and again and again.

His shots were hitting an armored window. He was trying to shoot an armored window! He was also trying to back up and get away.

The drone rolled; Zzt collided with a gas canister, tripped on its cable, started to fall, and threw out his paws to save himself. His gun went flying, hit the floor plates, slithered, and dropped out the open door into the waiting void below.

Skidding and catching his breath in sobs, Zzt got behind a distant frame to protect himself. He believed he was one dead Psychlo!

— 8 —

Jonnie came out of it. The shock of the crash had knocked him out for a moment. He guessed he was getting tired with the strain and the cold. A jolt like that shouldn't have knocked him out.

Then he found his left knee was bruised from hitting the console, the fingernails of his left hand were bleeding from stubbing on keys, and his forehead ached. He decided it must have been a harder crash than he thought.

The magnetic grip brake was on, but peering, he was having a hard time seeing it. He took off his air mask and found that his forehead had been cut on the mask faceplate rim and the blood was getting in his eyes. He reached back and got the tail end of a mining tarpaulin and staunched the blood and wiped out the faceplate. Now he could see.

The landing had been successful. An ancient gag he had found on a cartoon card over at their base occurred to him: "A successful landing is one you can walk away from." Well, he could walk, he hoped.

The ship was slewed. The wind pressure had come off the nose as it went in, but it was still on the tail. The tail was sticking way out of the door but was pushed over against the side of the doorframe. Was the ship hurt?

He looked around inside. The main motor housing and the two right and left balance housings seemed all right. He reached for the door latch to get out and then something tugged at his memory. Something about the crash. What was it? Ah, something must have exploded in the drone. He dimly recalled hearing a series of explosions. He reached over to the pilot window and touched it, intending to wipe some steam from it. It was hot! Yes, something had exploded in this drone.

Well, that was a good sign, maybe. It meant something could break in this place.

He looked at the gas canisters vivid in the plane lights. They looked sound. He saw that they were also armored and that all the cables to them were as well. He looked around through the ship's windows in dismay.

This place was as armored inside as outside!

What an unpleasant view. Structural rib frames, very deep. Floor plates for loading only, having gaps on both sides of the walkway. Cross-braces. Toward the tail there were a series of holes like a beehive—ah, additional gas canister spaces; the thing was only about a third full. But enough, enough to wipe out any place it was going.

How much time did he have? He looked at his watch and it was shattered. There were no clocks in these battle planes; the clocks were all down in the console cabinets and had no faces anyway. Only lapsed time dials on the dash. He realized he wouldn't know when radio silence ended. He tried to compute by sunrise but he didn't know where he was beyond a few hours short of Scotland. Abruptly he realized he was maundering. Still a bit dazed?

He put the air mask on and made sure it was snug in case a gas canister had cracked in the crash, which he doubted. He checked to see whether Terl's blast gun was still there. Yes, fallen on the floor. He might need it to try to cut cables. He put it in his belt and got out of the plane.

The thunder of these motors was deafening. Arctic wind curled in at the door. The night lay like a black pit below them.

He examined the gas canisters. No, the plane hadn't even touched them. Nothing could touch them, from the looks of it. They were covered with the crud of extreme age. He found a half-obliterated date, a Psychlo date. These things dated from the original attack! Spares? Not used in that attack? No, another date. They had been refilled about twenty-five years later. The hope that they were expended died. They were live, all right.

Where were the controls of this thing? Ah, way up forward. Best look at those. There just might be a chance that he could change setting and, in extremis, simply pull the wires loose.

He walked up along the plates. His plane's lights were bright even up front.

There was the setting box. A "preset," and there was the console one set the preset plates in. Fat lot of good the console was. Like a stamping machine. He looked at the preset box. One usually fed preset plates into the side and latched the box. Here, too. But this one?

It was armored.

It had a keyhole. He looked around but there was no key left behind.

Cables? All armored. And they even went into the preset box with an armored connection.

Crud was all around. Lord, this thing was old! It was only clean around the preset box. He supposed they had cleaned it up to set it.

A vague feeling of unease troubled him. Completely aside from his intentness on stopping this drone, there was something odd in this place. He looked down toward the plane. The deep recesses between the frames were in complete darkness.

Zzt, unseen in a recess not six feet away, crouched back in desperation. His wits were racing. What did he know about Tolneps? Shortly after he had graduated from Mechanics College on Psychlo he had done a duty tour on Archiniabes where the company had mines. It was in this universe. The system star was the double star he sometimes saw in winter on this planet; the smaller star of the "dumbbell" had a weight so dense that a half cubic inch of it here would weigh one ton. A minesite had been wiped out utterly by a Tolnep raid. They came from somewhere near the star cluster he often saw here. They had mastered time control and could hold it frozen and their ships made long piratical voyages. The company had analyzed several of their dead bodies. What did he remember about them? What weakness? He could think only of strengths. Their bite was deadly poison. They had a body density comparable to iron. They were immune to Psychlo gas. They couldn't be killed with an ordinary blast gun. Weaknesses, weaknesses, weaknesses? If he didn't recall them he would never get out of this alive. Never.

This one was walking back down past him now. He shrank against the ship skin. It didn't see him here in the darkness.

Then he remembered. Their eyesight! That was why they always wore face masks. They saw in infrared only and had to have a filter plate. They went totally blind when subjected to shorter wavelength light and they could be killed only with ultraviolet weapons. They were intensely allergic to cold and had a body heat of around two hundred degrees, or was it three hundred? No matter, he was on to it. It was eyesight. Without its faceplate that creature would be blind.

Zzt planned carefully. The instant he got a chance, he would knock off the faceplate, leap forward, and claw the thing's eyes out, somehow avoiding the poison teeth. Zzt's paw slid down to the side of his boot and he got out his trusty big wrench. He could throw it like a projectile. Don't hit the body, hit the side of the mask!

Zzt then drew from his breast pocket the small round mirror with its long handle that he used to look in the back of connections or the underside of bearings. He carefully extended the mirror around the edge of the frame, praying to the crap nebula the thing wouldn't notice it. He began to watch the creature.

Jonnie found it very hard to walk in the rolling drone. The floor plates were not meant for walking and had gaps on both sides.

He went clear to the back end of the drone, quite a walk in itself. He looked at the strange honeycomb. It was bottle racks for additional load. He crawled in the entry port. Maybe some cables or something overlooked would be in there. He could barely get through the port and wondered how a Psychlo could, until he realized it was just for canister loading of the racks. Clumsy. Just racks. Bad design. The ports were toward the center and it was only blank bulkhead on either side. Nothing else here.

He went back toward the forward end. He stopped just beyond the ship. He thought very hard. He could see nothing that could be pulled apart, nothing that could be blasted apart. He could even blow up his ship in here and nothing would happen.

No controls. The drone was not made to be flown but just set and launched. Not even the remote Terl had shown him would do anything now.

Rolling like a huge ungainly drunk, the thing continued on its way with death in its jaws. Insensate, invulnerable.

He wasn't seeing so well again. Blood had started flowing when he crawled into the hole back there and he'd knocked his mask. He lifted his hands to the mask, turning sideways to lessen the blast from the door. He was reaching for the edge of his jacket to wipe it off.

With the impact of a bullet the mask was hit!

It flew from his hand.

Something had almost broken his left thumb.

There was motion about thirty feet away.

Mountain training and a hunter's life had left nothing wanting in Jonnie's reactions.

The action of dropping to one knee, drawing, and firing the blast gun did not take more than a third of a second.

He fired at the mass that had begun to come at him. The shots drove it back with sheer force.

Again and again he fired.

The thing, whatever it was, moved back into the cover of the rib frames near the preset.

There was something or someone in here with him. He had walked right past it twice when he went to the preset box.

— 9 —

Jonnie protested a little at not heeding his instincts earlier. He had *felt* some presence. That was the worst part of wearing air masks. It denied one's sense of smell. And he could smell it now. Despite the cold air and the rust motes Jonnie could smell a Psychlo.

He rose cautiously, holding the gun, and backed toward his plane to get a bit more distant. A Psychlo was pretty strong stuff not only to smell but to deal with in any wrestling match. He recalled having to wait for Thor before he could approach within arm's length of Terl. Psychlos could crush one with ease. Which Psychlo was this? Did he know him?

Zzt, pressed up against the skin, was trying to keep from vomiting with contempt and disgust. Only what it would do to his breathe-mask prevented him.

It wasn't the blast gun shots. Yes, those that hit had bruised him and thrown him back, and a few feet closer they might have disabled him.

It was his own reaction to change. Here he had been in abject funk and all the while it was only the animal. Terl's animal!

A surge of hatred and fury followed his nausea. He almost emerged from the recess and plowed straight in. But a blast gun stung. And the dumb twit didn't even have it on penetration, only on blast. Typical.

That this animal had subjected him to such terror he could not forgive. Why, he had nearly killed it once on the tractor with a remote. He really should have killed it. He should have taken a blast rifle out that day. Who would have noticed in all that fire?

Nothing but the animal! A puny, soft, undersized, slug-white, stupid *animal* had scared him like that! He quivered with rage. His nausea faded.

Desire for information overrode his kill lust at this moment. Maybe this was some new plot of Terl's. Damn Terl!

Zzt got himself under control enough to speak. "Did Terl send you?"

Jonnie tried to place the voice. Hard to do the way they talked through a face mask. The masks had sound amplification patches on their sides but voices got muffled, low as they were. He could ask; Psychlos were very arrogant.

"Who are you?" said Jonnie.

"You went through all that at the tractor and you don't even remember who I am! Stupid dimwit. Answer me! Did Terl send you?"

Zzt! The times Terl had muttered and rumbled on about Zzt! Jonnie had his own score to settle with him.

He couldn't resist it. "I came to bust up the machinery," said Jonnie.

Another Psychlo might have laughed. Not Zzt. "That goes without doubt, animal! Answer me or I'll—"

"You'll what?" said Jonnie. "Step out and get killed? This blaster is set on penetration now." Jonnie was slowly pacing backward to the battle plane. He edged around it. He got up on its step and opened the door and got out the assault rifle with radiation bullets. He cocked it and, when he had it ready to fire, put the blast gun back in his belt and began to walk up the corridor again.

Zzt had gone silent.

Jonnie tried to step sideways far enough to angle a shot into a recess as soon as Zzt spoke again. Then he paused. Zzt was the master mechanic of the compound, the transport chief in fact. He would know far more about this drone than anyone else.

"How'd you get yourself trapped aboard here?" said Jonnie.

"Terl!" It was practically a scream. "The———," and there followed a string of Psychlo profanity that went on for minutes.

Jonnie waited it out. When it finally subsided into mere rumblings, Jonnie said, "So you want to get off. Just tell me how to land this and you can get off."

There followed a new string of Psychlo obscenities, so violent that Jonnie began to be convinced. Finally, "There *isn't* any way to change it or land it—" A pause, almost hopefully then, "Did Terl give you the keys to the preset?"

"No. Can't it be blasted open?"

Apathy. "No."

"Can't you tear out the cables?"

"That would just crash this thing, and you can't do that either. They're armored with molecular lamination metal. He didn't give you the keys." It was a groan. Then savage: "You dimwit! Why didn't you get the keys from him before you came out here?"

"He was a bit tied up," said Jonnie. Then, "You better tell me what *not* to do so I just don't stop its motors."

"There aren't any *nots* either," said Zzt. He was feeling sick again from the rolling of the drone.

Jonnie pulled far over to the side. He was wondering whether he could send some ricochets from the frame into the recess. He couldn't get over far enough. The frames were pointed-edged for strength and the edges angled out.

So Zzt was no help. Jonnie backed away toward the plane. He was going back for the copilot air mask. The Arctic chill was freezing his face. He glanced at the remains of the one knocked out of his hand. His thumb still ached.

Zzt had thrown a *wrench*. It was still imbedded in the side of the mask. If that had hit him in the head—

A wrench? Wait. What could one do with a wrench?

Jonnie picked up the wrench. Typically Psychlo, it was heavy as lead. It could open up to take a twelve-inch-diameter nut, a small nut in Psychlo machinery. Quite a weapon.

The second he started to straighten up from retrieving the wrench, Zzt tried to charge.

The gun was off target. Jonnie squeezed the trigger and shots flamed up the passageway. Zzt dove back. He wasn't hit or he would have gone into a pale green explosion from radiation bullets.

Jonnie eased back to the plane and got the other air mask, checked its valves, and put it on. It worked okay.

Zzt was scrambling around on the floor, trying to find his mirror. It had become wedged in a loose plate. A loose plate?

Zzt used the mirror to check where the animal was. Then he

got to work with his talons and a small metal ruler he always carried to pry up the fifty-pound plate. It was hard going, but what a projectile it would make!

The lethal drone roared on toward Scotland.

— 10 —

Jonnie held the wrench in his hand. He hefted it thoughtfully. Certainly, in setting up this drone to fire, mechanics would have to get into *something*. And they'd have to service something if it were ever to be fired again

Locked, armored preset box. Yes, but that was just a control box. He had seen nothing else that took a key.

He was finding it hard to think. It was cold! These ancient Air Force flying suits were supposed to be electrically warmed, but they had not been able to rig any batteries and the originals hadn't been made for a shelf life of a thousand years. The blood from his cut forehead kept messing up his faceplate quite in addition to the way it kept misting. What was the temperature where they were flying? A power zoom to get up to freezing, that was for sure.

This wrench . . .

He caught a flicker of movement up toward the front of the ship and fired a warning shot.

Two problems. No, three. Zzt, Nup and a Mark 32 on top, and how to disable this drone!

Old Staffor used to say he was "too smart." A lot of village people had thought that. He wasn't feeling very smart now.

He knew he should get rid of Zzt. But firing shots in this armored interior was not just dangerous to Zzt. It was dangerous to himself. All these frames sent every shot madly caroming about, and twice now one had whistled past his own ears and another had hit his plane on rebound.

Suppose Zzt were a puma. How would he go about killing it? Well, one didn't walk up to a puma; one waited for the puma to spring. No, now suppose Zzt were a bear in a cave. That was a more fitting example. Walk into a cave with a bear in it? Suicide.

He thought of setting a time fuse on a limpet and pitching it up there, getting in his plane, and depending on its armor to protect him. But there was a limit to the way magnetic grips held and he might blow up his own plane into an unusable state. He wished he had a grenade, but all the grenades they had found were duds and they hadn't worked out how to use them. He even thought of taking one of the fuel or ammunition cartridges—of which he had plenty for the plane—throwing it up there, and shooting into it. It would explode, that was for sure. But one cartridge might not kill Zzt. Psychlos were very tough, very tough indeed. Zzt had once beaten Terl, he had heard, and Zzt truly hated him—in fact, had almost killed him once. No, he was not going to try any stunt of walking up there even with an assault rifle firing. He did not know how deep that recess was or even what recess Zzt was in, and Zzt might very well be armed still.

Nup he had nullified for the moment.

Lord, it was *cold*.

One thing at a time. His job was not Zzt or Nup. It was to stop this drone. He had better get awfully smart. Fast!

Because of his misting and blood-stained faceplate, he had not spotted the tiny mechanic's mirror that watched him. He got busy untangling the problem of this drone.

Where Psychlos couldn't use a molecular parting and resealing tool, they used nuts and bolts. And he was sure that this armor wouldn't yield to a "metal knife," as they called the tool in Psychlo mechanic's slang. He had gathered from Zzt that this was molecular lamination, layer after layer of different but binding metals. Good. So somewhere here they had used nuts.

He caught a flick of motion and fired another shot. The bullet ricocheted three times and went whining out the door.

Maybe one of these floor plates . . . He laughed suddenly. Squarely in front of the ship, in a shadow the lights left between the skids, was a floor plate held down by nuts!

He reduced the jaw size of the wrench and got down between the skids. Another small adjustment and he had the size. There were eight nuts. They came off very easily—these had been removed recently. He put the nuts on one of the skid tops that had an inset groove. Heavy, they stayed there despite the roll.

One of the plane skids was on the far edge of the plate. He pounded it with the heel of the wrench and it loosened. He pried the plate up with the lip of the wrench. He intended just to set it aside, but as it came loose the drone rolled and it went sliding out of his numb hands, through the door and into the screaming wind and emptiness. Who cared?

He got out a torch and shone it down into the blackness.

He was looking at the top of the main motor drive!

The housing was as big as a one-story house. It made him realize that the whole underside of the drone was motors and additional gas canister storage. What tons and tons and tons of lethal gas this carried! The canisters glowed like monster fish in the darkness. But the housing!

Jonnie knew these drives in miniature. They were space translation cubicles, mostly empty but served by an enormous number of points that jutted into them. Each point had its own coordinate message, and these points had to be cleaned.

There must be an inspection and maintenance plate on this housing!

With a wary look up the long passageway, he slid down and braced his feet on the structural support members of the housing. He played the light around.

It was hard to keep an eye on the corridor from this position, and he alternated looks at the housing with looks at the corridor. Maybe he really ought to work out how to get rid of Zzt before he went on with this. He had to duck down to see the housing. But doing something with Zzt might put an end to himself and he reminded himself that too many lives—in fact the only human lives left—depended on him. Courage aside, he mustn't risk his neck. Bear in a cave. He decided he could chance it and ducked down.

There it was!

A huge inspection plate.

Held down by four twelve-inch nuts.

But what an unhandy place. Handy maybe for a Psychlo mechanic to reach down with huge long arms. Not handy for him.

He banged off another shot up the passageway. He ducked down and adjusted the wrench. He gripped the first nut.

Yikes, it was tight. No one-hand job with this big wrench. Psychlos didn't know their own strength when putting nuts on.

He inspected the corridor again. He had to lay down the assault rifle to do this. He made sure the place he put it braced it reasonably so it wouldn't slide out the door. He still had his revolver in its holster.

He eased down and, with two hands on the wrench, legs braced, heaved on the nut.

It turned!

He had learned enough about mechanics not to just undo and take off one nut. He'd find the last one wedged tight. So loosen all four about half a turn each. . . .

He had number two loosened.

He was straining at number three.

"What are you doing!" roared Zzt.

Jonnie came up. Zzt was still in his recess up there.

"You dimwitted, stupid slug!" roared Zzt. "If you monkey with those motors this thing will just crash!"

Thank you, Zzt, said Jonnie to himself.

"If you leave it alone, this thing will just land by itself in two or three days!" howled Zzt.

Actually, Zzt was getting panicky. There was something very peculiar about those shots the animal kept sending up the passageway. Right now the exhale valve on his breathe-mask had sparked slightly. For some minutes he had been aware of little tiny sparks around him. He had thought they were dust motes at first and then thought something was wrong with his eyes, that he was seeing tiny molecular flashes in his head. But this last exhale had actually sparked. Was there radiation around here? Was that animal throwing uranium dust around? Wait, were those slugs or was that gun he used operated by radiation?

He had decided he better act, regardless of consequences. Yes, there was another tiny flush when the mask exhaled spent breathe-gas into the air!

"You've got a mask!" roared Zzt. "This kill-gas won't blow back in the drone. Just wait until it lands!" The stupid, filthy animal. Damn Terl!

"How about other people down there?" said Jonnie.

That shut Zzt up for the moment. He could not work out how something happening to somebody else had any bearing on what one would do for himself.

"Leave those motors alone!" screamed Zzt.

The Psychlo was getting hysterical. Maybe he would charge. Jonnie waited, rifle in hand. No, Zzt was not going to charge. He better get back to work on these nuts. He laid down the assault rifle and ducked. He took a full turn on nut number one. He came up to be sure Zzt hadn't moved.

The fifty-pound floor plate, sailing in a deadly spin, traveling with the speed of a cannonball, struck a skid strut, glanced, and smashed into the back of Jonnie's head.

The assault rifle flew from his clutching hand and went out into the dark. Holding somehow on to consciousness he fumbled for the revolver. There was nothing but darkness in front of his eyes.

■

PART 14

— 1 —

They had the compound!

A final dive of Glencannon's battered plane had blown the air-cooling through into the compound breathe-gas pumps, flooding all the underground areas with air.

Glencannon had landed the ship safely. A hidden gun battery had blown out his instrument panel and radio, but he had not been burned and his controls still worked and he got the ship back to the ravine.

Scots, howling with joy, had pulled him out and pounded him on the back until sternly reminded by the parson that the pilot had broken ribs.

A few more bursts of assault rifles had cleaned off some snipers.

The pipe major had cut loose with bagpipes. The other piper and the drummer had thrown aside their rifles and picked up their instruments, and the high-pitched wail and low drone of pipes skirled across the compound to the beat of the drum.

The last remaining Psychlos came stumbling out of the underground with their paws on high. Oddly enough, they soon proved to be top-flight graduates of the various company schools and their female assistants. Breathe-masks had been in short supply, having been put on combat teams who were going out to fight. But as Robert the Fox noted, these top-drawer ones had had their own personal masks. There were about thirty of them left alive.

Hundreds of Psychlos had died in the fire fights and hundreds more in the air flooding. By eventual count there had been nine hundred seventy-six Psychlos in this compound.

Ker tried to get away by crawling through an exhaust vent and was captured alive.

They got the fire system water valves and shut them off. A

team raced around checking for radiation with open breathe-gas vials and it was found that water had washed it down into underground drains. The area was relatively safe.

Chrissie had been spotted by the Scots, and the news earlier rumored to that effect was now confirmed as she went about helping the parson collect wounded Scots on a flatbed that had been gotten running. She was a trifle taken aback by the enthusiasm that greeted her. She was not used to being a celebrity. And she did not realize that she had given the Scots an element called for in their romances. Everywhere she went, Scots, no matter what they were doing, rushed over to her, stared at her with glad eyes, and then rushed back to the work of getting the place handled. There was still a war on, but they could cheer and their pipes could skirl. And they could delight in the successful rescue of a fair maiden. But Chrissie, even though busy and very tender with the wounded, felt a suppressed terror that she masked. Jonnie was not here and she somehow knew Jonnie was not all right.

Scots under the direction of Angus were trying to get the tumble and jumble of forklifts operating. The whole hangar door was blocked solid with wrecked planes and they could not move any planes out. They told a worried Robert the Fox it would be hours before they could get forklifts running and get to work on that pile.

Terl tried to manage a last ploy. He got to see Robert the Fox by saying he had something urgent. They brought Terl up with hoist chains wrapped around him and held in four different directions by four brawny Scots while two others held assault rifles on him.

He told Robert the Fox that he had keys to the drone presets and would exchange them for a promise of an early teleportation back to Psychlo.

Robert the Fox said yes, if Terl could produce the keys. Terl thereupon asked for his boots.

A female Psychlo who said her name was Chirk had been found in a breathe-mask under the bed in Terl's old quarters. So Robert the Fox went to her where she was being held under the spotlights of an otherwise wrecked mine car and asked her whether she was Terl's secretary, and she readily said yes, she was. So Robert said he had a message from Terl for her to get the preset keys of the drone.

Chirk had had lots of time to think since Zzt sailed off on the drone for reasons of his own, and she had finally remembered about the keys. She got very cross and sent back the message that Terl must think she was very inefficient: he knew very well that he had given her a set of keys and told her to drop them in the recycling trash bin, and that had been ages ago and the keys were long gone, and if Terl was trying to blacken her company record by saying she disobeyed orders, she could do a little blackening on her own. There was something about promising her a huge home on Psychlo. She was very cross.

So Robert the Fox called for Terl's boots and examined them and found a false sole. He removed from it a very thin, small blast gun.

Right now, Terl was chained up with four separate chain strands in a well-lighted field with an assault rifle on him. He kept snarling something about females.

The compound was a litter-strewn bedlam of lights and noise. There were hundreds of Psychlo bodies lying around in everybody's way. Everything was soaking wet.

The Chamco brothers had gladly contracted for C15,000 a year with a C500 bonus for each major job. They were a little apprehensive about a counterattack from Psychlo, but pay was pay. They were laboring with the team of Scots to get radios back into operation but it didn't look like they would earn C500 right away. Water had saturated a lot of equipment and the transshipment area was a write-off. Nobody could get a plane out into the open where its radio could broadcast, and Glencannon's ship radio was just fused metal.

Robert the Fox walked up and down, his old cape flowing. He answered where he had to and gave orders where needed. But his mind wasn't on it.

The twelve-hour radio silence was up and he was out of communication on the planetary band. He could not order the ships that had attacked the remote minesites to go look for the drone. He had no ships to send.

He went over to where about twenty wounded Scots were laid out in a field, being handled by the parson and schoolmaster and four old women. And Chrissie.

His eyes and Chrissie's eyes met.

Robert the Fox felt very bad.

Jonnie had been right. It would not have done to wait for

minesite-bound ships to attack the drone. They had left long before it fired and they knew nothing of it. And he could not even tell them.

He had a feeling Jonnie was in trouble.

Robert the Fox gave his head a slight shake. Chrissie looked at him steadily for a moment, swallowed hard, and then went back to work.

— 2 —

Zzt felt triumphant.

The animal had been hurt and hurt badly. It could have been better. The roll of the drone had caused a slight miscalculation in the throw, and instead of totally severing the animal's head as he intended, the plate had hit a strut of the plane skids and then had struck the animal.

But the results had been very satisfactory. There was red blood all over the floor plates under there.

The animal had fired a new small weapon up the corridor. But in the mirror Zzt could see that the animal was passing out, coming to for an instant, and passing out again. Zzt had waited. The animal would pass out long enough for Zzt to dart forward and finish it.

However, it didn't quite come off as Zzt had planned. The animal had crawled backward toward the back end of the drone, halting and firing a shot, backward further, firing another shot.

It had crawled into a canister-loading hole in the rear cargo space. The hole it went through was almost too small for it. It disappeared.

Zzt waited a long time and nothing else happened. Finally he crept out of his recess and, ducking into other recesses and using his mirror, got all the way back to the rear cargo bulkheads.

He tried to look in with the mirror. It was too dark in there.

He shone a torch in there. Nothing. The animal must have crawled off to the side.

Zzt tied the torch to the mirror and looked to the right. He got one very short glimpse of the animal and then a bullet hit the torch and mirror and they went flying out of Zzt's hand. Lucky he hadn't tried to reach in there himself.

He listened all along the bulkhead. The roar of the drone was too great to hear any breathing.

For quite a while he expected the animal to pop out and shoot. But nothing like that happened. He finally concluded that the animal had crawled in there and died. There sure was enough blood. Bled to death, probably. Zzt beamed happily.

Well, enough! Zzt decided he better get to work.

He opened the door of the battle plane and switched on the local command channel and tried to wake up Nup. The dimwit certainly must be up there. Maybe asleep. Zzt impatiently threw on all the radio channels. That would blast the nincompoop out of his wits. Planetary had a habit of knocking in earbones at just a few hundred feet.

"Nup, you crap brain! Wake up!"

Nup's voice came back. "Who? Who's this?"

"Look, Nup," said Zzt with controlled patience, "I know you are short on sleep. I know they didn't teach you the exact solution to all this in mine school. But, I feel that under the existing circumstances you might try to cooperate!"

"Is this Zzt?"

What a dimwit, what a flutter brain with its bearings burned out! "Of course it's Zzt!"

"And you're down in the drone? Ah, I thought you were. But didn't Snit fly you out? If you were—"

"Shut up," roared Zzt. "Here's exactly what I want you to do. Take off and land that ship just above this door. Land it close to the edge above the door so it will break the wind."

Nup wanted to know break the wind from what?

Zzt told him very unpleasantly. Nup, with ten minutes of fuel left, hastened to comply.

Zzt intended to rob this damaged battle plane of its cartridges of fuel. He had been appalled at the skill it would take to fly it out this door. Then he had a happy thought. Maybe it carried some spares.

He got up on the seat and started to rummage in the back compartment. A whole bag of cartridges! Dozens of them!

But he saw something else. His breathe-mask exhale ports flashed. This stuff had radioactive dust on it! Of course, this wasn't surprising for packages that had been in a radiation-bullet battle, and it was not much, but it frightened Zzt. He flung the bag of cartridges out into the passageway and jumped out to stop them before they rolled into open spaces. Holding them at arm's length he shook the bag. He breathed on it cautiously. No flash. Good.

He opened both doors of the battle plane. He wouldn't go near the back compartment. He did everything now at arm's length.

He played a torch on the housings of both main drive and balance motors. His practiced eye detected a hairline crack in the right balance motor. Maybe it would run, maybe not. The crash hadn't helped. He reached underneath it and got a paw full of wires and tore them loose, scrambled them, and laid them back unconnected but out of view. One battle plane that wouldn't fly straight! Good.

He got down under the plane and looked at the drone's main drive. Ah, there was his wrench. And the animal hadn't removed the plate. Good. He put the wrench back in his boot where it belonged.

The pitch and roll of the drone changed drastically now. Nup had moved. The pitch was gone but the roll was much worse. However, it all had its good points. The drone was now crabbing and protecting the door from the wind.

Gingerly reaching for the microphone, Zzt stood well away from the plane. "You in position?" he demanded.

"It took a couple of times but—"

"All right. Do you recognize a cable ladder?"

Nup tried to explain that as a mining executive and a fully qualified pilot, he of course could recognize—

"Fasten your end of the cable ladder to the cleats opposite the seat. Drop the weighted end of the ladder down here. Then lower an ore net on a line. And then a safety wire. All into this door. Got that?"

Nup said he certainly understood it, but was there ore in the drone? He didn't quite understand—

"Fuel cartridges! I'm going to send you up fuel cartridges.'

"Oh, my. That's a relief! Will they fit?"

Zzt didn't bother to answer. Of course they fit! All plane fuel cartridges were interchangeable. It was tanks to planes that didn't match. What a crud brain!

The ladder's weighted end came whipping down. It fell on the wrong side of the tail that was jutting out of the door. The tail was wedged over.

Zzt, feeling quite brave, reached in, waited for a correct roll of the drone, released the magnetic brake, shifted the plane with a massive heave only a Psychlo could manage, and reset the brake. Good, now he could get the cable ladder end where it belonged. He had clearance between it and the door edge. He lashed the lower end to a floor beam.

The lowering safety wire gave trouble for it kept flying out into the windstream. Zzt radioed Nup to haul it back. Devil with it, he didn't need it.

Zzt reached into the battle plane and pulled out a coil of safety wire from it. Then he couldn't figure out how to use it. He tied it to the battle plane in its proper ring but he didn't like the idea of being tied here. Suppose the plane moved or something. He left the safety wire on the floor plates. Devil with it.

"Ore basket!" he demanded of Nup.

It came down. It was heavy enough not to fly around in the three-hundred-mile-an-hour blast of cold air. As Zzt tied the cartridge bag into it he realized he hadn't inspected it for fuel. It probably also had ammunition cartridges in it. Well, who knew, they might need both.

As soon as they flew off he was going to gun this interior, blow this battle plane to bits and just make sure. Damn animal. Damn Terl.

A new thought hit him. It was a long way down. He better grab the jet backpack. Very gingerly, he reached an arm into the compartment and got it. There were two there. He brought out both. He threw one over the side and put the other on. Left the animal with no out. But of course the animal was dead. And good riddance. Damn Terl!

"You all set?" he demanded on the radio.

Nup said he was, but where was the fuel.

Zzt let him pull up the fuel in the ore net.

"You got it?" demanded Zzt.

"Yes, I'm trying to check . . . just let me remove the spent empties and make sure the size—"

"Blast you for a dimwitted crud! Stand by to steady that ladder. I'm sick of being down here in this crap-infested, monkey-cursed drone! I'll take care of the refuel when I get up there.

Don't put an ammunition cartridge into the fuel sleeves! I'm coming up and right now!"

But he didn't come "right now." He looked at the radio and then took his wrench out of his boot and slashed the radio to bits. Of course, he'd be shooting this thing to pieces in just minutes, but caution was always best.

Zzt grabbed the cable ladder rungs and started up. He looked up. It was not a short climb. The Mark 32 cut off the windstream quite a bit but it was still a strong blast. He paused, made sure his mask wouldn't blow off, and climbed up the ladder.

— 3 —

Jonnie lay on the cross-members of the canister storage area of the drone, gripped in a nightmare. He was in the cage again, a collar around his throat, and a demon was crushing in the back of his skull. He kept trying to tell the demon he would shoot it if it didn't stop, but he couldn't get the words out.

He wrestled himself up from the nightmare. The roar of the huge drone engines beat against his head. He realized where he was. It wasn't the collar: it was the neck lanyard of the revolver; the heavy weapon was hanging down between the beams. He painfully retrieved it. There was a small amount of light in here and he swung the cylinder open.

Just one shot left.

He reached to his belt to see whether he had reloads. He didn't. The blast gun was lost.

Before he passed out he had opened the first aid kit and tied a wound pad over his head and under the face mask straps. That was all he remembered after he had shot the flashlight out of Zzt's hand. He could see it gleaming still, bent over a cross-member. No, that wasn't a flashlight. It was about four feet away and it seemed forty. What was it?

A mechanic's mirror. So that was how Zzt observed him.

What had awakened him? How long had he been out? Seconds? Minutes? The back of his head felt like it had been staved in, soft to the touch. Fractured skull? Or was it just swelling and blood-matted hair?

He heard something clatter. Noise around the plane had awakened him.

With a sudden feeling of urgency he made the effort and retrieved the mirror. He slid along the crossbeam and put the mirror to the hole.

It was Zzt.

His first impulse was to dart out and use this one last bullet. Then he saw the ladder end. And the ore basket going up. They were refueling the Mark 32!

The sudden thought of what they could do with the Mark 32 back at the compound shocked him fully alert. He knew what he must do. Just now—*wait!*

That was the hard part. He kept drifting off into a murky black sea of unconsciousness. He could hold on for a while but the wave would drown him again.

Zzt was on the radio. No, he was smashing the radio with the wrench.

Jonnie gathered himself up, tensing to dive out through the hole. He watched carefully with the mirror. Zzt went over to the ladder. He started up. He stopped with just his legs visible below the door.

In a wave of pain, Jonnie got out of the canister loading slot. There was a safety line on the floor plates. He grabbed it and gave it a tug. It was secured to his plane. In his condition he did not want to lapse unconscious and fall out that door. He rapidly swung the safety wire around his waist and secured it with a hasty loop.

Zzt's legs were gone.

Jonnie checked the revolver to make sure the one shot was going to come up under the firing pin when he cocked it.

He swung himself onto the ladder. It was blowing outward from the drone. The bottom end was fastened inside the door but he was now out over empty space, protected from the windstream by the tail of his battle plane. He went up several steps.

Jonnie had a clear view of the Mark 32. The cockpit lights were on; the door was being held open by Nup's foot. Zzt was a third of the way up to the plane.

For a moment Jonnie thought he was too late. He thought Nup had hoisted the fuel cartridges out of sight. But no. Nup had the caps off the fuel receptacles and was examining them. For numbers? And he had the whole ore basket in his lap!

Zzt was howling at Nup, something about opening the door wider and steadying the cable. Zzt climbed further. The ladder was protected by the angle of the Mark 32 but there was still a tearing wind. It was ripping Zzt's jacket. He roared again something about opening the door, the words lost in the roar of the drone and the scream of the wind.

Jonnie cocked the revolver. The face mask protected his eyes. He could have shot either Zzt or Nup. He didn't. He carefully allowed for wind and elevation. The already high muzzle velocity of a Smith and Wesson .457 magnum was increased by blasting caps in its cartridges. He must be very careful. Only one shot.

Nup kicked the door further open, the ore basket in plain view on his lap. Then Nup saw Jonnie and yelled and pointed, and Zzt looked back down.

Jonnie fired!

He tried to duck back inside an instant after the shot. He was not quite fast enough.

Enough fuel and ammunition for twenty battles not only went up, it also flashed down into the open fuel and ammunition receptacles!

The roar and almost instantaneous concussion hit Jonnie like a sledge hammer. He went outward over black space.

The safety line held and snapped him back inside the door.

In that confused instant, as though it were a still picture, he saw Zzt on fire just starting to fly out into space. He saw the whole Mark 32 leap in an exploding ball high in the air.

Jonnie hit the floor plates just inside the open slots so he wouldn't slide back.

The concussion had been too much for his head and he was passing out again.

An idiot phrase passed through his mind just before a deeper darkness blanketed his senses. "Old Staffor was wrong. I'm not too smart. I just cost myself the only target search beams can pick up."

The drone was not rolling now that it had been relieved of its unstabilizing weight.

The body on the icy floor just inside the door did not move.

The lethal cargo soared onward toward Scotland and the rest of the world, its goal the final obliteration of the remainder of the human race, the ones it had missed a thousand or more years ago.

— 4 —

The small boy sped on feet of fire through the underground passages of the dungeons of the castle. He was soaked with the rain that fell outside. His bonnet was askew. His eyes were glowing with the urgency of a message he had carried for a two-mile sprint through the dawn twilight.

He identified a room ahead and tore into it, shouting: "Prince Dunneldeen! Prince Dunneldeen! Wake up! Wake up!"

Dunneldeen had just settled down in his own room, in his own plaid blanket for a nice comfortable snooze, his first in quite some time.

The small boy was wrestling with excited hands to light a candle dip with a ratchet flint device.

So it was "Prince" Dunneldeen now. They only called him that on feast days or when somebody wanted a favor. His uncle, Chief of Clanfearghus, was the last of the Stewarts and entitled to be called King, but he never made anything of it.

The light was burning now. It shone upon the sparsely furnished stone-walled room. It showed the rain-drenched, excited black-eyed boy, Bittie MacLeod.

"Your squire Dwight, your squire Dwight ha' sent a message, who he say is mos' urgent!"

Ah, this was different. Dunneldeen got up and reached for his clothes. "Squire" Dwight. Probably Dwight had used that because "copilot" would be an unknown word to this child.

"Your gillies are afoot asaddling a mount. Your squire ha' said 'twas most urgent!"

Dunneldeen glanced at his watch. It meant that the twelve-hour radio silence was over, that was all. Probably a babble of news. Dunneldeen had no idea at all that things had gone other than successfully at the other minesites or that they'd succeeded at the compound. He got back into his flight clothes. No hurry. He took his time.

What a busy night it had been. His and Dwight's plan had been to bring the Chiefs across the sea to celebrate the victory. They had landed both ships on a flat place two miles off so as not to shock the people, and he had borrowed a horse from a startled farmer he had known and ridden in.

He had gotten his uncle, Chief of Clanfearghus, out of bed. and gillies had flown to light the fires on the hills to gather the clans to hear the news. The minesite in Cornwall was no more. They would be free to roam the whole of England!

The Chief was very fond of his nephew Dunneldeen who was, in fact, his heir. He liked Dunneldeen's style. A true Scot. He had listened enraptured as Dunneldeen had given him a thumbnail but torrential account of all their doings. And if Dunneldeen were a bit incautious, the Chief gave his attention while making very sure to reserve judgment and act in a wise way on the general scene, without spoiling Dunneldeen's flair. So he had ordered the beacons lighted. He was cautiously thrilled.

Dunneldeen had then gone to see a lass and had asked her to marry him, and she had said, "Oh, yes! Oh. yes! Oh, yes, Dunneldeen!"

That attended to, he had come home for a nice snooze.

Bittie seemed to be trying to remember something else. He was hopping from one bare foot to the other, squinting up his eyes, wiping at his nose. Then the boy seemed to abandon his effort. Dunneldeen was almost dressed.

The boy's eyes caught the sword on the wall. It was a claymore, used in battles and for ceremony. It was a real *claid heamh mōr*, five feet long, not just a basket hilt saber. Bittie was gesturing at it, indicating the prince should wear it. Dunneldeen shook his head to signify no, he wasn't going to take it this time.

When he saw the eagerness die in Bittie's eyes, Dunneldeen relented. He took it down and handed it to him. "All right, but you carry it!" The sword was a foot taller than the boy. Worship, awe, and joy sprang up in the boy again as he draped the hanger around his neck.

Dunneldeen checked his gear and went out. The castle passages and halls were aswarm with gillies. They had lochaber axes in their belts and were bustling around with a hundred chores in preparation for a gathering of the clans. Dunneldeen had really thrown a firebrand into the scene. Nobody had been briefed. They didn't know what was going on. Dunneldeen had come home. Orders had been given. Somebody said the Psychlo minesite was no more. There was an awful lot to do.

The ancient ruin had remained a ruin above ground so as to

attract minimal attention from drones that had gone over for centuries. Some said the place had once been the seat of Scottish kings. Its dungeons had been expanded and it was a fortress in itself.

Two gillies had Dunneldeen's own horse saddled and it was prancing about. The gillies were smiling broad welcomes to Dunneldeen.

He mounted, and at a signal they tossed the boy up behind him, *claid heamh mōr* and all.

It was raining. A storm apparently had moved in. It had been clear when they landed but now the dawn was thick with overcast.

It was at that moment that Bittie MacLeod remembered the rest of the message. "Your squire," he said to Dunneldeen's back, "also say to 'squiggle'!"

The boy's accent was thick, not the accent of an educated Scot. "To what?" demanded Dunneldeen.

"I misremembered, I couldna think of the word," apologized the boy. "But it did sound like 'squiggle.' "

"Scramble?" asked Dunneldeen. The word that meant emergency takeoff.

"Ah, so 'twas, so 'twas!"

Dunneldeen was off like a shot and two miles were never eaten up so fast by a horse.

They came plunging to a stop on the flat-topped knoll. Dunneldeen looked wildly about. Only the passenger plane was there. He flung himself off the horse and flung the reins to the boy. He opened the door and leaped into the passenger plane, reaching for the radio.

And then Dwight landed nearby, startling the horse into frantic plunging that lifted the boy and the sword off the ground at every rear.

Dunneldeen raced over to Dwight.

"It's gone now," said Dwight.

There had been no radio messages from the compound. Dwight, as arranged, had faithfully stayed on watch. He had waited for any break in radio silence and the end of the silence itself. The time period had ended, but pilots, not hearing from the compound and Robert the Fox, had not opened up.

But something else peculiar had happened. Dwight had picked up a Psychlo conversation on the planetary plane band, very loud and clear. It seemed loud enough to be within a thousand miles or so, maybe more, hard to tell.

"What did they say?" demanded Dunneldeen.

"I got it all on a disc," said Dwight. He started the disc. It said "Nup, you crap brain, wake up!"

Dwight said he had at once sent the boy to tell Dunneldeen to scramble and then he himself had gone straight up. Yes, the sudden roar of Dwight's own engines was there on the disc.

The disc played on.

"Drone?" said Dunneldeen. "Zzt? There was a transport chief named Zzt."

"Well, he was out there some place in a drone!" said Dwight. He had gone up as high as he could go. About two hundred thousand feet. As fast as he could go. "Almost tore my heart and lungs out with gravity," said Dwight.

Then he heard complete instructions in Psychlo about relanding on top of a drone in front of a door so Zzt could get out of the drone.

"There is no drone that big," said Dunneldeen. "Not that I know of."

Dwight had turned on every search instrument he had. The transmission had been coming from the northwest. He had sped in that direction. He had gotten it on his scope. It was traveling three hundred two miles per hour, a very positive blip. It was clear weather where the thing had been; this cloud cover and rain was ahead of it.

He played some more transmission. Somebody named "Snit" was still in the drone but no explanation why. This was mad because drones didn't have pilots. But how could anybody fly anybody out of a drone? And then somebody was taking fuel out of the drone in an ore basket and the other Psychlo said he was leaving the drone.

"Then why are you here?" demanded Dunneldeen, turning toward the passenger plane. "Why didn't you attack it?"

"It blew up," said Dwight. "I saw it *visual,* eyeball! It looked like thirty lightning storms! It curved down. It probably went into the sea. I scanned the whole area. There was a little blip left; probably when it sank it had some debris. And then that was gone. It just isn't out there anymore on any scope. So I came back here."

Dunneldeen played the disc through again. Dunneldeen pulled

out the instrument recorders. They told the same story. Heat and then gone.

Dunneldeen looked at the sky. "You better go back up there and patrol in that direction."

"There won't be any blip," said Dwight. "And this overcast is high. The thing was flying at about five thousand feet and you won't be able to see a thing visually. The overcast goes up to at least ten. There's no blip," finished Dwight.

Dunneldeen turned and looked at the castle ruin, gaunt and very old in the morning rain and mist. Two miles away and it was drifting in and out of visibility.

What was that all about? Had the battle of the compound been lost? What drone? And why had it blown up? The clan Chiefs would be assembling and he had a lot of things to do today.

— 5 —

Jonnie drifted up out of a pit of black pain. He tried to orient himself. The drone motors were like shouting anger in his ears. His arms were hanging down into a gap in the floor plating. Blood had run along the sleeves and dried.

With a start of alarm he thought of Zzt and reached for the revolver. It was gone, the lanyard snapped in the blast. The blast! Zzt was also gone and so was the Mark 32. And so was anything that would let this ancient monster be located on a screen.

He lifted himself up with considerable effort. He was still tied with the safety line. He found it very hard to think connectedly, and he wondered for a bit why he was tied to the line. His back hurt, one more pain in a confused welter of it. He realized the safety line had pulled him back inside.

It was awfully hard to think, and he recognized that he was getting worse, not better. He was nauseated. Hunger. It must be that he was nauseated from hunger.

He got to his knees. The drone was no longer rolling. That was a relief. He turned and then stared.

Through the door, bright tendrils of mist and fog were curling in. It was a storm. He was flying through a storm. Wait. It was light out there. Daylight. Well-advanced daylight.

How long had he been out? It must be hours.

He spun on his knees, thinking to see the gas canisters dropping gas. He had no way to tell that. Were they already past Scotland? Had the drone already done part of its work?

He got to the door and tried to spot a brighter area in the storm that might tell him where the sun was. It was too thick. He wasn't thinking well; he realized he had reverted to being a mountain man. There were compasses in the plane. He opened the door and saw the havoc Zzt had made with the radio smashup. It distracted him. Then he realized he had opened the door to look at the compasses and did so. When he leaned over it felt like somebody was hitting his skull with a sledge hammer. He felt for the compress on his head. It was still there. No, the compasses. Look at the compasses.

He was heading southeast. The course to Scotland would have curved over like that. He couldn't be sure. He went back to the door and tried to look down. He nearly fell. He couldn't see anything down there. All rain and mist.

Then he remembered the ship had gas ports in the bottom. He crawled painfully to the floor plate he had removed and looked past the motor housings. No daylight was coming up.

His air mask seemed to be suffocating him. He recalled it had been askew when he woke.

Of course! The drone had dropped no gas yet. He'd be dead.

Well, he wasn't dead. Pretty well on the way to it with this head, but he wasn't dead. Therefore the drone had not yet dropped gas.

Part of his trouble was that his air bottle was out of air. He got new bottles and put them in place. It made him feel a little less lethargic. He got a grip on himself; he was just dawdling around. What had he been at when he had been hit with whatever it was?

Maybe he didn't have very much time!

His industry faded when he recognized he didn't have the wrench anymore. He made himself think, to come out of his pain. He climbed down and checked the nuts on the inspection plate. They were loose but it would take an age to unscrew each one: the threads were too many.

He got into the plane and rummaged about. He found a bag of explosives and emptied it. He had six limpet mines, a long coil of blasting cord, some boxes of blasting caps. He looked for time fuses. None. He looked at the limpet mines. No time fuses, only contact buttons that would explode them when heavily jarred. No electrical cord.

It was an awful effort to think, to concentrate on just one thing. What could he do with this mess? Straight contact! Suicide stuff!

He found his own belt pouch. Some flints, pieces of glass . . . ah, a roll of long buckskin thongs. At least he could get the nuts off.

Encouraged, he somehow got down to the inspection plate again. He did a binding wind for the first turn and then wound the thong around and around the nut. He tied a hand loop onto the remaining end. He braced himself and gave a heavy yank. The nut spun off, leaped up, and vanished into the dark hold.

Even though the yank had almost torn his head apart, he repeated the action with the other three nuts. Gone!

He struggled to lift the heavy plate. He had intended to just lay it aside but it slipped from his gloved fingers and fell into the darkness of the drone's belly. Let it go!

Now he was staring into the black interior of the housing. There were some small electrical sparks arcing in there. He knew very well you were not supposed to get into a motor when it was running. And certainly not put a hand to one. It was said it gave a paw a funny feeling like it wasn't there, and then was, and then wasn't there. One could lose a paw, Ker had said.

He painfully lifted himself to the ship again and found a spare torch and went back and shone the light inside the housing.

There were all the thousands of coordinate points jutting out from the inside skin. They were smoothly arcing as they translated progressive space. It wasn't electricity really; it was energy driven up to the arc point, and then these arc points did a conversion to space coordinates in terms of pure space. The electricity just kept little motors running behind the points. This thing must have thousands of submotors behind those points. And they could be damaged. It wasn't armored in there.

The light shining into it looked funny. It was appearing and disappearing in a flutter. Well, a blast could wreck those translation motors and the points. Flicker or no flicker. A small submotor was a small submotor, and a blast would disable them. The space converter wouldn't convert anymore, and this thing would simply go unpowered and crash. He didn't think the balance motors could support the mammoth drone by themselves. Yes, it would crash.

He drew back. Leaning forward was bringing on the blackness again. He mustn't pass out anymore. That was final. He mustn't pass out anymore.

In the plane he gritted his teeth and stayed conscious. He had to work out a rig. Nothing but contact firing devices. What could he use to detonate them?

The plane's guns!

He would rig it so he would fire the guns and blow the plane backward out the door.

An inspection of the battle plane gun panel revealed no damage. The console was not damaged. He looked at the housings of the plane's main and balance motors. Was that a scrap of wire on the floor? But when he leaned forward to see closer he started to black out again and stood up.

Time! He had better work fast. He might even be too late now and crash this thing in the hills with the gas blowing all over.

This nausea was just hunger, that was all. He picked up some dried venison and lifted his mask. But chewing on it was an effort. It made him feel worse.

What was he doing? He must concentrate! Not just his mind but even his actions were wandering.

He got a spare safety wire and started to tie the mines together in a long string. They had magnetic grips to hold them to hulls. He had asked for them, thinking he could drop them in a circle on top of the drone and blow an entry hole in. Useless for that, but he would put them to work now.

A garland. Chrissie, when she was a little girl, used to make flower garlands and put them on his pony's neck. She . . . he was wandering again. He gritted his teeth and kept at his job.

The manual had said, "Do not pack mines with contact fuses in such a way that the fuses can be subjected to closure by the weight of another mine . . ."

A vision of the Psychlo belt buckle, as he had seen it many times on Terl, rose before him. The clouds of gas in the sky. How he had hated it!

A garland . . .

He had the mines strung. He then took a long length of blast cord and wove it through the holes in the limpet bases that let the mines cling to metal. He hoped they didn't cling.

Yards and yards of blast cord, looped past the contact of each mine and up parallel with the safety wire. It was all so heavy. So very heavy. He was starting to black out again.

He caught himself. He managed to get the long end of the safety cord through an upper I-beam support. Using its friction as a brake, he got the mines suspended over the inspection hole and lowered them carefully down into the housing. Down they went, deeper and deeper. Good thing this drone wasn't rolling or the mines would snap over to cling magnetically to the inside skin of the housing. Careful, careful, lower and lower.

There was a sudden jerk. The bottom mine had hit the bottom of the housing interior. Good.

No, not so good. Had the drone motor changed pitch? Or was that just part of the murky sea of semidelusion in which he was so slowly moving? Were the mines altering the space contour of the interior and affecting the motor drive? He didn't know. But there was no time. He tied the safety line fast to a beam.

The loose long end of the blast cord he threw up over the upper structural bars. Ow, but that hurt his head! Was it in front of the plane's guns? Near enough.

He got the blasting caps. "Percussion" it said on the box in Psychlo.

He started to fasten a single cap on the blast cord directly ahead of his guns. Then with a burst of finality, he tied the whole box to it.

He checked, thinking with difficulty. When he fired the guns it would set off the caps. These would fire the blast cord and that would fire the mines. He realized then it would have been smarter to have sealed it with the housing cover. He looked down into the depths. He turned a torch down there. Was it possible to recover the inspection plate cover and its nuts?

But he forgot about that. His light was playing straight on the full intake cap.

There were two caps. No, five tubes! Into these he knew would be stuffed hundreds of fuel cartridges, dropped in one after the other. A drone like this required an enormous number of cartridges. It must!

Waves of nausea and blackness were hitting him. He mustn't tip his head over and look down. That was the secret.

He wondered whether those big fuel tube covers would move. They were usually just screwed on.

With difficulty he got down to them. With both hands he gave one a twist. It spun easily.

Within a minute he had five fuel tubes open, the covers clanging down into the dark belly. For a while it wouldn't affect the drone, but if a blast fed into those open tubes, oh my!

He checked everything again.

The drone soared out. But not for long, he told himself grimly.

— 6 —

Not until then had Jonnie thought about what was going to happen to himself. He had a feeling that it didn't really matter. He knew his head was staved in. He had lost an awful lot of blood. But he ought to make a gesture, some rudimentary effort, just to say he had. Say to whom? He was out of radio contact. The drone was wave-neutralized to any screen. There was not the slightest chance of the drone being seen visually in this storm. Down under him would be sea or an even less friendly mountainside if the blast disabled his plane. Battle planes were pretty well armored, but firing his own guns in an enclosed space, *plus* the mines, *plus* the fuel of the drone, was going to make a pretty big bang.

His jet backpacks were gone. He rummaged about in the back of the plane. Must remember not to lean forward. That's what blacked him out. A brief moment of hope. A life raft. He pulled it out. The automatic inflation cartridges were long since duds. It had a little manual pump. He started to pump it up. Orange colored. Some tinsel on it. Then he realized he was being stupid. If he inflated it he couldn't get it back in the plane. He knew the plane would sink. He wouldn't be able to get it out. The wind was tugging at the half-inflated raft. A wave of blackness came over him and the door draft casually flicked it out of his hands. It went away into the storm. Gone. It had all been a waste of time.

He got into the plane. He had some blankets. He had been hurt in the earlier crash; the map case had not been enough. So he padded his knees and the windscreen with blankets.

He realized he had not checked for loose objects. They were deadly. He took the blankets away and looked in the rear of the plane behind him. Littered! A backward jolt of the plane would have made them into projectiles.

Wearily he got out and began to chuck things out through the door. Clip after clip of assault rifle ammunition. A shovel, whatever that was doing here. A sample pick. Odds and ends. He snugged down the cable ladder and ore net equipment of the plane. He put the food bag and his own pouch under the seat.

More nauseated than ever, he got back in the seat and restored the blanket cushions. He wrapped the oversized security belts around him twice and up so they would keep his head from snapping forward.

All set.

He reached out for the gun controls and put them on "Full Barrage," "Flame," and "Ready." They were aimed at that box of blasting caps.

Was the drone tilting or was he just dizzy? He couldn't tell with his dazed senses. He looked at the climb indicator of the plane. Yes! The drone was tilting, the door behind him lower now. Something had upset the coordinates. The magnetic fields of the limpet mines? But whatever it was trying correct, it was pointing its door down!

That meant if he shot backward and fired he would be shooting himself toward the sea or the mountains.

He better not delay.

He kicked off the magnetic grips. The plane started to slide backward to the door.

Hastily he hit his starter buttons. The plane was sliding backward faster.

He slammed his fist into the gun-firing button.

The battle plane fired full blast.

But the result was far more than just gun recoil.

Before his eyes the whole interior of the drone flashed a violent orange and green.

The battle plane was catapulted backward into space like a projectile!

The shock of sudden motion almost tore his head apart.

He could still see, still register. The drone looked like an old rocket missile must have looked. It was soaring upward as though the door was the jet!

Jonnie's hands fumbled over the battle plane console.

He punched in coordinates to arrest his backward descent.

With a jolt the plane slowed its rocketing, downward plunge.
But something else was happening. There was no response from the right balance motor.
In a slow roll, the plane began to rotate in the sky. The roll became faster.
The left balance motor could not hold it by itself.
Jonnie frantically battered the console keys.
The plane was now cartwheeling through the storm!

— 7 —

Badly shaken and feeling very ill, Jonnie tried to control the plane. There was a thin spot in the storm.
It was extremely hard to think. If he shut off the left balance motor, maybe the stricken ship would stop rolling. He managed it. Then he realized the guns must still be firing. He got a wad of blanket out of his vision and reached up to push the firing button off. And as he did he saw *it*.
The drone!
Almost straight at him it was tumbling out of the sky. Spent flames were licking out of the doorway and a vast plume of smoke was trailing behind it.
It was going to hit him if he didn't move.
His hands hit the console. He felt the plane move.
The drone went by so close the plane tumbled again in the air rush.
Abruptly a geyser of water smashed upward into the storm, a column two hundred feet high.
The battle plane spun about under the new impact.
Water? *Water!*
Jonnie felt a surge of relief. They were not yet over Scotland, still over the sea.
Water! He would hit it. He knew that pressure outside the doors would keep him from opening them. This battle plane would never float.
He brought a fist down on the window openers, both of them.
He looked at the console. What could he press to arrest his own descent?

The battle plane crashed into the sea.

The jolt threw him back into unconsciousness. But in a moment a wave of the coldest water he had ever felt rushed in on him, revived him. Bitterly cold water, colder than ice to the touch. And it was hitting him in a roaring torrent from both sides.

He fought with the huge, ten-pound Psychlo belt release. Everything seemed to be moving in slow motion. He unwound the belt from himself.

The water was getting darker. The battle plane must be sinking very rapidly. Or he was passing out once more?

The incoming rush eased. At least the plane was no longer spinning, he thought vacantly.

A sudden surge of energy. He got to his knees on the seat and thrust a floating blanket out of his way. The futility of it struck him. There was nobody to save him. He couldn't live in water this cold.

More by reflex than by intention he went out the window and began to rise to the surface. His air mask tanks were lifting him. Water was getting in the air mask, washing dried blood off the inside glass. The sea became lighter and lighter green.

Then a spatter of rain hit his head. *Rain!* It was welcome.

The sea about him, as he floated face-up, was a panorama of tossing, overwhelming waves, pockmarked with the rain. A wild scene.

The cold was getting to the very center of his being.

He knew he was going into a delusion again. As the waves covered and uncovered his ears he thought he heard a voice. They said dying men often heard angel voices calling them. He knew he was very close to death.

More delusion. Hopeful thinking giving rise to false sights. It was what he would have dearly loved to see, not what was. But the water-blurred vision stayed there.

Something hit him in the face mask. A line?

He became more alert. It looked like Dunneldeen on a cable ladder not four feet away! A Dunneldeen who was being submerged and uncovered by the waves.

Jonnie felt his arms being guided into safety line loops. Tension was being taken up on the line. His ears came free of the water and he could hear. It *was* Dunneldeen, a Dunneldeen who was smiling even though he was being doused repeatedly as the waves rolled past the cable ladder.

"Come on now, laddie," Dunneldeen said. "Just hold on and they'll pull you up to the plane. 'Tis a wee bit cold for a swim."

■

PART 15

— 1 —

Fleeting impressions, half-seen through a wall composed of darkness and pain. Dim consciousness of being in a ship and landing. Of someone spooning broth at him. Of being carried in a stretcher with rain on the blankets. Of a stone-walled room. Of different faces. Of whispered conversations. Of another stretcher. Of another plane. And a pain in his arm. He sank back into darkness. He thought he was in the drone again. He opened his eyes. He saw Dunneldeen's face. He must still be in the sea. But no, he was not cold, he was warm.

"He's coming around," said someone softly. "We'll be able to operate soon."

He opened his eyes and saw boots and kilts. A lot of boots and kilts standing beside what he was lying on.

A plane's motors? He was in a plane.

He turned his head a little and it hurt. But there was Dunneldeen's face.

Jonnie saw that he was on a sort of table. He was in a plane, a passenger plane. There was a tall gray man in a white coat on his left side. There were a lot of older Scots on his right side. Four young Scots were sitting on a bench. There was another table with some shiny things on it beyond the doctor.

Dunneldeen was sitting beside him and there was a tube and a sort of pump connecting Dunneldeen's arm with his own.

"What's this?" whispered Jonnie, indicating the tube or trying to.

"Blood transfusion," said Dunneldeen. He felt he should be very careful about what he said. He was smiling but he was worried and felt very bad. Keep a bright face on it. "Laddie, you are singularly fortunate. You are getting the royal blood of the

Stewarts, no less, which puts you into direct line, after me, of course, to the throne of Scotland.''

The doctor was signaling Dunneldeen to take it easy. They all knew that Jonnie might die, that there wasn't a thirty percent chance of his recovery, not with those two severe skull fractures and other injuries, as well as shock. His respiration was too shallow. In the underground hospital where they had operated for centuries, in a land where skull injuries were common, the doctor had seen too many die in less injured condition than this one. He was looking down at the big, handsome lad with something like pity.

''This is Dr. MacKendrick,'' said Dunneldeen to Jonnie. ''He'll handle you all right. You always overdo things, Jonnie. Most would be content with one skull fracture. But not you, laddie, you've got two!'' Dunneldeen smiled. ''You'll be right as rain in no time.'' He wished he could believe it; Jonnie's face bore the gray of death.

''Maybe I should have waited for you in the drone if you were so close,'' whispered Jonnie.

The older Scots let out an incredulous gasp. Chief of Clan-fearghus stepped forward. ''Naw, naw, MacTyler. The foul thing crashed just a mile north of Cape Wrath! 'Twas almost upon us!''

''How did you find me?'' whispered Jonnie.

''Laddie,'' said Dunneldeen, ''when you light a beacon fire to gather the clans, you don't do it halfway! The drone went up to ten thousand feet like a flaming rocket and like to have lit the whole of Scotland. That's how we spotted you.''

The Chief of the Argylls grumbled, ''That wasn't what your companion told us, Dunneldeen. They said your what-you-call-it detected a small object in the water and then got a look on a plane and then saw the fire.''

Dunneldeen was very composed. ''It makes a better story that way and that's the way the historian will write it. He lit a beacon fire in the sky!''

The other Chiefs nodded firmly. That was the way it should be.

''What day is this?'' whispered Jonnie.

''Day 95.''

Jonnie felt a bit confused. He had lost a day, two days? Where had he been? Where was he? Why?

The doctor saw the puzzlement. He had seen it before in head injuries. This young man had lost track of time. "They had to wait for me," he said. "I was not in Aberdeen at the moment. And then we had to type your blood and find someone with the same type. I'm sorry it took long. But we also had to bring you out of shock, get you warm." He shook his head sadly. "I should have gone with you all along. I'll help the others when we get there."

This upset Jonnie a little bit. "Were there a lot of Scots hurt? You shouldn't have delayed for me if you had a doctor."

"No, no," said the Chief of the Camerons. "Dr. Allen, who's so expert with burns, was sent two days gone."

"Twenty-one hurt," said Dunneldeen. "The one being you. Only two died. Very light casualties. The others will all recover."

"Who are they?" whispered Jonnie, making a slight motion with his hand to the four young men on the bench.

"Why, those," said Dunneldeen, "are four members of the World Federation for the Unification of the Human Race. The first one is a MacDonald and he speaks Russian now. The second is an Argyll and he speaks German. . . ." That wasn't why they were there at all. They were the others they'd found of Jonnie's blood type, waiting in case more transfusions were needed.

"And why am I in a plane?" whispered Jonnie.

That was the question they didn't want to answer. The doctor had told them not to worry this young man. They had him in a plane and were rushing him to the huge underground defense base in the mountains. There was some chance of a Psychlo counterattack. They had no idea at all whether the bombs sent to Psychlo had succeeded or failed. The Chamco brothers had told them about the force screen on Psychlo's transshipment area and that the early recoil had shown evidence of the screen's closing. The Chamcos had also told them that common salt neutralized the kill-gas completely. Angus had gotten mine ventilation fans into the old base and they'd found salt for filters of air. A group of excited, imported, awed Russians were at that very moment cleaning up the old base and the parson was burying the dead there. And they were not about to leave Jonnie MacTyler anywhere but safe in that base!

Dunneldeen answered, "What? Why not in the plane? You want to miss the victory celebration? We can't have that!"

A Scot helping Dwight up in the cockpit area came back and

whispered in Dunneldeen's ear. He was dragging a mike on a long cord. They had it on the planetary band.

Dunneldeen turned to Jonnie. "They want to hear your voice so they can believe you're alive."

"Who?" said Jonnie.

"The compound, the people. Just say something about how you are." Dunneldeen put the mike very close to Jonnie's mouth.

"I'm fine," Jonnie whispered. Then something told him he should try harder. He tried to speak louder. "I'm just fine."

Dunneldeen gave the mike back to the Scot who hesitated, not sure the message had gone out. Dunneldeen waved him away.

"I hear other planes," whispered Jonnie.

With a glance at the doctor for permission, Dunneldeen helped him turn his head. Jonnie looked through the plane ports.

There were five planes out there, stacked in a long echelon. He turned his eyes and looked out the other port. There were five planes out *there* in another echelon.

"It's your escort," said Dunneldeen.

"*My* escort?" whispered Jonnie. "But why? Everybody helped."

"Aye, laddie," said the Chief of Clanfearghus. "But you were the one. You were the bonnie one!"

The doctor disconnected the tube. He felt Jonnie's pulse. He nodded and motioned the others to silence. He had let this go on too long. The plane was not vibrating; the flight was very smooth. He had his patient out of shock. He wished he were in his own operating cave. But the others would not leave this young man there. And he himself, having heard but a small part of it, could share their awe and respect for what he had done.

"If you'll just drink this," said the doctor, "it will make things easier."

They held the cup to Jonnie's mouth. It was whiskey and it had heavy herbs in it. He managed to drink it. Shortly the pain grew less and he seemed to be floating.

The doctor signaled them all to be quiet. He had a trephine in his hand. The brain was being pressed upon in three places, not two, and the pressure must be relieved.

Dunneldeen went up to the cockpit to help Dwight. He glanced at their escort. Most of them were flying with one pilot. They had each smashed their minesites and come hammering back here when he put out the call for a massive patrol to the north of Scotland. They all should have gone home, but they wouldn't hear of it when they knew about Jonnie. They'd gone down with a Scot war party and gotten more planes from the Cornwall minesite after shooting the few Psychlos staggering around, and those not ordered back for urgent duty had been sitting, waiting for news about Jonnie. Now they were escorting him home.

"You better tell them he's all right," said Dwight. "They keep calling in every two or three minutes for news. And so does Robert the Fox. Takes one man just to handle the radio!"

"He's not all right," said Dunneldeen. And he looked down the long corridor to where the doctor had begun the operation.

Dwight glanced at Dunneldeen. Was the young prince crying? He felt like it himself.

— 2 —

Jonnie had been in a coma for three days.

They had brought him to the ancient underground military base in the Rocky Mountains where salt filters could be dropped into place at once if a counterattack materialized from the planet Psychlo.

The hospital complex was very extensive. It was all white tile, hardly any of it cracked. The Russians had cleaned it all up and the parson had buried the crumbling dead.

Fifteen of the wounded Scots were there, including Thor and Glencannon. They were in a separate series of rooms from Jonnie's, but one could hear them now and then, especially when the pipe major gave them an afternoon concert. Dr. Allen and Dr. MacKendrick had already discharged five of them as reasonably well and certainly too restless and impatient to keep idle when so many things were going on elsewhere.

Chrissie had been in constant attendance at Jonnie's bedside and she rose when Dr. MacKendrick and Angus MacTavish came in. They seemed angry with one another and Chrissie hoped they would go soon. MacKendrick put a hand on Jonnie's forehead and stood there for a moment looking at the ashen pallor. Then he turned to Angus with an expressive hand that seemed to say, "See?" Jonnie's breathing was shallow.

Three days before Jonnie had awakened and whispered to her

to send for somebody. There was always a Scot guard at the door, his assault rifle blocking out would-be visitors, of which there were too many. Chrissie had brought him in and watched worriedly while Jonnie whispered a long message to Robert the Fox, and the guard got it on a picto-recorder mike held close to Jonnie's lips. The message had been to the effect that if another gas drone appeared in the sky they could probably stop it by landing thirty recon drones on it with magnetic skids and racing their engines on reverse coordinates so the gas drone's motors would burn out. Chrissie didn't understand the message but she did understand that it was too tiring to Jonnie. He had relapsed back into a coma, and when the guard came back to say Sir Robert sent his thanks and would do that, Chrissie was quite cross with him.

The same guard was on again when Dr. MacKendrick and Angus were let in, and Chrissie vowed she would reason with him. MacKendrick, yes. Angus, definitely no!

MacKendrick and Angus went out and the guard closed the door behind them.

"Look," said MacKendrick, dragging Angus into one side room after another. "Machines, machines, machines. This was once a very well appointed and outfitted hospital. Those big things over there—I have seen them in an ancient book—were called ['X-ray machines']. It was a subject called radiology."

"Radiation?" said Angus. "No, man, not on Jonnie! Radiation is for killing Psychlos. You're daft!"

"Those machines let you look inside the body and find out what is wrong. They were invaluable."

"Those machines," said Angus, angrily, "were run by electricity! Why do you think we light this place with mine lamps?"

"You *must* get them running!" said MacKendrick.

"Even if I did, I see by that one they have *tubes*. The gas in those tubes is over a thousand years old. We can't get any more of it and couldn't get it into the tubes if we had any! You're daft, man."

MacKendrick glared at him. "There is something pressing on his brain! I can't just go plunging into it with a scalpel. I can't *guess*. Not with Jonnie MacTyler! People would slaughter me!"

"You want to see inside his head," said Angus. "Well, why didn't you say so?" Angus went off muttering about electricity.

He told a standby pilot at the heliport that he needed to get to the compound fast. The pilots were very few and they were being run ragged. They were zipping off to all parts of the world; they had a sort of international airline going that was beginning to visit every remaining pocket of men on the planet at least once a week. They were ferrying World Federation Coordinators and chiefs and tribal leaders as fast as they could. More pilots were in training, but right now they only had thirty plus the two in hospital. So a casual request, even from a Scot, even from a member of the original combat force, was not likely to get much heed. Travel from the underground base to the compound was usually by ground car.

Angus told him it had to do with Jonnie, and the pilot said why hadn't he said so and pushed him into a plane and said he would wait for him to come back.

With grim purpose, Angus went to the compound section where they kept the captive Psychlos. A small area of the old dormitory level had been rigged to circulate breathe-gas and "unreconstructed" Psychlos were there under heavy guard. They numbered about sixty now, for occasional ones were brought here from distant minesites when they surrendered peacefully. Terl was captive elsewhere.

Angus got an air mask and the Scot guard let him in. The place was very dim and the huge Psychlos sat around in attitudes of despair. One didn't walk in the place without being covered by the guard. The prisoners expected a Psychlo counterattack and were not too cooperative.

The Scot engineer located Ker and dug him out of his apathy. He demanded of Ker to tell him whether he knew of any mining equipment that would let one look through solid objects. Ker shrugged. Angus told him who it was for and Ker sat there for a while, his amber eyes thoughtful. Then suddenly he wanted to be reassured as to who this was for, and Angus told him it was for Jonnie. Ker was turning a tiny gold band around in his claws. Suddenly he sprang up and demanded that Angus give him an escort and a breathe-mask.

Ker went down to the shops and in a storeroom there dug up a strange machine. He explained it was used to analyze the internal structure of mineral samples and to find crystalline cracks inside metals. He showed Angus how to work it. You put the emanation tube under the object to be examined and you read the results on the top screen. There was also a trace paper reader that showed metals in alloys or rocks. It worked on some wavelength he called sub-proton field emanation, and this was intensified by the lower tube, and the influence went through the sample and you read it on the top screen. Being Psychlo, it was quite massive, and Ker carried it for him to the waiting plane. A guard took Ker back and Angus returned to the military base.

They tried it with some cats they had that were cleaning the rat population out, and the cats afterward seemed cheerful enough. The screen showed the skull outline very nicely. They tried it on one of the wounded Scots who volunteered and they found a piece of stone in his hand from a mine injury, and he too seemed fine afterward.

About 4:00 that afternoon they used it on Jonnie. By 4:30 they had a three-dimensional picture and the trace paper.

A very relieved Dr. MacKendrick pointed it out to Angus. "A piece of metal! See it? A sliver just below one of the trephine holes. Well! We'll just get him ready and I can have that out with a scalpel soon enough!"

"Metal?" said Angus. "Scalpel? On Jonnie? No you don't! Don't you dare touch him! I'll be right back!"

With the metal trace paper flying behind him, Angus fifteen minutes later charged in on the Chamco brothers. They worked in a separate breathe-gas dome at the compound, industriously trying to assist Robert the Fox to put things back together. Angus shoved the trace under their pug nosebones: "What metal is this?"

The Chamcos examined the trace squiggles. "Ferrous daminite," they said. "A very strong support alloy."

"Is it magnetic?" demanded Angus. And they said yes, of course it was.

By six o'clock Angus was back in the hospital. He had a heavy electrocoil he had just made. It had handgrips on it.

Angus showed MacKendrick how to guide it and MacKendrick worked out the best path to bring the sliver out with the least damage to tissue.

A few minutes later they had the broad sliver in their hands, withdrawn by the magnet.

Later the Chamco brothers identified it with closer analysis as a piece of a battle plane skid strut "which has to be very strong and very light."

Jonnie had not been conscious enough to tell anyone what he had done on the drone and Chrissie had shooed off the historian when he tried to find out earlier. So it was a bit of a mystery as to how a sliver piece of a strut could have been daggered into Jonnie's head.

But whatever they had done to him, Chrissie was extremely relieved. The fever he had had dropped. His breathing improved and his color got better.

The following morning he came out of the coma and smiled a little at Chrissie and MacKendrick and dropped into a natural sleep.

Planetary radio was not slow in crackling with the news. Their Jonnie was out of danger!

The pipe major paraded his pipes and drums all around the compound on the heels of the crier who was yelling it out to work parties. Bonfires blazed both there and in various other parts of the world, and a Coordinator in the Andes relayed the news that the chiefs of some peoples they had found there had declared this an annual celebration day, and could they come now and pay homage? A pilot standing by with a plane in the Mountains of the Moon in Africa had to get help from both Coordinators and chiefs of that small colony in order to get space to take off again, so mobbed had the field become with celebrating, jubilant people. The compound radio operators had to double up on shifts to handle the message traffic roaring in on them as a result of the announcement.

Robert the Fox just went around grinning at everybody

— 3 —

As the days wore on into weeks, it became obvious to the Council, originally composed of the parson, the schoolmaster, the historian, and Robert the Fox, and now augmented by several Clanchiefs who left deputies in Scotland, that Jonnie was brooding about something.

He would smile at them from his bed and talk to them when spoken to, but there was something deep in his eyes that was dull and moody.

Chrissie tried not to let them come very often, and when they did she was a bit impatient with them if they overstayed.

Some of the Russians and some Swedes were rebuilding parts of the Academy due to the desperate need for pilots. Until the ancient capitol building in Denver could be rebuilt, the Council had a room at the Academy. They could get to both the compound and the underground military base from there, and all their berthing quarters were there.

At this particular meeting Robert the Fox was walking up and down, his kilt flaring out each time he turned, his claymore held snug enough by an ancient officer's belt from the base—which also held a Smith and Wesson—knocking against chairs. "Something is bothering him. He is not like the old Jonnie."

"Does he think we are doing something wrong?" said the Chief of Clanfearghus.

"No, no, it isn't that," said Robert the Fox. "There's not a scrap of criticism for anyone in his makeup. It's just he . . . he seems worried."

The parson cleared his throat, "It just could be his side has something to do with it. He cannot much move his right arm and he cannot walk as yet. He is, after all, used to being about and very briskly as well. After all, the lad had a dreadful time of it, all alone, injured. I can't think how he managed. All that time in a cage, earlier. . . . You're all expecting too much, too fast, gentlemen. He is a brave spirit and I have faith . . ."

"Could be worry over the possibility of a Psychlo counterattack," said the Chief of Clanargyll.

"We must reassure him somehow," said the Chief of Clanfearghus. "Heaven knows, we are working hard enough on planetary affairs."

And they were. The World Federation for the Unification of the Human Race had been formed from those Jonnie had not accepted for the group that had come with him to America. Some two hundred young Scots and another fifty oldsters had done their beginning work well. In two dangerous but successful raids, one to the site of an ancient university named Oxford and another to a similar ruin at Cambridge, they had obtained language books and a mound of material on other countries. They had worked out where isolated groups of humans might still be and had formed up a unit for each language they thought might still be in use. Their selection was proving not far off, and ruler-bruised hands attested to the diligence of their study. They called themselves "Coordinators" and they were making a vital contribution all over the world where groups were being found.

The current estimate was that there were nearly thirty-five thousand human beings left on Earth, an astonishing number that, the Council agreed, was far too great for any one town. The groups were mostly survivors who had withdrawn to mountainous places, natural fortresses their forebears had mined, as in the case of the Rockies. But some were in the frozen north in which the Psychlos had had no interest, and some were simply overlooked strays.

The duty of the Council, as they saw it, was to preserve the tribal and local customs and government and install over all of it a clan system, appointing local leaders as Clanchiefs. The Coordinators spread the news and were extremely welcome and successful.

The hard-worked pilots were ferrying in chiefs and visitors and simply anyone who got on their passenger planes. If there were too many going or coming they simply told them to wait until next week and that was fine.

But there was no really organized forward motion. Local control of the tribes was often slack. Some had retained literacy in their language, some had not. Most of them were poor, half-starved, ragged.

The one incredible fact that after over a thousand years there was freedom from Psychlos, even if possibly temporary, united them in a wave of hope. They had once gazed from their mountains on the ruins of cities they dared not visit; they had looked upon fertile plains and great herds they dared not benefit from; they had seen no hope whatever for their dying race. And then suddenly *men* from the sky, speaking their language, telling them of the remarkable feats that led to possible freedom, had brought them soaring hope and reburgeoning pride in their race.

The Council's existence they accepted. They joined it and, with radios parked on rocks and in huts, communicated with it.

They all had one question. Was the Jonnie MacTyler of whom the Coordinators spoke a part of this Council? Yes, he was. Good, no more questions.

But the Council well knew that Jonnie was not an active part of the Council now. Completely aside from the political significance of it, every Council member was himself personally concerned for Jonnie.

There were all kinds of things happening over the world, most of the actions taken without even informing the Council. People were moving about. A group of South Americans, with baggy pants and flat leather hats, swinging wide lariats and riding almost as well as Jonnie once did, had suddenly walked off a plane with their women and lariats and saddles and said, through their Spanish-speaking Scot Coordinator, that they were "llaneros" or "gauchos" and they knew cattle—but would find out what to do with buffalo—and were taking over the management of the vast herds to preserve them and make sure the people at the compound and base were properly fed. Two Italians from the Italian Alps had shown up and taken over the commissary after making peace with the old women. Five Germans from Switzerland had shown up and opened a factory in Denver to salvage and service man-equipment such as knives and tools, you name it, and if you sent it to them they would make it shiny and working and send it back. This put a freight line into an already overburdened pilot zone. Three Basques showed up and simply started making shoes; the difficulty was that Basque as a language had been omitted by the Coordinators, and the shoemakers were learning English and Psychlo while they turned out shoes from the hides the South Americans dedicatedly furnished them. Many others came in.

Everybody wanted to help and simply helped.

"There is no control of it," Robert the Fox told Jonnie one day in the hospital room.

Jonnie simply gave him a small smile and said, "Why control them?"

The historian, except for Jonnie's account of the drone, which was too sketchy to be called history, was getting bogged down in assembling tribal histories of the last thousand or more years. The Coordinators sent him all kinds of stuff and he couldn't even keep it in order. Some serious-eyed Chinese from a mountain fastness there had shown up to help him, and they were furiously studying English but were not of much help yet.

It seemed at first that language would be an obstacle. But it soon became clear that the future educated person would speak three languages: Psychlo for technical matters; English for arts, humanities, and government; and their own tribal language if not English. The pilots chattered Psychlo at each other: all their equipment was in Psychlo as well as their manuals and navigation and related skills.

There was a lot of protest at speaking the language of the hated Psychlos until the historian learned that Psychlo as a language was really a composite of words and technical developments stolen from other peoples in the universes, and there never had been a basic language called "Psychlo." People were glad of that and thereafter learned it more willingly, but they liked to refer to it as "Techno."

The parson had his own problems. He had about forty different religions on his hands. They had one thing in common: the myths of the conquest a thousand or more years ago. Otherwise they were miles apart. He had witch doctors and medicine men and priests and such flooding his doorstep. He knew very well the wars that can develop out of different faiths, and he was not going to evangelize any one of them. Man wanted *peace*.

He explained to them that Man, being divided and internally at war, had advanced too slowly as a culture and so had been wide open to an invasion from elsewhere. They all agreed Man should not be at war with Man.

The myths—well, they knew the truth of it now. They were happy to abandon those myths. But on this question of which gods and which devils were valid . . . well . . .

The parson had neatly handled the whole thing for the moment. He would disturb no beliefs at all. Every one of these tribes was demanding to know what was the religion of Jonnie MacTyler? Well, he wasn't really of any religion, the parson told them. He was *Jonnie MacTyler*. Instantly and without exception, Jonnie MacTyler became part of their religions. And that was that.

But Jonnie was lying a bit wan, trying each day at Chrissie's and MacKendrick's persuasion to walk, to use his arm. And when the parson tried to tell him he was getting woven into the pantheon of about forty religions, he said nothing. He just lay there, not much life or interest showing in the depths of his eyes.

The Council was not having a happy time of it.

— 4 —

He lay half-awake in his bed, not really wanting to try.

The secret behind Jonnie's lethargy was the feeling that he had failed. Maybe the bombs hadn't landed on Psychlo. Maybe all this was just a brief interlude of peace for man. Perhaps soon the beautiful plains of his planet would once more be denied the human race.

And even if the bombs had landed and Psychlo was no longer a menace, he had heard of other races out there in the universe, savage races as pitiless as the Psychlos. How could this planet defend itself against those?

It haunted him at every awakening; it plagued his sleep. People now looked so happy and industrious, so *revived*. What cruelty if it were just a brief interlude. How crushed they would be!

Today would be just another day. He would get up, and a Russian attendant would bring in his breakfast and help Chrissie straighten the room. Then MacKendrick would come and they would exercise his arm and he would try to walk a bit. Something about there being nothing wrong, really, just having to learn to do it again. Then Sir Robert or the parson would come over and sit uncomfortably for a while until Chrissie shooed them out. A few more dull routine actions and another day would be gone. His failure oppressed him. He saw more clearly than they did how cruel a letdown this would be if the Psychlos counterattacked. He felt a little guilty when he saw a glad face: how soon it might turn to grief.

He had given the historian, Doctor MacDermott, a colorless outline of the drone destruction, all from the viewpoint of what one could or could not do if another one appeared, and Doctor Mac had well supposed there was far more to the action than that, but he had been chased out by Chrissie.

Chrissie had just washed his face and he was sitting at a trolley table when he noticed something odd going on with the Russian attendant. It really did not thoroughly challenge Jonnie's interest, for there were always Scots guarding him in the outside passage against intruders or disturbance—a guard he had at first protested and then accepted when they all seemed so upset at the refusal.

Jonnie had not seen this particular Russian in two weeks; others had been taking his place. Once this Russian had come in with a great big black eye and a triumphant grin on his face; questioned, Chrissie had explained that the Russians sometimes fought among themselves over the right to serve him. Well, this fellow looked like he could win any fight. As tall as Jonnie, heavyset with slightly slanted eyes, and dressed in baggy-bottomed trousers and a white tunic, he was quite imposing, his bristling black mustache standing straight out on both sides of his big nose. His name was, inevitably, Ivan.

After putting down the breakfast, he had drawn back and was standing there at the stiffest attention Jonnie had ever seen.

A Coordinator came slipping in the door, the Scot sentry scowling and privately vowing to send for Sir Robert by runner the moment the door was closed.

Jonnie looked at the Russian questioningly.

The Russian bowed from the hips and straightened up, looking stiffly ahead. "How do you do Jonnie Tyler sir." His was a very thick accent. He did not go on.

Jonnie went on eating oatmeal and cream. "How do you do," he said indifferently.

The Russian just stood there. Then his eyes rolled appealingly at the Scot Coordinator.

"That's all the English he knows, Jonnie sir. He has some news and a present for you."

Chrissie, with a broom in her hand, her cornsilk hair tied out of her eyes with a buckskin thong, bristled at this violation of proper announcement. She looked like she was going to hit both of them with the broom. Jonnie motioned her to be still. He was slightly interested. The Russian was so imposing and was fairly bursting with what he had to say.

Ivan barked off a long string of Russian and the Coordinator took it up. "He says he is Colonel Ivan Smolensk of the Hindu Kush—that's in the Himalayan Mountains. They are descended from a Red Army detachment that was cut off there and intermarried locally; there are about ten groups in the Himalayas; some speak Russian, some an Afghanistan dialect. They really aren't army units. 'Colonel' to them means 'father.' They're really Cossacks."

The Russian thought this was going on too long—it was more than he had said. So he rattled off another string. The Coordinator cleared up a couple of points and turned to Jonnie.

"This is very irregular," said Chrissie, her black eyes flashing.

The Coordinator was already in awe of Chrissie and Jonnie had to tell him to go on. "It seems like when they found they could travel around—the steppes there are huge—a troop—that's their name for a family unit—rode clear over to the Ural Mountains. They got on the radio to him—anybody can use a radio it seems—and they gave him some news. Our Coordinator there had told them about this base and that troop for some reason thought there might be a Russian base.

"They came back and radioed Ivan here about it and he took off—anybody can hook a ride on a plane; they schedule 'round the various tribes about once a week—and he rode like the wind he says on their very swift horses and he went to check it personally and he's just come back and wants to tell you."

"He should tell the Council!" said Chrissie. "Jonnie is in no condition to be holding what they call audiences!"

The Russian let out another string. The Coordinator timidly translated (he did not like crossing Chrissie; she was such a beautiful woman and such a celebrity herself). "There *is* such a base. It is as big as this one and just as full of atom bombs and hardware and dead men."

Jonnie was vaguely interested. Might serve them as a refuge if there were a counterattack. "Well, tell him that's fine and why not clean it up and use it."

A brief interchange between the Coordinator and the Russian, and then fireworks! Russian splattered off the very walls.

Robert the Fox came in; short of breath from hurrying, thoroughly disapproving of anyone disturbing Jonnie as well as short-circuiting proper channels. But he paused. Jonnie seemed interested. Not much, but more than Robert had seen for a while. The veteran leaned back against the wall and signaled the Coordinator to go on.

The Coordinator was getting overwhelmed. He was quite used to dealing with important tribal heads and notables, but here he was in the company of three of the most important names this planet had ever had, especially Jonnie sir. But Colonel Ivan was almost stomping his feet for him to translate.

"He says that's what ruined the whole human race. He says

the valiant-red-army, trying to fight the capitalist-imperialist-warmongers (these are just names to him, Jonnie sir, he doesn't have a political axe to grind) had their attention on each other and didn't cooperate when an invader landed, and he says while tribal wars will and do happen, international wars among whole peoples are against the good welfare of the people. He says he is for the people of Earth and people didn't stick together but fought, and this must not happen again. He's very emphatic, Jonnie sir, and he says all the other Russian tribes are also."

Jonnie pushed back the tray, and the Russian, suddenly remembering his duty, picked it up. He let out another broadside of Russian.

The Coordinator pulled out some papers. "They've retained literacy, sir, and he and some of the chiefs drew up some papers—they don't have much paper so excuse its condition, I think they found it in that base—and they want your agreement to it."

Jonnie looked tired to Robert the Fox. "This is Council business. The Himalayan chiefs are members of the Council."

The Russian seemed to divine what he was saying and rattled off more Russian.

"He says no," said the Coordinator. "This Council is over here on this continent and that base is over there on that continent. He says there are silos of nuclear weapons aimed at this continent and have been for a thousand years or so. And he doesn't want anything to happen to you, Jonnie sir. So he wants a force of South Americans and Alaskans—he knows there are almost no North Americans left—to take charge of that base over there on your authority. He says if the Russians have charge of this base here, they won't fire at Russia. And if people from this continent take charge of that base there they won't fire on this continent. They've got it all worked out, Jonnie sir. It's all here. They worked it out in Russia. If you say all right, and put a little initial here . . ."

Robert the Fox was watching Jonnie. This was the first thing he'd seen the lad take even the slightest interest in. Robert knew it would probably be all right with the Council. He saw Jonnie looking at him. He nodded. Jonnie took the offered pen and wrote his initials on the paper.

The Russian seemed to almost deflate with relief. Then he

rattled away at the Coordinator, who presently said, "He now has a present for you."

Ivan put down the tray and reached into his tunic pocket. He brought out a gold disc with a big red star in the center of it and two lapel tabs of ancient braid. He gave them to Jonnie, waiting for him to accept.

The Coordinator said, "That is the cap ornament they found on the Marshall of the Red Army who was in charge of that base and those are his lapel tabs. He wants you to know that they are yours. And *you* are in charge of *both* bases."

Jonnie smiled slightly and the Russian promptly kissed him on both cheeks and rushed out.

Robert the Fox was holding the papers and Chrissie put the gifts in Jonnie's buckskin pouch.

"If this had happened a thousand or so years ago," said Robert the Fox, "maybe things would have been different." Chrissie was shooing him to leave. Jonnie looked tired. "The Council will put this through and handle it. There might be vital materials in that base."

"You might get it cleaned up and filtered," said Jonnie. "It might help them if gas drones come again."

When Dr. MacKendrick came to exercise his arm and get him to walk, he told Jonnie he was improved.

Jonnie alarmed him. "Not improved enough!" said Jonnie, a bit bitterly. "I may not have been so smart after all."

■

PART 16

— 1 —

Terl sat in his dark hole and was gloomy.

He was not with the other Psychlos; they would have torn him to fur fluffs. He was here in a cubicle that had once been used for cleaning supplies on the dormitories. It had been rigged with a breathe-gas circulator; it contained a narrow, twelve-foot-long bed; there was a little port that had been rigged to push food through—one could see the outside corridor beyond its revolving panes; and there was a two-way intercom inset below the door.

The place was strong enough: he had already tried every means of opening it and escaping. He was not chained, but every hour of the day and night there was a sentry with an assault rifle just outside.

It was really the fault of the females, both the animal females and Chirk. His hindsight was a bit faulty, but not his conviction that it was correct. Always a master of self-delusion, Terl was at his best these days.

When he compared his present lot with the beautiful dream of being wealthy and powerful on Psychlo, being bowed to by the royalty and trembled at by everyone else, he quivered with suppressed rage. These animals were denying him his due! Ten beautiful gold coffin lids lay moldering in the company cemetery on Psychlo, of that he was utterly certain. The delicious thought of slipping out there some dark night and exhuming them was second only to the thought of the wealth and power that would ensue.

He had befriended these animals. And how had they treated him? A mop closet!

But Terl was nothing if not clever. He roused himself now and began to think hard and brightly. Now was the time to be the calm, cool, masterful Terl.

He *would* get to Psychlo. He *would* get these animals and this planet destroyed, finally and forever. He *would* dig up those coffins. He *would* be bowed to and trembled at. Nothing must stand in his way!

He began to tally up the bits and scraps of leverage he had. First, of course, it went without saying that his own cleverness was his chief asset; he agreed with himself on that. Second, he was almost certain the first animal he had caught had forgotten that there was a hefty charge of explosive left buried in that cage. Third, there had been *three* remotes: one was still in his office, one had been seized, but the third was just inside that cage door in case he somehow got tricked or trapped in there. That third one would have enabled him to blow up the females or shut off the power to the bars, and he was certain it had not been found. The fourth piece of leverage was a pretty big one and the fifth was gigantic.

Leverage!

Sitting there in the semidark he thought and thought. And after several days, he knew he had it. Every point in its torturous pattern of events was perfectly channeled, perfectly conceived, and ready to be put in train.

The primary stage was to get himself put in that cage. Good! He would do it.

So it was that a very mild, personable Terl noted one morning that the sentries no longer wore kilts. Gazing out through the revolving panes of the food slot, he carefully concealed his elation. He sized the creature up. It had long pants, strapped boots, and a half-wing insignia on its left breast.

Terl might be a top graduate of company schools but he was no linguist: that was part of the arts, and what self-respecting Psychlo had anything to do with those? So an element of luck had to enter in here.

"What," said Terl in Psychlo through the intercom installed in the door, "does that half-wing stand for?"

The sentry looked a bit startled. Good, thought Terl.

"I should have thought it would have two wings," said Terl.

"That's for a full pilot," said the sentry. "I'm just a student pilot. But I'll have my full wings someday!"

Terl laid aside his conviction that you couldn't understand animals. While arrogance demanded nonrecognition of them, necessity demanded he recognize them. This thing was talking Psychlo. Chinko accent, as would be expected, but Psychlo.

"I am sure you will earn wings," said Terl. "I must say your Psychlo is excellent! You should practice it more, though. Talking to a real Psychlo would help."

The sentry brightened up. Suddenly he realized that that was perfectly true. And here was a real Psychlo. He had never talked to one before. It was quite a novelty. So he told Terl who he was, that being easy to discuss. He said he was Lars Thorenson, part of the Swedish contingent that had arrived some months ago for pilot training. He did not share the ferocity of some of the Scots against the Psychlos, for his people, way up in the Arctic, hadn't had any previous contact with Psychlos. He thought maybe the Scots exaggerated things a bit. And by the way, was Terl a flier?

Oh, yes, Terl told him, and it was quite true. Terl was a past master in all types of flight, battle tactics, and stunts like flying right down into five-mile-deep mine shafts and picking up an endangered machine.

The sentry had drawn closer. Flight was very dear to him and here was a master. He said that their best flier was Jonnie, and did Terl know him?

Oh, yes, Terl not only knew him, but back in the old days before there had been a misunderstanding, he himself had taught that one a few tricks: it was why he was such a good flier. A very fine creature, actually; Terl had been his firmest friend.

Terl was elated. These were cadet sentries, standing watches in addition to their schooling to ease the considerable load on regular personnel.

For several days, each morning, Lars Thorenson improved his Psychlo and learned the ins and outs of combat flying. From a master and a one-time friend of Jonnie's. He was quite unaware that if he put some of these "tricks" into use he would lose the most elementary fight in the air, and later others would have to shake the nonsense out of him before he got himself killed. Terl knew well it was a risk to play this trick, but he just couldn't resist it.

Terl corrected the sentry's Psychlo up to a point. And then one morning he said he himself would have to exactly clarify certain words and really they should have a dictionary. There were lots of dictionaries, and so the next morning the sentry gave him one.

With considerable glee, Terl went to work with the dictionary when the sentry was off duty. There were a lot of words in the composite language called "Psychlo" that were never actually used by Psychlos. They had leaked into the language from Chinko and other tongues. Psychlos never used them because they could not really grasp their conceptual meaning.

So Terl looked up words and phrases like "atone for wrongs," "guilt," "restitution," "personal fault," "pity," "cruelty," "just," and "amends." He knew they existed as words and that alien races used them. It was a very, very hard job, and later he would look on this as the toughest part of his whole project. It was all so *foreign,* so utterly *alien!*

Soon Terl was satisfied he was ready to enter his next stage.

"You know," he said to the sentry one morning, "I feel very guilty about putting your poor Jonnie in a cage. Actually, I have a craving to atone for my wrongs. It was my personal fault that he was subjected to such cruelty. And I wish with all my heart to make amends. I am overwhelmed by guilt and I pity him for what I did. And it would be only just if I made restitution for it all by suffering in a cage like he did."

It made Terl perspire to get it all out, but that only added to his contrite look.

The sentry had made a habit of recording their conversations, for he studied them later and corrected his own pronunciation, and since he had never heard a lot of these words in Psychlo before, he was glad he had it all on disc. Terl was also glad. It had been an agonizing performance!

The sentry, having the evening free, digested all this. He decided he had better report it to the Compound Commanding Officer.

There was a new Compound Commander, an Argyll, very well noted for his prowess in raids in earlier days and very experienced—but not in America. The ease with which a radiation bullet could blow up a Psychlo had given him a bit of contempt for them in their current state. And he had a problem of his own.

Literal mobs of people from all over the world got off planes and took tours of the compound. The Coordinators showed them around and pointed out where this had happened and that had happened. Many-hued and many-tongued, they were a bit of a nuisance. And almost every one of them wanted to be shown a Psychlo Most had never seen one, no matter that they had been oppressed by them for ages. Some very important chiefs and dignitaries had enough whip with the Council to get special permission. That meant an extra detail of guards the commander did not have; it meant taking people down into the dormitory levels where they should not be; it actually meant a bit of danger to them for some of those Psychlos down there were *not* reconstructed!

So the commander toyed with this idea. He went out and looked at the cage. Evidently it could be wired—in fact it *was* wired—with plenty of voltage to the bars. If one put up a protector in front so people would not touch the bars and get hurt, he would be relieved of these nonsense tours into the dormitory.

Further, it appealed to him to have a "monkey in a cage." It would help morale. And it would be an added attraction. He could plainly see that somebody might want to make restitution and do amends. So he mentioned it sketchily to a Council meeting. They were very busy and had their minds on other things and he omitted to tell them it was Terl.

Technicians checked to make sure the cage wiring was live and could be shut off easily from the outside where the connections and box had been fastened to a pole, and that a barrier was erected to keep people from electrocuting themselves.

It was a very elated—but carefully downcast—Terl who was then escorted under heavy guard and put in Jonnie's and the girls' old cage.

"Ah, the sky again!" said Terl. (He hated the blue sky of Earth like poison gas.) "But I must take no pleasure in it. It is only just that I will be confined here, exposed to public view and ridicule," (he had looked up some new words) "and mocked. It serves me right!"

And so Terl went about his duty very honestly. The crowds came and he looked ferocious and leaped about, glaring at them through his breathe-mask glass and making little children scream and flinch outside the barricade. He had heard of gorillas—beasts over in Africa—beating their chests, so he beat his chest.

He was a real hit. The crowds came, they saw an actual Psychlo, they even threw things at him.

They had heard that he put Jonnie in a collar, and young Lars visited him one day and told him, through the bars, that the crowd wanted to know where his collar was.

Terl thought that a great idea. A couple of days later, five guards came in and put a heavy iron collar and chain on Terl and fastened him to the old stake.

The Compound Commander was quite happy about it. But he told the guards that if Terl showed any sign at all of trying to escape, they were to riddle him.

Terl's mouthbones wore a private smile as he capered and postured. He rumbled and roared.

His plans were working out perfectly.

— 2 —

Jonnie threw the book from him and pushed away his lunch untouched.

The guard at the door looked in through the glass, abruptly alert. Colonel Ivan whirled in an automatic response, combat ready: it had sounded like the thud of a grenade for a moment.

"It makes no sense," said Jonnie to himself. "It just makes no sense!"

The others, seeing it was no emergency, relaxed. The sentry returned to his usual position and the colonel went on wiping down the white tile.

But Chrissie remained alarmed. It was almost unheard of for Jonnie to be irritable, and for days and days now, ever since he had started to do nothing but study books—Psychlo books they seemed to be, though she could not read—he had been getting worse and worse.

The untouched lunch worried her. It was venison stew with wild herbs cooked especially for him by Aunt Ellen. Weeks ago she had rushed to the old base to give him a glad and relieved greeting and to tell him that though her fears for him had almost come true, here he was alive! She had stood around suffused with delight until she suddenly saw what they were feeding him. The old village was only a few miles away down the pass, and either personally or through a small boy mounted on one of the horses Jonnie had left, Aunt Ellen routinely sent him his favorite dishes to be warmed up and served from the hospital galley. The boy or Aunt Ellen usually waited to take back the utensils, and when

Aunt Ellen saw the food had not been touched she would be upset. Chrissie vowed to get the sentry to eat some and maybe gobble a few bites herself. It wouldn't be polite to send back an untouched venison stew.

Had he been able to walk easily, Jonnie would have gone over and kicked the book. Normally he had vast respect for books, but not this one! It and several similar texts were all on the subject of the "mathematics of teleportation." They seemed incomprehensible. Psychlo arithmetic was bad enough. Jonnie supposed that because Psychlos had six talons on their right paws and five on their left, they had to go and choose *eleven* as their base. All their mathematics was structured around the number eleven. Jonnie had been told that human mathematics employed a "decimal system" involving ten as the radix. He wouldn't know. He only knew Psychlo mathematics. But these mathematics of teleportation soared above normal Psychlo arithmetic. The book he had just thrown down had begun to give him a headache, and these days his headaches had almost vanished. The book was called "Elementary Principles of Integral Teleportation Equations." And if that was elementary, give him something complicated! Nothing added up in it at all!

He pushed back from the metal dolly table and rose shakily, supporting himself with his left hand on the bed.

"I," he said in a determined voice, "am going to get out of here! There is no sense just waiting around for the sky to fall in on us! Where is my shirt!"

This was something new. The colonel went over to help Jonnie stand and Jonnie brushed him away. He could stand by himself.

Chrissie turned around in a flurry and opened three or four wrong bureau drawers. The colonel picked up a handful of assorted canes and sticks that stood in the corner and knocked half of them down. The sentry, ordered to report any unusual happenings to Robert the Fox, got on the radiophone right away.

Jonnie chose a "knobkerrie." MacKendrick had had him practicing with a lot of different canes. It was difficult because both his right arm and right leg were seemingly useless, and carrying a stick in the left hand and hopping on the left leg didn't work very well. The knobkerrie had been brought in as a gift from a chief in Africa who didn't know Jonnie was crippled. The black wooden stick was beautifully carved; they used them as throwing weapons as well as canes. They must be big men down there because it was the right length. It also had a comfortable palm grip.

Jonnie hobbled over to the bureau and half-sat on it and got rid of the military hospital robe. Chrissie had found three buckskin shirts and some perverseness made him select the oldest and greasiest one. He got it over his head and let her lace the thongs across the front of it. He got into some buckskin pants and Chrissie helped him with a pair of moccasins.

He struggled with a drawer and got it open. One of the shoemakers had made him a left-handed holster and had more properly fitted the old gold belt buckle to a wide belt. He put them on over the shirt.

The holster had a .457 magnum Smith and Wesson on it with radiation slugs, and he lifted it out and laid it back in the drawer and got out a small blast gun, made sure it was charged, and dropped it in the holster. At the colonel's odd look, Jonnie said, "I'm not going to kill any Psychlos today."

He was engaged in stuffing his right hand into the belt to get it out of the way—that arm tended to dangle—when an uproar broke out in the passageway.

Jonnie was intent on leaving so he gave it little heed. It would be just Robert the Fox or the parson rushing over to fuss at him about Council business.

But it wasn't. The door burst open and the base officer of the day, a big middle-aged Scot in kilts and claymore, a man named Captain MacDuff, rushed in.

"Jonnie sir!" said MacDuff.

Jonnie had the definite impression they were objecting to his leaving, and he was about to be impolite when the captain sputtered the rest of the message: "Jonnie sir, did you send for a Psychlo?"

Jonnie was looking for a fur cap to wear. They had shaved his hair off for those operations and he felt like a singed puma bareheaded. Then the import of the question hit him. He got the knobkerrie and unsteadily hitched forward and peered out the door.

There stood Ker!

And in the glaring mine lamps out there he was a very bedraggled creature. Ker's fur was matted with the filth clinging to it; his fangs seen through the faceplate were yellow and stained; his tunic was all ripped down one side and he had on only one boot. no cap. Even his earbones looked messed up.

They had put four chains on him with a soldier at the far end of each one. It looked so overdone on the midget Psychlo.

"Poor Ker," said Jonnie.

"Did you send for him, Jonnie sir?" demanded Captain MacDuff.

"Bring him in here," said Jonnie, leaning back against the bureau. He felt amusement mingling with pity.

"Do you think that's wise?" said MacDuff. But he waved them forward.

Jonnie told the soldiers to drop the ends of the chains and leave. Four more soldiers he hadn't noticed backed up, assault rifles trained on Ker. He told them all to leave. The colonel was flabbergasted.

Chrissie wrinkled her nose. What a stink! She'd have to clean and air the whole place!

No one wanted to go. Jonnie saw the pleading look through Ker's breathe-mask. He waved them all out, and it was with enormous reluctance that they closed the door.

"I had to tell the lie," said Ker. "I just had to see you, Jonnie."

"You sure haven't put a comb to yourself lately," said Jonnie.

"It's a devil's cauldron they've got me in," said Ker. "I'm half-crazy these days. I dropped from His Planetship down to gooey dirt, Jonnie. I got only one shaftmate and that's you, Jonnie."

"I don't know how or why you got yourself here, but—"

"It's *this*!" Ker dove a dirty paw inside his torn shirt, oblivious of the fact that a more nervous Jonnie might have shot him. Jonnie could draw, if a trifle slowly, with his left hand. But Jonnie knew Ker.

Held before Jonnie's eyes was a bank note.

He took it with some curiosity. He had only seen these at a distance in the hands of Psychlos paying off wagers and he had never held one before. He knew they were a basic symbol of exchange and greatly valued.

It was about six inches wide and a foot long. The paper felt a bit rough but it seemed to glow. One side of it was printed in blue and the other side in orange. It had a nebula pattern and bright starburst on it. But the remarkable thing was that it was worded in what must be thirty languages: thirty numeral systems, thirty different types of lettering—ah, one of them was Psychlo. Jonnie could read that.

He read: "The Galactic Bank" and "One Hundred Galactic Credits" and "Guaranteed Legal Tender for All Transactions" and "Counterfeiters Will Be Vaporized" and "Certified Exchangeable at the Galactic Bank on Presentation."

It had a picture of somebody or something on the blue side. It looked like a humanoid, or maybe a Tolnep somebody had mistaken Dunneldeen for, or maybe . . . who knew? The face was very dignified, the very portrait of integrity. On the reverse it had a similar-sized picture of an imposing building with innumerable arches.

All very interesting, but Jonnie had determined to do other things today. He gave it back to Ker and started to fish out his own cap again. He felt sort of embarrassed with such a shaved head.

Ker looked a bit let down. "That's a hundred credits!" said Ker. "It isn't a Psychlo bank. The Psychlos and everybody else use those. It's *not* counterfeit. I can tell. See how it glows? And these little fine lines here around the signature—"

"You trying to bribe me or something?" said Jonnie, discarding the cap he'd found and looking for a colored bandana instead.

"Why no!" said Ker, "Look, this money is no good to me now, Jonnie. Look!"

Jonnie propped himself more comfortably on the bureau edge and obediently looked.

Ker, with a glance at the door to make sure he had his back to it and that only Jonnie could see, dramatically threw aside his lapels and pulled the tattered tunic apart.

There was a brand on his chest.

"The three bars of denial," said Ker. "The criminal scorch. I don't think it's any news to you I was a criminal. That's one of the holds Terl had on me. That's why he felt he could trust me to run around and teach you. If I was returned to Psychlo, having been found to hold false papers and employment, I'd be vaporized. If Psychlo recaptured this place they'd be sure those of us alive were renegades, and they'd examine us and find this. My papers are false. I won't burden you with my real name: not knowing it you can't be hit as an accessory. Got it?"

Jonnie didn't have it at all, especially since the Psychlos would kill him on sight and not be troubled at all about "accessory." He nodded. All this wasn't getting anywhere. Where had Chrissie put the bandanas they'd found?

"And if in addition they found two billion Galactic credits on me, they'd do a *slow* vaporization!" said Ker.

"Two billion?"

Yes, well it seemed old Numph had been screwing the company for the whole thirty years of his duty tour here. Things not even Terl had dug up; things like commissions from the female administrators who charged; things like double prices on kerbango; maybe even selling ore to aliens who picked it up in space shifts . . . who knew? But Numph slept on four mattresses, and Ker thought it was funny they crinkled like that and he liked only one mattress, so he'd ripped open an end and there it was!

"Where?" said Jonnie.

"Out in the hall," said Ker.

The midget Psychlo closed his coat and Jonnie beckoned at the guard in the small door window. Ker darted out through the door, loose chains dragging, alarming everyone out there, and came back lugging a big box which he dumped. Then he rushed out and got another box. Although a midget, only a bit taller than Jonnie, Ker was very strong. Before anybody stopped him and despite the flapping chains, Ker shortly had the room bulging with old kerbango boxes, and every one of them was overflowing with Galactic credits!

"There's more in his numbered accounts on Psychlo," said Ker, "but we can't get that." He stood there panting a big smile, very proud of himself. "Now you can pay the renegades like the Chamcos in cash!"

Captain MacDuff had been trying to tell Jonnie they'd checked the boxes and made sure there were no explosives while still asking what was this stuff? all the while wanting to know how Jonnie had sent a message to the compound without it being known to the sentries, and was it all right that they had let Ker bring it? He was flustered. He had a Pyschlo running around flapping chains and Jonnie was laughing.

"And you want—?" said Jonnie to Ker.

"I want out of that prison!" wailed Ker. "They hate me because I was over them. They hated me anyway, Jonnie. I know machines. Didn't I teach you to run every machine there is? I heard they have a machine school over at what you call the

Academy. They don't know anything about those machines. Not like you and me do! Let me go help teach them like I did you!"

He stood there so pathetically, so pleadingly, he was so convinced he had done the right thing, that Jonnie laughed and laughed and shortly Ker's mouthbones started to grin.

"I think it's a great idea, Ker," said Jonnie. At that moment he looked up and saw a frosty Robert the Fox in the door. Jonnie shifted to English. "Sir Robert, I think we have a new instructor for the schoolmaster. It's true he's a great machine operator and he knows them all." He smiled at Ker and said in Psychlo, "Terms of employment, a quart of kerbango a day, full pay and bonuses, standard company contract omitting only burial on Pyschlo. Right?" He knew very well Ker probably had buried a few hundred thousand credits on his own.

Ker started bobbing his head emphatically. He had held a few hundred thousand against a rainy day. He held out a paw to bash paws with Jonnie. That done, he was about to leave when he turned and came very close to Jonnie, speaking with the Psychlo equivalent of whispering.

"I got one more thing for you, Jonnie. They put Terl in a cage. You watch Terl, Jonnie. He's up to something!"

When the midget Psychlo had left, Robert the Fox looked at these bales and bales of money.

"Job bribery," said Jonnie, "comes high these days! Turn it over to the Council." He was laughing.

"This is Galactic money, isn't it?" said Robert the Fox. "I'm going to contact a Scot named MacAdam at the university in the Highlands. He knows about money."

But he was wondering at seeing Jonnie dressed. He was more than glad Jonnie had cheered up even though he thought the lad foolhardy for letting a Psychlo so close to him: one rake of a set of claws could cost one half his face. Then he realized Jonnie was hobbling forward, going out. He looked his question.

"I may not be able to hold the sky up," said Jonnie, "but I don't have to wait forever for it to fall either. I'm headed for the compound."

He had to talk to the Chamco brothers. He had heard they were making absolutely no progress on repairing the transshipment stage and without that they never would find out about Psychlo.

— 3 —

It was a long way to the heliport, and especially long when you had only one working leg and a cane on the wrong side. The elevators weren't working and probably never would again. Hobbling along, Jonnie had just begun to appreciate what a great job had been done cleaning up this place when he heard running feet behind him and a sharply barked order in Russian. Two men appeared, one on either side of him, who gripped each others' arms in a chair lift, boosted him into it, and were running with him down the stairs to the heliport.

Somebody must have alerted the standby pilot there, for he was standing beside a mine passenger plane with the passenger door open.

"No!" yelled Jonnie and pointed with his good arm at the pilot side. What did they think he was, a busted-up invalid?

Of course, he was just that. But Colonel Ivan popped up at the pilot door and opened it. The two Russians literally threw Jonnie into the pilot's seat.

A little confused, the standby pilot started to close the passenger door but was brushed aside by three Russians who, out of breath, had come tearing down the stairs. They leaped into the plane with a clatter of assault rifles.

Colonel Ivan was magically on the other side of the plane helping Robert the Fox and two kilted Scots into the ship and then got in himself.

The pilot was a Swede. He was getting into the copilot seat and saying something in a language Jonnie could not understand. Maybe a South African from the Mountains of the Moon? No, the pocket of whites there among the Bantu had been contacted too late for anyone to be fully trained yet. Then he realized the pilot was only there for local runs, really a cadet.

Jonnie wrapped himself up in the seat belt, pinning down his relatively useless right arm, and looked around at his passengers. The Russians were in baggy red pants and gray tunics and were finishing getting into their gear. As he turned, Colonel Ivan ripped the bandana off his head and clapped a round, flat, fur cap on him. Jonnie took it off to get it on straight and saw it had a red star set in a gold disc on the front of it.

"We charge!" said Colonel Ivan. Evidently he had worked very hard at his English.

Jonnie grinned. They sure were an international contingent!

The wide doors had been left open and sunlight streamed in. He sailed the plane out into a beautiful summer day.

Ah, the mountains, the white mountains, majestic and calm against the dark blue sky! The ravines with their black shadows, the trees with their soft, dark green. And there was a bear. Cantering along a slope, bound on some important errand no doubt. And a whole herd of bighorn sheep, looking up at what must now be the ordinary sight of a plane on this route.

With his left hand romping on the console Jonnie dropped the ship over the last hills of the eastern slope and down toward the plains. Summer. And evidence of a recent rain, for there were flowers. Stretching out to an endless horizon in the east, an undulating landscape spotted with browsing herds, seemingly inexhaustible space in which men could live.

What a beautiful planet! What a lovely planet! Well worth saving.

The standby pilot was watching Jonnie in awe. He was flying with his left hand and left foot only, better than he himself had ever hoped to fly with five hands.

A rider? Jonnie darted down in a swoop to see who or what. Baggy pants? A flat, black-leather hat? A coiled rope in his hands? Gathering up a small herd.

"A llanero," said Robert the Fox. "South America. They tend the herds now.

Jonnie flipped his window down and waved and the llanero waved back.

What a beautiful day to be his first day out.

And there was the compound. What an awful lot of people! Must be thirty or forty of them looking toward the ship.

Jonnie set it down with a lightness that wouldn't have cracked an eggshell. Thank heavens none of that huge mob of people had gotten onto the alert strip before he did, for now they were flooding over toward them, brown skins, black skins, silk jackets, ragged homespun, women, men . . . what an awful lot of people!

He opened the plane door and put the first and fourth fingers of his left hand in his mouth and blew a piercing whistle Above the babble his trained ear heard what it wanted to hear: hoofs! And there came Windsplitter.

Jonnie got out of the security belts and before anyone could interfere slid to the ground—a trick seeing as these Psychlo planes had high cockpits. His right arm got in the way and he shoved the hand in his belt.

Windsplitter was nickering and bouncing about, glad to see him, and almost knocked him down with a tossing nose.

"Let's see the leg," said Jonnie, kneeling and trying to get hold of the left front hock that had seemed injured in the run down the cliff. But Windsplitter thought he was trying to do a trick Jonnie had taught him—to shake hands—and almost reprovingly he hefted his right hoof and offered it, succeeding only in practically knocking Jonnie flat. Jonnie laughed. "You're all right," and shook the offered hoof.

Jonnie had worked out how he could mount. If he sprang up belly down and threw his left leg over fast he would make it. He did. Success! He didn't need all this help.

Now to ride around and find the confounded Chamcos. And find out about the delay in this transshipment rig.

But people were pressing around his horse. Black faces, brown faces, tan faces, white faces. Hands touching his moccasins, hands trying to give him things. And all talking at once.

He felt a twinge of guilt. Smiling faces, welcoming faces. It put a trifle of a blot on his day. If these people only realized it, he might very well be a total failure. And those lovely skies up there might soon go gray with death.

His lips tightened. He had better get about his business. Adulation was, if anything, a little embarrassing, particularly as he strongly felt he might not have earned it.

More hoofs. The voice of Colonel Ivan barking Russian at somebody. Leading six horses at a dead run, another Russian sprinted up. A barked command and Colonel Ivan and four Russians mounted up and Robert the Fox was mounting. There must have been a Russian and horses waiting at the compound.

The two kilted Scots pushed their way through the crowd to either side of Windsplitter's head and began to gently part the throng so Jonnie could get going. There must be fifty people there now!

Just as he thought he was going to get moving, a small boy in a kilt elbowed his barefoot way to Windsplitter's head and dropped a lead rope on it. His piping voice came out of the hubbub: "I am Bittie MacLeod. Dunneldeen said I could come and be your page and I am here, Sir Jonnie!" The accent was thick but the determination and confidence brooked no rebuke. The small boy started leading Windsplitter toward the compound.

Even though Windsplitter guided only with a heel and other signals, Jonnie didn't have the heart to say no.

Behind him came five Russians with long poles—lances?—in their stirrups, pennons on the poles, assault rifles across their backs. A llanero dashed up on a horse and took position with them. A squad of Swedish soldiers rushed into view from the compound and presented arms. Workers were coming out of the compound. A big passenger plane came into the landing area and thirty Tibetans on a pilgrimage to the compound spilled out and joined the mob. Two flatbeds roared up to the fringes and about forty people from the city just to the north tumbled off. Another flatbed tore up from the Academy.

Jonnie, his horse walking dead slow behind Bittie MacLeod, looked over this joyous mob. They were shouting and waving at him and cheering. He had never seen so many people since the gathering of Scotland. There must be three hundred here!

White hands, black hands with pink palms, yellow hands; blue jackets, orange dresses, gray coats; straight blonde hair, brown hair, fuzzy black hair; languages, languages, languages: all saying, "Hello Jonnie!"

He looked up apprehensively at the bright blue sky. For an instant he was startled by a drone . . . no, it was a recon drone; they had a lot of them constantly patrolling, watchful for any invader.

The voices were a continuous roar. A woman was pushing something into his hand—a bouquet of wildflowers—and she was shouting, "For Chrissie!" He nodded to thank her and didn't know what to do with them, so he put them in his belt.

The people of Earth, their hopes kindled, could rise and be alive again.

He felt more guilty than ever. They didn't know he might have failed. Aside from not enjoying adulation, he also felt he certainly didn't deserve it, not all this.

Robert the Fox had worked his horse up beside him. He saw that Jonnie was troubled. Robert didn't want the first day out spoiled. "Wave to them a bit, laddie. Just raise your left hand and nod."

Jonnie did and the crowd went wild.

They had been working their way up the hill toward the old Chinko quarters. There was the morgue over there. There was the dome behind which Terl used to have his quarters and where so often he had stood out the night. . . ."

Jonnie stared. There was Terl in a cage with a collar on. Terl was capering and leaping about. A vague unease took Jonnie and he persuaded the Scot boy to lead him over toward it.

— 4 —

There was plenty of time. His business with the Chamco brothers was important but a few minutes would make no difference. He had certainly better see whether he could find out what Terl was up to.

The size of the throng was growing. The bulk of the trainees at the Academy, when they heard Jonnie had appeared at the compound, demanded a few hours off instantly, and the schoolmaster, understanding but unable to do anything about it anyway, had let them off and here they were in a swarm. More people were in from New Denver. All work had stopped and machines were now deserted in the underground shops at the compound. Several Council members appeared on the outskirts of the crowd. They included Brown Limper Staffor, chief of this continent. More than six hundred people were now there. The din was nearly deafening.

Terl saw the animal coming toward the cage and capered more violently.

Jonnie saw the area was not much changed or damaged by the battle. The geysering water had cut a few furrows on the plateau in its runoff; a bar or two of the cage was nicked by bullets; water had tended to wash the cage clean rather than damage it. He looked up to the connector box on the pole and saw it had not been changed: the bars were electrically charged in the same way, by the same cables. Someone had put a barrier of mine fencing so people could not reach the bars. Yes, it was much the same cage except that green grass grew in tufts around the perimeter.

His attention came away from the crowd. How many months had he been inside looking out, and how many nights had he stood outside looking in. A lot of nightmare was mixed up in that.

He wanted to question Terl. He flinched from talking through those bars again. A normal voice volume could not reach anywhere in this hubbub and he was not about to sit here shouting. He caught the eye of a sentry and beckoned him over. But instead of the sentry coming, the Compound Commander pushed through to him.

Jonnie saw that the man was an Argyll by his kilt. He leaned over to him to be heard: "Would you please turn off the electricity up there and have a guard open the door of the cage?"

"What?" exclaimed the Compound Commander in astonishment.

Jonnie thought he might not have heard and repeated his request. Then he saw the man was refusing. There was always a little friction between the Argylls and the Clanfearghus—indeed it had often erupted in clan warfare, and he recalled that only his visit to Scotland had interrupted the last war. Jonnie was not going to argue with the man. And he wasn't going to yell at Terl through bars.

Robert the Fox looked at Terl, the cage, the Argyll, the crowd and the connector box on the pole. He reached out to check Jonnie. But Jonnie had already leaned forward and swung off his horse. Colonel Ivan breasted some people aside and thrust the knobkerrie into Jonnie's hand.

Hobbling, Jonnie made his way to the exterior pole switch and pulled it open, having to balance against the pole to free his hand. It popped an electric spark as the bus bar opened. The crowd parted for him when they saw in which direction he was trying to walk. Suddenly they became very quiet, the silence starting from where Jonnie was and going out like a wave to the very outskirts.

The cage sentry had not left his post in all this hubbub. He carried the door keys in his belt. Jonnie pulled the keys out of the guard's belt.

There was a ripple of excited questioning from people and then tense silence.

Terl took the opportunity to roar ferociously.

The Compound Commander started to rush forward but found himself halted by the huge hand of Colonel Ivan who had simply leaned down from his horse. The colonel wanted no extra bodies in a field of fire. The other Cossacks fanned out abruptly: there was the sharp clatter of assault rifle bolts being cocked, and four rifles were leveled at Terl in the cage. Some Scots sprinted to the roofs of the old Chinko quarters and the rush of running feet was replaced by the snicks of rifles being cocked and leveled on Terl.

The crowd surged back away from the barriers.

Jonnie heard the rifle bolts. He turned, speaking in a normal voice for it was now quiet except for the roaring of Terl, "A bullet could ricochet off these bars and go into the crowd so please put your guns up." He loosened the blast pistol in the holster and then as an afterthought checked to see that it was cocked and on "Stun" and "No Flame." But he was convinced he was in no danger. Terl had a collar on and was chained, and while it wouldn't be wise to get within physical reach of him, the only thing Terl would try would be some antic from the apparent mood he was in.

The door lock worked more easily than it used to. Someone must have oiled it. He opened it. There was an intake of breath from the crowd. Jonnie's attention was not for the crowd.

Terl roared.

"Quit clowning, Terl," said Jonnie.

Terl promptly did and hunkered down against the back wall, his amber eyes evilly amused. "Well, hello, animal."

The parson's voice rapped out from somewhere in the crowd: "He is *not* an animal!" Jonnie hadn't realized the parson spoke Psychlo.

"I see," said Terl to Jonnie, "that somebody clawed you up. Oh, well, it happens when one is stupid. How'd it happen, rat brain?"

"Be civil, Terl. What do you think you are doing in this cage?"

"Oh, that Chinko accent!" said Terl. "Try as I would, I could never make you into a polished, literate being. Very well, if it's courtesy you want and as you speak Chinko, why, forgive this ignorant intrusion of speech into your lordly earbones—" He was going to go on with a string of the old Chinko abasements. Then he laughed viciously.

"Answer the questions, Terl."

"Why, I'm ———," and he said a Psychlo word Jonnie had never heard before.

Jonnie had had another purpose in coming in here. He wanted to see what Terl may have set up that somebody else had missed. He hobbled around the cage, staying wide of Terl and keeping part of an eye on him. He looked at the inside walls below the bars, looked into the pool. Terl had a small pile of things wrapped in a tarpaulin. Jonnie motioned with his left hand for Terl to back up and went over to the loose package. He knelt and flipped it open.

There was a garment in there, no more than a wraparound—Terl was wearing another one now and was otherwise naked. There was a bent kerbango saucepan with a hole in it and no kerbango. And a Psychlo dictionary! What on earth would the very educated Terl—in Psychlo at least—be doing with a Psychlo dictionary?

Jonnie backed up out of the reach of the chain. What was the word Terl had just used? Ah, there it was: "Repenting: the action of being sorrowful or self-reproachful for what one has done or failed to do; a word adopted from the Hockner language and said to be actually experienced by some alien races."

"Repenting?" said Jonnie. "*You?*" It was his turn to laugh.

"Didn't I put you in a cage? Don't you realize that it could give one feelings of ———?"

Jonnie looked that word up: "Guilt: the painful feeling of self-reproach resulting from a conviction one had done something wrong or immoral; adopted from the Chinko language and useful to political officers in degrading individuals of subject races; said by Professor Halz to factually exist as an emotion in some aliens." He popped the book shut.

"You must have some, too, animal. After all, I was like a father to you and you labored day and night to shatter my future. In fact, I clearly suspect that you just used me so you could betray me—"

"Like the exploding truck," said Jonnie.

"What exploding truck?"

"The delivery flatbed," said Jonnie patiently.

"Oh, I thought you meant that blade scraper you got yourself trapped in, the one that blew up out there on the plateau. You animals are always hard on machinery!" He sighed. "So here I am, the ——— subject of your revenge "

Jonnie didn't bother to look up the word. He knew it would be another one no Psychlo would ever use. "I didn't order you in this cage or into that collar, you did. By rights I should ask them to put you back in the dormitory level. Capering around here, half-naked—"

"I don't think you will," said Terl evilly. "Why did you come down here today?"

It was better not to talk too much to Terl, but if he didn't he couldn't get him to leak data. "I came down to ask the Chamco brothers about the delay on the transshipment rig."

"I rather thought you must have," said Terl. He seemed indifferent. He heaved out a long sigh into his breathe-mask and stood up.

The crowd outside drew back with a frightened mutter. The monster was almost four feet taller than Jonnie. Claws, fangs visible through its mask . . .

"Animal," said Terl, "in spite of past difference, I think I should tell you one thing. You will be coming to me for help soon. And as I am ——— and ———," two more words Jonnie wouldn't bother to look up, "I probably will be stupid enough to help you. So just remember, animal. When it gets too difficult, come to see Terl. After all, weren't we always shaftmates?"

Jonnie let out a bark of laughter. This was simply too much! He threw the dictionary over on the tarpaulin, and leaning heavily on his knobkerrie, back to Terl, he walked out of the cage.

The moment he had closed and locked the door, Terl let out a dreadful roar and began prancing about beating his chest.

Jonnie threw the keys to the guard and went over and turned the electricity back on. He was still laughing to himself as he hobbled toward Windsplitter. The crowd was way back, making sounds of relief.

Not everyone was way back. Brown Limper Staffor was between Jonnie and the horse. Jonnie recognized him and was about to greet him. Then Jonnie stopped. He had never before seen such naked, malevolent hatred on anyone's face.

"I see there are *two* cripples now!" said Brown Limper Staffor. He abruptly turned his back on Jonnie and limped off, his clubfoot dragging.

— 5 —

There were people there who would be telling their great-grandchildren that they personally had been present when *the* Jonnie had gone into that cage, and who would gain no small importance and notoriety because of it.

Jonnie was on Windsplitter again, walking the horse toward the small isolated dome erected to house the Chamco brothers.

"That was not well done," said Robert the Fox, close beside Jonnie. "Don't scare these people like that." He himself had been worried stiff.

"I didn't come over to see the people," said Jonnie. "I came over to see the Chamcos and I'm on my way right now."

"You have to think of your public presence," said Robert the Fox, gently. "That frightened them." This might be Jonnie's first day out and Robert might want it to be a good day for him, but that visit to Terl had been hair-raising. "You're a symbol now," he continued.

Jonnie turned toward him. He was very fond of Sir Robert. But he couldn't conceive of himself as a symbol. "I'm just Jonnie Goodboy Tyler." He suddenly laughed in a kindly way, "That is to say, *MacTyler!*"

Any concern Sir Robert had felt melted. What could you do with this laddie? He was glad the day seemed a happy one again to Jonnie.

The crowd was much more subdued but it was following. Colonel Ivan had gotten over his fright and had his lance-carrying Cossacks in formation. Bittie MacLeod had successfully swallowed his heart and was leading in the direction Windsplitter seemed to be pointing him. The Argyll in command of the compound sneaked a quick and needed one from a flask and was handing it to his second in command.

Jonnie sized up the separate dome ahead. Well, they had done very well by the Chamco brothers. They had salvaged a dome canopy from some mine shaft not now working. It had been raised on a concrete circle. Its atmosphere lock was one of the better ones—a transparent revolving door to keep the breathe-gas in and the air out. There was a separate breathe-gas tank and pump. The transparent dome had shades and they were open now despite the sun's heat—Psychlos didn't seem to care much about heat and cold. Here the Chamcos were busy with plans and suggestions in return for pay—that could be paid now in cash thanks to Ker's discovery of Galactic credits.

Jonnie knew them from his training days around the minesite. They were top-grade design and planning engineers, graduates of all the accepted Psychlo and company schools. By report they were extremely cooperative and even polite—as polite as a Psychlo ever could be, which was not much. Their idea of politeness was a one-way flow—at *them*.

They could be seen in there now, working at two big upholstered desks, flanked by drawing boards. There was an intercom of the usual type so one could stand outside and talk to those inside without going through the lock. But Jonnie could not imagine trying to talk technical matters through one of those intercoms.

Colonel Ivan must have read his mind. He pushed forward and said in his limited English, "You go in there?" Then he looked around wildly for a Coordinator who spoke Russian.

The Coordinator interpreted, "He says that's bulletproof glass in that canopy. He can't cover you with rifles."

Robert the Fox said, somewhat desperately, "Haven't you been out long enough for your first day?"

"This is what I came over to do," said Jonnie, rolling off Windsplitter.

Doubtfully, Colonel Ivan handed him the knobkerrie and at the same time tried to get the interpreter to translate.

"The colonel says not to stand in the airlock," said the Coordinator. "To go inside and move over to the right. If you don't, his men can't charge in."

Hobbling toward the atmosphere lock, Jonnie heard the crowd behind him saying things like: "He's going in there, too! Doesn't he realize these Psychlos . . ." and "Oh, look at those awful beasts in there." Jonnie didn't like all this impeding of his actions. Being a symbol had its problems! It was an entirely new idea to him that he couldn't move about freely at his own discretion and that others would have a say in where he was going.

He guessed the Chamco brothers usually had their canopy

curtains closed, because even though the curtains were now open they had lights burning. He put on an air mask a pilot had handed him.

Jonnie hobbled through the atmosphere lock, experiencing a bit of trouble with it. These locks, built for Psychlos, were always clumsy for him. Too heavy, too hard to push.

The Chamcos had stopped working and were sitting still, looking at him. They were not in any way hostile but they didn't greet him.

"I came to see what progress you were making in rebuilding the transshipment rig," said Jonnie, using pleasant Psychlo intonations—as pleasant as Psychlo ever was.

They didn't say anything. Was the smaller Chamco brother looking a little wary?

"If you need any materials or anything," said Jonnie, "I will be happy to see they are furnished you."

The bigger Chamco brother said, "The whole rig was burned out. The console. Everything. Destroyed."

"Well, yes," said Jonnie, leaning on his cane in front of the atmosphere lock. "But I'm sure they are just common components. There's miniature rigs in these freighters that are not too dissimilar."

"Very difficult" said the smaller Chamco brother. Were his eyes a little strange or was it just a Psychlo being a Psychlo?

"We ought to rebuild it," said Jonnie. "We won't know what really happened to Psychlo until we do."

"Takes a long time," said the bigger Chamco. Were his eyes looking a little strange? But then the amber orbs of a Psychlo always had tiny flames in them.

"I have been trying to figure it out," said Jonnie. He looked over to the side where they had some textbooks. Right on the end was the one he had thrown down this morning. "If you could explain to me—"

The smaller Chamco sprang!

The bigger Chamco leaped up from his desk and charged.

They were roaring.

Jonnie stumbled backward. The cane was in the road of a draw. He threw it at the nearer Chamco, a weak throw; he was never left-handed.

He saw an enormous paw blurring in the air, coming at him.

He knelt and did a left-handed draw.

Talons raked the side of his face.

Jonnie fired.

The recoil threw him back against the door and he tried to push into the atmosphere lock. It seemed jammed, frozen.

Flat on his back, a boot stamping down to crush his ribs he fired up from the floor.

The boot blurred away.

A furry pair of paws were coming at his throat!

The roars were berserk.

Jonnie fired at the paws and then at a huge chest. He punched blast after blast into them, driving them back.

Somehow he got to his knee. The two gigantic bodies were falling back, falling down. Jonnie fired again at one and then the other.

Both of them were flat on the floor.

The smaller Chamco brother was thoroughly stunned. But just beyond him the bigger one was fighting with a desk drawer. He got it open and pulled out something.

It was all happening too fast. Jonnie could not see what he had due to the angle of the desk. He moved sideways to get a clearer shot.

The bigger Chamco had a small blast gun. But he wasn't trying to aim it at Jonnie. He was aiming it at his own head.

He was trying to commit suicide!

The howling maelstrom of action had passed. Jonnie coolly aimed and blew the gun out of the bigger Chamco's hand. It didn't explode. Part of the blast had hit the Psychlo and he flopped back, knocked out.

Damn, not having a right hand and arm! He couldn't at once recover his cane. He hopped sideways and leaned against the canopy wall.

Smoke was thick in the room, curling around the breathe-gas exhaust vents. He was half-deaf from all the roaring and snarling and the blasts of the gun in this confined space.

Whew! What was *that* all about? There they lay. But why the attack?

The atmosphere lock door revolved and Colonel Ivan and a sentry burst through.

"Don't fire those rifles!" warned Jonnie. "This is breathe-gas and radiation will blow us to bits. Get some shackles!"

"We couldn't find air masks!" howled the guard, hysterical. Then he tore out to find shackles.

Colonel Ivan adjusted his own air mask a hitch to better look at the two Psychlos sprawled on the floor. They looked like they were out, but Jonnie still had a blast gun on them.

He gestured at the breathe-masks of the Psychlos, which were hanging on a coat tree. Colonel Ivan grabbed them and put them on the unconscious Chamcos. Jonnie gestured at the breathe-gas circulator controls and Colonel Ivan went to them and shut them off, and then with a lot of battering with huge strength he got the atmosphere lock folded back on itself, flooding air into the place.

Sentries finally could rush in, chains and shackles rattling and clanging, and get them onto the Chamcos.

Jonnie hobbled outside. Only then did he realize the crowd had been there and had seen all this through the canopy glass. Some were pointing at his face and he realized for the first time that he was bleeding.

He hobbled to Windsplitter and mounted.

The crowd was talking to one another. Guards were trying to work. "Why did he attack those Psychlos?" "They attacked him." "Why did they fight?" "Look out, here comes a flatbed and forklift, please stand aside." "I don't blame Jonnie for shooting Psychlos." "Could we have some help here with these bodies?" "Why did they let him go in there?" "How come they attacked him?" "I have heard that these Psychlos . . ." "But I saw him; he was being very pleasant and they charged him. Why would they do that?"

Jonnie didn't have a bandana or a scrap of buckskin to staunch the blood dropping down on his hunting shirt. Some mechanic handed him a wad of waste and he held it to his cheek.

"They were supposed to be tame Psychlos! Why did they attack him?" More crowd talk.

Jonnie surely wished he knew. What had he said? He had a sudden thought. He called out, "Did anybody get a recording of that? The conversation must have been coming through the intercom."

Well, there had been about fifteen picto-recorders using up discs ever since he had stepped off the plane. An Argyll rushed up waving one. "Can somebody copy that for me?" asked Jonnie. "I have to know what was said that made them do it."

Oh, yes, sir, right away! And they had copies of it before he hoisted himself off Windsplitter and into the plane. He was going to study these.

"Wave," said Robert the Fox.

Jonnie waved. The crowd was looking at him, some faces quite white, even a black face a bit gray. "Please stand back," from the guards. "Clear the field, please."

Back at the base that night, just after dinner, Colonel Ivan got a Coordinator in. The Coordinator said, "He wants me to tell you that you live too dangerously."

There might have been more, but Jonnie cut him off. "Tell him, perhaps at heart I'm just a Cossack!"

The Russians laughed about that, repeating it for days and days thereafter.

It *had* been a rather energetic first day out.

There was a repercussion. Three days later he received a confidential written message from the Council. He did not think much about it at the time, not being unduly sensitive.

Later he would look back on it as a turning point and criticize himself for not realizing how ominous it was.

The message was very correct, very polite, passed by a slim majority. It was brief:

> By Council Resolution, in the interest of his personal safety and to curtail any embarrassment, realizing his value to the State, it is decreed that Jonnie Goodboy Tyler not again visit the Compound located in this place until such prohibition is formally rescinded by constituted authority.
>
> Duly passed on voice vote and certified as legal.
>
> Oscar Khamermann,
> Chief of the Tribe of British Columbia,
> Secretary to the Council.

Jonnie read it, shrugged, and tossed it in the wastebasket.

■

PART 17

— 1 —

Brown Limper Staffor came away from the compound utterly ill with envy—he called it "righteousness."

What a horrible, *vulgar* spectacle!

All those people crowding about, cheering even, touching his moccasins, absolutely fawning. It was more than a normal sane man like Brown Limper could tolerate.

He had felt he was losing ground lately, and he beat his head to think of ways and means, even criminal, to correct this gross mistake people were making about that Tyler!

Since Jonnie Goodboy Tyler had come to the village last year, prancing about, bribing people with gifts—while really only trying to do them out of their lands and houses—and since Brown Limper had realized that Tyler was not only not properly dead but apparently moving in a larger world and moving far too successfully—Brown Limper had been lying in wait.

When he recalled how he had been put upon and scorned and held up to ridicule by Tyler ever since they were children, he seethed. He had to be careful not to dwell on it too much, for then he would lie awake in bed and roll and toss and grit his teeth and bring on a fever. That the instances of Tyler's doing those things could not be directly recalled or isolated as actual incidents only made it grindingly worse. They must have happened or Brown Limper wouldn't feel this way, would he? It proved itself.

When he heard that Tyler was crippled and likely to die, a flood of relief had poured through Brown Limper. But here he was today, limping maybe but certainly making a nauseating spectacle of himself with those Psychlos.

It was not that Brown Limper had not been trying. Some time since when old Jimson had complained of rheumatism, Brown Limper had kindly shown him how beneficial locoweed was to aches and pains—Parson Staffor had left a supply. Brown Limper had performed this act of humanity right after he had been startled to find old Jimson inclining toward Tyler's criminal proposals to destroy the village and move the people to some desolate mountainside and abandon them there to starve and freeze. Jimson obviously could not be trusted to govern, due of course to his aches and pains. Mercifully now he had retired to his bed and awoke when his family brought him some food. It was so gratifying to see that the old man was out of his pain and not worried and harassed by village affairs. It was, of course, a bit of a burden to take all the work on himself, but Brown Limper was patient and enduring, if a bit pious, about it.

When the Coordinators had come from the World Federation for the Unification of the Human Race, Brown Limper had thought of them as interfering busybodies at first. Then they had shown him some books.

Old Parson Staffor, before he began to chew on locoweed day and night, had taken his responsibilities seriously, both to his village and to his family. He had sought to initiate Brown Limper into the church and had brought out from hiding a secret book no one else in the village knew about called [''The Bible''], and in strict privacy he had taught Brown Limper how to read. But Brown Limper had not much cared for a career as a parson, and he had thought it was better to aspire to be a mayor. A parson could only persuade, but a *mayor* . . . well now!

It was quite simple logic. There was Tyler, prancing around on his horses, ogling the girls, the young men following his lead and getting into trouble, the Council soft-headedly overlooking his criminal pursuits. And there was Brown Limper—wise, tolerant, understanding, and brilliant—overlooked and even scorned and cast aside. And hadn't Tyler's own father—if he really was Jonnie Goodboy Tyler's father—protested when Brown Limper was born clubfooted and mutated and was allowed to live. Well, maybe not just older Tyler but Brown Limper's mother used to tell him that some had protested but that she had prevailed and saved his life. She used to tell him that several times a week and Brown Limper had gotten the message: the Tylers had attempted to murder him!

So it was only sensible he should be upset and take measures to protect not only himself but the whole village as well. It would be utterly irresponsible not to do so.

These Coordinators had been delighted to find he could read and had given him some texts on "government" and one on "parliamentary procedure" called ["Robert's Rules of Order"]. They had astonished him by informing him that as the active and only mayor, he was the chief of the American tribe. Apparently nearly all the people in America (they had to show him where it was on the globe) had been slaughtered or died off; his was the principal tribe and, being near the minesite, the most influential group politically.

Getting right down to it, what was this Council? Well, it was the heads of tribes all over the world, and they met or sent their deputies to meet in a sort of parliament right here in his front yard, so to speak.

They mentioned that he of course should be very interested due to the fact that *the* Jonnie came from there. Brown Limper did not just become interested, he became obsessed!

Were there any other peoples in America? Well, there were a couple found in British Columbia and four found in the Sierra Nevadas—a mountain range to the west—and some Indians—not really from India but called that—in some mountains way to the south. There were Eskimo and Alaskan tribes but they didn't count geographically in America.

Brown Limper had been making progress. Since each Council member had one vote, he engineered the rescue of the couple in British Columbia and the four in the Sierra Nevadas (this was all humanitarian, of course) and settled them in his village as tribes and now claimed three Council votes. He was just now working on the Indian question to get a member of that tribe up here and so have four Council votes.

He hoped he was also making progress in other ways. At the Council he would casually and very truthfully drop remarks about Tyler. How the village had always considered him wild, rash, and irresponsible even though he personally had tried to correct such impressions. He mentioned how as a child Tyler was always running about playing and refused even to draw water for his family, an obligation all well-behaved, thoughtful children had. He made light of any rumor that Tyler had known about the tomb all the time and had hidden the information so that he, Tyler, could go there and rob the honorable dead: Tyler only went now and then, he said, and the parson of the village had once tried his best to correct him and had even taken some of the things the boy had stolen away from him as punishment. Tyler had eventually run away entirely and left his family and the whole village to starve for two winters. As to Tyler and Chrissie not being married, well, actually that was a village secret—the parson had found out certain things when they were children and had forbidden marriage. Not that Tyler cared much for authority—youth being what it was . . .

A lot of the older chiefs from far-off places did not know much of what was going on, and wasn't Chief Staffor the only one around who had been Tyler's own dear companion?

Just a couple of days before, Brown Limper had been argued with by some ignorant lout, a chief from the Siberian tribe, and Brown Limper had a feeling they didn't all quite believe him. So he had been morose. Didn't he *know* Tyler, the *real* Tyler? And now this disgusting spectacle of self-aggrandizement today. What a conceited oaf. Ugh! Spit! And now he had the nerve to go around pretending he couldn't walk. Just more mockery of Brown Limper.

Brown Limper had noticed that the Psychlo in the cage seemed to be on very good speaking terms with Tyler. While he did not know what they were saying, it was obvious that they were actually well known to each other. But he had detected some bit of frostiness there.

Grabbing at a straw, Brown Limper decided to look into this a bit further and returned that evening to the compound. The sentries, of course, would not dream of saying anything to a senior Council member wearing a bit of colored ribbon that denoted his tribe, and Brown Limper hung about, watching the huge Psychlo from a distance. And he saw something very curious. A young Swedish pilot trainee stood for a while outside the bars talking to him.

The sentry said yes, the cadet came quite routinely after the classes of the day; he was polishing up his Psychlo: all pilots had to be very expert on Psychlo, and the monster in that cage was a real Psychlo and there weren't many others around to talk to. No, he didn't know what they talked about for the sentry couldn't speak Psychlo, being part of the Argyll raiders on duty here, but the cadet's name, it says here in the log, is Lars Thorenson, and thank you very much chief, sir, for mentioning that sentries should have cloaks and promising to take it up with the Council.

So, using his influence, Brown Limper found in Academy

records that Lars Thorenson had been a member of a Swedish tribe that emigrated, way back, to Scotland; that he had originally been chosen as a Coordinator trainee because he spoke Swedish and English and had a gift for tongues; that his father was a fascist minister and had urged the boy to use the Federation to spread the call of fascism in view of the fact that it had been the state religion of Sweden and had had some important military figure named Hitler as its head and was needed by the world; that the boy had been dropped therefore by the Federation but had reapplied due to the scarcity of manpower and been accepted as a flying cadet; that he was doing horribly in stunt flying and was right now healing up from a bad landing and was temporarily suspended and probably would be sent back to the farm in Scotland on the basis that while he might have a gift for languages he didn't seem all right in the head.

Well! A senior Council member could easily get that threat of dismissal quashed.

Brown Limper began to take a very definite interest in Lars Thorenson, and through him, in that monster in the cage.

Things were definitely looking up. Certain crimes must be corrected even if the criminal were an old companion!

— 2 —

That day had left Terl feeling very optimistic.

It had gone off just like he knew it would. Someone sooner or later was going to get teleportation in operation again on this planet, and with what joy he had found that the animal himself was taking an interest in it!

Terl was a highly trained security chief, the best by his own admission, and he knew all about teleportation. *All* about it.

When the animal went over to the Chamco dome, Terl had even pleasantly waited for the shots. They came!

Terl was of two minds about the outcome. He was very pleased there was a fight and that the Chamcos had reacted exactly as predicted, and at the same time he was disappointed the animal had only received a scratched face. It was a difficult emotional conflict to be glad the animal had shot up the Chamcos successfully and to be unhappy to see the animal still hobbling around alive afterward. Well, one couldn't have everything.

He waited for two days for the news that the Chamcos had committed suicide. It finally came to him through the stupid cadet who visited him of an evening. Practicing talking a language required having something to talk about and so Terl got lots of news.

"You know those two Psychlos that used to work over in that dome," said Lars, talking through the barrier and bars. "Well, they put them in a cell down in the dormitory area, and this afternoon, despite a great deal of precautions, the two hung themselves with their chains. Over a crossbeam. They broke their chains apart and made a pair of nooses with them and they hung themselves. They could have escaped maybe, but instead they simply strung themselves up."

"No!" said Terl, pretending he didn't expect just that. "The poor fellows. Must have been hurt terribly badly by the animal. I saw it from here. He just stood there and kept firing into them. When a Psychlo is hit too badly and knows he can't recover, he is likely to commit suicide." Which was about as far from the facts as Terl would allow himself to stray. Without breaking down laughing.

"They're giving the sentry and the guard sergeant drumhead court-martials," said Lars. "Probably send them back to Scotland. They're Argylls. Clanargyll, that is."

Terl clicked his fangs in sympathy over this gross injustice and said so.

Lars could agree how unjust authorities could be. But he mustn't go too far. "There's someone here I'd like you to meet. He's very important, a senior Council member. I won't mention his name. He's standing over in the shadows under the pole. Do you see him?"

Terl had seen him the instant he took position over there. He said, "Where? Oh? What's a senior Council member?"

So Lars—it was great practice for his Psychlo—filled him in on the whole political background that was now functioning. And Terl said, well, certainly he'd talk through his friend the cadet to this very important official, it would be glorious practice for the cadet's Psychlo.

So, using a couple of mine radios (Brown Limper said the glaring lights in front of the cage hurt his eyes and he had had a fever lately), a considerable amount of conversation occurred with Lars in the middle.

Terl gave the politician a lot of very good, "factual" data. The Psychlos were actually a peaceable people, interested in commerce, and here, only in mining. A disaster had occurred a thousand or so years ago that made it possible for the Psychlo company to move in. No, he didn't know what caused the disaster, probably some natural cataclysm. The company had tried to save all the people they could but the inhabitants misunderstood their intentions and hid from the peace missions and rescue teams, and the company, being only a commercial company and not political, had been quite poor and unable to continue with the financial burden of rescue since profits were down and so the whole thing had gone on.

Yes, well, he could say that this animal (Tyler?) had provoked a crisis. Rash? Well, yes, come to think of it, pretty rash. Wild, too. He knew. He had tried to befriend him and now he, Terl, was in a cage—without trial too! But of course his feelings of guilt and desire for repentance were the real reason he wanted to be in the cage. This animal—what did you say its name was? Tyler? He didn't know it had a name; it was very secretive, bad-tempered in fact. Well, look what he had done to Terl's two best friends just a couple of days ago, and they had been so badly injured they had now committed suicide.

Oh, indeed the Psychlos were very peace-loving people. Honest, kind, good to their friends. Trustworthy. He, himself, made it a rule of his life never to betray a trust.

What? Oh, yes, it was too bad this animal Tyler didn't have the principles and morals of a Psychlo. Yes, he agreed someone should have taught him to be honest and upright when he was young.

Oh, no, the Psychlos would never think of counterattacking. They weren't a military nation and Intergalactic was only a mining company, only interested in struggling along and staying at peace with the universe. Badly misunderstood people, the Psychlos.

After they left, Lars was very gratified at all the Pyschlo practice he had had, and the shadow under the pole was seemingly desirous of further conversations. Terl hugged himself enough to crush his rib bones.

He would get off Earth, that was for sure. His plans were

really sparking! What a lucky break. He would have made it without the break, but how easy it all became. He was not only going to get home to his gold, he was going to blow this planet out of the sky. And he was going to take a prisoner with him. They had air chambers on Psychlo. They could question a captive from almost any system for weeks—and very painful weeks they were. Yes, he'd take a prisoner. Not this silly cadet who knew nothing, not that crooked self-serving politician who was too crap-brained to know valuable information from trash, not the animal Tyler since he could be awfully dangerous . . . well, maybe Tyler if he had no success with anyone else. But it better be somebody else, somebody who would know all their plans and military preparedness . . . who?

Terl was hugging his ribs to keep from laughing with delight. He didn't want the sentry to log something about his conduct. Maybe the sentry would think he had a stomachache.

Oh, it was too much!

His professors were absolutely right. He was easily the greatest officer they had ever trained!

The laughs finally erupted from him but the guard had changed by then and the new sentry thought he was just being more insane than usual. There was nothing in the log except that that cadet had been there for a routine visit to practice talking Psychlo. The new sentry walked about. He had an odd feeling of foreboding. Had the summer night turned cold? Or was it just that insane laughter from the cage?

— 3 —

"We," said Jonnie, "are going to Africa."

Dr. MacKendrick looked up from his task of removing the cast from Thor's arm, a little startled.

All the wounded Scots but Thor had left the underground hospital; Thor's arm had had to be rebroken and set but now it was fine, and with Thor gone, the hospital would be empty save for Jonnie. Dr. Allen had returned to Scotland to care for his practice and Dr. MacKendrick had been thinking of doing so as well.

As he finished cracking off the cast, Dr. MacKendrick said, "*We?*"

"Yes," said Jonnie. "You are a bone man but you are also a neurosurgeon, I think they call it."

Dr. MacKendrick looked at the tall young man, standing there leaning on his cane. He liked this young man. He liked him very much. His practice was being run at home by a competent young doctor and he supposed that arrangement could continue. He had thought a little vacation might be appropriate before taking up his tools in the Aberdeen cave. But Africa?

Thor was flexing his arm, looking very pleased. MacKendrick told him all about what exercises he must now do to keep his muscles from collapsing. It looked like a pretty good job of bone-setting this time.

Jonnie beckoned and MacKendrick followed him as he hobbled into a sickroom Jonnie had been using as an office. An old operating table was covered with papers, photographs and books.

"I need some dead Psychlos and I need some live Pyschlos," said Jonnie.

Thor, in the doorway, laughed. "I shouldn't think you'd have any trouble with the dead ones. There's nearly a thousand somewhere around the compound."

"Sorry," said Jonnie. "They dumped them in a mile-deep mine shaft and the shaft is so shaky it's a risk to fly down it. I've spent the whole last week looking for dead Psychlos."

"There is the Chamco pair," said Dr. MacKendrick.

"Sorry again," said Jonnie. "The Council for some reason of its own had the bodies burned."

"Just what is the problem here?" said Dr. MacKendrick.

"You ever stop to wonder why the Intergalactic Mining Company always shipped bodies home? They don't want dead Pyschlos lying about."

"The parson," said Thor, "cut up the pair we found in the plane."

"He wasn't looking for what I'm looking for," said Jonnie.

Dr. MacKendrick smiled. "Autopsies on dead Psychlos. Jonnie, it wouldn't be a full day unless you astonished me with something." He was referring to an incident a week ago when he was sewing up Jonnie's cheek: the needle had been a little dull, and Jonnie in reflex had reached up with his *right* hand and gripped his wrist to make him ease off.

MacKendrick had felt a bit contrite about the arm and leg; he had feared that he might have injured something when he operated. But the sudden movement of the arm and hand had told him that it was a matter of getting back into communication rather than physical damage: Jonnie had tried to do it again voluntarily and couldn't. "Must be like learning to wiggle your ears," Jonnie had said. "All you have to do is find the right muscles to pull, and how." MacKendrick supposed he really should stay around and help Jonnie recover.

"Well," said MacKendrick, motivated more by the possibility of being able to help Jonnie's arm and leg than by any real interest in autopsies on dead Psychlos, "I guess I could go along. But why Africa?"

Jonnie smiled and beckoned Thor nearer. "There's a live, operating, untouched Psychlo mine there!"

Thor gasped. "We missed?"

"It isn't a full-fledged minesite. It is a branch mine of the central minesite near what used to be called ['Lake Victoria']. Here." And he showed them on the map. "Over to the west of there, way deep in jungle, there was—and is—a tungsten mine. The Psychlos are mad for tungsten." He circled an area. "All this is jungle. On the pictures it looks like tall, tall trees, making a total umbrella. Thousands of years of growth. A recon drone doesn't even penetrate into that vast area of swamp.

"We chose our targets from recon drone maps. And yes, we missed. It's my bet they're still sitting there listening to the strange chatter on the pilot planetary, keeping their furry Psychlo heads down and waiting for a chance to break out.

Thor smiled. "That's sort of grim, Jonnie. We go down and shoot them just to get some dead bodies."

"I don't want just dead bodies, I also want some live ones. There's a graduate engineer or six at every minesite."

"And what," asked MacKendrick, "are these autopsies supposed to show?"

"I don't know," said Jonnie. "So will you gather up your scalpels and come along?"

"You're not telling me everything," said Dr. MacKendrick.

"Well, as a matter of fact," said Jonnie, "I'm not. This is very secret. We will state we are going to make a tour of some tribes. And if you go, Thor, you can even visit some, and pretend to be me the way you used to at the lode."

"This sounds very hush-hush," said MacKendrick.

"It is," said Jonnie.

Jonnie had not liked the way things were going with the Council. It was passing lots of laws—one couldn't keep up—and he wasn't invited there anymore.

"And you're trying to solve—?" said MacKendrick.

"Why the Chamcos committed suicide," said Jonnie. And why he was making *no* progress trying to untangle the mathematics of teleportation. For a week now he had been going round and round and getting nowhere. He didn't know exactly what he was looking for, but it had to be there whatever it was.

"So Africa?" said Jonnie.

"Africa," said Thor.

"Well, Africa," said Dr. MacKendrick.

— 4 —

The big battle plane lanced through the skies over the Atlantic. It was a type used for company marines and had seats for fifty Psychlos with space and lift capacity for tons of weaponry and gear. Jonnie in the pilot's seat flew easily and relaxed, flying with his left hand, straight on course.

Big as the plane was, they had had trouble keeping it from getting overloaded. It was all secret and would remain so. There would be no leaks. But friends and a small amount of activity attracted attention to them.

Dunneldeen had shown up with five Scots—just happened by that day from their regular run to Scotland. Colonel Ivan, whose total force was about eighty valiant-red-army Cossacks, had to be persuaded to leave half of them taking care of the base. Angus, just an hour before departure from the heliport, had casually plunked about a hundred pounds of tools into the back and quietly sat down, uninvited. A rather fearful stack of weapons and explosives had magically appeared in the hands of four of the original Scots led by Dwight. Dr. MacKendrick seemed to have brought anything he thought he ever might need in any practice.

There had been a bit of a flap just before take-off. Pattie, it seemed, had found the true love of her life in Bittie MacLeod and they wouldn't have known Bittie was also aboard except that Pattie came rushing down the stairs to the heliport to kiss him a childishly tearful goodbye. Chrissie had said nothing, feeling bad. But suddenly an old woman had come up with Chrissie's possessions and taken her in tow, and it turned out Robert the Fox was putting them on a regular run to Scotland. His family wanted to meet Chrissie, he explained. And then Pattie had to be packed up and sent with them. Then they were just closing the door when they had to open it again to take in Robert the Fox, complete with cloak and claymore.

Then just as they were passing the eastern coast of what had been the United States, two battle planes had shown up, and it turned out to be Glencannon and three other pilots. "Just finished with our regular ferrying runs, and where are you going, we have enough ammunition and fuel," on the local command radio channel.

They also had a Coordinator who was an expert on Africa and spoke French.

It was *not,* Robert the Fox said reprovingly in Jonnie's ear, walking up the wide aisle from the back, the best-planned raid he had ever participated in. And where was Jonnie going?

The Coordinator was a young lad called David Fawkes. He had recovered from having a Russian drag him out of bed before dawn, jumble his possessions into a bundle and his reference books into a pack, and spirit him to the plane. Sitting with the copilot and next to Jonnie, the Coordinator was babbling away happily.

"We have an operation going in that part of Africa. I think it used to be called the 'rain forest.' So if this is all hush-hush, you better stay clear of the Federation unit operating there. We didn't know there was a minesite up north of there."

"You're lucky you didn't get your heads blown off," said Robert the Fox, leaning over the back of the copilot seat.

"Well, you see," said David Fawkes, "we're not really a war unit. We don't operate like that. This is the first time we've felt a need for such hardware, as you raiders call it."

"You mean you were going to fight Psychlos?" said Sir Robert.

"Oh, no, no," was the quick response. "The Brigantes. Usually tribes are so happy to see us they're delirious but—"

'What's a Brigante?" said Robert the Fox. This certainly

wasn't a well-researched, well-planned raid. He didn't even know their target or purpose.

Well, it turned out that the "Brigantes," as they called themselves, were a pretty strange lot. A Coordinator had been dropped into a ruined city in that area to see whether anybody was alive and he'd almost gotten blown to bits with a grenade.

"Grenade?" said Robert the Fox. "Psychlos don't use grenades."

Well, they knew that. This was a *powder* grenade. Smoking powder, bright orange flash. And then the Coordinator was about to do battle with a club while bellowing into his radio for help when a very old man crawled out of a wrecked basement and apologized in French.

He was a very tattered old man, on his last pins. He'd been left to die by his squad because he was old now and couldn't keep up. Turned out he called himself a Brigante. He thought the Coordinator was a Psychlo at first glimpse. Then he saw he was human and now thought the Coordinator was part of a relief team sent by the bank.

"The what?" from both Thor and Sir Robert.

Well, seems like they had some kind of legend that they would be relieved by somebody, and they'd held onto it for over a thousand years. Incredible they could keep a tradition going that long—

"What exactly," demanded Sir Robert, liking his information a little more crisp, "is a Brigante?"

"Well, that's what's making it so hard to really get in solid contact with them, and right this minute they have three Coordinators in there in hopes of doing that. Oh, what's a Brigante? Well, it seems like at the time of the disaster—this is all according to this abandoned old man, of course—not confirmed—some big international bank wanted to overthrow one of those African countries that had gotten its freedom from some people called colonialists, and then it borrowed a lot of money and had a military coup and wouldn't pay the bank back or something like that.

"What's a Brigante? Well, I'm telling you. So this international bank collected up a lot of what they called mercenaries, soldiers for hire, and put together a thousand-man unit, and they were going to use nerve gas and wipe out this government and all these mercenaries were equipped with gas masks like our air masks only they filter outside air.

"Yes, I'm getting to it. These were also called 'soldiers of fortune' in ancient times. So they were just about to make their attack on the government of this new country and were lying out in some mines in the desert—old salt mines—and the Psychlos hit the planet. Well, they had these gas masks—"

"Salt," said Jonnie, "neutralizes Psychlo gas."

"Oh, well, fine. So anyway there they were in Africa, fully armed and ready to go, and their target was wiped out for them! A mixed-up lot: Belgians, French, Senegalese, English, American, all nationalities, anybody the bank could hire. But a full, skilled military unit. They didn't have any other name so sometime, then or later, they started calling themselves Brigantes."

"Well, thank you at last," said Robert the Fox.

"Wait, that isn't all of it. The natives in that area were mostly dead from the kill-gas, so this unit drifted south. The tall trees and jungles seem to have kept them masked from observation from recons and so on. They picked up women from missions and villages, white and black, and kept going.

"And that isn't all. This is why they're so hard to contact: after a couple of hundred years, they got into a working arrangement with the Psychlos. First you've heard of that? Well, us too. And it makes them edgy.

"Apparently what they used to do was capture people and deliver them to the Psychlos to shoot or torture or something. They never really went too close to the Psychlos but the Psychlos couldn't operate in those swamps: bodies too heavy to walk, ground too soggy for tanks, trees too tall to fly into. So these Brigantes somehow got into a working arrangement: they'd tie up some people and leave them near a compound and the Psychlos would come out and take the people for whatever—"

"Torture," said Jonnie. "They enjoy it."

"—and the Psychlos would leave some knickknacks like cloth or something on a log. A kind of trading arrangement. Well, all that was centuries ago and they ran out of people. But the Psychlos never hunted them down—swampy ground, tall trees and so on, like I told you."

"Sounds like pretty crazy people for unarmed Coordinators to be fooling around with," said Robert the Fox.

"Well, not really. We're pretty good on diplomacy and so on.

But we got this order from the Council just a few days ago to be sure and contact them and bring them in, and we are just doing our job.

"To tell the truth, the Brigantes are a bit strange. They keep their numbers down to a thousand men, leave their old ones to die, don't marry but just use women. They seem to have a high mortality rate among children. Also probably from hunting elephants with grenades . . .

"Oh, well yes, the grenades. They know how to make crude black powder—you know, charcoal and saltpeter from dung heaps and sulphur from a mine. And they put it into a baked clay receptacle that is studded with stones and stick a fuse in it and light it with a cigar. They have to get right up to an elephant to use one and I suppose that's part of the reason for the mortality rate.

"Rescue? Oh, yes. Well, it seems their ancestors once had a firm promise from the international bank to 'pull them out,' and they haven't a clue to what's going on in the outside world. Well, yes, of course; the Coordinators in there can use that. We'll get them out."

"And that's near this minesite?" asked Robert the Fox.

"To the south, to the south," said David Fawkes. "Just thought you had better know. From what I gather here your target is a branch mine compound with just ordinary Psychlos in it."

"Ordinary Psychlos," snorted Thor. "You got a handgun? No? You'll need it. Here's a spare. And don't try to find the tribal history of a Psychlo before you shoot. Got it?"

David Fawkes took the gun like it would bite.

They flew onward to Africa.

— 5 —

Jonnie lay behind a tree trunk, saturated with rain, perspiring from the heat, looking at the compound through infrared glasses that did not do much good.

For three soaking wet days they had been following a power line, the only sign of civilization. They had landed at the power dam well enough. It was automatic and self-maintaining, and

Psychlo machinery had been superimposed upon the ancient man-works. They had no actual clue as to the position of the minesite beyond its existence, but Jonnie knew this power line, huge cables on metal pylons—themselves ancient—would take them to it eventually. And "eventually" seemed to be the right word.

Usually power lines had trees and brush cleared out, but not this one. There for countless years, the power line provided no more open sky than any other part of this vast forest.

The old man-maps said this had been a country called ["Haut-Zaïre"] and that this portion of the extinct nation was the ["Ituri Forest"].

Here the equatorial sun never reached the ground. It was umbrellaed first by cloud cover and then by the crowns of mighty trees that locked together in a canopy a hundred feet above the ground. Great vines a foot or more in diameter wrapped like gorged serpents around the trunks. Underfoot the thick humus squished at every step.

And the rain came down! It dripped, it rivuleted down the trunks and vines, it poured through slight openings until one felt he was trying to progress through a constant warm waterfall of varying thickness.

It was all twilight.

The game blended in deceptively with the gloom, a dangerous fact. They had seen elephants and forest buffalo and gorillas. A giraffe-like animal, an antelope, and two kinds of cat were routinely started up by them. The snarl of leopards, the roar of crocodiles, the chatter of monkeys and the screech of peacocks—sounds muted by the rain—made Jonnie feel the area was hostile and densely inhabited.

The old man-maps said there were around twenty thousand square miles of this forest, and that even at the height of man-civilization it had never been completely explored. No wonder a minesite could go overlooked here!

The Ituri Forest was no place for buckskin and moccasins and a limp.

Trying to progress through it was made difficult by the uselessness of trying to overfly it and the need for some secrecy. They dared not use radios. Dropped lines from planes could foul power cables if they reached them at all. Streams infested with crocodiles made the crossings dangerous.

Well, a small party of them were here. Only twenty of their

force, scattered out among the trees and ready to call in reserves or the planes if needed.

The compound looked deserted, but then Psychlos never wandered around in the open. It had been built so long ago that it too was overshadowed by the streaming canopy of trees. What had an employee had to do to be assigned to this dismal, gloomy, saturated outpost, Jonnie wondered.

He was looking to the left of the compound for signs of truck passageways. There would be no road of tires, but ore truck floating drives would have crushed and killed vegetation. Yes, there was a road over there, headed east through the gloom. Ah, yes, more lights beyond an opening through the trees for the landing of freighters. Did the road go to that? No. Another road. One exit road through the forest and the other to the field.

"Never was there a more unplanned raid," Robert the Fox was muttering. But a well-planned raid took intelligence scouting first. He never could have imagined any terrain like this existed on the planet!

Now, Jonnie was thinking, what did they really want here? Not dead Psychlos, really. He wanted live Psychlos. That the Psychlos would fight he had no doubt, and that some would be killed was almost certain, but he was far more interested in live ones than in dead ones.

He was reaching to his belt to unfasten the miniature mine radio—to be used first in the hope that they had one on in that compound—when his infrareds strayed over to the right of the compound. There was a defined path and at its end what appeared to be the wreck of a flatbed truck, ages old and mostly overgrown. Hard to see in this twilight at noonday. The rain made it so hard to pick out details even with infrared.

Jonnie gave the glasses to Robert the Fox. "What do you see on that old truck bed?"

Robert the Fox squirmed over into a new position, his cloak as wet as a soaking sock. "Something under a tarpaulin. A new tarpaulin . . . a barrel? Two barrels? . . . a package?"

Suddenly Jonnie remembered the rambling story of David Fawkes. The Coordinator was back of them, hunkered down, dripping. Jonnie crawled back a short distance. "What was that about putting things on a log for barter with the Psychlos?"

"Oh, yes. Yes. They put people there for the Psychlos to see and then withdrew, and the Psychlos would come out and leave some trinkets. You mean the Brigantes, don't you?"

"I think I'm looking at an incomplete trade," said Jonnie. He hissed to a Scot, "Pass the word for Colonel Ivan!"

Ivan's English was improving remarkably fast under the interested tutelage of Bittie MacLeod, who "thought it a shame for the grand man not to be able to talk a human language." This was giving Colonel Ivan a thick accent but nevertheless he needed the Russian language Coordinator less and less. Jonnie found they had brought that Coordinator, too, leading Sir Robert to wonder whether they might not find an old woman or a couple of Psychlos on the plane as well.

"Scout way over to the right," whispered Jonnie, amplifying it with a descriptive circle of his left hand. "Watch it."

"What's this new maneuver on this unplanned raid?" said the very wet Robert the Fox.

"I don't like losing men," said Jonnie. "As the English say, 'It's bad form.' Precaution is all."

"Are we going to just charge that place?" asked Robert the Fox. "You can't get plane cover through these trees. I think I see an air-cooled housing for a breathe-gas circulator over there. I could hit it from here, I think."

"Well, have we got any plain bullets?" said Jonnie.

"Aye, but it surely is a no-plan operation!"

They waited in the dismal drip and cascade of the rain. Somewhere off to the left a leopard snarled and it set off a wave of bird sounds and monkey chitters.

There was an abrupt thud about twenty feet behind them. They snaked back. Ivan was standing back of a tree. On the ground at his feet lay a strange human. He was out cold.

He might have been any nationality, or any color for that matter. He was dressed in monkey skins cut in such a way that they looked oddly like a uniform. A strapped bag had fallen open under him and a clay-pot grenade had rolled out.

Ivan was pointing to an arrow in his canteen. He pulled it out and gave it to Jonnie. Over Jonnie's shoulder the Coordinator whispered, "Poisoned arrow. See where the glob was on its tip."

Jonnie took off Ivan's canteen and threw it away, making signs it was not to be drunk now.

Ivan detached the man's bow from his belt and offered it. But Jonnie was kneeling beside the man and picking up the grenade.

It had a fuse sticking out of it. He knew the type of fuse. Psychlo!

As soon as he had Jonnie's attention again, Ivan handed him a Psychlo mine radio and pointed at the man.

"He watch us," said Ivan. "He talk." He pointed at the radio.

Abruptly alert, Jonnie saw that they might have an enemy in front of them and another one in the forest behind them!

He passed orders swiftly through Robert the Fox, who whipped off to get their small force faced both ways.

Brigantes! The man at his feet had wide, hide crossbelts and spare arrows were arranged, points into flaps along the leather. He had an odd pair of crudely made, strapped boots reminding Jonnie of the remains of "paratrooper" boots he had seen in base storerooms. The man's hair was cut short and stood up. The face was scarred and brutal.

The fellow was stirring, recovering from the unexpected clout of a rifle butt. Colonel Ivan promptly put a foot on his neck to prevent his rising.

Robert the Fox was back with a nod that dispositions had been made. "They may have been scouting us for days. That's a Psychlo radio!"

"Yes, and bomb fuse. I think there's more here—"

A bomb exploded in an orange blast about fifty feet away.

An assault rifle hammered out.

There followed a period marked only by the startled rush of birds and monkeys through the drip of rain.

Jonnie got back to the log. Nothing was happening in the compound. Robert put two riflemen in position to cover it. "We're boxed," he said. "Nicely planned raid."

"Take the rear first," said Jonnie. "Clean them out back there!"

"Charge!" bawled Colonel Ivan. Then something in Russian.

There was an instant hammering of assault rifles.

Bursting grenades racketed and smoke poured through the rain.

Running feet of men covering each other as they went forward in alternate waves.

Screams!

Russian and Scot battle cries!

Then a lull. Then another furious hammer of assault rifles.

Another lull.

A voice, hoarse, rising way above the birds and rain, "We surrender!" English? Not French? The Coordinator looked confused.

Some distant running feet as Robert the Fox threw some of his men back of the voice to prevent a trap.

Jonnie grabbed a blast rifle from a Scot and threw himself down. "Pinpoint." "No Flame." He cut loose with a savage burst at the breathe-gas cooler housing. The ancient outside metal peeled away under the repeating impacts like hide.

There was a clank and a hiss over there. Jonnie gave it another burst.

They waited. No Psychlos came rushing out. The place must be flooded with air over there. But there was no reaction.

The rain came down and the birds and monkeys quieted. Drifting smoke, black powder smoke from the grenades, was harsh to the nose.

— 6 —

Jonnie looked toward the ore plane landing field beyond the short road. Deserted.

The Scot carrying radio equipment answered his beckoning. The covering scrap of a tarpaulin was cascading rain. Jonnie checked the set. Working. He flipped to planetary pilot band and picked up the mike.

"Flight to Nairobi, standing by," said Jonnie. It would sound like routine pilot traffic but a code had been prearranged with the two ships they had left near the power plant. "Nairobi" meant "Fly in to our beacon" and "Standing by" meant "Don't come in shooting, but be alert."

Dunneldeen's voice crackled back, "All passengers aboard." They were on their way.

Jonnie took the mine radio off his belt and turned it to "Constant Bleep," which was used by miners when trapped or caught in a cave-in. It would act as a radio beacon for the planes. He stabbed a finger at three of his force. As the men passed, he handed one of them the mine radio to put in a tree at the field.

Assault rifles held low, running wide of the compound,

pausing to give one another cover, they raced toward the landing field. Shortly, one of them, seen as a blur through the dull curtains of rain but brighter out there on the field edge, raised a hand in an "all clear." They would give the planes landing cover as they came in.

Jonnie slung the blast rifle over his shoulder and hobbled across the compound perimeter, his cane not sinking so deep on this more traveled ground. He could hear pumps going further south. That would be where the mine workings were. He saw that a branch of the power cables they had used to trace this place turned off halfway up the road to the field. He followed it.

A squat hut made of stone sat there in the trees, festooned with insulators and surrounded by pipes. He recognized it as a fuel and ammunition manufacturing unit. Ha! They had one at this branch mine; probably to utilize all the excess power available from the hydroelectric plant.

The ground around it was roughed up with recent foot and flatbed traffic. The door was ajar. He gave it a push with his cane.

What a jumble! Fuel and ammunition canisters were usually stacked neatly on racks in these places. Side bins usually contained the various minerals used in concocting the contents of the canisters. A recent flurry of activity had left minerals spilled on the floor, and damaged unusable canisters underfoot. This place had been very busy very recently. He knew it took a bit of time to stir up and charge the brews that became fuel and ammunition and seal them into canisters. Had they worked here flat-out for days? A week?

He made his way over to the exit road that must go to the main minesite, using a short cut between the two roads. He looked at the brush on both sides of the exit road. Ordinarily his educated eye would have been able to track this easily, but the pouring rain made it more difficult.

He bent, examining some twigs broken from the underbrush that bordered the road. Some breaks, the ones that pointed toward the compound, must be several days old. Others, very fresh, still leaking sap, were broken in the direction of the main minesite up near a lake that old man-maps said had been called [Lake Victoria].

A convoy had come in here many days—weeks?—ago and had gone out hours ago. A big convoy!

He glanced up the exit road, half-expecting to see trucks or tanks coming down it, back to the compound.

Their tactical situation was not ideal. They had a small force of Brigantes holding out in the woods back of them. Somewhere, near or far, there must be the better part of a thousand Brigantes. And up this road—he looked at the traces of the ground drives—there were a very large number of Psychlo vehicles. Ore flatbeds? Tanks?

He heard their planes now. That sound wouldn't matter after all the uproar of this recent skirmish. And any convoy on that road wouldn't hear anything above their own motor drives. The vast canopy of treetops that made this place a twilight not only prevented anyone from looking down at the exit road and seeing anything on it, but also prevented anyone on it from seeing up.

A poor tactical situation. They could not fight a convoy, probably escorted with tanks, in this water-saturated, hemmed-in forest. Their planes were of no use to them.

He made his way over to the landing field. Sky! Not much sky but enough to get ore freighters up and down through. Leaking sky, but sky! He hadn't seen any sky in three days.

The soldiers were in the trees, covering the field. The mine radio bleeper was set in a fifteen-inch diameter vine that coiled like a huge snake up a tall tree. Maybe this field had once been bigger, but the jungle and the trees had encroached deeply.

The big marine attack battle plane wound down from directly overhead, letting the smaller battle plane cover it from above as was proper. Then the plane mushroomed a puddle of field water into a geyser and came to a halt. It was Dunneldeen. He swung the door open and sat there grinning, glad to see Jonnie.

Robert the Fox came rushing up. The side door of the big plane swung open and the officer of the remaining part of their force looked questioningly. Robert waved to him to sit tight, no emergency, and got into the smaller battle plane with Jonnie and Dunneldeen.

Jonnie was rapidly filling Dunneldeen in on the events. "There's a convoy on that road headed for the main minesite," concluded Jonnie. "I think they came down here for fuel and ammunition and then went back."

"Ah," said Dunneldeen. "That explains it."

Typical Dunneldeen, he had not been sitting quietly waiting for their call. He could get that, he said, back at the dam or way

upstairs. So he'd left the big attack plane at the dam and on radio standby so they could recall him, and he'd been keeping the main minesite, up at what they used to call [''Lake Albert''], under surveillance by going way up and following normal traffic routes. His instruments and viewscreens could penetrate rain and cloud—even though they couldn't see a thing through the canopy of trees.

The main minesite, he recalled, had been knocked out on Day 92 by a pilot . . . MacArdle? Yes, MacArdle. And he'd had a bit of trouble. The Psychlos had attempted to loft two battle planes and MacArdle had nailed them right at the hangar launch door, blocking it. He'd blown their power lines to bits and knocked out huge breathe-gas and fuel and ammunition dumps. The Psychlos had gotten two batteries of antiaircraft into operation and he'd had to knock those out. This was the fight where the copilot had been wounded, if Jonnie and Sir Robert recalled. A very fighting minesite!

Anyway, Dunneldeen went on, on his overflights from one hundred thousand feet up during the last three days he hadn't found any current movement in the place *but*—he showed them the pictures he'd gotten from his screens—those apes had cleared away the hangar door—that's it there—and look over here, see? Those shadows under the trees at the edge of their field . . . no, over there. Ten battle planes on standby!

''Nobody ever came back to mop up that minesite,'' he concluded, ''and those gorillas have been busy!''

Jonnie looked at the several pictures. One had been taken with a lower sun. He examined the profiles of the planes half-hidden under the trees. He looked at Dunneldeen.

''Yes,'' said Dunneldeen. ''Just like you described the one you put on the gas drone. Mark 32 low-flying ground strafers, heavy, heavily armored. Not much range but they can carry extra fuel cartridges.''

''Those Psychlos,'' said Jonnie, ''are not setting up to defend their minesite. They are probably desperate for breathe-gas. They had their fuel blown up . . . see the dolly tracks in the grass in front of those Mark 32s. They were dollied there, not flown there.'' He pointed to the hut half-seen through the trees. ''They've been over there for days manufacturing fuel and ammunition like mad. They used what fuel they could scrape up to get that

convoy here; they grabbed all the breathe-gas, I'm sure. And they're on their way back."

"The only other big supply of breathe-gas," said Robert the Fox, "is over at the central compound in America! That's where they're headed."

"With those ten Mark 32s they could turn this whole war around the other way," said Jonnie. He opened a map, water still dripping off him and onto it, and traced out the exit road. He found it left the forest, ran across a plain and into a long ravine that was open to the sky. The road went on toward Lake Albert but there was a flat place as it left the ravine. He looked at some pictures Dunneldeen had taken.

"We've got a battle coming up," said Jonnie. He measured distances and turned to Sir Robert. "It will take them a day and a half to reach this spot; two days to the main compound since that road is awfully bad. Meanwhile we have to take care of the main force of Brigantes. Pack Colonel Ivan, four raiders, and a mortar into this place. Tell him he's got to hold that pass until relieved. And you, Dunneldeen, stand by up there to make sure that convoy doesn't get through. Remember, we're only after live Psychlos."

"We're after stopping a counterattack on the Denver area," said Sir Robert.

Thor had gone down to put in an appearance at the Mountains of the Moon as "Jonnie." He was a fair rider and would put on a bit of a show for them and say hello. He was scheduled to visit another tribe south of there. He was a bit far for recall and it would mess up their plans to expose where Jonnie really was.

"I'm sorry you've only got one battle plane," said Jonnie.

Dunneldeen smiled happily. "But there's only one battle, Jonnie lad."

Robert the Fox was rapping out orders, and very shortly Colonel Ivan and four soldiers struggled up through the rain carrying a bazooka and a blast mortar and other equipment. They'd forgotten about their Coordinator to translate for them and it was a very tight fit indeed to get all this into the battle plane.

Sir Robert briefed Colonel Ivan. He smiled cheerfully. Ambushes in passes of the Hindu Kush were *much* more complicated. Have no fear, Marshal Jonnie and War Chief Robert. That pass

would be held. *Live* Psychlos? Well, not quite as satisfactory, but have no fear, the valiant-red-army would perform.

The battle plane soared up, seven men and one battle plane to stop a convoy of dozens of Psychlos and battle tanks. Dunneldeen waved down at them through the rain and was gone.

— 7 —

True it was that the stockpiles of breathe-gas and ammunition had been stripped to the last cartridge. The grass and shrub had been crushed dead for years. A quarter of an acre had been the extent of the breathe-gas dump; half an acre the extent of the fuel and ammunition dump. And it was all gone.

Angus opened the lock of the compound's main door, and the reserve troops from the attack carrier went sprinting in, covering each other.

The place was empty. It had four levels of offices, shops, and hangars. Pumps were running. Lights were all on. And it was a jumble of hasty departure.

Jonnie stood in the corridor outside the recreation area. What a dismal, dank place; mold was growing on things. Water was dripping down the walls, only kept cleared out by the pumps. What an awful place to try to live, even for a Psychlo.

He thumbed through sheaves of radio dispatch forms that had been spouting out of a printer. Even the paper was wet in this hot, humid place. They had been monitoring all bands, particularly the pilot band. It was odd to see: "Andy, can you pick up that load of pilgrims in Calcutta?" and "Please bring me another flying suit and some fuel, MacCallister." The Scot pilots largely talked Psychlo with a jumble of English. It must have looked quite mad to the company employees, huddled here in this remote jungle, not knowing what was really going on but monitoring every scrap of it.

A Russian raced up to him holding a Psychlo breathe-mask he must have found someplace. It still had the bottle attached and was operating. Jonnie sniffed it and it burnt his nose passages. Let's see, it took about twelve hours for one of the flasks to run out. This was still . . . half-full? quarter-full? He shook it to see how much of the breathe-gas in liquefied form was still there. The Psychlos had left within the last eight or nine hours.

He hobbled along the corridor, sweat streaming off him. The pumps were running air into the place but it didn't make it any cooler. The usual Psychlo stink . . . no, worse, for it was mixed up with mold. Bubbles of sound floating in from various parts of the interior levels where his people were still searching. There was a mine phone off its buttons and he listened at it. Still alive. He could even hear the mine pumps running at the distant tungsten workings.

This minesite wasn't as old as most. Probably been moved here from elsewhere in the forest when they found another tungsten deposit. They were mad for tungsten. The viewscreens in the mine manager's office were on. Jonnie looked at the big electric roasting ovens at the mine. They conveyed and roasted ore there. Steam was coming off coils. They must have considered this upset on the planet temporary for they'd gone on mining.

He went down the stairs that led to the hangar. The usual Psychlo steps, twice the height of human steps, hard to negotiate with this leg. Well, he *was* getting better. He'd sure been able to use a blast rifle today. No speed in his arm. But it was improving.

The hangar was in the same disarray as the other parts of the interior. It still held vehicles.

Angus was poking around in the vast, overlit interior. He had a big crayon in his hand and was putting an "X" on vehicles he felt couldn't be readily made operational. Two small tanks. Angus had "X'd" them out. Several flying mine platforms. No "Xs," so okay. Several flatbeds, only half of them usable.

A Psychlo sign: "Ordnance" on a door. Jonnie went in. Blast mortars! Even a pile of shells for them, contrary to interior-storage-of-ammunition regulations. Well!

He came out and grabbed Angus. "Get two of those big flatbed trucks, get a flying mine platform on each of them. Put a mortar and ammunition on each of the flying platforms. Pile those tarps in wads on the front of the flatbeds for armor. Put one of the rigs outside, put the other one just inside the door of the hangar." Yes, there was fuel.

He told Sir Robert to get him four men and a driver for each of the rigs. And to dispatch one of the rigs as soon as made up to tail the convoy.

"That rig?" said Sir Robert.

"They can fly the mine platform off the truck and lay a mortar barrage down. They can block the road by blasting trees across it. Get the convoy tailed, not too close, and if they turn back, block their way."

"And if it doesn't work and they get chased back here?" said Sir Robert.

"The other rig inside the hangar door can be taken out to help defend the place. Put another four men and a driver with it. I'll be taking it when we return here from a visit to the Brigantes."

"You'll be chasing the convoy too!" said Sir Robert, adding with sarcasm: "Ranked among the best-planned and most carefully drilled operations of history, this one is undoubtedly the very finest!" He went off to get it handled, muttering about a flatbed handling tanks.

A Scot came racing up. "Jonnie sir, I think you'd better come down to the third level." He looked ashen.

Jonnie limped with difficulty down the next stairway. He was not at all prepared for what they had found.

It was a big room they apparently used for shooting practice, a sort of indoor range. Some Russians were standing around something on the floor, looking at it with varied expressions of distaste and disapproval. The Scot directing him stopped, mutely pointing down.

In the middle of a veritable lake of congealed blood lay what must have been two old women. It was hard to tell from the scraps. But strands of gray hair, brown skin, and ripped clothing lay, with scattered bone chips in two mounds. The mangled messes and some spent blast gun cases told their story.

Several Psychlos has stood here and bit by bit, inch by inch, with hundreds of carefully nonlethal shots, had carved two women apart.

What a hellish bedlam of shots and screams and laughter this place must have been just a few hours ago!

Dr. MacKendrick, summoned by someone else, came in. He stopped, avoiding standing in the blood. "Impossible to tell from temperature. Not enough left to check. Maybe four hours from the coagulation. Women . . . forty, fifty years old . . . worn out by hard work. . . . They carved their limbs off inch by inch and shot by shot!" He stood up and confronted Jonnie. "Why do Psychlos do that?"

"It gives them pleasure. They think it's delicious. The pain and agony." Jonnie looked at MacKendrick. "It's about the only time they feel joy."

The doctor's face set. "I feel much better about autopsies on Psychlos!"

A Russian had been moving something with a stick he had found.

"Hold it," said Jonnie. He stepped around the blood pool and picked the object up.

Robert the Fox had come in. He halted in shock.

The object that was being held up was a tam-o'-shanter, the bonnet of a Scot!

No body of a Scot. Just a tam-o'-shanter, fairly new. The kind the Coordinators wore.

— 8 —

Jonnie stood in the drenching rain and looked at the platform of the ancient, wrecked flatbed.

Here within the last two or three days or perhaps only hours ago stood three bound human beings: two old Brigante women and one young Scot, waiting for the Psychlos to come out and seize them, helpless to move or escape, probably covered from behind by poison arrows and grenades. How many Bantu and Pygmies had stood in this place the same way, captured and sold by the Brigantes?

And the Psychlos had come and taken them, bought them from the one-time mercenaries with the articles now lying there. The two old women had died in agony. The fate of the Scot was unknown.

A Russian lance had gingerly tested the flatbed and barter goods for booby traps. If Jonnie knew Psychlos, and if they felt this trade ended future relations, it would have been rigged to explode. It wasn't. The Psychlo employees must think that when they retook the planet they'd be back.

Jonnie examined the goods. Sealed metal containers: a hundred pounds of sulphur, another hundred of niter. Under the tarpaulin lay a big coil of mine fuse. Articles that could be used, adding only charcoal, to make grenades. In a smaller wrapped pack:

mine radio power cartridges. Such was the price of three human beings.

Jonnie turned his back on it and walked to where a Russian officer and men were holding the captured Brigantes. There were seventeen of them left alive. They sat with their hands gripped back of their heads, looking down at the ground, very still under the ring of assault rifle muzzles. Seven wounded Brigantes lay about, groaning and moving in the thick humus. Twelve dead Brigantes had been hauled in and lay in a heap.

One of the seventeen sensed a new presence and looked up. He was a barrel-chested brute: teeth broken long ago, face scarred and pitted, a huge jaw, short-cut hair. He was dressed in monkey skins cut in a military pattern. Two bandoliers slotted with poisoned arrows crossed his chest. His eyes looked like scummed pools.

"Why did you fire on us?" he demanded. It came out as "W'y ja fur awn oos?" English if you could unscramble it.

"I think," said Jonnie, "it was the other way around. What were you doing here?"

"By conventions and articles of war you can only get my name-rank-and-serial-number." Mush, but understandable.

"All right," said Jonnie, leaning on his cane. "What is that you said?"

"Arf Moiphy, captunk, fit'commando, occpaychun fierces, Yarmy of Hauter Zairey. Are you the relief fierce or united-nationsh?"

Jonnie turned to David Fawkes, the Coordinator, with a raised eyebrow.

"They have a myth, a legend, that someday the international bank will send a relief force. I think the United Nations was some political organization that looked after small countries and interfered when they were attacked. It's remarkable that they could keep a myth going that long . . ."

"Where is your main body?" said Jonnie.

"Doan hefta answer nuppin bot name-rank-and-serial-number," said the Brigante captain.

"Well, now," said Jonnie, "if we were this relief force we'd have to know, wouldn't we?"

"If yur purt of the relief fierce yu'd know where was," challenged the Brigante. "The relief fierce is alroddy dere, or gung be dere any day."

"I think we had better talk to your commander," said Jonnie.

"General Snith? He's inna main basecamp. Too far."

Jonnie shrugged and waved a hand at the Russian officer as though to go ahead. The Russians nosed up their assault rifles.

"Tup day's march ober dere!" said the Brigante captain, trying to point with tied hands and then making do frantically with his chin.

"How long ago did you put the captives over on that platform?" asked Jonnie.

"Pla'furm?" said the Brigante playing it dumb.

Jonnie turned to the Russian officer again.

"Yes'day afnoon!" said the Brigante swiftly.

The fate of the Scot was important, if he were alive. Jonnie cast around as to what he could do. He had a makeshift tail on the convoy. He had an ambush in front of it. There was no flanking in these woods: indeed, a ground car (much less a truck) would almost run into itself trying to get around these trees, or even be able to make headway over this soaking wet humus. No wonder the Psychlos had their own arrangements with the Brigantes. He decided he'd have to wait for the battle.

He told the Russian Coordinator the orders for the Russian officer. In a very gingerly, alert fashion they began to strip the Brigantes, going over their monkey skin uniforms for knives and concealed weapons, which abounded.

They were in the process of tying the descendants of the long-ago mercenaries when Captunk Arf Moiphy pleaded, "You min uf I attembt to my wounded?"

Jonnie let him go ahead.

Moiphy jumped up, grabbed a heavy club, and pounced on the seven wounded before he could be stopped. With expert swings that landed crushing thuds on their skulls, he killed them.

Smiling and gratified he threw down the club and turned to a Russian so his hands could be retied.

"Thanunk you," he said.

■

PART 18

— 1 —

Bittie MacLeod, carrying a blast rifle as tall as himself, followed along behind Sir Jonnie into the main Brigante encampment.

Sir Jonnie had sent him back twice, but wasn't the proper place of a squire to follow his knight with his weapons into a place of danger?

And Bittie admitted to himself that it did look dangerous! There must be twenty-five hundred or three thousand of these people scattered around this clearing deep in the forest.

They had landed at the top edge of the open space. The prisoners—ooh, how they had stunk up the ship!—had been held in a lump in the big marine attack plane, well separated from their weapons, and when they landed, the prisoners had been put on the ground first. Then Sir Robert had looked over the place and made some defense dispositions to cover their possible retreat as was proper for a War Chief.

Bittie had taken the opportunity of persuading Sir Jonnie into some dry clothes—all you had to do was touch him and the water splashed. The Russians had not been idle over at the dam, and seeing all this rain, they had cut up some camouflage cloth and made rain capes.

It had been hard to get Sir Jonnie to pay attention and take care of himself, to get some food down and change clothes. But Bittie had done it. He'd clasped up the rain cape with a badge with a red star on it and gotten Jonnie's dry shirt belted with his gold buckled belt and had found a helmet liner with a white star on it to keep the rain off him, and all in all, under these circumstances, Sir Jonnie looked pretty presentable even in this rain.

Sheets of water were marching across this wide clearing full of people. Somebody had cut down an awful lot of trees and burned them sometime past. The blackened stumps stood all about. A crop was half-grown but these people were running all about trampling it, a thing you shouldn't do to crops.

Bittie looked about him through the rain. These creatures did not fit into his sense of fitness of things. He had read quite a bit in his school—he liked the very old romances best—and he hadn't ever encountered anything like this!

There were no old men or old women. There were quite a few children in various bad, unhealthy conditions—potbellies, scabs on them, dirty. Shocking! Didn't anyone properly feed them or clean them up?

Men they passed gave them a funny salute with a raised finger. Ugly, contemptuous faces. Faces of all colors and mixed colors. And all dirty. Their clothing was a kind of joke of a uniform, and not worn with any style, just sloppy.

They seemed to speak some strange kind of English like they had oatmeal in their mouths. He knew *he* didn't talk really good English, not like university men such as Sir Robert, nor as good as Sir Jonnie. But anybody could understand him when he talked and he was trying to improve so that Colonel Ivan's English, which he helped him with, would be good. But these people didn't seem to care if the words even got out of their stinky mouths. Bittie almost bumped into Sir Jonnie, who had stopped in front of a middle-aged man. What language was Sir Jonnie using? Ah, Psychlo! Jonnie was asking something and the Brigante nodded and pointed over to the west and said something back in Psychlo. Bittie got it. Sir Jonnie didn't want to know anything, he just wanted to see whether the Brigante spoke Psychlo. Clever!

Where were they headed? Oh, toward that big lean-to that had a leopard-skin-sort-of flag on a pole in front of it. Bittie saw they had been following the prisoners who were still under guard, probably being taken to their chief.

This was a pretty awful kind of people. They simply halted wherever they were, right in the path, and relieved themselves. Awful. Over there a young man had thrown a girl down and they were . . . yes, they were! Fornicating right out in public.

Bittie turned his head away and tried to purify his thoughts. But the direction he turned showed him a man making a child do something unspeakable.

He began to feel a little ill and walked much closer to Sir Jonnie's heels. These creatures were worse than animals. *Far* worse.

Bittie followed Sir Jonnie into the lean-to. How the place stank! There was somebody sitting on a tree trunk they had built the lean-to over. The man was awfully fat and was yellowish with the yellow that Dr. MacKendrick said was malaria. The folds of the man's body made deep seams of dirt. He had a funny cap on that must be made out of leather; it had a peak in front; there was something set on it—a woman's brooch? some kind of stone—a diamond?

The creature they had captured, Arf, was standing in front of the fat man. With a fist beat on his chest, Arf was making a report. What was he calling the fat man? General Snith? Wasn't "Snit" a Psychlo common name? Wasn't "Smith" the common English name? Terrible hard to tell with that oatmeal accent. The general was chewing on a haunch of something and didn't seem much impressed.

Finally the general spoke: "Didjer gitcher serplies? The sulphur?"

"Well, no," Arf said and tried to tell it all again.

"Didjer bring bock yer stiffs?" the general said. Stiffs? Stiffs? Oh, bodies!

This "captunk" Arf seemed to get a bit scared and back up.

The general hurled the haunch straight at him and hit him in the face with it! "Howjer oxpect ter eat, den!" screamed the general. Eat? Stiffs? Bodies? Eat? Their own dead?

Then Bittie looked down at the thrown "haunch" that had ricocheted toward him. It was a human arm!

Hurriedly Bittie got out of there and got back of the lean-to and was very sick at his stomach.

But Sir Jonnie found him in a moment and put an arm around his shoulders and wiped his mouth with a bandana. He tried to get a Russian to take Bittie back to the plane but Bittie wouldn't go. The place of a squire was with his knight, and Jonnie might need this blast rifle among these *horrible* creatures. So they let him continue to follow.

Sir Jonnie looked into the lean-to in the edge of the trees and seemed very interested, and Bittie looked and saw a very old, very battered instruction machine like the pilots used to learn Psychlo, and this seemed to mean something to Sir Jonnie.

Who were they looking for now? The rain was coming down and these people were racing around and the blast rifle was very heavy and getting heavier. Oh, the Coordinators!

They found them in another lean-to, a pair of young Scots . . . wasn't one of them a MacCandless from Inverness? Yes, he thought he recognized him. They sat there, soaking wet even under cover, their bonnets like mops. They looked pretty white of face.

Sir Jonnie was trying to find out how they got here and they were pointing to a pile of cable—dropped by a plane.

So Sir Jonnie told them they'd better leave with them and they were saying no, it was a Council order to bring these people back to the compound in America, and even though the transports were overdue they had supposed it was trouble for the Council to be finding enough pilots for the lift.

After a lot of argument about their duty—on their side—and their safety—on Sir Jonnie's side, they were persuaded to at least come to the plane where they could be given a food package and maybe some weapons. So they all pushed their way through this mob of people back to where the Russians held a defense perimeter and got into the plane.

Sir Robert was there. He sat the two Scot Coordinators down in one of the big Psychlo bucket seats.

"Was there a third one of you?" Sir Robert wanted to know.

"Well, yes," said MacCandless. "There was Allison. But a couple of days ago he fell in a river and some scaly beast got him."

"Did you see this?" said Sir Robert.

Well, no, they hadn't *seen* it. The general had told them and there were plenty of rivers and lots of scaly beasts.

Sir Jonnie was saying something now: "Did Allison talk Psychlo?"

"He was in pilot training," said MacCandless. "The Federation needs its own pilots sometimes. I suppose he did."

"Yes, he did," said the other Scot. "He could talk some Psychlo. They pulled him out of the class to come here. The order to lift these people out came very suddenly from the Council and we were short—"

Sir Robert said, "Do you recall hearing him talk Psychlo to these ruffians around here?"

They thought for a while. The rain was drumming on the marine attack plane roof and it was awfully hot.

"Aye," said MacCandless finally. "I heard him talking to one of the officers that was finding it remarkable he talked Psychlo. They chattered away in it quite a while. I don't speak—''

''That's all we wanted to know,'' Sir Robert was saying. He looked up at Sir Jonnie meaningfully. ''Interrogation! They wanted him for interrogation!''

And Sir Jonnie was nodding.

Then Sir Robert pulled out something Bittie didn't know he had. A tam-o'-shanter with blood on it. He handed it to the two Coordinators.

They found some thread initials in it. Yes, it was Allison's. Where'd Sir Robert get it?

Sir Robert blasted them very proper. He told them, and Bittie was shocked to learn that the Brigantes had sold Allison to the Psychlos! And the Psychlos must have wanted him for interrogation and god help Allison now. Sold Allison? A human being? To the monsters? Neither Bittie nor the Coordinators could get their wits around that.

There was a dreadful row then. Sir Robert ordered the two Coordinators to come along with them. The Coordinators said this was their duty: to lift these people out; it was a Council order! And Sir Robert thundered at them that he was the War Chief of Scotland and he damned well wasn't going to leave them here. The two Coordinators tried to leave and Sir Jonnie and Sir Robert, using the cargo lashings Bittie hastily found, simply tied them up. They put them on top of the supplies at the rear of the plane.

They withdrew their defense perimeter and took off, and Bittie was not surprised to hear one of the pilots ask permission to strafe these creatures from the air. Sir Robert said no, if they tried that the creatures would just run under the trees; they weren't equipped to handle them right now and they had other things to do; but if they'd done what they appeared to have done, they'd have a bloody feud on their filthy hands. Everybody was pretty upset about Allison.

When they had taken off and were flying back to the compound, Bittie got to pondering those people down there.

He leaned over to Sir Jonnie and said, ''Sir Jonnie, how in all this rain can they be so *dirty?*''

— 2 —

The big marine attack plane landed in the night near the branch mine. It was still deserted. The rain still came down. But there were quarreling sounds of animals over where the skirmish had been fought. The snarls and spits of angry leopards, the shattering barks of some other beast, the eerie cackling laughter of yet another predator. They were fighting over the bodies of the dead.

The flatbed with the flying platform and blast mortar was where it had been prepared just inside the hangar door. There was no sign that the other flatbed had returned in retreat. It must still be following the convoy.

Jonnie looked through the deserted compound again. The lights were still on. The distant mine pumps still pounded away. Unless disturbed by some outside force, all such machinery would probably continue to run for decades.

The planetary traffic printer was still sitting there spewing out paper that recorded current traffic. Jonnie glanced through it. "MacIvor, can you please bring extra fuel to Moscow?" "This is the traffic controller at Johannesburg. Are there any planes en route this way? If not, I can close down for the night." "Isaac, please come in, Isaac. Listen, Isaac, were there any serviceable ore freighters left in the Grozny minesite? And can they be converted for passengers? Please let me know by morning. We're a wee bit shy of carriers right now." "Lundy, we're cancelling you on the Tibet run. We need you and your copilot back here to help with an airlift. Please acknowledge, laddie." Most of it in the pilot jargon of Psychlo.

It struck Jonnie that this stream of messages would give an attacker a pretty good idea of what areas were actively operating. It was almost a catalogue of targets for Mark 32s.

If the convoy got through and these Psychlos mounted an overall attack, they could take back the planet.

He wondered whether he shouldn't put out a general call on this set and order a seventy-two-hour radio silence. But no, the damage was done. These same messages were probably reeling out of the Lake Victoria minesite printer too. And any transmission he made here might be picked up by the convoy, alerting it. Well, he would just have to succeed with the attack on the convoy, that was all.

He walked back through the empty, echoing levels. The Psychlos, he noticed, had mainly stripped the place of armament. They were leaving no blast guns or portable weapons behind to fall into Brigante hands. Lucky they'd overlooked the mortars in their haste.

The flatbed was out of the hangar now, waiting in the dark yard. Jonnie shut the doors of the compound—no use letting in the leopards and elephants and snakes.

He went back to the big plane and did a rapid review of the actions that were about to occur. He told them to fly in very low indeed—hugging ground—from way over to the east and come in behind the ambush point. He didn't want that plane on convoy tank screens. Then deploy along this ridge . . . this one here that flanked the road . . . and when the convoy was well into the ravine, give them a flanking fire. What if they turned around and started back? Well, he'd be back there with a mortar on the flying platform to keep them from retreating.

What? an incredulous Robert the Fox was saying. One mortar against tanks? That's impossible. The convoy would be able to get back into the forest and they'd never get them out. Oh. You want this plane to take off and help block that. Well, that's all right. It *is* a battle plane.

"Just try to roll the tanks and trucks over without exploding them," said Jonnie. "Use no radiation bullets. Just blast gun force. Keep your weapons on 'Broad Blast,' 'No Flame,' and 'Stun.' We don't want to kill them. As soon as they're all strung out along this ravine, block the road from the ambush. I'll block it from the rear. The rest of you flank it from the ridge. This battle plane is to help if they get loose and head back toward the forest. Right?"

"Right, right, right." A Coordinator tried unsuccessfully to make up for the absence of the Russian Coordinator, who was now with Ivan, and then said, "I'll make sure the Russian Coordinator explains it when we get to the others. . . . Oh, I've got it straight. I can tell them then."

"Remember," said Jonnie, "there's a slim possibility that Allison is in that convoy, so keep your eye out for him and if he gets away in the fight, don't shoot him."

"Right, right, right." And they'd get it explained to these Russians here when they caught up with Ivan.

"Smooth," said Robert the Fox. "Oh, so very smooth. The bulk of our force can't be briefed because the translator is elsewhere. What stupendous planning and coordination! I wish us luck. We will need it."

Jonnie said, "But we've got the Psychlos outnumbered."

"What?" exclaimed Robert the Fox. "There's more than a hundred of them and only fifty or so of us."

"That's what I mean," said Jonnie. "We've got them outnumbered one-half to one!"

They got it, and some Russians more advanced in English than the rest explained the joke to the other Russians. They all laughed. The rain had been getting them down. They felt better.

Jonnie was getting down to the flatbed where a Scot and four Russians, one of them a driver, waited, when a scurry in the plane drew his attention. It was Bittie MacLeod, all set to go with him, draped around with equipment.

This was something Jonnie did not want. The coming battle was nothing to drag the boy into. But there was a problem—the boy's pride. Jonnie thought fast. This was almost harder to solve than the tactics!

Bittie's world was filled with the romances of two thousand years ago, when knighthood was in flower, with flame-breathing dragons and pure knights and rescued fair damsels. Nothing wrong with that. He was a sweet little boy and his greatest ambition was to grow up and become a man like Dunneldeen or himself. Nothing wrong with that either. But his dreams risked bruising against the brutal realities of this world in which they fought, a world with its own brand of dragons. He would never live to become like "Prince" Dunneldeen or "Sir" Jonnie if he were not protected. But there was his pride. And it was showing now when he saw Jonnie's pause, saw the search for an excuse to say no in Jonnie's ice-blue eyes.

Hurriedly, Jonnie grabbed a mine radio from a seat and thrust it into the boy's hands. Jonnie tapped the one in his own belt. He leaned very close to Bittie's ear and whispered, "I need a reliable contact on this plane who can tell me, after the battle is joined, if anything is going wrong. Don't use it until the first shot is fired. But if there's anything amiss after that, you tell me fast." He put a finger to his lips.

Bittie was instantly bright, if a trifle conspiratorial. He nodded. "Oh, yes, Sir Jonnie!" and he faded back into the plane.

Jonnie hobbled down the squishy road to the flatbed. It was sitting there, lights stabbing through the sheets of rain. He checked his crew, got in, and nodded to the driver.

The flatbed, with its flying mine platform and mortar, roared, drowning out the snarling fight over in the woods.

They were off in a truck to do combat with tanks.

— 3 —

Brown Limper Staffor sat in his new palatial office and stared down at the offending object on the desk. He was revolted.

Things had been moving well lately. The domed government building—some said it had been the state capitol building—had been partially restored and even its dome painted white. The halls had been refinished. A chamber had been provided for Council sessions—a very ideal chamber with a high dais and bench on one end and wooden seats before it. Huge, upholstered Psychlo executive desks had been carted in to furnish separate offices for Council members (they were a bit dwarfing to sit at, but if one put a man-chair on a box behind them they were all right). A hotel had been opened that provided living space for dignitaries and important visitors, and under the ministrations of a cook from Tibet it was serving very passable meals on real plates.

The tutelage he was getting while standing in the shadows of a post over at the compound at night was truly excellent. Utterly invaluable data about government. Terl hardly deserved the extreme conditions of living in a cage. The Psychlo had repented and was doing all he could to help. How misunderstood the Psychlos were!

The fruits of such learning were already showing up. It was taking a little time and it required a considerable amount of political skill. But Terl had traveled all over the universes as one of the most trusted executives of Intergalactic Mining, and the things he knew about governments and politics were far in excess of anything else available.

Take this matter of having too numerous a Council. The tribal chiefs from over the world resented having to come here and spend endless time wrangling in the chamber; they had their own tribal affairs to look after. They were also too numerous, thirty of them, to really get anything done. And it was almost with joy that they divided the world up into five continents with one representative from each. From an unwieldly throng of thirty, the Council had been reduced to a more easily handled five. And when it was explained to them that their own tribal work was far more vital than this humdrum paper shuffling at the Council, and that the most competent men were needed at home, they had gladly pushed some cousins and such into the five continental seats.

The five-man Council, of course, was a bit unwieldly, and it was in the process now of appointing a two-man Executive. With a little more work and the application of some invaluable tips Terl had given him, sometime in the coming weeks, Brown Limper would find himself the Council representative with authority to act independently in the name of the Council, assisted only by the Council Secretary who, of course, did not need to have a vote and would be required just to sign his name. It would be so much neater.

The Scots had been a bit of trouble. They had protested Scotland being included with Europe, but it was shown that it always had been. This made their representative a German from a tribe in the Alps. Well, majority votes of the old Council had handled that, and now there were no more of those accursed Scots around challenging every sensible measure proposed by Brown Limper.

The tribes were satisfied. They had been given title to all the lands about them with absolute right to allocate them as they chose. They had each been given the exclusive ownership of the ancient cities and anything contained therein. This had made Brown Limper quite popular with the chiefs of most tribes—but not the Scots, of course. Nothing could please *them*. They had had the nerve to point out that this gave all property and the whole continent of America and everything in it to Brown Limper. But that was quashed by simply indicating that there were *four* tribes in America now—British Columbia where two people had been found, the Sierra Nevada where four people had been found, the little group of Indians to the south, and Brown Limper's.

That they all now lived in Brown Limper's village had been quite beside the point!

The selection of a capital had been another victory. For some reason, some tribes thought the world capital should be in their area. Some even thought it should shift about. But when it was pointed out how much trouble and expense it was to maintain a capital and that Brown Limper Staffor, out of the goodness of his heart and with philanthropy as his only motive, would let *his* tribe pay all the costs, there was no further argument. The world capital had been decreed to be "Denver," although its name one of these days would be changed to "Staffor."

The resolution of the old Council, before it became only five, to establish a Planetary Bank, was what had started this trouble now before him.

A Scot named MacAdam had been called in, and he had advised them that the Galactic credits they had would be meaningless to Earth people at this time. Instead he proposed that he and a German now residing in Switzerland, a German who had an awful lot of dairy cows and home cheese factories, be granted a charter. They would issue currency to a tribe to the amount of land it had in actual productive use, and in return they would charge a small percent. It was a good idea for any tribe could only get more currency by getting more area into productive use. The currency was then backed by "The Tribal Lands of Earth." The bank was to be called the Earth Planetary Bank and the charter given it was quite broad and sweeping.

With amazing speed they had printed currency. The German had come in on it because he had a brother who had preserved the art of making woodcutting blocks that printed on paper. They had found warehouses full of untouched currency paper in an old ruin called London and hand presses in a town once called Zurich. In no time at all, they were issuing currency.

The notes only had one denomination: one Earth credit. Apparently they had made one trial issue and it didn't go. People didn't know what to do with it. They had been bartering with horses and suchlike and they had to be taught what money was. So they had made a second issue.

It was a specimen of this second issue that was lying on Brown Limper's desk and giving him much trouble. Not just trouble but a revulsion so deep it was making him ill. The woodblock bill was very nicely printed. It said Earth Planetary Bank. It had a figure [''1''] in each corner. It had [''One Credit''] spelled out in all the languages and calligraphy used by existing tribes. It had [''Legal Tender for All Debts, Private and Public''] on it, similarly repeated in the various tongues. It had [''Exchangeable for One Credit at the Bank Offices of Zurich and London or any branch of the Earth Planetary Bank'']. It had [''Secured by the Tribal Lands of the Tribes of Earth as Attested in Production'']. It had [''By Charter of the Council of Earth'']. And it had the signatures of the two bank directors. All that was fine.

But it had, squarely in the center of it, in a big oval, a portrait of *Jonnie Goodboy Tyler!*

They had copied a picture of him somebody had taken with a picto-recorder. There he was in a buckskin hunting shirt, bareheaded, a silly look on his face somebody thought must be noble or something. And of all things he had a blast gun in his hand.

Worse! There was his name curled over the top of the picture: [''Jonnie Goodboy Tyler''].

And even worse! On the scroll under the picture it said, [''Conqueror of the Psychlos''].

Nauseating. Awful.

But how could the bank make such a blunder?

Not fifteen minutes ago he had finished a conversation with MacAdam on the radio. MacAdam had explained that the first issue was not popular at all. So they had instantly gotten out this second issue. It seemed people might not know what money was, but they could comprehend Jonnie Goodboy Tyler, and in some places they were not using it as money but putting it up on their walls, even framing it. Yes, bundles of it now had gone to every tribe. No, they couldn't be recalled for it would hurt the bank's credit.

Brown Limper had tried to explain that this was totally against the Council's intentions in chartering the bank. There had been a unanimous Council resolution that there must be no more *war*. The resolution had meant ''War between tribes is hereby forbidden,'' but Brown Limper had seen that it was worded so as to include all war everywhere including interplanetary.

This bank note, he had explained with all the logic he could bring to bear, was contrary to that antiwar resolution. They had this . . . this . . . fellow brandishing a weapon and they were actually inciting war in the future against the Psychlos and who knew who else.

MacAdam had been sorry and so had the German in Zurich, but they really didn't sound sorry. They had their charter, and if the Council wanted to ruin its own credit, it would be unfortunate if funds were cut off to America in the future, so the charter must stay valid and unchanged and the bank must do what it saw fit to do in order to carry on its business. And it would be too bad when the World Court now in planning convened, if it had as its first suit a member of the bank against the Council for breach of trust and corollary expenses.

No, Brown Limper thought gloomily. They didn't sound sorry.

He would take no more advice from Council members about this. He would go down and get some while standing in the shadows of the post near the cage. But he didn't have any real hope.

"Jonnie Goodboy Tyler. Conqueror of Psychlos." Brown Limper spat on the bill.

He suddenly seized the bill and tore it frantically into little pieces.

Then he threw the pieces around with angry gestures.

After that he gathered them all up again and, with a set, malevolent expression on his face, burned them.

Then he pulverized the ashes with his fist.

But somebody came in soon after and said with a delighted smile, "Have you seen the new bank note?" And waved one!

Brown Limper rushed out of the room and found a place to vomit.

Later, calmer, he determined that even though they were all against him, he would continue to do his very best for Earth. He would really *get* that Tyler.

— 4 —

The flatbed rumbled and jarred through the soaking wet night. The ground drive of these things was supposed to keep them floating one to three feet off the ground. But when the ground varied eight to ten feet from level every few feet, the effect was far from floating. It was bone jarring.

The teleportation-type drive sought to automatically adjust itself to the sensed ground distance. It corrected and recorrected and the result was a whining, racing, dying, racing combination of rumbles and screeches that hurt the ears.

No wheeled vehicle could have traveled this "road" at all; so gullied and rock strewn a "highway" was fit only for wandering beasts, if that. The ore trucks that had traversed it for hundreds of years had worsened it rather than otherwise as they blew off the humus, the only thing that protected it from the gutting of the rain.

Jonnie was trying to get some sleep. He was dead tired. His left arm ached from constant use of the cane. His palm was calloused now but even it had rubbed raw. Four days of floundering through this forest, four days of constant sweating from the heat, four days of walking with a cane and four nights full of insects had taken their toll. If he wanted to fight a battle with any degree of success, he had better get some sleep.

The seat was, of course, huge. But it was not very cushioned. And when there weren't bumps and jolts, there were stops. Like right now.

He opened his eyes to look through the windscreen. The rumps of elephants! Tails twitching in the headlights, bedewed with rain, they were strolling along, used to these trucks and owning the road for themselves. Psychlo trucks had no car horns but they had bullhorns and the Russian driver was using one now. He was telling those elephants to get off the road. He was repeating some word that sounded like "suk-in-sin" and Jonnie divined it did not mean "elephant." He went back to sleep, bullhorn and all.

The next time he opened his eyes, a leopard was blocking the way. It had killed a mouse deer and was using the road for a dinner table. Jonnie took it that the leopard did not like its meals interrupted. The fangs and glaring green orbs of the eyes indicated it was ready to take on any number of trucks. The bullhorn was going again. Somewhere they had changed drivers and the Scot was at the controls. The leopard heard the Scot battle cry and leaped straight up and off the road and was gone. They passed over the dead mouse deer, once more on their way.

A flatbed could do eighty on the flat. It was straining now to get eight! No wonder it took days to get from the branch compound to the main minesite! Testimony that Psychlos didn't do it any faster lay in the little round-domed roadside houses that occurred every few miles.

Jonnie had stopped at the first one they came to. It was ideal for ambush, and even though he didn't think the Psychlos would leave anybody behind, one should know what lay ahead. But it was just a dome, big enough for four or five Psychlos to stretch out and rest or wait for a repair truck or have lunch. It was bare; a shelter that kept out wild animals and rain, nothing more.

There was no sign of the other flatbed and its crew so they were still following the convoy up ahead.

Toward morning Jonnie woke to find the truck stopped. The lights were on. The rain was still coming down. The driver was tapping Jonnie's shoulder and pointing to the road ahead. Jonnie sat up.

Somebody had hacked some vines and made a sign on the road. It was an arrow. From the clean cuts it appeared to have been done with a claymore or a bayonet. Psychlos would have shot the vines in two. So it was their own people. They'd left them a sign.

It was pointing to a roadside rest hut.

There was a clatter of weapons in the back as his crew made ready in case they dismounted. Jonnie pulled the rain cape around him, checked his belt gun, and picked up a mine lamp and his cane.

The rain drizzled down his neck as he got out.

The only thing different about the mine hut was evidence of recent foot traffic in front of it and a door slightly ajar. Jonnie pushed it open with his cane. The smell of human blood hit him!

There was a scurry of something in there. Jonnie drew his belt gun. But it was only a large rat that came charging out.

The Scot was behind him with an assault rifle. Two Russians were coming up.

Jonnie flooded the mine-lamp light into the place. There was something lying against the far wall. He could not make it out for a moment and stepped forward to find he was walking in blood.

He turned the mine lamp fully on the object. He went closer. It was hard to tell what it was beyond a mangle of shredded flesh. Then he saw a piece of cloth. Part of a . . . kilt!

It was Allison.

The Scot and the Russians stood petrified.

A closer examination showed that every artery and major vein had been left unsevered. Careful Psychlo claws had ripped away the flesh around them, slice by slice. The whole body had been shredded in such a fashion.

It must have taken hours for him to die.

They had left the throat and jaws until last and much of them still remained. Interrogation, Psychlo-style!

There was something in the remains of the hand. A sharp-edged tool Psychlos often carried in their pockets to clean motor points. A major artery on the inside of the leg was parted.

Allison had effected his own death. He must have seized the tool from an unguarded pocket and finished himself.

Could they have rescued him? Not in this forest and on this road, Jonnie thought sadly. The Psychlos must have started his torture at the compound and finished it here when they feared he might be dying.

And they would have learned nothing of any help for their own convoy. Allison had not even known of their own expedition. Ah, but Allison possibly could have told them the numbers and disposition of bases the humans now had. And Allison had probably talked, for there are limits to human endurance.

No, the remaining teeth were chipped with grinding, the jaws seemed to be frozen shut. Possibly Allison had not talked.

But it didn't matter whether he had talked or not. The convoy was doomed. It was doomed in the narrowed eyes of the Russians. It was doomed in the angry clench of the Scot's fist on a claymore.

After a little, the Scot went out and got a tarp and laid it gently over the mess that had been Allison. The Scot said, "We'll be back for ye, laddie. With blood on our blades, never fear!"

Jonnie walked back out into the rain. It came to him suddenly that the Brigantes now had a blood feud with Scotland.

The Psychlos? He was not too sure he wanted them alive now, and he had to make himself be very rational about it.

— 5 —

In the mid-morning twilight of the forest, they caught up with the other flatbed. It was the small beginning of the string of mishaps that were to dog them that day.

Running in the dark, the other flatbed had come to a river, one of the many that wandered through this forest on a more or less westerly course. Their own direction of travel had been to the east of south. The driver, possibly overly tired, had not slacked speed. These ground drives could run on water, if it were reasonably smooth, as the sensors under them could sense water as well as ground. A teleportation drive didn't rest the weight of a vehicle on the surface but held it suspended. But the driver must have hit a bump on the bank and had an unlevel vehicle when he reached the water, and there it sat, nose submerged in the water, disabled.

The crew was sitting there now on the flying mine platform, back in under the trees. They had flown it and the mortar off and put themselves in a posture of defense. They were very happy to see Jonnie. Crocodiles were all over the river bank in front of them and a ring of the beasts were circling around the flying platform—nobody had dared shoot for fear of pulling the convoy back on them.

Jonnie made room for the second platform on his own flatbed and they flew theirs the short distance. The roar of the motors and the bellow and roar of the crocs were deafening, and Jonnie was afraid they might be close enough to the convoy tail to attract attention.

They left the half-submerged flatbed where it lay, and double-loaded with two platforms and two mortars, they crossed the river and continued their pursuit.

Shortly after, the road got better, due possibly to a change of soil. They picked up speed. They had had about a twelve- to fifteen-hour travel gap between the tail and themselves. But a convoy tends to be slower than a single vehicle, particularly in such rough terrain.

They were traveling so fast by early afternoon that they did not see that it was getting lighter ahead. Abruptly they burst out of the forest and onto a wide savannah.

Three miles ahead, there was the convoy tail!

With a prayer they had not been seen, they did a U-turn and got back in the trees.

Jonnie directed them eastward within the thin border of the forest over very rough going. Then they stopped.

The savannah before them was covered with grass and some shrub. Here and there cactus-like plants dotted the wide expanse.

Jonnie got up on the cab to get a better look. Aha! The defile of the ambush was just ahead of the convoy. The lead tank was entering it now. That ravine seemed to be a cut through the southern shoulder of a range of mountains.

Mountains! Up to the northeast, their crowns above the clouds, reared two peaks, enormously tall. Was that ice and snow?

There was something else strange. Then Jonnie had it. It wasn't raining! There was cloud, it was very hot and humid, there was not much sun, but it wasn't raining!

The Russians were buzzing, looking at the convoy. It was impressive. Over fifty vehicles, most of them flatbeds loaded to the last pound with ammunition, fuel, and breathe-gas, were crawling along like some enormous black snake. Three, no five, tanks! The one in the lead was a Basher "Bash our Way to Glory." A nearly impregnable armored vehicle. There was another tank in the middle and three tanks at the end. Now that their own motor was off, the roar of that convoy even at this distance was like thunder.

If the ambush were in place, the ball would open when that whole convoy was in the defile and the mortar up front closed the road in front of them.

Jonnie turned to the Russian officer he had brought. The man spoke hardly any English at all, but with signs and a little relief map drawn in the dirt, Jonnie got across what he wanted him to do. The southern side of the defile ended in a knoll. The right side of the defile was a steep hill, a cliff in fact. If one of the flying platforms could just get behind that knoll and wait until all those vehicles were in the ravine, it could lob mortar shells into this end of the cliff and start an avalanche that would close the back door.

The Russian got it. He and his crew took off in the flying mine platform, flew along inside the border of the trees, and vanished.

Jonnie watched the convoy intently. It was struggling along into the ravine. This was a "set-piece battle," the kind he'd read of in old man-books. When the whole convoy got into that defile, the ambush would avalanche the road closed in front of them, and the mortar he'd just sent would close the road behind them. They would have a soaring slope on their right and cliffs on their left. They wouldn't be able to turn around. And one had only to fly over them and tell them to surrender and it would all be over, just like that. But set-piece battles seldom come off, as they were about to discover.

They waited for the convoy to enter fully. There was just a momentary glimpse of the platform they had sent in as it settled into position. Perfect. Now all they had to do was wait for the last tank to enter. The head of the convoy was now out of Jonnie's sight. Nearly all the convoy was in the ravine.

Then BLAM! The ambush mortar let go. BLAM! BLAM! BLAM!

But the last three tanks were not yet in the gap.

Jonnie dove for the console of the flying platform. His four-man crew scrambled up to hold on.

The flying platform soared into the air, Jonnie's fingers dancing on its rudimentary keyboard. He took it up a thousand feet, south of the road and near the forest edge.

He could see the head of the convoy now. A roaring avalanche was falling across the road in front of the Basher tank. He could see some Russians in a reserve group back of the ambush point. He spotted three Russians along the crest to the convoy's right, hundreds of feet above the vehicles.

The Basher sought to climb the roadblock. Its guns would not elevate high enough. It backed and then charged the dust-geysering rock pile. The tank's nose lifted and it began to fire.

Blast after blast arced up from the tank. It must be firing explosive shells! They soared in a glowing curve up and dropped in the area where the ambush command post must be. But the mortar up there was still firing down.

The last three tanks in the convoy were backing up. There was no way this end could be sealed!

Jonnie took the flying platform halfway between the convoy tail and the woods. The end tanks were now turning around. Let loose on this savannah they would be very hard to handle even with planes. Yes, they were also Bashers. No, a plane couldn't handle them.

At the head of the convoy the tank charged the rock barrier again, probably to elevate its gun muzzles. The tank in the center of the convoy was firing toward the ambush point but could not fire up the steep slope to the crest.

Jonnie yelled to the Scot. "Start felling trees across their road!"

The Scot got it and angled the mortar around. The Russians, holding on to the thin, tilting platform, began to drop mortar shells into the stubby barrel.

They landed a shell beside a giant tree near the road back into the forest and it began to topple.

Mortar blast after mortar blast flashed at the forest edge. Trees began to fall amid towering columns of dust. Jonnie was sighting the mortar in by tilting the platform.

The three tanks saw the road back closing in front of them. They knew they could not get through and into the forest. They started to fan out on the savannah.

Their guns opened up trying to hit the flying platform.

Jonnie dodged their misused vehicle about. It had no armor. It was really just a flat plate. There was even hardly anything to hold on to.

Dunneldeen flashed down with the battle plane. He must have been up there thousands of feet and out of sight.

Gouts of flame and dirt began to pound around the three Basher tanks.

Suddenly, the convoy in the ravine began to close up. Evidently thinking it was moving again, the three tanks swerved and raced back to the convoy tail, mindful of their duty to protect it. They stubbed right onto the trail. Then they too halted. They were trying to fire up at the ambush point. They could not elevate to reach the crest of the slope to their left.

The other flying platform opened up.

Blast mortar shells crashed into the cliff behind the last tank. The rocks and dirt flashed into the air. An avalanche roared down and closed the back door.

The lead Basher tried another charge at the rockslide blocking their forward progress. Just at the instant its nose reared up, a mortar struck under it.

The lead Basher flew up, rolled over in a back summersault, and lay upside-down in the road, helpless.

Jonnie drew a deep breath. He was just about to tell Dunneldeen to open up on a bullhorn and demand surrender and was reaching for his belt mine radio to do so, when their fortunes reversed.

— 6 —

Debacle!

Cutting in through the chatter of Psychlos in the convoy, but clearly heard because of its high pitch, the piping voice of Bittie said, "There's nobody left here speaks Russian! Sir Jonnie! There's nobody to tell the Russians anything!"

"What's happened?" barked Jonnie.

"Sir Jonnie, the tank shots wiped out the command post here! Sir Robert and Colonel Ivan and the Coordinators are knocked out! I was under a tarpaulin pile. I would have told you sooner but—" a wail—"I couldn't find my radio!"

Then static and a babble of Psychlo voices on the same wavelength.

Jonnie swung the flying platform north of the ravine and behind it, using it for protection.

Below in the ravine the jammed convoy clogged the road. It couldn't turn. It couldn't escape. But neither could they fire into all that ammunition and fuel and breathe-gas without blowing the whole thing a mile high.

There were only a few shots being fired down by the Russian soldiers. Only three of them were on the crest. The Psychlos must have thought the crest was not held.

There was a battery of commands on the mine radio.

Suddenly the Psychlos unloaded from their vehicles, grabbing blast rifles. They lined up along the bottom of the slope. Breathe-gas masks in place.

More Psychlo commands.

The line of huge bodies surged forward all along the slope bottom. It was four hundred yards or more, very steep yards, up to the crest. They were going to storm the crest!

But no real disaster yet. Dunneldeen was in place up in the

sky. It was very obvious that all he had to do was wait for those Psychlos to get halfway up that slope and then set his guns on stun and knock them flat and unconscious.

Then Bittie's voice again. "The Russians don't understand! They're rushing up to the crest!"

Jonnie lifted the platform a little higher to see. Bittie himself seemed confused. There was nothing wrong with the Russians manning that long top of the ravine's left side. In fact, they'd better.

Yes, the reserve group of about thirty Russians were sprinting from in back of the crest, their assault rifles ready. The upcoming line of Psychlos was about a hundred yards up now and still had three hundred yards of very steep slope to climb.

In just a few moments now, when those Psychlos were far enough up from their trucks, Dunneldeen could make a pass with guns and stun them flat.

Bittie's voice, "These Russians are awful mad about Colonel Ivan! They think he's dead! They're not listening!"

Jonnie slammed the flying platform down behind the Russians and jumped off. He started toward the cliff. The Russians had reached it. Several were firing down at the Psychlos.

"Hold off!" Jonnie yelled at them. "That plane will knock them down!"

Not one Russian face turned in his direction. He looked wildly about for one of their officers. He saw one. But the man was yelling something down the slope at the Psychlos and firing a pistol at them.

The officer roared something at his men. They rose up—good lord! They were going to charge!

Before Dunneldeen could make his firing pass, the downslope was loaded with charging, shouting Russians. They were angry, beserk! They stopped, fired, ran, stopped, fired!

The slope was a roaring sheet of flame going both up and down!

Psychlos tried to stem this avalanche of ferocity. Assault rifles were hammering and flaming. Blast guns were roaring.

Dunneldeen, unable to shoot without killing Russians, hung helplessly in despair. One pass and those Psychlos would be knocked into unconsciousness.

The Russians were in among the Psychlos, firing ceaselessly!

The remaining Psychlos tried to run back to their vehicles. The Russians were right on top of them!

Huge bodies went tumbling down the slope. Isolated groups tried to stand their ground. Assault rifles racketed into solid sheets of sound. Then one last Psychlo almost made it to the cab of a truck. A Russian knelt, sighted, and cut him in two.

A cheer went up from the Russians.

The slope went quiet.

Jonnie surveyed the ruin.

Over a hundred Psychlo bodies. Three dead Russians.

Smoke drifting up from clothing that still burned.

Disaster! They had been there to capture Psychlos!

Jonnie went plunging down the slope. He found the Russian officer standing there, obviously intending to shoot any Psychlo that twitched.

"Find some alive!" Jonnie shouted at him. "Don't finish off the wounded. Find some alive!"

The Russian looked at him with battle-glazed eyes. Seeing it was Jonnie, he began to unwind a bit. He fished about for some English. "That show Psychlo! They kill colonel!"

Jonnie finally got it across that he wanted them to find any live ones. Neither the officers nor the rest of the Russians thought this very sensible. They did finally understand it. They went poking among the recumbent Psychlos to find any that were still breathing, a fact that could be determined by a flutter of a breathe-mask valve.

They finally located about four that were shot up but still alive. They couldn't move the thousand-pound bodies very much but they straightened them out.

MacKendrick put in an appearance, walking, half-sliding down the slope. He looked at the four and shook his head. "Maybe. I don't know much about Psychlo anatomy but I can stop that green blood oozing out."

One of them had a different tunic from the rest. An engineer? "Do all you can!" he told MacKendrick and hobbled up the slope toward the ambush point.

Bittie was beckoning to him from the top of a rock, then scrambled down and vanished behind it.

Jonnie came up and surveyed the scene. The command post they had chosen was a hollow in the rocks and it was a mess. The Basher tank had scored a hit just above it.

The gear was all smashed up. Their radio was in bits.

Bittie was kneeling beside Sir Robert, lifting his head. The old veteran's eyes were blinking. He was coming to.

They were stunned with concussion. Some blood was coming out of their ears and noses. Jonnie walked closer. Probably some broken fingers, lots of bruises. None of it serious.

With water from a canteen on a bandana, he went about the work of bringing them around. Robert the Fox, Colonel Ivan, two Coordinators, and a Scot radioman.

Jonnie clambered up on a rock and looked down the defile. The convoy was all there. Nothing had blown up so the Russians must have been using plain, not radioactive, slugs. But they hadn't been after the material. They'd been after live Psychlos.

Three Russians and Angus were getting the lead Basher tank open, a trick to do for it was upside-down, which sealed its hatches. Angus got a side port open with a torch. The Russians looked in. Jonnie cupped his hands. "Any alive in there?"

Angus saw him up there, looked into the tank and back up to Jonnie: Angus shook his head negatively. He called back, "Crushed and suffocated!"

Sir Robert had made his way up to Jonnie, very shaky and white of face. Jonnie looked at him.

Sir Robert started to speak and Jonnie joined him in chorus.

"The best-planned raid in history!"

— 7 —

It took them three hard-working days to clean up the mess and occupy the Lake Victoria minesite.

The ore road had gone south to skirt the mountain ranges and turned back north to the minesite itself.

In full view when the overcast parted, to the northwest of the minesite, were the Mountains of the Moon. It was a long range that contained at least seven peaks up to sixteen thousand feet high. Right here on the equator, in all this heat and humidity, one didn't look for snow and ice, but there it was atop those peaks. There were even glaciers up there; now and then the towering tops were briefly visible, blazingly white.

At one time this range had been the border between two or three countries of ancient times. At the period of the Psychlo invasion or perhaps before, the passes had been mined with nuclear tactical weapons. Needless to say, close as the mountains were to the minesite, the Psychlos never went there. There were several small tribes in the Mountains of the Moon, brown and black and even some whites remaining; they were often starved despite the teeming forests and savannahs full of game below them, and although they could come down now, long tradition kept them from approaching the minesite.

An ancient dam the man-maps said was the [''Owens Falls Dam''] provided power for the minesite, power so plentiful that the Psychlos just left all lights blazing.

This was an extensive minesite with seven underground levels and many branches working for tungsten and cobalt, and it was plentifully supplied with machinery and equipment. But MacArdle in his original raid had blown up their fuel and ammunition plant and all their dumps.

The four wounded Psychlos were in a sealed-off section of the dormitory and breathe-gas was pumping into it. MacKendrick did not have much hope for them but he was working on it.

The problem of the other bodies they had solved. There was no morgue, and fighting time in this equatorial heat, they had hastily gotten forklifts and ore freighters from the minesite and lofted the Psychlo bodies up through the clouds to the freezing temperatures and crusted ice and snow of a mountain peak once called, the man-maps said, [''Elgon'']. They were up there now, ninety-seven bodies, around a thousand pounds each, neatly laid out in the frigid zone.

''We may have no diplomas,'' Dunneldeen had said when they finished, ''but it would seem we are pretty good Psychlo undertakers!'' And then he looked down from the dizzy altitude to the plains below and added, ''Or is it overtakers?'' The Scots scorned his joke, it was so terrible.

They had opened up the road with blade scrapers and righted the Basher tank with a crane and driven the vehicles the rest of the way to the minesite. Despite company regulations they stored the fuel, ammunition, and breathe-gas underground out of the way of attack. They were experts in attacking such dumps.

Thor had come back to help them. He said some of the people in the tribes had seen the flashes of the battle and when they heard the last Psychlos were mopped up they had named the day the Tyler Battleday. Thor had flown a hunting party down to the savannah and they had come back with game and there had been a lot of feasting and dancing. "It is sometimes very gratifying, Jonnie, to be taken for you! But I had to disappear during the battle. You can't be in two places at once." Thor had spotted the convoy exit from the forest and had discreetly stood by at two hundred thousand feet to assist if needed. He had full picto-recorder discs of the whole battle and was surprised that nobody wanted to see them.

Tired, glad to be out of the rain, they sat around in the huge chairs of the Psychlo recreation hall. Jonnie was looking through the pilot traffic that still spewed out on the printer. Nothing unusual. He threw it down.

"We better get to work," said Jonnie.

They *had* been working. What did you call what they'd been doing if not working? Robert the Fox shook his head. Angus looked at his hands, bruised by wielding heavy torches and twisting open oversized locks. Dunneldeen just stared and thought of the flight hours ferrying dead Psychlos to the snow. Colonel Ivan whispered back of a bandaged hand to the Coordinator who then told him what Jonnie had said, and he looked back frowning. Hadn't his people been killing every Psychlo in sight and driving trucks and cleaning a minesite and doing everything else?

"Well," said Jonnie, "I hate to have to tell you that we aren't here to do all that."

All right. But then what—

"We're here," said Jonnie, "to find out why the Chamco brothers committed suicide."

The devil with the Chamcos. They were just Psychlos and they'd tried to kill Jonnie—

So Jonnie made a speech. He paused now and then to let the Coordinator catch up for the Russians present.

He told them that they did not know whether or not Psychlo was still there as a functioning planet. He told them about the Galactic Bank note and all the races listed on it, and he remembered he had one and passed it around.

They realized what he was saying. Earth was wide open to counterattack. If the Psychlo planet were still there, it would eventually counterattack with new gas drones. And these other races possibly had means of reaching Earth swiftly. And when they found there were no Psychlo defenses here, they could slaughter the place if they had a mind to.

The only way to find out was to rebuild the teleportation shipment rig and get it cracking.

But the Psychlos put on the project had attacked him when he questioned them on that subject.

They got it. They also got the fact that no other group or organization was working to handle these problems or the defenses of the planet.

"Which elects us," Jonnie said.

They agreed.

"So, Angus, I want you to set up that machine they said you used on me to feel that steel splinter. And we're going to set it up and start looking in Psychlo heads! If we find something and if one of those Psychlos that are still alive can be operated on, we will have somebody we can make rebuild the teleportation rig and we're in! We can cast picto-recorders out and look at Psychlo and we can look at these other civilizations and then we'll know where we are. Right now we're listing in the cloud layers with no direction but down. Without knowing, I think we're dead men."

"We have all their mathematics and texts on teleportation," said Angus. "I've seen them, man. I've even held them in my hands!"

"But you haven't made any sense out of them," said Jonnie. "I tried for weeks to unravel them. I'm no mathematician but there's something wrong with those mathematics. They just don't work out! So we need a Psychlo who won't commit suicide if we ask him."

"Tell me, Jonnie," said Dr. MacKendrick, "I see no evidence of anything in their heads. You can't X-ray, or whatever you call it, thoughts!"

"When I was lying around trying to get back the use of my hand and arm," said Jonnie, "I got hold of a lot of man-books on the subject of the brain. And you know what I found?"

They didn't know.

"Way back when man had hospitals and lots of surgeons and engineers," said Jonnie, "clear back, maybe twelve hundred years ago, they were experimenting with planting electric capsules in the heads of babies to regulate their behavior. To make them laugh or cry and get hungry just by pressing a button."

"What a disgusting experiment," said Robert the Fox.

"They had an idea," said Jonnie, "that they could control the whole population if they put electric capsules in their heads."

The Coordinator translated for Colonel Ivan. He said there was a myth that that had been tried—controlling whole populations—in Russia, and nobody liked it.

"I don't know they ever succeeded," said Jonnie. "But when I looked this Chamco thing over, I had a clue about it. Why should two hitherto cooperative renegades, happily signed up on good contracts, suddenly attack me when I said certain words? I have reviewed the discs somebody cut. I was pressing them to rebuild the teleportation transshipment rig and they started to get upset and then I said these words: 'If you will explain to me . . .' and they both went crazy and attacked."

"Maybe they were just withholding information," said Robert the Fox. "They—"

"They committed suicide two days later," said Jonnie. "After that I asked Ker whether he had ever heard of Psychlos committing suicide and he said yes, one did, an engineer on a planet he'd served on. They used an alien race there and the Psychlo engineer had gone out drinking one night, killed an alien, and then two days later committed suicide. That was the only one he ever heard of. Also," he added impressively, "they return all corpses to Psychlo. There must be something in them they don't want found."

The group buzzed to each other and got their wits around it.

"So I am guessing that Psychlos, when they are babies," said Jonnie, "get something put in their heads to protect their technology!"

MacKendrick and Angus were very interested now.

"So that's what we've been doing," said Robert the Fox.

Angus went to their ship to assemble the device. MacKendrick went to a dormitory section to set up tables. Dunneldeen and Thor went off to the mountain peak to bring down a couple of corpses, Dunneldeen calling himself and Thor "the gruesome twosome."

If Jonnie was right or Jonnie was wrong, they would know more very shortly.

The planet *was* wide open to counterattack.

Robert the Fox went out and got an antiplane battery manned and arranged for twenty-four-hour alert and pilot scrambles. This tiny group, under half a hundred, only four or five pilots, and an antiplane battery that had already failed to shoot down one of the minesite attack craft, to defend a whole planet? Ridiculous! But he went through the motions. At least for local defense.

— 8 —

"Who are you?" said Terl. He had no trouble at all in seeing the figure who stood in the shadow of the post. It was a brilliantly clear, moonlit night, so bright that even the snow-capped peaks of the Rockies gleamed.

Lars Thorenson had brought the newcomer down to the cage at senior Councilman Staffor's request. Lars had totally flunked out of pilot training after trying a "combat maneuver" so impossible that it crashed him, wiped out a plane, and cracked his neck. He had been appointed "language assistant" to the Council. The plaster cast collar he was wearing did not interfere with his talking. He had been told to bring the newcomer down to the cage, turn off the electricity, hand in a mine radio, give the newcomer another mine radio, and then with no mine radio of his own withdraw. Lars was very punctilious about his duties—he had accepted the appointment on the condition that he could now also spread fascism among the tribes, which made both him and his father very happy. This newcomer had really stunk up the ground car! Suddenly Lars remembered he was also to tell the cadet on guard duty to go elsewhere, so he rushed off to find him and tell him just that.

Terl looked at this newcomer, hoping his contempt for the animal wouldn't show through his face mask or sound in his voice. He knew all about General Snith of the Brigantes. As security officer, war officer, and political officer of this planet, he was very well informed about this band. Like all security officers before him, Terl had accepted the situation of a human group in a rainy forest who couldn't be reached or observed and who had developed a symbiotic relationship with the Psychlos. The Brigantes had kept all other races wiped out and had delivered hundreds of thousands of Bantu and Pygmies to the branch minesite. The only attraction that place had was that you could occasionally buy a human creature to torture. Yes, Terl not only knew all about them but he had personally engineered their transport over here.

Terl had persuaded the creature Staffor that what he needed was a true and reliable corps of troops for this place. Staffor had vehemently agreed—you couldn't trust those Scots, they were too sly and treacherous; you also shouldn't use cadets who seemed to have some damnable and misplaced admiration for that Tyler.

The Brigantes had come but Staffor seemed to be having trouble with the negotiation with them, so Terl had suggested their chief be sent down.

"Who are you?" repeated Terl in the mine radio. Did the creature speak Psychlo as was reported?

Yes, the next words were Psychlo, but a Psychlo spoken as though the thing had goo-food in its mouth. "The question be, who the crap crud be you?" said General Snith.

"I am Terl, the chief security officer of this planet."

"Then what be you doing in a cage?"

"An observation post that keeps the humans out."

"Ah," said Snith, understanding. (Who did this Psychlo think he was fooling?)

"I understand," said Terl, "that you have had some difficulty coming to terms." (You crud brain: I pull you out of a jungle and you don't realize my power!)

"It be the back pay," said Snith. It seemed quite natural to be talking to a Psychlo over a mine radio. He had never talked to one any other way. So maybe this interview was on the level after all. This Psychlo knew the proper form.

"Back pay?" said Terl. He could understand somebody being concerned about that, but he thought it was a barter system of explosive ingredients for humans.

"We was hired by the international bank," said Snith. He knew his legends and he knew his rights, and he was very good at trading. Very good indeed. "At one hundred dollars a day per man. We ain't been paid."

"How many men, how long?" said Terl.

"I calculate in rough figures one thousand men for, let's say, one thousand years."

The rapid skill Terl had with mathematics told him this was 36,500 a year per man; 36,500,000 per year for all the men; and

36,500,000,000 in total. But he made a test. "Why," said Terl, in a shocked voice, "that's more than a million!"

Snith nodded gravely. "Just so! They won't agree to it." This Psychlo knew when he was in a boxed ambush. Maybe he could do business with him after all.

Terl had his answer. The piece of crap couldn't do common arithmetic! "You were hired, you say, by the international bank to take Kishangani of Haut-Zaïre and then take Kinshasa and overthrow the government and wait for bank representatives to come in and negotiate for proper payment of loans. Is that right?"

Snith had said nothing of the sort, not in that detail. The legends were a trifle vague. But he realized abruptly that he was talking to somebody who really knew his business.

Terl always knew his business. He hadn't even bothered to review any of this. It was a security chief joke and had been for more than a thousand years on this planet. They had had all the details from a captured mercenary, properly interrogated over several days way back when; it had made delicious reading. "But your ancestors," Terl bore on remorselessly, "only captured Kishangani. They never went on to capture Kinshasa."

Snith had dimly known that, but he had hoped it wouldn't come up. His ancient forebearers had been crudely interrupted by the Psychlo invasion. He wasn't sure what was coming now.

"You see," said Terl, "the international bank has been taken over." He hoped this crap brain would swallow this outrageous set of lies. "The Galactic Bank, located in the Gredides System, bought them out."

"Gredides System?" gawped Snith.

"You know," said Terl, "Universe Eight." This much was true, where the Galactic Bank was. Always sweeten lies with a little truth.

"Ah," said Snith, totally adrift. He better watch it. This Psychlo would swindle him. It had happened before. He was on the alert.

"And," lied Terl, "you will be glad to know that it took over all obligations of the international bank and that includes yours."

This quick reversal almost spun Snith.

"So as one of the agents for the Galactic Bank," (if he only were!), "I am authorized to pay you the back pay. But your ancestors only did half their job so you only get half the back pay. That would be five hundred thousand dollars.' He was wondering what a dollar was. "I'm sure that will be acceptable."

Snith came out of his fog like a shot. He had expected nothing! "Yes," he said deliberately, "I think I can persuade my men to accept that." Creepo! That would be ten dollars a man and the rest for himself. Riches!

"Now is there any other trouble? Quarters? They found you quarters?"

Snith said yes, they'd given them a whole "serbub" in the town up there, a square mile of old houses and buildings in the outskirts. Bad repair, but palaces really.

"You should also insist on some uniforms," said Terl. He was looking at this filthy creature over there in its monkey skins and crossed bandoliers of poisoned arrows and a diamond in a peaked leather cap. "You should also clean yourself up, comb your fur. Look more military."

This was rank criticism! Snith became very cross. He himself was spit and polish and so was his unit. All twenty of his commandos, fifty men in each, properly officered, trained to the nth degree! (He slowed down, hoping they wouldn't notice it was only thirty-five to the commando these days, the food situation being what it had become.)

"And food?" said Terl.

Snith was startled. Could this Psychlo read his mind? "Food is bad!" said Snith. "There be plenty of dead bodies in those houses but they be old and dried and unfit to eat. There would got to be a clause in any future contract about better food!"

Belatedly, Terl remembered that these Brigantes were reputed cannibals, a fact that had lessened their trade with the minesite over the centuries. Sternly he said, "There can be no such clause!" His whole plan could be wrecked if they threw these creatures out. His studies, when he was doing the lode plan, had isolated some data in Chinko books indicating that these human animals curiously objected to cannibalism. He had at one time considered using the Brigantes for his gold plan but they had been far away, and also they might have run around yammering about no food due to the scarcity of humans in these parts.

"For the duration of this contract," said Terl, "you will just have to put up with cattle as food."

"It tastes funny." said the Brigante chief. He was willing to concede the point. His brigade had had to eat an awful lot of water buffalo and monkey and elephant. But it wouldn't do to be too agreeable. Be a hard bargainer! "But all right, if the pay is good."

Terl told him then that he himself intended to go back to Psychlo very soon and he would personally collect their back pay at the Galactic Bank and return it here. And that meanwhile they should hire on as the sentries and military force of this compound and the Council.

"You'll bring the back pay back?" said Snith. "All half-million?"

"Yes, you have my word on it."

The word of a Psychlo? Snith said, "I and six of my picked men will go with you to see that you do!"

Although Terl didn't know whether the Imperial government would want to interrogate them—the Imperial government would want a very important, knowledgeable man—he readily agreed. Who cared about what happened to Snith once Terl's plan was executed!

"Of course, and welcome," smiled Terl. "Providing of course you help me all you can until we go. Anything else?"

Yes, there was. Snith fished out something and gingerly approached the cage. He laid it down between the temporarily de-electrified bars and withdrew as was proper.

Terl tugged his chain over and picked the item up.

"They want to pay us in that stuff," said Snith. "It's only printed on one side and *I* think it might be counterfeit!"

Terl took it closer to a cage light. What was this thing? He couldn't read any of the characters on it. "I doubt you can even read this!" he challenged.

"Oh yes, I did," said Snith. He couldn't read either, but somebody had read it to him. "It do say it is one credit and is legal for payment of all debts. And around the picture it says, 'Jonnie Goodboy Tyler, The Conqueror of the Psychlos.' " That was what disturbed him really, that the Psychlos were said to have been conquered.

Terl thought fast. "Indeed it *is* a counterfeit and a lie as well!"

"I thought so," said Snith. They always tried to trick you. His ancestors had known that very firmly. Trick before you are tricked, they used to say about all dealings.

"But I'll tell you what I will do," said Terl into the mine radio. "Just so you know who you are really working for, you accept this and say nothing, and when we get to the Galactic Bank, I will redeem it in cold, hard cash!''

That was fair. Now he knew who he was really working for. Made a lot of sense, quite proper. Paid by one group but working for another. This Psychlo was straight after all.

''That's fine,'' said Snith. ''By the way, I know that man in the picture.''

Terl looked closer. The light had been bad. By crap, it *did* look like his animal! He tried to remember whether he had ever heard its name. Yes, he dimly recalled the strange words. Yes, it was the damned animal!

''That bird just waltzed in and wiped out a whole commando of mine,'' said Snith. ''Not too long ago. Attacked them without even a salute, mowed them down. And then stole their bodies and a truckload of trade goods!''

''Where?''

''In the forest, where else?''

This was news! His intelligence said that this creature in the picture had been flying around visiting tribes! Or maybe this was how he visited tribes! That was probably it. Terl knew he himself would visit tribes that way. Ah, well, he knew Staffor would be very, very happy indeed to know that! The animal was not where he was thought to be and he was making war on peaceful tribes. Staffor was a very apt political pupil. Now he would make him a very apt military pupil: in the dumb way that was the only one possible.

But to business. He put the bank note back on the ledge between the bars, withdrew, and Snith retrieved it.

''So we've settled the contract matter and you can negotiate it further,'' said Terl. ''Get settled in and in a very few weeks or even sooner you'll be doing your duty here. Right?''

''Indeed so,'' said Snith.

''And as a bonus,'' said Terl, ''I'll persuade certain parties to authorize you to kill the animal who wronged you on sight.''

That was very, very good. And Snith was driven back to the old city by a dutiful Lars, who endured the stink in the name of spreading the righteous creed of fascism and the great military leader, Hitler.

— 9 —

The underground room at the Lake Victoria minesite was chilled. Angus had rigged heavy-duty motor cooling coils along the wall and the humidity in the air dripped from them and made dark pools along the floor.

The metal and mineral analysis machine hummed; its screen cast an eerie green light on everything around it. Five tense faces were turned to that screen: Dr. MacKendrick's, Angus's, Sir Robert's, Dunneldeen's, and Jonnie's.

Massive, more than eighteen inches in diameter, the ugly head of the Psychlo corpse lay on the machine's plate. Such a head was mostly bone. It bore considerable resemblance to a human head and could be mistaken for one in bad light, but where a human had hair, eyebrows, fleshy lips, nose, and ears, the Psychlo had bone whose shape was more or less the same as the corresponding human features, and the distribution and spacing were similar; the result was a kind of caricature of a human head. Until you touched the features, they did not seem to be bone, but contact proved them hard and unyielding.

The analysis machine was not penetrating the head. Not only were the features bone but the whole top half of the skull was bone. As the parson in his earlier, inexpert autopsy had discovered, the brain was low down and to the back; he had discovered nothing in the brain because he had not opened the brain of the cadavers.

"Bone!" said Angus. "It's almost as hard to penetrate as metal!"

Jonnie could attest to that from the negligible effects of his kill-club on Terl's skull back in the morgue.

Angus was resetting dials. The Psychlo letters were codings for various metals and ores. He swung the intensity dial up five clicks.

"Wait!" said MacKendrick. "Back it up one! I thought I saw something."

Angus backed the intensity of penetration dial back one, then two. It was sitting on "Lime" now

There was a hazy difference in density on the screen, one little spot. Angus adjusted the beam's "in depth" control, focusing it. The internal bones and fissures of the skull came clear on the screen. Five pairs of eyes watched intensely.

The Scot's fingers took another knob, one that swept a second beam to various positions in the subject.

"Wait," said MacKendrick. "Move the beam back to about two inches behind the mouth cavity. There! Now focus it again." Then, "That's it!"

There *was* something there, something hard and black on the screen that was not passing waves at this intensity. Angus touched the recorder of the machine and the whir-flap sound of registry of the images on the paper roll was loud.

"They *do* have something in their skulls!" said Robert the Fox.

"Not so fast," said MacKendrick. "We jump to no conclusions. It could be some fragment of an old injury, some metal picked up in a mine explosion."

"Naw, naw, naw," said Robert the Fox. "It's very plain!"

Jonnie had pulled out the recording sheets. They had the metal analysis trace squiggling down one side. He had left the Psychlo metal analysis code book, usually used to analyze drone transmissions as they hunted a surface for ore, outside. It was chill and dank and odorous in this room and he didn't care much for this job, vital as it was. He took this opportunity to go out and look it up.

Page after page he compared the squiggle he had with the illustrations. It took a long time. He was no expert at this. He couldn't find it. Then he got clever and began to compare composites of *two* squiggle illustrations.

The Psychlo engineers who would do this sort of thing could probably have told him with no code book. He cursed the anger of the Russians who, believing they were avenging their colonel, had slaughtered the Psychlos. The four in the guarded room of the dormitory were in very bad condition. Two of them were ordinary miners, one was an executive by his clothes and papers, and the other was an engineer. MacKendrick was very doubtful that they would make it. He had extracted bullets and sewn them up but they were all still unconscious or appeared so, and they lay there in the breathe-gas ventilated room, chained to their beds, breathing shallowly. There wasn't even a first-aid handbook for

Psychlos that Jonnie had ever seen. He didn't think there was one issued. The company might require all bodies to be returned but it didn't require that anybody keep them alive—a fact that tended to confirm that the sole reason for returning dead Psychlo bodies was to prevent examination by alien eyes—there was no sentiment involved. There were never even any hospital sections in these compounds, and mine accidents were very frequent.

Hold it. One of these squiggles in the book almost matched: copper! Now if he could find the little tail squiggle somewhere—here it was: tin! He overlaid the two squiggles. They seemed to match better. Copper and tin? Not quite. There was a tiny squiggle remaining. He searched for it. He found it: lead!

Mainly copper, some tin, and a little bit of lead! He put the patterns one on top of the other. They matched now.

There was another code book, very thick, called "Composite Ore Bodies for Drone Scan Analysis," and because it had about ten thousand characters in it he had shunned it. But this one he had just done made a look-up easy. He looked under "Copper Deposits," and then its subheading, "Tin Deposits," and then its sub-subheading, "Lead Deposits," and he found his squiggle. Not only that, he found, by comparing it to variations, that the analysis of "per-elevens" (Psychlos used the eleven integer) was five copper, four tin, and two lead.

He went further and looked this up in a man-book and it said ["Bronze"] for such a combination. Apparently it was a very durable alloy that lasted for centuries and there had even been a ["Bronze Age"] where implements were mainly ["bronze"]. Great. But it struck him as funny that an advanced technical race should be using ancient bronze in a skull. Amusing.

He went back inside with his findings to discover that MacKendrick, with a hammer and chisel-like instrument, had been taking the head apart. Jonnie was just as glad not to have been around to watch that.

"We searched all through the rest of the skull with the machine," said Angus. "That's the only odd thing in there."

"I went through its pockets," said Robert the Fox. "He is the lowest-class miner. His identity card says his name was Cla and he had forty-one years' service and three wives back on Psychlo."

"The company paid them benefits?" said Dunneldeen.

"No," said Robert the Fox, showing him the crumpled record,

"it says here the company paid him also for the female earnings in a company 'house,' whatever that is."

"The economics of Psychlo husbandry," said Dunneldeen, "are a credit to their morality."

"Don't joke," said Jonnie. "The object in his head is an alloy called 'bronze.' It is not magnetic, worse luck. It would have to be operated out. It can't be pulled out with a magnet."

Dr. MacKendrick now had the brain laid bare. With a surgeon's skill, he was parting things that looked like cords.

And there it was!

It was shaped like two half-circles back to back and the circles were slightly closed, each one around a separate cord.

"I think these are nerves," said MacKendrick. "We will know shortly." He was delicately pulling the objects off the cords. He wiped the green blood off it and put it on the table. "Don't touch any of this," said MacKendrick. "Autopsies can be deadly."

Jonnie looked at the thing. It was a dull yellow. It was about half an inch across at its widest point.

Angus picked it up with a tweezer and put it on the analysis machine plate. "It's not hollow," he said. "It's just solid. Just a piece of metal."

MacKendrick had a little box with wires and clips on it. It had a small fuel cartridge in it to generate electricity. But before he connected anything with his gloved hands he was distracted by the character of these cords in the head. It was a brain, but it was vastly different from a human brain.

He cut off a small cord end and a slice of skin from the cadaver's paw and went over to an old makeshift microscope. He made a slide from a thin specimen and looked into the eyepiece.

MacKendrick whistled in surprise. "A Psychlo isn't made of cells. I don't know their metabolism but their structure isn't cellular. Viral! Yes. Viral!" He turned to Jonnie. "You know, big as a Psychlo is, his basic structure seems to be clumps of viruses." He saw Jonnie looking at him askance and added, "Purely academic interest. It does mean, however, that their bodies probably hold together much tighter and have a greater density. Probably of no interest to you. Well, let's get to work on these cords."

He attached one clip to the end of a cord in the brain and grounded the other on an arm and, watching a meter, measured the resistance of the cord to electrical flow. When he had determined that, he stood back and touched a button to send electricity through the cord.

The others felt their hair rise.

The Psychlo cadaver moved its left foot.

"Good," said MacKendrick. "Nerves. There is no rigor mortis in these bodies and they're still flexible. I have found the nerve that relays walk commands." He put a little tag on the nerve. He had marked the places from which they had removed the metal with a spot of dye on each of the two nerves involved with it. But he wasn't checking those yet.

His spectators were quite horrified to see, as MacKendrick identified nerves with tags, a Psychlo cadaver that moved its claws, clenched the remains of its jaw, moved an ear, and lolled out its tongue, one after the other as various nerves were given an electrical jolt.

MacKendrick saw their reaction. "Nothing new in this. Just electrical impulses approximating brain commands. Some man-scientist did this maybe thirteen hundred years ago and thought he'd found the secret of all thought and made up a cult about it called 'psychology.' Forgotten now. It wasn't the secret of thought; it was just the mechanics of bodies. They started with frogs. I'm cataloging this body's communication channels, that's all."

But it was *very* weird. The depths of superstition stirred in them as they saw a corpse move and breathe and saw, for a couple of pumps, its heart beat.

MacKendrick's gloved hands were slimy with green blood but he moved in a very efficient and businesslike fashion until he had more than fifty little tags clipped to the nerve cords.

"Now for the answer!" said MacKendrick. He sent pulses through the two nerves to which the bronze item had been attached.

It was difficult work. The room was cold. The corpse stank, having gone even mustier than the common, rank smell of a Psychlo.

MacKendrick stood up, a little tired. "I'm sorry to say that I don't think that piece of metal would cause any of these monsters to commit suicide. But I can make a pretty good guess now as to what it does do."

He pointed to his tags. "Taste and sexual impulses branch off from that one as near as I can tell. Emotion and action branch off from the other one there.

"This metal clip was installed when it was an infant. See the faint, ancient scars in this side of the skull. At that time the bones would be soft and would heal fast."

"And what does it do?" said Angus.

"My guess," said MacKendrick, "is that it short-circuits pleasure with action. Maybe they did it to make a Psychlo happy only when he was working. But—and I can't tell fully unless I dissect a lot of these nerves further down—I think its actual effect was to make a Psychlo enjoy cruel action."

Suddenly Jonnie recalled an expression of Terl's. He had seen him do something cruel and heard him mutter, "Delicious!"

"The effort," said MacKendrick, "to make them industrious I think was miscalculated by their ancient metal specialists, and they made a race of true monsters."

Everyone agreed with that.

"That wouldn't make them commit suicide to protect technology!" said Robert the Fox. "You got another corpse here. He was an assistant mine manager by his papers and got twice the pay of the one you just did. Get him on the table, man."

MacKendrick got another table. He would have to picto-record and sketch the work he had just done.

They put the mammoth head of the second one on the machine. They had the setting now. And they looked into the dead brain of one who had been called Blo.

And Jonnie, who had been getting despondent, gruesome as this job was, suddenly smiled.

There were *two* metal pieces in this one's head!

The whir-flap of the machine took the recording and he rushed out to tear through the analysis code books.

There it was, bright and clear: silver!

When he reentered the room, MacKendrick, being practiced now, had the brain stripped down. He was spot-dyeing the connections of the second bit of metal before he took it out.

It was about three-quarters of an inch long. The lack of oxygen in a Psychlo blood stream had left it gleamingly bright. It was a cylinder. The nubs on each end were insulated from the silver.

Angus put it on the machine and it was hollow.

Jonnie made him adjust the equipment even more finely. There was a filament of some sort inside that cylinder.

They surmised they would find them in other executive corpses, so when MacKendrick had sterilized it, Jonnie cut it in half very delicately.

The inside of it resembled a component in remote controls but it was not a radio.

"I haven't identified these nerves," said MacKendrick, "because I can't tell exactly what they go to right now. But I'll work on it."

"Could it be a thought wavelength vibrator?" asked Jonnie.

"A difference measurer?" said Angus. "Like difference of thought waves of another race?"

Jonnie would let them go on working on it, but he had a very good idea it was designed to release an impulse under certain conditions and that that impulse could cause attack and suicide.

"There's only one thing wrong," said MacKendrick. "It was put in an infant. Getting it out of the head of a live, adult Psychlo, through all these bones, would be a task one could never guarantee the success of." Then he saw the look of disappointment on their faces. "But I'll try, I'll try!" He didn't think it could be done. And he only had four Psychlos—and they looked like they were dying.

■

PART 19

— 1 —

Brown Limper Staffor chaired the Council meeting in a black mood.

There they sat before the raised platform in the capitol room, wrangling, wrangling, wrangling. Disputing *him*, the senior Councilman of the planet. Objecting to his measures.

That black fellow from Africa! That yellow creature from Asia! That tan idiot from South America! That dull, bullheaded brute from Europe! Ugh, ugh, ugh, and UGH!

Didn't they realize he was doing the very best things that could be done for man? And wasn't he, Brown Limper Staffor, now representing *five* tribes since the Brigantes had come and he was indeed Senior Mayor America?

They were disputing the cost and contract terms of hiring the Brigantes. Of all things! The planet needed a defense force. And these clauses that he had so painstakingly sorted out—spending his valuable time hour after hour with that General Snith—were all necessary.

Senior Mayor Africa was challenging the pay. He was saying that one hundred credits per Brigante per day was excessive, that even Council members only got five credits a day, and that if they spread credits around this way they would make them worthless! Wrangle, wrangle, wrangle, taking up picky and unimportant points!

Brown Limper had been making good progress. He had the Council whittled down to five now, but it certainly looked like four too many!

He cudgeled his brains as to how to solve this dilemma.

Driven by Lars out to the Brigante suburb of the city that day, it is true he had been taken a bit aback by what the Brigante women were doing. Right in the streets and with no clothes on at anytime. But General Snith, during their conference, had said they were just frolicking.

Coming back, Lars had been talking about that wonderful, wonderful military leader of ancient times named . . . Bitter? . . . no . . . Hitler? Yes, Hitler. How he had been a champion of racial purity and moral uprightness. Racial purity didn't seem very interesting but "moral uprightness" had caught Brown Limper's attention. His father had always been a champion of it.

Sitting there listening to these endless arguments and objections, he recalled a conversation—purely social—he had had with that friendly creature, Terl. It had been on the subject of *leverage*. If one had leverage, one could do pretty well what he pleased. Sound philosophy. Brown Limper had grasped that. He truly hoped Terl thought him an apt pupil, for he was very happy to have his friendship and help.

He sure didn't have any leverage on this Council! He tried to think of some way he could maneuver them into appointing himself and a secretary as the sole authority for the planet. He couldn't quite come up with anything and he pondered other things Terl had said: good, down-to-earth advice. Something about it being the right thing to do to pass a law and then arrest the violators or use their violations as leverage. Something like that.

It came to him in a flash.

He rapped for silence.

"We will table the resolution to accept the Brigante contract for now," said Brown Limper in his best voice of authority.

They quieted down and Asia folded his robes with a gesture of—of what was that—defiance? Well, he'd take care of him!

"I have another measure," said Brown Limper. "It has to do with morality." And he proceeded to make a speech about morality being the backbone of all societies and that officials must be honest and true and that their conduct must be beyond reproach and that they must not be discovered in any scandalous situations or circumstances.

It went down rather well. They were all reasonably honest men and they saw that official conduct should also be moral even though their different moral codes varied.

They unanimously passed the offered resolution that scandalous official conduct should result in removal from post of any offender. They felt very upright about it.

At least they had gotten one resolution passed. They adjourned.

Back in his office, Brown Limper reviewed some data with Lars about "button cameras." Lars had some knowledge of them. Yes, he thought Terl could tell him where some were in the compound.

The following morning, when all the officials were out of their rooms at the hotel, Lars, in the name of decency, put some button cameras in unsuspected places in rooms and connected them to automatic picto-recorders. The following night, Brown Limper had a very confidential meeting with General Snith. As a result, a dozen of the better-looking Brigante women were employed at the hotel in various capacities by the manager, who was short of help and who agreed that such good-looking women should be in posts that directly contacted his guests to make their stay more comfortable.

The evening after that, Terl thought Brown's measures were very wise and said he was proud of him to have thought of it all on his own.

Brown Limper was very pleased and he went back to his office, to work late at night assembling the steps of his plans. Notable among them were charges to bring against Jonnie Goodboy Tyler when Brown Limper at last had a free hand. The list of charges were getting pretty long, and punishment was overdue.

— 2 —

It was the dark of the moon. The lights of the cage area had been turned out. The sentry had been told to stay elsewhere.

Brown Limper sat on the ground. Terl crouched close to the bars. Lars Thorenson, using a tiny masked light to occasionally resort to his dictionary, sat between them.

Their voices were very low. There must be no possibility of any of this being overheard. Tonight was the big one!

Terl's claws twitched and little surges of energy ran through him. This conference was so important, its successful outcome so vital to his plans, he was having trouble breathing. Yet he must sound indifferent, casual, helpful (a new word he had learned). Conflicting impulses had to be sealed off, such as reaching through the bars (which he had de-electrified, unbeknownst to them, by using the inside remote control hidden in the stones); the pleasure of tearing them with claws was very, very subordinate to what he was attempting tonight. He made himself tensely concentrate on the business at hand.

Brown Limper was relating in whispers that he had succeeded in exposing blatant scandal in the Council. He had taken each of the four other Senior Mayors aside and shown them certain recordings, and they had realized their conduct was a total violation of their own laws. Each had looked at himself performing perversions he had recently been introduced to by the Brigante women, as many as four women at a time, and had agreed with shame he was a potential disgrace to the government. (Lars had trouble finding "shame" in the Psychlo dictionary but at last discovered it in the archaic section as an old Hockner word, obsolete.)

A resolution appointed Brown Limper Staffor Executive for the Council, assisted by the Secretary (who could sign his name after much drilling but who otherwise could not read). The entire authority of the Council now reposed in one Brown Limper Staffor as Senior Mayor Planet from here on out and forevermore as the most deserving and competent Councilman. The others had packed and gone home. Brown Limper's word was now *law* for the whole planet.

Terl would have thought some note of elation would be detectable. That was how he would have felt. He whispered an approval and a commendation on how statesmanlike this conduct was. But Brown Limper did not brighten. "Is there something else I could help you with?" whispered Terl.

Brown Limper drew a long breath, almost a sigh of despair. He had drawn up a list of criminal charges against that Tyler.

"Good," said Terl in a very low voice. "You now have the power to handle him. Are they strong charges?"

"Oh, yes," whispered Brown Limper, brightening. "He interrupted a Council-ordered removal of a tribe, kidnapped the Coordinators, murdered some of the tribesmen, stole their goods, and violated their tribal rights."

"I should think," whispered Terl, "that that was serious enough."

"There's even more," said Brown Limper. "He ambushed a

Psychlo convoy and mercilessly slaughtered it, gave no quarter, and stole their vehicles."

"You have proof of all this?" whispered Terl.

"Witnesses from the tribe are right here. And picto-recorder pictures of the ambush are being shown nightly at the Academy right over there in the hills. Lars has made copies."

"I should think all that is more than adequate to bring about justice," said Terl. The word "justice" was another one they had to look up in the translations going back and forth.

"There's even more," said Brown Limper. "When he turned over the two billion Galactic credits found at the compound, it was over three hundred credits short. That's theft, a felony."

Terl gasped. He wasn't gasping at the shortage. He was gasping at two billion Galactic credits. It made the coffins he supposed were in the cemetery on Psychlo mere kerbango change.

He needed a few minutes to sort this out and he told Lars he needed a fresh breathe-gas cartridge for his mask. Lars got him one, not noticing the electrification switch had been reversed. Terl had to flip his remote, which he did in the nick of time to prevent an electrocution.

As he fitted the new cartridges in place, Terl thought furiously. Old Numph? Must have been. Why, the bumbling idiot wasn't so bumbling after all! He'd had other swindles going for . . . thirty years? . . . must be! Two billion Galactic credits! Suddenly Terl updated his plans. He knew exactly what he could do with this. Those two billion were going into three or four sealed coffins marked "radiation killed" so they never would be opened and they were going to go right into his cemetery. He had had slightly less workable plans. He abandoned them and a whole new panorama spread before him, one that not only could not fail but also would be enormously profitable. All in a flash he had things rearranged. A plan far safer than he had had. Far more workable. No desperation in it.

The close, dark conference got going again.

"What," whispered Terl, "is your problem really then?" He knew what it was exactly. This idiot couldn't lay his paws on the animal Tyler!

Brown Limper sagged once more. "It's one thing to have charges. It's quite another to get my hands on Tyler."

"Hmm," said Terl, hoping he sounded very thoughtful and considerate (a new word Terl had looked up). "Let me see. Ah

Hmm. The operating principle here is to *attract* him to the area.'' This was just common security chief technology. ''You can't go out and find him as he is elusive or too well protected, so the right thing to do is to lure him here, away from protection, and then pounce.''

Brown Limper sat up with a sudden surge of hope. What a brilliant idea!

''The last time he was active here,'' whispered Terl, keeping the twitches down to a minimum, ''was when we did a transshipment firing. If another transshipment firing were done and he knew about it, he would be here in a flash. Then you could pounce.''

Brown Limper saw that clearly.

''But,'' said Terl, ''you have another problem too. He is using company property. Company planes, company equipment. Now if you personally *owned* all that, you would really have him on grand theft.''

Brown Limper got lost. Lars repeated it and clarified it. Brown Limper couldn't quite grasp it.

''And,'' whispered Terl, staying very calm, ''he is using the *planet*. Now I don't know whether you know that the Intergalactic Mining Company paid the Imperial Psychlo government trillions of credits for this planet. It is company property!''

Lars had to look up things in both the Psychlo and an old English dictionary to get across how much was a trillion and then had to write it for Brown Limper. At last Brown Limper could at least grasp that it was an awful lot of money.

''But the planet,'' said Terl, ''is now mostly mined out.'' This was a flagrant falsehood but these two wouldn't know that. A planet wasn't ''mined out'' until you were almost through the crust to the liquid core. ''It just so happens that it is now worth only a few billion credits.'' It was still worth about forty trillion. Crap, he'd sure have to cover his tracks on this one! But it was *brilliant*.

''I am,'' whispered Terl, ''the resident agent and representative of the company and authorized to legally dispose of its property.'' What a lie! Oh, would he have to cover his tracks. ''You realized that, of course. The animal Tyler did, which was why he kept me alive.''

''Oh!'' whispered Brown Limper. ''That had puzzled me! He

is so bloodthirsty I couldn't understand how he let you live when he murdered the Chamcos that very same day.''

''Well, now you know his secret,'' said Terl. ''He himself was trying to negotiate with me to buy the Earth branch of Intergalactic Mining *and* the planet. That's why he feels he can go around using company equipment and stamping all over the globe. Of course I wouldn't hear of it, knowing his bad character.'' (The last was another word Terl had looked up.)

Brown Limper was suddenly engulfed by the trap Tyler had ''set'' for him. For a moment he felt the very earth he was sitting on was crumbling under him.

''He knows where this two billion is?'' asked Terl.

''Yes,'' whispered Brown Limper tensely. Good heavens, how blind he had been! Tyler was going to buy the company and the planet, and what would happen to Brown Limper then?

Terl had it all sized up. ''But I wouldn't sell. Not to the animal Tyler. I was thinking of you.''

Brown Limper whistled with relief. Then he looked around over his shoulders both ways and leaned forward, impatient at the delays of cross-translation. ''Would you sell the company and the planet to me? I mean us?''

Terl thought about it. Then he said, ''It's worth more than two billion, but if I have it in cash and a few other considerations, I will do it.''

Brown Limper had studied a lot of economics lately. He knew how to be cunning. ''With a proper bill of sale?''

''Oh, yes,'' said Terl. ''The bill of sale would be legal as soon as signed. But it would have to be recorded on Psychlo as a formality.'' Oh, devils, if he ever tried to record such a thing, if they even heard of it, they'd vaporize him the slow way!

He pretended the last cartridge had been spent and he bought time with another change. There was a condition where a planet was written off. The company never sold a planet. When one was abandoned, they had a weapon they used. Terl had already decided to destroy this planet. He'd already covered the ground. He got a grip on himself. Any bill of sale he signed would go up in smoke if he destroyed the planet. Good. It might take the company two years to counterattack. He had ıots of time. Yes, he could safely sign a bogus bill of sale.

Once more the close huddle was going again. ''To make such a concession, you would have to do the following: One, get my old office set up; Two, let me work in there freely to calculate and build the console of a new transshipment rig; Three, provide any and all needed supplies; and Four, provide me with adequate protection and force at the firing itself.''

Brown Limper was a little doubtful.

''But I will have to take the two billion to the company offices on Psychlo,'' said Terl. ''I'm no thief.''

Brown Limper could appreciate that.

''And I will have to record the deed of sale for both the planet and the company branch here for it to be totally legal,'' said Terl. ''I wouldn't want you holding an unrecorded deed. I want to be fair to you, too.'' (That was another word, ''fair,'' he had looked up.)

Yes, said Brown Limper, one could see he was leaning over backward to be fair and legal. He was still a little doubtful.

''And if you have a bill of sale to the company you own all the equipment and minesites as well as the planet, and Tyler won't be permitted to fly about.''

Brown Limper sat a little straighter. He began to get a little eager.

''Also,'' continued Terl, ''You can let it be known through various channels that you are going to fire a shipment to Psychlo. *And the moment he hears that, he'll be right over here and you've got him*!''

That did it!

Brown Limper almost reached through the bars to shake hands on it until Lars reminded him they were electrified. He got up, restraining an impulse to jump about.

''I'll draw up the deed!'' he said. Too loud. ''I'll draw up the deed,'' he whispered. ''All your conditions are accepted. We will do exactly what you say!'' He rushed off in the wrong direction to get to the ground car. Lars had to collect him and get him into it. Brown Limper had a wild look in his eyes.

''Now we will see justice done,'' Brown Limper kept repeating all the way back to Denver.

Terl, in his cage, couldn't believe his luck. Laughs and twitches fought to take over.

He had done it! And he would be—was!—one of the richest Psychlos alive!

Power! Success! He had done it! But would he ever have to be sure this accursed planet went up in smoke. As soon as he left.

— 3 —

Jonnie was pitching rocks down off the bluff and into the lake. The vast lake, really an inland sea, stretched out to a cloudy horizon. There was a storm building up out there now, a not uncommon thing for this huge expanse of water.

The bluff on which he stood rose nearly sheer, two hundred feet above the lake. Erosion or some volcanic cataclysm from the cloud-hidden peaks to the northeast had covered the bluff top with rocks the size of a man's fist. They were simply made for throwing.

He had formed the habit of daily trotting down here from the minesite a few miles away. It was hot and humid here at the equator but the running did him good. He was not afraid of the various animals around here, ferocious though they might be, for he never went unarmed and the beasts seldom attacked unless disturbed. There was a road of sorts to follow, and the Pyschlos must have made a habit of coming here from the minesite, perhaps to swim, for the road went across the bluff and down to a beach on the other side. No, not to swim. Psychlos didn't like swimming. Perhaps to go boating?

Once he had read that this lake area had been one of the most heavily populated on the continent. Several millions had lived here. The Psychlos seemed to have taken care of them long, long ago, for there was not even a trace of fields or huts, much less people, left.

He wondered why the Psychlos mainly hunted people. Dr. MacKendrick said it was probably a matter of sympathetic nerve vibration: animals might not suffer acutely enough to add to the enjoyment of the monsters, or perhaps it was just that man's nerve pattern, in a body with two arms, two legs, and upright, paralleled their own. Even their nerve gas specialized in sentient beings and was far less effective on four-legged creatures and reptiles. There was a Psychlo text on its use and it said as much. Something about its being attuned to "more highly developed central nervous systems." But whatever might be the reasons for that, these Psychlos at the minesite had not made much of a dent in the game. And the game, smelling him, did not go racing away. He suddenly realized that he didn't smell even vaguely like a Psychlo.

The storm out there was building up. He glanced toward the very distant minesite to see whether there was any rush getting back there to beat the storm.

Very tiny in the distance a small tri-wheeler ground car had left the mine. Somebody coming. To see him? Or just somebody out for a ride?

Jonnie went back to pitching rocks. The current state of affairs was a bit gloomy. One of the Psychlos had died; the other three were holding on. They had found about a third of the corpses had two items in their heads, and Dr. MacKendrick was practicing on the cadavers to find out how to bore in and remove them without killing a Psychlo—in case one of the last three made it. They still had two with two objects in their heads. Might even be a relief to them to get rid of the hideous things!

But Jonnie did not much like all this business with cadavers and he turned his mind to something more cheerful.

During the battle he had made an interesting discovery. He had been flying that mine platform with *two* hands. He hadn't recalled that until a week had gone by. MacKendrick said it was another part of his brain taking over the lost functions. Under stress, he had assumed, those "lost" functions and nerves healed because of a battle. But Jonnie didn't believe that.

Jonnie's theory was that *he* manipulated the nerves. And it was working! He had begun by simply willing his arm and leg to do what he wanted. Each day he had gotten a bit better. And now he could trot. No cane. And he could *throw*.

For a hunter trained as he was, the inability to sling a kill-club had made him feel helpless. And here he was pitching rocks.

He threw one out. It went arcing through the air, down off the bluff, and sent a small white geyser up in the lake, the "plunk" coming back to him a moment later.

Pretty good! If he did say it himself.

The storm out there was towering up a bit higher, grayish black, a bit ugly. He glanced toward the minesite and found the tri-wheeler had almost arrived. It stopped.

For a moment Jonnie did not recognize the rider and he stepped nearer to him, questioningly. Then he saw it was the third "duplicate" of him, a man they called Stormalong. His real name was Stam Stavenger, member of a Norwegian group who had emigrated to Scotland from Norway in ages past and who had preserved their names and lineage but not their customs. They looked and acted like Scots.

He was Jonnie's height and build and had eyes like Jonnie's, but his hair was a shade darker and his skin very much more tanned. Since the lode days he had not bothered to keep up the resemblance and had cut his beard square at the bottom.

Stormalong had stayed at the Academy. A skilled pilot, he enjoyed teaching the new cadets to fly. He had found an ancient flying coat, a white scarf, and a huge pair of goggles from a bygone age and he affected these. They gave him a bit of dash.

They swatted each other on the back and grinned at each other.

"They told me I'd find you down here throwing rocks at the crocs," said Stormalong. "How's the arm?"

"You must have seen the last one I threw," said Jonnie. "It might not have knocked down one of these elephants but it's getting there." He guided him over to a big, flat rock overlooking the lake and they sat down. The storm was building up but it was an easy run back.

Stormalong was seldom very talkative but right now he was full of news. It had taken some ferreting out, real badger digging, to find where Jonnie was. Nobody knew in America, so he had gone to Scotland to find him or some trace of him.

Chrissie sent her love. He'd already given Pattie's to Bittie. The Chief of Clanfearghus had sent his respects, mind you, not his regards but his *respects*. His Aunt Ellen sent her love; she was married to the parson now and in Scotland.

He'd gotten on Jonnie's trail through the two Coordinators who had gone back to Scotland, the ones sent out to bring in some tribe or other . . . the Brigades? . . . the Brigantes. Oh, that mob was up in Denver now. Horrible people. He'd seen some. Anyway, they'd brought Allison's body home for burial and Scotland was in an uproar over the murder of Allison.

But that wasn't what he wanted to tell Jonnie. The craziest thing had happened on his flight over.

"You know," said Stormalong, "how you said we could get invaded again here on Earth? Well, it does seem possible."

He'd been coming over to Scotland on the North Great Circle, flying an ordinary battle plane, making good time, and just as he reached the northern tip of Scotland, right there on his viewscreen and visual as well he had seen the biggest, most enormous craft he ever hoped to see. For a moment he thought he was running into it and would crash right then. There it was on his screens and through his windshield! But bang! He hit it but it wasn't there.

"Not there?" asked Jonnie.

Well, that was exactly it. He'd run into a solid object that wasn't there. Right in the sky, mind you. Big as all the sky but not there. Here, he had the screen pictures in this pack.

Jonnie looked at it. It was a sphere with a ring around it. Nothing like any ship he had ever heard of. And it looked *huge*. In fact, at the corner, the Orkney Islands were visible. It looked like it reached from mid-Scotland to the Orkneys. The next consecutive picture showed it enveloping the battle plane taking the shot, and the third one showed it was *gone*.

"The ship that wasn't there," said Stormalong.

"Light," said Jonnie, suddenly recalling some man-theories. "This thing could have been going faster than light. It left its image behind. That's a guess, you know, but I read that they thought that things that went faster than light could look as big as the whole universe. It's in some texts on nuclear physics we had. I didn't understand most of it."

"Well, that just could be," said Stormalong. "Because the old woman said it wasn't that big!"

The old woman?

Well, it's like this. When he had gotten over his scare, he had backtracked his screen recorders. He hadn't noticed it in approaching Scotland—you know how it is, you get groggy on a long flight, not alert, and he hadn't had much sleep lately, cadets being what they were, slow to graduate when desperately needed by the overloaded pilots.

The backtrack of the screens showed this little trace coming up from a farm west of Kinlochbervie. You know, on the northwest coast of Scotland—that little place? Well, he cranked down his speed and went in to that spot, expecting maybe the place had been raided or shot up.

But there was just a burned spot in the rocks—a farm raises mostly rocks around there—and he didn't see any other damage or hostile force so he landed near the house.

An old woman came out, all fluttery about two callers from the sky in one day when she didn't usually see anybody for months on end. And he was made to sit down and have some yarb tea and she showed him this new, shiny pocketknife.

"A pocketknife?" said Jonnie. This ordinarily very quiet Norwegian-Scot was taking his time about getting down to it.

Well, yes. They'd seen some in ruined cities, remember? They folded in on themselves. Only this one was shiny as could be. Yes, I am getting on with it.

So anyway, according to what the old woman told him, there she was combing her dog that often got burrs in him and it almost startled her witless. Standing right behind her was a small gray man. And right behind him was a big gray sphere with a ring around it parked right where the cow was usually staked out. Like to have frightened her silly daft, she said. There hadn't been a sound. Maybe only a bit of wind.

So she asked the small gray man in for a cup of yarb tea just like she asked me, except that I'd had the manners to come down roaring and announcing myself.

But the small gray man was very pleasant. He looked a bit smaller than most men. His skin was gray, his hair was gray and his suit gray. The only thing odd about him was he had a box he wore on a strap around his neck and hung on his chest. He'd say something to this box and then, presently, the box would speak English. The small gray man's voice was quiet and had different tones and the box only had one tone, a monotone.

"A vocoder," said Jonnie. "A portable translation device. A Psychlo text describes them but the Psychlos don't use them."

Well, all right. But anyway this small gray man asked her whether she had any newspapers. And no, because of course she'd never seen a newspaper; few people have. And then he asked her whether she had any history books. And she was disappointed to have to tell him she had heard of a book but didn't have any.

Well, apparently he thought she didn't understand, so the small gray man made a lot of motions to indicate something printed on paper was what he wanted.

So she got very helpful. Seems like somebody had bought some wool from her and given her a couple of those new credits in exchange. And explained what they were.

"What credits?"

"Oh, you haven't seen them?" And Stormalong fished in his pockets and found one. "They pay us now. With these." It was a one-credit note from the new Planetary Bank and Jonnie looked at it with casual interest. Then his attention riveted on the picture. A picture of *him*. Waving a gun. He didn't think it was all that good a likeness and also it embarrassed him a bit.

So anyway, Stormalong went on, the old woman had accepted them because of the picture of you. And she had one of them on the wall. And she sold it to the small gray man for the pocketknife because she had another one she could put on the wall.

"I should think that was a cheap price for the pocketknife, if it was as fancy as you say," said Jonnie.

Well, Stormalong hadn't thought about that. But anyway the small gray man finished his yarb tea and put the bank note away very carefully between two pieces of metal and put them in an inside pocket, and then he thanked her and went back to the ship and said something to somebody inside and got in. He called back for the old woman not to come close and shut the door. And then there was a curl of flame and it rose up, and then all of a sudden it got as big as the whole sky and vanished. Yes, as Jonnie said, probably a phenomenon of light. But it didn't fly like our ships and it didn't teleport. It didn't seem to be Psychlo what with the man being a *small* gray man.

Jonnie had become very quiet. Some *other* alien race? Interested in Earth now that the Psychlos weren't here?

He looked across the lake, puzzling about it. The storm was building even higher.

Well, be that as it may, continued Stormalong, that wasn't why he was here. He fumbled in a flat case he carried for maps.

"It's a letter from Ker," said Stormalong. "And he said I had to bring it personally and not let it get out of my hands. I owe him favors and he said if you didn't get it the whole shaft would fall in. Here it is."

— 4 —

Jonnie regarded the envelope. It was the paper cover used to package antiheat shields. The only writing on it was "AWFUL SECRET." He held it up to the light, darkening now as the storm drew nearer. It had no explosive in it that he could detect. He ripped it open. Ah, it was Ker's writing all right. The semiliterate curved hooks and loops might not spell correctly but they spelled Ker's idea of a Psychlo alphabet. He opened it up all the way to read it. It said:

AWFUL SECRET

To You Know Who.
As you know, Personal letters are forbidden by company policy and if I was caught writing and sending one it would cost me three months' pay. Ha. Ha. But you said before you left I should write you if a certain thing happened and give it to a pilot like you know who to bring to you fast. So no names as names is out-security. But it is going to happen so I am writing you even if the company docks me three months' pay. Notice this handwriting is disguised too. Yesterday that flunked-out ex-pilot knothead Lars the one who thought he was the world's greatest combat acrobactic pilot from talking to a party I won't mention because of out-security (*security*, get it?) and broke his silly neck and got promoted to assistant to you know who (no names) came down and asked all the Psychlos they got in stir to fix up the breathe-gas pumps and ventilators in you know who's old office. Well, they won't cooperate as I knew and you knew they wouldn't. They believe and I am sure they are drilling straight in that you know who killed old you know who by murder. Another one that was murdered afterward had figured it out and told them just before the semiannual firing and then he got missing down the shaft so they believe it. They ain't going to do a thing for you know who or have anything to do with you know who's old quarters because

the Psychlos are sure you know who would blow them up. So anyway the breathe-gas pumps and circulators in that section are all blown to bits as we both know and before anybody can go work in there without a mask they have to be fixed but they are broke. So this crazy idiot the universe's greatest combat pilot that never was in combat and broke his neck and we couldn't train come over to see me and I said yes I could fix up the offices of you know who but I would need certain parts maybe even from other minesites because the breathe-gas pump is so broke. And he said it was a Council order and he could make sure I got what I needed. So I am drawing up a very fancy repair design that needs lots of parts and I am delaying as long as I can. They said you know who on the Council said it was secret and urgent and they're going to ride me to get it done and pay me extra pay. Ha. Ha. So I am stalling and like you said you better get over here as I told them I needed assistants, but don't use your name as anything to do with you know who and you know who is poison gas in the drift. So there, you know now and I have about wore my paw out writing this and my ears out listening to how rush it is but I will delay and look for unnecessary parts as long as I can for the breathe-gas circulator that sure was broke and is now even more broke. Ha. Ha. This personal letter could cost me three months' pay. Ha. Ha. So you owe me if I'm caught at it. Ha. Ha.

—You know who

Addition: Claw this letter up so it don't cost me three months' pay—or my furry neck. No ha, ha.

Jonnie read the letter again and then, as required, tore it into bits. "When was this given to you?" he asked Stormalong.

"Yesterday morning. I had to trace you."

Jonnie looked out across the lake. The storm was huge now, towering with black turmoil. It was almost upon them.

Jonnie pushed Stormalong onto the tri-wheeler and started it up. Without another word he tore across the savannah to the minesite.

The growl of thunder sounded and the first stinging slashes of rain lanced the air.

Jonnie knew he had to get to America *now*. At once!

— 5 —

"It's a trap!" said Robert the Fox.

Jonnie had returned. He rapidly told them what Ker had said. He had given orders for the immediate refueling, check-over, and cleaning of Stormalong's plane to be ready within the hour. He had the copilot who had come with Stormalong in front of him now with Angus standing nearby, and he was comparing the two.

"Can you trust Ker?" demanded Sir Robert.

Jonnie didn't answer. He was satisfied Angus could be mistaken for the copilot if he darkened his beard, put on a bit of walnut stain, and changed clothes.

"Answer me! I canna think ye've got all yer wits!" Robert was so agitated he was pacing back and forth in the underground room Jonnie had been using. He was even lapsing into his colloquial Scot dialect.

"I must go. Now and fast," Jonnie shot at them.

"No!" said Dunneldeen.

"No!" said Robert the Fox.

There was a flurry of translations with his Coordinator and then Colonel Ivan shouted, "Nyet!"

Jonnie had Angus changing clothes with the copilot. "You don't have to go, Angus," he said. "You said 'yes' too hastily."

Angus said, "I'll go. I'll say my prayers and make my will but I'll go with you, Jonnie."

Stormalong was standing there and Jonnie pulled him over to a huge Psychlo mirror and stood beside him. Tropic sun had tanned Jonnie lately: their skin tone difference was not so great now. Stormalong's beard was a little darker: some walnut stain would fix that. There was the new facial scar, well healed now, that Jonnie had gotten: nothing could be done about that, and he hoped people would think Stormalong had had an accident; yes, wait, he could put a bandage on it. Ah, the square cut of the bottom of the beard: that was what was making the difference. He reached for the tool kit Angus always carried, got out some sharp wire snips and began to make his beard exactly the same as Stormalong's. That done, he changed clothes with him. Now a little walnut stain in the beard . . . good. He looked at himself in the mirror. Ah, yes. The piece of bandage. He got that and put in on. Now? Good. He could pass for Stormalong. The huge, old-fashioned goggles, white scarf, and leather flying coat: yes, they did it. Unless he was looked at too closely or their slight difference in accent was heard . . . .He made Stormalong talk, then he talked. No Scott burr in Stormalong's accent. Scot university? A little soft in pronunciation? He tried it. Yes, he could also sound like Stormalong.

The others were very agitated. The big Russian was cracking the knuckles of his huge hands. Bittie MacLeod was peering into the room. He came forward, his eyes bright with pleading.

"No," said Jonnie. Pride or no pride, this mission had death in it. "You cannot come with me!" Then he softened. "Take good care of Colonel Ivan."

Bittie swallowed and backed up.

Angus had finished and run out. The clang of cartridges being changed and the whir of a drill sounded from the hangar where they were readying the plane.

Jonnie beckoned to Colonel Ivan. He and his Coordinator came forward. "Get the American underground base closed, Colonel. Every door. So no one can enter but us. Close it so hard they'll never get into it. Do the same thing with the tactical and nuclear weapons area thirty miles to the north. *Seal* it. Secure every assault rifle not in use by Scots. Have you got it?"

The colonel had a group there now. Yes, he got it.

Jonnie beckoned to Dunneldeen and Sir Robert and they kept pace with him as he went toward their commissary. Jonnie, in terse, brief statements, told them exactly what to do to carry on, if he were killed. They were very sober, worried for him. The hairbreadth daring of his plan left an awful lot of room for slip-ups. But they got it. They said they would carry on.

"And Dunneldeen," concluded Jonnie, "I want you over at the Academy in America in about twenty-four hours, coming in from Scotland to take over the pilot training duties of Stormalong who by then, with luck, will be on 'other assignment.' "

For once Dunneldeen just nodded assent.

The old woman who had come down from the Mountains of the Moon tribe—with her whole family—to run their commissary must have heard rumors in the wind. She had a food package gathered up for two, some gourds full of sweet water and a big sandwich of roasted African buffalo meat and millet bread, and she stood right there in front of Jonnie until he began eating it.

Sir Robert picked up the food package and Dunneldeen the gourds and they walked past the old Psychlo operations office. There was hammering and drill whirring still coming from the plane area, where Angus was making sure it was all operational. Jonnie picked up a few yards of radio printer paper and glanced at current traffic, looking for any unusual weather in the pilot cross-talk.

Well, well! One . . . two . . . yes, two mentions of the craft that got as big as the sky. Stories similar to the one Stormalong had told him. The small gray man mentioned in both. India. South America.

"The small gray man gets around," murmured Jonnie. Dunneldeen and Sir Robert craned around to the printout to see what he was talking about. "Stormalong will tell you," said Jonnie. Earth certainly was of interest to some other civilization in space. But the small gray man didn't seem hostile. At least not yet. "Keep this or any other base you go to defended on a twenty-four-hour basis," said Jonnie.

The whirring and hammering had stopped and they went to the plane. It was being dollied to just inside the open hangar door.

Stormalong was standing there with his copilot. "You stay here," said Jonnie. "Both of you. You," he jabbed a finger into Stormalong's chest, "be me. Go on that same route every day in my clothes and throw rocks. And you," he pointed a finger at the copilot, a Scot they called Darf, "be Angus!"

"I'm na good at a' the things bonnie Angus kens!" wailed the copilot.

"You do them," said Jonnie.

A Russian came running in from outside and told them it was all clear, no drones coming. Not on screens or eyeball. His new English had a colloquial Scotch accent.

Jonnie and Angus got in the plane; Sir Robert and Dunneldeen threw the food and water in. Then they both stood there looking up at Jonnie. They were trying to think of something to say but both of them were unable to talk.

Bittie stood back. He waved a timid hand.

Jonnie shut the plane door. Angus gave him a thumbs-up. Jonnie signaled the dolly crew to shove them out and pushed the heavy starter buttons with his fists. He looked back. The crews and people in the hangar door weren't waving. Jonnie's fingers shoved into the console buttons.

Stormalong watched breathlessly in the door. He had known Jonnie was a flier unequaled, but he had never seen a battle plane vault upward so fast and sharply and rush into hypersonic so quickly. The bottom of the broken sound barrier rocketed back at them as it echoed against the African peaks. Or was that the boom of the storm that engulfed the speeding ship?

A roll of thunder and a lightning flash.

The group in the hangar door still stood there, looking at the place where the ship had vanished into the cloud-boiling sky. Their Jonnie was on his way to America fast. They didn't like it. Not any part of it.

— 6 —

It was dark when they landed at the old Academy. They had flown close to the North Pole, rolling back the sun and arriving before dawn.

There were few lights. No one had lighted the field for it was not the operational field of the area, and they had slipped in on instruments and viewscreens.

The cadet duty officer was sound asleep and they woke him to get themselves logged in: "Stormalong Stam Stavenger, pilot, and Darf McNulty, copilot, returning from Europe, student battle plane 86290567918. No troubles, no comments." The cadet duty officer wrote it down. He didn't bother to get them to sign it.

Jonnie didn't know where Stormalong and Darf had been berthed. He had not remembered to find out. Stormalong probably in senior faculty berthing. Darf . . . ? He thought fast. "Darf" was still carrying the overgenerous, heavy food bag and a tool kit. After all, Stormalong was their ace here.

Abruptly Jonnie grabbed the food bag and tool kit and shoved them at the cadet. "Please carry these up to my room for me." The cadet looked at him oddly. Even Stormalong did his own fetching and carrying in this place. "We've been flying for days with no sleep," said Jonnie, faking a reeling motion.

The cadet shrugged and took the bundles. Jonnie waited for him to lead off and he did.

They arrived at a separate bedroom and went in. Stormalong's, all right. It had a Norwegian woven picture on one wall. Stormalong had made himself comfortable.

The cadet dropped the food bag and kit on the table and would have left. But although Angus was the one who had put this base together originally and knew it inside out, he wouldn't have known where Darf was berthed. Hastily Jonnie grabbed half the food and the kit and put them back into the cadet's arms. "Help Darf get to his room."

The cadet looked like he was going to protest. "He hurt his arm playing skittles," said Jonnie.

"Looks like you hurt your face, too, sir," said the cadet. He was quite sullen at losing his sleep but they went off.

Fine beginning, thought Jonnie. About now Sir Robert definitely would be talking about planning raids right. You *plan* a raid, he would be saying. One as dangerous as this one might be, certainly hadn't wasted any planning time.

The cadet and Angus didn't come back and he had to suppose it had been successful. He stripped off his clothes and rolled into Stormalong's bunk. He forced himself to go to sleep. He would need it.

It seemed like only seconds later that he was alarmed awake with a shake of the shoulder. He sat up suddenly, hand going under the blanket to his blast gun. A face mask. A breathe-mask. The "hand" was a paw.

"Did you deliver my letter?" whispered Ker.

It was broad daylight. A late-morning sun was streaming in through the discolored glass of the window.

Ker stepped back, looking at him oddly. Then the midget Psychlo catfooted over to the door to be sure it was closed, looked around the room for bugs or other surveillance devices, and came back to the bed where Jonnie had swung his legs down.

Ker guffawed!

"Is it that plain?" said Jonnie, a little cross and smoothing his hair out of his eyes.

"Not to an unobservant idiot," said Ker. "But to one who had sweated on as many driver's seats and in as many shafts with you as me, I know you, Jonnie!"

He swatted his paw into Jonnie's palm. "Welcome to the deep

pit, Jonnie . . . I mean Jonnie logged in as Stormalong! May the ore fly and the carts roll!''

Jonnie had to grin at him. Ker was always such a clown. And in a way he was fond of him.

Ker stepped very close. He whispered, ''You know you could get yourself squash killed around here. The word trickles out through the cracks in the bunkroom doors—top, high-level bunkrooms. You and me, too, if they trip the latch on us. Caution is the word. You ever have a criminal background? No? Well, you will have when they get through with you. Good thing you're in the hands of a real criminal, me! Who came with you? Who's Darf now?''

''Angus MacTavish,'' said Jonnie.

''Oho! That's the best news of the day next to your being here. Angus has a way with the nuts and bolts. I keep track of things. What's first?''

''First,'' said Jonnie, ''I get dressed and eat some breakfast. I'm not showing my face in that dining room. Stormalong trained most of these flying cadets.''

''That he did, while I trained the machine operators. You know I've been doing a great job on that, Jonnie.'' Jonnie was dressing but Ker the chatterbox rattled on. ''This Academy is the most fun I ever had, Jonnie. These cadets . . . I tell them stories about teaching you and things you did—mostly lies of course and made up to make them do better—and they love it. They know they're lies. Nobody could blade scrape thirty-nine tons of ore an hour. But you understand. You know me. I love this job. You know, it's the first time I've been really glad I'm a midget. I'm not much taller than they are and I got them—Jonnie, this will kill you unless somebody else does it first—I got them believing I'm *half-human*!'' He had taken a seat on the bed, which sagged under his seven hundred pounds, and now it almost collapsed as he rolled around in laughter. ''Ain't that rich, Jonnie? Half-human, get it? I tell them my mother was a female Psychlo that raped a Swede!''

Jonnie, in spite of the seriousness of their mission, had to smile. He was getting into Stormalong's clothes.

Ker had stopped laughing now. He was just sitting there, looking pensive. ''You know, Jonnie,'' and he sighed so that his breathe-mask valve fluttered and popped, ''I think this is the first time in my life I ever had friends.''

Eating a few bites of breakfast and chasing it down with some water, Jonnie said, "First thing you do is go down to the Academy Commandant and tell him you want Stormalong and Darf assigned at once to your special project. I'm sure they gave you authority from upstairs."

"Oh, I got authority," said Ker. "I got authority running out of my furry ears. And upstairs is all over me to finish that breathe-gas circulator. But I told them I needed help and parts from the Cornwall minesite."

"Good," said Jonnie. "Tell them Dunneldeen will be over in a couple of days to replace Stormalong in the training schedule. Say you arranged that, too, to keep the school from disruption. Then you get a closed ground car out in front of this building, get 'Darf' in it, and come back here and knock on my door and we're away."

"Got it, got it, got it," said Ker as he went rumbling off.

Jonnie checked his blast gun and put it inside his coat. He would know within an hour or two whether Ker was playing this straight. Until then . . . ?

— 7 —

They got to the car without incident beyond a couple of sly cracks from passing cadets such as, "Had a crash, Stormy?" in reference to the bandage, and "Wipe one out, Stormalong? Or was it that lass in Inverness? Or her daddy?"

There was a big package in the car, making seating tight even in Psychlo seats. Ker swept the car out across the rolling plain with the effortless skill of one with years and tens of thousands of hours on a console behind him. Jonnie had not remembered how well Ker drove. Better than Terl on ground cars and machinery. "I told them," he said, "that it was you two that had gone to fetch the housing needed from Cornwall. I was even seen to unload it from your plane."

Nothing like having an experienced criminal along, Jonnie commented. It tickled Ker and he cranked up the ground car to a hundred fifty. On this rough plain? Angus had shut his eyes tight as the shrubs and rocks whooshed by.

"And there's two air masks and bottles I brought," said Ker. "We'll claim breathe-gas is leaking in the pipes, not enough for me, too much for you. Put them on."

They deferred it, however, until they were near the compound. Chinko air masks, cut down to fit a human, were a mite uncomfortable at any time.

Jonnie didn't care about the speed. He took an instant to glory in the beautiful day. The plains were a bit brown and the snow a trifle less on the peaks at this season. But it was *his* country. He was tired of rain and humid heat. It was sort of good to be *home*.

He snapped out of it suddenly as they screeched to a slow in billowing dust on the plateau near the cage. Ker didn't care where he went in a vehicle. Ker leaned out the window and yelled at the cage, "It came. I don't think it's the right housing but we'll see!"

Terl! There he was, paws on the bars. They had the electricity off.

"Well, speed it up!" roared Terl. "I'm tired of being roasted in this sun. How many days yet, you crap brain?"

"Two, three, no more," yelled Ker. He shot the vehicle into a perilous reverse and it spun up in the air about seven feet and came down diving toward the other side of the compound to enter the garage doors.

Ker shot in and spun the car down a ramp into a deserted sector and stopped.

"Now we go to his office," he said.

"Not yet," said Jonnie, hand on the blast gun inside his coat. "Remember that old closet where they first imprisoned Terl?"

"Yes," said Ker, doubtfully.

"Is it still rigged with breathe-gas?" said Jonnie.

"I guess so," said Ker.

"First drive by the electronics storeroom and pick up a mineral analysis machine and then drive to that closet."

Ker was a bit uneasy. "I thought we wanted into his office."

"We do," said Jonnie. "But we got a little business first. Don't be alarmed. The last thing in the world I would want to do is hurt you. Relax. Do what I said."

Ker revved up and shot the car through the mazes of ramps on its way to do as Jonnie said.

The place had not been much cleaned up since the battle, but hundreds of planes were still there, the thousands of vehicles and mining machines, the dozens of shops for various types of work and hundreds of storerooms—the bric-a-brac as well as the valuables of a thousand years of operation. Jonnie looked at them speculatively—they were wealth for this planet in the way they could be used to rebuild it. And every minesite had huge and similar stores of material. These things should be preserved and cared for—they were irreplaceable, since the factories that had made them were universes away. But plentiful as they were, they would run out and wear out eventually. Another reason to join the community of stellar systems. He doubted that much of this was made on Psychlo: the Psychlos were exploiters of alien races and terrain; hadn't they even borrowed their language and technology? Teleportation seemed to be the key to their power. Well, he was working on that.

They drew up before the old closet and Angus struggled in with the mineral analysis machine. Jonnie fiddled with the breathe-gas circulator. They checked their own air masks and shut the door. They told Ker to take his mask off.

Ker, a trifle apprehensive, yet had the presence of mind to pull out a wad of black waste and block the view port.

Jonnie and Angus went right to work. They persuaded Ker to put his head on the mineral analysis plate. He did but he kept rolling his amber eyes up at them sideways as though he thought they were a bit crazy. He recalled the machine's use on Jonnie and he tried to tell them he had never been shot in the head much.

They worked. Angus had become very expert in adjusting these machines and he twiddled knobs for different depth settings and focuses. Ker was getting a crick in his back bending over and said so. They shushed him. They turned his head in every direction on the plate. At the end of a sweating thirty-five minutes they let him up.

Ker stood there rubbing his neck and trying to get his spine straight again.

Jonnie looked at him. "Tell us about your birth, Ker."

Ker thought this was a bit mad. He opened his mouth to speak and then glanced at the door. He took a device out of his pocket and plunked it against the area beside the view port. It had a little light sphere on it and would tell them whether anyone was standing outside. Angus checked the intercom set into the panel and turned it off.

"Well," said Ker, "I was born of wealthy parents—"

"Oh, come on, Ker," said Jonnie. "Truth, we want the truth, not some fairy tale!"

Ker looked a little offended. He sighed in a martyred fashion. He took out a miniature box-flask of kerbango and chewed off a small piece. He needed that. He hunkered down against the wall and began all over again.

"I was born of wealthy parents on Psychlo," said Ker. "The father was named Ka. It was a very proud family. His first female gave birth to a litter. Usually a Psychlo litter is four pups, sometimes five. In this case it was six. Well, it often happens that when there's that many pups, one of them is a runt—not enough space in the female organs or something.

"So anyway, I was the sixth pup and a runt. Not wanting the family disgraced, they threw me out in the garbage, that being the usual treatment for such.

"A family slave, for his own reasons, fished me out and took me away. He was a member of an underground revolutionary organization. There are miles of abandoned mine shafts under the Imperial City and slaves escape into them and nobody can keep them policed, so there I was. Maybe that's why I'm at home in the mines. The slaves were of the Balfan race, blue-colored people. They aren't exactly ordinary-looking—they can breathe breathe-gas, the Psychlo atmosphere, and don't have to wear masks and so they can be seen easily in the streets. Maybe they had an idea they needed a Psychlo of their own to plant bombs or something. But anyway, they brought me up and trained me to steal things for them. I could slip in and out of small places, being so small.

"When I was about eight, which is pretty young for a Psychlo, an Imperial Bureau of Investigation agent named Jayed infiltrated the group with what they call agents provocateurs, to provoke them to commit big crimes so they could be arrested. The I.B.I. raided the underground after a while.

"Being small, I got out through an old ventilator shaft. I was hungry after that and just wandering in the streets. So I found a small window in back of a goo-food ship; it was too small to be barred for no normal Psychlo could get in. So I crawled through and tripped an alarm system—a fact that encouraged me later to learn all about such things."

Ker paused and took another small chew of kerbango. Actually it was a welcome break for him: one can't handle kerbango wearing a breathe-mask for you can't spit out the small grainy residue. It was kind of a relief to him as well. He'd never told the story before.

"Anyway," Ker continued, "they tried me and found me guilty and sentenced me to be branded with the three bars of denial and a century of service in the Imperial pits. There I was, eight years old, at hard labor with hard criminals.

"I was too small to fit any of their shackles so they just let me run around and that's why I haven't any shackle marks on my ankles. I don't have to be careful when I take off my boots.

"Because I was foot-loose (ha ha), the older criminals could use me to carry illegal messages between the chain gangs and cells and they educated me pretty thoroughly in crime.

"When I was about fifteen, there was a plague hit the pits and a lot of guards died, and having no shackles I escaped.

"By this time I knew my business, even though fifteen is pretty young for a Psychlo. Being small, I could get in and out of windows and cubbyholes nobody thought to bar and I collected myself a lot of ready cash.

"I bought false identity papers, bribed an Intergalactic Mining company personnel clerk, and got myself employed as a shaft man because I could get in and out of small places.

"I served in various systems for the company and have somehow gotten along for the last twenty-five years. I'm only forty-one and a Psychlo lives to be about one hundred ninety, so I got one hundred forty-nine years to go. The immediate problem is how I plan to spend it (ha ha)."

"Thank you," said Jonnie. "What leverage does Terl have on you?"

"That ape? None now. He did have, but not now. None. Praise the devils!"

"Were you ever trained in math?" asked Jonnie.

Ker laughed. "No, I'm dummy at it. All I am is a practical engineer—no education but experience . . . and crime of course."

"Do you like cruelty, Ker?"

The midget Psychlo hung his head. He looked ashamed in the reflected light from the machine. "As long as I'm being honest, which is a novelty I can tell you, I have to pretend to like cruelty, to get my fun out of hurting things. Otherwise other Psychlos would consider me abnormal! But . . . no, I don't like it, I'm sorry to say." He roused himself. "Say, Jonnie, what's all this about?"

Angus and Jonnie looked at each other. This Psychlo didn't have any objects in his head. None at all!

But Jonnie was not going to let go of vital data. Ker didn't know about such objects and probably very few Psychlos did. "You've got a different skull structure from other Psychlos," said Jonnie. "You are completely different."

Ker jerked into alertness. "Is that a fact? Well, well. I often felt there was some difference." He became pensive. "Psychlos don't like me. And actually I don't like them. I'm glad to have the reason."

Jonnie and Angus were very relieved about their test. They didn't want Ker attacking them and committing suicide when he realized they were seeking the answer to the riddle of teleportation.

They were just gathering up their gear when the telltale on the door flashed. Somebody was just outside.

— 8 —

Ker got on his breathe-mask. He tiptoed over to the machine and picked it up, using only one arm. Then he tiptoed over to the door and suddenly swung it open as though walking out.

A wave of breathe-gas burst out of the room.

Lars was standing there, frozen in the act of attaching a listening device to the door. He wore no air mask.

The invisible puff of breathe-gas hit Lars full in the face.

He must have been in the act of taking a breath at that moment for he rose on his toes like someone being strangled.

He gagged. He reeled back. He fought for air. He started to turn blue. In another few seconds he would start into convulsions.

Jonnie and Angus grabbed him, one on each arm, and rushed him back to clearer air. Angus fanned him with a metal plate he'd found on the floor.

Gradually Lars came back to life. The blue tinge faded. But what he said was, "What were you doing in there?" and he said it angrily.

"Now, now, laddie," said Angus soothingly. "Here we are saving of your life and ye're making mean sounds. Tch. Tch."

Lars was looking at Jonnie with a peculiar expression on his face. Jonnie went over to where Ker was rattling the housing around in the car as though he had just put it there.

"It's all right now," said Ker. "No cracks or metal faults in the housing. We better go see if it fits."

They drove off and left Lars lying there, gazing after them with that peculiar look.

"Why's he looking at me that way?" asked Jonnie.

"You better be careful," said Ker. "He's a crazy one. And he's the Council's long nose and pry. He's got some idea that somebody named Bitter or Hitter was the greatest military leader in your history, and if you stand still for ten seconds he'll begin on you. It's some church. There's nothing wrong with religion but plenty wrong with what *he* says. Terl wrecked his wits. But there wasn't much there in the first place. Ha. Ha."

"But why that peculiar look at *me?*" asked Jonnie.

"Natural suspicion," said Ker. "Say, you know I feel a lot better since talking to you creatures! I sure am glad I'm different."

They stopped and got out below the top compound level where Terl's office was. They removed the housing from the car and struggled up the ramp with it.

Just before they went in, Angus stopped them. "Why couldn't Terl fix this place up himself?"

Ker laughed. "When Jonnie left here he said to spread it that the place was booby-trapped. But that isn't all of it." He indicated the door to Terl's office with a paw wave. "If the Psychlos got out from the dormitory section they could come here and kill anybody working here. Terl's pretty sure they'd kill him if they got loose. They *hate* him."

"Wait," said Jonnie. "That means Terl will get them killed before he moves in here." He put a hand on the door latch to the office. "You did debug this place and look for booby traps?"

"Ha. Ha!" said Ker. "I had been tearing this place to bits waiting for you!"

They went in and set the housing down. Indeed the place *was* a wreck. Wires pulled out, the old breath-gas circulator scattered in bent pieces on the floor, desks and chairs askew, paper thrown about.

Jonnie looked it over. At once he saw that in Terl's inner

office the whole lower section of the wall to the right of Terl's desk as he would sit at it was lined with large, locked compartments. "Been into those?" he said.

Ker shook his head. "No keys. A security chief loves his security."

Jonnie sent Angus out to find a sentry. The cadets were still the guards in this compound. Ker, with his blanket authority, repeated what Jonnie whispered to him and sent for Chirk.

They got to work sorting out wires and papers and trash and presently three cadet sentries showed up with Chirk.

She was a long way from the smart-looking secretary of the old days. They had her on three chain links attached to a collar. Her fur was all the wrong way. There was no powder on her nosebone and no polish on her triple-jointed claws. She wore just a cloth thrown around her shoulders, no other clothes.

"Where's the keys?" said Ker, as prompted.

Keys! Everybody wanted keys! Her voice was punctuated with fang clicks and snaps and hisses. It wasn't enough Terl brought them all to this and sought to ruin her company record by saying she was disobedient and didn't follow orders, but she had to be dragged all over—in chains!—just to say *what* keys now? That day of the battle Terl provoked, everybody had been after the keys, keys, keys. Her company duties—

Jonnie was quietly whispering in Ker's ear. Ker whispered back, "You trying to start a riot?" But as Jonnie insisted, Ker said loudly to Chirk, "Shut up! Just because Terl plans to murder all of you down there is no reason to take it out on us!"

Chirk went very still. Through the face mask glass her eyes got very round. The flutter valve of the mask started pumping rather quickly.

Jonnie whispered again and Ker said, "It might or might not make any difference, but when he moves in here and has free reign of this whole compound, he will be furious with you if the keys aren't found!"

The muscles in the middle of her body where her heart was were twitching and leaping. The flutter valve stopped totally for half a minute. Then started again. "He's moving in here?" she said so quietly it was hard to hear her though the mask.

"Why else are we fixing it up?" said Ker. Then menacingly, "Where's the keys to those wall doors?"

Chirk shook her head. "He never let anybody have them. They're maybe gone!" Was that a sob in her breath?

"Well, take her away," said Ker gruffly to the guards.

They dragged her off.

"What's going on here?" demanded Lars, popping up in the door.

"We're trying to find the access panels to the wiring," snapped Ker. "It's all shorted out!"

There were breathe-gas vials scattered around. Jonnie reached behind his back and turned one on. Angus, Ker, and himself were wearing masks.

Ker was reaching in his pocket. He pulled out a handful of items and shoved them at Lars. "This is a dangerous job! I demand a higher bonus! These were in the first wiring recess!"

Lars looked at them. Three were dented bullets that looked like radiation ammunition but weren't. Another was a bent time fuse of the kind set in small blast holes. The biggest was a wad of malleable explosive compound.

"Somebody has been getting into this office!" said Ker. "After this I want the door *locked*. I want nobody in or out of here but *us* and I want *you* miles away before you kill yourself and get me blamed for it. I know how you work!"

Lars was beginning to cough again from the new breathe-gas coming out of the vial.

"See?" said Ker. "These ducts are still loaded with breathe-gas and it leaks!"

Lars was backing out into the hall, still coughing. He lifted the objects that had been put in his hand. "Are these dangerous?"

"Take them and throw them at your betters and find out!" said Ker. "And if I see you around here again, I'll tell them you are slowing down this job by issuing orders to take it easy. Get out, go away, stay out, and if I see your face again you will just have to find another expert! Got it? I'll quit!"

Lars looked at Jonnie in a very peculiar way. But at that moment, from the direction of the distant dormitory three levels down, came some angry howls and snarls. Lars rushed off.

"Did you really find those items in here?" said Angus.

"Of course not," said Ker. "Shut, lock, and bar those doors out there and let's get to work. The last place Terl will want to be for now is in this compound. After we're finished and he's sent somebody else to see whether they get blown up is the first he'll want to see of this place." He listened to the distant howls and roars. "You sure started a riot, Jonnie. Terl will hear that clear out in the cage. That Chirk really told them!"

Jonnie barred and locked the outer doors and then gestured from Angus to the wall cabinet locks and Angus whipped out a small set of picks and went to work on them.

They were in business!

■

PART 20

— 1 —

Their problem was really bugging the place more thoroughly than any place had ever been bugged while still preventing the bugs from being discovered by one who, although quite mad, was one of the sharpest security chiefs ever to walk out of the mine schools.

If they did this well, they would have a total record of the technology of teleportation and its mathematics. They would know what happened to Psychlo because they would be able to cast out picto-recorders. They would know the whereabouts and possibly the intentions of other races. They would be in communication with the stars and universes and could defend themselves on Earth.

Terl would have to work out and build from scratch a whole transshipment console, for the one out there near the old platform was a burned-out ruin.

They needed devices that could read over his shoulder every book he opened, every page of figures he made. They needed to fix up his workroom in his office and rig it so that every resistor he picked up, every wire he put in, would be recorded exactly.

It was certain that he would sweep the place with a probe before every work period and possibly after every day of toil. He would be meticulous in his bug detection.

If Terl had any inkling the technology would be observed he would not start. If he thought it had been taken away by an alien, he would commit suicide. For there was no doubt that Terl had in his skull both the devices they had found in the dead Psychlos.

Before they had left Africa, Dr. MacKendrick had been very pessimistic about being able to remove such brain devices from all that bone and still have a live, functioning Psychlo on his hands. That chance was not entirely gone. But it was nothing to be counted on.

Angus had lately begun to understand why Jonnie had kept Terl alive, why they didn't just get out some battle planes and wipe this new political mess out. It was a very delicate situation. It was a thin chance. It had to work. But with what risks! Angus had no doubt whatever that Jonnie was holding his own life at stake. A huge and dangerous risk. But what a prize. The Psychlo technology of teleportation. Earth depended upon it.

Jonnie was a cool one, Angus thought. He himself would never have that much patience or be able to retain that detached an overview of the entire scene without permitting personal considerations from entering in.

Angus looked up from the locks. He was in awe of Jonnie as he thought about what they were doing. These people or Terl would kill Jonnie in a flash if they found him or knew what he was up to. Robert the Fox had denounced it as folly and a hopeless, unwarranted risk. Angus didn't think so. It was a brand of courage he had never seen before.

He got the cabinets opened. They contained all the paraphernalia a security chief ever thought he would need. They contained papers and records Terl would consider vital.

Jonnie was looking for superconfidential notes on teleportation or its odd mathematics. On his inspection he did not find anything on those subjects beyond normal tests. But he did find an item of interest.

It was a record of all the mineral deposits left on Earth. The company had not made a mineral survey for itself for centuries, content with their originals. But Terl had.

Jonnie smiled. There were *sixteen* lodes of gold on the planet almost as good as the one they had mined! In the Andes and the Himalayas—they just weren't that close to home and it would have been more public to have mined them. Ah, yes. All these other lodes were also associated with uranium.

There were thick records of Earth's existing mineral resources. Hundreds of years of security chiefs had continued to log the findings of the drones, which were used for security but were essentially mineral spotters.

The company, with its "semicore" methods of mining, could go down almost to the molten core, to the very bottom of the crust without breaking through. And they were content to mine what they had and conserve their assets of unmined wealth.

Terl had simply removed the records from company view for his own purposes.

Ores, metals! The planet was still wealthy in resources.

Jonnie recorded every page rapidly. This was not what he was here for, but it was nice to know their planet had not been bankrupted of minerals. They would need them.

Angus had found what they were really looking for just now—Terl's bug probe. It was an oblong box with an aerial sticking out of it and a disc cup on the tip of the aerial. It had on/off switches for various frequencies and light domes and buzzers.

Jonnie had done his apprenticeship well in the electronics ship. He knew that no wave this could detect would pass through lead or a lead alloy. Ordinarily this would not be a factor since any bug of any kind whatsoever would also not pass through lead. Therefore, why detect it since it wouldn't work as a bug or button camera if it had lead over it?

The first job was to rig these switches.

Jonnie made a trip to electronics stores and got what he wanted. He came back to find that Ker had swept the area for bugs and found none.

They chose where Terl would do his shopwork: in Chirk's former reception office. It was big enough to work in and the size console it would be would go in and out of the door.

While Jonnie, at his desk, worked on the bug probe, the other two rigged a workbench out of a metal slab and welded it to the floor and then armor annealed the welds so it would be an awful lot of trouble to move. They even got a stool and put it in front of it. When they had finished, they had a very nice layout. Jonnie moved his work over to it.

He had made excellent progress. Using microbutton transmitters employed normally in remote controls, he had rigged every switch in the probe so that when it was turned on it would send out an impulse from the remote relay. These relays took a microscope to see properly. They were fastened in with a small molecular spray. The worst part was getting them to stay where one wanted them while spraying them down. But the eye that could detect them unaided had never been made.

Using a scope set at a distance from the probe, he clicked each switch on in turn and the scope bounced in response.

The next part was hard because it involved the adaption of iris leaves taken from tubes of plane viewers. These were small devices that automatically adjusted the volume of a light path. They would close their concentric leaves from wide open to shut.

They had to take these delicate things apart and spray them, molecules thick, with lead and reassemble them so they would not only work but would go on working, opening and closing. Angus was the best at this sort of work.

They then got some contraction rings and put them around these leaded irises and installed microbuttons in them to activate them.

When they had built about fifteen of these, they made a thorough and extensive test. When the probe was clicked on the iris instantly closed. When the probe was turned off the irises sprang open.

In other words, the leaded irises would be shut whenever the probe was on, thus putting a lead screen over any bug and making it undetectable and for the moment unable to "see" and "hear." But when the probe was off, the screen would be off and any bug or device could "see" and "hear."

So far so good. They now went on an extensive tour of storerooms—telling Lars, who showed up, that they were looking for "spindle-buffers"—and located not only every other bug probe in the compound but also every other key component it took to make a bug probe. They put these in a box and put the box in their car to be transported out of the country.

They now had a probe that wouldn't probe while obviously working and fifteen irises they could put in front of bug devices.

Lars popped up again, saying they sure were quiet, and they told him to get lost. But presently Ker took a disc recording of hammering and pounding and drilling and let it play.

They cleaned up traces of their work so far and hid their products.

Suddenly they realized it had been a long day. They hadn't eaten. They had a long way to go, but that, they agreed, was enough for now.

Jonnie and Angus, not wanting to tempt the fates by running into too many cadets at the Academy, elected to bed down in Char's old quarters. Ker was going to drive back to the Academy and get them something to eat and bring them some work clothes.

Dunneldeen should be there now and Jonnie had a message for him about the Psychlos. Jonnie typed it out on Chirk's writing machine:

> All's well. In three days engineer the transportation of the thirty-three Ps now in compound jailhouse to stated destination Cornwall. Report them crashed at sea. Deliver to the doctor. Not before three days. You will have no trouble with them. They'll be screaming to leave. Eat this note.

Ker said he'd deliver it and rushed away.

Jonnie and Angus stretched out to unwind. So far it was okay. They had a ways to go.

— 2 —

A bit lost in Char's twelve-foot bed, a bit tense in this echoing, empty compound, Jonnie was waiting for Ker's return. It was getting very late and he was wondering what the delay might be. But to pass the time he was reading.

Char, in packing, had tossed out odds and ends that he hadn't cared to take back to Psychlo with him, and one of them was a Psychlo infant's "History of Psychlo," maybe from Char's own early schooling, for it said under the coverleaf, in an immature scrawl, "Char's Book. You Stole it so give it back!" and then below that, "Or I'll claw you!" Well, Char wouldn't claw anybody now: he was dead, by Terl's thrust, quite a time now.

Because Ker had mentioned underground mines, Jonnie was mildly interested to learn that the whole of the Imperial City on Psychlo and all the surrounding area was a maze of deep and abandoned shafts and drifts. As long as three hundred thousand years ago, Psychlo had exhausted surface minerals and had developed semicore techniques. Some of the shafts went down as far as eighty-three miles and in some cases that was within half a mile of the liquid core. How awfully hot those mines must have been! They could only be worked by machines, not living beings. The labyrinth was so extensive that it caused some buildings on the surface to sag from time to time.

He was just reading about the "First Interplanetary War to End Mineral Starvation" when Ker came back.

Ker looked a bit grave, even through his face mask. "Dunneldeen's been arrested," he said.

Dunneldeen, related Ker, had arrived in a battle plane just at sunset and had gone to find quarters and supper. As he came out of the mess hall, two men in monkey skins with crossbelts stepped out of the shadows and told him he was under arrest. A squad of several more were at a distance.

They had taken Dunneldeen in a ground car driven by Lars up to the big capitol building, the one with the painted dome up in the ruined city. They pushed him into the "courtroom" and the Senior Mayor Planet started to charge him with a whole lot of crimes like interrupting Council projects and committing war and had then looked at him more closely and said, "You're not Tyler!" And had called for the guard captain and there'd been a row. Then this Senior Mayor made Dunneldeen promise not to incite a war with Scotland over this and had let him go.

Dunneldeen was back at the Academy after taking Lars' car away from him and he was all right. Ker had had to wait to give him the message and Dunneldeen said to warn Jonnie.

"It means," concluded Ker, "that they expected you to come in and they've got their eyes out all over the place. We got to work fast, be careful, and get you out of here as soon as we can."

Jonnie and Angus ate a bit of the food Ker had brought and then went to sleep for four hours. Ker had turned in in his old room, sleeping in a breathe-mask for there was no breathe-gas circulation in the general compound.

They were at it again before dawn, working fast. Ker had another disc recording of hammering and pounding and he put it on. The kind of work they were doing didn't sound at all like duct work.

What they had to do now was plant "eyes" and picture transmitters so they could not be seen or detected.

They attacked the lead glass dome and bored "bullet holes" in it in the exact right places; getting around the problem of their being covered by the blinds if drawn. The very top of one of these upper-level domes was much more thickly tinted than the sides, so the detectors ("readers," Ker called them) had to be up pretty high.

The ' bullet holes' also had to be starred out, which is to say, given hairline cracks to make it look like they had come in from the outside. For good measure they put some in other domes and didn't repair them so that the condition appeared more general than in just Terl's quarters.

They sank readers and transmitters into the holes. Then they repaired the holes with one-way, see-through "bubble patch." They put more glass repair sealing roughly on the "cracks."

Each reader had a leaded iris in front of it and was in a little lead box. The result looked like a crudely repaired hole fixed up in slovenly fashion by careless workmen. Each of these was focused on a different part of the work areas in the two rooms.

"He won't fool with that," grinned Ker. "He'll be afraid he'll let his breathe-gas out and air in!"

It was afternoon by the time they completed the dome readers. They tested them with the probe and receivers. They went blind and undetectable with the probe on and read everything in their path with the scope off.

They took a short lunch break and turned off the disc that had been blasting their ears in. There was suddenly more din outside.

Ker went to the door and unbarred it. Lars got a whiff of breathe-gas and backed up. He demanded Ker to come out and talk to him right now.

"You're interrupting our work." said Ker. But he went out in the hall.

"You ve got your nerve!" said Lars. quivering with rage. "You gave me a handful of junk that had radioactive dust on it! You got me in trouble! When I showed it to Terl this morning, it started to explode when it got near his breathe-mask. You knew it would! He almost bit me!"

"All right, all right, all right!" said Ker. "We will clean up everything in here before we turn on any big amount of breathe-gas."

"Those were radioactive bullets!" shouted Lars.

"All right!" said Ker. "They came in through the dome. We'll find them all. Don't get so excited!"

"Trying to get me in trouble," said Lars.

"You stay out of here," said Ker. "It rots human bones, you know."

Lars didn't know. He backed up. He left.

Angus said, when Ker had come back in and barred the door, "Were they really radioactive bullets?"

Ker laughed and began to shove goo-food in his mask. Jonnie marveled. Ker was the only Psychlo he had ever seen that could chew kerbango with a mask on and now he was eating goo-food and talking with a mask on.

"It was flitter," said Ker, laughing. "It's a compound that throws off blue sparks when sunlight hits it. I dusted some of it on the bullets. Harmless. A kid's toy." He was laughing even harder. Then he sighed. "We had to explain the bullet holes, so we had to 'find' some bullets. But that Terl—he is so clever that he sometimes can be awful dumb!"

Jonnie and Angus laughed with him. They could imagine Terl seeing the sparks when Lars held out the "finds" Ker had given him and the sunlight setting off the blue sparks. Terl's conviction that the world was after him must have driven him halfway through the back wall of the cage! He would have thought his own breathe-mask exhaust was setting off uranium!

They were into the duct work now and they really did start hammering and pounding. The trick was to inset lead-irised readers into the duct vent intakes and exhausts around the room so that they could not be seen and yet, peering out of the dark depths of the vents, could read an exact portion of the workrooms. The ducts actually required some very fancy work of their own. Although Ker was a midget, he could bend sheet iron with his paws like it was paper.

Ker fixed it so the ducts, as they entered and left the room, were rickety. If you touched them they appeared to be in danger of coming apart and falling out. But in actual fact the final fittings were armor-welded.

They set the readers into these, made sure the irises worked, put the ducts in place, and began on the circulator pumps. It was late evening by this time, but they worked straight on through. By about one in the morning they had completed a usable circulator system that would go on working.

They felt they were running behind in time so they didn't stop. They had the problem now of centralizing the transmissions of all the readers and getting them clear over to the Academy miles away.

None of these readers could be powered and picked up from

more than a few hundred feet away. They all had different frequencies to keep them apart and this meant a bulky feeder system.

Jonnie worked on the probe some more and put an on/off remote in it that would turn off and on the multichanneled feeder box. That was the easiest part. One mustn't have radio waves flying about with a probe on.

The tough part of it was getting the transmission through to the Academy. They solved it by using ground waves. Ground waves differ from air waves in that they can travel only through the ground. The "aerial" to send is a rod driven in the earth and the "aerial" to receive is simply another. It takes a different wavelength band so there was no danger of anything detecting it. Since ground waves were not in general use by the Earth Psychlos it required a feverish fabrication of components, converting normal radio to ground wave.

It was the fall of the year and it was still dark when Angus and Ker went screeching off to the Academy to install the receivers and recorders, one unit in a toilet, one in an unused telephone box, and the third under a loose tile in front of the altar in the chapel.

Jonnie meanwhile buried the feeder outside the dome in the ground. He had the pretext ready of "looking for power cables" but he didn't need it. The world slept. He shoved in fuel cartridges to run it for half a year or more, wrapped it in waterproofing, buried it in the hole, pounded in the ground aerial, and restored the turf. Nobody could detect the grass had even been touched—a hunter's skill in making deadfalls came in handy.

Inside again, he checked. Every lead iris was working flawlessly. The readers were powered. They went on and off at the feeder. He let them run to give Angus and Ker a signal to set their recorders to, over at the Academy.

Jonnie busied himself with placing and armor-welding the desks and drawing board in place. No molecular cutter would ever dent those welds!

At eight o'clock Angus and Ker sauntered in as though just arriving for the day. They bolted the door and both turned huge grins on Jonnie.

"It works!" said Angus. "We watched you laboring away and

even read the serial number of your welding torch. We got all fifteen readers on the screen!" He thrust out his hand. "And here's the discs!"

They replayed them. They could even see the grain in material, much less read numbers!

They heaved a sigh of relief.

Then Angus took Jonnie by the shoulder and pointed to the door. "We needed your skill and ideas up to now. But from here on, it's just putting cream on the oatmeal to convince Terl. Every minute you stay here is a minute too long."

Ker was already putting the rigged probe back in exactly the same place, arranging the cabinet just as it had been. "When I took on this job and suspected you'd be coming," he said as he worked, "I fueled a plane. It's the one exactly opposite the hangar door—93 is the last of its serial numbers. All waiting for you. They don't want us, they want you!"

"It will take us only forty-five minutes or an hour to rig the rest," said Angus. "You get out of here and that's an order from Sir Robert—to get you gone the moment you can leave."

Ker now had relocked the door of the cabinet and was prying at the corner with a Jimmy to make it appear it had been unsuccessfully tampered with without being opened. "Goodbye!" he said emphatically.

Yes, it was true. They could handle the rest and were in no danger. But it was also true that it had to be completed. He would get ready and stand by in the plane. "Come down and tell me when it's all done," he said.

"You *go!*" said Angus.

Jonnie gave them a salute, and went out. They locked the door behind him. He went down the passage to Char's room to get his kit. It was 8:23 in the morning. Already two hours too late.

— 3 —

By five o'clock that morning, Brown Limper Staffor knew he had found Tyler.

For days now he had been unable to sleep, to even sit down quietly or eat. Forgotten were all other cares of state, forgotten were all other tasks that ordinarily occupied his time. With a wild, intent glare in his eyes, for nearly twenty-four hours a day, he had concentrated only upon closing the trap which had been set. Crime must be punished! A malefactor must be brought to book. The safety and integrity of the state must be given priority. Almost every text he had studied on government, all advice he had been given, proved to him only one thing: he had to *get Tyler!*

Victory had begun to beckon with a drone picture he took off the machine at 3:00 A.M. He had trouble with these machines. Ever since these recorders had been moved to the capitol, he had been irritated by their incomprehensible complexity, and he often hit them when they failed to spit out what was wanted. It made him feel martyred having to do all this work with so little help. But he had been scanning the tray of drone takes that were rolling out from Scotland. The pilot who handled drone control and these machines was not here at this time of day. A nuisance.

And there was Tyler! Dancing one of those insane prances the Highlanders did. By bonfire with half a dozen others. Although the pictures were silent, a pain went through his ears as he imagined the crazy pipe music that must have been playing. Yes! Hunting shirt and all, it was Tyler.

The machine gave him a lot of trouble trying to backtrack its trace. He never could tell one Psychlo number from another. But he managed it and got a blown-up view.

It wasn't Tyler! He realized then he was not being logical. Tyler would not be dancing and flinging his arms about. The last time he had seen him down at the compound, Tyler had been limping heavily on a cane and had no use of his right arm.

But at 4:48 A.M. a picture from another drone, then overflying the Lake Victoria area, spewed out and showed a man by the lake throwing rocks in the water. A man with a hunting shirt, same hair, same beard. Tyler! But it couldn't be Tyler because he was using his right arm to throw and as he drew back it was obvious he had no limp.

He had no more than thrown the picture down on the floor when Lars Thorenson rushed in as though he had news. Brown Limper let him have it *but good*. What were two Tylers doing visible on two different drones in such a short time apart, yet so widely separated on the Earth's surface?

"That's what I am trying to say," cried Lars. "There are three Scots who look like Tyler. But that isn't it. You know what Terl told us to look for? Scars on Tyler's neck from the collar he wore so long. I couldn't understand why Stormalong was wearing his scarf so high around his neck. He never did before. And just five minutes ago I woke up with the whole thing plain as daylight! He's hiding those scars! Tyler is down in that compound right now posing as Stam Stavenger! Stormalong!"

For all the wrong reasons, they had reached the right conclusions.

Brown Limper went into immediate action. Time and time again Lars had told him about this great military hero Hitler and his faultless campaigns. Terl had impressed foresight upon him. He had been ready for this moment.

Two days before, he had finalized the contract with General Snith. One hundred credits a day per man was a lot to pay, but Snith was worth it.

Two commandos had gone by truck to the village in the high meadow. There was no town meeting. The villagers had been swept up regardless of any protest. They had been hastily relocated in the distant village on the other side of the mountain Tyler had once chosen for them. The five youths who might have said something were at the Academy, three of them learning machine operation and how to keep the passes open in winter with blade scrapers, the other two learning to be pilots. Old people and young children didn't have to be listened to and their pleas that their preparations for the coming winter were now ruined could be ignored. As a concession to political sagacity, they had been told they were being moved so the old tactical mines could be dug up and disposed of. These mines—they knew now that they were explosives buried long ago and Brown Limper had shown them this was just another instance of Tyler's lies—had their own role to play in this clever strategy.

Tyler's old home had then been booby-trapped with grenades and blasting caps and Brown Limper had been assured by the Brigante explosive experts that all Tyler would have to do was open a door and he would be blown to bits.

The story would be that Tyler had gone to his house despite warnings about the old mines and that one had blown up. In this way there could not possibly be any outcry or blame attached to Brown Limper. The Senior Mayor Planet was a bit hazy on whether this had been his own idea or Terl's. But no matter, it was brilliant political thinking. The state and nation must be freed of the scourge, the arch-criminal Tyler, and with a minimum of repercussion to the body politic. Also Brown Limper had read someplace that the end justifies the means and this seemed to be a sound basic policy. Brown Limper realized, when he thought about it, that he was becoming a statesman ranked with the most stellar figures of ancient man.

At 6:00 A.M. he ordered General Snith to begin changing the guard at the compound. The cadets were to be permanently relieved on the grounds they didn't like the duty and it interrupted their studies, and the state now had a proper standing army. Brigantes were to be on guard duty there by 8:00 A.M.

A hasty call had ascertained that the other two with "Stormalong" had left some time ago for the Academy and it was so logged by the duty officer at the compound.

Thompson submachine guns had been issued to the Brigante commando. Somehow assault rifles were not available but Thompsons were all right for this duty.

Lars had been briefed. He had been given two picked men armed with submachine guns. He was to go to the compound. He was to lie in wait inside until "Stormalong" appeared and then, with a minimum of disturbance, was to take him in custody. Lars was to bring him here to the courtroom. He was not to alarm Tyler into combat. When Tyler had been formally charged, he would be told his case would be tried by the World Court to be formed in a couple of weeks, and then taken to the old village. "House arrest" and "awaiting trial" were terms Brown Limper had looked up. He would inform Tyler that he was under house arrest. Then it was up to Lars to get him to the meadow. There must be no chance taken of alerting cadets or some Russians holding out at the old tomb.

Lars had said, "I think I should grab him while he's still in Terl's office."

Brown Limper said, "No. Terl has assured me that he can undo any mischief Tyler may get up to if he gets in the office. He has probably remained behind to do something criminal after the others finished. You want to take him alone. The other two might help him. We are after the criminal Tyler. We must get him here smoothly, charge him, and get him up to the meadow. Be polite. Grant any ordinary request. Be smooth. Cause no disturbance. And don't damage the office. That is a request Terl made."

It all seemed a bit muddy and out of sequence to Lars in the briefing, but he got the essential points. He got his two Brigantes, made sure they had their submachine guns, got an executive armored ground car, and left.

Brown Limper told General Snith, "Keep your mercenaries out of sight at the compound, but be alert for trouble this morning. Tell them not to start shooting unless they are attacked."

General Snith got it. His men were ready to earn their pay.

Brown Limper had found the pattern of judicial robes judges used to wear and he had one made for this occasion. He got into it, hopping over to the window and looking out between times, and finally gazed at himself in an old cracked mirror.

The time of reckoning for a lifetime of abuse and insult was at hand!

— 4 —

Jonnie strode two paces inside the door of Char's room.

The muzzle of a submachine gun jabbed into his left side!

A Brigante rose from behind a chair holding another Thompson grimly leveled.

Lars stood up from behind the bed, a blast pistol pointing at him.

"We are not here to kill you," said Lars. He had worked this entire campaign out and added a few embellishments of his own. From all he had heard, this was a treacherous and dangerous criminal liable to do anything. To carry out his principal orders it was necessary to be very intelligent about this, as intelligent as

Hitler would have been. "Just do as we request, and no harm will come to you. This is an entirely legal proceeding. You are under arrest by order of the Council and these are Council troops."

Jonnie, as he entered, had been in the act of removing his air mask or he would have smelled the badly tanned skins and body stench of a Brigante.

An hour. Angus and Ker required an hour to put the vital finishing touches on that office. These creatures might go up to the office and might even have arrest orders for them. He would buy Angus and Ker that hour.

He realized then that Lars and these two Brigantes had been here for a while. Ker, when Jonnie asked for work clothes, had simply bundled up all of Stormalong's gear. It had been in a neat kit by the bed. Now it was strewn about, thoroughly searched. The food bags from both Africa and the Academy were there. They had also been ransacked. Angus's gear had been very slight and he had his tool bag with him, so there was no trace that two men's gear was in this pile.

The Brigante behind him, with a glance at his mate to see that the action was covered, whisked the blast pistol out of Jonnie's belt.

Jonnie shrugged. Buy time! "And you are taking me somewhere?"

"You are to appear this morning before the Council to be charged," said Lars.

Jonnie casually swung the door shut behind him, closing out any view of the corridor. Angus and Ker would not come out that way to go to the hangar but they might make some noise. And worse, might foolishly abandon what they were doing and take these fellows on!

"I haven't had anything to eat since yesterday," said Jonnie. "Do you mind if I have a bite first?"

Lars stepped back to the wall. The Brigante behind him backed away. The one behind the chair stepped to another position and Jonnie collected up the food bag contents and water gourds and sorted them out. He sat down and drank some water out of a gourd. There were some bananas there and he broke some off the small bunch.

The Brigantes hadn't seen any bananas since leaving Africa and eyed them. Jonnie offered them some and they would have taken them, except that Lars barked a reprimand and they quickly snapped back to military duties.

Jonnie ate a banana. Then he found some millet bread and made himself a sandwich from local beef. He had quite a hard time selecting the exact right slices. The huge Psychlo wrist watch on his wrist was whirring off the seconds and minutes. He had marked it for the hour.

"What are these charges all about?" said Jonnie.

Lars smiled very thinly. He was being pumped for confidential Council information. "You will be told in the proper time by the proper people."

Jonnie finished the sandwich and found some wild berries. He ate these. The wrist watch whirred along. Forty-nine minutes to go.

He looked into the food bags and discovered some wild sugar cane from Africa. He peeled it with care and chewed on it, sipping from a gourd between times.

Then it occurred to him if they were all silent, Angus or Ker might come busting in here to see whether he was gone. Angus would suppose Jonnie had taken his kit to the plane, but still, they might just come barging in and get arrested or shot. Very shortly now he had better start this Lars talking so they would hear a strange voice in here.

Forty-two minutes to go.

"You sure messed up my clothes," said Jonnie. "I'll have to repack."

But Lars was intent on something else. He wanted a real double-check on identity and in his haste he had forgotten it. He wanted to make doubly sure about the collar scars. He became clever. A military maneuver was needed here. He didn't want this Tyler to be able to seize a Brigante and use him as a shield. Right now the collar of the work jacket covered his neck.

"There is no idea of inconveniencing you," said Lars. "You are in your work clothes and I should think you would want to appear at your best before such an august body as the Council. You can change your clothes if you wish. We've removed all knives and weapons. So go ahead."

Jonnie had smiled wryly when "august body of the Council" was mentioned. What pomposity! But he said, "Oh well, in that case I suppose I had better."

He began to sort the scattered clothes into piles, making noise. It would be better if he could keep Lars talking. Thirty-nine minutes to go.

Ker certainly had brought all of Stormalong's kit. He folded it all neatly and then began picking up items and looking at them critically as though deciding which he should wear, saying, "Would this do?" and "How about this?" and "How do they ordinarily dress when appearing before the Council? In something like this?" He got Lars advising him. The Council was very formal, very strict and mindful of its dignity, and its power was enormous and men were expected to realize it. Twenty-eight minutes to go.

Jonnie suddenly saw that Stormalong, who was always very neat as well as a bit dashing about clothes, had preserved the costume he had been issued in lode days to look like Jonnie. Chrissie had made several sets, pushed into it by Jonnie to take her mind off her imprisonment, and Jonnie had handed out sets to Dunneldeen, Thor, and Stormalong to improve their duplication. He unwrapped the buckskin hunting shirt and breeches and belt. Yes, even the moccasins. Twenty-three minutes to go!

Jonnie took off his jacket, intending to sponge off a bit before dressing.

Lars leaned forward eagerly. Terl had told him that a good security chief always depended upon body marks for identification. How right! There were the small scars of the collar. He had his man. He became inwardly jubilant. Cheerful.

"You can hurry it along now, Tyler," said Lars. "I know you for sure. The collar scars!"

So that's what he had been looking for, thought Jonnie.

"The others left hours ago, didn't they?" said Lars.

"Well, yes, as a matter of fact they did," said Jonnie. It came to him that the others had been logged out when they went to the Academy to install the recorders and must not have been logged back in. Great! Twenty minutes to go.

"And you stayed behind to rig some little tricks of your own, didn't you?" said Lars. "We'll find them later, never fear. Your masquerade is over, Tyler." Lars thought that was pretty good. He had thought it up himself. "Get dressed."

Jonnie took a piece of buckskin and gave himself a sponge bath, a procedure looked upon with total amazement by the

Brigantes. They had never seen nor heard of anyone ever taking a bath.

"How did you get onto me?" asked Jonnie.

"I'm afraid," said Lars, "that that is a state secret."

"Ah," said Jonnie. Seventeen minutes to go! "Something you learned from Hitter or Bitter or whomever that was?" He recalled Ker mentioning this fellow was crazy on the subject.

"You mean Hitler!" corrected Lars angrily.

"Ah, 'Hitler,' " said Jonnie. "That doesn't sound like a Psychlo name. Psychlo names aren't two syllables, usually. Sometimes they are, though."

"Hitler was *not* a Psychlo!" said Lars emphatically. "He was a *man*. He was the greatest military leader and the holiest church member man ever had!"

"Must have been a long time ago," said Jonnie. Fifteen minutes and seventeen seconds to go! They were almost in the clear for their forty-five minutes. But it could be an hour.

Well, yes, said Lars, it was a long time ago. How'd Lars ever find out about Hitler? Well, his family was from Sweden and they were very literate. In fact his father was a minister. And they had some old books the church had kept that had been printed by the "German War Propaganda Ministry" in the purest Swedish and it really was inspirational. It seems that to be really religious, one had to be a pure Aryan and an Aryan was really a Swede. Most people in the tribe had the colossal nerve to scoff at such holy creeds, but it had been the state religion of Sweden.

"I wish I'd heard about him sooner," said Jonnie. Twelve minutes and seven seconds to go! "Was he really a great leader?"

Oh, indeed he was, make no mistake about that. Hitler had conquered the whole world and enforced racial purity. You should really read those books. They are truly marvelous. Oh, you can't read Swedish? Well, I could read them to you. What's some parts of them? Oh, well, it would take weeks to cover it all, but for instance there's a part of a book called "Mein Kampf" that outlines the whole destiny of the race. You see, there are really supermen and just plain men. And to be a superman one has to study and know the religious creed of fascism.

"Did they worship god?" said Jonnie. Seven minutes and twelve seconds to go. He began to dress, taking care with the thongs.

Well, of course. God's real name was Der Fuehrer but Hitler

had taken his place on Earth to make a world of peace and goodwill. Now Napoleon was also a military leader and before him was Caesar and before him was Alexander the Great and before him was Attila the Hun. But these men were not holy. One really had to know history to tell the difference. Now even though Napoleon was a great military leader, on many points he didn't favorably compare with Hitler. Even though Napoleon had conquered Russia, he did not show the finesse Hitler showed when *he* conquered Russia. Now all this was very ancient and a long time ago and man had come to grief since, though not through any fault of Hitler's. So it was obvious that if man were to rise and be great again they should follow the creed of religious fascism, and who knew but what some new Hitler might arise to bring peace on Earth and goodwill toward men like Hitler had. It's a funny thing, you know, but his mother used to say when she looked at the old pictures that he, Lars, quite closely resembled—

The distant roar of a car starting up. The snarl of its going around the ramps to exit. The unmistakable mad driving of Ker! They were gone.

Jonnie finished dressing, packed the kit, especially Stormalong's favorite coat and scarf and goggles, and bundled it all up.

"You will be sure this gets to Stormalong," said Jonnie. But as Lars said nothing, Jonnie decided to take it along.

They had done it!

How he would get himself out of this mess he didn't know. He was a little puzzled as to why the other two had driven off when the battle plane must still be down there. But he was grateful they were out of it.

"Let's go," he said.

— 5 —

They exited from a different ground-level door, one that was usually locked. Jonnie glanced around for a cadet to give Stormalong's kit to and saw no one.

"I'll see that it's taken to the Academy," said Lars, divining his purpose. He must not see too deeply into the dispositions Lars had made, most of which prevented them from being seen by anyone lest Lars find himself with a battle on his hands from cadets or Russians, some of whom had just arrived at the underground base in the mountains and were a considerable force.

A storm was coming in from over the mountains, rolling black clouds, studded with lightning around the distant Highpeak. The wind was picking up and bending the tall brown grass. A few dead leaves fled through the air. Autumn was here. There was a chill in the air on this mile-high plateau.

It gave Jonnie an eerie feeling, almost a premonition. He had left Africa in a storm and here was a storm again. He threw the kit in the back and got in. The windows were darkened so no one could see in. With submachine guns trained upon him, they drove toward the capitol.

Lars was a bad driver and Jonnie could see how he must have gotten the cracked neck the plaster cast advertised. Jonnie despised him. Jonnie had known lots of Swedes and they were good people; he had even gathered from Lars' conversation that *they* despised him too.

The man tried to chatter on about the ancient military leader but Jonnie had had enough. "Shut up," he said from the back. 'You're nothing but a turncoat traitor. I don't see how you can stand yourself. So shut up." It was unwise but he couldn't go on listening to this insanity.

Lars shut up but his eyes slitted. He suddenly enjoyed the fact that this criminal would be dead in a few hours.

The ground car squatted down at a side entrance to the capitol, never used. There were no people to be seen. There were no people in the corridor either. Lars had seen to that.

They thrust him toward a door. Unseen Brigantes in the shadows kept their guns trained upon him. Two more were in the courtroom, in the corners, Thompsons cocked and ready.

And there sat Brown Limper.

He was at a high desk on a dais. He was in a black robe. Ancient law books flanked him on either side. His face had an unhealthy sheen. His eyes were too bright. He loomed like a vulture about to attack a corpse. Just himself, the Brigante guards, and this Tyler in an otherwise empty room.

It *was* Tyler! He had recognized that the moment the fellow strode through the door. There was an air about this Tyler one couldn't miss. He had hated it since they were children. Hated that easy confident walk, hated that set of even features, hated those light blue eyes. He had hated everything Tyler was and he could never be. But who had the power now? He, Brown Limper! How he had daydreamed of this moment.

"Tyler?" said Brown Limper. "Come stand in front of the court bench! Answer me: is your name Jonnie Goodboy Tyler?" Brown Limper had a recorder running. Such proceedings must be regular and legal.

Jonnie came to a bored stand in front of the bench. "What is this farce, Brown Limper? You know my name well enough."

"Silence!" said Brown Limper, hoping his voice was resonant and deep. "The prisoner will answer correctly and properly or become guilty of contempt of court!"

"I see no court," said Jonnie. "What are you doing in that funny dress?"

"Tyler, I am adding contempt of court to these charges."

"Add what you please," said Jonnie, bored with it.

"You will not consider this lightly when I read you what you are charged with! This at present is just a hearing. In a week or two, a World Court will be established and the trial will take place at that time. But as a felon and criminal you have the right to hear the charges so that you can organize your defense when tried!

["Now hear ye, hear ye. You are charged with a count of murder in the first degree, the victims being the Chamco brothers, loyal employees of the state, feloniously assaulted with intent to kill and later dying by their own hand due to pain of their wounds.

"Kidnapping in the first degree, the said Tyler assaulting and feloniously seizing the persons of two Coordinators going about their legal dutics as agents of the Council.

"Murder and felonious assault upon a peace-loving and unoffending tribe called the Brigantes including the slaughter of half a commando.

"Massacre of a convoy of peaceful commercial people going about their business and viciously and maliciously slaughtering them to the last man."]

"Psychlos," said Jonnie. "They were Psychlos organizing an attack upon this capital."

"That's stricken from the records!" said Brown Limper Indeed, he would have to erase it from this disc. "You are not on trial.

These are just the charges that have been brought against you by decent and deserving citizens of this planet. Remain silent and hear the charges!

[''It is noted by the court,''] continued Brown Limper—how he had slaved over this parlance from ancient books; he hoped he had it all right and legal—[''that numerous other charges could be brought but at this time have not been brought.'']

''Such as?'' said Jonnie, indifferent to this clown.

''When you seized the remote control panel from one Terl and launched the drone against man, it has also been stated that you then and thereupon shot down said Terl when he was in the act of trying to shoot down the drone. However, there being witnesses, undoubtedly perjured and extorted by you to speak false testimony, who speak otherwise, the charges have not been included at this time, though of course they may be brought at some later date.''

''So that's all you could come up with,'' said Jonnie, with irony. ''Nothing about stealing babies' milk? I'm surprised!''

''You won't be so arrogant when you hear the rest of this,'' threatened Brown Limper. [''I am an impartial judge and this is a legal and impartial court. In the interim time pending your trial, you are forbidden to use any more of my] . . . I mean, [Council property such as planes, cars, houses, equipment, or tools!'']

Brown Limper had him! Quick as a flash he pulled out the bill of sale of the Earth branch of the Intergalactic Mining Company and thrust it at Tyler.

Tyler took it and looked at it. [''For a sum of two billion credits, one Terl, duly authorized representative of the party of the first part which shall hereafter be called the party of the first part, did hereby convey all lands, mines, minesites, compounds, planes, tools, machinery, cars, tanks] . . . on and on . . . [to the Council of Earth, the duly elected and authorized government of said planet, to have and to hold forever and from this day forward.''] It was signed ''Terl,'' but Jonnie, who knew Terl's signature, saw that it must have been written with the wrong paw. He started to put it in his pouch.

''No, no!'' shouted Brown Limper. ''That is the original!'' He fussed around in the papers on his desk and handed over a copy and exchanged it for the original. Jonnie put the copy in his pouch.

''And not only that,'' said Brown Limper, ''the whole planet was the property of Intergalactic and there is a deed for that as well!'' He started to hand over the original, thought better of it, found a copy, and handed it over.

Jonnie glanced at it. Terl had actually sold these fools their planet!

''The deeds are valid,'' said Brown Limper pompously. ''That is, they will be when fully recorded.''

''Where?'' said Jonnie.

''On Psychlo, of course,'' said Brown Limper. ''Out of the goodness of his heart and in spite of the trouble, Terl himself will take these deeds there and get them fully recorded.''

''When?'' said Jonnie.

''Just as soon as he can rebuild the apparatus you feloniously and maliciously destroyed, Tyler!''

''And he's taking the money with him?''

''Of course! He has to turn it in to his company. He is an honest man!''

''Psychlo,'' corrected Jonnie.

''Psychlo,'' corrected Brown Limper, and then instantly became furious with himself for permitting this judicial proceeding to assume other than a judicial tone.

[''So therefore,''] said Brown Limper, reading, [''and as stated nothwithstanding, in accordance with the legal tribal rights of the said Jonnie Goodboy Tyler, he is hereby placed under house arrest in his own home in the meadow and is herewith and hereby not to quit said home and said vicinity until hailed before a World Court, duly to be constituted under the authority of the Council, said Council being duly elected and invested with the total authority of total government of Earth. Hey man!''] He had thought the last religious note gave it style and he now sat proudly on the bench. ''So unless the prisoner has some last request . . .''

Jonnie had been thinking hard and quickly. He had never before paid much attention to Brown Limper, and such malice, falsehood, and evil was a little surprising. There was a fueled battle plane in the hangar at the compound.

''Yes,'' said Jonnie. ''There is a request. If I am going to the meadow, I would like to pick up my horses first.''

''Those and your house are all the property you own now, so it is only fit that you do so. Out of courtesy and feelings for the rights of the prisoner, and possibly even out of a fatherly feeling for him as his own Mayor, I grant request so long as you go at once from there straight to the village in the meadow and into your house!''

Jonnie looked at him with contempt and strode from the room.

Brown Limper, eyes overbright, watched him go. That would be the end of Tyler! He let out a shuddering sigh. What a relief all this was! And how long sought? Twenty years. No, this was not revenge. He had to do it. Duty demanded it! The peoples of Earth would now be wholly in good hands—his, Brown Limper's. He would do his very best for them, as he was doing now. Despite the toil it cost him.

— 6 —

The incident that would later become known as ''The Murder of Bittie MacLeod,'' which would bring the planet toward war, cost many men their lives, and later become the subject of ballads, romances and legend, began at noon that day with Bittie's unfortunate spotting of Jonnie in the capitol area of Denver.

When the head of the Russian contingent had been given orders in Africa to close the American underground base, it was very plain to the Russians that neither they nor Jonnie would thereafter be resident in America, which brought up the subject of horses. Horses were wealth to the Russians; they had developed a small herd of their own in America and they were not going to abandon them.

Bittie MacLeod considered himself responsible for Jonnie's horses. He informed Colonel Ivan in no uncertain terms that he must go along with them to bring back Jonnie's horses. When objections were raised, he doggedly countered them: he was with the Russians and he would be safe; the horses knew him; Windsplitter, Dancer, Old Pork, and Blodgett would be frightened on the long plane ride unless they had somebody soothing them they knew they could trust. After hours of this, Colonel Ivan gave in.

The Russians, just before dawn of that day, had thoroughly closed the American underground base as well as the nuclear missile store. If anyone tried to get into them now who didn't know the way or have the keys, they would be blown to bits

Planes had been arranged for the return, any material they were taking back abroad was already loaded, and before dawn that day they had left the base in a small convoy of trucks and cars to do their last job: pick up the horses from the plains.

The way from the base led through the ancient ruins of Denver and few of the Russians had ever been there. Further, recently they had begun to get paid. They were going home and they had sisters and wives and sweethearts, mothers and friends.

A few tiny stores had opened lately in Denver, the proprietors from other places, the customers the people of the world making pilgrimages to the minesite. The goods were salvaged and repaired items from the ruins of sprawling cities and even some new products of native tribes. Dresses, shoes, cloth, jewelry, utensils, souvenirs, and relics were the main stocks in trade. The stores were few and widely scattered.

The Russians decided that since they were many hours early for their departure time that evening from the Academy field, and since they did not favor sitting around in the grass waiting, they would spend a little shopping time in Denver.

They had parked their vehicles near the capitol for there was much space there, and its dome could be seen from all around as a landmark and gotten back to easily. They had scattered out, each on his own errands.

Bittie had been given a special guard, a strong, tough Russian who was a special friend of Bittie's named Dmitri Tomlov, and Dmitri had been charged by Colonel Ivan to stay close to Bittie and not be careless and to carry his assault rifle and magazine pouch wherever he went. So it seemed all right.

Bittie and his guardian had found a little jewelry and trinket shop that had been opened by an old Swiss couple and their son. The old Swiss had found and repaired an engraving machine; he was also clever with repairing items found in ancient wrecked stores—where and when they had been overlooked by metal-hungry Psychlos.

The son was in a back room of the shop recovering from trying to defend the store from being robbed by the Brigantes—it seemed the Brigantes would go around telling everyone they were "police" and they carried clubs and would pick up anything that took their fancy and put it in their pockets. The Council, when approached by the few people now in Denver, had admitted that yes, the Brigantes *were* "police," and that law and order was vital and that it was a felony to resist "police." Nobody really knew what "police" meant as a word, but they had come to realize it was something very bad. So the old Swiss had decided to move away and a lot of his items were for sale at very low prices.

The wife was waiting on Dmitri. He had lots of relatives. But his first purchase was a little silver-headed riding crop for Bittie. Although Bittie would have been aghast at the idea of hitting a horse, the crop looked very nice. It was about two feet long, about the length of a Brigante bow although no one noticed this at the time.

Despite all these very low prices, Bittie was having a rough time. He wanted something special for Pattie. He thought he would be seeing her shortly. He looked and looked, helped by the old man. Also Bittie did not have very much money with him: his pay was only two credits a week whereas a soldier's was a credit a day. Pay had not been going on very long so Bittie only had four credits and the better items were as much as ten. Bittie's problems were also complicated by the limited command of English on the part of the Swiss people, who spoke a combination of German and French. The Russian was no help—he had practically no English and nobody spoke Russian there, including Bittie. But they were making out with signs and count marks on scraps of wrapping paper and raised eyebrows and pointing fingers.

At last Bittie found it! It was a real gold-plated locket in the shape of a heart. It had a red rose, still bright red, inset on it. It opened and you could put pictures inside and it had had its hinge nicely repaired and it had a thin chain. Also it had enough space on the back to engrave something, and yes, the old Swiss would be happy to engrave it. With one credit for the engraving, it all came to six credits. It was the very thing. But six credits! He only had four.

Well, the old Swiss was selling out, and when he saw the disappointment on Bittie's face, he relented and let him have it, with a box thrown in, all engraved, repolished and ready to go.

When given a card to put the message on so it could be copied, Bittie fell into more difficulty. What was he going to put on the back of the locket? Jonnie and others had told him that he and Pattie were far too young to get married and that was true. So he couldn't put "To my future wife" really, for people might smile and this was no smiling matter. He didn't want to simply put

"To Pattie Love Bittie" as the old Swiss seemed to be suggesting. The Russian was no help at all. Then he had it! "To Pattie my ladye faire, Bittie." The old Swiss then said that was too long to fit on the back. So he had to come back, after all, to "To Pattie, my future wife." The old Swiss counted that up and said he could fit that in. It wasn't too satisfactory and people might laugh, but he couldn't do any better and the old Swiss set up his engraving machine and had at it.

All this was taking time and Bittie was getting edgy. He might miss the Russians, and after all Jonnie's horses were *his* job as squire and that's why he had come over to America. He hopped from one foot to the other and pushed at them all to hurry. The Swiss finally finished and put the locket in a nice box and wrapped it in some old paper, and the Russian finally got all the things he wanted and they paid it all up and went rushing out to get back to the trucks.

It was a cold day. There had been a frost and dead leaves were blowing about. A storm was rumbling over the mountains. It all seemed to tell Bittie to hurry.

But when they got back to the trucks, the position of the sun, seen through scudding cloud, said it was only noon. There were no Russians returned.

The guard got into the driver's seat of their cab and began to sort out the presents he had bought. Bittie, almost engulfed by the huge Psychlo passenger seat, closed the window against the chill wind and dead flying leaves and sat there impatiently twiddling his new riding crop and looking out the window, his eyes just above the level of the bottom, keeping watch for the rest of the Russians.

From where he sat he could see a side entrance to the capitol building. There was a big executive ground car sitting there with blacked-out windows.

Suddenly he saw Sir Jonnie! There he was, dressed as usual in buckskin, unmistakable. He walked out of the side entrance of the capitol. The door of the executive ground car was swung open from inside and Jonnie got into it.

Bittie scrambled to get down the window and shout. He got it open partway. He couldn't get it all the way down.

Then somebody else came out of the capitol, somebody dressed like a cadet A plaster cast around his neck This second person stopped and called back into the capitol stairway where somebody must have asked a question.

The man in cadet clothes yelled back, "He's just going down to the compound first to pick up his horses." Then he too got into the ground car and it started up.

Bittie was wild! He hadn't been able to get the window down and call to Sir Jonnie. Get the horses! That was why he was here what he'd come all the way to America to do!

He tried to get his guard to just start up the truck and follow. But Bittie's command of Russian was not up to it. Gestures and motions and repeating the sense of what he was saying got no place. This Russian was not about to go after that executive ground car. He was here to wait for the rest of the contingent.

But Bittie got him out of the cab and they went sprinting around looking for the rest of the Russians. Minutes went by and they couldn't find them. This ruined city was too big, too spread out, too filled with rubble.

Suddenly they spotted one Russian. He was walking along the edge of a park by himself, eating some nuts he had bought. He was a man named Amir, and he had no reputation for being quick in the wits, although he was a nice fellow

Bittie reeled off the situation to him, using gestures and a Russian word he did know, "Skahryehyee!" meaning "Hurry up!" and trying to get the man to understand he was to find the others and tell them to come along right away.

He was not at all sure the man got it for he looked blank, but the action was enough to convince Dmitri that it was now all right to follow the ground car so they got back to the truck and the Russian started it up, and they went roaring out of the city to catch up to the vehicle Bittie had seen Jonnie enter.

— 7 —

Lars Thorenson had taken every precaution. He had gone over it very carefully. If there was no public display of arms and guards, while making sure that this Tyler was thoroughly covered at all times by adequate weaponry, then no alert would go out and no misguided friends of this felon would come pouring around to rescue him.

Lars had left guards in the car, had let no other Brigantes appear on the streets or openly in corridors, had sent word to the commando now posted at the compound to keep out of sight but ready and not to shoot unless attacked.

He had a little surprise for this Tyler at the compound, but all should go smoothly and well. He thought even Hitler would have approved of the tactical skills Lars was displaying. They would pick up the horses, drive up through the pass to the meadow, order this Tyler to go into his own house, and that would be that. The scourge and menace to the stability of the state would be ended. Thoroughly and with no blame at all to the Council.

The day had gone gray. The sun was more and more overcast. The wind was picking up and billows of dust and clouds of dead grass were running before the approaching storm.

Lars' driving was not all that good to begin with and gusts were buffeting the ground car, swerving it from already badly chosen courses. He was not driving fast.

Jonnie was considering his chances. He had no idea they intended to let him out of this alive for all their smooth assurances. What point of that plaster cast, if hit, would finished the job of breaking this traitor's neck? How familiar were these two evil-smelling Brigantes with a Thompson submachine gun?

The weapon, deadly though it was, had been obsolete for a century at the time of the Psychlo attack. It fired pistol ammunition that was too heavy for a hand-held automatic weapon and caused it to kick upward furiously so that you had to hold the muzzle down with great force. These weapons they had were not equipped with "Cutts Compensators" that used some of the muzzle blast to help hold down the upward kick. They were loaded with sixty-shot drums and the springs of those drums were often weak and failed to feed. A certain percentage of the very ancient ammunition failed to fire and one had to know the trick of recocking rapidly to keep the gun shooting on automatic. Jonnie knew these things for he had fired a lot of practice rounds with them when Angus had first dug them out of the old camion where they had laid through the ages, protected by heavy grease and airtight ammunition packaging. But did the Brigantes? Probably they had fired a few rounds with them, the first firing of powder missile weapons they had ever done in their lives. The improbable and rapidly discarded ploy had occurred to him to talk to them about the weapon and then take one to explain a fine point and blow their foul matted heads off.

Unless he thought of something, this was going to be his last ride. It was in Lars' manner. It was in the looks the Brigantes gave him. They were very, very confident.

The compound appeared in the distance ahead of them. There was some stock scattered about in the plains. Lars narrowly avoided a group of buffalo, dodged a scrub tree, nearly dumped them in a gully, jolted them over some boulders anyone who could drive would have avoided, and finally halted about a hundred feet short of the beginning of the rise that ended in the plateau near the cage.

It was not as close to the compound as Jonnie had expected them to stop. And then he saw the reason for it. The ground, aside from some boulders, was open, and a man trying to run away could be cut down.

There were his horses, three of them standing with their heads away from the wind. Where was Dancer? Then he saw her. She was up on the plateau and she seemed to be wearing a lead rope, not too unusual. She wasn't facing away from the wind. What was that? Ah, her lead rope was caught in some rocks. Just beyond her was a large boulder, and beyond that the compound itself offered numerous points of cover for a marksman as they had learned to their concern in the old battle here. Jonnie looked at it through the windscreen. What was this, some kind of ambush or trap? Where one expected some cadet sentries, there wasn't a soul in sight.

Now Lars chose his moment to spring his little compound surprise. He had read in the works of Hitler—or was it Terl?—"If you want someone to remain inactive, crush their hope. Then guide false hope into a new channel where you can finish them off!" It was an extremely wise military maxim.

Lars, lolling easily now over the console, said, "You know that battle plane, the one with the serial ending in ninety-three that was parked and refueled just inside the hangar door? I'm sure you know the one I mean. Well, it isn't there anymore. The fuel was removed from it and it was put way back in the hangar out of sight this morning."

So that was why Angus and Ker didn't stop when they left, thought Jonnie. They saw no battle plane and thought he had flown safely away. This accounted for no one's showing up to trace him. Well, he hadn't expected any help anyway. And it was a very good thing they had not walked in on these nervous Brigantes and their submachine guns.

The traitor let him digest the surprise and then said, "But we won't be riding horses to the meadow. I will go down to the garage and get a stake truck and we can load the mounts in and I might even be persuaded to let you drive up into the mountains." He had no intention of doing that. But it was a good false hope. In fact, masterful! Hitler—or was it Terl?—would have approved. "You can get out and start collecting the horses. The two Brigantes here will keep you covered."

Lars got out and jogged off in the direction of the garage entrance on the other side of the compound.

Jonnie was pushed out with gun muzzles and he stood on the left side of the car, a Brigante on either side of him with their guns on him and fingers on the trigger. He was studying the apparently unpeopled compound. Was this the assassination area?

— 8 —

Jonnie heard the rumble of a truck above the wind. He looked to the north. An empty truck was approaching at considerable speed, the occupants of the cab invisible to him in this light. From behind that truck to the horizon in the north it was only empty plain, no other vehicles.

He heard another rumble. A plane? He spotted it in the east, approaching slowly just below the overcast. Only a slow-flying drone scanning for its endless millions of pictures.

Well, no real help was coming from those directions. He was on his own. The truck, now quite near, was probably one of theirs and part of this snare.

Jonnie looked back at the compound. He had a feeling of watchful eyes and danger there.

The two Brigante guards were on either side of him about a pace to the rear. They seemed to be watching this new truck. That they held guns was masked from the truck's view by the ground car's bulk.

The huge vehicle roared on by them on the other side of the ground car. It went a short distance up the rise toward Dancer. It stopped suddenly, banging to earth in a cloud of dust as its suspension drive cut off.

Somebody leaped down through the dust from the eight-foot height of the cab floor and began to run up the slope toward Dancer.

Jonnie couldn't believe his eyes.

It was Bittie MacLeod! He was carrying something in his hand. A crop? A switch?

"Bittie!" shouted Jonnie in alarm.

The boy's voice floated back to him, carried by the wind: "I'll get the horses, Sir Jonnie. It's *my* job!" Bittie was racing up on the hill.

"Come back!" shouted Jonnie. But the throb of the drone and a rumble of thunder in the mountains drowned his voice.

The Russian had had trouble getting his truck level. It had tilted on a boulder. But now he flung open the door and shouted toward Bittie, "*Bitushka! Astanovka!* (Halt!)" A sudden spurt of wind and the drone muted his words. "*Vazvratnay!* (Return!)"

The boy ran on. He was almost to Dancer to free the lead rope.

"Lord god, Bittie, come back!" screamed Jonnie.

It was too late.

From behind a boulder, just beyond the horse, a Brigante stood up, raised his submachine gun, and fired at full burst directly into the stomach of the running boy.

Bittie was slammed back, pummeled by bullets that drove his body into the air. He crashed to earth.

The Russian was running forward, trying to unsling the assault rifle from his back, trying to get to Bittie.

Two more Brigantes rose into view in different places and three Thompsons roared. The Russian was cut to pieces.

Jonnie went berserk!

The two Brigante guards stood no chance. With one backward stride, Jonnie was behind them. He sent them slamming together like egg shells.

He caught the gun of one as that Brigante went down and stamped his heel into the side of the mercenary's skull, crushing it.

He reversed the gun and battered the other Brigante with bullets from a range of three inches.

Jonnie dropped on one knee, turned the Thompson on its side so its kick would fan the bullets, and blew the two last Brigantes who had risen to bits.

He spun to find the one who had shot Bittie. That one was not in sight.

Five Brigantes rushed from a door in the compound and sent a hail of lead in his direction.

The Thompson he had used was jammed. It would not recock. He threw it down and picked up the other one.

Totally unmindful of the slugs ripping up the ground, running low and firing as he went, he raced forward toward the fallen Russian.

He knelt behind the body, turned the Thompson on its side, and fanned a storm of bullets into the five. They crashed back against the compound, bodies jerking as a second spray of slugs hit them before they could even collapse.

Jonnie got the assault rifle off the Russian and yanked its slide to get a bullet in the chamber.

He was after the Brigante who had shot Bittie.

To his left and behind him eight mercenaries who had been lying in wait in the ravine rushed into view.

Jonnie whirled. Then he stood there braced until the last one was out of the ravine.

They came on firing.

Jonnie raised the assault rifle to his shoulder and took careful aim. He shot the last in the line first so the others would not see him go down and then fanned a barrage of shots from there to the first one in the lead.

The squad came sprawling forward in an avalanche of dead men.

Down in the garage, Lars heard the firing. He sprinted up toward the plateau. Then he heard the assault rifle's sharper bark racketing against the compound. Instantly he knew that Jonnie was not dead. No Brigantes had assault rifles. This intermediate ammunition, halfway between a pistol and a rifle, was far more accurate than a Thompson. He knew. He had tried to get some and he could not. He halted.

There was another prolonged burst from the assault rifle. The heavier staccato thud of the submachine guns had dwindled. Lars suddenly hit upon a better course of action for himself.

He scuttled backward into the garage He sprinted into its

depths. He found an old wrecked car and he crawled under the heaps of damaged body plates stripped from it. A far-off hammer of the assault rifle again. He burrowed deeper, sobbing with terror.

Jonnie raced over to the side to get a view behind the boulder, still trying to nail the mercenary who had shot Bittie.

A group of Brigantes sprinted into sight on the other side of the compound, firing submachine guns as they came.

Jonnie braced himself on a rock, fired over its top, and riddled them.

Terl in his cage had dropped down below the parapet that held the upright bars, lying flat to be out of the path of bullets. He raised himself cautiously now. It was the animal! He ducked back. At any moment now he supposed the animal would charge over here and riddle him. It's what Terl would have done. He wondered whether he could get to the hidden explosive charge in the cave and make a grenade out of it, and then he saw he would expose himself if he did so and abandoned the idea. He lay there, panting a little in fear.

Taking advantage of trees and boulders, running from one to the next with deadly purpose, Jonnie was still trying to get the Brigante who had shot Bittie.

The wind was rising. Thunder was sounding amid the gunfire. The slow-flying drone was very near overhead now.

Where, where was that Brigante?

Two mercenaries jumped into view in a door and bore down on him with Thompsons. A bullet flicked the side of his neck.

Jonnie pounded them into rolling balls of dead flesh with the assault rifle.

He snapped in a fresh magazine from the bag. The ape he was looking for must have taken refuge back of a wrecked tractor. Jonnie probed it with bullets fired to ricochet behind it.

Running, he rushed it, firing as he went.

There he was!

The Brigante ran away. Jonnie sighted in on him. The Brigante turned and started to shoot.

Jonnie sliced him in two with the assault rifle.

The sound of the drone grew less. There was no thunder at the moment. Save for the moan of the wind it seemed strangely quiet.

Jonnie put another magazine in the assault rifle. He quickly walked over the ground, glancing at one or another of the strewn dead.

A mercenary was crawling, trying to get his hands on a Thompson. Jonnie put a burst into him.

He waited. There seemed to be no sound or movement in the area that would be dangerous.

Dancer had broken free in the firing and fled down the slope.

Jonnie held the assault rifle ready in the crook on his arm. His battle rage died.

He went down the slope to Bittie.

— 9 —

The little boy lay on the blood-stained ground, his head back and in the direction of the lower slope.

Jonnie had been certain he was dead. Nobody could take that many submachine gun slugs in the middle of his body—and a small body—and live.

He felt awful. He knelt beside the torn boy. He was going to pick the body up and he put his hand under the head and lifted it slightly.

There was a light flutter of breath!

Bittie's eyes trembled open. They were glazed in shock but they saw Jonnie, knew him.

Bittie was moving his lips. A very faint whisper of a voice. Jonnie bent closer to hear.

"I . . . I wasn't a very good squire . . . was I . . . Sir Jonnie."

Then tears began to roll sideways from the boy's eyes.

Jonnie reacted, incredulous! The child thought he had failed.

Jonnie tried to get it out, tried to speak. He couldn't make his voice work. He was trying to tell Bittie, no, no, no, Bittie. You were a great squire. You have just saved my life! But he couldn't speak.

The shock was wearing off in the boy; the numbness that had held back the pain vanished.

Bittie's hand, which had risen to clutch Jonnie's wrist, suddenly clenched bruisingly in a spasm of agony. The body did a wrenching twist. Bittie's head fell to the side.

He was dead. No heartbeat. No breath. No pulse.

Jonnie sat there for a long time, crying. He hadn't been able to speak, to tell Bittie how wrong he was. He was not a bad squire. Not Bittie. Never!

After a while, Jonnie picked the boy up in his arms and went down the hill. He laid the body very gently on the seat of the ground car.

He went back and picked up the dead body of the Russian and carried it to the car and put it in.

Windsplitter had seen him from a distance and came up, and the other horses, over their fright now, approached.

Jonnie put the dead boy on his lap and drove very slowly toward the Academy. The horses, seeing him go at that pace, followed. The little cortege crossed the plain.

It took them a long time to make the trip. Jonnie stopped at last beside the trench where the sixty-seven cadets had fought the last battle so very long ago. He just sat there holding Bittie's body.

A cadet sentry had seen them approach. In a little while cadets started to come out of the buildings. Word spread further and more came. The schoolmaster, from an upper window, saw the crowd gathering around the ground car and went out. Dunneldeen and Angus and Ker came up to the fringe of the crowd.

Jonnie got out, holding the dead boy. He wanted to talk to them and he couldn't speak.

Several truckloads of Russians suddenly roared up to a halt and they spilled out, joining the crowd.

Several cadets raced back to the armory and came out with assault rifles and shoulder bags of magazines and began to pass them around to men who were looking in the direction of the compound.

An angry mutter was rising higher and higher among them.

Several cadets raced back to their rooms to get personal side arms and came back, buckling on belts and loading magazines.

The thunder in the mountains reverberated now and then across the plain and an angry, cold wind whipped around the mob.

A truckload of Russians who had swung over by the compound arrived back and stopped in a geyser of dust. The Russians were shouting and pointing toward the compound, trying to say what was over there now. No one could understand them.

A small ground car raced up from the direction of Denver, spraying clods of dirt as it screeched to a stop. The pilot officer in charge of drones jumped out, a stream of drone printout pictures crackling in the wind as he forced his way into the crowd, trying to tell them it had all come through on a drone overfly, trying to show people what had happened. He had ripped the printouts and the discs out of the machines and come at once.

A Coordinator was finally able to make himself heard. He had gotten now what the single Russian truck had seen at the compound. "The Brigantes are all dead over there! A whole commando!"

"Is that Psychlo Terl still alive over there?" somebody shouted.

There was an angry roar from the crowd. Several surged forward to see whether Terl was visible in the pictures.

"He's still alive," shouted the Russians' Coordinator who had gotten the information from the truck.

The crowd surged and some started to climb into the Russian trucks. The Russians had been drawn up in a line by a Russian officer and they were checking their rifles on command.

Colonel Ivan, who had come to stand near Jonnie, was gazing, stricken with guilt, at the face of the dead boy. "The Psychlo dies!"

Jonnie had finally gotten a grip on himself. Still holding the boy he climbed to the top of the ground car. He looked down at them and they quieted to hear him.

"No," said Jonnie. "No, you must not do anything now. In the star systems of the universe around us there is a far greater danger than Brigantes. We are fighting a dangerous battle. A bigger battle. We have made a mistake and it has resulted in the death of this innocent boy. I killed his murderer. We cannot undo the mistake. But we must go on.

"In that trench there, sixty-seven cadets died, fighting the last battle of the Psychlo invasion over a thousand years ago. When I first saw that trench, it gave me my first hope. It was not that they lost, it was that they fought at all against hopeless odds. They did not die in vain. We are here. We are fighting again. You and your fellow pilots control the skies of Earth.

"I will make a request of one or another of you in times to come. Will you honor those requests?"

There was a massed stare. Did he think they would not? Then

there was a concerted roar of assent. It took minutes for it to quiet.

Jonnie said, "I am leaving you now. I am taking this boy to Scotland. To be buried by his own people."

Jonnie got down off the car.

The pilot whose ore carrier had been readied for the Russians was pointing it out to the Russian Coordinator. They loaded Jonnie's horses. They found Stormalong's kit in the ground car and put it aboard.

The Russians took over the body of Dmitri Tomlov to take it home.

Jonnie climbed to the cockpit of the big ore carrier, still holding Bittie.

Before he closed the door, he looked down at the crowd and said, slowly and clearly, "It is not the time for revenge." And then he added a bitter, grim "*Yet!*" The crowd nodded. They understood. Later it would be an entirely different matter.

The huge plane rose and turned in the gray, storm-discolored sky.

It dwindled and was gone.

— 10 —

A much more serious crisis awaited him in Scotland, one that threatened to wreck all his plans.

Pilots on the ground talked the ore plane down through the dark swirling mists of autumn. The Scots had begun to rebuild Castle Rock in Edinburgh, cleaning up and trying to restore the ancient buildings that two thousand years before had been the seat of Scottish nationalism and that was now being called its original Gaelic word: Dunedin, "the hill fort of edin." Jonnie landed in a park below the Rock, just in front of the ruins of the ancient National Gallery of Scotland.

Swarms of people had been there to meet him and gillies had been hard pressed to clear space in the throng for the plane to land.

Unfortunately, the drone pictures of the compound fight had come in on the Cornwall minesite recorders, and they had been rushed by mine passenger plane to Scotland long before Jonnie's arrival. The Scots were making good use of the vast amounts of transport taken from the Psychlos, and flatbeds were being used as buses now that trainee machine operators were back home.

Bittie's mother and family were there and Jonnie gave over the corpse to them to dress and prepare for a funeral. Pipers were wailing a lament, drums beating its slow and doleful cadence. Women in the crowd were openly crying and men were beating their fists together as they dwelt on what they conceived to be the necessity of war.

It was nearly dark. An honor guard of kilted Highlanders approached and its officer courteously told Jonnie he was there to escort him through the crowds to a meeting of the Chiefs. They had not yet restored the parliament house on the Rock; the Chiefs, brought hastily in from the hills, were meeting in the nearby open park before the ruined Royal Scottish Academy.

To the mournful cry of pipes, Jonnie walked toward the space. It was lit with a towering bonfire in its center. The flame's glow was flickering over the buckles and swords of Clanchiefs and their retainers. It was an assembly with only one, single-minded purpose: WAR!

Belatedly, Robert the Fox, just in from Africa, rushed to Jonnie's side. They were already on the outskirts of the assembly, the honor guard opening the way, heading for some raised stone slabs that served as a rostrum. Clanchief Fearghus was coming forward in courtesy to escort him to this rostrum.

"Do you want war?" said Robert the Fox into Jonnie's ear. "I think not! It would ruin all your plans."

"No, no," said Jonnie. "That is the last thing we want. Without it we have a chance."

"Then why," said Sir Robert, "didn't you change your clothes before this meeting? You might have known it would take place!"

Jonnie had not thought about his clothes. He glanced down. The buckskin shoulder was dark red from the bleeding of the superficial wound at the side of his neck, long since staunched by coagulation. The entire front of his shirt and his trousers down to the knee were saturated with Bittie's blood.

At that very moment the Chief of the Campbells was speaking to the assembled Chiefs. ". . . and I say this is a blood feud that can only be settled in *war!*"

There was a savage roar of agreement. "War!" "War!"

Lochaber axes were flashing in the light of the leaping flames. The slither of swords coming from their sheaths was a deadly, martial declaration.

Jonnie stepped up on the stone rostrum. He held up his hand for quiet. They gave him a silence electric with tension and punctuated by the crackling flame of the bonfire.

"We want no war," said Jonnie.

It was the wrong thing to say. A clamor of disagreement rolled at him.

"By the very blood on his clothes," shouted the Chief of the Argylls, "this cries out for war!"

"The murderer of the boy is dead!" said Jonnie.

"What of Allison?" cried the Chief of the Camerons. "His vile murder has not been avenged! The chief of the Brigantes, he that brought it about, still lives! These are matters of blood feud!"

Jonnie realized they were out of control. They were demanding pilots and transport. Their target was the obliteration of the entire force of Brigantes. And now! He knew this had all been decided before his arrival on the slow ore carrier. He could see all their labors going for nothing. If that area in America were wiped out, that would end their plans!

He looked for the face of Robert the Fox and found only this sea of enraged Chiefs and retainers. He did not dare tell them so openly and in public of his plans. Lars had shown there could be traitors.

He tried to tell them the planet was under a much greater threat, that they did not really know what had happened to Psychlo, that there were other races out in the stars, but not one single word he said was heard in the tumult.

Finally the big and lordly Chief of Clanfearghus leaped up beside him and bellowed at the throng: "Let the MacTyler speak!"

They quieted under that, tense, determined.

Jonnie was tired. He had not slept for days. He summoned up reserves of energy and spoke in a strong confident voice: "I can promise you SUCCESSFUL war! If you will let me guide you, if you will each one contribute men and time to a daring enterprise, if you will but plan with me and work in preparation for the next few months, we will have war, we will have revenge, and we will have a chance of everlasting victory!"

They heard that. After a moment, while it sank in, they burst into a savage din of agreement. The lochaber axes were raised higher; claymores flashed back the light of flames. The pipes suddenly burst into the stirring tunes of war. They hailed Jonnie until they were hoarse. As he stepped down and was led away by Robert the Fox, big hands clapped him on the back as he passed, others sought to grip his. Men leaped before him, claymores held before their faces in devoted salutes. Somebody started a chant of "MacTyler! MacTyler! MacTyler!" The pipes screamed and drums added to the din.

"Count on you, laddie," said Robert the Fox fondly as he led Jonnie off to temporary quarters in an old house, a bath, clean clothes, and rest. "But I'm only hoping we can deliver!"

They buried Bittie MacLeod the next day in a crypt in the old Cathedral Saint Giles. The funeral procession was over a mile long.

To the Chief of Clanfearghus Jonnie had said, "He died a squire. We must bury him as a knight."

Placing a robe on the corpse, Fearghus, as titular King of Scotland—and now the entire British Isles—knighted Bittie with the tender touch of a sword.

A rock carver had worked straight through to complete a sarcophagus—a stone casket—and it was ready.

The parson read the funeral oration, and to the doleful mourn of pipes, Bittie was laid away.

On the plaque, beneath the new armorial bearings they had given Bittie, was carved:

[Sir Bittie]
[A True Knight]

They knew Bittie would have liked that.

Pattie, her face frozen in shock since she had first heard the news of his death, at the funeral's end was given the small packet they had found in his pocket. It was the locket. She numbly read the engraving on it: "To Pattie, my future wife."

The dam of her tears broke and she collapsed across the sarcophagus, weeping uncontrollably.

But Bittie was not really gone. He had become a legend. Future generations, if they survived, would hold in song and story the memory of Sir Bittie who they said had saved the life of Jonnie.

■

PART 21

— 1 —

The spacecraft Aknar II rode in orbit four hundred twenty-one miles above the planet Earth.

The small gray man sat in a small gray office in the ship. He was looking at small gray instruments.

He was only partly finished with a critical analysis and he was not even vaguely satisfied with it.

A bottle of pills sat on his desk, pills for indigestion. His job had its drawbacks. Drinking all manner of hospitable offerings including yarb tea had upset his stomach.

The small gray man was deeply troubled. The problems which assailed such a position as his were never easy: they required the most conservative possible judgment. He had faced many situations in his long life, a large number of them involving the most dangerous and overwhelming elements. But at no time—he did a hasty calculation with a rolling calculator—in three hundred thirteen thousand years had he or his predecessors ever been confronted with the ruin potential of this one.

He sighed and took another indigestion pill. This last packet of information that his communicator had given him contained elements which defied even the most expert mathematical dissection and reassembly. There were explosive elements in all this which could well wreak havoc.

For one thing, a lightning storm had grossly interfered with the clarity of the first item. An infrabeam sound transmitter, no matter how narrowly it could be focused, was after all an electronic device, and interference was not only possible, it had happened. He considered himself no technician; that was not his role. But his technicians aboard could not get it clarified either. Compounding his trouble was this delay in all communications to competent labs. He was two and a half months in travel time away from any such help.

Wearily, he ran the data of the first item through the display machine for the seventh time.

There was the compound, the old central Psychlo minesite of the planet. There were some men in hiding behind rocks holding weapons. There was the arrival of the car, the departure of the first man into the compound. Then three men getting out of the car, two of them with weapons held on the third.

He had tried and tried to get a clearer picture of the third man but the interference due to the lightning was really bad. He once more got out one of the several "one-credit bank notes" he had managed to procure and studied the picture. But he could not be sure it was the same man. It was useless to call in a technician again. He had already done that.

He let the signal decode into running visual again and spin forward. Then there came this second car. Truck. A small figure leaping out holding some sort of weapon. The small figure racing forward to attack. It didn't really look like an attack. The man behind the rock might have thought it was an attack. Then the firing . . .

He skimmed through the battle. Yes, it really must be the one on the bank note. What a perfectly poor transmission! They were usually so clear.

Then the car followed by horses and the man getting up on the car and talking to a crowd and holding the small body. . . .

This was where he *had* to have clarity and he didn't have it. The vocal was so interrupted by the lightning that it was just sparks. Only a few bits came through. The picture showed arms being broken out. But not used. Was it a plea for no war by the man on the car?

Who had that small body been to cause all this? A prince of a reigning sovereign?

Well, thankfully the infrabeam transmission from the island country was better and the speech there came strong and clear. And it promised a war!

But against whom? Why?

It was the same man. The ship he had gotten into had been carefully tracked as it went over the pole of the planet.

One could not be absolutely sure, however, that it was the

same man as on the bank note—firelight was a very long band and almost went off the bottom of the infrabeam spectrum.

The small gray man sighed again. He could not be sure at all. Not sure enough for a vital critical analysis.

He was just reaching for another pill when a light blinked from the people up on the flight deck—there was nothing much to do while in orbit and a warning signal was a rarity. He tapped a button to light a screen and get the picture being relayed to him. And then he looked out the port.

Ah, yes. He had half-expected this. A war vessel! There it was, settling into orbit near them. Bright and shining against the black sky. Always unnecessarily dramatic, these war vessels. Let's see, diamond with a slash, the insignia of the Tolneps. He had wondered when they would arrive.

He flittered a rolling, lighted list in a round indicator on his desk. Tolnep . . . Tolnep war cruisers . . . did that one out there have a diamond-shaped bridge? Yes . . . Vulcor class. Vulcor . . . specifications . . . ah, here it was. "List weight two thousand tons, solar powered, main battery 64 Maxun blast cannons. . . ." How dull these endless specifications, who cared about the number of blast-tight bulkheads . . . ah. ". . . complement five hundred twenty-four Tolnep marines, sixty-three operating crew. . . ." Goodness, wouldn't one think that the computer clerks would realize the important items one would really want? ". . . commanded by a half-captain, autonomous authority over local tactical conditions but without authority over strategic decisions!" *That* was what the small gray man was looking for.

The local space communication buzzer went on. The small gray man turned a visio screen on. The hard face of a Tolnep topped by a small shield helmet appeared. A half-captain insignia on the helmet. The small gray man knew he was talking to the vessel's commander. The small gray man flipped a little switch so the Tolnep's screen would show his own face.

"Good spacing to you, sir," said the Tolnep. "I am Rogodeter Snowl." He was speaking Psychlo, which was pretty universal. He adjusted thick glasses to better see the small gray man.

"Greetings, half-captain," said the small gray man. "Could we be of service to you?"

"Why yes, Your Excellency. You might possibly oblige us with any vital information you might have regarding this planet."

The small gray man sighed. "I am very much afraid, half-captain, that anything I have to give you has not yet resolved itself to critical analysis. It would not be complete, and while we are always happy to be of service, I fear we might erroneously advise you."

"Ah. Well, it won't take very long to organize things here," said the Tolnep. "It's been a very long voyage and my crew is still in deep sleep, but we can launch a party in the next few hours and obtain preliminary data."

The small gray man was afraid he would say that. "I, of course, would not presume to thwart your intentions, half-captain, but I should think it would be very inadvisable."

"Oh? But a quick smash-bash, a few beings seized from here and there, and a rapid interrogation should give us all we need."

"Half-captain, I feel I should advise you that I do not think it would yield fruit. I have been collecting information for some time now and have here anything you would get. I can transmit it over to you, whatever I happen to have."

"That would be very thoughtful of you, Your Excellency. But why not a quick smash-bash minor raid? I detect some thoughts on this."

"Well, as a matter of fact," said the small gray man, "you do detect some reservations and it is very acute of you. It might be important to stand off and wait."

"Do you think they're the ones?" asked Snowl.

"My dear fellow," said the small gray man, "I believe there are three hundred different planetary suspects."

"Three hundred two, I think," said Snowl. "At least that is the rumored figure.

"We cannot tell you that this *is* the one," said the small gray man, "and I can't give you comparative evidence about other planets and systems for I am, of course, concerned with simply this sector, as you are. But it is my belief, based on very thin evidence, that this just *could* be the one."

"Oh, I say!" said the Tolnep. "That's promising!"

"We are not in a position to adjudicate at this time. But it could be that a raid by you might disturb what appears to be a very critical political situation down there and possibly disturb it to our disfavor."

"You're advising us to wait, then," said the Tolnep.

'Well, yes," said the small gray man. "I will send you across any file data I have been collecting and I think you will reach the same conclusion.''

''It's difficult,'' said the Tolnep. ''No raids, no prize money is our position. But we do have this other strategic thing.

''Yes, and we should not make any tactical move that might upset it.''

''Ah,'' said the Tolnep. Then, ''How long would you think we should delay? Days, months, years?''

''Months, I should think.''

The Tolnep sighed. Then brightened and smiled—a Tolnep smile was a bit frightening since their fangs were poison—''All right, Your Excellency. It is very courteous of you to offer the information and I shall be very happy to review it. By the way, can we offer you escort and protection? I should think a Hockner ship might show up and they are quite nasty, you know.''

''I do thank you, half-captain,'' said the small gray man wearily, ''but as you know, we have no quarrel, ourselves, with the Hockners.''

''No, of course not,'' said the Tolnep. ''Any supplies, anything like that we can provide?''

''Thank you, not just now. Possibly later. Your courtesy is always appreciated.''

''We're already in your debt,'' said the Tolnep and laughed. ''Come across for some tea sometime.'' He clicked off.

The very thought of more tea made the small gray man's stomach hurt. He reached for another indigestion pill. All things considered, this really was the worst hard-core problem that had ever come to his desk.

The indigestion pill was about to take effect when he suddenly realized that the Bolbods, the Hawvins, and who knows who else might show up. He hoped they wouldn't quarrel with one another. In the situation he was in, it took months now to get proper reports home and months to hear anything. He felt very much on his own.

He looked out the port again at the gun-bristling monster of a war vessel, flashing along beside them in the glaring sunlight. Tough beings, the Tolneps. But really not much worse than Bolbods or Hockners.

He glanced down at the planet face below them. Was it really the one? If it were, in one way it would be a relief. But if it were, what violence could go shooting down at it!

His sigh was very deep.

— 2 —

Terl was purring. He was moving into his office today!

There had been a few bad moments. This morning he had sent Lars into it to make sure it was not booby-trapped—better Lars blew up than he.

The compound in general had been in a bit of a turmoil. General Snith had come down and commandeered all the dead bodies of the slaughtered commando and had had a fight with a couple of his officers, apparently concerning mess table allocations. But Snith had resolved all that. There were twenty-eight bodies, eighteen active commandos. So he had hit on the masterful solution of one body to be issued to each commando, two to the officer's mess, six to the women and children, and two to his own table. So that had died down.

The thirteenth commando had cleaned the place up and the fifth commando had taken over the duty, all very smooth and military. They were all very polite to Terl and so it was obvious they knew who their boss was.

But right after things had smoothed out, Lars came screaming back to the cage to tell Terl that the place *was* booby-trapped. Worse, he didn't have a clue how to disarm a booby trap. Knowing he had better not let any of these Brigantes loose in the place—they'd stink it up and maybe blow it up—Terl himself had had to go in to handle the trap.

It was right inside the kneehole of the desk. Knowing that one booby trap could have another under it to explode when the top one was removed, he had taken a lot of care to remove it.

When he had disarmed it, he was about to throw it out when he saw that it had hairs stuck in it. They were gray Psychlo wrist hairs! Ker's fur was orange. And somebody had broken a claw tip while pushing the plastic explosive down around the edges: it was too big a tip for it to be Ker's.

On hearing about this booby trap the first time, Terl had supposed it would be the animal's doings. According to what he had learned, the animal had remained behind after the other two left and probably had planted this trap.

The fact that the animal had not come up and killed him too when the animal had wiped out this commando had troubled Terl. This was the second or third time the animal had had a chance to kill him but had not done so. Eerie. Unnatural. So he had figured out that the animal, having planted this booby trap, thought it was all cared for.

These bits of fur and the claw tip changed that. Once more, the animal had not killed him or tried to. Very abnormal behavior. Terl finally came to a conclusion, however. The animal had been so beaten about by Terl that the animal was afraid of him. *That* was the right answer!

Terl was comfortable with this until he realized that it was the Psychlos down in the lower dormitory who had sneaked up here and planted the trap.

Instantly he demanded their slaughter. He didn't want them around anyway. But Lars had come back and said that that very morning all thirty-three of them had been removed under cadet guard and had been shipped overseas—and here was the requisition for goo-food, kerbango, breathe-gas, etc., to prove it. So Terl got over his fright and began to collect the odd bits such as the dictionary and extra breathe-gas vials from the cage, walked out of it forever, and went back to his office.

What a relief to be out of the sun and air of this accursed planet!

He locked the door and turned on the breathe-gas circulator and soon he could take off his mask. What a relief to have a mask off.

Terl looked around. Some things had been moved out. No drone recorders. Who wanted them? No radio links. So what? Compound intercoms all dead. Who cared?

But the place was all set up to work. He thought one table was out of position and sought to move it and found it was welded down. Even welded down with an armor weld! Ho, ho! Somebody wanted that table in exactly that place! Ah, ha! That was why the animal remained behind. The place was bugged!

They hadn't moved his clothes out. Later, he would dress and become civilized again. But just now he wanted his green dress boots. There they were. They even had dust on the floor around them and hadn't been moved an inch. He turned the right boot upside-down, twisted the heel, and the cabinet keys fell out.

He went back into the main office room. Ah, hah! They had

tried to jimmy the cabinets. There were the jimmy marks and one door slightly bent. But Terl knew you couldn't jimmy security cabinets open. He unlocked them all. Everything all in its same old place! Better and better.

He picked up the bug detector, inspected it. He turned it on. And right away a buzz! Lights flashing! Devils but this place was really bugged!

For a solid hour, Terl did nothing but remove bugs. Micro-microphones, button cameras, scanners. All in very hidden places, all focused to zero in on the key work areas.

Thirty-one of them. He had been tossing them, when found, onto his desk. He counted again. Thirty-one. Oh, that animal had been busy! And stupid! Terl bet every other detector had been removed from the compound.

Finally he put on a tunic. Somebody had stacked a whole crate of kerbango pans against the wall and he was eyeing it. He was about to indulge when he thought, "Just one more sweep," and passed the bug detector around again. It whined!

For fifteen minutes he searched and searched. And then he found it. It was a micro set into the design of the top tunic button. He was wearing it.

Thirty-two.

He checked out all his other clothes. No more.

He thought he had better look into the ducts visually. They didn't register on the detector but who knew? But when he tried to steady himself on a chair by touching the duct frame it was wobbly. No more of that! He could let air into this place. Shoddy work. But what could one expect?

He surveyed the place again. He stood and laughed when he saw the components rack. Every assorted type of component, each with a big label above the box. And one of the button cameras he'd found hidden in a light fixture had been trained straight on it. Stupid animal!

Then he suddenly realized there must be a planted feeder unit to power these bugs and relay their coverage.

He put a mask on and got Lars. They went up and down the passageways. And there it was! A whole feeder unit, all wired up, right inside a recess closet for fire apparatus. He pulled it out and turned it off. Such a thing could run for half a year.

And recorders? It must have been relaying to recorders. Within a few hundred feet. He went back and got a mine radio, turned the feeder on, and very shortly ran down the recorder. Just inside the garage door where anyone could pass in and out to change its discs without much observation. Stupid animal!

He turned the thing off and took it away. Who cared about any others? They were blind now that they had no bugs to feed or record.

Happily, he went back into his office, barred it, rechecked with his detector. Beautiful silence. No lights. Wonderful. Privacy at last.

He put on some pants and boots. He opened up a pan of kerbango and sank back in his chair, luxuriating.

Home to wealth and power. That's where he was going now. And this time he would set such a trap that the animal would be gobbled up if he even came near it.

After nearly an hour, he thought he had better get to work.

But first things first. He had better calculate how much time he had to get this job done. And then start on the construction of a weapon so lethal and deadly that the company never used it except in the extreme emergency of planet destruction. After he fired, this place would be just a smudge in the sky.

He went to the cabinets and opened a false bottom.

— 3 —

Since his return to the African minesite, Jonnie had had trouble getting to sleep at night. He would roll and toss on the oversized Psychlo bed in the underground room he now used, uncomfortable in the overly hot and humid dark, going over and over again the steps and planning of recent past events, spotting where he had gone wrong in this and where he should have done something else in that. The life of a boy seemed far too much to pay for the information they had to have.

Sir Robert was not here. He remained in Scotland organizing a perimeter antiaircraft defense for Edinburgh. MacKendrick was not here. He had taken a trip home to see to the movement of his underground hospital to more suitable quarters now available and to check up on how his assistant there was getting along. Colonel Ivan was in Russia.

Stormalong had been detained here, for they were afraid some revenge might be taken upon him for lending his clothes and identity to the recent enterprise. Finding himself at loose ends, the Norwegian had kept himself busy inventorying the "flying hardware"—a name he had gotten from somewhere or invented for planes.

Through Stormalong's efforts Jonnie had begun to divine the true character of his African base. Because it shipped very little bulk ore—they had roasted the tungsten down on the site—it had had none of the bulk ore carriers, a fact which made it necessary to truck out fuel and breathe-gas from the branch minesite in the Ituri Forest. But this African central did have a great many other types of planes which had led Stormalong to conclude that the base had also had a defense function. From some old Psychlo manuals they had found, it seemed that in event of attack upon the minesite near Denver, this African base had the function of launching a counterattack to take an enemy by surprise. And this is exactly what these Psychlos had been engaged upon when annihilated.

It greatly intrigued Stormalong to find several types of flying hardware he had never seen before and which weren't listed in current Psychlo manuals. They were not battlecraft as such, however. They were dual-purpose machines brought in to perform a specific task, and then, that task done—rather typical of company policy—they had simply been dollied to the back of the hangar and forgotten. Too costly or too much trouble to return them to Psychlo.

According to flight logs still with them they had been used to "mine out" an enormous amount of material which was found in orbit around this planet, a circumstance unusual in Psychlo experience. Some of the metals in these objects were priceless, being very scarce elsewhere, and the company had taken the unusual step of sending in some machines.

If properly gasketed in its doors, due to its teleportation motors which had no dependence upon air for lift, any common battle plane could fly to the moon and back without too much trouble. But they were not equipped to *mine* in space. You couldn't take objects in and out of a battle plane while flying in a vacuum. So some factory on Psychlo or on a planet controlled by the Psychlos had converted some very heavy duty, armored, marine attack planes. With atmosphere locks and remote control grapplers, they could fly alongside some object in space, seize on to it, and put it in the hold. Some scraps of such recovered objects were still in the holds of these things, bits which had broken off, like nameplates. One said [''NASA''] and Stormalong tried to look it up in planetary lists and couldn't find it. Therefore he had to conclude it had once been a local something.

Jonnie had looked at the old relics with some indifference. The gaskets on the doors were deteriorated—you can't expect a gasket to last for eleven hundred years and still be airtight, he pointed out. Every hinge and ball joint in their cranes and doors was too stiff to operate properly. There were even some spider nests in them and the spiders had dined, for countless generations, on another breed of insect that had dined upon the upholstery. The things were a mess. Jonnie had been more interested in another craft which mounted a blast cannon.

But Stormalong, having some idle and recently-trained mechanics and three spare pilots on his hands and full shops available, had put these relics in operating condition. He had even painted a burning torch on either side of its nose which he said was a symbol of freedom. Stormalong had a lot of artistic style in him, Jonnie had to admit. But he privately hoped the symbol didn't forecast the thing going down in flames.

Not detecting the expected amount of enthusiasm, Stormalong had smugly pointed out, ''Do you have anything else that could go up and visit those things orbiting four hundred miles up there?''

For some days now there had been four bright objects in orbit. First there had been one, then two, and now four.

''Visit them!'' Jonnie had said, aghast. ''This thing doesn't even have guns anymore!''

''We put them back,'' said Stormalong. ''And every screen and instrument in it works now. There were spares.''

''You better test fly it,'' said Jonnie, ''with a jet backpack close to hand!''

''I did,'' said Stormalong. ''Yesterday. The console buttons are a bit old-fashioned but it flies great.''

''Well, don't go flying up to those objects!'' said Jonnie.

''Oh, I didn't,'' said Stormalong. ''I just took pictures of them.''

He had them. One was a big craft with a diamond-shaped bridge and a lot of blast-gun snouts. One was a cylinder with a control deck in the front, flat end. One was a thing which looked like a five-pointed star with a sort of gun on each star point. And the fourth was a sphere with a ring around it.

"Hey," said Jonnie, "that answers the description, the last one, of the small gray man's ship, the one you did, but didn't, crash into."

"Precisely," said Stormalong. "We're under surveillance."

Jonnie had known they were under surveillance. No enemy had a monopoly on that. They had shifted their own drone pattern and control to Cornwall and there were repeaters here. Twelve drones, flying slow around the globe, were passing the American minesite every few hours. They were also recording the objects in orbit, though not so well for drones were basically down-looking. No, a potential enemy had no monopoly. And ground defenses were also alert. But it was minimal defense and Jonnie knew it.

Tonight he couldn't sleep at all. Dunneldeen was overdue with the first recordings of Terl's activities, and Jonnie didn't even know yet whether they would get recordings. Radio chatter about their project was forbidden. He was in the dark.

He got up restlessly at last and paced about. Then he went outside the compound. Hot, muggy. A lion was roaring down by the lake. The sky was overcast. Suddenly he was overcome with the desire for some cool air and a look at stars.

There were a couple of battle planes on standby, ready for a scramble if needed, but they were defense items. The ancient relic Stormalong had repaired was near at hand, a dull green in the glow of compound lights. On impulse, wanting only to do something besides brood, he went in to the duty officer and told him where he was going and got a mask and flight suit.

True enough the controls were a bit old-fashioned. The lift-balance buttons were bigger and in a different place. The gun trips had been moved to make way for the crane controls. But so what? He put on a jet backpack, strapped himself in, closed all the windows tight, and vaulted the old wreck skyward.

He burst through the overcast and there were the stars. Jonnie could always get a thrill from flying. Since that first enchanting day he had been aloft, he had never lost it. The black sky and bright stars, half a moon, some snow-capped peaks close by shoving their crowns up through the overcast and into the night sky. Jonnie felt some of his tension ease away.

He simply enjoyed it. It was certainly cooler now.

Out of habit he scanned his screens. Some blips! He looked through the screen for a visual check. Four objects in orbit was what should be there. No, there were *five*. One new object was approaching the four old ones, all brighter and steadier than stars. About four hundred miles up.

The last thing he was going to do was go up and "visit" them. Unknown ships there; he was flying a relatively untried ship here. He had no support. And even if this old relic could fly clear to the moon and back, he needed no additional incidents at this time, thank you.

But maybe he could get some better pictures. Stormy's, taken in daylight, had been fuzzy with ultraviolet. He threw his plane up to a height of two hundred miles and closer to the objects, his attention mainly on putting the recorders on standby.

What was that? A flash from the new fifth ship? Yes. Another flash? Were they shooting at him?

Ready to take evasive action, he suddenly saw a wild flurry of flashes coming from one of the four objects and a splash of light on the fifth. Hey! The fifth ship was shooting at one of the original four and that one was firing back!

He quickly battered away at the old controls and closed the distance to about a hundred fifty miles. He was so intent on getting his recorders working he didn't realize he was shooting in toward those ships at hypersonic maximum.

Astonishing! The fifth ship and one of the original four were really having at it. Blast streaks were sheets of blue-green and red between them. Orange splashes of hits!

Abruptly he realized they were getting awfully big in his viewscreens. A Psychlo-numbered digital was rolling up the narrowing distance. Seventy-five miles.

An instant before he pressed the console for a reverse role and drive, the firing among the ships ceased abruptly.

Jonnie put his old wreck into a full power fall and got out of there. That was not his war. He didn't even know whether he had working guns.

At about a hundred miles above the Earth's surface he eased off. He was about fifty miles up when he was flying level again.

He looked back. They were not firing now. Just sitting up there. The fifth ship seemed to have closed in on the others.

Jonnie shook his head at himself. This was not the time to be doing crazy, reckless things. He had almost done exactly what he had warned Stormy *not* to do—go visiting.

The old relic he was flying had become heated from air friction. It was built to take it but he had come up for a cool breath of air and now the flight deck was hot. If he'd really wanted to go up there he would have taken just an ordinary battle plane, making sure its gaskets were tight around the doors. And making sure its guns were loaded and working. Sir Robert would not have been proud of him!

Another blip on his viewscreens. Down low at about a hundred thousand feet of altitude. Coming on a route from Scotland? America over the pole?

Warm cabin or no cabin, he streaked down to intercept and identify. He flipped on his local command channel, and just as he did so a voice from the nearby plane came through:

"Don't shoot! I'll marry your daughter!" It was Dunneldeen.

Jonnie laughed. It was the first time he had laughed since returning from America.

He spun the old relic around and flashed after Dunneldeen as the Scot roared down toward the minesite.

— 4 —

The small gray man in his small gray cabin was sighing patiently. Well, not too patiently. His indigestion had not improved at all, and now this.

Things were distressing enough without the military people getting into fights among themselves. But it was a military matter, not political, not economic, and not strategic, so he was perforce out of it, a mere observer.

He now had four faces on his separate viewscreens. And if it kept on going this way, he'd have to ask his communications officer to break more screens out of stores and put them in on a rack. It made one's office so cluttered.

The face of the Tolnep half-captain was quite angry-looking and he kept adjusting his glasses in an agitated way. "But I don't care if you *were* surprised to see me here. I have no advices at all that our nations are at war!''

The Hawvin's face was the light violet Hawvins got when they were very provoked. The square helmet was crushed down on his oval head, bending his ear antennae. His untoothed but blade-gummed mouth was distorted in the lifted attitude of biting. ''How would you know who was at war and who wasn't at war! You cannot be less than five months out from any base!''

The Hockner super-lieutenant who commanded the star-shaped craft looked a little supercilious with his monocle and excessive amount of gold braid. The long, noseless face portrayed what passed for disdain among his people in the Duraleb System.

The Bolbod was just plain plug-ugly, as they always were, bigger than Psychlos but sort of shapeless. One wondered how they ever handled anything at all—their ''hands'' were always clenched into fists. The high sweater neck almost met the bill of his exaggerated cap. The Bolbods considered insignia beneath their dignity but the small gray man knew he was Gang Leader Poundon, commanding the cylinder-shaped spacecraft. He certainly had a low opinion of all the rest as effete degenerates.

''All right!'' snapped the Tolnep. ''Are our races at war or aren't they?''

The Hawvin said, ''I don't have any information that they are or aren't! But that doesn't mean that they aren't. It would not be the first time a Hawvin ship came peacefully onto station only to be raked by a sneaking Tolnep.''

''Your Excellency!'' snapped the Tolnep, suddenly including the small gray man. ''Do you have any information that the Tolneps and Hawvins are at war?''

It was a military matter but this could fringe on the political. ''The courier ship that met me here did not mention it,'' he said tiredly. Maybe one of the crew had some different brand of indigestion tablets. No, he didn't think they would. Mello-gest was all that was sold these days. He wished they'd stop wrangling.

''You see!'' hissed the Tolnep half-captain. ''No war exists Yet you come in here denting my plates in an unprovoked assault—''

''Did I really dent your plates?'' said the Hawvin, abruptly interested.

''Here,'' said the Hockner super-lieutenant. ''Here now. You are both completely off the subject of the strange interceptor. If you two fellows want to draw off somewhere and batter away at each other, that's your business, isn't it? But who and what was that interceptor?''

The Bolbod snorted, ''Couldn't be anything but Psychlo.''

''I know, old fellow,'' said the Hockner, adjusting his monocle, ''but I've looked it up and it isn't listed under Psychlo military craft.'' He held a recognition book to the screen: ''Known Types of Psychlo War Craft.'' It was of course in Psychlo. All of them spoke Psychlo and the whole of their cross-communication was in Psychlo, since they didn't speak each others' native tongues. ''It isn't listed here.''

The Hawvin was glad to drop the subject of his attack on the Tolnep, no matter how surprised he'd been to find a Tolnep ship here. ''I've never seen one like it.''

The Bolbod was more practical. ''Why did it veer away the moment you stopped shooting?''

They pondered that for a while. Then the Hockner adjusted his monocle and said, ''I rather think I have it! He supposed that our attention would be distracted and that this,'' he snorted, '' 'battle' would knock out some of us and he'd be able to mop up the damaged remainder.''

They talked about this for a while. The small gray man listened politely to their military theories. It was none of his concern. They finally came to the conclusion that that was what it was all about. The interceptor had come up, ready to take advantage of the ''battle'' and destroy the remainder left over when they were in a damaged condition.

''I think they must be very clever,'' said the Hockner. ''Probably they have other interceptors here and they're ready and waiting.''

''I could have eaten that one with one bite,'' said the Hawvin.

''I could have knocked it out with one punch,'' said the Bolbod. ''If they were strong they would have come up here and smashed us up some days ago. I don't think they're Psychlos and I never before heard of any race that had that torch insignia. So I say they are very weak. I don't know why we just don't go down and wipe them out. As a combined force!''

A combined force was a brand-new idea. The three others had always considered Bolbods rather stupid, if strong, and they looked at him on their viewscreens with a dawning respect.

''We've never, any of us,'' said the Hockner, ''made any real dent in the Psychlos. But it does seem to me that they are not really Psychlos. Strange ship, strange insignia. So possibly it would just be an afternoon's work to go down as a combined force—''

''Knock them out and divide the loot,'' finished the Tolnep.

This was verging on the political. So the small gray man said, ''And what if they are the one?''

This was what they were here to determine. They chewed it over. They finally came to a unanimous conclusion: they would operate as a combined force. Any newcomer would be invited. They would wait for the return of the courier ship the small gray man had sent out even though it might not return for months. If it brought news that *the one* had been found elsewhere, this ''combined force'' would go down, knock the planet out, and divide the loot among them to recompense them for their time. They didn't lay out any system for dividing the loot for each had his own ideas of what would happen when that moment came. The plan was agreed to.

''What if something happens in the meanwhile to prove it *is* the one?'' the small gray man asked. Violence, violence; all these military people ever thought about was violence and death.

Well, they decided, that was sort of political, and they would play it by ear. But also if it were the one, probably it ought to be knocked out so the same plan applied.

It was the first time the small gray man had ever seen independent commanders of traditionally hostile ships reach a firm agreement on something. But these were very unusual times.

When they clicked off their viewscreens, the small gray man reached for another pill of mello-gest to help his indigestion and then put it back in the bottle.

He thought he'd go down and visit that old woman again. Maybe she had an *antidote* for yarb tea.

— 5 —

Their heads were bent together in the dull green reflection of the viewers. They were in a small, converted, lead-lined storage room in the lowest level of the African minesite. Jonnie was getting his first look at the fruits of earlier work.

There were ten days' worth of discs and it was a considerable pile. Dunneldeen had explained that he couldn't come earlier: there were lots of pilots graduating and needing their final check-out flights and it would have been suspicious to leave America at a busy peak. He had also brought fourteen new pilots to Africa and Jonnie and Stormalong could nurse them through their advanced combat here. They were good lads—Swedes and Germans. Ker was going full blast training machine operators; every tribe seemed to want a blade scraper and flatbeds for buses. Brown Limper was selling the tribes equipment even from their own nearby minesites and they had to have operators. Ore carriers were busy lugging machinery over the globe and they had to have pilots. Angus had come back with Dunneldeen for he was finding it too hard not to shoot Lars Thorenson on sight.

There was also the matter of page *one*.

Jonnie skimmed through the beginnings of Terl's reoccupancy. It was enough to know that that crucial hour after he had left had really been pay dirt. They'd planted thirty-two false bugs and even feeders and recorders, and there was Terl big as life dumping them on his desk, convinced. When he saw that Terl was apparently using a mine radio to detect feeder channels to the recorders, he had a moment's qualm, but then he realized their main feeder was a ground wave.

A false bottom to the cabinets! He hadn't suspected that, for they simply looked armored. And this huge, thick book he was bringing out . . . about three feet wide and two feet high and seven inches thick and on the thinnest paper he had ever seen. Thousands of pages!

Each page was divided into about forty vertical columns. Over at the left, the widest column gave the name of a system, and below it the names of planets in that system. From left to right in the columns followed every movement of the system such as its speed of travel and direction, precession, torque, and the weight and quality of the sun or suns if double or treble.

In the columns beside every planet of that system were noted that planet's own weight, rotation period, atmosphere, surface temperatures, races, city coordinates, relative mineral estimate by symbols and value in Galactic credits, and the location of its minesites, if any.

All speeds and directions of travel were based on the zero center of that universe and three-dimensional compass coordinates, using the inevitable Psychlo numeral eleven, and parts of eleven and powers of eleven.

Terl had sat there, day after day, turning pages of it, one by one, running a claw down one particular column. He had gone through the whole book. They had every page!

"Except page one," said Dunneldeen. "I don't understand several of these symbols because they're so abbreviated. Look at how tiny these figures are. We reviewed it and found we didn't have page *one*. We figured that would be the symbol key code and Terl knew it all so well that he never referred to it. But look at the last disc there."

Jonnie was a bit dazzled. He had had no idea there were that many populated systems, much less planets. Thousands and thousands and thousands. It would take somebody a month or two just to count them! Sixteen universes! And these were only the ones the Psychlos had an interest in. This accumulated knowledge must have taken several millennia to compile. He looked very closely at the writing. He could swear it was Chinko. He came out of it a bit. "I don't understand some of these symbols," he said.

"That's what I'm trying to tell you. That was part of the delay. I didn't want to put you in the frying pan waiting for the key to the symbols. So we did the waiting. Look at the last disc."

Jonnie did so. Terl had thrown the whole book down and the ventilator had blown up the cover by accident and there was page one! All the symbols listed and what they meant.

"We've got all the positions and firing coordinates of sixteen universes!" said Jonnie. Then he sobered. "What was he looking for?"

Terl had thrown the book down in disgust, that was plain. Jonnie played the disc a little more. The sound on it, which was not of much use, was very colorful Psychlo cursing.

For those whole two days a blank piece of paper had been lying there with not a mark on it. Now Terl almost ruined his pen as he wrote a figure on it.

Jonnie went back to an earlier disc and looking more critically at what column Terl's claw was moving down. By the symbol at the top of it, the column was "Transshipment firing times to/at Psychlo." Jonnie understood it. Terl was trying to find an open period at Psychlo so that nothing he shipped would collide with something some other planet was shipping. Jonnie recalled from his machine training days that the Psychlos never changed these tables for decades on end. Looking at the number of planets sending and receiving, the Psychlo platform must run constantly, day and night. He also had gotten the impression that one planet couldn't have two platforms operating for it made interference. The nearest second platform for transshipment had to be about fifty thousand miles away, and since the diameter of Psychlo was only about twenty-five thousand miles, they only had one platform.

So, if Terl didn't want to collide with somebody else's ore arriving or smelted metal going out to some buyers or maybe military hardware, he had to be careful to find an open period.

If one fired ore or machinery one could be quick about it. But live personnel required a longer time period or it shook them up. Terl was taking no chances with his own neck.

The figure he so disgustedly wrote, almost breaking his pen, was "Day 92"!

He had been forced to choose a time more than five months from now. It was quite evident from the amount of kerbango he then consumed that the thought of spending all that additional time on "this accursed planet," as the sonic recorded him saying, was upsetting.

He had had to choose Earth's next scheduled semiannual. And finally, by the next day, he had reconciled himself to it.

Expecting the next discs would show the beginning calculations and circuits of a transshipment console, Jonnie was amazed not to find it.

Terl had gone to another cabinet and opened up its *back*. Using both paws he removed a package. It appeared to be a bit heavy.

He opened up the wrappings and then got a big pair of tongs, big enough to lift a huge boulder. He screwed the gap down to about a quarter of an inch and reached into the package.

The picture didn't show what he was lifting out at first. Then he dropped it and it hit the floor. Terl's curse was very sharp.

He got down with the tongs and lifted a gray something about the size of a pea. For an instant the spot on the floor showed. Jonnie still-framed it. The metal floor was dented, deeply.

Terl managed to pick up the small object again with the tongs, a hard job because it had sunk in the floor. He lifted it back up to lay on the side of the table. Jonnie did a very quick calculation. He knew how strong Terl was within rough limits. The amount of effort, when you subtracted those big tongs, made that little pea-sized piece of metal weigh about seventy-five pounds at a wild guess.

Jonnie got busy. He called Angus and had him set up the mineral analyzer that should transfer traces from the disc and enlarge them. He went and got the trace code books.

For the next three hours they tried to find that trace. It wasn't there! The Psychlos didn't list it or any composite trace of it in any of their code books. They were dealing with a metal the Psychlos had but didn't list.

Jonnie tried to estimate by weight and volume and periodic tables what its atomic number was.

The Earth tables were of no value at all. This thing would be way off the bottom of them.

He looked over the Psychlo periodic tables, so different from the old Earth ones. There were a lot of elements that would have atomic numbers as high as this one, maybe even higher, but if they didn't have its name. . . ? Jonnie suddenly realized it probably wasn't on the Psychlo table either if it wasn't in their analysis books.

"I wish I were some good at this," said Jonnie.

"But, laddie," said Dunneldeen, "I think you're a plain wizard. I fell in the mine shaft about two hours ago and haven't been heard of since!"

Jonnie said, "These are atomic numbers. An atom is supposedly composed of a core with energy particles in it, some of them positively charged, some of them not charged at all. The number of positively charged particles is what they call the 'atomic number,' and these particles, together with the uncharged particles, make up the 'atomic weight.' Also, around the core are negatively charged particles that circle the core in what they call 'rings' or 'shells,' but they're not; they're more like envelopes. Anyway, the core and the negatively charged particles around it gives one the different elements. That's about all there is to a periodic table, to oversimplify it.

"But ancient man here on Earth constructed his tables on oxygen and carbon, I think, because those were important to him. He is a carbon-oxygen engine. But a Psychlo has a different metabolism and burns different elements for energy so the Psychlo table is different. Also, Psychlos had a lot more universes to work in and they had metals and gases Earth's old scientists never heard of.

"The ancients here on Earth also omitted *distances* of spacing between the core and the ring and between ring and ring, as a variable. So they didn't realize that one core and one ring at one spacing could be quite something else when the spacing changed. Got it?"

"Laddie," said Dunneldeen, "that thump you just heard was me hitting the bottom of the shaft!"

"Don't be lonely down there," said Jonnie. "I hit it every time I get tangled up in this. But the point is, what *is* he up to? This is *not* a transshipment rig component!"

They looked at other discs. Terl considered metal like a man would consider paper—easily worked with.

He had bullied Lars into getting him a sheet of a beryllium alloy and it almost hurt their ears when Lars couldn't find it anywhere in the compound and Terl told him the ——— stuff was what they used for panel metal in vehicles and to go down to the ——— garages and get into that ——— Zzt's repair supplies and get him a ——— sheet of the stuff!

Lars trotted back shortly, his panting clear on the disc sonic, bringing a sheet of beryllium alloy that rumbled as it was waved about. Terl kicked him out and locked the door.

They did a quick analysis of the metal and even Dunneldeen had no trouble with the traces. It was beryllium, copper, and nickel, sort of rough for it had not been polished.

On the disc Terl took some shears and cut expertly. Then he folded some edges. He annealed the edges shut by molecular bind. Then he had a top which fit very well. He put a little knob on the top for lifting it. Then he cut a hole in the bottom of the box and made a screw-in access plate. He had begun to laugh so it was easy to divine that this was something quite nasty.

It was a pretty box when he finished. He polished it up and buffed it and it looked like jewelry, a gold color. Pretty. It was hexagonal, each one of the six sides and corners geometrically precise. Quite a work of art. The top came off easily. The bottom hole access plate was left unscrewed. It was about a foot across and about five inches high.

The next day he went to work on the inside. He made some very precisely hinged rods, quite intricate. He fitted them into the box and tested them. There was a hinged rod in each of the six corners and it was fastened to the lid. When you raised the lid, these rods pushed sockets, empty as yet, to the center of the box. He tested it several times and laughed louder as he gazed up into it from the access hole in the bottom. The cover came off very smoothly; each of the six rods pushed an empty socket to the center.

Then he chased Lars all around finding different, common substances and eventually he had three different metals and three different nonmetals in a pile. They were just ordinary elements, the analyzer said: iron, silicon, sodium, magnesium, sulphur, and phosphorus.

Why? To what end?

Jonnie tore through some books. Sodium, magnesium, sulphur, and phosphorus had one thing in common. They were of use, one way or another, in explosives. Knowing Terl, that was the first thing Jonnie looked up. But this combination he didn't think would explode, because there they lay, right on the table in an earlier frame, right together and they didn't explode. Iron and silicon? It seemed that they were very common indeed in the composition of the Earth's crust and core.

He looked at a later frame, quite apprehensive. What if Terl made something and then hid it outside and they couldn't find it? What was this devil up to? Ah! Terl might have jumbled up the six elements but the strange pea-sized mineral had vanished. Jonnie backtracked on the disc.

Terl had taken the heavy bit of strange metal and measured it and then had wrapped it all up and put it back in the false cabinet. The place where it had lain now had a dent!

He made a braced basket to hold the pea in the center. But he didn't put it in for it was now back in the cabinet. Then he put the six common elements, each one, in the slots on the rods.

When one opened the lid, the rods pushed them all in to the center. They would go into contact with each other and with the pea.

Jonnie knew something about radiation and elements after their early battle. He knew that all you had to do was *stimulate* the atoms to get a chain reaction going.

But Terl was not working with uranium radiation. He couldn't. Not with the overstimulation radiation gave to breathe-gas!

So that pea thing must be some higher order of stimulation.

Knowing Terl, it would be deadly. He was sure that when that heavy, heavy pea-sized piece of metal was in the center and somebody opened the lid and all those metals pushed together and against it, something ghastly was going to happen.

Terl locked the pretty box away, cleaned up things, and opened a mathematics text entitled "Force Equations," which had nothing to do with teleportation! What was he up to now?

And that was as far as the discs went.

Their own clock had moved up to noon as they had gone nonstop, no sleep, no food.

"Now I know who made Satan," said Dunneldeen. "His name was Terl."

— 6 —

Since Terl seemed to be working on other things than teleportation, which was the key to this entire dilemma, Jonnie, for the time being, turned his attention to other things.

He had not entirely lost hope of unraveling the Psychlo technology through the restoration and possible cooperation of the remaining Psychlos. If he could get the two pieces of metal out of the head of a trained Psychlo engineer, there was a possibility that some of these mysteries would be solved, and solved they would leave them in better control of the planet's future.

Dr. MacKendrick had returned. One or two of the African base people had come down with a touch of what MacKendrick said was "malaria," carried by mosquitoes. MacKendrick had procured "chinchona bark" from South America and had made them mop up standing pools of water in the base and put nets over the air intake vents and all that seemed to be under control.

MacKendrick's three remaining Psychlo patients, two of whom were rated engineers, were not, however, so easily handled as the malaria. They were not getting well. They remained barely alive.

The thirty-three live Psychlos from the American compound arrived in Africa without incident and were put in a prepared dorm section. They had been duly reported as "lost at sea in a plane crash."

But the doctor did not have much hope for it. "I have tried every way I can think of," he told Jonnie one evening in his underground African surgery, "and one can't get through the intricate skull structure to the items without severely damaging it. Every Psychlo cadaver I have worked with so far plainly shows that critical skull bone joints would be very damaged and vital brain nerves would be severed. Those things were put into the soft skull of a newborn pup, and even within a few months the skull would have been hardened to a point where they could not be removed. I will go on working with Psychlo cadavers but I cannot hold out any real hope."

Jonnie wandered off from the conference, trying to think of some solution to that problem. It seemed these days he had a lot more problems than he had solutions. He felt that if he didn't come up with some solutions fairly soon, the human race might well be a write-off.

He heard his name called. He was passing by one of the doors that housed the new Psychlo arrivals and he stopped and went over. There was a small view port and an intercom inset into the door panel.

It was Chirk!

He had never had anything against Chirk. A rattlebrain and dedicated to wrong conclusions though she might be, the times when he had seen her they had not fought.

"Jonnie," said Chirk, "I just want to thank you for saving us."

Jonnie realized somebody had been talking to the Psychlos, maybe Dunneldeen.

"When I think of what that awful Terl planned to do—murder us all, you know—my fur crackles! I always thought you were kind of cute, Jonnie. You know that. So I know you saved our lives."

Jonnie said, "You're welcome. Can I do anything for you?" She looked pretty forlorn, really. No clothes but a wraparound, fur all matted.

"No," said Chirk. "Just thank you."

Jonnie walked off and was halfway down the passage before the weirdness of it struck him. A Psychlo being thankful? Expressing appreciation? Not wanting something? Impossible! He had never had much to do with female Psychlos. They were not numerous in the company. But a grateful Psychlo? Never!

He acted fast. Ten minutes later they had a mineral analyzer rigged and Chirk's head in it. Twenty minutes of investigation and they had an answer.

Chirk did not have any bronze object in her head. She did have a silver capsule, but it was of different shape and size.

There were twelve females from the American compound, and after a great deal of hustle and bustle and assembly line treatment, they had established that none of the females had a bronze object in their brains but they did have silver ones of the same pattern as Chirk's.

Two pilots took off for the morgue in the clouds, accompanied by a fur-wrapped MacKendrick, and they soon established, working in the icy blast of a keen wind, that they had three females in that lot.

That night MacKendrick held out the different capsule to Jonnie and Angus. He had removed it from the female corpse that had been brought back.

Careful examination showed it to have a less complex internal filament but that was all they could tell.

"I don't think that could be cut out either," said Dr. MacKendrick. "The structure of the female skull is even more complicated than the male's. All I can contribute is that it probably puts out a different message when activated."

That seemed to be pretty well that.

However, the bronze cruelty factor was missing in a female, so the following morning Jonnie had another talk with Chirk.

"How would you like a job?" said Jonnie.

Well, that would be wonderful. It just showed he was cute. Because she couldn't go back to Psychlo now. Terl had ruined her company record and they would never reemploy her with the black marks of disobedience all over the file. And if he promised not to send her back to Psychlo and paid her usual wage of two hundred Galactic credits a month, a job would be a very good thing for she was going mad from inactivity and no cosmetics.

For a long time now they had been taking Galactic credits out of company payroll offices, out of the wallets of dead Psychlos, out of canteen cash drawers, and they had a couple of million credits kicking around. So it was feasible. They struck a bargain.

Loosed with a breathe-mask and a sentry, Chirk promptly found a few yards of cloth in supply, was escorted down to the lake, and, oblivious of crocodiles, took a bath. She then demanded access to the minerals sample room of the compound.

She got some white gypsum, put it in a mortar and finely pulverized it, and put it in a sample bag. She threw some copper in a retort, added some acid, boiled it all away, washed the residue, and mixed it with some clear motor grease. She put it in a can. She got some tractor paint out of the storeroom, deepened its color to a brilliant purple by boiling it and added simple stain dye, and then poured in a pungent thinner. She put the last in a bottle.

Then she went to the tailor shop and slashed and annealed dress uniform cloth. She took some seat covering and cut it and annealed it into a pair of flare-topped boots and demanded to be taken back to her room.

Shortly there emerged the most stylish female a Psychlo street had ever seen. Although the breathe-mask hid the face makeup, one supposed that it was there for morale. And if you looked closely through the leaded faceplate you could see that she had brilliant green lipbones, a glaring white nosebone, and white and green circles around her eyebones. Her claws were a glaring shade of purple. The white dress uniform cloth was topped with a flaring gold collar and bound about by a gold-colored belt, and her boots were gold with purple sole lines.

Chirk then demanded access to another room where the other females were kept, and thereafter the current base commander was beseiged with demands for more contracts at two hundred Galactic credits a month *and clothes!*

Although Jonnie had not really expected much help from that quarter, he got it unexpectedly. Shortly he would get trouble, but to begin with it was revelatory.

Chirk made a trip out to find some mud. In that area there was lots of mud but she was looking for a certain kind of mud. She chattered away at Angus as they tramped about. She was carrying a two-hundred-pound scope under her arm like it was a handbag. Jonnie saw them walking around the edge of a swamp, Angus dwarfed by the eight-hundred-pound female, two sentries following, mostly in case of wild beasts.

Jonnie went over to them. She was looking for mud. She would stick in a paddle and put a dab on the scope plate and shake her head and walk on. She didn't seem to be getting anywhere.

Jonnie noticed something odd in animal behavior. When he went out, the game ignored him. But Chirk? You couldn't see game as far as you could look. Not an elephant, not a lion, no deer, nothing! He reasoned it must be the smell of a Psychlo. Where once animals fled at the smell of a man, over the centuries they had transferred their survival instincts. They wouldn't let a Psychlo within miles of them. Still, this area hadn't been hunted out and neither had any other area.

"Oh, Psychlo men don't mass hunt," said Chirk, busy with her paddle and scope. "The silly things find just one animal and follow it and then they sit around in a circle and take three days to kill it little by little. So they don't often get three days off. Not in this company. Silly things, males."

Jonnie did not enlighten her as to what made them "silly."

After a while she found her mud. She filled a mine bucket with it and easily carried the two-hundred-pound scope and the four hundred pounds of mud back to the compound.

She put the mud in glass bottles and added some green liquid goo-food and then rinsed the mud out. She handed the bottles to MacKendrick who gazed at them in mystery.

Chirk said, "Put that in the wounds, you foolish creature. How can you expect them to heal up if you don't use a counter-virus! Any child knows that!"

MacKendrick got it. His treatments were all aimed at bacterial control on beings who were basically virus-structured. Within the next three days all his Psychlo patients began to get well, their festering wounds closed, and it appeared they were going to have three completely cured ones soon.

Chirk got to work on the library. It shocked her that the volumes were so strewn about and for two days she did nothing but collect Psychlo books into huge piles. The other females helped and also began to clean up large areas of old Psychlo berthings.

Jonnie was working one day in the old Psychlo operations room when Chirk suddenly presented herself. "Your library," she said, "is in disgraceful condition. According to company regulations, certain booklists must be in every minesite and you can see by this form that the manager here has been negligent and should be given a black mark on his record. But I am working for you now so I must call to your attention Form 2,345,980-A. If you place this order with Psychlo, they will send them out on the next shipment. It is a very serious matter. An incomplete library!"

Chirk might not be in present time about the company but she certainly had filled out the form.

Jonnie hadn't even known the form existed. And he found himself staring at one item checked as missing: "War Vessel Recognition Tables of Hostile Races." And another, "Individual Troop Combat Capabilities Catalogued by Alien Races."

Chirk went back to work putting books in order on shelves, but within minutes, Jonnie had thirty people including two pilots ransacking the place. The "visitors" upstairs could be identified, and some means of defense might exist!

Sir Robert had returned from Scotland that morning and it was he who guessed it: "Jonnie, that group here didn't know who was attacking. Anyone in command here would have been tearing through those books. Have you looked on the corpses?"

That's where they were! In a shoulder bag on the body of the former mine manager up in the snow.

Not more than three hours later, comparing his own and Stormalong's pictures and the texts, he knew he was dealing with Tolneps, Hockners, Bolbods, and Hawvins. And he knew what they looked like and what their capabilities were—all dangerously nasty. There was no listing for the globe-shaped ship with the ring around it or any race of small gray men.

But the following day his luck ran out with Chirk. She had been doing very well. But he made a mistake.

She was sitting, all eight hundred pounds of her, at a desk in the library making some lists. Jonnie was looking at a sheet of figures he had drawn up.

The sheet concerned distances from Earth to various hostile bases nearest to it and the speeds of the types of alien ships. They had different types of drives. For the most part they ran on energy accumulated from suns, but they handled it differently. He was trying to calculate how many months those ships were from their relative bases. Terl's lists of inhabited planets had now been copied off in sheet form and it was evident they didn't include all systems or suns but only those in which Psychlo had an interest.

Jonnie had been amazed to find in other texts that there were four hundred billion suns in this galaxy alone and that this universe contained more than a hundred billion galaxies. And he had *sixteen* universes to look at.

The possible bases of hostile peoples were easier to mentally encompass. From Earth to this galaxy's center was about thirty thousand light-years. And one light-year was about six trillion miles. All these enemy ships exceeded the speed of light one way or another, but this still made it necessary to compute by how much they exceed it against what base where.

It was an awful lot of Psychlo arithmetic. He was not too patient doing it by hand. Thoughtlessly, he said to Chirk, "Could you help me add these figures up?"

She looked at him, totally blank for about a minute. Then she said, "I don't know how."

Jonnie smiled. "It's just arithmetic. Here, I'll show you—"

Chirk's eyes glazed. She fell forward across the desk.

There was no response from her. She was totally unconscious. They had to get a forklift in and take her to her room and put her to bed.

Three days later, MacKendrick told Jonnie, "She's just lying there in a coma. Maybe in time she'll come out of it. She seems to have had a heavy shock."

Although he felt bad about it, Jonnie had an idea now of what the silver capsule in the females was. They were not to be taught any Psychlo mathematics ever!

The key to the whole Psychlo empire must be mathematics. And aside from their arithmetic, he couldn't make head or tail of their equations. It seemed to be a dead end.

— 7 —

They had just completed the installation of a radio telescope when the courier came in.

Angus, his face red, first from sun at lake level and then from wind and snow up at the summit of nearby Mount Elgon, was very proud of himself. The German and Swedish pilots, with something to do besides train under the relentless Stormalong, had helped find and install the huge reflector bowls and relays from the peaks and down to the minesite.

Now that they had the frequencies, Angus was saying, they would soon be hearing everything those monkeys up there were saying to each other. He'd even have them on the screens!

Jonnie's ear caught the far-off approach of the plane above the overcast. He thanked Angus and the pilots and said they had done very well, and yes, now maybe they would know more about the intentions of their visitors.

Glencannon had taken over the ferrying of the vital discs from America. A copy was now going to Doctor MacDermott to bury in a deep underground vault and the originals were coming through to Jonnie in Africa.

Glencannon had lots of news. Pattie had been extremely ill for weeks but Chrissie was nursing her and there was hope. And Chrissie sent her love and said she'd found a lovely old house right near Castle Rock, and some of the Chiefs' wives were helping her find real furniture in old ruins, and she sent her love and when was he coming back?

Castle Rock was now so surrounded with antiaircraft blast cannon it made one fair nervous to fly near it.

Dunneldeen? Oh, he was flying the pants off new recruits but there weren't as many coming in now. Mostly machine operators were getting trained. Ker was fine and sent him some brand-new air masks he'd made that fit better and said not to turn him in for stealing company materials, ha, ha. And here were some personal letters for Sir Robert. And here was the latest set of you-know-whats.

Jonnie went deep underground and got the discs rolling. They had the place well set up now. Watching the female Psychlos, while not letting them handle anything vital, they had learned the use of some of the office machinery they had earlier ignored, and they could copy discs and make blowups of sections with a fine-line accuracy they had not thought possible. They had cabinets for files and all in all they could make the discs "talk" much better.

Terl! He was sitting there doing force equations. Incomprehensible. The equations didn't balance and didn't make any sense. He was filling pages and pages with them. Still nothing to do with teleportation.

Jonnie almost skimmed by it. He backtracked. The pictures showed Terl getting up, going over to the cabinet, and opening up *another* false bottom. He took out a huge sheet of paper, so big it would take three scanners' views to encompass it. The paper was very old, creased until it nearly fell apart, stained brown and faded.

Terl spread it out, looked at it and then shook his head over it. He traced one claw along the north side of the big dam, way to the southwest of the American minesite. He nodded.

Then he wadded the paper up and threw it at the shredder bin. He wrote down some footage figures and some voltage figures and then went back to his equations, and it was just equations for the next two days. And that was all there was in the discs.

It took an hour of patching from three different scanner channels to get it. But Jonnie recovered the huge piece of paper in its entirety and got a half-dozen huge copies of it.

It was entitled, "Defense Installations of Planet Number 203,534." Jonnie knew already that was the Psychlo name for Earth.

It showed every minesite, every dam, every gun battery, and every ———? A little symbol that trailed around each dam and below each power line from dams to minesites and branch minesites. Jonnie had no idea what that symbol was.

But there was a goody he had never, never dreamed of. Marked clearly was a firing, transshipment platform!

He compared the Psychlo mass of numbered locations with a man-map of ancient times. The second platform was alongside a dam which had once been named ["Kariba"] in a country which had once been called ["Rhodesia"] and then ["Zimbabwe"].

The platform was marked "Emergency Defense Armament Receipt Point." Obviously, if the main minesite were ever knocked out, Psychlo could send in another force or the Psychlo command on the planet could demand troops or at least inform the home office.

Hopes soaring, but a little held down by the age of the map and Terl's treatment of it, Jonnie had a marine attack plane on the line and Scots piling into it. Robert the Fox boarded hastily. Just as they were about to close the door, MacKendrick piled in with a medical kit. Jonnie sent the plane racing to the south.

It was only about a thousand miles away, and it only took them thirty-five minutes to spot the huge dam and lake and the mammoth installation. Some distance to the south and east of that they saw what had been called ["Victoria Falls"], one of the biggest waterfalls on the planet. Spectacular country!

Because the area had been marked "heavily defended," Jonnie approached it cautiously. It was another branch mine they hadn't known the existence of.

They found the compound some distance to the east and landed a platoon with assault rifles and radiation ammunition to make a cautious approach. A half-hour later they had the report on mine radio. The place was deserted and, the platoon officer reported, not much different from the one in the Ituri Forest to the north.

The map had not shown the second platform at the minesite but it was quite close to the huge dam. They took the platoon back aboard and Jonnie began to cruise the area.

Trees, trees, trees. This was a high plateau, but not an open plain. Trees had been knocked down in swaths where elephant herds had passed through.

There were lots of little hills. Everything was masked with undergrowth except a few open places.

Cruising along, elephant and African buffalo looking up at them, Jonnie searched and searched. He had found before that it was one thing to look at a map and quite another to be on the ground, and he was experiencing it again.

Time after time, he studied the map while Stormalong in the copilot's seat kept them cruising above the treetops. Jonnie finally got out some dividers and very carefully measured the distance from the dam edge and then, taking the plane to that point and cruising it at the speed a horse walks, finally got them in the center of what must have been the point. Stormalong threw out a smoke flare to mark it and a couple of big elephants took off.

It was a bowl in the ground, the edges of which rose about two hundred feet above the middle. It was like a crater, possibly even made with a bomb blast. It was about a thousand feet in diameter.

The bowl itself was so overgrown one could not see what was in it. But as the white smoke spired up, the truth hit Jonnie.

For centuries, perhaps, the company security officers of this planet had paid no attention to maintaining the elaborate planetary company defenses which once existed. No wonder Terl had thrown the map away. He looked so disappointed that Sir Robert tried to cheer him up. "We won't really know until we look closer." But it certainly was wilderness, receiving no care for centuries.

Jonnie put them down on the upper edge of the crater, and with riflemen ready to handle any hostile game, others got axes and began to hack their way down.

"Be careful around here," said Dr. MacKendrick. "This area

had an insect called the tsetse fly that brought on sleeping sickness. Also the water had a worm in it that got into the blood stream. I don't have much in the way of medicines but wear nets and stay out of the water."

"Great," said Jonnie. That was all they needed.

They cut their way down to the center of the bowl. They passed one of the transshipment poles three times before they spotted it. They paced out in various directions and located another two. The fourth was easy.

Jonnie took a shovel and started down through the humus. He was hoping the company maxim of "never salvage anything" would hold true. Two feet of dead leaves and humus down, he hit the platform.

Axes ringing, they were getting trees and brush out of the way. They found the concrete base of the operations firing dome and then finally the dome itself, upside-down and some distance away.

No console!

Wires were eventually uncovered within the concrete base. Typically Psychlo, they were still well insulated when you scraped the mold off.

Jonnie was struck by the absence of the power lines. There should be power lines coming in from the dam. There was a power channel marked on the map and also that old squiggle he couldn't identify.

Light was failing and they would have kept on but MacKendrick made them get up to high ground. They spent the night listening to elephants trumpeting, lions roaring, and all the other cacophony of a very live jungle. But the night was quite cool since this plateau had a fairly high altitude.

In the morning they dug a crosscut trench and found the power line, being careful not to cut into it. They cut another trench and found the same line went on underground to the distant minesite.

And there was another cable they couldn't identify that went along with the power line.

Flogging their way through the brush, they went over to the huge dam. It was a real soaring monster of a dam. It seemed intact. The spillways were running. There were signs that Psychlos had landed near it and gone in and out the access door to the powerhouse in some recent time.

Jonnie had never been inside one of these dams before. They

vibrated with sheer, raw power. The thunder of the water and the high whine of generators made it impossible to be heard.

It was the usual Psychlo conversion, he supposed. It was very, very old and some bits of the original man-equipment that had been cast aside were very much older.

Angus found the switchboard and bus bars—a vast, towering affair in a separate control room. Only two of the handles were clean and it didn't need a little tuft of fur caught in one of them to tell that Psychlos had come here to shut power on and off.

But what were all these other bus bars? They got some mine sacks and tried to wipe the panel down without causing short circuits. There were Psychlo letters inset into it. A whole row said, "Force Stage One, Force Stage Two, Force Stage Three." A second row said, "Transshipment One, Transshipment Two, Transshipment Three."

Jonnie gingerly rubbed some more with a mine sack, careful of closing any gap. "They're color-coded." He tried to tell Angus this but there was no talking in this place. They went back out.

"Terl," said Jonnie to Angus and Sir Robert, "is working on force equations. There is something on the north side of the American dam I think he must want. The squiggles on this map must have to do with force." He sent Angus back into the power control house and placed some Scots along the underground line of squiggles and connected every one up with mine radios.

"Close Force Stage One!" he radioed to Angus.

The effect was far more drastic and dramatic than anything they expected.

All inferno broke loose!

Along the squiggle line of the map, all around the crater, trees erupted, splintered, soared, crashed.

It was as if a bomb had exploded.

Trunks and leaves and branches were falling for over a minute afterward.

Sir Robert was running to find out what had happened to their spotters. Were they all killed? Their radios had gone silent!

It took them an hour to dig the Scots out. One had been knocked unconscious, the rest were bruised and slightly cut. Six had been involved.

MacKendrick collected them and assessed the damages and began applying the antiseptics and tape. Jonnie made his way over to them from the dam. It looked like a first-aid station after a battle. The one who had been knocked out had come to now He had been blown in the air. Jonnie apologized to them.

The Scot that had been knocked out was grinning. "A little thing like that isn't likely to ruin a Scot!" he said. "What was it?"

Yes, indeed. What was it?

"Did I do something wrong?" Angus's voice came over the radio.

The Scots were all taking it as a joke so Jonnie said, "I think you did something right!" They were out of the area now. "Close that switch again!"

A bit of the tree wreckage stirred and moved and then was still. Jonnie cautiously moved toward the bowl. And couldn't leave the dam area!

He walked straight ahead and then he couldn't go any further. He could *not* walk through the air before him!

He threw a rock at it. The rock bounced! He tried again, throwing harder. Same result.

He had Angus open the bus bar again. No barrier! Closed. Barrier!

For the next two hours, by opening and closing the first and second row of bus bars and throwing rocks, they found that the dam itself was surrounded by a protective screen. The bowl had a screen all around its top and was completely enclosed!

Riflemen even fired shots at it and they glanced off.

At Stage Two the air got a bit shimmery, and Angus reported the power output meters were lower. At Stage Three there was a strange electrical smell in the air and the output meters of the total dam power dropped way down.

Defense and more defense. A transshipment platform operating in that bowl could not be interfered with by attack. Not from the sides and not from above. And neither could the dam.

The amount of raw power it took to operate it was a large portion of the total output of this huge dam, and Jonnie surmised that they changed stages of output to repel extreme attack and then eased them off to Stage One when they needed power to transship.

Jonnie had them booby-trap the entrances in case their visitors upstairs came down for a look and prowl. And they took off in the early afternoon for home.

A glimmer of hope. Not much, but a glimmer, Jonnie told Sir Robert on the way home.

He wanted Sir Robert, Jonnie said, to take charge in the African area for the moment for Jonnie had some other things to look into elsewhere. He rebriefed the grizzled War Chief on the existing situation: they were threatened by a possible counterattack from Psychlo; the visitors upstairs were waiting for something—he did not know what, but he was certain they would eventually strike; the political scene in America was a lesser menace but existed and they had to let it go on for now. The thing that would solve their troubles, Jonnie said, was to get control of teleportation or at least an operating console; with that they could operate far more widely, but it seemed to be the most closely guarded secret the Psychlos had, and avenues to cracking it were not very hopeful.

The main problem, Jonnie said, was protecting what was left of the human race; they were no longer very numerous; a wide attack by the visitors or a counterattack by Psychlo could, either one, finish them as a race forever. Jonnie, as soon as they landed, was going to leave for Russia to begin to handle this point.

Would Sir Robert, Jonnie concluded, take a few local protective measures which Jonnie then named.

Robert the Fox said he was honored and certainly would. Such things were easily done, but did Jonnie much care what happened to any visitors who might wander down?

Jonnie said no. And Sir Robert smiled.

■

PART 22

— 1 —

The Bolbod punchcraft was quite clear on the screen. Cylindrical, a small miniature of the Bolbod war vessel from which it came, it was about to make its landing near the dam.

The small gray man sat in his small gray office and watched. He was mildly interested in a detached sort of way.

He was very glad he had asked his communications officer to install the racks and extra screens. A Jambitchow war vessel had joined them—commanded by an officer in glittering gold scales and eyes where his mouth ought to be—had been informed of the situation, had been told that they didn't know yet whether this was the *one,* had agreed to join the combined force, and was now in orbit with the rest. The Jambitchow face was now on its own viewscreen, watching, like the rest, the outcome of this "punch" as the Bolbod called it. Six screens, five of them with intent faces, the sixth carrying the long-range view of this raid.

For the last few days the small gray man had felt much better. It had been a good idea to go down and see that old woman again. She was certain it could not have been her yarb tea that had caused his indigestion. Had he drunk anything in some heathen country? Well, never mind, drink this "buttermilk."

He had drunk the buttermilk. It was quite cold and good to taste and shortly his indigestion had greatly eased. But the old woman had not let it go at that. A cousin in some distant past had sent some plants to some ancestors of hers and they were still flourishing up the hill near the spring. It was called "peppermint" and she would go get some, and she had, steering a bit wide around the parked spaceship. The green leaves had a pleasant aroma and he had chewed some, and astonishingly, his indigestion eased even more! She had given him a whole pocketful of the leaves.

The small gray man had tried to pay her but she wouldn't have it; she said it was just the neighborly thing to do. He had persisted however, and she finally said, well, there was a Swedish colony up the coast she was never able to talk to, and that thing around his neck, the one he talked into and it talked English, would it talk Swedish? He'd been happy to give it to her—he had several—and had changed its microplates while sitting pleasantly on a bench outside her door with both the dog and the cow seemingly quite interested in what he was doing. It had been a pleasant afternoon.

The Bolbod punchcraft banged down near the overgrown walkway at the dam. They were carrying a demolition kit.

"I thought this was just a probe," said the Hawvin. "Didn't we agree they were just to discover what those people had done down at that dam?" They had watched the terrestrial antics around them, had seen them blow up a bunch of trees, and their curiosity had been greatly aroused. No heat had accompanied the eruption of trees and nothing had burned. "If we use demolition on the dam, it could become political."

"I command my own crew," rumbled the Bolbod on his screen. That was the trouble with combined forces, everyone tried to run everybody else's ship! But combined force had been his idea so he couldn't say much more.

There had been three Bolbod crewmen in the punchcraft. The first one, carrying the demolition kit, was followed at some distance by the other two.

The faces on the viewscreens were very intent as they followed this operation. It was their first probe down to the surface. The small gray man had tended to advise against it but this was a military matter. They all knew that one must test the enemy's defenses.

The leading Bolbod was now about fifty feet from the powerhouse door. The roar of the spillway was coming back up the infrabeam, very strong. That was an awfully big dam.

Abruptly there was a flash!

A rolling ball of flame rocketed skyward.

The image on the screen jittered from the concussion.

The first Bolbod had vanished, blown to bits. Whatever he tripped had also detonated his own demolition kit.

The other two Bolbods who had been well behind him had been knocked flat.

"Aha!" said the Hockner super-lieutenant as though he had known it all the time.

But the "aha!" wasn't for the explosion. A marine attack plane that a moment before hadn't been on their screens landed clear of the explosion area. A small unit of people leaped out.

Swedes, thought the small gray man, seeing their blonde hair. Led by a black-bearded young officer in kilts who carried a claymore and a blast pistol.

A ramp went down on the attack plane's side and a forklift rolled to the ground.

The Swedes had some chains in their hands and were wrapping up the two recumbent Bolbods. Thin little shouts of command were coming back up the infrabeam, almost engulfed by the roar of the dam spillway.

The Scot officer was trying to find pieces of the exploded Bolbod, picking up items of bloody cloth. He seemed to find something. He put it in a bag and waved to the forklift. They now put the huge Bolbod bodies into the plane with the forklift. The lift came back and put the punchcraft inside.

The plane took off and went back north. The terrestrial group went into the powerhouse and vanished from sight.

The faces on the viewscreens were hard to read. They were grappling with this situation.

They didn't have too much time to ponder for their second probe was now in progress, and infrabeams shifted to the snowy crest of Mount Elgon which gleamed above the clouds far below.

It had annoyed them to see an old device they took to be an ancient radio telescope mounted up there. It seemed to be tracking them as they orbited.

A Hockner probe ship with five Hockners had been assigned to disable the device. And there was the Hockner probe now, nearing its destination. A Hockner probe carried no artillery itself but the men did. The noseless, overly ornamented crew members were visible under the probe canopy. It was little more than a sled and was jet-powered. There seemed to be very high winds and it was having trouble setting down on a broad, icy shoulder of the peak. There was a precipice there that dropped down into the clouds. Yes, it was a high wind; plumes of snow were blowing away from the peak. Just ahead of them but set well back from the edge was the offending radio telescope. Beyond that object, out of the view of the probecraft, a glacier fell away.

The faces watching it on their separate screens were quite different in reactions. It was taking the probecraft so long to get down to a landing, going out and back again time after time, that their attention was drifting.

The Tolnep half-captain was doing some calculations about slave prices. He knew an air planet where you could get a thousand credits a slave if you could get them there alive. He estimated that he had a potential here of about fifteen thousand, landed live, out of maybe thirty thousand shipped. That was fifteen million Galactic credits. His nineteen percent of that, the prize money he would get personally, would be two million, eight hundred fifty thousand credits. His loaners were owed fifty-two thousand, eight hundred sixty credits in gambling debts (the reason he was happy to undertake a very long cruise) and this left him two million, seven hundred ninety-seven thousand, one hundred forty credits. He could retire!

The Hawvin was thinking about all the silver and copper coins that must be in the ruins of old banks—the Psychlos valued neither metal but he knew a market for it.

The Bolbod had been thinking about all the Psychlo machinery down there up until the time his punchcraft was captured. Now he was thinking about punching terrestrials.

The Jambitchow commander was wondering how he could do the rest of these aliens out of slaves, metal and machinery.

Finally the probecraft made it and sat down on the ledge and their attention riveted on it.

The five Hockners got out, bulky in their fancy space suits and clumsy in swinging their blast rifle straps off their shoulders.

Suddenly the voice of the Hockner landing control officer in orbit crackled out of their radios down there and came back up the infrabeam.

"Alert to the battle plane!"

There *was* a battle plane up at about two hundred thousand feet. But it had been there for an hour, doing nothing. And it was doing nothing now. The five Hockners were looking at it way up there, a tiny speck to them, hard to find in the blue sky they saw

"No, no!" barked the Hockner landing control officer. "Around the corner from you! Coming up the glacier!"

Only then did the watching faces see it. From their viewpoint it was just a line on the glacier, just the top of its body showing, the rest cut off by the jutting crag above the telescope. The battle plane had hugged the glacier all the way up! It was almost a hundred yards back of the telescope when it stopped. No one here could see whether anyone got out of it. It must be holding in that position on its motors. The glacier was *steep*.

The five Hockners, alert now but seeing no one yet, crouched, guns ready. Then they sprinted forward.

A hammering burst of blast guns flared just behind the telescope.

One Hockner, near the edge, was hit, thrown out into space, and went spinning down through the clouds.

The Hockner sled, struck by a burst, slithered backward, teetered, and dropped into empty space.

The four remaining Hockners charged through the snow and wind, guns going.

The relentless pounding of blast rifles racketed up the infrabeam. The whole area under the telescope seemed to be erupting continuous, green gouts of thundering energy.

One Hockner down. Two down. Three down! The fourth almost reached the telescope and then thudded into the snow.

The only sound now was the whistle of wind around the peak.

Several terrestrials sprang into view from beyond the radio telescope. They rushed forward, their red and white high-altitude suits looking like splashes of blood against the snow. They turned over the Hockners, took their weapons. One terrestrial looked over the edge where the fifth Hockner and the probecraft had fallen but the only cushion down there was the tops of the clouds far below.

The Hockners were picked up and lugged off by the terrestrials. Using safety lines and slipping and sliding down the glacier, they loaded the Hockners into the marine attack plane which was now more visible.

One terrestrial came back and checked over the radio telescope and then he went sliding down the glacier, grabbed the door of the plane, and swung aboard.

The plane took off and went down through the clouds. The infrabeam shifted to penetrate the overcast and followed it back to the minesite.

"That proves it," said the Tolnep half-captain. "It was just as I thought all along."

He ignored the comments to the effect that he had favored the probes.

"It was a lure," he continued. "It is quite obvious that at the dam yesterday they went down and made a harmless eruption of trees to intrigue us. Then they lay in wait and succeeded in capturing two Bolbod crewmen.

"The radio telescope," he went on, "is just a dummy as I suspected. They have not been used for centuries. Everyone uses infrabeams to pick up faint signals and broadcasts. So they put it there in an elaborate charade to attract down a probe. None of the Hockner crew besides the one so clumsy as to fall off the cliff were killed. The guns were all on 'stun.' Thus they succeeded in luring four Hockners."

"Should you be talking so plainly?" said the Jambitchow commander, stroking his polished scales. "They may have us on monitor."

"Nonsense," said the Tolnep. "Our detectors show no infrabeams and we are just on local. I tell you no one has used radio telescopes since . . . since . . . the Hambon Sun War! They have far too much clutter; they are too bulky. That's just a dummy down there. And did you notice the cute way that officer came back and 'adjusted' it. They're just hoping we'll try again."

"I shouldn't think they need to," said the Hawvin. "They now have two Bolbod crew and four Hockners to interrogate at leisure. Knowing Psychlo methods of interrogation, I shouldn't care to be those crewmen!"

"They're not Psychlos!" said the Hockner super-lieutenant, covering up the fact that he was aghast at the fate of his crewmen.

"Yes, they are," said the Bolbod. "You saw that Psychlo with the terrestrials the other day down by the lake. The Psychlos are using aliens as a subject race. They've done it before. I vote we go down in an actual mass attack and pound out any installation they have, now! Before they are further prepared."

But at that moment they were startled when a hazy image appeared on all their screens. It was a gray black-haired and bearded human visage. The eyes were blue. The being seemed to be wearing an old cloak.

"If you will turn up your transmission to planetary strength," this newcomer said in Psychlo, "I would like to discuss returning your members to you. The two Bolbods are shaken up but not hurt. The four Hockners are just stunned, though one has a broken arm.''

They turned up to planetary strength, but their response was an emphatic uniform no!

The Tolnep half-captain managed to get his voice above the uproar. ''So you can capture the rescue party? Emphatically, no!''

''We can put them all out on a slope—over by that black volcanic cone. All in the open and no ships of ours in the air.'' The terrestrial was persuasive. ''Call it a truce. Your pickup ship will not be fired upon or molested.''

''You haven't interrogated them *that* fast,'' said the Jambitchow, ''so they must be dead!''

''They are quite all right,'' said the terrestrial. ''Are you sure you won't pick them up?''

Emphatically, no!

''Very well,'' said the terrestrial with a shrug of his shoulders. ''At least tell us what they eat.''

The Tolnep gave a signal on his screen to the others. Let him speak. ''Why, of course,'' he said smoothly, smiling. ''We will make up a food package and send it down.''

They went off planetary. ''I told you,'' said the Tolnep, ''that those incidents were a lure. Now two of you have bungled, so let me handle this.''

Presently a rocket-borne package went out of an airlock of the Tolnep ship. It was very well aimed and its parachute burst open below the overcast. It went drifting down and landed just short of the lake shore.

Presently a vehicle went speeding away from the compound toward it. The faces on the viewscreens smiled. If those were Psychlos down there, or whoever they were, they were in for a surprise!

Then suddenly the Hockner super-lieutenant, who had been leafing hurriedly through a recognition book, said, ''Oh, I say! That's a Basher 'Bash our Way to Glory' tank! Totally armored!''

The tank went down near the package, lowered a turret gun, and fired a mild stun shot into it. The package, being a bomb of course, exploded in a geyser of flame. The tank fired a second shot at the remains. Then somebody got out of it and collected the hot fragments.

"We even gave them bomb fragments for analysis!" shouted the Hawvin.

They held a hasty conference. The small gray man listened to them. Military minds, he thought to himself, could be quite remarkable at times. They decided that anything those terrestrials did was just a lure; that the strategy of those people was to take the invader to bits piecemeal and then pulverize him; that they should now wait for the courier the small gray man said was coming sometime, the one that might tell them if the *one* had been found; meanwhile only the safest type of probes should be attempted in areas obviously not guarded or covered. Then the moment they *knew*, one way or the other, whether this was the *one*, they would plunge in with a mass war vessel attack and defeat and gut the place.

All the commanders agreed except the Tolnep. He was still in a rage about his bomb failing.

"I should go down there right now," hissed the Tolnep, "and bite the lot of them to death!"

"We think that's an excellent idea," drawled the Hockner, adjusting his monocle.

"Yes, why don't you do that!" the rest agreed. And, "We're sure you should."

The Tolnep realized they would only be too happy to get rid of him. He subsided for now. Later would be another matter.

— 2 —

Jonnie had gone on his trip to look at bases but he found himself looking at people.

The flight had been pleasant enough. A new pilot had thought he would be flying Jonnie, but the very idea of having to be flown about amused him: he didn't have a broken arm! But an escort of three Mark 32 battle planes, long-range ones that also were designed to carry a squad of Psychlo marines or employees, got into the air behind him when he took off and stayed right with him. He had flown northeast over Africa, the Red Sea, and the Middle East and into Russia, making good time two hundred thousand feet up and looking for a pattern of lakes and rivers

Colonel Ivan had shown him with a finger in sand. He had expected to find snow, but although it was late autumn, the only snow was on towering peaks below and to the east. He found his landmarks, found his preplanned landing space, and found himself in the middle of a sea of surging people! Colonel Ivan was holding them back with a dozen mounted lancers so that he had a place to land. There must be five hundred people in that throng.

He opened the door and was blasted with sound. They were cheering themselves hoarse! He couldn't even understand what they were saying, such were the rolling waves of sound. He couldn't really distinguish individual faces among so many.

Colonel Ivan dismounted as Jonnie got down from the plane. The Colonel was a little stiff and too formal, thinking possibly Jonnie blamed him because of Bittie—the Colonel was wearing a black band around his sleeve. But Jonnie threw an arm around his shoulders and it was abruptly all right.

They had brought him a horse, a golden-colored stallion with a sheepskin saddle, and he swung up. The crowd cheered. He only knew one word of Russian and that was "zdrastvuitye," which meant "How do you do, hello." So he called it loudly and the crowd cheered.

Jonnie looked around. They were close to, in fact right up against the mountains, fairly high mountains . . . fourteen thousand feet? They had snow on them. The ancient Russian base must be nearby. He had thought they would go right to it and he could get his observation and estimation done right away. But no, everybody seemed to have other ideas. There were some skin and felt tents, and fires put their smoke in the air, and suddenly Jonnie realized this crowd was in their best clothes. This was a holiday! And the way they pressed in upon him, he certainly was the reason. He wondered fleetingly whether Thor had been up here, for if he had then a lot of these people would think he knew them. Well, his one word of Russian would have to get him by.

The Colonel's horsemen were opening the way. Every time Jonnie raised his hand and nodded there was a new ear-bashing burst of cheering. Colors, faces! He knew the sound of Russian well enough to know it was Russian, but he was also hearing scattered words like "Bravo!" and "Bueno!" and "Viva!" Sounded like the llaneros. Yes! There was a flat-crowned, black-leather hat. Several of them. And some huge straw hats.

The smell of roasting meat and the tang of dung fires was in the air. A band made up of balalaikas and Spanish guitars and Andean flutes and Mongol drums was splitting the air.

The colonel got him to a skin tent that had been set up for him and with a final wave of the hand and his one word of Russian—now no longer adequate—he got inside.

A Coordinator had also come in and through him Jonnie wanted to know, couldn't they go to the base now?

The colonel was aghast. Nyet, nyet, there was time for all that. One had to think of the people! Many of them, in fact most of them, had never met Jonnie before, had never even seen him.

Jonnie said he *was* thinking of the people! To get them safe from possible harm.

Well, harm was always around, according to the colonel, but not every day was an opportunity to meet Jonnie. Vyehrnah? (Right?)

At that, Jonnie was glad to get out of his heavy flight suit for it was much less cold here than he had thought. The colonel had brought his kit in but he ignored it. He had a near-white buckskin suit he had had made—not quite like the one on the credit bank note—those loops there on each side of the breast were cartridge loops—but the village girls had done very well. Those moccasins should fit, but here were some military boots and red baggy pants if he preferred. This gold helmet? Well, it wasn't really gold. It was a lightweight Russian helmet, armor-proof aluminum no less, and somebody flying through here had taken it down to the old minesite at Grozny and plated it with beryllium. See? It didn't have any star or ornament on it, but this chin strap with the heavy ear pads, and the colored beads all over it, had been done by one of the Siberian tribes, and wasn't it nice? And besides Dr. MacKendrick had told Jonnie to be careful of his head after the fractures. So wear it! Jonnie said he couldn't hear with it buckled. Wear it!

Jonnie washed his face and got dressed and told the colonel he was a bully and the colonel confessed he was far worse than that.

It was this way: his original plan to have Americans man this base had been passed by the old Council—before it went funny. They'd recruited some South Americans and sent them over. But there was a tribe up in the Arctic descended from political prisoners in Siberia and they spent most of their time starving to death, so they had come down en masse, dogs and all, and they were here—the Siberians were the ones out there in white bearskins. And then there was a little tribe they'd found in the Caucasus that had survived and they were here. So it really was getting pretty manned up with Russians. But they had an American here. Yes! You want to see? He's right outside.

The American was ushered in and he was pulling a young girl behind him. He stood there grinning. It was a boy from Jonnie's own village! Tom Smiley Townsen. They were very glad to see each other. Tom Smiley was a big lad, almost as big as Jonnie and a year younger. He said he had graduated from machine school and heard they didn't have enough operators over here for this job and had caught a ride, and he'd been working here for over a month running mine sweepers and teaching others and fixing things that broke down.

This was his girl, Margarita. "*Margarita, permiteme presentarte al Gran Señor Jonnie.*"

The girl was very pretty, very shy, and overawed. Jonnie bowed. He had seen Sir Robert do that. And she bowed.

Tom Smiley said they were going to get married in a few weeks. And Jonnie said he hoped they had lots of children. And Margarita blushed when Tom Smiley translated it but nodded her head with enthusiasm.

For the first time, Jonnie learned the village had been moved. Tom Smiley had been trained so he could keep the passes open in winter using a blade scraper, and they wouldn't have the usual winter starvation, but now that they were moved, there was less snow. It was to the town Jonnie had recommended, but Brown Limper had sent troops to force them to go to it. They had even had to leave their belongings behind, but he thought by now the other boys—two more were machine operators now and two were pilots—would have collected those up for them.

The colonel pushed them out and gave Jonnie a sip of the "finest vodka ever brewed," and it almost took the top off Jonnie's head. What a cure for flight fatigue! Must have been out of bears' teeth!

The colonel said that was absolutely correct, how did he guess the formula, and took him outside again.

Most of the people were going about their business getting ready for a big party and dance but they smiled and smiled as they passed Jonnie.

Two German pilots from the African base were sitting in front of a fire drinking something. The third pilot was upstairs flying patrol, the rumble of the motors faint due to his extreme altitude. Jonnie told them in Psychlo they should relax and enjoy themselves, and they just looked at him respectfully. Jonnie knew they had completely different orders: two on alert for scramble, sleeping in their planes with the radio on, one ship always in the air. Jonnie realized all this good cheer and festivity in the air was dulling his awareness of the facts of today—they were at war with powerful forces.

The colonel led him to a small knoll and with an expansive hand showed him how great this country was. There was wild cotton, enough to clothe thousands, there was wild wheat and wild oats and herds of sheep and cattle enough to feed hundreds of thousands. Those ruins way over there had been a city full of factories, and although the machines didn't work with existing motors, Tom Smiley thought he could get some looms running—which made Jonnie wonder whether they didn't have another Angus on their hands in Tom Smiley.

Did Jonnie know there was a tomb over to the southeast, way over, where the emperor of the world was buried? A Mongol named Timur i Leng. Nearly two thousand years ago he had ruled the whole world. It was a fact. He would have to take Jonnie over there and show him the tomb. It said so right on it.

Jonnie had heard quite enough about Hitlers and Napoleons and such. He had often wondered whether—if such vermin had not been so intent on personally ruling the world—man might have had the cultural advancement to repel the Psychlo invasion. He had heard some theory that it required war to invent technology and he thought that must be a Psychlo maxim. But he didn't tell Colonel Ivan that. He admired the truly beautiful view.

The base? The colonel responded to Jonnie's question. It was up there, not very far away from here. He'd give him a whole tour tomorrow.

As they started down, a big, jolly-looking Scot and two aides met them. It was Sir Andrew MacNulty, the head of the federation and Chief of all the Coordinators. He had gotten the word Jonnie was here and had just flown in. He had a pleasing manner and cheery laugh, very admired by his extensive and busy corps of Coordinators. Jonnie was very glad to see him for the business he was here for involved the movement of tribes. He complimented Sir Andrew on the magnificent work the Coordinators were doing and Sir Andrew thanked him for saving the lives of that pair in Africa. Jonnie knew he could get along with this man. Good.

About sunset the party was ready, and the big square box constellation in the sky was well down before it finished. Dances and music and more dances. Spanish dances. The Dance of the Bear Hunt from Siberia. Wild leaping dances from the Caucasus. Firelight and laughter. Good food and drink. Since it seemed everyone had to clink a cup with Jonnie and since he had never done much drinking, he had quite a head the next morning when the colonel, all bustling efficiency, broke him out.

After a bit of breakfast they trooped off in a mob to see the ancient defense base. The colonel said that they had all worked on it and they were all going along to make sure he liked it and to straighten anything up he didn't like. They were no longer in their party clothes. They were here now to go back to work as needed.

The ancient base was entered through a tunnel that was masked by overhangs. Built to resist nuclear bombing and to serve as a command post, it was deep. Due to occasional earthquakes in this area, it had been built very strong. It lacked the polish and finish of the American base but it was even bigger.

They had lighted it with Psychlo mine lamps. They had buried the vast numbers of dead with honors. They had swept everything up with Psychlo mine sweepers flown in from Grozny. Tom Smiley had gotten the water lines working. The colonel said he really hadn't intended for him and his men to help so much for this should be an American base but they had the experience and so they had pitched in.

The amounts of stores were vast. Uniforms were not as well packaged and sealed as the American ones had been but much of the stores were useful. Possibly the quality was even better. Look at these portable "flame throwers." They still worked!

A hundred thousand assault rifles called AK 47 had been found totally preserved and they had retailored the ammunition with and without radiation. They presented Jonnie with one that they had chrome-molecular-plated down at Grozny and five thousand rounds of guaranteed no-misfire ammunition in clips.

The Russian premier had apparently never gotten here but his command post had been ready. Jonnie thought that must be a picture of him, that big one on the wall, but he was told no, that was a picture of a former tsar named Lenin. Possibly in the time of Timur i Leng, they were not sure, but it was evidently a very respected picture so they had left it.

Level after level, passage after passage, they trooped through the vast base, stopping now and then to show Jonnie things, smiling at his praise, very happy that he was pleased with it.

But the main thing Jonnie was happy with was the underground hangars. Here was room for thousands of planes. The very thing. Storage. Exactly what he had hoped to find. They had used blade scrapers to push out the crumbled ruins that they said were "migs" and other craft. Jonnie could not read the alphabet but many of them could, and they showed him some of the labels they had salvaged before pushing the mounds of warplanes out. "Migs" meant "airplane" in Russian, they said.

The hangers had their own ports and entrances. Just what Jonnie wanted!

They showed him the tactical nuclear and other nuclear manuals. They were all in Russian but one old fellow from the Hindu Kush assured Jonnie he could read them.

There was a lot of nuclear weapons storage to the north and they were not going near it until they got the manuals read. There were a lot of "silos" too that had powder rockets still in them but the powder was dangerous to handle. It had gone bad but little pieces blew up if you hit them hard with a hammer. Not very useful.

They also showed him a coal mine nearby where the black rocks burned. So heating and fuel were handy.

Now they were going to get a lot of these black rocks. They were going to harvest a lot of that wild wheat. They had plans. Jonnie said the plans were great and they had done so very well that they were great too. He was very, very pleased. He shook the hands of hundreds of people.

It was not until dawn the following day that he could leave for Tibet. What had been intended as a two-hour check of a base had developed into a two-day tour. He was amazed what people could do if you let them just get at it, without a lot of government restricting them.

He was wearing the new helmet when he left. The colonel

saw to that. Buckled down too! The colonel didn't care if he couldn't hear. Motors were bad for the ears and at high altitudes his ears would get cold. Jonnie laughed at him but he wore it.

— 3 —

As an experienced if not always lucky gambler, Half-Captain Rogodeter Snowl of the Tolnep Elite Space Navy considered that he knew a sure thing when he saw it, no matter how bad his eyes were lately.

A week ago he had discovered a radio band down there on the planet that the others of the combined force did not seem to be aware of—and he was not going to tell them. It was apparently termed "The Federation Channel" and it gave news and orders and carried reports of some creatures called "Coordinators." It dealt with *tribes*. As an officer of a navy that depended mainly on slavery for its prize money, he felt anything to do with people down there was of vast interest. This was a trade Tolneps were good at, well equipped to handle, and happy to engage in.

He had told the other ships that there really should be a guard on the opposite side of the planet and had separated from them, taking a position in orbit out of their direct view.

Two days ago he had been amazed at the security those potential slaves down there omitted. They chattered away in a language called "English"—which he had vocoder circuits for from ages back—and they were making advance arrangements for the visit of a notable.

It had been too late to do anything about a visit this notable made to a flat plain in the north, but not too late to observe it. He had been amazed to see that it was the man on the one-credit note. And even easier to identify by a gold helmet.

The Federation network was chattering away about his next intended visit. It was an ancient city in the mountains they called "Lhasa." The Coordinators were to gather up some tribes at that point for a reception and do this and do that. From there on it was easy. Careful search of those huge mountains down there showed movement of people converging on just one city. The site was protected all around by mountains and was itself at a high altitude. Lhasa!

Half-Captain Snowl made his plans quickly but well. Without informing the others, take that notable captive, interrogate him as only Tolneps—or maybe Psychlos—could interrogate, get the priceless information, use what was left of the notable to negotiate a planetary surrender, and to blazes with sharing anything with the rest. Pick up the population, pay his gambling debts, and retire! He had the time, the place, and the opportunity. Act!

On his diamond-shaped bridge, Snowl went over the Vulcor vessel's watch officer list and found an officer to whom he had lost 2,021 credits—which Snowl still owed. It was Double-Ensign Slitheter Pliss. If this failed, that was one gambling debt the half-captain would not have to pay. But it could not possibly fail. Too standard an action.

He called Double-Ensign Pliss to the bridge, told him exactly what was wanted, ordered two marines broken out of deep sleep, authorized the use of a small strike launch, and got the kidnap underway.

It was a clear, beautiful day and Jonnie turned the controls over to the German copilot. Jonnie was entranced with those mountains far below. He had never seen the Himalayas before. Impressive! Some of them were five miles high and a few nearly six. Snow and glaciers and wind plumes, deep valleys and frozen rivers, they were very emphatic mountains. And such a vast extent of them.

They were flying on a general southeasterly course and very high. They were only a bit above sonic since they were beforehand in their planned arrival time. It was relaxing not to listen to the heavy roar of their motors. The helmet ear pads were quite soundproof, much more so than the usual domed helmets. Strange to be flying without sound. Maybe the colonel was right—maybe it did hurt the ears.

The copilot had spotted a key towering peak to their right. They were right on course. Jonnie relaxed—it had been quite a visit. After a while he got interested in the assault rifle they had given him: they had put it on the floor plates under his feet. A chrome-plated rifle! He wondered whether they had also chromed the inside of the bore—if they had it would be dangerous to fire. He worked out how to field-strip the weapon and looked down the bore. No, they hadn't chromed it, so it was fine. He put the weapon back together and practiced a bit with the cocking bolt. Then he put a magazine in it and working the cocking bolt, ran a whole clip through it without firing. It all worked just fine. He reloaded the clip and checked the other clips. They worked too. He tested the balance of it by sighting on a peak. The sights took a little getting used to and he practiced with them.

He didn't hear the copilot trying to tell him they would shortly land and was taken by surprise when he looked down and saw Lhasa. They were coming right on in.

What an impressive city it must have been once. A huge palace ruin went up the side of a red mountain. The palace was so big it was more than the mountain. There was a wide-open expanse just below the palace and a lot of other ruins stood around what must have been a park. The whole city was in a sort of bowl surrounded by high mountains.

Yes, and there was a little mob of people waiting at the far side of the park, most of them in furs, some in yellow robes. There was lots of space to land and Jonnie let the copilot bring the ship in over the top of a tumble of rubble that had once been a building and set her down. The huge ancient palace reared up on their right, the crowd was a hundred yards in front of the plane, and an ancient ruin was two hundred yards behind it.

Jonnie undid his security belts and swung the door partly open.

The crowd was simply standing over there. Perhaps two hundred people or more. They didn't rush forward. They didn't cheer. Oh, well, Jonnie thought, one can't be popular everyplace.

The sling of the AK 47 caught on the console before him and he lifted it up, swung the door wider, and dropped to the ground. Usually the copilot would shift over to the pilot's seat and Jonnie glanced up. The German was just sitting there, staring straight ahead.

Jonnie looked at the crowd again. Nobody came forward. Nobody moved. Eerie! There they were across the park, about a hundred yards away. He could make out three Coordinators. They were also just standing there as though rooted.

They looked like people with a gun trained on them.

An outdoorsman's instinct caused him to whirl and look back of the plane, back toward the tumbled ruin two hundred yards behind his ship.

Three running figures were racing toward him, blast rifles held low.

They were gray They were about the size of men. They wore big faceplates.

Tolneps!

They were closing the distance fast. Only seventy-five yards away.

Jonnie started to grab for his belt gun and realized he was holding the AK 47. He crouched cocked the weapon, and sent a spray of fire at the figures

They checked as though surprised. Then they began rushing at him in a crouching run.

The AK 47 slugs had not halted them.

Tolneps! What did he know about Tolneps? He had read the Psychlo manual only a few days ago. Eyes! They were half-blind and without faceplates couldn't see.

He fumbled with the single-shot lever.

They were strung out the nearest was now only fifty yards, the furthest about sixty.

Jonnie dropped to one knee. He sighted. He squeezed off at the farthest one's faceplate. He shifted to the second. He sighted on the faceplate. He fired.

It had taken too long.

The leading one was almost upon him

Fangs!

Faceplate!

No time to fire.

Jonnie leaped up and slammed the butt of the AK 47 into the Tolnep's face.

He completed the movement with a slash of the barrel.

The Tolnep didn't go down but he swerved.

Poison fangs. Mustn't get too close.

Jonnie leaped backward, shifting the rifle to his left hand, and drew his belt blast gun.

He fired and fired at point-blank range The force shots pounded the Tolnep to the ground.

Jonnie walked nearer, still firing. The blast pistol was literally pounding the Tolnep into the ground. Geysers of dust blurred the view.

He hadn't had the handgun on "Flame." But the sheer force

of it had knocked the Tolnep out. The faceplate was shattered; the strange eyes were glazed and rolled up into the head. Obviously knocked out.

The others! Where were they? One was running off toward the high ruined palace, obviously unable to orient himself. The other one was making his way back to something in the tumbled wreck of a building. Jonnie could see the bright nose of a small craft jutting from its hiding place in a rubble cavity

That one was trying to get back to a ship!

Jonnie leaped up to the cockpit and pulled a blast rifle out of its rack, throwing the AK 47 inside.

Back on the ground he knelt, steadied himself, and fired a single well-aimed shot at the Tolnep trying to get to his ship. No effect!

Jonnie threw the switches to "Flame" and "Maximum." The Tolnep was inside the ruin, almost to his ship.

Jonnie sighted and squeezed the trigger.

The Tolnep erupted in a pillar of fire!

Swinging to the other one, Jonnie sighted in and squeezed off. A flash as the bolt struck and then a blast of fire as the Tolnep's own rifle exploded.

Jonnie peered at the ship. Nobody else in it apparently. He looked down at the Tolnep at his feet. From insignia he must be an officer.

Getting a safety line from the ship, Jonnie wound the Tolnep up in a tight series of loops and windings and tied the end behind his back. He had not carried a rifle, only a handgun. The shots Jonnie had fired had messed it up but he threw it far away. Then he dragged the Tolnep clear of the ship. Good lord, he was heavy! Jonnie tapped the Tolnep's "flesh." Like iron. He looked human but he was so dense no wonder the AK 47 had had no effect. The slugs had just glanced off.

He felt the situation was in hand. It had happened too fast for the three escort planes to do anything and they were up there, circling now. He supposed they had been too far behind him to have seen the Tolneps begin their charge.

Jonnie looked around further. Then he was amazed. That crowd was still standing there, a hundred yards in front of the plane, unmoving. Nobody had come forward. He looked up at his own ship. The German copilot was just sitting there staring straight ahead.

Jonnie reached in and grabbed the local radio. "Don't come down here!" he told the other pilots.

That ship over there. Was it about to fire or blow up or something?

Jonnie hefted the blast rifle and, running in a wide detour, approached the ship.

They had certainly hidden it well. They had used a deep recess in the rubble and pushed the ship in until it was invisible from the air, maybe flown it in backward.

He approached it gingerly. It had blast cannon mounted on its nose. It was a bright silver color. It was shaped like a diamond. It had a canopy, now thrown back, that dropped over it to make an air seal. It had places for three and a sort of cargo space in the rear of it.

Jonnie, keeping his distance, rocked it with the barrel of the blast rifle. It didn't blow up. It rocked very easily, surprisingly light to carry such heavy beings.

He put his hand on its side to climb into it. The ship was vibrating. Something on it was running.

He peered at the panel. Several lights were blinking. The controls were totally strange. He had no idea what alphabet those letters were part of. He didn't know what kind of power it had beyond the generality in the Psychlo manual that they were usually "solar powered."

Better not touch those controls. It might take off.

He glanced out at the crowd about three hundred yards away. They were just standing there, fixed in place.

For a moment he felt sort of fixed in place, too. But maybe that was just battle reaction.

Something in this ship was running! With his hand he traced the vibration. What he thought was a cannon was more than a cannon. It had *two* barrels, one over the other. The upper barrel had a flare at the "muzzle."

The lethargy he felt was increasing.

Well, anything that ran had to have power one way or the other. Where was a power cable? He found a big thick one under the panel. It led down to an exposed accumulator.

There was a coil of line in the back of the craft and Jonnie tied it to the cable just above the accumulator connection. He got back, braced himself, and pulled hard.

The cable snapped off the accumulator.

There was a ferocious flash of sparks.

At once, three things happened. The craft stopped vibrating The lethargy Jonnie had felt vanished. And the whole crowd out there collapsed. They fell to the ground and lay there.

Jonnie tied the cable away from the accumulator so it couldn't short again and then ran out toward the crowd.

As he passed his plane, the German copilot was fumbling his way out of the door. He called something but Jonnie couldn't hear him.

Reaching the crowd, Jonnie found a Coordinator struggling to his knees. Others were stirring, sitting up groggily. The place was a litter of fallen banners, musical instruments, and odds and ends of what must have been a planned celebration.

The Coordinator's mouth was moving and Jonnie thought the Scot must have lost his voice. He couldn't hear anything the Coordinator was saying. Jonnie turned and saw an escort plane had landed. He hadn't heard that.

Suddenly he realized it was this confounded helmet of Ivan's Jonnie unfastened the chin strap and got the huge, thick ear pads off his ears.

". . . and how did you get here?" the Coordinator was saying

"I flew in!" said Jonnie, a bit sharply. "That's my ship right over there!"

"There's a creature on the ground!" said the Coordinator. He was pointing at the tied-up Tolnep. "How did he get there?"

For a moment, Jonnie was a trifle exasperated. All this shooting and running . . . it dawned on him: none of these people had observed a thing that had gone on.

The people were confused and embarrassed. The three tribal chiefs there were coming up, bowing, upset. They had "lost face." They had planned a very fine reception—see the banners, the musical instruments, the presents there—and he had already landed. So please excuse them. . . .

The Coordinator was trying to answer Jonnie's questions. No, they hadn't seen anything strange. They had all come out here shortly after sunup to wait and then here he was and their schedule was all out of kilter now and it must be nine of the morning . . . what? Two of the afternoon? No, that can't be. Let's see your watch!

They wanted to start the reception up now even though they

didn't feel that well. Jonnie told the Coordinator in charge to hold it off a bit and got to the radio.

On local command, he told the two planes still holding to be very alert to any ship in orbit. Then he switched to planetary pilot band, knowing well it could be heard by the visitors. He got Sir Robert in Africa.

"The little birds tried to sing here," said Jonnie. They didn't have a code. They surely needed one. But he was making do. "All okay now. But our friend Ivan in his new hole must have a ceiling. Got it?"

Robert the Fox got it. He knew Jonnie meant him to get air cover to the Russian base and he would right away.

"Have our own band play Swenson's Lament," said Jonnie. There was no such Scot piper lament. Planetary radio silence, if you please. If the visitors had known he would be here, they were monitoring unguarded speech. "I may play a note or two but otherwise Swenson's Lament."

He turned off. The situation was more dangerous than he had thought. For all the people on this planet.

Only he had been "deaf." Only he had been able to act. Therefore that bell-mouthed barrel had been emitting a sound wave of high intensity that produced a total paralysis. So that's how the Tolneps did their slave trade

— 4 —

The escort pilot who had just landed didn't understand what had happened either, and he was trying to explain it to the Coordinator who didn't speak German. Jonnie asked the German whether he had recorded the action and the pilot said he had. Jonnie explained it to them both, in English to the Coordinator and in Psychlo to the pilot, that it was a device on the nose of that hidden patrol ship over there. And they had better gather this crowd up and take them into a room of one of these ruins and explain and play the discs for them so they wouldn't think the place was full of devils. Soothe them down. They could have a reception later.

The crowd was trailing after the Coordinator into a nearby interior. Jonnie walked over to the Tolnep.

The creature was conscious now. His eyes without his faceplate looked blind. They saw in some different light band and needed correction filters. Jonnie looked around and found the half-shattered plate and, keeping well away from the creature's teeth, dropped it over his eyes. It tried to snap at him.

Jonnie hunkered down and said, "We will now begin your narrative, the long sad story of your youth, how circumstances drove you to crime, and how that fateful trail led you to this pitiful ending."

"You're mocking me!" snarled the Tolnep.

"Ah," said Jonnie. "We speak Psychlo. Very good. Continue your story."

"I will tell you nothing!"

Jonnie looked around. It was quite a drop from the top of that huge palace down to the valley. He carefully selected the spot and pointed it out. "We're going to carry you up there and drop you. See the place just at the end of the long gable?"

The Tolnep laughed. "Wouldn't even dent me!"

Jonnie was thoughtful for a while. "Well, we're not really enemies of yours, so I am going to reconnect the wiring on your ship, put a little remote control I have in it, and send you back up to the Vulcor-class war vessel."

The Tolnep was silent. Rather alertly silent.

"So I just better get to work on the remote control—" and Jonnie got up as though to go to his plane.

"Wait," said the Tolnep. "You really wouldn't do that, would you? Return me to my ship?"

"Of course. It's the civilized thing to do!"

The Tolnep screamed, "You rotten foul Psychlos! You would do anything! Anything! There is no limit to your filthy sadism!

"Why, what would they do to you?"

'They'd shoot me down and you know it! And I'd sizzle and burn in the air friction!"

"But why wouldn't they want you?" said Jonnie.

"Don't play around with me!" raved the Tolnep. "You think I'm stupid? You think they're stupid? I notice you don't mention sprinkling virus powder all over me to infect the crew. You are a fiend! Coughing my lungs out all the way there, writhing in agony as I fall, burning slowly mile after mile with the build-up of air friction heat! You just plain go to hell!"

Jonnie shrugged. "It's the civilized thing to do," he said and started toward the ship again.

"Wait! Wait, I tell you! What do you want to know?"

So Jonnie heard about the travails of this Double-Ensign Slitheter Pliss and his Half-Captain Rogodeter Snowl, and how stupid it was not to let a superior officer win at gambling. He heard a lot of other things, not really relevant, and then the double-ensign said, "Of course Snowl hasn't told the crew, because he'll take the whole prize himself, but it's rumored that there's a hundred-million-credit reward for finding the *one*."

"What *one?*" said Jonnie.

But Double-Ensign Slitheter Pliss didn't have anything more on it than that. He explained they were waiting to make sure, but either way the combined force would eventually attack en masse. The commanders of the ships were gambling via viewscreen for shares of the loot, and Rogodeter Snowl had already won the planet's people, he thought, though Snowl often lied and one didn't really know. But for certain they would need transport and maybe have to go home for it. Home? Did he ever notice a bright star—really a double star? Must be very bright from here. Constellation above it looked like a square box from this angle. Well, that was home. Ninth planet in the rings. The Tolneps only had one planet. They were raiders of other planets. Slaves.

That seemed to be all just now, so Jonnie told him he wouldn't send him back to his ship. Not yet, anyway.

Jonnie had read that once a Tolnep bit, it took six days to develop more poison. So he got a mine sample bottle and a rag out of the plane and told the Tolnep to bite the rag a few times and the Tolnep resignedly did so. Jonnie put the rag in the bottle and put the lid on tightly. MacKendrick knew about snakebite serums. Maybe he could make one for Tolnep bites.

Another escort plane had landed. It had a copilot. There was a minesite down the mountain, smashed now, but it would have an ore carrier and they had spare fuel, so Jonnie sent them down to check one out and fly it up here. He was taking this Tolnep and the patrolcraft back. He also told them to see what the minesite could supply in the way of passenger carriers.

Jonnie looked up in the afternoon sky. He couldn't see anything in orbit but four hundred miles and daylight would make it invisible. An uneasy day.

The Coordinator and the German pilot had shown the pictures and had taken the crowd over to see the ship and explain the gun to them. The throng was leaving it now. Coming back toward Jonnie, who was standing by the plane, they were within talking distance.

Abruptly, as though on signal, they all dropped down to their knees and began bowing their heads to the ground. And then they stayed down.

Jonnie had seen quite enough people falling down today. "Now what's the matter?" he said to the Coordinator.

"They are deeply ashamed. They planned a great welcome for you and it all went splat. But more than that," said the Coordinator, "they have developed a lot of respect for you. They had it before, but now—"

"Well, tell them to get up," said Jonnie a bit impatiently. Adulation was not any pay he was after.

"You just saved their lives or maybe more," said the Coordinator.

"Nonsense," said Jonnie. "I was just lucky to be wearing a helmet with ear pads. Now tell them to get up!"

The German pilot was near at hand. It seemed that this was the day for embarrassment. He was explaining to Jonnie again that he had dared not fire: a Mark 32's guns might have blown half that palace right down on the crowd and Jonnie. It was an enclosed bowl here and the blow-back of the blast— Jonnie shook his head and waved him away.

The Coordinator was introducing chiefs. A small man with a smiling Mongol face, wearing a fur hat, came forward. Jonnie shook his hand. The Coordinator said this was Chief Norgay, head of what remained of the Sherpas. They were famous mountaineers and used to run salt caravans clear across the Himalayas in Nepal above India. They used to be very numerous, maybe eighty thousand, but there were only a hundred or two now: they had hidden high up in inaccessible places. There was very little food; even though they were good hunters the game was scarce in high places.

And this was Chief Monk Ananda. The man was wearing a reddish-yellow robe. He was big with a very peaceful face. He was a Tibetan and they had a monastery in caves. Any other

Tibetans that remained in the country considered him their chief: You see, even before the Psychlo invasion, the Chinese had driven the Tibetans out of their country and they had gone to other lands. The Chinese had suppressed Buddhism—Ananda was a Buddhist—but the caves were very hard to reach, being way up a ravine in a peak, and the Psychlos had never succeeded in rooting them out. The Tibetans were pretty much starved. They were unable to come out to flat places and grow much food and even in this last summer had not been able to grow much due to lack of seeds.

And this man here was Chief Chong-won, head of all the Chinese that were left. Did Jonnie know there used to be six or eight hundred million Chinese? Imagine that! There was another tribe up in North China who had taken refuge in an old defense base in the mountains. The base? The Chinese never finished it. It wasn't very much. There were only a hundred or two up in North China. But Chief Chong-won here had three hundred fifty people. They were in a valley that probably had been mined and the Psychlos never went near them, but there was hardly any food. Nothing much would grow up so high. Awfully cold. No, we don't have any trouble talking with the Chinese. They preserved a lot of their university records and are quite literate: they speak Mandarin, an old court language.

Jonnie shook hands. They would *bow!* So he bowed and this pleased the Chinese enormously.

"Speaking of languages," said the Coordinator, "they had a little show for you. They're all over there, so would you see it now?"

Jonnie glanced a bit uneasily at the sky. An escort was up there, very alert. He himself was not too far from the plane. He sent the German over to stand by his. Yes, he'd see the show. He felt bad; all their banners were on the ground, their musical instruments upside down in the turf.

About eighty people in reddish-yellow robes were sitting now in precise rows. They were some of Chief Monk Ananda's people. As Jonnie approached he could see that they were anywhere from eight years old to fifty. They all had shaved heads. They were boys, girls, men, and women. They were trying to be very solemn as they sat with legs folded under them but a gleam of mischief was in their eyes An old monk was standing in front of them with a long scroll.

"We had trouble last spring," said the Coordinator. "Nobody, absolutely nobody could talk to these people. Not in India or Ceylon—that's an island—or anywhere could we find any trace at all of the Tibetan language or this one. We really looked. But we solved it. Listen!" He gave a signal to the old monk.

The Buddhist read a line from the scroll. The whole group sang out as one, a singsong but not a repeat.

It was Psychlo!

The old monk read another line.

The group sang out the translation in Psychlo.

Jonnie was incredulous. The performance went right on, singsonging along.

"He's reading a language that was once called 'Pali,' " whispered the Coordinator. "It's the original language in which the canons of Buddhism were written. The monastery for some reason had in its possession a huge library of all the quoted tenets and words of Gautama Siddhartha Buddha, the man who started that religion about thirty-six hundred years ago. And they are literate in that language. But it is extinct. So we got a Chinko—"

"—instruction machine," finished Jonnie, "and taught them Psychlo from scratch!"

"And they converted it back to Pali! That Psychlo minesite down there is pretty smashed, but it had a dictionary and some other books in a fireproof safe and they've been going like a race horse ever since. So we can talk to them."

The singsong was going on. They were speaking with a Chinko accent, just like Jonnie and the pilots!

"You like that, Lord Jonnie?" said Chief Monk Ananda in Psychlo. "They not only sing it out, they also talk it really well."

Jonnie applauded them loudly and they cheered. He knew what he was going to propose here.

"Is this all of them?" said Jonnie.

No, there were about forty more, but it was quite a scramble down here from the monastery. It took ropes and climbing skill and help from the Sherpas.

The idea of a religious teacher's words of peace, as he had heard them in that singsong, being put into Psychlo, where all such sentiments went unused, was marvelous to Jonnie.

Some musicians had recovered their instruments and began to play on small horns and long horns and drums. Some women had gotten fires going and their slight amounts of food were being warmed.

The pilots came back from the minesite with an ore carrier. Jonnie got massive amounts of help and they manhandled the patrolcraft into the big plane and put the Tolnep in it, very securely strapped down.

"There's a lot of aircraft down there," said Jonnie's copilot. "The Scots that hit it must have set off an explosion in the compound. They must have blown the breathe-gas—the domes are scattered in pieces over about five acres. They didn't bother to blow up the ammunition and fuel dumps. The hangars are on a lower level. There are about eighty or ninety battle planes in there. Some are singed but they look all right. There's a lot of tanks and machinery. And there are about fifty of these ore carriers, lord knows why. Bunch of shop and storehouse material. Looks like they shipped a lot of bauxite from here. No live Psychlos."

Jonnie made up his mind. He went to his plane and put the radio on planetary. He called the American base—Dunneldeen.

Jonnie remembered Dunneldeen's joke. "You didn't know I had fifteen daughters. It's quite urgent they wed."

"Got it," said Dunneldeen and broke the connection.

Jonnie knew he would have fifteen pilots—even though not all were graduated—within the next ten or twelve hours. Dunneldeen knew where he was.

The reception had gotten going now. People were over their shock. They were serving food. They were smiling as they passed him. More bows.

Two escort planes were aloft. Jonnie's and the third plane were ready to scramble.

Evening had come and they had found enough wood to make a fire. But an enemy would show on a viewscreen up in the sky.

They made speeches. They were grateful to Jonnie many times and he was a welcome guest. Then it was Jonnie's turn.

He was flanked by a Coordinator who knew Chinese and a monk who also knew Sherpa. Jonnie had to speak in English for the Chinese-speaking Coordinator and in Psychlo for the monk, and the monk had to translate into Sherpa or Tibetan or whatever it was so it took a bit of time waiting. But not too much.

After some pleasant responses to their speeches, Jonnie got

right down to it. "I can't leave you here," he said and pointed at the sky. "And you can't leave any you have left at home."

Oh, they surely agreed with that!

Jonnie looked at their firelit faces as they sat in their different groups. "It is cold in these mountains." They certainly agreed with that, particularly the Chinese. "There apparently isn't much food." Oh, he was so very right; Lord Jonnie was very perceptive and he knew how thin their children were. "There are ways you can help. Ways you can help to defeat the Psychlos, possibly forever, if they come back. Ways you can help defeat the aliens in the sky."

One could have heard a snowflake fall, it was so still. He thought they hadn't understood him. He opened his mouth to repeat. And this orderly throng became totally disorderly. Forgotten were manners. They surged forward; they pressed so tightly close to him he had to stand up.

Only one eager question was being roared at him now in at least three tongues. "How? How can we help?"

These beaten people, these ragged, starved remnants of once-great nations had not really dreamed they could be of value. That they could assist. That they might have a role to play besides to hide and starve. It was a mind-shattering thought. To help.

The Coordinators and chiefs somehow got them back in their places around the fire but they couldn't sit down. They were too excited.

When Jonnie could speak again, it was into a new stillness. But he suddenly realized he might have more audience than he intended. Could the visitors upstairs monitor this? Probably. He held a hurried consultation, low-voiced, with a senior Coordinator. Yes, the man whispered back. There was a large hall beneath the palace. It had been cleaned out.

Jonnie spoke to Chief Monk Ananda. Wild-eyed with excitement, the Buddhists went into the hall. Jonnie got a mine light from the plane. He closed the door. This was an atmosphere they loved.

Jonnie spoke to them very quietly. They spoke Psychlo. They spoke Pali, a dead language. They also spoke some tongue known as Tibetan. Yes! they whispered back. Jonnie told them he would see their library was flown out to a safe place. They could have a deep section of the Russian base for it and their temple. But were they afraid of heights? They laughed; that was a silly question to ask mountain people. Did they mind being scattered all over the globe and living with other tribes? No, no. That was fine. They were not really withdrawn from the world just because they lived in a monastery. They had to live in the caves because of danger.

He told them what a communicator was. If people gave them a message in Psychlo, they could put it on the radio in Pali and the Buddhist at the other end could put it back into Psychlo. And the enemies upstairs would never understand. They thought it was marvelous. A whole worldwide Pali-speaking network. Yes, yes, yes!

But now there was a sobering thought. At some time one of them might be captured and made to give messages. And if so they would give the message in Tibetan, and that was their secret. It was dangerous.

All life was dangerous. They accepted, every man, woman, and child of them and accepted for the ones at home too! Jonnie tried to tell them their pay would be a credit a day, which was fair pay in most tribes, but he didn't get a chance. They would go and that was that. And they knew it was secret and they would tell nobody. They even tiptoed out the door.

The next were the Sherpas. There was a lot of hunting to be done; there were even occasional peaks to climb elsewhere. There were huge plains in Russia, teeming with sheep and cattle. There was an awful lot of meat drying and preserving to be done. Could they, all of them, go to Russia and help stock that base with food? Food? They themselves were starving. Yes, indeed, they would hunt and stock the base with food.

Then Chief Chong-won brought in his people. Secrecy was a breath of life to them. Jonnie began by telling them there was a place that was not too healthy, that had a fly that carried a sickness, but proper precautions and nets could handle it. There were also savage beasts but there would be armed guards and they too could learn to shoot. Insects? Beasts? They didn't care about those! Where was this place? What did he want them to do? They would leave right away. Was it a far walk?

Jonnie told them they would go by plane. But there was another thing. Although the place was a mile high, it could be hot there.

Hot? A place that was hot? How marvelous! How absolutely marvelous! Who cared how hot?

Jonnie asked them whether they could build things. They

proudly told him they had kept up their studies. Some of them were engineers. They could build anything.

Now all this was very secret, said Jonnie, but he had a place near a large power dam that had to be cleared up and cleaned out and the hills dug into and bunkers made. They would get technical assistance. They would even get machines and operators and could themselves learn—

They had eight trainees over in America right now learning about machines! Why were they delaying here talking? Where was this place?

Jonnie told them they would get a credit a day each and bonuses for completions. And they could have land afterward.

Chief Chong-won asked the people whether they agreed. And they thought he was just delaying things. Of course they agreed!

Jonnie returned to the celebration. But it was not a celebration now. Little groups had their heads together working it all out but whispering and in incomprehensible tongues. Jonnie told them good night and they all faced him and bowed and he bowed back.

En route to pass the night in his plane, just in case, he stopped by the ore carrier where the Tolnep lay. He had an impulse to call Half-Captain Rogodeter Snowl and chew on him. But he didn't. Let the half-captain stew. That was a future battle.

— 5 —

In Scotland, Jonnie delayed a meeting with the Chiefs as long as he could. He was expecting discs and further progress from America. But Glencannon had not arrived.

Finally Robert the Fox, who had come up for the meeting from Africa, told him the Chiefs were getting restless so Jonnie accompanied him.

The house Chrissie had found was just by Castle Rock and it was only a short walk. They didn't talk en route, eyeing the overcast sky above them.

Two gillies armed with lochaber axes and blast rifles let them into the entrance of an underground passage. The Chiefs had found the remains of powder magazines and air-raid shelters from some ancient wars and had suspended reconstruction of their parliament house and had refurbished the deep caverns instead. Mine lights burned in niches and cast the shadows of clan banners upon the domed roof.

The Chiefs were all there. They had been there for hours. But they gathered around and shook Jonnie's hand and clapped him on the back. Finally the Chief of Clanfearghus brought the meeting to order.

Robert the Fox played them some discs of the radio telescope intercepts. Aside from other items in them, the Chiefs were amazed at the dissimilarity of faces in the combined force. They were also very interested in a game these creatures were playing by viewscreen: one of Robert's prisoners had identified it as "klepp." Each player had a board of six sides and six different sets of pieces, and when one of them made a move, the other players would make the same move on their boards. The pieces were little spaceships and tanks and marines and soldiers, and they had different movements and were held down magnetically to a board of six-hundred-sixteen hexagons. It wasn't the game that interested the Chiefs but the fact that the announced stakes were different items of loot from this planet. It sobered them.

Then Robert told them about infrabeams and that it would be unwise to discuss things out in the open. Sir Robert had gotten a full description of them from a Hockner prisoner. If you had to talk in the open you should turn on an "interference generator," but they didn't have those.

The Chiefs tried to pass a motion to forbid talking in the open air or telling people things they would then discuss in the open. It was also proposed that they begin a campaign with the slogan "The Enemy Has Long Ears." But the Chief of the Argylls took the floor and informed them that they could not pass legislation affecting all tribes because they were not the government of all tribes—that was located over in America, even though they would be at war with it eventually. What they proposed was usurpation of the powers of state.

This was Jonnie's cue. He got up and reminded them that the first government actions had been taken by them up in the Highlands, beside the lake and in the meadow, that they *were* the original legislative body. They must preserve the semblance of a government in America and not act as though that government didn't exist for this would ruin his plans. But action must be taken to protect the people of the planet. This ruling body here controlled the World Federation for the Unification of the Human Race. He was sure that body would take their orders and ignore those from America. They could call their orders "Federation Orders" and they would be international in effect.

"Hear, hear!" said Sir Andrew MacNulty, head of the Federation.

Dunneldeen, continued Jonnie, was a titular prince of Scotland named, he thought, after this very Rock, Dunedin. He controlled the pilots or could control them—

"Dunneldeen and *you* control the pilots," the Chief of the Campbells corrected him.

Jonnie told them that this legislative body controlled the pilots. And the War Chief of Scotland controlled all effective troops—omitting only the Brigantes. So in actual truth it was this body that controlled the planet. If his argument prevailed with them they should pass confidential resolutions to this effect and then make dispositions as they saw fit.

They discussed it a bit and then so resolved it. Sir Andrew MacNulty was to carry out their wishes with the tribes, Sir Robert was to execute their directives in the military sector. And due to the peculiarities of the situation, orders from the American governing body were to be ignored without creating suspicion. The American body had supported enemies of Scotland, enemies with whom Scotland had a blood feud. The present emergency required emergency actions.

It was what Jonnie wanted.

Sir Robert then got up and described the spread-out character of the few people remaining on the planet and put forth the principle that one must collect the population into a minimum number of strong points that could be defended. He had a plan that would do this.

They wanted a summary of the situation as the MacTyler saw it. Since the MacTyler was part of and a member of every clan and for innumerable other reasons, his estimate would be valued.

Jonnie privately had hoped to have further word from America before meeting such a question. So much depended on what Terl was doing, and there seemed to be a long blank period in which he had heard nothing. He was not going to give some of the data he needed to this body anyway for he wanted no chance of leaks. But this body had quite a role to play.

He rose and told them (a) they did not know for certain what had happened to Psychlo and there was some possibility of a counterattack; (b) the visitors were a heavy threat—he did not know why they were holding off and it was worrisome, but they were buying time with it and must be ready and should work fast; and (c) the primary concern was the preservation of the people of Earth—they were not just endangered as a race; they could quite abruptly become extinct.

They thanked him and passed Sir Robert's plan. They were very sober.

There was other business.

They called in Dr. Allen who was deeply involved with Federation tribal movements. In his opinion it was a danger to combine tribes and bring them too close together, due to the fact that their immunities to various diseases might have diminished. The tribes had long been separated from one another and epidemics of smallpox or typhoid fever and other diseases could occur. He had several assistants. He had been flying about doing what he could. He had read all available man-texts on vaccination, innoculation, sanitation, insect control, and such matters and they had prepared serums. He wanted two measures: the first was compulsory isolation of every person who seemed to have signs of illness; the second was compulsory innoculation and vaccination. He was getting excellent cooperation from Coordinators and tribal chiefs but he wanted his program made official.

The Chiefs passed it as a Federation Directive with their approval and the order was to be issued by Sir Andrew MacNulty.

Then MacAdam of the Planetary Bank was ushered in. He had requested an audience with the Chiefs for three reasons. Short and gray-haired and conservative, MacAdam was very courteous to them and very precise. He had a portfolio of papers and he put it down on the table.

To begin with, that government in America was throwing money around and creating local inflation which could then spread to other areas; the Brigante troops were being paid a hundred credits a day, each one; there were supposed to be about seven hundred sixty of them and this made seventy-six thousand credits a day which was about double the *yearly* budget of most other tribes; they didn't value the money, threw it around in the streets; there was not much to buy in America now and no product to absorb the funds. He was not there without a solution: he wanted authority from somewhere to issue a special American bank note which could then devaluate against the currency of the rest of the world. He had reason to believe the government there would accept it, if the issue omitted the picture of Tyler and replaced it with one of Brown Limper Staffor for that issue. The caption would be "Brown Limper Staffor, Senior Mayor Planet Earth." In his opinion the omission of the Tyler picture would also cause the currency to further deflate in value but he didn't think Tyler should be on a devalued issue. What did they think?

Tyler smiled. The Chiefs laughed and gave MacAdam their blessing.

MacAdam wanted more than that. He wanted a second charter, much like the first, but from this body. It wouldn't be publicly displayed but he wanted it in his safe.

They read it and passed it.

Then MacAdam objected to some private, preliminary discussions he had had with Sir Robert to the effect that he should move his bank from Zurich to Luxembourg. It was inconvenient and difficult. They would also have to move presses and find staff housing in Luxembourg.

The Chiefs called on Sir Robert. He told them that there was a Psychlo minesite at Luxembourg where the Psychlos had gotten their local planetary iron supplies. Close by it was a fortress from ancient times; in fact Luxembourg meant "little fortress"; it had been a crossroads of banking and trade for a couple of thousand years. It was a temporary measure. Luxembourg could be defended. Zurich could not be.

They told MacAdam he better move.

MacAdam resignedly said he would. But he had another matter and that was the expenses of war preparation. Certain costs were being incurred that were not covered by tribal budgets or guaranteed by tribal lands. He had a solution to it which was to make loans against something else.

Jonnie asked to speak. He said he knew of quite a few mineral deposits (he did not say how he knew), and once things were calm again, they could be mined. They were quite extensive. They knew his earlier connection with mining and should be able to take his word for it. These could serve as a loan guarantee if held as property of the chiefs and not of tribes.

MacAdam said did they know Brown Limper claimed to own the whole planet? The Chiefs said they knew of that. Also that he claimed to own the whole Earth branch of Intergalactic Mining?

The Chief of Clanfearghus said that valid or not, part of such deeds belonged to them, and they would pledge their share of these mineral deposits to guarantee the war expenses.

MacAdam had a quiet smile. He knew which way the wind blew. He accepted that. He would not violate their confidence.

The Chiefs passed a resolution to that effect and gave Sir Robert the right to draw against this open account at his discretion as a "war chest."

Much later, it was a very sober group that broke up.

Gillies escorted Jonnie to his door.

Chrissie was up and waiting for him and served him some tea and what she said were "crumpets."

Legs stretched out, shirt thongs unlaced, feet in soft moccasins, Jonnie sat in the drawing room. He was worried about events in America but he forced his attention onto domestic things.

Chrissie was telling him that the parson and Aunt Ellen would be here for lunch tomorrow and she hoped he would be at home. Aunt Ellen was doing so well here in Scotland—her cheeks had filled out and she had lost a cough she had had. She was looking quite young, really.

Jonnie said you could say that about Chrissie. She looked very pretty with her long cornsilk hair piled up on top in a big puff, her eyes were brighter and blacker, her tunic cloth that had been made into a gown set off her figure even better than buckskin. The collar scars had almost vanished. Chrissie blushed over the compliments he gave her.

Pattie was better. She had gotten terribly thin. She was still in bed from her fever but it had subsided, leaving her weak. Jonnie should visit her in the morning. The only worry was that Pattie did not seem to take any interest in anything. Maybe Jonnie could tell her a story about something.

Jonnie asked whether the house had a basement and she said yes, a strong deep one. Jonnie told her she had found some very nice furniture and if things got rough she should put the better pieces in the basement, well protected. And did she have a safe place in the underground shelters at Castle Rock? Chrissie said she had thought of all that and he mustn't worry about her. She had been around in the world now and had her share of experience. And wouldn't he like some more of this tea? And another crumpet?

He found it all very pleasant. It was a lovely old house, so different from those decayed ruins in the old village. If they could just win through somehow and if his luck held, maybe someday the rather remarkably pleasant fact of sitting in this drawing room and talking about calm matters with Chrissie or friends would become routine.

Then the gong at the door was struck and Chrissie went to open it.

With a shout, Jonnie jumped up to greet Glencannon.

■

PART 23

— 1 —

Damn Terl!

At first, Jonnie had thought he had data on the point positions of the poles. He had no adequate viewing equipment in his house in Scotland; he had only taken a quick scan and a glance at a box Ker had sent that seemed to have just a piece of cable in it. It was months to Day 92 and so he was happy to stay for lunch and see Aunt Ellen and the parson again. And to try to cheer up Pattie.

He had flown back to the African minesite in good spirits. He had gotten up this morning all ready to really plow into it. And now this!

Glencannon had said the delay was occasioned by Terl's spending most of his time outside measuring. Terl apparently didn't like to stay outside very long: Glencannon hinted that a bit of air had been injected into breathe-gas vials when the office was set up in order to discourage Terl from developing too much of a fondness for wandering around. Also, Glencannon had told him, they had omitted something in their original planning—they didn't have a picto-recorder to record what went on around the platform itself. But they had rigged one in a tree now and the Brigantes hadn't noticed and they didn't have to depend on drone overflys anymore.

Looking at them now, Jonnie saw how meticulous Terl had been in measuring distances to poles. He had almost used a micrometer. But he had *not* been measuring point positions for teleportation firing!

Here it was, the full layout and plan, complete with the exact dimensions: the firing platform, the new position for the console, *and* a squiggly line.

Jonnie knew now why Terl had spent so many days on force equations. He had been calculating exactly how close you could put the squiggly line to the firing platform without messing up the teleportation! There it was on his final plan: seven and eight-elevenths feet. All around the firing platform and the new console.

The box Ker had sent contained a little note, written with his wrong paw if Jonnie knew Ker.

> To You know who.
>
> Here is a chunk that got sawed off by accident—ha, ha. I am digging it up for them from beside that dam to the southwest where it ain't used anymore. In case you don't know it's called ''atmosphere-armor ionization cable.'' I won't include the parts order number because you won't be ordering any from Psychlo. Ha, ha. Also it is a fine of three months' pay to give away company property so if I'm caught, you owe me another three months' pay. You're going to go broke at this rate. Ha, ha.
>
> —You know who
>
> Added: They are paying me a fortune to dig this up. You get your split when we swap lunch boxes. Ha, ha, ha!

Jonnie inspected it. The cross-section was obviously the same as that around the dam and site in Kariba. But now he had a look at what it was composed of. It had to be put in right-side up and be pointed in the direction you wanted the screen to go. It itself was armored, and how Ker had cut it, he did not have any idea.

The way it worked seemed fairly obvious: the bottom insulation interior was really a reflector. Just above that went the main current source. Then above that there was another wire and above that a third and so on up. A stack of fifteen wires. Each apparently amplified the charge of the one just below it. Out at the end it must be fastened together with a box, not included here, which assisted amplification. The resulting fabulously boosted charge must be tuned to the fields of the core and ring particles of air atoms. Hit, the molecules of air realigned themselves into molecular cohesion. The final product was an invisible curtain wall entitled ''atmosphere-armor ionization cable.'' They had proved it at Kariba. Not even a bullet would go through it.

It wasn't a ''force screen.'' Those were used in space and the Hawvins employed them on major war vessels. It was air armor.

And Terl was going to put this seven and eight-elevenths feet all around the console and platform?

Jonnie's tentative plan had been to let Terl build the console and set up the firing platform and then somehow seize it.

But this changed things.

How could one get through a solid curtain like that?

Damn Terl!

Dully, Jonnie made quite a few copies of the firing platform plan. He got out the Intergalactic Mining Company map of their one-time defenses and noted where Ker must be digging up cable for reinstallation at the platform.

The map was so old and creased that he hadn't really noticed before that all minesites had these cables around their dams and along their lines. He saw now that this African minesite had a second underground power transmission line and that what had been known as the Owens Falls Dam back in man-days was protected. He called for Angus and told him to go down there and check, and if the cable was still there, to get the trees removed from above it, using a blade scraper, and then if the switchboard at the dam still worked, to shift over to underground transmission and drill the sentries on turning it on and off so one could get in and out of the dam and in and out of the minesite.

Jonnie, trying to work his way through this new one, wandered around the compound. He saw Sir Robert had just arrived and showed him on the old map that all minesites had these and that he should probably use them.

Jonnie wandered on, troubled.

Teleportation! The secret of the Psychlos. With it they had controlled universes. Without it he didn't see how he could defend this one planet.

He saw MacKendrick. Yes, the wounded Psychlos were all well now. Except Chirk who just lay there. No, he hadn't figured any way to get those things out of a Psychlo's head—disturbance at that bone structure would kill the monster. Yes, he realized that if they tried to consult Psychlos on technical matters they would attack and kill themselves, or, if female, probably go into a coma like Chirk.

What MacKendrick was really worried about was the diet of the prisoners. The Psychlos in their manuals didn't consider it valuable information, being Psychlos; the prisoners themselves knew what they ate but didn't know the names for it that applied to this planet, and if he didn't solve it, they'd shortly have no prisoners.

Did Jonnie know they now had three Jambitchows? It was last night. Evidently a scouting party had been sent down to investigate all the new activity that was going on at Kariba, and the Scot officer there, the moment he got word a small craft had detached itself from the Jambitchow cruiser up in orbit, had put into action something dreamed up by the Chinese. They called it a "tiger net." They put a dummy dressed like a Chinese down near a pool away from the camp and the Jambitchows went right in to grab the dummy and a big net had been tripped up in the trees and they'd been caught. Evil-looking brutes.

MacKendrick wanted to know whether he'd heard what they ate. No? Well, the old woman from the Mountains of the Moon was helping and maybe they could work it out.

Jonnie wandered on. Damn Terl! It was getting too chancy! Somewhere, somehow he should be able to get the information on some other channel.

Once before he had thought of exploring a teleportation motor to see whether he could get some sort of answer out of it. A motor wasn't a transshipment rig, but it did work on space-position change.

He had a motor and console to fool with: the ones from the wrecked tank in the battle of the pass. It had been carted in to the garage repair shop. Maybe if he just tore it apart . . . a thin hope, for he'd already looked at such rigs. But he got into some work clothes and went down to the repair level.

The Basher was sitting there, badly scarred and with a couple of plates sprung. He got into it, checked the fuel, and started the motor with a "right here" space coordination punched in on the console. It ran! One thing you could say about the Psychlos, their stuff lasted forever.

He shut the motor off and took a screwdriver to the top screws of the console. He loosened them a half-turn, each one.

Jonnie was distracted by a sentry appearing at the tank port and handing him some ear pads, asking him to put them on. Jonnie stood up and looked out the turret port to find out what was going on.

It was Stormalong and the Tolnep, Double-Ensign Slitheter Pliss, surrounded by guards.

"What's up?" called Jonnie.

They didn't hear him. They all had ear pads on. Then Jonnie saw that the Tolnep patrol craft had been dollied in here and he could guess the rest of it. Stormalong probably wanted to know how it flew so he could teach pilots how to handle Tolnep craft. Probably Angus wanted to know the cycles of vibration of that paralysis beam.

Slitheter Pliss seemed quite amiable. He had obviously written himself off as a Tolnep. He saw Jonnie and hissed a greeting.

But if they were going to let the Tolnep near that lethal sound vibrator, they were taking no chances that he would turn it on, paralyze the lot of them, and escape. Jonnie didn't think so for the Tolnep had nowhere to go. But he put the ear pads on anyway.

The Tolnep seemed to find it a bit provoking that the accumulator terminals had been bent. They responded to his dumb-show signs and gave him some tools and he straightened them and rehooked the power cable. The craft promptly began to run and he shut it off. With more dumb-show he pointed the switches out to Stormalong, indicating what they connected to, and Stormalong seemed to find it quite elementary; he nodded to the Tolnep and signaled the guards to take him away.

Once Pliss was away from the craft, Jonnie cautiously removed the ear pads and started to duck down out of the turret to resume his work.

The Tolnep alarmed the guards by pausing and swinging open the side door of the tank. He almost got himself shot. But Jonnie gestured for them to back up. He could shove the screwdriver into the Tolnep's teeth if he tried to bite.

"You people aren't Psychlo-commanded, are you?" said the Tolnep, hanging in the door. Getting no answer—since Jonnie was not going to volunteer information to a potential escapee no matter how remote escape might be—the Tolnep said, "What are you trying to do with that tank motor?"

Jonnie just looked at him for a moment and then it occurred to him that as a Tolnep officer, Pliss might have been trained on these things. "You know how this works?"

"Blast no! And neither does anyone else in any universe that I ever heard of," said Pliss. "We've never raided this planet but we have raided other Psychlo bases. According to the textbooks, we've brought in thousands of these things just for the experts to look at." He smiled a rather frightening smile. "I'll bet my next month's pay, which I'll never get, that you people are up against the same thing that everybody else is up against."

Allowing for possible malice, Jonnie looked encouraging.

"We've gotten their textbooks, their mathematics texts even. We've actually captured a transshipment console intact. It said in the text that it worked once and then as soon as they tried to find how it was built, pop, no console.

"The very best Tolnep commanders have interrogated Psychlo engineers," continued Pliss, "and nothing happened. Some use that is. They chew you up and kill themselves. Been going on, I read once, for three hundred and two thousand years!"

The Tolnep changed the subject. "You got a metals sample room around here? I'm hungry and maybe I can find something."

Jonnie told the guards to take him there.

"So good luck," said the Tolnep with a sarcastic-sounding hiss. They took him away.

Possibly it was just malice, Jonnie thought. But he didn't believe it.

He'd lost track of the sequence of actions he had been involved in when interrupted. So he started all over again. He put the console buttons in "right here" and tapped the power switch to start the tank motor.

Nothing happened.

He checked the connections. All usual.

He tried to recall whether the Tolnep had touched anything and the Tolnep hadn't.

He once more tried to start the motor. Nothing

What had Ker told him once about consoles? They'd had a blade machine back up. The canopy had been open because Jonnie didn't need breathe-gas and a torrent of dirt had come spraying down on the console and the blade machine wouldn't start afterward. Oh, yes. Ker had said to leave it, that he'd get an engineer on it. Not a mechanic but an engineer! And an engineer had come down and disconnected the console and taken it off to an underground workshop with a small traveling crane.

Jonnie had been more interested in the crane at the time. The cranes had magnetic plates in a circle with springs between them. They didn't have any motors. The arms of the crane moved by applying power to the magnets. Jonnie wished he had watched when they pulled the console out.

What had he done before the Tolnep arrived? Let's see. He had loosened the top-plate screws. Psychlos once in a while used screws. Most of the time they just annealed metal with a molecular adhesion/cohesion blade. But they were a bit unusual.

He now took all the screws out and lifted off the plate. The screws went into a black material that held, on its underside, all the complex components of the console.

The screws. They must connect something to something in addition to holding the cover on. But he couldn't find any switch. They just seemed to be screws. But turning one or another of them had certainly disabled this console.

He put it back together. He looked at another console and found the angle the screws were supposed to be set at. He set the Basher's console screws at the same angle.

It would not start again, no matter what he did.

It *must* be the screws. When that blade scraper quit, maybe a dirt clod had hit a screw and turned it.

He went through all the motions for the fifth time, trying to align screws.

But that was it. He had a dead-motor Basher tank.

Jonnie finally gave it up.

He went down to the lake and threw rocks at the crocodiles. Then he became ashamed of himself for teasing the beasts.

They were very amiable creatures compared to Terl.

A tri-wheeler came down from Sir Robert who wanted to tell Jonnie it was unwise to be in the open without air cover. The visitors might send somebody down.

"Would you like to shoot a Psychlo?" Jonnie asked a startled messenger.

Damn Terl! Damn all Psychlos!

And it wasn't any comfort to know that thousands of races had been saying the same thing for three hundred and two thousand years.

He'd have to think of something, some plan, no matter how desperate or dangerous, or this planet was finished!

— 2 —

Winter had come to Denver.

But the cold wind and snow flurries could not dampen the elation of Brown Limper Staffor.

The new bank note had arrived.

A packet of them lay on his desk and four of them were spread out before him. How beautiful! They were bright yellow, printed on one side, and there, right in the middle, was an oval picture of Brown Limper!

What an awful lot of trouble they had had getting that picture. Brown Limper had tried innumerable poses, facing this way and that; he had tried countless expressions, frowning or scowling; but none of these would do.

Lars Thorenson had finally had to give him a hand. Lars had explained that it was the beard that was wrong: Brown Limper had a black mustache and beard, and whereas the mustache was all right, the beard was thin and scraggly. So the thing to do was shave off the beard and trim the mustache until it was a bushy tuft just under the nose; that was the sort of mustache the great military hero Hitler had had and so it must be correct.

Then there had been the problem of a proper costume. Nobody seemed to find anything proper. General Snith came to the rescue. He had heard one of his men report that there was an old graveyard that had air-sealed coffins in it. Several had been dug up, looking for a corpse that had been properly dressed: but after more than a thousand years the fabric wouldn't hold together. The only outcome of all that was a sickness that had hit the Brigantes: two had died and a doctor, passing through, had said it was "formaldehyde poisoning," whatever that was.

Somebody had finally found a bolt of gray cloth in a basement that didn't tear very much and somebody else had found a pattern that said "chauffeur's uniform" on it and some Brigante women had sewn it up. They had also found a black-visored cap that lasted long enough for the picture.

Snith had a handful of jewelry he'd found—which Brown Limper knew couldn't possibly be rubies or diamonds and was probably colored glass—and they'd put that on the left breast of the coat so he would have "medals."

The final posing was solved by using a picture Lars had of somebody called "Napoleon," also a great military hero of ancient man. The pose had the fingers of one hand tucked into the coat edge on the breast.

MacAdam had been a bit difficult. He had asked Brown Limper whether this was what he really wanted by way of a portrait and Brown Limper had been cross about it. After all that trouble. Of course that was what he wanted!

So here was the new bank note at last. It was a hundred-credit note: MacAdam had said he could only print one denomination and it had to be a hundred credits. Brown Limper realized that that made this a far more important bill. It had the bank name on it. It was only printed in English and no other tribal language. And right there, loud and clear, it said ["One Hundred American Credits"]! And it said ["Valid for the payment of public and private debts in America"].

One of the conditions MacAdam had made was that all earlier money in the country be collected up and exchanged for these new bills. It was hard to do because the earlier issue was a one-credit bank note and this American issue was a one-hundred-credit bank note. But the dream of having all Tyler notes *gone* was so alluring, Brown Limper had made up the differences in exchange out of his own pocket.

This victory was doing much to improve Brown Limper's spirits: they had been very low as of late.

When that Tyler had not only not gone to his booby-trapped home in the meadow but had walked right out of the country, Brown Limper had been so dispirited he had wanted to call off the whole Terl project.

But Lars had talked to him. Lars seemed to have developed a hatred for Tyler. (He did not say it was from the degradation of hiding under scrap metal in the garage and envy over the way Tyler could fly, but the emotion was very well understood by Brown Limper who considered it natural.)

Lars had said that if they went ahead and actually transshipped, Tyler was certain to reappear.

Terl had talked to him. Terl said that when they fired a shipment to Psychlo, Tyler would be right there, and he had traps for him that even Tyler could not get around.

So Brown Limper had continued with the project.

Other things were going wrong, though. He did not hear much anymore from the tribal chiefs. Lars explained it was natural—they trusted him to run things. No pilgrims came anymore to the minesite. But that was natural—it was winter.

People had been disappearing.. First the hotel cook. Then some Swiss shopkeepers. Then another and another until now the hotel was no longer operating and no shops were open at all.

The shoemakers had vanished. The Germans who repaired things were no longer to be found. The llaneros had driven the large herds south—where they would have better winter feed, they said—and then they had vanished.

Brown Limper had taken it up with Snith. Did this have anything to do with Brigantes? Even Terl put the question to him. But Snith swore up and down he and his men had behaved.

The Academy was still there and operating. There seemed to be a vast number of pilot trainees and a vaster number of machine operators. But they stayed down at the Academy and all one saw was an occasional plane doing practice flights.

All his office radios and teleprinters were gone. They broke down and had to be taken away to be repaired and then they never came back. But never mind, Brown Limper couldn't operate them anyway and couldn't really trust anyone else to.

This new bank note was making a world of difference to his morale. He decided he would not pay the pilots in it. He'd get even with them.

People would be hanging *him,* Brown Limper, on their walls now!

On sudden impulse, he decided he had better mend his political fences with his own tribe—and show them this bill, of course. He called Lars and General Snith and they got into a mine passenger plane Lars kept in the parking lot and took off for the new village he had put his people in.

Brown Limper was still admiring one of the bank notes he held in his hand. The thought of showing it off to the village people warmed him. He did not even mind the harrowing way that Lars Thorenson flew.

Narrowly missing snow-covered peaks that were not even on their route, Lars set them down near the old mining town.

But it all seemed deserted.

Not a single plume of smoke rose from a fire. Not even the smell of it remained.

Carrying a Thompson, Snith scouted the place. Empty! Not even a trace of belongings. Nothing.

Brown Limper searched, looking for a clue, dragging his clubfoot through the smooth snow from building to building. Finally he found where they must have had a meeting. There were some torn scraps of paper lying about. And then, under a table where it might have fallen off a pile of papers unnoticed, he found a letter.

It was from Tom Smiley Townsen.

Brown Limper looked at it and went into an immediate rage. Not at what it said, but at Tom Smiley's having the effrontery to know how to write. What arrogance! But then he saw it was not really written, it was printed, and rather crudely at that. Even the signature was printed. So he decided to be tolerant and read it.

The letter went on and on about how nice some area known as "Tashkent" was. Big mountains, endless plains of wild wheat, lots of sheep. And a mild winter climate. And how he had gotten married to some . . ? Some *Latin!* Disgraceful. No blood purity there.

Brown Limper threw the letter down. Well, maybe the village people had gone back to their old home. They had not wanted to move. But he was surprised that the Indians and the people from the Sierra Nevadas and the other British Columbian fellow had not remained here for they hadn't cared for the old village—too cold and too heavy a prospect of starving every winter.

They flew to the old village. Lars had trouble setting down and almost landed in the middle of one of those uranium circles. When he could let go his grip on the seat, Brown Limper looked around.

No smoke here, either.

Brown Limper poked into some of the houses. When they had moved at such short notice people had had to leave most of their personal possessions behind and Brown Limper thought they must still be there. But no. Every house was empty. Not ransacked the way Brigantes left places. Just neatly empty.

With a bit of fear—because it had been booby-trapped—he approached the old Tyler house. It was still standing. Maybe the booby traps hadn't gone off.

Then he saw that some of the roof was bulged and he went

around to the other side to where the front door had been. The door had been blown off. Lars and Snith were poking at something in the snow.

It was the remains of two Brigantes. What hadn't been burned had been torn apart by wolves. It was obvious they had tripped the booby traps and quite a while ago.

General Snith poked at the scraps of money, skin, and bones with thc muzzle of the submachine gun. "Mus hab come oop here browling fer loot!" said Snith. "Waste of good meat!"

Brown Limper wanted to be alone. He dragged his foot up the slope to the place they once had buried people. He turned at the top and gazed down at the empty village, falling apart and now abandoned forever.

Something had been nagging at him and now it hit him.

He was a tribal leader without a tribe.

From five tribes he had descended to one—the Brigantes! And they were not native to America.

Numbly he realized he had better keep this awfully quiet. It undermined his whole position.

Something caught his eye. A monument? A small stone shaft sticking up out of the ground. He moved around it. It had an inscription:

TIMOTHY BRAVE TYLER
A good father
Erected in Respectful
Memory
By his loving son
J.G.T.

Brown Limper screamed! He tried to kick the monument down. It was too firmly planted and he only bruised his foot. He stood and screamed and screamed, tearing the echoes of the valley apart.

Then he stopped. It was all Jonnie Goodboy Tyler's fault. Everything that had befallen Brown Limper all his life was totally and wholly Tyler's fault!

So Tyler would come again, would he? Terl might have his plans and they might be all right. But Brown Limper was going to make very, very sure.

If Tyler ever hit that firing platform again he was a dead man.

Brown Limper went down to the waiting plane. He said to Lars and Snith—they mustn't know what he really intended—"For our mutual protection, I think you should teach me how to use a Thompson submachine gun."

They agreed it would be wise.

Terl had said time and again you didn't dare shoot off a gun during a transshipment. But who cared about that? Two guns. He would use two guns. . . . Brown Limper planned how he would do it all the way back to Denver.

— 3 —

The small gray man sat watching the strange antics of a terrestrial craft several miles above his orbit.

The combined force had learned over a month ago to leave such a craft alone. Half-Captain Rogodeter Snowl, already in disgrace over trying to sneak a kidnap and cut them out of the potential loot, had charged his Vulcor-class cruiser, guns blazing, at a ship doing exactly what this one was doing. The strange craft had sidestepped neatly; there reportedly had been a series of clangs against the cruiser's hull.

Snowl had pulled up, mystified as to what the "clangs" betokened. He had sent crewmen out on lines to inspect his hull and they had been horrified to discover they had about twenty limpet mines on it, held solidly by magnetism to the hull.

The terrestrial craft had apparently mined the orbit they used.

Snowl had been further embarrassed to discover that the mines did not explode. They had atmosphere pressure fuses, which meant that if he brought the Vulcor-class cruiser within a hundred thousand feet of the planet's surface, the air pressure would explode them there.

Every commander had hastily examined his whole ship to see if he had picked any up. They hadn't, but it meant to them that if you chased that terrestrial ship it threw a cloud of mines in your path. Very unnerving! So they left it alone.

The ship had a huge door in the side and a lot of cranes. The small gray man was no miner or military expert, but the ship was obviously collecting space debris. It wasn't using its cranes so it must have a big magnet inside that door.

Apparently it would spot something on its screen—there were a lot of odd bits in orbit just now as a large, strange comet had entered the system lately, evidently from some other system, and bits of it were floating around and occasionally hitting the meteor shielding of most of these ships. Then the terrestrial would go out and pace the object—many of them were moving as fast as nineteen miles a second—and suddenly dart sideways. The apparent magnets inside that door would collect it.

Rather interesting, the small gray man thought. Somewhat like a hummingbird he had once seen, darting about after insects, stopping around a flower, and then zooming off. He needed something to occupy his mind.

There was no word yet. Probably wouldn't be for another couple of months. No new courier had come to him, which seemed to mean that the one had not been found elsewhere. These were very troubled times.

His indigestion had begun to act up again. About three weeks ago he had gone down to see the old woman—he had run out of peppermint leaves. She had been glad to see him and so had the dog. She had used the vocoder to start up some trade with the Swedes and she had sold them some oats and some butter and she was rolling in money—look, six credits! Enough to buy an acre of ground or another cow! And she had been busy evenings. Cold weather had been coming on and it must be an awful lot colder up there in the sky, and she had knitted him a nice gray sweater.

The small gray man had the sweater on now. It was quite soft and warm. He touched it and felt a little sad.

He had told those military men that it was politically inadvisable to try to operate in the Highlands of Scotland and he thought they had listened. But just a week ago he had gone down to get some more peppermint and the old woman was gone. The house was closed up. The dog was gone. The cow was gone. There seemed to be no sign of violence but then you never knew with these military men: they could be very sneaky and thorough at times. He had dug up a few sprigs of mint from under the snow but was quite troubled. Anything like sentiment was a foreign thing to him. But he had felt troubled nonetheless

These military men! They were so obsessed with finally smashing up this planet that they were quite restless when asked to wait for his courier.

They got such silly ideas. They had noted that every plane and every installation down there now seemed to have a little creature in an orange-yellow robe. They couldn't understand the messages now being sent on the planet's radios. They had tried language machines and none worked. Then they tried all their coding and scrambling machines and none worked. All the messages seemed to begin and end with "Om mani padme om," like a sort of chant.

That place in southern Africa near the big dam—the one the terrestrials had used to lure in and trap two raiding parties—was being all cleared out and it gave them their first clue. A pagoda-like structure—several in fact—were being erected. They found in some old reference texts that the design was a "religious temple." So the military men had agreed that the planet had now experienced a new political upheaval. Some religious zealots had taken over. Religions were very dangerous—they inflamed people. Any sensible government and its military should stamp them out. But they were not concerned with politics and religion just now. They would wait.

The small gray man turned his attention from the terrestrial craft to the combined force. It had increased in number now to thirteen. New arrivals. Other races. They had brought the news that there was a hundred-million-credit prize offered now to the ship or ships that discovered the *one*. Thus they were more eager to raid and collect evidence than they were to gut the planet.

Half-Captain Rogodeter Snowl had become quite incensed with this place, obsessed with it in fact. But his military sense was telling him that he was outnumbered by the rest of the combined force, and he had left a couple of weeks ago to return to his planet and bring up additional war vessels. It would get quite crowded in the orbits. His own captain had asked the small gray man whether he could draw off a bit from the rest. This was going to be an awful mess when these military men "found out" and could split the prize and then gut the planet. The small gray man had agreed.

He returned to idly watching the terrestrial ship. It seemed to be finished now, possibly had a full hold. It was slowly going down into the atmosphere, making its way to the African base.

— 4 —

Jonnie watched Stormalong's old orbit miner come in. A sentry turned off the atmosphere armor shield and let the plane through, and they turned it back on. There was always a faint sizzle from it when the power went on, but after that it was silent. Aside from some luckless birds and insects that hit it and sometimes left a feather or feelers, one wouldn't know it was there. All pilots had had to be warned and a complex set of guard signals had had to be developed lest some pilot crash his ship.

Stormalong put the old ship alongside a metal pulverizer. The Psychlos used a device which first "softened" metal by breaking down its molecular cohesion and then let it go through armored rollers that really tore it apart and smashed it. The result was a metal powder so fine that if one threw a handful into the air, a lot of it stayed there like fine dust. The Psychlos needed it that way for part of their fuel and ammunition processes.

Using the ship's own cranes, the copilot began unloading the "catch" into the metal pulverizer. Stormalong got out and came over. "Fifty-five tons this trip," he said smugly. "There's plenty up there, trapped in orbit. Think we'll need any more?"

Jonnie wasn't sure. He had been onto other things. They walked down into the compound to verify.

One of the Buddhist communicators came up. They had a way of moving which always intrigued Jonnie. They would put their right hand into their left sleeve and their left hand into their right sleeve and then they would move their feet in a sort of fast trot-shuffle. Their shoulders didn't bob. The result made them look like they were floating or scooting. Until yesterday many had continued to wear their reddish-yellow robes; these and their shaven heads made them too easy to single out from above. A huge batch of packages and uniforms had come in from Ivan: people there had been reworking cloth sent to them from some looms now operating in Luxembourg. They were green uniforms with an armored, aluminum helmet, also green. Jonnie supposed that all their forces would be in these soon. The Buddhist was wearing his now. He bowed—always a bow—and handed Jonnie a package. He was so very sorry. There was so much in, distribution was delayed. Jonnie bowed back. It was contagious.

He and Stormalong walked on through the compound looking for Angus. Jonnie was opening his package. It was from Ivan. A helmet. Plain green like everyone else's. Ear pads put on that would lift. There was a letter (some Coordinator had written it for Ivan) on top of the helmet:

Dear Marshal Jonnie:

Your village people arrived and are very happy and so are we. Dr. Allen got the old man Jimson off some weed he was eating and he looks like he will live. Your people all say how do you do, hello. Tom Smiley also says how do you do, hello. Your horses got shipped over here and they are now learning to speak Russian (joke). But they are fine. I worked on Blodgett and she can run pretty good now. You must always look after horses. We got the Buddhist library down deep now and it's safe. On the helmet, I wish I could tell you I had an angel visit me the night before you left that told me you had to wear it. Your letter thanking me is received with embarrassment. I was not trying to save your life but I would anytime, anyway. So I can't accept your gratitude. It was no angel. I just knew that in those high mountains you can freeze your (scratched out) ears off. This helmet is less conspicuous. I didn't even put a star on it. Give my best to Chrissie when you write. I hope somebody is looking after your clothes.

Your comrade,
Ivan
(Colonel Commanding
Russian base until you can
dig up some Americans)

It was a nice helmet and it fit. There were a couple of small creases on it they hadn't quite rubbed out. Ivan must have fired some shots at it to make sure it would stop bullets.

There was also a package of ammunition for the AK 47s. Jonnie had advised them to bore a hole in the ends and put some thermit explosive powder in them so they would be useful against Tolneps. They said it worked and they were converting.

Stormalong and Jonnie had arrived at the 'meteorite powder

washing area.'' Four Psychlo females were working hard, sloshing pans of metal powder around in huge tubs of mercury. They were gloved and clothed to protect them from mercury poisoning.

When Stormalong had begun this orbit mining it had been with an eye to training pilots and, Jonnie suspected, to gratify a craving for wild flying. The stuff collected was odd enough. Meteorites and such got caught in orbit or perihelion and before they sizzled down through the atmosphere they were often crystalline and quite amazing. Jonnie was about to put a stop to it—it had served its purpose scaring the visitors half to death with limpet mines. But Angus, always prowling into something, had noted some pieces in a recent batch that were of different chemical structure.

An outer space comet, not native to the system, had been blasting across the skies for some time Angus pointed out to Jonnie that it contained the tiniest traces of the unknown element Terl had used for the center of his device. Angus had shown him on the analyzer: there they were! Microscopic traces of it. If the material had burned down through the atmosphere like meteorites usually do, the element might have vanished from the heat. But these ''virgin'' bits did contain it.

Jonnie had gone in circles for a day on how to extract it, and then remembered you could ''pan'' gold because it was heavier than dirt and rock.

The Psychlos used literally tons of mercury in some mining process. So they got pans of it and tested it. Iron, copper, nickel, most elements now in powder form, were lighter than mercury and floated off or combined. But this strange element went to the bottom with a thud. It was terribly cohesive and clung to itself. It took an awful lot of powdered metal to get any.

They could have rigged some machines to do the panning but these Psychlo females couldn't care less about a big pan of mercury and they happily sloshed it about, panning the powder. They smiled at Jonnie. They were all right unless somebody foolishly mentioned mathematics—you would lose one Psychlo female, right then It had happened with Chirk and again with another one.

They said Angus would be back and they waited for him He reappeared presently and they asked him: did he need any more? Angus shook his head and beckoned.

In the shop where he was working, Angus had duplicated

Terl's box with one exception: it didn't push all the elements together when you raised the lid. A timed piston did that. You set the time and then the piston closed the rods.

Angus had six of them. The center bit was probably not as pure a metal as Terl's but they were sure that was of no importance. The weights were varied a bit but all around seventy-five pounds for the center bit. Angus had not put the centers in place: he had those sitting well apart and every one was making a dent in what it sat on.

"Unless you've got in mind to blow up the universe," said Angus, "don't you think about eight will do? The load you just brought in should give us two more."

"But what does it do?" begged Stormalong.

Jonnie shook his head. "We don't know. But if Terl made one with that expression on his face you can be very sure it is the deadliest weapon the Psychlos have. One thing you be sure of, Angus: pack the core separately and don't let anybody combine them on this planet! When you're all done, send them down to the underground armory in Kariba."

Jonnie went out. He was feeling fairly cheerful. Lots of good things were happening. The Chinese in Kariba said they had engineers and they did, but they were engineers expert in wood and stone and bridges and things. They also had some painters and that small bowl and its surrounds looked pretty strange—but artistic. They lined internal bunkers with tile they made. It was all very neat. They even had a little village of their own between the atmosphere armor cable and the shore of the lake made by the dam. Their antiaircraft pits had little pagoda rain domes over them.

Good progress was being made in America.

He was almost cheerful. They might have a chance. Thin but possible.

Of course there was the mathematics thing. Lately all Terl seemed to do was scan pages and pages and pages of incomprehensible mathematical equations. He had not started building a console but he was obviously figuring it out from scratch. The old one was burned out. He had demanded it anyway for its case and they had brought him all kinds of scrap but none was it—it couldn't be for Jonnie had the original console, a burned-to-a-crisp wreck, down in the garage here. So Terl would even have to do the metal case.

Jonnie saw a couple of Hockners being taken to another room. These prisoners fought each other, race to race, like wildcats. The tallest Hockner, not too bad-looking in spite of having no nose, was a lower-grade officer but educated. He was showing vast interest in the vehicles parked around. Jonnie stopped the group, intending to ask some questions.

The tall Hockner was grinning superciliously at the vehicles. Ordinary Hockner crewmen didn't speak Psychlo but their officers did. He recognized Jonnie. "You know," said the tall one, "that none of these vehicle frames are built on Psychlo, don't you?"

"I didn't know," said Jonnie.

Although it made the sentries wary, the Hockner went over to a ground car and looked around under the edge of one of the bumpers. "There," he said, pointing.

Jonnie looked at it. It was one of the alphabets on the Galactic bank notes.

"That's Duraleb," said the Hockner. "It says 'Made in Duraleb.' The Psychlos import all their plane bodies and tank bodies and machinery from other systems and peoples. The Psychlos only furnish metals and then motors and consoles. Nobody can use this stuff except Psychlos, since nobody has the drives. These other planets build other things for other peoples. But this Psychlo stuff is useless if you don't have consoles. They make those on Psychlo and only on Psychlo."

Jonnie thanked him. He said, "Don't thank me, old fellow. If you ever start running out of consoles and motors, while you can buy all the bodies you want, you won't have a thing. It's the way the confounded Psychlos run things! They've got a throat-choke monopoly on every universe. You can't go up against them. Hockners have tried. You'll just lose."

Jonnie knew these prisoners, while cooperative, tended to be malicious, but he had heard this too often for it to be just a guess. He changed the subject: "Did you fellows ever capture any Psychlo mathematics texts?"

The Hockner gave a laugh. It sounded like a horse neighing. "My dear fellow, every wizard brain in the universe for three hundred and two thousand years has tried to figure out Psychlo mathematics. It can't be done. Oh, it isn't their arithmetic. An eleven-numeral system is not too strange. There's a race that had twenty-three different numerals. It's their silly equations. Nothing ever balances. Texts? Anybody can pick up their texts. They're meaningless! Pure rubbish! Balderdash! Rot! Now will you order them to give me and my crew something to eat like you did the Tolnep?"

Jonnie told them to see MacKendrick.

He went to his viewing room and looked at Terl's vast numbers of worksheets again. He wasn't feeling so good now.

Jonnie had a bomb to land on Psychlo if necessary. Great! He didn't have a thing to land it there with.

He had a rapidly growing force of visitors overhead. Terl was dawdling.

Jonnie had a very desperate plan to seize the console before it could be destroyed, but even if he got it, it might work just once and quit if the Tolnep was right.

He looked over Terl's equations again. They didn't balance. They didn't proceed one to the next logically. Yet the whole fate of this planet depended, in the final analysis, on solving them.

Maybe other people of other races had met this impasse, this same problem before. And lost. Maybe another being had sat here, like this, staring at texts and worksheets of Psychlo math, uneasy, and with a feeling of hopelessness, and then gone out to be destroyed by the Psychlos, his personal courage meaningless.

— 5 —

Terl was getting suspicious.

It was a whole series of little things.

First, there was the trouble with the money, and trouble with money was one thing Terl would *not* tolerate.

They had his contracts and Terl had supposed they would simply hand it over in due course. But no. It seemed the two billion Galactic credits had been safeguarded in the Denver branch of the Earth Planetary Bank. Worse, it also seemed that this Brown Limper Staffor was running up huge bills and loans with the Earth Planetary Bank. The most recent had been one to build a castle up on a hill. He wanted to call it "Bergsdorfen" or some such thing.

Brown Limper Staffor, to get the money, had offered as collateral the Terl contracts.

Directors of the Earth Planetary Bank, a man named MacAdam and a German, had turned up here at the compound with new documents for Terl to sign. And unless they were signed, then the Galactic credits could not be turned over.

The last thing Terl wanted was valid evidence lying about. But there was no help for it. MacAdam said the original contracts were not properly notarized and no one had attested to the signature. Terl had signed them with his left paw since he hated the idea of all this evidence. He could have claimed the first contracts were forgeries he knew nothing about.

But these bankers had typed up brand-new, much more valid-looking contracts. The new ones attested that Terl was political officer, war officer, security officer, and acting head of Intergalactic Mining Company. True enough, locally.

It was pointed out that there was no Earth branch of the company, that there was just the company as a whole. So Terl had to sign as acting for the whole board of Intergalactic Mining Company, and the contract sold "the company and any interests the company might have that could be sold, transmitted, conveyed. . . ." You could read this contract in a way that sold all of Intergalactic everywhere! And all its planets. Or you could read it that it was just this planet and this branch. Very general.

It made Terl's claws curl in fear. If the Imperial government of Psychlo learned of this they would take days to torture him to death. Not in over three hundred thousand years had Intergalactic ever sold any part of itself or its interests.

They had brought a Swiss notary and witnesses. The contract was in English, German, and Psychlo. It had fifteen originals that had to be signed.

But no sign, no money. Terl, rage and fear suppressed, had signed every copy and then Brown Limper had signed as the "Custodian of Interests for Any Legally Constituted Government of the Planet, said contract binding on all Successors" and then had also signed an addition to it conveying the contract to the Earth Planetary Bank "to have and to hold and to execute or convey in return for sums advanced."

With horror Terl saw this document witnessed, stamped, covered with red seals, covered with gold seals, and packaged in wax seals. Fifteen separate copies of it!

But they gave him his money. They said the Denver branch of the bank was closing and they could not keep it there and Terl had to take it right now. Terl raised no objection to that.

They brought the boxes on a flatbed truck and put them in his bedroom.

They gave Terl his copies of the contract and he signed a receipt for those and the money. They all left, and the moment they were out the door, his first act was to shred, burn, and destroy the ashes of his copies. If Psychlo ever got word of it—!

He felt soothed then and he sat and petted the money for a while. Then he realized he couldn't go to bed amid all these boxes.

He got the guards to let him go out to the morgue and get three coffins. It seemed to him that there were fewer coffins there than there used to be. However, he brought the coffins in and put them in the bedroom and got to work putting the money into them, counting it by bundles.

It was late and he still hadn't finished the job so he spread some blankets on one of the coffins and went to sleep.

The next day, still working on packing the money—he had never realized before what an enormous lot of money two billion credits was—he found he was short one coffin. It was going to take four.

Accordingly, he got the guards to let him out and he went to the morgue to get another coffin. On his last visit, there had been one quite close to the door. Now it was no longer there. Somebody was doing something with these coffins.

Only a security chief of Terl's talents and training ever could have gotten to the bottom of it. That he was sure of.

First he questioned guards. Then he questioned a Captunk Arf Moiphy. And he found these Brigantes, these allegedly reliable, trained mercenaries, had been trafficking in coffins with the cadets.

The night duty commando had been selling coffins to the cadets for whiskey. Whiskey was some drink made in Scotland. Intoxicating.

Oh, Terl got the whole story. Late of an evening, some cadet, different ones, would come to the compound with an open pail of whiskey and trade it for a coffin. The guard would simply open the morgue and hand one over and take the whiskey.

It did no good for Captunk Arf Moiphy to show him that the cadets used the lead to make little cast-model spaceships and soldiers. Moiphy even had a couple. Terl knew those. They were for a game called klepp. Those cadets were selling game pieces and game boards made out of melted-down lead coffins. Company coffins!

Terl had demanded to see Snith. He ordered him to put a stop to it.

Three days later, Terl had gotten himself escorted down to the metal supply storeroom to get some needed sheets of material when he noticed that the hangar was nearly empty. There were a few ore carriers and a half-dozen battle planes and that was all that was left in those vast hangars. He had promptly gone to the garage, and that, too, was nearly empty. There were just a dozen flatbeds and a couple of Basher tanks left in there.

The place was being stolen blind!

He got hold of Lars and raged at him.

Lars said there had been a lot of crashes and the cadets were simply replacing the lost machines from the hangar.

Just as he was about to rip Lars to bits, it suddenly occurred to Terl that company property was no longer his responsibility. So he let it go.

Three days later there was a tearing argument with Ker.

Sometime since, they had begun to clear away the wreckage and fused wires of the old transshipment rig and now that it was gone, Terl wanted to be sure that the points would be at the correct distances on the poles. He went out and he found . . .

Ker using the most sloppy, inexperienced machine operator trainees he had to dig the trench for the atmosphere-armor ionization cable! There was the trench half-dug. But these trainees had been digging all over the place!

And more! There was equipment scattered everywhere. Cranes, blade scrapers, you name it. Whenever one of these stupid animal trainees had dug something, he had simply left the machine there. Whenever he lifted something, he left the magnetic crane right there.

What a mess!

Standing on the platform, hating the bright winter sun, half-sick from the rotten-quality breathe-gas that was available, Terl had felt like clawing the midget to bits.

"You know better than this!" raged Terl.

"Can I help it if these animals break machines?" shouted Ker.

"Can't you follow a straight, plain plan?" shouted Terl.

"Can I help it if these animals can't follow a straight, plain line?" shouted Ker.

Terl realized Ker had a point. They weren't going to get anywhere standing here shouting. "Look," said Terl, "it is in your own best interest that I get safely to Psychlo."

"Is it?" said Ker.

Leverage, leverage, Terl told himself. "I'll tell you what I will do," said Terl. "I will put ten thousand credits to your account in the Galactic Bank. You have a numbered account there with quite a bit in it already. But I will add—"

"Brown Limper Staffor paid me a hundred thousand Earth credits just to dig up that cable for you, that cable right over there. It was no easy job and I considered the pay cut-rate!"

Terl thought fast. "All right, I'll pay you a hundred thousand Galactic credits to help install this firing rig and cooperate."

"I can get double that from this Brown Limper *not* to do it," said Ker.

"You can?" said Terl, suddenly alert. He thought hard. Yes, that Brown Limper had been acting furtively lately, like he was hiding something.

"He wants a certain party!" said Ker. "He doesn't care if you get to Psychlo or not!"

"But doesn't he know I have to record the deeds?"

"He's only interested in getting one man!" said Ker.

"Look," said Terl, "I will put half a million credits in your account if you cooperate in getting me to Psychlo."

Ker thought about it. Then he said, "If you will get me new papers and destroy my old company records *and* deposit seven hundred fifty thousand credits to my account, I'll see all goes smoothly."

Terl was about to say he agreed when Ker spoke again: "You will have to make it all right with this Brown Limper Staffor also. Tell me how you intend to trap this man so I can reassure this Staffor. He controls these workers. So add that, and it's a deal."

Terl looked at Ker. He knew how money-hungry he was. "All right. I'm going to string five hundred Brigantes around outside that atmosphere armor, armed with poisoned arrows. Arrows won't make a concussion if fired and they can shoot that animal to bits if he comes! You whisper that to Staffor and he'll also cooperate with you. It's a deal then?"

Ker smiled.

Terl went back inside, glad to get his breathe-mask off. He got some kerbango to soothe his nerves.

He reviewed this strange scene. It *was* Staffor. That was the one who was going to mess this plan up. Terl would take care of the animal: he hadn't told Ker he also intended to have Snith and a squad on the platform armed with poisoned arrows or that he had a beautiful beryllium box to hand Staffor. The box would destroy all the evidence, the contract copies, everything.

And Ker, too!

He would have a hostage to handle the animal.

He felt quite satisfied about everything until three nights later when he noticed there were no guards in view. He went out and there they were, sprawled around the morgue, dead drunk.

It was obvious that Snith had used the information just to get a commission in whiskey.

Well, he could handle Snith when the time came.

The one to keep an eye on was this Staffor. His suspicions were right. It was Staffor that was plotting, plotting, plotting. Sneaky rat! It was plain he would try to steal this money back.

Warned, Terl was confident he could outsmart them all.

He went in and checked the money coffins, sealed them, marked them "radiation killed" so nobody on Psychlo would want to open them, and put his private "X" on the bottom of each one.

He would be a wealthy tycoon on Psychlo!

He spread his bedding out on top of the coffins and slept a beautiful sleep with beautiful dreams where royalty bowed when they met The Great Terl on the street. And all evidence and this planet would have been totally destroyed behind him.

— 6 —

Deep in the African minesite, bent over the viewscreens in the half-lit dark, Jonnie was taking a loss.

Day 92 was coming up on them like a whirlwind.

At first he had hoped that he could get a separate console built using Terl's plans and install it down at Kariba. Such would bypass any real necessity for a hopeless attack in America to seize that one. It looked as if it remained their best chance but it was hardly any chance at all. He would have had to stop Terl from using that strange bomb but he could not do that without the almost foolhardy risks of letting it go right on up to firing time on Day 92 and trying to attack the platform and grab that console at the last moment.

Other news was not good. There had been two more raids by the visitors in different places and casualties had been suffered. An ore plane, returning empty from a ferrying trip, had been swooped down upon by the Hawvins and blasted out of the sky with the loss of both pilot and copilot. A hunting party from the Russian base had been gunned from above and three Siberians and a Sherpa had been killed before their air cover had shot down the intruder.

Also the Edinburgh defense planning had gone wrong. Sir Robert had wanted to bring in a couple of miles of atmosphere cable and surround Castle Rock with it. The power dams in Scotland of long ago were not in shape or converted to Psychlo power. The Cornwall minesite power supply was a tidal dam at Bristol in the Bristol Channel, and while it worked well on the ebb and flow of those gigantic tides, it was not possible to run a line clear up to Edinburgh—and that line would have been open to attack in any case. The hauling of that much cable, itself, was a formidable block, for it would have had to be flown in sections to Scotland. No other means than antiaircraft fire was available to protect Edinburgh. And the Scots, having regained it, were not going to abandon it. It was the center of the most ancient Scottish nationalism. Moving the whole remaining population down to Cornwall, as proposed by Jonnie, had not been approved, and it was true it would be pretty crowded. Jonnie knew Edinburgh was going to catch it.

Terl was going about his job in a way that seemed backward. He spent a lot of time measuring up poles and stringing outside wire and putting in firing points. Everything he did was being duplicated exactly down at Kariba. They now had the wires up and all the points in, down at that base. Angus, each time they got a new item, would go tearing down to Kariba and install an equivalent in the secondary defense platform there.

It had looked very hopeful for some days. Terl had gotten a lot of metal and had built the console case, a heavy, massive thing about a yard square. They had built the same case here and it was sitting down in a locked room, an empty shell, waiting.

But after all this spurt of energy, Terl for the last several days had just been fooling with fuses. He wasn't getting on with construction.

Reams of mathematics had been worked out by Terl. But a lot of good they were. Who understood them.

Now it was just fuses. Jonnie had gotten duplicates out of supply here of all the fuses Terl was working with and tried to figure out what he was doing.

Jonnie had learned one thing: that some of the items in a console that would appear to be different components were fakes. They were not resistors or capacitors. They were actually fuses made up to look like other things.

Terl was doing something Jonnie had not heard of before. With meters and such, he was working with an "underload" type of fuse. The circuit would be connected only so long as current was going through it. When the current ceased to flow, the fuse burned out. It was an odd kind of circuit breaker, made of a filament so tiny and thin it had to be worked under a magnifying scope.

Well, that seemed to be all Terl was doing.

Jonnie's attention was drifting when he suddenly realized that the filament Terl was using looked awfully like the ones in the silver capsule in Psychlo heads.

Forgotten was his stiff neck. He went tearing out and got one they had removed from a corpse. Yes, the same thing!

Abruptly he added it all up and rushed out to find MacKendrick. The doctor was working with a Psychlo skull he had cleaned and whitened. He was trying to find some means of entering it with instruments. He put it down on the table before him where the sockets stared sightlessly at him and composed himself to listen to Jonnie.

"That isn't anything very mysterious!" said Jonnie, pointing excitedly into the silver capsule he held. "It's just a fuse! It doesn't vibrate or put out radio signals or anything. It's just a *fuse!*"

Jonnie grabbed some pictures of one inside a Psychlo brain. "Look! You said the nerves this was fastened between were the primary impulse channels of their thought.

"All right. Mathematics is logical thought! It is the approximation of being sensible! Now even if a Psychlo has a soul and does his thinking with a soul, or even if he doesn't have, mental action works between those two channels.

"So long as a Psychlo is thinking logically, there is a constant current between those two nerves. Even asleep there would be a current, a very slight one.

"Now up comes an alien. The Psychlo knows his whole race and empire depends upon keeping his mathematics a secret. And the alien wants to know about Psychlo mathematics. The Psychlo instantly shuts off thinking about them. Or a surge occurs and then a shutoff. Pop. Blown fuse!"

MacKendrick was quite interested. But he said, "That doesn't explain suicide."

"All right! Look at this picture and look at this fuse. The silver capsule is very close to that bronze item that short-circuits pleasure and pain and action. Look at this fuse filament! When it parts, the ends drop down inside the capsule and you get a short circuit into the bronze item.

"The Psychlo has an instant impulse to kill! If he can't right then, the short circuit between the silver and bronze items acts as an obsession to kill that doesn't let up. He has to kill something and he winds up killing himself!"

MacKendrick thought it over and nodded. "But," he said, "that doesn't explain the females."

Jonnie got that type of capsule and looked at it. 'It's another kind of fuse. Since mathematics is logical thought, it would cause a concentration of current to begin. They probably are taught not to teach females mathematics—it's part of their moral code. And the females are noted for being illogical. When they start to think in mathematical terms or even try to, a current gets too heavy and they blow the fuse. They don't have a bronze object and they just go into a coma. Their wits won't connect anymore and they go out of communication with the nervous system."

Jonnie paused. "My explanation may not be complete. But I know these are just fuses and short circuits. And that's how they protected their empire!"

"And why they're so crazy," said MacKendrick. "I am sure you have the explanation and that those things are what you say they are."

MacKendrick turned the Psychlo skull around on the table. It was a huge, massive, heavy thing. A complex mass of bone and joints. "There's only one thing wrong."

Jonnie was all revved up with having gotten that far. He listened.

"We're no closer to getting those things out of their heads than we were," said MacKendrick.

Jonnie laid the pictures and the capsules down on the table beside the skull and walked quietly out of the room.

It was definitely not a hopeful day.

— 7 —

Jonnie lanced northwest in the Mark 32 battle plane.

The alert had come just over half an hour ago. Glencannon was in trouble.

It was Day 78, only fourteen days before Terl had scheduled himself to fire. He had not begun his panel on the last discs Jonnie had had. There had been a delay.

And now this! Glencannon was under attack en route.

The visitors, four hundred miles above Earth, had increased. There were eighteen of them now. Half-Captain Rogodeter Snowl had come back and with him he had brought four heavy war vessels. One of them at least, if not more, was a plane carrier. It was probably from this that the attack on Glencannon had been launched.

Jonnie had no communicator with him. He had simply been outside when the alert came. Stormalong and two other pilots had scrambled and Jonnie had simply grabbed an air mask and a plane. All the communication in the air right now was in Pali—both Glencannon and Stormalong had communicators with them and were using them. Thus Jonnie could not tell what was happening. The singsong of the Buddhists never showed excitement even in combat, so their voice tones told him nothing.

He was gaining altitude and widening his viewscreens. He had Stormalong and the other two ships just ahead of him. He had not yet picked up Glencannon.

Jonnie threw a scanner upward. Three of their visitors were way up there, not as clear in this bright daylight as they would be on scanners at night due to daytime ultraviolet in the air.

Was that the Vulcor-class vessel? The other two with it were larger, more bulky. Yes, that was the Vulcor-class: diamond-shaped bridge. Half-Captain Rogodeter Snowl himself.

The three weren't coming down—apparently it took a lot of solar accumulation to do that and they tended to reserve themselves. The other two must be plane carriers.

Yes! From one of them came a new launch.

Six needle-like craft were coming down like arrows.

Clearly, using Psychlo, Jonnie said, "Six new hornets from above!" That would warn Stormalong.

There was Glencannon. Streaking along at about one hundred thousand feet, flat-out, heading for the minesite. Where was his escort? He should have an escort. No sign of them!

Four needles were shooting along behind Glencannon. Occasionally a long-range flash of fire laced out from them.

There went Stormalong!

In tight formation, the three planes cut straight through the pursuing Tolneps.

An explosion! A second gout of hot blue flame. And a third.

There was only one Tolnep racing out of the smoke.

Jonnie turned up to intercept the six coming down. They grew larger and larger in his sights.

He centered on the nose of the leader. His thumb hit the firing trip as he wildly swung sideways, sweeping his awesome firepower into the Tolnep's tight formation.

His viewscreen flared out with the explosions ahead.

A slight thump as a broken piece of a Tolnep plane touched his wing.

Jonnie flipped around as they went by him. He sighted in on

the tail of the last ship. He hit the trip of the blast cannon. He was skidding so wildly from his turn that he missed.

Four Tolneps left to go.

He flashed ahead of them and spun about. He was almost head-on with the Tolnep now leading. An instant before they would have collided, Jonnie's shots stuffed the Tolnep's own fire up his cannon barrels. The ship exploded.

Three Tolneps left. They looped and came on, firing in formation. The air about Jonnie was slashed. The Mark 32 took a hit in the windscreen. Half of it went black.

Jonnie's guns were going. One Tolnep! Two Tolneps!

The last one tried to make a run for it, shooting back into the heights.

Jonnie steadied his battle plane. He threw the firing sets onto "Flame" and "Maximum Range." He sent searching needles straight up.

The Tolnep shattered into a ragged ball of fire.

Where was Glencannon?

There he was, racing down to the minesite, almost there.

He had a Tolnep right on his tail.

Stormalong and his other two ships were slashing down on the Tolnep.

The guard opened the atmosphere armor curtain and Glencannon flashed through. He was safe!

A scythe of fire hit the Tolnep as Stormalong and the other two pilots let drive from extreme range.

The guard got the atmosphere curtain on. The Tolnep hit it and slammed through.

The air had not had time to reionize enough.

The Tolnep ship exploded in a ball of flame in the scramble area, narrowly missing Glencannon's ship as it landed.

Jonnie and Stormalong scanned the skies for more enemy. There was none. Some smoke palls rose in the distance where enemy ships had disintegrated.

The guard opened the atmosphere curtain. A fire-fighting crew was there now spraying the burning wreckage of the Tolnep ship. Jonnie, Stormalong, and the other two landed.

Glencannon was sitting in his seat still. His Buddhist communicator was trying to calm him. Glencannon was crying. His hands were shaking. It was a reaction of total frustration.

"I had orders to come through," Glencannon was repeating

over and over. The communicator waved the others away and then came to them.

"There are many things for the Academy of pilots to do in America," the Buddhist told Jonnie and Stormalong. "They also have to maintain their air cover. There were no escort pilots and we delayed coming for days. Then Glencannon felt he could not delay anymore.

"A Swiss pilot, a close friend of his but a very new pilot, volunteered. The Tolneps hit us just after we crossed the coast in northern Africa. It was too far away for Cornwall or Luxembourg to help us.

"The Swiss fought them off. He shot down three. But he needed help and Glencannon had orders to keep going in such an event and he kept going.

"He feels that if he had turned back to help the Swiss, they wouldn't have got him. The Swiss pilot was alone, he had no communicator, but he also told Glencannon to keep going.

"The Tolneps shot the Swiss to pieces. When he ejected and tried to get down by backpack they closed in and killed him in the air.

"Glencannon wants to go up and shoot down those ships in orbit. They would murder him. Please help."

They got Glencannon calmed down. Stormalong said that he would call Sir Robert and get the vital communication line made more secure. Sir Robert was going over to move the Academy out of America and to the Cornwall minesite in a few days but meanwhile better arrangements should be made. The ferrying of innumerable planes and equipment to safe places was now all complete. The tribes were centralized. Stormalong also said he would take over the run.

Glencannon handed over the pouch of discs.

Jonnie looked at the packet.

He hoped it was worth it.

— 8 —

It was!

Minutes after Jonnie opened the courier pouch and got a disc on a viewscreen, he realized that for the first time in all of Psychlo's long and sadistic history, non-Psychlo eyes were looking upon the actual construction of a teleportation transshipment console.

Terl, having no models or patterns, was working from scratch. And crazy though he might be, his workmanship was exact. Of course, his own life depended upon its being so.

He had already made the console case. He had fitted the rows of buttons, spares from the storerooms, all properly marked, into the panel top. He had made the screw holes which held the top on to the bottom case.

Watching the view discs, fascinated, Jonnie saw him take a yard-square piece of common black insulating board, the kind that was used to back all electronic assemblies, and fit it into the area between the top panel and the case sides. It was this board, evidently, which would hold the various components of the circuit he would build. He carefully and precisely drilled the holes in this insulating board so it would fit between the top panel and the case and be held in place by the same joining screws.

He temporarily fastened down the board in the case and put a smear of powder over it and then pressed each button so the location where it touched the board was exactly marked. Then he took it all apart again and made more exact marks with a red pencil wherever the powder had been dented. He drilled small holes in each one of these points and put in a metal plug. Now the buttons of the top panel, when pressed, would come down and touch a metal plug.

Terl now turned the insulating board over. The little metal plugs showed on the underside. He marked which was the top and which was the bottom of the board and really went to work.

Scarcely consulting his notes and formulas at all, he began to cover the underside of the board with various electronic components:

resistors, capacitors, tiny amplifiers, relays and switches. It was actually a rather crude and old-fashioned sort of layout. It seemed to match up to the metal plugs the buttons would hit from above and often connected to it.

But there was an oddity. He was putting fuses in places where, if you used the board at all, they would certainly blow. In fact, for every metal plug through the board, there was a fuse that would disconnect it from the circuitry now being built. It looked to Jonnie that all you had to do was hit one button on the upper console and a fuse would blow. Dozens of such fuses.

In a dumb kind of way, this mysterious circuit he was building made sense. All except these fuses. Why would one put fuses all through a piece of electronic circuitry?

Terl neatened up this whole complicated circuit. He color-coded it and polished it. And at last it was complete. It really looked marvelous, if one admired all the complexities of an electronic circuit board. It almost made sense—you pushed a top console button and current went here, you pushed another and current would go there.

The board was complete. Terl admired it, even took a break and bit off some kerbango.

Then he did the strangest thing imaginable.

With a flourish of his paws, he hooked up some leads to a power source, snapped the clips to the terminals of the very artistic board circuit he had just built, and *blew all the fuses in it!*

They went with little glowing pops and smoke puffs.

He had just made the whole circuit inoperational.

Now he really got down to work. He pulled over his vast pile of equations and worked-out formulas, got out micrometer measuring tools, cleaned up a set of drafting triangles and rulers, sharpened up white marking pens to a hairline point.

He turned the board he had just made over to the blank side, made some reference points on it, and for the next two days, meticulously consulting his notes, he *drew in* a circuit. Aside from matching up with the metal plugs for the console buttons, this new circuit had nothing whatever to do with the one he had so laboriously built on the bottom side of the board.

He drew in the resistors and amplifiers and capacitors and every other electronic component. All in tiny lines and squiggles and curls.

Terl consulted his equations and worksheets and duplicated the measurements with enormous exactitude in white on the board. It was a long and complicated procedure and it was a very complex circuit that emerged. The console buttons, when pressed, would activate it if it were composed of wire.

He got that finished. Then he dusted the whole drawing with a thin coating of reddish paste. You could see the circuit through it but when you put something on the paste like a pencil it would show that that bit of the circuit had been traced.

Terl now got a thin-bladed annealing knife. One end of these knives, by the process of separating molecules through destruction of their cohesion, cut metal. The other end was used to restore the molecular cohesion and "sew" the metal up.

He took the sewing end of the knife and began to trace his circuit with it. Wherever he followed a line, the thin red paste showed he had followed it. Thus, he could keep track of where he had traced and work without any skips.

Jonnie stared at this activity. Then he rushed out of his viewing room, raced up to one of the compound storerooms, and got a piece of insulating board and an annealing knife.

He made a diagonal mark across the board with the sewing end of the knife. He put clips at both ends of his mark and put current through it.

The current flowed!

By aligning usually insulative molecules in a straight line, one had a path, a "wire."

He had seen that Psychlos, in cutting these boards to size to install circuit breakers, always sawed them. He had just thought knives didn't work on them. True enough, knives were not efficient in cutting them. But by aligning molecules, the insulating board conducted electricity at the points of touch.

Jonnie, starry-eyed, went back to further view this activity Terl had been engaged upon.

It had taken Terl two days just to trace that circuit. Finally he finished.

And then Terl took some solvent and a rag and wiped the whole board clean.

There was not one visible trace left. But that "insulating" board now contained all the alignments of a complex circuit.

The underside's visible components were a total fake. They weren't ever intended to work. And anybody examining one of these boards would think he had blown its fuses. Scientists of many races had probably spent hundreds of years of time trying to make that false circuit make sense and agree with Psychlo math.

Terl was doing something in the upper left corner of the board. Unfortunately he had carelessly dropped a text open in such a position that its cover obscured much of what he was doing. It had something to do with the installation of a switch. It was a switch which would appear in the top panel. All Jonnie could see on the discs was that the switch probably had to be changed with every use of the board. Up one firing, down the next, up the next, and so on. The switch was misleadingly labeled, "Dimmer." The component it was attached to was visible enough.

If activated by a wrong turn of the switch, that component would send a surge through the board and erase the invisible circuit.

Jonnie couldn't see what position the switch was rigged to be in at the first firing.

Terl now was putting the board together.

And Jonnie found why loosening the screws which held it all together made the board inoperational.

Terl took a large electromagnet and put it around the case. Then just inside one screw, where it went through the insulating board, he inserted a fuse.

Jonnie went down and got one. It was a "magnet fuse." As long as a current went through it, it stayed whole. The moment a magnetic current was absent, it blew. To remove a console top, one had to put a magnetic field around the console.

When the screw was touching the top edge of the console, the magnetic top edge kept a tiny current running forever. The moment that screw was loosened, the magnetic current ceased and the fuse blew.

More: when it blew it activated one of the components just under it and wiped the invisible circuit out of the board.

But to take a panel top off all you had to do was put a magnetic field generator near that screw and the fuse wouldn't blow.

An invisible circuit, two booby traps to wipe it out, a completely false circuit to distract.

And that was the secret of the Psychlos.

A sober Jonnie made plentiful copies of Terl's circuit. One could simply put it on a piece of insulating board and trace it in.

The metal plugs through it activated the invisible circuit. They could duplicate it.

All except for one switch. And that was why he was sober. Exactly how it was rigged he did not know. The position it would have to be in for each sequential firing he did not know.

He reviewed the discs again.

No, he could not make it out.

He speculated on the possibility of just making several boards and working it out. No, it might do something else too.

He made a full file and plenty of notes.

They couldn't make teleportation motors from this, but possibly they could open them and trace the circuit. Maybe. But without that one switch . . .

Jonnie knew they would have to go over and seize that console just to see where Terl set it.

It was an appalling risk and might cost men's lives.

He knew they would have to do it.

— 9 —

Jonnie quietly and efficiently neatened up his scene.

In case anything happened to him, which he felt was more than likely in this American raid, he carefully briefed Angus in all the intricacies of the console. He made copious notes especially for Angus, so that he could duplicate and operate such a console. He told him some of the things that could be done with it.

Angus objected violently to Jonnie's going on the raid. Jonnie said he was not going to risk anyone else's life, for the actions he had to take were too dicey. He would have the backup of thirty Scots, ten drivers, and fifteen pilots. Angus was still trying to protest but it didn't do any good. If Robert the Fox had been there the two of them might have prevailed, but Sir Robert was over in America moving the Academy and Angus gave in reluctantly.

A Scot aide of Sir Robert's was there and Jonnie briefed him on the military aspects of their situation: the visitors were waiting for something—he was not sure what. Jonnie felt it had to do with whether or not they got a transshipment rig operating. An analysis of their chatter among themselves showed they were observing the American compound, waiting for something to happen: the visitors had seen Psychlos there (probably Terl and Ker) and seemed to think the American scene might still be in Psychlo hands, or in any event might be political. Jonnie expected the sky to fall in right after that transshipment rig was fired and an alert should be out, then, for Day 92, which was approaching very quickly.

Jonnie briefed another Scot officer and arranged a decoy platform to be hastily built in the Singapore area. There was a minesite there northwest of the ancient, deserted man-city where the Psychlos had mined tin, titanium, and tungsten; it had full hydroelectric power, atmosphere armor, and a certain amount of stores and planes left in it. A handful of Chinese, three pilots, a communicator, a Coordinator and this officer were to lay out a platform and poles. Jonnie gave them the old burned-out console which they repainted. Under the protection of the cable they were to make like they were busy firing, complete with things appearing and disappearing on the platform. When the flights left the American area with the real console, the heaviest part of the escort would streak to the Singapore area and pull any pursuit of the real console away. The Kariba platform had been under camouflage nets from the beginning and chatter from the visitors showed they thought it was a temple. He warned the officer that the attack would be heavy there in the Singapore area. But the Scot just smiled and grabbed his allocated men and left.

Jonnie made a fast tour of Kariba. The Chinese had done wonderfully well. There was a roof under the screen but over the firing platform, all held together with wooden pegs; swooping gables and points made it very artistic. They had a lot of dragons around, carved from wood and cast in clay, that pointed out from the beam ends with flaming mouths and scaly tails. They had bunkers inside the protected cone. They all had tiled interiors. They even had a little hospital. Their own village was inside the protective cable over by the lakeshore. It was all very colorful and attractive, more like a garden than a war area.

Dr. Allen had gotten some juice of plants from up in the old Nairobi area—he called it "pyrethrum"—that killed insects very efficiently, and despite the number of animals in the woods thereabouts that attracted flies, they had had no trouble with tsetse sleeping sickness.

Jonnie heard them singing and playing on strange string and wind instruments that evening so he recorded a lot of it and had them rig loudspeakers ready to play it when they activated the area—it would foul up any listening beams from upstairs. That plus the interference the armor cable posed would keep them ignorant of what was going on here.

When he returned to the African compound, it was Day 87. He found Stormalong there with more discs that showed the color codes of the cables and the pole wires. They could simply hack off the console's cables and reconnect them at Kariba. He gave the code to Angus.

Stormalong said this would be his last run so Jonnie briefed him carefully on the military situation. It was Jonnie's belief that the visitors would attack in force after any American firing. Stormalong had better be prepared to take control of air defenses on the planet. Jonnie would not let him go on the raid. Dunneldeen was handling air cover for them on that. Thor would be with them in the raiding party. Jonnie missed Robert the Fox who usually handled these briefings and actions.

Stormalong, like Angus, did not want Jonnie to go. He said America was stripped now. The Academy was empty. Jonnie would have only his own raiding party, and though he knew it had been drilled within an inch of the participants' lives, there were an awful lot of Brigantes over there. Just after they had pulled the recorders out of the three places at the Academy, Brigantes had begun to systematically loot the place. But with no Sir Robert to support his objections, Stormalong did not prevail.

Jonnie was going up to an upper level of the compound and he ran into Ker.

The Psychlo midget was all smiles. They swatted "paws." He had been looking for Jonnie to show him the silly money they were now printing for America and in which he had been "paid." Jonnie pulled him into a deserted office and shook his head over the hundred-credit note and the picture of Brown Limper Staffor.

"The stuff is worthless!" said Ker. "The Brigantes just throw it into the street!"

Ker was so happy to be out of that area. He told Jonnie all about it. "And he offered me seven hundred and fifty thousand Galactic credits that I'll never see. He's one crazy Psychlo. Not sane like us half-humans!" Ker laughed over that.

Ker gave him the final layouts of the firing platform area.

There was nothing new. Ker had dug and done exactly according to plan. It was the same plan on which his raiding team had been drilled and Ker assured him everything was in place.

But Ker hadn't realized Jonnie was going over there. When he heard that he got very serious. "This Terl is a very bad one. He's liable to have surprises. I don't like your going, Jonnie."

Jonnie said he had to go.

"What if you get a Psychlo war party back on that platform in return?" said Ker.

"I don't think we will," said Jonnie. "And we have a present for Psychlo."

"I hope so," said Ker. "It's my furry neck if they ever turn up here again. The I.B.I. would take days to kill me!"

"I don't think you have anything to worry about," said Jonnie. "But you stay here among these defenses. There's quite a few enemy prisoners in the place and all the Psychlos that are left. Maybe you can teach them to play cards!"

Ker laughed. And then he said, "Did the one you call Sir Robert come back here?"

"Why?"

"Well, right in the middle of the Academy move to England, we didn't see him anymore. I wanted to check a couple of points with him and I couldn't find him. And Dunneldeen put in calls. He isn't in Edinburgh or Luxembourg or Russia. I thought he must be here. The reason I ask is he knows all your dispositions of forces and even some of your raid details."

Jonnie was very concerned about Sir Robert. He threw off Ker's question with, "They could never make him talk."

"The I.B.I. could make anybody talk," said Ker.

"We don't know the enemy has him," said Jonnie.

Shortly afterward he instituted his own queries. There was no sign of Sir Robert in any area. A couple of ferry planes had gone down lately from enemy attack. They had been en route from America to Scotland. Had Sir Robert been on one of them?

Sir Robert had not handled many of the details of this raid. There was no reason to change planning this late.

Jonnie spent his last day at the Lake Victoria minesite neatening up what there was of his personal life. He was under no illusion that this raid was not dangerous

He wrote a letter to Chrissie that he knew the parson would

read for her and put it in plain sight on his desk, the envelope marked "To Chrissie in Case of Something Happening to Me."

He had heard one wrote wills to leave personal possessions. He started one. All he had was his horses and some odds and ends of clothes. He couldn't think of anything else he owned. Then he thought maybe Chrissie had occupied the Edinburgh house in his name, so he put down any interest he had in that or its contents and left it to Chrissie. Then he remembered he had a few books so he left those to Pattie. For the life of him he couldn't recall anything else he owned. But maybe people would think he owned gifts like the chrome AK 47. They weren't very many. Still, they might be. So he added a clause, "And anything else I am found to own shall be equally divided among . . ." and he listed the names of those men who had been closest to him. He thought for a while and then added Ker.

He had also heard that you signed these things and got them witnessed so he did that. Then he put it in an envelope and put it alongside the letter to Chrissie.

Feeling he had made things very orderly, he spent that evening making sure all his weapons and gear worked, that his radiation suit had no holes in it, that his air mask tanks were full and that half a dozen kill-clubs were in throwing condition. He put copies of the latest sales contract Terl had signed into his pouch. He checked the beryllium bomb case for safe carrying. He tested the edge of a hatchet to cut console cables.

He felt he was ready and got a good sleep on his last night before the American raid. He had done everything he could. Now it was in the hands of the gods Or a devil like Terl.

■

PART 24

— 1 —

At the American minesite, Day 92 had dawned windy and cold. And then in midmorning, four hours before the firing time, it had begun to snow. It was not too late for snow but this snow was a heavy one. It came down in huge soft flakes that swirled here and there in the wind puffs.

Terl did not care. He was jubilant. This would be his last day on Earth.

So far things had gone smoothly. From sunup to the moment it started to snow he had been outside, checking the wiring and cables. Almost lovingly he had put a final polish on the firing points on the poles, the points which would change space and transport him once again to his homeland.

He had a wonderful story all made up. He would come in with the tale of a mutiny, of a sellout to an alien race. And how he, Terl, fighting hard, had saved the company technology and was forced, alas, to use the ultimate bomb to make certain the company was not further betrayed. They would believe him on Psychlo. They would of course fire a camera back and check but it would record a black smudge.

Then he would retire, saying that the strain of it all had been too much. And one fine night, he would go to a cemetery and do a bit of quiet digging and become richer by ten gold coffin lids and two billion credits that he would expose bit by bit, saying he had profited on the exchanges of the various universes.

It was a perfect plan.

He had been idling about for a few minutes wondering when the Brigante special squad would come down from the mountains. He didn't like to stay outside. He hated this planet too much. But today, the breathe-gas didn't seem to make him ill, and after all, it was a great day.

And here they were, the Brigante special squad. They had their bundle with them just as ordered. It was long and made to look like baggage. Just before the firing, Terl would open the end of it and one of Snith's bodyguards would pop an air mask on it. And anybody seeing it would think twice about charging the platform!

He told the special squad to just dump it on the middle of the platform and then stand by.

Now for the next step. Terl went back into the compound and got the small forklift he had had parked there in the corridor, got on it, and went into his office.

It was really a tossup whether he took the coffins first or the console. The coffins could stand the weather better. With a Brigante squad there, nobody could come up and steal them. They were too heavy.

He paused for a moment, looking at his rug. There was a dust tread mark there. But then he thought he must have made it himself. His "X" mark was there on each coffin.

With four rapid runs and very expert machine handling, he got the four coffins outside and dumped them on the platform—four trips. On each trip he cautioned the squad to be alert and watch them.

Now for the console. He tipped it up on edge to get at the hollow bottom. He unlocked a cabinet and got the booby trap and put it under the front edge of the bottom. He would not set it yet. He would give it ten minutes from when he operated the console at firing time. The length of the firing would be three minutes—he had decided to take it easy on himself—and the recoil time would be about forty seconds later. So six minutes and twenty seconds after he fired—bang! No console!

He took it out and put it down on the oversized metal platform made for it, a platform about ten feet by seven feet, just inside the atmosphere armor zone. All nicely figured out. The big bus bars which operated the atmosphere armor cable had long since been installed on a raised board. He hadn't expected snow but he had put a weather shield on the cable board. He hadn't put a shelter for the console itself so now he had to throw a piece of tarpaulin over it to keep snow off the buttons.

Terl adjusted the console's position and then got the forklift out of there. He simply dumped it. What did it matter? Those animals had left machinery all over the place—big magnetic cranes, blade scraper, diggers. What a mess!

He got busy connecting the power cables from the poles to the console. It was quite a massive lot of cables. He didn't want to trip on his way from the console, when he punched in the coordinates to the platform, so he bundled them all together. It made a snake about six inches in diameter.

Terl double-checked the color codes. Yes, he had them all correct.

He checked the armor cable by turning it on. A lot of new snow flew into the air in a circle. Yes, it worked. He turned it off.

He checked the juice input to the console. All live.

Terl looked at his watch.

It was a full hour to firing time. Time to go in for a mouthful of kerbango.

He surveyed the office. Last time he would ever see *this* place. Thank the devils!

Terl opened his cabinets and began to dump anything and everything into the recycling bin. He opened the false backs and bottoms and consigned anything in them to oblivion. The habits of a security chief were too strong. He dumped all his reams of notes and formulas into the maw of the recycler. Then he noticed it wasn't running. Ah, of course, he must have blown the compound fuses when he put that armor cable on. Who cared? This planet was going up in smoke anyway.

He went to his closet and got his dress uniform and boots out and quickly changed. He put on his parade cap. He looked at himself in the mirror. Pretty good!

Terl threw a few things in a travel bag. He looked at his watch. Twenty minutes to go.

The snow, he could see through the compound roof, was coming down even heavier. Who cared?

He put on a breathe-mask with a fresh pair of cartridges, picked up the beautifully wrapped—and very difficult to unwrap—ultimate bomb, picked up his travel kit, and left his office for the last time.

All was ready outside!

Five hundred Brigantes, bows protected from the weather, looking a bit huddled and cold even in their buffalo coats, had been marched up and now stood in the formation he had carefully pointed out. A total ring with its back to the atmosphere cable, a nearly solid wall of Brigantes.

Captunk Arf Moiphy seemed to be the officer in charge of them all. Terl addressed him sternly: "Now you and your men all understand that you are only to use bows and poisoned arrows and knives or bayonets. There must be no firing of powder or blast weapons."

"We's gart orl dat!" called General Snith.

Ah, good! General Snith and an honor guard of six Brigantes, all of them in air masks, were on the platform, armed with bows which they were protecting from the snow.

Terl looked around. It was a bit hard to see through these snowflakes and gusts of wind. He had heard a chattering from somewhere.

What was that? By the crap nebula, the whole Brigante tribe was gathered down by the morgue to see General Snith off! Amazing! The women were all bundled up against the snow and off-duty mercenaries were in among them. What a filthy mob! Good thing he was wearing a mask for he knew they smelled awful.

And there was Brown Limper Staffor and Lars Thorenson. They had come up on the plateau with a ground car and were standing there. The very people he wanted to see.

Terl walked over to them.

Instead of saying "Goodbye" or even "Nice to have known you," Brown Limper Staffor said, "I don't see Tyler."

Terl stopped before him. Brown Limper was all bundled up in some kind of expensive fur. Snow was falling upon his hair and collar. His eyes looked feverishly overbright.

"Oh, he'll be here," said Terl. "He'll be here."

Terl looked down at Brown Limper's feet. There was a case there, a fat case about three feet long. Aha! Terl stooped and before Brown Limper or Lars could stop him picked up the case and, with a cuff of his paw, broke the locks.

A Thompson submachine gun! So he was right to distrust this animal. One shot from this thing during a firing could blow up the platform!

Terl took the weapon by the barrel and with his paws bent it in a half-circle. He threw it aside. "That was not nice," said Terl. "You could have blown up the whole place!"

Brown Limper didn't seem upset. His eyes still looked furtive.

Terl took Lars' belt gun, took the cartridge canister out of it, and threw it fifty feet away. "No firing!" said Terl, waggling a cautionary claw in front of their faces. Did Brown Limper have something else? Terl wondered. He looked quite unhinged but not about the guns.

"Here," said Terl, in a cajoling tone of voice, "here is a nice present to make it up to you."

He handed Brown Limper the thoroughly wrapped ultimate bomb. It weighed about eighty pounds, and as Brown Limper took it, he almost dropped it. Terl, in some apprehension, caught it before it could fall. Terl managed a smile as he restored it to Brown Limper.

"It's a nice gift," said Terl. "Open it when I'm gone and you'll find the answer to your most golden dreams. Something to remember me by." No danger in giving it to them: it would take them an hour to get the wrapper off. Then one lift of the lid and bang—no planet!

Terl patted Brown Limper on the head. He glanced at his watch. Still plenty of time. He walked over toward the platform. Captunk Arf Moiphy called his men to attention. Terl marched on by.

With a bold and martial step, Terl walked to the console.

He reached down and closed the bus bar on the atmosphere armor cable. Snow flew up all along its length. Good! He was now safe! A solid wall enclosed the console and platform and beyond that a solid wall of armed bodies.

He glanced at his watch. He had plenty of time. He walked over to the baggage and kicked his own kit into the pile. The Brigantes had brought quite a mound of air bottles for themselves.

General Snith, militarily dressed in a buffalo coat, his "diamond" in his cap, his crossbelts jammed with poisoned arrows, gave him a chest-pound salute. But he asked, "You gonna change de money fer tsure?" He pointed to a huge mound of money, Brown Limper notes.

"Absolutely," Terl reassured him. "Credits go where credit is due! Besides, you have me hostage, don't you?"

Snith was reassured.

And speaking of hostages, Terl leaned over the long bundle and opened the top of it. Black, glaring eyes pierced him. He beckoned to the Brigante so assigned and the man pushed an air mask on the face and shoved the bottle onto the chest. He buckled the bottle on. He had almost gotten bit!

Terl looked at his watch. The time was coming up. He walked over to the console.

He moved the toggle switch in the upper left-hand corner to the up position. He threw on the activating bus bar. The console's top buttons glowed.

Terl sat there counting down the seconds. Then he punched in the long-since-memorized coordinates. He checked his watch for the exact instant. He punched the firing button.

He reached down and activated the ten-minute time bomb.

The wires began to build up a hum.

Out of the tail of his eye he saw a man rise up beyond the Brown Limper car. Somebody jumping up. Somebody in a radiation suit. Terl looked hard and suddenly realized it looked like and must be the animal.

Ha! Brown Limper had gotten his Tyler after all.

Terl walked over to the center of the platform.

The hum was building up. What joy to think of being safe on Psychlo in just under three minutes!

— 2 —

Brown Limper Staffor had seethed when Terl discovered the submachine gun. But the sight of the barrel being bent almost double had caused him to hold his peace. This huge monster was *strong*.

So he stood there and accepted the gift. Actually it must be gold, it was so heavy. He had no qualms about accepting gold even if it looked like a bribe. He had earned it. But his mind was only slightly on all that. He was still looking avidly for Tyler.

But he decided he would wait until Terl was safely at that console.

He saw Captunk Arf Moiphy salute. Saw the Brigantes draw up and begin to take poisoned arrows from the crossbelts. Saw the performance on the platform. Terl had somebody else there in the bundle. Tyler? No, it couldn't be Tyler or Terl would have called out. Maybe it *was* Tyler. Maybe Terl was double-crossing him! No, it couldn't be Tyler. Who was it? But yes, it might be

Tyler. They put an air mask on whoever it was. They meant to take somebody to Psychlo!

No, it couldn't be Tyler.

But maybe it was.

When the snow had jumped up from the ground, Brown Limper had been slightly startled. But nothing had happened except that Terl went over to that bundle.

Ah, finally Terl was going back to the console. Brown Limper had been told the wires would begin to hum.

He would wait for that.

It was hard to see in this snow. The white glare of it and the swirls in the wind gusts kept blanking out things.

But he could listen.

He thought he heard the hum start. He couldn't be sure. The wind was making sounds and that Brigante mob was yelling goodbyes to General Snith. Brown Limper thought he had better wait until Terl walked back to the platform center before he moved.

In the back of the car was another submachine gun. Brown Limper had thought of everything.

The moment Terl reached the middle of the platform, Brown Limper would dive into the back of the car, get the Thompson submachine gun, load it, and race to that platform edge and spray the whole place. It must be Tyler in that bundle!

Brown Limper stood there, holding the "gift," waiting for Terl to walk away from the console. The yells of the Brigante tribe and the whir of the wind made it impossible to tell whether the hum had started. He would have to be sure.

He had better wait for the last moment. Then Terl couldn't rush off the platform to stop him.

He didn't hear the thud of running feet behind him.

Suddenly two hands reached out and grabbed at the "gift!" A radiation-masked face and an air mask under the radiation mask.

Then he saw the blonde beard through all that leaded glass.

Tyler was right on top of him!

"Run!" yelled the face.

The hands whipped the "gift" away from Brown Limper.

"Run for your life!" came from the half-hidden face.

Then the man turned and, carrying the package, sprinted toward the hangar side of the compound. The figure was growing thinner in the snow, hard to see.

"Shoot him!" screamed Brown Limper to Lars.

He whirled. Lars was running away! He was already a hundred feet away and half-hidden in snow flurries. He was running as hard as he could toward Denver.

But then something registered with Brown Limper. That voice! He knew Tyler's voice. Even through masks and shields he did not think it was Tyler's voice. It had sounded Swedish.

But Tyler must be around. Around someplace.

Brown Limper tore his way to the door of the car to get the other gun. The door on that side was locked.

With the whimper of despair, Brown Limper raced around the car. He had to get to that other gun.

And even as he went, above the snow, above the yells, he heard Tyler's voice from the platform. Unmistakable! He must hurry.

— 3 —

Dwight rose cautiously just behind the lip of the ravine. He was dressed in a radiation camouflage suit with an air mask behind its lead glass faceplate.

As Terl first entered the platform area, Dwight held the mine radio close to his shield glass and said, "First alert!"

Dwight had been chosen as officer of the outside raiders because he could be depended upon to follow orders exactly, without deviation, and as one of the lode mine crew chiefs, he could handle men.

They had lain since shortly after midnight in the lead coffins buried at spaced intervals around the platform's perimeter. The coffins had been positioned long since by Ker and cadets in the night while they laid the armor cable. They had been covered with dirt and now were also covered by a layer of snow.

It had been no trick to slip in last night. The Brigante guards, drunk on drugged whiskey as they had been every night for two months, had detected nothing.

Dwight had a streak of superstition. It all had gone almost too smoothly. Jonnie was inside that atmosphere cable area, buried in a coffin just at the edge of the firing platform. Fire from outside would not hit him: they had tested that. But the thought of Jonnie in there, alone with those savage beasts, made Dwight numb. He had tried to get Jonnie to let somebody else do it but Jonnie had said no, he would not put a man to that risk: somebody had to be in there to shut off the armor cable, use a remote control to complete the action of the crane, and lower an armored dome down over the console to protect it. The crane could not get the dome cover through the atmosphere armor unless it was shut off. Something about a switch position that had to be determined at the firing, a switch that might automatically shift once the humming stopped. And somebody had to cut the cables away from the console. Dwight had wanted to send three men in—Jonnie had said that many wouldn't fit in the dome with the console.

Terl had now walked to the console. Dwight said, "Second alert!" into the mine radio. The third would come when Terl pushed the firing button. Action would be called when he was at the platform center and the wires had begun to hum.

Dwight and his team had only one and a half minutes to do their entire job. They had drilled and drilled in Africa. But one never knew.

The snow flurries made the visibility sporadic. But he could see what he had to see. My god, that was an awful lot of Brigantes! They were a solid line all around the perimeter of the platform, backs right up against the atmosphere ionization cable. They looked lumpy in buffalo coats. They were protecting their bow strings but their crossbelts bristled with poisoned arrows.

Dr. Allen had briefed them on those arrows. The poison was slow but deadly. It caused the nervous system to speed up faster and faster until it killed. He had developed an antidotal serum for it. He had given them all a small shot of it, but he said any wound would need speedy treatment all the same. They each carried a small ampule of the serum. Dwight hoped it worked.

Then he saw that there would be seven Brigantes on the platform. Was that the one they called General Snith? And a squad? They had not counted on that. What a fool Snith must be to permit himself to be fired to Psychlo. But Jonnie! He wouldn't have added that into the plans. Was it too late for Dwight to do something? His orders were very positive. To do nothing but his job.

They had somebody else on the platform, bound. Who was

that? My god, Jonnie's plan wouldn't work! He would be in there all but defenseless! Dwight gritted his teeth. His orders were to do his job only. He would. But he had a feeling of despair for Jonnie.

The Brigante tribe was noisy and cheering over there by the morgue. They were no problem. Dwight turned his attention back to Terl. The Psychlo pushed the firing button.

"Third alert!" said Dwight into the mine radio.

The weapons they would use would not interrupt the firing. They had tested them. They also had nuclear weapons in case Psychlos came in on the platform afterward from Psychlo.

Terl walked over to the center of the platform. He halted. The humming had begun, heard above the shouting and wind. Dwight heard Jonnie's voice in that enclosure. That was not on schedule.

Dwight would do his job.

"Action!" barked Dwight into the mine radio.

Thirty Scots threw off their coffin lids. Twenty-five hit their igniters. One made ready to rush for the crane. Four were up to form a reserve.

Flash! In a ragged outer ring, pointing in at the massed Brigantes, twenty-five Russian flame throwers spewed out their deadly orange spray.

Like twenty-five hoses the roaring inferno slashed into the Brigantes.

"For Allison!" came a Scot battle cry.

"For Bittie!"

"Scotland forever!"

Dwight hit the button of a planted loudspeaker. It was a recording of charging, trumpeting elephants, the sound that would bring terror to the Brigantes.

The mercenaries surged forward, trying to get their bows into action. Scything flame shriveled the bowstrings. The Brigantes were drawing bayonets to charge.

The tribe by the morgue screamed, adding to the din. They turned and ran with all their might out into the plain, trampling one another as they sought to get away.

A Scot had a flame out. A group of Brigantes were charging him with bayonets.

"Cover Andrew!" barked Dwight.

The Scots on either side of the dead flame thrower widened

their arcs. Andrew had a claymore out. He cut down the Brigante officer and then he himself went down. Two of the reserves hacked their way into the mess with lochaber axes and slaughtered the Brigantes stabbing at Andrew.

Dwight glanced at his watch. Fifty-eight seconds to go.

Flame throwers were sending boiling flame into Brigantes. Their buffalo coats and monkey-skin suits were balls of fire. Another attempted charge by them.

Dwight tried to see through the flame and snow. The crane. It should be moving now!

Yes, the operator had gotten to it. One of the reserves was protecting him with a flame thrower.

They had buried the dome cover for the console in the ground with the cable already attached. It was evidently frozen in. It was made of the armor from a discarded tank. The bottom of it was equipped with plane skids which would anneal to the metal on which the console sat and seal it.

Dwight could see the top of the crane dipping. The operator was rocking it to break the dome loose from the ground.

There it came.

It rose with a rush. It swung. The operator steadied it.

Brigantes were rushing the crane. The Scot there blasted at them with a roaring flame thrower.

The operator was coolly swinging the dome over to position. It could not go further than the atmosphere armor screen. Dwight could see the operator throw the controls over to remote. Jonnie had the remote there in the cage and would have to do the rest of it if and when he shut off the current to the armor cable.

Dwight tried to see what was happening on the platform. Snow flurries, smoke, and roaring arcs of savage orange flame barred his view. He was sure Jonnie needed help. He gritted his teeth and did his job.

Here and there along the perimeter the flame throwers were now off. Changing bottles? No. The Brigantes within their reach were burning piles. Black, greasy smoke was rising up through the white snow.

Dwight glanced at his watch. They had time. His own cue to dive back into cover was when Jonnie turned off the cable and the dome began to lower. Then he was under orders to get back in protective cover in the coffin.

Scots were mopping up with flame throwers. Two of the reserves were speedily putting Andrew in his coffin. They were shoving wound pads hastily under the radiation suit.

A Brigante rose out of a pile of corpses. He had a bayonet. He charged. A thrown dirk hit him. A flame thrower erupted and he went forward as a spinning ball of fire.

The crane operator was out of his crane and running back to his coffin foxhole.

"Ten seconds to withdraw!" said Dwight into the mine radio.

It was suddenly quiet except for flame crackles and the wind. Nothing was moving in the Brigante ranks but smoke and small tongues of fire. Allison and Bittie had been avenged.

The fleeing remains of the tribe were way out on the plain, still running.

The smoke was very thick. Dwight could not see what was happening on the platform.

Numbers were coming back to him from his mine radio; a number was a signal that a man was back in his lead coffin in a foxhole and had fastened the lid down from within. Dwight was checking them off. All reported except Andrew and he knew he had been put inside his coffin. Dwight hoped it wasn't his coffin for real.

Dwight couldn't see the platform for the smoke.

He watched the crane.

Wires were still humming. They must all be under cover before the recoil, Jonnie had said.

Dwight looked at his watch. The armor curtain had not gone off. The top of the crane had not begun to move.

He was in an agony of indecision. But he could not get inside that cage with the atmosphere armor curtain still on. He wanted to disobey orders. He knew Jonnie was in trouble for the curtain had not gone off on time.

But he had been chosen because he would obey orders. Time was up. The humming had almost ended. Dwight crawled back to his coffin foxhole, scrambled in, and fastened down the lid from within.

— 4 —

When he heard, "Alert three!" from the mine radio in his belt, Jonnie had slid out of the coffin buried close by the platform and inside the atmosphere armor curtain. He was dressed in a camouflage radiation suit and wore an air mask under its face shield. His pouch was hanging from a wide belt. He was armed with three kill-clubs, a dirk, and a flame thrower. He had a couple of other things for contingencies.

He had not expected the Brigantes to be inside on the platform. Six guards and General Snith! He hadn't thought even a Brigante would be crazy enough to let himself be fired to Psychlo. Money! They had bundles of money on the platform.

They were all looking at Terl. Terl was turning away from pushing the firing button. The Brigantes had not noticed Jonnie thirty feet away and slightly behind them.

Well, it would not matter. Jonnie started to ignite the flame thrower.

And then he saw a movement. They had something in a long bundle. The end of it was open. They had somebody there. A hostage they were taking to Psychlo? Gray hair, the scrap of a cloak.

Sir Robert!

Jonnie had to abandon any thought of using the flame thrower. It would kill Sir Robert as well!

Terl was walking easily and confidently back from the console to the platform center. The wires were humming. He halted, thunderstruck. Just a moment ago he had seen what he had thought was the animal, *outside*. Way over by the car.

And here he was inside the armor curtain!

Was the curtain off? No, he could see it shimmer through the snow. How had the animal gotten through it?

Just as Terl was about to charge, he saw the animal drop a long rod weapon he carried. The animal's hand darted toward a pouch at his belt.

Jonnie withdrew the contracts Terl had signed. He skimmed

them to the platform center, the red seals glaring in the falling snow. Unmistakably the contracts Terl had signed!

Jonnie shouted as loud as he could to be heard through masks and faceplates: "Don't forget to record these on Psychlo!"

Terl was horror-struck. The last thing he wanted to appear on Psychlo's platform were those phony contracts! Terl started to dive toward them and pick them up. He collided with Snith just as the general sought to give orders to his bowmen.

Reaching down, Jonnie picked up a beryllium ultimate bomb. He had intended to just throw it on the platform. It was wrapped with a cord. The golden glow of its metal, its size, and its hexagonal shape made it totally recognizable. The cord was not a fuse. The fuse was inside it set for eight minutes by a timing device on the top. It had an access plate in the bottom that was purposely jammed.

Jonnie touched the igniter he still held to the carrying-cord end. Two poisoned arrows whizzed by him.

"Grenade!" shouted Jonnie.

He pitched the eighty-pound weight straight at Terl. It struck the Psychlo a glancing blow and bounced down under his feet.

One glimpse of a lit grenade, their own favorite weapon, caused the Brigantes to run.

At that moment trumpeting elephants sounded outside. The Brigantes hit the atmosphere armor curtain and were thrown back from it.

Terl took one look at the bomb and any thought he had about papers fled as his horror turned into terror.

It was the bomb! But it had a time fuse. How had the animal gotten it away from Brown Limper, unwrapped it, and changed the fuse all in no time at all?

But Terl knew what he had to do. He had to get rid of it fast!

He was about to pitch it off the platform when the Brigantes came thudding back in recoil off the curtain. He knew that if he threw it, the bomb would just bounce back.

The wires were humming!

Terl knew he had to get that access plate off and remove the core and do it fast! He could even see the time fuse closing.

He crouched down and began to claw at the access plate in the bottom. It was stuck! He fought with it.

Jonnie sprinted past Terl. He had to get Sir Robert and get him over to the console.

A Brigante was up on one knee. A poisoned arrow slapped past Jonnie's head.

Jonnie dragged Sir Robert clear of the long case. His hands and feet were tied. Sir Robert was shouting something, something like, "Leave me and save yourself!"

All chaos had broken out beyond the curtain. There were Scot battle cries, and the roar of stampeding elephants.

Flame splashed against the other side of the atmosphere armor. The falling snow, even inside the platform, was converting to rain. Heat!

Terl was clawing at the access plate. He had no annealing knife to cut the metal. He was trying to scrape a circle and cut it with his claws. He was bellowing in frustration and adding to the uproar.

Two Brigantes charged Jonnie. He let go of Sir Robert, snatched a kill-club from his belt, and struck twice. They went down.

He was able to drag Sir Robert a bit further. It was a long way to that console!

Another Brigante was up. Jonnie threw the kill-club. It hit the mercenary's forehead and his head went back at an incredible angle.

Snith was up, shouting and pointing at Jonnie.

The din was deafening outside this cage.

A Brigante tackled Jonnie in the legs. Jonnie got another kill-club and smashed his brains out. He got Sir Robert a little further. The Scot was heavy!

Snith was trying to get the last two of his guards to fire. Their bowstrings were too wet. They snatched out bayonets and charged.

Jonnie threw a kill-club and one Brigante was catapulted backward. The other came on. Jonnie took his last kill-club from his belt. He parried the bayonet and struck the Brigante alongside the head. The kill-club flew out of his hand.

He got Sir Robert a bit closer to the console. He was trying to pick Sir Robert up and carry him.

For a moment Jonnie's back was turned. General Snith snatched a poison arrow out of his crossbelt and rushed.

The heavy impact of the body hit Jonnie's pouch. General Snith raised the poisoned arrow and drove it into Jonnie's upper left arm, drove it in through the radiation suit, and deep into the flesh.

Jonnie went down. He rolled, pulling a dirk. He came up and drove the knife into Snith's heart.

The pain of the wound was savage. Jonnie grasped the arrow shaft and pulled it straight out. But he knew the damage was done. The ferocious fire in the wound was almost more than he could bear.

He gritted his teeth and rallied his strength. They had said it was a slow poison. He still might have time to save Sir Robert and the console.

He grabbed the hilt of the knife and tried to yank it out of Snith's heart. It was stuck. He looked at Terl.

The Psychlo, still raving, was clawing at the access plate. Tearing his claw points he was actually cutting into the hard metal to make a circle and remove the core.

It was quieter outside. Dwight's voice came out of the mine radio at his belt, "Ten seconds to withdraw!"

Jonnie knew he was late.

The wires were still humming.

Jonnie made himself concentrate. He still had a job to do. He could feel his heart revving up.

He got a hand under Sir Robert's armpit and dragged him through the slush. He got to the console. He knew it had a bomb in it he would have to disarm fast. But he tucked Sir Robert in close to the console so the dome coming down would not amputate his arms or legs.

He glanced at the console. The switch was in the up position. It would have to be in the down position when next this was fired. He wished he had time to tell somebody.

He fumbled for his remote control box. There was broken glass in his pouch. His arm felt like it was on fire. That broken glass was the serum ampule! He had no serum.

The remote shook. No, it was his hand shaking. He threw the switch and swung the crane. No. He had to turn off the armor curtain first. He was getting flashes of blackness. His heart was beating faster and faster.

The armor curtain! He crawled to the bus bar and got it off. Back at the console he looked up at the dome. He operated the remote, positioning the dome exactly above them so it would come down correctly. He threw the switch to lower it. It was coming down too slowly. The cables must be stiff. He could not help that.

He got a hatchet out of his belt for the cables. He would have to be ready to hack them off the instant the humming stopped.

Jonnie lost track of time. He could still hear the humming of the wires.

He looked toward Terl over on the platform. The monster seemed to have succeeded in opening the access plate. He was handling the bomb with great care, extracting the heavy metal core.

Suddenly Jonnie knew what Terl was going to do. He would throw that core at him. It would travel like a bullet! It could go straight through him.

Abruptly Jonnie saw something else.

Brown Limper!

He was rushing forward with a Thompson submachine gun in his hands. He had gone through where the armor curtain had been at the far end of the platform. He was trying to get so close to Jonnie he couldn't miss.

The dome was not yet down.

Terl had the core in his paw now. He was going to throw it at Jonnie.

It was quieter. There was only smoke and falling snow and the creak of the cables lowering the dome. Jonnie pointed at Brown Limper.

"Terl! He's going to shoot!" he shouted.

Terl spun around and saw Brown Limper. He saw him raising the Thompson to aim it. One shot at this moment would shatter the firing.

Terl threw. He threw with all his strength.

The core hit Brown Limper in the side. It ripped through and hit his spine. The Thompson clattered to the ground.

Brown Limper fell in a jerking tangle of arms and legs, screaming: "Damn you, Tyler! Damn you!" He laid still.

The wires were still humming.

Terl yelled at Jonnie, "I still win, rat brain!" He knew better than to move now.

Jonnie's head was pounding. His heart was going too fast. But he could shout back. And he felt he had to pin Terl there, distract him.

"Those coffins are full of sawdust! They were changed in your bedroom this morning!" shouted Jonnie.

Terl whirled to look at them.

"And the gold never went to Psychlo! We changed those too!" yelled Jonnie.

Terl opened his mouth to shout.

The platform cargo shimmered. The coffins full of sawdust shimmered. The Brigante corpses on the platform shimmered. Terl shimmered. And it was all gone. The platform was empty, clean even of slush.

The humming stopped. Jonnie took his hatchet and slammed the blade down across the cables. It wasn't a full severance. He struck twice more. All the cables parted.

Things were going blacker. No, it was the dome.

The reworked plane skids on the bottom of it hit the metal. Jonnie reached out to the dome interior and pulled closed the locking lever which annealed them to the metal the console sat on.

It was very dark.

He felt his time sense must have gone out and then a fleeting thought that maybe Terl had extended the time for his own firing.

Jonnie had had a small mine lamp in his pouch. He made an effort to reach it. His whole body was beginning to shake as if everything was drawn too taut.

A voice was talking to him. It was Sir Robert. "Hurry. Cut my hands loose."

Jonnie had the hatchet. He made himself feel about for Sir Robert's hands. The blade was dull, the cord was resistant.

Then he remembered with a surge of panic there must be a time bomb under that console. It would blow Sir Robert to bits. He dropped the hatchet and put his hand to the console side. It was terribly heavy. He only had one working arm but he put his agonizing shoulder against the metal. He got the bottom of the console lifted.

He fished along the lower edges. Then a little higher. He felt it. It was taped on. Working with one hand he got it loose and pulled it out. He let the console tip back in place. In the dark he extracted the fuse from it.

Jonnie felt he was going unconscious. His heart was revving up. Faster and faster.

He had one more thing to do. The switch. The position of the switch.

Jonnie felt like he was being torn to pieces by his nerves pulling tight.

"Sir Robert! Tell them the switch . . . the switch has to be in a down position . . . a down position for the next . . . ."

The outside of the dome was struck a blow so hard the whole platform rocked!

It was as though a dozen earthquakes had hit at once. As though the planet had been torn apart.

Jonnie stiffened out into blackness. He no longer heard the chaos going on outside.

— 5 —

About an hour before the firing, the orbiting group of ships had just come over the horizon that put them into position to view the American compound.

A small Hawvin spycraft in the orbit ahead of them had already reported some activity there earlier in the day. The report had only said that in the middle of the night a group had been seen on infrascreens entering the compound area and that the group had vanished, leaving only the usual sprawled about and apparently asleep night guards.

The scanners of the orbiting combined force were now picking up something unusual down there on the approaching horizon. There seemed to be a more than normal number of people at the site.

There was a local snowstorm in progress down there and infrabeams were a bit blurred.

The attention of the combined force was not yet fixed on the compound as it shortly would be. The command network of viewscreens was occupied by an interview that was going on.

When Half-Captain Rogodeter Snowl had gone back to Tolnep for reinforcements he had contacted his uncle, Quarter-Admiral Snowleter. Rogodeter believed in keeping profit in the family. The quarter-admiral had come along gladly with a flotilla of five ships, the largest of which was the Terrify-class battle-plane-launching capital ship *Capture*. Snowleter had not become a quarter-admiral without some skill and he had brought part of that skill with him: a reporter.

Roof Arsebogger considered himself the ace reporter of the Tolnep "Midnight Fang." Even among news media of other systems, the "Fang" was envied as the very epitome of inaccuracy, corruption, and biased news. It always printed exactly what the government wanted even while pretending to be antigovernment. And Roof Arsebogger enjoyed the reputation of being the most poisonous reporter on a staff that specialized in them.

The interview was being conducted by Arsebogger on the *Capture* and was addressed to Half-Captain Rogodeter Snowl. It was just a background interview and things were dull so others were listening in. They had various opinions. The quarter-admiral was not well liked. Other commanders contested Snowleter's contention that he was the senior commander and therefore the head of the combined force. And that he was the uncle of the even less popular Rogodeter Snowl made him even less acceptable. They detested Snowl.

"Now getting back to the man on this counterfeit one-credit bank note," Arsebogger was saying, "would you say that he was dishonest?"

"Oh, worse," replied Snowl.

"Would the description, 'He is a known pervert,' fit him?"

"Oh, worse," replied Snowl.

"Good, good," said Arsebogger. "We must keep this to a totally factual interview, you understand. How would 'He steals babies and drinks their blood,' do?"

"Fine, fine," said Snowl, "exactly."

"I think you mentioned," said Arsebogger, "when you filed dispatches, that you had several times met this . . . what is his name . . . this defiler of established governments . . . er . . . Tyler? Yes. That you met him in personal combat."

Other commanders were hearing this and Rogodeter had not thought it would become public property. He had reckoned without the publicity hunger of his uncle. "Not exactly," said Rogodeter quickly. "I meant to say that I tried but he always ran away."

Quarter-Admiral Snowleter's voice came from the background behind Arsebogger, "But he won't get away again!"

"Now in your opinion, Rogodeter, do you truly think this is 'the one'?"

The small gray man had been watching all this on his viewscreens. He detested reporters and this Roof Arsebogger had earned his particular dislike: the reporter's fangs were stained nearly black, there were blotches of some disease on his face, and one could almost smell his unwashed condition over the viewscreen.

Unfortunately or fortunately, whichever way you looked at it, his courier ship had come in just yesterday. It had brought lots of odds and ends but among them was the clear-cut statement that the *one* had *not* been found.

Along with that, there was a prize addition. The one hundred million credits originally offered by the Hawvin Interrelated Confederation of Systems had been doubled by the Bolbod Equality Empire. The small gray man did not know what was going on in other sectors, much less other universes, but he could suppose that the same mad scramble was in progress.

The courier dispatch box contents, when viewed as a whole, said that these were indeed very strange and troublesome times, that a problem like this had not existed in any past history they were aware of. And there had been some hints about the vital necessity of his presence "where he could do some good" instead of out here sailing around "a twelfth-rate rim star's only planet." There was no direct criticism, of course. There were just hints, an undertone.

But actually, it would not matter whether he were home or not. Unless some solution presented itself, the chaos that was going to ensue would be so vast that neither he nor others could hope to control it.

He was going on listening absently to this asinine reporter interview an asinine military mind when his bridge buzzer sounded and his watch officer's face appeared on the screen.

"Your Excellency," said the watch officer, "there is something going on down in that capital city area. The infrabeams are scrambling. We cannot tell what is happening. There are no clear pictures."

The "interview" cut off suddenly. Other commanders seemed to have noticed it.

The Hockner commander appeared on the small gray man's screen. "Your Excellency, I believe you said that was the central seat of government. We are getting pictures of massed troops and recordings of excessive heat. In your opinion, is this political?"

The small gray man looked at his own screens of the area.

Bad as they had been before, due to a local storm, they were incredibly bad now. One couldn't make out a thing. Some sort of interference was blasting them off the air.

Wait! That jagged traveling line on the screen.

A teleportation trace.

Hastily the small gray man thought of an answer. "I believe," he said conservatively to the Hockner, "that it is probably political in some connected way. All the information that—"

His screens almost caved in!

There was a tremendous flare, then nothing.

A squawk horn was going. "Screen overload! Screen overload!"

Good heavens, you never got *that* except in a major battle area.

The small gray man rushed to his port as he knew the commanders must be doing.

He stared down.

There was a babble of incredulity on the remaining voice channels from the other ships.

The storm there had almost been exploded away.

A fireball was climbing heavenward. Spreading, rolling masses of coiling smoke and flame were rising to incredible heights.

Daylight was dimmed by the flash.

It looked like the world had been torn apart!

— 6 —

Sir Robert hardly waited for the earth to cease rumbling. He did not even ask himself what it could be. He had only one idea in mind: to get his hands loose and help Jonnie.

He had seen the arrow strike Jonnie. He had seen the lad pull it out. Sir Robert knew it was a poisoned arrow and he had some idea of the consequences. After such venom entered, physical exertion would spread it all through the body much more quickly. And Jonnie had been moving violently.

When the hatchet had cut the cord, it had not gone all the way through. Sir Robert strained every sinew to part the remaining strands. It was dark as pitch in this dome. He could not even see where Jonnie had fallen or which way he lay. But these confines were very close. He could and must get to him! Even though it was probably already too late.

He almost tore the skin off his wrists. The cord parted!

In feverish haste he reached out, felt around, and found Jonnie's arm, the wounded arm. Sir Robert closed his huge hand around it just below the armpit and held it tight, shutting off the blood flow.

The hatchet had fallen here somewhere. The rocking must have sent it skidding. Moaning with urgency, Sir Robert felt around the metal floor, under the console, under Jonnie. Suddenly his fingers contacted its handle in a corner.

He got hold of the head just back of the blade. He tried to cut through Jonnie's radiation suit sleeve.

It was so hard to work with just one hand.

And in the dark.

He was also trying desperately not to cut into Jonnie's flesh.

He got a fold of the suit and sawed through it. The hatchet had been dulled and chipped while cutting the cables. The leaded sleeve material was very resistant. He was not making it. Not with one hand.

Suddenly he remembered that Jonnie always had thongs in his pouch. It lay under his body but he got it loose. He reached in and found broken glass that sliced his fingers. He paid it no attention.

He found the end of a long thong and drew it out.

He put a piece of twisted mine lamp metal under the arm and against the artery and wrapped it around and in place with the thong. He drew the thong as tightly as he could and tied it.

Now he could work.

He cut the radiation suit sleeve away just below the tourniquet. He stripped it off the arm. The cloth was matted with blood. The arm was slippery with it.

It was hard to find the wound because of the blood.

He found it.

He took the edge of the hatchet blade and cut an "X" across the wound hole.

He got out of his air mask and put his mouth to the wound. Anything to get all the poison out that he could.

Time and time again he sucked the wound dry and spat. The

taste of the blood was stinging and bitter. There was venom in it all right

Finally he thought the blood was cleaner. He did not know how deep the arrow had gone but there was no way to probe.

He worked the flesh of the arm in a way he thought would force more poison up to the surface of the wound. He again applied his mouth to it. Yes, there was more bitterness. Then it seemed cleaner.

Sir Robert felt around Jonnie's belt for a wound compress pack. He didn't find one. Well, the bleeding was slightly less now. Maybe no vein had been hit. It was probably better without a compress.

He felt the pulse of Jonnie's other wrist.

Devils in hell! It was *racing!* The pulse was way above anything he could count.

Jonnie's body was stretched taut. There was a tremble in the limbs.

Sir Robert, in the dark, tried to find the ampule in Jonnie's pouch. Planning dictated there should be one. That broken glass might have come from the mine lamp. He found the bottom half of the ampule.

Although he couldn't see what he was doing and it was just a gesture more than anything else, he opened the wound and upended the broken bottle over it, close to it, pouring in anything that might be in it. He held and massaged the flesh in such a way as to let any liquid drop lower in the wound. It was probably just his imagination, he thought, but the arm area felt slippery.

He felt the pulse. It was racing faster if anything, and the limbs were trembling more.

Had he done all he could? He couldn't think of anything more.

The air was getting used up in this close space and he put his air mask back on. Jonnie's radiation mask was in the way and he took it off and checked the air mask under it. The flutter valve was moving slightly but very rapidly. In briefing, they were supposed to put in a new bottle just before the first alert If Jonnie had done that, he had two hours of air.

Sir Robert sank back. He worked the bonds off his ankles and then straightened Jonnie's body out and raised Jonnie's head to his own knee to keep the head higher. Double devils in hell but the limbs trembled!

He thought the situation over. He had not been in on the last briefings; he did not know whether there had been anything he should know now.

Bitterly, Sir Robert cursed his own stupidity. Since things had been going so smoothly with the Academy move, one night he had walked by himself—like a daft sheep—to a knoll to look at the compound. Not really any purpose in it. Just a review of a field where a battle would soon be fought. And Brigantes had grabbed him. They must have been watching him for days.

They had trussed him up and kept him in a cavern. They had tried to interrogate him and had beaten him. His nose was broken and full of dried blood even now. But he was too old a campaigner to talk. He did not know what they wanted with him until they brought him into the compound area and dumped him.

He had not really thought they would take him to Psychlo until they put the air mask on him. The thought had made even him sweat. He had an excellent example of how the Psychlos interrogated—Allison.

Sir Robert had been braced to stand up to it. He had known of this attack but he could not see how he could be fished out. A flame thrower was supposed to sweep that platform clean.

And then this lad had thrown his flame thrower down and attacked! It looked like such a hopeless effort.

Because of Sir Robert, this lad had thrown away his own chances. His own life?

Sir Robert felt the pulse again. Good god, how long could a pulse race like that without a person dying?

He began to get uneasy about the silence outside. There was supposed to be a standby rescue crew deep in the old compound, waiting with flatbeds and planes with both Dr. Allen and Dr. MacKendrick. All in radiation suits and air masks.

It was so silent in here. Was that a slight crackling sound?

Jonnie would have had a mine radio. Sir Robert felt around Jonnie's belt and then scrabbled around the floor.

He had it! A crackling sound was coming out of it.

It was live, but no voices. Were they all dead out there?

He pressed the transmit button. "Hello. Hello." Not clever to say more. Who knew who might be out there?

Silence.

"Hello, hello." Then he thought he better give them a location. Not clever but he had to do it. "Console talking."

Was that the click of a transmit switch?

Then a voice in a whisper as though from far away, "Is that you, Sir Robert?"

It was Thor's voice! Sir Robert almost wept with relief.

"Thor?"

"Yes, Sir Robert."

"Thor, Jonnie is in here. He has had a poisoned arrow in him. You've got to get him out quick!"

Then Dr. Allen. "Sir, do you have a radiation suit on?"

"No, blast ye! I've no suit! To heil wi' thet! Get the lad out!"

"Sir, is his suit whole?"

Sir Robert realized he had torn the sleeve off. "No."

"I'm sorry, sir," whispered Dr. Allen over the mine radio, "to open that dome would kill you both. Have a little patience. We're trying to find out what we can do."

"Patience be domned!" stormed Sir Robert. His extreme urgency was throwing his speech into dialect. "Git th' lad oot!"

There was no answer. Sir Robert was about to start banging on the inside of the dome. Didn't they realize Jonnie was probably dying in here?

Then a tiny, piping, whispering voice took over. "Sir Robert?" It was one of the young Buddhist communicators. Probably the youngest they had. They had turned him over to a child!

The War Chief was about to thunder a damnation at them when the child whispered, speaking Psychlo, "Sir Robert, they're doing all they can, honored sir. It is pretty bad out here."

"Where are you?" demanded Sir Robert, reverting to Psychlo.

"I am just outside the dome, honored sir. My mine radio is inside my air mask under my radiation face shield. Excuse me that I whisper. We want nothing picked up by the visitors above. They can't hear this and the mine radio won't reach them."

"What are the visitors doing?"

"I don't know, Sir Robert. The snow clouds have closed in again. I see a pilot communicator. I will ask. I will be right back."

There was a long pause. Then the tiny, shrill little voice, "Sir? The pilot communicator says they have moved in orbit and are somewhere above us. They have this place being looked at. But our battle planes are standing by. Dunneldeen is up there. He wants to know how we are. How is Lord Jonnie?"

Sir Robert felt the shaking limbs of the body resting against him. But he knew morale was a factor up there in the sky. He could not tell them he thought Jonnie was dying. But Jonnie was still alive. "Tell them they should not worry just now."

The child was gone for a bit.

Then the tiny whispering voice, "The pilot communicator passed it on."

"What are they doing here to get us out?" demanded Sir Robert. What hell it was sitting here in the dark waiting. Jonnie's breathing was too rapid, too rapid by far!

"It's very bad out here, Sir Robert. Very bad. If you hear crackling, it's the power lines. They are all shorted out and burning on the ground, throwing sparks."

"Are there any casualties in the raiding party?"

"Oh, we don't know that, Sir Robert. The rescue team is using blade scrapers to uncover the coffins. I'm standing beside a hole where the platform used to be. It's smoking. Is it hot in there?"

Sir Robert had not noticed. Then he realized that the dome was warm to the touch. He said so.

"I'm told to tell you not to release the annealing lever on the dome skids. It is a wonder that they held. So don't release the lever. They will move the whole metal platform."

Somebody else was coming through on the channel. "Dwight? Can you hear us? Dwight!"

The tiny voice of the child said, "They found his coffin under the ravine bank just now. The bank caved in on it. They have found a forklift in the garage that operates and they are lifting the coffin. They are opening the lid. Dwight looks stunned but he is sitting up."

"They should be working on this dome!" raged Sir Robert.

"Oh, there's a whole other team working on it, honored sir. They are bringing a small crane out of the lower levels of the compound now. I see a man throwing clamps on the big crane. It is on its side and they have to lift it upright."

Sir Robert was getting an idea of what it was like out there.

"We were down in the sixteenth level," said the tiny voice. "The concussion was bad. It grabbed air out of the place but nothing was heard."

"Well, what was it? What happened?" demanded Sir Robert.

"We don't know, honored sir."

"They had some nuclear weapons on standby. Did they explode?"

There was a pause. The child had gone off somewhere. He came back. "No, sir. Thor says they are intact and he is awfully relieved. They didn't explode."

"Then what was it?"

"I am so very sorry, sir. None of us knows. Oh, here comes a blade scraper to loosen your platform so it can be lifted. The first one they had broke down after they got the fire out of it. I am told you must be patient, sir. We are doing all we can." Then, "They've got three more coffins out now." A pause. Then sorrow. "The one they call Andrew is dead."

The platform gave a jolt as a blade scraper seemed to pry under it. Sir Robert could hear a motor roar.

There was a shout of alarm and then a crash.

Then the piping little voice, "One of the poles fell in the crater. No one was hurt. Here comes your flatbed truck, sir."

"Flatbed!" barked Sir Robert. "It's supposed to be a plane! We're supposed to airlift out of here!"

There was a pause. The Buddhist communicator had gone off somewhere. He came back, "They have found a river to the south. It is the Purgatoire. The pilots told us."

Sir Robert felt Jonnie's pulse. Racing!

"I don't understand!" cried Sir Robert. "Time is everything here! I need serum! Can't we lift this dome and push some serum in here?"

"I am sorry, Sir Robert. The Purgatoire is one hundred twenty miles south of here. It's on an ancient man-highway." He rushed on so Sir Robert wouldn't interrupt. "They have mine pumps out. All our equipment and planes are contaminated. They have to be hosed down to get rid of radiation. When that's done they can open the dome."

Sir Robert clenched his fists. One hundred twenty miles! How long would that take?

The child must have been reading his thoughts. "I'm told they will drive very fast; they can on the ancient highway. Thor himself will drive your flatbed. They know how important it is. Your flatbed will be the first to leave. They have your crane standing up now."

There was another chunk from the blade scraper. Something under the platform seemed to tear loose.

"They have found fifteen coffins now," said the child. "The Scots in them were all alive except one. The coffin was blown into the air and smashed his skull. The lead on the outside of the coffins is all melted. The tops, I mean. They're hot to the touch and it's hard to handle them.''

There was a groan and a squeak as the crane hook on top of the dome tightened. They were being very careful from the sound of it not to drop the lower platform off.

The annealing skids held. Sir Robert felt them swinging in the air. Then a thump as they hit the top of the flatbed body. They picked it up again to let it drop down more squarely.

The child must still be standing on the platform overhanging. The tiny voice calmly came through. ''I can see better from here. It's not snowing. Way out on the plain over there I see some bodies. Must be the Brigante tribe. And I can see more coffins.'' He yelled to someone and must be pointing. ''The whole top of the old compound had blown off. It's wide open to the winds.''

Sir Robert was feeling Jonnie's pulse. Was it weaker?

''Thor is turning over to someone. He is climbing in your truck now. He says he's a good driver, don't worry. He will go as fast as he can. Excuse me but I am supposed to get in the cab and tie a seat belt.''

The flatbed started up with a roar. It jolted and banged over the uneven terrain. Sir Robert steadied Jonnie's head. Was he still breathing?

They hit the ancient man-highway. The engine revved into a high-pitched scream.

Sir Robert remembered Jonnie had had a watch. He tried to find its illumination button. The numbers were rolling.

They were driving so fast Sir Robert could hear the wind roaring outside the dome.

Time, time, time! Fifty minutes. Fifty-two minutes. Fifty-nine minutes!

The flatbed abruptly slowed. It jolted down some rough ground. It halted with a surge. It dropped to the earth.

The small piping voice again: ''We are at the riverbank. There is plenty of water. They are rigging a mine pipe. I must get away from the dome while it is washed down. I have to get washed down myself and so do the others. Then they will test with breathe-gas.''

Water was suddenly pounding against the dome. It roared and reverberated inside. The sound went all around. And then the water went all over the flatbed, apparently.

There was silence then. Then the piping voice. "Sir Robert? The truck with the small crane has arrived and has been washed down. So have I. Can you find the release lever in there? The one outside is bent."

Sir Robert had already located and indeed had been on the verge of pulling it an hour ago. He yanked it open. There was a roar and a clank as a crane was moved closer and connected. The dome lifted!

Murky daylight hit his eyes. Jonnie was lying there. Was he breathing?

The owner of the small voice was standing there, dripping water, visor and air mask off. He was about thirteen. "My name is Quong. Thank you for being so patient with me, Sir Robert. I was as worried as you."

Dr. Allen jumped up on the flatbed. He had a syringe in his hand and was grabbing Jonnie's arm. A woman nurse took over. She was holding Jonnie's head.

Sir Robert stood up unsteadily. He was drenched with sweat and the wind was cold.

He looked to the north.

The sky was glowing there.

"What's that?" he demanded.

Thor was there. Another member of the rescue team. More trucks were arriving further downstream.

Thor said, "That's Denver."

Sir Robert stared. They had just come from hell.

■

PART 25

— 1 —

For the first time in what had been a dreary, wearisome year, the small gray man was intense and interested. Hope, to which he had become a stranger, struggled to rise in his breast. Faint still, but it was there.

He had no real interest in the overpowering flash they had seen and almost did not bother to watch the roiling, filthy mass of violent cloud which rose above the earth.

It was that momentary trace on his screen. A teleportation firing! A trace he had never hoped to see again.

His immediate reaction was to see whether any of these military minds in the ships around had seen the flickering trace. He listened anxiously to their chatter.

"It was obviously a nuclear explosion," said the Bolbod. That settled it for him. He thrust his pugnacious face forward from his collar until it was almost visible as though daring somebody to dispute him.

The Tolnep half-captain made an immediate proposal to go down there and "really wipe the place out!"

The Hawvin speculated that the situation might be political and sought to pull the small gray man into it. But the small gray man was noncommittal: he was waiting to see what the others knew.

It was the Hockner super-lieutenant who summed it up. He put his monocle to his eye and sniffed at them. "You fellows are missing the point, rather!" he said. "Earlier intelligence told of a night raiding party vanishing in the area. Quite obviously, what we have just seen is the culmination of a political surface war. And I rather say that the government has now changed hands. As we know, the political scene was unstable: a priesthood earlier took over the planet, those yellow fellows in the robes. But they lost out, perhaps, and were driven back to that temple in their southern hemisphere.

"Some military group," he continued, "has now obliterated the former capital of the planet with nuclear weapons. With two separate revolts in just the last few months, the political climate is highly unstable and the time is ripe for a concerted attack by us."

"Yes!" rumbled the Bolbod. "We should go right down and smear them!"

The Jambitchow commander laughed lightly. "I am afraid you will have to count me out, gentle sirs. For the moment at least. Have you looked over there at that shoulder on the mountain peak—the one just to the west of the capital?"

There was silence and then some startled gasps.

Fifteen assorted battle planes and marine attack carriers were just now rising into view.

"It was an ambush!" said the half-captain.

"Bah," said the Bolbod. "Their firepower does not compare to even one of our major vessels!"

"They could be quite nasty," said the Jambitchow in his lilting voice.

There was a lull. Abruptly a face filled the viewer of the small gray man. It was Roof Arsebogger of the "Midnight Fang" calling from the Tolnep Terrify-class battle-plane-launching capital ship *Capture*.

"Your Excellency," drooled the reporter, "could we take advantage of this lull to get your personal reactions to this general situation?"

The small gray man was always calm, never emotional. All he said, and in a quiet voice, was, "Get out of my viewscreen."

"Oh, yes sir, Your Excellency. Indeed, sir, Your Excellency. At once, sir!" The diseased face vanished.

The small gray man made a grimace of distaste and then went back to considering the rest of them. Sooner or later they would come to some conclusion and take some concerted action. So far none had mentioned the teleportation trace. None of them was coming to any logical conclusion. Was each one privately hungering for prize money and keeping the rest in the dark? He would listen. It was always safe to listen.

The combined force had come alive and was changing position in orbit so as to maintain its location above this area. Flashes of engine exhausts were apparent in the sky around and a mutter of internal ship commands trickled through the channels. They were readying themselves.

It was the Hawvin who finally expressed something that must have been on all their minds—the rewards. "I have just worked out that they might be the one and don't know! There is a report here of a big Psychlo walking around a firing platform down there earlier this day."

"Well, if it was a Psychlo, don't you think he would have known?" said the Jambitchow commander.

This brought the Hockner super-lieutenant into it. "If the silly fool didn't know, he still might have been the one."

"But if he had been the one," said the Hawvin, "he would know. And he didn't know, so this isn't the one."

The quarter-admiral chipped in, tapping a tooth thoughtfully. "As the possibility now exists that they are the *one*—" other faces looked at him on their viewscreens, unable to figure out how he had gotten to this conclusion "—why then I see no reason to hold off further from simply raiding the place and gutting it and then clearing out.

"But on the other hand," continued the quarter-admiral in a brilliant spurt of logic, "if they are the one, then they constitute an extreme danger to us and should be raided. Either way, we simply raid it, divide up the loot, and clear out."

"And the reward money?" said the Jambitchow.

"Why," said the quarter-admiral, "we can best find out about that with an extensive interrogation of the resulting prisoners. As commander-in-chief of this combined force—"

There were instant protests. They agreed that in any event they should attack, gut the place, and clear out. But they didn't agree that the quarter-admiral was their commander-in-chief!

This produced a very sour effect on Quarter-Admiral Snowleter. Roof Arsebogger being aboard, he wanted to get the best possible image. This disagreement didn't fit with it and it made him quite cross.

The ensuing wrangling took considerable time and the small gray man returned to studying the scene below.

He had spotted a small convoy racing south. It was in two sections. The first, smaller section was streaking down what must have been an ancient highway. The second was larger and driving nearly as fast. At first it might appear that the second was chasing the first. But now they had come together without a fight on the banks of a river. They must all be the same group.

The stream was in spring flood, and shortly after the arrival of the first section, water pumps were placed and huge sprays of water were visible. They were spraying down their vehicles and themselves.

The action was not known to the small gray man so he consulted some reference books. Radiation! The way to get rid of contamination was copious use of water. The particles could be washed down and away due to their weight. Then that *had* been a nuclear blast. The Psychlos down through the ages had remorselessly suppressed anyone seeking to use such weapons. It was a nearly forgotten chapter of ancient warfare.

The small gray man had his communication officer tune in his viewscreens better. There was haze and overcast down there, a little difficult to see through. The city to the north had begun to burn quite fiercely, a glow under the clouds of spiring smoke. The wind was from the south and even though this left the river area where the trucks had arrived clearer, there was a lot of interference. Ah, it was that shorting power line to the old minesite. It made the viewscreen jump and distort.

It took some time for the group at the river to sort itself out. What were they? Refugees? The remains of an attack force?

And then he saw it: under that dome they had raised with a crane, a teleportation console.

He began to piece this situation together. He did not know why or how, but that fight and explosion had to do with teleportation.

One or another of these commanders in the ships about him would invite his advice. He would answer noncommittally. For once he would not be helpful at all. He hoped and prayed that they would not see that console down there.

The group apparently had some wounded and were caring for them and their attention for quite a span was not on security. The console was sitting there, plain as day.

Finally six marine attack battle planes flew in and landed. There was heavy air cover over this group quite in addition to the landed planes.

The small gray man kept his eye on that console. They finally shrouded it and moved it into one of the marine-attack planes.

The Hockner super-lieutenant suddenly said, "Wasn't that a

transshipment console they transferred from truck to plane? I'm playing back my screens."

The small gray man sagged. He had not wanted them to see that. He had hoped they wouldn't recognize one if they did see it.

Vain hope. "It *is!*" said the Hockner.

It took them quite a while to load down there. Some of the marine attack planes were quite empty; two were very fully loaded. The small gray man looked up capacities. Yes, two marine attack planes could handle that entire party.

The commanders were now chattering at a great rate. Some had seen pictures of such consoles. There was a rising tide of excitement, a rising vision of sharing in two hundred million credits of reward money.

Then the group down there abandoned the flatbeds and pumps and a crane and what might be a couple of coffins. Six marine attack planes took off.

And then they did a very puzzling and confusing thing. Instead of assuming an orderly formation, they began to crisscross each other's bows and circle and dart. It was quite impossible even on a screen playback to tell which marine attack carrier was which!

Four of them landed again. Which four? Which were the loaded ones?

The commanders really chattered over this. They were playing back screens, looking for identifying marks. Not possible in this static.

Abruptly the Hockner solved it. Two of the planes, with only a small part of the additional air cover, took off at a leisurely pace—only a thousand miles an hour—on a northeasterly course. The other four and the remaining but majority air cover planes stayed at the river.

"It's a lure!" cried the super-lieutenant. "They want us to follow that northeast group!"

They watched, plotting the course of the northeast group. It would pass over this side of the pole and, unless it stopped before that, would wind up at that pagoda place in the southern hemisphere and at that speed would get there in about nine hours.

As if to confirm the Hockner's suspicions, the remaining four marine attack planes and the rest of the air cover suddenly streaked away on a course slightly to the west of north. They were traveling at two thousand miles an hour.

A hasty extrapolation of their course gave their only possible destination as an ancient minesite near a place which had been called [''Singapore''].

''That does it, old fellow,'' said the Hockner. ''There is a report here that there has been heavy activity in that area and some sort of platform being laid out. They're taking that console to 'Singapore'!''

The quarter-admiral tried to disagree. As the senior officer he had a right to be obeyed. He explained that it must be the pagoda. The reason was that he hated all religions. Religious people were zealots and upset governments and always had to be crushed. This obviously was a religious revolt and they even had evidence of it. A religious order had upset the government of the planet and had now stolen a console. This planet *was* the one and he ordered them all to head for the pagoda objective.

His order did it. The combined force streaked into controlled motion, in full cry after the Singapore-bound group.

But the mighty Terrify-class battle-plane-launching capital ship *Capture* did not follow them.

Egged on by Roof Arsebogger into independent action that would make better copy and by a scathing hatred of all religions, Quarter-Admiral Snowleter turned his ponderous and overwhelming ship, with its belly full of battle planes, toward Kariba.

— 2 —

Jonnie awoke with a start of alarm. The ground had shaken! A woman nurse who must have been at his bedside left the room.

He stared around him, for a moment unable to place the unfamiliar surroundings. Then he recognized them. It was the bunker room at Kariba that the Chinese had fixed up especially for him at the inner edge of the hollow of the firing platform. They had ringed the inside hill with deep bunkers and even tiled some of them. They were lit with mine lights.

This one was tiled in yellow. It was furnished with a bed, chairs, and a wardrobe. They had even done a portrait of Chrissie in the tiles, taking it from a picto-recorder shot—it looked quite like her except that they had slightly slanted her eyes.

The ground jolted again. Bombs?

He was just about to swing out of bed when Dr. Allen came in and soothingly pushed him back. "It's all right," said Dr. Allen. "They have things under control out there.". He was taking Jonnie's pulse.

Sir Robert showed up in the doorway. He had a bandage across his nose which Dr. Allen had set. He was obviously waiting for Dr. Allen to finish.

"You had a nasty one," said Dr. Allen. "But your pulse is normal now. That prevention shot of serum you had handled some of the venom reaction. But you really owe it all to Sir Robert: he got the poison out and even gave you a few drops of serum."

Jonnie's huge Psychlo wrist watch was lying on the sidetable. He stared at it. He had been asleep for eighteen hours! Lord knows what had happened in that time.

Dr. Allen anticipated him. "I know, I know. But it was necessary to put you on an opiate to slow your heart down." He had a stethoscope on Jonnie's chest. He listened. Then he folded it up. "I can't detect any heart damage. Hold out your hand."

Jonnie did.

"Ah, no tremble," said Dr. Allen. "I think you're fine. A few days in bed—"

At that moment the ground jolted again. Jonnie tried to get up and Dr. Allen pushed him back again.

"Sir Robert!" called Jonnie. "What's happening?"

Dr. Allen nodded to Sir Robert that it was all right and then left. Sir Robert came over to stand beside the bed. He was not answering Jonnie's question. He just stood there beaming down at Jonnie, glad to see him alive. The lad even had color in his cheeks.

"What is happening?" said Jonnie, spacing each word.

"Oh," said Sir Robert. "That's a Tolnep ship up there. It's at about two hundred miles but it keeps sending down planes to bomb this place. We have air cover. Stormalong is here and directing air defenses. So far the enemy is giving Singapore its main attention."

Angus was at the door. Jonnie called to him, "Have you set up the console?"

"Oh, aye," said Angus. He came in. "That's why they didn't disturb you." He pointed a finger up. "With all that firing, our antiaircraft outside the screen, and the motors of our own planes, we wouldn't dare use the firing rig. It's all connected. The Chinese set that place up very nice."

"The next firing position of the switch is *down*," said Jonnie.

"Yes, Sir Robert told us that. It's all ready to go if this firing ever stops! Get a rest." Angus left and passed Thor.

Thor said, "How do you feel?"

Jonnie waved his hand negatively. "Unimportant. The last I remember was being in the dome. You better bring me up to date."

They told him what had happened and what they had done.

"A recoil that bad!" said Jonnie.

"Worse," said Thor.

"How many men did we lose?" said Jonnie.

"Andrew and MacDougal," said Thor. "But we have fifteen of them here in this little hospital they have. Couple of concussions, broken arms or legs. Mostly bruised, very badly bruised. The lead of the coffins protected them. No radiation burns. Andrew was badly bayoneted by the Brigantes and couldn't fasten his coffin lid from inside, and it blew open."

"And MacDougal?" said Jonnie.

"Well, that one is sort of bad. He had the station over by the old cage and the coffin was jolted out of the ground. We couldn't find his body for a while and that's what got us looking." Jonnie noticed Thor was holding a heavy package: he had steadied it against the table. "We had to start looking for corpses. They had been blown all around, most of the flesh burned off. We followed the blast line, thinking his body had been blown directly away from the platform, and we got into what was left of Terl's office—the whole top of it had been blown off. Four or five bodies from the platform edge had been blown into that area. We didn't want to leave anyone listed simply as missing so we were trying to identify bodies. We found MacDougal's body.

"And we found this." He was unwrapping the heavy package. "I know you will be relieved to have it. One of the corpses had all the flesh burned off and the vertebrae were exposed and this was sticking in them."

It was the pea-sized pellet of the unknown core material of the bomb.

"Brown Limper," said Jonnie. "Terl threw it at him. Like a bullet. Yes, I am very, very glad you found it!"

"We got the other package Terl handed to him," said Thor. "We gave it to Angus and he disarmed it. What does it do?"

"We don't really know," said Jonnie. "But knowing Terl—"

"We got his whole recycling basket," said Thor. "We figured he'd try to use it and we cut the power off. It's really full! It's out here on a dolly if you want it. We had it in a radiation-proof mine sack, fortunately." He beckoned toward the door. "We grabbed it right after he left his office."

A gillie wheeled the dolly in. They had stacked the material neatly on it.

"Don't try to fire those assassin pistols," said Thor. "Ker put a plug in them so they'd shoot out of the back at the user. Ker said to tell you and that he'd fix them back."

They handed Jonnie some of the booklets and papers that had been in the false backs and bottoms of the cabinets. Jonnie had a lot of it already. His eye was caught by a pamphlet: "Known Defenses of Hostile Races and Surveys of Their Homelands." He thumbed through it. Lot of planets here. He looked under Tolnep:

> This planet is a planet of a double-star system. (See coordinate chart for location.) The system itself has only three inhabited planets, the seventh, eighth, and ninth. The Tolnep homeland is the ninth planet. It has five moons. Of these, only Asart is important. It is used as the launch of major war vessels. No Tolnep vessel can operate in atmosphere due to the great inefficiency of its star energy drives which, being essentially reaction engines, use up too much of their power in atmospheres. After construction, such vessels are based on the moon Asart and their crews and material are ferried to them from planet surface. Since plans have been proposed from time to time to occupy and mine the Tolnep planet, and since usual offensive tactics are thought to be adequate in the event of such a war, the moon Asart has not been assaulted up to the time of this writing.

Jonnie looked at the Psychlo date. It was only a couple of years old. The catalogue went on. Jonnie laid it down.

Another thud and ground shake.

Suddenly, Jonnie was aware of the underlying tension in all those who had come in. They were just trying to make him feel easy! Thor had received an urgent summons while he had been reading. And now a communicator rushed in with a sheaf of dispatches for Sir Robert and rushed out. Jonnie saw the frown flicker across Sir Robert's face as he read them.

"The situation is worse than you're letting on, isn't it?" said Jonnie.

"Naw, naw," said Sir Robert. "Dinna fret yersel', laddie."

"What *is* the situation?" demanded Jonnie. Sir Robert never dropped into dialect unless agitated.

The grizzled old Scot sighed and recovered his university accent. "Well, if you must have it, we have lost the initiative. For whatever reason, the enemy has decided to attack in force." He tapped the reports. "Singapore is holding so far and right now has tied down about three-quarters of their forces. But they won't be tied down there forever. The Russian base is getting the attention of planes from a large war vessel. Edinburgh is getting hit. Neither of the last two places have any armor cable coverage. And up there," he pointed, "is a huge monster of a battleship that has been sending planes and bombs down for several hours. It could also launch up to a thousand Tolnep marines and we aren't that well equipped to handle an assault force by land. So there you have it. It can only get worse, not better."

"Call Dr. Allen," said Jonnie. "I'm getting up!"

Sir Robert tried to protest but he finally called the doctor in.

Dr. Allen did not like it. "You're full of a drug we found called 'sulfa' that will prevent infection and blood poisoning. You'll feel dizzy if you get up suddenly. I don't advise it."

Nevertheless, Jonnie insisted. He knew they were doing all they could. But he wanted to look over the situation. He just couldn't sit still and be pounded to bits.

Jonnie couldn't see any clothes. A Coordinator showed up with an elderly, gray-headed Chinese man. "This is Mr. Tsung," said the Coordinator. "He has been in charge of fixing up your room. He has been learning a little English so he can help you."

Mr. Tsung bowed. He was obviously pleased to see Jonnie but the thudding bombs also held some of his attention. He had a bowl of soup for Jonnie to drink and his hands shook a bit as he held it out. Jonnie would have laid it down but Mr. Tsung shook his head. "Drink! Drink!" said Mr. Tsung. "Mebbe so no chance eat later."

Another communicator beckoned to Sir Robert from the door and the old Scot rushed out.

Mr. Tsung was getting his nervousness under control. The novelty of meeting Jonnie was wearing off, and now that he was doing something, the sporadic thuds of bombs seemed less. And then a conviction came to him that if anybody could do anything about this it would be Lord Jonnie. As he laid out weapons he began to smile with more confidence.

It was true what Dr. Allen said about being dizzy if he moved too suddenly, Jonnie discovered as he dressed. His arm was very sore and stiff. It was a bit hard to dress.

Mr. Tsung got him into the plain green uniform they all wore. He buckled the Smith and Wesson with the left-hand holster and a blast pistol with a right-hand holster around Jonnie's waist. He rigged a black silk sling for his arm and then adjusted it so that Jonnie could get the arm out of it fast and draw the Smith and Wesson if he had to. He made Jonnie check it to make sure he could do that. Then he gave Jonnie the plain green helmet.

"Now you shoot them," said Mr. Tsung. He made his hand into a pistol and fired it twice. "Bang! Bang!" He was very confident now, smiling. He tucked his hands in his sleeves and bowed.

If it were only that simple, Jonnie thought. But he bowed and thanked the little man. Good lord, he was dizzy. Made the room spin to lower his head.

An unusually large explosion shook the ground.

They *were* catching it.

— 3 —

As Jonnie left his room, he saw that the underground passage also led past the hospital. Although his intention had been to go out to the cone where the platform was, concern about the wounded of the raiding party halted him by that door.

A clatter was coming from the place. The click of bolts being cocked and the slap of slings? Arms? He stepped inside the door. There were about thirty beds and over half of them were occupied. But two Chinese, whose armbands showed they were from the armory, had a dolly with assorted weaponry, and they were passing out blast rifles, AK 47s with thermit ammunition, and handguns to the wounded Scots.

A gray-haired Scot nurse came up to Jonnie. She obviously did not approve of this commotion in her ward. Then she recognized Jonnie and choked back whatever she was about to say, probably to tell him to get out.

Jonnie had been counting. "There's thirteen in here from the raiding party and two gunners. Are there any more?"

"The two lads with concussions are in surgery," said the nurse. "Dr. MacKendrick says their operations went well and they'll be fine. Are you supposed to be up, MacTyler?"

By now one of the injured Scots had seen Jonnie at the door and barked his name. Jonnie had been about to go from bed to bed with apologies. It appeared there were seventeen casualties out of the raiding party of thirty-one. No, eighteen including himself. Heavy! These men were badly bruised; black eyes predominated. Several broken limbs. He felt that better planning could have averted this.

But the other Scots had seen him and they began to put up a yell. Sounded like "Scotland wei heigh!" They were sitting up and yelling. Nothing wrong with *their* morale!

Suddenly Jonnie realized that these lads had slaughtered the Brigantes and settled the blood feud of Scotland. They were victors. Their injuries were badges of honor. They would be heroes to the whole Scottish nation.

No apologies needed here. He tried to shout into the din and then simply saluted them and, with a smile and wave, withdrew.

He could hear loudspeakers outside playing solemn religious music to prevent infrabeam surveillance.

He came out of the passage from the bunkers and gazed into the bowl. The daylight was made murky from drifting smoke. The slight odor of the atmosphere armor at Stage Three mixed with charcoal's tang. The bowl seemed unusually crowded.

It was a thousand feet in diameter at the level of its floor. Before, he had thought that was a lot of space, about three-quarters of a million square feet he had guessed. But it did seem crowded now.

The pagoda structure in the center extended well beyond the platform on all sides. All around the bowl, with the pagoda at its center, was a sort of wide paved road.

When he had seen it before, it had almost been deserted. Over there to the right were two Italian-Swiss electricians rigging more wires into some bunkers. A German and a Swiss pilot were sorting out a dolly load of air masks. Near to hand a Scot officer was giving some instructions to a Russian soldier. Way over to the left a group of Swedish soldiers were sorting out ammunition on a dolly. There, just coming out of a passage which must lead outside, were two Sherpa hunters pushing a dolly load of African buffalo meat toward what must be a kitchen. Here and there a Buddhist communicator was moving with a floating walk from one bunker to another. And scattered all about, along the inner bank, were Chinese families and their children and belongings. On one of the big posts which held up the pagoda roof, the Chinese had hung tribal shields representing the remaining tribes of Earth.

A truly international scene—the peoples of Earth.

Jonnie was about to move on when a voice speaking Psychlo sounded behind him and to his right.

"I am so sorry." It was Chief Chong-won, head of the Chinese tribe and principal architect of this place. "We had to bring in all the people from the village by the lake. The lake is so broad, the cable protection is thin in the center, and some bombs have come through above the dam. Waves from the explosion have made the village unsafe. And the smoke from cooking fires does not escape through the screen."

He was bowing. Jonnie nodded. "But see," continued Chong-won, "my engineers are digging air ducts through the hill under the cable."

Piles of dirt and rock on either side of the bowl showed where the Chinese were using spade drills to cut a channel to the outside air.

"They will use intake fans in one and exhaust fans in the other. They will be curved so no bomb blasts come through. I am so sorry for the oversight."

"I think you have done splendidly," said Jonnie. "You say bombs fall in the lake above the dam. Is there any dam injury?"

Chief Chong-won beckoned a Chinese engineer and they chattered for a moment in Mandarin. Then Chong-won said to Jonnie, "Not so far. But some have sent water over the top of the dam and they have put in the flashboards to reduce the spillway. If the lake were to drop in volume, we would have no electricity."

The whole lowest floor of the "pagoda" was wide open on all

four sides. The pagoda was really just a fancy roof. The metal transshipment platform was in plain view. The Chinese had polished it until it shone even in the subdued light.

Jonnie walked under the high roof to get a better look at where they had put the all-important console. Then he smiled. Over on the other side of the platform they had built a stand with sides in the shape of a huge, savage-looking, winged beast!

Angus was there at the console and he waved. "It's something, isn't it?" said Angus.

Yes, it really was. A huge head, two wings, a curling tail. Armored metal. Painted gold and red.

"A dragon," said Chong-won. "Once it was the emblem of Imperial China. See, it is laminated molecular armor."

Not only that, but it had a top! The console was set into the dragon's back and a cover was made of dragon scales so the operator could work the console without anyone's observing what he was really doing. There were two stools on the raised console platform and a side shelf for papers and a computer. And all armored. Nothing was going to hurt *that* console. Or see what was being done with it either.

Such a far cry from the materialistic Psychlo, who was without paintings or art. And what these Chinese could do!

"See?" said Chief Chong-won. "It is the same as those other dragons." He pointed to a dragon that formed the roof point of the pagoda nearby. Each corner had one. And then the chief pointed to some unfinished work over by the bank. "Each bunker was supposed to have its dragon over the entrance. We have not had time to put them up." They were much smaller dragons, made of baked clay and painted in gold and red.

The console looked fine under the protective cover. Angus had a copy of the coordinate book there and was drilling himself without punching anything. He was figuring how to convert the figures in the book to this moment of time and the console buttons. "I've got it pretty well," said Angus. "It just takes quite a bit of time to do the calculations. There are eight separate movements listed for each planet and you have to pick where on the planet. But it is not too hard."

Jonnie looked up. Another bomb had just hit somewhere. "If all that would stop, we'd be in business. I don't have any idea when it will or exactly what we can do with this console yet."

Chief Chong-won was pointing at the inside of one of the huge posts that held up the pagoda roof and protected the platform and console from rain. They had rigged mine spotlights on each post so that they spotlighted the platform center. "At night," he said, "they won't shine outside."

Jonnie wanted to go over to the operations bunker, but the chief detoured him into a large underground room in the side wall of the bowl. It was nicely tiled and had a platform at the end for a speaker. It had chairs and would hold about fifty people. Very nice.

Then Chief Chong-won showed him a sample of thirty little apartments they had made for guests and visitors. They were in addition to pilot and personnel berthings. These Chinese engineers could certainly build in wood and tile and stone, particularly when assisted by Psychlo machinery.

Jonnie was interested in gun emplacements all around that could cover the platform and the bowl interior. Given troops, the place could really be defended. But they did not have all that many troops.

He finally got to the ops room. It was a busy place. It was a miniature of the one they had found in the American underground base. A huge map of the planet was in the center. As reports came in from the adjoining communications office, men with long poles were pushing about small lead models of planes and the war vessels in orbit. Enemy vessels were red with tags. Their own planes were green with tags.

Stormalong was there in his white scarf, leather coat, and oversized goggles. He had two Buddhist communicators on either side of him and they were talking into close-to-the-mouth microphones that excluded any speech but theirs. Their shaved heads gleamed under the too-large headphones they wore.

Jonnie was told they were operating a planetary battle channel—used by Stormalong—and a planetary command channel used by Sir Robert. The Scot War Chief had a thirteen-year-old Buddhist boy operating his channel.

Nobody had to brief Jonnie. It was all there on the big operations board. Singapore was really catching it. There was a lot of antiaircraft being used at the Russian base. Dunneldeen was flying air cover for Edinburgh. Thor was flying air cover for Kariba. Nothing was happening at the Lake Victoria minesite or any of the rest. But where it was hot, it was very hot.

Jonnie listened in to the babble on both battle and command channels. It was all in Pali which he didn't speak.

There was a third station, manned by a Scot officer, that was monitoring enemy traffic.

Down at the end of the room where there were some spare desks, Glencannon was hunched over a pile of pictures. Jonnie glanced at them. They seemed to be viewscreen runoffs of an air battle. The one he had when the Swiss was killed? Glencannon had another stack, apparently just taken. They were of the huge monster overhead.

Glencannon seemed very agitated, his hands shaking. He had not really recovered from that courier run, seemingly, for Stormalong didn't have him flying. He didn't answer when Jonnie spoke to him.

The operations board was not good, but Jonnie did not have anything to contribute. It was simply a slugfest. He wondered how long places not protected with atmosphere armor cable could hold out. Edinburgh was particularly vulnerable. A worry about Chrissie passed through his mind. He hoped she was safe in a bunker under Castle Rock. Sir Robert answered his question. Yes, they were all in bunkers up there. It was mainly antiaircraft that was protecting the place. Dunneldeen was taking care of strafing planes that tried to come in. The antiaircraft was taking care of bombs.

Jonnie thought he had better look at this antiaircraft they had here. He had never seen the Psychlo guns in action. Not up close.

He went out. Chief Chong-won had vanished, attending to other duties. Chinese families with their children and an occasional dog were sitting about, mostly in and near rifle pits. They looked a bit worn, a bit worried. Some of the children were crying. But the parents smiled broadly, and got up and bowed as Jonnie passed. It made him hope their confidence was not misplaced.

The exit from the bowl was a curving underground passage under the cable so it wouldn't have to be turned off each time anyone went in or out. The curves were to prevent bomb flash and fragments from getting in.

He went to the first antiaircraft gun emplacement. The gun was shielded. The two gunners were in Russian bulletproof battle dress. A Scot officer saw him and got out of a pit.

"We don't have enough of these," said the Scot, pointing at the gun. "We can't cover the lake. It's all we can do to cover this bowl."

Jonnie went over to the gun. It had computer sights that zeroed in on anything moving. What one had to do was hit a trigger and the gun calculated the speed and direction of a moving object, sent a blast concussion into its path, then found the next moving object and hit that.

He looked up. An enemy plane at about two hundred thousand feet was barely discernible. Jonnie knew the range of this gun was short of that by about fifty thousand feet. So did the enemy apparently.

That plane was dropping bombs.

The gun bucked five times rapidly. Five bombs exploded in midair, direct hits by the gun. The explosions up there came back down to them.

"The ones you feel land," said the Scot officer, "go into the lake. They're beyond our sector. And of course the ones that fall way out in the woods. We don't bother with those."

Jonnie looked toward the woods. Seven or eight miles away there was quite a fire going. No, three separate fires. Every animal within fifty miles must have left the country. The African buffalo the Sherpas had was probably killed by bombs earlier. Well, the woods wouldn't burn very long. It was pretty wet just now.

He looked back at the gun. What havoc one of these things would have made with their attack on the minesites over a year ago if the attack had not been a total surprise. And if security chiefs like Terl had not let the company defenses go neglected.

Another bomb hit on a hill about ten miles away, and even from here one could see the geyser of smoke and trees. That battleship up there was dropping pretty heavy bombs. If one hit this cone, he didn't know whether the atmosphere screen would repel it.

He was walking back to the entrance when he saw Glencannon come out. He was buttoning up a heavy flying suit. He didn't have a communicator or copilot with him. He was walking toward a plane that was surrounded by sandbags. Jonnie thought he must have special orders and did not stop him.

Glencannon got into the plane, a heavily armored Mark 32 that had been converted to high-altitude flying.

Just as Jonnie started down into the passage, Stormalong came racing out of it.

"Glencannon!" shouted Stormalong.

But the pilot had taken off.

— 4 —

For days Glencannon had brooded over this. His sleep was tortured with nightmares.

In his mind he could still hear the voice of his Swiss friend, "Go on! Go on! I will shoot them down! Keep going!" And then his scream when he was hit just before he ejected. And back of Glencannon's eyes he could still see the viewscreen of his friend's body being shot to pieces in the air.

He had his own playbacks of the war vessel that had launched those planes. And he had the shots taken of this monster overhead.

It was the Terrify-class battle-plane-launching capital ship *Capture*. There could be no doubt about it. That was the vessel that had butchered his friend.

He felt he should have gone back, regardless of any orders. The two of them could have finished the Tolnep attack plane, he was certain. But instead he had followed orders.

He had suppressed the urge to go up and destroy that ship, and he felt that if he did not go ahead and do it now his whole life would be a nightmare.

He heard Stormalong's voice in clear Psychlo on the local command channel: "Glencannon! You must come back! I order you to land!" Glencannon clicked the channel off.

This was Stormalong's own Mark 32 he was flying. It had been in "emergency reserve." It was rebuilt for high altitudes, the doors and ports sealed tight. It had huge firepower and even side bombs that could destroy half a city. It was armored to take a ferocious beating. And while its guns may or may not be able to penetrate the skin of a capital ship, there were other ways.

They could not follow him from the ground. All other Mark 32s were at Lake Victoria and here they were only using interceptors. No, they could not follow him. Not to the heights he was going.

He vaulted skyward higher and higher. He adjusted his air mask so it was snug: he was going to go out of the atmosphere.

The *Capture* was swinging in a slow and ponderous ellipse, three hundred fifty miles above Kariba. It was fifty miles above the termination of the Earth's atmosphere. It was operating on reaction engines and was no longer simply sailing in orbit.

Planes would leave it, streak downward to targets, and then return to be rearmed. One spotted him and dove. Almost with contempt, Glencannon centered him in his sights and pressed his fire button. The Mark 32 bucked in recoil.

The Tolnep burst into fire and plummeted earthward like a comet.

It alerted the *Capture* to his presence, and as he neared it the gunports winked and long laces of flame streaked the sky about him. One splashed on the side of the Mark 32. It made the flight deck hot.

Glencannon danced back out of range. He saw the steering ports of the ship jet fire and anticipated its course.

Twenty-five miles in front of it he began to tap his console to hold his position. It was just out of the Tolnep's range.

He adjusted his viewscreens and began to watch.

The stars were glaring bright in the blackness above him but he had no eye for them. The Earth spread out its curves below him but he saw them not.

His whole, concentrated, obsessed attention was on the *Capture*, studying it.

The ship resumed operation after a bit, believing his mission must be surveillance, not attack. The arrogance of such a ship was plain. It did not believe it could be hurt. It was once more launching and taking aboard planes.

Glencannon saw that just before they opened the huge front ports of their hangar deck, a small exterior warning light winked, probably to warn approaching planes to stand clear and not get in front of the ship as it was about to open the door and launch.

Each time the door opened he studied the enlarged viewscreen of the interior. The entire hangar deck was cluttered with planes. Tolneps in pressure suits were racing about, fueling ships and loading bombs. They had gotten out much larger bombs now.

They were leaving the interior magazine open. Fuel cans, probably liquid gases, littered the hangar deck. The Tolneps were overconfident and sloppy. But what could one expect of a slaver?

Glencannon shifted his attention to the rearing diamond-shaped bridge. There were two figures there, moving back and forth. One was not in uniform. A civilian, probably. The one in the naval cap seemed to have attention only for the civilian. No, they were not being alert.

He turned his attention back to the outside light and the hangar door. He timed it. He calculated his own position. In the back of his mind he could hear the voice of his friend from time to time: "Go on! Go on! I will shoot them down! Keep going!"

That was exactly what Glencannon was going to do: shoot them down!

For the first time in quite a while he felt calm, relaxed, confident. And totally determined. He was doing exactly what he had to do.

The next time. . . .

The light went on!

His hands hit the console.

The Mark 32 streaked ahead, almost smashed him through the back of the seat with acceleration.

Guns flamed in the *Capture*.

Balls of orange glare racketed against the Mark 32.

It sliced straight through the barrage.

Just as it entered the open hangar door Glencannon's hand hit all guns and bombs.

The explosion was a sun blowing apart!

Jonnie and Stormalong saw it as they stood outside the cone, back of a gun viewscreen. They saw the plane enter the hangar door with all guns blazing.

But it required no viewscreen to see the flash. The abrupt glare lit the fading daylight for fifty miles around. It was painful to the eyes.

It would be soundless in the void above the Earth. But it was not motionless.

The giant capital ship began to fall. A flaming arc began to draw its way down the sky, slowly, very slowly at first, but building up speed.

And then it hit the atmosphere and began to burn more brightly

Down it came, further and further, lower and lower.

"My god!" said Stormalong. "It's going to hit the lake!"

Down it came, faster and faster, like some huge comet painting the sky.

It was dropping at an angle.

Stormalong's muscles strained as though by will alone he could push it into the hills and away from the water above the dam.

Down it came, a blazing incandescent wreck, traveling at great speed.

Five miles uplake from the dam it struck.

The heat and speed of passage thundered in the air. Then came the screeching crash of the strike.

Steam and water geysered a thousand feet in the air.

There was an underwater flash as some remaining part of its fuel exploded.

The shock concussion raced ahead of the wave as great as any tidal wave.

The deserted Chinese village was snuffed out as though it had never been.

The concussion wave hit the back of the dam.

The water wave inundated the structure, smashing flashboards, flying in a mighty cascade into the air at the dam front.

The ground underfoot shook.

Breathless, they steadied themselves and stared. Would the whole dam go?

Waves subsided. The dam was still there. But there was new sound in it.

The lights were still on. The generators were running.

Guards who had been in the powerhouse came staggering out.

Water was roaring down the river as the excess sped away, tearing down banks, ripping through islands.

Engineers came racing from the cone.

Most of the machinery which had been parked near the lake had been swept away. They were racing about trying to find a flying platform.

They found one imbedded in the bank, half-covered with mud. They freed it, swept the mud off it, and got it flying.

The engineers and a machine operator went flying along the top of the dam.

Jonnie and Stormalong stood by beside a plane, waiting to see whether the engineers needed help. Their voices, in Chinese, were coming over a mine radio.

The atmosphere armor over the cone was still sizzling in Stage Three. Guards got back into the powerhouse and turned off the dam protection cable and reduced the cone armor to Stage One.

Although this dam lake was one hundred twenty miles long, it seemed lower in level.

Jonnie and Stormalong were about to take off to see what the engineers had found when they came back. They landed and were reporting to Chong-won. There was a lot of excited and upset talk and Jonnie went over.

"They say the dam did not break," Chong-won told him. "Flashboards are broken all along the top and even some concrete along the walkway and the guard rails are gone. But that is nothing. They can see no cracks. However, at the far end of the dam abutment, over there on the other side of the dam, it seems to have shaken loose from the bank and there is water escaping. They say water is erosive and it could get bigger. It could even greatly lower the level of the lake to a point where the water turbines will not run."

"How many hours?" said Jonnie.

Chong-won asked them. They could only guess. Maybe four, maybe five hours. They would do all they could to stop the water and plug the leak. They did not have much grouting to seal it. The whole far end of the dam seemed to have torn out of the bank. They wanted to get back over and do what they could.

Angus came running out of the passageway seeking Jonnie. "We can fire now! There is no shooting."

"Maybe you can fire the rig," said Stormalong, appalled at Glencannon's sacrifice. "But for how long?"

"At least he bought us that," said Jonnie, sadly.

— 5 —

The small gray man had followed the pack to the Singapore area. He had instructed his ship captain not to get in the way of military craft for they were inclined to be impetuous and prone to accidents, to say nothing of poorly aimed shots. Thus they were a little late on the scene and the battle had already begun.

The minesite was not at all hard to locate—it was a brilliant cone of defensive fire, its guns arcing up and converging upon target after target. It was quite a distance north of the ancient ruined city, and just north of the minesite was a hydroelectric dam. The gunfire was quite intense and disturbed his infrabeams, preventing for the moment a closer inspection of what they had down there.

The small gray man did not consider himself much of a military specialist, and things which a military man might know at once, he usually had to look up. He wanted the maximum/minimum height which would give him a safe altitude from which to observe and it was quite laborious to identify those guns. At last he had it: "Local defense perimeter, computerized antiassault craft, and bomb predetonation atmosphere/nonatmosphere beam projection cannon; rate of fire 15,000 shots per minute, maximum 175,000 feet, minimum safe limit 2,000 feet; crew two; barrels and shields manufactured by Tambert Armaments, Predicham; computers by Intergalactic Arms, Psychlos; Cost C4,269 freight on platform Predicham." My, my, what cheap guns. But that was Intergalactic Mining: "Profit—first, last, and always, profit." No wonder they had trouble! One would have thought they would have orbit cannon.

So it was safe to remain two hundred miles up so long as they did not get in the road of launched craft from the non-atmosphere major war vessels riding at three hundred fifty miles high. He told his captain and then asked his communicator to focus beams very sharply on what appeared to be a firing platform under the shield cable below.

He spotted it almost at once and had a surge of hope. It was a console! A transshipment console right there near the platform! There were even some men about it as though working it.

Intently, he watched his viewscreens for a teleportation trace. He watched for quite a while. There was none. He wondered that the military men in the war vessels had not noticed this lack. Maybe they did not know the telltale trace existed. Maybe they had a different make of viewscreen. But the probability was that they had never seen one because they were always shooting and you couldn't shoot—

The small gray man sighed. He was no detective, and the evidence so plain before him had gone unnoticed. Those men down there could not be using a transshipment rig. They even had their own planes in the air. And either one, planes or shots, would prevent any use of teleportation. The rig itself would blow to bits with distortions.

The military had begun to give attention to the power dam lake now and were trying to drop bombs into it to cut off the minesite power supply. This gave a respite to the minesite itself and the small gray man had been put onto that console.

He looked up the mineral traces which resulted.

Carbon!

That settled it. That thing down there was a burned-out console.

It was *so* disappointing!

He drew off and watched for a while. Combined force planes were not having much luck with the dam lake due to atmosphere armor cable around it and they were now giving their attention to the air cover planes from below. There was a boiling fight and he saw two Jambitchow combat battle planes blown to bits.

He had his ship moved up higher. Down to the south the combined force bombers had begun to drop bombs into the deserted ancient ruins of Singapore. A fire blossomed up. Then another. He wondered at the military mind that would bomb an undefended city with no military value but which might contain some loot that they so valued. But they always did it.

His indigestion was bothering him again. These were such awful times. There seemed to be no hope at all.

He knew there was a base in the northern continent man had once called ''Russia'' and he had his ship captain move up there.

One of the attacking-force war vessels was launching planes over that base. They were personnel carriers. The small gray man observed a force of about five hundred Hawvin marines deploying on the plain before the base. Behind fire shields they began to move forward. It almost seemed that the base was not defended. No answering fire came back to the advancing force. It got closer and closer to the base. Several fires erupted. Then the force began to move up a mountain slope toward what must be an underground defense point. The force was within a hundred yards of it now, pouring a hail of fire into it.

Abruptly the ground under the attacking force erupted.

Mines! The whole terrain was flaming.

Flashes of weapon fire blasted down the hill from the base. The attacking force withdrew in haste beyond the village. Officers were shouting and regrouping their marines. But they had left over a hundred dead or wounded on the ground before the base.

The attacking force formed up again and advanced on the base.

Planes streaked out of base hangar doors and ground-strafed the assault force.

The small gray man had seen no traces on his viewscreens. He had not really hoped to see any, not in all that firing.

Since it was not far out of the orbit course he now had, he told his ship captain to pass over the American minesite at a height of four hundred miles.

It took a while and the small gray man napped a little. A buzzer told him they were over it and he turned to his screens.

Way down below, the ruin of the minesite was utterly dead. The abandoned trucks and pumps still lay beside the river. What a desolate, lifeless scene! The dome which had covered a console was still lying there, still attached to a crane hook but tipped over.

The city to the north was still burning.

His mineral tracer showed the whole area hot with radiation.

He directed his ship captain to change orbit to pass over Scotland. It was in his mind to stop and see whether the old woman might have come back, but then down on the horizon beyond, the sensors picked up heat and then a clear view of a Drawkin war vessel. He looked at his maps. They were not very good maps for they were just pages of schoolbooks, but he easily identified the city. It was [''Edinburgh'']. And it was burning.

His radio was crackling and the communicator tuned it in more finely. What a rushing barrage of sound! Some of it was Drawkin and the small gray man could not understand that tongue even though they controlled twenty planets. It was a sort of hysterical-sounding language. He could take a vocoder to it, for he had the vocabulary circuits somewhere, but they would just be commands to pilots down below. The other language he had heard an awful lot of lately. It was a sort of smooth, meditative tongue. He had even dawdled over a frequency decoding table to try to get a grasp of it but it seemed to defy that.

But he didn't need to understand the language. The phy facts were plain enough. There was a heavy air battle in pr

He looked down through the port. A big promont above the city. Antiaircraft fire was coning up from stood in a sea of fire as the city burned.

A Drawkin bomber exploded in midair and fell to add its bursting gouts of green flame to the orange of the burning city.

No teleportation traces possible there. That was for certain.

He felt very depressed, even sad. He wondered at himself. Was the strain of this past year making him *emotional?* Surely not! Yet the old woman in the north of Scotland, and particularly his finding her gone, had stirred *sentiment*. And here he was feeling a bit of *anxiety* lest she be down there in all that flame.

All this was quite unlike him. Quite unprofessional.

He thought he had better have a little nap so he could awake thinking more clearly, less clouded and blurred. What an absolutely terrible year it had been.

He went to his cabin and lay down. And it seemed only moments later that he woke with the whole thing bright and plain before him.

That criss-cross dance those terrestrial marine attack planes had done. How dull of him! Of course he was no military tactician, but he should have realized it long before now. That high-speeding group that flashed off to Singapore was the *lure*. The burned-out console was just *bait*.

He went to his small gray office and did a very efficient playback of that "dance of planes" and then plotted the course of the real group quite accurately. Yes, on that course they would arrive at that pagoda in the southern hemisphere of the planet.

He gave his orders to his ship captain and away they sped, right up to 2X light.

He was just in time to see the death of the *Capture*.

It startled him.

He was not sure how it could happen. A Terrify-class battle-plane-launching capital ship? Exploded in orbit?

With a cautionary word to the bridge to draw off, the small gray man watched the huge vessel disintegrate down through the atmosphere and strike the lake of the dam. For a bit he watched to see whether the dam would give. It might be damaged, he decided, but it appeared to be holding for the moment. A huge amount of water was rushing down the river channel in an overpowering flood. But there was nothing down there.

He telephotoed his viewscreens on the dam itself. Yes, it had [illegible] damaged. Quite a bit of water was escaping on the lower [illegible] side, much of it under the dam there. A big hole from [illegible] it.

There had been quite a fight here. The woods were burning. Yes, and there went a squadron of the *Capture*'s planes, streaking off over the horizon in the hopes of being taken aboard some Tolnep ship in the Singapore area. They must have been outside when the *Capture* exploded. Well, they probably wouldn't make it. They didn't have the range. They'd wind up in the sea.

But he better watch this pagoda. There were no planes around it now. His infrabeams couldn't pick up anything but religious music. It drowned out any voices.

From a respectful distance he watched his screens intently. He did not have too long to wait.

A teleportation trace!

Yes, yes, yes! He played it back.

Hope surged.

Then he felt this was too good to be true. Consoles when captured had been known to fire once and then that was it. They never fired again.

It seemed absolutely ages that he waited.

There it was again.

It had fired twice. It had fired *twice!*

Joy surged up in him. Then he found an instant to wonder at himself. Sentiment? Anxiety? And now joy? How very unprofessional! Get to the urgent business at hand.

How could he communicate with them?

The radio channel was full of the calm, religious-sounding speech. What would they speak down there?

He grabbed a vocoder. He threw on his transmit and put the vocoder in front of a microphone. But what language? He had several in the vocoder bank. One called "French"—no, that was utterly dead. One called "German?" No, he had never heard that in their channels. "English." He would start off with English.

He muttered into the vocoder and it said, "I am requesting safe conduct through your lines. My vessel is not armed. You may train your guns on it or on me. I have no hostile intentions. It might be mutually beneficial were you to grant me an interview. I am requesting safe conduct through your lines. My vessel is not armed. You may train your guns on it or on me. I have no hostile intentions. It might be mutually beneficial were you to grant r an interview."

The small gray man waited. He hardly dared brea awful lot of things depended upon the reply.

PART 26

— 1 —

Jonnie and Angus were straight up against it.

They had their heads bent over the worktable in the console enclosure. Before them lay an open technical manual Angus had found in Terl's recycler basket. Psychlo technical manuals were bad enough but this was exceptionally bad. There is nothing worse than a cloudy operator's handbook produced for an already informed reader which omits basics and essentials.

It was ruining Jonnie's half-formed plans and introducing a tactical dilemma. Entitled "Cautionary Examples for the Instruction of Trained Transshipment Console Operators," it, of course, made no mention of the essential switch position. But it did discuss what was called the "samespace" phenomena.

The manual warned against firing a transshipment item *nearer* than twenty-five thousand miles.

Jonnie had hoped he could somehow lay a tactical nuclear weapon inside each of those major war vessels and get rid of them.

The "samespace" phenomena informed them that space "considered itself" identical on the principle of nearness. By a law of squares, the farther another point in space was away, the more "different" it was from the point of origin. Total difference did not occur until one reached a point approximately twenty-five thousand miles away.

Teleportation motors used this to run and they were quite different from transshipment functions. A motor ran on the principle that "samespace" resisted distortion heavily. The shorter the distance, the more the distortion. Thus the motor thrived on the refusal of space to distort. But here one was not moving an object; one was moving merely the position of the motor housing.

You could even run a dozen motors in the same room and though they would cross-distort, they would function.

But to move an object cleanly, without destruction of it or harm to the transshipment rig, one had to have two spaces to coincide with each other, and space would not do that so long as it "considered itself" "samespace." You would just get a mangled mess.

It was all quite obtuse and Jonnie did not feel well. Every time he leaned over, he felt dizzy. Dr. Allen came out and insisted he take some more of this sulfa.

"We can't bomb the ships with this," said Jonnie. "And if we bomb their home planets with this rig, the attacking force won't find out about it for months. They're all just reaction drives and they're months from home." He sighed. "This rig won't serve us offensively!"

The rig worked. They knew that because they had just proven it. They had taken a gyro-mounted camera from drone spares. It was the type of picture-regulating device which a drone used to look for things and it moved any kind of a recorder around through any degrees of a sphere according to how you set it. You could put any picto-recorder in it and they had done just that.

The rig could "cast" an object out and bring it back or it could "cast" one out and leave it. You moved "this space" out there and brought it back in order to just send out an object and recover it. Or you moved "this space" out to the coordinates of "that space" and "that space" now would hold the object and you brought this space back empty. Actually nothing moved through space at all. But "this space" and "that space" were made to coincide.

They had put a picto-recorder in the gyro-mounted camera and sent it to the moon's surface, an easy one since the moon was up and in their line of sight. They had gotten back some very nice pictures of glaringly bright craters.

They had then "cast" the picto-recorder out to Mars, of which they had the path and coordinates, and had just looked at a huge valley that could be imagined to have a river in it.

The rig worked. They had had no doubts of that. But they weren't here to take pretty pictures. They could hear the mutter from the nearby ops room and they knew their friends were being hammered mercilessly. There must be *something* they could do with this rig.

And it didn't help to feel lightheaded and dizzy.

One might threaten the invaders by saying their planets would be destroyed but more than likely they would just attack this place again.

Suddenly the strung intercom from ops buzzed. Stormalong's voice: "You better hold up firing. We have an unknown vessel about four hundred miles up and to the north. Stand by. Will advise."

At the end of the line, Stormalong took his finger off the intercom and started to put the gun trace that had just come in through his playback resolver to get a picture from it.

His communicator, a young Buddhist woman on this shift, touched his shoulder. "Sir," she said in Psychlo, "I've got a message on the battle line I can't make out. It's in a monotone but it sounds sort of like the language I hear you and Sir Robert use to each other. I've got the recording of it, sir."

Stormalong didn't pay much attention. He was pulling the paper transfer out of the trace resolver. "Play it," he said.

" 'My vessel is not armed. You may train guns on it or on me'. . . ."

Stormalong blinked. English? A funny kind of machine English?

He had the picture out of the resolver now. He looked at it, grabbed the recorder, and raced out to the console.

Jonnie and Angus looked up in alarm.

"No, no," said Stormalong. "I think it's all right. Look!"

He put the picture in front of them urgently. It was a ship shaped like a ball with a ring around it. "Remember the ship I ran into that wasn't there? And the old woman on the Scottish coast? This is the same ship!" He looked at them demandingly. "Do I let it through?"

"Might be a trick," said Angus.

"Any way you can be sure?" said Jonnie. "You know that it's not a different ship?"

The Buddhist had followed Stormalong with a cable mike. He grabbed it away from her. "Hello. Hello up there. Do you read me?"

A metallic, monotone, "Yes."

"What did the old woman serve you?" demanded Stormalong.

The monotone, metallic voice, "Yarb tea."

Stormalong grinned. "Land in the open field north of this

place where guns can be trained on you. Leave your ship by yourself and come unarmed. You will be met by sentries."

Metallic voice, "Very good. Safe conduct accepted."

Stormalong sent the needful orders to the guns and guards outside.

He played Jonnie the whole message.

"Who is this guy?" asked Angus. He spoke for them all.

— 2 —

The small gray man was escorted into the pagoda area by two polite, but alert, Scottish guards. He was about as high as Jonnie's shoulder. He was dressed in a neat gray suit. He looked like a human being except that his skin was gray.

Angus looked at him. "That's a Scottish-knit sweater," said Angus suspiciously.

"I know, I know," said the small gray man through his English speaking vocoder. "I am very sorry that we have no time for social amenities. We must conduct our business right now and rapidly!"

One of the guards said, "He has a white flashing light blinking on and off on top of his ship."

Sir Robert's communicator, the boy named Quong, whispered to Sir Robert, "He has a radio signal going on the battle frequency that is saying, 'Temporary local safe conduct.' " He said it, of course, in Psychlo.

The small gray man must have had very sharp ears for he promptly said, "Oh! You speak Psychlo!" He was speaking it and he took off the vocoder and put it in his pocket, saying, "We can dispense with this then. They are sometimes inaccurate—they misword critical clauses that lead to disputes."

As he did this and before they could stop him he took a quick step up on the pedestal before the open console and looked in. "Ah! A standard transshipment console, I see. You have only one."

Jonnie felt they were being criticized in some way. "We can build others." He meant it to mean, don't try to steal this one for we can replace it fast enough.

But the small gray man positively beamed with joy. He stepped down and looked quickly about. "We really must hurry. Is there an authorized representative of the planetary government here?"

"That would be Sir Robert," said Jonnie, indicating him.

"Do you have the power to sign on behalf of your government?" asked the small gray man, crisply.

There was a delay. Sir Robert took his communicator out of their hearing and was quickly in communication with Chief of Clanfearghus in embattled Edinburgh. They were going through their communicators in Pali. Chief of Clanfearghus said he didn't see why not since they were the original government and there was no other.

The small gray man called over, "Record his brief statement in clear, if you please. We must have nothing irregular. Nothing that won't stand up in court or litigation."

They didn't like to put it out on the air so Chief of Clanfearghus said it in the Gaelic language and they recorded it.

The small gray man was all business. He took the recording and said, "Do you have any money? Galactic credits, I mean."

Well, usually one or another of them had Galactic credits they had taken off dead Psychlos as souvenirs. But Jonnie's pouch had been ruined and Angus was carrying only his tool kit and Robert the Fox had never bothered to pick any up. But the communicator Quong went tearing around to guards and came back in a moment with a one-hundred-credit bank note the guard said Sir Robert could have and welcome.

"Oh, dear," said the small gray man. "We are so rushed I should have been more explicit. Five hundred credits is the minimum amount."

Jonnie knew where there were probably several hundred thousand of them—in Ker's baggage! But that was all the way up at Lake Victoria. There were about two million more in a safe but that wasn't here either.

Quong went tearing around to the pilots. Bull's-eye! They had been taking them off pilots they had shot down. One had a five-hundred-credit note, six one-hundred-credit notes . . Sir Robert could have them, yes indeed.

"Ah, twelve hundred credits!" said the small gray man. He had been making out a card form "And what is your title?" he asked Sir Robert.

"War Chief of Scotland."

"Ah, no. Shall we just put down here 'Duly Authorized and Empowered Signatory.' And here at the top we will put 'Provisional Government of the Planet Earth.' Date. . . . Address, Call Number . . . no, we can just leave those as they have no legal value. Please sign here at the bottom."

Sir Robert signed.

The small gray man meanwhile had extracted a small pad from his pocket. He opened it and wrote "Provisional Government of the Planet Earth" inside the cover. And then he wrote on the top line of the next page: "C1,200" and his initials, and handed it to Sir Robert. "Here is your passbook. Keep it in a safe place and do not lose it." He shook hands.

The small gray man drew a long sigh. Then he became brisk again. He turned over the lapel of his gray jacket and said something into a button-sized radio.

The guard post outside said into the intercom to them, "The top lights on his ship just went blue."

Quong said, "His radio signal is saying now, 'Local conference. Do not interrupt.' "

The small gray man beamed at them, rubbing his hands together in small quick motions. "Now that you are a customer, I can give you advice. And my first advice is *act fast!*"

He was hauling a book out of his inside pocket. It said "Address Book" on it in Psychlo. "Cast to these addresses as quickly as possible. We will give the belligerents priority. The first would be Hockner . . . home planet Hockner . . . coordinates . . . coordinates . . . yes: Fountain Garden in front of Imperial Palace. . . . Basic coordinates are. . . ." He rattled off a series of numbers and Angus hastily scribbled them down. They were in the same order as Terl's huge book of planets.

Angus said, suspiciously, "Can you operate a console?"

The small gray man shook his head vigorously. "Oh, dear no. Good heavens no, much less build one! I just have the addresses!"

Then he noticed that Angus was about to bring the coordinates up to date with a pen and sheets of paper. "Goodness gracious! Don't you have a coordinate computer? This would take forever by hand! We haven't any time!"

He lifted the lapel but before he spoke he looked for permission to Sir Robert. "Can I have one of my crew bring in a computer? I'll also need the red boxes. Could you send out a guard to escort him in and back out? It won't explode and I'm here."

Sir Robert nodded and the small gray man rattled off something into his lapel radio and a guard raced out. The small gray man waited quite impatiently. But he patted the side of the console housing and beamed. "Quite ornamental. Usually they are so plain, you know."

A gray-uniformed crew member raced in with the guard and deposited a rather impressive computer in the small gray man's hands, laid down a stack of what appeared to be red cardboard, and was escorted out.

With a deft, repeated flick of his hand, the small gray man was working a ratchet on the right side of the computer. They could see different keyboards appearing and disappearing. He overshot and came back one.

"Now here is a coordinate computer," he said, laying it down before Angus. "You feed in the exact firing time on these keys here. It must be the actual moment you will press your firing switch. Then you feed it whether it is just 'cast' or 'cast and recall' or 'exchange' on these buttons here. And then you simply punch in the universe and the eight basic coordinates of time zero on the table on these keys here. Quite simple. You may have this one as a new-accounts gift. I have several. Now let's see. I imagine we can begin firing by twenty-two hundred, sidereal, base universe." He looked at his watch. "That is in eight minutes. A cast requires about two minutes. We have thirty casts to do. We will call in the basic civilized nations and omit Psychlo which makes twenty-nine, but we will add Lord Voraz—good gracious, I hope he is not in bed. That will take an hour. Then we will wait three hours and do a 'cast and recall.' That will take six minutes each—we will make it easy on them so they won't arrive upset and cross—which is three hours. So in about seven hours, plus a little organizing time, you should be able to get them here."

He was quite out of breath. He grabbed a stack of cards that sat on the red stack of cardboard and shoved them at Sir Robert. "Just sign each one at the bottom and I'll fill in the rest. Let me have them as fast as you sign."

Sir Robert looked at the form. It was all in Psychlo:

URGENT

You are courteously requested to send an authorized minister with powers plenipotentiary in all matters relating to political and military relationships with other races and with powers to negotiate and arrange final and binding treaties. His person is guaranteed and any effort to hold him as a hostage shall result in his immediate revocation of all agreements and his instant suicide.

Appear____________________hours at place of arrival.

TO:________________________________

CONFERENCE PLACE:____________________

DURATION OF CONFERENCE AT MINISTERIAL DISCRETION.

PLANET NAME:________________________

ATMOSPHERE OF PLANET:________________

MEAN TEMPERATURES:____________SUN TYPE:__

GRAVITY OF PLANET:___________________

METABOLISM OF RACE:__________________

FOOD SUPPLIES: Available for your race__________

Not available___________________________

Return of emissary guaranteed, safe and in good condition, with copies of all relevant proceedings.

Recommended____________________(Initial and seal)

Authorized representative for the legal government of this planet.

____________________________________(Signed)

All relevant diplomatic costs will be borne by this planet.

____________________________________(Signed)

Sir Robert studied it a bit too long for the small gray man. "Sign it, sign it" he said. "Twice. On the last two lines. I will initial and seal it and fill the rest in."

The small gray man was popping together slabs of cardboard. He would hit them on two diagonal corners and they became a fairly large red box. An unignited smoke pot and flare were on the top of each box and a small gong which would keep sounding.

In a tearing hurry, the small gray man took the first card Sir Robert signed, filled it in with a flurry of entries, initialed it, banged a seal on it, and popped it into the box. "Hockner!" he said to Angus and trotted over to the center of the firing platform, dropped the box, and came back quickly and started to work on the next box.

Jonnie looked at his watch, took the coordinates and marks Angus had drawn out of the computer with a tape, punched them in. "Time!" He punched the firing button.

The first box shimmered an instant and vanished.

"Tolnep!" said the small gray man. "Front steps of their House of Plunder."

Angus rattled the computer. Jonnie set the console. The small gray man raced over and put the second box on the platform. The moment he was off, Jonnie punched the firing button. That red box vanished.

Two Buddhist communicators saw the drill and relieved the small gray man putting the boxes out on the platform. The small gray man was getting quite out of breath. The boy, Quong, noticed all the cards were the same except for the addresses and helped him fill those in so he just had to initial and seal them and pop them in a box. The small gray man caught up and everything was ready to fire forty minutes before the last one would go.

Panting a bit, the small gray man stood aside and let them get on with it.

Sir Robert said to him, "Are you going to conduct this conference too?"

The small gray man shook his head. "Oh dear, no. I'm just helping out. When they get here, it's all up to you!"

Jonnie and Sir Robert exchanged a look. They had better think of something fast! Six and a half hours from now authorized ministers of twenty-nine races, which apparently made up about five thousand separate planets, would be here!

The small gray man said something into his lapel.

A guard outside intercommed in, "The lights on his ship just changed. The blue one is flashing faster and now they have a big flashing red one going."

A communicator said to Sir Robert, "The radio message that keeps going out just changed. It is saying 'Local truce area. Security and safety of your own representatives would be endangered by gunfire, motors, or attack. Keep five hundred miles clear of zone.' "

Sir Robert said, "Can't you just call a general truce for the planet?"

"Oh, my no. I couldn't do that. It would be a protest

producer—an usurpation of the powers of state. I am sorry. Your people in other places will just have to hold out."

Sir Robert went to ops to put messages on the command channel to tell them what was going on. They were encouraged. They reported there was no diminution of the attack's ferocity. They were holding out, but just barely. For some foolish reason the enemy, per pilot reports, had set ancient ruined London on fire.

Angus had tapes punched now for the bulk of the firings. But the small gray man said he could do the rest for him and then do those necessary for the "fire and recall" after the three-hour wait.

A Chinese engineer and Chief Chong-won had been hanging back but were trying to attract Jonnie's attention. He saw them and turned the console over to Angus.

"Forgive us," said Chief Chong-won. "But it is the dam. The water level is dropping and you can now see the tops of the generator intake ports. My engineer here, Fu-ching, says that you won't have any electricity in another four hours."

And they had another six and a half to go!

— 3 —

Jonnie sent for Thor and some maps, including a copy of the old Psychlo defense map.

While he waited, he watched the small gray man working the computer beside the console. His fingers were flying. The handling of that computer compared to the skill of a very experienced pilot on a console. Then he realized the small gray man wasn't even looking at the computer keys. His fingers seemed to move in rapid blurs all by themselves. Jonnie thought that there was more to this small gray man than had surfaced so far. Not just his name and identity, for they didn't know those yet either. But he had some much greater reason to help than he had let on. It was not that Jonnie distrusted him. It was just a feeling Jonnie had that even back of any information the small gray man gave them, there would be much deeper reasons for his presence. He decided that whatever the small gray man might tell them later, he, Jonnie, was going to really get the reasons which underlay all of this. Just a feeling. No, a certainty.

Well, one thing at a time. He had the dam to worry about, for if power failed, that would be the end of all this! And he only had, really, two working hours coming up. Repair a dam that size in two hours? Ow!

The maps came. One was a sketch the Chinese engineers had lately made. They had put the village location in. They had done a sketch map of the lake and aside from the Chinese character notations and numbers, it was all quite nice and comprehensible. They had even taken soundings.

He looked at the defense map and noticed for the first time that it was "copied from the original survey." And from the Psychlo dates, the original survey was nearly eleven hundred years ago. By means of a glass he read the original dam data.

The original Kariba dam, as modified by the Psychlos when they first took over and installed this defense installation, was shown to be about two thousand feet long. The structure height was about four hundred and twenty feet, backed by a lake one hundred seventy-five miles long and about twenty miles wide at its widest point. A truly big dam. It had even had a road for vehicles running all along the top of it.

Jonnie compared the maps. The original had no place for any village! What was this? Had the planet changed its face?

He grabbed a man-map of the area. The river had been named the ["Zambesi"], about twenty-two hundred miles long and one of the world's major rivers. It had flowed through ["Kariba Gorge"] and here it had been dammed for hydroelectric power, an immense undertaking. The sides of the gorge at this place had been steep too. No place for any village! He compared the maps.

The top of the dam that had been a road, even before the ship hit the lake, had been awash.

Then Jonnie knew what had happened. The floods of the Zambesi, year after year for eleven hundred years, had been silting up this lake.

No wonder the water level had dropped so incredibly fast. The crash must have blown a million tons of silt over the dam. And now there was not enough water flow to replace it so fast for there wasn't that much lake! It was now only about one hundred twenty miles long, and the water at the dam itself was only about a thousand feet wide. The rest had been mud.

He said to Chong-won and the Chinese engineer, "This dam had six generator intake ports where the water entered from the lake, fell through the dam, and turned the generators. Right now, I want all six of them closed. The instant they are through firing, in about twenty-five minutes, we're going to cut all power. Do that, then close the ports. When they need electricity to start firing again we will omit lake defense cable to get rid of its power drain and we will open up only two generator ports. Can you do this?"

"Ah, yes!" Then a repeat. "You want us to shut off all power in about twenty-five minutes, close all generator ports, and about two hours later omit defense cable at the lake and open only two ports to the generators. We will also close all spillways?"

Jonnie nodded. The excess dam water hadn't ever before gone over the top of this dam. It spilled through spillways under the dam and reentered the river far below. Conserve water. That wouldn't handle the whole situation but it might help.

Thor was there. "Get Dwight!" Jonnie said.

"He's in the hospital. Broken arm, bashed up."

"He was also our best explosives man at the lode," said Jonnie. "Get him."

They were still firing at the console but he could use this time to organize.

Dwight came. He had two black eyes and a plaster cast on his arm. He was limping. But he was grinning like a lighthouse.

Jonnie wasted no time. "Dwight, collect two one-thousand-foot rolls of blast cord, about three one-hundred-pound drums of liquid explosive, three of those port-a-pack drill rigs with a hundred feet of shaft for each, and fuses and things."

"What are you going to do?" asked Thor. "Blow up the planet?"

Jonnie said, "You, Thor, collect every man here we had with us at lode and a lot of Chinese."

Stormalong was there. "Get ready to transport explosives and men across that lake," Jonnie told him. "The instant they are through with this first hour's firing, we've got to be ready to roll."

He scribbled a note for a communicator to give to Angus the instant he was finished with firing boxes: "You are going to lose all power for two hours. Inform us when you are through with this first run as we'll be running motors and blasting. Don't start firing again until you get an all-clear from us. Communicate with me by mine radio."

Men were being sent through the passage to the outside. Some of them were veterans from the raid, and hospital cases. Dr. Allen looked on with disapproval, especially at Jonnie. But he said nothing.

Jonnie got outside. It was daylight now, thank heaven. He could see what he was doing. He looked at the dam. Yes, indeed. Silt! There was silt splattered all over the place. What a muddy job *this* would be. Where the top of the dam had been broken, piles of silt lay there. There was silt all up the cliff sides. Splattered as if with a gigantic paintbrush. Wet silt. One of the biggest dangers here was slipping and sliding.

He had his mine radio on so he could be told when they were done with the first hour's firing. Men were running dollies out of deep magazines, getting explosives to a plane. Pilots were standing by. Two mine passenger planes were loading personnel. A dozen Chinese raced into the powerhouse equipped with big wrenches: they would need them to move levers and controls frozen in place for a thousand years.

Jonnie walked to the dam edge and looked up the lake.

He couldn't believe his eyes. He would have thought the plunge through the atmosphere would have destroyed more of it than that.

There was the capital ship, a gigantic wreck, dug sideways into the silt five miles uplake from the dam.

And it was contributing its share to the disaster.

The twisted, charred hulk was blocking fresh water flow to the dam! Above it, a new lake was forming.

He got Dwight. "You pick about three men. Put them on a flying platform. Lay blast cord on the east side of that wreck and blow a new water channel around it. I'll give you the time to fire the cord. Get it laid and come back to me."

Dwight rushed off to find his men and more explosives.

Jonnie walked over to a point where he could see the opposite end of the dam. It was a very curved dam, its lake side jutting into the lake like a half-moon. Yes, there sure was water escaping. Because of the shape of the dam, a hard push of concussion against it would cause the ends to thrust much more strongly into the banks. The far end over there was firm enough against the cliff, but the *bottom* of the dam must have moved. Water was roaring out under that far edge like a gigantic fire hose.

Possibly ancient cracks at the far base had been filled with silt until now. But the blast had torn them open. The only thing that would plug that was about half a million tons of rock dumped upstream from it. And this was no time to be dumping rock with blade scrapers and cranes.

The half-formed plan he had made had been right. He looked at the cliffs on the far side of the gorge. If he blew one of them down to fill the breach. would the concussion also rip out the rest of the dam?

The defense cable also ran along those cliffs. He did not dare sacrifice that too.

Angus's voice on the mine radio. "First stage of firing is complete. Ready to shut down!"

"Shut down!" said Jonnie into his mine radio. "Powerhouse! Take the power off! Stormalong! Fly them!"

The sizzle of the armor cable vanished. There was a patter of burst shell fragments, dead birds, and leaves and they dropped to the ground, no longer held there by the ionization armor.

The planes took off with a blasting roar.

Jonnie had spotted an unused flying platform and he stepped aboard and hit the console. He went streaking out over the dam and lake, heading for the tops of the far cliffs.

Dwight was there. Jonnie eyed the texture of the rock in the cliffs. He estimated the rush and flow of water which must be occurring at this side bottom of the lake. His task was to dump enough rock off these cliffs into the lake and get it carried into that break to plug it. A tricky calculation.

Three holes. He needed to drill three holes, each about a hundred feet deep and each at an exact angle. These would be at the points where the cliff must be sheered off.

He pointed, racing along back of the cliff edge. One two, three. About two hundred yards uplake from the dam. Down at an angle of about fifteen degrees from the vertical.

Men got the port-a-pack drills in operation. They were usually used to deep-core a vein. But they could drill a fast hole. Fast enough? He only had two hours.

The cable! This section lay closer to the lake than they were drilling. He mustn't sacrifice it. If left where it was it would get severed by any blast and slide into the lake.

"Stormalong!" yelled Jonnie. The pilot had just climbed out of a mine passenger plane. "What's the biggest motor we've got here now?"

Stormalong looked at the planes. They had brought over four. One was a marine attack plane. Stormalong pointed at it.

"Get some technicians down to this end of the dam. There's a cable junction box there according to this old defense map. Get them to unhook it. And then you put a heavy line on that end and fly this whole section of it out of the ground and dump it up there."

This was right where Stormalong lived. What a crazy idea! To take the unfastened cable end and secure it to a plane and fly the plane southwest up the lake and tear the cable out! He needed no further instructions. He knew the weight of a tenth of a mile of cable might well crash the plane. He'd put a quick release trip on it. He sent technicians racing to disconnect the dam end of it.

Jonnie looked at the drills. There were armored bits and they could stand an awful lot of heat. But they were smoking. How fast could they drill? He looked at his watch and saw how many sections they were down already. This was going to be close!

Up the lake, five miles away, the old mine hand that Dwight had sent and two assistants were sliding and slithering around in the silt beside the battleship wreck. They were sinking almost to their hips. The flying platform they had taken had to be reflown by its operator every few minutes to prevent it from simply sinking out of sight in the ooze.

What a gigantic wreck! No wonder they couldn't put those down in atmosphere. They must assemble them on that moon, Asart, above Tolnep. Probably they flew the pieces up there section by section. Only intricate calculations of planetary gravity and gravitic force flows would let those things fly at all.

He wondered for a sad moment whether Glencannon's body was in there somewhere. But even a Mark 32 couldn't stand up to that internal blast. That ship was really a graveyard. There must be charred chunks of fifteen hundred Tolneps in that twisted, blackened wreck. How long was it? Two thousand feet? Three thousand? Hard to tell from here, so much was buried. But it was sure making a great dam. One would have thought it would have buried itself deeper. Then he saw what really was the case. It had made a sort of crater and it was the crater *edge* that was restraining the water.

He took a small scope from his pocket to see exactly what the men were doing. Yes, they were doubling up blast cord over the far crater edge and then another one of them was doing the same thing on the near crater edge. They needed no advice.

The drills were screaming through the rock, steam shooting up from their overheated water-coolant jets. Twenty men were rigging a line from the lake water to a mine pump. They were getting more cooling water.

Ow, the silt! It was hard to walk without sliding and nearly all the crews by now were caked with mud.

He looked at his watch. It would be very touch and go. To drill a hundred feet of hole in three hours would be a bit of a feat; they had to do it in about one and a half! They were really leaning on those drills. Four men on each were adding their weight to the handles.

He hoped that flashing signal on the small gray man's ship would hold good. They had skeletonized their defense force to handle this dam and they were wide open to attack with no cable armor.

His mine radio came alive. It was the party at the wreck calling Dwight. They were ready to fire. Dwight looked over to Jonnie.

With his scope, Jonnie tried to see the generator intake ports in the dam. Were they closed? Muddy, muddy water. He couldn't see from here. He called the Chinese engineers inside the dam. Chief Chong-won was in there.

"It needs five minutes to close the last port," the chief's voice came back. "They've got the excess spillway ports closed. I am sorry, Lord Jonnie. I don't think these levers and wheels have been moved for years."

"Make it a thousand," said Jonnie. "How many men have you got in there?"

"Seventy-two," said the chief.

Good lord, he had half his force inside that dam.

"You're doing great. Finish it up and then get everyone out of there. That dam could go, the whole thing, with these blasts."

"We'll hurry," said the chief.

There was a roar and Stormalong took up slack on the defense cable. He was using his plane's bullhorns. "Ready to rip!" he yelled. "Tell me when everyone is clear!"

The big marine attack plane was hanging in the air at the dam end. Grapnels had the cable and it was loose from the junction box. Men were scrambling away there.

Jonnie yelled to the men on the port-a-packs. "Stand clear!"

Unwilling to leave their drills, they nevertheless shut them off and went slipping and sliding away from the cliff edge.

Jonnie checked it. They were in the clear all along what must be the cable path. "Let her rip!" he yelled into his mine radio.

In the plane, Stormalong poured it on. The cable, like a gigantic snake, jerking and resisting, began to come out of the ground. It was stalling the plane. Stormalong began to dance the huge ship up and down, yanking at the cable. Foot by foot and yard by yard it worked free of the ground. The plane rose higher and higher, working along the cliff edge.

He had almost half of it out of the ground!

There was a ripping pop.

The cable parted!

Stormalong's ship catapulted toward the sky, trailing two hundred yards of cable.

He checked the rise. That Stormalong could fly. He took the broken piece up the lake and laid it on the shore. He triggered his quick release and dropped it.

Stormalong came back overhead. Someone in the plane was lowering the grapnels. "Hook me up!" yelled Stormalong through the bullhorn above.

Men went slithering down to the cliff edge. They caught the grapnel and got it securely fastened to the torn cable end.

It could be patched. But all this was taking time and the drill crews weren't drilling.

They got it fastened again and once more Stormalong was pulling the remaining length from the bed in which it had rested for centuries.

He got it free of the blast area and dropped it.

The men raced back to their drills.

"We're all finished here!" came Chief Chong-won's voice on the mine radio.

"Excellent," said Jonnie. "Now clear every man out of there and tell me when they're gone, including you!"

He could see them streaming out of the powerhouse and up the far roadway, tiny figures in blue work clothes. At last they were safely away from the dam. "All clear, Lord Jonnie," said Chief Chong-won.

It wouldn't stop the drilling. Jonnie signaled Dwight. Dwight gave the crew at the wreck their orders. "Fire in the hole!" yelled Dwight. Jonnie could see them setting fuses. Then they slipped and slithered and plowed through the ooze to their flying platform and boarded it. They had to bodily haul the last one onto it by his collar and fly off with his legs still dangling. The platform went over to a safe area and landed. Jonnie watched the wreck area.

Blowie! Blowie! The sharp cracks of blast cord exploding.

A long line of mud catapulted into the sky. Smoke and spattering goo obscured the wreck for a moment.

A shock wave made the ground tremble. A small roll of water ran down the lake. Twenty-four seconds after the blast the sound of it reached them like a hard buffet with a big hand.

The smoke was clearing away up there. The enormous wreck had not moved but a channel had been cut through the upper and lower crater edges. A trickle of water started through the farther one. Just a trickle?

Jonnie held his breath, eyeing it with a scope, afraid that in their shortness of time they would have to shoot again. "Come on! Come on!" he was saying. "More, more!" He knew water was very erosive and tended to chew and widen its own way. "Come on!"

The farther side was at least two feet higher than the lake at the dam. It should have more push than that!

Right then some object in the way of the flow was worked out by the water. It was a big blast gun. It twisted in the swirl and then at last went tumbling away.

The water burst through the far crater wall. It swirled and surged in the crater, a boiling, frothing churn of discolored mud. Water thrust the upper channel wider. More water burst through.

Now it was working at the nearest ditch the blast cord had dug. It gnawed at obstruction and debris. And then it started through!

A third surge in the upper crater. Pieces were tearing loose. There was a roaring torrent there now. The bowl was filling; it was emptying into the lower lake.

They had gotten the river running again. Jonnie told Dwight to give them a very well done.

The drills were raving and smoking. Jonnie looked at his watch. They only had about twenty minutes left. Where had the time gone? "How many drill sections have you gotten into those holes?" asked Jonnie to Thor.

"Five. That's seventy-five feet."

"It will have to be enough. Get those drills out of there. Stormalong!" he barked into his radio. "Start pulling these crews and equipment out of here!"

He could see Chief Chong-won, a speck way over on the far side. He spoke into his mine radio. "Chief, you are going to see one awful flash over here in a few minutes. Wait to make sure the whole dam doesn't go out, and the instant it's safe, send a picked crew in there to open two generator ports and get the power back on to the cone cable and pagoda area only. Got it?"

"Yes, Lord Jonnie."

"And be sure to be under cover for this blast," added Jonnie.

They had the port-a-packs out and were clattering them in plane holds.

"Dwight!" said Jonnie. "Take those three drums of liquid explosive and pour them in those holes and then set the empty drums on top of them. Fast!"

Dwight pointed with his good arm and got men running. They began to pour a big drum of explosive into each hole. The holes were still so hot, the explosive was almost boiling. It was hard to get it to flow down against the trapped air. The air came bubbling and steaming back up.

Jonnie raced along, stringing blast cord. He put a big loop of it around each place where they would set a drum. The drums would be like bombs with the explosive vapor still in them.

"Fuses!" yelled Dwight.

"We've got no time," shouted Jonnie. "I'm going to set this off with a plane's guns!"

"What?" gawked Thor.

They had the barrels empty and were putting them in place in the circle of blast cord at each hole. A shot into any one drum would set off the lot.

"Leave me that plane!" Jonnie pointed at a single battle plane they'd brought. "Get the rest of them out of here with all men right now!"

Stormalong started to protest and then started hurrying men into the remaining ships. As their equipment went slamming into the planes, Stormalong yelled over to Jonnie, "Shoot it from way up! This thing is going to skyrocket!"

Jonnie was looking at his watch. They only had nine minutes left.

The planes were taking off, Dwight was being dragged into the last one. Jonnie looked at this setup. All okay.

He rushed to the battle plane and got ready to start it.

There was nobody left in the area.

He took off. He jumped the ship to about two thousand feet. The dam still looked big.

The planes were landing in sandbag abutments on the other side. Stormalong had really gotten across and slammed them down in an awful hurry.

Chief Chong-won and his men were under cover.

"Fire in the hole!" said Jonnie on his mine radio.

He flipped the guns to "Flame," "Narrow," and "Maximum." He checked his security belt.

Now for some nice gunnery. At this moment it all looked pretty peaceful down there. The blackened wreck was spilling flotsam as water went through its broken girders. The river was flowing right up to the dam lake.

But the increased water was spilling under the dam below the lake and it would be tearing that hole wider and wider.

Jonnie closed all windows with a flick of switches, made sure doors were all secure. Should he back up to three thousand? No. This was the best range. A battle plane could take a lot. But he had never heard of anybody setting off a hundred fifty gallons of liquid explosive before. Plus a thousand feet of number five blast cord.

He put his sights carefully on the center barrel. He pushed the gun trip.

There was a flash across the whole sky before him. A curtain of green fire three thousand feet high.

Crash!

The recoil hit him and the plane went spinning skyward like a thrown toy.

The yank of the security belt was like a blow. It knocked the wind out of him.

Three seconds later he found he was upside-down. He punched the console. The plane's balance motors caught up and righted it. He was flying backward.

The whine of engines fought against the wrong direction.

The plane steadied. Somebody would have to replace the windscreen. It had a diagonal crack in it.

And then he saw the cliff. The smoke had cleared. And the whole cliff front was sliding down toward the lake in slow, slow motion.

Half a million cubic yards of rock, moving down.

A lot of it was apparently still in one piece. But that was an illusion. It was a clean slice of cliff, knifed off neatly. But inside it the rock was cracked and shattered and just before it hit the water it lost shape and tumbled in fragments. It had looked at first like it hadn't left the bank. But there had been distance. Some of it struck nearly at the center of the lake.

He watched the dam. Would it, too, crumble in slow motion and this whole lake go roaring down the gorge? He had set it up so the shock wave would go into the air, not down and through the ground. It had gone into the air, all right; witness what happened to his plane.

The first wave hit the dam and a splatter of water soared a hundred feet above the dam top. Had he lost too much water there? No, that was just spray.

Was the dam holding?

He could not tell whether the underwater currents were carrying the rock into the low hole. He darted the plane sideways. Water was still roaring out under the dam. He watched.

Was it his imagination that it was lessening?

His attention was yanked off it by blue figures racing down to the powerhouse. They certainly had not waited!

He looked at his watch. He only had two minutes to get this plane out of the air.

With a pound on the console keys Jonnie lanced the plane down to an empty abutment. He killed its motor. He had to make sure it was off—his ears were ringing.

Thirty-three seconds left to go. *That* was cutting it close!

He went through the underground passage into the cone. He looked at the pagoda. Not even a tile had moved in that blast.

Angus was at the console. The small gray man at the computer. Angus waved and shouted, "Power's on! We're firing!"

— 4 —

Somebody else had been busy in the last two hours. A different music was playing. It was very noble and dignified. It sounded vaguely familiar to Jonnie and then he remembered that a cadet had found a pile of what he called "records," big things: if you ran a rose thorn held in a paper box around an endless circular groove and put your ear close, it sounded like twenty or thirty instruments playing; the ancient label on the record, mostly faded out, said the name of the piece was ["The Cleveland Symphony Orchestra. Lohengrin."] This music was much like that but deeper, fuller, quite impressive! Jonnie suspected the small gray man had had a hand in that. Something from his ship? Music for the delegates to arrive by, of course.

And something else that must be from the small gray man's ship: there was a screen, meshed so you could see through it, all around the firing platform, and Dr. Allen was finishing putting it up. "Disease control," he said cryptically as Jonnie passed by.

Sweaty Chinese engineers crawled out of a duct hole with cheery faces. They had air circulating in and out now. The smoke had already cleared away. A good thing, thought Jonnie. A lot of different atmospheres would momentarily be whiffing across the platform at the instant of coincidence of spaces and during recoil especially.

And the mobs of Chinese refugees from the village had changed, too. They may have lost their village but they had saved their possessions and these had been scattered about. Now the untidy bundles had vanished. Children and dogs were quiet down in the rifle pits and parents and others that had no immediate duties were standing about. They had on what must be their best clothes.

An honor guard came out of a bunker and finished neatening themselves up with a tug here and a buckle there. Six of them, different nationalities; all in their best uniforms. No weapons but the shafts of pennons. An aged Chinese gentleman—no, a

Buddhist communicator dressed to look like a Chinese, wearing a silk robe with designs on it and a small cap—was taking position at the head of the honor guard. Of course, somebody who spoke Psychlo to greet the arrivals, yet who looked like a dignitary.

It would be three or four minutes until the first one appeared and Jonnie walked toward the ops room. He didn't get in. The boy, Quong, sprinted out, going somewhere fast, and Sir Robert popped out of the door and called after him, "And tell Stormalong to bring that other recognition book too!" The boy hardly checked his pace, nodding in full run.

Beyond Sir Robert the ops room was boiling with sound and movement as people worked.

Jonnie opened his mouth to ask how it was going. But Sir Robert answered before he could speak. Sir Robert shook his head bleakly. "They're using a new kind of bomb. The guns sometimes don't explode it. And the idiots are burning deserted cities! Our drones are still running. Why would they want to burn an empty place that used to be called 'San Francisco?' The last drone shot we had of it, there were just two bears walking down the street. We're dealing wi' daft imbeciles!"

Jonnie made to go in past him and Sir Robert shook his head again. "You can't do anything more than we're doing. Have you thought what we're going to tell these emissaries?

"No idea," said Jonnie. "Shouldn't we get Clanchief Fearghus down here?"

"Naw, naw," said Sir Robert. "No e'en a wee chonce! Edinburgh is gang up in flames!"

Jonnie felt a contraction of his heart. "Any news of Chrissie?"

"They'd a' be doon in the shelters. Dunneldeen is giving them a' the air cover he can."

Stormalong raced in with the book.

Sir Robert took a look at Jonnie. "Go get yersel' cleaned up. And think of something to tell these arrivals!" He shooed Jonnie off toward his room and vanished into ops. He closed the door behind him so the frantic sounds wouldn't come into the platform area.

Jonnie walked on toward his room. Just as he was about to duck into the passage the humming of the wires, which had been going on underneath the music, made itself known by stopping. There was a space of time and then a slight recoil.

The Hockner emissary was on the platform. Noseless, holding a monocle on a stick, he was dressed in shimmering robes. He had a gold-colored hamper beside him.

A bell on the screen pinged. The screen top edge lit with a purple glow all around. The Hockner picked up the hamper, looked about through his monocle and minced off the platform. The honor guard saluted and dipped pennons.

He halted well clear of the disease control fence. A messenger took the hamper from him. The Buddhist in Chinese clothes bowed.

In a supercilious tone of voice, the Hockner emissary said, in Psychlo, "I am Blan Jetso, extraordinary minister plenipotentiary of the Emperor of the Hockners, long may he reign! I am empowered to negotiate and arrange final and binding amendments to agreements or treaties in all things political or military. My person is inviolate and any molestation cancels any agreements. Any effort to hold me hostage shall be in vain for I shall not be redeemed by my government. At the threat of any torture or extortion, you are warned that I shall commit suicide instantly in ways unknown to you. I am not the carrier of any disease nor weapon. Long live the Hockner Empire! And how are you today?"

The communicator dressed as a Chinese bowed and made a brief, fast speech of welcome, very pat, told him the conference would begin in about three hours and led him off to a private apartment where he could rest or refresh himself.

Jonnie had an idea these arrivals would all be about the same, different only as to races, persons, and clothes.

He was trying to think of something to tell the emissaries. It was a bit of a shock for Sir Robert to infer that it was up to *him*. When that grizzled old veteran didn't have any ideas— But then he must be terribly distressed over Edinburgh. So was Jonnie.

— 5 —

Jonnie ducked under the door beam to enter the passage to his room and a wave of dizziness hit him. So far, in trying to handle the dam, he had carried himself along on willpower and he had pushed the feeling aside. But now, with worry about Edinburgh and Chrissie, he felt he was not in very good condition to handle much of anything. He had taken quite a battering these last couple of days.

He was not prepared for what he found in the passage just outside his room. There were four people there and they were working on things he couldn't quite make out. They had low benches, they were sitting on the floor, their heads were down, and their hands were flying.

Mr. Tsung sensed his presence and bobbed up from the floor. He bowed. "Lord Jonnie, meet my wife!"

The second person, a gray-haired Chinese woman with a kindly face, bobbed up, smiled, bowed. Jonnie bowed. It made his head feel bad. The woman popped down and went right back to work.

"Meet my daughter," said Mr. Tsung.

The third person bobbed up, bowed. The daughter was a very beautiful Chinese girl, very delicate. She wore a flower in her hair. Jonnie bowed. It made his head feel worse. The girl sat down and went frantically back to work.

"Meet my son-in-law," said Mr. Tsung.

A good-looking Chinese bobbed up from his bench with a clatter. He bowed. He was in the blue work uniform the mechanics wore. Jonnie bowed, very slightly so the room wouldn't spin. The young man popped down and sparks again flew from his tools.

Jonnie looked at them. They were working dedicatedly and with near ferocity on whatever they were doing. Jonnie felt a pang of sorrow. If this conference failed and if they lost, what suffering would await these decent people! These and the rest of the thirty-five thousand that were all that remained of the human race. He could not face the prospect of letting them down.

He went into his room. Somebody else had used those two hours. Angus, probably, and an electrician. A rack with three viewscreens now stood against the wall beyond the foot of his bed. A button camera had been placed in the ops room for one screen and he could see the huddled groups there, faces strained as they handled microphones and drone pictures and the operations board. Another button camera was trained on the conference room to broadcast to the second screen—the conference room was empty. The third button camera was on the platform and console and served the third screen.

Even as he looked, the Tolnep emissary arrived. He was in shimmering green; even his cap was green. But he had on dirty blue boots. Huge glasses hid his eyes. He carried a sort of scepter with a large knob at the top and a green hamper on green wheels for his food and supplies. A reptilian creature although he walked upright and had a face and arms and legs. A genetic line from dinosaurs that had become miniature and sentient?

He made his speech much like the Hockner, accepted the reply with an evil smile, folded his shimmering green cloak about his steel hard body, and was led away to a private apartment. He looked like trouble.

Jonnie was about to throw himself down on the bed when he was suddenly obstructed. Mr. Tsung had followed him in. "No, no!" said Mr. Tsung. "Bath!"

Two Chinese had followed Mr. Tsung in. They had a steaming bath sitting on a mine dolly which they pushed to an empty spot on the floor before vanishing.

"I happen to be just about exhausted," said Jonnie in protest. "I will just wash my face—"

Mr. Tsung slid around in front of him with a mirror. "Look!" demanded Mr. Tsung.

Jonnie looked. Mud. Explosive stains. The black silk sling he had been wearing was a tatter of light tan. Silt was all through his beard and hair. He looked down and saw that somewhere he must have walked up to his waist in ooze. He looked down at his hands and he could not even tell the color of his skin. He looked like something no dog would have dragged out of the village garbage dump.

"You win," said Jonnie and wearily began to get out of his clothes. Mr. Tsung had a big mine bucket and as each garment was removed he dropped it with some distaste in the bucket, even the helmet and boots and guns.

Jonnie climbed into the bath. It was not long enough to stretch out his legs but the water came up to his chest. He had never had a hot bath before, only rivers and cold mountain streams. He felt the exhaustion oozing out of him. Indeed, he found with some surprise, there was much you could say in favor of hot baths!

Avoiding the bandage on the arm, Mr. Tsung scrubbed industriously with a lathering soap and a brush. Suddenly he stopped work and there was a whispered consultation back of Jonnie. Then a touch on the top of each of Jonnie's shoulders. Another consultation and one of Jonnie's arms was held out by Mr. Tsung and a piece of string was stretched down the length of it.

Jonnie was momentarily horrified to realize the daughter was behind him and he was naked in a tub! He turned his head but the daughter was gone. Mr. Tsung scrubbed on. He washed Jonnie's hair and beard.

Twice more the bath was stopped. Once to put a string around his chest. The second time to put a string down the side of his leg.

Eventually Mr. Tsung dried his hair and beard with a towel and then wrapped a bigger one around Jonnie as he stepped out of the tub. He dried Jonnie off, having to jump up a bit to really get the shoulders now that Jonnie was standing. He put Jonnie in a soft, blue robe and only then permitted him to lie down on the bed.

Thankful to stretch out at last, avoiding even looking at the screens, Jonnie was interrupted again.

It was Dr. MacKendrick and Dr. Allen. The robe was loose and they got his arm out. Dr. Allen cut off the bandage, cleaned the area with alcohol that stung the nose—probably whiskey of not too good a distillation—poured some white powder in the wound and then made him eat some of it. More sulfa! Mr. Tsung was there with a bowl of soup while Dr. Allen put on a fresh bandage.

Then the two doctors stood back. Jonnie, wise in such medical manners, began to suspect they were up to something. They had that false joviality doctors assume just before they take you by surprise and do something gruesome.

"I always thought," said Dr. Allen, "that Dunneldeen and

Stormalong were wild. But I was out there when you blew that cliff in. *You* are the wild one, Jonnie Tyler. Do you always use a battle plane to light fuses?"

Jonnie was about to inform him somewhat austerely that there had been no time at all to rig fuses when Dr. MacKendrick moved closer.

"I suppose," said MacKendrick, "it just seemed more natural to him." A remark calculated to distract.

And he took the long needle he had been holding behind him and, seizing Jonnie's wrist, slid two inches of steel into a vein and pumped a full syringe of something into Jonnie's blood.

"Ow!" said Jonnie. "That wasn't fair! You know I don't like your needles." The stuff burned like fire in his vein.

"That's for your dizziness," said Dr. MacKendrick, smugly cleaning the needle. "It's some stuff we found called 'B Complex.' The venom and the relaxant and this sulfa all rob the system of it. You'll feel much better very shortly."

"I've got enough to do," said Jonnie, a bit cross, "without being shot full of holes."

Dr. Allen laid a hand on his shoulder. "That's just it," he said. "You've got far, far too much to worry about and to do. You've got to learn to let others help you. Let them contribute as well. You do splendidly. Let others help too!" He gave Jonnie a pat on the shoulder and they left.

The soup had made his stomach feel better. After a bit he raised his head and bobbed it. He wasn't as dizzy as he had been.

Another couple of emissaries had arrived on the platform. The ops room looked frantic. He was worried about this coming conference. Jonnie thought he had lain around long enough.

"Tsung!" he called. "Please get out my best buckskin suit." Yes, he would let someone else contribute. Mr. Tsung could dig up his buckskins.

The result was totally unexpected. Mr. Tsung flashed in, drew himself up to his full five feet, and said, "No!" Then he struggled to find more words from his meager store of English. "They lords!" He couldn't say what he wanted to say.

An amazed Jonnie saw Mr. Tsung tear out of the room and come back in a moment with a Coordinator for the Chinese, one who spoke Mandarin. Mr. Tsung was blazing away at the

Coordinator with every shot in his magazine. Mr. Tsung died down. The Coordinator opened his mouth to speak. Mr. Tsung thought of something else, battered the Coordinator with it, and only then stood back with a "so there" expression and put his hands in his sleeves and bowed.

The Coordinator, a black-bearded Scot, took a deep breath. "You're maybe not going to like this, MacTyler, but you have gotten yourself a diplomatic manager. I know these Chinese, and when they get their minds set on something, they're worse than my old woman!"

Jonnie had lain back. He addressed the ceiling. "And what is wrong with my simply asking for my best buckskin suit to be laid out?"

"Everything," said the Coordinator. "Just everything." He sighed and began to explain: "Mr. Tsung is a descendant of a family that served as chamberlains to the Ch'ing Dynasty—those who ruled China from the mandate 1644 A.D. to about 1911. Maybe eleven hundred years ago. That was the last dynasty before China became a People's Republic. The court and emperors were not Chinese; they were a race called 'Manchus.' And they needed a lot of advice. Tsung says his family served them well but times changed and because they *had* served the Manchus his ancestors were exiled to Tibet. It was the western powers that overthrew the Manchus, Tsung says, not his family's advice. So Mr. Tsung here is really a 'Mandarin of the blue button' according to ancestry, a lord of the court.

"He says all the family records and scrolls are with the Chinese university library you put in a vault someplace."

"Russia," said Jonnie. "They're in the Russian base, though lord knows how it's holding out right now!"

"Well, good," said the Scot. "He says he could read you some of it but he doesn't have it here. But his family always kept up on its background, expecting someday a dynasty they could serve would come back into power. They have long memories, these Chinese—imagine waiting eleven hundred years to get back a job!"

Mr. Tsung detected this was wandering off track and he nudged the Coordinator's arm and made gestures that clearly said, tell him, tell him!

The Coordinator sighed. He was not sure how Jonnie would

take this. "He says you are 'Lord Jonnie' and"—he got it all out in a rush—"you can't go around looking like a barbarian!"

If Jonnie had not been so worried about other things he would have laughed.

The Coordinator was relieved that this had not been received as criticism. He continued. "He says he knew there would be a diplomatic conference and that a lot of lords would be arriving and that they would be very uppish and snobbish and fancy. And it's true enough. I've seen them coming in on the platform. Jeweled breathe-masks, glittering cloth, ornaments—one even had a jeweled monocle. Pretty fancy dudes!"

He then swallowed and said the rest in a rush, "And if you go out there and talk to them in *hides,* they'll think you're just a barbarian and won't listen to you. He says if you look and act," he swallowed again, "like an uncouth savage, they'll hold you in contempt." He stopped, relieved to have gotten through it. "And that's what he was trying to tell you. Don't be upset with him. I could add that quite in addition to a genuine affection for you, about thirty-five thousand lives—no, less than that now, but a lot—depend on this conference. Otherwise I wouldn't have translated it for him because to me, MacTyler, ye're no barbarian!"

Jonnie thought all he would have to do was reassure Mr. Tsung he would be polite and not slap anybody and that would be that. But not so!

Mr. Tsung made the Coordinator stand right there and translate everything he said exactly with no changes. Mr. Tsung hunkered down close to the side of the bed and started talking. The Coordinator translated at each pause.

" 'It is one thing,' " translated the Scot, " 'to be a mighty warrior . . . but although you have won every battle . . . and driven the enemy to rout . . . from a field of slaughter . . . the entire war . . . can be lost . . . at the conference table!' "

Jonnie digested that. They actually hadn't won the war yet by a long ways, but even if they did, they *could* lose the whole thing in that conference room. He had known that, but he was impressed. Mr. Tsung had obviously sought this job, not as somebody who cleaned up a room, but as an advisor. Well, heavens knew he needed advice. He had come up with no ideas.

" 'Your attitude,' " the Coordinator continued to translate as the little Mr. Tsung spoke on, " '. . . must be calculated to impress. . . . A lord is used to handling inferiors. . . . He is impressed by being handled as an inferior. . . . Be haughty. . . . Do not be polite. . . . Be cold and disdainful. . . . Be distant and aloof.'

"Say, this old man is really wringing out my Mandarin. That's real court Chinese he's talking!"

Mr. Tsung motioned him not to add his own comments.

" 'Do not,' " the Scot obediently translated, " 'agree or seem to agree to anything. . . . Your words can be tricked into seeming to agree . . . so avoid the word: yes. . . . They will make preposterous demands they know they cannot attain . . . just to gain bargaining points . . . so you in return should advance to them . . . impossible demands even if you feel they won't agree, and who knows, you might win them. . . ! All diplomacy is a matter of compromise. . . . There is a middle ground between the two opposite poles of impossible demands . . . which will become the eventual treaty or agreement. . . . Always work for the most advantageous position you can get.' "

The Scot paused. "He wants to know if you've got all that."

"Yes, sir!" said Jonnie. "And welcome."

He was feeling this was useful even though it didn't give him the idea he needed.

"And now," said the Coordinator, "he wants to give you lessons in deportment. Watch him."

Well, they were dealing with creatures from many another race, and their ideas of deportment and those from ancient Imperial China might not agree at all. So Jonnie felt a bit tolerant as he watched the Chinese. But almost immediately he felt he was wrong. These manners fitted any race!

How to stand. Feet apart, tall, leaning slightly back. Firmly fixed to the earth. Position *dominant*. Got that? Then do it!

How to hold a sceptre or wand. One hand on grip end, other end laid in the other palm. Grip both ends to show control. Tap one end into palm to hint the small possibility of punishment when one might wish to seem a bit offended. Wave idly in air to show that the other's argument was of no consequence and was like the wind. Got that? Here is a wand. Do it! Not quite right. Be easy, lordly. Now do them all again.

Walk as though not caring what lies before you. Suggest power. Steady, unstoppable. Like this. Got it? Do it!

For half an hour Mr. Tsung worked on Jonnie. And Jonnie realized that his own walk was like that of a panther whereas for this conference it must be stately.

Mr. Tsung made him go through the whole lesson and then the postures and walks again before he was satisfied. Jonnie, who had always had a sinking feeling about being a diplomat, began to feel a bit more confident. There was an art to this thing. It was like hunting game but a different kind of game. It was like a battle but a different kind of battle.

He thought he was all through. He could see on the screen that more and more emissaries were arriving. But Mr. Tsung said they would all have to present their credentials at the first meeting in the conference room and that there was lots and lots of time. Had Jonnie thought of a strategy? A strategy was very necessary. How to approach the diplomatic battle, what one intended to use to maneuver. Well, Jonnie could think about it. It was like a battle but your infantry and cavalry were ideas and words. Maneuvered wrongly, it meant defeat!

Meanwhile, they had to handle this other matter, and leaving Jonnie a bit mystified, Mr. Tsung went out in the hall.

Seeing that for the moment Jonnie wasn't busy, Chief Chong-won slid in the door. He was beaming and bobbing his head. "The dam!" And he made a tight grip with both fists and gestured with his hands. "The hole. The outflow is decreasing. The level of the lake is rising." He bobbed his head vigorously, bowed deeply, and vanished.

Jonnie thought, well that was one thing that had gone right. The power wouldn't go off and leave some diplomat parked in some wrong space! All he had to worry about now was a burning planet, the fate of its people, and this conference.

That shot had worked. He wasn't dizzy.

— 6 —

The "other matter" turned out to be a haircut. The daughter came in and sat him in a chair facing the viewscreens and got to work with a small pair of scissors and a comb. The idea was rather novel to Jonnie—he usually just hacked his hair off with a knife when it got too long.

She seemed to be very practiced and expert and no doubt took care of the tonsorial requirements of many, for she just sailed in with her scissors moving so fast they sounded like an ore belt running at high speed, clip, clip, clip.

So diplomacy was like a battle, Jonnie was thinking. Watching these lords arrive one could see that they practically oozed authority and power. The visitors attacking Earth were almost local small fry, controlling at the most a few dozen planets. Some of those arriving, he knew from earlier readings, were from other universes and controlled hundreds of planets in just one governmental sphere. And they were very arrogant, very sure of themselves. Whatever their physical form, there was no doubt that they were ministers plenipotentiary to powerful heads of state. What wealth and striking power they represented! Behind them were collective populations numbering trillions in just one state alone. They were the veterans and victors of hundreds of such conferences. Yes, a conference *was* a battle and an even more important one than a war.

And what chance did he and Sir Robert have against these experienced diplomats? They were both warriors, not glib, smooth, cunning courtiers with a thousand parliamentary tricks up their sleeves. With no guns or battalions, but with only his wits and the tips Mr. Tsung had given him, he felt quite outnumbered. And so far he had no strategy at all.

The girl had a small mirror she was holding up so he could see. She had cut his hair to collar height in back and combed and rolled it at the bottom. It looked kind of like a helmet he had seen with a back neck guard. And the hair was shiny. His beard and mustache looked very precise much shorter. He hardly knew himself—had she seen some old paintings of men with beards and mustaches cut like this? Indeed she had—there was an ancient man-book, English, open on the bed to a picture of somebody named [“Sir Francis Drake”] that had defeated somebody called [“the Spaniards”] long, long ago.

His attention was attracted by something and he took the mirror from her. His neck! The scars had been quite faint for they were really callouses. And they were gone.

He had to look very hard to see the remains of the Brigante grenade scar on his cheek. That would probably vanish too.

Somehow he felt freed with the collar scars gone. He understood the irony of it and would have smiled but his attention was pulled to the ops room screen. The sound relay had been off and he gave the girl back the mirror and hit the button.

“. . .can't think what they're up to!” Stormalong was saying as he angrily finished pulling another picture out of the drone resolver. “I've lost count!”

“Fifteen,” said somebody else.

“Look at this! A spray of fire bombs going down into this deserted . . .” he looked at a map. “Detroit! Why set Detroit on fire? There's been nobody in Detroit for over a thousand years! Are they trying to pull defenses over to that continent? They're insane.” He threw the picture down. “I'm not providing any air cover for a bunch of ruins! What's the latest from Edinburgh?”

“Antiaircraft still replying,” said someone at the ops board. “Smoke interfering with visual firing. Dunneldeen just shot down his sixteenth Hawvin strafing plane.”

Jonnie touched the button to “sound off.” He felt an impatience taking hold of him. These diplomats coming in one by one . . . it was too slow!

The Coordinator had come in with Mr. Tsung, who was holding a lot of things in his arms. It was obvious that Jonnie was under strain. Mr. Tsung said something in his singsong voice. The Coordinator said, “Mr. Tsung reminds you that even a lost battle can be redeemed at a conference table, to be patient and use skill.”

Mr. Tsung had other things now. He took the haircut cloth off Jonnie and showed him a tunic.

It was a very plain garment at first glance. It was cut from shimmering black silk; it had a stand-up collar. It was supposed to be a tight form fit. But it was the silver-colored buttons that attracted Jonnie's attention.

He knew what they were. He had once remarked to Ker that it was surprising to see such pretty metal on a Psychlo emergency switch. It looked like silver at first glance but the least amount of light striking it made it glow in rainbow colors. Ker had said, no, it wasn't used for emergency switches because it was pretty. It was used because it was *hard*. It was a one-molecule-thick metal spray of an iridium alloy, and no matter how many claw points hit it, it wouldn't wear off. And when you were in a dark mine with little light, the emergency button was visible because it looked like it flashed in colors. He knew what the son-in-law had been doing—plating buttons. Enough to blind you!

Mr. Tsung had him put it and the black silk pants on and buttoned the tunic all up—iridium buttons every couple of inches down the front.

Then Mr. Tsung made him put on a pair of boots. They were Chinko boots but they had plated them with iridium alloy.

A belt was fastened around him, a wide one, and it was also plated. All except the buckle. And that was his old gold-colored "U.S. Air Force" buckle, shined until it gleamed. He remembered thinking once in the cage he might be the last surviving member of a long-gone force. A strange thing to think. But right now it sort of cheered him up.

He had thought he was getting dressed and was a bit dismayed to find that Mr. Tsung did not like a pucker on the shoulder and a certain gather in the tunic back and took it all off him and sent them back.

Mr. Tsung had something else now. It was his twisted knobkerrie with the carved figures. But they had plated it with iridium. It flashed like a length of flame. He knew he couldn't use it that way but he was glad not to be going into that conference totally without a weapon.

Then the son-in-law came in. He was carrying a helmet. Basically it was just a Russian helmet they had smoothed down. But what had they done to it? The chin strap was plated with iridium alloy. So was the whole helmet. But what was this? The son-in-law turned it, a bit proudly, so Jonnie could see what was on the front.

How had they done this? Then he saw that the son-in-law was

holding the paper patterns he had laid down on the helmet front and sides, one after the other, and sprayed through the open holes with different metal sprays.

It was a dragon.

And what a dragon!

Gold wings on the side of the helmet, clawed paws that seemed to grip the lower helmet edge, scales and spikes from the spine edged in blue, a ferocious face with what appeared to be real rubies for flaming eyes, white fangs in a scarlet mouth. Ferocious. And a round, whitish ball in its scarlet, otherwise gaping, mouth.

It looked three-dimensional. It was similar to the dragon at the console and the clay dragons lying on the building pile except for this big white ball in its mouth.

At first Jonnie felt it was far too fancy. And just then another emissary arrived on the platform wearing a towering gold crown. This was far less fancy than that. But still. . . .

Jonnie looked at it. It was a bit different from the other dragons. "Very beautiful," said Jonnie so the Coordinator could tell the son-in-law.

They were fixing his clothes. It wasn't time yet by a long way. Jonnie looked at the helmet. Via the Coordinator he said to Mr. Tsung, "Tell me about this dragon."

Mr. Tsung tossed it off and via the Coordinator told Jonnie that the throne of China had been called the "Dragon Throne." "Lung p'ao" or "Chi-fu" patterns or robes were court dress. It was an Imperial . . .

Jonnie knew all that. "Tell him to tell me about *this* dragon. It's different."

Mr. Tsung sighed. There were a lot of other things, far more important, that he should be telling Lord Jonnie, and he didn't think it was very applicable just now to embark on myths and fairy tales. But, well, yes. This dragon was different. The whole story? Oh, my. Well, it went this way. Once upon a time. . . .

Jonnie lay back on the bed with the helmet on his stomach and listened. Unfortunately he did have time. So he listened as Mr. Tsung went on telling him the long and involved fairy tale.

Suddenly about halfway through it, Jonnie abruptly sat up and said to the Coordinator, "I thought so! Please send for Sir Robert."

It startled Mr. Tsung and Jonnie said, "Thank you. Very good story. Thank you more than you know!"

As Lord Jonnie seemed pleased and things were a bit rushed, Mr. Tsung happily went out to make sure the silk suit was altered correctly.

Jonnie looked around to see whether there were any button cameras in the place. He couldn't really tell. He didn't think so, but he would be very brief and cryptic to play it on the safe side.

A couple minutes later Sir Robert came in. He too had been grooming himself. He was wearing a cloak with the Royal Stewart colors, a matching kilt, and Scottish white spats. The wool was made of shining hairs. He was the complete Scottish soldier and lord, excepting only weapons. Jonnie had never seen him dressed in full regimentals before. Quite impressive. But the old man looked a bit hollow-eyed and worried.

"This is going to be a tough one," said Jonnie.

"Aye, lad. Did ye ken thet Tolnep? I be no diplomat, laddie, and there's nae chonce of bringing Fearghus oot. The danger lies in antagonizing them lords and states thet isna involved as yet. A false step and we'll be adding them tae the enemy!"

He *was* upset. Even talking in dialect.

Jonnie never thought he'd have to soothe Sir Robert. "We have a chance. A good one. Now here's what I propose we do: you go in there by yourself and do all you can." Sir Robert didn't much care for that but he listened. "And then when you have finished or think you have gone as far as possible, you call me in. Introduce me however you please but not too specifically."

"The communicator they've been using as host will do a' the introductions," said Sir Robert.

"Well, tell him what I said. All right?"

"Verra good, laddie. I'll do whativer I can. An if I havna a cease-fire, I'll ca' you."

The old War Chief turned to leave. "Good luck!" said Jonnie.

"Aye, lad, that's exactly what I'll be a needin'! We're nae a doin' weel at a' in the field!"

Jonnie looked at his watch. It wouldn't be long now.

Chief Chong-won popped in, grinning. "The hole in the dam has stopped all but a trickle! My men are replacing the armor cable, patching and replacing it. The lake will be armored again before nightfall." He threw his arms up simulating the earlier explosion Jonnie had made. "Boom!" he said and vanished.

Jonnie thought, boom indeed. We'll all go boom if this conference fails.

— 7 —

Sir Robert had not been in the conference room three minutes before he realized that he was fighting the most difficult duel of his life.

And he was in no shape for it. He had hardly slept at all since their return and he recognized now that this was a huge error. For all his nickname, "the Fox," he felt sluggish mentally. That nickname had been earned in physical combat and not in a conference room. Had this been a matter of troop dispositions and tactics, he could have coped with it. He would have laid an ambush for this Tolnep and transfixed him with arrows and hacked him to pieces with lochaber axes.

But there stood the Tolnep, elegant, poised, and deadly, already pressing Sir Robert back toward defeat.

Sir Robert's morale was very bad. Half the antiaircraft cover of Edinburgh had been wiped out by a desperate charge of Tolnep marines. Russia was not answering at all. And his own wife was unreported after a cave-in of passages to the bunkers. It was desperate that he get a cease-fire!

Yet this Tolnep was dithering around, posing, fiddling with his scepter, flattering the emissaries, and acting like he had all the time in the world!

His name was Lord Schleim. He had a tittering laugh that alternated with insidious, acid hisses. He was a master of debate much like a swordsman became a master of his blade.

"And so, my worthy colleagues," the Tolnep was saying now, "I really have not the faintest idea why this assemblage was convened at all. Your own time, your physical comfort, even the dignity of your august persons, representing as you do the most powerful lords of the universes, should not have been assaulted and insulted by an upstart lot of barbarians involved in a petty, local dispute. This is a purely local affair, a minor spat. It involves no treaties and so your presence was well known to be unneeded by this weak band of outlaws and rebels who seek to call themselves a government. I propose that we simply dismiss this gathering and leave it up to the military commanders."

The august body stirred, bored. And they *were* an august body. Jewels glittered on the breathing masks of some. Brilliant cloth rippled as they moved. Some even wore crowns as tokens of the sovereign power they represented. Twenty-nine arbiters of the fates of sixteen universes, they were quite conscious of their power. They felt that if they so chose, they could flick this small and unimportant planet into eternity with no more than a careless gesture of a claw or finger tip. They were not really paying too much attention to Lord Schleim, but tittering and whispering to one another, possibly about trivial scandals that had occurred since last they saw one another. They were evidence, physically, of what happens when different genetic lines, moving up from different roots, became sentient.

Off to the side sat the small gray man. Another man, quite similar to himself but with a better-quality gray suit, had arrived. They were quietly watching Sir Robert. It was very plain they were not going to intervene or help further.

Sir Robert loathed courtiers. Weak and corrupt and dangerous—that had always been his opinion of this breed. His contempt, he counseled himself, must not show. "Shall we get on with this meeting?" he said.

The emissaries stirred. They muttered responses. Yes, let's complete the formalities. Must have come for something or other. Let's get it over and done with—I've a birthday party waiting for my pet lizard (a remark followed by laughter).

They had all shown their credentials earlier and these had been acknowledged by the group, all but Sir Robert's.

Lord Schleim had seated himself off to the side, in front where he could appear to be addressing them all as their leader. "We have not actually examined the credentials of this . . . this . . . soldier? who called this meeting," he offered. "I move that he be removed as the principal speaker, that I be appointed in his stead."

Sir Robert offered them the disc. It was played. It was in Gaelic, a tongue they didn't know. And he might have been called ineligible to conduct the meeting had he not looked beseechingly at the small gray man and if one of the disinterested members had not asked the small gray man whether *he* had accepted these credentials. The small gray man nodded. Bored, the rest of them accepted the credentials.

That one had been touch-and-go for Sir Robert, for just prior to his entrance he had gotten word that the Chief of Clanfearghus had been wounded in repelling an attack on the guns and he did not know whether he could get a confirmation from Edinburgh.

"I fear," said Lord Schleim, "that I must raise another critical point. How can we be sure that this upstart planet can afford even the small costs of convening such a meeting as this? Your lordships surely would not want to remain unpaid and have to bear such expenses yourselves. They guaranteed the diplomatic costs but we have no way of knowing that they will ever pay them. A scrap of paper saying that one is owed does not fit well in the pocket."

The emissaries laughed at the joke, poor as it was.

"We can pay," glowered Sir Robert.

"With scraps off dirty plates?" said Lord Schleim.

The emissaries laughed some more.

"With Galactic credits!" snapped Sir Robert.

"Taken, no doubt," said Lord Schleim, "from the pockets of our crewmen. Well, never mind. Your august lords have a perfect right to declare that the meeting should proceed. But I, myself, feel it is demeaning for the representatives of such mighty and powerful sovereigns to meet just to determine the conditions of surrender and capitulation of some felons—"

"Stop!" bellowed Sir Robert. He had had enough. "We are not here to discuss our surrender! Also there are other planets than your own involved and we have not heard from them!"

"Ah," said Lord Schleim with a leisurely, airy rotation of his scepter, "but my planet has the most ships here—two for every one the other planets have. And the senior officer of this 'combined police force' happens to be a Tolnep. Quarter-Admiral Snowleter—"

"Is dead!" roared Sir Robert. "His flagship, the *Capture,* is lying right out there in the lake. Your admiral and that entire crew are carrion."

"Oh, so?" said Lord Schleim. "It had slipped my mind.

These accidents happen. Space travel is a perilous venture at best. Probably ran out of fuel. But it doesn't alter what I have just said at all. Captain Rogodeter Snowl is the senior officer, then. He has just been promoted. So it remains that the senior commander and the greatest number of ships are Tolnep, which leaves me in the position of principal negotiator for the surrender of your people and planet after their unprovoked attack on us."

"We are not losing!" stormed Sir Robert.

Lord Schleim shrugged. He cast a negligent glance over the assemblage as though pleading with them to have patience with this barbarian and drawled, "Would the assemblage give me leave to confirm certain points?"

Yes, of course, they muttered. Reasonable request.

Lord Schleim's head bent over the round ball atop his scepter, and with a shock Sir Robert realized it was a disguised radio and that he had been in communication with his forces all along.

"Ah," said Lord Schleim as he raised his head, showed his fangs in a smile, and fixed his glass-hooded eyes on Sir Robert. "Eighteen of your major cities are in flames!"

So *that* was why they were burning deserted cities. To make an appearance of winning. Just to terrorize and have a bargaining position in any surrender talks.

Sir Robert was about to tell him those were just deserted ruins that hadn't been lived in for a millennium, but Lord Schleim was pressing on. "This august assembly needs proof. Please have this trace run off!" He pulled a tiny thread from the base of the radio, a trace copy of the type they received from drones.

"I will not do it!" said Sir Robert.

The assemblage looked a little shocked. It began to dawn on them that maybe this planet's forces *were* losing.

"Suppression of evidence," laughed Lord Schleim, "is a crime punishable by this body by fines. I suggest you mend your attitude. Of course, if you have no modern equipment. . . ."

Sir Robert sent the trace out to a resolver. They waited and presently a stack of pictures came back.

They were spectacular air views, in full color, of twenty-five burning cities. The flames were roaring thousands of feet into the air, and if you passed a finger down the right border the sound turned on, the sound of rushing flames and crashing buildings cut through with the howl of furnace winds. Each picture had been taken at a height best showing the conflagration and the resulting effect was devastating.

Lord Schleim passed them around. Paws and jeweled hands and inquisitive feelers made them roar.

"We offer," said Lord Schleim, "very liberal terms. I am quite sure I will be rebuked by a motion of our House of Plunder for being so liberal. But my feelings of pity prompt me and my word here is, of course, binding upon my government. The terms are that all your population be sold into slavery to meet the indemnities it incurred when Earth brought on this unprovoked war. I can even guarantee that they will be well treated—over fifty percent survive such transportation on the average. Other belligerents—the Hawvins, Jambitchows, Bolbods, Drawkins, and Kayrnes—to divide up the rest of the planet to meet the expenses incurred in defending themselves against this unprovoked attack upon their peaceful ships. Your king can go into exile on Tolnep and even be provided with a spacious dungeon. Good fair terms. Too liberal, but my feelings of compassion prompt them."

The other emissaries shrugged. It was obvious, it seemed to them, that they had been called here just to witness some surrender terms in a petty war.

Sir Robert was thinking fast, trying to see a way out of this trap. At the start of the meeting he thought he had heard the hum of the transshipment rig two or three times. He could not be sure. He could not count on anything right now. He was tired. His king was wounded. His wife might be dead. All he could really think of was leaping on this horrible creature and taking his chances with those poisoned fangs. But he knew such an action before these emissaries would be fatal to their last glimmering chances.

Seeing his indecision, Lord Schleim said with a harsh, acid hiss, "You Earthlings realize that these mighty lords can make an agreement to force your capitulation! I believe the other combatants of the combined police force agree to my terms?"

The representatives of the Hawvins, Jambitchows, Bolbods, Drawkins, and Kayrnes all nodded and said, one after the other, that they certainly agreed to these liberal terms. The rest of the assembly was just watching. A local dispute. But they could swing over and support the Tolneps if it meant ending this useless consumption of their time.

"I came," said Sir Robert, "to discuss *your* surrender. But before we go any further with this, I shall have to call in my fully authorized colleague."

He made a signal in the direction of where he knew the button camera was and sat down. He was tired.

The slowness and delay of these deliberations had eaten into him. Didn't these gilded popinjays realize that while they dawdled about, good men were dying out there in the field! But urgency never touched them. They were not even really interested.

He knew he had failed miserably. He hoped he had not hurt any chances Jonnie might have.

Forlorn hope. It was all up to Jonnie now. But what could the poor lad possibly do?

PART 27

— 1 —

Music began to be heard in the conference room. It was slow, dignified music. Ponderous. Impressive. The emissaries looked about with some interest, wondering what was going to happen. So far this had been a deadly dull conference on an apparently deadly dull planet that didn't even have any night life or dancing or singing females to serve up. The conference had begun right away as though there was something urgent or important to take up: not even a customary round of hot spots to get acquainted; so far no one had even offered any bribes! Instead just some boring, minor squabble that concerned combatants of just this one universe and just a sector of it at that. Nice music. Fit for regal functions, much less a conference.

A huge man entered the door. He was about six and a half feet tall, stripped to the waist, wearing a scarlet sash, with yellow skin, shaved head. (It was one of the Mongols from among the Chinese.) That in itself would not have been very interesting. But his muscles were huge and swollen with the effort of carrying something on his head that would seem to be very heavy indeed. But from all they could see, he was carrying *nothing!* There were his arms and gripping hands, there were his bulging back muscles and biceps. Although he was walking in cadence with the music, there was even a slightly perceptible tremor in his legs. But they could see nothing being carried.

The man went up to the platform and with great care set the nothing down. They even heard a bump. (It was a glassine electronics table used by Psychlos for small electronic work that required light from every angle. It had been sawed down and sprayed with lens spray that passed light one hundred percent and so reflected nothing.) He arranged the nothing with great care.

There was a bit of flurry in the audience as emissaries craned about and peered, amused and interested. The communicator acting as host (he had a stripped-down mine radio in his ear) said, "You have the solemn promise of this planet at the risk of heavy indemnity that no lethal, destructive, or harmful object will be entered into this conference room."

Several emissaries laughed. They were quite cheerful. A good joke to put nothing on the platform and then say it was harmless. It quite took their fancy.

But something else was happening now. The huge Mongol had withdrawn. To the stately music, two beautifully gowned Chinese boys, faces impassive, came down the aisle. Each was carrying a gorgeous red satin pillow with gold tassles and on each pillow was a huge book. Solemnly, first one, then the other, approached the host. He took each book from its pillow and laid it upon the heretofore invisible table, spine titles toward the audience.

So there *was* something on the platform. An invisible table. New interest. Those with better eyes could read the titles on the spines up there: one was a "Dictionary of the Psychlo Language"; the other was "Intergalactic Laws By Treaties of Governing Nations."

But Lord Schleim, with his weak Tolnep eyes, was not even trying to read any book titles. He was tense and crouching back. Theatrics! They were pulling theatrics on him. Ah, well. He would corner whoever this was and bite him to death with wit-fangs! *Sssst* on theatrics! They would change nothing.

The two boys withdrew in a stately fashion, carrying away their now-empty pillows.

The music suddenly stopped.

There was a roll of drums.

The host drew himself up and cried out his announcement in a strong, sonorous voice above the drums, "Masters of all planets! Lords of the great and powerful realms of sixteen galaxies! May I now introduce to your august presence, LORD JONNIE! He who embodies the spirit of Earth!"

A trumpet fanfare cut through and rose above the drums. The clear, piercing notes rose into the air.

Jonnie came walking down the aisle. He was walking slowly, heavily, commanding as though he weighed a thousand pounds. He was dressed in black and silver and he carried a silver wand.

But it wasn't silver; it looked so, but when the light caught it on the slightest movement it flashed with blindingly bright rainbow colors.

He came to the platform, stepped up, moved behind the table, and turned.

At that instant a mine spotlight placed just above the door flamed on. He stood there in black and silver and yet a blaze of living color.

He did not speak. Feet apart, not blocked from their view by the table, he held the silver wand between his two hands and simply looked at them with a stern and even disdainful expression. Dominant.

This was impressive enough to the emissaries. Even though they were used to pomp and tended to discount it, they would have been respectful of this display. But there was something else.

That beast on the helmet! It looked alive. The trick of the light, the play of the silver metal that flashed, the glowing red coals of eyes, whatever it was it looked *alive*. Was he wearing a live winged beast on his helmet?

Lord Schleim would have none of it. Unfortunately there had been a slight slip which played directly into his hands. When one word meant several things in Psychlo, it required a slight change of inflection or tone to make it have the different meaning. The word "spirit" in Psychlo could also mean "mind," "angel," or "devil," and although the communicator had used the right inflection for "spirit," Lord Schleim chose to accept a different inflection.

The Tolnep sprang up as though striking from cover. "Lords and august emissaries," he said with an acid hiss, "I challenge the right of this *devil* to speak! We have seen no credentials. We—"

"Sir," said Jonnie. "I could not quite hear you. What did you say?"

Lord Schleim whirled on him. He began savagely, "I said—"

"Ah, yes, yes, yes," said Jonnie, waving his wand. "I beg your pardon, your lordship. It was merely your uncouth Tolnep accent. Quite provincial. Can you understand him, my lords?"

They laughed. It was true that Schleim had a bit of an accent, due probably to his fangs and having to hiss. Tolneps were really quite rural; they had only one planet and that was quite distant from the center of things.

"You devil!" hissed Schleim.

"Uh, uh, uh," said Jonnie. "No violence in such a meeting. I am quite certain I nor the truly worthy emissaries in this gathering desire your ejection from it."

Then before Schleim would retaliate, something else happened. The wand, which had been tapping Jonnie's palms, suddenly pointed in the direction of Schleim's feet. It had a small beam of light set in the end of it and it flashed on. (It was a light used to show dust in a mine shaft and it made a very thin white pencil of light, like a pointer.)

Jonnie looked a bit incredulous. Then he turned his head clear off to the side as though to hide a laugh. The light switched off.

Schleim looked down. He had to stretch for he had a bit of a paunch. What had this devil seen?

Then Lord Schleim saw them. His boots! Instead of wearing his proper, scaled, glittering green boots, he was wearing old, rough blue boots. Dirty blue boots. His valet! In the rush of getting him off, his clumsy, damned valet had put the wrong boots on him. Oh, when he got home . . . when he got home he would have the oaf punctured! Worse. Dragged through the streets and bitten to death by small children.

But Jonnie was addressing the emissaries. "I must apologize to you, my lords. I pray you to overlook my discourtesy in arriving late. But I am sure you will understand when I tell you that I was looking for a point of *law*." He looked at them in a kindly and deferential fashion, laid down the wand on the invisible table, and tapped the top of the law book. (The manners and phrases of the old Chinko instruction discs were coming in handy now! At first when he entered he had felt stiff and unnatural, artificial and affected, but suddenly it felt as though he had been doing this sort of thing all his life.)

"No one," he continued, "could possibly expect such noble and such highly titled and credentialed lords to experience an uncomfortable trip, nor to convene upon such a lowly and undeserving planet, for the petty purpose of adjudicating the minor differences of some back planet squabble."

The delegates sat up. This was more like it. This is what they had been thinking all the time. Hear, hear!

Sir Robert was thunderstruck. What was this lad up to? The

war not important? Their strong points caving in, their friends dying, and he could say it wasn't important? He looked at the two small gray men. They were both sitting there smiling, a bit vacant but smiling. They hadn't been smiling before and Sir Robert knew for a fact that Jonnie hadn't talked with them, so they knew no more than he. But he had to restrain himself from jumping up to cry out that this *was* an important war. One point: these emissaries in their jewels and flashing clothes, strange faces and feelers, were all bobbing their heads and settling down for a real conference.

"No," continued Jonnie. "It would be an insult to the mighty states you represent to call you here on something as trivial as repelling pirates!"

Lord Schleim started to slither up out of his chair. He was about to shout this devil down and force him to mend his language when he saw those eyes looking again at his boots. But it wasn't really the glance at the boots that stopped Lord Schleim. He recognized with diplomatic shrewdness that this devil could fall into a trap of his own digging. It was a very simple matter to prove that the attacking Tolnep ships were fully commissioned, legal ships and officers of the Tolnep navy. So let the devil plow on for now. He'd fang him shortly. Hah, the fellow was no real opponent after all!

"Such regal representatives of kings and governments," continued Jonnie, "should—and if I am wrong, please correct me—convene on real points of treaties and Intergalactic law. And on these their expertise cannot be seriously challenged or questioned."

Hear, hear. True. Naturally. You have a point. Pray continue! The emissaries, all except for the combatants, were sitting up, interested. And all combatant representatives began to look uneasy. All except Lord Schleim who was beginning to feel confident—this devil was going to dig a hole for himself. There was one trouble here for Lord Schleim: each time that devil moved it made lights flash off his buttons, and Tolneps had to wear filters to convert to ordinary visible spectrum, so every flash of a button overwhelmed the power of the filter and he was getting a headache. He wished he could make them turn off that spotlight they had on this creature.

Jonnie was sweeping on. "The definition of the category of 'pirate' as opposed to the definition of 'military force' is a critical question. I am sure that, from time to time, even in the best-organized, paid, and regulated military forces, elements of navies or even merchant ships have mutinied or gone astray or been misled and have turned pirate, defying the benign and responsible authority of their own governments."

Oh, yes. Many instances. Just last month in these troubled times, a squadron of spaceships had mutinied at Oxentab. Lots of them in history. An old point, the emissaries agreed. Lot of stories written about it. Go on.

"So," continued Jonnie, "to protect legitimate authority such as that which you represent," (pleased faces except for the combatants), "and to really be able to cope with piracy when it occurs, the definition must be clarified. And this can only be done by an august body such as yours in the form of a formal treaty."

Good idea. Correct. Right. Very glum combatants, except Schleim who was certain now this devil would shortly be sent down in flames.

Jonnie opened the Psychlo dictionary to a marked place. "We know that the Psychlo language is a composite of many tongues, even your own individual languages, and was not in fact a language generated solely by the Psychlos. It is a universal tongue because it was taken from many universes, which is the only reason we so generally speak it."

That was true. Real scholarship. The Psychlos picked up everything from others including language. Shouldn't even be called "Psychlo." The emissaries buzzed about it.

"This dictionary," said Jonnie, "is the standard recognized work, is it not?" He held it up. Yes, they nodded. Jonnie laid the book down and read from it. "It states: 'Pirate: one who preys upon commerce or communities or planets in a vessel or spaceship or group of ships not under the regulation of a national or planetary government; also any commander or crew member of such a ship.' "

Right, right. That was a pirate. But Lord Schleim was feeling very smug. He felt he really had this devil now. He could see exactly which way he was trying to go. It would be child's play to fang these arguments to pieces and then proceed with the surrender talks. What a letdown the devil was going to get. Every Tolnep ship was under the direct orders of the Tolnep government. Totally legal.

Jonnie had turned to the book on Intergalactic law. "However, according to treaties, of which Intergalactic law is composed, we have a different definition. With your permission I will read it: 'Article 234,352,678. Based on the treaties of Psychlo vs. Hawvin signed at Blonk, Psychlo vs. Camchod signed at Psychlo, a pirate shall hereinafter be defined as one who feloniously steals or mines minerals.' " Jonnie tapped the book and laughed lightly. "I guess we know who and how and why *that* misdefinition occurred!"

They laughed. Psychlo was not very well liked, and a Psychlo would pass anything to protect Psychlo interests.

"Therefore," said Jonnie, "this august body, I feel, should define 'pirate' and 'piracy' among systems and planets and, after due deliberation, envisage the execution of treaties to forbid it!"

Sir Robert groaned. The lad was proposing days of wrangling over stale things like treaties when the planet was being torn to bits with a flat-out assault, undoubtedly egged on by this Tolnep through his hidden radio. But his groans were drowned in the general assent.

Jonnie had now drawn back from the books. He took up the wand. He tapped it in his palm. "I feel in my humble opinion," (he certainly didn't look humble), "that we must work upon this now in order that we should know whether the Tolnep fleet officers and crewmen are to be slowly vaporized individually as pirates or simply shot as military men when court-martialed."

Lord Schleim slithered up with a scream. "Stop!" He glared around at the other combatants. They sat just behind him. They were saying nothing. They simply looked stunned. Then he realized that the devil had said "Tolnep"; he had not said "combined forces." Venom splattered as Lord Schleim hissed his protest. The devil had gone too far! In a moment Lord Schleim would tear down his house, but just now there was another point.

"You are selecting out the honorable Tolnep forces for your venomous insinuations!" said Schleim ravingly. "This is a clear case of prejudice and has to be dismissed as such by this body! There are other combatants. I demand these statements to be stricken from our recorders as biased, slanted, and an intentional insult to the Tolnep planetary forces."

Jonnie calmly smiled at him and looked at the Tolnep boots

and back up to the fanged face. "Bombastic conduct will right no wrongs here. Your conduct insults these lords. Behave yourself."

"I demand a reply!" screamed Schleim.

Jonnie sighed tolerantly. "Very well. You shall have it. It is my opinion that the Hawvins, Bolbods, Drawkins, Jambitchow, and Hockner forces were simply coerced, probably with false statements, into cooperating with the Tolneps. Since by your own testimony your ships vastly outnumber theirs, and since your own senior officer, as you state, commanded the so-called combined force, and when killed, was succeeded by another Tolnep who is now their senior officer, it seems very evident they were forced to cooperate in this attack by the superior firepower of the Tolnep fleet. So we cannot hold these other races or forces guilty. And we are not charging them. They are only victims and cannot be regarded, in my opinion, in any other way when we apply the word 'pirate' on a clarified definition."

Now! Now was the time! Lord Schleim knew the ripe moment when he saw it. He would crush this devil. He slithered himself up to his full height. He assumed the grandeur of dignity.

"Your arguments, devil, drop into the rocks and fall like dust into the grass. The Tolnep admiral and the Tolnep captain and all the Tolnep ships and crews were never in any way acting outside the command of the Tolnep central government. So enough of this claptrap about 'pirates' and let us get on with the proper business of surrender!"

The taste of triumph and victory was sweet as poison in the Tolnep's mouth. In a few moments now, this whole thing would be finished.

Sir Robert groaned.

He saw the two small gray men were looking down, nervous now Regretting perhaps they had helped?

— 2 —

Jonnie looked at the Tolnep.

He shook his head sadly.

He looked at the assemblage. They were leaning back, beginning to lose interest. For a while there it had appeared that something would occur that would concern them.

"My lords," said Jonnie, "please do forgive this distraction from the main purpose of this meeting. This . . . this Tolnep is absolutely demanding that we finish this minor concern of a raid upon a peaceful planet. So with your permission, I feel I have no other choice than to settle this slight disturbance."

Yes, oh, well, go ahead. One doesn't see where this is going now but go ahead. I suppose the Tolnep will just keep interrupting. So go ahead.

Jonnie sighed. "Thank you, your lordships. You are very tolerant." Then he turned to Lord Schleim. Jonnie took a very firm stand with his feet. He had picked up the wand and was now tapping it in his palm.

"Lord Schleim," said Jonnie, "for I believe that is what some call you, please produce the orders given to your admirals and captains."

Schleim laughed. "You know very well an emissary cannot carry with him the whole files of a military establishment. Furthermore, although you, as a barbarian, would have no inkling of this, a Tolnep commander is at liberty to exercise autonomy on military expeditions."

"As I suspected," said Jonnie. "There were no legal orders."

"I did not say that!" hissed Schleim.

"I'm afraid you did," said Jonnie. "I have no choice now but to proceed for you are delaying more important proceedings."

Jonnie smacked the wand into his palm twice. It sounded like two pistol shots.

There was an instant rush down the aisle as two uniformed technicians came, pushing a mine cart. The cart had been plated in gold. It looked very sleek. On it rested a projector of some size and it too was gold-plated. It was an atmosphere screen projector. Its general use was to project pictures of mine shafts or tunnels. It used a projection light based on the same principle as an atmosphere armor cable with a variation. The light, striking atmosphere ions, made them condense to greater or lesser degree and reflect back. By putting a stick for scale in the original scene, one could then take the projected picture and actually measure distances in it from point to point. It put, in this way, a three-dimensional picture on thin air.

The technicians moved it into place where it would project into the large, empty space to Jonnie's left. They placed a multiple-button switch on the invisible table close to Jonnie's hand. They bowed, about-faced, and withdrew.

They had come in so fast and left so quickly that Lord Schleim had not had time to get in an objection. Now he did. "I must protest this display of foolish flimflam! I will not permit you to hoodwink this august body further—"

"Schleim!" said Jonnie severely, "it will do no good for you to seek to suppress evidence when you well know it will work to your disfavor."

Mutters from the emissaries. Sit down, Schleim. Be quiet. This looks like it will be interesting. Hush, Schleim.

Jonnie pressed two buttons. The spotlight at the door went out and simultaneously a picture flashed on it. It was a three-dimensional, remarkably detailed closeup of Roof Arsebogger. He seemed to the emissaries to be standing right there in what had been empty space. There was no sound. But they had never before seen a mine atmosphere projector for the simple reason that the Psychlos never marketed entertainment gadgets and this was mining equipment.

Roof Arsebogger's face was patched with the sores of disease. His fangs were black and one was broken. He was dressed in something that looked like it had been discarded from a slum. It was part of a long series of pictures shot by pilots flying air cover at the Purgatoire River. It had been taken with a radio telephoto camera. The shots had been left in Jonnie's room to help do the briefing of the time he had been out of action.

Jonnie said, "Is this man a member of your government? Now answer carefully, Schleim. Is this a minister of any department, an official of the military?"

Several emissaries tittered. The figure was so *disgusting* that if this were a member of the Tolnep government . . . well!

Schleim was stung. He looked at the picture. What a disgusting creature! Vomitous! Eyes still dazzling a little bit from the lights flashing off the devil, he pawed at his filter and stared again. Was there something vaguely familiar about that figure?

That he was peering so hard made it seem that maybe the Tolnep government *was* composed of such riffraff. Several emissaries laughed out loud.

That did it. Schleim lashed out, "Of course not! That filthy creature would be thrown out of any government department on Tolnep! You are insulting me. You are insulting Tolnep! You are running a calculated campaign to degrade the dignity and importance of my office and my planet. I must protest—"

"Quiet," said Jonnie, soothingly. "Just pay attention here. You have said he is no part of your government and has no official capacity. Is that right?"

"Absolutely! If you think—"

"Then," said Jonnie, "what is he doing giving orders to Quarter-Admiral Snowleter?"

He pressed another button. The camera seemed to draw away. Motion occurred in the scene. The bridge of the *Capture* came into view, along with the diamond with a slash, the Tolnep insignia. And there was Quarter-Admiral Snowleter facing the horrible creature Roof Arsebogger.

Jonnie touched another button. Sound came on. The rumble of a capital, nonatmosphere ship as picked off the vibration of its bridge window glass was clearly penetrated by the voice of Roof Arsebogger.

"You must act independently, Snowleter! You must do whatever gives you the best chance of private profit! What I am telling you to do is rush on down to that base and grab it all for yourself! Once you have this planet under your personal control you can tell everybody else to buzz off and be damned. Smash the place. Seize the people and sell them for your own profit. I will cover you. And like it or not, that is what you must do! The power is mine! And we will split the profits! Understood?"

Snowleter was smiling. He touched his quarter-admiral's cap in a salute. "I am at your orders!"

Jonnie hit another button. The camera seemed to draw further away. It showed the whole combined force in the sky over the Purgatoire River. The sound was off.

"That is your admiral, that is the fleet." Jonnie hit a pair of buttons. The picture was gone and the spotlight back on.

The emissaries were enthralled. They had never seen atmosphere projection before. It was like looking at a totally live scene. Yes, that was the Tolnep fleet all right. That was the admiral. Schleim's attitude said clearly it was.

Suddenly Lord Schleim exploded. "Doctored pictures. Anyone can doctor recordings. This so-called evidence—"

"Oh come now, Schleim," said Jonnie. "Bombast and hysteria won't cancel this. The pictures were too clear to be 'doctored' as you call it."

He turned to the emissaries. "So you see, your lordships, the Tolnep admiral was not acting under the orders of his government but under those of a private individual. He was acting for personal profit and not for his planet. Be quiet, Schleim; you can't cover up evidence with shockingly bad temper. My apologies for his conduct, my lords. One can sympathize with his position. This Quarter-Admiral Snowleter, by the way, is the uncle of Half-Captain Rogodeter Snowl and was brought into the venture by his nephew according to discs and traces we have available. It was a family matter and the piratical venture is obviously being continued by the nephew."

Jonnie didn't tell them there was a lot more in the views just shown which did not necessarily carry out his point. But very clearly Roof Arsebogger had been the one to egg the admiral on.

"So the point of piracy," said Jonnie, "has been proven. Here we had a fleet operating by another authority from that of its government. If you will indulge me a moment longer, I will simply ask this Schleim for the surrender of those ships and then we can get about our more appropriate business of piracies and treaties. Schleim, will you please call whoever is in command now and tell him to gather his ships in a meadow I will name—"

"You must be mad!" screamed Schleim. "Our fleet is in full command of your skies and you ask us—"

"To help end a pirate venture," Jonnie finished for him. "My lords, forgive me, but this Schleim is going to occupy a little more of your valuable time before you are rid of him. With your permission, we will complete this odious business."

Yes, yes. By all means go ahead. We can take up the treaty later. They agreed. The combatant-planet emissaries were looking at one another, a bit frightened. What had they gotten themselves mixed up in?

The small gray men looked less hangdog.

But Sir Robert, studying Schleim, knew he was far from finished. He was using the moment to hiss into his radio. He was giving orders, something about making suicide crashes. He must be a bit rattled for he was speaking Psychlo.

Sir Robert excused himself and stepped quickly over to operations to tell their forces what was going on, to tell them to be alert, to double their efforts to fight back.

The first small gray man slipped out and passed an order to his ship to turn on two red lights and change the radio signal to "Alert! Alert! An interplanetary, intergalactic conference is taking place within this area. Any capital ship or vessel of any kind entering this zone will be branded an intergalactic outlaw and its government or owner subject to all penalties that can be imposed. Alert! Alert! An interplanetary, intergalactic conference is . . ."

— 3 —

Lord Schleim was not the least bit rattled. He knew exactly what he was doing: he was now applying a maxim of diplomacy which stated that when diplomacy failed, one resorted to military means.

It had become obvious to him in these last few minutes that if he continued along the previous course, he would lose. So he had shifted his entire planning suddenly and irrevocably.

These were very troubled times. He felt the power of the small gray man had crumbled and that things were not what they used to be. Therefore, any threat of retaliation from the small gray man could be ignored. This was the first emissary meeting in over a year and he was completely certain that the power of the emissaries and collective governments had become a shadow that was no real danger to Tolnep—these empires and states were too far away.

He had just given Half-Captain—now Captain Snowl just today—

very specific orders. He had used a word code known only to officers of flag rank and executives high in the Tolnep government. Using one set of words, one could convey quite another meaning. Additionally, the radio band used was hyper-nondirectional, known only to the Tolneps, and could not be picked up on any other radio except those used by flag officers and the diplomatic service, a band which was constantly running on the bridge of every Tolnep major war vessel. And if that weren't safe enough, the transmissions were also scrambled.

Schleim had just ordered Rogodeter Snowl to send the ships of other combatants to the terrestrial points being defended by the Earthlings, to gather up all Tolnep forces, and to proceed with all speed to the conference location. He had told Snowl to totally disregard any and all conference warnings of the small gray man.

Since the bulk of the Tolnep vessels were at Singapore, a little over forty-five hundred miles away—quite close, really—they would arrive over this spot in about two hours.

Schleim had, in the bottom of his scepter, on the opposite end from the radio, a paralysis beam. All he had to do was give the end of it a twist and every person or creature within hearing would become instantly paralyzed except himself: a tap on his own ears first would close his deaf-flaps. This entire conference was at his mercy. All he had to do was get them all outside in the bowl on some pretext so that any and all guards were also within hearing distance, listen for the first signs of the arrival of his fleet, tap his own ears, and twist the bottom of the scepter.

Tolnep diplomats were chosen for bravery as well as wits. He would pick up a gun and shoot his way to the switches of the armor cable if necessary, turn it off, and let his fleet marines in.

As to this teleportation console, he really couldn't care less. Tolnep would be better off if it were destroyed—a nation that based its economy on slavery was always under some kind of threat and this teleportation had interfered with Tolnep far more than it had helped.

He himself was within flying distance of home. The other combatants were also and would have to bow to his commands or be killed. As for the rest of these emissaries, how they got home if ever was no concern of his. And dead emissaries and a dead litter of terrestrial personnel told no tales, especially when buried.

He would of course go through the motions of torturing this devil and try to get the teleportation design out of him. If the devil died in the process, it did not matter.

But the cream of the jest was that, if anything went wrong, he would use the devil's own arguments to defend himself. He would claim that Rogodeter Snowl had turned pirate, that he had acted contrary to orders and that his approach to this conference was an outlaw act. He knew he could depose and execute Snowl and still command the Tolnep crews. Snowl would simply be sacrificed for the greater good of the state—a common expedient in such diplomatic circles.

Schleim could even mop up the other belligerents using the Tolnep fleet if it came to that.

It was very neat planning.

The only thing he had to solve now was how to get this entire conference out into the bowl.

He was now feeling so confident he was hardly even listening to this devil as he resumed his actions. Whatever the devil did would be useless, without avail.

Tolerantly, Lord Schleim sat back and lent half an ear to the continuing proceedings.

Diplomacy was, indeed, quite an art. But if it failed, there was always force.

He fingered the bottom end of his scepter.

He tuned the rest of his hearing in to catch the first rumbles of his fleet in the sky.

— 4 —

There had been a delay while a technician changed the cartridges in the atmosphere projector.

The emissaries, seeing that Jonnie was again about to speak, settled down.

"My lords," said Jonnie. "I do appreciate your indulgence in permitting me to clean up the remaining bits of this odious Tolnep matter. Indeed, I am impressed by your patience. I assure you we may soon be able to proceed with the legitimate concerns of such an authoritative group." The influence of the polite instruction discs of the Chinkos was coming in very handy now. These lords, except for the combatants, were definitely on his side.

Jonnie stood tall in the mine spotlight. His buttons flashed. The dragon on the helmet seemed to move as he turned his head to Lord Schleim.

"Tolnep," said Jonnie, with disdain and contempt in the word, "I have some views that were taken while the conference was verifying credentials. I am going to ask you to identify certain things for me."

Schleim sat back easily, quite composed now. "Go ahead, devil," he said almost airily.

Jonnie looked at him closely. What had caused this sudden calm? Was it just an exhibition of diplomatic supercontrol? Schleim was, after all, a clever and well-trained diplomat.

With a deft touch of switch buttons, the mine spotlight went off and a new view appeared, filling all the empty space in the room to Jonnie's left. It was a remarkable shot. The emissaries sat up and peered, very interested.

There, just as though seen from the port of a spaceship, bright and clear, projected in three dimensions upon the empty air, was the whole system where the Tolnep planet rode in the ninth ring. The huge combination sun, a double star with the small companion circling the larger orb, shed its double-shadowed light upon the vast system of planets and their moons. The name of the system was Batafor in the Psychlo coordination books, ["Sirius"] or the ["Dog Star"] in the ancient man-constellation charts.

"Is this Batafor?" Jonnie asked Lord Schleim.

The Tolnep laughed. "If you took the shot, you know what it is. Why ask me?"

Jonnie searched out the Hawvin in the second row with his wand as a pointer. "Perhaps the regal emissary of the Hawvins might care to assist us. Is this the Batafor System?"

The Hawvin had been regretting his involvement in all this for some time. His nation was a traditional enemy of the Tolneps and had suffered much in times past from their slave raids. He had begun to suspect that there were penalties and reparations coming up sometime soon. This "spirit of Earth" seemed to have been taking pains to exclude the other combatants, and he had seen a possibility of escaping censure if it all went wrong here—as it definitely seemed to be doing. Best curry some favor. He could see no danger in it.

He rose and came forward and Jonnie handed him his wand with the pointer beam turned on.

The Hawvin waved the beam generally across the system. "I recognize and attest this is indeed the Batafor System. That is the old Psychlo name. We locally call the double sun 'Twino' which stands for 'Mother and Child' in the Hawvin tongue."

He tapped the planet ring nearest the sun. "This is Jubo, uninhabited due to its extreme heat and gravity pulls." He pointed rapidly to the second, third, fourth, and fifth rings. "These have names but are not important. Uninhabited, for they are subject to earthquakes and volcanic upheavals." He tapped the sixth ring, the planet almost hidden behind the double sun. "This is Torthut, a Psychlo mining planet: it had a population once but they were annihilated."

The Hawvin looked inquiringly at the Hockner. "My lord, do you mind if I go on?"

The Hockner shrugged, then gave a strained laugh. "As you have already as much as said so, my dear colleague, you may tell them it is a possession of Hockner!"

"Very good," continued the Hawvin. "This seventh planet is Holoban, part of the Hockner Confederacy. The eighth planet is Balor, one of our own Hawvin planets."

He lowered the beam and looked at Lord Schleim. But Lord Schleim simply shrugged and said, "You make a very fine astronomy lecturer, lord of the Hawvins. You have omitted some of the fauna and flora but go ahead."

The Hawvin put the pointer on the ninth ring. "And this, I can attest, is Tolnep." He peered more closely. "Yes, these specks about it are the five moons, though one is hidden from this angle. Tolnep is remarkable for its moons in a system where planets seldom have more than one. The reflective quality of these moons is a bit remarkable due to their composition. The double sun can give out the normal light spectrum but on reflection from these moons, the light shifts upward in the spectrum. The Tolnep civilization prefers to work by moonlight and normally sleeps in the direct sun. It is said they are not indigenous—"

"Oh, spare us, spare us," said Lord Schleim. "You'll be telling us about Tolnep egg-mating next! Keep it clean, Hawvin!"

Some of the uninvolved emissaries laughed. Schleim was wriggling his way back into their good graces.

"The tenth planet," the Hawvin went on, "is a Psychlo mining planet, Tung. The population existed once but had actually been removed by the Tolneps before Psychlo occupation. The eleventh—"

"Thank you very much, lord of the Hawvins," said Jonnie. "You have been very helpful."

The Hawvin stepped down and would have gone back to his seat but Jonnie checked him. Jonnie hit another button.

A clear view of the city magically appeared in the air. It was just as though one were suspended in space well above it.

"That is Creeth," said the Hawvin. "The Tolnep capital. Very distinctive. See how the streets wind their way and entwine." He came back up and took the pointer. "This is the House of Plunder, their legislative center; see how its sections wind around and come back together. Unmistakably Tolnep in its architecture. This is Grath, their famous combined public park and slave auction center. This rock hill with the holes in it—"

"Thank you," said Jonnie. "And now this is what I really want you for." He pushed a button and the picture changed. It swooped down at the park and gave the emissaries the feeling they were free-falling in space. The park stayed still but all the surroundings swooped sideways and away, making it look for a moment like a bowl. The camera had steadied. The view now showed just the park.

One could see the long slave auction blocks, the comfortable seats and boxes for the buyers. But what was remarkable was the huge clock face laid out in the hill at the edge.

"The clock," said Jonnie.

"Ah, yes, the clock." The Hawvin sighed and glanced at Lord Schleim, but his lordship was sitting there, a smile on his mouth below his glasses, fingering his scepter. "The clock is built of slave bones, it is said. Huge masses of them have been inset into wheels that turn and show through the windows. It is said that fifty-eight thousand female slaves were killed to make up the border you see—"

"I meant the time and date," said Jonnie. "They are in Tolnep script and I suppose you read it."

"Ah," said the Hawvin, glad to be off the hook. He was afraid Lord Schleim might rip into him. "The hour, the date.

Why yes. I do know the Tolnep number system. This was taken about two hours ago.'' He glanced at his own watch. ''About one hour and fifty-one minutes ago, to be exact. Remarkable. Was it taken with the teleportation rig out there just today?'' He stared at it. ''Must have been.''

''I do thank you,'' said Jonnie. He took the pointer from the Hawvin lord who then stepped down, casting a somewhat fearful look at Schleim.

Jonnie hit another button. Into view flashed the Tolnep planet and its five moons. It was remarkably detailed.

''Lord Schleim,'' said Jonnie, ''is this the Tolnep planet and its moons?''

Schleim laughed. ''It wouldn't do me any good to say no, would it? Yes, devil, it doesn't take an astronomy professor like our friend the Hawvin here to detect that that is Tolnep and its five moons.'' He laughed easily.

''Very good,'' said Jonnie. ''Then, as a native of Tolnep and someone undoubtedly fond of its moons, could you tell me which moon you like best?''

This sudden dive sideways made Schleim wary. He was only giving it half his attention. There would be a while before the fleet could arrive, he supposed, but they might send a scout racing ahead. He glanced at his watch. He fingered the bottom of the scepter. He was preoccupied with how to get these emissaries outside so both they and the guards could be all taken in at one twist of the scepter bottom.

''Well,'' said Schleim, ''I'm afraid I have better things to do at home than stand around gazing at moons.''

''Which one do you like the least?'' persisted Jonnie.

''Oh, any of them,'' said Schleim easily.

Jonnie smiled. The dragon on the helmet flashed and seemed to move as he turned to the emissaries.

''As Lord Schleim has no preference,'' said Jonnie, reaching out with the pointer beam, ''we will choose this one. Asart!'' And he tapped it with the light. ''Notice the peculiar crater patterns, these five ellipses, that make this moon distinctive.''

A sudden chill hit Schleim. Asart! Covered under its surface were the huge shops and hangars of the entire Tolnep navy. To this place local freighters took the parts of space vessels and on Asart they were reassembled. The mighty nonatmosphere ships of Tolnep could not even take off from a planetary surface

Before every material or crew delivery, all the heavens were combed for hostile surveillance. Before every war vessel launch, surface-fired spy ships rose from Tolnep itself and scanned the skies. The function of Asart was a hard-kept secret. How had this devil come upon such data? Or was it a lucky choice? Schleim felt a crawling unease.

And then abruptly any worry he had was dispelled. The devil with the strange beast on his helmet said, "Could I ask all your lordships to come outside? Seats have been placed for your ease. And there will be what I think you will find an interesting demonstration."

He had just unwittingly solved Schleim's problem!

— 5 —

Lord Schleim was making very sure that he was the last to leave the room. He wanted nobody left in here. He had noticed that the room had a door and that it had a lock. By leaving last he could quite naturally close the door and turn the lock. That would be one less door he would have to watch and he could be certain that nobody lurked in this nearly soundproof room to see what would go on and leap out to surprise him.

All the other emissaries filed out. As the one deepest in the room, it was natural that he be the last to leave. The devil had tagged after them and he was gone. The small gray men had departed.

But this confounded host! The elderly man in the fancy Chinese gown seemed to have accumulated some papers and they were on the floor beside the chair where he had sat. Guest lists, of course! And one must have fallen back of the chair for he was searching it out. He finally found it and then stood there going over it, evidently rehearsing some hard-to-pronounce names. So Schleim had to pretend that *he* had misplaced something and stood there going through his pockets and looking thoughtful. It was a bit of a strain waiting the host out. The man did not seem to notice him but just stood there, running a finger down a list and muttering. Fine time to rehearse, thought Schleim acidly. In another few moments his own delay would become noticeable. But he *had* to be sure this was an empty room. Too soundproof!

And it might have screens in it—he looked about. There was a device in one upper corner. Could it be a viewing device? Hard to tell. Bad light. This projector might also be a viewer. No, he better wait in case somebody should look in here.

At last! The host moved with a sort of sailing walk up the aisle to the door, still muttering over his list. Schleim went along right behind him.

The Tolnep was almost to the door, was even reaching to close it, when the host stopped.

Lord Schleim, almost in the doorway now, eyes only for the door, was distracted by two technicians appearing. The same technicians who had set up the projector. They were rushing in to move it.

The collision was sudden and violent.

The scepter flew from Schleim's hand.

A technician caught a glimpse of fangs right in front of his face and raised his arm. Unable to check its forward crush, the technician's heavy sleeve banged into Schleim's mouth.

The reaction of a Tolnep was inevitable. He bit! He bit hard and repeatedly, hissing in rage as he struck!

With a yell, the technician reeled back. He staggered away, holding his sleeve close to his body with the other hand, and vanished into another doorway.

The second technician was chattering horrified apologies in some tongue. Chinese? He reached down and picked up a gold object from the floor and shakingly handed it to Schleim.

Schleim gripped it. He felt the perforations at the top and the rings at the bottom. He straightened up his glasses and heaved a sigh of relief. At least the scepter was secure!

The host was brushing him off with heavy, frantic apologies. The host took a second to gesture impatiently at the second technician and only then did the hovering man go in and get the projector and wheel it out.

Managing to hang back and seem offended, Schleim at last got the room empty and, without the concerned host remarking it, closed and locked the door. Schleim even pretended to limp a bit. He told the host not to mind. And he went to join the others.

In the hospital, Dr. Allen and a nurse were getting the Chinese "technician" out of his jacket. They did it very delicately. Dr. Allen took the padded sleeve and, without touching it, cut it off the jacket and let it fall into a wide-mouthed jar. Drops of poison were visible on the cloth, oozing back up out of the padding.

Dr. Allen looked at the arm. In Psychlo, he said, "Not a scratch, but a good thing we put the leather lining in. That was a brave thing to do, Chong-won."

The chief ignored his compliment. He threw down a thin knife and a small blast gun. "He had the knife in the back of his neck and the gun in his boot. I thought we might as well have them, too."

"Are you sure he might not have had something else?" said Dr. Allen. "I don't want to patch up any more holes in Jonnie than I have to."

"Nothing else," said Chong-won, "unless he bats somebody over the head with that scepter."

"I'm sure Jonnie can duck that if it comes to a fight," said Dr. Allen. "This Lord Schleim is a very dangerous creature." He gestured toward the jar which held the sleeve. "Nurse, add that to our collection so we can develop some antivenin for it."

— 6 —

Colonel Ivan lay in the dark, a flame thrower resting on the sandbags piled before him. He was at the first turning of the underground passages that labyrinthed down into the base. At every turn behind him lay more sandbagged abutments, every one of them manned.

His beard was singed off. His hands were covered with blisters.

In front of him, fifty feet away, the main entrance door, steel armored, had begun to glow from the pounding it was taking. Hot blast shots were hitting the outside every few seconds.

He had pulled his planes back in—when was that—yesterday? They were out of fuel and ammunition and of no further use in the air. Pilots were scattered below, behind the abutments.

His radio antennae had gone out. Was that yesterday too? It seemed like half a year ago.

Every mine they had planted out front had now been exploded. A thousand mines? And although the terrain out front was carpeted with strange, dismembered corpses, it had not stopped the attack.

The door was growing hotter now, gone from red to blue in

some spots. How long would it last? How long could he stand the searing heat of it?

He wondered what Marshal Jonnie was doing.

Chief of Clanfearghus lay on his unwounded side, looking along the face of the rock. There was no retreat. The tunnels had caved in behind him.

They had the last antiaircraft gun that would fire. They were not using it to shoot upward now. They had it trained on the spot the enemy would most likely attack to breach the last barricade to the rock.

The firestorm that had been Edinburgh roared ceaselessly above the din of small arms fire. How long could old buildings burn?

They had thought they had the enemy halted until just now. A new ship was high, high up there. It had just arrived and it was now sending down plane after plane of troops.

There was only Dunneldeen flying now. There he came from the direction of Cornwall where he had gone to refuel.

Why hadn't they listened to MacTyler and crowded everyone into the old Cornwall minesite? Sentiment for Edinburgh. Well, what would Edinburgh be now but ashes?

A wave of enemy troops was gathering now, getting ready for an assault upon that other entrance. He hoped Dunneldeen would live through this. The Scots, if any were left, would need him. The Chief of Clanfearghus did not think that he himself would. Too much blood was coming from his side.

He wondered what MacTyler was doing now.

"Fire low into that first wave," he told the gunner. "And keep firing as long as you have ammunition left. At least we can gae oot i' a blaze o' glory!"

At Singapore, the Scottish officer turned to the blaze-blackened communicator and lowered his infrabeam binoculars. "I don't understand it.".

Tolnep marines had been using artillery to pound a hole under the atmosphere armor cable to the north. It had cost them very dearly. They had lost twelve tanks trying to do just that. But a running group of them had rushed up to that distant cable before they could be stopped and had blown a hole wide open beneath it at a cost of five marines.

The Scottish officer had fully expected that with the next wave some of them would get to the powerhouse and turn all their power off and leave them defenseless.

But they had suddenly withdrawn.

For the past twenty minutes they had been picking up wounded and salvaging equipment and boarding launchcrafts, harassed continually by the terrestrial battle planes.

Now they were soaring up out of reach.

The Tolnep fleet was circling. Some minutes ago, the antiaircraft control men had reported all non-Tolnep ships up there had pulled out, one for Edinburgh, three more for Russia. Now there were just Tolneps up there.

"They're leaving!" said the Scottish officer. Well, this point at the Singapore minesite *had* served as a diversion that pinned enemy forces down. And for quite a while with very light losses. The cost to the enemy had been great.

While he watched, the last of his own planes pulled back. None were equipped with door seals to let them fly out of the atmosphere.

His planes were landing now. The last one came in. When its motor went off, the silence after all the constant din almost hurt the ears. There was only the sizzle of armor cable.

Way to the south and east, black smoke still soared above the ancient ruins of Singapore.

"Those ships up there are heading west!" the antiaircraft control officer called across to him. "Slightly south of west."

"Speed?" said the Scottish officer.

"They're still accelerating. Wait. I'm plotting this. On that course they are going to arrive at Kariba minesite. They must be low on solar charge because their speed is only about two miles a second. They would get to the Kariba site . . . in thirty-seven or thirty-eight minutes."

The Scottish officer said to the communicator, "Warn Kariba ops they're about to have company."

The smoking terrain all about them showed the hell that flotilla could raise. Without the armor cable the defenders here would have been dead ten times over.

A bird sang somewhere. Funny in these charred ruins.

The Scottish officer wondered what Jonnie was doing just now. Whatever it was, they had better get a move on at Kariba. God, he was tired. Those Tolneps played rough games! If they had not pulled out so strangely, the whole force here at the Singapore minesite, armor power off, would have been slaughtered in another twenty minutes. Yes, they better look alive at Kariba.

— 7 —

It had taken a little while to get the emissaries settled back down outside. Some had wanted to change their breathing cartridges, another one or two had wanted a bite of something. Others had just strolled around, looking over the inside of the bowl, curious but friendly enough. One of them had gone so far as to haggle with a Chinese among the village refugees over buying a dog. He had never seen a dog before and he thought it was cute, especially after it snapped at him. He couldn't understand that the Chinese, who spoke no Psychlo, refused. Five thousand credits was a lot of money to pass up. It would buy a house and farm on Splandorf, his home planet.

But they were all settled down now. Even Lord Schleim, who had done an awful lot of wandering about, chin parked most of the time on thc rounded top of his sceptre.

It was night. The platform was lighted with mine spots. The emissaries were seated on benches and in chairs which had been arranged in a half-circle just out of the danger range of the huge metal square. Some were still talking to one another but they were interested.

Jonnie was standing in the middle of the platform and for a bit they wondered whether he was going to send himself someplace or something like that. The spotlights flashed off his buttons and the creature on his helmet seemed to be alive. Interesting even to a bored lord.

"My lords," said Jonnie, "may I ask further forgiveness for absorbing your valuable time. But to settle this thing with Schleim, I fear we have to have a demonstration. It is a demonstration of excessive appetite. With your permission?"

All but the combatant lords and Schleim laughed. A demonstration of appetite. Some sort of eating contest? They'd seen those before. But yes, by all means go ahead.

Jonnie slapped the wand into his hand twice. Two mechanics came rushing out of the shadows with a very splendidly decorated mine cart.

And on the cart sat a dragon like the one on his helmet. It was about five feet long. It had wings. It had a neck. And it had a very ferocious head, a gaping fanged mouth, glaring red eyes, and horns. And from head to tail it had spines jutting out all the way along. A gold-scaled, scarlet-mouthed dragon.

The mechanics made as if to lift the dragon down off the cart but Jonnie warned them back as though the dragon might bite.

Schleim guffawed. Engrossed as he was in listening and knowing well it didn't matter what the devil did, he still could not restrain himself. "That's not a live beast!" he hectored. "That's just a painted figure made of clay! There are more like it right over there!" And he pointed toward the unfinished works where they lay unmounted. "It's just a hollow image!" Theatrics, good lord; the poor fool thought he could take these lords in like they were children!

But the lords looked at him a bit reprovingly for interrupting, particularly the one behind him who leaned over and said, "Hush." Schleim looked at him. He was a huge creature who must have had a genetic line back to trees. His skin was bark-like and he had masses of leafy-looking "hair." His arms were about a foot in diameter. Schleim decided he'd have to watch this one when he made his move. Not long now.

"Forgive Lord Schleim," said Jonnie. "He has been under a strain and doesn't see well."

The lords guffawed now.

"This beast on the cart," continued Jonnie, "is called a 'dragon.' If you look, you will see his mother at the console over there."

The lords looked at the bigger dragon that wrapped around the console. They laughed. His mother!

Sir Robert was standing in the door of the ops room. Behind him Stormalong, with reports in his hand, was arguing with him in a low voice. But Sir Robert was shaking his head. Finally Sir Robert said audibly, "Let the lad alone!" And Stormalong went back inside.

Lord Schleim had noticed it. Somebody had reported the flotilla somewhere? Maybe he'd have to act faster than he had planned. He cocked an ear at the sky. They would arrive and launch something into the atmosphere he could hear. That was his instruction.

"Now if you will notice," said Jonnie, "the dragon on the cart is different from the dragon on my helmet." He pointed to his forehead. "The tiny one has been fed."

Yes, that one on his helmet *did* have a small round ball in its mouth. A small, round, white ball.

"And the one on the cart is hungry!" said Jonnie. "For your collection of data on the flora and fauna of various worlds, you should have these facts. This is an Imperial Dragon! It eats moons and planets!"

They thought it was a pretty good joke. Rulers were always eating up planets. Imperial diet! Get it? Good joke. The emissaries laughed. They understood it was an allegory they were watching. Clever.

Jonnie cautioned back the mechanics again, petted the clay dragon on the head soothingly. Then he suddenly put his arms under the neck and belly, the way you might catch a wild beast by surprise, and staggered back. That dragon was heavy!

The mechanics whisked away the decorated mine cart and vanished. Schleim carefully watched them as well as he could see into the shadows. Oh, they just went back and stood there watching. All right, no problem when the paralysis beam was turned on.

Jonnie had set the dragon down on the center of the platform. And now he did a most interesting thing. He leaned over the dragon's head and he was talking into its ear.

"Very good," said Jonnie. "I *know* you are hungry. SO GO EAT UP ASART!"

Out of their sight on the other side of the dragon, he reached in, heard a soft "now" from Angus at the console, and ratcheted down the time fuse lever of the ultimate bomb, lying in the dragon's hollow belly, to five minutes. With the thumbnail of his other hand he pierced the cap of a smoke bomb used in mines to trace currents of air in shafts.

White smoke began to pour from the dragon's mouth in jets. Ferocious!

Jonnie skipped back off the platform. Angus hit the firing button. Jonnie's wand pointed at the dragon. "Go! And don't come back until you have devoured Asart! Go!"

Wires hummed.

The dragon, smoke and all, shimmered and was gone.

There was a very small recoil.

Jonnie looked at his watch. Three and a half minutes to go.

He walked back across the platform. There was a cold, cold hangover on it where it had doubled with the icy space of Asart.

"Now do any of you lords have a picto-recorder you can trust?" said Jonnie. "I do not want to use our own since you might not trust it. I want to borrow a picto-recorder, one that you can seal, that can't be tampered with."

The lord from Fowljopan, an empire of seven hundred worlds, said he'd oblige. He went to his apartment and got it out of his hamper. He came back and checked the loading. Jonnie made him wrap a metal seal around it and clench it and make sure it couldn't be tampered with.

The two mechanics now rushed to the platform and laid down a gyrocage from a drone. Jonnie asked the lord from Fowljopan to lay the recorder in the gyroslots. The lord glanced at the console to make sure it wasn't being operated, glanced up at the poles to be sure they weren't humming, and walked to the center of the platform and put his picto-recorder inside the cage, and, as Jonnie requested, locked it down. He left the platform.

Jonnie glanced at his watch. Seven minutes had gone by. That dragon had been laid exactly on the surface of Asart. The bomb should have gone off two minutes ago. This next shot would put the picto-recorder well up from that moon and to the side.

"Now!" said Angus.

The wires hummed.

The picto-recorder and cage shimmered and vanished.

There was no recoil.

Numbers on Jonnie's watch whirred. Thirty-nine seconds.

There was a change in the humming. There was a shimmer on the platform.

The picto-recorder and cage reappeared.

The humming went off.

There was a slight recoil.

Two mechanics rolled up the dolly the projector sat on so that it was among the emissaries.

"Now if you please, my lord," said Jonnie to the Fowljopan, "would you please retrieve your recorder and take it to the projector and unseal it. And please be certain that it *is* your disc by putting a few words on the end of it. Then make sure there is no other disc or trace in the machine and put your disc in. If you please.''

Lord of Fowljopan did exactly as requested. ''The recorder is ice cold!'' was all he said.

Jonnie held his breath. He had a pretty good idea of what the bomb did. But he was not sure. This was the touch-and-go moment!

He hit the remote. Off went the spotlights. On went the recorder picture.

There in the dark before them was Asart, three-dimensional. There were the five ellipses which identified it.

Used to bombs and explosions, they had indifferently expected to see some high tower of dust or smoke. Actually, they had not thought, most of them, that much would happen. Jonnie had been so calm, so polite, certainly not a mood in which one engaged in war.

They didn't see anything strange for a moment. And then as the picture rolled off the disc, they saw a *hole*. A hole occurring in the upper right surface of Asart. Just a hole. No, there was a bit of black around the edge of it.

Schleim, ear cocked at the sky, felt a jar of alarm. What in the name of fifty devils was going on here? But he relaxed. Bombs went boom. There were no bombs that made just a hole. The picture went off and Fowljopan's ''My voice here,'' came on.

''Theatrics!'' laughed Schleim. ''You're engaging in nonsense!''

''My lords,'' said Jonnie. ''Does another one of you have a picto-recorder I can borrow?''

Yes, my Lord Dom had one. He went and got it and they went through the same procedure as before.

Angus updated the time, cast the recorder to a new angle, and got it back.

Lord Dom, a little bit frightened at the implications of this to the twelve hundred worlds of his republic, had a quaver in his voice when he put it on the disc.

Jonnie hit the switches.

Asart gleamed in the dark before them.

About a hundredth of the moon had become a hole edged in

curling black clouds. And just before the view went off, down in the lower left, it looked like a door had opened in the crust, not part of the growing hole.

A breath of terror trembled through the gathering. But Jonnie was not going to let it become a riot.

"You see, my lords, the dragon *was* hungry." He laughed lightly. "He is also a very obedient dragon. Told to eat the moon, he is eating Asart! A very controllable dragon after all."

Had he hit them with ice water he could not have produced a more chilling effect. Their eyes focused on him in growing horror.

Schleim broke the spell. It had occurred to him that he had a new way to guarantee success. He had a spare gun in his hamper as well as a recorder. He had just felt in his boot and discovered the weapon gone. Damn that valet! Hawvin slaves were never any good.

"All you are doing," said Schleim, "is casting that recorder out somewhere to a model you've made in the hills. And you have people regulating a model for it to photograph! You're a fraud!" And Schleim really believed it. But he had to make sure before he went off the edge. "There's a recorder in my hamper."

"Go get it," said Jonnie.

Schleim rushed to his apartment. He scrambled through the hamper. Ah! Not just a spare gun but also a spare scepter hidden in the bottom, a spare with another paralysis beam in its heel. He could leave one on in a chair while he carried the other one out to turn the power cable off. Ha-ha! Three blast grenades! After he turned the beam on he'd pitch one into the ops room and use the other two to silence anyone rushing out of another door. Perfect! He wouldn't torture the Hawvin slave after all. Good fellow!

Schleim carried the whole hamper back to the gathering and set it beside his chair. Cautiously opening it so they wouldn't see what else was in it, he removed the picto-recorder. It was a different make and type but it played a disc.

"Devil," said Schleim, "we will end your fraud here and now. You would not know, not being a native of a proper planet, that on the back of Asart is a huge diamond with a slash. It is done with hyperband nullifying material to act as a navigation and identification marker. It is unknown to practically everyone except a fleet officer. The marker will not show up on your standard recorders. And you have none like this one that takes the hyper-spectrum as well as what you call visible light. It will show that diamond and slash. Yours won't. So of course you didn't put one on your fake model. I am about to expose you as the fraud of all time!''

He sounded confident. But before that rig was destroyed he really had to know. Was it a model up in the hills or was that Asart? If it *was* Asart . . . should he be sure his torturer got the secret of teleportation? What a weapon!

He slithered over and put his recorder into the gyrocage, sealed the cage shut with a claw pattern, and walked off the platform.

Angus had heard it all. He shifted coordinates so that the recorder would view both the back of Asart and the hole.

He fired it and recalled it, and when the recoil died, Lord Schleim raced up to it, checked the claw pattern. It had not been broken.

He came back to the projector. He made absolutely sure it was not projecting something else. He put, ''This is Lord Schleim!'' on the disc and put it into the machine.

Did his ear detect a far-off whine in the sky?

— 8 —

Lord Schleim felt there would be no diamond and slash beacon in the picture that would, in a moment, be shown. Only Tolnep eyes would ever detect that and only a Tolnep modified picto-recorder could film it. He would use this moment to distract the others.

Yes! That was a whine in the sky. The fleet would be over them in moments. The timing was just right. How clever of him. But he had a well-deserved reputation as a slippery diplomat. Formidable in fact.

He walked over to his chair, made very sure his hamper was well within reach. He glanced back at the assembled emissaries. They were all craning forward tensely, waiting for the picture to come on—totally off guard. He spotted exactly where the devil was standing, slightly in front of them all and well clear of the projector. Schleim fingered the bottom ring of the sceptre.

"Turn on the latest picture of your fake model!" jeered Schleim.

Jonnie hit the buttons. Off went the mine spotlights. On went the three-dimensional picture of Asart.

It was a new angle. It showed the back side of the moon as well as some of the front. Filtration gave it a bluish hue, but it was Asart. It seemed to float hugely before them.

And right there in the center, massive and unmistakable, was the diamond and slash insignia of Tolnep, jet-black on the surface of the moon.

Schleim gasped. It was real. That really was Asart.

One of the ends of the slash was supposed to point to a hangar door. And even as they looked, that door finished opening. The huge, yawning mouth of a Tolnep-made cavern!

The moon had deflated further now. It resembled a blue balloon with one side being poked relentlessly in, a great pucker that was growing bigger now and at a more rapid rate.

What appeared to be black gases were eddying up to fill the sunken part.

And then out of that yawning hangar bolted a war vessel! Although it must have been traveling very fast, the enormous size of it caused it to seem to move in slow motion. At least thirty thousand tons of Tolnep capital ship was seeking to escape into space.

But it was too late. It had already been touched by the pucker within the moon. A whole back section of the ship was gone!

Before the fixated eyes of the delegates, the vast space vessel was eaten up from tail to nose, its massive metal turned to gases.

Other hangar doors were starting to open.

But that was the extent of the picture. One last puff of black gas as the final bit of capital ship was overtaken by disaster and the recorded voice said "This is Lord Schleim!"

Schleim screamed! Then he acted.

He popped his earplugs shut. He leaped up. He wrenched at the bottom ring of the scepter and, as though it were a machine gun, swept it in an arc from left to right to freeze them all.

"Paralyze!" screamed Schleim. "Stand dead! Damn you, stand dead!"

It wasn't happening fast enough! There was a surge of emissaries away from him, some falling.

He snatched the other scepter from the basket. He twisted the bottom ring and swept it all around, taking in guards in rifle pits.

They were not falling quickly enough.

Schleim dove into the hamper and came up with three grenades. With all his considerable might he hurled one into the open door of the ops room. He sent another at the bowl entrance. He hurled the third at the devil.

Before they could even land, such was his speed of reaction, he had the gun out of the hamper. He lined it up on the devil, square at his face thirty feet away. With joy he pulled the trigger.

It did not fire.

Lord Dom, a bulbous creature from a mostly liquid world, was bouncing to his feet and coming at him.

Schleim raised the pistol on high, preparing to bring it down on Dom and splatter him. A Tolnep could physically smash them all.

Straight as a sizzling arrow, Jonnie threw his knobkerrie. The hard butt end smashed into Schleim's eye filters.

Lord Browl, the massive tree-like emissary who had sat behind him, wrapped Schleim in foot-diameter arms and held him from behind in a creaking vice.

"Hold him still!" shouted Fowljopan. "Don't let him touch his body!" With a flick of his wrist, Fowljopan snapped a beaklike knife into his right claw and advanced upon Schleim.

The Tolnep struggled but the huge arms held. Fowljopan peered with beady eyes all around the steel-like neck of the Tolnep. "Ah!" he said finally. "There is the half-healed incision!" His knife moved in and began to cut. Grey drops of Tolnep blood oozed from the shallow gash that was being made. Fowljopan squeezed the wound and a fragile glassine capsule popped out of it. It was intact.

"His suicide capsule," said Fowljopan. "All he had to do was strike the side of his neck and he would have been dead." He looked reprovingly at Jonnie. "Had you hit this with that throwing stick, we would have had no defendant!"

It was Jonnie's first intimation that all was not going to go exactly as planned, and that all was not well.

Fowljopan turned to the others now crowding around. He

shouted in a squawling voice, "Is it the will of the conference that this emissary be under conference arrest and be brought to trial?"

They thought. They pondered. They looked at one another. One said something about "invoking Clause 32."

Jonnie could only think of getting in there and getting the war stopped *now*. Didn't these lords realize people were dying? And as for Schleim, hadn't they seen him try to use weapons on all of them? But he had collided with the ponderous idiocies for which governments and courts were renowned. There was even a growing whine in the sky. It threatened their own safety.

"I move that he be properly tried," a lord at the back called out.

"All those in favor?" shouted another.

All noncombatant lords said "Aye." The combatant ones said "No!"

"I hereby declare," said Fowljopan, "that the emissary of Tolnep is a prisoner of the conference and is to be duly tried under Clause 32, threatening physical violence to the conference!" That whine in the sky was much louder now. Jonnie shouldered his way through. He got right in front of the Tolnep. He pushed a sceptre at his face.

"Is this what you were looking for, Schleim? This is the real one. The others were just copies we made. Duds like the rest of your weapons."

Schleim was struggling and screaming. "Get me some chains!" shouted Fowljopan.

Jonnie came close to the Tolnep's face. But Fowljopan was prying in among Schleim's teeth to make sure there were no other capsules to bite down on. The moment that was done, Jonnie spoke again.

"Schleim! Tell your captain up there to draw off! Talk or I'll shove this radio down your throat!"

Lord Dom tried to push Jonnie away. "This is a conference prisoner! He may not be communicated with until tried. Clause 51, governing trial procedures—"

Jonnie somehow controlled his temper. "Lord Dom, this conference is at this very instant under threat of bombing! For its own safety, I demand that Schleim—"

"Demand?" said Fowljopan. "Here now, those are very strong

words! There are certain procedures that must be observed. And you are hereby officially informed that you yourself threw an object at an emissary. The conference—''

''To save his life!'' cried Jonnie, pointing at Dom. ''This Tolnep would have crushed his skull!''

''You were acting then,'' said Fowljopan, ''as master-at-arms of this conference? I do not recall any appointment—''

Jonnie took a breath. He thought fast. ''I was acting as the appointee of the host planet which is responsible for protecting the lives of invited delegates.'' He knew of no such procedure.

''Ah,'' said Lord Dom, ''he is invoking Clause 41, responsibilities of the planet responsible for assembling emissaries.''

''Ah,'' said Fowljopan. ''Then you cannot also be charged. Where are those chains?''

A Chinese guard was running up with coils of jangling mine-hoist chains. Two pilots followed him with another tangle of heavy links.

''Under Clause 41,'' said Jonnie desperately, ''I must demand of the prisoner that he surrender his offensive forces at once.''

Lord Dom looked at Fowljopan. Fowljopan shook his head. ''All that can be arranged, per Clause 19, is a temporary suspension of hostilities where warfare threatens the physical safety of a conference.''

''Good!'' said Jonnie. He knew he was at risk. These emissaries were not as friendly now. But he would push it all he could. He had to save lives. Not only theirs but those of any survivors of Edinburgh. He shoved the radio close to Schleim's mouth. ''Declare an immediate suspension of hostilities, Schleim! And tell that captain up there to draw his forces off!''

Lord Schleim simply spat at them.

They were wrapping him in chains now. Somebody had found a spare filter in the hamper and replaced the shattered ones over his eyes so he could see. They had him on the ground and he looked like a huge coil of hoist chain. Only his face was visible now. His lips were drawn back and nothing but hisses were coming out of him.

Jonnie was about to rage at him that if he didn't talk into this radio, the planet of Tolnep would get one big dragon. The thought that this, too, might violate something made him hesitate for a moment, searching for words.

Lord Dom accidentally solved it before Jonnie could speak. "Schleim," said Lord Dom, "I am sure it will go much easier with you at your trial if you call off your forces."

This was the bit of grass that Schleim had been wriggling to get. "On that condition, and if the captain of that fleet up there will forego his piratical venture and follow my orders, give me the radio."

It was promptly shoved to his mouth by a Jonnie who would rather have smashed his fangs in with it. "No codes! Just say, 'I have hereby declared a temporary suspension of hostilities' and 'You are ordered to withdraw into orbit remote from all combat areas.' "

Schleim looked at the faces above him. When Jonnie pressed the hidden talk switch, Schleim surprised them all by saying exactly what Jonnie had told him to say. But was there a lurking smile on the Tolnep's mouth?

Some prearrangement or regulation must be going into effect up there in space. Rogodeter Snowl's voice came back through the sceptre, "It is my duty to inquire whether the emissary of Tolnep is under any physical threat or duress."

They looked at each other. It was obvious that Tolnep naval regulations covered such sudden and otherwise inexplicable orders.

Schleim, wrapped to the chin in heavy mine-hoist chain, smiled. "May I speak to him again?"

"Tell him to comply at once!" said Jonnie. He didn't want to make an overt threat against the Tolnep planet in this company and at this time.

Again, Schleim said exactly what Jonnie had told him to say

Rogodeter Snowl's voice came back, "I can only comply if I am assured that the personal safety of the emissary of Tolnep is guaranteed and that the conference promises to return him unharmed to the planet Tolnep."

Fowljopan said to Lord Dom, "It simply precludes execution."

"By Clause 42," said Lord Browl, "a trial can still be held. It is quite normal. I move we guarantee this emissary's safe return as a personal matter. All those in favor?"

The ayes came back, unanimous this time.

Fowljopan was looking around. "Where is . . . where is . . . ?"

The small gray man appeared among them. He took the scepter from Jonnie. He looked around at the faces of the lords and then, as they nodded, he spoke into the mike. First he gave a code word followed by a peculiar buzz which seemed to come from the lapel of his gray suit. Then he said, "Captain Snowl, it is certified that the emissary of Tolnep will be returned, physically unharmed, to his planet in due course but not with any unreasonable delay."

Snowl's voice came back: "Thank you, Your Excellency. Please inform the emissaries that I will honor a temporary suspension of hostilities and at this moment am withdrawing to an orbit clear of this and all combat areas. End transmission."

Jonnie was pointing at the emissaries of the other combatants. *They* were the ones wrecking Edinburgh and Russia! "Lord Fowljopan," said Jonnie, "I am certain any temporary suspension of hostilities includes all combatants."

"Ah," said Fowljopan. He thought. "We have no guarantee that only Tolnep ships were up there. It would be irregular for these others not to agree."

But the Bolbod, Drawkin, Hawvin, and other combatant lords were pointing at Sir Robert who was standing outside the ops room.

"We agree!" shouted Sir Robert with an expression of disgust for their delays.

The combatant emissaries started to look around for communication facilities. A mob of communicators with mikes rushed out and almost knocked them down.

With a spatter and batter of many tongues, the other combatants ordered a temporary suspension of hostilities for all their ships.

Good god, thought Jonnie. All this while men went on dying. It was still very touch-and-go. No one had said hostilities would not be resumed and with even greater ferocity.

And who was this small gray man who exerted such power over them? Where did he fit in? Who was he? What would *he* want out of all this? Another threat?

— 9 —

The emissaries were dragging Schleim off when Quong, Sir Robert's Buddhist communicator, ran up to Jonnie.

"Sir Robert asks me to tell you," whispered the boy, "that there will be a sudden exodus in a moment and not to be alarmed. They have been working it out in ops for the past half-hour and the orders are being issued this instant. There are hundreds of people trapped in shelters in Edinburgh. The tunnel corridors and entrances fell in under heavy bombs. They do not know how many are alive or anything else. He says it is like a caved-in mine. They are leaving in minutes and he wants you to carry on here. If needed he will come back."

Jonnie felt like a cold hand had gripped his heart. Chrissie and Pattie were part of that. If they still lived.

"I should go!" said Jonnie.

"No, no," said the boy Quong. "Sir Robert said you would say that, Lord Jonnie. They will do everything that can be done. He said to tell you he is leaving all this in your hands."

At that moment pandemonium broke loose. Sir Robert raced out of the ops room. He had somewhere changed his clothes and the gray cloak billowed as he donned it on the run.

"Goodbye, Lord Jonnie," said Quong and raced away.

Sir Robert was at the passage, waving his arm with an urgent swing, "Come on!" he bellowed. "Come on!"

Doctors MacKendrick and Allen sped out of the hospital area, shutting valises as they ran. Allen turned and shouted something at the nurse and then sped on.

The walking wounded hobbled and limped out, heading for the passage.

Four pilots raced by.

Guards who a moment before had been covering Schleim from pits were yelling to one another and a soldier carrying several packs raced toward them and then they were gone.

A crowd of officers and communicators slammed out of ops and headed for the passage exit.

Suddenly, Jonnie was aware of the turmoil and commotion among the Chinese. Mothers were dumping babies and a screech of instructions at older daughters and then running to the exit. The Chinese men were snatching up bits and pieces from the personal baggage, shooing smaller children into the vicinity of the half-grown girls, yelling at each other to hurry. Dogs, snapped on to leashes that were pushed into the hands of young boys, set up a cacophony of barking and howling at being made to stay.

A plane motor started up. Then another.

Three Scot pilots ran out of the ops room, getting into flight clothes and gripping maps.

And all the time Sir Robert was at the exit shouting, "Come on! Come on!"

From the open door of ops, Stormalong's voice was rising above the din. "Victoria? Victoria? Damn it man, keep your radios manned! Take every mine pump you've got. Every atmosphere hose and pump. Got that? I know it's in clear! All right." A woman communicator in there was taking over. She started to chatter Pali.

"Come on!" Sir Robert was shouting at the delaying few. "Damn it, Edinburgh is burning!"

A plane took off. Sir Robert was gone. Another plane. Another, another, another. From the whip of sound they were lancing up to hypersonic in seconds. Jonnie wondered whether they were leaving any aircraft at all.

Lord Dom came over to Jonnie. His big, liquidy face looked a bit concerned. "What's happening? Are you abandoning this area? You realize that in a temporary suspension of hostilities it is irregular to use it to arrange the redisposition of military forces to achieve the advantage of surprise when hostilities are resumed. I would caution—"

Jonnie had had just about enough of being Chinko polite for one day. He was worried about Chrissie and Pattie. And very concerned about his village people who had gone to Russia. "They are on their way to try to dig hundreds of people out of collapsed shelters," said Jonnie. "I don't think your rules apply to noncombatants, Lord Dom. And even if they did, not even you could stop those Scots. They're on their way to save what they can of the Scottish nation."

Jonnie walked into ops. The place was in a shambles left by

the hasty departure. Only the Buddhist woman communicator and Stormalong were there. She had finished her messages and was sitting back, head bowed, exhausted. They had been on straight duty for days without rest. This was the first lull.

"Russia?" said Jonnie to Stormalong.

"I sent the whole contingent at Singapore there over half an hour ago. They took everything they had. It's just a flight over the Himalayas and they'll be there in another couple of hours. I don't know what they'll find—we haven't heard from Russia for a couple of days."

"Edinburgh?" said Jonnie.

"Nothing for the last hour."

"Did I hear you sending everyone at Victoria to Scotland?" said Jonnie. "What about the prisoners there?"

"Oh, they gave Ker a blast rifle." He saw Jonnie's look. "Ker says he'll blow their heads off if they so much as move an eyebone! They left that old woman from the Mountains of the Moon to handle their diets. And all your vital notes are safe—" He was about to add "here" when he saw Lord Dom at the door and looked at him.

Lord Dom said, "I didn't wish to intrude but I couldn't help overhearing. Haven't you left this whole conference area, maybe this whole continent, maybe the planet, without air cover?"

Jonnie shrugged and pointed to Stormalong. "There's he and I."

This startled Lord Dom. He quivered a bit.

Stormalong laughed and said, "Why, that's twice as many as there used to be! Not long ago, there was just *him!*" He pointed at Jonnie.

Lord Dom blinked. He stared at Jonnie. The young man didn't seem worried at all.

Lord Dom went off and told his colleagues about this. They discussed it considerably among themselves.

They decided they had better keep a careful eye on Jonnie.

— 10 —

Jonnie stood outside the ops room door and looked around the bowl. How quiet it seemed.

The older Chinese children had quieted the younger ones and gotten them to bed. The dogs were silent, exhausted from the excitement of a while ago. The emissaries had all gone off to their apartments or guard duty over Schleim. There were no sentries in sight. The place seemed deserted. Even though it was not late yet.

To one brought up in the silences of mountains, the calm was welcome.

It might be the sort of calm that is followed by blasting storm. But it was a moment's calm.

Too many situations were running all at the same time for him to have any peace of mind. Who knew what would happen as a result of the emissary trial: he did not trust them. What would occur after this "temporary suspension" of war? What would they find in Edinburgh? In Russia? He told himself he had better not let his mind dwell long on these last two places or he would edge over into anxiety and grief.

That book he had read—that said you could handle things if you did one of them at a time: good advice.

Psychlo! He had been living in such a tornado that the question of Psychlo had become a sort of dull pain like a toothache. Was there any danger of counterattack? Or was that just a shadow?

Ha! This was a thing he had been waiting for. He had a transshipment rig. It was in fine working order. There were no planes in the air, no motors running. Psychlo! He would end right now that question of threat.

He strode over to the console and almost fell over Angus. The Scot was sitting in a pool of light, working intensely with some rods and wheels. He didn't look up but he knew Jonnie was there.

"While you were settling up with Schleim," said Angus,

fingers flying around his work, "I parked a picto-recorder on a peak on Tolnep to watch that moon. Reaction motors don't mess up a firing—only teleportation motors do. So I just fired it. But that was the only gyrocage assembled. I'm putting together a spare.

"Angus," said Jonnie, "we are going to find out what happened to Psychlo! We've got the machine, we've got the time."

"Give me about half an hour," said Angus.

Jonnie saw he needed no help and he wasn't going to stand around here and wait.

En route to his room he looked in at the hospital. They had left a woman nurse, an elderly Scot, and she resented being left behind. She looked up from a patient as Jonnie entered. "It's time for your sulfa and your shot!" she said threateningly. Jonnie knew he shouldn't have come in here. He had just wanted to see how the wounded were doing.

The two fractured-skull cases were lying in their beds. They seemed all right. But being Scots and left behind, they eyed him dully. The two burned antiaircraft gunners seemed all right but, being Scots, they didn't want to be there with Edinburgh burning.

"Take off your jacket!" snapped the nurse. Then she took the bandage off his arm and looked at the arrow wound. "Hah!" she said, sounding disappointed, "it won't even leave a scar!"

She made him take sulfa powder and wash it down with water. She jabbed an inch of needle into his good arm and squirted B Complex stingingly with a savage thumb. She took his temperature and counted his pulse. "You're perfectly well!" It sounded like an indictment.

Jonnie had had a lot of practice in diplomacy that day. He felt sorry for these people. Jacket and helmet dangling from his hand he said, "I sure am glad you people stayed. I may need lots of help defending this area."

After a moment of amazement, they all came alive. They said he could count on *them!* And when he left they were all chattering about what they could do and smiling—even the nurse.

With the exodus of the adult Chinese, he hadn't really expected to find Mr. Tsung. But there he was. He had laid out a blue jacket on the bed along with some other items for change. But he was bowing and beaming. With his hands tucked in his sleeves, he was going up and down like a pump.

He was trying to say something but his English wasn't up to it and suddenly he bolted and came back with Chief Chong-won.

"Well, at least you're here," said Jonnie. "I thought the place was near empty!"

"Oh, no," said the chief. "The Coordinators are all gone. But we have guests, you know. The emissaries. So I'm here and the cook; there's an electrician and two antiaircraft gunners." He started counting off on his fingers. "Must be a dozen people left. We do have one problem." He saw Jonnie go alert. "It's the food. I thought we'd be feeding all these emissaries and we got ready to fix the fanciest Chinese food you ever heard of. But they don't eat our food! So we have all this food and nobody to eat it! Too bad!"

To a people who had been pressed starving into the snowy mountains for centuries, it must look like quite a tragedy. "Feed the children," said Jonnie.

"Oh, we have, we have," said the chief. "Even the dogs. But we've still got lots too much food. I tell you what we'll do. There's an empty apartment and we'll set it up for a dining room and we will feed you a beautiful dinner."

"I've got something to do," said Jonnie.

"Oh, no problem, no problem. It is very stylish to eat late. The cook will be so pleased. Here," and he made a dash outside to the hall and brought back a tray with some soup and small patties of dough and meat. "These are . . . no Psychlo word . . . between-meal-bites. Help us out!"

Jonnie laughed. If that was all the problems they had, life would be a basking in the sun! He sat down in a chair and began to eat the snack. Tsung, after setting up a small table, was back to bobbing again.

"What's he bowing about?" said Jonnie.

The chief waved his hand and Jonnie saw that a fourth viewscreen had been installed, making two for the conference room. "He's been in here all the time you were on that platform, working a Coordinator half to death translating. They've got discs of everything that went on. The second screen was so they could see both you and the emissaries. I looked in here a time or two—''

Mr. Tsung was volubly interrupting him. The chief translated, ''He wants you to know that you are the fastest pupil he has ever seen. He says if you had been an Imperial Prince of China and his family had still been chamberlains and not exiled, China would still be there.''

Jonnie laughed and would have acknowledged with a return compliment but Mr. Tsung was talking very fast and drawing something from his sleeve. ''He wants something,'' said the chief. ''He wants you to put your 'chop' on this paper. That is, your signature.'' He was unfolding it. It was a considerable expanse of Chinese characters.

The chief raised his eyebrows and translated the sense of it for Jonnie. ''This says that you approve the cancellation of exile of his family from the Imperial Court and that you recommend its reinstatement as chamberlains to the principal government of this planet and yourself.

''I'm not a member of the government,'' said Jonnie.

''He knows all that, but he wants your chop on it. I warn you that he has two brothers and several relatives. They're all educated in diplomacy and such. Oh, he tells me there's a second paper here. Yes. This one restores their rank as Mandarins of the Blue Button—lets them wear a round cap with a blue button on top—noblemen, actually. It's valid. They are noblemen.''

''But I'm not—'' began Jonnie.

Mr. Tsung sang off into half-a-dozen trills of protest.

''He says you don't know what you are. Put your chop on these and he'll do the rest.''

Jonnie said, ''But I have no authority. The war isn't over yet. Not by a long ways! I—''

''He says wars are wars and diplomats are diplomats and there is no point in the game when it ends. I'd sign them, if I were you, Lord Jonnie. They're all studying Psychlo and English. It's his chance to attain an eleven-hundred-year-old goal. I'll read these word for word for you.''

Well, Jonnie felt they might not have made it without Mr. Tsung, so he was given a brush and he signed them and Chief Chong-won witnessed them.

Mr. Tsung reverently folded the pieces of paper into a cover of gold brocade and laid them away like they were crown jewels.

"Oh, yes," said Jonnie as he left. "One more thing. Tell him how much I enjoyed that tale about the dragon who ate the moon."

■

PART 28

— 1 —

Psychlo!

The home planet of two hundred thousand worlds.

The center of an empire that had ruled and ruined sixteen universes over a period of three hundred and two thousand years.

Psychlo. That had been the cause of man's destruction.

What had happened to its empire, if anything?

What had happened to Psychlo? And if it still existed, what did it plan?

Was it a danger or not?

For a grueling and turbulent year they had wondered. It lay like a nagging barb under their thoughts.

Now they were going to find out.

Pale light lit the bowl. The metal of the platform shone dully. Not a motor to be heard in the sky. The stars were bright above.

Angus and Jonnie looked at each other. Now they would know.

"First," said Jonnie, "we will inspect minesites and see what transshipment rigs are active. Perhaps there is some indicator somewhere that would alert them to this. We will be cautious, not get too close to anything."

The coordinate book told them of a transshipment rig at Loozite, a Psychlo mining world without population other than Psychlo miners. It was a large planet but distant from Psychlo.

They put the new gyrocage down, put a picto-recorder in the armored case, calculated the coordinates for a point forty miles from the Loozite transshipment site, punched the console buttons, and fired.

The wires hummed.

The cage came back.

There was a slight recoil.

Jonnie put the disc in the atmosphere projector that still stood there.

He pressed the button.

For a moment both he and Angus thought they must have miscalculated and shot a mine instead. Forty miles was a long way off for detail and Jonnie adjusted and recentered the scene before them.

It was a hole!

But not a mine. There stood a transshipment pole at a drunken angle.

But it was otherwise just a hole in the planet surface. No trace even of compound domes.

Jonnie wondered whether they had different compound layouts on different planets. Perhaps that Loozite platform had been miles from anything else. Still, the Psychlos were demons for standard layouts. Usually the whole central administration of the planet was at the transshipment rig. For there was where the ore came from all over the planet. There was where the books were kept, where the main shops existed, where the top executives were.

Just that hole. It was pretty big, but a hole is a hole.

They chose another firing site: Mercogran in the fifth universe. It was shown as a planet five times the size of Earth but of less density.

They fired and recalled the gyrocage.

When Jonnie turned the projector on, they saw at once they had something different. They had to widen the view on the projector to see better.

Mercogran had been close to a mountain range and avalanches had apparently come down. They would have covered much of the space of any compound.

Jonnie brought the view in closer. There! At the lower right! The inverted bowl of a compound dome. It was lying like a broken soup plate. There was a transshipment pole and attached charred wires sitting in the middle of it. But nothing else.

So far no tight conclusion could be reached beyond the fact that those central compounds and transshipment rigs were certainly no longer working.

At random they took another planet: Brelloton. It was an

inhabited planet, another reference told them, with a population of its own, governed by a Psychlo "regency," enduring such rule for sixty thousand years.

They calculated the coordinates for a spot forty miles from the transshipment rig and fired the gyrocage.

They were not prepared for what they got. The atmosphere image showed a city. The transshipment rig there had apparently been on a raised plateau in the center of town.

Buildings that once must have been massive were blown to bits. They made a spreading pattern that radiated out from the plateau. Buildings that must have been two thousand feet high in a city that must have held a million beings or more had fallen outward like dominos.

The remains of the rig were plain. The platform was a hole. The poles were all leaning outward.

The compound domes had lain under the edge of the plateau and had been lifted by concussion and blown away, leaving the familiar underground layout plain in view.

Bringing the compound in closer one could see what must be a year's growth of grass in crevices.

There was no sign of life.

Jonnie went back and sat down and thought. He asked Angus to find some views the air cover had taken at the Purgatoire River. Views of the American compound.

Angus got them and Jonnie looked at them: the hole where the platform had been, the outward lean of the poles that still stood, the blasted city fifty or more miles away.

"I know what happened," said Jonnie. "We could go on looking at Psychlo planets all night and get the same answer. Give me that computer. We're going to look at Psychlo on Day 92 last year!"

Light. It traveled approximately 5,869,713,600,000 miles a year. The light which came from Psychlo on that hour and date was still traveling in space. They would get just ahead of it, and with a picto-recorder from a star drone set for 6,000,000,000,000X magnification, they would look at Psychlo at the instant it occurred. Whatever had occurred.

It had been just a few days ago over a year ago.

Choose a sidereal angle to aim the scope. Avoid nearby heavenly bodies so that the cage would not be influenced by gravity and would stay there for two or three minutes. No, let's be brave and put it there for fifteen minutes and hope it doesn't move and we get it back.

It took a while to set up. They had to readjust magnification, tune in heat sensors, and blind them to other bodies. Calculate seconds.

They fired the cage.

The wires hummed in holding for the long required time. They called the cage back.

It arrived!

It was a little misplaced on the platform. Jonnie would have touched it in his eagerness but Angus grabbed his hand. It would be cold enough for the metal to take one's skin off! They had to wait and let it warm up, for if they opened it cold they might warp a disc with the abrupt temperature shift.

It was like teasing a thirsty man by withholding a water skin from him.

Finally they projected it. What a brilliant picture! They had thought it might be fuzzy such as you get with heat waves. But the light that had traveled for over a year was crystal-clear and straight.

There was the Imperial City of Psychlo. Circular tram rails, streets down from its cliffs like conveyor belts. They even carried the idea of mining into their city design.

Huge, bustling Psychlo! The center of power of the universes. The hub of the great, cruel claw that raked the bones from planets and peoples everywhere. There was the three-hundred-two-thousand-year-old monster itself, spread out in its sadistic and ugly might!

Neither Jonnie nor Angus had ever seen a live city of that size before. A hundred million population? A billion? Not the planet, just the city above the lower plain. Look at the trams. Rails that ran in circular spirals. Cars that looked for all the world like mine cars but full of people. Mobs in the streets. Mobs! Not riots. Just Psychlos. You ever see so many beings? Even in such a tiny size one could see *mobs!*

They were daunted.

They compared it to their own towns, even to their own ruined cities. These didn't measure up to it at all.

What arrogance to attack anything like that.

They were so awestruck and impressed they hadn't even been looking at the transshipment rig of Psychlo. They missed the beginning and had to track back.

They adjusted the projector lens and position to get the transshipment platform of Psychlo more centered and enlarged.

And then they saw the whole sequence, just as it had occurred right after Jonnie and Windsplitter had raced across the Earth platform.

First, there were the Psychlo workers racing out to leave the platform clear for the incoming semiannual from Earth. There were flatbeds lined up to receive coffins and personnel.

There was the first shimmer of arrival of the Psychlos Jonnie and Windsplitter had knocked down.

Then a small puff.

There were the Psychlo workmen flinching back.

A force screen had gone on! A dome over the platform had closed instantly to contain that small explosion. It could not have been an atmosphere armor cable. Some sort of shimmering, sparkling screen. Transparent but very much there.

Trucks had time to start up before anything else occurred. One huge emergency truck had lunged nearer the platform, evidently to handle the minor blast. A whole minute went by.

Then the first lethal coffin exploded! A big "planet buster" nuclear bomb, nestled into a bed of dirty mines.

The force screen held.

The holocaust was contained. The boiling, ferocious blast had not even bulged the screen.

Then another shock as the second coffined "planet buster" went off.

The screen held! Good lord, what technology to build a screen like that. What power it must take to hold it.

Another shock inside that dome. The third planet buster. It and all its ancient, very dirty atomic bombs.

The screen held.

Psychlos were racing toward it from far off. Those near the platform were flattened by concussion transmitting through the screen.

The fourth contained bomb went off.

The screen still held.

But the transmitted concussion had hurled the emergency truck backward. Nearby buildings lost their glass.

The ground was shaking as though hit by gigantic earthquakes.

A nearby building suddenly dropped downward as though sucked from below. Other buildings began to go the same way.

The fifth bomb went off!

And seen in slow motion, first narrowly, then more broadly, the entire scene went into a churning, boiling mass of atomic fire.

No, something more! Molten, flaming fire was erupting in spots all over the plain.

They widened the angle quickly.

The whole Imperial City of Psychlo was sinking and all about it sprayed up rolling oceans of molten fire.

The circular trams, the mobs, the buildings, and even the towering cliffs were drowning in a tumult of liquid, yellow-green flame.

They hastily widened the view.

And they saw the entire planet of Psychlo turn into a radioactive sun!

The recording ended. They sat limp.

"My god," said Angus.

Jonnie felt a little sick. Psychlos or not, he had just watched the end product of all their planning and risk a year ago, and he was hit with a feeling of guilt. It was not easy to take responsibility for that much destruction.

He had thought the bombs would wipe out the company headquarters and perhaps the Imperial City. But they had created a new sun.

"What happened?" said Angus.

Jonnie looked at his feet. "I pulled ten tabs out of those coffins. We didn't want to set a time fuse and then have them go off on Earth. We knew the bombs were a bit contaminated. Had radiation leaks. They were old and their cases were old. We handled them in radiation suits."

He made a dropping gesture with his hand. "In the fight, I dropped the fuse tabs on the platform. I forgot them. They must have been slightly radioactive, and when they hit the Psychlo platform, they made a small puff of explosion. They are what caused the minor recoil last year.

"They triggered the force screen on Psychlo that the Chamcos mentioned. And that force screen was good enough and strong enough to contain the blasts.

"I read in a book Char had that the crust of Psychlo is riddled with abandoned mine shafts and tunnels, a complete sieve. They call it semicore mining. The blasts went down. One after another they pounded deeper and deeper toward the molten core of Psychlo.

"The fifth explosion penetrated the core. The next five exploded in that.

"I think all a nuclear weapon does is *stimulate* a chain reaction into existence. And in addition to blowing out the planet crust, the fusion continued. And is probably still going on and may well go on for millions of years.

"Psychlo is no longer a planet. It's a flaming sun!"

Angus nodded. "And all the transshipment rigs in the whole Psychlo empire, keeping schedule, not knowing about it, fired into that radioactive sun and blew themselves to bits!"

Jonnie nodded, a bit spent. "Just like we did in Denver a year later." He shuddered. "Terl fired himself into a holocaust. Poor Terl."

That's what it took to yank Angus out of it. "Poor Terl! After all the rotten things the demon did? Jonnie, I sometimes wonder about you. You can be cool as ice and then all of a sudden you come out with something like 'poor Terl'!"

"It would be an awful way to die," said Jonnie.

Angus straightened up. "Well!" he said just like he had popped up out of a dive in the lake. "Psychlo is gone! The empire is gone! And that's one thing we don't have to worry about anymore! Good riddance!"

— 2 —

Despite emotional reactions, Jonnie had been raised a hunter. His had been a life in the mountains, much of it spent alone on trails where pumas and grizzlies and wolves could lurk. There were times when you could feel a planning predator behind you, watching for a false move, concentrated on intentions of its own.

For the last fifteen seconds he had had that feeling. *Danger!*

He spun about, tensed for action.

The small gray man behind him said, "Oh, didn't you know?"

Jonnie let his hand fall away from his gun butt.

The small gray man appeared not to have noticed. "A lot adds up now that I didn't understand before. Yes, I fear Psychlo is gone. We knew *that*, of course. We weren't sure how."

Angus said, "Are there *any* Psychlos left? *Anywhere?*"

The small gray man shook his head.

The other small gray man, who had arrived by teleportation, had been lurking in the shadows. He came forward now. "We checked it and checked it. Probes told us Psychlo was gone only a couple of weeks after it happened. We've had ships out everywhere. . . ."

The first small gray man had glanced at him. A cautionary glance?

The other small gray man smoothly shifted what he was going to say. "The transshipment rigs were all at minesite centrals or at regency palaces: that was company custom. All their executive personnel and high-ranking officers on planets were quartered near the platforms—pure laziness, really, so they wouldn't have far to walk and could get dispatches sooner. And the bulk of their breathe-gas storage was also in the same area.

"The first word they got—they never went in much for space travel as such, since they had a monopoly on teleportation—and it wouldn't have gotten back to them soon enough anyway—was when they fired into Psychlo.

"We of course couldn't examine all universes, but knowing Psychlos, we are positive there are no transshipment rigs or central compounds or executives left. We ourselves gave it up over five months ago. The time limit would have been six months for breathe-gas to last. And that expired six months ago."

Jonnie had been watching them carefully. These men were hiding something. And they wanted something. They were a threat. Down deep he knew that. Their manner was easy. They were very pleasant and smooth. But their frankness was a pose.

"How can you be sure," said Jonnie, "that some Psychlo engineer didn't build a transshipment rig?"

"Oh," said the second small gray man, "he would have fired straight to us at once if he avoided firing into Psychlo. The rig nearest us blew to bits. Took half a city with it. Horrible. Just by a freak, I was out sailing with my family that day, miles away. However, our own offices are fifteen levels underground."

Was the original small gray man giving him a warning sign? In any case, he got interested in his pointed fingernails.

Angus said, "I don't see any planets listed that have the same atmosphere as Psychlo. Are there any other planets that have that breathe-gas?"

The two small gray men thought it over. Then the one who had come latest said, "Fobia. I don't think they'd list it." The two of them laughed about something.

The original one said, "Excuse us. It's kind of a joke. The best-kept state secrets of Psychlo are all a kind of open book in our business. That they would omit listing 'Fobia' is so typically Psychlo. It's where they exiled King Hak about two hundred sixty-one thousand years ago. It's the only other planet in that system, and it is so much further out than Psychlo, you can't even see it from the home planet with an unaided eye. It is so cold, its atmosphere has liquefied and lies in lakes on the surface. They built a little dome there and exiled Hak and his fellow conspirators and then got so scared he'd escape they sent assassins in and killed them all. Typically Psychlo. They cut the whole thing out of their schoolbooks. Let's see your astrographic tables." He took them, looked a while, and then laughed and showed his companion. "Not there! An omitted planet right in their own system!"

In response to Jonnie's look, the second one said, "No, not even any Psychlos there, and nothing going on there either. It's nothing but breathe-gas ice and very tiny anyway. As of a couple of weeks ago, probes showed it totally deserted. No, you can be certain that's the end of the Psychlos. I saw on scans I reviewed here that you have a very few still alive, but you didn't get them to build this!" He patted the side of the console dragon. "For reasons best known to Psychlos they'd kill themselves first!" He shook his head. "There were a few alive. Engineers in branch minesites. And don't think one didn't try to persuade them! They're all dead now."

Was the original one trying to turn the other one off? But the new one was a bit better dressed and appeared to be the superior of the other.

"I think," said the original one, "that we really ought to get together for a formal conference. There are some things to take up."

Ah, thought Jonnie. Now we get to it. "I'm not a member of the government," he hedged.

The newest arrival said, "We're aware of that. But you do enjoy its confidence. We were thinking that possibly if you and the two of us could have a talk, you might assist us to arrange a conference with your government."

"A talk about having a serious talk," said the other.

Jonnie had an inspiration. He recalled the first gray man had drunk yarb tea. "I'll be having dinner in half an hour. If you can eat our food, I'd be pleased to have you join me."

"Oh, we eat anything," said the newest small gray man. "Anything there is. We would be so pleased."

"Half an hour it is," said Jonnie. And he left to tell Chong-won he had dinner guests after all.

Now maybe he'd find out the threat that these two posed. He wasn't imagining it. These two were *dangerous!*

— 3 —

The small gray men could really *eat*.

Jonnie had been surprised at how well the chief had decorated the main room of the spare apartment. Colored paper lanterns—with mine lamps in them—had been hung about; two paintings, one of a tiger coming toward you in the snow, the other of a bird in flight, decorated the walls; side tables for serving had been set up; the large center table where they sat even had a cloth on it.

Mr. Tsung had insisted Jonnie don a gold brocade tunic—after Jonnie refused to wear a robe of green satin—and Jonnie looked quite nice.

Some very subdued but kind of squeaky music was coming from someplace. It and the click of dishes that Chief Chong-won kept hauling in and the jaws of the small gray men were the only sounds.

Jonnie had tried to invite Angus but he had said he had to keep an eye on that moon gyro. He had wanted Stormalong to come but the pilot was dead tired and catching naps in the ops room. He had asked Chief Chong-won and Mr. Tsung to also eat with them but they said no, they had to serve. So just Jonnie and the two small gray men had wound up as the diners. Jonnie felt that this was a pity for there was an awful lot of food. And Jonnie, so far, had no one to talk to. The small gray men just ate. And ate and ate!

The dinner had begun with appetizers—egg rolls, barbecued loin ribs, and paper-wrapped chicken; these had been served in mounds and had all been eaten up by the small gray men. Then various noodles had been served—pancake noodles, yat ga mein, mun yee noodles, war won ton, beef lo mein, yee fu noodles, and gorn lo won ton, tubs of them! And the small gray men had eaten them all up. Large platters of chicken had been served—almond chicken, cashew chicken, button mushroom chicken, and lichee chicken. And the small gray men had eaten all that up. Then there had been beef dishes—Mongolian beef, sauteed eggplant with beef, tomato beef, and chili pepper steak. And they had gotten around that! Massive platters of Peking duck, cooked in three ways, had, in its turn, disappeared down their gullets. They were working now on egg dishes—chicken egg foo yung, precious flower egg, and mushroom egg foo yung.

Jonnie wondered where Chief Chong-won had gotten all the ingredients until he recalled that game had been plentiful, including lots of fowl in the lake, and that the Chinese had had time to plant and harvest gardens, using an area protected by the dam armor cable to keep the wild beasts out of it.

He himself had not eaten very much. Mr. Tsung had had it relayed to him disparagingly that most of these dishes were southern Chinese cookery and that true cookery had evolved in the north during the Ch'ing Dynasty when his family took care of things. The Peking duck and Mongolian beef should get his main attention. Jonnie had complied. It was pretty good food. Not as good, of course, as his Aunt Ellen's venison stew, but quite edible. The nurse had sent in word he was not to have any rice wine because of the sulfa but that was fine—Jonnie didn't much care for drinking anyway.

These small gray men were eating the entire banquet that had been planned for thirty people! Where did they put it all?

Jonnie took the time to study them. Their skin was gray and kind of rough. Their eyes were a dull gray-blue, maybe like the sea, and had heavy lids. Their heads were round and hairless.

Their noses took a sharp upturn just at the tip. The ears were a bit odd—reminded one more of gills than ears. They had four fingers and a thumb on each hand, though the nails were very pointed. They really looked quite like men. The main difference was their teeth: they had *two* rows of teeth, the second set just behind the first.

Watching them eat so voraciously and hugely, Jonnie tried to figure out what genetic lines such creatures might come from. They reminded him of something and he sought to place it. Then he recalled a fish that a pilot who was passing through Victoria had shown them. The pilot had been downed by fuel failure in the Indian Ocean and had ejected with a life raft. While waiting to be picked up he was attacked by these fish. When he was rescued, they had shot one of the fish with a cannon and picto-recorded it. It had been pretty big. What had he called it? Jonnie tried to think. They had looked it up in a man-book. Ah, a *shark!* That had been the name! Yes. These small gray men had a similar skin, similar teeth. Maybe they were evolved from sharks that had become sentient.

It finally came down to tea. It wasn't that the small gray men couldn't eat any more. It was that Chief Chong-won had run out of food! The tea was served, and the first small gray man asked with just a trace of worry whether this was "yarb tea." He was reassured that it was just plain green tea, a fact that seemed to bring relief.

They sat back and smiled at Jonnie. They said that was the best dinner they had had in some time, maybe ever, and Chong-won slid out to tell and please the cook.

Under their gaze, Jonnie thought to himself that now they were finished with all the food in sight, they were going to try to eat him! But no, that was vaporing. They were quite pleasant, really. Now maybe he could find out what they were all about, what they really wanted.

"You know," said the original small gray man, "about these hostile forces—your trouble here was really your defenses. Cheap trash. But that's the Psychlos for you. They never put their money in good defenses. Personnel were cheap. They'd rather buy half-a-dozen new females or a ton or two of kerbango than proper armaments."

He looked at Jonnie as though about to apprise him of something utterly devastating. "You know how much those antiaircraft guns you use cost? Less than five thousand credits. Cheap trash! They won't even shoot up to two hundred thousand feet. Bargain-basement, rummage-sale armaments. They probably bought them from some war surplus, used. And some executive put the new price on the books and pocketed the difference."

"What should a proper antiaircraft gun cost?" said Jonnie to keep it going.

The newest small gray man thought a moment. Then he brought a small gray book out of his vest pocket and opened it. The page seemed to get bigger and he scanned down it with a little reader glass. "Ah, here's one. 'Surface/space combination repulsion, multicomputer firing defense cannon: maximum range 599 miles, 15,000 shots a minute, simultaneous tracking of 130 vessels or 2,300 bombs, destruction potential A-13 (that's capital ship penetration), cost before discounts, C123,475 plus freight and installation.' Now batteries of those located around your strong points would have handled that entire combined force or kept them so high up they could not have launched atmosphere crafts."

The original small gray man agreed. "Yes, that was the main trouble. The Psychlos were both improvident and credit-pinching at the same time. I don't think they even kept up this planet's defenses."

Jonnie could agree with that. He felt he was going to find out something about these fellows now that they were talking. Keep them talking! "Well, just at a guess," said Jonnie, "what would you say proper defenses for this planet would cost?"

He had started something!

Both small gray men put their heads together. The original one started pulling all sorts of little things out of his pocket, looking into them and finding things. The newer arrival had a large ring on his left finger and at first Jonnie thought he was simply fiddling with it: not so; he was twisting and tapping it with sudden little jerks, and a long thread, so thin as to be nearly invisible, was coiling out of the ring.

They were very intense and their voices murmured and blended together. ". . . thirty space probes . . . maintained carrier wave probe warning beams . . . fifteen space drones, automatic firing at all nonsignal identified craft . . . cost of equipping terrestrial craft with identification beacons . . . 2,000 atmosphere beacons . . . 256 Mark 50 combat fighters . . . 400 fly-away, antipersonnel tanks . . . 7,000 antipersonnel road barricades . . . one hundred city cable defenses with rectractable gates . . . fifty heat/color search drones . . . fifty automatic target destroy surface drones. . . .''

They were finished. The newer one snapped off the thread at the ring and tapped it at the end, and with a little pop! the thread expanded into a long sheet of paper like a tape. He gave it a small flick and it landed in front of the original small gray man. He picked it up, scanned the figures on it, and then looked at the end.

''With spare parts and freight,'' he said, ''it comes to C500,962,878,431 at two parts in eleven annual interest rate, plus an estimated C285,000,006 annual military and maintenance personnel salaries, housing and equipage.''

He tossed the long tape across the table to Jonnie and concluded, ''There it is. An efficient and economical planetary defense system. All top-of-the-line merchandise. Good for a hundred years. *That's* the sort of thing you should have had! And you can still have it!''

That was C498,960,878,431 more than Earth had! It had made him realize how broke Earth was. Now was the time to find out more about these two. ''I surely appreciate your information. If you will excuse me, what are you two gentlemen? Arms salesmen?''

He might as well have dropped a bomb on them, they looked so startled! Then they looked at each other and both of them laughed.

''Oh, I am so sorry,'' said the original small gray man. ''It is so terribly impolite of us. You see, we are quite well known in our respective areas. And we know so much about you, in fact, know you so well, that it just never occurred to us that we never introduced ourselves!

''I am His Excellency Dries Gloton. And I am very pleased to meet you, Sir Lord Jonnie Tyler.''

Jonnie shook his hand. It was a dry hand, quite rough.

''And this,'' said His Excellency, ''is Lord Voraz. Lord Voraz, Sir Lord Jonnie Tyler.''

Jonnie shook *his* dry, rough hand and said, ''It is really just Jonnie Tyler, Your Lordship. I have no titles.''

"We choose to doubt that," said Lord Voraz.

His Excellency said, "Lord Voraz is the Central Director, Chief Executive Officer, and Overlord of the Galactic Bank."

Jonnie blinked but bowed.

Lord Voraz said, "Dries here likes to call himself the chief collections executive but it is a sort of bank joke. He is actually the Branch Manager of the Galactic Bank for this sector. You might have noticed a time or two that I stepped on his toes accidentally. A Branch Manager has total authority for his sector and is a bit jealous of his prerogatives." He laughed, teasing his junior. "Your planet comes in his sector and dealings about it are entirely up to him. He's the one who has to show a profit for his area. Now I, I am simply here because the emissaries have met. These are very troubled—"

Dries Gloton cut him off sharply. "His Lordship can't be expected to know all the ins and outs of sector business. He does very well to keep up with universes."

Lord Voraz laughed again, "Oh, dear, I am really sorry we worried you. Why, we have been looking—"

Dries cut him off again, "We're just here to help, Sir Lord Jonnie. By the way, would you like to start an account? A personal account?" He was fishing in his pockets for the materials. "We can give you a very low number and absolute confidence assured."

Suddenly Jonnie realized that he had no money. Not just no money in his pockets. He didn't have and never had had any money at all. He'd even given the gold coin away. He thought maybe he got pilot pay that was given to Chrissie, but he had never seen it. He steered off apprehensive thoughts of Chrissie quickly. He had better keep his mind on this talk. But he was broke. Penniless.

"I'm sorry," he said. "Perhaps later if I ever get any money to deposit."

The two gave each other a quick look. But Dries said, "Well, just remember, we're not enemies of yours."

"I think you would be very bad to have as enemies," said Jonnie, still fishing. "That fleet wouldn't go away until you talked to Snowl."

"Oh, that!" said Dries Gloton. "The Galactic Bank has lots of services for its customers. What you saw there was just notarial services. They needed a radio notary code trace to attest and verify that it was a valid conference order. He wouldn't take their word, of course. They trust the bank."

"Was calling the emissaries here a bank service, too?" said Jonnie.

"Well, no," began Lord Voraz.

"You could call it so, if you like," said Dries. "For sometimes such a conference *is* arranged as a service. It's in the interest of the Galactic Bank to have civilized planets do business together smoothly."

Jonnie was not at all satisfied but he put an easy face on it. "These emissaries do seem to obey you, though. They call you 'Your Excellency' and they call Lord Voraz 'His Worship.' What do you do if they don't obey you? You know, not come to the conference or do what you say."

The thought shocked Lord Voraz. Before Dries Gloton could stop him, he said, "Unthinkable! Why, the bank would call in their loans, shut off their credit. Their economies would shatter. They would go bankrupt. Their whole planet could be sold right out from under them. Oh, they would think several times before—"

Dries finally got his attention and shut him off. "Now, Your Worship," he said softly, "I know you feel strongly about these matters but we must remember that this is *my* sector and things that concern this planet are *my* worry. Forgive me. I think possibly Sir Lord Jonnie doesn't really know too much about the Galactic Bank. We haven't reprinted the information leaflets for ages. Would you like to know more about it, Sir Lord Jonnie?"

Jonnie definitely would. He privately had become very alert about "the whole planet could be sold right out from under them."

— 4 —

Chong-won poured more tea.

"You mustn't get the impression we are violent people," said Dries, taking a large swallow from a bowl.

Just powerful and deadly, Jonnie thought.

"Our race is called the 'Selachee,'" continued Dries. "We are indigenous to the only three habitable planets of the Gredides System. The planets are mostly water—nine surface parts of water to only two parts of land on the average. And we have only banking as our industry."

He smiled and drank more tea. "We're ideal bankers. We can eat anything, drink anything, breathe almost any atmosphere, live on almost any gravity. By tribal mores, we worship total honesty and the righteousness of obligation."

Jonnie thought that was probably true, but he also thought they were not telling all they knew and especially what they intended to do. "Honesty" might not include the whole truth, and there might be some real clues here as to what was going on. He smiled politely and listened closely.

"We have about five billion inhabitants on each planet," continued Dries, "and it is quite a busy population. Although mostly devoted to banking, we have, of course, our engineers and specialists and, naturally, lots of mathematicians. Nearly five hundred thousand years ago we developed space flight. That's about the right figure, isn't it, Your Worship?"

Lord Voraz was still a bit out of sorts at the idea of planets going back on obligations. But he put a good, professional banking face on it. "Four hundred ninety-seven thousand, four hundred thirty-two years this coming Sidereal day one hundred three for this universe," he said.

"Thank you," said Dries, having gotten His Worship back into the discourse. "And three hundred two thousand years ago—"

"Three hundred two thousand three," said Lord Voraz.

"Thank you. . . . We ran into the Psychlos! Now, don't be alarmed. We were not conquered. We didn't even fight a war. In those days the Psychlos were not as bad as they became about a hundred thousand years later. In that time, they had not begun killing for the love of it—I'm sure I don't have to go on to you about Psychlos."

"No indeed!" said Jonnie. This was all going somewhere that was going to wind up as bad news. He could feel it despite their smiles.

"Precisely," said Dries. "Where was I? Anyway—and this will amuse you—they were not interested in us really for we did not have any metals to amount to anything. Being mostly water, our planets would have presented formidable mining problems.

"We needed metals and the Psychlos needed some computer technology we had, and so we became a *market*. This was something brand-new in Psychlo experience. They had a lot to learn about finance and that sort of thing. So we taught them.

"Internally, they were pretty bad off. They breed like . . . what's some fish of this planet you'd know . . . like herrings! They have always been terrified of founding actual Psychlo colonies for fear they'd rise and revolt against the home planet. They had mobs and unemployment. Heavy, heavy depressions. They were an economic mess.

"So we helped them build markets for metals. With their teleportation shipping arrangements, it was very easy for them to do this. They became prosperous and developed even more ways to mine and we saw to it they were economically stable.

"Then suddenly, from the Psychlo viewpoint, an awful thing happened. It terrified them. That was about two hundred thousand years ago."

"Two hundred nine thousand, four hundred sixty-two," corrected Lord Voraz.

"Thank you. Another race stole or invented teleportation!"

"The Boxnards, Universe Six," said Lord Voraz.

"It is unclear what happened then," said Dries. "We don't always have access to military files and we never had access to these, not ever. But I think the Boxnards tried to put teleportation to military use. The Psychlos got there first and the entire seven planets of the Boxnards and every single Boxnard were wiped out. It took the Psychlos years."

"Three years and sixteen days," said Lord Voraz.

"They even slaughtered people and races which had been

associated with or allied with the Boxnards, for we never afterwards found any trace of them.

"That war," said Dries, "also seemed to change the Psychlos. For nearly half a century they all but cut contact with other worlds. It was a bad time for us as well. Our economy was wrapped up in their concerns. They also must have engaged in some internal slaughter because the next records we have show their own population to have decreased by six-elevenths.

"It took another century for the Psychlos to become busy again. But they were a very changed people."

Aha, thought Jonnie. I have the time they began to use those capsules in baby Psychlos' heads! And why. To protect their teleportation technology and mathematics.

"They had burned all their books," said Dries. "They had lost any aesthetic arts they had had. You can tell from their dictionaries that the language they had accumulated over the ages ceased to be in full use. They dropped words like 'compassion' or 'pity' and it even seemed they had dropped the term 'good sense.'

"Although we refer to them now as 'Psychlos,' that name didn't come into use until that time. Previously they called themselves after whatever king might chance to be on the Imperial Throne.

"Anyway, not to bore you for I see you know something of this, the ensuing centuries were very, very bad for everyone, especially the Psychlos. They built a reputation of being the cruelest, most sadistic oppressors any universe had ever seen.

"But they were in internal trouble. Their population was bursting. They were in economic chaos. They were nine parts in eleven unemployed. The royal house was terrified of revolution and as a matter of fact, experienced, I think, four assassinations of princes—"

"Seven," said Lord Voraz. "And two queens."

"Thank you," continued Dries. "And in total desperation, they came to the Gredides and actually begged the Selachees for help. They wanted money to hire soldiers and buy arms. But our parliament, the Creditable Body, along with every other race in sixteen universes, wanted nothing to do with them and it looked like outright war. But somebody in the Creditable Body—"

"Lord Finister," said Lord Voraz.

"Thank you. Had the good sense to turn them over to us. We were as big a bank then. The current head of it—"

"Lord Loonger," said Lord Voraz.

"Thank you. Brought them to the bargaining table and really got them on the signature line! The bank would handle *all* economic connections they had with other races, handle *all* transfers of Psychlo funds, handle *all* peace conferences. And in return every Selachee would be held inviolate, the Selachee planets and the Gredides System were totally hands off, and the Psychlos would furnish teleportation facilities throughout the universes for the bank. They signed, they got their money, they stabilized."

Lord Voraz spoke up, "The only two times they ever sought to violate those agreements, they went into a nose-dive splash and they hastily reformed at once."

"So there," said Dries Gloton, "you have the whole background of the Galactic Bank. We call it 'Galactic,' you know, even though it should be 'Pan-Galactic,' covering sixteen universes as it does. But 'Galactic' makes customers look on it as *their* galaxy's bank. More neighborly, don't you think?"

What Jonnie thought was that he was dealing with an outfit more powerful than the Psychlos. With the galactic organization that could give orders to monsters and be obeyed. He was very alert. There was trouble here somewhere.

"Then possibly," said Jonnie, "you want to talk with the government here about teleportation service."

Dries and Lord Voraz looked at each other and then back at Jonnie.

"Not with the government," said Lord Voraz. "I doubt it owns any of that. Teleportation would be quite another subject and really we aren't engaged in having a talk to arrange a talk about it just now. You see, there *is* space travel. It is slow and time-consuming but it does exist."

Jonnie felt he was not saying everything but he wouldn't push that. It evidently wasn't where the danger lay—for certainly it lay someplace! He could *feel* it. He sat easily and said, "Maybe it's about the payment of fees for this conference. They might be much larger than we had anticipated."

"Oh, heavens, no!" scoffed Dries. And *he* went to work with a ring *he* wore. The fingers flew, a thread came out and popped into an expanded tape, and he looked at it. "Negligible. The fees vary for emissaries because their governments vary in size and even pay them differently. But they only add up to about C85,000—it could, of course, be more if they delay. But not much. The bank fee is standard: only C25,000. There is of course the matter of my yacht—"

"The bank," said Lord Voraz, "pays the space yacht expenses when he uses it on bank business. I think it would be fair, Dries, for you to charge up all the months you searched—"

Dries cut him off sharply. "The yacht would only be charged from the Batafor planet of Balor—that's the Galactic Bank branch office for this sector," he added for Jonnie's benefit. "It's a Hawvin planet. They're not such bad people really. Honest enough individually. So call it C60,000. The total is only around C170,000."

They had that much, thought Jonnie.

But Dries was hesitating. "We're not entirely sure yet that you would get this bill. It sort of depends on the outcome of the conference."

Something here, Jonnie told himself. He was now getting a finger on it.

— 5 —

They looked at Jonnie with their heavy-lidded eyes. They were very serious now.

His Excellency Dries Gloton leaned forward. "It's a question of clear title. The bank would never have anything to do with a clouded title."

"*Never!*" said Lord Voraz.

"The whole reputation of the bank, indeed, the racial reputation of the Selachees," said Dries, "is based on absolute honesty and impeccable legality."

"Always legal," said Lord Voraz. "It would be our ruin if we ever did anything illegal. We never bend rules. That's why uncounted quintillions of people trust us."

Jonnie was not among those quintillions of people. There was something cold, hard, and horrible here. "Perhaps you had better explain further," said Jonnie. "If I am to arrange a meeting for you, I really have to know the background of what will be taken up."

Dries leaned back. "Ah, well. That's true. Where shall I begin? Well, the point of discovery of this planet is a good place.

"The sixteenth universe," he continued, "was the last one to be discovered, possibly less than twenty thousand years ago. It was never wholly mapped. The Psychlo Imperial government introduced probes into it to do further charting but for a very long time they found nothing new.

"This planet is part of what might be called a 'rim star system' way out at the edge of a galaxy. It might have gone overlooked had it not sent out some probes of its own. It gave its exact location, an Imperial probe picked it up, and the rest is history.

"The Psychlo Imperial government obtained title, quite valid, on the right of discovery. And this system's title was entered on the books for the first time.

"That government sold the planet to Intergalactic Mining which, being short of cash, borrowed the purchase price from the Galactic Bank. All this is very routine, ordinary, and usual. Intergalactic Mining has done this countless times.

"Such loans are secured by lodging the deed of title of a planet with the Galactic Bank. The interest rate is usually two parts in eleven. Or, in non-Psychlo arithmetic, roughly eighteen percent per annum. The term was twenty-five hundred years.

"Intergalactic in the past always paid such loans off smoothly—they knew better than not to. In fact, this was the only planet they had bought in recent times; all the others had been paid off. Such a transaction is called a 'mortgage.' Are you following me so far?"

Jonnie was. He had begun to guess what was coming.

"There was a second mortgage also," said His Excellency. "It was to pay for the expenses of military conquest by Intergalactic. But that was a minor matter and, being at a higher interest rate, was paid off in only five years."

Jonnie got it. The Galactic Bank had financed the invasion of Earth. Financed the gas drone.

They must have detected that something had changed in his attitude.

Lord Voraz said, "It is just business. The bank tends to banking and the customers tend to their own affairs. It does not mean the bank was ever hostile to you. Actually we are not hostile now. This is all just routine. Ordinary banking business."

"So anyway," said Dries easily, not bothering to assert his prerogatives, "the basic mortgage has fourteen hundred years to run."

Jonnie digested that, very warily, very alertly. 'But I should think that a war and so on would tend to wipe out that mortgage."

"Oh, dear no!" said Dries. "The simple fact of military take-over does not change the basic debt structure of a planet. That a government changes does not relieve the property of debt. Why, if that were true, then governments would just arrange to change hands every day and they would be rid of all their financial obligations." He laughed. "No, no. A change of government or a military take-over does *not* change a country's debts. The new owners have to pay."

"The original conquest," said Jonnie, "when Intergalactic took over Earth, did not assume any debts."

"They would have been internal," said Dries. ' Internal debts have nothing to do with international debts. No, the planet was properly discovered, properly bought from the Psychlo Imperial government by Intergalactic Mining. The mortgage papers were all properly executed. Everything was totally legal."

"Totally," said Lord Voraz.

"The debt is not in question," said Dries. "Who pays it *is* in question."

"You called this conference to see who pays the debt?" said Jonnie.

"Not precisely, but close. You see," said Dries, 'so long as combat was threatened and so long as one could not really determine who was and who would be the actual responsible government of this planet, I could not serve this paper."

He was holding a big legal-looking piece of paper. He did not hand it over. Jonnie reached out his hand for it but Dries said, "No, you are not a member of the government, by your own statement."

"What happens when you do serve it?"

"Why, we have a meeting to arrange the possibility and terms of payment, and if no agreement can be reached, we foreclose."

"And then what happens?" said Jonnie.

"Why, the planet is put up for public auction and sold to the highest bidder."

Jonnie began to understand the feeling he had had about these two.

"And what happens to the planet's people?" said Jonnie.

"Why, that is up to the buyer, of course. The title would not be clouded in any way. He could do with them pretty much as he liked. That is wholly outside the province of the bank."

"And what do such buyers usually do?" said Jonnie.

"Oh, it all depends. Ordinarily they would pay cash or use their credit to pay for the auctioned planet—such buyers usually have credit or other collateral and they assume the balance of the mortgage. They often just move in, but if there is local protest, they get a short-term loan from the bank and engage in a swift military suppression of the population. Sometimes they sell the original population as slaves to meet their payments. Such buyers want to move in their own people, you know."

Jonnie sat and looked at them. "I don't think a buyer would find it so easy to take this planet."

"Oh!" said Dries, brushing it away. "The planet has no defenses worth mentioning. You have very few people. Modern arms could do it in a few days. This combined force you had here was just a buzzing of insects. The real fleets of these combatants weren't even involved. But be calm. There is no reason to become alarmed. It is just business. Just a matter of a mortgage and paying one's obligations. A banking matter."

"So you are waiting now to see whether we win so you can serve that paper," said Jonnie.

"Oh, I think you *will* win," said Dries. "That is why we are talking with you tonight. We want you to arrange a meeting with your government the moment we know it really *has* won. And then we can serve this paper and discuss things. That's all."

"If I'm going to arrange a meeting for you," said Jonnie, "you had better show me the paper so I will know what I am talking about."

"I'm not serving this on you," said Dries, "but you can look it over."

Jonnie took it.

It had pages and pages of legal details, tracing the discovery, the loan, the payments made. And then it had a huge, single page attached to it. Jonnie had held each page of it up to catch the light better (and to expose it to the button camera that had been going in the upper corner of the room all evening), and he now held up the final one. It said:

NOTICE OF DELINQUENCY

To:__________(legal owners and occupiers of planet at time of service) Date:__________You are hereby summoned to a meeting with the duly appointed officials of THE GALACTIC BANK to: (a) Discuss terms for the discharge of this pressing financial obligation forthwith, well understanding that it is overdue by "one year and days" without any payment of any kind and without any arrangements to extend or discharge.

(b) If such arrangements are found unsatisfactory by THE GALACTIC BANK, to surrender title, occupancy and use promptly to avoid further penalties, WITHIN ONE WEEK FROM ABOVE DATE. The undischarged amount of said loan and mortgage being FORTY TRILLION, NINE HUNDRED SIXTY BILLION, TWO HUNDRED SEVENTEEN MILLION, SIX HUNDRED FIVE THOUSAND, TWO HUNDRED SIXTEEN GALACTIC CREDITS (C40,960, 217,605,216), being the unpaid remainder and interest of the initial loan, advanced in good faith to THE INTERGALACTIC MINING COMPANY of Psychlo, of SIXTY TRILLION GALACTIC CREDITS (C60,000,000, 000,000), and paid by GALACTIC BANK TRANSFER at the order of said INTERGALACTIC MINING COMPANY to the account of THE IMPERIAL GOVERNMENT OF PSYCHLO, being, in full, payment for purchase of said planet "Earth, Solar System, Universe Sixteen."

____________________ DRIES GLOTON
(Signed and sealed) Branch Manager
THE GALACTIC BANK
Balor, Batafor System
Head Offices of Sector 4
Universe Sixteen

Jonnie said, "And what would be satisfactory 'terms' for its discharge?"

"Oh" said Dries Gloton easily, "a payment of five trillion at once and some arrangement like five hundred billion a month would do. You see, legally, a whole loan becomes due and payable instantly if payments are missed. So you will really find the bank very easy to do business with, for we could require the whole amount instanter! We really are your friends, you know. We always pride ourselves, not just on our total honesty and integrity, but on our customer relations."

Five trillion! thought Jonnie. Five hundred billion a month! They only had two billion, two hundred million. They had no industry or income. No resources they could dig out of the ground would match the amount needed in that time period.

Dries saw through his fairly well-hidden consternation. "You'd have a whole week! It is very liberal."

"And as soon as this conference decides the fate of Schleim," said Jonnie. "And the relationship to the other combatants—"

"Why, the planet will have a clear title!" said Dries triumphantly. "And you can arrange the meeting for us. And we can serve this paper and the whole thing will be handled!"

"The winning government," said Lord Voraz, "would have *days* to discuss it and find where they were going to get the money."

"You couldn't lend it to us?" said Jonnie.

"Oh, dear no. It's already been lent."

"And who might buy this planet?" said Jonnie.

"Why, any one of the combatants would be glad to have it. They, unlike you here, have industry and credit and collateral."

"So after we win this war, if we win it, then we might lose it totally, even to the Tolneps!" said Jonnie.

"Well," said Dries Gloton with an expressive hand gesture, "banking is banking. Business is business."

— 6 —

Stormalong, folded across a desk in the ops room, was jolted out of the sleep of exhaustion. Groggy from days of directing battle, it was with alarm that he saw Jonnie.

"Wake up!" Jonnie was saying urgently. He was trying to shake the Buddhist communicator, Tinny, into some sign of life.

"What's the matter?" Stormalong surged up. "Have they started attacking again?"

"Worse!" said Jonnie. "These small gray men! . . . Tinny, please wake up!" The woman was almost senseless after days of combat communication, all without sleep.

Jonnie had bowed the guests out. He had walked a full circle around the night-shrouded bowl. MacAdam! He knew he had to get hold of MacAdam of the Earth Planetary Bank in Luxembourg and get hold of him fast. He would arrange no meeting with the government. But he sure would arrange one with somebody who should know banking!

Tinny was coming wake. "MacAdam!" said Jonnie. "Get MacAdam on the radio!"

"What's up?" said Stormalong. Jonnie was usually pretty cool and calm. "What can I do?"

Jonnie shoved a pair of discs at him, the recordings of the whole party. "Get me duplicates of these. It's a dinner party."

It made no sense at all to Stormalong but he went over to the disc duplicator and ran them off.

Tinny was trying to wake up Luxembourg, sleepily singing out the code call signs in Pali.

"If you're calling Luxembourg," said Stormalong, "they're all gone." Then he realized Jonnie had not had much briefing.

"It's Russia," said Stormalong. "The Singapore people got there and they can't get near the place. It's all on fire."

Jonnie didn't understand. An underground base on fire?

"You've been there," said Stormalong. "I don't know why but they had some material, some black stuff, inflammable, outside the main entrances. Do you know what it was?"

Coal! The Russian base had been piling coal up for the winter. "It's coal," said Jonnie. "A black rock that burns."

"Well, whoever built that base built it next to or on or under a mine of this stuff and in the fighting it must have ignited. The Singapore team couldn't get near the base. They were very few and they didn't take any mine pumps, and even if they had there was no water near there. They yelled for help. They had to get the fire out to get near the base. Luxembourg was the only defense area that was never hit and they had flying tankers there. About two hours ago they filled those tankers and flew to Russia. We have no further reports on the fate of the Russian base. And there's no defense team left in Luxembourg."

"Surely the Earth Planetary Bank had a radio!" said Jonnie.

"Yes," said Stormalong doubtfully, "but at this hour of the night, I don't think it would be manned. They're not part of the defense network."

"I've got to go then," said Jonnie. "What planes are left—"

"Whoa!" said Stormalong. "I had direct orders from Sir Robert that *you* stay *here!*"

"But MacAdam can't fly down here if there are no pilots. Not even one pilot left in Luxembourg?"

"Not one."

Jonnie felt desperate. "Then how about detaching a pilot from Edinburgh and getting—"

"Not a chance," said Stormalong. "They're arrived there and it's a screaming mess. The whole tunnel network under the rock has collapsed. You can't get into the place to see whether there's anyone still alive in the shelters. They've got atmosphere hoses and equipment to get air in to any survivors and they are bringing mine diggers up from Cornwall. But they need the pilots they have as machine operators. I don't think I could persuade even one of them—"

"Do you have a plane here?"

"Of course I've got a plane here. I've got five planes here! But you are not leaving!"

The woman turned from the mike. "It is dead. There is no one answering from the Luxembourg mine site or the bank. And after all, it is two in the morning there."

"I'm going," said Jonnie.

"You're not!" shouted Stormalong.

"Then you are!" shouted Jonnie.

Stormalong blinked. After all, he had had about two hours worth of catnaps. "You'll have to handle anything here by yourself," he said. "Be in the air and at that mike at the same time if you have to fly defense."

"I'd take Tinny and handle the network from the plane," said Jonnie, "if I had to go up and fight. But that isn't where the fight *is!* It's right down here with these small gray men! Can you stay awake to Luxembourg?"

Stormalong shrugged and then nodded.

"All right," said Jonnie. "You take those copies you made of the dinner party and you fly to Luxembourg and find MacAdam. Blast him out. Tell him I said it was vital he review those recordings right now. And he's *got* to find some way to handle a debt. You tell him that."

"A debt?" said Stormalong.

"Yes, a debt. And if we don't pay it or handle it, we've lost this whole war! Even if we win it!"

■

PART 29

— 1 —

The next two days were the most horrible in Jonnie's life—cage, drone, and all!

Stormalong had simply flown into thin air and vanished.

He didn't answer on radio even when Jonnie said his name in clear.

The bank office in Luxembourg was open and answering but there was just a girl there, and she didn't speak any tongue anyone at Kariba could speak—French?—and even though they said ''MacAdam'' and she tried to tell them something back, they couldn't make it out.

Jonnie could not leave here.

The emissaries in the conference room would go in and out. They were working on and on with the trial. They didn't pay much attention to him.

Jonnie slept in the ops room and only got out when Chief Chong-won would spell him for a few minutes by standing in in case anything urgent came through.

Truth told, there was not too much coming through that Jonnie had to handle. Even had he gotten urgent requests, he couldn't have done anything about them, for he had no available pilots, troops, or defense forces. He was actually the only one defending the planet. The woman, Tinny, was lots of help, but there was a limit to the number of hours anyone could stay awake, even a Buddhist nun.

Angus was spending some time with the transshipment rig. He had left the gyrocage on a Tolnep mountain to learn the full fate of the moon Asart. ''I wanted to see whether there were earthquakes on Tolnep,'' he told Jonnie. ''When you change mass in a system, you could expect changes in gravitational stresses. I read someplace that if our own moon got knocked out into space or something, it would cause earthquakes here. But Tolnep didn't shake up our gyrocage."

A few hours later, Jonnie had heard a motor running in the bowl and, edgy, had gone out to check. Angus was running a blade scraper. He was pushing a huge piece of the capital ship through the under-cable entrance; it was a piece that had hit the shore. Chief Chong-won was very sharp with him for it was scraping up the pavement and Chief Chong-won had no men to repair the scars.

Angus said something about wanting to see whether the ultimate bomb were still active.

"Well, don't bring anything back here that touches that area," said Jonnie and went back in to answer a radio query.

The next morning Angus had come in to eat a bowl of noodles with him and tell him about it.

"I put that scrap metal way out beyond Asart," said Angus. "I thought it would fall through the gas—"

"What gas?" said Jonnie.

"Oh, Asart just seems to be gas now," said Angus. "Just a huge cloud of gas. It was blackish for a while but then it cleared up. You can *see* it is a cloud of gas but you can see through it. It's pretty obvious now why the Psychlos never used that bomb. As mining people they needed metal, not gas!"

"So what happened to the scrap iron?" asked Jonnie.

"I thought it would fall through the gas and go on down and hit the surface of Tolnep. It didn't. It fell all right, but it just went to the center of the gas cloud and it's still there. Want to see a picture of it?"

"Just don't fire into that cloud and bring any of that stuff back here on recoil!" said Jonnie.

"Oh, I won't," promised Angus. "But what I believe is, once that ultimate bomb converted everything to gas, it went null. It doesn't have anything to work on and the reaction isn't self-starting again once it's complete. The metal trace says that it's all very low-order gases now. Hydrogen."

"Then the ultimate bomb brings about low-order fission," said Jonnie. "It stimulates a split of the atoms of heavier metals. I'm no expert, but that's what it seems you're describing."

"Anyway," said Angus, "all I'm trying to tell you is that the mass of the moon didn't change so far as gravitic influence is concerned. In that coldness, the resulting gas has kind of gone liquid and the moon is a sort of bubble with a much bigger diameter. I think you could fly through it."

"Great," said Jonnie. "Don't."

Angus finished up his noodles. "I just thought you'd like to know that destroying that moon won't upset our coordinate tables. A shift of mass could throw every coordinate out eventually."

"Ah," said Jonnie. "You *do* have a point! That was clever of you."

Angus thought so, too.

But news from other areas was not so encouraging. It was not that anything bad was adding up. It was just the nonexistence of news so far as the fate of Chrissie and the people in Scotland was concerned, and the fate of his people in the Russian base.

They had found the Chief of Clanfearghus outside, very close to death, and after emergency transfusions had rushed him up to the old underground hospital in Aberdeen. There was not much hope.

They had drilled holes through rubble that blocked the tunnels and they hoped they had gotten air hoses into the shelters. There were rumors they had heard voices, but there had been no mine radios in those shelter areas to begin with and you couldn't tell much while trying to shout down an air hose, pumps running and all.

The city was just towers of smoke, as was Castle Rock.

They were having a terrible time trying to open the approach tunnels, working around the clock.

The Russian-base news was not much better. They had put the surface coal fires out but the mine was burning underground, and they did not know whether it was reaching the actual levels of the base. The huge doors were so warped they could not be opened even with burning torches, and they were now driving in a brand-new entrance to bypass them, a drift through solid rock, working over ground that was still burning under them down deep. The ventilator shafts were too torturous and too barred with armor and filter to be of any use.

To add to the tension in Kariba, the original small gray man, Dries Gloton, had vanished. The one antiaircraft gunner on duty said that the man had simply come out about dawn, ordered a new set of signal lights and radio beacon signals near where his ship was parked, and sailed off, wham, into the sky, and they couldn't even track where he had gone to. The lights were out there now, two reds flashing, and the radio beacon was telling all ships to stay clear from a conference area.

Lord Voraz, when asked, had shrugged and said it probably came under the heading of prerogatives of a branch manager and was probably bank business, and he had gone on eating the perpetual bites-between-meals the cook served him up. He was no help.

But what gave Jonnie a shock in those two days was the sudden arrival of Captain Rogodeter Snowl.

The conference had called him in as a witness and they didn't tell Jonnie and didn't tell the antiaircraft gunner.

The first Jonnie knew of it was the antiaircraft gun going off.

Lord Dom came rolling into operations like a liquid jelly fish, roaring and rumbling to cease fire!

Jonnie got the gunner to quit. Fortunately, it had been at very extreme range and Angus had not been using the rig. But Rogodeter Snowl, omitting to ask permission to land a small launchcraft, almost got himself shot down.

"He's been called as a witness!" shouted Lord Dom. "Don't you know there's a trial going on?"

Trial or no trial, Jonnie stuck a Smith and Wesson with thermit bullets in his belt and plugs in his ears and went out to personally con the launchcraft down with a hand radio and make sure the Tolnep remained blind to their defenselessness.

Suppressing an urge to shoot Rogodeter on sight, he limited himself to confiscating his vision filter, making sure the Tolnep had no spare, and personally escorting him to the conference room. He left the Tolnep there but told them that when they were through with him, they better call ops to escort him out because Rogodeter was going to be stone blind all the time he was around Kariba.

About five hours later they did call him again and he collected Rogodeter and guided him out to the launchcraft. But before he gave him back the filter faceplate, he had Chief Chong-won smear the inside of the launchcraft dome with black water ink. Whether Rogodeter complained or not that he would have to wipe holes in it somehow to find his orbiting ship was unknown to Jonnie: he still had his earplugs in.

Jonnie gave Rogodeter back the filter for his eyes, and from the look of his mouth, the Tolnep, staring at him, said "You!"

So Jonnie said, "Me. And just as a personal goodbye, the next time I see you on this planet's surface, you won't like it at all. So get the hell out of here!'' And slammed the canopy down on him.

When the launchcraft was gone, Jonnie took the earplugs out and found that the single antiaircraft gunner had been begging him for ten minutes for permission to ''accidentally'' shoot the ship down. Jonnie sympathized with him. He felt the same way himself.

And still not a whisper from Stormalong. And not a bit of sense from Luxembourg.

No word of Chrissie. No word of his village people. No word of his friends.

It was a horrible two days.

Inaction, he was finding, was a far, far heavier load than the whirlwind existence to which he was accustomed. He was nearing a breaking point of apprehension for the people and planet he had fought so long to save.

At eight that night, it didn't make things any better to be stopped by Lord Voraz who offered him a job at fifty thousand credits a year to come to the Gredides System and make teleportation consoles for the bank for the rest of his life. Jonnie had to walk away quickly to keep from becoming violent.

A very horrible two days!

— 2 —

Things began to change the following day.

Jonnie had spent the night in ops and was sprawled over a table when Lord Dom came in to wake him.

''In two hours,'' said Lord Dom, ''the trial findings will be read and voted upon.''

''I'm not a member of the government,'' said Jonnie.

''We know that,'' said Lord Dom. ''But you are personally concerned and should be present. Reparations will also be announced. So be there!''

Ah, reparations. A sudden surge of nope. Would they be enough to cover this debt to the Galactic Bank? Or at least enough to make arrangements or first payments or something?

Tinny had had as good a night's sleep as one could get in a

chair, there was very little traffic, and so Jonnie asked Chong-won to stand in for him and went to get dressed.

Mr. Tsung was wearing a little round black-satin pillbox cap with a blue button on the top of it and had not ceased grinning since he had recovered his rank. He bowed and got a bath wheeled in on a mine cart and generally worked to get Jonnie dressed and fed.

Then Mr. Tsung picked up a little thin box on a silk neck cord and put it on and whispered at it, and Jonnie was startled to hear English coming out of it in a flat, electronic monotone.

In response to Jonnie's raised eyebrows, using the box, Mr. Tsung explained it was a gift from the small gray man, Dries Gloton, before he had left on a trip. A gift for starting a bank account! It seemed that Mr. Tsung's daughter was painting tigers and birds on big sheets of handmade rice paper and selling them to the emissaries for fifty credits apiece; the lords said they were "primitives" and collector's items. And his son-in-law had been making pictures of dragons on round metal plates with a molecular sprayer and selling those to the lords for a hundred credits each, and like a good father, even though he despised merchants and the merchant class, he was taking care of their money for them.

Mr. Tsung explained that His Excellency had found the language "court Mandarin Chinese" in his library on the ship and had done the necessary microcopy of it and—you see this little switch here? That's Mandarin to English in the up position, Mandarin to Psychlo in the middle position, and English to Psychlo in the down position. And didn't it sound funny when it turned English into Chinese tones?

But that was not all: it was a vocoreader. See this little light on the end? You passed that over Mandarin characters and it read them aloud in English or Psychlo. And it also read Psychlo and English in Mandarin. So now he couldn't be fooled or led into mistakes by wrongly worded speeches.

It ran on body heat so it didn't need any batteries and now he could talk straight to Jonnie! Of course, he'd still learn the languages himself, for he didn't want to sound so monotone. But wasn't Dries Gloton a nice man!

He was glad Mr. Tsung could now talk to him without a Coordinator, but all the same, it made Jonnie feel surrounded by the Galactic Bank.

Mr. Tsung put it to work right away. "I am told you are going in to hear the sentence and that it somehow includes you. Now since you don't know whether you are going to be found guilty or not, you just sit respectfully and listen, and if they ask you anything, you just bow—you don't answer. Just bow. That is how you open the way to demand a new trial."

It was good advice, but it did not do much to calm Jonnie's nerves.

Chief Chong-won said the radio was quiet. No, no news of Stormalong, nor Edinburgh nor Russia.

The lords were all assembled. They had rearranged the room. They had a high desk on the platform and Lord Fowljopan was sitting at it. The lords themselves were in orderly rows facing it. Down the side of the room was a line of chairs. Schleim was lying on a mine cart, totally wrapped up in hoist chains, with only his face showing above the links. They had him between the desk and the audience.

Lord Dom indicated that Jonnie should sit on one of the side chairs where Lord Voraz was sitting. It was obvious to Jonnie that they didn't consider him part of their deliberations. The lords didn't even look at him. But at least he wasn't there alongside that mine cart with Schleim!

"They have already discussed all this," whispered Lord Voraz to Jonnie. "But they have to review and vote on each finding. It's really more of a treaty than a trial. I'm surprised the Earth emissary isn't here. But they can proceed without him right up to the signing."

Lord Fowljopan signaled Lord Browl to call the session to order, which he did.

"We have already agreed upon and committed to treaty form," said Fowljopan, "the redefinition of the word 'pirate.' I wish to call to your attention, however, that the redefinition can have no bearing on the present findings for it was passed upon *after* the incident under trial. Is that correct, my lords?"

They signified that it was.

"Therefore," said Fowljopan, "we are basing this trial on existing findings and clauses. Testimony of Captain Rogodeter Snowl has been heard and duly entered in the record to the effect that he was *ordered* to disregard the sanctity of the conference area by the Tolnep then-emissary Schleim. I believe it is the desire of this conference to accept the testimony and evidences of the said Snowl, particularly in the light of the fact that he considered he was bound to protect the Tolnep emissary. This absolves Snowl. Do you so vote?''

The lords so voted.

''Therefore,'' said Fowljopan, ''it is considered established by this conference that the said Tolnep emissary, by name Lord Schleim, did willfully and maliciously order the military forces of Tolnep to attack the conference area. Do you so find?''

They voted unanimously that they so found and Schleim in his chains hissed and spat.

''It was further witnessed and established,'' continued Fowljopan, ''that the said Tolnep emissary did seek to paralyze, shoot, and otherwise injure other emissaries engaged in their lawful and time-honored duties, contrary to specific clauses numbered here but too numerous to read. Is that your finding?''

They definitely so found and Schleim hissed and spat some more.

''Therefore,'' said Fowljopan, ''it is adjudicated by this conference, lawfully assembled, by the power of treaty hereby made among planets, that Tolnep shall hereinafter, for a space of one hundred years, be regarded as an outlaw nation! Do you so vote?''

They so voted and with deep scowls of determination.

''All treaties with the planet and nation of Tolnep are canceled herewith,'' said Fowljopan. ''Do you so vote?''

They so voted.

''All embassies and legations and consulates of the Tolnep planet and nation shall be closed and their diplomats expelled, and for the space of the next hundred years, diplomatic functions in minor matters shall be undertaken by the Hawvins' embassies, legations, and consulates at usual charges. Do you concur?''

They concurred.

''Since the personal safety of the said Schleim was promised by this conference and since it guaranteed to return the said Schleim unharmed to his planet, it is the decision of this conference that the said Schleim be deposited naked and in chains in the public slave market of the city of Creeth, Tolnep, as an expression of disfavor of this conference. Is this your wish?''

It was their wish. Schleim hissed and spat. Jonnie wondered when they were going to get around to ''reparations.'' It was a thin hope but it was a hope.

Fowljopan was continuing. "Since Tolnep had the majority of war vessels and since its officer was, according to the testimony of Schleim himself earlier in this conference, the senior and commanding officer of the combined force, it is the finding of this conference that the non-Tolnep nations, which complemented the combined force, are nationally absolved of the offense. But that, as the presence of their forces poses a continued threat in the skies above this conference, this absolution is dependent on the following conditions: (a) that they ensure that the Tolnep fleet deposits any and all prisoners taken unharmed, undamaged, at a spot to be designated by the Earth military commander; (b) that they themselves deposit any prisoners they may have taken, unharmed, undamaged, at the same or similar place; (c) that they then escort, with the use of any military persuasion necessary, the Tolnep fleet back to Tolnep; (d) that they direct the Tolnep fleet to land on the surface of Tolnep, it being known to the conference that the Tolnep fleet cannot, thereafter, take off again; and (e) that they then return to their respective homelands. The forces mandated by this clause are those of the Bolbods, Hawvins, Hockners, Jambitchows, and Drawkins, and any and all forces retained by them and any and all forces of any other planet or nation from outside this system. Is it so decreed?"

There was some discussion as to whether the emissaries representing these forces should vote or abstain.

"I suppose," whispered Voraz, "you can designate a deposit place for the prisoners in the absence of other authority."

"Yes," Jonnie whispered back, "but they don't say what we do with any prisoners we may have of theirs."

"This isn't a peace treaty," whispered Lord Voraz. "This relates to offenses against this conference. I . . . uh . . . put in a word about Earth prisoners. They're planetary assets, you see. Prisoners you have from the fleet up there would only be mentioned if this were a peace treaty. And I doubt they'd take them back due to possible contamination—you might want to get even through biological warfare. You're covered since they included 'unharmed' and 'undamaged' in the clause."

Assets, thought Jonnie. You're just concerned about the value of the property you're trying to repossess. But he didn't say it He was glad they'd get any Earth prisoners back.

They had finally decided the emissaries of other combatants

had better vote for it would look better on the record. The conference was then unanimous.

"By conference law," Fowljopan then said, "mention must be made of personal violence used against a then-emissary, Lord Schleim."

Lord Voraz touched Jonnie's knee. "This is you."

"One designated as Jonnie Goodboy Tyler was seen to throw a cane or sceptre at the said Lord Schleim, striking him. It is the wish of this conference to exonerate the said Tyler. Do you so vote?"

They voted to do so and Schleim *really* spat.

"Now comes the nice part," whispered Lord Voraz.

"In accordance," said Fowljopan, "with Clause 103, which covers services in protecting and saving the lives of conference members, for predetermining the intentions of the said Schleim and for disarming him so that his attack was to no avail, one designated as Jonnie Goodboy Tyler is hereby vested with the Order of the Crimson Sash. Is this the wish of the conference?"

There was a spatter of applause, a buzz of comment.

Lord Voraz whispered, "The Empress Beaz of the Chatovarians created that order eighty-three thousand, two hundred sixty-eight years ago when an attendant saved the life of her lover at a conference. Someone tried to assassinate him and the attendant prevented it but got a superficial knife slash in the process. Hence 'Crimson Sash.' " He whisked from his pocket a little book which expanded and he looked up something. "It entitles you to be addressed as 'Lord' and it carries with it a pension of two thousand credits a year. We manage the trust fund for it. I must make a note."

They were still applauding a bit and Lord Browl indicated Jonnie should stand up and bow. Jonnie thought sourly he'd put the sash on Windsplitter. He didn't want their honors. He sat down. They sure were taking a long time to get around to reparations. Ah, here they were!

Fowljopan was unreeling a long roll of paper with figures on it. "It has also been found that the dignities of the emissaries and their planets have been offended by the unseemly attack or attempted attack upon them by the said Schleim. A fine and reparation in the sum of one trillion Galactic credits is hereby levied upon the planet Tolnep by the conference."

Fowljopan rattled through the papers. "The emissaries who

had ships in the skies at the time of this incident are not to be included as recipients in this indemnity because of a witting or unwitting taint of conspiracy. The sum, as already discussed in previous deliberations, shall be allocated to emissaries in accordance with populations they represent.'' He rattled off a lot of figures. ''Does the conference so agree?''

They corrected a couple of calculations.

''Earth,'' Jonnie whispered to Lord Voraz, ''is getting almost nothing!''

''Some of these emissaries have populations of hundreds of billions,'' Lord Voraz whispered back. ''The Chatovarians have almost thirty-nine trillion beings on their seven hundred planets. What have you got here? Thirty-three thousand?''

The emissaries accepted the amended figures. Jonnie held his breath. Were damages to Earth going to enter in here?

''Any and all financial arrangements to be made in accordance with the practices of the Galactic Bank,'' said Fowljopan. He didn't ask for any agreement on that. Lord Voraz simply nodded.

''This concludes our findings,'' said Fowljopan. ''Is it the wish of this conference that these be scrolled in finished form, as voted, so that they can be signed and attested?''

Jonnie whispered urgently to Lord Voraz, ''Wait. They claimed they burned a lot of cities. There are all sorts of war damages.''

''I tried to get it in; it would have increased the value of the property,'' Lord Voraz whispered back, ''but this isn't a peace conference, you know. It's a trial and treaty about offenses to the conference itself.''

No reparations for Earth? Jonnie felt like jumping up and protesting. If Sir Robert or MacAdam had been here—

''A trillion credits fine,'' whispered Lord Voraz, ''is *stiff*. It will crash the whole Tolnep economy. Even if Earth were awarded city damages, Tolnep could never pay them after *that* huge fine. Be happy about it. You got rid of all the hostile forces.''

And got rid of all challenges to a clear title, thought Jonnie sourly. Now they were wide open to the bank foreclosure with no real money to meet it.

But Fowljopan was coming down on Jonnie. ''Your emissary was not here! This is highly irregular. It does not void or change these findings. But if he is not here to sign them, they will not be valid. Your war will go right on. So you better advise your government to get him here quick. These papers will be ready for signature tomorrow afternoon. Are you going to see he is here?"

"I'm not a representative—" began Jonnie.

"You have influence," said Fowljopan. "Use it! We want to finish up here and go home."

"You better do as he says," whispered Lord Voraz.

Jonnie looked up to see Dries Gloton standing at the door. He'd come back!

As Jonnie walked out, Dries asked Lord Voraz, "Is the Earth representative coming?"

Voraz pointed to Jonnie.

"Will you get him here?" Dries Gloton asked Jonnie.

Jonnie said he'd try, and Dries and Lord Voraz looked at each other and grinned.

He was too disheartened about no reparations for Earth to give much thought to them.

— 3 —

A few feet from the door of the conference room, Jonnie started to get mad.

War! Any one of those lords in there, or their governments, merely had to say the word and their fleets pranced off to bash somebody's head in!

And when they'd bashed it in, they could just sail off tra-la, without a thought of what they'd done to people's homes and lives, and then maybe come back another day to bash some more!

Jonnie took a walk around the causeway of the bowl. It was a sunny noontime and the mine entrance and exhaust fans made a gentle breeze as they changed the air.

The little children lay in the rifle pits, shaded with bits and pieces of cloth. They followed him with their eyes. The dogs whuffed and snuffled at him from the ends of their leashes and, somehow recognizing him as a friend, wagged their tails. The older children, having fed the younger ones, were sitting cross-legged and eating from bowls: they grinned and nodded as he went by.

Jonnie thought, why shouldn't these children have a chance? Why couldn't they have a future that was happy and safe?

War! What right did cold, impersonal nations have to murder and rampage, to smash and crush and gut their more helpless fellow beings?

Call it "national policy," call it "necessities of state," call it what you will, it still amounted to an action of the insane.

Psychlo! What right did Psychlo have striking this planet down? Couldn't they have bought what they wanted? Couldn't they have come in and said, "We need metal. We will exchange this or that or technology for it." No, it suited them better to murder and steal it like a thief.

He thought about the time before the visitors came, when first they had been free from the oppressive tyrants. The people had been trying to get on with it, had been happy, had been working with a will. And then the visitors came. And with them the bank.

Organization might be necessary. But it gave no one the right to create a government that was an inhuman, soulless beast!

He thought of Brown Limper and his idiocies in the name of "the state." Yet Brown Limper had been almost sensible compared to those lords in there.

Jonnie looked at the children. And he made up his mind. Whatever happened, there would be no more war. Not anywhere.

He had been so engrossed in his thoughts that Chief Chong-won had to shake his arm to get his attention.

The chief was jumping up and down and waving at Jonnie to come on and at last practically pushed him into the ops room.

Tinny was *beaming!* A chatter of Pali was spraying out from around her headphones. She said something into her mike and turned to Jonnie.

"It's the Scot officer in charge of rescue in Russia!" said Tinny. "They spotted some green smoke coming from a ventilator in puffs. Somebody inside had gotten the armor off the ducts. They've got mine hoist gear going right this minute hauling people out!"

Minute by minute the reports came in. Then Tinny turned to Jonnie: "It's Colonel Ivan! It's for you! He says 'Tell Marshal Jonnie the valiant-red-army is still at his command!' "

Jonnie was about to reply. He was finding it hard to talk. But Tinny said, "Here's another one for Jonnie. He wants to hear your voice!" She pushed the headset at Jonnie.

Security or no security, the voice said, "Jonnie? It's Tom Smiley Townsen!"

Jonnie couldn't talk.

"Jonnie, the village people are all okay. Everybody is all right, Jonnie. Jonnie, are you there?"

"Thank god," Jonnie forced himself to say. "Tell them that for me, Tom. Tell them all. Thank god!"

And he sat down in a chair and wept. He had not realized how worried he had been about them. He had suppressed it with an iron will so that he could work.

The reports were still coming in and after a while he got busy. They wanted to know where to go and he in his turn had the glad news for them of the departure of the enemy and the terms, and shouts and cheers began to leak through from the background of the communicator's voice there.

They had five wounded pilots and a lot of burn cases and they wanted help from Scotland. He learned the old underground hospital in Aberdeen had been set up and he got the badly wounded ones flown through to it and pried a nurse loose in Aberdeen to be flown back to Tashkent to care for the minor burns and injuries.

He had gotten so busy with these problems that he had forgotten all about Sir Robert until Dries Gloton got Chong-won to remind him of it.

Jonnie had been avoiding it a bit. They had not yet succeeded at Castle Rock and he knew that trying to pry Sir Robert loose was going to take some doing. He had even wondered whether he couldn't get Lord Fowljopan to put off the signing a day. Sir Robert was going to be a handful.

Even so, he put the call out and got busy arranging for all prisoners to be put down at Balmoral Castle about fifty miles to the west of Aberdeen, easily found from the air because of three noticeable peaks nearby, because of a river, and because it itself was a prominent ruin. It was only about fifty miles from Aberdeen on a road that was in fair condition, but Thor said he could pick any up in a marine attack plane and get them to the hospital at Aberdeen if they needed it. Jonnie gave him some precautions and then went out and got the Hawvin emissary, who seemed to be the contact now with the orbiting fleet, and gave him a trace map so he could transmit it to the Hawvin commander. They said they could do it this afternoon without waiting for the final signatures. Nobody knew how many prisoners there were but they'd be flown down in different launchcraft. Jonnie left it up to them and to Thor in Scotland.

Doing all that had given him a pretty distinct impression that things were very hectic around Edinburgh and he was even less inclined to call Sir Robert.

Once more, Dries Gloton got Chong-won to push him. Good lord, those small gray men were anxious to get Sir Robert here!

He finally persuaded communicators up there in Scotland to track down Sir Robert, and when he finally got him on the radio, every misgiving he had had was fully justified.

"Coom doon there!" Sir Robert had rapped back via communicators. And so far as it could be translated and relayed, he told Jonnie off properly!

Didn't Jonnie know that there were twenty-one hundred people in the various ancient shelters beneath the Rock—if they were still alive? That heavy bombs had smashed in every possible entrance? They had gotten atmosphere hoses drilled in here and there, but who could talk through those? The Rock cliff sides had been pulverized and shattered so that every time they got a drift going in, they had landslides.

Yes, Dwight was there! Yes, Dwight had gotten tunnel casings from Cornwall and tried to drive them in. Did Jonnie think they were all standing around doing nothing?

It was all right for Jonnie to be sitting around with those la-de-da lords drinking tea. Go right on and drink tea but let people get on with this, this—

It took Jonnie half an hour to impress on Sir Robert that without his signature, the matter of the "visitors" wouldn't be ended.

Finally, with considerable blasphemy that the communicators couldn't handle well in Pali, Sir Robert said he would pry a pilot loose and fly down.

Jonnie sat back, feeling exhausted. He didn't like to fight with Sir Robert. And he could understand his position completely. His Aunt Ellen was in those closed-off shelters. And Chrissie! It was all he could do himself to sit here handling things when he felt he should be up there, digging with his bare hands if necessary.

The small gray man looked very pleased when Chong-won told him Sir Robert was coming.

— 4 —

Out of the night sky from the north, rushing far ahead of its sound, seen at first as just another star, a plane approached Kariba.

The antiaircraft gunner intercom sounded: the plane was friendly and requested permission to land.

Jonnie went to watch it set down. The door opened and somebody jumped out. The face was a white blur in the night. Jonnie peered more closely: bandages—somebody with his face totally bandaged.

A finger pointing at Jonnie's beard. "The very thing!"

It was Dunneldeen!

They swatted each other happily. Then Dunneldeen pushed Jonnie back into better light and looked at him. "The very thing! Somebody cut your beard half-off! And mine's burned half-off! Make an appointment for me with your barber!"

"Did you get shot down?" said Jonnie, looking a little anxiously at the swathe of bandages on his face.

"Now, laddie, don't be insulting!" said Dunneldeen. "What Bolbod or Drawkin or Hockner could shoot down the ace of all aces? No, Jonnie boy, it was helping fight fire. It's not too bad a burn, but you know Dr. Allen. Never happy unless he's swaddled you up like an innocent babe."

"How is it up there?" said Jonnie.

"Bad. We got the fire out but that's all you can say for it. Dwight and Thor are trying to open tunnels but the rock slides. There's lots of hope but that's all I can give you. Say, did that small gray man come back here? Is that his ship over there?"

"Was he at Edinburgh?"

"Oh, that he was. Went all around bothering everybody asking questions. Got in everybody's way. And then he seemed to get what he was looking for and went swooshing up to Aberdeen. Almost got himself shot down! He was looking for the king—you know, Chief of Clanfearghus."

"How is he? The Chief?" said Jonnie.

"Well, he's a bleeder. You know, doesn't stop bleeding once

he's cut. I'm always telling him to stay out of wars—they're unhealthy! Anyway, we found him outside and rushed him to the Aberdeen hospital and they gave him transfusions. This small gray man tried to get in to see him and of course the gillies threw him out. But then Dr. Allen got cornered by him. Seems like this guy," he indicated the ship where the lights were flashing, "has been collecting books and libraries all over the place. He pictographs them. And he got Dr. Allen to tell him what was wrong with the Chief and they looked it up in a lot of old man-books, and Dr. Allen found there was a compound called Vitamin K that made blood coagulate and they synthesized some and what do you know . . . the bleeding stopped! The Chief's recovering. What is this small gray man, a doctor?"

"No," said Jonnie. "He's the Sector Branch Manager of the Galactic Bank. I'll tell you more later, but he was up there making sure this planet had a government!"

"Well, it was a nice thing to do, anyway," said Dunneldeen.

Jonnie was glad for the Chief but he sure was beginning to feel surrounded by the bankers. He didn't tell Dunneldeen they were about to foreclose on them. "You see Stormalong?"

Dunneldeen shook his head. "Let's get Sir Robert. He's dead to the world in the plane."

And Sir Robert really was dead to the world. Singed and gray-faced where his skin wasn't blacked with soot, his hands torn, his clothes in burned rags, Sir Robert looked exactly what he was—an old man who had been going through hell for days without rest.

They tried to lift and carry him between them but the old War Chief was a very heavy man, especially when dead weight. They got a mine cart and wheeled him into the hospital.

Jonnie got the nurse up and she examined Sir Robert. He was not injured except for his hands. She gave him a shot of B Complex and he never stirred at the punch of the needle.

Mr. Tsung and his family were suddenly up and hovering around and they ran off to get things organized. Shortly, they were giving Sir Robert a bath and trimming the burned areas in his beard and hair so they looked more even. They soon had him in a bed. He had never opened his eyes!

Jonnie went back to the hospital where he had left Dunneldeen and found him sitting in a chair sound asleep while the nurse changed his face bandages. The burns were not disfiguring. His beard sure was tattered. Jonnie stopped the nurse from putting on fresh bandages and called Mr. Tsung's daughter, who came in with her scissors and neatened the Scot by cutting his beard like Jonnie's.

Jonnie had hoped Dunneldeen could spell him in ops while he went to look for Stormalong. But Dunneldeen was really in no condition to do anything but sleep. Jonnie turned him over to the Tsung family and they gave *him* a bath and put him to bed.

It must be hell in Edinburgh!

Jonnie got on the radio to Russia. They had had several thousand people stuffed into that old base. Smoke or no smoke, some of them must be functional. There were two hundred fifty Chinese there from North China. There were the Siberians and the Sherpas. Tinny got some of her own messages in: the rest of the monks and the Buddhist library, the Chinese library and such things were safe. She had to run out and tell Chong-won and Mr. Tsung. Late at night it might be, in both Tashkent and Edinburgh, but Jonnie started shuffling people.

The most vital question now was: where *was* Stormalong? Where was MacAdam? The only thing they ever got out of Luxembourg was a girl saying something that sounded like "Je n' comprempt pas!" and that sure didn't spell Stormalong or the Scot banker. Was he going to have to handle this foreclosure thing with no help?

— 5 —

The treaty signing, Jonnie was told, would be that afternoon.

They came, Lord Dom and Dries Gloton, to the ops room. Dries seemed extraordinarily pleased. "I hear," he said, "that the Earth representative arrived last night. Be sure he is at the signing."

Jonnie glanced at his watch. It was mid-morning. He went to the room where they had put both the old War Chief and Dunneldeen.

Dunneldeen was up and dressed and seemed bright enough for all his bandaged face. Sir Robert was just groggily opening his eyes so Jonnie took Dunneldeen back to ops.

"I want you to take over this post," said Jonnie. "I'll stay for the signing but right after that I'm getting out of here to search for Stormalong." He spent some time genning Dunneldeen in and then went back to Sir Robert.

The old Scot was as grumpy as a bear. He was sitting on the edge of bed with nothing much to cover his bony limbs and eating something Chief Chong-won had brought him.

"Treaty signing!" he grumped between bites. "Waste of time. They'll never keep any treaties. This is a beautiful planet here and they want it! I belong right up in Edinburgh helping dig those poor people out. Oh, you were right, MacTyler, they all should have been at Cornwall!"

Jonnie let him finish his food and then, while he was having some tea, went out and got an atmosphere projector. And although Sir Robert spent much of his time muttering and railing about being absent from Scotland, Jonnie briefed him carefully on events and what they could possibly do. When he had finished, he stood back.

"I'm no diplomat!" said Sir Robert. "I proved that! And I'm no lawyer and I'm no banker! 'Tis a thin chance, but I'll do what you say."

That was all Jonnie wanted.

In mid-afternoon they went to the conference room. Sir Robert was in his regimentals, Jonnie in his helmet and black tunic. Nobody paid them much attention.

The emissaries had drawn up the treaty Jonnie had heard voted and they had it on a big scroll, laid out in such a way that each emissary could walk up to the table where it lay, sign it, affix his seals, get the signature and pattern or print attested by the bank, and then go back to his seat.

It was a sort of parade. Dries Gloton and Fowljopan were the only ones who stood at the table.

Sir Robert sat and fumed about wasting time, but he did so only in a very low voice and only to Jonnie. They signed and signed. It took them almost an hour.

Earth was the last signature, and Sir Robert went up and put down his name, got a match and melted some wax, and then smashed his big seal ring onto it. Dries drew a bank trace around it and held it up.

"I hereby certify," said Dries, "that the Galactic Bank has attested the authenticity of this Treaty of Kariba, Earth. It is complete. May I suggest that immediate copies of it be transmitted to all ships concerned.'' He spread the treaty out, pulled a small picto-tracer from his breast pocket, and scanned it down the scroll.

Jonnie passed it to Dunneldeen in ops for transmission and copies for themselves and all delegates and the bank.

The lord of the Hawvins stood up. ''I have received word that all prisoners were put down at the designated place and signed for by the Earth representative there.''

Dries looked at Jonnie. Word had come from Thor in midmorning. There had been seven pilots, three Russian soldiers, two Sherpas, and one Scot. Thirteen in all. They had been in fair condition. But since none of these invading ships had the kind of food terrestrials ate, they were suffering badly from starvation and certainly would have died in months-long space travel. They had been rushed to Aberdeen for intravenous feeding and treatment of minor injuries. Thor had had a row with the Hawvin officer in charge of the landing for one of the pilots remembered another pilot he was sure the Tolneps had picked up. After sending the first group off Thor had stood by, and sure enough, the Tolneps had another pilot, a German. It had taken two hours to get him set down. They swore that was all. Thor had then believed them.

''Our officer attests we have the prisoners back,'' said Jonnie.

The emissaries who had ships in orbit then passed their orders to their respective commanders.

There was a wait. Then Dunneldeen came in to report that according to sightings from Russia, the whole flotilla in orbit had flamed up, gotten into formation around the Tolnep vessels, and left. The phenomena of their getting very big and vanishing had been observed. Radio contact was lost.

The whole group went outside and Angus fired a spitting, naked, and chained Schleim to the slave market in Creeth.* The emissaries came back to the conference room.

*There was a curious aftermath to this treaty. Lord Schleim, arrived back in Tolnep, used the owners of the Creeth newspaper, the leading Tolnep journal ''Midnight Fang,'' who were incensed at the loss of their ace reporter, Arsebogger, to conduct a smear campaign on Captain Rogodeter Snowl, blaming him for the entire disaster, Schleim claiming it was

Sir Robert thought that was all. He was sitting in the front row, grumbling.

Dries Gloton smiled. He walked over to Sir Robert and he drew a thick paper from his pocket.

"My lords," said Dries to the assemblage, "are witnesses to the fact that there is no further dispute over the ownership of Earth. The government of the planet is intact. The king is recovering. The Earth representative here is legally empowered to act for the government.

"The title to the planet is clear!" he said triumphantly. "Emissary of Earth! I hereby serve you with a notice of delinquency of payments! If, after a discussion, but in no case later than one week, this mortgage remains unhandled or unpaid, it will result in foreclosure on the planet and all its assets and peoples."

He dropped the paper in Sir Robert's lap. "Consider yourself legally served with due process!"

Sir Robert sat there, staring at the paper.

Dries Gloton smiled a shark-like smile at Jonnie. "Thank you very much for getting him here and into the open so that he could legally be given this paper. In addition to being branch manager, I also usually act as my own collections department."

He went over to a chair and picked up a foot-high stack of large booklets. He returned to the platform and addressed the assembled emissaries.

Snowl's "false testimony" which had brought about Schleim's and Tolnep's disgrace. Rogodeter Snowl was set upon in the streets of Creeth by a mob which bit him to death. A relative of the slain officer, Agitor Snowl, in his turn blamed Lord Schleim for the attack and murder. He and a group of fleet officers waited until Lord Schleim next addressed the government and then blew up Schleim and the entire assembled House of Plunder in an incident which became known as "The Great Schleim Plot." Soon thereafter, its fleet gone and no longer able to engage in the slave trading which had formed the basis of its economy, Tolnep was unable to meet its indemnity payments. Its income tax department, always corrupt, fell behind in its bribe quotas to higher officials and, one by one, seized Tolnep citizens for tax delinquency, had their fangs drawn, sterilized them, and sold them into slavery. The Hawvins eventually bought the planet and completed the extermination and the Tolneps became extinct.

(Excerpted from Galactic Bank, Customer Service Summaries, Vol. 43562789A.)

"Honored lords," said Dries, "the primary business of this conference—to clear the title of Earth—is complete. However, I know each one of you has full authority to acquire territories for your state. There are other means than war."

The lords shrugged. War was the surer method, said one. The mental health of the people depended upon war, said another. How was a state to demonstrate its power without war? said Browl. The Galactic Bank would have a hard time surviving without making war loans, quipped Dom. Rulers only became famous when they prosecuted war, laughed another. They were all in a jovial mood.

Jonnie listened to all this with a kind of horror. The impersonal cruelty of large government was brought home to him.

"Get on with it, Your Excellency," chuckled Fowljopan. "We all know what you're going to say."

Dries smiled and began to hand out the booklets. "Here are some brochures I made up while waiting for a clear title. You will find data like mass, surface area, weather, numbers of seas, heights of mountains, and you will also find some scenic views. It is a very pretty planet, really. It would support several billion people, providing they could breathe air. But most of you have air-breathing colonies that even now are overcrowded."

He finished handing the brochures about and the lords began to scan through the colored pictures. "You have collateral and credit and, many of you, cash. It would take a minimum mercenary force to occupy it for, as you know, its defenses are quite antiquated and it has minimum personnel to resist an invasion. Conveyance of title would include all people and assets.

"Therefore, should you care to linger, there will be an auction of this planet as a bank foreclosure and repossession in the next seven days unless suitable arrangements for payments of its debts are made—which hardly seems likely for they are without other adequate cash or collateral or credit. Thank you, my lords."

They were all chattering to one another and examining the brochure and seemed quite in a holiday mood. It was obvious they would stay around, even those from distant universes.

Jonnie said to Dries Gloton, "So it was all just a question of money!"

Dries smiled. "We have not the slightest feeling of hostility toward you. Banking is banking and business is business. One must pay one's obligations. Any child knows that."

The banker turned to Sir Robert, "Arrange a meeting for negotiations as soon as possible. will you? Then we can get this thing over with and done."

Sir Robert and Jonnie walked out.

— 6 —

There was a lot of activity in the bowl. Chief Chong-won's tribe of Chinese had, for the most part, been replaced in Edinburgh by the North Chinese Jonnie had sent there from Russia.

The returning people were smudged and singed. Some were in a state of obvious exhaustion that not even rest on the flight from Edinburgh had eased. They rushed gladly to their children, scooping them up, embracing them, throwing questions to the older children. The dogs were straining at their leashes and barking joyously. It was a scene of glad reunion.

Jonnie was glad he had gotten them replaced on the rescue team. They had worked without ceasing and soon would have been unable to carry on. Yet they had worked until they nearly dropped. Watching fathers in happy chattering exchange with their youngsters, watching mothers anxiously verifying whether this or that had been done properly as to feeding and naps, Jonnie thought of those disdainful and arrogant lords and the soulless haughtiness of government. What did they care what happened to people like these? Yes, such governments might go through gestures of justice and perhaps even social work, but they remained cold, hard forces that could disrupt and shatter lives and people without conscience, without a second thought.

Chief Chong-won was getting them organized. He told Jonnie, as he rushed by. that he was moving them all to the old minesite dome that had been cleaned up: it had rooms underground and the armor cable was working there now.

Well! Jonnie was free of the signing conference. Dunneldeen was available to take over.

In ops he asked Dunneldeen, "Any news from Edinburgh come in with this tribe?"

Dunneldeen shook his head.

Jonnie grabbed an air mask and flight jacket. "Then I'm off to find Stormalong!"

He got no further than the exit to the bowl. He collided head on with Stormalong himself.

"Where have you been?" cried Jonnie. "I have called and called and called!"

Stormalong pushed him into a bunker where they could not be overheard. "I have been fighting and flying my goggles off for days!" He looked it. He was gaunt and hollow of eye; his white scarf was dirty, his jacket stained with sweat and grease. He even had a gun burn in his shoulder.

"You're hurt," said Jonnie.

"No, no, it's nothing. A Drawkin officer wouldn't surrender. I had to chase him with a marine attack plane! Imagine it, him on foot running up the side of a mountain, Ben Lomond, and me having to stun him, not kill him, just stun him, mind you, with a blast cannon! And then when I landed and got out, he was just playing dead and he shot me and I had to stun him again with a handgun. Oh, laddie, it has been a wild time!"

"What have you been *doing?*" demanded Jonnie, making no sense of it.

"Catching prisoners! They left marines and pilots scattered around the Singapore site, some wounded, some not. They didn't bother to pick up their wounded in Russia. Dunneldeen must have shot down thirty enemy planes around Edinburgh and pilots that ejected are scattered to the west and in the Highlands. It takes some doing, let me tell you, to pick them up. They think they'll be tortured or sprinkled with virus or killed. And they don't surrender easily!"

"All by yourself?"

"Except for half-a-dozen bank guards. And they're French, Jonnie. They're not soldiers. They can maybe guard a vault or carry valuables—"

"Stormalong, I had radios in all those places! You must have had your set on. People must have seen you!" None of it made any sense to Jonnie.

"It's MacAdam, Jonnie. He wouldn't let me answer. And anybody we saw, he told them they mustn't put on the air they'd seen us. I told him you would be worried. But he said, no, no. Radio silence utterly and absolutely! I am sorry, Jonnie."

With careful patience, Jonnie said, "Begin at the beginning.

Did you deliver the copies of the talk I had with the small gray men?''

Stormalong sank down on an ammunition box. He verified they were out of sight and hearing of everyone. ''I got there about dawn and I went right to MacAdam's bedroom, and when he heard I was from you, he put the whole thing on a projector. Then he called the German and grabbed six bank guards and a whole basketload of Galactic bank notes, and he told a girl in his office not to give out any information at all and we got airborne. He just plain kidnapped me!

''We've been to every battleground looking for officers. He had a list of nationalities and he wanted several of each. Jonnie, those French bank guards are no help! I had to do all the flying and fighting. But I did get some rest. Every time we'd collect some officers . . . did you know both he and the German speak excellent Psychlo? I was surprised they'd been studying so hard . . . they'd interrogate them and I'd get a couple of hours of catnap. Then we'd load the prisoners aboard, all tied up . . . the bank guards could sit there with a gun on them . . . and off we'd go to another location.''

''What was he asking them?''

''Oh, I don't know. He didn't use torture. Sometimes he handed out a fistful of Galactic bank notes. They talked.''

Jonnie looked out the bunker entrance at the plane. There were the bank guards all right. They were dressed in gray uniforms. But they weren't pushing prisoners. They were unloading boxes and some Chinese were bringing up some mine carts and rushing loads into the bowl. ''I don't see any prisoners,'' said Jonnie.

''Oh, well,'' said Stormalong, ''we came back to Luxembourg and picked up some boxes and he got a couple more bank guards—Germans this time—and we flew down to the Victoria minesite. I got a pretty good rest there because he spent so much time talking to the captives we already had there. Then we dumped out prisoners and came on and here we are. And that's the whole thing.''

It was a long way from the whole thing, Jonnie thought. He told Stormalong to go get some food and rest and went out to find the banker.

MacAdam, short and stocky, his black beard flecked with gray, was pointing this way and that and rushing people along. He stopped abruptly when he saw Jonnie and shook his hand vigorously. Then he turned and beckoned another man to come over.

"I don't believe you ever met Baron von Roth," said MacAdam, "the other member of the Earth Planetary Bank."

The German was a huge man, as tall as Jonnie and heavier. He was bluff and hearty, red of face. "Ach, but I am pleased!" he bellowed and promptly gave Jonnie a huge hug.

MacAdam had vanished into the bowl and the German picked up a heavy box and rushed after him.

Jonnie knew something of the German. Although he had made a fortune in dairy and other foodstuffs, he was descended from a family that was supposed to have controlled European banking for centuries before the Psychlo invasion. He looked like a very tough, capable man.

The last of the baggage from the marine attack plane was being wheeled into the entrance. Jonnie couldn't figure out what they were up to.

Inside, a crew of Chinese and some bank guards, under the direction of Chong-won, were hanging huge mine tarpaulins all around the pagoda eaves to completely hide the firing platform itself. Some more Chinese were stringing mine cables and hanging tarps on them to make a covered passage from a bunker to the console. They were totally hiding the platform and all operation of it.

MacAdam was talking with Angus, and although they smiled at him when Jonnie came up, MacAdam was very rushed and he said, "Later, later."

All the baggage had vanished into the covered bunker. The Chinese children and dogs were all gone. Some Chinese were cleaning the bowl up. Some emissaries wandered out and watched what was happening with the tarpaulins and then, showing little curiosity, wandered off showing each other bits and points in the brochure.

Dunneldeen was on the job in the ops room and told Jonnie that he'd talked Stormalong into getting his beard trimmed like "Sir Francis Drake." No, nothing new from Edinburgh except that the North Chinese now working there were doing fine. Did Jonnie know they were much bigger men? Oh, yes, and Ker and two bank guards were holding blast rifles on fifty new prisoners at Victoria.

Jonnie glanced up at the sky. If worse came to worst, he had his own way to handle this: a way which might make a fatal future but which might have to be done.

He went to his room to get into less spectacular clothes. They had a few short days. But days had a habit of passing awfully fast when you needed them.

The final confrontation, the last battle, was all too near.

— 7 —

The fateful moment of the bank meeting arrived.

Five days had passed.

Jonnie sat alone in the small meeting room that had been prepared and waited for the others to arrive.

There was not the slightest doubt in his mind that this was going to be a battle bigger than he had ever fought before.

Being Jonnie, he had been unwilling to simply sit idly by while MacAdam and Baron von Roth prepared.

They had been busy enough. For five days and nights, the hum of the teleportation rig had resounded through the bowl. Things had come and things had gone on the platform behind the tarpaulins.

But they did no talking less they be overheard and the only words that sounded were, "Motors off!" "No planes approaching!" "Stand by!" and "Fire!" Whenever anyone, especially emissaries or the small gray men, had come near the tarpaulins or the curtained corridor to a bunker, stern bank guards had pushed them back peremptorily. All Jonnie got from MacAdam was, "Later. Later!" Not even Angus was talking.

He had gotten an estimate that it would be several days. Mr. Tsung had told Jonnie that the negotiations of finance and banking were very specialized things. He had added one phrase that had stuck in Jonnie's mind: "The power of money and gold over the souls of men passes all wondering."

The predawn sky of the day after MacAdam's arrival had found Jonnie in the air. He had heard of a university outside the ruins of an old city named Salisbury about one hundred seventy-five miles southeast of Kariba. He had tried to get Sir Robert to come along but the old Scot was hanging on to the radio in the ops room, doing what he could for Edinburgh. Instead, Jonnie had taken a couple of Chinese soldiers to shoo off the lions and elephants when they threatened to interrupt his studies.

The university was a ruin but the library could be sorted out amid the dust and debris, the roof and walls having stood. Camped out in the wreckage, Jonnie had pried congealed packs of catalogue cards apart and had pretty well found what he was looking for. It had been a well-endowed library once. It included lots of economics texts, probably because the relatively new nation had had a dreadful economic struggle of it. The texts were in English and they covered the history of economics and banking pretty well.

Mr. Tsung had been absolutely right! It was a highly specialized subject. And when one went wrong, like some nut named Keynes they had all become mad at, it really messed things up. What Jonnie got out of it was that the state was for *people*. He had suspected that was the way it should be. And individuals worked and made things and exchanged them for other things. And it was easier to do it with money. But money itself could be manipulated. The Chinkos had been great and patient teachers and Jonnie knew how to study. And with a mind like his, he got things as quickly as a traveling shot.

Four of those five days had been spent ears deep in books, nose full of dust, with Chinese guards warning off black mamba snakes and African buffalo.

Sitting there in the meeting room, waiting for the others, he had the satisfaction of knowing that, while he was no expert, he would at least have a grip on what this battle was all about.

Sir Robert came in, grumbling and cross, and took a seat over to the side with Jonnie. Even though the small gray men had indicated it was between Sir Robert and them, the War Chief of Scotland knew that claymores and lochaber axes weren't going to win this one and as far as he was concerned it was all up to the experts. Basically he was very concerned about Edinburgh. They had gotten food and water through into the various shelters with thin hoses but rock was still crumbling in on their tunnel efforts. They had been driving in huge, heavy pipe casings for days now and the only hope was that they were not crumbling this time.

Dries Gloton and Lord Voraz came in. A table for four had been set in the middle of the room and they took two of the places on one side of it. They were very neatly dressed in gray suits. They had their arms full of papers and attaché cases and they put them down. They looked exactly like hungry sharks.

Neither Jonnie nor Sir Robert had acknowledged their arrival.

"You don't seem very pleased this morning," said Lord Voraz.

"We be men of the sword," said Sir Robert. "We ha' sma' truck wi' the money changers i' the temple."

Sir Robert's sudden use of English caused both small gray men to turn on their vocoders.

"I noticed," said Dries Gloton, "when I came in that there were half a hundred soldiers in white tunics and red pants all around in the rifle pits in the bowl."

"An honor guard," said Sir Robert.

"They had an assortment of weapons," said Dries. "And one huge fellow certainly looked more like a brigand than an officer in charge of an honor guard."

"I wouldn't let Colonel Ivan hear you say that," said Sir Robert.

"Do you realize," said Dries Gloton, "that if you killed the emissaries and us, you would become an outlaw nation? They know where we are. You would have a dozen fleets in here smashing you to bits."

"Better to fight fleets than be a' cut up with bits o' paper," said Sir Robert, gesturing at their piles of it. "There's na thrat i' the Roosians if you tell the truth and behave. We ken this be a battle o' wits and skullduggery. But it's a battle a' the same and a bloody one!"

Lord Voraz turned to Jonnie. "Why do you regard us in so hostile a fashion, Sir Lord Jonnie? I assure you we have only the friendliest feelings for you personally. We admire you greatly. You must believe that." He seemed and probably was sincere.

"But banking is banking," said Jonnie. "And business is business. Is that it?"

"Of course!" said Lord Voraz. "However, personal regard sometimes enters in. And in your case it most certainly does. I tried several times in the last few days to find you. It is unfortunate that we could not have had our talk before this meeting here. We are actually your personal friends."

"In what way?" asked Jonnie coolly.

A grizzly bear or an elephant would have backed off when Jonnie sounded like that. But not Lord Voraz. "Do you realize that when a planet is sold, all its people and all its technology are sold with it? Didn't you read the brochure? You and your immediate associates are exempted in the sale and so is anything you may have developed."

"How generous," said Jonnie with cold sarcasm.

"Since we had no chance to talk and the others seem to be late," said Lord Voraz, "I can tell you now. We have worked out an offer. We will create a technical department in the Galactic Bank and make you the head of it. We will build a fine factory in Snautch—that's the capital of the system, you know—provide you with everything you need, and give you a lifetime contract. If the figure I already offered seems too low, we can negotiate it. You would not lack for money."

"And money is everything," said Jonnie bitingly.

Both bankers were shocked at his tone. "But it *is!*" cried Lord Voraz. "Everything has a price! Anything can be bought."

"Things like decency and loyalty can't be," said Jonnie.

"Young man," said Lord Voraz sternly, "you are very talented and have many other fine qualities, I am sure, but there has been some radical omissions in your upbringing!"

"I wouldn'a talk to him like that," warned Sir Robert.

"Oh, I'm sorry," said Lord Voraz. "Forgive me. In my effort to help, I permitted myself to be carried away."

"That's better," growled Sir Robert and loosened his grip on his claymore.

"You see," said Lord Voraz, "a scientist is supposed to be hired by a company. What he develops belongs to the company. It's quite disastrous for a scientist to try to go it alone and manage his own developments and affairs. All companies and all banks and certainly all governments agree on this totally. A scientist is supposed to quietly draw his salary, turn over his patents to the company, and go on working. It's all been arranged that way. Why, if he tried to do anything any other way, he'd spend all his life in law courts. That is how it has been carefully arranged."

"So the shoes a cobbler makes belong to him," said Jonnie, "but the developments of a scientist belong to the company or the state. I see. Very plain."

Lord Voraz overlooked the sarcasm. Or didn't hear it.

"I am so glad you understand. Money is everything and all things and talent are for sale. And that's the heart and soul of banking, the very cornerstone of business. A first principle."

"I thought making a profit was," said Jonnie.

"Oh, that too, that too," said Lord Voraz. "So long as it is an honest profit. But believe me, the heart and soul—"

"I'm so glad to know," said Jonnie, "that banking and business have a heart and soul. I hadn't been able to detect one thus far."

"Oh, dear," said Lord Voraz. "You are being sarcastic."

"Anything that destroys decent people has no heart and soul," said Jonnie. "And by that I include banking, business, *and* government. These concerns can only exist if they are for *people*. If they serve the wants and needs of the ordinary being!"

Lord Voraz looked at him searchingly. He thought for a bit. There was something in what Sir Lord Jonnie was saying. . . . He gave it up. He was a banker.

"Indeed," said Lord Voraz, "you are a peculiar young man. Perhaps when you get old enough to understand the ways of the world—"

Sir Robert's tensing was halted by the arrival of MacAdam and Baron von Roth.

"Who's a peculiar young man?" said Baron von Roth. "Jonnie? Indeed he is. Thank gott! I see you two were early," he shot at Dries and Lord Voraz. "Never saw anybody so anxious to collect their pound of flesh! Shall we begin?"

■

PART 30

— 1 —

Andrew MacAdam and Baron von Roth put down piles of papers and attaché cases on the floor on their side of the table, briefly shook hands with Dries Gloton and Lord Voraz, and sat down.

Jonnie blinked. MacAdam and the baron were wearing gray suits! They were expensive tweed and the individual fibers sparkled, but they were gray suits!

The four of them sat there at the table for a bit, just looking across it at one another. Jonnie was reminded of some gray wolves he had once seen, prowling back and forth, eyes alert, teeth ready, sizing each other up before they plunged into a snarling, slashing fight to the death.

And it was a fight to the death, for if MacAdam and the baron lost, that was the end of the people of this planet and all they held dear. He didn't have the least idea what MacAdam and the baron had been doing, and it was with a sinking feeling that he heard MacAdam fire the first shot of the battle.

"Are you sure," said MacAdam, "that you gentlemen couldn't give us a little more time? Say another month?"

Dries showed his double row of teeth as his lips curled back. "Impossible! You have waited until the last moment. There can be no extension."

"Times are very bad," said the baron. "There are economic upsets everywhere."

"We know that," said Lord Voraz. "It cannot be used as an excuse. If you were unable to pay your just debts and settle your obligations, you could have said so days ago and spared us this wait. I can't imagine what you were doing."

"I was interrogating abandoned crew members of the departed ships," said MacAdam. "It was a bit difficult to find an officer of each race that attacked this planet."

"And they told you there were economic upsets," said Dries. "You might as well sign this quitclaim to the planet now and get it over with." He pushed a form at Sir Robert, who didn't get a chance to take it.

MacAdam pushed the form back to the table and let it drop. "I found that these crewmen did not want to go home. They had been conscripted, actually press-ganged into their services. Some felt that on return they might have to take part in revolutions or civil wars and did not want to fire on their own people. Some felt that if they went home they would just be discharged and have to join the mobs of unemployed that were starving and sometimes rioting in the streets of many capitals."

"This is nothing new," said Lord Voraz. "All this past year there has been unrest. That's why these emissaries here are planning wars of foreign conquest—to take the peoples' minds off all this. You could have asked me. I would have told you."

"This changes nothing," said Dries. "I advise you to surrender the planet tamely. For any of these emissaries would like nothing better than to buy this planet and mount a military expedition to wrest it from you. The ships that were up there were nothing compared to what could be sent against you. So if you will just—"

The baron fixed him with a bayonet stare. He said, "Having collected all the data available locally, we went to see for ourselves."

Jonnie came alert. Ah, so that's what all that firing was about. This pair had been traveling all over the place! He'd noticed faint air mask marks on their jaws. Had they been doing something else than just traveling?

"There is economic chaos!" said the baron. "When Intergalactic Mining Company ceased to deliver metals, the scarcity caused their prices to soar. Factories are closed. People are out of work and rioting. To distract them, the governments are planning wars that are not popular. To get metals to build weapons, they are even commandeering peoples' cars and the pots and pans of housewives."

Dries shrugged. "This is not news and it is totally off the subject of your unpaid balance. Does the Earth emissary sign this or do we resort—" He let the threat hang.

The air seemed charged with electricity for a moment.

The baron's pale gray eyes bored into Dries Gloton. "You are in severe trouble, Your Excellency."

The branch manager shrugged. "Internal concerns of the bank have no bearing on your paying up as you are obligated to do."

Baron von Roth turned to Sir Robert. "His Excellency here committed his sector branch bank to some very unwise personal loans to the high executives on the Psychlo planets Torthut and Tun in the Batafor System and some even bigger personal loans to the Psychlo regent governors of sixteen Psychlo-owned planets in four nearby star systems. Those loans were secured by holdings in real estate on Psychlo itself."

"How did you find that out?" snapped Dries. "It is confidential bank information!"

"A disgruntled employee you sacked," said the baron. "The real estate on Psychlo went up in smoke and the debtors are dead. An unwise bank risk. Psychlos were renowned for bad faith."

"The depositors could bring pressure on the bank," said Voraz, defending his branch manager. "But that does not change your loan—"

"Indeed they *could* bring pressure," said the baron. "The basic profit income of the Galactic Bank came from handling fund transfers for Psychlo planets. Not from loans, but from the high percent charged by the bank for handling their funds. And with those regency planet transfers shut off, Your Excellency, your regency banks had to dismiss their staffs and close their doors. The senior branch bank in Balor, your own personal office, fired nearly everyone.

"So *that*, Sir Robert," continued the baron, "is why you are being pressured. Dries figured the only route he had out of going bankrupt was to repossess Earth. It's the only planet in any universe that Intergalactic Mining Company owed any money on. He thought if he could auction this planet off, if only for a little cash, he could prevent total insolvency."

"Pointing to the mud on someone's fins," said Dries, "does not improve your own swimming! You had better sign over or you yourself will drown!" This rehearsal of the last year's troubles was making him edgy. "Pay up and pay up *now!*" He picked up the form and rattled it in front of Sir Robert. It crackled like a machine gun.

MacAdam reached over and pushed Dries' arm gently back down to the table. "We'll come back to that later."

The small gray man trembled. He could never remember being so upset before. It had been a very terrible year. What were these fellows up to? If they didn't have the money, why were they delaying? He sat back. Never mind. The end would be the same. Let them ramble.

"Now let's take up the main bank in the Gredides," said the baron. "We went there, right to Universe One. The capital city Snautch was damaged by the transshipment recoil and so were the capitals of the other two Selachee planets. The whole top floors of the bank buildings were very badly damaged."

"They can be rebuilt," said Lord Voraz.

"The blasts knocked down the huge Galactic Bank signs, the ones you can see from all over the cities in each capital, and they're still hanging there shattered. You can see what they said but that's about all."

"They can be hung up again," said Lord Voraz smoothly.

"But for a whole year," the baron bored in like a mine drill, "you haven't done it! Now, all three Selachee planets depended upon banking. Those banks affected millions and millions of people. When you lost teleportation, you were thereafter unable to reach the other fifteen universes, space travel or no space travel. You have millions of Selachees stranded in branch banks all over those universes, banks as broke as His Excellency's, that you can't bring home. Families and relatives don't think they'll ever see their fathers or brothers or sons again. There are mobs rioting outside your bank doors. Rioting very loudly and howling for blood!"

Lord Voraz shrugged. "There are strong bank guards."

"And how will you pay them?" said the baron. "Your bank income did not really come from loans but from Psychlo fund transfers. The instant Psychlo and Intergalactic Mining were blown up, there was no further fund flow. You started to go broke and you began to lay off employees. You know from Dries here that many of your branch banks have had to close their doors."

"We have gone through economic difficulties before," said Lord Voraz.

The baron leaned closer to him. "But not as bad as this one, Lord Voraz. The Psychlos were hated bitterly by peoples everywhere. When your Lord Loonger, whose face you carry on your bills, made a deal with the Psychlos a couple of hundred thousand years ago to handle all their finances, he refused to let any Psychlo sit on the bank's board of directors.''

''It would have hurt the bank's reputation,'' said Lord Voraz. ''A sensible move. People would have claimed it was a Psychlo bank.''

''Ah, yes,'' said the baron. ''But the Psychlos then insisted that forever thereafter the bank's reserves would be kept in vaults on Psychlo. They're gone!''

Lord Voraz dropped his heavy eyelids for a moment. He passed his hand across his face. Then he rallied. ''It is true. This still does not alter the fact that you are a debtor.''

''It certainly does!'' said the baron. ''You're insolvent. *And if you don't find assets to back you fast, you will go under!*''

''All right!'' said Lord Voraz. ''But this just proves the fact that we must repossess this planet!''

''This one planet won't save you,'' said MacAdam.

''Why,'' said the baron smoothly, ''don't you just grab some old Psychlo mining planets or regency planets. There are over two hundred thousand of them lying about.''

''Oh, here now!'' said Lord Voraz, horrified. ''It is quite one thing to run down our credit and expose our troubles. But it is an entirely different thing to suggest the bank would ever engage upon piratical seizures of things to which it has no title!''

''Goodness,'' said Dries, shocked. ''Those planets were all properly paid for! You simply can't engage in theft!''

''Their titles would be in dispute!'' said Lord Voraz. ''It would open up the bank to wars and the bank is not a military organization! Anybody who touched those planets would wind up in court. No title to them! I must say, you know very little about intergalactic law governing nations!''

''Oh,'' said MacAdam, ''I think we do. Have you ever read the original Psychlo Imperial Royal Charter of the Intergalactic Mining Company?''

''Exhaustively!'' said Lord Voraz. ''You can't do business with a company that doesn't file its charter. It was granted three hundred two thousand, nine hundred sixty-one years ago by King Dith of Psychlo. Why, there's a copy of it—or was—on the wall of every Intergalactic Mining central compound. Required by law. I have read—''

The baron threw a copy of it on the table. ''You should read the fine print.'' He turned the copy around so Voraz could read it, though Voraz didn't bother to, knowing it almost by heart.

"Note this clause here," said the baron, "Number 109: 'In the absence of a director or directors, the head of a planet owned by the said Intergalactic Mining Company shall have the power to make resolutions and his resolutions shall be binding.' "

Lord Voraz shrugged. "Of course. They had only one additional planet then and the head of it was a royal prince. The directors at that time couldn't be bothered with business. I don't see—"

"But it is a valid clause," said the baron.

"Right, right," said Voraz. "But you are just delaying—"

"Now take this next clause," said the baron. "Number 110: 'In time of emergency and/or threat to the company, and especially at a time of disaster, the head of a planet may dispose of company property.' Note that it is not further limited nor qualified."

"Why should it be?" demanded Voraz. "It was the same royal prince. He wouldn't take the job away from home otherwise. He was afraid of communication cutoffs or palace revolutions. He could have been left out there holding a claw full of company bills. It was Prince Sco."

"But you agree," said the baron, "that these are valid clauses."

"When do I get to repossess this planet?" said Dries wearily. "Nothing in that charter will permit you to wriggle out of paying forty trillion credits!"

Lord Voraz corrected him, "Forty trillion, nine hundred sixty billion, two hundred seventeen million, six hundred five thousand, two hundred sixteen Galactic credits."

"So there's nothing inaccurate in this royal charter," persisted the baron.

"Of course not!" said Lord Voraz.

Baron von Roth and Andrew MacAdam looked at each other and laughed, startling the other two.

MacAdam reached down into the papers beside his chair and drew up a thick pack of documents. "This was fully signed and witnessed eleven months after the destruction of the planet Psychlo." He threw down the stack and it landed like a cannon shot.

It was all embossed with seals and glaring with huge official red ribbons and scarlet and gold discs.

It was the Terl contract!

It sold in full the entirety of Intergalactic Mining Company, all its equipment, assets, planets, and accounts.

MacAdam plopped another document on top of it. "Here is the attest by the last Planet Head of the company that this is a true and valid contract and it adds his total conveyance of the company. It was signed just a few days ago."

Another paper was slapped down on top. "And here is the receipt and it says 'Paid in full.' "

Dries and Lord Voraz stared, open-mouthed. They had never been that startled before in their whole eventful lives. Seconds went by.

Then, as one, they seized upon the pile and began to go through it. They read it. They looked for holes in it.

Finally Lord Voraz said in awe, "It's valid all right. I even see that it was assigned by the legal government of this planet to the Earth Planetary Bank in payment for loans. Quite regular. Stand up in any court."

But Dries shook his head. "To be legal and for it to be of any use to you in preventing the repossession, it would have to be recorded and put on file in the Hall of Legality on Snautch!"

"Oh, but it is, it is," said the baron sweetly. And he drew the file copy of the Hall of Legality form from his pocket and threw it down. "Fully recorded just three days ago! In fact, it was the first thing I did when I got through the mobs!"

Dries had gotten over his shock. "It may give you planets and equipment. It might even give you collateral to borrow money on. However, the bank would take time to make the loan. And we wouldn't lend on top of an unpaid loan. The document simply proves that now you *really* owe the debt. I will have to demand instant cash—"

"We'll come back to that," said the baron. "Lord Voraz, how much would you say the Galactic Bank was worth? You know, assets and liabilities as per your last balance sheet?"

Voraz bristled. "We are under no obligation to show our bank balance sheets! Particularly in the middle of collecting a debt from a debtor!"

"You do have a copy of one as of two weeks ago," said the baron.

Voraz almost choked. "Have you been riffling my hamper?"

"Ach, gott, no!" said the baron. "No reason to. I was told you had one. In any event, here is a current copy from your accounts office." He pulled the immense, closely tabulated machine copy from his pile of papers and tossed it on the table. "Counting all buildings, real estate owned, and accounts actually collectible and subtracting bills owed, taxes yet to be paid, and all that, it seems to come to roughly one quadrillion credits."

"They had no right to give this out," said Voraz. "But I admit it is correct. Roughly, one quadrillion."

"Providing we overlook the fact that you are about to go broke," said MacAdam.

"The bank would liquidate for that!" snapped Voraz.

"If you could get to the branches in other universes, which you can't," said MacAdam.

The baron waved a big hand airily, "But we are in a generous mood, aren't we, Andrew?" He smiled at Jonnie. "Aren't we?"

Jonnie had his eyes riveted on the scene. It was like watching a bullfight.

"Our two friends here," said MacAdam, indicating the small gray men, "don't seem to be very generous."

"But we'll be big," said the baron. "Voraz, you desperately need somebody to back you, you need visible assets. Without them you will fold. Right?"

Voraz looked at him, glaring. Then he hung his head. "True."

MacAdam said, "So we're willing to bail you out. Right, Jonnie?"

Jonnie shrugged. Let them go ahead. There was going to be more to this fight.

Voraz looked from MacAdam to the baron, very watchfully.

The baron said, "So the Earth Planetary Bank is offering to buy two-thirds of the Galactic Bank."

"What?" cried Voraz. "That's a controlling interest! You would control the whole vast empire of the Galactic Bank!" He thought about it for a moment. "And with what?"

The baron smiled. "We will buy it with two-thirds of a quadrillion credits worth of planets." He drew another sheet from the papers beside him. "Pending further evaluation, a planet is worth a minimum of sixty trillion credits."

Voraz said, "To be honest, most are worth considerably more."

The baron said, "You'd have assets, then. You could back your currency with reserves which you don't now have. The Psychlos never let you own planets but you can now. We will turn over eleven planets that are worth sixty trillion credits for the ownership of two-thirds of the Galactic Bank, all its assets, debts, everything."

Lord Voraz was wavering. But he had not said yes.

MacAdam leaned back easily. "And we will put 199,989 planets and all company assets into a trust to be managed by the Galactic Bank. That gives you back your fund transfer profits. That lets you lease out mining rights. That surely saves your bank!"

"Wait," said Lord Voraz. And they thought he was going to turn it down. "I must be honest with you. You took your list of planets from the Intergalactic Coordinate Firing Table. It does not include the mine reserve planets. To push off all the planets it could on Intergalactic, and to bleed the company, there was an Imperial Decree that Intergalactic Mining Company had to own five planets for every one it actively mined. There is a list of one million additional planets recorded in the Hall of Legality, with their coordinates, unexploited by Intergalactic. Also I am afraid Dries never gave you the actual purchase contract for this planet. You keep speaking of it in the singular. It includes nine other planets in this system and all moons, mentioned in passing because they are deemed worthless. There are also suns and nebulae and clusters. There is obviously an awful lot of Intergalactic property you don't know about. Would you leave it up to us to ferret it out and include that in the bank-managed trust also?"

MacAdam smiled. "Seem all right to you, baron? Find any flaws in that, Jonnie?"

Jonnie thought about it. There was another situation here they were evidently overlooking. But he saw nothing wrong with what the Earth bank was doing.

With a hand outstretched to Lord Voraz, MacAdam said, "We agree."

Voraz had made his point. He started to reach for the hand and then he drew back. "Such a deal has to be ratified by a Galactic Bank board meeting."

The baron laughed. "Good. Let's hold one. They can be convened anywhere in sixteen universes according to your charter."

"Ah, wait," said Lord Voraz. "There are twelve other board members: rich, influential Selachees who are—"

"Scared to death," the baron finished for him. "The state of the bank and the riots made them believe that they would lose all their personal property and fortunes if the bank went under. So they thought this was a great offer!''

Voraz gaped. ''But they can't hold a board meeting behind my back!''

''Oh, they didn't,'' said the baron. ''They gave me all their proxies and these delegate to me the right to place their votes.'' He reached down and threw another pack of documents on the table. ''There they are.''

Lord Voraz stared at them. He recognized the personal seals. They had even been filed at the Hall of Legality.

''So as chairman,'' said the baron, ''would you please convene a board meeting of the Galactic Bank at once and move that the Earth Planetary Bank buy two-thirds of the Galactic Bank—''

''It will have to be a typed resolution,'' said Voraz. ''I do hereby convene the meeting. I even have my seals. But—''

''Here's the resolution,'' said the baron. ''All typed. I'm awfully glad you're convening the meeting for it saves the trouble of going back to Snautch and getting you fired.''

Voraz laughed suddenly. ''You are a pair of hard rock eels! That was typed by my own secretary! That's her initial!''

''Right, right,'' said the baron. ''A charming girl. She was trying to save your and her jobs! Now just sign there as Chairman of the Board and President—''

''Wait,'' said Voraz, suddenly sober and worried. ''This is all very well. But there are three things that could ruin this whole deal and all of us.''

Dries interjected, ''The first is how do I get my money, cash right now, for the mortgage here!''

''Oh, *that,*'' said MacAdam. He scooped up a huge sheet of paper which unfolded yards long. ''This is the Intergalactic Mining money transfer summary from your bank. It says that on day ninety-two of last year, there were certain Intergalactic funds in process of transfer. They were given over to the bank for further relay but the bank, of course, was thereafter unable to relay them. Payments for metals, salaries . . . they're all listed here. They are still in your bank. It's all Intergalactic money. When we were in Snautch we started an account for the Earth Planetary Bank. Let's see, the total of received and unrelayed funds from two hundred thousand planets for their past month was C209,438,971,438,643 credits. That's our money. Just subtract the mortgage from it and it still leaves us about one hundred sixty-eight trillion."

MacAdam rummaged around in his pile of papers. "Here's our letter of authorization and here is the receipt for you to sign, Dries."

The small gray man was sitting there, speechless. He was trying to realize he was solvent. He had not thought to recover more than ten trillion in a forced sale. He sat up and grabbed a pen to sign the receipt.

Lord Voraz stopped his hand. "That's all very well," he said in a worried voice. "But there are two other matters." He turned to Jonnie. "Can you forgive us for trying to treat you as a hired hand, Sir Lord Jonnie? It is quite true that we cannot operate at all without transshipment rigs and consoles. We are cut off. We used to ship all bank business on the Psychlo rigs, using our own bank boxes. They charged us heavily but to deliver a dispatch by spaceship can cost fifty thousand credits and takes ages! Are you going to help us in this?"

"That's all Jonnie's," said MacAdam. "We at the bank don't own any part of it. Jonnie, we can make you a loan at low interest and help you set up a manufacturing plant. A separate company that you own. How about it?"

— 2 —

Jonnie roused himself. He had been so intent upon finance that he had to consciously force himself to think about technical matters.

It would be dangerous to Earth to have these consoles scattered through sixteen universes—thousands, possibly hundreds of thousands of rigs in not always friendly or well-meaning hands, run by other races.

You could do a lot of things with a console. You could transport people, send dispatch boxes, ship ores, ship finished goods, send food. But you could also send bombs as he himself had proven so fatally to the Psychlos, and as would have been the end of the Tolneps.

He had not thought much about the problem. Many other

things had been very urgent. Yes, one console out there, much less half a million, could be very dangerous to this planet.

"Give me a moment," he said.

Mr. Tsung also had his uses for the moment and brought them some tea and a tray of bites-between-meals. It was nearing lunchtime. It also, as he had wisely noted, gave Jonnie a needed moment to think.

The Psychlos had had Psychlo operators. It didn't make much difference about the platform and rig.

The same security measures could be used in the console itself. Possibly even improved a bit.

If he put a camera in the armored front of the case that would shoot a picture of every cargo. . . .

Aha! Metal analysis detectors. If they were built into the platform itself, they could analyze a cargo from all sides, above and below, and if that were connected to a circuit no one could get at in the console and if that circuit had a metal tracer. . . . Yes. If anything in a cargo matched forbidden traces like uranium or this ultimate bomb heavy element, the match of the circuit would separate a relay and the console would not fire. . . .

It was a trifle difficult to think with all these faces staring at him, waiting. He didn't have to be told the fate of the banks depended upon it. And they hadn't mentioned a thing which could queer the whole deal.

If he got with Allen and MacKendrick and worked out disease . . . they said it had an aura. Anyway, there were disease viruses and bacterial traces and he could work those in, whether disease had an aura or not, and if anything on the platform matched, they would trigger that relay and the console wouldn't fire.

He could rig it so if any of such items were put on platforms for Earth, he could tie in the coordinates of Earth so that the console would blow up.

Then if a sign were put on every console in plain view like, "Any attempt to fire contraband cargo with this console will render it inoperative. . . ." No list of things or else somebody might try to mask the trace. And if one added, "Any attempt to use this console in an act of war against Earth will cause it to explode. . . ." Maybe even put out that the console could read evil intentions. . . .

Yes, he could build a foolproof console.

And if the console seemed to be finally assembled in a place which was not known, by people who could not be found . . .

He could make the construction areas very heavily defended. He would let only a very trusted, unbribable few do the final assembly. . . . Start a school for extraterrestrial operators who knew only how to operate it. . . .

"I think I can do that," he told them.

They all brightened up. Mr. Tsung took the tray away.

"However," said Jonnie, "the rigs will be a bit expensive."

Unimportant.

"And I will not sell them. I will only lease them. Every five years a console will have to be exchanged for a new one." That would keep going an Earth that had no real income, and it would permit an inspection of views of cargos that had been shipped. "Some extraterrestrial firm will have to be brought in to make components and cases. Otherwise it will take too long to build one."

"You can provide consoles?" asked Lord Voraz.

"He said he could," said the baron. "If Jonnie says he is going to do something, watch it! He will!"

"All right," said Lord Voraz. "That brings us now to the most serious block of all." He pointed in the direction of the big conference room. "Those emissaries!"

Voraz looked very gloomy. "You are almost in the intergalactic banking business now and will be if this resolution is signed. You had better understand that it is very tricky business handling such as those!

"As you noted," he continued, "right now they have countries in riot. Their economies are in rags. But they are of such a nature that they will just sit there square in the middle of their prejudices, cling to their most arrogant opinions, and ignore everything else.

"Right this minute, I have better reason than you to know, they are absolutely counting on war to save their economies and their states. They think that war powers and war hysteria will distract the people and secure their own positions. It is their only formula.

"This bank lived in the shadow of the powerful even if hated Psychlos. They are gone. You, and even the Gredides, are small planets. You have no great military force. To be blunt, those lords will not respect you.

"I read the ripples in the water with Lord Schleim. He

supposed the bank was no longer the power it had been. He thought he could violate a conference. He failed. But that kind of thinking couldn't have existed a mere thirteen months ago. Others among those haughty lords will get the same ideas sooner or later."

He pointed to the papers. "You have here more than one million, two hundred thousand habitable, useful worlds. It is very tasty bait for very big fish.

"Since these lords are bent on war to save their regimes, they will find a pretext not to respect the ownership of Intergalactic, Earth, or the bank. They will raid these planets. They will quarrel over them. They will throw good sense and order to the winds and waves. The harder they are driven at home by economic chaos, the more they will seek a pretext to take outlaw actions."

Jonnie was listening to him. He had wondered for some time now when they would get around to this point. It was the key problem. And if it were left unhandled, all the doors they were trying to open would jam shut in their faces.

"Since I have been here," said Lord Voraz, "not one of those elegant aristocrats has failed to draw me aside and try to discuss his nation's chances for a war loan. Of course, we seldom make war loans. All we do is issue the bonds for them and let them sell them to each other. There's no real money in war loans. With economics this shaky, the chances of their being paid back are poor. Wars are not as popular with the people who fight them as with the lords who run them and profit by them! Revolutions could occur and revolutionaries are notorious as bad risks.

"So before you commit yourselves to these risks, you should understand them."

Jonnie stood up. These small gray men had not signed anything yet. He had been afraid there would be a quibble. He picked up his helmet and silver wand.

"Sir Robert and I discussed this. We rehearsed it. It is risky. But I believe we have no choice. Do I have the temporary right, granted by all of you, to set bank policy for the next couple of hours? If it is successful, you will not be the losers. If I am not successful, you won't have lost anything."

"You set bank policy?" gaped Lord Voraz.

"Let him do it!" said the baron.

"But he might commit us to some course of—"

"You just better say yes, Lord Voraz," MacAdam said. "That's Jonnie Tyler there who's talking."

Lord Voraz looked numbly from MacAdam to the baron. "I've not yet signed—"

"Nor have I," said Dries.

The baron reached over and made Voraz's head bob. "He said 'yes,' Jonnie. Go ahead."

"But he might do something dangerous," Lord Voraz was trying to sputter. "He is a very peculiar young man!"

Jonnie had already left with Sir Robert. A Sir Robert with a grim expression on his face.

— 3 —

The bowl of the firing platform area had been stripped of tarpaulins. A Russian trooper stood in each rifle pit, the noonday sun harsh on their white tunics and glittering weapons. A few emissaries lounged in the shade under the pagoda eaves.

Jonnie called for the host and ordered him to get the lords into the conference room.

Stormalong, hearing the stir, popped out of the ops room with a dispatch in his hands, intending to rush over to where Sir Robert and Jonnie stood. But the broad arm and bandaged hand of Colonel Ivan stopped him.

"Leave them alone," Colonel Ivan managed in English. He had his orders. He stood and watched the emissaries going in the conference room door. He knew Jonnie would be going in there in a moment and he knew what Jonnie was going to do. It made him a little nervous for Jonnie, since he would have no direct protection in there. A casual glance had told him that many of these lords were secretly armed for all their fine clothes and arrogant ways. When Jonnie gave them the shock that was planned, they might react in violence. It would be like swimming in a river full of crocodiles! Colonel Ivan made up his mind: if they hurt Jonnie, not one of these fine lords or these bank people would leave Earth alive. But that was no immediate help for Jonnie if they turned on him. And that they well might do.

Angus was kneeling by the atmosphere projector, putting some final touches to the adjustments. He glanced across the bowl, saw what was happening, and speeded his work up. They would need it in a moment.

Stormalong, frustrated, fluttered the dispatch in his hand and, still restrained by Ivan, watched the last of the lords file in. Then there went Sir Robert and Jonnie, following them.

Inside the conference room, the host was adjusting chairs and helping the lords get settled.

The small gray men and MacAdam and Baron von Roth entered and took seats along the wall.

Sir Robert stood with Jonnie alongside the raised platform. Sir Robert was shooting glances at the lords from under bushy gray eyebrows. Somehow these mighty powers had to be brought to heel. He did not much mind tearing into them. He just hoped the final outcome would not be disaster.

Martial music came on.

The host stood up. "My lords, this final stage of the conference has been called by the emissary of Earth. I present Sir Robert!"

It did not start well.

There was a buzz among the lords. They looked askance toward Voraz. Wasn't this supposed to be an auction? What was the Earth emissary doing talking to them?

Sir Robert in his regimentals took the center of the platform. The mine spotlight came on.

"My lords," he said in a heavy, sonorous voice, "we have something else to discuss besides auctions!"

"You mean," called Fowljopan, "that we have been delayed here for days for nothing?"

"Our food and atmosphere supply is running out," shouted Lord Dom, "and we are long overdue! Is all this just a waste of time?"

They were turning ugly. Voraz was signifying nothing, just sitting there, expressionless. He had a very poor opinion of this whole action.

"My lords," said Sir Robert, loud enough to be heard across a battlefield, "of recent times there has been talk among you of a reward!"

They quieted instantly. A reward was something to engage one's attention.

"Two sums of money," said Sir Robert, "each amounting to

one hundred million credits, have been put out to encourage a certain search!

"It was," he shouted, "to find the *one!*"

The lords went very alert.

"*There* is the *one!*" and his hand shot out pointing at Jonnie!

The mine spotlight shifted to Jonnie and his buttons and helmet flashed fire.

It was dramatic. A sudden intake of breath from the lords.

It was not exactly as Jonnie had planned it. Sir Robert had let his own feelings change it. Still, it was very effective.

Sir Robert resumed in a strong, triumphant voice. "With the help of a few Scots, *he* put a total end to the most powerful empire in sixteen universes!

"That man," cried Sir Robert, "put a finish on an empire that had crushed and awed you all!

"Among you, you have five thousand planets! *He* put an end to an empire of over a million planets!"

The delegates sat very still. They were afraid of what might be coming. But they were impressed.

"Now do you want to see what he did that ended Psychlo forever?"

There was no wait for an answer. Four Russians and Colonel Ivan raced into the room with the mine cart that carried the atmosphere projector. They put it smartly in place and then drew back to the wall and stood there at attention.

Sir Robert touched a remote relay. The mine spotlight went off, the projector went on.

The view of the Imperial City just before the cataclysm leaped up over the platform. There, as though in visual sight, lay the moving, brilliantly etched ramparts of mighty Psychlo.

Few of the emissaries had ever seen full pictures of it. It would have been worth their lives ever to have set foot in the place. But they recognized the domes of the palace from Psychlo seals. Just seeing Psychlo was an experience.

And then the catastrophe rolled on.

They held their breaths.

Never had such widespread, violent disaster met their gaze.

Psychlo, engulfed in a hellish, molten death, before their staring eyes, turned into a scorching, blazing sun.

The picture went off. The mine spotlight did not come on. Sir Robert's voice battered them from the dark.

"Think of the oppression of Psychlo! Think of how it altered every part of the lives of nations! Think of what its tyranny has done! And realize now it is over and ended, finished forever!

"You owe this man," the mine spotlight hit Jonnie, "a huge debt for freeing you from a monster!"

The emissaries were not accustomed to fear. They felt afraid.

Sir Robert bored on. He had discarded Jonnie's orders. He felt too strongly himself. And he hated these pitiless lords who had possibly ended Scotland. "You have seen what he can do to such a planet as Psychlo!

"*Now* I am going to show you what else he can do!" Sir Robert killed the mine spotlight. He hit the projector remote.

The complete sequence of the Tolnep moon came on. They had viewed bits of this before. But they had not seen the whole finish of that moon, for it had been taken after the fight with Schleim.

Before them, the moon began to crumble and pucker in. The great ship that had tried to escape was eaten up before their eyes once more. And then the views from the Tolnep mountaintop came on.

Jonnie, too, had not seen these. Unless one looked hard, the moon seemed to be turning into gas. And then the gas began to liquefy in the intense cold of space.

The scenes of the piece of scrap iron falling in had a part in it Jonnie had not seen. Just before it entered the surface of the moon, a tongue of lightning roared at it. For an instant it went red hot and then, striking the liquefying gas, crumbled as it visibly drifted down to the still-fluid core.

That moon was now a ball, not just of gas, but of uncountable quintillions of megavolts of electricity. The separation of atoms had generated enormous charge, but there being no oxygen and no second pole to cause flow, the intense cold of space had frozen the resulting electricity. Jonnie realized this was how Psychlo fuel worked, but it had no heavy metal in it, only the more base metals. And that moon would kill any ship that came near it, not by disintegration but by huge powerful charges of electricity. Ah, there came a meteor! Lightning flashed out and melted it.

The emissaries had seen a planet roar into the heat of a sun.

Now they were seeing a moon vanish and then congeal into a cold, deadly, frigid mass of destruction.

Sir Robert's voice went into them like shock waves. *"He can do that to your home planet at will!"*

Had he hit them with a stun gun he could not have produced a more frozen effect.

"And," cried Sir Robert, *"there is nothing you can do to stop it!"*

Jonnie had not planned it this strong. But Sir Robert was getting his revenge.

The mine spotlight hit Jonnie.

Sir Robert shouted at them, "He is going to put twenty-eight firing platforms in twenty-eight separate places—none of them on this planet. *Your* home planet coordinates are going to be set. Those twenty-eight platforms are going to fire, all twenty-eight of them, if any one of you turns hostile!"

This was not what Jonnie had told him to say. The twenty-eight platforms, yes. But not—

"All you have to do," Sir Robert bellowed at them, "is get one small inch out of line, and *all* your home planets will become exactly like that moon!"

They were in paralyzed shock.

"You," cried Sir Robert, "all of you are going to sign a treaty, a treaty that forbids war with us and war between yourselves. If you don't, your home planets, all of them, will disintegrate just like that moon, and you and all your people will go with them!" He pointed again at Jonnie. "He *can* do it and *will* do it! So get right to work and sign a treaty *now!*"

Bedlam!

Every emissary came out of his seat, screaming with rage.

Colonel Ivan and the troopers tensed.

The din almost caved in one's ears.

Sir Robert glared at them, feeling triumphant.

Jonnie walked to the center of the platform. The spotlight followed him. He raised his hands to quiet them. The tumult eased off a bit.

A final cry from Browl expressed the sentiments of them all. "This is a declaration of *WAR!*"

Jonnie stood there. Gradually his presence brought silence.

"It is not a declaration of war," he said. "It is a declaration of *peace!*

"I know that your economics are geared to war. I know that

you consider the best way to get rid of excess population, which you feel you all have, is to engage in war.

"But in wars, one or another of the combatants is going to lose. Each one feels that it could not be he. But there is an even chance it will be.

"So, in declaring peace, we are only protecting you from each other."

Fowljopan suddenly shouted, "When we get home we can send vast armadas against you! Even if you slay all of us, those fleets will still come and destroy you. And as for you, you have laid yourself open to assassination!"

Sir Robert was suddenly in front of Jonnie. "Your fleets will not save your own planets. There is no defense you have against these platforms. Only this one man would know where they are. And if thirty days passed without his resetting them, if anything happened to him and he was not there, those platforms would fire automatically. If something happened to him or to Earth, the home planets of every one of you would be destroyed.

"Also, he has doubles. They look exactly like him; you cannot tell the difference. If you thought you were assassinating him, you would probably only be assassinating a double. And if any double is harmed or touched, those firing platforms fire. All of them!

"It is up to *you* to protect Earth and to protect *him*. The lives of you, your rulers, and your people depend upon it.

"And as to your fleets coming and destroying us, they might well do so. But if you don't get home, they won't know. They would attack here and have no base or people or rulers to return to. Think about that!"

"You are threatening emissaries!" shouted Browl.

"He is *protecting* emissaries!" snapped Sir Robert. "With your war industries tooling up to go full blast, there is more than one in this room who will be representing a government conquered by another!

"You should look at a principle known as [force majeure]. It means that an unexpected and uncontrollable event has suddenly entered upon the universes. A superior force!

"This man and what he can do is an event of [force majeure]. It changes the way things were. It determines how the future will be.

"I am a man of war. You are diplomats! You have it in your

power as of this moment to exert an influence on this [force majeure]. If you do not avail yourselves of it, you are not diplomats but fools and suicidal fools at that!"

"How can we control this?" said a small lord at the back.

Jonnie gently guided Sir Robert to the side. It had not gone as planned. Sir Robert had his own ideas. But Sir Robert had actually done very well. They were listening.

"Before the platforms fired," said Jonnie, "a conference of emissaries would be called. Any unjustness in the action, any mistaken idea, could be handled."

He saw he had some interest.

"The platforms could operate as an arm of such a conference as this," he said.

He could see them sorting it out. He could see that at least some of them were edging toward the idea that this might give them, as individuals, a new power in their governments. It was in their manner. They were not speculating on him but on themselves. They were looking down at their fingers or talons. They were casting their heads to one side or another. But he knew he didn't have them yet.

"It's still an awesome threat," said one.

"It solves nothing in our economies," said another. "On the contrary, it will produce chaos."

Jonnie looked at them. Then he began to realize what he was really dealing with. Every one of these lords and all their peoples had been bred for eons in the shadow of the cruel and sadistic Psychlos. They may have remained politically free but they were stamped with the Psychlo philosophy—all beings are just animals. Greed, profit, and corruption were understood to be the nature of every individual. There were no decencies or virtues. The brand of the Psychlo!

Such sentiments were the ideas of madmen. The Psychlos had tailor-made life this way and had then said, see? this is the way life is.

How could he reach these mighty lords?

"Our industries," another cried, "are geared to war. An intergalactic peace would ruin us, every one!"

Yes, thought Jonnie. The Psychlos wanted any they did business with at war with one another. Who cared what these "free planets" did so long as they bought metal? The Psychlos could crush them at any time. The Psychlos wanted them fighting like animals, believed they were only animals!

Jonnie said, "There are other ways of handling economies. You could phase every war industry you have over to what is called 'consumer production.' You make things for the people. The people are employed. They make things for one another. Your people are your best market for your industries.

"In the near future there will be cross-shipping between your worlds. The Psychlos had it worked out that everything was first shipped to Psychlo. By that very fact, they throttled trade. It will be worked out so that you can quickly and cheaply exchange goods from one system to another. Out of that alone will come prosperity.

"Your people, now starving and rioting, can become gainfully employed in peace industries. They can have things for themselves. Such things as better houses and furniture, better clothes, better food.

"You have a golden chance here to herald an age of prosperity and plenty!"

He wasn't quite reaching them. They were listening, which was all you could say.

"That doesn't handle riots going on right now!" said Dom.

Jonnie looked at him. Now for the big plunge that would make Voraz shudder. "I am sure the Galactic Bank would be pleased to make huge and ample loans to governments that would use the money to buy food for their peoples and tide them over to a time when peacetime industry could be phased in. That and the news of no war again would halt your riots and stabilize your governments."

Browl looked at Voraz. "Would you do that?"

Voraz found he had MacAdam on one side of him and the baron on the other. They both were jabbing him to say yes. He just sat there.

Jonnie was talking again. "And I am sure the bank would make available all necessary loans to convert your industries over to consumer production. Not only that, I am quite sure that the bank would engage in making loans to the private sector: to small businesses and even to individuals so they could purchase new products."

Voraz ignored the jabs he was getting. He was looking at Jonnie. This young man was talking about "commercial banking," a thing usually relegated to petty little stalls on streets, a half-credit here and a quarter-credit there sort of thing.

Jonnie went on. "And I also wish to inform you that many new planets will be on the market. You will be able to borrow money to buy them and ample funds to colonize them with what you now consider 'excess population.' " Jonnie raised his voice a bit and spoke very levelly at Voraz. "Isn't that correct, Lord Voraz?"

The head of the Galactic Bank felt like he was in a tidal wave. He hadn't really agreed he would let this young man set bank policy. Should he get up and denounce it?

The Galactic Bank had dealt with nations. Then suddenly he realized they had depended upon the Psychlos.

Voraz thought furiously. The bankers of the Gredides knew how to do these things. He thought of their own vast population, much of it always unemployed. Suddenly he had a vision of small offices of the Galactic Bank springing up in every town, every continent, every planet, manned with Selachees . . . neighborhood banks! Lending money to small businesses and all comers, even employees. Hadn't they done that once? Before Lord Loonger? Yes. . . he recalled. . . . It would employ an awful lot of Selachees!

And these planets to colonize. Lending money to buy them. . . . He was abruptly hit with the fact that he would have to do *something* with one million, two hundred thousand planets! They couldn't just sit in trust idle. And getting them into production would keep pace with the money supply so as to avoid inflation. This young man was trying to get these excess assets busy.

But, but, but! he protested to himself, this idea of lending money to governments so they could buy food for their people and just give it away. . . . That was *social* banking! It was not unknown. But this phase-over period he was talking about would be long. These governments would be in debt up to their gills.

Suddenly Lord Voraz shot an awed look at Jonnie. Did he really know what he was doing to these haughty lords and their governments—if they approved it all?

Yes! He could see it in his eyes. He did!

"Answer, Voraz!" said Browl. "Is it true you would do those things and on that scale?"

Voraz stood up. "My lords, it so happens that the Galactic Bank has just come into possession of assets a thousand or more times greater than anything it ever controlled before. It will be necessary to put those assets to work. You have all been good credit risks. The answer is, yes. With the proper papers and formalities and commitments, the Galactic Bank stands prepared to make those loans as described.''

The lords sat for a while. This expansion of policy was very sweeping.

''And now, my lords,'' said Jonnie. ''Could we discuss this treaty of intergalactic peace?''

They were hesitating. Worse, some of them looked negative. Mr. Tsung's quote flicked through his mind: ''The power of money and gold over the souls of men passes all wondering.'' These were not men, but it fit. Dominated by Psychlo materialism over the long ages, they had come to think like Psychlos. He would have to treat them like Psychlos, appeal to their personal greed.

It was slightly repugnant to his own ethical sense to do what he knew now he would have to do. But there were too many lives, too many civilizations at stake to fail here.

Jonnie moved to the front of the platform. He knelt down to get his head at the level of theirs. ''Turn off that spotlight!'' he called to the back. It died. ''Turn off all recorders!'' he barked at the button cameras.

''They're off,'' a small thin voice came back.

Jonnie looked at the audience. ''Turn off any recorders you are holding.'' And to the small gray men, ''There must be no bank recorders on and you must so attest!''

The small gray men tapped their lapels with a twist. ''We attest they are off.''

He certainly had their attention now. They were riveted.

Jonnie turned his head to the lords. In a conspiratorial tone that they had to strain forward to hear, he said, ''You didn't think I would leave each one of you personally out of this, did you?''

They were very alert.

''What do your major firms manufacture?'' whispered Jonnie.

''Armaments,'' came whispering back.

''And what do you think will happen to interests in those firms, to their stocks and bonds?''

The lords wondered that he didn't know. ''They'll crash!''

''Precisely,'' said Jonnie, still whispering. ''Let me tell you what this is really all about. If you went home and talked loudly and widely about a treaty forbidding all war, the stocks and bonds and interests in those armaments firms would go out the bottom. And if, without mentioning yet any plans to convert those firms to consumer products or the promises of the bank to make adequate loans, you and your friends let those armaments firms crash and then bought up all their shares and interests, possibly even with loans from the bank, you would own them utterly. Meanwhile, you would be heroes to the people for giving them money for food and the rioting would stop. Then, when you were fully in control, the bank would make conversion loans. Those firms would boom. The merely wealthy would become millionaires, the millionaires would become billionaires."

He crouched there for a moment longer. Then he said, "You must forget that I mentioned this or even spoke of it."

He stood up.

He waited. Had he been wrong? He couldn't be. Their thinking had been conditioned too long by the oppression of the Psychlos.

They began to buzz to one another. Then there was a little tittering laugh behind one hand, a drawing closer together of heads.

Whispered remarks began to drift up to Jonnie. "I can get a new mistress." "My wife always hated that old castle." "I won't have to sell my yacht."

Their heads were together again, whispering. Jonnie couldn't make it out.

Then suddenly Fowljopan stood up among the mob. "Lord Jonnie, we have forgotten what you said. None of it will be repeated by us."

Fowljopan seemed to grow in size. "Build your platforms! We are going to write the toughest, clawproof, iron-hard, most vicious antiwar treaty you have ever heard of!"

He turned toward the back. "Turn on the lights! Turn on the recorders!"

Almost as one being the audience stood. They began to shout.

"Long live Lord Jonnie! Long live Lord Jonnie!"

The applause was enough to knock one down!

Colonel Ivan let out a gusty sigh of relief and took his finger off his gun trigger. Then he hastily formed up troopers in a zone of protection to get Jonnie out of there and back to the small meeting room. These lords were pounding Jonnie on the back, almost knocking him down. Bedlam! He didn't know what Jonnie had said or how he had turned it around. He didn't speculate; he just concentrated on getting Jonnie out of there before they smashed him with good intentions. Knowing Jonnie, the reversal did not surprise him. That was life living around Jonnie Goodboy Tyler!

— 4 —

The Russians had gotten them safely back to the small meeting room and they had seated themselves once more.

Dries Gloton was almost purring as he verified the wording and signatures of the transfer check from the Intergalactic-held funds over to his bank. It was not the biggest check he had ever heard of, but it was the biggest that had ever come to deposit in his branch bank. And it wasn't just a check. It meant solvency, reopened doors in the lesser sector offices, employees back on the job. Actually, he didn't have to verify it at all. He knew it was good. But he just liked to read it.

With a flourish, he drew the receipt to him. With an expert flip of his hand he signed it. And then he picked up the mortgage papers and with great, big letters scrawled across it wrote "PAID IN FULL!"

My, but this was worth all those worried months of waiting.

He put the check safely in his pocket and then sailed the receipt and papers with a gay spin back to MacAdam. "Our business is finished. It is a pleasure to do business with you."

But as he let go his grip on MacAdam's hand, Dries saw Lord Voraz was still sitting there, staring blankly at the table. An instant of alarm touched Dries. "Your Worship! Is something wrong?"

Voraz turned to him. Ignoring Jonnie's presence, such was his preoccupation, Voraz said, "Didn't you understand what he did?"

Dries said, "Speculative loans? The lords will try to borrow money to get those shares when they crash. But that is a small matter. Those loans will be good."

"No, no," said Voraz. "What he is doing to those lords and

their governments. No, you don't see. Let me explain. By providing widespread employment and by making it possible for the little creature on the street to borrow money, he is creating an independent working class. In years to come they won't have to stand around, cap in hand. They will become financially independent. The state will depend on them as a market and not be able to neglect them anymore. And huge quantities of bank business will be with that working class."

"I see nothing wrong in that," said Dries. "With all the money those governments will owe us, they'll have to do pretty much what the bank tells them."

"That's just it," said Voraz. "And the bank will tell them more and more to pay attention to the working class because that's where the bank's main interest lies! Those lords and their existing governments will have less and less power. To all intents and purposes they will vanish as a special class."

"Ah," said Dries, remembering his school days. "Social banking."

Jonnie lounged back in his chair at the side. He was a little bit spent. He wished they'd finish up. "It's called 'social democracy,' " he said. "It will work as long as there are lots of new frontiers and room to expand. But we have those and in a few thousand years somebody can think of something else."

Voraz was looking at MacAdam and the baron now. "Do you know what he just did? In that short period in that room in there he freed more people than have been freed in all the revolutions in history!"

"I know he gave us the power to hold those lords in check," said MacAdam. "Shall we finish this bank resolution so we can end this conference?"

Voraz came out of it. He picked up a proxy. "This mentions a second resolution."

The baron came to life. "That's about Lord Loonger."

"Yes," said Voraz. "How long has he been dead, now? Two hundred—"

"Listen," said the baron. "The Psychlos are about the most hated people any universe ever saw. A couple of hundred thousand years ago, your Lord Loonger saved them with the bank. Today, that's not a very popular act."

"Indeed not," said Voraz.

The baron said, "The definition of money is 'an idea backed

with confidence.' It isn't helping your money any to have Lord Loonger's face on all your bank notes!''

Jonnie suddenly stirred; a premonition based on what had happened with Earth money hit him. He was about to speak. Sir Robert's huge hand closed over his mouth and silenced him.

Dries had been looking at Jonnie for the last minute. Without taking his eyes off him, Dries said, ''Your Worship, has it occurred to you that this young man could be part Selachee?'' There was no humor in his voice at all.

Jonnie was absolutely glaring at them above Sir Robert's big hand. He wouldn't fight Sir Robert. But he really had his eyes boring into the rest of them.

''It's his eyes,'' said Dries. ''They've got gray in them. Another color, yes, somewhat like the sea. But look at those eyes. Gray!''

''I certainly see what you mean,'' said Lord Voraz. ''He does resemble a Selachee.''

''I have several picto-recordings of him,'' said Dries. ''From a lot of angles. We can get that painter Rensfin to use them and make an idealized portrait. With the helmet in color. There is a special ink that can make the buttons flash. And we can do the helmet in full color, three-dimensional view. But what should be put on the scroll? 'Jonnie Goodboy Tyler, Conqueror of the Psychlos'?''

''No, no,'' said Voraz.

'' 'Who brought freedom from war'?'' said the baron.

''No, no,'' said Voraz. ''That word 'freedom' would antagonize lords and such. We have to have this really good and final, you know, for we'll be reprinting all currency and retiring all old issues everywhere. We have to add along the bottom, 'Backed by the assets of the Earth Planetary Bank and Intergalactic Mining' or something like that. We can make the picture a bit larger in the center. But the wording . . .'' he trailed off.

MacAdam brightened. ''We've got to get in there what he did. The painter should put in the background a picture of Psychlo exploding. And on the scroll we can put 'Jonnie Goodboy Tyler,' and right under that put 'who brought happiness to all races.' ''

''The very thing!'' said Voraz. ''It doesn't relegate it to just destroying Psychlo. Because that isn't all he really did. People will know fast enough. His popularity will be not just in the stars but all over the stars and planets in sixteen universes!''

Lord Voraz sat forward and drew the resolution to him. He penned in the wording for the bank note. And then he shot his cuffs, raised his pen in a flourish, and signed the resolutions.

It was all finished. The small gray men got up. They were all beaming smiles. Sir Robert let go of a morose Jonnie and they shook hands all around.

"I think," said Voraz to MacAdam and the baron, "that we can work together splendidly! It is banking right after my own heart!"

They laughed. The small gray men gathered their papers and left.

"Wheeoo and whuff!" said MacAdam, grinning from ear to ear. "We're free and clear and sailing like birds!" He looked at Jonnie. "Thanks in no small part to you, laddie!"

— 5 —

MacAdam and Baron von Roth were picking up their papers, admiring the signatures, getting ready to leave.

Jonnie said, "How did you get those directors in Snautch to pay enough attention to you to listen?"

The baron boomed a laugh. "It was the way we started our account. It went all through the bank in seconds. Since the Psychlos hogged it and it was already scarce, gold in the Gredides is soaring at half a million credits an ounce. We opened our account with gold. Your gold, Jonnie. Near a ton of it. We melted it into ingots some time ago. Almost broke our back lugging it into the bank. They hadn't seen that much gold in a century!"

Jonnie laughed. "So even Terl's gold came in handy."

"After all that work at the lode," said MacAdam, "that gold belonged to you and the crews! We'll bring it home, if you want. But it's on exhibit right this minute behind armored glass in what's left of the main foyer of the Galactic Bank in Snautch! Historic gold, Jonnie."

"Another thing," said Jonnie, "what did you do with Ker that got him to sign those papers?"

"Ker?" said the baron. "Well for one thing, he's your friend,

Jonnie, and we said it would help you. But Stormalong saw your views of Psychlo that night and he told Ker it was one dead planet. You never saw such relief! He's always felt hunted by them. So as the last official Planet Head—he even had his appointment papers and they're attached to the deed—he was really glad to be rid of it. We promised him a standard employment contract minus the clause to ship the body home. We let him keep the few hundred thousand credits he hooked out of the loot of his predecessor and guaranteed him breathe-gas for the rest of his life. I hope we can fulfill the latter."

Jonnie thought of the moon, Fobia. Yes, they could pump tons of it into bottles with the transshipment rig. "No pain. Easy."

Jonnie watched them packing up and then said, "You two certainly did a brilliant job! Really extraordinary."

They grinned at him. "We had a good example. You!"

"But," said Jonnie, "how did you know to word that Intergalactic sale contract that way for Terl to sign?"

MacAdam laughed. "When Brown Limper Staffor tried to use it to secure his new currency issue, we saw that it wasn't a legal contract. Terl had even tried to forge his own signature!" He had a copy of the original and it *was* a ridiculous mess. "So the baron and I got to thinking. It had been nearly eleven months since you sent those bombs to Psychlo and there had been no counterattack. If Psychlo were gone, then according to Ker, there wasn't much chance of other mining planets having enough breathe-gas left. They'd all be dead."

"So," said the baron, "we took a banker's chance and worded it so that it was valid either way."

"And there's one additional reason," said MacAdam, "knowing how you operate. If you set out to destroy Psychlo, which you did, we put our bets on the fact that you had really done it. And we were right!"

"You can't go very wrong putting your chips on Jonnie," said the baron. He hitched a stack of documents under his arm and picked up a bulging brief case, looking around to see if they had everything. "Then, we're all set."

"Oh, no, we're not!" said Sir Robert. His tone was so positive and censorious that they stopped and looked at him, startled.

"I think," said Sir Robert, "that it's a wee bit disgraceful, the way you use this poor lad!"

"I don't understand!" said MacAdam, shocked.

"You use his picture on Earth currency, you use his energy and ideas to further your own ends. You own the bulk of sixteen universes. You're now plotting to put his face on Galactic money. And here he is, poor as a church mouse. Why, he doesn't even collect his own pilot pay that I know of! I know you're going to lend him money for a factory. But what's that? just a plan to get him in debt. You should be ashamed of yourselves!" And he meant it.

He couldn't have had more effect on MacAdam and the baron if he'd shot them with a stun gun.

Jonnie had tried to stop Sir Robert the moment he had gotten an inkling of what the old Scot was saying. Jonnie didn't think he needed any money: if he was hungry he could always go out and hunt. But Sir Robert's hand had stopped him.

The baron looked at MacAdam and MacAdam looked at the baron. Clearly they were two very puzzled men.

Sir Robert just kept on glaring at them. It was very uncomfortable. Finally, Sir Robert said, "You might at least give him a little payment for using his picture!"

Suddenly a light seemed to dawn on MacAdam's face. He dropped his bundled documents on the table and began to riffle through a near-bursting attaché case. He found what he was looking for and, holding it, sat in a chair before them.

"Oh, Jonnie, Jonnie, please forgive us. It is plain you don't know." He began to open up some documents.

"When you never mentioned it," said the baron, "we thought you didn't want it known."

MacAdam was holding out the information announcement of the charter of the bank. "The Earth Planetary Bank was chartered by the original, valid, thirty-Chief Council. This was the information sheet that was released about it." He took the second document he held and opened it. "But this is the actual charter as passed. The actual charter is the only one valid under law and the baron and I have wondered many times why they were different. But do you remember who was sometimes acting as secretary of the original Council?"

The information sheet on the charter mentioned only MacAdam and Baron von Roth.

The baron and MacAdam looked at each other and in chorus said, "Brown Limper Staffor!"

"For reasons of his own," said MacAdam, "he miscopied the

resolution for public release. We stupidly thought you didn't want it disclosed.''

He opened up the original charter and there at the top, ahead of the names of Baron von Roth and Andrew MacAdam, was the name, bright and clear: Jonnie Goodboy Tyler!

''Haven't you ever noticed we always try to ask your opinion of any big deals?'' pleaded the baron, very contrite.

''You were doing so many things more important that we just carried on,'' said MacAdam. ''But Sir Robert! This lad is the owner of a third part of the Earth Planetary Bank. By charter!''

The baron said to Sir Robert, ''Jonnie now owns two-ninths or about twenty-two percent of the Galactic Bank and a third of Intergalactic Mining Company.'' He turned to MacAdam. ''Maybe we *should* make it more.''

MacAdam looked at Sir Robert. ''Did you think we would leave the poor lad, as you call him, out in the cold? He also owns part of that ton of gold. And altogether you'd need a computer to add up his money. It's in the quintillions! He's the richest poor lad these sixteen universes have ever seen, including the late Emperor of Psychlo!''

Sir Robert let go of Jonnie and suddenly began to laugh. He punched Jonnie in the shoulder. ''Get along with you, you church mouse in disguise.'' He looked at the others. ''Aye, gentlemen, I'll let it be and say enough's enough. Just barely, mind, just barely! Say,'' he added, ''maybe you should go out there and buy him half a dozen of those fancy lords for his gillies!''

''He already bought them,'' said MacAdam. ''Down to the last bauble in their boots!''

All but Jonnie boomed out laughter. His head was going round. Quintillions? The number was unreal. Maybe he could buy one of those woven leather lead ropes for Windsplitter. Or buy some new furniture if Chrissie had lost all hers. . . .

The thought of Chrissie hit him. He had been keeping it suppressed so he could keep on going.

MacAdam and the baron collected up their things again and walked out shaking their heads and muttering, ''Brown Limper!'' And, ''Made trouble clear to the end!''

A wailing, petulant voice cut into the room and Sir Robert looked up. Stormalong was behind two Russians at the room entrance who were stolidly blocking him out of it. ''Sir Robert!

Please come out here! I've had a dispatch that's been waiting for you for hours and hours and hours!''

Sir Robert pushed past the Russian guards and vanished.

Jonnie sat there, a little bit spent, trying to get oriented to what the rush of events added up to, trying to decide what he should do now. He made up his mind. Nothing was holding him here. He would go out and get a plane and get to Scotland to help. He grabbed his helmet off the floor. The two Russians at the door parted to let him through.

He collided with Sir Robert. The old Scot was standing there, a written message in his hand. He was crying and laughing all at the same time.

Sir Robert pushed the dispatch into Jonnie's hand. ''Ah, weel! 'Tis quite a mess. But Jonnie, Jonnie, th' auld Rock protected them a'!''

Edinburgh! They had gotten through the last tunnel at dawn today. They were half-starved, some injured, all in a state of greater or lesser shock, but they had gotten them out! All twenty-one hundred of them.

Jonnie felt dazed with relief. There were no specific names mentioned in the radio dispatch. He stumbled out into the bowl, meaning to go to ops.

There was someone across the bowl, someone covered with dust but wearing the domed helmet they used in high-speed flying. It was Thor!

Thor was beckoning to him gladly. Thor shouted, ''Look who we got here for you, Jonnie!''

Somebody was rushing toward him. She threw her arms about him, crying his name.

It was Chrissie! Gaunt and pale, her black eyes flooding with tears.

''Oh, Jonnie! Jonnie!'' she was saying. ''I'm never going to leave you again! Never! Hold me, Jonnie!''

Jonnie did. He just stood there, almost crushing her ribs. He held her for a long time. He couldn't talk.

■

PART 31

— 1 —

Jonnie was riding Windsplitter along the banks of the Alzette River in Luxembourg. He was leisurely wending his way home.

It was a lovely summer day: the sunlight spattered down through the leafy trees along the trail, making patterns of green and gold that shifted gently and seemed to slowly echo the soft music of the purling stream.

Windsplitter snorted and tried to rear. It was the bear. The same bear they had seen there several times during the three months they had been in Luxembourg, using this same trail from the old minesite to Jonnie's house. The bear was fishing. He stopped now and tested the environment with his nose and saw them. He was a pretty big bear, brown, about six and a half feet tall as he stood up.

"It's just the bear, you old fraud," said Jonnie.

Windsplitter sort of laughed and settled down. He did what he could to make life more exciting. And ever since the horses had been flown down from Russia they had been getting fat from idleness. Jonnie always rode him down to the minesite mornings and left him to poke around the strange doings there until Jonnie rode home. Just now he would have been far happier with a good old flat-out run through these interesting, summer-dressed woods. But he stood still, obedient to a heel command.

Jonnie sat and idly watched the bear. It had resumed its fishing, seeing no menace in the horse and rider on the other bank of the shallow stream. Jonnie bet if he had been a Psychlo, that bear would have left the country! And would have still been running all the next day. Jonnie indifferently wanted to see if the bear would catch any of the big trout with which the stream abounded.

For all this beautiful day, Jonnie had a small feeling of

disappointment. He had awakened that morning with the odd conviction that this new day was going to bring something really eventful, some piece of good news. And all day he had been anticipating it.

He reviewed what had happened so far to see if any bright event had been missed by him.

He had gone, pretty much as usual, down to the old minesite to find the routine bedlam in progress. Three months ago he had bought the old Grand Duchy of Luxembourg from the Intergalactic holdings. The Psychlos had had an iron mine there which they had worked in a lackadaisical fashion. They had also built a small steel mill and a forge which they used to turn out hooks, ore buckets and such for their mines on Earth.

The invaders had not touched the place, already well defended, and the deep underground levels had been ideal for doing the final setup of consoles. Angus MacTavish and Tom Smiley Townsen worked there, behind vault doors. They had streamlined assembly so all they had to do was implant the pattern of the circuit on the insulating board, assemble the console, and shove it into a shipping case. Everything else was preconstructed practically out in the open since it gave away nothing.

In fact nobody but Jonnie, Angus, Tom Smiley, and Sir Robert knew that the consoles were completed at Luxembourg. The preassembly even included boxing. People who did it thought Angus and Tom Smiley were just inspectors. But these two, working only a couple of hours a day, using designed patterns and tools, withdrew the "preconstructed" console out of the case, finished it, sealed it, and then lined it up in the rows of them.

A heavily guarded convoy of trucks then drove them an incredible distance down to an ancient tunnel, once called Saint Gottard, about nine miles long. There the boxes were unloaded onto mine platform cars and sent on the ancient rails to the tunnel center. An automatic machine stamped them "completed" as they were passed through a blocked chamber and put them onto a new set of mine platform cars.

A brand new set of trucks, much more heavily guarded, then rushed them to the new firing platform that was now located in a mountain bowl outside Zurich. There, they were routed and shipped.

As Jonnie, Angus, and Tom Smiley had set up the tunnel and

as it was heavily gunned and guarded, nobody knew who did the final assembly. Some thought there were special personnel or gnomes or something that lived in that tunnel and did the work.

They were batting out about two hundred consoles a day. The preassembly people were making the whole platform and poles and wiring since none of that was secret, and they were being shipped right along with the consoles.

No, mused Jonnie. There was nothing startlingly new in all that today. It was last week when Tom Smiley had told him Margarita was going to have a baby.

The bear had gotten his first trout. He batted it way up on the bank, looked around, and then went back to fishing. Windsplitter had found some young grass and was noisily pulling it up and eating it.

There had been nothing new with the Chatovarians. The bank had informed Sir Robert the moment all arms and related firms had crashed but good in the Chatovarian Empire and Sir Robert and Angus and half a dozen Selachees had sped there.

The Chatovarians had the reputation of being the best defense builders. It was their boast that no Psychlo attack had ever broken through in the entire seven-hundred-planet empire. They had even shot down gas drones. So, for that and other reasons, the new teleportation company—now called "The Rig Industry" after Jonnie rejected using his name on it—had done business with the Chatovarians. The Selachees had helped Angus find the right companies and had helped Sir Robert do the purchasing and they now owned eleven Chatovarian firms, each one specialized in what they needed. There had been no dearth of firms for sale and no lack of engineers and workers in that heavily overpopulated empire—forty-nine trillion!

They had left the main offices in Chatovaria and only working sections were here.

No, there'd been no new good news about all that! Rather, a bit of bad news. The main offices of those firms were costly to maintain as they couldn't fire key staff there. And the problem of what they should now manufacture at home was coming up.

Their technology and ability were good. Jonnie had a little trouble with their math—they used a binary system as everything they had ran on computers and circuits. But everything they built was just great. With one exception.

Jonnie could not abide reaction engines. Flying one was a

drag. And they required special runways and pads to land. They were fine out in space but not for atmosphere transport. You couldn't even stunt them really.

The Chatovarians themselves were all over the place at Luxembourg. They were nice people. They stood about five feet tall, had somewhat flat heads and big buck teeth. They were a bright orange-tan. Their hands were a trifle webbed but very nimble. And they were strong. Jonnie had found that out when he was fooling around wrestling with one of their engineers. Jonnie had come within an ace of not being able to throw him. And they were always going fast. Work, work, work!

They ate wood. And the first thing they did when their crews arrived was plant about fifteen thousand acres of assorted trees, planted with the speed of machine guns into what they called "catalyst pots." This was so they could have something to eat.

They had a bit of conflict with the three Chinese engineers that were here. The Chinese like to build out of wood and the Chatovarians thought that was an awful waste of good food. The Chatovarians loved to work with stone: they had small beam tools, like swords, and they cut stone with splice-notches so it would hang together with no mortar. Then they annealed the stone and made it join molecularly so it was armor-hard. And the whole grain of the stone came out in bright, glossy colors. Very pretty. They taught the Chinese how to do it and the Chinese taught them how to weave silk, so all was forgiven and it came out with smiles, but it was touchy for a while.

Going to a Chatovarian dinner was like walking into a lumber yard. Jonnie had to make them promise not to gnaw down all the trees in sight.

The Chatovarians tended to overstaff. And unless Jonnie dreamed up some consumer product for the home offices to build, the red ink on their balance sheets would splash into blood.

He wanted to get them building teleportation motor cars and planes. But he didn't know how to make a teleportation motor and all efforts to work it out failed. Those blasted Psychlo mathematics! Nothing ever balanced.

The thought made him restless. The bear had caught another fish. The sunlight played over Jonnie's buckskin shirt.

He had been *sure* something nice would happen today. Well, the day wasn't over.

He touched Windsplitter's shoulder and the horse decided it was a signal to run, which it wasn't, and went tearing up the trail for home.

— 2 —

They burst out of the forest and rushed toward the palace and then Windsplitter made a huge show of how hard it was to stop—it wasn't—and reared and pawed the air.

"Show-off," Jonnie accused him.

It hadn't been all that much of a run—only half a mile. But Windsplitter was content. The row that was going on in the middle of the ten-acre lawn attracted him.

Stormy, the lame Blodgett's colt—he looked just like Windsplitter even with his much-too-long legs—and a huge tan dog that had recently trotted out of the forest and adopted Chrissie, were romping and plunging and racing away and pretending to stomp and bite, always missing. Blodgett was looking on without much concern and Windsplitter walked over to her.

Jonnie slid off and raised his hand to the Russian in the control turret hidden in the right-hand tower. A flick of a white sleeve as the guard waved back.

This place had really changed. The only trouble with it was, it looked too new and shiny and it certainly now would never age. The Chinese engineers had understood, but the Chatovarians just couldn't grasp that a place should show a little age.

Jonnie remembered when Chrissie had first spotted the place. They were in a small plane and Jonnie, having just bought the duchy, was trying to get some idea of its layout. Chrissie had all of a sudden leaned out the window and shouted, "There! There! There!" and nothing would do but that he land and let her look at the place. She had still been gaunt and he couldn't refuse her much.

The building had stood in the middle of a wilderness that might have once been parks. Hard to tell. Hard to tell even that the piled ruin of stone had ever been much but rocks.

Chrissie had raced around, heedless of the briars that plucked at her buckskin leggings, shouting back at him in wild excitement. She pointed to a fifty-acre plot crying, "And that's *just* the place for a cattle yard!" And to another place, "*Ideal* for your horses! And spreading her arms, indicating some pits, "*Perfect* for tanning vats!" And then tracing a stream that was bubbling along minding its own business, "And this can be diverted to run right by the kitchen door and we can have running water all the time!"

She had gone tearing around on the cracked remains of what might have been room floors and pointed to outlines Jonnie could not see, "A fireplace here. And one here! And another there!"

Then she had stood in front of him and said, "Here we will never be hungry, we will never be snowed in, we will never be cold!" And then defiantly, as though he might say no, "*This* is where we are going to live!"

Jonnie got the Chatovarian chief engineer who had arrived with the two-hundred-Chatovarian first construction contingent and told him to build something modern on the site. He thought he was rid of the problem but the following day he found himself confronted by a very irate Chatovarian architectural team.

When a Chatovarian became incensed he sort of whistled through his teeth, quite distinct from the gurgling sound, like air coming up through a water bottle, when they laughed. The leading architect was whistling his indignation.

It didn't matter whether Jonnie owned the company, but Jonnie was really a Chatovarian, proven by the fact that he had his title direct from the Empress Beaz. And he had to be told that he should know better!

Completely at sea, Jonnie was treated to a dissertation on architecture. They had studied Earth forms and many were all right. Classic Greek and Roman were known in other systems and, if impractical, were still acceptable. Gothic, neo-Gothic, and Renaissance architecture they actually thought quite novel. They could even strain their artistic sensibilities by going along with Baroque.

But *modern?* They quit. Send them back to Chatovaria. Send them back even though they would starve there. Some things one just couldn't do!

It was only then that Jonnie found that "modern" had been a type of architecture prevalent on Earth about eleven hundred years ago; that it consisted of plain, straight up-and-down walls on a rectangular base; that it often was a vast expanse of glass windows; that it had been conceived by somebody dedicated to stamping out all indigenous architecture of an area. In short, "modern" was an architecture that wasn't architecture but just a cheap way to throw rubbish in the air and get paid for it.

The Chatovarian, with a quivering, pointing finger in the direction of the old city of Luxembourg and backed up by the serious nods of five assistants, wailed that that whole town had been built in modern, and on his artistic soul, no such abominations would be perpetuated while he lived!

Jonnie had apologized. The Chatovarian said maybe it came from having to talk in Psychlo. And Jonnie asked what *they* recommended.

Five assistants presented a huge plan instantly.

This building, they said, had been the palace of the Grand Duke of Luxembourg in ancient times. And even though Jonnie did not think so, he didn't say so.

The indigenous architecture, from the castles that lay about, probably had been Gothic and neo-Gothic. And this palace should be like this. Jonnie had delayed long enough to ask Chrissie, but all she gave him were the items she had found that made the place charming, and he had made sure those were included and had told them to go ahead.

Chrissie and he had camped out in the woods, happy to be away from the din, cheerful in a buckskin tent and eating good food cooked on an open fire.

The Chatovarians had cleared the site and erected an armor steel shell. They had then flown down to a couple of marble quarries north of Leghorn in Italy and operated a ferry of ore freighters until they had piles of green and rose and other colored slabs. They had spliced them together into an exterior and interior of polished, armored rock. They had underplated the stream so that it did what it was supposed to do. But they had also installed full plumbing. The fireplaces would burn wood but since this was a waste of good food they also put solar driven infraheaters in them and a simulated flame.

It was a palace all right. And it might be Gothic. But it sure was colorful! Chrissie had been enthralled with it.

Jonnie, as he walked to the arches on the other side of the drawbridge, could hear in the distance the crash and bang of the Chatovarians ripping the old city of Luxembourg into chips.

They had gone through it with historical and artifact survey teams and then the rams had been turned loose. That was the one piece of modern that would not survive.

The bank had already moved back to Zurich and Jonnie would have liked to live there too because of the nearby mountains.

Jonnie halted. Dries Gloton must have been here today for there was a burned spot in the lawn. Dries, after turning over his sector branch office, had been appointed Galactic Bank Liaison with the Earth Planetary Bank. He had been the finder of the "one," but a bank executive couldn't accept such rewards—they would undermine customer confidence—and Voraz had raised Dries' salary to a hundred thousand credits a year—quite enough to maintain his yacht and anything else. Dries had left the yacht here and teleported home, and while he was gone his Selachee crew had been teaching the Chatovarians gambling games and winning a lot of their pay. But the Chinese engineers had been winning it back from the Selachees so Jonnie had kept out of it.

Dries rambled all over in his yacht—an oddity to use a spacecraft to go to the corner store for a bottle of schnapps, but that was Dries. He had taken the job on the condition that he would have long weekends and he seemed to always be going to northern Scotland. He said he was starting a "peppermint industry" on the side, but Jonnie didn't believe him. He was sure something else was involved. Today he had probably brought Chrissie some butter or something.

On the other hand, he might have been settling some accounts with Mr. Tsung. Dries kept certain customers and Mr. Tsung was one of them. Jonnie's account was cared for by fifteen Selachees who worked down at the minesite, and Dries had nothing to do with that—it ran about a trillion a day income now and was growing. Mr. Tsung's account was, however, somehow interesting to Dries: Jonnie had offered Mr. Tsung a salary and Mr. Tsung had been very surprised for he said a chamberlain usually paid his boss, from which Jonnie got the explanation of how some guests were always invited and some weren't. But it was Mr. Tsung's daughter that was making money. She was named Lü, after the last Empress of the Han Dynasty, and she was becoming famous. She worked in a little pagoda-like structure out back that was really a disguised antiaircraft pit, and she turned out pictures of tigers in the snow and birds flying and things like that on both silk and rice paper, and they were collector's items, bringing in a thousand credits at a crack. She also worked around the house and helped Chrissie and cut hair.

Jonnie decided he'd better have a metal pad installed for Dries to land on. He got along fine with him now. No use to tell him off.

He couldn't get through the courtyard. Lin Li, Mr. Tsung's son-in-law, had all the banquet hall furniture out and was working it over with molecular metal spray. The young man had an audience of a couple of awed Chatovarians. He could "paint" pictures, freehand, with a metal spray gun and a piece of cardboard to catch the splatters. He was very quick. Right now he was doing a scene Jonnie knew he must have gotten from pictures of tapestries—a lot of knights. He was putting it on the huge banquet tabletop.

He had stopped doing dragon medallions by hand. As they were all the same, a couple of Chatovarian mechanics, awed by his ability, had gotten him to do a perfect one and then had made a machine to turn them out at about ten thousand an hour. The demand out in the universe was such that they were back-ordered even so.

Jonnie couldn't get through without interrupting Lin Li. So he stood there watching. Chrissie and Mr. Tsung had been talking about the possibility of some of these Chatovarians getting out of hand at a party and eating up the furniture. That must be what this metal plating was all about! They had to suit the dwelling to the many guests they always had.

The vague feeling of disappointment hit him again. He had been certain, when he rose, that this was a sort of special day. That something wonderful was going to happen. It hadn't.

Lin Li had just started on a ferocious figure of a charging knight. He was using a scarlet metal, putting blood on a blade. It made Jonnie think of the red ink coming in so far on the Chatovarian company, "Desperation Defense." If he could just unravel motors he could put them over into passenger transport. But he was condemned if he would continue with reaction engines.

Lin Li was guiding the molecular spray, now gray, to make the armor. The Chatovarians were looking on with awe. One of them was holding a spare gun, ready to hand it to Lin Li. They weren't assistants. They just wished they could do things like that. The Chatovarian closed the trigger of the gun to test it.

Suddenly Jonnie knew it had happened. The nice thing!

He sped back out the arch and raced all around the palace side and jumped the creek and popped into the back door.

Chrissie, hair tied back, was filling a big bowl, held by Mr. Tsung, from a pot on the fire.

"Chrissie!" said Jonnie. "Get your things!"

Pattie was sitting over in the corner. Pattie never said anything these days. She just looked down. Tinny, the Buddhist communicator, had been trying to talk to her as she often did.

"Tinny!" said Jonnie. "Call the minesite! Get me a marine attack plane on the pad in twenty minutes! Call Dr. MacKendrick in Aberdeen and tell him to come right away to Victoria!"

"Pattie doesn't feel well," said Chrissie.

"Bring her along!" said Jonnie.

"Is it a diplomatic conference or a scientific one?" said Mr Tsung, monotone through the vocoder.

"Medical!" said Jonnie.

Mr. Tsung put down the bowl and raced off to put a white coat and a pair of spectacles—which had no glass in them—in a sack. That was proper dress he had seen in ancient pictures.

"Jonnie!" said Chrissie. "This is venison stew!"

"We'll eat it on the plane! We're headed for Africa!"

— 3 —

Jonnie headed the marine attack plane slightly east of south and turned on his viewscreens. This copilot was new, from the French refugees in the Alps, named Pierre Solens: he was quite young, recently trained; he still had a little trouble speaking Psychlo. Usually his duties consisted of simply shifting the minesite planes about, but as compound duty pilot it had been up to him to deliver the ship to Jonnie's house; he had not dreamed that in the next few minutes he would be flying copilot to *the* Tyler and heading for Africa. He had started out all right but when he saw how Jonnie took off he had become overawed. He had never seen a plane lofted that way, like firing a bullet! And now they were flying hypersonic at only fifteen thousand feet. Would they clear the French and Italian Alps?

"We're awfully low," he timidly offered.

"People in back," said Jonnie. "Can't let them get too cold. Get to work with those viewscreens so we won't be running into any drones."

Drones, drones, drones! All his life Jonnie had been being looked at by drones! It was no exception now. The Chatovarian defense system was only half-complete: despite buying the company, it was an expensive system, almost three times as costly as the one the small gray men had described, but it was about ten times as good. Automatic blast cannon that fired fifteen hundred miles into space could shoot down a space fleet with one salvo; atmosphere drones that fired; space drones that patrolled orbits; probes that scanned anything moving within ten light-years. Real armor cable would make every city untouchable.

As the system was incomplete, a lot of emergency stand-in drones were about and they were attracted to anything flying. A huge green flashing light was going on top of the plane, and the box there, newly installed, was sending out the "code of the day," which was so fast and so scrambled and changing microsecond to microsecond that an attacker could not hope to duplicate it. If the drones didn't see and hear it, they'd shoot.

Ah, yes, here came the Mediterranean emergency drones, three of them, shooting over to "have a look." The copilot was slow and Jonnie tuned a knob to focus them.

Chatovarian drones, all right. Each one had a big eye painted on its nose. But those big, staring eyes were not a Chatovarian fixation on decoration: a pilot would instinctively shoot into the center of them, and if a pilot did, the drone used the shot as a return carrier wave to send a surge back that blew up the attacker's own ammunition and thereby his ship. Don't shoot at one of those eyes!

Nevertheless they were a bit disconcerting, glaring out of the viewscreen. They nudged in like sniffing dogs, and then satisfied by automatically cross-verifying with each other, they fell away and returned to their patrol sectors.

The French pilot was looking back at the Alps. They hadn't hit any!

But Jonnie had his screens on the orbit drones now. They seemed to be disinterested, satisfied by the code of the day.

And what was this? He had a space probe on the screen. He hadn't known you could see one. Was it hostile?

Like any star drone or probe, these things had a "lens" that was made of a "light magnet." This reacted on light beams and pulled them in from a zone many miles in diameter and concentrated them, magnetically corrected for aberration, into a spot smaller than a dot on paper. In effect, it made a lens many, many miles in diameter. The problem was too much light rather than too little, and they had blinders or filters that dropped into place to keep them from burning out their receivers or recording discs should they turn toward a sun too close. In that way one could get magnifications into the tens of trillions.

One of the contractors had drilled Jonnie in on command controls and a box of these existed overhead. Jonnie flipped a switch and tapped the probe's receiver and shifted the image to his own central viewscreen.

It was their own space probe all right. He was looking at the copilot and himself behind their own viewscreen. Yet that space probe was over ten thousand miles away. It must be at the near end of a run. Friendly, so he threw the tap off.

He didn't really think anybody would attack Earth now. The peace treaty had gone in, as promised, with claws! Very, very popular. The delegates had even taken home copies of the end of Psychlo and the death of Asart. The bank was shoveling out food loans like a waterfall. Consumer products had not yet begun to roll. That would take time. He hoped he could get at the secret of how one built a teleportation motor: that would open the door to a lot of consumer products. And even more important, keep the vehicles they had here operating. These planes wouldn't last forever.

"Take over," he told the French pilot, Pierre, and went back into the body of the plane.

Chrissie stirred herself and unwrapped a bowl. "I'm afraid the venison stew might be cold now."

Jonnie sat down in one of the huge bucket seats. Pattie was down at the back of the plane, just sitting there, looking down. It worried him. Sometimes she went for walks at night. Sometimes he could hear her in her room, crying. Because she was only ten he had thought she would recover. But she hadn't.

Mr. Tsung, he saw, was going to use this time-space to catch up with his diplomatic and social duties, for here he came with about ten pounds of paper. Jonnie put his attention on the stew. It wasn't cold.

"The week's dispatch box came in from Snautch," he said.

So that was what Dries was doing coming down from Zurich. "Send the business matters down to the minesite office; it's their job."

"Oh, I did, I did," said Mr. Tsung. "These are all social and diplomatic. Invitations to weddings, banquets, christenings. Requests to address meetings—"

"Well, thank them or tell them no," said Jonnie.

"Oh, I have, I have," said Mr. Tsung. "We don't have any trouble. We use a vocoreader, a vocoder, and a vocotyper. We can handle correspondence in about eighteen thousand languages now. But this is going to get heavier."

Here it comes, thought Jonnie. Mr. Tsung's elder brother had been appointed chamberlain to the court of the Chief of Clanfearghus. His younger brother was busy starting up a diplomatic college in Edinburgh.

"You got another brother?" said Jonnie around a mouthful of stew.

"I am sorry that I don't," retorted Mr. Tsung. "I'm talking about the nephew of Baron von Roth. He wants to apprentice as a diplomat in my office."

"Fine," said Jonnie.

Mr. Tsung adjusted the vocoder volume higher as the plane was roaring more with Pierre at the console. "I want to hire about thirty more Russian and Chinese girls to train as clerks and vocotyper operators. It's really very simple. One reads invitations with a vocoreader into one's own language and then one uses a vocoder to talk to the vocotyper and it types the answer back into the tongue of the original letter—"

"Go ahead," said Jonnie.

"I think there should be a new building to take care of all these people and files. Something more on a Chinese—"

"Go ahead," said Jonnie.

"There was one letter that I pulled out that you should see," said Mr. Tsung. "It's from Lord Voraz to MacAdam with a copy to you, and Dries said MacAdam had to hear from you before he answered."

Trouble, thought Jonnie.

"Voraz wants a formula to determine the validity of a commercial loan."

"That's not diplomatic or social," said Jonnie.

"It's kind of diplomatic," said Mr. Tsung, "Voraz and

MacAdam being who they are, one does not wish to see tensions. The whole problem is *what* consumer products should arms companies convert to. If they convert to the wrong ones, the whole program will fail and the bank will have granted useless loans."

His own problem in a different dress, thought Jonnie. He thought of the red ink of Desperation Defense.

"Intergalactic Mining," said Mr. Tsung, looking at the Voraz letter, "was sitting on hundreds of thousands of inventions that were on file in the Hall of Legality to prevent other nations from using them. I know this isn't diplomatic, but it could make a big diplomatic mess if the bank lends money to make the wrong products. Also, all the invention formulas are in Psychlo math."

Jonnie had finished the venison stew and he gave the bowl back to Chrissie. There was something in the old man-books about this. What was the subject? . . . Marketing as a factor in profit. "You tell MacAdam to have banks get out survey teams—people that go around and ask people questions—and find out what people in each planetary area think they would want to buy: not what they *should* buy, but what they *want* to buy. Don't offer suggestions. Just ask them. For all they know it might be as little as a . . ."—he recalled his own discovery that glass would cut—". . . as something to skin hides more easily. The subject is 'marketing surveys.' And I'm working on Psychlo math right now."

Tinny had been listening. She was already punching phone buttons. This was a new system. But it was kind of overdone. The smallest exchange the Chatovarians made for a planet had two billion individual radio channels, and since the war, they only had about thirty-one thousand people. There were radiophone printers everywhere. She was on to the Zurich bank, plugging in the recording she had just made of his voice. Tsung saw Jonnie wasn't going to say more and nodded to her and she let it start. The printed reply would be rolling off onto MacAdam's desk right now. She fed in the reference letter Tsung gave her.

"Dries left you this," said Mr. Tsung. He handed Jonnie a little blue disc with a pin on the back of it. It said "Galactic Bank" on the front of it. When he saw Jonnie looking at it but not taking it, he added, "The Chatovarian deadly-device officer passed it."

Jonnie took it. "He give you anything else?"

"Oh, you know Dries," said Mr. Tsung. "He said there was

an excess supply of butter up in the Highlands now and he brought Chrissie a whole bucket of it. Some old woman has fifteen Holstein cows and he says he's financing a butter business."

Jonnie laughed. There had been no Holstein cows in Scotland that he knew of. Dries must have persuaded a pilot to fly them up from Germany or Switzerland where they roamed wild. Another "peppermint industry." "Do we give him anything in return?"

"Oh, yes," said Mr. Tsung. "We always feed him a tub of fried rice. He loves it! And my son-in-law found a book of colored plates of fish and he made up some fish medallions and we give him one of those each time. He says they're valuable."

"And you pay Lin Li," said Jonnie, wise to the ways of commerce and the Chinese.

"Of course. From your social petty cash."

The term "petty cash" could be pretty general. The Earth Planetary Bank was paying for Earth's defense system out of petty cash.

But Mr. Tsung was going on. "That button is a pre-run of prizes they are giving out in their new neighborhood bank program all through the universes—you know, to people who open up accounts. It will in each case be in the local language. You put it on your color tab or a place like that and then you hum a note and as long as you move your mouth, the button will sing. They are gathering up all the folk songs of each local region."

Jonnie got a kit out of his bag. He had brought it to help the project he was on right now. He took a microannealer and opened the button up and looked at its insides with a microviewer. It was just a molecular-sized set of storage cells with little triggers and relays. A tiny battery charged itself from room heat. An electron vibrating prong set atmosphere molecules in motion to make sound. Simple, rather cheap.

But that wasn't what Jonnie was looking for. He often suspected the bank acquired information in peculiar ways and he checked vocoders and suchlike to make sure they didn't contain a radio mike or a recording thread that could be taken back later. He had never found one so far. But that was the world he now lived in.

He microannealed it back together and hung it on his buckskin collar.

"That isn't a standard one, he said to tell you," piped Mr. Tsung through his own monotone vocoder. "He collected some old records of American ballads and put them in it. There aren't very many Americans, so it won't be manufactured for them."

Jonnie cleared his throat and moved his mouth. The button hummed a wordless tune. Hadn't he heard that tune before? Scottish, German? Ah . . . it was called "Jingle Bells." Then the button sang:

"Galactic Bank!
"Galactic Bank!
"My friend so tried and true.
"Oh what fun it is to have
"A neighbor such as you!"

And then in a proud voice it said, "*I* am a customer of the Galactic Bank!"

Well, that certainly wasn't any "American ballad!" Was Dries having a joke? He never joked, really. A very serious, small gray man.

Jonnie was about to take it off. But his laugh started it up again.

"Home, home on the range,
"Where the deer and the buffalo play. . . ."

Jonnie remembered you had to keep moving your jaws to make it sing. Saliva pops or muscle tension or something. He started moving his jaws again.

"Where there seldom is heard
"A discouraging word. . . ."

"Mister Tyler!" came through the intercom from the nervous Pierre, "I can see Lake Victoria on the viewscreens through the overcast. It's totally clouded in ahead. Hadn't I better go on to Kariba?"

Jonnie went forward and took over the console. It was always overcast at Victoria.

Jonnie opened his mouth to call in for clearance. But the button sang:

"And the skies are not cloudy all day!"

What a lousy forecast, thought Jonnie, and put the button in his pocket.

— 4 —

After glancing over the flying conditions, Jonnie could not much blame Pierre. For a while now they had been flying through the night: a fact which an experienced instrument pilot would not have thought about twice, and indeed, Jonnie had scarcely noticed it.

By looking very hard, and only then with trained pilot's eyes, one could just barely make out Mount Elgon rising above the black cloud carpet, for there was no moon and such a peak became mainly visible because it blocked out certain stars.

It was the screens which caused Jonnie to forgive Pierre. So thick was the cloud layer below them that the viewscreens, aimed at it, were more snowstorm than image. You would actually have to know the shape of the lake and the compound to have any notion of what you were looking at. A lot of electrostatic disturbance; it must be raining like fury at the compound, rain flicked with lightning.

Pierre, however, was in a state of mind that wasn't asking for anything but to stand on solid ground. He could not read the screens. He could not see anything but some stars above them and blackness below them, a blackness lashed now and then by some internal flash. He thought they were done for if they tried to go down through that. Who knew what hill they would run into? He would have been petrified had he known that Mount Elgon was higher than they were flying but mercifully he did not know that. Nor, even more frightening, that they had passed by a couple of peaks even higher. Magnifying his alarm, Monsieur Tyler had come back to the pilot seat and hummed a strange song. Mon dieu, one did not sing when one faced certain death. Lunacy!

Victoria gave them permission to land and Jonnie felt his way down through the rain clouds. His screens didn't clear up, but knowing the area, he could identify the scraps of image he sometimes glimpsed. It was useless to look through the screen: it looked like it had a fire hose being played on it.

Jonnie felt for the ground with his skids, more concerned about a bump affecting his passengers than about where he was. He did it very smoothly and Pierre was again alarmed when Jonnie turned off the motors—he thought they were still in the air!

The rain was actually making it hard to talk in the cab of the plane. Jonnie threw open the door and there was Ker standing there, water cascading off him in the plane lights.

Even allowing for the deluge, Ker was awfully glum-looking. He was usually very glad to see Jonnie.

The last time Jonnie had been in Africa, he and Ker had spent three nights working the Kariba rig. The planet Fobia had been very elusive: they had no coordinates for it beyond "somewhere around the Psychlo sun," and for a while it had seemed they would never discover it and Ker would eventually die from having no breathe-gas.

The planet was, however, located: it was doing a squashed ellipse. Fobia's perihelion (the point in its orbit where it was nearest its sun) was so much closer to its sun than its aphelion (the point in its orbit where it was furthest), and the distance to its sun from these two points was so vastly different, near and far, that anyone trying to live on Fobia would have perished, even a Psychlo.

Fobia went through three states: as it swung away from its sun, its atmosphere chilled and became liquid; as its distance increased, the liquid froze to solidity; as it again approached its sun, the sequence reversed and the atmosphere became gaseous again. But this long period of having a "summer"—and the Fobia year was about eighty-three of Earth's—permitted moss and other plants to grow and these flourished for a time and then, as the atmosphere liquefied, remained in a state of suspended animation until summer came again.

Although they had an awful time with camera triangulation to estimate its orbit, the end product had been beyond Ker's wildest dreams. The planet was well into "autumn" and it was no real trick to pump huge cable tanks full of liquid breathe-gas. Not only that but they had brought back about fifty tons of the material needed to make real goo-food. Yes, Ker had been acting like a Psychlo gone to heaven, a most unlikely event, when Jonnie and he had last met.

And here he stood, glum in the rain.

"Hello, Jonnie," he said woodenly.

"What's the matter with you?" said Jonnie. "Lost your loaded dice?"

"Oh, it's not you, Jonnie. I'm always glad to see you. It's that Maz. He was chief engineer here when the place was operating. One of the wounded ones. I got about seventy ex-prisoners from all over and I'm trying to earn my pay by getting this tungsten mine going again."

He moved nearer, the rain cascading down his breathe-gas mask, his tunic sodden with the hot rain that battered him. "I'm no engineer!" he suddenly wailed. "I was an operations officer. We ran out of ore body and the next one is just beyond it someplace. That ——— Maz and all those other ——— Psychlos just sit down there on their butts and gloom! Some ——— fool showed them the pictures of Psychlo blowing up and they just won't do anything!

"I don't know any ——— math and I can't calculate the next ore deposits!"

That's two of us, thought Jonnie. He was glad the girls didn't speak Psychlo. The ex-underworld midget could really swear. But he almost never did unless he was terribly upset. "That's why I'm here," he said.

"Really?" Ker brightened up like a mine charge had gone off in him.

"Has MacKendrick arrived?" said Jonnie.

"Control got a drone report on a plane from Scotland. That MacKendrick? He'd be about three hours behind you."

Three hours! Jonnie had wanted to get to work right away. Well, there was something else he had to do first anyway—get some Psychlo corpses.

"There's people in the back. Do me a favor and get them into the compound."

"Right," said Ker, cheered up. He had a folded mine tarp on his arm he could use on the others as a rain shield. He sloshed toward the rear door unfolding it.

Pierre had been recovering. But now he was horrified to find that Jonnie was rummaging around in a locker for high-altitude suits. Jonnie threw one at him and began to pull on another one.

Jonnie heard the door slam in back and saw dim figures running toward the compound in the rain. He finished zipping up his suit and checked his fuel. Plenty.

Twenty seconds later they were hurtling into the sky again. Pierre was still struggling into the unfamiliar high-altitude suit. Mon dieu, life around Monsieur Tyler was hair-raising!

Jonnie was unperturbed about it all. Up above the rain clouds the screens were clean and by seeing what stars were omitted he could even eyeball the peaks. He left the plane lights on, heading for the glacial snows where they had left the Psychlo corpses. He needed two, he thought. A workman and an executive.

It did not help Pierre's frame of mind at all not to be told where they were going, nor why. Charging into the ink at such speeds appalled him. He did not even look at the viewscreens. His eyes were riveted through the now-streaked windscreen.

Very shortly Jonnie was in the right location. He knew they had left a forklift up here. He would use that to guide in. He supposed that after all this time, the corpses would be pretty well covered with snow.

But Pierre, not knowing what was being looked for or where or why, simply looked through the windscreen, his eyes dilated with something that was getting up close to terror.

Suddenly Pierre saw a whiteness. It had puffs blowing off it in the plane lights. With horror he heard the engines wind down for a landing.

"Don't!" he screamed. "Don't! Don't! You're landing on a cloud!"

Jonnie glanced up through the viewscreen. It did look like a cloud at that, seen from this angle. A high wind was blowing snow about.

Ah, there was the forklift! Up to its seat in snow and ice. The corpses would be lying, covered up, just beyond it.

He had been flying by screens only. They were a long way from the nearest drop-off. He let the ship crunch down into the snow and shut off the motors. The wind was screaming up here; enough to make the plane tremble.

Jonnie settled his air mask on tighter. "Get out and give me a hand!"

Pierre was in a total confusion. He had clearly seen them land on a cloud and he could not understand what was holding the ship up. He knew from their earlier course that they must be close to, if not on, the Earth's equator, and recent studies had told him that the equator was very hot. So snow was the furthest thing from his imagination.

His small tribe had been under the domination of Jesuit priests and they had controlled by instilling a heavy fear of heaven and hell, mostly the latter. The reputation of Monsieur Tyler was itself a matter of growing superstition and awe. It surprised him less that they had landed on a cloud than it did to be told to get out.

Pierre looked at the puffs of white in the ship's light. Yes, a cloud! He fingered the image of a crucified Christ that hung about his neck; he felt he was too young to be a martyr. But there was a solution. He snatched the jet backpack from the compartment behind the seat and hastily shrugged into it. Monsieur Tyler quite probably was able to walk on clouds but that didn't include Madame Solens' son Pierre.

It took a lot of courage to open the door but he did so. He closed his eyes tightly and sprang out, hand on the backpack firing trigger. It was about eight feet down from a seat of such a plane to the ground. But Pierre had been nerved up to fall twelve thousand. When he hit the ground, despite snow, he almost broke his legs. Pierre fell backward in total confusion and lay propped on his elbows in the snow. He could not understand why he had not fallen through the cloud.

Jonnie, intent on his project, was oblivious of all this confusion. He had taken a mine crowbar from the plane's tool kit and was prospecting through the snow for the corpses. They certainly were covered up.

The tip of the iron bar found one. He knelt and brushed away some snow, the particles flying away in the wind. He uncovered the tip of a breathe-gas mask and then the ornament of a cap. Yep, an executive!

He felt around under the monstrous shoulders to see where he had to insert the flat end of the crowbar to pry the monster loose from the adhesions of ice. One of these Psychlos weighed about a thousand pounds, more in all this snow and ice.

Jonnie inserted the crowbar deeper and heaved down on it. The monster was so stuck that the top end of the bar slipped and tore open his high-altitude jacket fastenings.

He tried again, this time giving it all the strength he had. With a creaking, low-pitched sound, the monster moved upward.

But the sound must have been close to that of clearing one's throat. The bank's singing button in his pocket gave out a ballad line with a baritone voice:

"Ghost riders in the sky. . . ."

Pierre, already badly shaken, beheld a demon rising from out of the cloud. And not only that, it was singing in a sepulchral voice.

It was a lot too much. With a low moan, he fainted dead away.

— 5 —

Jonnie loosened a workman's corpse with the bar and then went to the forklift and knocked the ice out of its cogs and ratchets. He was about to start it up when he noticed the absence of Pierre. He had expected him to open the loading doors of the plane at least.

He spotted the man, lying in a shadow made by a balance motor. The snow was already blowing over him. A bit anxiously he checked to see if he was injured, puzzled by the presence of the jet backpack, wondering why he was lying there unconscious. Well, this was no place for even first aid.

Jonnie got the forklift moving and scooped up Pierre. He ran the machine down the length of the ship to the doors and, standing on the seat, got them open.

But the wind, coming from the tail of the plane, was trying to bang the door closed. Jonnie jumped up to the fuselage flooring in hopes of finding something to block the door and stopped in his tracks.

Pattie! She was still in the plane. They must have overlooked her in their scramble to get through the rain. She made so little sound and motion these days she easily went unnoticed.

She must be freezing. Jonnie opened an equipment locker and dragged out a blanket and threw it around her. She hardly even looked up.

All he could find to block the door open was the stick from a map roller and he tried to make it do by butting it against a floor equipment ring and pushing it against a hinge.

He got down and operated the forklift to boost the inert body of Pierre into the plane. He had almost made it when a powerful gust of wind banged the door shut. Once more he climbed into the plane to try to make the stick prop the door. But this time the frail wood splintered.

A soft voice sounded behind him. "I will hold it open for you."

Pattie, gripping the blanket to her with one hand, put the other on the door and braced it open.

This was the first time he had seen her volunteer anything for months.

Jonnie jumped down onto the forklift and raised Pierre up and dumped him on the floor plates. He got into the plane once more and began tugging the man over to the side out of the way and was a bit amazed to see Pattie pulling on the body to help.

So, with Pattie to hold the door open, Jonnie was able to fork the two monstrous bodies out of the snow and dump them into the plane. Pattie was watching him and what he was doing intently.

Shortly he parked the forklift, closed up the plane, and got into the cab out of the cutting wind. He phoned the compound to have a flatbed and forklift waiting and then, checking to see if Pattie was strapped in, shot the plane up into the sky.

He had been prepared to feel his way down through the overcast with half-blind screens and was very happy to see that the worst of the storm and all of its electrical interference had passed by.

It was no longer raining at the compound and they had every pole spotlight on. Quite a crowd had gathered around the waiting vehicles to see the plane come in. The last time Jonnie had seen some of these ex-marines and ex-spacemen had been through gunsights, and it was a trifle strange beholding Jambitchows and Hawvins and such standing around, but they seemed inoffensive enough. Three Chatovarian engineers in bright orange work suits that had "Desperation Defense" written on their chests were in the crowd, probably there doing preparatory surveys to convert this minesite protection over to the new system.

A new plane was there with nobody around it and Jonnie realized that MacKendrick must have arrived. He called Pattie forward and with her under one arm jumped down from the plane.

Ker was sitting on a forklift. "The copilot is in there. He is breathing but he must be injured or something," said Jonnie. "Get him and the two Psychlos down to the hospital."

Jonnie, still carrying Pattie, rushed into the compound to find MacKendrick.

Ker promptly got busy with the forklift and, with an expertise only Ker could achieve with a machine, scooped all three bodies off the floor of the marine attack plane and swooshed them over to the flatbed.

The driver, a newly trained Jambitchow, looked on in wide-eyed shock as he saw two huge Psychlo bodies plump down on the truck with a small human body dropping on top of them.

The first impulse of the crowd, seeing Psychlos, was to retreat, and fast! All the snow and ice had melted off them and to all appearances they might be alive.

The driver was about to get off the truck and put distance between himself and anything that had to do with Psychlos that might suddenly come to life.

Ker withdrew the forks and realized he was in the middle of a commotion and was about to have no driver. "No, no," he shouted. "They're dead!"

Timidly the Jambitchow got back on the flatbed seat. Cautiously the crowd crept forward to get a closer look. Eyes went questioningly to Ker.

"Didn't you hear what Jonnie told me?" said Ker.

No, they hadn't. Too far away.

"Those Psychlos," said Ker, "have been hiding out in the jungle. They rushed out of cover and started to claw the copilot to bits. And it made Jonnie so mad he charged them. He grabbed the throats of both of them at the same time and just plain strangled them to death!"

Mouths were open and eyes were popped. The evidence was right there before them.

After a moment a Hawvin ex-officer said, "No wonder we lost this war."

"Yes," said Ker. "When you get to know Jonnie better, you'll realize that when he gets mad, he gets mad!"

He signaled the flatbed to follow and drove off in the forklift. He just couldn't resist doing what he'd done. But the hardest part was to keep from guffawing in their faces.

— 6 —

Jonnie, when he got into the compound, put Pattie down and went looking for MacKendrick. He found him in the hospital.

"Where's the epidemic?" demanded MacKendrick. "I got your call in the middle of a medical lecture. I brought a whole medical team! And when I get here, I find you've taken off—"

"This time," said Jonnie, "we're going to *do* it!"

"Oh," said MacKendrick. "You mean the capsules. Jonnie, I have tried every way I can think of and there's no getting in those skulls. Too much bone! I thought I showed you!"

The doctor went over to where he'd last left the huge Psychlo skull. He knocked his knuckles on it. "It's just plain, solid bone! The brain is clear down under the lower back plate. If I drill out enough bone to get to it, you'll just have a dead Psychlo.

"Ah," said Jonnie. "You used the word 'drill.' I didn't."

He walked over to the skull and picked it up, all half a hundred pounds of it. MacKendrick had wired on the joints and Jonnie opened the jaw. "Now watch the earbones." He got a better grip and held it up to the light, an action something like juggling a medicine ball. "Watch." He opened the jaw again.

The hinge, not the place a Psychlo heard through, but the place where the earbone met the back jawline, opened to show a hole about a thirty-second of an inch in diameter.

"You showed me this once," said Jonnie, "and explained you couldn't get an instrument through it. But it leads right to the spots where the capsules are embedded in the brain."

MacKendrick was skeptical. "Jonnie, I got a whole team in there cleaning the place up for a possible operation. I thought something serious had occurred. But as it's no emergency, why don't we just get some sleep—"

Jonnie took the skull over to the table they had used before for dissection and put it down. "It may look like no emergency to you. But the truth is that we don't know how to make a Psychlo motor and we don't know how to work their math. If we don't know those things we could come unstuck. We must have hundreds of planes right this minute that are inoperative. We need consumer products out in the planets and the Psychlo motors are tops. It's an emergency that'll do for now. But watch!"

Jonnie took a thin insulated wire from his pocket and inserted it in the tiny skull hole. He took the other end of the wire and pushed it through the tiny hole on the other side.

"What are you doing?" demanded MacKendrick.

"Now the question you must answer is, will these wires, pushed in, tear up any jaw or ear muscles?"

"Oh, they might hit some tissue, but the main muscles aren't there. That hole occurs because the jawbone, when extended to the extreme lower position, would have to leave a hole: otherwise there would have to be two additional bone plates and lord knows, there's enough already! I don't think—"

Jonnie reached for the kit he had hastily packed. He drew out a molecular plating gun. "This thing pours a stream of molecules from a rod onto a surface."

MacKendrick was at sea. "You can't get a gun like that in a head!"

"The gun unit goes outside." He dug out an electrical terminal plate. "Where is one of those capsules we removed?"

MacKendrick got one, the two half-circles of bronze.

Jonnie snipped off some lengths of insulated wire. He took the molecular plating gun and connected a length to the electrode that ordinarily fed current to the rod of spray metal. Then he laid the other end on the bit of bronze. He took a second piece of wire and laid it from the bronze to the electrical terminal plate. Then he connected the back of the terminal plate with a long wire to the current input terminal of the gun. He was simply going to substitute the bit of bronze for the gun's usual spray rod and then bypass the spraying component but instead make the molecules flow on a wire to a receiving plate. And just to make sure electrolysis would occur, he was completing the circuit back to the gun.

He pressed the trigger.

The terminal plate began to be plated in bronze.

A tiny hole appeared in the capsule taken from a Psychlo head.

No electrician, MacKendrick said, "It's disappearing!"

"We're flowing the metal molecules up the wire to the plate. I think it's called 'electrolysis.' We're just not letting the metal molecules spray. We're flowing them onto a plate."

He adjusted the wires to the bit of bronze so that an inflow hit a different spot and the outflow occurred from a new place.

MacKendrick gawped. "That piece of metal is disappearing!"

"It's reappearing over on the terminal plate," said Jonnie. "But that will be outside the head!"

He picked up a new bit of wire and with a small torch melted the end of it round. "If we take the sharp point off, can you wiggle this wire in through that hinge hole, around the various nerves, and touch the bronze bit in the skull? And then do the same thing from the other side?"

This was something MacKendrick knew about. The corded nerves of a Psychlo brain were easy to push around. The cortex, or covering of the brain, could probably be pierced in a couple of tiny places without much damage.

"We'll see!" said MacKendrick, giving up all thought of waiting for morning.

The Psychlo bodies were lying on two mine carts outside the door. Pierre seemed to have vanished. MacKendrick called in two nurses and another doctor and they wheeled the workman Psychlo into the dissection room. It was about five times as much body as they were used to handling, but with everyone helping, they got it on a table.

"It's probably still frozen inside," said Jonnie.

"No problem," said MacKendrick. "You forgot we've been through this before. A couple of times I was all hopeful we could even operate." He took a stack of microwave emanating pads and plopped them on either side of the head to thaw it out with a quick defreeze.

The room seemed awfully populated. Mr. Tsung was giving Jonnie a white coat and a pair of lensless glasses. Jonnie wondered what they were for and put them in his pocket. He was about to order a repositioning of the body when the singing button started up. It sang:

> "Gone are the days,
> "When my heart was young and gay.
> "Gone are the days. . . ."

The medical team was startled and a bit shocked. The scene was macabre enough without somebody singing a doleful dirge!

Jonnie pushed the button at Mr. Tsung. "Get rid of this thing!"

Pulling other bits out of his kit, Jonnie got to work making a more easily handled setup. Dr. MacKendrick was getting the metal analyzer they used for an X-ray machine in place. He put the head of the corpse on it and tuned the dials so that he had a sharp, clean picture of the bronze capsule. He was testing the jaws of the corpse to see if they were flexible and, finding they were, propped them open with a metal expansion tool.

The other doctor was mopping up water that had run off the cadaver's head and was getting the lower wave-emanation plate wet.

A nurse leaned over to Jonnie and whispered, "I don't think this little girl should be in here during all this."

Jonnie turned and there was Pattie. She must have followed him in. She was looking with interest at the bleached skull.

This was the first day in all these months he had seen Pattie noticing her environment. He was not going to suppress her by telling her to get out. "Let her stay," he whispered to the nurse. The woman was a bit disapproving but she did not push it.

Jonnie had his rig ready. MacKendrick was looking at some sketches he had made of Psychlo brain nerves. He laid the drawings down, took the offered wires, and got to work.

Watching the viewplate and checking the sketches he began to work a blunted wire end in. He finally, with a few minor detours, got it to the embedded bronze. Then he got the other wire through to the other side of the metal.

Jonnie verified they were ready and threw the switch.

The exterior terminal plate began to turn bronze.

MacKendrick worked very delicately, feeding in electricity to one side of the plate and taking it from the other. It was, looking at the viewplate, sort of like cleaning up a blot.

The bronze in the skull became less and less. MacKendrick steered the wires around. After about half an hour, he could find no further shadows or traces of the bronze in the skull. He carefully withdrew the wires. "Now to see if we burned nerves," he said.

The team went into immediate action. They broke out aprons and gloves and a set of instruments including a spinning-disc bone saw.

The nurse leaned over to Jonnie again and whispered "I do

really think that little girl ought to go. This is too much for anyone that young. How old is she? Ten?"

Pattie was sitting on a stool, overlooking the proceedings. She was very interested.

Nothing could have made Jonnie banish her. "Leave her alone," he whispered back.

They removed the viewers and put down pans and cloths. And in a moment the bone saw was whining and screeching into the skull. Shortly, green blood began to flow and the team mopped it up.

MacKendrick had done this so often that it seemed only minutes before they were looking at the place where the bronze had been. MacKendrick mopped up a bit more blood and got out a glass and inspected the nerves.

"The tiniest amount of burn," he said.

"I'll reduce the amperage," said Jonnie. He got busy installing a rheostat in the circuit.

The team was throwing the bits of the dead Psychlo back together. They heaved him off the table and back onto the mine cart and shoved him out in the hall. Two minutes later they had the former executive on the table.

They repeated the molecular flow operation on the bronze and got rid of it.

Jonnie did a test on a silver capsule they already had from times past. MacKendrick consulted his drawings again.

The doctor pulled the wires back and fished them in again on the silver capsule in the cadaver's brain.

It went along all right until they got to the fuse in it. It was so tiny and so quickly melted that it took quite some time to pick up all the bits. The wires, manipulated around, were more likely to touch each other than the scraps left.

Eventually that was gone too. Once more the gloves and saws, and presently the brain interior—mopped of green blood—was exposed. MacKendrick went over it with the greatest attention. Then he stood up.

MacKendrick was looking at Jonnie with awe. The lad had invented a new way to operate! MacKendrick was thinking of the bullets and metal bits that could be removed with this, and without making huge incisions or holes. Electrolytic surgery!

"It works on a corpse," said Jonnie. He glanced at his watch. "It's near midnight now. Tomorrow let's see if it works on a live one!"

— 7 —

At seven the following morning, MacKendrick's team began to set up an entirely different room for operating. "We don't know enough about Psychlo diseases," he told Jonnie, "and their cadavers might be very infective to them when decayed. They are built of viruses and there may be a virus smaller than viruses. So change your clothes and get brand new wires and equipment."

Jonnie did, and when he came back—having given Mr. Tsung the problem of digging up another white coat—and was laying out new wires, he was astonished to hear MacKendrick tell his nurse to go get Chirk.

"She's almost dead," said MacKendrick. "Psychlo females have been feeding her for months with a stomach tube. The brain structure is similar and the hole in the jaw is bigger. She's already in a coma and we won't have to give her much methane. That's the anesthetic that knocks them out."

"I better go get her," said Jonnie.

He took a mine cart and an air mask and went down to the rooms which were always circulated with breathe-gas.

Two Psychlo females came over at once when he pushed the cart toward Chirk's bed.

There she lay, eyes shut, unmoving. But she was *thin*, almost skeletal. Poor Chirk.

The two hefty females had no trouble at all laying her on the mine cart. Jonnie thought he might have been able to do it himself. Her bones almost rattled.

"Give me a breathe-gas mask for her," said Jonnie.

The two females looked at him blankly. "Why?" one said.

"So she can breathe!" said Jonnie impatiently.

The other female said, "It won't do any good to try to torture her first. In her state, she won't feel it."

Jonnie was trying to wrap his wits around this, and seeing his confusion, the first one explained, "We have been waiting for someone to come down to kill her. They always do. We wondered and wondered why you waited months."

"That's the only treatment the catrists ever permitted for lapsin."

What were these words? Well, "catrist" was the medical scientist cult that really ran Psychlo. Didn't he know that? And "lapsin" was a common disease which child females sometimes got, and although it was rare for one of Chirk's age—she's thirty, you know—to get it, it was undeniable that she had lapsin. And, naturally, sooner or later, she had to be killed.

"I'm not going to kill her!" said Jonnie, indignant. "I'm going to try to cure her!"

They didn't believe him. In the first place it was against the law to cure lapsin. It was also against the law for an unauthorized person to trifle with the mind. So it followed that he was lying to them just like a catrist would. But it still wouldn't do any good to try to torture her before she was vaporized as she wouldn't feel it and he wouldn't enjoy it.

Jonnie had to get the breathe-mask himself, put it on Chirk, and wheel her through the atmosphere lock. Behind him the two females were telling each other, "Torture, I told you so."

Even getting his toe back into the "civilization" named Psychlo had upset Jonnie. But he soon had Chirk in the improvised operating room. Thin as she was, it still took three of them to get her on the table.

MacKendrick had drilled all this out long ago and his team was quite efficient. The new doctor lifted the mask enough to slip an expander into the mouth. A nurse slipped a methane tube under the mask edge and then stood with a stethoscope on Chirk's heart to detect beating changes. The heart evidently slowed down enough to suit her and she nodded to MacKendrick.

The jaw holes were outside the mask edge and MacKendrick soon had the wires inserted through the tissue and into the brain. He positioned the head on the viewscreen very carefully. Jonnie regulated the gun trigger for him. The nurse listened carefully to the heart and regulated the methane/breathe-gas mix.

The capsule in her head got less and less. The metal on the plate terminal got more and more.

One hour and forty-five minutes later, MacKendrick stood back, the extracted wires in his hands. A trickle of green on each side of the head was staunched by a nurse. The methane tube was taken away. The expander was removed from the mouth. The nurse turned up the breathe-gas valve to maximum on the mask vial.

"We tried this on a workman a few months ago without

operating," said MacKendrick. "It will take her about four hours to come out of it. If she does."

Jonnie was going to make sure nothing got in the road of her doing just that. He pushed the mine cart and its burden out of the room and back to the lower atmosphere lock.

The two Psychlo females were still inside and very surprised to see him. They gave him a hand putting her back onto the bed. As Jonnie was taking off her breathe-gas mask, one of the females said, "I suppose you brought her back here to order us to kill her."

That did it. Jonnie kicked them both out. He got a chair and sat down outside the atmosphere lock. He was going to sit there all four hours and make very, very sure nobody else got any odd Psychlo ideas! At the end of that time, he hoped Chirk would come to. But in any event he was prepared to wait until she did.

— 8 —

Unfortunately for Jonnie it proved to be a rather well-traveled passageway—or people found excuses to travel it just so they could see him there.

Chrissie found him. "I'm awfully sorry we overlooked Pattie. I thought you were coming right behind us and had her, and then when I saw she wasn't there, I ran out again but you had taken off." Pattie was standing behind her looking at Jonnie.

"But that isn't what I *must* talk to you about," said Chrissie. She produced from behind her an envelope and began to take things out of it. One glimpse of them told Jonnie that Dries had been up to something else. They were the proof sheets, all marked "Specimen, not valid for exchange," of the new Galactic Bank money. There were four coins of different size and four bills of different size. The coins were different geometric shapes, well stamped. The paper and printing were excellent. Jonnie couldn't imagine what was wrong with them.

"This eleventh-of-a-credit coin," said Chrissie, "is not too bad. It's green and you can't see it. The three-elevenths coin, this blue one, is not too awful because you can't see it either. This red metal, five-elevenths coin is barely passing. The yellow, six-elevenths coin just won't do."

Hearing Chrissie expound upon money *was* novel. She had probably never used it in her whole life.

"But the smallest to the largest paper bank notes are what you should be concerned about. I told Dries I was *very* upset! This is the one-credit note. And this here is what they call the eleven-credit note but it says, 'ten.' "

"Psychlo number system," said Jonnie. "It's based on eleven, not ten. 'Ten' means one unit of elevens plus zero units of ones which equals eleven. So an eleven-credit note would be written in numbers as 'one-zero.' "

"I'll take your word for it," sighed Chrissie, "but that's not what I'm mad about. Here, look at these. This one is . . . the . . . one-zero-zero credit note. It says 'one hundred' but it's the same as a hundred twenty-one one-credit notes. Yes, yes, I know . . . Psychlo numbers." She showed Jonnie one more. "And this one is the one-three-three-one credit note."

Jonnie had been looking at them. The coins had larger and larger stamps on them. The bank notes looked startlingly glossy with their shimmer paper. "I'm sorry," he said, "I don't see anything wrong with them."

"It's the face!" said Chrissie. "Look. On the coins they have your face in profile and you can't see it on the smaller ones but you can on the yellow one because it's big enough. The nose! Your nose isn't turned up at the end!"

Jonnie took the coins. Yes, it sure was a turned-up nose.

"And these bills. I don't care," said Chrissie, "if it *is* hard to reproduce accurately like Dries said. They made your skin grayish. The eyes have too big a lid. And Jonnie, your ears aren't like that! These look more like gills!"

Jonnie took the bills. Sure enough, they had changed the portraits! Then he barked a laugh. He still looked enough like himself for no real dispute to rise. But they had shifted it over so he slightly resembled a Selachee.

Great! Less chance of being pointed at in the hills. But Jonnie had learned a lot about diplomacy. "I'm sorry you don't like them, Chrissie."

"Oh, it's not that! It just doesn't look like *you*."

"I'm afraid it would cost an awful lot and make a lot of

trouble to change them now," said Jonnie. "Maybe the next issue!"

That seemed to mollify her and she put them back in the envelope and walked off, noting from the way he seemed to have nailed himself down that he might have to be fed lunch there.

Pattie stayed behind and sat down on the floor. She still seemed very thoughtful but she was not as dull as she had been.

Ker came up the ramp, followed by about thirty assorted ex-marines—Jambitchows, Drawkins, and a couple of Hockners. Ker went on by with a friendly hello. But when the others got abreast of Jonnie they suddenly realized who was sitting there. They recoiled so hard against the far side of the passage that they bounced. They instantly raced up to be in front of Ker.

Jonnie had not missed it. He called out, "Ker!"

The midget Psychlo walked back to him, leaving his group standing up the passageway. "Ker," said Jonnie, "what have you been telling those ex-soldiers?"

"Nothing," said Ker, amber eyes glowing with innocence back of the faceplate. "They're just kind of hard to handle sometimes."

"Well," said Jonnie, "whatever that 'nothing' was, you straighten it out."

"Of course!" said Ker. He turned and yelled up at the group. "It's all right! He isn't mad at you right now!"

They all seemed so relieved, Jonnie gave Ker a very suspicious eye. The midget yelled at the Hockner ex-officer to take them to the garage and get busy washing down machines and then turned back to Jonnie. "You had me scared there for a moment," he said. "I thought you'd really caught up with me."

"Something else?" said Jonnie.

Ha. Ha. Well, it wasn't true that he had been the only one here when everybody including the Mountains of the Moon people had taken off for Edinburgh to help. They'd left their old ones and their kids. And he'd gotten bored just sitting with a blast rifle in his lap up the corridor there and he'd found one of the old ones spoke a funny kind of Dutch—that's an Earth language, or was. And Ker had found a vocoder in the Chinko bin that had had Dutch in it, so he'd amused himself by telling the old one stories to relay to the kids that were always hanging around.

The children had been pretty shy at first, thinking he was a monster and all, so he'd told them that he was really human

That he had a human mother and father. But his mother had been scared by a Psychlo and so when he was born, he looked this way.

But he'd be honest with Jonnie and level with him because he was a boyhood friend and Ker confessed he was only half-human.

"Not to change the subject," said Ker, doing it, "but I heard you say something about handling a problem. I can't wash vehicles forever. When are you going to get busy and nail Maz so I can get this mine going again?"

"I'm working on it right now!" said Jonnie. He looked at his watch. Another hour and a half to go. And then he'd have an idea whether it would fully work or not.

— 9 —

Perhaps because she had been so weak, it was five hours and Chirk had not stirred.

Jonnie had moved his chair in to the foot of the bed and sat there with an air mask on. Pattie had tried to come in but Jonnie had blocked her until he could find another mask. Breathe-gas could send one into convulsions. So Pattie now sat with her back to the wall, cross-legged on the floor, watching Chirk.

The Psychlo's breathing seemed to be less shallow, or was he just being hopeful?

No, he wasn't! Chirk had moved a paw. Very slight, but she had moved it.

After a long time, Chirk let out a fluttering sigh.

She opened her eyes and looked dully about her.

She finally focused on Jonnie. She simply looked at him for quite a while.

Then abruptly Chirk hitched herself up on her elbows and said with some authority, "Jonnie, did you send that library form in like I told you? The home office is going to be pretty cross if it finds you've got an incomplete set of books down here!"

Jonnie heaved a sigh of relief. Part of it was for the practical value of this. Part of it was for Chirk herself.

He was about to answer when she caught sight of her arms. Puzzled, she said, "What am I doing so thin?"

She hitched herself up a little higher. "Why am I so weak?"

"You'll feel stronger when you've had something solid to eat. We have some very good goo-food now. And even some chew-roots."

Her interest was immediate and then faded. "I've been here for some time, haven't I, Jonnie?"

"A while," said Jonnie.

She thought about it. Then she stiffened. "I've had lapsin! It's incurable!" She let out a wail.

"It's cured," said Jonnie.

She thought about it. Then another upset took her. "But why didn't they vaporize me? The catrists?"

"I think you'll get well," said Jonnie. "In fact, I think you'll be healthier than before."

She thought she understood. "You're sitting there so they won't come in and vaporize me. Jonnie, that's brave and I should thank you, but you can't stop the catrists! They're the law. They're beyond any law! They can do anything they please, even to the emperor. Jonnie, you better get out of here before they come."

Jonnie looked at her for a while. What a world of terror and cruelty these Psychlos had lived in. He said, "I'm sitting here to tell you the news, Chirk. I fired the catrists." Well, it was true, wasn't it? Even if he didn't really know what a catrist was, if they'd been on Psychlo, they were fired. Radioactively.

Chirk sat up higher, shedding the dullness. "Oh, Jonnie, that was awfully nice of you!"

She swung her legs to get off the bed. "Where are my clothes? I better get to work or I'll have another black mark on my record." She tried to stand.

"I'd take it easy," said Jonnie. Then, an inspiration. "It's your day off."

She sank down on the bed, shaking with weakness and evidently dizzy. "Oh, that's lucky. Will it be all right if I come in tomorrow?"

Jonnie assured her that it was. He went out and found the two females, and perhaps because of his reassociation with Ker, he told them he had an order that exempted Chirk from being vaporized and that if they harmed her he'd dock their pay and put black marks all over their records and they better go get her some goo-food and chew-root and help her take a bath. They did not misunderstand him. Whatever else he said, he had a palm resting on his belt blast gun. They understood that.

■

PART 32

— 1 —

With all the weight hanging on the outcome of this project, Jonnie was in no frame of mind to be told that it would be three days before they could be sure they had succeeded with Chirk. MacKendrick said there were dangers of infection, of relapse. He had to observe the reactions before he could proceed.

In vain Jonnie told him that unless they solved Psychlo math, he might find himself back in a conference room with very angry emissaries whose economies had remained stagnant, that he might be pushed into a new demonstration of force. MacKendrick said it wouldn't help to rush it.

And Chirk did not instantly rebound. On the second day she was still in bed, too weak and dizzy to get up. It made Jonnie wonder whether the removal would disturb their sense of balance, even their ability to think.

Other things occurred. Pierre Solens had vanished and it took Jonnie hours to find that he had been seen boarding a plane that had come through, sky-hiking his way back to Europe.

Pattie seemed to have undergone a change. Jonnie was sitting in the old library, impatiently thumbing through books, when he became aware of Pattie. She obviously had something to say. He sat quietly, giving her his attention.

"Jonnie, please tell me the truth. Did Bittie live very long?"

It startled Jonnie, hurled him back to that fatal day. A wave of grief choked him. He could only nod faintly.

"Then he could have been saved," said Pattie, not accusing, just stating a fact.

Jonnie looked at her. He couldn't talk. Dear God, no! The boy was blasted half in two; his spine was shattered. Nothing could have saved Bittie. Nothing. But he couldn't say that to her.

"Jonnie, if I had known how to be a doctor and if I had been there, he wouldn't have died." She said it as fact, conviction.

He waited. He couldn't talk.

"When the doctors leave here, I want to go with them," said Pattie. "I will be very good. I will not bother them. I will go to a school and study real hard and I will learn everything I have to know to be a doctor. Will you help me, Jonnie?"

He couldn't talk. He put his arms around her. After a while he was able to say, "Of course I will, Pattie. You can stay with Aunt Ellen. I will speak to MacKendrick. I will see you have all the money you need."

She stepped back, her eyes bright with determination. With dignity she said, "Thank you," and went away.

After a little, he felt a sense of relief for her. He had thought she would never recover. But she had. There was a direction for her to go and she had found a path to travel on, a path that led out of despair and back to the world of the living.

On the following day he had been down in the electrical shop organizing equipment and needing a reference on molecular gun current values. He raced up to the library to get it.

And there was Chirk!

She was sitting at a desk, surrounded with books. "Jonnie," she said, a little severely, "you let this place get in an awful mess. You must learn to put things back when you pull them off the shelves!"

He looked at her. Inside her breathe-mask, her jaws were chomping away on chew-root. Her amber eyes seemed totally clear. She had already put on a bit of weight. "The company is very strict about orderly libraries," she said. "You must remember that." She went back to getting volumes in order. Her coordination seemed very exact as she stacked things with sure paw motions. The resulting piles were very even. Not even a tremble.

He was about to go tearing off to spread the news.

"Jonnie," said Chirk, pensively, "I've been thinking about mathematics. If you still need me to help you, I'll try to learn to add and subtract and all that sort of thing. But, Jonnie," and she fixed him with a very questioning stare, "truthfully, why should any intelligent person want to *do* mathematics? I mean, what use are they, Jonnie?"

Three minutes later an excited Jonnie was telling MacKendrick they could roll.

— 2 —

They had taken time and worked it all out.

There was always a risk in handling Psychlos, even in just being around them. One rake of a paw's claws could tear one's face off. MacKendrick had actually started on Chirk because there was less danger of it. The worker he had tested earlier had been a risk: the Psychlo had surged up when half-anesthetized, and had it not been for straps, somebody would have gotten hurt. So putting a Psychlo under and operating when that Psychlo was apprehensive, believing perhaps he was about to be killed, was a thing to be avoided.

The younger doctor had been trained, as many general practitioners were, in rudimentary dentistry. He examined a couple of skulls, studying the fangs and back teeth. They were caked with a coating from goo-food which seemed to turn black in time. There were a couple of cavities evident.

Jonnie got him some silver and mercury so the doctor could make an amalgam for filling. He also fashioned a breathe-mask for them which used the nosebones and made some plugs which could block the mouth air passages and force the Psychlo to breathe only through the nose. He also found some small drills.

The plan was to tell all the Psychlos that it was a new regulation that they have their teeth repaired and polished. They said it could be painful so it was being done under an anesthetic. The Psychlos, as a group, when being briefed, were a little dubious, mostly because the company had never had any concern for employee health. But new place, new ways.

The team set it up as an assembly line. The Psychlo would be brought in, put under, and have the capsule or capsules removed, and then would be pushed down to another table where the younger doctor, taking advantage of the anesthesia, would fix and polish up the fangs and back teeth.

In this way, after the first one, each Psychlo entering would see another Psychlo lying there, unconscious, getting his teeth fixed on another table. The metal analyzer on the first table was explained as necessary to find cavities.

They rolled up their sleeves and began to roll.

The assembly line went off without a hitch. A Psychlo would come in, get the metal removed from his brain, be shunted over to get his teeth fixed, and then be wheeled back on a mine cart to the Psychlo area of the compound to recover.

It took one hundred forty-four working hours, twelve days, to get the whole lot through.

The early ones were all up and about before the last one was finished. They had had a lot of cavities, even some minor extractions. But their gleaming fangs! My, were they impressed. Walking about, whenever they passed a reflective surface, they could be seen holding their breath, lifting their breathe-masks, and inspecting anew their beautiful new "smiles."

A Psychlo admiring beauty was a major change in itself.

They did not become more polite. But they became more pleasant and agreeable.

Ker couldn't stand the others getting all this without himself getting into the scene. He didn't even know he didn't have any capsules, but he did know his fangs weren't shiny bright. So they had to pull him in, put him under, and polish his teeth. And that finished the lot.

The medical team took the cricks out of their backs and began to pack up.

"It's all over to you now, Jonnie," said MacKendrick. "Be careful as we have no guarantee they won't retain some residual behavior pattern based on tradition and education. I hope you finally solve their math."

And the team went back to Aberdeen.

Jonnie was on his own.

— 3 —

Chirk collected the company personnel records for him, and Jonnie went through them, one by one, as they were handed to him. Just now she had a big, thick, tattered folder that was all water-stained and mildewed.

Jonnie took it. It was the record of one named Soth, an assistant mine manager who had served in the compound near

Denver. Jonnie had never seen him there: he must have kept to his room or his office. Some of the reason was visible in the record: Soth was one hundred eighty years old; a Psychlo life span was around one hundred ninety and it meant that Soth could not have been feeling all that spry.

But there was more in the record. Since the age of fifty, Soth had never returned to Psychlo. He had been shipped all over the universes, serving two years here, four years there. But never a return to Psychlo. He had even been cross-fired on rigs every time, a thing that was very unusual as almost all cargos went via Psychlo and Jonnie had thought that all personnel did. In fact, this insistence on using Psychlo as a transfer point was the main bottleneck on the expansion of the Psychlos: the transshipment platform there could only handle so much cargo and firings in a day. Jonnie had already started doubling up platforms in places, one to receive and one to fire.

Jonnie studied the record. Soth, after graduating from mine school, had been an under-professor of "ore theory." It all seemed quite usual right up to the age of fifty when abruptly he had been assigned as an assistant mine manager to a very remote planet. And for the next one hundred thirty years he had been shifted continually, always retaining the same rank.

It was an oddity. Jonnie went through the reams of records on him. And finally found one of the same date as his original transfer from Psychlo. It said, "Unsuitable for teaching profession Fla, Chief Catrist, Gru Clinic, Psychlo."

That little slip of paper had condemned a being to obvious exile for a hundred thirty years! No other black marks evident. Always seemed to have done his work, nothing negative otherwise.

Instead of going straight to Soth, Jonnie instead made a test with Maz. This Psychlo, at whom Ker was mad, was one of the biggest Jonnie had ever seen. He had been the local planning engineer.

Remembering the Chamco brothers, Jonnie loaded up a hand blast gun just in case, positioned himself in a room where he had lots of space to back up, and had Maz brought in.

Maz's teeth were *gleaming* behind his faceplate. He sat down easily enough. He was a bit surly.

"I hear that Ker clown has been saying I won't work," began Maz with no preliminary. "Contract or no contract, if you think you can put a midget operations officer over the head of a planning engineer, you think trouble!''

"He just wants to get the tungsten mine going,'' said Jonnie.

"What's the point? You can't ship it to Psychlo. You finished that!''

Jonnie thought he might as well dive in now rather than drag it out. "If you'll give me the mathematics to compute the location of the next ore body, I'll work it out.''

Maz scowled. Jonnie prepared to draw.

"Somehow,'' said Maz, and his scowl deepened, "I don't think I'm supposed to talk mathematics with an alien.'' He thought it over. He lifted a back strap of his breathe-mask and scratched under it.

A considerable time passed.

"I can't think where I got that idea. Mine school? Yes, mine school. Say, this is funny. I got a picture of somebody holding a whirling spiral in front of me. . . .'' He yawned. He thought a while. "Hey!'' he said explosively. "That's the catrist in charge of our group. You know, I haven't thought of him for years. Funny old———. He used to spend hours with the youngest males—when he wasn't down in the sex shops of the old town. Yeah, it was him. What were we talking about?''

"Showing me how to do mathematics,'' said Jonnie.

Maz shrugged. "Why bother? Take a lot less time for me to do the calculations myself. What's he going to do with the ore?''

"Cross-fire it to other planets,'' said Jonnie.

"That's kind of illegal. How much bonus? For me, I mean.''

"The usual,'' said Jonnie.

"Tell you what. You tell that Ker he ain't no boss of mine and mind his manners and you double my planning bonus per ton and I'll calculate the ore body.'' He laughed. "There's a lot more tungsten there than I ever told the company! Is it a deal?''

Jonnie said that it was and Maz left. It was an inconclusive test. But he hadn't been attacked. He waited for two days for Maz to commit suicide. But he didn't. He just went out and started giving Ker a hard time, but in the process he broke out his analyzers and instruments and stakes and shortly was shooting "glow-stripes'' into the earth to give workers lines along which to dig.

Jonnie used the time otherwise as well. He went down to Salisbury and, with Thor to back off the elephants and black mambas, dug into the man-books trying to find anythıng about "whirling spirals" being held in front of people's faces.

He found one reference to it in a booklet named, ["Hypnotism for the Millions"]. Seemed kind of silly. He made one and, with Thor holding a small deer, spun it in front of its face and all the deer did was stare at it. Thor said to try it on him and he did, but Thor just went into gales of laughter.

According to the book, you put people to sleep and told them things and then the people would do them afterward without knowing it was an order. Jonnie guessed Psychlos must be different if it worked on them.

Anyway, he had an idea of what the "catrist" had been attempting with Maz. There had been some effect but not enough without the capsule.

What a weird world those Psychlos had lived in! Imagine putting a whole population under a mental cloud! But the idea wasn't solely Psychlo's, for there it had been among the spiderwebs of the old man-library! And it had been a man-book which had led him on to the capsules.

How could any being consider itself so *right* as to think it should make all other beings into robots to do its bidding? He thought of Lars. Had Hitler been doing things like that?

As Maz, according to a call to Victoria, was still going strong, Jonnie went back to tackle Soth. If anyone knew math, he should.

Jonnie was determined to get motors into production. And after all this time of getting trouble from Psychlo mathematics he was feeling quite willful about it. This *had* to be revealed. There were no two ways about it. Terl and his condemned equations that wouldn't balance, that never made any sense! Why, if something happened with a console, he'd never know what was wrong with the circuit. He couldn't figure one out. Not with Psychlo math.

Suddenly he remembered the Voraz letter. Hundreds of thousands of inventions and the formulas all in Psychlo math. To really get the crashed arms companies converted over to consumer products, those hundreds of thousands of inventions—even though accumulated for millennia and probably stolen by the Psychlos from now defunct races—could very well spell the difference between booming prosperity across the galaxies and having to face a new conference of emissaries howling for his blood. Nobody would be able to figure them out unless he could pry the secret of Psychlo math out of these ex-company employees. Mr. Tsung had been right. It could become a "diplomatic" matter. It could even become war.

— 4 —

Soth, Jonnie found, did not live in the dormitories. Apparently he coughed at night and kept other Psychlos awake, and they had insisted he be berthed in a small former storage room that was hooked into the breathe-gas circulating system. And that was where Jonnie found him.

The room wasn't too bad. The old Psychlo had cut down the original storage shelves and fabricated some bookcases and tables from them; the cases were utterly jammed with books and the tables covered with a litter of paper.

Soth was sitting on a high stool as Jonnie entered. His fur was splotchy with blue hairs, sign of an aged Psychlo. The amber eyes were a bit blurry with white matter at the corners. He was dressed in a wraparound robe and he had a small cap on his head.

He peered near-sightedly at Jonnie, evidently seeking to see who it was. Then he remarked the belt gun.

"So you have come to ship me on," said Soth. "I was wondering when someone would notice."

"You seem to have a lot of books here," said Jonnie, seeking to change the subject.

"I was fortunate," said Soth. "When that attack first came on the compound, I was in my office and I heard the fire gongs going. I knew there'd be a lot of water so I ran down to my room and put everything I had into waterproof ore bags. Then when we were to leave for here, I asked a nice young human if I could go get them and bring them. And he permitted it."

Jonnie was looking at the titles. He couldn't read most of them. They were in scripts he had never seen before.

"They usually let me keep my books," said Soth. "In cross-firing, they don't much care what weight or cubic space there is for there's nothing else going. Will you let me keep them when you cross-fire me this time?"

Jonnie was afraid for a moment that this old Psychlo must be in his dotage. Then he realized they wouldn't really know that there were no other Psychlos alive; they might think there were other captives elsewhere.

"I'm not here to cross-fire you. We're sure there are no Psychlos on other planets now."

Soth digested this. Then he let out a little snort. "Funny way to end a hundred thirty years of exile. But it's not ended. I'm still exiled even if I stay here."

Jonnie had him talking. He had better keep him talking. "How did it start?"

Soth shrugged. "The way it always starts. Being impolite to a catrist. Isn't it in my record?" As Jonnie shook his head, Soth went on. "You might as well know. Lately I have had this strange feeling that I should be more honest. And I do appreciate your fixing my fangs for me. Two were quite painful. Anyway, we had this young Psychlo in school and he got confused about his lessons and wanted a better explanation—"

"About mathematics?" said Jonnie.

Soth looked at him for quite a while. "Why do you ask that?" he said finally. A sort of a cloud had passed over him and gone away. Then, as Jonnie didn't reply, he went on. "Well, yes, it was about mathematics in a way, I suppose. It was how you calculate ore bodies in semicore mining." He sighed. "Somebody must have reported him because the catrist of that school wing came in and started shouting at him and then started shouting at the whole class. It was very disruptive. There's no excuse for what I did really, but for years I used to think it was because my mother was a member of an underground church group. They believed that sentient creatures had souls and they felt very strongly about it.

"It wasn't that she was caught or anything. But some of it must have rubbed off on me to make me do what I did. This catrist was standing there screaming at the class that they were all animals and they better remember they were animals. And he was making so much noise I must have gotten confused. I did want him to quiet down because I had a class to teach. And it just slipped out."

He sat for a long time. "It's sort of painful to talk about this. I never do. If word of this got back to the—" Then he let out a slight gasp. "I just realized. They're all dead. It's all right if I talk about it!'' Then he looked closely at Jonnie. ''It *is* all right, isn't it?''

''Sure,'' said Jonnie. 'I don't even know what a 'catrist' is.''

''You know,'' said Soth, ''I've come to believe I don't either, really. But because of what it did to my life, I pieced a lot of it together. There's lots of books on lots of planets. Two hundred fifty thousand years ago, Psychlos were really a different people. They didn't even have the name 'Psychlo.' I think sometime or other they must have gotten frightened of somebody invading them or something.

''As near as I could piece together, there was this group of carnival performers—you know, mountebanks, frauds. *They* were the original Psychlos. They used to hypnotize people on the stage and make them do funny things to get the audience to laugh at them. Just trash. Actually, just criminals.

''When this panic came on, they went to the emperor and told him something or other because the next thing anyone knew, they were in charge of the schools and medical centers. The race before that had been called after the current emperor according to books on other planets. Well, right at that time, they began to be called Psychlos. *That* was the name of these carnival performers. So instead of being called after the ruler, the race was now called after the 'Psychlos.' It means 'brain,' according to some old dictionaries. Another form of the word also means 'property of.' Everyone became the property of the Psychlos.

''Anyway, members of this mob of cutthroats began to call themselves 'catrist.' That means 'mental doctor.' So the people became 'Psychlos' or 'brains' and the 'catrist' or 'mental doctor' was the real, hidden government. They taught all the children. They inspected every citizen. They suppressed religion. They told people how to think.

''Oh, I was stupid. There's no excuse for what I did.'' He fell silent. ''But this catrist was raising so much row! I should not blame my mother. I should never have blamed her.'' He paused again and drew a long breath. ''It just blurted out. I said, 'They are *not* animals!' ''

He shuddered and after a while said, ''So that began my exile. Now you know.''

What Jonnie now knew was that that mob of frauds was stark staring insane.

''Well,'' said Soth coming out of his despondency, ''if that isn't why you're here, why are you? An old ruin like me has nothing to offer."

Jonnie decided to dive in. "You obviously know mathematics.'

Suspicion clouded Soth's already rheumy gaze. "How did you know my hobby was mathematics? It isn't in my record. I paid a female clerk five hundred credits once to see it and I know." The mystery of it threw him. Then he solved it. "Ah!" he swept his paw down the bookshelves. "My books!" Then he clouded over again. "But they're mostly outer-language books and very few people can read them. A lot of the races are even dead! Come," he pleaded, "tell me why you're here!"

"I want you to teach me about Psychlo mathematics," said Jonnie.

There was a sudden tension in Soth. He seemed to become confused. Then it seemed to clear away. "Nobody has asked me to teach them anything for a hundred thirty years You're an alien race, but what does it matter? There are hardly any Psychlos left. What do you want to know?"

The tension slid out of Jonnie. He'd made it!

— 5 —

'In the first place," said Soth, after he had made himself more comfortable and taken a small bite of the kerbango Jonnie had produced, "there are an awful lot of different kinds of mathematics—different races you know. I sort of kept my interest in life by collecting them.

"There have been existing systems for lots of different whole numbers. There's the 'binary system' like the Chatovarians use: it has only two numerals in it, one and zero; that's so they can use them in computers, in which the electric current pulse, or the direction of magnetization of an element, has one of two values. One value corresponds to the numeral zero; the other to numeral one. Any number in any system can be translated to the binary system using only zero and one. Unwieldy for beings, but understandable for the computers.

"Then there's a system based on the integer three, an entirely different one based on four, another on five, another on six, another on seven, still another on eight, yet another on nine and so on. There's even been one on twenty and one on sixty.

"For paper computation the best system is called the 'decimal' system, based on ten." (Jonnie knew about this from man-books.) "Psychlo mathematics are based on eleven; some people call this the 'undenary' system. It's difficult so I won't try to teach you that."

"Oh, I would love to know about the 'undenary' system!" said Jonnie. His use of the words 'love to know' gave him a twinge of conscience. He *hated* this confused mess!

"I can teach you the 'decimal' system much more easily," said Soth. "Whenever they discover it on some planet they engrave the discoverer's name among the heroes." He saw Jonnie wouldn't buy it and sighed. "All right," he said. He got a sheet of somewhat crumpled paper. "I will write down the 'undenary' numerals for you."

Jonnie said he already knew the Psychlo numerals but Soth shook his head.

"No, no," said Soth. "I doubt very much if you do. To really understand a symbol, you have to know what it came from. Now all numerals as symbols were originally either the first letter of the word that spelled them or a number of dots or lines. Or they were pictographs that then became stylized until they were only a part of the original picture or a shorthand version of it.

"Now Psychlo numerals were originally pictographs. And then as time went on, they were written in a more and more simplified form until they now are what you see as the eleven separate Psychlo numerals. They were once called 'the road to happiness.' "

Jonnie had not known that. He saw these numbers, these symbols, every time he flew. He began to get interested.

Soth was writing the numerals as pictographs, little pictures. "Zero is an empty mouth; see the teeth? One is a claw; just one talon. Two is a being and a pick. Three is a being, a shovel, and a rock. Four is a mine cart; see the four corners? Five is what we call the 'off' paw, the one with five claws. Six is what we call the 'on' paw, the one with six claws. Seven is an ore chute. Eight is a pot smelter; see the smokestack and the smoke? Nine is a pile of metal ingots made like a pyramid; nine of them originally but now just the pyramid. Ten is a lightning bolt; symbol of power, now just a slash. Eleven is two paws clasped; that represents contentment.

"It's a little moral lesson, you see. If you dig and smelt ore, it lifts you from starvation to power and contentment." He laughed. "Very few people know this All they know is what time and haste boiled them down to." And above his pictures, he rapidly wrote the eleven Psychlo numeral symbols as they commonly appeared. They still bore the traces of the pictographs.

"I'm very glad to know that," said Jonnie. And he was amused by it. The Psychlos had been miners from the start! "I can do a little arithmetic in this system." He decided to really push it. "Where I get hung up is the Psychlo force equations." And that was *no* lie. They gave him headaches. Nothing ever balanced.

Soth was looking at him very keenly. "I think you are digging for the teleportation formulas."

Jonnie shrugged. "We have a rig running. We are making rigs."

"Yes, I heard that," said Soth. "That's where all the new breathe-gas and goo-food came from. I heard there was a planet, Fobia, nobody could live on." He was plainly puzzled. "Ah!" he exclaimed. "One of your scientists reevolved it in some other mathematics and you are trying to verify it against Psychlo equations." He laughed and laughed.

Jonnie gave him another bite of kerbango.

"Ah, well. Not that it will do you much good. But it's small wonder you can't work it out. He laughed again. "You'd have to be a native of Psychlo!"*

He laughed so hard he had to wipe his eyes.

"Oh, well," he said at last, "you already have teleportation so what's the difference." He took another big piece of paper and drew a huge circle on it. Then he had second thoughts and sat back and looked at Jonnie. "If I give you this," said Soth, "what's it worth?"

"Money?" said Jonnie.

"A separate dome, access to compound libraries, and tools to experiment with computers. And *not* to be cross-fired elsewhere!"

*For the Earth and several other editions of this book, translation liberties have been taken throughout, but especially with the explanation that follows, due mainly to the temporary unavailability of print fonts which include Psychlo numbers and letters. —*Translator*.

"All right," said Jonnie.

Soth made a fast list of what he had said. Then he added, "Breathe-gas and proper food for the rest of my life. I'm sorry to have to add this. But I've only ten years or so to go so it's only ten years' worth. I won't add anything else."

Jonnie signed it. He even put a paw print on it, using his fingernails. Soth looked like he had lost ten years of age.

With a flourish, Soth pulled the circle to him. Then he put another piece of paper on top of it. "Do you know anything about codes and ciphers? Cryptography? Well anyway, here is the Psychlo alphabet." And he wrote it out. "And here are the Psychlo numerals." And he wrote them under the letters and then started the numerals over again until there was one written under each letter. "Do you see, here, that each letter has a number value?"

Jonnie said he did. Soth laid aside the top sheet and again addressed the big circle.

"This," said Soth impressively, indicating the circle, "is the perimeter of the Imperial Palace of Psychlo." He made a series of small slashes around the circle. "These are the eleven *gates*. A lot of people even on Psychlo never knew they had names. But they do:

"Going counterclockwise, the names of these gates are: 'Angel's Gate,' 'Betrayer's Gate,' 'Devil's Gate,' 'God's Gate,' 'Heaven's Gate,' 'Infernal Gate,' 'Monster's Gate,' 'Nightmare Gate,' 'Quarrel's Gate,' 'Regal Gate,' and 'Traitor's Gate.' Eleven gates, each with a name."

He took a book, "Force Equations" off his shelf. "It doesn't matter which types of equations in Psychlo higher math. They're all the same. You mentioned 'force equations' so we'll use those. No difference."

With a dig of his claw, he opened the book to the point where all the equations were summarized and pointed to the top one. "Now you see this 'B'? You might think it is a symbol for something in Psychlo mathematics. But there is no 'B' that represents anything mathematical except 'Betrayer's.' "

He pulled the first paper back. "So where that 'B' occurs, we see that the letter 'B' has a number value of *two*. So we just have to add or subtract or whatever it says to do to 'B,' the number *two*.

"When we get to the second stage of the equation, there is no letter but a Psychlo mathematician knows you must take the second letter of 'Betrayer's,' which is 'E' and then look up the number value of 'E,' which is *five*, and factor the second stage of the equation with *five*. Now you get the same equation to its third stage and a mathematician knows he has to factor it with the number value of 'T' which is *twenty*. And so on.

"If the letter in the original equation were 'I,' then we would use its number value and follow right on down with the number values of the letters for 'Infernal.'

"You always have one of these letters in the first equation, so you always have the gate name. And you have to use it. When they put the equations together, they constructed them backward from the answer so a gate name would fit. Got it?"

Jonnie got it. A code and cipher mathematics!

No wonder nothing ever seemed to balance. This made even the original equations rigged.

And add to that all the complexity of a base-eleven math and you had what would appear to any outsider to be an utter mess.

He was glad he had the recorder running under his lapel. Completely aside from his being no native of Psychlo, the gate names themselves were weird.

"I have to be honest with you," said Soth. "I don't know where I am getting all this impulse to be honest. But all this will be of limited use to you."

— 6 —

Jonnie sat very still. Something else? You mean, he'd gotten all this way and he still wouldn't attain it? But he didn't speak. He waited.

Soth fiddled a bit with his papers. He picked up the contract Jonnie had signed and then laid it down again. Obviously he was having qualms about the honesty of accepting it.

"You have to understand how crazy they were on secrecy," he said at length. "Although what I have given you applies to Psychlo math in general, there is another circumstance. When equations are applied to the calculation of teleportation, you won't find all the answers in the texts."

Soth sighed. "The government was afraid of a lot of things. Among them was the possibility that Intergalactic Mining employees, out in some far planet, might get ideas or go into business for themselves. So the exact sequence in which you use the force equations is not revealed in the texts and I think there are dummy equations there as well. I could not work you out a console."

Jonnie objected, "The Chamco brothers seemed to be working on it!"

"Oh, the Chamco brothers!" said Soth impatiently. "They might have monkeyed about. They might even have tried. But they wouldn't know!"

He swept a paw in the general direction of the other Psychlo dormitories. "These clods here," he said with contempt, "could none of them build a console. They would know what I have told you and it would work for other things. But not consoles!"

He looked at the contract longingly. Then he confronted Jonnie. "There was a special class of trainee at mine school. The catrists went over each incoming class with the greatest of care, looking for the most brilliant new students. They were quite rare, really. And when found, they trained them lengthily in every branch of mining activity, theory, and practice.

"The Imperial government was determined that only one personnel on any planet would be able to build a teleportation console for use in times of emergency or to repair one. So they specially trained this group of students. We used to call them the 'brain-brains.' They weren't always the best people to know but the catrists thought they were.

"And as the government and company were so crazy on the subject of secrecy, of course the post to which these 'brain-brains' were appointed was that of security officer.' "

Terl! thought Jonnie.

And almost as if he was reading Jonnie's thoughts, Soth said, "Terl was a 'brain-brain.' Darling of the catrists. Trained in every branch of anything. Sly, evil. A true catrist product. Only Terl could have built a firing console from scratch and he's gone."

Jonnie's mind was racing. He had all Terl's work papers! They would tell him the sequence!

And then his hopes were dashed. Soth said, "That also applies to computing motors. Only Terl could have computed out the full circuits for motor consoles.''

Jonnie had no such papers.

''They are,'' said Soth, ''quite different, you know. The firing console overrides and gets around the 'samespace' principle. The motor runs on the resistance space puts up to being changed.''

Soth was dangling the contract in his claws. ''What I have told you about Psychlo math applies to all of it and can be used in solving anything but teleportation.''

Jonnie brightened. At least it would apply to the hundreds of thousands of patents. Still, it meant no motors. It condemned him to eventually flying reaction engines. It meant Desperation Defense wouldn't have an easy conversion to peacetime. Then he recalled something.

''But executives used to repair motor consoles,'' he said.

Soth sat up. He looked at the contract and then at Jonnie ''You just want the circuit itself? I thought you were interested in the mathematics. Mathematics is a pure subject,'' he added with the vehemence of any dedicated hobbyist. ''But if you want just the circuit. . . .'' He was fishing around under books and papers. ''Where's my breathe-gas mask?''

In minutes they were outside and Jonnie was issuing the orders Soth wanted relayed.

A console was to be removed from a plane, one from a ground car and one from a flying platform. And they were to be brought at once to the repair shop without being further tampered with. Mechanics went racing about.

Presently the three consoles were sitting on the floor of the repair shop.

''These are the three different types of consoles for motor drives. All other motor consoles are one or another of these types. Now you will have to give me a hand. I am not as strong as I was once.''

Soth closed the door, barring everyone else. He reached up on a shelf and brought down a ''poison ore bag.'' Jonnie had seen them often enough. They were transparent. They had two very tight armholes you could put your hands and arms into. He thought they were used when one sorted out arsenic compounds used in ore refining.

Soth, with a little help from Jonnie, struggled the ground car console into the bag. Then he stuffed in all the trailing connection wires that had just been severed from the vehicle. He sealed. the bag tight. He connected an air hose to the fitting at the bottom and the bag around the console began to inflate.

He picked up a pressure gauge and a tool kit and shoved these through the armholes. Then he put his own arms in and snapped seals around his elbows.

Through the transparent top he watched the pressure gauge he had put in. "One hundred pounds is what you want," he said.

The bag inflated. The gauge went up to one hundred. He checked his elbow seals. The pressure was holding.

Soth picked up a screwdriver from the kit he had put inside and swiftly took out the screws of the top plate.

Jonnie looked on, fascinated. He had done that once with a tank console and it had promptly ceased to work!

But Soth simply took the screws out. He lifted the top of the console, which contained all the buttons, completely off and bunched the cables which led to it.

He then looked into the console itself. There were all kinds of components in there, but unlike a rig, it had no insulating board. Soth selected a wire with clips on both ends and fastened it on either side of three components to bypass them.

"Pressure fuses," said Soth. "The whole inside of one of these consoles is carried at high pressure. If the pressure drops, any one of those three fuses expands and blows! If anyone monkeys with the cover, it lets the atmosphere out very silently. That blows these fuses.

"Except for the fuses and the erase-surge components, everything else you're looking at there is garbage. Sensible seeming. But really just garbage. It has nothing to do with the console operation. I have jumped a wire across the fuses. They will blow and I'll have to replace them. But the wipe mechanism won't work now. The *real* circuit is still intact."

Jonnie was wondering where the real circuit was if that vast area of components was just "garbage."

But Soth knew what he was doing. He kicked the pressure hose with a foot and the bag deflated. He withdrew his arms and pulled off the fasteners. The bag fell away.

Soth turned the console over. "These buttons would appear to go down, like ordinary keys, and hit the false circuit. But that isn't how it operates. The whole circuit is in the cover. When you push a button, it cuts off an internal light path and makes the circuit operate. Each button works like that."

A totally hidden circuit, done with molecular alignment in the cover plate. And if you fooled with it, it wiped the circui ɔut. One cover screw loosened and you had no console anymore.

"Where's some paper?" said Soth. He found a big sheet of it, larger than the console plate. "Where's some powdered iron?" He found some, the dust-like brown-black powder, almost capable of floating in the air, so fine was it.

Soth dusted the powder on the white paper and spread a thin coat of it. Then, struggling to keep the bunched cables from tangling, he laid the console cover right-side up on the paper.

He took some jump wires, found a battery, and linked the battery to the console amid a flash of sparks. He was fixing it so that the cover and buttons would have juice running through it.

Soth exactly positioned the cover on the paper and then rapidly tapped each console button.

Jonnie suddenly understood what he was doing. He held up a hand to prevent Soth from removing the cover. Jonnie got a metal analysis camera off a shelf, stood up on a stool, and shot a picture straight down.

When Jonnie had finished, Soth gently lifted up the cover.

There on the paper, drawn in magnetically grouped iron filings, was the whole circuit! Activated by pushing the buttons, each part of it had grouped the iron filings.

On the removal, a tiny part of it had gotten blurred. But Jonnie had it in the camera. To be sure, he now took another picture of the tiny, thin, brown-black lines.

They had that circuit!

Soth put it all back in the bag, inflated it to a hundred pounds, replaced the blown fuses, checked the plate gasket, and then screwed the console back together.

Two hours later, they had all three types of motor console circuits. They put everything away, called the mechanics, and had the consoles put back in the vehicles and connected.

Jonnie made a test. They all started the motors.

Very different from a firing rig. Very different indeed.

— 7 —

Back in his room, old Soth was tired and coughing a bit from having overexerted himself this day. Jonnie sat on an improvised bench and waited for him to get his breath.

Eventually Soth said, "I can't dismantle or put together a teleportation shipping rig; only Terl could do that. And I surely can't build one either. So maybe I shouldn't take this contract." He held it up between a couple of claws, looked at it longingly and then handed it to Jonnie.

Jonnie couldn't help but wonder how this race might have been if it hadn't been for the catrists messing up their brains.

"No, no," said Jonnie, pushing it back at him. "You've done fine. In fact, the key you have given me to routine Psychlo mathematics has probably unlocked the door to a parade of inventions intergalactic was sitting on. You may have helped bring prosperity to many, many worlds."

"Really?" said Soth. He thought it over. "That's nice. Yes, that's very nice." He was pondering something.

'You know," Soth said after a while, "you have something of a security problem too. An awful lot of people of an awful lot of races would do anything to get their hands on Psychlo mathematics and some developments they stole. You know, don't you, that Professor En who developed teleportation was a Boxnard? No? Well he was. Yes, people will be trying to get this data. But I think I can help."

He thought for quite a while. "Yes, I think I can do it." He smiled. "Like any hobbyist, I like to fiddle around, and about fifty years ago—I was on a dreadful planet, not even a tree—I set myself the problem of putting Psychlo higher math into a computer. The company and the government would have had fits had it been reported. But I remember the circuits I devised. It would work all right but I'd need some facilities and components."

A computer! Jonnie had been dreading solving hundreds of thousands of formulas to get whatever inventions they'd found into use. If he had a computer, anyone on his staff could rattle them off!

"If you do that," said Jonnie, "I'll give you a million credits out of my own pocket."

"A million credits?" gawped Soth. "There isn't that much money!" He was fumbling around through his litter of paper. Jonnie thought he was trying to find some reference but then saw he was trying to locate a kerbango saucepan. Soth obviously felt he needed a stimulant! The saucepan was empty and Jonnie got a package of kerbango from his pocket and put it in the pan.

Soth chewed a small bit of it thankfully, remembered his manners, and offered Jonnie some, which was, of course, declined.

"You startled me." said Soth. "But that wasn't all I was going to tell you." He chewed for a bit, got his heart beating again to his satisfaction. "I have been fooling about converting simpler Psychlo arithmetic to the decimal system." He went into the litter of papers again, found what he wanted on the floor, and showed it to Jonnie. "It's quite an amazing system. Children and people learn it quite easily. The Psychlo Empire actually held onto the eleven system just so others could get more mixed up."

"They mixed *me* up," said Jonnie.

"Well, I should think they did, but that was all part of the security program. Anyway, all the basic arithmetic functions and the lesser formulas can be converted over to the decimal system. Then maybe they'll even put money into the decimal system—as I see the Galactic Bank's new issue remains in the eleven system. Now here is the good part:

"The decimal system will go into general use. Nobody will want anything to do with the clumsy eleven system and it will go into disuse!"

He sat back triumphantly. "You'll have your computer. The eleven system will phase out. People will consider it some old curiosity and forget it. And that in itself is a kind of security precaution."

Jonnie had found a piece of paper and was writing on it rapidly.

"A second contract!" said Soth, reading it upside-down.

"In addition to the first contract," said Jonnie. "Two million credits if you make the computer and another million if you convert basic Psychlo math to the decimal system."

"Oh, dear," said Soth. "I could collect a warehouse full of mathematics texts with that! Ten warehouses Fifty! Quick, don't change your mind. Let me sign it!"

When they had finalized it, Soth looked at it for a while. "You know, on Psychlo, that would make me very rich. One would have a dozen females, raise a huge family, become almost a noble dynasty. But it's all finished."

"There are still some Psychlos here," said Jonnie. "There are several females. The race isn't finished."

"Ah," said Soth. "You don't know." He sagged. "The catrists long ago pulled back the only Psychlo colonies that had begun. They convinced the throne that colonies on other planets might mutate, be able to live in other atmospheres, and constitute a threat to the crown. So they insisted that all babies born be born only on Psychlo."

Where they could put capsules in their heads, thought Jonnie.

"Occasionally, very rarely," continued Soth, "a royal noble could take his own females to other planets but only with a whole catrist team along. All female employees of the company, by long-standing order from the catrists, had to be permanently sterilized before being shipped away from the home planet."

"You mean . . . ?" Jonnie gestured to the rest of the compound area.

"Yes," said Soth. "All these females are sterilized. They cannot have any pups."

He sat for a while, pensive. "You might think I hold it against you for destroying that planet. I don't, you know. From the moment the catrists began to gain power, the race started to go bad.

"The way I look at it," he continued, "their program of degrading everyone, suppressing any group who sought a new morality, calling everybody animals, turned Psychlo into a beast. People all over the universes, all through the ages, prayed for the end of that empire. It was *hated!*"

He looked at Jonnie. "Sooner or later someone was bound to rid the galaxies of Psychlo. Whole races have dreamed that dream.

"You," and he pointed a talon at Jonnie, "may think you did it. You didn't. That whole civilization was doomed the moment the catrists began to influence it. It wasn't you. It was *they* who destroyed Psychlo and the whole empire.

"Terl was their product and I believe he had a hand in their destruction in some way. You know, I've heard he used to sit around in the recreation hall and tell people that *man* was an endangered species.

"Because of the catrists, the Psychlos have been an endangered species for millennia. And now they're not just endangered. They're extinct!"

He sighed and looked at his litter of papers. "Well, maybe I can help make up for some of the crimes they have done."

Then he looked at Jonnie. "As for you, Jonnie Goodboy Tyler, have no qualms about it. When you destroyed Psychlo you gave all the galaxies a chance to return to better ways. I didn't need these contracts. You have offered them and I will keep them. But it is a privilege to help you and I thank you for the chance."

— Epilogue —

A few months later, Jonnie heard that the government in Scotland was going to introduce taxation in order to rebuild Edinburgh. He knew that taxation had been unknown in the earliest days of the Scottish nation—the king had just paid for everything way back then. And he doubted Scotland had the resources to do it. Also he felt a taxation, as a government way of life, was a sort of silly business: couldn't a government earn its keep? Why did it have to go around robbing people?

So he talked to Dunneldeen and got him to sell the idea to the Chief of Clanfearghus that Edinburgh would be rebuilt by "contributions." To foster the illusion that the Scottish people were paying for it, he and Dunneldeen put little red boxes along trails where Scots could drop in small coins and they even emptied some of them.

But what really happened was that Jonnie paid for it. He sent in his Chatovarian construction company, Buildstrong, Inc. They had finished all the industrial requirements at Luxembourg and banking requirements at Zurich anyway.

The Chatovarians, being Chatovarians, sent a research team all around Scotland and the government to find out what people wanted at Edinburgh and then went on and did what they thought was right, regardless.

They decided Edinburgh would be in three businesses: planetary government, extraterrestrial training, and Scottish handicraft. It was a real headache to them to reconcile such divergent actions into architecture, which they always maintained must be (a) indigenous and (b) suitable for the purpose.

The city itself, their research team found, had once been nicknamed "Auld Reekie" because it smelled so bad. They also found no Scot had lived in it for eleven hundred years. This gave them a totally free hand: they rammed down everything except Castle Rock; they got several Highland hydroelectric plants back in operation rapidly and then called in their companion company, Desperation Defense, and had them make their installations and emplacements; they then put in sewer systems and filtration plants; and then they rubbed their hands and really got to work.

They put the northern section of the town into industrial—for business and handicrafts—and gave it the overall look and landscaping of stone cottages such as the Scots were used to in the Highlands. They sweepingly planned out a large number of specialty schools: outside they were all Scotch baronial with the little projecting turrets, castles right out of the old fairy tale books, but the whole of the interiors were adapted to extraterrestrial living. They spread these all over the terrain with big parks.

Castle Rock itself they saved for government. It had been so battered and fractured they had to get early engravings of it to see how to shape it; shaping and armoring rock was no problem to the Chatovarians but what it had been like a couple thousand years ago was. They got an indication that a castle of an early Scottish king, [Duncan], who apparently had been killed by [Macbeth], had stood there—where they got this was a mystery. Somebody said an old play they had found in the wreckage of the British Museum.

They reassembled the Rock, rebuilt its interior shelters, covered the whole thing with blue Italian marble, got it all armor hard and glowing, and then put Duncan's castle on it in gleaming white. They found a cathedral they liked in an ancient city called Rheims that they said agreed with the architecture of the castle and put it up on the rock in shimmering scarlet and called it "Saint Giles" again.

The Scots were enraptured with the result of what they had "financed."

Jonnie thought it looked pretty good, too. But it did produce a problem. The Chatovarians, being overpopulated at home, always overhired and as this job had been "rush" and "for the boss himself," they had accumulated a very huge crew. They also had a policy that you never fired anybody ever. It left him with a swollen city-building team almost the size of Earth's entire population. So he put them to work rebuilding the cities the "visitors" had burned.

This, too, gave the Chatovarians a problem. What were the cities for? Nobody had lived in a city for eleven hundred years. So their research teams had to figure out what future use the cities *might* be put to, based on resources, proximity to rivers and the sea, what crops grew in that climate, who they might someday trade with, how many people would have to be housed for what industry. It was very complex and quite difficult.

Establishing the indigenous architecture was easy in Asia, fairly easy in Europe, impossible in America: this last continent had gone madly modern and the Chatovarians couldn't abide it. So they just had to take the most interesting landmark sort of buildings they found on the sites, duplicate those, and make lots and lots of parks. The parent company in Chatovaria had overbought zip monorails on another job so they shipped those in and internally connected the cities up high so their parks wouldn't be spoiled with roads.

They had to get a Hawvin company in to clean up the radiation around Denver—they did it with flying magnetic sweeps. Then the Chatovarians rebuilt that whole area, including even Jonnie's village.

There were no populations, so when they would finish a city, they would just seal up the doors and windows, put a caretaker crew in, and leave it.

Oh, well, Jonnie thought, when he saw all these empty cities going up, maybe somebody would live in them someday.

Ker took charge of the mine school in Edinburgh and the Psychlos that were left alive moved there and gave lectures and demonstrations. Absolute hordes of extraterrestrials were pouring in to learn how to mine their own planets and get the metals moving again. Ker pictographed all the lectures so the technology wouldn't be lost. He used Cornwall and Victoria for practical training and it kept him pretty busy, tearing around with Chirk who had the job of building up the libraries. Ker had a trick of wearing breathe-masks with the face of the race he was training painted on it. It made for friendlier relations, he said.

There was an awful lot of ex-Psychlo planets that had slave populations or people withdrawn to mountains, and the Coordinators were very busy running their Coordinator College in Edinburgh, showing former subject races how to get organized and prosper. Their enrollment was greatly assisted by the fact that the Galactic Bank gave much more favorable interest rates to such planets when they had Coordinators trained in Edinburgh.

The new Earth government claimed that Chief of Clanfearghus was King, probably due to the influence of Mr. Tsung's brother. This made Dunneldeen the Crown Prince, but from all Jonnie could see, neither the Chief nor Dunneldeen took his elevation very seriously. The government was very reluctant to pass laws and generally left things up to tribal chiefs in their own areas, intervening only when there was no other way to end a dispute among them. They were very popular.

Colonel Ivan, with the title of "The Democratic Valiant-red-army People's Colonel," ruled Russia. Jonnie's village people helped him, and then some of the younger ones went back to America to try to get it started again.

Chief Chong-won and the North Chinese tribe made an alliance and began to build up China. Handicraft and silk for export handled their economic needs. They also had a cooking school that became widely attended, for the Selachees, spread all over the galaxies even farther due to their "neighborhood banks," swore it was the best cooking anywhere, particularly for fish dishes, and were quick to finance any extraterrestrial who wanted to start a Chinese restaurant in his area providing he sent some cook trainees to learn how. There were usually more cook trainees in China than Chinese. They not only had to learn to cook but also had to learn how to grow much of the food. The extra labor and machinery boomed Chinese agriculture and fisheries, and, as Chief Chong-won remarked every time he saw Jonnie, which was often, starvation was no longer the main product of the Chinese. Jonnie often wondered how an extraterrestrial, who ate quite another diet, could learn to cook food he would never eat. But the power of the bank and the appetites of the Selachees were similarly wonderful.

Pursuant to wide galactic conversion to the decimal system, the bank distributed new issues of money. These upset Chrissie considerably: the coins and bank notes looked even less like Jonnie. She went on for some days about how they looked even more like a Selachee and even less like Jonnie. But Jonnie didn't tell her he had carefully maneuvered things in that direction: these days he could walk right down a street and hardly anybody pointed. A couple more issues and no stranger would know him on sight at all.

The bank in Snautch never did return their gold. When they built the huge new bank complex there, they put the gold behind armor glass in the main lobby with a multilanguage sign on it: "This gold was mined personally by Jonnie Goodboy Tyler and some Scots. He has left it with us because he TRUSTS us. So can you. If you start your new account today, you can reach through a slot and touch it!"

When Jonnie wanted some gold to plate the inaugural display model of a new teleport car Desperation Defense was now converting to build in Chatovaria, Dwight had to go to the Andes with a team of the old crew and open up a mine there to get it.

After the surveys on what people wanted were done by the bank as Jonnie suggested, the conversion of ex-arms companies to consumer products went very swiftly. Few of the Intergalactic patents were in any demand for a while. They found the people on civilized planets wanted pots and pans and such like, all of which were easily made and quite profitable.

The original emissaries were now becoming very wealthy and powerful and backed Jonnie's measures to the limit, even guiding their countries toward social democracy. Jonnie seldom attended their conferences, but they often rushed dispatch boxes to him to get his opinion on something. As they often told each other, antiwar was the most profitable venture they had ever heard of.

The Hawvin Commercial Intelligence Service circulated a secret report on the twenty-eight platforms without knowing it had been planted on them by the Galactic Bank. They had been chosen for the "leak" because they were the most infiltrated intelligence service in any universe. The report was rapidly and secretly relayed all over the galaxies.

It alleged that the original twenty-eight had been increased to fifty-three to allow for new nations and that the platforms were actually located in the seventeenth universe.

The report created a new flurry of antiwar. But it also created astrographic turmoil as it upset the stable datum that, as the number four when squared made sixteen, there could only be sixteen universes.

Immediate action resulted. Several scientific bodies began searching, not necessarily to find the firing platforms but to see whether there *was* a seventeenth universe.

The Democratic Royal Institute of Chatovaria did find an additional universe, but since it was just forming and had no evidence of sentient life in it, and since there was no trace of anything to put platforms on, it concluded it must be the eighteenth universe.

The seventeenth universe, containing the platforms, remains undiscovered to this day. And as Jonnie sometimes told himself, this was not hard to understand. It was in his head. He never built the platforms.

MacAdam had told Jonnie that quite a few of the old intergalactic Mining Company reserve planets, even though habitable and currently uninhabited, were a drag on the market. So Jonnie, by special Selachee couriers from his own staff, secretly informed the original emissaries of different groups of planets on the list. They promptly made deals with the company and then rushed the planets into the real estate market with the slogan, "Enjoy peaceful, untargeted, suburban living," and they made even vaster fortunes for themselves and their friends. They swore by Jonnie. Peace was one of the most profitable discoveries ever made!

During that period the only sour bit of news that came Jonnie's way was brought to him by his accounts staff. It had increased to two hundred Selachees to keep track of his income. They told him that the Earth division of Buildstrong, Inc., was now the only company he had that was running in the red. All the rest were way up in the black. Jonnie said he'd have a word with its general manager and he did. He found that they had added to their payroll another two hundred thousand Chatovarian workers. The general manager explained they were not just building the burned Earth cities now but had branched out and were rebuilding all the others and had a two-hundred-year construction program they had all planned out and didn't want interrupted. Jonnie told him—and his six assistant general managers—that he was building cities for which no populations existed nor would exist in the next several centuries, and that they better start figuring out how to show a profit. They said they would. But in return, he insisted they keep on with their program. No, they didn't have any plans to settle Earth with Chatovarians; they knew that would engulf Man. It was just that when they got going doing something they built up an awfully big momentum. Jonnie thought it didn't much matter anyway so he forgot about it.

Sometime after that Stormalong got bored with demonstrating the new teleportation-motored atmosphere transports Desperation Defense was selling all over the galaxies and training pilots for, and he talked Jonnie into letting him rehabilitate an old company orbit miner with cranes and fly to the moon. Jonnie talked Stormalong into first getting some pressure suits and then getting three other pilots as crazy as Stormalong, refitting *four* orbit miners and doing it right.

Stormalong had the excuse that he wanted to go see whether he could find some more of that heavy metal. He figured that flights of meteorites had now hit the moon. It took them two months to get ready and to make the trip and return.

They found the meteorites with heavy metal traces, all right, and mined them and brought back about two hundred tons of ore to process. But Stormalong brought back startling news:

"There's footprints up there," he told Jonnie. "And tire treads!"

This being in the world of tracking, Jonnie was very interested. They speculated on the possibility they had invaders. But the Desperation Defense people pooh-poohed it: nothing could get through *their* defenses. They then wondered if it might not have been the visitors putting down there during the war.

Jonnie wasn't going to spend weeks in space in an orbit miner so he chartered Dries Gloton's space yacht for a weekend and he and Stormalong were taken up to have another look.

Yessir! Footprints! Tire treads!

Then the sharp, trained eye of Jonnie spotted a paper wrapper that must have been discarded and lay almost covered with dust. It said ["Care*free Sugarless Gum, Spearmint, 15 sticks, Life Savers, Inc., New York City"]. Stormalong thought it must be some salvage gear from a wreck maybe. But there was no wreck. Dries thought that maybe it was used to repair holes. Gum, you know.

Jonnie wouldn't let them mess up the tracks with their own He pictorecorded them and then backtracked them and found a cairn with the very faded remains of what might have been a flag. Then, although he had trouble walking with almost no weight, he hiked around and found another cairn with another flag in it, also faded beyond recognition. That was all they found. But Jonnie showed them that the exposed edge of the wrapper was *much* more faded than the buried part and from that he deducted that these tracks and cairns were hundreds of years old. So they decided it was not an immediate danger and started back home.

The real discovery was made on the way back. Jonnie was admiring Dries' communication gear and Dries showed him the first pictures he had taken of the planet and Jonnie noticed there seemed to be much more cloud cover now.

He did more comparisons. They were flashing down toward Europe, of course, but they could still see northern Africa and the Middle East. The latter was *green*. And the former had a new sea in the middle of it.

Landed again, even though he was late for Sunday night supper, Jonnie got right onto the Desperation Defense duty officer and wanted to know if he was aware of planetary changes. He was and referred Jonnie to the general manager of Buildstrong.

"You ordered us to show a profit," the general manager said defensively. "So we hired some more Chatovarians and started a Health Subsidiary. We figured 'Buildstrong' could also be interpreted to mean strong bodies."

Jonnie wanted to know what the devil he had done now. And it seemed there was a below-sea-level spot in the dry wasteland of the Sahara Desert so they let the Mediterranean in and made an new sea that would furnish rainfall. And they had machine-gun-planted eighty-five quadrillion trees there, and also in the Middle East where they wouldn't require much water. Good varieties, slow growing, but very tasty. And they'd planted another sixteen quadrillion in the middle west of the American continent . . . oh, Jonnie hadn't seen that part of the continent? Well, there used to be trees on that huge, central, flat plain; they could prove it by fossil remains. Anyway, he was sorry if it had changed the climate. But it usually did, you know. Cleaned up the air, too.

Jonnie wanted to know how spending that much money and hiring that new army of Chatovarians was going to make a profit. And the general manager showed him the balance sheets now. They were all in the black. They were exporting food trees to food-short Chatovarian planets. Jonnie forgave him, raised his pay, and went home to a very late Sunday dinner.

Another incident worthy of note happened about that time.

Jonnie, wearing an extraterrestrial atmosphere mask to keep from being stopped on the street and gathering crowds, attended a fair in Zurich, and there he saw Pierre Solens. The ex-pilot was in beggar's rags and holding forth to an audience about how he personally, with his own eyes, had seen Jonnie Goodboy Tyler walk on a cloud and, not only that, pull a demon out of it and sing a duet with him. When he had finished his story, he passed around a battered cup for offerings. It seemed he made his living this way. When he got to Jonnie, Jonnie pulled his mask down and Pierre nearly fainted again.

There were so many exaggerations and lies going around about Jonnie that he figured he didn't need another one. So he forced Pierre into a plane, took him right down to Africa, and made him get into another plane at Victoria and by himself fly it up to the peak where the Psychlo cadavers still lay in the snow, land, look, fly back down through the overcast, and land. Pierre made it without wrecking himself and Jonnie took him back to Luxembourg. Pierre said "Thank you" and he meant it. He went back to his old job of moving the compound planes around the hangar and in time became an acceptable pilot.

There was a bizarre incident that occurred in Edinburgh. The sarcophagus of Bittie MacLeod had been miraculously preserved in the bombings: three beams of the collapsing cathedral had fallen across it almost protectively; the Chatovarians had repositioned it in the new cathedral crypt in a row of dead war heroes which included Glencannon's recovered remains.

When she was sixteen, Pattie demanded that she be taken to the crypt and married to Bittie MacLeod. Nothing could dissuade her and she stood there beside the sarcophagus in a white wedding dress, holding Bittie's locket with "To my future wife" on it. The parson, who could find no law against it, went through the wedding ceremony. She then changed to widow's weeds and after that called herself Mrs. Pattie MacLeod.

Still continuing with her medical training, she founded the MacLeod Intergalactic Health Organization. Jonnie funded it and it became a standard stop-point on and off all firing platforms throughout the galaxies. It also provided instant medical service.

Two other events had occurred. Jonnie and Chrissie had a boy born to them, Timmie Brave Tyler, an absolute carbon copy of Jonnie as everybody swore. And two years later they had a girl, Missie, that everyone affirmed was a mirror-image of Chrissie.

When Timmie was six, Jonnie blew up. They boy was *not* getting properly educated. He had "uncles" by the absolute score. "Uncle" Colonel Ivan, "Uncle" Sir Robert, "Uncle" Dunneldeen. And every Scot who had mined or served with Jonnie was an "uncle." They spoiled the child rotten. They brought him things from all over the world. But were they seeing to it that Timmie was properly educated? No! He did speak several languages after a fashion—Russian, Chinese, Chatovarian, Psychlo, and English. He could do sums in his head when it suited him. And he could drive a teleportation gocart Angus and Tom Smiley had made for him. But Jonnie was faced with the specter of a son who would grow up totally ignorant of the vital things in life.

Jonnie had made up his mind. Affairs were running fine—handled mostly by others anyway. So he took a few bare necessities, bundled Timmie and Chrissie and Missie and four horses into an old marine attack plane, and flew to southern Colorado. He disconnected the plane's phone and radio and hid the ship in a clump of trees and made camp.

For the whole of the next year, rain or shine, Jonnie worked on Timmie. Missie was fine and she helped her mother very well and learned all about real tanning and cooking and things like that. But it was Timmie who got the attention.

At first Jonnie had it a little rough for the boy obviously was getting a delayed start. But after a few months he saw he was making real progress. The boy learned to track, to spot different animals and their immediate intentions. He learned to round up wild horses and train them and he didn't need a sissy thing like a saddle. He came right along and was quite cheerful about it. Jonnie got him to throw kill-clubs with considerable accuracy and he even nailed a coyote with one. Jonnie was just beginning to feel some security about the boy's future and was about to post-graduate him into stalking wolves and then pumas. But on the very first day of this, he heard a plane in the afternoon sky. It wasn't a drone. It was a plane. Heading for the plume of smoke that marked their current camp.

Jonnie and the boy trotted back, Jonnie with uneasy forebodings.

It was Dunneldeen and Sir Robert.

Timmie sprang at them like a small windstorm, shrieking glad shrieks of welcome. "Uncle Dunneldeen! Uncle Wobert!"

Jonnie's manners let Chrissie fix them some supper. They

didn't seem to be in any hurry to get on with their business. Evening came and the two of them and the family sat around the bonfire singing Scottish songs. Then Timmie showed them he hadn't forgotten the Highland fling and danced it for them like Thor had taught him.

Finally, when the children and Chrissie had gone to bed, Dunneldeen made the wholly unnecessary statement, "I suppose you're wondering why we're here."

"What's the bad news?" said Jonnie.

"It isn't any bad news," grumped Sir Robert. "We've been holding sixteen universes together like glue. Why should there be any bad news?"

"It's been a year," said Dunneldeen.

"You came for something," said Jonnie suspiciously.

"Well," said Dunneldeen, "as a matter of fact, come to think of it, we did. A couple of years ago you made a tour of all the Earth tribes. It's been proposed that you make a tour of the major civilizations of the galaxies. A lot of governments want to bestow honors and estates and medals and things on you because galactic conditions are so prosperous."

It made Jonnie very cross. "I told you I was taking a year off! Don't you realize I have family responsibilities? What kind of father would I be to let my son grow up like an educated savage!" He really let them have it.

Dunneldeen heard him out and then laughed. "We thought you'd say that, so we sent Thor instead."

Jonnie studied that over. Then he said, "So if you handled it. why have you come?"

Sir Robert look at him. "Your year is up, laddie. Doesn't it ever occur to you that your friends miss you?"

So Jonnie went back home, and while Timmie learned to speak fifteen languages and do five kinds of math, while he learned to drive a ground car like Ker and drive and fly anything the company made, on any planet, including Dries Gloton's new yacht, his education was never finished. It was probably the one failure in Jonnie Goodboy Tyler's life.

·

Doctor MacDermott, the historian who considered himself expendable, lived on and on.

He wrote a book: [The Jonnie Goodboy Tyler I Knew, or The Conqueror of Psychlo, Pride of the Scottish Nation]. It was not as good as this book, for it was intended for semiliterate people. But it had three-dimensional pictures that moved in full color—he had access to several archives—and it sold two hundred fifty billion copies in its first printing. It was translated into ninety-eight thousand different galactic languages and went into many editions.

Doctor MacDermott received royalties so far in excess of anything his simple life needed that he endowed the Tyler Museum. It is the first building you see, the one with the golden dome, when you leave the MacLeod Intergalactic Health Organization exit at the Denver terminal.

Not too long after his return from America, Jonnie disappeared. His family and his friends were very concerned. But they knew that he disliked adulation and being unable to move about without attracting crowds. He had remarked that he was not needed now and that he had done his work. A pouch, two kill-clubs, and a knife were also missing. The dragon helmet and bright-buttoned tunic were still there on a peg where he had last hung them.

But people in the galaxies do not know that he is gone. If you ask almost anyone on a civilized planet where he is, you are likely to be told that he is *there*, just over that hill, waiting in case the lords or the Psychlos come back. Try it. You'll see. They will even point.

■

C O N T E S T   R U L E S

1. All entries must be original works of science fiction or fantasy. Plagarism will result in automatic disqualification. Submitted works may not have been previously published.

2. Entries must be either short story length (under 10,000 words) or novelette length (under 17,000 words).

3. Contest is open only to those who have not had professionally published a novel or novella or more than three short stories or one novelette.

4. Entries must be typewritten and double-spaced.

Each entry shall have a cover page with the title of the work, the author's name, address and telephone number, and state the length of the work. The manuscript itself should be titled, but the author's name should be deleted from it in order to facilitate anonymous judging.

5. Entries must be accompanied by a stamped (with sufficient International Reply coupons), self addressed envelope suitable for return of manuscript. Every manuscript will be returned.

6. There shall be three cash prizes for each contest: 1st prize of $1,000.00, 2nd prize of $750,00, and 3rd prize of $500.00.

7. There will be eleven quarterly contests commencing from January 1, 1984 and ending September 30, 1986.

a. Jan. 1—Mar. 31, 1984
b. Apr. 1—Jun. 30, 1984
c. Jul. 1—Sep. 30, 1984
d. Oct. 1—Dec. 31, 1984
e. Jan. 1—Mar. 31, 1985
f. Apr. 1—Jun. 30, 1985
g. Jul. 1—Sep. 30, 1985
h. Oct. 1—Dec. 31, 1985
i. Jan. 1—Mar. 31, 1986
j. Apr. 1—Jun. 30, 1986
k. Jul. 1—Sep. 30, 1986

To be eligible for a quarterly contest, an entry must be postmarked no later than midnight of the last day of the quarter.

8. Only one entry per quarter.

9. Winners of a quarterly contest are ineligible for further participation in the contest.

10. The winners of the quarterly contest will be eligible for trophies or certificates.

11. A 1985 grand- prize winner will be selected from among the quarterly winners from the period October 1, 1984 through September 30, 1985. Similarly a grand prize winner will be selected for the 1986 contest from among those quarterly winners from the period October 1, 1985 through September 30 1986.

12. Should the sponsor of this contest decide to publish an anthology of science fiction and fantasy works, winners will be contacted regarding their interest in having their manuscripts included.

13. Entries will be judged by a panel of professional authors. Each contest may have a different panel. Entries will not be judged by L. Ron Hubbard or his agents. The decisions of the judges are final.

14. Winners of each contest will be individually notified of results by mail, together with names of those sitting on the panel of judges.

This contest is void where prohibited by law.

ABOUT THE AUTHOR

Born in 1911, the son of a U.S. naval officer, L. Ron Hubbard grew up in the great American West and was acquainted early with the rugged outdoor life before he took to the sea. The cowboys, Indians and mountains of Montana were balanced with an open sea, temples and the throngs of the Orient as Hubbard traveled through the Far East as a teenager. By the time he was nineteen, he had traveled over a quarter of a million sea miles and thousands on land as he prodded and asked and recorded his experiences in a series of diaries mixed with story ideas.

Returning to the United States, Hubbard's insatiable curiosity and demand for excitement sent him into the sky as a pilot where he quickly earned a reputation for his skill and daring before he turned his attention again to the sea. This time it was four-masted schooners and voyages into the Caribbean as Hubbard mixed adventure with an education that was to serve him later at the typewriter.

While Hubbard's first articles were nonfiction and based upon his aviation experience, he soon began to draw from his travels to produce a wide variety of stories: adventure, mysteries, travel through the Far East, westerns, detective and finally, science fiction.

In 1938, Hubbard was already established and recognized as one of the top-selling writers of the field, but a new magazine wanted new blood. Hubbard was urged to try his hand at science fiction. The red-headed author protested that he did not write about "ray guns and rockets" but that he wrote about people. "That's just what we want," he was told.

The result was a barrage of stories from Hubbard that changed the face of science fiction and excited intense critical comparison—then as now—with the best of H. G. Wells and Edgar Allen Poe. Today, Hubbard is recognized as one of the "founding fathers" of the great Golden Age of Science Fiction who, like Robert Heinlein and a few other grand masters, continues to develop and significantly enlarge the contemporary literature genre he helped to create.

At the same time, Hubbard's prodigious and continuing creative output over more than half a century as a professional writer has assumed the proportions of a true publishing phenomenon—with more than a hundred novels and novelettes, more than two hundred short stories (published under his own name and such no-less-celebrated pen names as Rene Lafayette, Kurt Von Rachen and Winchester Remington Colt, among others), and more than twenty-two million copies of his fiction, in a dozen languages, sold throughout the world.

Battlefield Earth becomes one more milestone in a fabled career that has made Hubbard one of the most prolific and influential authors of the twentieth century.

"I AM ALWAYS HAPPY TO HEAR FROM MY READERS."

L. Ron Hubbard

These were the words of L. Ron Hubbard, who was always very interested in hearing from his friends, readers and followers. He made a point of staying in communication with everyone he came in contact with over his fifty-year career as a professional writer, and he had thousands of fans and friends that he corresponded with all over the world.

The publishers of L. Ron Hubbard's literary works wish to continue this tradition and would very much welcome letters and comments from you, his readers, both old and new.

Any message addressed to the Author's Affairs Director at New Era Publications will be given prompt and full attention.

NEW ERA PUBLICATIONS U.K. LTD
Dowgate, Douglas Road,
Tonbridge, Kent, TN9 2TS, U.K.